Erica James

Three Great Novels

Precious Time
Hidden Talents
Paradise House

ORION

This omnibus edition first published in Great Britain in 2005 by
Orion
An imprint of Orion Books Ltd
Orion House, 5 Upper St Martin's Lane, London WC2H 9EA

ISBN: 0 75287 196 X

1 3 5 7 9 10 8 6 4 2

A CIP catalogue record for this book is
available from the British Library

Typeset by Deltatype Ltd, Birkenhead, Merseyside
Printed and bound in Great Britain by
Clays Ltd, St Ives plc

www.orionbooks.co.uk

Contents

Precious Time

To Edward and Samuel,
whose time with me is
ultra precious

Acknowledgements

Heartfelt thanks to all my new and old friends at Orion, in and out of the office.

I shan't single anyone out for preferential treatment (not even my wonderful dancing partners from Bournemouth) because you're all special. But just to make his day, this is for Andrew Taylor: 'Thank you, Mr Taylor, for all your help. I wish I could say it's been a pleasure!'

Take good care of time, how you spend it
For nothing is more precious than time.
In one little moment, short as it is,
Heaven may be won or lost.

> From *The Cloud of Unknowing*,
> fourteenth-century mystical prose work

1

Clara Costello's friends were all of one opinion: that she was mad. Away with the fairies, crazy, doolally, Harpic, not the full shilling, and two bricks short of a load was just a random sample of what they had to say about her. And just for the record, Harpic was her favourite: it was their cute way of saying she was clean round the bend.

They had reached this diagnosis six weeks ago, at the end of January, when she had announced she was giving up her job – her well-paid and secure job, as was repeatedly pointed out to her – to take to the road in a second-hand camper-van with her four-year-old son.

Louise, her closest friend and biggest critic, had been disappointed that her gallivanting was to be restricted to the shores of Britain. 'Well, if you must indulge yourself with an early mid-life crisis, you might at least have come up with something a little more adventurous,' she had said. 'Backpacking round south-east Asia in search of spiritual enlightenment would sound so much more interesting.'

'That's because you and David are such dreadful snobs and want nothing but the most exotic postcards adorning your kitchen noticeboard,' Clara had responded good-humouredly.

'And what about Ned? You've only just got him into St Chad's. You'll lose his place, and even I know the waiting-list for that school gets longer the older your child becomes.'

'I don't care. He's only just turned four and he'll learn more doing this than he would stuck in a boring classroom every day. This will be fun for him, something he'll always remember. And, anyway, school will be waiting for him in the autumn. If I don't do it now, I'll never do it. This chance will never come round again.'

The car in front braked sharply and Clara did likewise. The carrier-bag of good-luck cards and presents she had been given during her farewell lunch slid forward on the passenger seat and dropped to the floor. She left them where they were, her attention caught by the sticker on the rear window of the rusting Fiat Panda in front of her. 'No Fear', it read. Did that mean 'No fear' as in 'Not likely', or 'No fear' as in 'Hey, look at me, I'm a free-falling daredevil who's not scared of anyone or anything'? Either way, Clara fancied a sticker like that. Her friends were always saying how fearless she was. 'You're too intrepid for your own good,' David had said, more than once.

'Not true,' she had argued. 'I always reason everything out before I dive in head first.'

But what neither her friends nor her parents knew was that they were all partly to blame for this rush of blood to the head, as Louise had so charmingly referred to Clara's shift of perspective.

It had started in the new year, when Clara's parents had embarked on their trip of a lifetime to Australia, where they would be spending an open-ended amount of time with her brother Michael, his wife and their newborn baby. Kissing them goodbye at the airport, Clara had felt the sting of being left behind.

It wasn't jealousy, more a case of acknowledging that it was too easy to stand still, too easy to let the glorious opportunities of life slip by without catching hold of them. For as long as she could remember her parents had talked about travelling the world, but it was only now, since her father had retired, that they felt they could justify such an extravagant trip, as if it was his reward for all the years he had put in at the insurance company he had worked for. But what if, after all that patient anticipation, one of them had fallen ill at the last minute or, worse still and heaven forbid, died? What would have been the point in all that waiting? Why, oh why, did we spend so much time putting life on hold?

Pondering this in the busy airport, she had suddenly realised Ned was crying. His tearstained face was pressed against the smeared glass of the window as he tried in vain to see his grandparents for one last time – they had promised to wave to him from their plane on the tarmac. She bent down and held him tightly, wondering how she would ever fill the vast gap in his world created by Nanna and Granda's departure.

The following evening she had gone for dinner at Louise and David's. It was their usual fivesome: David and Louise, Guy and Moira, and herself. At around midnight, the time when Guy was most likely to start philosophis-ing, once he'd progressed from wine to liqueurs, he had asked, 'If you only had a year left to live, what would you do?'

'In your case I'd donate the time to Help the Aged,' David had laughed. 'You'd fit in nicely now you're losing your hair.'

'And, knowing you, you'd waste your year.'

Helping herself to a grape, Louise had said, 'I'd stop dieting. I'd let myself become as fat as a pig and die happy.' She sighed and, with her teeth, peeled a tiny length of skin off the grape. She was going through another of her weigh-myself-and-hate-myself phases.

'I'd buy the house I'd always wanted,' Moira said, 'my dream home, and to hell with the expense.'

'So what's wrong with the one we've just bought?' Guy frowned. 'I thought it *was* your dream house.'

'It doesn't have a conservatory and the garden's too small.'

'It's got five bedrooms and very nearly an acre of paddock. What more do you want?'

'I just said what I wanted, a conservatory and—'

'Well, I know what I'd do,' David interrupted. 'I'd give up work and travel.'

'No, you wouldn't,' smiled Louise. 'You'd be bored to death within a week. 'You can't even go on a fortnight's holiday without reporting in. Besides, seeing too much of each other might send us over the edge.'

It was daft, drink-loaded, late-into-the-night talk, no one giving a sensible answer, no one giving the question the thought it deserved. They were a group of thirty-somethings, with no children (apart from Clara) and no real responsibility to anyone other than themselves. But driving home later, Clara did give it some serious thought, and after she had paid the babysitter and watched her drive away, she had gone upstairs to check on Ned. Kneeling by his bed she had experienced the fierce tenderness of love that she always felt for him in moments like this. As she stroked his smooth, rounded cheek, she knew exactly what she would do if her days were numbered. She would spend her time with Ned.

As a single mother and working long hours as a production manager for an international pharmaceutical company, she was all too aware of how little time she had with her son. It was hard to admit, but somewhere along the line she had got her priorities wrong and had ended up squeezing Ned into her busy schedule when and how she could, giving him the tired, worn-out bits of herself rather than the best.

How had she allowed herself to become the kind of person she would once have despised? The kind of person who, at the age of thirty-four, couldn't stay awake long enough to watch the ten o'clock news through to the weather, who perpetually worked late because there was yet another problem on the packing line. The kind of person who justified it all by saying there was a mortgage to pay, nursery-school fees to find, and a voracious pension fund to feed.

The reality was that, like her friends, she had confused success with happiness. And having built that happiness on the shifting sands of material success, she was feeling the strain of sustaining it. Financial security was a severe taskmaster, and she knew that only a monumental change of heart would alter her outlook. It had happened to her when she least expected it.

With her parents away, taking care of Ned had become even more of a juggling act. They had looked after Ned for her most days. They were wonderful with him and adored him, and were as much a part of his life as she was. They would pick him up from nursery, drive him to the park where he could play on the swings and ride his bike, then take him home to give him his tea and generally spoil him. But since they had gone to Sydney, to make the acquaintance of their new grandson, Clara had had to persuade Ned that he had to go to a new nursery school where he could stay in the after-school activity club until she came to collect him.

On his first morning his dark eyes had pleaded with her not to leave him, his tiny hand squeezing hers, sending her silent messages that this wasn't what he wanted. It wasn't what she wanted either, but she didn't have any choice. She helped him wriggle out of his stiff new blazer and hung it with his satchel and plimsoll bag on his hook, which was level with her waist. She stooped to kiss him goodbye and saw to her horror that, beneath his shiny fringe, his eyes were filling. 'It'll be okay, Ned,' she said, her throat so clenched she could hardly get the words out. 'You'll have so much fun that the day will whiz by and before you know where you are I'll be here to take you home.'

He swallowed. 'I want to go home. I want Nanna and Granda.'

'Oh, Ned,' she whispered, 'I wish they were here too.' Then, all business-like, she tilted up his chin and straightened the knot of his red and grey tie, although it was already perfectly straight.

Two bigger boys cruised by, and gave Ned a contemptuous once-over. One said, 'What's that in your hand?'

He smiled his best engaging smile, the one that his grandmother said was a gift from the angels, and proudly showed them what he was holding. It was a small plastic mermaid that had belonged to Clara when she was little and had gone everywhere with her. Now it went everywhere with Ned: it was his talisman and he was never without it. 'It's old,' he said brightly, 'nearly as old as my mummy.'

The boys drew in close for a better look. 'It's a doll,' one sneered. 'Dolls are for girls.' Sniggering, they sauntered away.

'Shall I look after Mermy today for you?' Clara asked, wanting to scoop Ned up and get him out of this place and away from bigger-boy superiority.

He shook his head, and pushed Mermy back into his pocket. With her heart fit to break she watched him square his shoulders ready to brave the day ahead.

That day, she had worried about Ned constantly. She didn't care a jot about the production of the latest infertility drug, nor about the rumours that, once again, Phoenix Pharmaceuticals USA were thinking of selling their UK division in Epsom, Surrey, to a French company. From their offices on the floor above her, Guy and David had e-mailed her with what was allegedly going on. Both suggested that she brush up on her French: 'Zut alors! Avec les Frenchies, nous will be out of le pan et dans le feu,' Guy had messaged, which had probably stretched his linguistic repertoire to its limit.

She left as early as she could and drove like the wind, dreading to find Ned in a crumpled heap of misery.

What she found was a tired-looking little boy sitting cross-legged on the floor with a group of glassy-eyed children watching a cartoon on a large-screen television. She was approached by one of his teachers who said she wanted a *little word*.

'He's been all right, hasn't he?'

'Oh, he's an absolute delight,' the woman said. 'He's fitted in just fine. But – and I know it's only his first day with us – goodness, what a disorganised little boy he is. A head full of clutter. And he never stops talking. But don't worry, I'm sure that between us we'll soon have him licked into shape.' There was laughter in her voice and Clara could see that she wasn't speaking unkindly. Even so, she could have slapped her face. For heaven's sake, he was four years old. What did she expect? A personal organiser tucked into his briefcase? Looking around her and seeing the orderly rows of blazers, satchels and plimsoll bags hanging from their hooks Clara felt angry. This was the future for Ned. At the age of four he was already on a conveyor-belt of uniformity. His next stop would be an office where he could hang his jacket and the rest of his life.

It was while she was driving home, with Ned almost asleep, his head tipped to one side, his hands wrapped around Mermy, that Clara made her decision. It was now or never. She had until September to give Ned what he deserved. She would use the precious time available and give him her undivided attention and, hopefully, a little adventure into the bargain.

2

More than two hundred and fifty miles away, in Deaconsbridge, a small market town in the Peak District where luscious hills of tranquil beauty gave way to peaty moors of savage wildness, a man sat brooding restlessly on an uncomfortable orange plastic chair. His name was Gabriel Liberty, and at the age of seventy-nine he believed he had earned the right not to be kept waiting.

Half an hour he had been stuck here, confined in this airtight room, exposed to any number of germs. He stretched out his stiff legs and knocked over a tower of building bricks, which an ugly, snivelling brat had just spent the last five minutes constructing.

'Watch it, can't you?' the child's mother said. She put down her magazine, shuffled a handbag and a small baby on her lap, and bent to the brat who was now producing an annoyingly loud wail.

'It serves him right for being in my way,' Gabriel said. 'And while you're down there, wipe his nose. It's disgusting.'

A shrill ring sounded, followed by an even shriller voice announcing that the doctor was ready for patient number sixteen.

Gabriel hauled himself out of his chair. 'And about time too,' he muttered.

'I think you'll find I'm number sixteen,' said a hesitant voice from across the room.

Gabriel glared at a pasty-faced man in a flat cap, daring him to mount any kind of a real challenge.

'Oh, let him go,' said the mother of two, 'give us all some peace.'

Without bothering to knock, Gabriel entered Dr Cunningham's surgery. 'Humph, not seen you before,' he said, sitting down in front of the fake teak desk with a computer on one end and a shiny brass statue of a dancing woman with too many hands at the other. Sandwiched between the two was a spry little Indian man in his shirt-sleeves. His name was Dr Singh, if the engraved plaque in front of him was to be believed. 'What happened to Dr Cunningham?' asked Gabriel.

'He died.'

'Mm ... that doesn't surprise me. He never did strike me as a good advertisement for his profession. Always looked overworked and underfed.

Clearly wasn't practising what he preached. What got him, then? Every doctor's weakness, the booze and fags?'

'No. A car crash in Portugal while he was on holiday with his family. Did you not read about it in the local paper?'

'I've no time for local rags. Nothing but a load of old cods about jumble sales and potting-shed break-ins. The Portuguese are the worst drivers on earth, aren't they? Mind you, your lot aren't much better. I was in Delhi once, never seen anything like it. Just passing through, are you?'

Dr Singh gave him a thin smile. 'No, I'm here for the duration. How about you?'

'All depends.'

'On anything in particular?'

'Yes. On how soon I can get out of here. I'll either die of boredom being cooped up in this surgery a moment longer, or I'll catch something fatal.'

'Well, let's see if I can oblige you and send you on your speedy way.' Dr Singh turned and stared into the computer screen. 'I see it's some months since you last paid us a visit, Mr Shawcross. How's that lazy bowel of yours?'

Gabriel bristled at the man's effrontery. 'I'll have you know my bowel is in perfect working order, nothing remotely lazy about it. And the name's Liberty. Gabriel Liberty. You could at least get that right.'

Dr Singh frowned and tapped away at his keyboard. 'I thought Mr Shawcross was next on my list.'

'Oh, him – he wasn't fast enough. Probably that lazy bowel of his holding him back.'

Gabriel snorted at his own joke, but Dr Singh attacked his keyboard once more. 'Ah, here we are. Gabriel Liberty of Mermaid House, Hollow Edge Moor, Deaconsbridge. Is that you? Have I got *that* right?'

'It'll do right enough.'

Another glance at the screen gave Dr Singh his next question. 'So how are you getting on with your diet? Still keeping an eye on your cholesterol?'

'A weather eye at all times,' Gabriel answered. He almost licked his lips at the thought of the steak and kidney pudding with chips that he would be tucking into as soon as he got out of here.

Another glance at the screen. 'And your arthritis?'

Gabriel waved his distorted large-knuckled hands. 'I'm giving them a rest, decided to ease up on the fiddly work of brain surgery. Truth is, I can't find the brains. Not round here anyway.'

Dr Singh rested his elbows on the desk. 'So what can I help you with?'

'I was wondering when you'd get to the point. It's this . . .'

Lunch wasn't proving as enjoyable as Gabriel had hoped it would be. For a start his usual table was occupied by a couple of day-trippers, and then there had been no steak and kidney pudding on the menu; he'd had to make do with egg and sausage instead. He didn't like change. And he didn't like having to make do. Besides, egg and sausage he could do at home. Nothing to it. But steak and kidney pudding was another matter.

He was sitting in the Mermaid café overlooking the square where Friday's market was in full flow – local people were going about their business while tourists, brought out by the warm spring weather, were getting in their way. He sprinkled extra salt on to his chips, folded the newspaper that the café supplied and prepared himself for a satisfying assault on the crossword. To his annoyance someone had beaten him to it. He pushed it aside. The day was not going well.

As pathetic as it was, coming into Deaconsbridge had become the high spot of his week. It was the only day that had any structure to it. He came here every Friday to browse in the antiquarian bookshop, to pick up the odd item of food – kippers for his supper that evening – and to go to the bank and the post office. And, of course, to have his lunch cooked for him.

He munched a mouthful of sausage slowly and wondered at the tedium of his life. It wasn't an easy confession for him to make, but he was bored. Other than his younger son, Jonah, who did the bulk of his shopping for him, he rarely saw anyone during the week. And Jonah only ever made a fleeting visit. As for Caspar and Damson, well, if it hadn't been for Val's funeral, he might not have seen them at all these last couple of years.

It was strange, but since the death of his second wife eighteen months ago, he had thought more and more of Anastasia, his first wife. The memory of her had grown sharper as Val's faded. Anastasia had been the mother of his children and had died thirty-four years ago.

He had been away on business in Nigeria when it happened and had missed her death by twelve hours. In those days communication wasn't what it is today, and he had arrived home to be told that he was the widowed father of three children – Anastasia had died giving birth to Jonah. Help was brought in to take care of the children, but nothing was ever the same again. As the years passed, it was clear that the children, in particular the twins, Caspar and Damson, who were growing wilder by the day, needed a mother. So he married Val. It was a union of convenience on both sides: he had needed someone to organise the house and his family so that he could devote himself to the running of Liberty Engineering, and Val had wanted the security a husband could offer. They never deluded themselves that the arrangement was perfect, but he liked to think that it had worked well for the most part.

His plate had been cleared away some time ago and he was ready for his dessert now. He banged his spoon sharply on the table and caught the eye of a waitress. Fellow diners looked his way and he returned their stares disdainfully. Someone muttered how rude he was, but the waitress came over with his bowl of apple pie and custard, just as she always did when he summoned her with his spoon.

'Everything all right?' she said.

She asked this every time she served him. He supposed it was her equivalent to 'Have a nice day' and went with the ridiculous outfit she and the other waitresses wore – silly red baseball caps with short red overalls, which made them look as though they belonged in a theme park.

'No,' he said, 'everything is far from all right. I'm at the wrong table, there was no steak and kidney on the menu and what's more,' he thrust the paper at her, 'someone has completed my crossword.'

'We'll have to see if we can do better next Friday,' she said breezily. 'Tea or coffee?'

'You know I always have tea.'

He spent the rest of the afternoon doing his errands before awarding himself an hour of browsing in the bookshop.

Eventually he drove back to Mermaid House in a foul mood. He had had to abort his first attempt because he had forgotten to call in at the chemist's. With Dr Singh's words echoing in his ears he had turned the Land Rover round and gone back into town. The man was probably overreacting but he had said it was imperative that he started the course of antibiotics as soon as possible. He had also said that Gabriel would have to come into the surgery again in a couple of days to have the dressing changed.

A lot of fuss and bother about nothing.

Even so, it wouldn't hurt to take the quack at his word, seeing as the pain in his arm had been getting worse. It had been so bad the last two nights he hadn't been able to sleep.

'That's a very nasty burn, Mr Liberty,' the doctor had said, when Gabriel had rolled up his sleeve. 'It's also infected. When and how did you do it?'

'Some time last week. I . . . I was careless with the kettle.'

'And you didn't think to get it seen to?'

'I thought it would heal on its own.'

'Do you live alone, Mr Liberty?'

'What's that got to do with the price of eggs?'

Once again the doctor's eyes had scanned his computer screen. 'Your wife died not so long ago, didn't she?'

'She might have. What else have you got stored on there about me?'

'You'd be surprised. Now, push your sleeve right back as far as it will go and let me have a good gander.'

'You know, for a foreigner your English isn't bad.'

'And for a man with a burn the size of a chapati, you're lucky you're not in hospital. Any family to keep an eye on you?'

'Mind your own business.'

The approach to Mermaid House was almost a mile long and the bumpy track made for hard going; it was a toss-up whose suspension would give out first, the ancient Land Rover's or Gabriel's. Cursing as each bump jolted his arm, he knew he would rather die than be forced to move. What was a little discomfort when he had perfection on his doorstep?

Perched high on Hollow Edge Moor, and about a thousand feet above sea level, his home was surrounded by unrivalled scenery. The best in England, for his money. From the front of the house, and beyond the expanse of moorland, Deaconsbridge nestled in the shallow plateau of the valley with its old mill and factory chimneys just visible, but turn to the right, to the south, and you had the swell of the dales of the White Peak. Walk round to the side of the house, and on a clear day, the windswept hulk of Kinder Scout dominated the skyline.

When he let himself in, Gabriel saw that Jonah had been and gone. There were three carrier-bags of shopping on the table with a note saying he had put away the perishable items in the fridge and freezer.

Damn the boy!

It had become Jonah's habit to call when he knew his father was out.

3

The nature of Archie Merryman's work meant that he saw more than his fair share of bereavement. A house-clearance job usually meant that he was tidying up the loose ends of someone's life and death, and it never failed to touch him. Stripping a property of its furniture and possessions, hearing the echoing footsteps on floors where once there had been carpets, always made him feel that he had personally removed the heart from the house. No longer was it a home: it was an empty shell. It was only the thought of the next family moving in that kept him from becoming maudlin. He liked to visualise them taking up residence, children crashing down the stairs, doors banging, chairs scraping, cutlery rattling, the radio playing.

He was glad that after twenty-five years in the business he hadn't become hardened to it, and not just because it gave him a good reputation and the edge on the other second-hand dealers in the area, but because it proved to him that he was still the same old Archie. 'You always were a soft beggar,' his mother used to say to him, 'soft as cottongrass, that's what you are.'

He climbed into his van, smiled goodbye to the two women whose father's house he had just cleared. What wouldn't he give to hear a sentence as coherent as that from his mother these days?

He reversed the van slowly, mindful of the load in the back. None of it was particularly valuable – the best stuff had been taken away for auction – but to mistreat it seemed disrespectful to those who had once owned it. Some of it would end up at the tip – even he couldn't sell perished bath mats and crumbling cork tiles – but he would shift most of it.

It had been a big job and had taken him longer than he had expected. He preferred smaller houses, not because he was lazy but because he didn't like to get too involved. If you spent too long clearing a house, you ended up thinking like the family, unable to be objective. He had done it yesterday. 'Are you sure you wouldn't like to hang on to this?' he had asked the two sisters. From the expression in their eyes he had known he'd said the wrong thing. They had probably already put themselves through countless emotional hoops deciding what to keep and what to part with, and here was this outsider making it worse for them.

He trundled the van slowly down the hill, away from the stone-built farmhouse and its For Sale board. In his rear-view mirror he could see the two women still standing where he had left them. They were crying. It didn't surprise him – he had seen it all before. While there had been business to conduct they had held themselves together, but now that they were alone, they could go back to mourning the death of their father.

It was warm in the van and he lowered the window. Immediately he felt his spirits drag themselves up from his boots. At last it felt like spring was really here. He loved March: in lush green fields criss-crossed with a network of drystone walls, sheep grazed while skinny newborn lambs hopped and skipped on bandy legs. In the distance he could make out a kestrel hovering above something on the ground that had caught its eye. He sighed expansively. Despite all the sadness the world wasn't a bad place, and until someone came up with anything better, he'd stick with it a while longer.

He drove on and wondered what he would find at home that evening. Since his mother had moved in with them after her stroke, things between him and Stella had gone from bad to worse. 'Over my dead body' had been her exact words when he had suggested it, and he hadn't been surprised by her hostility: Stella and his mother had never hit it off – but he had hoped she would come round to the idea. Thankfully she had, and Bessie had moved in last month.

When Archie had invited his mother to come and stay with them, as he had euphemistically put it to her, she had agreed quite readily – to his relief: he knew how independent she was. 'We'll treat it as a holiday,' he had said, 'but without the sunburn.' He suspected that she knew she would never go back to her house in Derby. Meanwhile, her neighbours were keeping an eye on it so that she could return when she was able. The fact that a second stroke was likely to follow the first, and that it would probably be more debilitating, was not mentioned.

She had had the stroke just before Christmas, not a massive one but bad enough to knock the stuffing out of her. The tough, uncompromising woman he had always known became fragile and unsure. The stroke had robbed her of nearly all the strength in her right arm and hand, and her right leg had also taken a beating, which made walking slow and difficult. Making herself understood had been a problem too. Her speech was a lot clearer now, and that was down to weeks of diligent speech therapy, although at times it was still a puzzle to know what she was saying. If she was tired or anxious the words came out slurred or just plain jumbled – 'hum-dryer' for tumble-dryer, 'rare hush' for hairbrush. He had tried to turn understanding her into a game, calming her frustration with light-hearted humour, but Stella didn't have the patience for this and recently had shown signs of losing her temper. He didn't blame her – Bessie wasn't her mother after all.

The strain of being caught between a rock and a hard place – wanting to keep the peace with his wife and do the right thing by his mother – was taking its toll. Initially things had gone smoothly, but then the niggles had turned into rows and recently he and Stella had both said things that should never have been voiced. Until then their skirmishes had been conducted in low voices. 'She's my mother,' he had whispered one night in the kitchen, as Stella slammed cupboards and drawers. 'She's not well. What do you expect me to do with her?' It was a dangerous question, given that he knew exactly what Stella wanted him to do with her. But he would never do that. He saw too often the hurt and sense of betrayal as families, as well meaning as they were, shepherded their elderly relatives out of the houses they knew and loved and into nursing homes. Sometimes they went willingly, looked forward to giving up the reins of running a house in exchange for having everything done for them. But more often than not they were sad and confused, not quite understanding that they would never see home again.

No. He would not do that to Bessie Merryman.

What saddened him most was that his mother apologised frequently for having become a burden and there was nothing he could do to convince her that she wasn't. The woman who had brought him up single-handedly, and taught him always to see the best in others, would never be a burden to him.

His shop, Second Best, was situated on the corner of Millstone Row and Lower Haye in Deaconsbridge. It was a double-fronted Victorian building of stone that originally had been honey-gold but which was now blackened with age. Positioned just off the market square, it had the bonus of convenient parking to the side where, with Samson's help, Archie unloaded the van. Samson – his real name was Shane – was the extra brawn Archie relied upon for those larger items of furniture he couldn't manage on his own. At six feet two, Archie wasn't a small man, but Samson dwarfed him. His conversational skills were restricted to a nod and a grunt, but he was a godsend with a wardrobe on his back and a horsehair mattress between his teeth.

On the occasions when Samson was on a house-clearance job with Archie or they were delivering furniture to a customer, Comrade Norm – so-called because his parents had christened him Norman Lenin Jones – kept a part-time eye on the shop. There were days when they could have done with another pair of hands, but business wasn't consistently good. It could stretch to two and a half salaries, but any more and the financial knicker elastic would snap.

He said good night to Samson, checked that all was locked and secure, and set off for home, a ten-minute walk across town. The low evening sun brought a soft glow of light to the square, and now that everything was shut, apart from the Mermaid café, which stayed open until seven o'clock, a pleasing calm had descended. The market traders had gone, leaving behind a vacant cobbled square splattered with squashed fruit and veg and discarded hot-dog wrappers. Over by the war memorial, a blue and white carrier-bag was swept along by the breeze until it came to rest at the foot of

19

a litter-bin. It was only a few yards out of his way so Archie strolled over and popped it in. Straightening up, he waved to Joe Shelmerdine, who was just locking his bookshop.

Further along the street was the Deaconsbridge Arms, and although it had been done up by the brewery to draw in tourists, it was still where the old die-hard drinkers gathered to sup their beer and indulge in local gossip. Archie rarely showed his face in there. He wasn't a drinker: he had seen alcohol turn his father into a vicious bully and had grown up with a horror of it doing the same to him. He had come home too many times from school to find his father drunk and ready to take out his anger on the first person to hand. From a young age Archie had known that it was better for him to take the beating than his mother.

He carried on briskly – it was the nearest he got to working out like Samson did – but slowed when he got to Cross Street: it was one of the steepest roads in the town and it always took him by surprise, squeezed the air out of his chest and turned his relatively healthy fifty-five-year-old body into that of a wheezing ninety-year-old. He paused to catch his breath, leaning against the painted handrail on which generations of small children had swung upside-down like rows of multicoloured fruit bats.

He and Stella had wanted children, but sadly it wasn't to be, and as the years passed they had resigned themselves to being one of those childless couples who never quite fit in. They had moved to Deaconsbridge not long after they had married and had lived in a rented flat until they had enough money to put down a deposit on a three-storey end-of-terrace house in Cross Street. They had been here ever since. They could have moved, and Stella had been keener than him to do so, but somehow they had never got round to it.

When he reached home he let himself in at the back door and was surprised by how quiet it was. Usually the radio or the television was on, sometimes both competing to be heard.

A sixth sense told him something was wrong – the same sixth sense that had dried his mouth and made his hair stand on end just before Christmas when he had found his mother's home dark and silent. She had been lying on the floor by the side of her bed, her face twisted, her nightdress exposing more of her than was fair. When she saw him her eyes had filled with tears. She had been there since morning, unable to move, unable to call for help.

He moved fast now, calling her name as he took the stairs two at a time. He burst into what had been the spare room, but which was now her room.

She wasn't there.

Into the bathroom next.

Nothing.

He was just about to go into his and Stella's room when he heard her voice. He bent over the balustrade and saw his mother looking up at him from the bottom of the stairs.

'Ser-late,' she said, pointing to her watch.

He put his heart back where it belonged and joined her in the hall. 'Only a little late tonight,' he said, adrenaline still pumping through him. 'I had a busy day. Where were you? Didn't you hear me calling?'

She took his arm for support and led him slowly towards the front room. Once again the hairs on the back of his neck warned him of an impending shock.

On the mantelpiece, between a pair of decorative china plates, was an envelope with his name on it. He knew without opening it what it would say.

Stella had left him.

4

It was Sunday morning and Ned and Clara were being treated to a brunch-party send-off. While Moira helped Ned to the last of the chipolatas and crispy bacon, Clara watched the goings-on outside where Guy and David were putting the finishing touches to Winnie, the three-year-old camper-van that was soon to be Ned and Clara's new home.

Parting with her lovely Mazda MX5 yesterday morning had been a wrench for Clara, and even Ned had looked sad when they had watched the smart two-seater sports car being driven away by its new owner – it had always been a source of pride to Ned that he was the only child he knew who got to sit in the front of his mother's car. He had brightened, though, when the camper-van arrived.

It was second-hand, but in excellent condition, and unlike a brand new car it seemed to have a highly developed personality. There was a cosy feel to it that suggested happy times ahead.

When Clara had first seen it, the salesman had explained that its previous owners were a nice couple who had only parted with it because they were upgrading to something bigger. 'I had no idea camper-vans could be so well kitted out,' she had said, as they stepped inside and she felt the soft fitted carpet beneath her shoes.

'This is actually what we call a motorhome, and quite a modest one at that. You should see what we have at the top end of the market. The Winnebago, now that's what we call deluxe.' He pointed through one of the side windows to a massive bus-like vehicle that looked as if it might accommodate at least two touring rock bands.

'Heavens! How many does that sleep?' she asked.

'Eight. One of the beds is queen-size. There's even a washing-machine and tumble-dryer on board.'

Then, feeling disloyal to the modest camper-van they were supposed to be viewing, she said, 'Well, how about you show me what this baby has to offer?'

While Ned carried out his own inspection – opening doors, trying the driver's seat complete with armrests – the salesman had filled her in on the superior coachbuilt workmanship, the elegant interior, the spacious dinette, the two-burner combination cooker, the tilt-tolerant fridge and the swivel

22

cab seats. Ned had already discovered those – one minute he was facing the front, the next the back. With growing enthusiasm the young man showed her rattle-free lockers and cabinets. There were recessed halogen reading-lights, upholstered bench-seats, two surprisingly large wardrobes, a drop-down contoured hand-basin in the ingenious bathroom that contained a flushable toilet as well as a shower. He left the sleeping arrangements till last, showing her, with a magician's flourish, the double bed over the cab, complete with little ladder, and the two single beds in the dinette area that could also convert to a comfortable double.

'Did the previous owners have a name for it?' she asked, when at last he drew breath.

He gave her an odd look. 'Not that I know of. I could check the registration document if you want – it's in the office.'

'No, that's okay.' She sensed he was humouring her, probably thinking that after everything he had just gone through, she was just another time-waster. 'May I have a test drive, please?' she said, keen to re-inflate him. 'I'd like to see how it handles.'

He was immediately back into his stride. 'Certainly. Have you driven one before? It will feel quite different from what you've been used to.' He cast an eye in the direction of her sports car.

'I'm sure I'll get the hang of it.'

'Is it ours now?' asked Ned, climbing down the ladder from the bed above the cab while the salesman went to fetch the keys.

'Would you like it to be ours?'

He slipped into the driver's seat, grabbed the steering-wheel and *brrmm*ed noisily, trying to reach the pedals.

'I'll take that as a yes.' She smiled.

It was while they were driving home, after she had written a cheque for the deposit, that the camper-van had been christened. Clara had been thinking of the ridiculous eight-berth monstrosity and had said scornfully, to no one in particular, 'Winnebago. What kind of a name is that?'

'Winnie, Winnie, Bago,' chanted Ned. 'Is that what we're calling our camper-van?' he asked, looking up from the pile of glossy brochures he'd gathered from the salesman's office.

'We could shorten it to Winnie,' she said. 'What do you think?'

He considered her suggestion earnestly, then smiled. 'Pooh,' he said.

'Oh dear, can you hang on until we get home?'

A grin extended across his face. 'Not that. Winnie-the-*Pooh*.'

Apart from filling Winnie with provisions, clothes, books, toys, games, cassettes, a basic tool kit, and anything else they might need for the next five months, they had also had to pack up other possessions. During their absence, a young professional couple would be renting their house and were moving in on Monday. Initially Clara hadn't wanted to let it, but common sense had dictated that she might as well have the money coming in to pay off the mortgage. Then her savings wouldn't receive such a large dent. It also meant that she would be committed to what she had started. With no house to come back to until the end of August, she would have to make a go of the trip.

Her friends had been concerned about money. 'I just don't understand how you'll manage,' Moira said.

'I've got a PEP that's just dying to be let loose,' she had said. 'I know that would only get you through a long weekend, Moira, but our needs will be quite modest while we're away. And if the worst comes to the worst we could resort to busking.'

'I wouldn't put it past you.'

'Oh, and since when did I become such a rebel?'

'You've always been a rebel, Clarabelle,' Guy had said. 'You've never been fully in step with the rest of us.'

Though Clara knew that there was an element of truth in what he had said, she was hurt to hear it voiced so openly. She and Ned had not yet travelled a mile, but already a gap was opening between her and the gang. 'You mean I'm different from you lot because I'm not married and I don't trade in my house every other year for something bigger and better?'

'Now, don't get nasty with Guy,' Moira had said. 'It's not his fault he still hasn't forgiven you for spilling the beans about Margaret Thatcher not being the Tooth Fairy.'

Suddenly everyone had an opinion about her.

David said, 'You know jolly well that you're the resourceful one of us. For goodness' sake, you're the only one sitting round this table who knows what to do with a power drill. When was the last time you had to have a "little man" in? Eh?'

'Nothing ever fazes you, Clara,' Louise put in. 'While we've become childishly self-indulgent as we've grown older, you've turned into a sensible adult.'

'That sounds worryingly like a criticism to me,' Clara said defensively.

They ignored her and carried on, warming to their theme. 'You're a natural facilitator,' Guy said. 'A doer who has to do things her way.'

'Are you saying I'm bossy?'

'Well, you do like to be in charge, don't you?'

'Not always!'

'Face it, Clara,' David said. 'You put us all to shame. Just look at what you've achieved single-handedly. You've carved out a great career for yourself, you have—'

'A great career I'm wilfully throwing away,' she chipped in, wanting to redress the balance of this cringe-making conversation.

He had waved her interruption aside. 'And you have a fantastic son, who even you would admit is your crowning glory.'

'Enough!' she had cried.

Clara was still watching the antics of her friends outside when Louise came and joined her at the window. 'Just look at them! Anyone would think you were getting married.'

Decorated with party streamers and shaving foam, Winnie indeed looked like the archetypal honeymoon getaway vehicle.

'You know, it's not too late to change your mind about this hare-brained caper,' Louise said.

Without turning her head, Clara said, 'And why would I want to do that?'

'Oh, you know, now that it's the day you're finally setting off, it might be dawning on you – the extent of your madness and the terrible mistake you're making. Only you're too proud to admit you might have been a little hasty.'

Now Clara did turn and look at her friend. 'And you're too proud to admit that you're envious of what I'm doing.'

'Me? Jealous of being cooped up in a box on wheels for five months with a chemical loo? You must be joking!'

'Come on, Louise. Admit it! Aren't you just a teensy-weensy bit envious that I'm escaping, taking time out so that I can enjoy each day as it comes?'

'No, I'm not. I'm more concerned with living in the real world, not this frothy concoction you've invented for yourself.'

'It feels real enough to me.'

'Mm . . . let's see how it feels in a week's time when you're bored of your own company and Ned says he's homesick.'

Clara looked across Louise and David's sitting room to where Ned was on the sofa with Moira. A momentary pang of uncertainty made her wonder if she wasn't being entirely honest with herself. Who did she think would benefit most from this trip? Herself or Ned?

Both of them, she told herself firmly. She needed a break from work and to be with Ned. 'Boredom and homesickness won't be an issue,' she said. 'What we'll experience will be just as real and valid as anything that's going on round here.'

'But it will only be as real as a holiday, which, when it comes to an end, will bring you back to where you started.'

'Maybe it won't. Maybe I'll find my personal Utopia out on the road and never come home.'

'And you can take this as a first official warning. If you stop washing your hair, pierce yourself just once and turn into a New Age hippie, I'll publicly disown you.'

Clara smiled. 'Is that a promise?'

'Oh, come here, and give me a hug. I'm going to miss you. You will write, won't you? I'll need the occasional phone call, too, to keep me going.'

Clara hugged her back. 'I'll miss you too. And of course I'll keep in touch. You don't think I'd pass up the opportunity to brag about what a wonderful time I'm having, do you? Rubbing your snooty nose in my happiness will give me the greatest pleasure.'

They drew apart. 'And don't you dare quote me,' Louise said, 'but, yes, part of me is jealous of what you're doing. Who wouldn't be?'

Clara embraced her again. 'And that happy thought will be with me every time I clean out the Chemi-loo!'

A bang on the window made them both jump. Guy and David's open-mouthed faces were pressed against the glass; it wasn't a pretty sight.

'And there's another happy memory for you to take with you,' laughed Louise. 'A matching pair of gargoyles!'

At last they were ready to go.

'Come on, you intrepid explorers,' David said, lifting Ned down from his shoulders, 'that's enough of the goodbyes. It's time you were on your way.'

'Glad to know you're eager for us to be gone,' said Clara. She settled Ned into the front passenger seat.

'That's because the sooner you go, the sooner you'll be back, sweetie-pie.'

'I wouldn't count on it.'

'You're all talk, Clarabelle. A hundred quid says you'll be crawling back to us within the month and applying for your old job.'

She held out her hand to Guy. 'Two hundred says I won't.'

He grasped it firmly. 'Done!'

Clara hugged everyone all over again and received their unhelpful words of advice with good grace. No, she wouldn't talk to strangers. No, she wouldn't hold the traffic up too much. And yes, she would remember to respect the countryside.

Louise moved in to have the last word. 'And don't do anything stupid while you're away.'

'Such as?'

'Such as taking any unnecessary risks. We want you to come back in one piece. Okay?'

'This may come as a shock to you, Louise, but that's something I'm keen to do myself.'

An hour into the journey and with Walton-on-Whinge – as she and the gang referred to Walton-on-Wineham where they all lived – well behind her, Ned had fallen asleep: the combination of excitement and anticipation had caught up with him. She turned off his story tape, and now that she was used to driving Winnie and had more or less mastered the vagaries of the gear-lever – roadworks and stop-start traffic on the M25 had seen to that – she relaxed a little and thought how wonderfully free she felt chugging along in the inside lane of the M40 with High Wycombe soon to be ticked off on her mental route-planner. She loved the idea of being able to stop at a moment's notice, park up wherever and feel instantly at home. It was this that had appealed to her when the idea had first occurred to her to take Ned travelling. A camper-van would provide a home-from-home environment that would give them a comforting sense of self-sufficiency. And certainly, right now, with Ned at her side, she felt as if she had everything she would ever want in the world.

A car overtook her and the driver gave her a wide smile. She wondered why. But then she remembered what Guy and David had done to the van – most of the streamers had blown away, but the balloons were still tied to the wing mirrors and door handles.

She switched on the radio. A song came on that she recognised – it was Nanci Griffith singing 'Waiting for Love' – and it tugged painfully at her heart. She had first heard it when she was living in America, and it would be for ever synonymous with that period in her life.

She had only recently arrived there, single and carefree, looking forward to the challenges of a year-long secondment at Phoenix's headquarters in Wilmington. Determined to work hard and further her career, she had wanted to make the most of the opportunity.

But it hadn't been quite the career move she had thought it would be. She had returned home before the end of her secondment with a bruised heart and a pregnancy to explain to her friends and family.

5

Gabriel was up earlier than usual. Last night when he had drawn the curtains the track had fallen down. Dust and bits of plasterwork had showered over him and something had got into his eye. He had tried bathing it with an old eye-bath he had found in the medicine cupboard, but it hadn't helped. Now, after a sleepless night, his eye hurt like hell and every time he blinked it felt as if the lid was coated with sandpaper.

Before going downstairs to make himself some breakfast he went into the bathroom and had another rummage in the cabinet, hunting through the shelves of old pill bottles and pots of gunk Val had sworn by. Right at the back, on the top shelf, he found what he was looking for: an ancient eye patch. The elastic had perished but he tied a knot in it, and it held firmly enough around his head. His hands were so annoyingly stiff and clumsy that it took him a few minutes to achieve this. He closed the cabinet door and took a long, hard look at himself in the dirty, black-spotted mirror.

He was presented with an unshaven, grey-haired old man wearing a black eye-patch.

He smoothed down his thick uncombed hair, which was sticking up all over his scalp, then he turned his head, and decided he looked no better sideways on. The long straight nose Anastasia had described as proud and regal had turned into something that didn't fit on his face any more; it looked too big, as though he had borrowed it from an older brother in the hope that he might grow into it. His cheeks had lost their firmness and sagged under the weight of so many lines. His mouth had withered into a rigid downward curve. Thick drooping earlobes hung at either side of his face and abundant bristly tufts sprouted from them. Dear God, when had he become such an ugly brute?

He walked the creaking length of the balustraded landing, avoiding the rucks in the threadbare runner, and paused, as he did every morning, to look down on the garden. The sun was still low in the eastern sky, but a pale light shone on the sloping lawn, planted sporadically with daffodils. It stretched down to a thick bank of rhododendrons that were yet to burst into flower, and beyond was Hollow Edge Woods, a copse where generations of foxes and badgers had lived. Way off in the distance, the swell of sheep-grazed hills rose up to the morning sky. He rested his hands on the stone sill and thought that Byron had got it right when he had compared Derbyshire with Greece and Switzerland, saying it was just as noble.

It had been love at first sight for Anastasia when she had seen Mermaid House. She had been an incurable romantic who acted on impulse and was inventively quirky, hence their children's bizarre names. But she had had her work cut out in convincing him to buy the house – he was so conventional and analytical. It cost much more than they could afford, and was miles from where Liberty Engineering's factory was situated, but eventually he had given in to her. He could still see her bright eyes flashing with delight as she whirled him round the room when he agreed to put in an offer.

It was only when they moved in that they appreciated the state of the place. It dated back to the mid-nineteenth century, and it was a wreck: dry rot, wet rot, any rot you cared to think of, Mermaid House had it in spades. Busy with work, he had left Anastasia to deal with it – it was her baby, after all. She threw herself into its restoration, determined to see the job thoroughly well done – and their bank balance just as thoroughly depleted. He had never regretted it, though. To see her happy was enough. And then Caspar and Damson had arrived. The upheaval in their lives was colossal, but Anastasia took the twins in her stride. She never complained of being tired, when night after night she sat in the nursery in the rocking-chair with one or other of the blighters on her shoulder. She never minded how little they slept, or how mischievous they were once they began to explore their surroundings, pulling themselves up on to their chubby legs and ransacking cupboards, drawers, shelves, constantly searching for something new to play with – and break. They were an inseparable two-man destruction derby: nothing was safe with them around. Gabriel had wanted to employ a nanny to help Anastasia, but she wouldn't hear of it, claiming that she loved the challenge of two such lively children.

It was five years before they took the plunge again and tried for another child. Then Jonah was born.

And Anastasia died.

By craning his neck to the left and pressing his head against the window, which was cloudy with dirt, Gabriel could just see the spire of the church in Deaconsbridge; it was where both of his wives were buried.

He tightened the belt of his dressing-gown and continued along the landing, passing closed doors to dusty rooms he hadn't been inside for months. He took the stairs slowly: his one-eyed view gave him a misleading impression of the floor – it wasn't as close as he thought it was. The staircase was yet another reminder of Anastasia: she used to refer to herself as Scarlett O'Hara as she swept down it in a graceful rush of laughter, her long hair tumbling around her shoulders.

The kitchen didn't catch the morning sun, and even in the height of summer it was the coldest room in the house. Val had had an Aga installed and had stoked it with coal morning, noon and night. It had been worse than a demanding baby: as she shovelled in fuel at one end, it deposited ashes at the other. She had soon tired of that and had had it converted to gas. Not long after her death it, too, had given up the ghost – something to do with a faulty thermostat that couldn't be replaced.

Since then Gabriel had bought himself a bog-standard electric cooker and one of those portable heaters on wheels with a large gas cylinder inside it. He switched it on now – he had to keep clicking the button until eventually a spark ignited the gas and a whoomph of flame shot across the blackened panels. It had been when he was doing this, the other week, that he had burned his arm. He had deliberately lied to Dr Singh about being careless with the kettle because he had thought that otherwise it might seem that he couldn't be trusted with a gas fire. Scalding oneself sounded less dangerous, somehow.

It was four days since he had been into Deaconsbridge and had his arm seen to. He hadn't been back to the surgery; he had decided there was no point. He had finished the short course of antibiotics several days earlier than he should have, working on the theory that the pills would take effect faster if he tripled the dosage on days one and two. What was more, he had changed the dressing himself, swapping the bandages and gauze for a clean handkerchief and securing it with a couple of safety-pins. By rights the doctor should be grateful for being let off the extra work. If more people were like Gabriel, the National Health Service wouldn't be in such a mess.

But now he had this wretched eye to deal with. He would give it a day or so, and if there was no improvement, he would go into Deaconsbridge – make his Friday visit on Thursday perhaps. He pressed the heel of his hand against the eye patch, resisting the urge to give it a damn good rub. It was so itchy and sore. To distract himself he set about making a pot of tea for his breakfast.

For such a large kitchen, there was little space to work in: every surface was crowded with crockery and paperwork that lay in untidy piles awaiting his attention. As did all those things that needed mending, but which he never got round to: an Anglepoise lamp that wouldn't stay in position; a battery charger he'd ordered from one of those junk catalogues and had dropped and broken; an iron that needed a new plug; a wobbly mug tree; a wooden bread bin that wouldn't open properly; and several shirts that were down to just a few buttons. But the mess was getting to him; there was something tidal in the stealthy manner in which it was creeping up on him. He would have to do something about it soon.

But not today.

Domesticity didn't suit him. He wasn't cut out for defrosting freezers or knowing how to get a crease-free wash out of the washing-machine. Val had taken care of all that. It had been her domain and he had willingly left her to it. He wasn't ashamed to admit that he was old school when it came to defining the boundaries of a husband and wife. The system had worked perfectly until the world had gone mad and everyone had become obsessed with equality and role reversal.

He switched on the wireless to listen to the *Today* programme, sweeping aside several days' worth of plates, cups, knives and forks, dirty pots and pans and a couple of empty pilchard tins, until at last he had cleared a space around the kettle and toaster. His breakfast made, he added a tot of twelve-year-old Glenlivet to his tea, just a drop to kick-start his day. Time was when a new day for him had been like cracking an egg – short, sharp, and he was off. Now he had to ease himself into it. He sat at the cluttered table and answered the wireless back, dishing out his objections and criticism with a fair hand: he disagreed on principle with everything the presenters or politicians said.

He was still sitting at the table when he heard a knock at the door. He checked his watch, as though it would tell him who was bothering him at such an unsociably early hour. But it was later than he had thought, almost ten o'clock. Even so, who could it be? Callers at Mermaid House were rarer than hens' teeth.

There was another knock, louder this time. Whoever it was seemed determined to summon him to the door. He pushed his feet into his slippers and shuffled off reluctantly to deal with whoever had come to bother him. He slid the bolts back, top and bottom, turned the key and opened the door.

'What the hell do you want?' Gabriel growled, when he saw Dr Singh standing before him. 'And don't tell me you were just passing and thought you'd see if I was in.'

'No, Mr Liberty, I wouldn't dream of lying to you. I am here because you didn't keep your appointment with me. You didn't return to the surgery for me to check your arm.'

'Very considerate of you, I'm sure. But (a) I didn't make an appointment, and (b) you've wasted your time in coming here because my arm is better.'

'Perhaps you would be good enough to let me be the judge of that.'

Gabriel gave him a hard stare. 'Persistent, aren't you?'

'Professional is how I like to view myself. Now, then, are we to conduct surgery business on the doorstep, or am I permitted to come in?'

'Suit yourself.'

Gabriel showed him through to the kitchen and realised at once that this was a mistake. He could feel Dr Singh's dark eyes appraising the situation, and the mess seemed a hundred times worse. The bottle of Glenlivet on the table didn't give quite the right impression either, especially as he was still in his shabby old pyjamas. Damn! He should have taken him into the drawing room. In fact, any room but this. He pushed up the sleeve on his dressing-gown, deciding that the sooner the infuriating man had examined his arm, the sooner he would be gone. 'There,' he said, removing the makeshift bandage, 'just as I told you. Practically as good as new.'

Dr Singh gave the handkerchief a disapproving look, but nodded at the improvement in Gabriel's arm. 'You're right, it's healing nicely. But since I'm here I might just as well apply a proper dressing, and while I do that, you can tell me what you've done to your eye.'

'I got something in it last night,' Gabriel said airily. 'It's a bit sore, that's all. There's no need for you to have a gawp at that too.'

But Dr Singh insisted that he be allowed to do his job. 'And how did you come by this?' he asked, when Gabriel had removed the patch and the eye began to water at the sudden brightness.

'A curtain track fell on top of me, if you must know.'

After pulling a small-beamed torch on him, Doctor Singh said, 'I don't like the look of it. You need to see a specialist. It's inflamed and you might have damaged the retina.'

'Don't be absurd. I've just got dust in it, that's all. Can't you give me some drops or something?'

'The "something" is a trip to hospital, Mr Liberty. Do you really want to risk going blind in that eye?'

'God! You foreigners make me sick. You're all the same, you come over here, you get yourselves an education at our expense, then start telling us what to do. Well, you know what you can do with your trip to hospital, don't you?'

Dr Singh put away his torch and snapped shut his medical case. 'Mr Liberty, listen very carefully to what I am about to say. Either you do as I say or I shall inform Social Services that you are living in squalor and that you are incapable of looking after yourself. And, trust me, they will descend upon you faster than you can say Enoch Powell and you will rue the day you ever ignored my advice. So, *old chap*, what's it to be?'

Gabriel's jaw dropped. 'You wouldn't dare.'

'Care to put me to the test?'

'Couldn't we just try the eye drops first?'

'No. Now, if you would be so good as to get dressed, I will drive you to the hospital. I was going there anyway.'

'What? Right now?'

'No time like the present.'

'I don't approve of blackmail,' Gabriel said, as he folded himself into the doctor's Honda hatchback. His knees were almost tucked under his chin, the top of his head jammed against the roof. Typical of the bloody Japanese to build cars for midgets then inflict them on the rest of the world.

'It wasn't blackmail,' Dr Singh said, 'it was a straightforward deal. We negotiated quite openly. There was nothing underhand about it. But tell me, why don't you have any help around your mausoleum of a house?'

'Who said I didn't?'

'Your standards must be low if you let a cleaner off so lightly.'

'If it's any of your business, I got rid of the last woman after I caught her stealing from me. I didn't object to her helping herself to the odd bit of loose change lying about the place, but I drew the line at her sneaking out of the house with my best single malt whisky stuffed up her knickers.'

'How long ago was that?'

'Nearly a year.'

'And no other help since then?'

'What is this? Twenty questions and then you file your report to Social Services?'

They juddered over the cattle grid at the end of the track where two stone pillars marked the entrance to Mermaid House, then joined the main road. 'Tell me about your family. Do they live nearby?'

Gabriel shifted the seat-belt that was cutting into his neck. 'Are you asking me why they don't act the part of doting children and pop in every other day to see how the old man's doing?'

'I might be.'

A slight pause hung between them before Gabriel said, 'We have a perfectly balanced relationship: they can't stand me and I can't stand them.'

Dr Singh slowed down for a sheep that was nonchalantly crossing the road. 'Those are harsh words,' he said. He turned to face Gabriel, looked at him gravely. 'Do you not feel the heavy weight of them? Do you not wish it could be otherwise?'

Seconds passed.

'The sheep's gone now,' Gabriel muttered. 'You can drive on.'

6

With no class before lunch, Jonah decided to bunk off school. He pulled on his jacket and took the stairs two at a time. At the bottom, pressed against the lockers in a slobbering, face-washing clinch, he found Tim Allerton wrapped around Shazzie Butler. They hadn't heard him coming, so he stood perfectly still, just long enough to induce in them the right level of embarrassment when they noticed him. He gave a discreet little tap on the locker beside them. 'A-hem.'

They sprang apart, which wasn't easy, given the tangle of arms and legs.

Assuming a deadpan expression, he said, 'On the basis that by now you've fully explored each other's dental work, perhaps you would be so good as to find your way to whatever lesson you should be attending. You know how I value your input as regards helping the school to sprint up the league tables.'

He strode off, leaving them to wipe themselves down.

Outside in the car park, he opened the rusting door of his J-reg Ford Escort, wondering, as he always did, why he bothered to lock it. Half the kids he taught at Deaconsbridge High – or Dick High, as its inmates affectionately referred to it – would have it open without the aid of a key in seconds flat.

He turned right out of the school gates and took the Lower Moor Road towards the centre of town, passing a dismal housing estate and an even uglier industrial complex. Back in the early 1970s, liberal town-planners had been assiduously fair with their unimaginative architectural handouts and had given Deaconsbridge High the same ugly status as its immediate neighbours. At roughly the same time as decimalisation had made its mark on the country, the evils of cheap flat-roofed urbanisation had hit Deaconsbridge. Since then, and in the last decade when restoration had become the watchword, money had been lavished on the small town centre so that it might compete with rival tourist attractions like Castleton and Buxton, but the outlying areas had received no such philanthropic gestures. Occasionally there were calls for a bypass, since the hordes of lucrative trippers had been successfully drawn to the town, but the seasonal density of traffic didn't yet warrant such outlandish expenditure.

And it was just as well that the traffic was so light, as Jonah was in a hurry. In the centre of the town, he joined the one-way system, drove along the war memorial end of the market square, then up towards Hollow Edge Moor. He was going to see his father, and had planned it this way deliberately. With only an hour and a half available to him, he would be able to say what he needed to say then get out. Direct and to the point, that's what he had to be. Above all else he must not flinch at his father's response, which would, of course, be of the ballistic variety. Many times he had witnessed, and been on the receiving end of, one of his father's furious dressing-downs, and on this occasion he was preparing himself to be stripped to the bone.

In his mind he had every line of the conversation already figured out, with every vindictive word his father would throw at him.

For starters he would be accused of being devious and too big for his boots, not to say conniving. Next he would be told he was the messenger of his cowardly brother, and that he was weak and too stupid to make a proper life for himself. It wouldn't be the same if that old line wasn't given an airing. Jonah was quite used to the torrent of scorn that was regularly poured on his teaching career.

'It's only those who can't get a proper job who teach,' his father had said, when Jonah had graduated from university and announced that he was applying for a year's teacher training course.

He didn't discuss it further with Gabriel, and certainly he didn't look to him for financial support. He paid his own way through college by working shifts in a meat-processing factory and as a consequence hadn't been able to look a meat and potato pie in the eye since.

That had been thirteen years ago, and still Gabriel hadn't forgiven Jonah for settling for such a 'second-rate' career.

Jonah always felt a chill run through him when he came home to Mermaid House. A knot of anxiety formed in the pit of his stomach, with the desire to make his visit as short as possible. He tried to kid himself that it was the bleakness of the house and its remote situation that made him feel like this, but he knew it wasn't. It was the memories.

Mermaid House was of an unusual, almost whimsical design, with a tower, four wings and a central cobbled courtyard. It was built of locally quarried stone that had turned depressingly dark and dreary with the passing of time. Now, as Jonah drove through the wide stone archway, the rumble of his car engine was amplified: it bounced off the walls and came back at him louder than it normally did. It confirmed what he had suspected earlier that morning when he had driven to work, that his exhaust was blowing.

He parked next to his father's mud-splattered Land Rover in front of what had always been known, rather ostentatiously, as the banqueting hall: it boasted original timbers, trusses and a massive fireplace.

Getting out of his car, he noticed that the tax disc on the Land Rover had expired and that the tread on one of the tyres looked borderline legal.

He crossed the courtyard and found the back door unlocked. He knocked cursorily, let himself in and nearly took a flyer over a pair of old boots lying on the floor. He pushed them to one side, called to his father, and walked through to the rest of the house. He passed the laundry room, noting the piles of unwashed clothes, bedding and towels in front of the washing-machine, and kept going, past the gun room, until he came to the kitchen.

These days, the mess seldom shocked him; it shocked him more that he had grown used to the conditions in which Gabriel was prepared to live. There was the unappetising smell of gone-off fish and he located the source of this as an empty tin of pilchards in tomato sauce on the draining-board. He went to throw it in the swing-bin but found that it was full to the brim. It was indicative of the scale of the problems at Mermaid House. No job was ever in isolation. There was always a knock-on effect. To change a light-bulb, you had to find the stepladder, and to find the stepladder you had to find the key to the cellar, and the key was anywhere but where it should be on the row of hooks in the kitchen.

It hadn't always been like this. When Val had been in her prime she had run the house with military precision, determined, against the odds, to instil in the three children a sense of shared duty. 'It's a large house, so I would be grateful if you could all pull your weight,' she had told them. On the first day of their holidays, when they were home from school, she would line them up and go through the running order. 'Damson, I'd like you to do the dusting and polishing in the dining room, and Caspar, you can clear out the ashes from the grate in the drawing room and bring in some fresh kindling. Jonah, I've put the silver on the kitchen table for you to clean.'

'Why does he always get the easy jobs?' Damson had pouted mutinously.

'Because he's the youngest. He's not as big and strong as the pair of you.'

Just as rebellious as his sister, Caspar would argue frequently that their father was rich enough to have a host of servants to do the work. But Val would have none of it. 'We no longer live in an age of servants, young man. We have Mrs Harper to help us, but she is not a servant.'

Ignoring whatever scornful comment Caspar would make, she would clap her hands and send them on their way. And always there would be the same music played at full volume while they did their chores. Even now, Jonah could never hear a piece of Gilbert and Sullivan without wanting to reach for the silver polish.

The meticulous order that Val so prized was lost when she suffered the first of a series of minor heart-attacks. As she slowly slipped away from them, she took with her the smooth running of the household. Mrs Harper, who was well past retirement age, handed in her notice and a succession of local cleaners proved unsatisfactory: the sheer size of Mermaid House overwhelmed them: ten bedrooms and three bathrooms was more than they wanted to take on.

It was more than any sane person would want to take on, thought Jonah, as he stood in the middle of the chaos. Suddenly he had the urge to hire the largest skip he could get hold of and throw everything into it. How tempting it was to clear the decks and start again. He would give his stubborn, sore-headed father the clean slate he needed. But he knew that that would never happen. Only a nuclear bomb would clear these particular decks.

But it was a bomb of sorts that he had come here to drop.

He called to Gabriel again, and helped himself to an apple from the bowl of fruit he bought religiously every week for his father, and which Gabriel rarely touched, then wandered out of the hall. He checked the drawing room, the dining room, and finally the library, where the curtains were drawn to protect the shelves of books from being damaged by sunlight. But there was no sign of his father. He stood at the bottom of the stairs and shouted, his voice echoing in the musty emptiness of the high-ceilinged house. There was no answer.

The irony was not lost on Jonah. Every week he did his father's shopping for him, and tried to time his appearance at Mermaid House for when he knew his father would be in Deaconsbridge so that he could avoid speaking to him. Now he wanted to talk to him and he couldn't.

Where was he?

Perhaps he had gone for a walk. Well, if he had, there was no point in looking for him. Jonah didn't have time to mount a search party. He would have to come back another day.

To his shame, he felt relieved as he retraced his steps the length of the house, knowing that, for now, he wouldn't have to go through with what Caspar had asked him to do.

He was about to use his own key to lock the back door – Gabriel really shouldn't leave the house unlocked – when he thought better of it. His father might have forgotten to take a key with him.

Outside in the pleasantly warm sun and taking another bite of the apple, Jonah looked at his watch and decided he had time to see to the balding tyre on the Land Rover. But when he checked the spare, he found that it was in an even worse condition.

Sometimes there was just no helping Gabriel Liberty.

7

It was four days since Stella had left him, and while Archie wasn't entirely surprised by her departure, he had been taken aback by the way she had gone about it. It was the coward's way out and he had never thought of Stella in that light.

The note had been blunt and to the point. It seemed that the affair he had thought was over had picked up again and Stella had decided, at last, where her future lay. And it was not with Archie, the man to whom she had been married for twenty-six years and who had failed to give her the children she had always wanted.

Indicating right, he pulled off the main road and turned sharply into the hospital car park. He felt angry. It was always Stella who was supposed to feel the loss of not having children. What about him? Why hadn't his feelings been taken into account? After all, it was he who had to live with the knowledge that he wasn't man enough to become a father, he who had taken the jibes when Stella's disappointment turned to bitterness. He had wanted children, too, but no one had thought he was bothered by his and Stella's incompleteness as a couple and no one had thought to ask.

Next to him, now that they were parked, his mother was struggling with her seat-belt. 'Here, love,' he said. 'Let me.' He pressed the red button and released the strap.

She straightened her hat and smiled at him. 'Ready now,' she said.

'Ready.' He smiled back.

She had dressed specially for the occasion – a trip to the speech therapist was a big day out for her. Archie had been roped in as chief style guru. 'Pink or glue?' she had asked, holding out two dresses as he sat on the edge of her bed eating his cornflakes.

'Definitely the pink,' he had said, trying to sound decisive. A hint of dithering on his part and they'd never get out of the house this side of sunset.

It seemed to work, and she held the dress against her in front of the long mirror. Then, lowering it, she said, 'Or maybe the . . . the . . . the . . .' She squeezed her eyes shut, pursed her lips, and at the back of her mind, where some prankster was rewriting the English language for her, she located the word. She snapped her eyes open and said, proudly, 'Or the cheese?'

38

He proceeded carefully. If he gave the wrong answer, the limited supply of good words available to her this morning would shrivel to nothing. He gave the matter serious consideration before he tapped the air with his spoon. 'No, I still think the pink would be best. Very Liz Taylor, when she was at her best. Shall I help you?'

He helped her now to take her seat in the hospital waiting room, and could feel the heavy tiredness in her body: the short walk from the car park had sapped most of her strength. But it did nothing to dampen her desire to enjoy her big day out. She smiled at the woman opposite, who also looked as if she was dressed in her best party frock – she had overdone the makeup, though, and the red lipstick clashed with the frilly purple neckline. The man sitting next to her, presumably her husband, looked dog-tired, and Archie wondered what unearthly time the pair of them had got up to get ready for their appointment.

But the woman didn't respond to the warmth of his mother's smile. Disappointed, Bessie turned to Archie and, in a voice that should have been a whisper but missed the mark by several decibels, she said, 'Cobbly cow.'

He tried not to laugh, and was still trying to contain himself when it was Bessie's turn to see the young girl who was patiently teaching her to speak again. Though with a phrase as beautiful as 'cobbly cow' – so much better than 'snobby cow' – he wondered whether it wouldn't be more fun to teach the rest of the world to speak as Bessie did now. He left them to their phonetics and flashcards and went in search of a polystyrene-flavoured cup of tea that would scald the top layer of skin clean off his tongue.

The vending-machine was situated in a bright, airy space where pieces of artwork from the local comprehensive were displayed on the stark white walls. There was an atrium-style roof to this modern extension – opened by a local soap star last year – and it felt more akin to a fancy hotel than a hospital. Not that Archie had had any first-hand experience of fancy hotels: the nearest he had got to one was when he and Stella were celebrating their twenty-fourth wedding anniversary. He had planned it as a surprise. He let her think he had forgotten about it, then on the day, while she was getting ready for work, he had presented her with tickets for the train to London and a show.

But it hadn't turned out the way he had hoped it would. She was moody and distant with him, and found fault with almost everything: the train took too long, the hotel was too small, the food too expensive and the show too loud. During the journey home he had wondered if everything would have been to her liking had she been with someone else. He kept the thought to himself, but he soon knew the answer. He found letters and a couple of photographs. He hadn't gone snooping, they had been left casually in a drawer, not even covered up; it was as if she had wanted him to find out. If she had been hoping for a confrontation, he must have disappointed her: he simply carried on as though everything was normal, convincing himself that if he ignored it she would get it out of her system and things would soon be okay again. Plenty of marriages had glitches; it was all about riding the storm. After a while he thought he had done the right thing. She stopped inventing reasons to be out of an evening, there were no sudden trips to see her sister, and the phone no longer rang with no one on the other end when he answered it. But she wasn't happy. If anything, she was worse – tearful, or irrationally angry. He almost felt sorry for her, imagining that her lover had decided to call a halt to the affair. Perhaps he, too, was married and hadn't wanted to jeopardise what he already had.

Stupidly, Archie spent more time than was healthy putting together a background for this unknown man. Was he younger than Archie? Better-looking? Funnier? More intelligent? Rich?

With the benefit of hindsight, he had been nothing but a coward. Instead of wasting time dwelling on her lover, he should have been talking to Stella, making an effort to understand where he had gone wrong.

But he had left it too late. All the talking in the world wouldn't make things right now. She was gone, no doubt to this perfect man who understood her. Who didn't . . . who didn't have an ageing mother to care for.

He swallowed the last of his tea and suddenly felt weary.

How would he manage Second Best and look after Bessie on his own? She wasn't so bad at the moment, but he could see that in the future she would need a constant eye on her. He crumpled the empty cup, dropped it into the nearest bin, and cursed himself for having taken advantage of Stella in the way that he had. In relying on her to be at home during the afternoons – she only worked mornings – he had felt that he was doing the right thing by his mother. It served him right that Stella had left him. He had given her a gold-plated final straw.

With ten more minutes before Bessie would be finished, he went for a stroll. He was just passing a couple of pretty nurses who were chatting about a hen party they'd been to last night when he caught sight of a face he recognised. It was that nice Indian doctor from the surgery in town, the one who was always so good with his mother. He was friendly without being overly familiar, which Bessie liked. She always used to say that if you had to undress for a doctor, the least he could do was look the other way, and Dr Singh was wonderfully courteous and proper with her.

Archie went over to say hello. 'Touting for business, Dr Singh?'

'Ah, Mr Merryman, how good to see you. Are you here with your mother?'

'Yes. She's with the speech therapist. It's slow going.'

'Patience, Mr Merryman, she'll get there in the end. Remember what I told you, there's life after a stroke so long as everyone involved pitches in. You just have to keep the faith.'

'I know. Some days she's quite clear, but others I can't make head nor tail of what she's saying. So what brings you here?'

'An errand of mercy. And here he comes right now.'

A tall, spectacularly grizzled man came towards them. A white dressing covered one of his eyes but not the scowl that darkened the rest of his face. 'Bloody hours I've been stuck here, and it's all your fault, you interfering little man!'

Not missing a step, Dr Singh was the epitome of politeness: 'Do you know Mr Liberty, Mr Merryman?'

'Er . . . no.' Archie held out his hand. 'Pleased to meet you, Mr Liberty,' he said affably. But when the other man made no attempt to shake it, he said, 'Well, then, I ought to be getting back. Bessie will be wondering where I am.' He turned to go.

Behind him, he heard, 'A bloody waste of time. Nothing that eye drops wouldn't have sorted. Just as I told you!'

'So aren't you the lucky one, Mr Liberty!'

After calling in at the shop and checking that Samson had everything under control, Archie took Bessie for a cream tea at the Mermaid café. A treat to round off the day for her.

'We should do this more often,' he said, when Shirley had served them with her customary good humour. She was a good sort, was Shirley; nothing seemed to bring her down, not even the break-up of her marriage several years ago. He passed his mother a cup of tea then set to work on the scones. He cut one in half, spread a dollop of strawberry jam on it then topped it off with a layer of cream, but when he gave it to her, his heart fell. From her pained expression he could see that he had assumed too much. He had treated her as an incapable invalid and robbed her of her dignity. 'I'm sorry,' he murmured, appalled at his lack of thought. 'Would you rather do it yourself?'

She shook her head. 'I'm well,' she said softly. 'Not ill, Archie.'

'Of course you are,' he agreed. 'You're absolutely fine. Now, tell me what the speech therapist said to you. Did she give you any gossip about that cobbly cow with too much lipstick?'

She brought her eyebrows together as she always had when she rebuked him as a child. 'Serious,' she said, pointing a finger at him. 'No fish pies. Tell me the truth about Stella.'

'What about?'

'Why?'

He knew what she was asking, but he didn't want to go down that route. Not yet.

When he had read the letter Stella had left him, he had shoved it into his pocket and gone out to the kitchen to make a start on their supper. Minutes later Bessie had appeared in the doorway and gone along with his need to pretend that nothing out of the ordinary had happened. Helping her into bed that night he had made up a story that seemed to satisfy her.

But now, four days on, she wanted to know what was going on.

'Why?' she repeated.

'Stella's left me, love,' he said. 'She's not coming back. I lied when I said she'd gone to her sister in Nottingham for a few days.'

For once Archie was glad that his mother's speech was so limited. They sat in a long, awkward silence, their eyes cast down as they concentrated on their scones. Then he heard her say, 'Is it me? Left you because of me?'

He looked up and saw that his mother's eyes had filled with tears. One of her hands had started to tremble and crumbs were scattered around her plate. His heart went out to her. 'No, love. She didn't leave because of you. It was me. I should have been a better husband.'

He had to turn away. He knew exactly what she was thinking: that she had become a burden to him, and that she had wrecked his marriage. She was wrong.

8

When the phone rang Jonah was standing on the top rung of the stepladder. He knew straight away who it was. Caspar was the only person he knew who could make the telephone ring with menace, and could be relied upon to do it at the worst possible moment.

He put the brush between his teeth, picked up the pot of paint, and made his descent. By the time he had found the phone under the dust-sheet by the side of his bed, and had switched off the Haydn piano sonata, he could easily picture his brother's tight-lipped face at the other end of the line. Just for the sheer hell of it he let it ring three more times before he put the receiver to his ear.

'Liberty Escort Agency, how may I help you?'

'Yeah, very funny, Jonah. Now, if you could act like the adult you're supposed to be and quit fooling around like one of those idiots you teach, perhaps you'd tell me how you got on. What did the old man say?'

'Absolutely nothing.'

'I find that hard to believe.'

'Not a word.'

There was a pause.

'Oh, I know what happened, you didn't see him, did you? You lost your bottle just as I thought you would. You always were a coward.' Caspar's voice was hard.

'You could always talk to him yourself,' Jonah said mildly. 'It *is* your idea.'

'Look, we've been through this before. These days, you're the only one who can get anything sensible out of him. He'll listen to you.'

Exasperated, Jonah pushed a hand through his hair. Too late he realised there had been a smear of Windsor Blue emulsion on his palm. He turned to look at himself in the mirror above the chest of drawers and saw that his wavy dark hair – the bane of his life as a boy – now had a blue streak running through it. Better than yellow, he thought, with a rueful smile.

'Jonah? Are you still there?'

'Sadly, yes. And I don't know why you think I'm any different from you and Damson.'

A loud snort told Jonah that if he didn't divert his brother, he would be subjected to the familiar lecture on what it was to be the hard-done-by Caspar Nobody-loves-me Liberty. 'Actually, I did go and see him this morning, but he wasn't there.'

'So what was wrong with trying again when you'd finished work?'

'This might come as a surprise to you, but when I'm not carrying out your dirty work, I do have a life of my own.'

'But you fetch and carry so well, brother dear. Who else can I rely on in this splintered family of ours?'

'It's not a family you need, Caspar,' Jonah said, 'it's a battalion of henchmen. Now, if there's nothing else, I'm in the middle of decorating, so I'd appreciate it if you would let me get on.'

'Good God, why do you insist on living like a peasant? Get a genuine peasant in to do it for you.'

'Caspar, was there anything else?'

'Yes. Speak to Dad as soon as you can. Every day you botch this up, is another day of . . . well, never mind that, just do it.'

Back on the stepladder, Jonah resumed painting his bedroom ceiling. If ever a child had been born to upset the sibling apple cart, it had been him: Caspar and Damson had never let him forget that his birth had precipitated their mother's death. As children they had been cunning and wilful, had taken pleasure in setting him up as the fall-guy and enjoying the spectacle of him being punished. If anything went missing, you could bet your bottom dollar it would be found in his bedroom, hidden at the bottom of the wardrobe. If anything got broken, you could guarantee that he would be positioned right by the smashed window-pane or the shattered vase.

Their devious schemes worked every time. They would pretend they had decided to let him be a part of their coterie and, like the fool he was, so desperate to be accepted, he would go along with whatever dare or initiation ceremony they felt inclined to put him through. He fell for it time and time again, hook, line and sinker. He was the perfect stooge, trailing behind in their contemptuous wake, needing their approval, wanting to be just like them: the mysterious, all-powerful twins who were at the centre of their own universe where, stupidly, he also wanted to be.

That was before he became scared of them.

Once, when they had said he could join in with their latest game, they had put a blindfold around his head and shoved him into cold water. He was only six and they said all he had to do was swim to the other side of the river. It had rained constantly for the last week and the river was higher than usual; as the force of the water rushed pell-mell down the hillside, the strengthening swell had swept him away. He could still remember their laughter as they ran along the bank beside him, and it wasn't until he banged his head on a rock and began to scream that they hauled him out. They shook him hard, pulled his hair and slapped his face to make sure he didn't pass out, then marched him back up to the house. 'We found him down by the river,' Caspar told Val, 'causing trouble again. It was lucky for him we happened to be passing, otherwise he might have died.'

Caspar was the most convincing liar Jonah had ever come across, then or since.

By the age of nine he had wised up and kept his distance from his brother and sister, shutting himself away in his room. But whenever they got the opportunity they played their games with him. They would sneak into his room late at night when he was asleep and steal whatever was precious to him – stamps, comics, books, pocket money. Gradually, though, he learned to outwit or second-guess them. He discovered that he was smarter than they were, and by the age of eleven he was spending more time in their father's library than anywhere else. He discovered that trying to gain Gabriel's approval and respect was infinitely more worthwhile than being accepted by Caspar and Damson.

Until then his father had been little more than an occasional visitor in his life, forever away on business, immersed in his own affairs, an autocratic figure. But when Jonah showed an interest in the books Gabriel had collected over the years, the two almost connected.

Jealousy caused the twins to step up their bullying campaign but they soon found themselves in more trouble than they could have imagined. Late one night Gabriel discovered them in his library, defacing two of his most highly prized first editions. Their plan had backfired. They were grounded for a month, their allowance was stopped, their combined birthday party cancelled, and they were put to work by Val to clean out the attic. It was then that Val began to question the previous crimes Jonah was supposed to have committed.

They never discussed any of these things as a family, that would have been far too open and communicative, much better to sweep it under the mat and pretend it never happened.

On one occasion, aged thirteen, Jonah had behaved completely out of character. It only happened once, but it was such a shocking act of violence that, even now, the memory made him flinch. He had been away at school, and the bully of his year had picked on him once too often: he had stolen a fountain pen Val had given Jonah for Christmas. Incensed, Jonah flung himself at the boy, pushed him to the floor and beat him mercilessly. With no teacher in the classroom, everyone else had left their desks and grouped around to watch the mild-mannered swot bashing the living daylights out of the boy who, in Jonah's mind, had become Caspar and Damson rolled into one. But while he was hailed by his peers as a hero, the headmaster was less inclined to praise him: Jonah was caned and made to write a five-page essay, answering the question 'Which offers man the greater chance of survival: pacifism or violence?' Ironically, his essay was so good that he was awarded a prize for it at the end of term.

If Jonah had a less than generous opinion of his brother and sister, the regard they held each other in could not have been higher. In Caspar's view

Damson could do no wrong, but as far as Jonah could see she had spent most of her adult life switching from one good cause to another with intermittent bouts of selfabsorption. Of the three, she was the only one to have married. She was also the only one to have divorced twice, and lucratively so. She was currently going through what she called her 'centred space' phase and was living, in peace and harmony, in a commune in Northumberland, which she had described as a self-help therapy centre in a hand-crafted Christmas card to Jonah last year.

This latest search for her inner self was just another in a long line of explorations from which she would doubtless emerge to plunge back into the hedonistic lifestyle she enjoyed: men, partying, shopping, and whatever else made her think she was happy.

Jonah didn't think she had ever been truly happy.

On the stroke of midnight, Jonah called it a day. It was handy living next door to a church: there was no danger of losing track of the time when the bells rang out every hour and slipped in a quick chime on the half-hour too.

He had moved into Church Cottage last August when he had come back to the area as head of history at Deaconsbridge High. Before then he had been living over yonder border – as die-hard Deaconites called it – in neighbouring Cheshire. He had been ready for a change and had followed his instinct when he had seen the post advertised. It had seemed the right thing to do, given that his father was now on his own with little sign of Caspar or Damson offering any help around the house.

And it was the house that was at the bottom of Caspar's insistence that Jonah speak to Gabriel. Caspar could dress it up any way he liked, but Jonah knew his brother too well. Caspar didn't give a damn about their father's welfare: all he was concerned about was getting his hands on the capital that would be released if Mermaid House was sold. Jonah had no idea what Caspar did with the money he earned – he owned one of the most prestigious car dealerships in south Manchester and had to be ripping people off for a decent amount – but however much it was, it clearly wasn't enough. Jonah had dared to query this the other day when Caspar had hinted that money from the sale would come in handy. He had been told in no uncertain terms to keep his nose out of things he didn't understand. 'Money is hardly your area of expertise, Jonah, so butt out! Just convince the old fool that he needs to move into something smaller and we'll all be better off.'

Much of what Caspar had said was true. Jonah wasn't a financial pundit and their father had reached an age when he might be better off living in a property a tenth of the size of Mermaid House. He had been thinking the same thing ever since Val had died, but had never found the right time, or the courage, to broach it with Gabriel, not when he knew how insincere and grasping it might sound to their father. It was annoying, though, that Caspar's thoughts had coincided with his, albeit for different reasons.

What his brother didn't know was that Jonah intended – if his father would listen to him – to make it clear that if Mermaid House was to be sold, Gabriel should not siphon off a penny of what it brought to his children to avoid inheritance tax, which, naturally, was the main thrust of Caspar's argument for selling up now.

Caspar would capitalise on a third-world disaster if he thought he could get away with it. And there were many things Caspar had got away with over the years. Just as he had stolen from Jonah as a child, he had continued through adulthood to help himself to anything else to which he took a fancy. So far Jonah had lost two girlfriends and a fiancée to his brother.

Admittedly the loss of the girlfriends had taken place during his teens, but Emily had been another matter altogether and he wasn't sure that he could ever forgive Caspar for what he had done.

Downstairs in the kitchen, while he washed the paintbrush under the tap and squirted a dose of Fairy Liquid on to the bristles, Jonah wondered if a family as bitterly divided as his could ever be reconciled.

9

With Ned's help, and with the aid of a simple device that turned the white plastic barrel into a mini garden roller, Clara was pushing their fresh supply of water across the dewy grass of the Happy Dell campsite towards Winnie. It was one of the many things about camper-vanning that Clara enjoyed: the multitude of unexpectedly clever gadgets that made life a little easier.

This was their fourth day on the road, and already Clara and Ned considered themselves old hands at it. They were perfectly at one with the intricacies of their cassette toilet, could turn a dinette seat into a double bed with the speed and professionalism of a Formula One pit stop, could knock up mouth-watering meals on the two-burner stove at the flick of a hand and, perhaps more importantly, they could do it all without once feeling as though they were living on top of each other. It was extraordinary how quickly they had adapted to living life in miniature. It reminded Clara of when she'd been a little girl and had played constantly with the doll's house her father had made for her. She had been fascinated with the scaled-down world he had created, and it was the same for her now with Winnie. Everything was so incredibly well designed, and appealed to her logical way of thinking and her need for order. As a child she had been ridiculously organised: her mud-pies were always neatly prepared, her bedroom was tidier than any other room in the house, her schoolwork immaculately presented – and always handed in on time – her social life thought out with every consideration given to when, how, where and with whom. And woe betide anyone who interfered with this carefully ordered infrastructure. At the age of ten, she had spent hours drawing cut-away sections of houses, each room in minute detail, and people joked that one day she would become an architect, or maybe an interior designer. When she expanded her repertoire to sketch the roads the houses occupied, then mapped out whole villages and communities of harmonious synchrony, they suggested town planning. Her brother accused her of being a control freak.

But if Winnie appealed to Clara's desire for pigeon-holed regularity, it was a joy to see how Ned, too, loved their new home, especially his bed over the cab. He would lie up there with Mermy and his battalion of cuddly toys, pretending to read to them from his favourite storybooks, and Clara was relieved that, so far, he had shown no sign of missing anything he had left behind. But, as Louise would have been quick to point out, it was early days yet.

Much as Ned loved the bed to which he had to climb up, there was a disadvantage in the arrangement, which had come to light on their first night. At three in the morning he had woken needing the toilet. It was the kerfuffle of him sitting up, bumping his head and letting out a cry that had woken Clara. It took her a few seconds to gather her wits, switch on the reading light and climb up to him. Parting the curtains, she had helped him down and carried him to the loo. He was so drowsy that she had had him tucked in again and fast asleep before she was back in her own bed.

But he had always been a good sleeper, even as a baby. At two days old he had slipped straight into a comfortable, convenient routine of feeds and napping that had rendered her parents nostalgically envious. 'Why weren't you and Michael like this as babies?' her mother had said, bending over the Moses basket and itching to smother her first grandchild with love as he slept on, his tiny hands balled into fists the size of walnuts, his lips quivering like butterfly wings. 'You both had me up at all hours, never gave me a minute's peace. Ooh, look, he's opened his eyes. Do you think I could . . . ?'

Clara and her father had exchanged a smile. 'Go on, Mum, while I make us a cup of tea; he's all yours.'

'And you can stop right there, young lady,' her father had said. '*I* will make the tea. And if I catch you moving just one inch from that chair, there'll be trouble.'

'Better do as he says, Clara, you know what a tyrant he can be.'

For years it had been a family joke that her father was a tyrant: the truth was, he was the biggest softie going. And he had been particularly kind and loving with his grandson. Once Ned was walking and talking, her father had come into his own, reading to him, teaching him to do simple jigsaws and taking him to the park. 'Come on, my little pumpernickel,' he would say, helping Ned into his hat and coat, then strapping him into the pushchair. 'Time for some man-to-man business down at the park. Let's go and feed the ducks.'

Clara knew that Ned's lack of a father tapped into her parents' old-fashioned instinct for a nuclear family, but she was happy to let her own father fill the void created by the man who could never be in Ned's life. He did it so well, never overstepping the mark, just quietly providing that indefinable extra for which Clara would always be grateful.

In the last few days she had noticed a change in Ned: he was fast becoming what her mother would describe as 'quite the little man'. He was forever insisting that he help her with everything he could. He particularly liked doing the washing-up. He would stand at the small sink on the step that was supposed to be used for getting in and out of the camper-van, up to his elbows in sudsy water. The job took a lot longer than if she did it herself, but it was such a pleasure to see him so involved that she didn't have the heart, or inclination, to stop him. And what did it matter how long anything took to do? They were in no hurry now.

Since leaving home on Sunday they had slowly made their way north. Their first night had been spent at a campsite in Stratford-upon-Avon, where the following day they had immersed themselves in all things Shakespearean and, more to Ned's liking, had visited a museum devoted to teddy bears. They had seen the original Sooty, and Clara had reminisced about her first pantomime, when she had sat in the front row and been soaked by Sooty and Sweep with water pistols.

From Stratford they had moved on to the West Midlands, taking in Cadbury World and the Museum of Science and Industry in Birmingham. Ned had been as pleased as punch when their guide picked him out from the crowd to press the button to start the steam engine. He was happier still when they left an hour later with a model of it, and he had spent the evening back at Winnie explaining enthusiastically to Clara how it worked.

Until now, they had decided together where to go each day while curled up in bed and flicking through touring books and maps. But their next port of call was to be a surprise for Ned, which Clara hoped he would enjoy.

When they had packed everything neatly away, and had paid the man in the campsite office, they were ready to go.

'Chocks ahoy,' said Ned, as he did each morning when they set off.

She smiled. She had given up telling him it was 'chocks away'. 'Chocks ahoy' sounded just fine to her. The people on the next pitch waved goodbye. They were an interesting couple in their mid-fifties who called themselves 'full-timers'. They lived all year round in their camper-van, which they had personalised by painting Ron's name on the driver's door and Eileen's on the passenger's. Over a glass of wine late last night, when Ned was asleep, they had given Clara their list of the top ten campsites in Britain. They were out of the way, not always listed in the touring guides: it was to one of these that Clara was heading today. Ron and Eileen had also shared with her how they had become 'full-timers': after giving up secure jobs, they had spent the last two years fruit picking in the summer and early autumn, then hooking up with fellow full-timers and travelling south to Spain and Tunisia for the winter.

Now, as she tooted Winnie's horn at them, Clara wondered what Louise and the rest of her friends would make of Ron and Eileen.

With the map spread open on his lap, his elbows resting on the armrests at either side of him, and his finger planted firmly on the streak of blue that was the motorway they were following, Ned looked every inch the seasoned navigator. That the map was upside down was neither here nor there. By Clara's reckoning they had about thirty miles of motorway driving left before they would strike out cross-country.

'Shall we stop at the next service station to stretch our legs?' she asked.

Ron and Eileen had said that if there were free facilities to be had it was their duty to take full advantage of them rather than waste their own resources.

Ned looked up from the map. 'When Nanna says that, Granda says his legs don't need stretching. He says he's tall enough already.'

Clara smiled. 'It's called a euphemism.'

He tried the word out for himself. '*Eu-fer-miz-um*. What does that mean?'

'Well, it's when we use a word or phrase to disguise what we're really saying, to make it sound more polite. I was really asking you if you wanted to stop and go to the toilet.'

He thought about this. 'Like when Nanna asks me if I want to spend a penny?'

'Exactly.'

'*Eu-fer-miz-um*,' he said again.

Ned's vocabulary was quite advanced for his age, and Clara put this down to his having spent more time with adults than children. Neither her parents nor her friends had ever talked down to him: they had always treated him as a mini-adult and he had responded accordingly, absorbing information at a phenomenal rate. With so much adult company around him, she had dreaded him turning into a precocious brat, but thankfully there seemed little likelihood of that.

After they had euphemistically stretched their legs and spent their pennies, they joined the motorway once more, and, with the map the right way round, Ned looked at it hard and asked where they were going.

She gave him a sideways smile. 'You're not catching me out that easily. I told you, it's a surprise. Wait and see.'

'But will I like it? Surprises aren't always nice.'

'I'll make you a promise. If you don't like it we'll move on somewhere else.'

An hour later, and with the M6 behind them, Clara took the B5470 out of Macclesfield and found herself driving through rolling hills of lush green farmland criss-crossed with a threadwork of drystone walls. It came as such a surprise that she slowed down to take a better look. It was beautiful, just as Ron and Eileen had said it would be. 'If we could get the work up there, that's where we'd spend our summers,' Ron had said. 'Believe me, you'll love it. It's terrific walking country.'

But it wasn't hill walking that had drawn Clara to this part of the Peak District, it was what, according to the guide books, had also drawn Victorian day-trippers from the neighbouring industrial towns and villages: the chance to see a mermaid. Not a live one, but an underground cavern that claimed to have a rock formation that looked just like the real thing and granted wishes for those prepared to dip their fingers into the clear still water of its pool. Given Ned's love of Mermy – who was currently in his hand – and his desire to meet a real one, this was probably as near as she could get to fulfilling a dream for him.

They drove on, the road becoming steeper, the houses fewer and the scenery even more stunning as it stretched before them beneath a picture-postcard blue sky with puffy white clouds. Suddenly, making her jump, Ned pointed Mermy at the window to his left and cried, 'Mummy, look at all the sheep on the green mountains.'

'Those are what people round here call hills, Ned.'

'Even that big one over there?'

Clara smiled. 'A mere Brussels sprout. Perhaps later on our trip we'll go up to Scotland and see some real mountains.'

'I like it here. Is this my surprise?'

'Not quite. Now, I'm going to have to concentrate on the road. I'm looking for a sign that says Deaconsbridge. Shout if you see anything with a big D on it.'

The road climbed higher and higher, until eventually they reached the summit of a hill. Dropping into a lower gear, Clara took the descent steadily, with extra care on the tight bends.

Their first sighting of Deaconsbridge revealed a small town nestling in the shallow dip of a valley. From a distance it looked a soft shade of industrial grey with rows of terraced houses tucked into the slope of the hillsides, their uniformity broken by a scattering of old mills and stately chimneys. A church with an elegant spire stood self-consciously to one side of the town, surrounded by a cemetery, whose gravestones seemed to flow out into the expanse of moorland behind. As final resting places went, Clara thought it was pretty spectacular.

With a queue of cars itching to overtake them, they trundled ever nearer, and just as the road began to level, narrow and guide them to the centre of the town and its one-way system, Ned bounced in his seat and let out a loud, excited cry. 'Look, a mermaid! And there's another. Over there! Mummy, there's lots of them!'

Once Clara had squeezed Winnie into the pay-and-display car park – no mean feat, given how busy the small town was and the lack of space available – she could see that Ned was right: Deaconsbridge was awash with mermaids. Almost every shop front in the market square where they were parked had a sign depicting a mermaid, and each one was different. They ranged from shy lovelies coyly submerged in water, showing just a modest hint of scaly tail, to pert blonde bathing belles posing on rocks, and buxom Page Three beauties flaunting themselves shamelessly. But the sign Clara liked best was the one above the antiquarian bookshop, which portrayed a sylph-like creature reclining in an armchair reading – the spectacles were a nice touch, she thought.

Across the square, and opposite where they were parked, a sign showed a rosy-cheeked mermaid wearing an apron and holding a large wooden spoon. It was a convivial and inviting sight. 'Welcome to Deaconsbridge, Ned,' Clara said. 'Ready for some lunch?'

10

The Mermaid café was busy and at first glance Clara thought they would have to try somewhere else. But in the furthest corner, and beneath a large mirror flanked by two prettily stencilled mermaids on the wall, she could see a waitress clearing a table that had just been vacated by a couple of intimidating-looking leather-clad bikers now queuing at the counter to pay their bill. One smiled at Ned, who stared at his pony-tail, earrings and the shiny studs on his fringed jacket, then smiled back, revealing two rows of perfect milk teeth.

The waitress continued to add dirty plates to a tray already stacked high with an assortment of crockery and metal teapots, and for a few moments Clara and Ned were forced to stand with the two bikers. The one who had smiled at Ned did so again, this time adding a wink. Then he turned to Clara. 'He's a cute-looking kid,' he said. 'A dead ringer for his mum, or his older sister, perhaps? If you want a worthwhile tip,' he went on, 'we can recommend the chef's special. You can't go wrong with it.'

'Insider knowledge,' said his friend, tapping his long straight nose. He reached into a small basket of lollipops for younger diners and gave one to Ned. 'Here, have this on us.'

Ned's face lit up. 'Thank you,' he said.

'You'd better keep it for when you've had your lunch, though. We don't want any trouble from your big sister.'

Clara was about to add her thanks to Ned's when the waitress came over. 'Sorry to keep you waiting, dear,' she said, 'but these leather joy-boys make so much mess.' She gave the two bikers a broad grin.

The one who had spoken first to Clara gave the waitress's red cap a light flick. 'Mum, I've told you before, keep the wisecracks for when we're at home. Do you want me to take that tray through to the back for you?'

'No, Robbie, I want you to pay your bill and sling your hook. You're cluttering the place up. Now, are you or are you not going to make a start on the spare room for me this evening? I've got the wallpaper and paste for you.'

'Wouldn't miss it for the world.'

Thanking the two young men for the lollipop, Clara shepherded Ned towards their table, and quickly, before anyone else nipped in ahead of them to claim it.

'Those men were nice,' said Ned, settling himself into his chair and placing his unexpected gift on the checked plastic tablecloth. He propped Mermy against a bowl of sugar.

'They were, weren't they?' she replied, letting him get away, just this once, with pilfering a sugar cube. She could see that he was now wondering how to slip it into his mouth without her noticing so she bent down to her bag on the floor. She thought about the two young men, one of whom had treated her to some friendly flattery. He must have been at least ten years her junior. Big sister indeed!

Catching sight of herself in the mirror above Ned's head, she supposed the new haircut made her look younger. She had gone for a radical change in Stratford, deciding that her shoulder-length hair would be a pain to take care of while they were away. In the salon, everyone had agreed that the new style took years off her, that her dark hair now framed her small oval face perfectly and accentuated her brown eyes.

She turned away from the mirror and, with the two bikers – who admittedly had not been her type – still on her mind, asked herself when had been the last time a man had paid her an unexpected compliment?

She couldn't remember and wondered when she had become so unaware of or immune to male charm.

Since Ned had been born, she had had little time, inclination, or opportunity to seek out a boyfriend, although there had been one or two skirmishes, in particular a disagreeable incident on an industrial-relations course eighteen months ago. Then a pushy type with groping hands and gin-soaked breath had tried his luck with her in the bar one night. She had blown him clean away: 'What makes you think an intelligent woman like me would be interested in a prat like you? Now, push off before I throw my drink in your face.'

It wasn't that she didn't feel comfortable with men, far from it, she usually preferred their company to that of a crowd of women, but she knew that to embark upon a series of going-nowhere relationships would do her no good. Also, she didn't want to confuse Ned by bringing home a succession of men. And, perhaps more importantly, she had a very real fear of accidentally getting pregnant again.

Not that she had ever regretted having Ned. She loved him just as much as if she had planned his conception down to the last detail.

Through the café window she watched the pair of swaggering lads in their leathers cross the road to the car park where two powerful-looking motorbikes were waiting for them, their well-polished chromework glinting in the afternoon sun. She watched them strap on their helmets, then heard the throaty roar of the engines, and though she had never before had any desire to sit astride anything more dangerous than a tricycle, she thought she could detect a change in her view now. Goodness, less than a week on the road and she was considering a wind-in-the-hair experience!

She plucked the menu from its wooden holder, and saw that the chef's special they had recommended was not a body-building tough-boy three-pounder burger but a vegetarian lasagne.

'What are you smiling at, Mummy?'

She raised her eyes from the menu. 'Myself, Ned. Now, what would you like to eat?'

They feasted on sausages, beans and chips, followed by the best Bakewell tart Clara had ever tasted. When she commented on this to their waitress – biker-Robbie's mother – she was told, 'I'll tell my sister that, she'll be well pleased. It's an old family recipe.'

'Is this a family business, then?'

'No. It's just a coincidence that we work together. Are you here for the day, or staying longer? The weather's supposed to be breaking by the weekend, so you'd best do your walking sooner rather than later.'

'Is that what everyone does round here – walk?'

'That, and go down the cavern to see the mermaid. To be honest, there's not a lot else to do.'

Ned leaned forward in his seat. 'A mermaid? Is it real?'

The waitress's eyes flickered over Mermy on the table. She sucked in her breath. 'Well, now, it's as real as you want it to be, I suppose. But if you've come to see it, you're too early. It doesn't open for another week. The tourist season round here hasn't got into full swing yet. You could always go across to Castleton or down to Buxton. Between them they've got more caverns than they know what do to with.'

'Do they have mermaids?'

'No, my fine little fella, it's only us that can boast something as special as that.'

They left the café unsure what to do next. If the Mermaid Cavern wasn't open for another week, should they move on somewhere else and come back, or stay put and use Deaconsbridge as a base for visiting the surrounding area?

Keeping her options open, Clara decided they would inspect the campsite Ron and Eileen had raved about and take it from there. She put this to Ned as she unlocked Winnie and stood back to let out the fuggy warmth that had built up inside the van while they had been having lunch. But now that Ned had heard about the Mermaid Cavern, he clearly didn't want to move on. 'If we don't like the campsite,' he said anxiously, climbing into his seat, 'we could find another, couldn't we?'

'If that's what you'd like to do, then yes.'

She started the engine, reached for the map, then regretted not having thought to ask their friendly waitress for directions to the Hollow Edge View campsite. It wasn't mentioned in the *Touring Parks* magazine she had used so far on the trip, but Eileen had said it was somewhere off the Hollow Edge Moor road. The road, or what Clara thought was the right road, was marked on the map and, with hope rather than solid conviction, she manoeuvred Winnie out of the market-square car park and went in search of a pitch for the night.

Nearly an hour had passed before she gave up. 'This is ridiculous,' she said, exasperated, when they found themselves, yet again, on irritatingly familiar ground. 'We've been up and down this road so many times we're on first-name terms with all the sheep. I'm sure they're laughing at us behind our backs.'

'Sheep don't laugh,' Ned said seriously. 'They go *baa*.'

'And I'll go *baa*-ing mad if I don't find this wretched campsite. I could also do with going to the loo. I'll just drive down this handy little track and park up.'

Ignoring the 'Private – No Entry' sign turned out to have been a mistake. The handy little track was longer and narrower than Clara had expected, and with drystone walls almost touching Winnie's sides there was no space to turn round. She had no choice but to keep going until it either branched off into another road, or offered her the opportunity to do a ten-point turn – reversing was not a viable proposition: it was the only trick of driving a camper-van that she hadn't yet mastered.

However, as mistakes went, it presented them with some of the best views they had seen so far and confirmed what Clara had read in the guide book last night, that Deaconsbridge, sandwiched as it was between the Dark Peak of Derbyshire and its southern White Peak counterpart, was home to an interesting combination of the two. Way off in the distance, and after checking the map, she could see the bleak windswept moor of Kinder Scout to the north. Referring to the map again, she could see that if she carried on along this road they would eventually come to a belt of trees and a dwelling called Mermaid House. It looked as though the road widened sufficiently by the trees to allow her to turn and drive back to join the main road once more.

Her guesswork proved right, and in the shelter of the trees, she brought Winnie to a halt. 'Time to stretch my legs,' she said, smiling at Ned as she climbed out of her seat to go through to the toilet.

When she came out, Ned said, 'Can we go for a paddle? I can see a bridge over a stream and there might be some fish we could catch for our tea.'

'They'll have to be very lazy fish, the type we can catch with our bare hands.'

He slipped out from his seat. 'It's easy. I saw it on the television. This man had a stick and he watched until the fish came right up to him and then he—'

'Yes, I get your drift,' she interrupted, not wanting the gory details. 'Couldn't we just shake hands with them and invite them in for a fish supper?'

He rolled his eyes. 'Fish don't have hands, Mummy.'

'You sure about that? What about octopuses? I thought they had eight hands.'

'Now you're being silly. Everyone knows they're called testicles.'

She laughed. 'Tentacles, Ned. Come on, my little genius, let's see if there's a nice bit of smoked salmon just waiting to make our acquaintance. But it will have to be quick. I really do want to find that campsite before the light goes.'

Taking a rolled-up towel with them they approached the bridge and the length of river Ned had spied. It twisted along the lower edge of the screen of trees, tumbled down the slope under the bridge and, gaining speed, gushed on further down the hillside.

'It'll be cold in there,' Clara said, looking doubtfully at the clear shallow water as it rushed over the stones. 'Wouldn't you rather play Pooh sticks?'

Beside her Ned was already sitting on the grassy bank and tugging at his laces. 'We could play that after. Help me, please, Mummy. This one's in a knot.'

She untied the lace for him and rebuked herself for sounding so old and boring. Where was the spirit of adventure that had brought her here in the first place?

Despite the warmth of the spring sunshine, the water was icy cold, just as Clara had predicted; it made them both gasp and squeal as they dipped in their toes. They rolled up their jeans, and bravely went in deeper. Clara held Ned's hand as they waded out, and now that she couldn't feel her toes, she joined in the game of looking for their supper. 'Do you think there are sharks here, Ned?'

'Ssh!' he whispered. 'I can see something.' He let go of her, bent down to the water, cupped his hands, and made a sudden scooping movement. 'I've caught something!' he cried. He peered through the gaps between his fingers.

Amazed, she lowered her head to see what he had.

He shrieked with delight and splashed her face. 'Fooled you!'

'Why, you little monkey! For that, you can have a taste of your own medicine.'

The water fight was noisy and spectacular, and left them both drenched. Shivering, but still laughing, they slipped on their shoes and went back to Winnie to change into some dry clothes. They were soon warm again, and just as Clara was about to make them a drink – tea for her and blackcurrant juice for Ned – they heard an engine. Ned, who was sitting in the driver's seat, stuck his head out of the window.

'It's a car,' he said. 'A green one. It's got two men in it and it's stopped behind us. They're getting out.'

Clara decided it was time to investigate. After all, she had ignored that 'Private – No Entry' sign. Maybe the owner had come to move them along. She stepped outside and didn't like what she saw. Two lads of about the same age as the bikers came towards her. One had a baseball bat and was smacking it against one of his palms. They both looked her over. She swallowed, every instinct in her screaming that these two meant trouble. She moved back a pace to shield Ned who was still leaning out of the window. 'Get down,' she whispered, turning her head to the side, 'and don't say a word.' They came in close and, one on either side of her, they pushed her hard against the driver's door: they smelt of sour beer and stale cigarette smoke.

'Please,' she said, conscious of Ned behind her and their gaze flickering from her to him, 'just take what you want and leave us alone.' Outwardly she was doing her best to appear calm, but inwardly she was frantic.

They both laughed, and a coarse, fleshy hand stroked her throat. For a split second she considered bringing her knee up into the youth's groin, but as the hand began to exert more pressure on her windpipe, squeezing it painfully, she heard another man's voice say, 'Take your hands off that woman and get the hell out of here.'

The grip loosened. Twisting her head, Clara saw an elderly man dressed in a flat cap and a waxed jacket coming towards them. A patch covered one of his eyes and raised to the other was a double-barrelled shotgun. Her legs began to wobble and she hoped to God that the old man knew what he was doing with it.

The gun still held high, he drew nearer. 'And do it before I lose my patience and blast both your heads off!' The voice that had started with a low warning rumble, had now pitched itself forward into a snarl of intent. 'Go on, get out of here!'

11

The hand dropped from Clara's throat. 'Take it easy, Granddad, don't go giving yourself a heart-attack.'

'Less of the lip, you scum. You're on my land and I want you off it. Pronto! Do you understand that, or do I have to spell it out into simple words that louts like you can understand?'

The two lads started backing away. 'Bloody cocky with your words, aren't you, you stupid old git?'

Tightening his finger on the trigger and lowering the shotgun until it was aimed directly at the youth's crotch, the man growled, 'So tell me, just how cocky do *you* feel? Get out of here.'

They fled to their car and, with the gun still trained on them, they turned it round and shot off down the track, leaving a dusty cloud hanging in the air.

Clara realised she had been holding her breath and let it out now, in a long sigh of relief. Her legs were still shaking and the sky spun. She leaned against the van, steeled herself, then opened the door and reached in for Ned. His face was as white as she felt hers must be. He trembled in her arms and she hugged him to her.

She turned to face the formidable man who had come to their rescue. 'I'm so grateful to you,' she said. 'If you hadn't turned up . . .' She swallowed, then tried again. 'Well, I'm not sure how I would have got out of that. Thank you very much.'

To her surprise, the man made no attempt to offer any further reassurance. He simply stared at her, bristling with disapproval. Then with a loud crack, he broke the gun and shoved the butt under his arm. 'You can save the fawning pleasantries,' he growled. 'I'm not interested. Maybe in future you'll think twice about trespassing on private property, especially somewhere as remote as this. Damn stupid of you to put yourself and the child in danger. Women! Bloody fools, the lot of you!' He turned his back and started to walk away.

Clara was outraged. 'Why, you miserable old bugger!' she burst out angrily. 'Come back here and apologise this instant.'

He slowed his step and twisted his head round. 'What did you call me?'

'You heard. And if I wasn't holding a terrified child I'd call you a lot worse.'

'If that child is terrified, then you have only yourself to blame.'

'Oh, because I'm a woman on my own I'm not allowed to take my son paddling. Is that what you're saying?'

'Paddling?' he echoed. 'Paddling in *my* water? I ought to bloody charge you for that.'

'Do that, you old skinflint, and I'll report you to the police for behaving in a threatening manner with a dangerous firearm. It's crazy old fools like you with guns who get innocent people killed!' Her voice was filled with rage.

'I'll wager that wasn't what you were thinking a few moments ago. I bet you'd never been so pleased to see a crazy old fool with a gun.'

'If I'd known it would be you, I'd sooner have taken my chances single-handed.'

'The hell you would have!' he guffawed.

They stared at each other. In the silence that followed, Ned lifted his head from Clara's shoulder. 'I need a wee,' he murmured, and started to sob. Then Clara felt a wet warmth run down her front.

The grumpy old man lowered his one eye to the puddle forming on the ground at her feet. 'Poor little beggar,' he said gruffly. 'Get him changed and I'll make you some tea.'

Near to tears herself, but determined to hang on to her self-respect, she said, 'I can manage, thank you. I wouldn't want to take up any more of your valuable—'

He silenced her with a fierce one-eyed stare. 'Don't look a gift horse in the mouth, young lady, until you're sure you can really do without it.'

Winnie seemed terribly cramped with the three of them inside it: their guest, as he fumbled around making a pot of tea, was too tall and bulky for such a confined space. By the time Clara had calmed Ned and changed their clothes, and they were sitting at the little table with their tea, she thought she should introduce herself. An apology seemed appropriate too.

'My name's Clara Costello, and I'm sorry for some of the things I said out there. This is my son, Ned.'

He took off his cap and laid it on the table. 'Well, Miss Costello, the name's Liberty, Mr Liberty, and I never apologise for anything I say.'

In spite of herself, she smiled. 'You know, that doesn't surprise me. Do you often go for an afternoon stroll with a gun?'

'When I feel like shooting something, yes.'

'Well, much as I disagree with the ownership of guns, I'm glad you felt the need to shoot something today.'

'Don't be so bloody patronising. Drink your tea and be quiet. That goes for you too, young man.'

'But it's got sugar in,' Ned said, taking a sip from his mug and screwing up his face that had now resumed its usual healthy glow.

The man gave a snort of derision. 'Hell's bells and buckets of blood! Don't tell me your mother's one of those new-fandangled creatures who doesn't believe in sugar.'

'I'm allowed sugar on cornflakes,' Ned said proudly. 'And grapefruit,' he added.

'Very generous of her, I'm sure.'

'What's wrong with your eye?'

'And what's wrong with your manners, Mr Nosy Parker?'

Unabashed, Ned carried on, 'You look like a pirate.'

This seemed to amuse their guest. 'A black-bearded, buccaneering, lash-him-to-the-mainmast-m'hearty type of pirate, I hope, not some white-frilled, swashbuckling nancy-boy.'

The distinction was lost on Ned. 'If you chopped a hand off, you could be Captain Hook.'

The man looked down at the badly swollen fingers that were wrapped around his mug of tea. 'I'll bear that in mind.'

'Come on, Ned,' Clara said gently, 'drink your tea and leave our guest alone.'

'Do I have to? It's horrible. It's too sweet. Can't I have some blackcurrant juice? Please.'

Sliding out from the seat she was sharing with Ned, Clara went over to the fridge, poured a cup of blackcurrant juice, and reached into a locker for a packet of biscuits. She had no desire to prolong their rescuer's stay with them, but she felt she owed him a Jaffa Cake at the very least.

He was a funny old stick, shabbily dressed in a moth-eaten green pullover with frayed cuffs and the elbows worn through. The points of his shirt collar were also worn and his brown corduroy trousers were scruffy and dirty. His shoes were unpolished and the stitching had been redone recently, but in the wrong colour. She sat opposite him and offered the packet of biscuits. His distorted fingers poked clumsily at the plastic wrapping as he helped himself and she wondered just how good a shot he would have been if he had fired that wretched gun. Thinking of it now, she gave it a censorious glance. It was resting against the wardrobe at the far end of the van, along with its owner's smelly old waxed jacket.

'Stop worrying,' he said, seeing her face. 'It's safe enough. I've taken the cartridges out. They're in my coat pocket.'

She made no comment, but thinking that she could take advantage of his local knowledge, she said, 'We're trying to find a campsite for the night. Perhaps you know where it is.' She got to her feet to fetch the map.

'I doubt that very much,' he said, when she returned. 'Camping's hardly my scene.'

'Heavens, are you always this helpful?'

He swallowed the last of his tea. 'You've got me on a good day.'

'Lucky old us.' She put the map down on the table between them and pointed to where Ron and Eileen had said the campsite was. 'It's called Hollow Edge View. I was told it was—'

'It's gone,' he interrupted. 'The owners beggared off down south last winter. Bankrupted themselves. Not an ounce of business sense. Softies from London who thought it would be an easy option playing Old Macdonald Had a Farm. I knew they'd never make a go of it. I told them so too.'

'Wow, and to think they didn't stick around to enjoy more of your warm neighbourliness. What were they thinking of?'

He looked up sharply, nostrils flaring. 'Nothing wrong in speaking one's mind.'

'Depends on the state of the mind. Can you recommend anywhere else for us to stay?'

'No.'

'Well, then, and since we've clearly exhausted you of your charm, you can leave us to sort ourselves out. I wish I could say it was a pleasure meeting you. Close the door after you, won't you, *Mr* Liberty?'

Gabriel was smiling to himself as he trudged home across the fields in the late-afternoon sunshine. He hadn't enjoyed himself so much in a long while. It wasn't often he came up against somebody brave enough to cross words with him, but that spiky, sharp-tongued young woman had made more of a go of it than anyone else ever had. Dr Singh had tried it on, although he was too conscious of his professional status to take a real verbal swing. But that Costello girl hadn't cared a jot for what his response would be. And fair play to her. Though he still maintained that she was a damned fool to go wandering about the countryside on her own with a young child. Asking for trouble in this day and age. One never knew who or what was around the corner.

Back at Mermaid House he let himself in and went through to the gun room. It was only then, as he stood in front of the locked glass-fronted cabinet, that he realised he didn't have the gun with him.

Damn and blast! He had left it behind with that girl and her son. A shiver of unease crept over him as he recalled the cartridges he had put into his coat pocket, which he had also stupidly left behind. He hoped to God that just as that little boy had been indoctrinated with the evils of sugar, he had been instilled with the belief that guns were a no-go area for children.

He was about to retrace his steps across the fields, to see if the camper-van was still there, when the telephone rang.

To his surprise he heard Jonah's voice at the other end of the line. Now what was this about? When was the last time any of his children had phoned him?

It was Ned who spotted it. 'Look, Mummy, Mr Liberty's forgotten his coat and gun.' He reached out to the twin barrels and Clara shouted, 'Don't touch!'

Ned jumped. 'I was only looking,' he said, hurt.

'I'm sorry,' she said, 'but those things can kill, and it's better that you never get within touching distance of something as dangerous.'

'What shall we do with it?' he asked, anxiously.

'We could either wait and see if Mr Liberty comes back for it, or we could go and find him.' She turned and looked at the map that was still laid out on the table. 'My guess is,' she mused, 'and since he claimed to own this land, that our friend Mr Grumpy-Pants Liberty lives here.'

Ned climbed on to the seat to see what she was pointing at. 'Where? Show me.'

She indicated with her finger.

'If we go back the way we came, join the main road, then turn right, just here, it's likely we'll find ourselves once again in the company of the rudest man on earth. What do you think? Is it worth the trouble?'

He stood up on the bench seat so that he was eye to eye with her. 'I thought he was funny.'

'I didn't. He was rude to us.'

Ned looked thoughtful. 'He stopped those horrible men from hurting you. And he made us tea because I was frightened.' He lowered his gaze beneath his long lashes. 'I'm ... I'm sorry I wet myself.'

At the poignant reminder of what the old devil had done for them, Clara put her arms around her precious son. 'I nearly wet myself too,' she admitted. 'It was scary. And you're right,' she added decisively, 'it's time I learned to be more tolerant of other people's shortcomings.'

After Clara had put the gun inside a wardrobe, they washed up their cups, stored them away and set a course for Mermaid House.

As to be expected, there was no helpful sign at the end of the track that Clara was convinced would lead them to where Mr Liberty lived. She turned off the main road, juddered over a cattle grid, and pressed on. She soon realised that she had to slow to a steady crawl. They rattled along for almost half a mile before they set eyes on the most extraordinary sight. Clara whistled. 'Now that's what I call a house.'

Ned was impressed too. 'It's a castle, Mummy!'

There weren't any battlements, but there was a tower built into one of the corners of the house and it didn't take much imagination to picture a cursing Mr Liberty standing at the window, shotgun in hand, ready to defend his home from the onslaught of double-glazing salesmen.

They came to an archway that led to a central courtyard. Clara parked alongside a battered old Land Rover, pulled on the handbrake and turned off the engine. Close up, the house was gloomier than it had appeared from a distance. The sun was low in the sky now, and the cobbled courtyard was in shadow. The stonework was almost black in places and looked to be in need of a good restorative clean. One wall was almost covered in ivy, which helped to soften the grim effect of so much discoloured stone, but otherwise the house was as saturnine and forbidding as its owner.

But how different it must have been when it was originally built, Clara thought, as she hooked Mr Liberty's coat over her shoulder and picked up the gun. She and Ned walked towards what she hoped was a regularly used door – a deduction based on the pile of rubbish bags grouped around a collection of dustbins. A nose-wrinkling pong of rotting detritus floated out to them. 'Home, not-so-Sweet Home,' she muttered, under her breath, as she stood on the doorstep looking for a bell. Not finding one, she rapped loudly with her knuckles.

'No doubt he's preparing the hot oil and flaming arrows,' she said to Ned.

'Shall I call him?' he said, pushing open the letterbox.

'That's probably not a good idea,' Clara said.

But it was too late. Ned was already peering through the gap. 'Ooh,' he exclaimed, 'it's really untidy. There's things everywhere. Oh, I can see Mr Liberty. Hello, Mr Liberty, it's us, you forgot your gun and we've brought it for you.'

'No need to make such a song and dance about it, young man.'

Bending down, Clara could see that Ned was nose to nose with the formidable one-eyed owner of the house.

'We've brought your coat too,' Ned carried on, as though it was the most reasonable thing in the world to be holding a conversation through a letterbox. 'Your house is nice. It's just like a castle. Can I come in and see it, please? I'll be very good. I'll take my shoes off like I have to at Nanna and Granda's so I won't spoil your carpets. And I promise I won't run about and knock things over.'

It was time to intervene. 'It's okay, Mr Liberty,' Clara said. 'We're not here to bother you. I'll put your gun and coat here on the step and leave you in peace. Thanks for your help earlier this afternoon. Ned and I really appreciated what you did.' Taking her son's hand, she lowered her voice. 'Come on, Ned, we mustn't make a nuisance of ourselves. Besides, it's getting late and we have to find a campsite.' She turned to go.

The door opened suddenly. 'You're too early.'

'Too early for what?' asked Clara.

'There's only one campsite in this area and it doesn't open for another two weeks.'

She sighed. 'Oh, that's brilliant. Just what I needed to hear. Why didn't you tell me that before?'

'Oh, so it's my fault you didn't do sufficient background research before you came here, is it? How typical of a woman to blame her inadequacies on the nearest man to hand.'

She sighed again. But now it was edged with a spark of annoyance. 'Mr Liberty, do you realise just how rude you are? Because if not, let me tell you here and now that I have seldom come across a more cantankerous and mean-spirited man.'

He smiled. Well, she thought it was a smile. It was more a case of his lips stretching into what she assumed was an unaccustomed position, resulting in the baring of two rows of large, uneven teeth.

'And I have seldom come across a woman with as much ungracious impudence as you, Miss Costello,' he snarled, 'so I know that if I were to suggest you use one of my fields for the night, it would be a pointless gesture. You would only throw it back in my face.'

Astonished, Clara hesitated. It was getting late, the light had almost gone and she was tired. Embarking on a lengthy search for somewhere to hitch up for the night didn't appeal. Also, the incident that afternoon had left her more rattled than she cared to admit. Just thinking about it again caused her heart to beat faster. It seemed eminently sensible to be within shouting distance of help. Even if it came in the person of this misogynist old-timer with a serious attitude problem.

'Perhaps we could come to some other arrangement,' she said, choosing her words with care. 'Rather than spoil one of your fields by driving across it, how about we stay right where we are in the courtyard?'

He considered this. 'Just the one night?' he reiterated.

'Just the one night,' she confirmed. 'In fact, we'll be gone first thing in the morning. It will be as though we'd never been here.'

He switched his gaze to Ned. 'And you, young man, you promise you'll behave? I don't want any trouble from you. No crying. No running about the place. And definitely no shouting through my letterbox. I like things nice and quiet round here. If I hear so much as a snore out of you tonight, there'll be trouble. Got that?'

Ned gave a solemn nod. And then one of his most engaging smiles. 'Would you like to have tea with us, Mr Liberty? We're having pancakes. Oh, Mummy, please say Mr Liberty can have tea with us.'

Clara pushed her hands into the pockets of her jeans. Oh, well done, Ned, she thought. A cosy evening with Mr Misery. Perfect. 'You're more than welcome, Mr Liberty,' she lied, 'but it will be very simple. Nothing fancy, I'm afraid.'

Mr Liberty's enthusiasm for the idea seemed as great as her own. He said, and dismissively so, 'Pancakes? I can't stand them. I've got a nice bit of rump steak and a glass of claret I'm looking forward to.' He turned back towards the house, but before he disappeared, he tossed them one last piece of invective. 'And remember, no noise or trouble.'

12

Gabriel went to bed early that night. He often did. Sleep was a welcome antidote to boredom. And, thank God, it was something he was still good at. The rest of his body might be betraying him – his hands, his bladder, his heart and the occasional limb given over to an attack of tremors – but sleep was a nut he could still crack.

He stepped over the mess of plaster and curtains that he hadn't done anything about since he'd pulled the track off the wall two nights ago, and got into bed. The sheets felt cold and damp. He didn't turn out the light straight away, but sat for a while to contemplate his day, a habit of Anastasia's that had rubbed off on him. 'Every day is a challenge,' she would say, 'but the real challenge is reflecting on the bad aspects of that day and learning from them.' It was another of her idealistic foibles that had contrasted with his more pragmatic approach to life: anything he didn't like about his day he wrote off. 'I haven't got the time to dwell on what's past,' he had said once.

Smiling her knowing smile, Anastasia had stretched out beside him in bed and stroked his cheek. 'Gabriel Liberty, I promise you that one day, when you're old and grey, you will find you have more time on your hands than you know what to do with and then you'll understand.'

'We're never going to be old,' he had responded fiercely. 'I would rather be dead than ancient and decrepit.'

He hadn't been much older than the age his children were now when he had said this, but as he shifted his pillows against the mahogany bed-head, Gabriel could remember uttering those words as though it were yesterday. Anastasia had shushed him with a finger against his lips. 'Yesterday, today, tomorrow, young or old, what does any of it matter so long as we're together and making the most of what we have?' Then she had kissed him. One of those long, lingering kisses that had promised him the world. With his eyes shut he could still feel the warmth of her moist mouth against his.

He snapped his eyes open. This was absurd. What did he think he was doing? He reached for the book by the side of the bed – a heavy tome of political memoirs guaranteed to see off such sentimental nonsense. But it remained closed as his train of thought was distracted again. Not by the

67

distant past, but by the events of today. He wondered how his guests were getting on.

Thinking of the pancakes they must have enjoyed, he thought of his own supper – a lukewarm tin of Heinz tomato soup. He had lied about the rump steak and claret just as he frequently lied to Jonah about what he ate. Often he didn't eat what Jonah fetched from the shops for him. The fresh fruit, the vegetables, the chicken breasts – it was too much trouble. Cooking for one was bad enough, but eating alone was worse.

So why hadn't he accepted the invitation to join that well-mannered little boy and his mother for supper? Especially as their appearance down by the river had provided him with the highlight of an otherwise tedious day.

Since Val's illness, and her death, he had got out of the habit of being sociable, not that he had ever been gregarious. Val had been the driving force when it came to showing one's face at local functions; he had gone along with it to keep the peace. He had preferred to devote himself to work. But even that had palled as the years went on. And then came the day when, finally, he had had to resign himself to the truth that none of his children was interested in taking over the business he had inherited from his own father. It had been a bitter day indeed when he sold up and retired. He had never forgiven Caspar and Jonah for letting him down – in his heart, Damson had never really been in the running. They could not have found a more hurtful way to snub him. Everything he had worked for and hoped to pass on to them, they had, by their actions, despised and rejected. A solid engineering company with a name that was known and respected around the world wasn't good enough for them, was it? Oh, dear me, no.

And what had they chosen to do instead?

Not much.

After dropping out of university, Caspar, whose colossal self-regard far exceeded his willingness to get his hands dirty with real work, had thrown himself into a series of get-rich-quick scams that had all turned into financial disasters. During the eighties he had fancied himself one of Thatcher's boys, but his entrepreneurial skills were never going to sustain that ideal. He was an idle beggar who thought the world owed him a favour. His worst commercial disaster had been selling time-shares in Spain. When the bottom dropped out of the *hacienda* market the banks foreclosed, investors lost their money and one of Caspar's partners was sent to prison for fraud. But what else would you expect from the Costa del Crime?

No two ways about it, Caspar was a dreadful businessman and an even worse judge of character. Now he peddled overpriced cars for a living.

As for Jonah, the brightest of the bunch, he was wasting what talents he had been given by teaching in a third-rate school and earning buttons.

It went without saying, of course, that Damson had never held down a proper job. She had been too preoccupied with enjoying herself.

So Gabriel had entered the twilight zone of retirement. It hadn't suited him, isolated from the only world he had been interested in – industrial engineering: pipes, gaskets and valves – he had soon realised he had few friends. The people he had mixed with had been business associates in the steel-producing heartlands of Sheffield, and other than his love of books, he had nothing else to occupy him. Without meaning to, he had allowed the days to run through his fingers like sand. Anastasia would never have let him do this: for her, every day had counted. Val had tried to persuade him that they should explore the world together, but because he had travelled so extensively on business, he had ignored the brochures she left lying about the house and withdrew to his library.

Then she had died, and it was easier to retreat further still: to batten down the hatches and let the world go hang.

He knew the house was a mess and that he should do something about it. But where to start? It had got so out of hand that the task now seemed insurmountable.

He knew, too, that at times he was offhand and acerbic, but he didn't have the patience to be polite. He had always been direct and to the point – that was how one survived in business. Fannying around with false pleasantries would have got him nowhere. If a spade was a shovel, what the dickens was wrong in declaring it so? When had mealy-mouthed insincerity become the alternative to good old-fashioned honesty?

That was what he had liked about the Costello woman. She had said exactly what she thought. She had had the guts to call him a miserable old bugger. Good for her. That was what he approved of and could respect. He hated it when his children took whatever he dished out to them. It made him want to shake them and shout, 'Why can't you be more like me? Where's your bloody backbone?'

She was smart too. He could tell that by her waspish, quick-witted manner. Take the way she had sized up the situation down in the courtyard. He had offered her the use of a field, but she had wanted somewhere better and hadn't been afraid to ask for it. She was a determined woman who was used to ploughing her own furrow. Though he doubted that she would have been able to talk her way out of that ugly situation with those two nasty pieces of work. Lucky for her that he frequently went down to the copse; lucky, too, that he had been seized with the urge to take a few pot-shots at the crows. He had hated those birds ever since, as a boy, he had seen one pluck out the eyes of a newborn lamb. Armed with his gun he had been intent on an afternoon's sport when he spotted the camper-van parked on his land. He had quickened his pace, preparing to give the trespasser a piece of his mind, when the car had appeared. It had been satisfying to see the expression on the two yobbos' faces change as they'd looked down the business end of a double-barrelled shotgun. And even better seeing them run off. Rotten cowards, picking on a young mother and her child.

Perhaps he had gone too far when he'd shouted at her, but anger had fuelled his words. Anger that this was the kind of world in which he lived, where young women and children weren't safe to set foot in the countryside for fear of being robbed or subjected to God knew what else. He thought of that poor mite wetting himself and wished now that he'd scared those bully-boys even more.

He hated the idea that the disease-ridden scum of the big towns and cities was now infiltrating what had always been a place of sanctuary to him. Anastasia had loved to walk alone in the hills, and so had the children. Jonah in particular had relished the solitude of the moors, disappearing for hours at a time.

He had offered Miss Costello and her son the field because he had been genuinely concerned about their welfare. What if she was too tired to find a decent campsite and had dropped anchor in any old place and attracted further trouble? He might be considered in some quarters to be a bad-tempered old devil, but he was not the kind of man who would let a young woman go without somewhere safe to stay.

Smiling to himself, he thought of all the names he had been called that day.

A miserable old bugger.

An old skinflint.

A crazy old fool.

A cantankerous and mean-spirited man.

Not bad for starters.

He switched off the light and wondered what he might be in for tomorrow morning. Then he remembered that his feisty little guest had said they would be gone by first thing in the morning – 'It will be as though we'd never been here.'

He turned the light back on, reached for his clock and set the alarm for six thirty. Just in case he overslept. It would be a shame to miss out on a parting shot.

13

That night, unable to sleep, Archie stared at the ceiling above his bed. The curtains at the window were thin and unlined, and from the street-lamp outside, a glow of orange light shone through the cheap fabric. It was sufficient, though, for his eyes to follow the cracks in the plasterwork as if he was tracing a route on a map. That's me, he thought tiredly, I'm looking for the way out. Or, at least, some kind of direction.

He turned on to his side, hoping sleep would come if he lay in a different position. It didn't. Now he could hear a gang of youngsters coming back from the pub: they were kicking a tin can between them and their carefree banter jarred on his troubled thoughts.

He had received a letter from Stella's solicitor. The grey paper with the overly pedantic language had told him what he already knew, that more than two decades of marriage was to be reduced to *Mrs S. Merryman versus Mr A. F. Merryman*. The tone of the letter suggested that the matter could be brought to a swift conclusion as Mrs Merryman was happy to leave her husband's business concerns out of the negotiations, but the house was another matter. As Mr Merryman no doubt understood, Mrs Merryman had been a party to the original purchase of the property as well as a regular contributor to the mortgage payments, so she was entitled to her share of the matrimonial home.

Archie had no argument with that. It was all true. And as much as he wanted to avoid the upheaval of selling the house, he knew he had no choice: he had no other means to pay off Stella.

Still restless, he rolled over on to his left side and tried to relax. But his mind was racing through the years he and Stella had shared. The good times, and the bad times.

It mattered to him that the past was kept intact, just as it mattered to him that, for now, there were still traces of Stella's presence in the house, painful as they were. Like the brush she had left on the dressing-table with hairs caught among the bristles; the clothes she hadn't taken with her; the magazine on the kitchen worktop, still open at a page showing some film star with the new love of his life.

Ten minutes later, as sleep continued to elude him, he let out a sigh of defeat.

Insomnia was a new phenomenon to him, and other than getting out of bed and making himself a brew, he didn't know what to do. He slipped on his towelling dressing-gown and went downstairs quietly, not wanting to disturb his mother. She had taken to waking during the night and thinking it was time to get up. She had done it last night: at three o'clock, he had heard a noise coming from the kitchen, and had shot downstairs ready to confront whoever had broken in. What he found was Bessie setting out the breakfast things: plates and bowls, packets of cereal and slices of bread ready to go under the grill. His appearance in the kitchen had startled her so much that she hadn't been able to get a coherent word out. It had taken him some time to convince her that it was still the middle of the night. As he led her back to her room, she had launched into a long, heartfelt and impassioned speech, not one word of which could he understand. He had sat on the edge of her bed, coaxing the words of lucidity from her, soothing her frustration, until gradually he had realised that she felt guilty Stella had left him and was trying to help by seeing to things around the house. 'But, Mum,' he had said, 'I can manage perfectly well. I don't want you to worry about anything like that.' He had wanted to add that Stella had never made the breakfast anyway, that it had always been his job.

He had spent an hour reassuring his mother that he could cope, before he got back to his own bed. But by five o'clock she was up again, running herself a bath.

When it came to Bessie having a bath, the golden rule was that somebody had to be on hand to help her ... just in case.

Just in case she slipped.

Just in case she fell asleep.

Just in case she scalded herself.

But if Archie's golden rule was that her bath time had to be supervised, her own golden rule was that he was not allowed in the bathroom while she was in a state of undress. With the door ajar, he could sit outside on the landing, keeping up a steady flow of conversation about the shop, Samson, Comrade Norm, and the customers that came in to haggle over a stainless-steel egg-cup.

Now, in the harsh glare of the overhead strip-light, he stood in the kitchen, listening to the kettle coming to the boil. The speech therapist at the hospital had said that Bessie was improving, and he hung on to this glimmer of hope, wanting to believe that his mother would make a good, if not full, recovery.

He poured boiling water into the badly stained teapot, thinking how unfair it was that Bessie should now be cheated of enjoying life. She had worked hard down the years, had accepted and overcome every challenge thrown at her. Most had been a direct result of Archie's father having walked out on her when she was pregnant, leaving her to cope with the daily grind of making ends meet while struggling to bring up a child on her own. If he had stayed away for ever, it would have been better all round, but he took advantage of Bessie's generous nature and returned to sponge off her when the mood took him. It was always a relief when he grew bored of regular meals and her willingness to forgive, and left them alone.

Archie sat at the kitchen table to drink his tea, and tried to remember what Dr Singh had said about there being swings and roundabouts to face. He'd heard a snippet on the radio, too. Something about keeping the stroke patient as active as possible, not just physically, but mentally. Apparently the precariously balanced mental capacities had to be exercised and shored up. Boredom was to be avoided at all costs. Loneliness too.

It occurred to him that maybe he could get Bessie into the shop for a few hours a day. She might like that. As kind as the neighbours had been, Bessie hadn't made a lot of effort to get to know them and, anyway, it wasn't easy for her to talk to strangers now. Her speech embarrassed her, and she knew that it embarrassed them.

No, the solution was to get her involved in the shop. Give her little tasks to do, such as polishing some of the small pieces of furniture. And those horse brasses from the house-clearance job he'd done the other day would come up a treat with a bit of tender loving care. As would the box of commemorative plates, which were covered in dust and grime. If he planned it carefully, there would be any number of little jobs he could find for her to do. But he would have to be subtle about it: his mother was no fool. He would have to make out that she was doing him a big favour, that he needed her help. There again, one look at Samson's huge clumsy hands would tell her that the big guy wasn't made for cleaning delicate china.

He swallowed the last of his tea, rinsed the mug under the tap, put it ready for his breakfast in the morning, and went back upstairs to bed. As he pulled the duvet over him, life didn't seem so bad after all.

He had always believed that for every problem there was a solution. It was just a matter of reasoning it through.

Drifting off to sleep, he felt better than he had in days. Maybe things would start to pick up now.

14

Clara woke to the sound of rain pattering on the roof of the camper-van. Stretching beneath the duvet, she opened her eyes and looked at her watch. It was eight o'clock. Goodness, as late as that. Still, there was no hurry, and as Ned was sleeping soundly, she could savour a rare lie-in. She closed her eyes, listened to the rain, and hoped it wouldn't develop into a full-blown downpour. Sadly, it seemed that the waitress's prediction at the café yesterday had been less than accurate: the rain had come early. They had been lucky so far on their trip: this was their first wet day. 'Captain's Log, Star Date 29 March,' she thought, with a smile, 'Day Five – rain.'

She should be keeping a diary. In years to come, when she was slogging away on the treadmill, it would make interesting reading. It would be nice for Ned, too. A keepsake to prove that they had been brave enough to flout convention.

Well, it wasn't too late to start. She would buy a book in Deaconsbridge and encourage Ned to play his part too. He could write his own entries, draw a few pictures, and maybe stick in postcards of where they had stayed. Another oversight. Postcards. She was supposed to be keeping her friends and parents up to date with their travels, but somehow she just hadn't got round to it. Nor had she phoned Louise. But that had been a conscious effort on her part to distance herself from home: to get the most out of this trip, she had wanted to separate herself from what she had left behind.

So, buying some postcards was another job for today, she thought, her orderly mind now putting together a list of things she had to do. They needed a supermarket, and a launderette would be useful. She didn't mind handwashing a few pairs of pants and socks, but larger items were a drag. After yesterday, and their several changes of clothes, she could do with throwing everything into a machine, while she and Ned had a nose round the shops in the market square. Maybe they could have another meal at the Mermaid café and decide what they were going to do next. If it looked like the rain was going to settle in for the day, they could perhaps drive across to Castleton and visit the underground caverns, some of which, according to the guide books, were open all year.

She stretched again, and sighed contentedly. How pleasant it was to know that one's only concern for the day was to find a washing-machine and something to eat, with a little amusement thrown in. It was a far cry from worrying about meeting the latest production-line quotas. She didn't miss any of it – except, perhaps, the silly e-mails from the boys – Guy and David – and their antics. Guy had lifted the tension on many a head-banging-against-the-wall day. He would burst through her door like a member of the SAS, rolling across the floor and jumping up to declare that he had her covered – usually with a staple gun. The first time he had done it she had nearly fallen off her chair in alarm. It was also the first time she had met him. 'Hi,' he'd said, slipping the staple gun into the waistband of his suit trousers. 'I've been sent to introduce myself, seeing as you're new to the department. How're you getting on, Miss Clarabelle Costello?'

'Fine until you burst in and tried to staple me to the spot. Could you try knocking in future? You never know what I might be doing in here. And my name's Clara, not a ding-dong to be heard.' He never did knock, but she soon got used to his entrance – and the pet name.

She smiled at the memory. It was the camaraderie she missed, not the job. Already she was discovering that, away from home, her sense of perspective was undergoing further change. Though she and Ned had had holidays before, this one was different. There was no rush to their days. They did not have to cram everything into a week.

Even yesterday's horrible incident hadn't dampened her enthusiasm. She wasn't nervous by nature, but last night she had been grateful to Mr Liberty for allowing them to stay here – for her own peace of mind and Ned's. But she need not have worried about him: Ned had tucked into his supper with relish and gone to bed happily. The campsites they had stayed at previously had never been free of noise – of caravan doors clicking shut, toilets flushing, radios and televisions playing. Here, in the courtyard at Mermaid House, it had been the quietest night she had known. Other than a faint rustling of leaves on trees and the occasional distant animal noise, it had been as silent as the grave.

Which probably accounted for the good night's sleep she'd had. Overcome with a general sense of well-being, she thought that perhaps when she and Ned went into Deaconsbridge that morning they would buy a small present for Mr Liberty to thank him. She also wanted to try to make amends for being so rude to him – fear and tiredness must have got the better of her. She wondered if he was a one-off, or whether there were more like him inside Mermaid House. A whole family of eccentric Libertys slowly driving each other round the bend. If so, it was straight out of *Cold Comfort Farm*.

Putting aside its cranky, eccentric owner, the house was a veritable piece of whimsy. She had never seen anything like it before. She hoped there would be a chance, if she made peace with Mr Liberty, to have a look round. Maybe she could get Ned to ask him. It would sound less intrusive coming from a four-year-old boy.

Thinking of Ned, Clara rolled onto her side and looked towards his sleeping compartment. There was still no sign of movement from behind the curtain. He must have been shattered last night to sleep so long. It's all the fresh air, she thought. That would meet with her mother's approval. As babies, she and Michael had been put outside in their prams in all weathers. 'Toughened you up nicely,' said her mother, who had tried to do the same with Ned. 'Just airing him,' she claimed, when Clara arrived to collect him after work and found him on the patio with a strong wind buffeting the pram.

'Airing him or freeze-drying him, Mum?'

Though she had made her views clear on how she wanted her son treated, Clara knew that while her back was turned her mother did as she pleased, but so long as Ned thrived Clara couldn't complain. Anyway, she was glad to have parents prepared to help out. Without them, she wouldn't have coped nearly so well.

When she had discovered she was pregnant there had been no dilemma over whether or not to keep the baby. She had loved her unborn child's father, so it had seemed natural to want his baby. Telling her parents that she was pregnant had been one of the hardest things she had ever done. She knew she had let them down.

'Is there really no chance of the father taking on his responsibility?' her mother had asked, stricken.

'No, Mum. He's already married.'

That had been the second shock they'd had to cope with: that their sensible, well-brought-up daughter had been stupid enough to have an affair with a married man. Initially they had wanted to blame the despicable rotter for tricking her into a relationship with him when he should have known better, but she told them, 'I knew all along that he was married. At the time, though, he was separated from his wife.'

They had seized on this glimmer of hope.

'Is he divorced now?' her father asked.

'No. He and his wife are reconciled.'

Her father had picked up on the one aspect of the tale she had tried to gloss over. 'Did you tell him you were pregnant?' he asked.

'No.'

'But, darling, why not? He's the father, he should know,' her mother remonstrated.

'You only think that because you want to believe he'll wave a magic wand over my pregnancy and make it nice and respectable.'

'That's a little hard on us,' her father said.

'But it's true, isn't it? Imagine this year's Christmas cards: "Oh, and by the way, Clara's expecting our first grandchild but we don't know who the father is."'

'You haven't told us his name,' her mother said, pushing this uncomfortable home truth to one side.

'There's no need to. You won't ever meet him.'

In the end, and once the shock had worn off, her parents made it clear that they would be standing right by her. 'It's your life,' they told her, 'and we'll do all we can to help.' Their love and solidarity was just what she needed. It still brought a lump to her throat when she thought of their support and devotion.

By the time Ned was due, they were ready to fend off the merest hint of criticism from anyone and drove her to the hospital when she went into labour. She had never seen her father drive as fast as he had that night, crashing through red lights, the horn blaring. In the back of the car, next to Clara, her mother was breathing so hard it was difficult to know which of them was about to give birth. Louise met them at the hospital. She had been co-opted into being Clara's birthing partner, much to the rest of the gang's relief. 'You know I'm your biggest fan, Clarabelle,' Guy had said, 'but to see you flat on your back and screaming like a banshee would dispel the beautiful illusion I have of you.'

In the early hours of the morning, Ned made his appearance. He was the most amazing, tiny, wide-eyed, dark-haired bundle of wonder Clara could have imagined. She couldn't take her eyes off him. As she gazed into his little face she felt as if she had always known him. 'So there you are,' she almost said. 'I was wondering where you'd got to.' Even Louise, the world's biggest child-hater, had been moved to tears when he had wrapped his tiny fingers around her thumb – though she claimed later that hunger and exhaustion had overwhelmed her.

Clara's parents had been equally moved by their grandson. Her father had hidden his wet cheeks behind a brand new Pentax – specially bought for the occasion – saying that somebody had to capture the moment, but her mother had sniffed and gulped quite openly, holding Ned in her arms and posing proudly for the camera.

At visiting-time later that day the gang were in her ward, presenting her with flowers and champagne, chocolates, and a huge teddy bear.

'It'll scare the poor mite witless,' Moira had said, taking a cautious but curious peek at Ned, who was asleep in Clara's arms. 'Was it as bad as Louise told us it was?'

Louise held up her hands. 'Sorry, Clara, but yes, I'm guilty of giving the sordid details. Frankly, from where I was standing, it was bloody awful. You've done me an enormous favour in putting me off for life.'

Four years on, Louise said that the moment she ever felt her hormones creeping up on her, she only had to think of that night in hospital with Clara and they shrank back into line without another word.

Though none of her friends had ever wanted children, they loved Ned, and went out of their way to spoil him. He might not be in possession of a full deck of parents, but in all other respects, he was a lucky boy: devoted grandparents and a set of the most doting aunts and uncles a child could wish for.

Clara slipped out of bed and filled the kettle. As she set it on the gas ring, she made a mental note to top up the water barrel before leaving. It held enough for two days of showers, cooking and washing-up, but she hated the idea of running out, so she kept a sharp eye on it. And while she was about it, she'd check their gas supply.

After wiping away the condensation that had formed on the window above the cooker, she opened one of the large vents in Winnie's roof, just enough to freshen the air but not to let the rain in, by which time the kettle had boiled and the van had acquired what she called a comforting happy-camper smell of burning gas. She made a pot of tea, then, surprised that the whistling of the kettle hadn't woken Ned, she stepped on to the first rung of the ladder and poked her head through the curtains.

Her heart leaped into her mouth.

Ned's bed was empty.

15

It was every parent's worst nightmare. Cold, debilitating fear consumed her, then sick panic took hold. She leaned across Ned's rumpled bed and flung back the duvet as though he might be there after all. She threw aside his pillow, too, and rummaged through his collection of cuddly toys.

Next she stumbled down from the ladder and checked the rest of the van, spurring herself on with the faint hope that in the night, and without disturbing her, Ned might have used the toilet and fallen asleep in there. No sign of him.

She stood for a moment to gather her thoughts. Had someone sneaked into the van while she slept and abducted him? She recalled a harrowing case several years ago of a young girl who had been taken from a tent and murdered.

No. Ned must simply have gone for a walk. In the rain?

Without bothering to change out of the oversized T-shirt she had slept in, she pulled on a pair of jeans and pushed her feet into her trainers. She opened the door and stepped outside. The rain was coming down heavier now and splashed against her face as she scanned the courtyard. If she had thought Mermaid House gloomy yesterday, it was even more so in the pouring rain. Beneath a pewter sky, the walls seemed darker than ever and water was cascading from a broken section of guttering. She made a dash for the door and, not caring that she had promised Mr Liberty they wouldn't cause any noise or trouble, she banged on it loudly. If she was going to find Ned, she needed his help. He would have some idea where a curious child might wander on his land.

Impatiently, she crashed her knuckles against the frosted-glass panel of the door again. 'Come on, come on,' she cried frantically. Then, just as Ned had done yesterday, she bent down, pushed open the letterbox and peered inside. 'Mr Liberty,' she called, 'I'm sorry to disturb you, but I need your help. Please answer the door.'

Still no response.

Desperation set in, and with no shelter from the rain, she was now thoroughly wet and cold. Fear was making her nauseous, and conjuring up yet more disturbing images, of Ned lost in this unknown landscape, wandering across the fields and finding his way down to the river where they had paddled yesterday. The water hadn't been deep there, but what if he had discovered a more dangerous section where ... where a small boy could drown?

She hammered wildly on the door. At last, and almost in tears, she heard the familiar, but welcome sound of Mr Liberty cursing. 'Hell's teeth, what's all the rumpus?' he growled, throwing open the door and staring at her fiercely.

'It's Ned.' She gulped. 'He's missing and I don't know where to start looking for him. Will you help me? Please. I thought you might know—' From behind him a head appeared, followed swiftly by the rest of Ned in his slippers, pyjamas and stripy dressing-gown whose belt was trailing on the ground. Clara went weak with relief. He was safe. She pushed past Mr Liberty, knelt on the stone-flagged floor and hugged Ned. But hot on the heels of relief came irrational anger and, to her shame, it was all she could do to stop herself shaking him. 'You know you're not supposed to leave the camper-van on your own,' she said, as calmly as she could. 'I was so worried. I thought something terrible had happened to you.'

'Please don't be cross with me, Mummy,' he said, tremulously. 'Mr Liberty said it would be all right.'

If Clara had felt like shaking Ned, she now felt like punching Mr Liberty's good eye right out of its socket. She got to her feet. 'Let me get this straight. This was all *your* idea?'

He cleared his throat. 'Saw the little lad peering out of his window and thought he might appreciate some company. Which he did. Isn't that right, young man?'

His cavalier attitude pushed Clara's anger to its zenith. 'What gives you the right to think you can encourage my son to break a rule? What did you think you were doing?'

'Mummy—'

'Ned, please, I'm talking.'

'But, Mummy, Mr Liberty showed me a secret door and the tower. He said there used to be a ghost up there. He told me that—'

'Ahem, possibly not the time, young man,' Mr Liberty murmured. 'Maybe we both ought to be apologising to your mother. She's looking a mite bothered to me.'

Clara flashed him a look of pure fury. 'Bothered? I was out of my mind with worry. I thought—' She stopped. She didn't want to relive the horror of thinking Ned might have been kidnapped by some perverted beast, that he might be lying dead somewhere, that she might never see him again and never feel his little body crushed against hers. That she might never stroke his soft cheek and silky smooth hair. Her anger subsided, and the heart-thumping pain of relief returned. 'I thought you didn't go in for making apologies.'

He looked uncomfortable. 'On this occasion I'm prepared to make an exception.'

'So what are you waiting for?'

'Miss Costello, I meant you and your boy no harm, and I'm very sorry that I caused you a moment's concern.'

'I'm sorry too, Mummy.' Ned's hand crept into hers. 'Don't be cross,' he added, shooting down any remaining vestiges of anger with one of his heart-melting smiles.

Suddenly she couldn't speak, but Mr Liberty filled in the silence. 'Well, if we're through with the sentiment, can you decide what you want to do next?' Contrition dispensed with, he went on, 'You can either stand here for the rest of the day letting in the rain and freezing to death or you can warm yourself by the fire in the kitchen while I make you some tea. A task I've proved myself more than capable of doing once before.'

Clara decided to accept, and she and Ned followed as Mr Liberty led the way. She was appalled at what she saw. Mess and clutter lay everywhere, piles of junk as far as the eye could see. The house smelt too. She had imagined a comforting old-fashioned kitchen with a massive fireplace where once upon a time a whole pig would have been roasted on a spit with a lowly scullery-maid to turn the handle. This dingy, bone-chilling room, with its grimy walls and flaking paintwork – especially above the cooker, which was covered in a thick film of grease – was not what she had envisaged. Nor was the gas-fired contraption with which Mr Liberty was now fiddling. She wondered why on earth he used such a device when behind it stood an Aga the size of a small car.

'It's the very devil to get going sometimes,' Mr Liberty complained, as he clicked away at a button on the side of the heater in an effort to ignite the flame. At last it caught and he straightened up triumphantly. 'There! That showed it who's boss.' She could see from his face that the coaxing of the heater into life was a daily battle of wills.

'Don't stand on ceremony,' he commanded. 'Sit yourself down.' He scraped one of the heavy chairs away from the long table and put it a few feet short of the heater. She crossed the room reluctantly, her shoes sticking to the scummy floor with each step, and sat in front of the meagre source of warmth. Mr Liberty threw a tea-towel at Ned. 'Don't stand there idly, young man,' he said. 'Help your mother to dry her hair. We don't want her catching her death, do we?'

'You wouldn't be spoiling me with your best Irish linen, would you?' she said, taking the grubby cloth from Ned.

He harrumphed loudly, turned away from her and set about the business of making tea.

A dubious brown crust on the tea-towel made her wonder if a mug of tea was such a good idea. Lord knows what she might catch. She tried to lose the tea-towel discreetly by folding it to slip it under some conveniently placed object, but Ned took it from her and tried helpfully to dab at her hair. She ducked out of his reach. 'No, Ned,' she whispered. 'It's dirty.'

'Shall I ask Mr Liberty for a clean one?' he whispered back. He might as well have placed a megaphone to his lips and relayed the message for the whole of the Peak District to hear.

Mr Liberty was rinsing mugs under the tap, and whipped round. 'Complaining again, Miss Costello? And there was me on the verge of offering you something to eat.'

The very idea made Clara want to gag. But, to her horror, Ned said, 'Breakfast would be nice.' He smiled at Mr Liberty. 'What have you got to eat? I'm very hungry.'

Clara stepped in fast. 'Why don't I cook us all a fry-up in the van?' She'd do anything to avoid being laid low with gastro-enteritis – even cook for this vinegary old man. 'We've got plenty of eggs and bacon.'

He looked at her shrewdly. 'Are you implying that my house isn't good enough for you? That it's not clean?'

'I'm not implying anything of the kind,' she said, rising from the chair to escape the gas heater and its noxious fumes. 'I'm telling you straight. The house, what I've seen of it, is a health hazard.'

He flared his nostrils. 'For one so young, you have quite a nerve, Miss Costello. Are you always so direct with people you hardly know?'

She gave him a conciliatory smile. 'Like you said earlier, sometimes there are occasions when one is forced into a position of making an exception. Which means I'm being unusually restrained with you. You should think yourself lucky.'

He gave a short bark of a laugh. 'Ned, m'boy, you have an extraordinary mother, did you know that? And just to prove that I don't harbour any ill feelings, I'm going to take up her offer of a cooked breakfast. That should teach her a lesson for shooting her impertinent mouth off, shouldn't it?'

Inside the camper-van, Gabriel tucked hungrily into his plate of bacon and eggs, relishing every mouthful. He couldn't remember the last time he had eaten a cooked breakfast.

'Would you like some ketchup, Mr Liberty?' asked Ned, from across the narrow table, a piece of streaky bacon dangling from his fork.

'Ketchup's for *caffs*,' Gabriel replied tersely. 'It's the opium of the common folk.'

'What's opium?'

'He doesn't need to know,' his mother chipped in, 'and don't speak with your mouth full.'

'Are you referring to me or your son?'

'To both of you.'

'Why don't I need to know?'

'Yes, Miss Costello, come along now, don't be shy. Surely you have an answer for your naturally inquisitive son. You seem to have an answer for just about everything else.' To his delight, a slightly raised eyebrow indicated that he had scored a point.

'It's a drug made from poppies, Ned,' she said, 'and it's highly addictive.

It melts your brain. And before you ask what addictive means, it means that you want it all the time.'

'Like chocolate?'

'Yes. But you want it even more than chocolate.'

'But how does it melt your brain? And if I ate too much chocolate, would my brain melt? Would it pour out through my ears, going gloopy-gloopy-gloop if I shook my head?' He gave them a demonstration, his eyes swivelling.

Gabriel was reminded of Caspar and Damson as small children. They had always been on at him, question after tiresome question. There had never seemed enough answers in the world for them. Jonah had been the opposite, hardly opening his mouth. If he wanted to know something he found it out for himself. 'Jonah's an intelligent boy, Gabriel,' Val often said. 'You should do more to encourage him. Try to show how proud you are of him.' But Jonah had thrown away his potential.

Sighing inwardly and feeling his good humour drain out of him, Gabriel stabbed a piece of toast into the yolk of his second egg. He could remember the stinging blow Jonah had dealt him when he had announced his intention to become a teacher. They had been in the library, the setting sun turning the room amber, shafts of light catching the motes of dust in the warm air, music coming from some other part of the house. 'Please, Dad,' he had said, his hands stuffed into his trouser pockets, 'don't make this any harder for me than it already is. Just hear me out and respect my decision. That's all I ask.'

'And all I've ever asked of you is your respect, loyalty and duty, as my father expected them of me.'

'And maybe your father was wrong to expect so much of you. Perhaps if he had treated you differently, you might have treated *us* differently.'

Incensed at the doubled-edged criticism levelled at both himself and his father – a man he had both feared and idolised – Gabriel had done the unthinkable: he had lashed out and struck Jonah, knocking him clean off his feet. In shock he had watched his younger son pick himself up from the floor, then touch the bloodied corner of his mouth. But something more than anger was raging inside Gabriel, something far worse that made his fists itch to strike Jonah again. He never knew whether Jonah had done it deliberately, but his gaze, as he dusted himself down, moved from Gabriel's face to the portrait of Anastasia above the fireplace. It was as if he was saying, 'And what would she say of your behaviour?' But in a quiet, and wholly restrained voice, he had said, 'Why can't you trust me to cock up my own life, Dad? Why try to do it for me?'

Not another word passed between them. Not for the rest of that evening, that week or the months that followed. When Jonah walked out on him that night, Gabriel didn't set eyes on him again for a year. He had never thought of his younger son as stubborn – that was more Caspar and Damson's style – but his absence from Mermaid House during those twelve months proved beyond measure that he was as stubborn as Gabriel himself. He could almost respect his son for that.

The sound of an engine jolted Gabriel out of his thoughts. 'Shall I go and see who it is?' asked Ned, already slipping down from his seat and opening the top half of the camper-van door so that he could peer out. 'It's a car,' he announced, standing on tiptoe. 'There's someone to see you, Mr Liberty.'

'Top marks, young man,' said Gabriel, using his hand to wipe a peephole through the steamed-up window and recognising, with annoyance, the mobile Japanese torture chamber that had pulled into the courtyard. Didn't the wretched man have the sick and the dying to attend to?

'Shall I invite him in, Mummy?'

'No, Ned, I'm sure Mr Liberty would rather entertain his guest in the comfort of his own home.'

Gabriel put a last piece of sausage into his mouth and rose stiffly to his feet. He had a nasty feeling that he knew why Dr Singh had called today, and if he was ever going to get the irritating quack off his case, he was going to have to engage his brain in some nimble thinking.

Dr Singh was already knocking on the back door by the time Gabriel made it across the courtyard in the rain. 'You know what your trouble is,' he said to the doctor, 'you've got too much time on your hands. I suppose you want to come in?'

'Good morning to you, Mr Liberty. Yes, entry to your fine house so that we can both get out of this terrible rain would be in both our interests, I suspect.'

'And I suspect you of foul play,' Gabriel said when they were standing in the kitchen, and Dr Singh had removed his wet coat and was requesting a look at his arm. 'You're keeping a close watch on me and I don't like it.'

'Mm . . . that's good. It's improving nicely. Eye next. Foul play? In what way?'

'You're biding your time before you start insisting that I do something about getting help around my house. You'll pull another of your blackmail stunts on me if I don't do as you say.'

'Tsk, tsk, Mr Liberty. I can't think what you're referring to. Mm . . . yes, your eye looks much better. But you do need help and I'm determined to make you see that. It's a big house you have here. And you're not—'

'And I'm not getting any younger,' Gabriel finished for him. 'Blah-di-blah-di-blah. You're just dying to get Social Services on to me, aren't you? You'd like nothing better than to have me rehoused in a tiny box with a warden banging on the door every ten minutes to check I haven't gassed myself through boredom. Why don't you just have done with it and measure me up for a coffin?'

'A tempting suggestion, and certainly something to consider. As risky as it is, may I wash my hands?' He pulled out a small hand towel from his medical bag, along with a tiny bar of wrapped soap.

'Oh, please, be my guest.'

'Talking of which, would I be correct in thinking you have one?' The doctor looked through the window, out across the courtyard. 'A member of your family, perhaps? Or are you about to take to the road and broaden your horizons?'

'My horizons are plenty broad enough, thank you. If you must know . . .' But his words petered out. 'Family,' he repeated, 'why did you say that?'

'A shot in the dark.'

Family, echoed Gabriel privately. Now there was an idea. But would it work? Surely it had to be worth a try? 'Actually, your stab in the dark is spot on. My daughter's come to stay with me.'

Dr Singh turned off the tap with the tip of a forefinger, picked the small white towel from his shoulder, and dried his hands. 'You've had a change of heart, then?'

Gabriel looked at him blankly. 'What do you mean?'

'The last time we spoke you gave the impression that your family meant little to you. Has a reconciliation taken place?'

'Ah . . . something like that, yes.'

Dr Singh smiled. 'That is wonderful news. So, will you be allowing your daughter to play a more active role in your life from now on?'

'Oh, do me the honour of getting to the point. What you're really asking is, am I going to let her help me clean up my act?'

'You put it so well, Mr Liberty.'

'And if that were to happen, would you leave me alone? Would you stop turning up here with spurious excuses to check on my welfare with blackmail on your mind?'

'I might.'

'Well, you stay right there while I go and fetch my daughter for you to meet. You'll soon see that I'm now in thoroughly good hands.'

Crossing the courtyard, Gabriel had no idea if Miss Costello would play ball with him, but as he had just reasoned with himself, it had to be worth a try. All he had to do was inveigle her into telling a white lie or two and everyone would be happy.

Or, more precisely, *he* would be happy.

16

As she stacked the dirty plates to be washed, with Ned at her side on his little step ready to help, Clara listened to Mr Liberty's extraordinary proposal. Amused, she let him grind on until at last he came to a halt and his words were left hanging awkwardly in the confined space between them. Waiting for her response, he shuffled his big feet from side to side like a naughty schoolboy up before the headmaster. 'Now let me get this straight,' she said, 'you want *me* to pretend to be your daughter?'

He shuffled again. 'I thought I'd just made that abundantly clear.'

'Would it be too much of an imposition to ask why?'

'I might have known you'd make matters difficult. Why can't you just accept what I've asked you to do?'

'Because it's not in my nature. I like to be presented with all the salient facts before I make up my mind about anything. If I'm going to play along with your curious game of subterfuge, I think I ought to be allowed to know the whys, the hows, and the whats. So divvy up the information or leave Ned and me to get on. We have a busy day ahead of us.'

'God *damn* it! You're the most infuriating woman I have ever had the misfortune to meet, Miss Costello.'

'With all due respect, Mr Liberty, it strikes me that you need my help more than I need your impertinence, so if you're through with the name-calling, perhaps—'

'All right, all right. I need you to pretend to be my daughter so that annoying quack will leave me alone. I need to prove to him that I have a loving member of my family clasped to my bosom who is eager to keep a watchful eye over me.'

'And if you can't prove that is the case?'

'I'll probably have Social Services snooping round here faster than you can say meals on bloody wheels. And they won't leave it there. You've seen the state of the house – their next move will be to have me rehoused, claiming I'm incapable of taking care of myself.'

'You don't think you're overreacting just a touch? They couldn't do that unless you allowed them to.'

'If it was your freedom in the balance, would you want to risk it?'

She considered what he had said. Okay, maybe he was being paranoid, and perhaps he might be better off in a more wholesome environment with a regular supply of meals, but who was to say, other than the man himself, whether he would *feel* better off living that way? If he wanted to spend the rest of his life, until he died from bubonic plague, surrounded by his own mess, wasn't that his right? She didn't know anything about taking care of the elderly and what powers Social Services had, but she knew enough to understand that a matter of principle was at stake. Clearly Mr Liberty felt that this Dr Singh, who was currently waiting to meet his patient's loving, caring daughter inside Mermaid House, wasn't going to leave him alone until he had been convinced that his patient was to be looked after. If a couple of fibs was all it would take to make everyone happy, why not tell them?

'Okay,' she said, 'I'll do it. And given that your doctor has been kept waiting long enough, we ought to get this over and done with immediately. We don't have time to concoct anything elaborate so we'll have to keep our story simple. Agreed?'

He nodded. 'If he asks, I thought you could tell him you were coming to stay indefinitely.'

'And Ned? What do we say about him?'

Mr Liberty hesitated. 'I hadn't thought of him. I suppose he'll have to be my grandson.'

At this last remark, and with his hands cupping an enormous bubble, Ned turned from the sink. He beamed and gave the bubble a long, steady blow. It moved slowly from his hands, drifted up towards Mr Liberty and came to rest on his shoulder. Where it burst.

'Let's hope that's not what's going to happen to our story when we meet your Dr Singh,' Clara remarked.

Dr Singh was absorbed in a three-month-old *Daily Telegraph* that was lying on top of a box of old shoes and jam-jars when Gabriel and his newly acquired family entered the kitchen. He raised his head when he heard their footsteps.

In a loud, jovial voice, Gabriel said, 'Dr Singh, I'd like you to meet my daughter, Damson, and my grandson, Ned.'

'I'm very pleased to meet you,' the doctor said, coming forward to shake hands. 'But, Mr Liberty, you didn't tell me you were fortunate enough to be a grandfather. And such a fine-looking boy. So like his mother. The resemblance is uncanny.'

'You're not my priest, I don't have to confess everything to you.'

Dr Singh shared a conspiratorial smile with Miss Costello. 'Your father is a very unusual man. His sense of humour is not to everyone's taste, I think.'

'Oh, he's always been a quirky old devil, but that's his charm. Affectionately curmudgeonly, is what we say about him. Isn't that right, *Dad*?'

She's enjoying every moment of this, thought Gabriel, with a half-smile.

But then, truth to tell, so was he. It was particularly satisfying knowing that he was getting one over on this interfering quack. 'If you say so, *dear*.'

'He tells me that you're coming to stay with him,' Dr Singh said.

'Yes, that's right. I thought I'd take him in hand, you know, tidy the place up a bit, maybe even encourage him to find himself a housekeeper.'

Dr Singh smiled again. 'I wish you luck in those tasks.' He cast his eyes meaningfully around the kitchen.

'Oh, I think I'm more than up to the task of whipping my rascal of a father into shape. No worries on that score.'

'Well, if you've both finished discussing me as though I were a dimwit,' Gabriel said tersely, 'perhaps you'd be kind enough to show the doctor to the door, *Damson*. There's a whole world of terminally ill people out there who must be desperate for a good dying scene in the arms of their local GP.'

'Yes, *Dad*, of course.'

Thinking how easily they'd got away with it, Gabriel watched the doctor being led out of the kitchen. He heard the back door open and was on the verge of a congratulatory pat on the back when the doctor reappeared. Gabriel froze. Damn! Had the wretched man merely been playing along with them?

'Dear, oh dear,' the doctor said, 'you would think I'd know better by now.' He came towards Gabriel and reached for his medical bag, which he'd left on a chair beside the table. 'I've been told so many times that I would lose my head if it were not joined to the rest of me.' He laughed brightly.

Gabriel forced himself to join in. 'Got everything now?' he asked.

'I do hope so. I certainly don't want to have to make another trip out here today. Your drive is murder on my little car's suspension.'

'You'd better keep away, then.'

Despite the rain, Miss Costello walked the doctor to his car. Through the window, Gabriel could see that they were deep in conversation. No need to ask who or what they were discussing. Doubtless the good doctor was pumping the prodigal daughter about her pathetic old father.

'Well?' he said, when she came back into the kitchen.

'Well what?' she asked, shaking the droplets of rain from her hair.

'Did we get away with it?'

'For the time being, yes.'

'Uh?'

'You've earned yourself a reprieve until next week. He said he's going to try and pop in on Monday to make sure your eye has recovered.'

'This is victimisation,' Gabriel roared. 'I won't stand for it. It's outrageous!'

'A lot of people would give their back teeth for such a caring doctor.'

'Well, I'm not one of them! I'll – I'll pretend I'm not in. Or, better still, I'll go to the surgery. That'll show the stupid little man.' Then, in a less acerbic tone, 'Why can't people understand that I just want to be left alone? Is that really too much to ask?' He slumped into a chair at the table.

With her hands resting on Ned's shoulders, Clara observed him from across the room. The poor man made a desolate picture. And for the first time since meeting him, she saw not a growling, teeth-baring tyrant but an elderly man who wanted to preserve his dignity. It was just that he was going about it in the wrong way.

The modern world didn't work by the old rules of dictatorship. Nowadays it was run on different lines, by compromise, tact, guile, and subtle manipulation. She should know: she had used them well enough during her time with Phoenix. She had lost count of the number of management training courses she had been on where she had been told that there is no such thing as a problem: problems are challenges, and challenges are to be shared.

But how could this old man ever adapt? How could he ever wise up to the great universal truth that it was all about give and take?

17

There was nothing else she could say so Clara took Ned's hand and turned to leave. 'Why is Mr Liberty so sad?' Ned asked, his voice too loud and too clear.

'I'm not sad,' rumbled Mr Liberty, his head still in his hands. 'I've never been sad in my life.'

Pulling his hand out of Clara's grasp, Ned went back to the table, stood next to the old man and peered at him. 'Why are you hiding behind your hands?' he asked. 'Are you playing a game? Granda does that with me. He sits very still, makes gaps in his fingers, then suddenly goes, *boo*! It makes me jump every time. Shall I show you?' Before either Clara or Mr Liberty could stop him, Ned let out an almighty boo! Mr Liberty jumped, but Clara could see that he was trying to pretend he hadn't. 'Do you want to play that game with me?' asked Ned. 'It might cheer you up.'

'Ned, I don't think Mr Liberty wants to play anything right now. He's not in the mood. And, anyway, we've got to keep our part of the bargain.'

At this, Mr Liberty raised his head. 'Bargain?'

'You generously gave us a place to stop for the night on the understanding we wouldn't cause you any trouble and that we would be gone first thing.' She looked at her watch. 'First thing was several hours ago, but by lunchtime we should be out of your way.'

Mr Liberty seemed to pull himself together. 'Of course. Well, I mustn't keep you. An agreement is an agreement. Where are you going? Have you sorted out a campsite?'

'Not yet, but I thought we'd go into Deaconsbridge and stock up on supplies. I also need to find a launderette.'

'You've as much chance of finding one of those round here as tripping over a crock of gold.' He was sounding much more his indomitable self. 'We used to have one, but it was turned into a fancy art gallery selling tacky paintings to dumb tourists who wouldn't know art if it jumped up and bit them on the nose.'

Clara smiled. 'We'll make it our first port of call, then.' Once more she turned to go, then hesitated. 'Would you like us to fetch you anything? It wouldn't be any trouble.'

He regarded her uncertainly. 'You're coming back in this direction?'

'Not specifically, but I don't mind making the trip. You're not that far out of the town, are you?'

'That's good of you,' he said gruffly. He took a ballpoint pen from Ned, who was making an irritating noise by repeatedly clicking the top of it with his thumb. 'But there's nothing I need.'

She looked at him thoughtfully. 'You're not used to kindness, are you?'

He squared his shoulders and straightened his back. 'At my age, kindness and charity become indistinguishable.'

'So you'd be much happier if you believed my offer was born out of a desire to interfere, rather than accept it as a genuine offer to help?'

He didn't say anything, but removed from Ned's hands a magnifying-glass he had unearthed from an overflowing shoebox of junk on the table. He had been using it to inspect Mermy at close quarters.

'Look,' she said, trying to be conciliatory, 'I'm sorry things didn't pan out better with your tenacious doctor, but the only way you're going to get him off your back is to meet him half-way. Clean the place up and prove to him you can fend for yourself. Can't you enlist your real daughter's help?'

Mr Liberty brought the magnifying-glass down on the table with a sharp bang. 'Damson doesn't show her face here unless she has to.' His voice was hard, scornful.

'Damson's an unusual name. I meant to ask you about it earlier.'

'Sounds more like a cat's name, doesn't it? Which is quite appropriate. Damson can be as sleek and cunning as any feline creature I've ever known. Scratchy too, when she wants to be.'

'Was the name your idea?'

He shook his head. 'The credit goes to my first wife. She had a fondness for the eccentric.'

Clara realised that this was the first time he had referred to his family. 'Do you have any other children?' she asked.

'A pair of sons who are both two shades of stupid. Caspar is a conman with as much head for business as a watermelon. He's a chippy brat who, like Icarus, hasn't yet learned the hazards of flying too close to the sun. My other son, Jonah, is a weak-willed idealist.'

'And what terrible crime did he commit to gain such familial approval?'

'*That*, Miss Costello, is none of your business. And while we're on the subject, why have you started asking me so many questions? I thought you said you were going.'

'I was simply wondering why you don't ask for their help. And you've given me the answer. You've scared them off, haven't you? But, like you said, it's none of my business so I'll say goodbye. It's been an education meeting you.' She held out her hand.

He stared at it hard, rose to his feet, and took it in his large distorted paw. Then he withdrew it, looking as if he was about to say something important. 'Tell me, Miss Costello,' he said slowly, 'you strike me as a woman who enjoys a challenge. Am I right?'

'It has been said of me, yes.'

'And you told me over breakfast that you don't have any real plans, that you and your son are just drifting from one place to another. Is that so?'

'Absolutely nothing wrong with your memory. Your point being?'

'I'd like to make you an offer. Help rid me of that interfering quack by pretending to be my daughter for a while longer.'

'Are we talking more lies? And perhaps you'd elaborate on what *a while longer* actually means. Another day? Another two days?' She watched him swallow and sensed that he was hoping for more than that from her.

'It depends on how long you think it would take to sort out this mess.' He indicated the kitchen.

Clara was stunned. He couldn't be serious. 'Whoa there, I'm not sure I like where this is going. What on earth makes you think I would be remotely interested in dealing with this little lot? Ned and I are on holiday. Cleaning up after somebody else doesn't feature on our itinerary.'

'But you do owe me a favour.'

'Since when?'

'Since I rescued you from those goons when you were trespassing on my land.'

The breathtaking cheek of the man! 'Oh, nice try,' she said derisively. 'You think you can toss that one in and hold my conscience to ransom. Well, think again, buddy, because you've got me all wrong. Anyway, I've already carried out one favour for you by lying to Dr Singh about being your daughter.'

'If I can't appeal to your good nature, then maybe your purse will be a better option.'

'Sorry, still not interested. Try flaunting your money at the *Yellow Pages*.'

'I'd sooner flaunt it at a person I know and trust.'

'How can you be so sure I won't fleece you?'

'I pride myself on being a good judge of character.'

'The flattery, even from you, won't work. Get hold of a firm of contract cleaners with a good reputation.'

'I don't want strangers in my house. Please, won't you even consider my offer? I'm willing to pay you whatever it takes.'

She held her ground. 'Look, you might be used to bullying people into doing what you want them to do, but you can't do the same with me. And, for your information, I'm not for sale.'

'Come, come, everything is for sale, surely you know that. And just think of the challenge.'

'The answer is still a resounding no.'

It was the most monstrously ludicrous idea Clara had ever heard, and as she and Ned packed up Winnie, she didn't know whether to feel flattered by Mr Liberty's proposal, that he clearly approved of her, or downright insulted that he had thought she might want to waste her holiday cleaning up his mess.

'Completely off his trolley,' she muttered under her breath, as she moved about Winnie, putting packets and jars into their respective cubby-holes and slamming the locker doors. 'Just who does he think he is?'

It was a power thing, she suspected. Old Laughing Boy needed someone he could treat as a skivvy. That was what this was about. Well, not this girl. She was nobody's skivvy. No sirree. And how dare he think she could be bought off? She hadn't given up a well-paid job to become a cleaner for that miserable old goat!

Gabriel watched the camper-van trundle slowly along the drive until it was out of sight. He turned from the rain-lashed stone mullion window in the tower, angry and disappointed: angry because he had been reduced to the humiliating level of begging somebody to help him and disappointed because he knew he was going to miss having that Costello woman and her son around. They hadn't been with him long, but there had been something about them he had liked, something about their company that had appealed to him.

The woman's forthrightness had been a refreshing change from the patronising sycophancy with which he was frequently treated, and the boy had been as bright as a button, not missing anything that was going on around him. He had forgotten how honest children could be. How they could put their finger on a raw spot and prod it mercilessly. Sad, was how the youngster had described him. Well, yes, in that moment he had felt sad. Weary too. Worn out. Shrivelled up. A husk of his former self. Old, and ready to throw in the towel.

He knew he was bucking against the system, which held all the trump cards. It was only a matter of time before Dr Singh and his kind would have their pernicious way with him. It was his greatest fear that the time would come when he would be carted off to live the remainder of his life among a crowd of insufferable strangers whose only excitement would be a change of incontinence pad after a game of bingo. It was, he knew, a fear that was bordering on the pathological, and not one based on personal experience of these places. But he had read enough horror stories in the papers to know that dreadful things went on in retirement homes. Last year, before the television had broken, he had watched an appalling series of programmes about a bunch of poor old dears and ageing Jack the Lads living out their lives to the tune of 'It's a Long Way to Tipperary' and 'The Hokey-Cokey'. Sometimes he had nightmares about this from which he woke in a sweat, heart pounding, terrified that he would end his days with sickeningly motherly women calling him 'dear' and offering to take him to the lavatory. Dear God, he'd rather take one of his shotguns to his head.

That was why he had resorted to pleading with the Costello woman. He had seen in her someone capable and strong, someone he could trust to help him sort out Mermaid House. He knew it had to be done, and if somebody could just get the job started for him, he felt confident he would see it through.

Nothing had been done since well before Val's death, and all of her things were still lying about the place – clothes, jewellery, perfume, books, stuff he didn't need, but felt he couldn't discard. It seemed sacrilegious to dismantle her life like that.

It had been the same when Anastasia had died. It had been years before he had emptied her wardrobes and dressing-table. But then it had been different: he hadn't wanted to part with Anastasia's belongings. Having them around had kept her alive somehow. For a long time after her death, and before going to bed at night, he would open a cupboard and run his hands through her dresses, holding the smooth fabrics against his face, breathing in her sweet, sensual fragrance. One night, when he had thought the children were asleep, Damson had crept up on him and asked what he was doing. She had stood in the doorway, her head tilted to one side, looking at him as though he were quite mad. 'You should throw everything away,' she had said matter-of-factly, 'or burn it. Caspar and I could make a bonfire for you.'

He could scarcely believe what he was hearing: seven years old and she was offering to burn the few tangible keepsakes they had of her mother. The cruelty of her words had horrified him. 'Why are you being so disgustingly insensitive, Damson?' he had asked.

She hadn't answered, just stared at him until he closed the wardrobe door.

He had told the twins that no amount of tears would bring their mother back, and he could not recall seeing either Caspar or Damson cry for her. Not even at the funeral, when they had stood beside him beneath the hot summer sun, perfectly composed, their dry-eyed gaze on their mother's coffin as they held hands, united by something that had excluded him.

He crossed the dusty wooden floor to the narrow staircase that led back to a short, unlit passageway, then on to the library, where a secret door opened to the right of the fireplace. It was this that he had shown Ned that morning. The little lad's eyes had grown as large as hub-caps when Gabriel had shown him the hidden handle that made the lower half of the bookcase swing open. 'Where does it go?' Ned had asked, peering cautiously into the darkness.

'It goes up to the tower you can see from the front of the house.'

'Will you take me to see it, please? I'll be very good.'

'If you promise to take care where you put your feet,' Gabriel had told him, as he dipped his head and led the way. 'It's as black as pitch, so stay close to me.'

'Are there any spiders?'

'Lots.'

'Big ones?'

'Enormous, and wearing hobnail boots and carrying sawn-off shotguns. So mind you don't look them in the eye or they'll have you for breakfast.'

He had enjoyed seeing the look on the lad's face as he tried to figure out how much to believe, and it had made him spin even more yarns of mysterious intrigue, of ghosts who lived in the tower, shook their chains and slammed doors at dead of night. All nonsense, of course, but it was what children lapped up.

When he had looked through the kitchen window first thing that morning and had seen Ned's face staring back at him from the camper-van, he had acted on a rare impulse and gone outside to see if the boy wanted to go round the house. He knew now that it had been a mistake to encourage him to go against his mother's rule – that he wasn't to leave the van without her permission – but it had seemed harmless at the time. She had been sound asleep and it had seemed better to let her enjoy a lie-in while her son had a bit of fun.

Which he had. He'd been thrilled by the secret passageway and had loved the tower, asking politely to be held up high so that he could look out at the view.

It had been ages since Gabriel had been to the tower and it had looked worse than he had remembered it. The last time he'd ventured up there had been to let out a bird that had got in through a broken window – droppings were still stuck to the floor and walls.

As children, Caspar and Damson had regularly holed up in the tower. Jonah had never been allowed in. Even when Val had intervened, they had refused him entry. 'He's a stupid baby,' they had yelled through the door, 'and we're not having him in here with us. He'll spoil what we're doing.'

Back in the library, and shutting the secret door behind him, Gabriel sighed. So many memories contained in one house. Some good. Some not so good. And some plain awful.

Perhaps if he could get rid of some of the rubbish from the house he might cleanse it of the memories he would rather forget. Selective memory via a damn good spring-clean, that's what he needed.

When he'd been widowed for the second time he had imagined he would more than cope with all this domestic malarkey. Nothing to it, he had thought, so long as he could boil himself an egg and remember to fill the washing-machine once a week. But he hadn't bargained on things going wrong, or fiddly, time-consuming jobs piling up until they had the better of him.

He cursed under his breath that the Costello woman hadn't accepted his offer. Now she and her son were gone.

Well, good riddance! Coming here and cadging off him for free!
Pah!

18

Clara had hoped to prove Mr Liberty wrong, but so far her search had revealed that Deaconsbridge was a launderette-free zone, just as he had said. It hadn't been a complete waste of time, though: she now had the lie of the land and knew that there was a modest supermarket a short distance from the market square where they could stock up on supplies.

'Ho hum,' she said to Ned, as they circled the market square one last time, the rain coming down harder still and the long wiper blades swishing across the windscreen, 'I guess this is one of those rare occasions when I'll have to admit defeat. Perhaps the next campsite we stay at will have a machine we can use. Shall we get the shopping done now?'

'Then can we go to the Mermaid café for lunch?'

'Good thinking, and while we're there, we'll make our plans. We'll look at the map and see if we can find a campsite we like the sound of. Oh, and something else we need to do before we leave. We must buy a large notebook and some postcards.'

Taking the next left, Clara told Ned about her idea that they should keep a diary. He liked the sound of this. 'Ooh, can we buy some new crayons, please?'

She smiled. What was it with children and crayons? It didn't matter how many packets you bought them, they could never have enough new ones. From the moment Ned had been old enough to grasp a crayon between his fingers, he had turned into a stationery fiend. At home, he was forever setting out his stash of felt-tip pens, rubbers, paper-clips and pads of paper. Her mother claimed that Clara had been the same as a child, except her collection had boasted several hundred pencil-sharpeners. Apparently she had always been striving for the ultimate sharp point. 'I think the budget will stretch to that,' she said.

'I'm going to draw Mr Liberty and his castle.'

'Steady on, Ned, this is a diary we're writing, not a horror story.'

'And next I'll draw the secret passageway and the tower he showed me,' Ned said enthusiastically. 'He told me it was full of spiders, but I didn't see any. He also said they wore boots and had guns, but I knew he was joking. Spiders aren't big enough to carry guns, are they, Mummy?'

'They might need to, living with a man like Mr Liberty. Right, here we are. And thank the Lord, it's free parking if we're only here for an hour. Life just gets better and better, Ned.'

The supermarket was a small independent one that Clara had never heard of. Built of local stone and tinted glass, it was conspicuous among the old buildings that surrounded it.

They dashed through the rain from the van to the front of the store, grabbed a trolley and made a start. But with Ned at the helm it was only a matter of time before they crashed into someone or something. He gave the job his entire concentration, and their first target was a freezer offering two packs of chicken Kiev for the price of one and placed inconveniently in the middle of an aisle. Next they scored a direct hit on a large wire basket of Walker's crisps. And finally, coming into the home straight, through wines and spirits, they rammed a trolley being pushed by a long-faced man in an expensive suit. Miraculously they arrived at the checkout relatively unscathed and with everything they'd gone in for, except the notebook and crayons.

There were only two checkouts in use, so they joined the one with the smallest queue. To Clara's embarrassment, the long-faced man pulled in behind them. She noticed that his trolley contained a dozen bottles of champagne that was on special offer. For a Champagne Charlie, he looked wildly out of place. 'Come on,' he muttered irritably after a few minutes. He tapped an expensively shod foot impatiently. 'What's the hold-up?'

The question was directed at nobody in particular, and Clara had no intention of answering it. Instead, she finished loading their shopping on to the conveyor belt, and looked at the woman in front of her. She was in her mid- to late seventies, Clara reckoned, and was wearing the type of felt hat Clara's grandmother used to wear. She looked upset and was glancing from the checkout girl to the purse in her trembling hands. She said something that Clara didn't catch. In response an over-plucked eyebrow hitched itself skyward. 'You what?'

Whatever the older woman had said, it wasn't getting her anywhere, and the girl – a sullen piece of work dressed in a pink and white overall – drummed her sparkly false nails on the till and rolled her eyes at Clara as if to say, 'Got a right one here.'

'Will you please get a move on?' the suit demanded from behind Clara. 'Unlike most people round here in Hicksville, I don't have all day to waste.'

Queue rage, thought Clara, with disgust. She left Ned scaling the side of their trolley and went to see if she could help. 'What's the problem?' she asked the checkout girl.

'Search me. The daft old bat's not making any sense.'

Clara turned to the older woman. 'Can I help?'

A pale anxious face, brimming with confusion and distress, looked at Clara. Trembling hands showed her the snap-fastened purse: it was empty. Oh, Lord, thought Clara, now what?

'Oh, for heaven's sake, this is ridiculous. Will somebody *do* something?'

Clara turned and smiled sweetly at the suit. 'For a start, you could try piping down, mate. No, better still, take your bargain-price bubbly and go and join the other queue.'

He stared at her furiously. 'And *you* should try keeping your brat under control. He's stepped on my foot three times since I've been standing here.'

She did the adult thing, poked her tongue out at him, then turned back to the woman and her empty purse. 'How much is it?' she asked the girl on the till.

'How much is what?'

'This customer's *bill*,' she said, slowly and with sarcastic emphasis. 'Please, do stop me if I'm going too fast for you.'

'It's three pounds seventeen.' The girl pouted.

'Goodness, a king's ransom.' Digging into her bag, Clara offered her credit card. 'Right, stick it on this and put my shopping through as fast as your helpful little fingers can manage it. *Okay?*'

'Stuck-up bitch,' the girl muttered, as Clara turned to explain the situation to the woman. She was looking even more confused and distressed.

'There's no need to worry,' Clara said. 'It's been taken care of. I've paid it for you.' But her words seemed to add to the poor woman's anxiety and she started speaking so fast that Clara couldn't understand what she was saying. 'Here,' she said slowly. 'This is your bag of shopping. Will you be all right now?'

But the head shook again, and a hand squeezed Clara's arm. After an agonising pause, she said, 'You ... with me.'

'You want me to come with you?'

A smile of relief and a nod confirmed that she had understood correctly. 'But where to?'

Another chaotic burst of words brought forth no further illumination. 'Do you want me to take you home?'

Clara didn't understand the answer, but after she had bagged up her shopping, paid for it, and insisted that she, not Ned, push the trolley, the three left the store. It was slow going as their newly acquired friend had something wrong with one of her legs and took each step, with the aid of a stick, as if she was picking her way through a minefield. They had run out of time in the car park, so Clara explained to the woman that they would have to drive to wherever it was that she lived. Getting directions was going to prove interesting, though. Then she had the idea of asking the woman to write down her address.

But when she gave the woman a piece of paper and a pen, it became evident that her hands lacked the dexterity to hold anything firmly. Nevertheless, after she had made a huge effort, Clara read the word 'stroke'. Ah, so that was it. She asked the woman where she wanted to go. It took a long time, but 'Second Best' and 'Son' appeared.

Following the woman's hand signals, they drove back into the market square, past the bookshop and the Deaconsbridge Arms, then took a side road called Millstone Row and there, on the corner, they saw a double-fronted shop called Second Best. There was just room to park in front of it, and through the windows Clara could see an Aladdin's cave of bric-a-brac and second-hand furniture. Seeing that her passenger was struggling to release her seat-belt, Clara did it for her, then called through to Ned, 'Okay, you can get out now.'

They entered the shop, their arrival heralded by a tinkling bell. It was jam-packed with corner cupboards, wardrobes and three-piece suites. There were coffee tables, bookcases, lamp-stands, mirrors, ornaments, and any number of chairs – dining chairs, kitchen chairs, garden chairs, even a rocking chair, which drew Ned like a magnet – and bar stools. Despite the quantity of furniture and knick-knacks crammed into the confined space, there was a surprising degree of order to the shop and Vivaldi's Four Seasons was playing on a radio.

'I'll be right with you,' a man's voice told them. 'I'm just on my knees with Des O'Connor and Val Doonican, and how many blokes do you know who would admit to that?'

Before she had set eyes on the voice's owner, Clara had decided she would like him: he sounded so cheerful, a real blast of fresh air.

The old woman took a few painfully slow steps through the shop and disappeared behind an old gas cooker.

'Hello, Mum, you back already with Samson? He found you all right, then? What's wrong?'

This was progress, thought Clara. They'd found the son. After a torrent of jumbled words, he appeared with his mother. In his arms he carried a cardboard box of old LPs.

Clara explained who she was and what had happened in the supermarket. At the man's side, his mother kept muttering something that sounded like 'Bunny. Blow bunny,' and twice showed him her empty purse. Then she started to cry. Her son placed the box of records on the floor and put his arm around her. 'Hey, it's okay, Mum, it doesn't matter. You took the wrong purse, that was all. It could have happened to anyone. Now, why don't you sit down, and I'll make you a cup of tea?'

Helping her out of her coat, he hung it on a convenient coat-stand and settled her into a chocolate-brown leatherette sofa. Clara was struck by his kindness and patience and that he didn't seem at all embarrassed that his mother was crying in front of a stranger. He was well over six feet tall and struck Clara as very much the gentle giant. She put him somewhere in his mid-fifties. He was overweight, but his bulk seemed to emphasise his naturally warm-hearted manner.

'Would you excuse me for a minute?' he said to Clara, when the worst of the tears were over. 'I'll just go and put the kettle on for a brew.' In his absence, Clara joined his mother on the sofa. The woman reached out to

Clara's arm, squeezed it as she had in the supermarket, and eventually produced, 'Bes-sie. Name ... Bessie.'

'I'm pleased to meet you, Bessie. We forgot to introduce ourselves earlier, didn't we, what with all those rude people at the checkout? My name's Clara, and in the rocking chair is my son, Ned.'

The anxious expression gave way to a smile. 'Juggly poy. Juggly pies.'

'Juggly poy?' Clara repeated, hoping for enlightenment.

'She's saying he's a lovely boy, and has lovely eyes.'

The son was back. He set a mug of tea on a small reproduction sherry table beside his mother, even rustled up a coaster from somewhere.

'I'm Archie Merryman, by the way,' he said, holding out a large, strong hand to Clara, 'and I'm extremely grateful to you. My mother had a stroke not so long ago and the words don't always come out as they should.'

'So I understand. I had what I thought was a brilliant idea of getting her to write things down, only I didn't realise it would be so difficult for her.'

'The stroke did its worst down your right side, Mum, didn't it?' he said, turning to his mother to include her in the conversation.

In the silence that followed, Clara realised that the music had stopped, as had the creaking of the rocking chair. She looked to see where Ned was, and located him on the other side of the shop where he was inspecting a commode. 'What's this for, Mummy?' he asked, his voice echoing slightly.

'I'll tell you later.' She glanced back at the owner of the shop, who was smiling. 'Children,' she said, with a shrug, 'questions, questions, questions. And at the least appropriate moment.'

'Eshooks berryou,' Bessie said.

Clara looked to Archie for help.

He interpreted, without a second's hesitation: 'She said he looks like you.'

'Yes, poor lad, there's no disputing his pedigree. You don't mind him poking around, do you?'

'Of course not. It's good to see someone enjoying themselves. He's a grand little chap. Are you here visiting Deaconsbridge?'

'Is it that obvious we're interlopers? I thought we were blending in rather nicely.'

He laughed. 'I've been here more than twenty years, and I still stick out like a sore thumb. But where are my manners? I should have offered you a drink. What can I get you?'

'That's kind, but no thanks. I've promised the chip off the old block lunch in the Mermaid café.' Ned had moved from the commode to a coffee table where he'd found a *Star Wars* jigsaw. 'No, don't tip it out, Ned,' she called, seeing him ready to settle in for the afternoon – there were enough things here to keep even the most hyperactive child amused. She stood up to go. 'Goodbye, Bessie, it was lovely meeting you. You take care now, won't you?' Then to Archie Merryman, she said, 'I know it's a cheek, but would it be all right if I left our van outside your shop while we have something to eat? We won't be very long.'

'Sure. It's the least I can do for you, sweetheart. Enjoy your lunch.'

The bell tinkled merrily behind them as they left, and while they waited for the traffic to pass so that they could cross the road to go back to the market square, Clara thought how nice Archie Merryman was. 'A juggly man,' she said to herself, with a smile.

'It's beginning to feel like home, this place,' Clara said to Ned, when they were sitting at the table they had used yesterday and had been served by the same waitress, whose name was Shirley.

'Why couldn't that lady speak properly?' Ned asked, while they waited for their food.

She told him that Bessie Merryman had had a stroke, and tried to explain what that was without frightening Ned. 'It can happen when you're young, but usually when you get older.'

He thought about this, tracing a finger along the squares on the checked tablecloth. 'Will it happen to Nanna and Granda?' he said, when his finger reached the salt cellar and knocked it over.

'I hope not, but we never know what's round the corner for any of us. It's what life is all about.'

'Why was she crying?'

'Well, in the supermarket people weren't treating her very kindly. The man in the smart suit probably doesn't think about anyone but himself, and the young girl on the till was probably worrying about what she ought to wear that night to go out. To them, poor Bessie was a nuisance who they couldn't be bothered to understand or help. She knew that, and it was horribly embarrassing for her and made her very upset.'

'I didn't like that man.'

'Was that why you kept stepping on his foot?'

He looked at her coyly from beneath his long lashes.

'I thought so, you little rascal.'

The café was even busier today and it was a while before the waitress brought them their meal. She explained that it was always like this when the weather turned wet. 'It brings the walkers down from the hills and moors in search of something warm to stick their ribs together,' she said. 'It'll be crazy like this for some days.'

'I thought you said the weather was breaking at the weekend. What went wrong with the forecast?'

She wiped her hands on her red overall. 'I was only out by a couple of days. And any road, we have our own climate round here. We're a law unto ourselves.'

'It means that, like any true Deaconite, she makes it up as she goes along.'

The three turned to see who had spoken.

'Ah, and what would you know about the weather, Archie Merryman? Are those flowers for me by any chance?'

He gave her a wink. 'Another bunch, another time, Shirley. Mind if I join you for a couple of seconds? I won't keep you,' he said to Clara.

'No, no, of course not. Please, sit down. What's wrong?'

'Nothing. It's just that I forgot to pay you back for my mother's shopping. And . . . and I also wanted to give you these, to say thank you for what you did.' He handed the flowers across the table.

Clara was touched. 'I don't know what to say except thank you. They're lovely.' She breathed in the heady scent of the purple freesias. 'Mm . . . wonderful. But there was no need for you to go to all this trouble.'

'I'll have to disagree with you on that point. And this is for you, Ned.' From a carrier-bag that Clara hadn't noticed until now, he pulled out the *Star Wars* jigsaw Ned had been looking at in the shop.

'Ooh, thank you,' he said, putting down his knife and fork with a clatter and kneeling up on his chair for a better look.

'This is very generous of you,' Clara said, 'but really—'

'No buts, sweetheart. Definitely no buts.' From his shirt pocket he retrieved a roll of money. 'Now, then, how much was my mother's shopping?'

'Glory be, do you always carry that amount of money round with you?'

'In my trade, cash is the best currency.'

'Well, you can put it back in your pocket. I don't need reimbursing.'

He frowned. 'That arrangement really doesn't suit me. I'm used to paying my whack.'

'It was hardly anything. I was just pleased I was there to help.'

He turned to Ned who, while tracing the outline of Luke Skywalker on the lid of the jigsaw box with a finger, was working on a long strand of spaghetti. His cheeks were sucked in hard and his lips were pasted with Bolognese sauce. 'Ned, you have a peach of a mother. You take good care of her, won't you?'

Clara laughed. 'Please, stop it, you're embarrassing him. To say nothing of what you're doing to me.'

'In that case, I'd better go.' He stood up abruptly.

Disappointed to see him leave so soon, she said, 'Have you left your mother on her own in the shop?'

'No, Samson's with her now. He got held up in traffic and didn't make it in time to fetch Mum from the supermarket as we'd arranged. I'm trying to give her as much independence as possible, but it's not easy. Anyway, enough of the moaning from me. Are you leaving Deaconsbridge today or will we be lucky enough to see you around town for a few days yet?'

'If I can find a suitable campsite nearby, there's every chance you might see us again. Our plans are fairly flexible.'

'We're going to see the Mermaid Cavern,' Ned piped up. 'And I've got a mermaid of my own. She lives in my pocket. Do you want to see her?'

'A mermaid in your pocket? Now, this I have to see.' He watched as Ned dug around inside his pockets. 'You know the cavern's not open yet, don't you?' he said to Clara.

'Yes, Shirley gave us the bad news yesterday.'

'Mummy,' Ned said, his voice wavering and his face crumpling, 'I can't find Mermy.' His lower lip wobbled. He got down from his chair, came round to Clara and buried his tomatoey face in her lap. 'I've lost Mermy,' he wailed.

19

Ned was inconsolable. He had only ever mislaid Mermy once before, during an overnight stay with Nanna and Granda when Clara was away on business. He was so distraught that his grandparents had ransacked the house, combed every square inch of the garden and turned the car inside out. When, in desperation, they emptied the kitchen bin they had found Mermy hiding inside a crushed tea-bag box. Nobody knew how she had got there, but her reappearance had instantly dried Ned's tears.

Clara knew now that if she was going to calm her son, she would have to convince him that, no matter what it took, she would find Mermy.

With most of the occupants of the crowded café looking sympathetically in their direction, Clara lifted Ned on to her lap. She took a paper napkin from the holder on the table and wiped his eyes. 'It's okay, Ned,' she soothed, 'we'll find her. Don't worry. She probably slipped out of your pocket in the supermarket.'

'Or she might be back at my shop,' Archie said, bending down so that he was eye to eye with Ned.

But Ned was far from consoled. 'Someone might have taken her,' he whimpered, his breath catching in shaky gulps. He buried his face in Clara's shoulder.

Shirley came over. 'You been upsetting the little boy with your ugly mug, Archie?' she asked.

Clara explained what had happened.

'Oh, dearie me,' Shirley said. 'Nothing for it but to retrace your steps. Where've you been today?'

Ned peeled himself away from Clara's shoulder. 'Mummy, I think I know where she is.'

'You do?'

He sniffed loudly. 'I left her at Mr Liberty's house.'

Clara didn't know whether to be relieved or disappointed. A return visit to Mermaid House and its splenetic owner – just how much fun could a girl cope with? 'Are you sure?'

Another messy sniff and a nod. 'I was playing with her at the table when you were talking to Mr Liberty.'

Clara vaguely remembered Ned inspecting Mermy with a magnifying-glass. 'And you haven't seen her since?' she clarified. 'Not in Winnie, perhaps?'

'I don't think so.'

'Well, that looks like it's settled,' Archie said. 'Where does this Mr Liberty live, by the way? Will you have far to go?'

'He lives in a castle,' Ned said, wiping his eyes with the backs of his hands. 'He has a tower and I've been up it. *And* he has a secret passageway.'

'This wouldn't be Mr Liberty of Mermaid House, Hollow Edge Moor, would it?' asked Shirley.

'You know him?' Clara said.

'Probably safe to say that most folk know of him,' Shirley answered. 'He comes in here every Friday lunchtime. None of the others,' she tilted her head in the direction of the kitchen, 'will serve him. I'm the only one thick-skinned enough. The man never has a civil thing to say for himself. If I was being polite I'd say he was a poor old fool who was losing his marbles. But if I was being honest, I'd say he was a disagreeable old crosspatch who ought to learn some manners.'

'You don't think he's just a lonely old man who's a touch eccentric?' Clara wondered why she felt the need to defend him.

'Try serving him in here when you're rushed off your feet and he's banging his spoon on the table to grab your attention.'

'She's a sweet, tolerant little thing, isn't she?' Archie said, when Shirley had moved on to clear another table.

'So what's your opinion of Mr Liberty?'

'If he's the same chap I ran into at the hospital the other day, I'd say he's a man of elusive charm and has a way to go in the tact and diplomacy stakes. What will you do? Go up to Hollow Edge Moor now and see if the little lad's toy is there, or would you like a hand checking out places closer to home first?'

Touched again by his thoughtfulness, Clara said, 'Ned seems pretty sure that he's left Mermy at Mermaid House, so we'll start our search there. If we draw a blank,' she added, lowering her voice, not wanting to dash Ned's hopes, 'we'll come back and have a look at the supermarket. Thanks for the offer of help, though.'

'I'll give the shop a good going-over as well, just in case. If I find it, I'll put it somewhere safe for you. Anyway, I'd better be getting back. Take care now. And thank you again for what you did for Bessie.'

It had stopped raining by the time they left the café and crossed the market square to where they had left Winnie. Through the window of Second Best, Clara could see Archie talking to an enormous young man with a pair of weight-lifter's shoulders. As she started the engine, they both turned. In response to Archie's wave, she waved back and pipped the horn.

'Right,' she said to Ned, 'fingers crossed that Mermy is where you think she is.' And fingers crossed, she thought, joining the flow of traffic, that Mr

Liberty hasn't done something unspeakable to her. And there you go again, she told herself. She was badmouthing a man she scarcely knew. Perhaps she ought to stop and ask herself why he was such a misery? What had happened to him to make him so unlovable? Why had he lost his respect for and pleasure in the world around him? And why was he deliberately isolating himself from it and those who should have given him the most reward: his children?

Having experienced nothing but love and support from her own close-knit family, and been lucky enough to have such wonderful friends, Clara couldn't imagine what it would feel like to be so alone. As for cutting herself off from Ned, she might just as well consider lopping off a limb.

Before she conceived Ned, she had never been one of those naturally maternal women who go all gooey at the merest glimpse of a Mothercare catalogue. Not once had she been conscious of her biological clock ticking away its indubitable message that time waits for no woman who wants to start a family. Perhaps it was because she had always thought that she would get married before she had a child. And with her not being married, or in any hurry to be so, she had not felt the lack of a baby in her life.

But then she had met Todd and she began to think that marriage might be something she could entertain, maybe even children. Being in love had made her think and act quite differently. She had thrown caution to the wind and tripped headlong into a passionate affair with a man recently separated from his wife. If she had been at home, her friends and family would have told her she was mad to get involved with a man on the rebound. But she was not and she gave no thought to the consequences.

Todd Mason Angel was his name and he was as attractive as his name sounded. He was seven years older than her and had a smile that lit up his face and softened the lines around his mouth. He was from Wichita, Kansas, and had worked for Phoenix at their headquarters in Wilmington since graduating from Harvard. He was ambitious and dedicated to his career, but he wasn't ruthless and hard-nosed as his position within the company might have implied. He was honest and up-front, and never hid the facts from her about his marriage, which had recently broken down, or the emotional tie he still felt to the woman he had been married to for nearly ten years, and who was the mother of the two daughters he adored. Clara had insisted they kept their affair secret at work because she didn't want anyone to accuse her of getting on by sleeping with someone so senior. He had gone along with this, but she had always felt that it was less out of respect to her than because he hoped that one day he would be reconciled with his wife. To put it bluntly, she had known all along that she was playing with fire and that she would have no one to blame but herself should he end their relationship.

Ironically, the day of reconciliation came twenty-four hours after Clara discovered that she was pregnant. She and Todd had arranged to go away for a long weekend, during which she planned to tell him her news.

On the day they were due to set off, he had come into her office an hour before lunch, closed the door behind him, and told her that Gayle had phoned him to say that she wanted to give their marriage another try. Though he had tried his best to let Clara down gently, and to conceal his happiness, the thud with which her heart had hit the floor had rocked her world and she had known she could never tell him she was pregnant. She had smiled bravely and said she wished him well, that if there was a chance of his marriage being put back together, he had to take it: he owed it to himself and his children.

'I'll never forget what we had, Clara,' he had said, rising from his chair, already wanting to get on with rebuilding his marriage. He added, 'I've only ever loved two women, and you're one of them. I just hope you don't feel that I've used you, because I haven't. I'm really not that kind of a man.'

With an airy wave of her hand, she had said, 'Go on, get out of here. You've a family to get back to.'

'No hard feelings, then?'

'You know us Brits, stiff upper lip right to the finishing line.'

He had leaned over her desk and kissed her forehead. 'I'm sorry, Clara. I wish we didn't have to end it like this.'

Another shrug. 'Hey, it was always going to have to end. We both knew that. And I'm really pleased about you and Gayle. Now, let me get on with some work.' She had wanted him gone from her office. A moment longer, and her resolve would have been shattered. Much better to stay in control and nurse a shattered heart that no one could see.

Some might say that she had behaved heroically, but she saw it differently. Such was her love for Todd that she knew she had to sacrifice her own happiness for his by letting him go.

She had spent the rest of that day going through the motions at work, until eventually she gave up and went home early, claiming she was feeling sick. It was true. She did feel nauseous. For the next two months, her morning sickness was so bad the weight fell off her. A month later she returned home.

Louise was the first person she told and, predictably, she was horrified. But no amount of questioning would make Clara reveal who the father was. She tried lying to preserve Todd's anonymity, but made a poor job of it. Louise said, 'Don't give me any of that "it was just a casual fling" business. I know better than anyone that you're not into one-night stands, Clara Costello. This man must have meant something to you, or why would you want to keep his child?' But Clara held firm. It was the one area in her friendship with Louise, and the rest of the gang, that remained a closed subject. Much as she loved Louise, Clara knew that she was a blabbermouth and would be sure to tell David, who would tell Guy, and before long, the whole of Phoenix Pharmaceuticals would know that Todd Mason Angel, the company's newly appointed finance director, was the father of Clara Costello's baby.

And every time Clara's mother said that Ned had a smile straight from the angels, she had no idea how close to the truth she was. Todd's could warm the coldest heart and Ned had inherited it.

Now, as she drove over the cattle grid to Mermaid House, Clara hoped that Ned's face would soon be its normal smiling self when he was reunited with his pride and joy.

Whether Mr Liberty would be smiling when he saw them again, was another matter altogether.

When Gabriel looked out of the kitchen window as he washed his hands at the sink and saw the camper-van drive through the archway, his face broke into a wide, sardonic smile. So she was back, was she? The insolent little shrew had a price, after all. Well, now they were in for some fun.

He dried his hands on the back of his trousers and went to meet them. 'Looks as if you can't keep away from me, Miss Costello,' he said, as she climbed down from the driver's seat. 'But I knew you'd reconsider, that it would come down to a simple act of bartering. So, what figure have you in mind?'

But his words went unanswered. Ned came barrelling up to him: 'Mr Liberty, have you got my mermaid? Is she in the kitchen where I left her on the table?'

And then he understood why they were back: not to help him but to help themselves.

'You'd better go and take a look,' he said to the boy. 'You know the way. But be careful not to touch or disturb anything of mine,' he called after Ned as the little boy shot inside the house.

Embarrassed at his mistake, and staring down at the cracked leather of his shoes, he said, 'It seems I've just made a colossal fool of myself, haven't I?' His voice was mute with despondency and his shoulders sagged.

Clara felt a pang of sadness for him. How hard he made life for himself, she thought. And what a contrast he was to Archie Merryman, who would go out of his way to help anyone. 'Perhaps only a mild fool of yourself,' she said softly. 'But tell me, just as a matter of interest, when was the last time you bought anybody flowers?'

He raised his one-eyed gaze. 'I beg your pardon?'

'It's a simple enough question. But what I'm really getting at is, when was the last time you made a spontaneous gesture of kindness to another person and felt good about it? Because if you did it more often, I'm sure you wouldn't be in the position you are now – bullying a stranger into helping you. If you were nicer, people would be queuing up with offers of help.'

'Are you saying that if I was nicer you would want to help me?'

'I was talking generally, about you being nice to your fellow man.'

'I'm not interested in talking generally. And as for my fellow man—'

'Don't split hairs.'

'Why not? You are.'

'Look, Mr Liberty, stop being so quarrelsome. Be more gracious and see where it gets you. For instance, instead of blackmailing me this morning by saying I owed you a favour, you should have just asked me politely if I would help you. As it was, you got my back up. I suspect that's what you do to people all the time, isn't it?'

'A man should be allowed to be himself,' he said stubbornly, drawing in his breath and pulling himself up to his full height.

'I couldn't agree more with you, but some common courtesy wouldn't go amiss.'

The sound of Ned's voice made them both turn. 'Mummy,' he cried, 'I've found Mermy. She was on the table just where I left her.' He came running towards them, and threw himself against Clara, who scooped him up and hugged him. You see, she wanted to say to Mr Liberty, it doesn't take much to be happy, does it? Then a more dangerous thought occurred to her. What effort, what *real* effort on her part, would it take to make Mr Liberty happy? Why had it been so simple earlier today to help Archie Merryman's mother in her hour of need but so difficult now to help this pugnacious old man? Okay, his demands were on a different scale, and he might not seem such a worthy cause, but who was she to judge? Here she was lecturing him on how to be more gracious, so why wasn't she leading by example?

Because she was on holiday! His problems were not hers.

But it would still be a holiday, she argued with herself. And Ned would enjoy himself just as much here as somewhere new. Besides, if she agreed to help him for a week, how big a hole in their schedule would that make? On the up-side, it would be a week of earning some money as well as landing themselves free lodging, and by then the Mermaid Cavern would be open. She thought of what Ron and Eileen had told her about their lifestyle, which they so enjoyed, about taking each day as it came, of rising to the myriad challenges that crossed their path and of always being the richer for having experienced them.

But it was a decision that couldn't be made in isolation. Still holding Ned, whose legs were wrapped tightly around her hips, she whispered in his ear, 'How do you feel about staying on here for a short while?'

'Will we still go to see the mermaid in the cave?' His lips tickled her ear.

'Of course.'

He nodded and smiled.

She lowered him to the ground. 'Mr Liberty, I'll do you a deal. I'll give you one week of my precious time, and in return you have to agree to certain conditions, the principal one being that you must promise me you will try to be less disagreeable, so that when Ned and I have gone, you will be enough of a human being to attract further offers of assistance. How does that sound?'

'Sounds to me as though it's a deal heavily weighted in your favour. What are the other conditions?'

She smiled archly. 'We'll sort those out as we go along. For now, though,

I need to hook the van up to an electricity supply. For which, I'd like it made clear, you will not be charging me. I also need water.'

'Anything else?'

'Yes. I want an up-to-date copy of the *Yellow Pages*.'

'I'm not having any contract cleaners in. I told you that. You do the job, or no one does it.'

'It's a skip I'm after. My guess is you have a lifetime's rubbish lying about this place and ditching it will be the only way forward. Well, don't just stand there, let's be about our business.'

'I'm not going to regret this, am I?'

'Let's hope that neither of us does.'

20

It was raining again as Jonah drove home from school, the light already fading. Other than a stack of essays to mark on the rise of the Nazi Party in the 1920s, he was looking forward to a quiet, uneventful evening. Supper and the pleasure of listening to the latest recording of Mahler's Symphony No. 5 was all he had in mind.

Despite the dreary weather, he was in a relaxed and happy mood. The day had been constructive and rewarding. With the exception of a couple of students, he was pleased with his GCSE students and had high hopes for them when they sat their exams next term. If he could keep them motivated, crank them up another gear, and make them believe that education was power, he reckoned he could get the best history results Dick High had had in years. Already a large number of his students were saying that they wanted to take the subject on into the sixth form and it was particularly gratifying to know that within his short time as head of the department, he had turned it round so dramatically. His predecessor had long since lost the plot: he'd grown tired of battling against cuts, damning league tables and hostile Ofsted recommendations. Worse than this, he had lost the will to cope with disaffected pupils who, once they knew they had the upper hand, could grind a vulnerable teacher into the ground faster than a pile-driver. Last autumn a group in year eleven had tried it on with Jonah during his first week. They had sat in the back row with their feet on the desks, their ties no more than a stubby two inches long. Passing round copies of *Loaded* and *FHM* they had pretended to ignore him as they shared with the rest of the class the details of the previous night's excitement on the estate where they lived. Modern world history had as much relevance to them as the FTSE index to their future giro cheques, or so they thought.

'Warfare,' Jonah had announced, slipping off his jacket and putting it on the back of his chair. 'Anyone up for it?'

Their attention caught, just for a second, he wrote on the white board 'No Man's Land', 'War of Attrition' and 'Going Over the Top'. He then asked for a volunteer, specifically from the back row, to come and draw a rough map of the estate he and his mates lived on.

'Don't be shy, ladies and gentlemen,' he said, his eyes resting on one lad in particular. His name was Jase O'Dowd and Jonah had heard nothing but bad reports of him since he had arrived at Dick High. Like a lot of the boys in the class, he wore his hair intimidatingly short, but with the most extraordinary gelled-up quiff at the front. He gazed insolently at Jonah, tucked a half-smoked cigarette behind his ear, and said, 'I thought this was a bleeding history lesson. Maps is for geography.'

The others urged him on. 'Go on, Jase,' they chorused. 'Show Sir where we live.'

'Yeah, and don't forget to make it look pretty. We don't wanna be shamed with Sir thinking we're not as lah-di-dah as him.'

Whistles and chants accompanied Jase as he lumbered to the front of the class. He snatched the marker pen out of Jonah's hand, and drew two large rectangles facing each other separated by a thin strip. With stabs and slashes of the pen on the whiteboard, he marked off little boxes within the two rectangles.

'For that extra-artistic touch, can you put arrows where you and your friends live, please?' Jonah asked. Just as he knew they would be, they were all congregated in the one rectangle. 'And who lives here?'

To the side of the other rectangle, Jase drew a skull and cross-bones and wrote underneath it, the Tossers.

'Okay, so tell me what this space between the two rectangles is.'

'It's a friggin' road, Sir – what d'yer think it was? *Durr!*'

'So, would I be right in thinking that when you're in the mood to give someone a good kicking, you have to cross it?'

Jase smirked. 'Yeah, got it in one. You're not as stupid as you look, Sir, are you?'

'Well, Jase, you'll be delighted to know that the tactics you use to exert your reign of terror on your neighbours are based on the same rules employed by the generals who devised trench warfare on the Western Front in 1915.' Taking the pen from him, Jonah drew a German flag over one rectangle and a Union Jack over the other, then an arrow from the words No Man's Land to the road Jase had drawn. 'Now, one more job for you, Jase. While I draw a slightly more detailed map of Belgium and northern France, can you rig up the TV and video for me, please?'

A loud cheer went up. 'What're we watching, Sir? *Hot Mammas Spank My*—'

'I'm afraid not, you'll have to save that for your role-play sessions in Drama. For now you're going to watch *Blackadder Goes Forth.*'

By the end of the lesson, he knew he had achieved what he'd set out to do: he'd got their attention. It was all the start he needed. Six months on, and a class of low achievers who had long been dubbed in the staffroom as tomorrow's social misfits could now make a reasonable fist of an essay and display an above-average interest in a subject they had previously dismissed – just as *they* had been unfairly dismissed.

Skirting round the centre of town, he swung the car into Church Brow and took the steep, cobbled road slowly. A row of cars was parked on the right-hand side, and as he drew near to his cottage, at the top of the narrow road next to the church, the easy-going evening he had planned evaporated. Outside his front door, in a flashy electric-blue Maserati, was his brother, Caspar.

What was *he* doing here?

Jonah parked alongside the cottage, gathered up his old leather briefcase from the back seat of his dilapidated Ford Escort and approached the immaculate sports car, the latest in an ever-changing range. This one, even at trade, must have set his brother back a small fortune: the numberplate alone – *Caspar 1* – had probably cost him more than Jonah's heap of mobile rust when it had been showroom new.

The only thing that Jonah and his brother had in common was their love of classical music, although Caspar's penchant for the pretentiously esoteric works of some latterday composers was where their commonality divided. It was a piece of this shrill, discordant music that Jonah could hear now as he tapped on the driver's window to attract his brother's attention. Caspar's head was resting against the smooth cream leather of the headrest and his eyes were closed as his fingers conducted an imaginary orchestra lined up along the dashboard.

The electric window slid down. 'You're getting wet, brother dear,' Caspar said, above the excruciating ting, ping and scrape.

'Could be something to do with the inclement weather. Are you coming in, or are you happy to stay out here showing off your new car to my neighbours?'

Caspar gave him a look of disdain. 'You mean these little shacks are occupied by real people? Heavens, whatever next?'

Jonah let them in. He shed his leather jacket and hung it up in the understairs cupboard, then took his brother through to the kitchen. He knew Caspar hated his house, that he found the old weaver's cottage cramped and claustrophobic. Caspar lived alone in a stark loft apartment in Manchester that was a temple of clean lines and minimalism. To Jonah's knowledge, he never entertained there, never encouraged visitors. The only time Jonah had been allowed in had been when Caspar wanted to show it off. He had come away feeling that whatever his brother had paid to live in such superficial splendour, it wasn't money well spent.

He watched his brother prowl uneasily round the tiny, low-ceilinged kitchen, his cold grey eyes seeking out the least offensive spot on which to stand. He was dressed in an expensive dark blue suit with a crisp white shirt, a red silk tie and black lace-up shoes. His fine hair was a light-brown version of Michael Heseltine's, and showed signs of grey just above the ears. The contrast between the two brothers could not have been greater. Jonah wore baggy corduroy trousers, a loose-fitting shirt with the odd splash of paint on the shoulder, and a tie he'd owned for more years than he cared to recall. His dark brown hair was thick and wavy, the opposite of Caspar's smooth well-cut locks. The kids at school often teased Jonah that his tousled mop made him look like David Ginola on a bad-hair day.

'I see you haven't got round to doing anything about the state of this kitchen,' Caspar remarked, still prowling and trying to avoid hitting his head on the pans hanging from one of the beams. He came to a stop in front of a bookcase crammed with paperbacks and CDs. Giving the handpainted cupboards a dismissive glance, he added, 'It really is the last distasteful word in folksy charm. You should gut it and start again. Maybe extend it into something worthwhile.'

'Actually, Caspar, this *is* done. Are you stopping long enough to warrant me offering you a drink?'

'Depends what you've got.'

'You'll have to be a lot more honey-tongued if you want anything better than instant coffee.'

'What do I have to do for a decent glass of Chablis? Fawn all over you?'

'No, go out and buy one. I don't have anything here of the ilk that would agree with your sensitive nose and palate.'

Caspar gave him a pitying look. 'Ha, ha, as droll as ever, I see.'

'I like to keep my hand in. One never knows when one's older brother is going to come calling and wreck one's evening.'

'You had plans? You do surprise me. A night of unbridled passion with a colleague from the staffroom? A lissom games mistress fresh out of college? Oh, do tell.'

Jonah turned his back on Caspar and reached for a bottle of Merlot from the wine rack. 'An evening of marking essays on the rise of the Nazi Party is what I had in mind,' he said. 'Just think, if you'd been around at the time as one of Hitler's right-hand men, he might have made a go of it.' He poured two glasses of wine and passed one to Caspar.

Caspar sniffed his suspiciously, then made a great play of picking out a rogue piece of cork. 'Not bad,' he said, giving the wine a swirl. He took a sip. 'Better than that acidic, enamel-stripping Sauvignon you gave me last time I was here. Argentinian, wasn't it?'

'Chilean.'

'Whatever.'

Did he have any idea how ridiculous he was, thought Jonah, standing here in his expensive suit, pretentiously appraising a bottle of plonk that had cost three pounds from the local supermarket? How could anyone become such a monumental prat and assume such an affected air of moneyed arrogance? Sadly, affecting the right air had always been of paramount importance to his brother. Having the right credentials, knowing the right people, owning the right car, it was all part of Caspar's carefully projected image. For what it was worth, Jonah suspected that Caspar had become a victim of his own arrogance: he didn't have any real friends, only hangers-on.

'What are you doing here, Caspar?' he asked. 'The phone not good enough for you, these days?'

Caspar shifted position. He went and tried out a space by the old Rayburn that Jonah had bought second-hand and patiently restored. 'I've been sampling the heady delights of Deaconsbridge,' he said, 'in particular, Mainwaring's, the estate agent. It's just as I thought. It's the perfect time to sell Mermaid House. I spoke to Mainwaring, and he's of the opinion that by the end of the summer the property boom will be over. It's now or wait another year, maybe longer, until things pick up again.'

'Anything wrong in doing that?'

Caspar narrowed his grey eyes. 'I told you, Jonah, we need to move on this sooner rather than later. If we let the old man stay put, the house will slide into a total decline. It's bad enough as it is, but another year and God knows what the place will be like.'

'And how do you know what state the house is in now? When was the last time you paid Dad a visit?'

Caspar banged his glass down on the table between them, his cool imperious manner giving way to temper. 'That is hardly the point! Why do you always have to be so damn picky? Can't you just accept that I'm right? *God!* You always were a bloody pain in the backside. I should have known better than to come here and expect a civilised conversation with you!'

Jonah leaned against the sink, casually crossed one ankle over the other, and considered his brother's outburst. He was used to seeing Caspar flip, but this struck him as different. Usually he could keep up the act of supercilious prig for at least two glasses of wine before he launched into an attack. What was the urgency about selling Mermaid House? Had he, yet again, got himself into a financial mess? He decided to push. 'Seeing as you're in the area,' he said blandly, 'why not go and see Dad this evening? If it's money you're short of, he might find it in his heart to bung you a few quid.' He knew his remarks would incense Caspar, but he didn't care. If it got his brother out of his house, so much the better.

Predictably, Caspar rose to the bait. 'Who the hell said anything about me being short of money? That's an accusation I find vaguely absurd coming from someone who knows nothing about business.'

'It was a logical assumption. You've been on at me to go and see Dad and—'

'Yes, and I'd like to know why you haven't.'

'I've been busy. If you must know, I've arranged to see him tomorrow.'

This seemed to mollify Caspar and he reached for his glass again. 'Oh. Right. Good. Well, it's about time too. But mind you be firm with him. Don't give in to his bullying.'

The amusing irony of this instruction stayed with Jonah, long after Caspar had left. The essays dealt with, his supper coming along nicely, and Mahler well into his stride, Jonah reflected on his brother's unwelcome visit.

He's desperate, he concluded, stirring the pan of mushroom risotto, then adding more stock. He must be, to have forced himself to drink cheap plonk in a house he hated with a man he despised. Caspar's need for money must be greater than it had ever been, which might mean that he was even more determined than usual to get what he wanted.

It was a grim prospect.

Caspar's scheming skulduggery over the years would make humorous reading if there wasn't always some poor soul who had lost out to his ruthlessness. Lying, cheating and trampling over other people's feelings to get what he wanted – it all came quite naturally to Caspar. It was a sport for him.

The most breathtaking example of this had occurred two and a half years ago when Jonah had unwisely, and against his better judgement, decided to introduce Emily to his family. He had been putting it off for nearly six months, but now that they were planning to marry, it seemed only right that Val and his father should meet his future wife. Val had been forever trying to bring them together as a family, and had insisted on a full Liberty turn-out with everyone spending the weekend at Mermaid House. Damson was in her most recent post-divorce state and Caspar came with his latest girlfriend, a model of half his age with a fake tan, whom he ignored for the entire weekend. He was much more interested in Emily.

It was just what Jonah had been terrified of. Until then he had deliberately kept Emily away from Caspar; he had even told her why. She hadn't taken him seriously, though, and had said he was being paranoid: 'It's you I love. Why would I be remotely interested in your brother?'

But that evening during dinner, he had seen Caspar working his charm on Emily, and that she was flattered by his attention. And why wouldn't she be? He was good-looking, and when he wanted to be, he was erudite and witty. He was the perfect dinner-party guest, regaling Emily with stories of Jonah growing up, telling her what a great kid brother he had been, what hilarious and companionable larks they had had together.

'You make your childhood sound so idyllic,' Emily had said, 'like something out of *Swallows and Amazons*.'

Looking across the table with his steely-eyed gaze on Jonah, Caspar had said, 'She's right, isn't she, Jonah? We did have a glorious childhood.'

To have told the truth would have seemed churlish and petty, so he had said, 'It had its moments.'

Caspar had laughed. 'Just listen to him.' Then, 'But what I don't understand, Jonah, is why the long face? Anyone would think this was a wake and not a celebration of your forthcoming nuptials with this heavenly creature. For heaven's sake, cheer up.'

While they were getting into bed that night, Emily had said, 'Your brother was right, you did look miserable during dinner. Are you sure you haven't exaggerated the stories you've told me about him?'

'Why would I do that?'

'Because you're jealous of him.'

'*Jealous?* You have to be joking!' He had tried to laugh off her accusation, but she had pursued the subject doggedly.

'You kept looking at him as though you hated him, Jonah. I've never seen you like that before. It's very worrying. You're showing me a side to you that I didn't know existed.'

All he could say was, 'You've never seen me in the bosom of my family before.' He had tried to make love to her, to reassure himself that her feelings for him hadn't changed. But it hadn't worked. He had been too anxious, too convinced of his own failings. Defeated, he had slept with his back to her.

The next day, after breakfast, Caspar had suggested they treated themselves to some fresh air by going for a walk. Val said she wanted to go to church and their father said he had more important things to do. Damson said she needed to be alone so that she could meditate and realign her aura, and Caspar's girlfriend, who was getting the message that she was history, pouted and said she didn't have any suitable footwear. But Emily had reacted as though she had just been invited to fly to Paris for lunch. 'What a wonderful idea, Caspar. You must have been reading my mind. A walk is exactly what I need to blow away the cobwebs.'

'Cobwebs, Emily? Don't tell me my brother doesn't take you out enough and he's allowed you to collect cobwebs.'

It was no kind of joke, yet Emily seemed to find it hysterically funny, and Jonah knew that the only thing being blown away was his chance of marrying Emily.

Caspar and Emily strode on ahead, leaving Jonah to plod along with the sulky model, who was wearing a pair of Val's boots as well as a borrowed waxed jacket.

'Is Caspar always like this?' she said, pausing for the umpteenth time to catch her breath as they climbed the gentlest of slopes – she might have been racehorse thin, but she had as much stamina as a soggy Ryvita.

'Always like what?'

'So rude. And why don't you stop what he's doing with your girlfriend? Or are you so stupid you haven't noticed?'

Oh, he'd noticed all right, and if the skinny, lettuce-nibbling girl hadn't stopped every few hundred yards, Caspar and Emily wouldn't have got so far ahead. Way off in the distance, and in the shelter of a rocky outcrop, he could see Caspar standing behind Emily, an arm over her left shoulder as he supposedly pointed out the landmarks to her – Kinder Scout, Cracken Edge and Chinley. Then he saw the hand stroke her windblown hair. When Emily turned to face him, her face tilted upwards so that he could kiss her, Jonah knew it was over.

Leaving Caspar's girlfriend to sort herself out, he took off back to Mermaid House. He packed his things and left without telling Val or his father what he was doing.

Another man – a real man, as his father would have been quick to say – would have confronted Caspar and beaten the living daylights out of him. But apart from that one incident at school, Jonah had never resorted to violence and preferred to keep it that way.

That evening, Emily called to tell him what he already knew, that their engagement was off. Riding high on the euphoria created by Caspar's attention, she told Jonah she hadn't realised until now how dull he was. She told him that she was moving in with Caspar, that she had never known anyone so amazing. 'It was love at first sight,' she went on. 'I hope you can understand that. He's literally swept me off my feet.'

But in less than a month, she discovered what it felt like to be swept aside. As was to be expected, Caspar had lost interest in her. She wrote to Jonah, apologising for what had happened, saying that she had been a fool, that she didn't know what had come over her. She even asked if there was any chance of them getting back together.

He never replied to her letter. What was there to say? He had warned her that Caspar liked nothing better than to play games with other people's emotions.

There was no point in him asking why Caspar had done it. His answer, as it had been the first time he had taken a girlfriend from Jonah, would have been, 'Because I can, Jonah.' When the dust had finally settled, all he said on the matter was, 'She clearly wasn't in love with you, Jonah. If she had been, I wouldn't have been a temptation for her. Think of the episode as my having done you a favour. You're better off without her. No need to thank me.'

Now, as he tipped his mushroom risotto on to his plate, and poured himself another glass of wine, Jonah wondered if anything, or anyone, could shame Caspar into behaving like a decent human being.

21

Archie had been too tired to face cooking supper that evening, so he had picked up fish and chips on the way home from the shop. He unwrapped the two parcels and tipped the contents on to the plates he had warmed under the grill, then put them on the table where Bessie was doing her best to butter some slices of white bread. Her movements were heartbreakingly slow and clumsy, and all at once he was reminded of past Christmases, when Bessie would cook the largest turkey they could afford and invite any neighbours who were on their own to share it with them. One Christmas morning, she had sent Archie out on his bike to round up Miss Glenys Watson, a retired music teacher, who was so proud she would rather sit on her own listening to the radio than admit she couldn't afford to celebrate Christmas. Nor did she want it known that, other than her ageing cat, she didn't have anyone to spend it with. 'Please, Miss Watson,' he had said, after knocking on her door, 'Mum says she needs your help. She wants us all to sing carols after lunch and you're the only one she knows who can play the piano without her getting a headache. Will you come?'

Miss Watson must have known what his mother was up to, but she never let on. She had accepted the invitation graciously, pulled on her hat and scarf, her gloves and coat, locked the door and walked alongside him as he pushed his bike. They had almost reached home, when she said, 'Do you play the piano, Archie?'

'Oh, no, Miss Watson. I'm not at all musical.'

'Perhaps it's time someone taught you. I could give you lessons after school.'

He had said he would like that very much, but he didn't think his mother could afford it. 'But you mustn't tell her I said that,' he had confided.

She had smiled and said, 'I'm sure we can find a way round that little problem.'

At ten years old, he didn't understand that he had just become a bridge between his mother's warm-hearted generosity and an old lady's pride. All he knew was that it was Christmas morning and a whole day of seeing his mother happy lay ahead of him. She liked nothing better than having people around her, especially those she thought she was helping. 'The world is full of sad and lonely people,' she would say to Archie, 'so it's down to the rest of us to put a smile on their faces.' One of her favourite games was to sit on a bus and see how many people she could make smile during their journey. The bigger the challenge, the more she enjoyed herself. 'See that poor old soul just getting on, the one in the tatty gabardine and the rucked-up face to match,' she whispered to him one day. 'Two peppermint humbugs says I can have her lips twitching by the time she gets off.' And, of course, she had, and with so little effort. 'It doesn't take much to spread a little happiness,' she always claimed.

The first Christmas Miss Watson spent with them was also the year his father had turned up unexpectedly on Boxing Day. They had heard nothing from him for years, then out of the blue there he was, sprawled on the settee, throwing peanuts into the air and catching them in his mouth, expecting to be fed before he strolled down to the pub to pick up where he had left off with his drinking cronies. In bed that night, Archie had heard his mother telling his dad that, for the sake of their son, if he was back, it had to be for ever or not at all. Archie had held his breath. He didn't want his father around: he knew it would make his mother unhappy, that it would mean more drunken, violent rages. There would be no more amusing bus rides together, no more cosy evenings by the fire while his mother read to him. His heart had crashed to a stop when he heard his father say, "Course I'm back for good, Bess. What can I do to convince you I'm a reformed character? I'm gonna take the first job that comes along and prove to you I'm as good as my word.'

That first job never did come along and he lay on the settee smoking and drinking beer while Bessie worked at the bakery. He even suggested, since he was around to see to the boy – he always called Archie 'the boy' – that she ought to work more shifts because the extra money would come in handy.

Archie had never been able to understand why his mother, when she could be so strong – she was known as the rock of the neighbourhood – was so weak when it came to dealing with a husband who treated her so badly. Perhaps her feelings for him overruled common sense and allowed her to compromise where otherwise she would have held firm.

And wasn't that what he had done with Stella? Even when he had known she was having an affair, he had held on to the hope that she would once again feel for him what he still felt for her.

When he had met Stella, she had bowled him over: she was tall, elegant and knew how to dress to make the most of her long legs. How proud he had been to catch such a stunner. She could have had anyone, but she had settled for plain old Archie Merryman. 'It's because you're going to take me away from all this,' she would laugh, when he asked her why she loved him. 'All this' had been the noisy, robust family in which she had grown up. Archie had thought her parents, brothers and sisters were full of fun and knew how to enjoy themselves, but she said they embarrassed her, that they didn't aspire to anything. There was so much Stella wanted out of life, and that was one of the reasons he had started up his own business. Nobody in her family had done that: the men had all been employed at the local steel works in Sheffield, while the women had cleaned and had babies.

'Archie?'

He looked up from his plate, realising that his mother had been trying to talk to him. 'Sorry, Mum, what did you say?'

'Sad?'

He shook his head. 'No, just tired. It's been a long day.'

She forked up a chip with her good hand. 'Sorry.'

'What for?'

Her words came out in a long jumble, but eventually he disentangled them. 'I told you earlier, there's nothing to apologise for. It was great that you felt strong enough to go shopping, and it was a simple mistake you made, taking the wrong purse with you. It was only because you got flustered that your speech went all to cock. Remember what the therapist said? It's when you get upset that the words get clogged up inside your head.'

And if those people at the supermarket had been more understanding, she wouldn't have got into such a pickle, he thought, and stood up to put the kettle on. Thank heavens that young woman and her little lad had been on hand to help. He didn't like to think what would have happened if they hadn't been there. It broke his heart to think how distressed Bessie must have been at not being able to explain what was wrong with her.

Water was gushing over the top of the kettle and he turned off the tap as his sadness turned to anger. His mother had been treated as if she was batty, until a stranger had come to her aid. Not so long ago, Bessie had been as strong and capable as any of them.

His mother was still eating her fish and chips when he sat down again with their mugs of tea. She never had been one to rush her food, but now she took twice as long. He wasn't bothered. He didn't have anything else to do that evening and was happy to sit with her. He reached for the local paper and flicked through to the classifieds to make sure his regular house-clearance advert had gone in. The 'What's On' section caught his eye. It was years since he had been to the cinema – Stella could never sit still long enough to watch a film – and he was seized with the urge to go. 'What do you think to seeing a film at the weekend?' he asked his mother.

Without needing to disentangle her response, he could see that she approved of the idea. In the old days, going to the flicks had always been something of a treat for her. Clark Gable, Rex Harrison, Audrey Hepburn and Omar Sharif had provided her with a much-needed touch of glamour and excitement.

He folded the newspaper and laid it flat on the table so that they could make their choice. Today's movie stars might not be as glamorous as they'd been in Bessie's day, but they might give her a chance to escape the unfairness of her life for a little while.

22

Their breakfast eaten and everything tidied away, Clara was keen to make a start on Mermaid House. Her only concern was keeping Ned occupied while she got down to work. Though he could amuse himself for quite long spells, she wasn't sure how soon it would be before he was bored. And, like any parent, she knew that boredom might lead him into danger or mischief.

The answer was to keep him busy, and having already glimpsed some of the ground-floor rooms, she felt there was enough relatively safe-looking junk lying about the place with which Ned could play for hours.

Mr Liberty had offered to give them a tour of the house last night, but Clara had declined. Instead she and Ned had driven back into Deacons-bridge and made a return visit to the supermarket where, with a sub from Mr Liberty's wallet, she had bought several carrier bags of cleaning products, rubber gloves, cloths, tins of polish, air-fresheners, and several rolls of bin-bags.

She never did anything by halves, and having made a deal with the old man she was determined to see it through. There had been no danger of her waking this morning and regretting her decision. That was not her style. She had always been the same, even as a child – so her mother had frequently told her. If she had wanted to come top in French she went all out to achieve it. Conversely, if she didn't want to do something, like finish a piece of embroidery for a needlework lesson, there was no making her do it.

Louise and the gang had always teased her that she saw life so clearly. 'Nothing ever muddies the water of your vision and thinking, does it?' Guy had said to her one day at work, after she had dealt with a dispute on the packing line between two women who claimed they couldn't work together. And she supposed he was right. She wished, though, that he hadn't made it sound like a criticism.

Much to her amusement, and Ned's delight, Mr Liberty had joined them for supper in the van last night. 'No steak and claret this evening?' she had asked, when he had accepted her offer of grilled lamb chops and easy-cook noodles. His gruff reply had got lost somewhere in his rattling throat and confirmed what she had suspected: that it was a while since he had cooked himself such a meal. If ever.

Over supper he had brought up the subject of how much she expected to

122

be paid. 'I'm nobody's fool,' he said, pointing his knife at her. 'You're not going to con me.'

'And I'm no mug, either, so you'd better brace yourself. This won't be cheap. If you want the best – me – you're going to have to pay accordingly. I assume you have sufficient funds.'

'That's damned impertinent!'

'Just making sure we both know where we stand. For all I know, you might be a penniless old codger who's down to his last shirt button.'

'I resent the implications of that last remark. I'll have you know that I'm not an old codger and, what's more, I'd bet my last shirt button that I'm better off than you.'

'I'm glad to hear it. So why haven't you got around to throwing a wad of cash at some other idiot to do the job for you? Or are you just mean with your money?'

'I've never been mean with money, just prudent. If I was a Scrooge, do you think I'd be providing you with free electricity and water while you're here? And I didn't replace my last cleaner because I saw no reason to put up with another light-fingered woman helping herself to my belongings.'

'So what changed your thinking?'

'That blasted doctor started poking his nose in.' He went on to tell her how he had burnt his arm and reluctantly paid a visit to the surgery. 'I knew I was in trouble the moment that doctor started asking me how I was coping after my wife's death. Fine, I told him. But they don't want to believe that, do they? And then he turned up here and I'd got something in my eye and he blackmailed me into going to the hospital to have it checked.'

'Blackmailed you?'

'It was what happened, true as I'm sitting here. He threatened me with Social Services if I didn't get into the car with him there and then to go to the hospital.'

Clara had wanted to laugh at the doctor's audacity, but refrained, and again she felt sorry for Mr Liberty. He was clearly terrified that he was going to have his independence taken from him. It convinced her that she was doing the right thing in helping him and that her main objective was to make him see the sense in getting regular help once she had gone. If he didn't, he would be back to square one within weeks with the threat of Social Services still hanging over him. If indeed they were a real threat.

She had smiled at the thought of the days ahead when she would be giving Mr Liberty a taste of his own medicine – a generous dose of bullying.

Carrying the bags of cleaning things, Clara let Ned run on ahead to knock at the door. It was opened almost immediately, as if her employer had been waiting for her to arrive and clock on. 'Is your eye better now, Mr Liberty?' asked Ned. The patch had gone and without it he looked a little less fierce.

'It's as good as new,' he replied starchily, and stood back to let them in. 'Where will you start? The kitchen?'

'We'll start first with improving labour relations,' Clara said. '*You* will bid *us* a good morning, then *you* will offer to put the kettle on. And while *you* are making *us* some coffee, I will survey the wreckage and assess the extent of the damage.' She handed him one of the carrier bags. 'There's a jar of instant in there, along with a packet of biscuits which will add to your onerous duties as tea and coffee-maker.'

He grunted and led them through to the kitchen.

'Ever thought of buying a dishwasher?' she asked, when she saw once more the piles of dirty crockery still untouched on the draining-board.

'A waste of money just for one person.'

'There are some reasonably priced ones on the market, small machines designed for people on their own.'

'Reasonably priced,' he repeated. 'I don't need things to be *reasonably priced*. I told you, I have money.'

'Well, try spending it! Or are you hell bent on leaving it to the family of whom you've spoken so highly?'

He snorted, then reached for a pen and a used envelope. He handed them to Clara. 'Make a list of all the things you think I need.'

'I'll put "new heart" at the top of it, shall I?'

Her first job was to clear the decks by shifting most of the junk on to either the table or the floor so that she could get at the work surfaces to scrub them clean. Once she had done the sink, she tackled the washing-up, then moved on to the cupboards, which were chock full of things she doubted were ever used. At the back of one she found a two-year-old bag of self-raising flour crawling with weevils. Cringing, she threw it into a bin-bag, along with a dozen pots of out-of-date Shippam's paste, two opened jars of pickled cabbage, another of horseradish sauce that was a dubious shade of yellow, and a tin of rock-hard Oxo cubes. It wasn't difficult to work out what the poor man was eating on a daily basis: the stockpiled cans of pilchards and tomato soup were a dead give-away.

With Ned helping to empty the lower cupboards of old pans, buckled lids, steamers and fish kettles, the like and size of which Clara had never seen before, she called Mr Liberty. He appeared in the doorway and looked aghast at the mess. 'You've made it worse,' he said, as he surveyed the scene.

'Oh, bring on the gratitude, why don't you?' said Clara sharply. 'Now, listen, I need you to decide what you want to keep.'

He shrugged. 'You decide for me.'

She took him at his word, and deciding that it was highly unlikely that he would be cooking a whole salmon in the near future, or steaming enough vegetables to feed an army marching on its stomach, or making vats of jam and marmalade, she put together a modest collection of pans for his basic cooking needs and instructed Ned to take them over to the sink. He could mess around with soapy water under the guise of washing them.

'What will you do with the others?' asked Mr Liberty.

'Some are fit for the dustbin – which reminds me, that skip I ordered should be here around lunchtime – but the better ones could go to a charity shop. Do you have such a thing in Deaconsbridge?'

'There was one, but when the rents on all the shops in the market square went up, it closed.'

'It seems a shame to ditch them when they're in pretty good nick. Put the kettle on again and I'll have a think.'

With a bucket of hot water dosed liberally with disinfectant, she started to clean inside the cupboards. There was something satisfying about bringing order to chaos, and though she would never admit it to Mr Liberty, she was enjoying herself. By the end of the day she would have the pleasure of knowing that she had personally conquered this grubby wreck of a kitchen. She would have it shipshape and Bristol fashion, or her name wasn't Miss Clara Costello.

Calling herself by her full name made her think about the formal way in which she and Mr Liberty referred to each other. It amused her, and if she wasn't mistaken, it amused him.

Behind her, she could hear Ned talking to Mr Liberty as he spooned coffee into mugs. He was chattering nineteen to the dozen, just like he did at home with Granda, and she realised that as long as Ned had someone to talk to, he would not get bored.

When Mr Liberty handed her a mug of coffee, and she indicated for him to place it on the floor next to her, he said, 'You've been working like a Trojan ever since you got here, why don't you take a break?'

She wrung out the cloth into the bucket and doffed an imaginary cap. 'Gawd bless you, guv'nor, for taking pity on a humble scullery-maid. I'm touched.'

She was even more touched when he held out a hand and helped her to her feet. 'Bring your coffee with you, and I'll give you a guided tour,' he said gruffly.

She tugged off her rubber gloves and, Ned following with the biscuits, Mr Liberty led the way. He stood for a moment in the vast hall, as though getting his bearings – it was a large house, after all.

'Do we need a map?' she asked, good-humouredly.

He threw her a disparaging look. 'Suggesting I'm so far gone I don't know how to get round my own home?'

'Not at all. I was merely implying you live in an above-average-sized house. How many bedrooms are there?'

'Just the ten.'

'Just the ten,' she repeated. 'A bit cramped, then?'

'I know the way,' said Ned, and sped off down the gloomy length of the hall, whose panelled walls were decorated with an incongruous mixture of African masks, a barometer, a large, heavily worked brass plate that looked Indian, and a moth-eaten bear's head. Everything was covered with a peppering of dust, including the ornate gilt frame of a massive oil painting depicting a Highland stag.

'Where's he taking us?' she asked. 'And do you mind?'

'To the library, and it doesn't look as if I have much choice.'

When they caught up with Ned, he was swinging open a heavy door. 'Slow down, partner,' Clara told him. 'And you've had enough biscuits.'

She took the packet and handed it to Mr Liberty. For the first time she noticed his arthritic hands, how swollen and clenched they were. Slipping a thumbnail under the top biscuit, she raised it so that he could easily get at it. He caught her eye. 'Don't go putting yourself out on my account,' he muttered.

'Don't flatter yourself.'

The library felt cold and damp, but was comparatively tidy, in as much as it contained a few basic items of furniture: two leather armchairs either side of a stone fireplace, another two in the bay window either side of a large rent table, a footstool, and a lampstand with a dented shade and an unravelling gold fringe. Two of the walls were lined from floor to ceiling with books. But it was difficult to make out anything in any detail: the curtains were drawn, keeping out the light – and holding in the musty smell of age and soot. Clara guessed that the chimney needed sweeping. 'Do you always have the curtains like this?'

'Not always.' He went over to the window and gave the burgundy velvet drapes a hefty tug. 'But it stops the light destroying the books.'

So the man had a weak spot. Books above humans, by the looks of things.

She changed her mind when light flooded the room and she saw the painting above the fireplace. 'Who's that?' she asked.

Mr Liberty stood beside her. 'My first wife, Anastasia.'

Clara stared at the young woman, her confident gaze and the beguiling gentleness in her expression. The eyes were full of warmth and humour and were as dark as her thickly tousled hair, which was painted so luxuriantly and with such depth that Clara could almost feel the silky curls in her fingers. 'Is it a good likeness?' she asked softly.

He took a noisy swallow of his coffee. 'Yes.'

'She was very beautiful.'

'And I suppose you're wondering what she saw in someone like me?'

Before she could deny or refute this, Ned called, 'Mummy, come over here. This is where the secret passage is.'

She went to where he was standing. She stared at the rows of leatherbound books that he was pointing to. 'Are you sure?' she asked, playing along with him. 'All I can see is a load of old books.'

His eyes danced with excitement as he glanced at Mr Liberty. 'Shall I show her?' he asked, his hand already reaching to the shelf where, presumably, the handle was hidden.

Mr Liberty sucked in his breath, then let it out slowly with a doubtful shake of his head. 'I don't know, lad. Can she keep a secret? We don't want her blabbing all over the county, do we?'

Ned's face grew solemn. 'Mummy, you won't tell anyone, will you? Do you promise?'

'Hand on heart,' she said, as seriously as she could. 'I promise not to tell a living soul about Mr Liberty's back passage.'

Mr Liberty snorted. But the hint of a smile on his face didn't escape Clara.

Despite the misty rain, the views from the tower were spectacular. They would be even better if the windows were clean, thought Clara, wondering if there would be sufficient time in the coming week to add the tower to her agenda. But was there any point? Dr Singh was hardly going to rate his patient's ability to stand on his own two feet according to whether this extraordinary piece of whimsical architecture was spick and span. Stick to the essentials, she told herself.

'When was the house built?' she asked.

'In 1851. John Temple, a local quarry owner, had it built for him and his family. He called it Temple House, but when his son inherited it, and later discovered an underground cavern in the area with its dubious rock formation, the whole ridiculous mermaid saga was set in motion. As a consequence, and to plump up the son's ego, the house was renamed.'

'You sound like you don't approve.'

'I don't approve of scams.'

'What's a scam?' asked Ned.

Not wanting Ned's anticipation spoiled, Clara gave Mr Liberty a warning look. To her grateful surprise, he said, 'Nothing you need worry about, young man.'

'Any particular reason why the secret passageway was built?' asked Clara. 'The age of the house precludes priest-holes, and the geography's certainly wrong for smuggling.'

'No real reason as far as I'm aware, other than that John Temple wanted something none of his neighbours had. Now, if you've seen enough, shall we get on?'

He took them down the creaking narrow staircase, along the dark corridor and back into the library. From there he showed them the rest of the ground floor: the dining and drawing rooms that, like the library, both smelt of soot, the gun room, where Clara had no wish to linger, and the laundry room, which was a glory-hole with bells on. Piles of yellowing newspapers and boxes of empty whisky bottles littered the stone-flagged floor, with dirty clothes, towels and bed-linen. Mr Liberty kicked at the heap of washing. 'Machine's not working,' he muttered, embarrassed. He picked up a wooden clothes horse and set it against one of the damp-spotted walls.

'Do you know what's wrong with it?' She bent down to investigate.

'Haven't a clue. It's too modern and fancy for me. Jonah bought it last year and it's been nothing but a damned waste of money. It's supposed to dry as well as wash. All it does is bang about a lot.'

'I'll take a look at it later,' she said, 'though presumably it's still within its guarantee.'

He looked at her scornfully. 'You can mend a washing-machine?'

'Sure. So long as it's not the electronics, they're usually straightforward enough. Sounds like the drum belt may have worked itself loose.'

'Mummy can mend all sorts of things,' Ned said, helping himself to an empty whisky bottle and unscrewing the lid. He pulled a face when he held it to his nose. 'Pooh!'

'Is that right?' Mr Liberty said, taking the bottle from him and replacing the lid.

'I don't like things to get the better of me,' she responded.

'Or people, I should imagine.'

'How astute of you. Now, then, shall I get back to work, or will you show us the rest of the house?'

The tour continued upstairs, and mercifully the mess didn't get any worse. As far as she could see, the damage was relatively superficial, but it was the scale that was so awesome. That, and the poignancy of some of the bedrooms.

'This was my second wife's room . . . It was where she died.' Mr Liberty unlocked the door and let them in. It was strange the way he said it, and prompted Clara to ask how many wives he had had.

'Just the two. And don't look at me as though I was careless with them.'

It was a long oblong room with a view over the garden and the moors beyond. 'Val loved to look across to Kinder Scout,' he said, moving to the window, 'which is why she chose this room. We never shared . . .' He cleared his throat. 'We didn't have that kind of relationship.'

Clara would have liked to pursue this tantalising confidence, but wisely held back. Instead, she said, 'What did she die of? Ned, don't touch!'

They both looked at Ned, who had settled himself on a stool in front of a dressing-table. Set out before him was a dusty array of scent atomisers, pots and tubes of cream, lipsticks, powder compacts, necklaces, and bottles of nail varnish. At his mother's words his hands, which had been hovering over a pair of reading glasses, dropped to his sides.

'It was heart trouble,' Mr Liberty said, joining Ned. He picked up the glasses and slipped them inside a tapestry case. 'I should have got rid of this lot, but I couldn't bring myself to do it. Makes me look like a sentimental old fool, doesn't it?'

Without answering him, she said, 'Would you like me to sort it out for you?'

'There's clothes too.' He indicated two large mahogany wardrobes and a matching pair of chests of drawers.

'Just let me know what you want to keep, and I'll bag it up for you . . . if that's what you'd like.'

Next he showed her the rooms that had belonged to his children. It was at this point, standing in what had been his daughter's room, that Clara realised it was what Mr Liberty didn't say, coupled with the emptiness of some of the rooms in this huge house, that revealed most about him. She realised, too, that she hadn't seen a single photograph of any of his children. Other than the portrait of the first Mrs Liberty, and the second wife's belongings, there was no record of anyone else having lived here. She thought of her parents' modest little semi-detached house and the rogues' gallery of pictures they had of her and Michael growing up, with treasured photographs of Ned and their latest grandchild. As a teenager she had been mortified at the number of photos around the house recording her transition from gummy baby to spotty adolescent. But by the time her graduation photo adorned the wall of the dining room, along with Michael's, she had come to terms with her parents' pride, and knew that when the time came she would probably do exactly the same.

Which she had. From his birth, Ned's likeness had been framed many times over. When she had been clearing the house ready for the young couple who would be renting it, she had spent hours removing them, wrapping them and storing them in a box to go in the attic. Ned had been captured in every conceivable pose: smiling, frowning, chewing, laughing, crawling, clapping, sitting, walking, even sleeping.

Caspar, Damson and Jonah's bedrooms were shabby and bare. Each contained an uncovered wooden-framed bed, a rug, a few pieces of functional furniture and a series of ghostly marks on the walls where once there had been shelves and pictures. It struck Clara that someone had gone to a lot of trouble to strip these rooms. It seemed such a callous act. Vindictive. Almost a threat.

But as Mr Liberty went on to show them the rest of the bedrooms, which were piled high with trunks and huge ugly pieces of furniture, with faded wallpaper coming away from the walls, she began to think it was no wonder he was so miserable. If she had to live in this mausoleum, she too would turn into a crabby old devil. Suddenly she felt angry with his children. How could they have left him to rot here? Okay, he clearly wasn't an easy man, but why hadn't they persisted and won him over? Because it was easier to turn their backs and forget him. They were a bunch of idle, pathetic cowards and they ought to be ashamed of themselves.

This thought was still with her when Mr Liberty showed her his bedroom. It was almost thirty feet long with a spectacular view over the garden and the moors beyond. She made a mental note to deal with the curtains, which were lying on the floor.

When he made a surprising offer to take Ned off her hands and play a game with him, she returned to the kitchen with renewed vigour and determination. She switched on the radio, moved the dial to Classic FM and pulled on her rubber gloves. Her plan now was to tackle at least one room a day, so that by the end of the week, a minimum of seven would have been scrubbed and polished, which would go some way to restoring the house to what it had been.

She turned her attention to the Aga and hoped it wasn't a lost cause. If she could get that running smoothly, it would make all the difference to the dreary atmosphere in the kitchen.

23

Gabriel passed Ned the pack of playing cards and told him to shuffle them.

'I'm not very good at that,' Ned said, kneeling up on the chair and taking the pack uncertainly in his small hands.

'I'm sure you'll make a better job of it than I would.'

As he jumbled the grubby cards, Ned said, 'Why are your fingers so funny, Mr Liberty? They're all knobbly and crooked.'

'That's because I'm the crooked old man who lives in the crooked old house.'

'No, you're not. And your house isn't crooked at all. What are we going to play?'

'What can you play?'

'Um . . . Pairs. But we usually use picture cards. Nanna gave them to me for my birthday.'

'Well, let's try it with these. Have you finished messing them up yet?'

'I think so. Shall I spread them out for us?'

'Be my guest.'

Leaning across the dusty table, placing the cards face down, Ned said, 'That's what Granda always says to me.'

'Uh?'

'If I ask him if I can play outside, he says, "Be my guest."'

'I'm surprised Granda ever gets a word in edgeways with you around. Don't you ever stop talking?'

'Nanna and Granda are in Australia,' Ned carried on. 'Granda sometimes calls me his little pumpernickel. I have a baby cousin now. I've seen pictures of him on the Internet. Do you think Nanna and Granda will see any kangaroos? Kangaroos are funny. They go *boing, boing, boing*.'

Just as Gabriel was despairing of ever keeping up with such a butterfly brain, the child got down from his seat and gave an impromptu demonstration of how he thought a kangaroo would bounce around the library of Mermaid House: ankles together, elbows tucked in and hands sticking out in front of him.

'And you'll go *boing* in a moment if you don't get back into your chair. I thought we were playing Pairs.'

Gabriel watched the boy climb up into the leather armchair and resume setting out the cards. At least he wasn't cheeky and constantly running about the place, smashing into the furniture. He had an enquiring nature, and Gabriel approved of that. His spitfire of a mother was doing a good job of bringing him up. Just as she was doing a good job of sorting out the kitchen. He was still surprised that she had changed her mind about helping him. Perhaps, after all, the money had swayed her.

But she didn't seem the sort to be strapped for cash. People like her – quick-witted, intelligent, well-spoken and confident – didn't usually struggle to make ends meet. They knew where they were going; they had a goal and went for it. They weren't drifters who sponged off others in the hope of handouts. Which brought him right back to where he had started: why the dickens was she mucking out his kitchen?

He hoped it hadn't been an act of charity. Charity was for those too weak to help themselves. That wasn't him. And it never would be.

He caught the sound of music coming from the kitchen – blast the woman, she'd gone and fiddled with his radio – and his gaze moved from the boy to Anastasia's portrait above the fireplace.

She was very beautiful, had been Miss Costello's words earlier, but they didn't cover half of what Anastasia had meant to him.

Her inner strength, humour, and dazzling candour had attracted him to her when they had first met at a mutual friend's wedding. Compared to his contemporaries he had left marriage relatively late. He claimed it was because he was so busy, but until Anastasia he had never met a woman with whom he had wanted to spend more than a night, let alone the rest of his life. She had changed that as soon as he had taken his seat beside her at the back of the church. During the excessively long sermon on the sanctity of marriage, delivered by a vicar who plainly liked nothing better than a captive audience, she had leaned into him and whispered, 'I know one is supposed to be awfully generous in these moments but, goodness, don't you just want to heckle the man down from the pulpit so that we can get on and enjoy ourselves at the reception, which, hopefully, will be a lot more jolly?'

He had smiled and agreed.

'I can't tell you how tempted I was a few moments ago to leap to my feet and say I had a just cause and impediment as to why the marriage shouldn't be taking place,' she had added, her wide-brimmed hat knocking his head as she leaned closer to him.

'What is it?' he had asked, amused.

'That I know they'll split up within the year. I can't think of a more unsuited couple.'

When they were outside the church, watching the ill-fated bride and groom pose for the photographer, she said, 'Do you think anyone would object if I removed my hat?'

He had wanted to say that if anyone did, he would personally knock them to the ground. He had watched her take it off, remove several pins and let an autumnal rustle of curly brown hair fall around her shoulders: it enhanced her long, slender neck and made her even more alluring. 'I don't think you should bother with hats. You look perfect without one,' he said.

She had given him a brilliant smile. Not one of those brittle, glued-on social smiles, but a flash of sunny brightness. 'Do you really think so?' she said. 'Between you and me, I paid a ridiculous amount of money for that one, and all to disguise my unfashionable hair. Every other woman here, including the bride, is dyed blonde like Grace Kelly. Had you noticed?'

Truth was, he hadn't noticed a single woman until he had sat next to her.

'I went all the way to London for that hat. It seems a shame to let it go to waste,' she said.

There was no vanity in her, just a mild touch of irony. It was something he soon came to love. She was at her best when she was being entirely herself.

'Have you seen Grace Kelly's latest film, *The Country Girl?*' she asked. 'For such a natural beauty, she was surprisingly good as a plain girl.'

'No. I don't go to the cinema. I don't have time.'

'What *do* you have time for?'

'Work mostly. Sorry if that sounds dull.'

'You need someone to change that for you.'

He stared at her to see if she was mocking him, but she wasn't. Her smile was genuine and he knew in his heart that there was no guile or cunning in her. He didn't know her name or where she lived, but suddenly he wanted to know everything about her. More importantly, he wanted to know that he would see her again. He said, 'What are you doing when this tortuous shindig is over?'

Confident brown eyes as dark as her hair had gazed at him, and he had momentarily lost his nerve. Why would this dazzling young beauty be remotely interested in a man whose friends described him as a confirmed, gone-to-seed bachelor?

'Having dinner with you, I hope,' was her answer.

A year later, in 1956, her prediction that their mutual friends' marriage would end in separation was proved right. They heard the news two days before their own wedding, and it prompted him to say, 'Do you know any just cause or impediment why our marriage should not go ahead?'

'None whatsoever. We are the best suited couple I know.'

She had been right. They had been the best of companions, the best of lovers. She was reassuringly self-sufficient, which suited him: being so busy with work and travelling as extensively as he did, he had needed to know that she wouldn't be lonely without him, or unable to cope with the running of such a large house on her own. Too often he had seen marriages collapse because one half of the couple relied too much upon the other. He and Anastasia relished being independent spirits, but the welcome he received when he came home after a long trip away never left him in any doubt that his wife loved him as passionately as he loved her.

Still staring at the portrait above the fireplace, he sensed that, in many ways, Miss Costello was from the same mould as Anastasia. She was a confident young woman who would glide through life on the strength of her own determination. She was just the kind of person to take everything in her stride and make the most of it. Anastasia had never made a drama out of anything that went wrong – not even when the tower had been struck by lightning while he had been in Canada. No doubt about it, they were two of a kind, and perhaps that was why he had felt compelled to seek Miss Costello's help. He had known instinctively that because she saw things so simply, she would be able to cut through the chaos of Mermaid House so that he could take control again.

But while he could appreciate her many strengths, he realised that he knew little about her. What did she do when she wasn't roaming the countryside in a camper-van with her young son? Where did she and the boy live? *How* did they live? Where was the boy's father? Was he her husband? And why had he himself made the assumption that she wasn't married? He tried to picture her left hand to see if he could recall a ring. He couldn't, but observation had never been his strong suit.

He knew he shouldn't do it, but with his curiosity fully aroused, and with the means to satisfy it sitting opposite him, he saw no reason not to ask a few questions.

'Finished!' Ned said, sitting back in the large chair and admiring his handiwork. The circular table was now a patchwork of blue and green tartan. 'Shall I go first?'

'As Granda would say, be my guest.'

A short while later, when Ned's pile of successfully matched cards was greater than his own, Gabriel said, 'You're not bad at this. You sure you didn't look at the cards before you put them down?'

'No!' Ned's voice rang with indignation. 'I just have a better memory than you.'

'Depends what one uses one's memory for. I can remember things very clearly a long time ago—'

'But not where the Queen of hearts is!' Gabriel turned over the wrong card and Ned claimed the pair. 'I'm beating you, aren't I?'

'Do you play this a lot at home with your mother?'

'I do now. But not when we were at home. Mummy was too busy then.'

'Oh? Busy with what?'

'Work. She had a very important job. She told lots of people what to do.'

Gabriel caught the past tense – *had* a very important job. Redundancy, eh? Well, there was a lot of it about.

'She gave up her job to be with me,' Ned said, with unashamed pride. He claimed another pair of cards. 'She said she wanted to give me an adventure I wouldn't forget.'

'And here you are playing cards with an old man who can't remember where the nine of clubs is ... Aha, got it.'

'You're getting better, Mr Liberty. But I'm still winning.'

'So who looked after you when your mother was busy telling people what to do?'

'Nanna and Granda. And I went to nursery too. Nanna and Granda are in Australia.'

'You said. Do you miss them?'

He nodded. 'Yes. But not so much now.'

'Why's that?'

'Because I see Mummy all the time now.'

'And you prefer that, do you?'

'Ooh, yes. I wish it could be like this for ever and ever. I wish I never had to go to school.'

'But you'll have to go home some day, won't you?'

'I suppose so.'

'And your mother will have to go back to bossing people about. I can see she'd be good at that.'

'She's not bossy with me.'

'She isn't? You sure?'

'She loves me.'

When he heard the boy express himself so simply and honestly Gabriel was jolted by something he didn't understand. It was a faint stirring of an emotion that was buried deep. There was a squeal from across the table.

'Look! I've found the Jokers.'

'And what about your father?' Gabriel ventured, after he had watched Ned rapidly unearth another series of pairs. There was hardly anything left on the table now: the child's memory was extraordinary. 'You never speak of him.' As soon as the words were out, he regretted them. The boy, normally so bright and open, looked confused, as though he didn't understand the question or, perhaps, didn't know how to answer it. Gabriel suddenly felt horribly unworthy. Supposing his father was dead?

'There's lunch on offer if anyone's interested,' said a stiff voice.

It was the boy's mother and Gabriel reddened with shame. *Damn!* How long had she been standing there? And just how much had she heard?

His guilt was multiplied many times over when he stood in the kitchen and saw the transformation.

The surfaces were all cleared and scrubbed to a high sheen and the cupboard doors were so shiny that reflections bounced off them. The floor was no longer sticky underfoot, the windows looked as if the glass had been removed, and the cobwebs that had been hanging from the ceiling like last year's Christmas decorations were gone. There was no sign of grease or burnt-on stains on the cooker, the fridge door looked as if it had been given a coat of white gloss paint, the rubbish that had covered the table had vanished, and lunch had been set for three. There was a white embroidered tablecloth he didn't recognise, and in the centre of the plates of sandwiches and glasses of orange juice, there was a small vase containing some purple flowers. He could just about discern their delicate scent above the more powerful odour of cleaning fluids.

It was as if he had walked into someone else's kitchen. He wouldn't have thought that just a few hours could have wrought such a change. 'I don't know what to say,' he murmured. A lump was firmly wedged in his throat. The more he looked, the more he was staggered.

'"Thank you" would be a start.'

He could hear in her voice just how very cross she was with him.

'Ned, do you want to go to the loo before we eat?' she said, in a more kindly tone. 'It's down by the laundry room, where Mr Liberty keeps his empty bottles. Be sure to wash your hands. I've put a clean towel in there.'

Gabriel walked awkwardly over to the Aga, which had also been given a clean and a polish. He ran his hand over the smooth green enamel and caught a distorted view of a bulbous-nosed face in the shiny chrome of the hot-plate cover. 'Miss Costello, I'm truly amazed at what you've done. Thank you very much.'

She gave him a steely glance and turned off the radio, which she had moved from the top of the fridge to the window-sill. 'And if you want me to stick to our agreement I'll thank you not to interrogate my son. Got that?'

He hung his head. It was a long time since he had felt so ashamed. 'I'm sorry,' he mumbled.

'At least have the decency to look at me when you're apologising.'

'I'm sorry,' he repeated, more clearly this time and looking straight at her. 'Shouldn't have done that to the little lad. Not on at all. Not my business.'

'Good,' she said briskly. 'Should you feel the disreputable need to play the part of grand inquisitor, please just ask *me* what you want to know. Okay?'

'Agreed.' Contrite. Meek. These were strange feelings to him, but that was exactly what he felt. That and the need to put things right with another person, whom he'd clearly upset. But how?

What could he do to make her think better of him? And when was the last time he had ever been concerned with what anyone thought of him?

24

Still beside herself with barely controlled fury over Mr Liberty's scurrilous behaviour, Clara was putting the surge of energy to good use. After lunch, and after she had instructed him – rather curtly – to wash up the plates, cutlery and glasses, she took the grimy curtains she had earlier unhooked from the kitchen windows and took them outside into the courtyard. She wanted to get the worst of the dust and sticky cobwebs off before washing them. The fine misty rain had stopped, and as she shook the curtains her anger began to subside. 'Just let him try a stunt like that once more,' she muttered, 'and I'll be out of here faster than . . . well, faster than anything he's ever seen move!'

Marching through to the laundry room, she threw the curtains on to the floor. Then, with the contents of the toolbox she had fetched from Winnie, she started to take the washing-machine apart.

To her satisfaction, her diagnosis was correct. Fortunately nothing was damaged and in no time at all she had it in working order. Not only that, but she soon had two loads of washing pegged on a line she had rigged up in the courtyard. While a third load was sloshing around inside the machine, she went outside to catch her breath. The sun was making a valiant effort to shine now, and while she stood in the courtyard, watching the clothes and curtains billow in the light breeze, the skip arrived.

'Sorry I'm late,' the man said, when he had lowered it into position and she was signing the form confirming its delivery, 'but it's been one of them days.'

'Tell me about it,' she said, with feeling.

Ned and Mr Liberty came to investigate just as the man was driving away. 'You don't do anything by half, do you, Miss Costello?' Mr Liberty said, when he had surveyed the scene – a large yellow skip and a line of his freshly laundered clothes, including some items he would perhaps rather not have had on show quite so visibly.

'Not if I can help it,' she said. 'Aren't you going to thank me for mending your washing-machine?'

'I was just about to. But why aren't you using its dryer?'

'No need – not when we can dry your unmentionables for free. Looks to me as if you could do with investing in some new ones.'

He scowled in embarrassment.

Enjoying his discomfort, she said, 'Now then, as you're both here you can help me ditch some of the rubbish I've collected. First to go will be those boxes of bottles from the laundry room.'

Under her directions, they worked steadily for the next hour and a half, until Mr Liberty suggested he made some tea. 'Got to keep the workers happy,' he said, and sloped off.

The moment Jonah had driven through the school gates that morning and the exhaust had dropped off on to the tarmac, he knew that it was going to be one of those days.

Now it was three o'clock and he was accompanying Jase O'Dowd to the doctor's surgery in Deaconsbridge. He had been in the staff room, drinking a cup of coffee while standing over the temperamental photocopier and thinking about year eleven's parents' evening next week, when Larry Wilson, the design-technology teacher, poked his unwashed head of grey hair round the door and asked if anyone would mind taking O'Dowd to the vet's to be put down. 'The bloody idiot's tried to chisel off a finger,' he grumbled, when Jonah agreed to forgo his hour of free time. 'If I've told him once not to muck around in my lessons, I've told him till I'm blue in the face. Serve the time-wasting blighter right if he's done himself some serious harm.'

Jonah found Jase waiting outside the secretary's office, and while he looked his normal cocky self as he leaned against the wall, kicking it idly, his face was as white as the notices on the board behind him. He raised his temporarily bandaged hand at Jonah. 'I'm gonna sue,' he said. 'It's not safe making them chisels so friggin' sharp. I'm gonna get the best lawyer Legal Aid can give me.'

'A cracking idea, but first things first. Let's get you stitched up, shall we?'

Exhaustless, they roared unceremoniously through the school gates, through the town and into the surgery car park, where Jonah pulled on the handbrake, switched off the engine and said, 'I'm not doing much for your street cred, am I, Jase?'

'Could've been worse. Could've been old Ma Wilson bringing me here.'

'I was referring to my car, not the status and quality of one of my colleagues.'

'Yeah, but you agree with me all the same, don't you? He's a right poxy old woman.'

Jonah kept his expression unreadable. 'I couldn't possibly comment.'

They reported to the receptionist, then took a seat in the empty waiting room. Jonah said, 'By the way, Mr Wilson did contact your parents, didn't he?'

'Nah, I told him there was no point.'

Jonah sighed. 'Jase, school has to let them know. You know that as well as

I do. We have to do things by the rule book or that hot-shot Legal Aid lawyer of yours will be down on us like a ton of bricks.'

His face set, Jase said, 'Leave it, Sir.' Then, 'How long do you think it will take for this to get better?'

Jonah looked at Jase's bandaged hand. 'Depending on how badly cut it is, a week or two. Why? Worried it might get in the way of your love life?' He knew from corridor and playground gossip that, since last Christmas, Jase was devoting less time to fighting on the estate where he lived and more to Heidi Conners, an anxious girl who was painfully thin – Jonah thought she might be anorexic.

Jase's face coloured, all the way to his sharp-curled quiff. He got to his feet and went over to a table where there was a pile of pamphlets on family planning. 'Friggin' hell, Sir, you ain't 'alf got a filthy mind! I was thinking of my exams next term and whether or not I'd be able to write.'

Suitably put in his place, and mildly surprised, Jonah apologised. 'I expect it'll be fine by then.' He knew that Jase could now put together a history essay that covered enough salient points to get him a C grade, possibly even a B with a bit more attention to detail and the wind blowing in the right direction, but as to his other GCSE subjects, he wasn't so sure. Occasionally he heard mutterings in the staff room that Jase O'Dowd was nothing but a load of trouble and Jonah was annoyed that the youngster could be so easily written off.

'Sir?'

'Yes?'

'What d'yer think my chances are of getting a job when I leave in the summer?'

'Do you have something in mind?'

Jase gave him a withering look. 'I thought with the qualifications I'm likely to get I'd start off with something easy – investment banker, summat like that.'

Jonah ignored the sarcasm. 'You don't think you might want to stay on in the sixth form, then?'

'What? *Me?* Have you flipped or what?'

'Heidi's staying on, isn't she?'

Another flush rose to Jase's face. 'Yeah, well, it's okay for her, she's got brains.'

'And so have you, Jase. You're just a bit more selective about how you use yours. I think you should consider it.'

He came and sat down again. He chewed at a grubby thumbnail. 'No point in considering it. It's too late.'

'Says who?'

'Old Ma Wilson for one.'

Jonah mentally cursed Larry Wilson, remembering now that he was Jase's form teacher. What hope was there for this disillusioned sixteen-year-old boy if the person who was supposed to be offering support and guidance was consigning him to the burgeoning number of disenfranchised young people the length and breadth of the country?

A shrill bell announced that whoever would be attending to Jase was ready to see them. Looking at his watch and seeing that they had only been waiting a short while, Jonah was glad that Dick High's policy was to use the local surgery in Deaconsbridge rather than the hospital.

Expecting a nurse to stitch up Jase's finger, Jonah was surprised to be greeted by a slightly built man, who introduced himself as Dr Singh.

'I've heard of educational cutbacks,' the doctor said, unravelling the bandage from Jase's hand and focusing his attention on his patient, 'but removal of a pupil's finger is going a step too far in my opinion. Ah, there we are, and what an impressive attempt has been made to slice through this fine finger. And what a lot of blood you have to spare.'

It was at this point that Jase's eyes rolled back and he fainted.

Jonah caught the boy before he slid off the chair and helped the doctor resettle him. Then, at his instruction, he went over to the small sink in the corner of the room and filled a paper cup with cold water.

Conscious again, Jase took the cup from Jonah, but without meeting his eyes. Jonah knew that he was embarrassed by what had happened and would have liked to reassure him that nobody would hear of it from his lips, but the doctor was gesturing for him to get out of the way.

'Now, Mr O'Dowd, to avoid a repeat performance, I suggest you avert your eyes while I tidy you up.' While Jase studied a poster that advocated a healthy diet of fruit and vegetables, the doctor completed his task with speed and efficiency. His small-talk never once dried up as the needle dipped and rose, and a layer of gauze and a finger bandage were expertly applied. 'I see from your notes that you're up to date with your injections, which means you'll be spared the ignominy of a tetanus jab, so it's not all bad today, is it? Now, tell me, is school as awful as I remember it? Are your teachers, present company excluded, of course, as sadistic as they were in my day?'

Jase shrugged. 'Some of them are, but Mr Liberty's okay.'

Standing at the sink now and ripping off his surgical gloves, the doctor looked at Jonah. 'Either the young man is terrified of you, or you have a loyal and devoted fan.'

'He's terrified of me,' Jonah smiled. 'Terrified I'll do a better job of chopping off a finger next time.'

Coming back to his desk, the doctor paused. 'Forgive my inquisitiveness, but are you by any chance related to Mr Gabriel Liberty of Mermaid House?'

Surprised at the question, Jonah confirmed that Gabriel Liberty was his father.

The doctor sat down and rearranged his sleeves. 'Well, how extraordinary. And isn't life strange? Suddenly the world is full of Libertys. They are crawling out of the woodwork, so to speak.' He laughed at his own joke.

'I'm sorry, Dr Singh, I'm not with you.'

'Forgive me again, please. But in one week I meet first your father, then your sister, and now you.'

'You've met my sister?' It was news to Jonah that Damson was in Deaconsbridge. What had brought her here? Then he remembered Caspar. Of course, the two of them were planning a pincer move on their father.

'Oh, yes,' Dr Singh said. 'I met her yesterday, your nephew too. They're staying with your father, didn't you know?'

Jonah gaped. Nephew? Good grief, Damson had had a baby!

There was no point in going back to Dick High – school had finished twenty minutes ago. Jonah dropped off Jase at home, and headed back towards town and the supermarket, as he usually did at this time on a Friday afternoon. Next he went to Church Cottage where he left his own shopping, then drove on to Mermaid House, still unable to get his head round the idea that Damson was not only staying with their father but was a parent herself. He hadn't seen her since Val's funeral, but he couldn't imagine she had changed in the interim to the extent that she was now a doting mother.

The light was fading when Clara remembered to bring in the washing. It was dry enough to be ironed, so she folded it neatly into the pitiful excuse for a laundry basket, thinking that if she wasn't too tired, she might tackle it later that evening. She was just adding the last of Mr Liberty's threadbare underpants to the pile when she heard an almighty racket. The throaty rumble grew louder and nearer. Someone's car was in need of a new exhaust.

She went inside the house to find Mr Liberty, to warn him that he had a caller. It was probably Dr Singh again. And if it was, she needed to know if Mr Liberty wanted her to keep her head down, or to be a visible presence in the guise of helpful daughter.

Interrupting a rumbustious game of Snap in the library, she told Mr Liberty he had a visitor. Like her, he assumed it was Dr Singh. Instantly every inch of him was bristling, ready for battle. She followed a few steps behind him, but stayed out of sight when they reached the kitchen. Peeping round the doorframe, she saw that they had leaped to the wrong conclusion. Standing beside the table, and with several plastic bags at his feet, was a tall man in a leather jacket. His collar-length hair was thick and wavy and, as he stared round the kitchen in obvious amazement, his profile and stance reminded Clara of a Renaissance painting.

'Good God, Jonah, what are you doing here?'

He turned. 'It's Friday, Dad, the day I always go shopping for you, and the day we agreed I'd come and see you. What's been going on here? It looks fantastic. Has Damson done this?' He plonked the bags on the table, carefully avoiding the vase of flowers.

Mr Liberty looked incredulous. 'Damson?' He snorted. 'Damson be damned!'

Having sized up the situation, that this was the youngest of her employer's uncaring darlings made flesh, Clara decided to leave them to it. She turned to join Ned, who was still in the library, but a commanding voice bellowed, 'Oh no you don't, Miss Costello. You come right back here and take the credit for all your hard work.'

She stepped into the kitchen. 'I'm in no need of credit,' she said briskly, making her tone hostile. Irrationally she wanted this casual-looking Renaissance man to know that she disapproved of him. That she despised him for being too weak to take his father by the frayed scruff of his neck and whip him into shape.

'Miss Costello and I have what one might call an arrangement, Jonah,' Mr Liberty explained, a wry smile twisting his mouth. 'For an exorbitant sum of money, she is staying with me for the week to do my bidding.'

'What your father is trying to say, in his clumsy way,' Clara said sharply, 'is that I'm here to tidy up Mermaid House.' She gave them both an accusing look. 'And since you're clearly about to settle in for a family bonding session, Ned and I will be off.'

Mr Liberty guffawed loudly.

But his son continued to stare, confused. 'Could someone please explain exactly what's going on here?' he said. 'And where's Damson?'

'Hell's bells, what makes you think she's here?'

'I was told she was. Apparently I have a nephew, who I'm curious to meet.'

Clara exchanged glances with Mr Liberty. She said, 'Have you been talking to a certain Dr Singh?'

'Yes, this afternoon. I was at the surgery with a pupil and he told me—'

'That your sister was staying here,' interrupted Mr Liberty. He smiled triumphantly at Clara. 'Didn't I say we'd taken him in? Hah! We reeled in the poor stupid fool good and proper! What a team we make.'

But Clara wasn't so triumphant. 'Hang on a moment. Before you start ringing the bells of victory, hadn't you better check with your son that he didn't dispute the matter and blow your little scam out of the water?'

Liberty Junior held up his hands. 'Whatever scam it is that you've got going here, I'm not guilty of trying to spoil it.'

His father needed convincing. 'You sure about that?' His tone implied he might reach for a shotgun if the answer wasn't to his liking.

'I played my part beautifully, dumb schmuck, right to the end.'

'Now why doesn't that surprise me?' muttered Clara.

Even by her standards the remark sounded more caustic than she had intended, and Liberty Junior frowned at her. He started to unpack the bags of shopping, and said to his father, 'I'm sorry to run the risk of repeating myself and appearing doubly foolish, but would it be too much to ask you why you've gone to the trouble of duping Dr Singh into believing that you have a daughter staying with you?'

'I would have thought that was obvious.'

'Please, indulge me.'

A short while later, the shopping put away, a pot of tea made and explanations given, Jonah watched his father leave the kitchen to fetch Miss Costello's son. Standing in front of the Aga, and running his fingers over the shiny surfaces, he was overwhelmed by the shame this acerbic one-woman dream-team had made him feel. He wanted to thank her for what she had done, and for what she was prepared to go on doing for the rest of the week, but he was mortified that a stranger had walked into his father's life and achieved what no member of his own family could do. Or, more precisely, what none of them had even tried to do.

Behind him he could hear her opening a packet of biscuits he had brought. He turned and watched her tip the chocolate chip cookies on to a plate to form a perfect spiral. He wondered if things always turned out so well for her. 'This must seem strange to you,' he said. 'From the outside looking in, it must appear as though we, his children, don't care.' He hoped she wouldn't judge him too harshly.

She gazed at him severely. Astutely. Assessingly. 'You probably *don't* care. Not enough, anyway.'

'That's not fair,' he said, defensively.

She crumpled the empty packet into a tight ball and put it into the swing bin. 'Okay, then,' she said. 'I'll be generous and say you've simply got used to the chaos and squalor in which your father has been living and turned a blind eye to it.'

'Are you always so blunt?'

'Yes.'

'Then that's probably what my father likes about you. Few people ever gain his approval. And just because one is related to a person, it doesn't mean you understand each other. Or even get on.'

She surveyed him steadily, her eyes cool and measuring. Unnerved, he turned away.

As unlikely as it was, Jonah had never seen his father talk to a child before, and intrigued, he watched him with Miss Costello's young son, Ned. He was a sweet-faced boy, whose expression ran the gamut from solemn to bright as if at the flick of a switch. He was immensely confident, not at all shy, and seemed extraordinarily comfortable with Gabriel, whom Jonah would have expected to terrify the child senseless. He had a shiny cap of dark brown hair, the same colour as his mother's, intensely dark, alert eyes and an engaging smile. Jonah had no way of knowing if his mother had passed this on to him, too, because he had yet to see her smile. But from the disapproving glances she flung at him, Jonah was getting the message that she despised him for not doing more to help his father.

Though Jonah was more used to teenagers, he had to admit that, for four years old, Ned was remarkably well behaved, never once spilling his drink or dropping crumbs. The nearest he got to making a *faux pas* was when he had told his mother with his mouth full that Mr Liberty was going to teach him to play draughts tomorrow morning. 'He says I can be white and go first. He's shown me the board, it's very old.'

'Mr Liberty won't teach you anything if you spray everyone with biscuit crumbs, Ned,' his mother reprimanded him gently. 'Finish what's in your mouth, then talk to us.'

His lips tightly sealed now, he was chewing extra fast, his miniature eyebrows rising up and down. He swallowed hard and continued excitedly, 'But he says I might not be clever enough to play draughts because I'm so young. Do you think I'm clever enough to play, Mummy?' Suddenly he looked grave, his eyes wide.

'You're as clever as you need to be, Ned,' she said reassuringly. 'No more, no less.'

'Another of your inscrutable replies, Miss Costello. Bravo. Do you lie awake in bed at night practising them when you can't get to sleep?'

'Not at all, Mr Liberty. I'm naturally inscrutable. Moreover, I never have trouble sleeping. I put it down to having a guilt-free mind.'

As he got up to add more hot water to the teapot, Jonah felt strangely isolated. There was a level of light-hearted repartee going on between this woman and his father that seemed designed to exclude him. It was as if he had walked in on the middle of something – which, in a way, he had. Oddly, he felt as though he was playing gooseberry to their extraordinary double act of sparky lovebirds.

He stared out across the darkening courtyard to where the yellow skip stood and, beyond, to where Miss Costello's camper-van was parked. Lifting the kettle, he poured freshly boiled water into the pot and wondered what was really going on here. Who was this confident, efficient woman who could sit so at ease at his father's table playing verbal pit-pat with him? And why did their obvious rapport rankle so much with him? Why did it make him feel even more of a failure than he usually did at Mermaid House? It was the same every visit, as if the bricks and mortar contained a magnetic force that made him revert to the anxious boy he had once been.

Hearing his father laughing behind him – and not the usual scornful barked-out guffaw he was more used to but full-throated good cheer – an ugly thought occurred to him: he was jealous. Jealous that this stranger with her sharp, no-nonsense way of talking, who had probably never suffered a moment's doubt, could make his father happy and he could not.

Suddenly he felt a flash of searing pain. He hadn't been concentrating on what he was doing and had poured boiling water over his hand. Stifling a yelp of pain, he moved to the sink and shoved his fist under the cold tap.

'Here, let me see.' It was the efficient Miss Costello.

'It's nothing,' he said, but he allowed her to inspect his hand.

'Keep it under the tap while I go and fetch my first-aid kit,' she instructed.

While he watched her through the window as she hurried across the courtyard, his father joined him at the sink. 'You wouldn't be attention-seeking, would you, boy?'

And you wouldn't be making a fool of yourself over a pretty young girl, would you? Jonah wanted to retort.

Within minutes she was back and showing him a tube of cream. Slightly out of breath, she said, 'It will sting at first, but then it will feel quite cool.'

'What is it?' he asked, turning off the tap and reaching for a clean handkerchief from his trouser pocket to dry his hand.

'A homeopathic remedy for burns. Works every time. Now remember, I said it would sting at first—'

'*Ouch!*' He pulled away his hand.

'You're worse than a baby. Honestly, men, you're all the same. Merest hint of pain and you go pathetically weak-kneed.'

'Whereas you brave women lap it up and ask for more.'

'No, we simply grin and bear it.'

He forced a grin and held out his hand again. 'Go on, then. I'll bear the agony just to prove to you that I'm no coward. I'm sure inflicting pain on a mere man will give you great pleasure.'

She smiled unexpectedly and for the first time he registered that there was more to her than the prim, judgemental woman he had thought her. 'Sorry to disappoint you,' she said, 'but I get my kicks in a much more satisfying way. There, that's it. And not one tear shed. Give yourself a pat on the back.'

'I would if I had any feeling left in my hand.'

'You have two hands, Mr Liberty Junior, or is the glass always half empty for you rather than half full?'

Before he could answer, she was screwing the top back on the tube of cream and had turned to his father. 'I think Ned and I have earned ourselves the rest of the day off. Eight o'clock suit you tomorrow morning? I want to finish sorting out the laundry room. Then I'll make a start on getting the dining room into apple-pie order.'

He grunted. 'Eight o'clock? Working part-time already, are you? Thought you were too good to be true.'

'And you're too full of sweetness. Come on, Ned. Time for some supper and our own more congenial company.'

Suppressing a yawn, Ned climbed down from his chair. 'Goodnight, Mr Liberty,' he said. 'You will teach me that game in the morning, won't you?'

'A promise is a promise, young man. Now be off with you before you fall asleep and I have to carry you across the courtyard to your bed.'

Both Jonah and his father saw them to the back door and watched them go. When a soft light glowed from the windows of the camper-van, giving it a warm, cosy look, Gabriel shut the door, led the way back into the kitchen and said, 'Right, then, what was it you wanted to talk to me about?'

Remembering why he was here, Jonah suddenly felt every inch the coward that only moments ago he had denied.

25

It didn't matter how many times Jonah replayed the scene at Mermaid House, or how often he tried to convince himself that he was overreacting, he knew that last night he had been judged by the snappish Miss Costello and, worse, that he had been found wanting.

It was Saturday morning, and he was lying in bed, trying to enjoy the slow, potentially relaxing start to the day. But it wasn't working. His enjoyment levels were at an all-time low. He laced his hands behind his head and stared up at the ceiling. His mood took a further nose-dive when he noticed that the indigo-blue paint he had applied earlier that week looked patchy in the bright sunlight shining through the uncurtained window.

No doubt that would never happen to Miss Costello. Anything she painted would be perfect.

Irritated that she had come into his thoughts again, and that he was forced to refer to her so formally – as though she were an old-fashioned school-marm – he reminded himself that what she didn't know, and could never understand, was that there were other dimensions to the truth about his family. A whole kaleidoscope of dimensions that no outsider could appreciate. But far from making him feel better, this added to his guilt. He was making excuses for himself.

He closed his eyes, then opened them again, hoping he had imagined the flaw in the paintwork. No, he hadn't. Haphazard criss-crosses were clearly visible. It was an infuriating mess. Why hadn't he noticed it before? And why hadn't he done something about his father instead of leaving him to turn to a stranger?

Frustrated with going round in this same futile circle, which kept dumping him where he had started, he launched himself out of bed. He went to the window and gazed down at the long stretch of garden at the back of the house, which he was in the process of taming. It ran parallel to the churchyard and fell away to merge with the landscape of gently rolling hills. At the bottom of the garden there was a tangle of brambles, which for years had got the better of a beautiful old rose that must once have reigned supreme. Against the wall of the brick-built shed there was a forsythia that had also taken more than its fair share of space, and that, too, needed his attention. He had always thought it was just the kind of space in which Val would have liked to potter. The garden at Mermaid House had never lent itself to a quiet afternoon's pottering. It was too big, much too wild and exposed for anything tender to flourish in it.

Normally the view from his bedroom window cheered him: the lush green pastureland had a pleasantly soothing effect. But this morning his mood was still clouded by the severity of Miss Costello's words and the reproachful way in which she had treated him. There had been something unnervingly proprietorial in her manner towards his father. He had wanted to explore this with Gabriel after she and her son had left them alone last night, but there had been no opportunity to steer the conversation in that direction, not without annoying his father. He had soon sensed that the proprietorial thing went both ways. Gabriel hadn't been prepared to divulge any information about her. Or maybe he hadn't anything to divulge. Certainly he didn't seem to know much about Miss Costello.

'What does it matter where she's from?' he had said, in response to Jonah's probing. 'She's on holiday with her son and doing some work for me. What more do I, or *you*, need to know about her?'

'But I still don't understand why you wanted to play a practical joke on Dr Singh.'

'And frankly, Jonah, I don't understand why you're suddenly paying me so much attention. Do I interfere in anything you do? No. I leave you to get on and cock up your own life, just as you told me to do when you walked out on me.'

Those words reminded Jonah too poignantly of the scene in the library when his father had struck him, so he had changed the subject and suggested that he cook them supper. But Gabriel had turned the offer down flat. 'I'm quite capable of getting my own supper. Why don't you stop wasting our time and get to the point as to why you've come here?'

Which he did, but only when his father was searching the cupboards for a bottle of whisky, banging doors and muttering, 'Where the hell did that infernal girl put it?'

'Dad, have you thought that maybe it might be a good time to think about selling Mermaid House?'

The last of the cupboard doors crashed shut and his father turned round, a bottle of single malt in hand. He banged it down on the table, spun off the top, poured himself a large measure and, without saying anything, raised it to his lips. He took a long gulp. 'And why would I want to do that?' he asked finally.

'Because you might be more comfortable in something smaller, easier to manage.'

Gabriel topped up his glass. 'How small were you thinking? Coffin size?'

'Don't be ridiculous, Dad.'

'That's rich! You don't think *you're* being ridiculous by coming here and suggesting I change my lifestyle to suit your conscience?'

'It's got nothing to do with my conscience.'

'No? Then perhaps it's more to do with lining your pockets. Caspar and Damson's bottomless pockets as well, no doubt. Have they bullied you into coming here tonight to convince the old duffer that it's in everybody's best interests for him to sell the house so they can get their hands on the loot?'

'Of course not!'

He gave a contemptuous snort. 'You never did have any talent for lying, Jonah. Unlike your brother. So what's the line he's taking? Death duties? Am I expected to sell my home and make a gift of the proceeds to my beloved children in the hope that I would live long enough for there to be no heavy tax penalties to pay? A happy-ever-after scenario for everyone . . . except me.'

'Whatever Caspar may or may not have in mind, you don't have to go along with it.'

He snorted again. 'What's this? Rebellion in the ranks?'

'Look, Dad, you might get some kind of vicarious thrill from pitching me against Caspar, but the truth is, I've come here tonight to suggest that it might be in *your* interest to think about moving to a house that would be more convenient for you to live in. No one else should come into the equation. What's more, what you chose to do with the proceeds of Mermaid House would be your affair. Personally, I'd rather you used them for your own pleasure and satisfaction, or gave them away to someone a whole lot more deserving than anyone with the name of Liberty.'

'A dog's home, perhaps? Or how about Miss Costello? She strikes me as being eminently deserving.'

In spite of himself, Jonah had looked up sharply at this. 'It's your money, you can do with it what you will. If you think Miss Costello would benefit from it, then give it to her.' Slipping his jacket on, he'd added, 'I've said all I came to say, so now I'll go before either of us says anything we'll regret. Goodnight.'

It wasn't until he was driving home that he knew he had omitted to say one important thing: that above all else, he cared about his father's welfare and happiness.

Downstairs in the kitchen, eating a piece of toast and scanning his mail, Jonah thought of how his father could never resist fanning the smouldering flames of a difficult conversation into a roaring argument. His comment that Miss Costello was an *eminently deserving case* had been a blatant attempt to keep their heated exchange going. Even so, he couldn't help wondering how Caspar would react if he thought there was a chance that the threat might be carried out.

The thought stayed with him for the rest of that day. So when the telephone rang later that afternoon and Caspar demanded to know the outcome of his visit to Mermaid House, he couldn't stop himself pursuing what could only be described as a wanton act of malicious stirring.

It was petty and foolish, but none the less he relayed the goings-on at

Mermaid House to his brother, labouring the point that their father seemed very taken with the attractive woman who had appeared from nowhere to work for him.

To hear the taut shock in his brother's voice and visualise his fuming face was worth every second of the ear-bashing to which he was then subjected.

26

Caspar gave the matter no more than a minute's thought. He cancelled his plans for that evening – the opening of a new restaurant in Manchester – and phoned Damson. Not that he held out much hope of speaking to her.

Poor deluded Damson, so fully immersed in mystical mumbo-jumbo that she was away with the fairies at the bottom of some sacred garden, getting high on pungent candles and herbal tea-bags while extolling the merits of Celestial Sex.

It vexed him that he couldn't remember the last sensible conversation they had shared. She was constantly on about biorhythms and her karma. It was like being with her in an Edward Lear poem at times: the words came out fluently enough but he was damned if he could understand a word she was saying. As far as he was concerned, she was going from bad to worse. 'It's all New Age funk, Damson,' he'd said, 'shallow and meaningless. Dare one ask how much you're paying for the privilege of being brainwashed?'

'Darling Caspar, I know you only have my best interests at heart but, please, the reward of finding one's centred self is beyond measure. You should give it a try.'

Yes, he'd thought, when hell froze over. The idea that she could be taken in by such a massive con appalled him, though part of him admired the person who had set up the scam: as commercial ventures went, it had the potential to be a lucrative money-spinner.

Still waiting for some idiot in Northumberland to get off his or her backside and answer the phone, he crossed one leg over the other and stared around him. Of all the things he had ever possessed, his loft apartment was the one from which he derived the most pleasure. It was a conversion of an old brewery warehouse in close proximity to Manchester's gay village, and though a high percentage of his neighbours were gay, they had good taste, were tidy, and seldom gave him much trouble – so long as they kept their mattress-wrestling behind closed doors, he had no complaints. The local restaurants and wine bars weren't bad either, pandering to the strength of the local currency, the vibrantly pink pound.

Since the day he moved in, he had felt at home: the stark barrenness of the place appealed to his keen sense of the aesthetic. Not for him the wild confusion with which he had been surrounded while growing up at

Mermaid House. He preferred everything stripped back to the purity of line and form. And that was exactly what he had achieved here: polished wooden floors, white-painted brickwork, large sheets of plate glass, stainless steel and slabs of granite gave him the austerity he craved. He had kept away from colour too, never straying into the garish palette of vulgar tones for which so many people opted. The only relief to this hard-edged simplicity was a large cream leather sofa and a specially commissioned circular bed on the mezzanine level.

But unless he could work a miracle in the next month or so, there was a danger that he would lose it. His car too. In his line of business he didn't need to own a car – a perk of the job was that he could have the use of more or less whatever he fancied – but such a transient arrangement didn't suit him. Outright ownership was what counted, and selling his Maserati would be a last resort. And he'd be damned before he did that. That was why his father had to see the sense in selling Mermaid House and freeing up its considerable capital. It was going to happen one day, no matter what. The old man couldn't stay there much longer, not at his age, so why not get it over and done with now and let his children have the benefit of the money that would come to them anyway?

It was spite that was stopping him from selling. It had been the same earlier that year when he had approached his father for a loan to get the bank off his back. 'Enough is enough!' Gabriel had roared. 'Not another penny, Caspar. So long as I'm breathing, you'll not scrounge another bean out of me.'

At last somebody in Northumberland answered the phone. 'Rosewood Manor Healing Centre,' announced a reedy voice, which sounded as though it needed a boot taking to it.

'This is an emergency,' lied Caspar, sitting upright and uncrossing his legs. 'I need to speak to Damson Liberty. Tell her it's her brother and that it's imperative she comes to the phone.'

'Damson who?'

'Damson Liberty – I mean Damson Ackerman,' he repeated impatiently. He never could keep up with the changes to her surname. Peevishly he added, 'Just how many Damsons do you have there?'

'Oh, you mean *Damson*. Hold the line and I'll see if she's available.'

'You do that. Now trot along quick as you can and find her for me. Meanwhile, I'll cope with the pain of your absence by slipping a rope around my neck and pulling it tight.'

Drumming his fingers on the smooth leather arm of the sofa, he listened to the woman's footsteps recede down what he imagined was a dark, draughty passageway, and in the minutes that passed, he went over what he was going to say his sister. He had to attract her attention in the first nanosecond of their conversation. Let Damson run so much as an inch with the ball and he would never get a coherent word out of her. She would be off on one of her surreal planes of fantasy.

What he needed to get across to her was that they had to work together on their father, persuade him to sell Mermaid House now, while the property boom was still at its height. Leave it till next year and they would lose out. Despite what Jonah thought, every pound counted. For some annoyingly perverse reason, his brother seemed intent on missing the crucial point that they must cash in on a buoyant market. Just as he was woefully naïve about the appearance of this unknown woman at Mermaid House.

What the hell was their father up to? And just who was she? A gold-digging opportunist who had caught the whiff of money?

He brought the flat of his hand down on the arm of the sofa with a loud smack. As if he didn't have enough to worry about without his father getting involved with a travelling New Age hippie! He could picture her perfectly. An irresponsible single mother who was shaven-haired, pierced all over, and who clomped around in boots and khaki trousers that were three sizes too big for her. It was the thought of her getting her unwashed feet under the table at Mermaid House that was causing him to act without delay.

He wanted Damson to understand that unless they took immediate action they might find themselves out in the cold with a scheming new step-mother calling the shots. Gabriel Liberty wouldn't be the first or last old man to make a fool of himself over a much younger woman.

Footsteps in his ear told him Damson was about to pick up the receiver. He felt himself relax and realised how tense he had become. He knew that once he had his sister on board, it would be like old times, and they would be invincible.

But he was wrong. They weren't Damson's footsteps he had heard. They belonged to the woman with the reedy voice. 'Are you still there?' she asked.

'More's the pity, yes. Where's Damson?'

'I'm afraid she can't come to the phone just now. I've been told to tell you she's in the middle of a very important holistic—'

'But I need to speak to her!'

A timid silence seeped down the line, followed by the sound of a loud gong. 'I'm terribly sorry,' the woman simpered, 'I'm going to have to go. I should ring back later if I were you.'

'And if I were you, I'd have a full-frontal lobotomy!' He slammed down the phone.

Now what?

He'd have to deal with the problem direct. Scooping up his keys from the glass bowl on the table by the front door, he locked his apartment, took the lift down to the garages on the ground floor and slipped behind the wheel of his Maserati. He nosed the car into the early evening traffic and tried to steady his temper by switching on the CD player, at the same time focusing his thoughts on the smoothness of the drive.

It worked.

By the time he had picked up the A6 and had driven through Disley, he could feel the knots easing in his neck and shoulders. He knew he shouldn't let things get the better of him, and knew, too, that as long as Damson was under the thumb of those hippies up in Northumberland, he could no longer rely on her. But old habits died hard: he still saw her as his rock. As children she had always been the more daring and cunning of the two of them. If ever he thought he was losing his nerve, it was always Damson who reassured him that nothing could go wrong.

But where was she now when he needed her support and reassurance?

Hanging around with a bunch of navel-gazing screwballs who had as much chance of finding their inner selves as he had of becoming the next Queen of England.

The tension was building again in his shoulders, and he tried not to think of how much he missed Damson. It was ages since he had last seen her – Val's funeral probably.

He pressed his foot down on the accelerator and sped on towards Mermaid House and the devious woman who had designs on his father.

She might have met his younger brother and concluded that he was as much of a threat to her plans as a wet paper bag but she hadn't reckoned on coming face to face with Caspar Liberty.

27

The day had gone well for Archie. The shop had been busy from the moment he had opened. A cold north-easterly wind had provided him with a steady flow of day-trippers coming in for a browse and a warm. There had also been a number of more serious customers, like the well-dressed couple who wanted to furnish a cottage in Castleton, which they were letting to the holiday trade. 'Naturally we don't want to fill it with anything new and expensive,' the wife had said, in a tight, haughty voice, 'not when cheap tat will do the job perfectly well. And what a lot you seem to have. I suppose it's all clean?'

Ignoring the implied slur, Archie smiled and got on with offloading as much furniture and knick-knacks as he could and arranging for its delivery on Monday morning.

Another couple had come in soon after them, a husband and wife in matching fleeces, whom he recognised from their monthly trawl of his shop. They were dealers from Buxton who made it their business to check out the bottom end of the market for the antiques of tomorrow. It always surprised him what they picked from his shelves. Last month it had been an ugly chrome ashtray – one of those silly things on a stand that always got knocked over. Today it had been a Bakelite clock. He couldn't see the attraction in Bakelite; in fact, he hated it. It reminded him of when he had been in his bedroom as a child, listening to his father shouting at his mother downstairs. To keep himself awake, just in case his mother needed his help, he would leave his bedside lamp switched on. But then it would overheat and give off a horrible fishy smell.

Alone in the shop now, he was locking up. Samson had given Bessie a lift home earlier so that she could take her time to get ready for their big Saturday night out at the pictures. Just as he was slipping the last of the chains and bolts across the door, the telephone rang. Because Archie was thinking of his mother, he rushed through to the office and snatched up the receiver, fearing the worst.

'Is that Mr Merryman at Second Best?' asked a woman – an assured young woman.

'Yes, it is. What can I do for you?'

'You might not remember me, but my name is Clara Costello and my son and I—'

'Of course I remember you. How are you? Still enjoying the delights of Deaconsbridge?'

'Yes, but not quite in the way I thought I might. I know it's a bit late in the day but I've got a proposition for you. Have you got a moment?'

'I'm all ears.'

When he'd heard what she had to say, he laughed. 'Well, I think I could manage that. I'll put it in the diary for Monday afternoon, around three o'clock. That soon enough for you?'

'Yes, that'll be fine. Do you need directions?'

'No, thanks. I've a nose on me like a bloodhound.'

After he'd rung off, he reached for the diary to make a note of his appointment with Clara Costello at Mermaid House. It was only then that he remembered he'd be delivering an entire house's worth of 'cheap tat' for Mr and Mrs Hoity-Toity over in Castleton that morning. Oh, well, he and Samson would just have to make sure they got through the job in double-quick time.

Feeling surprisingly chipper, he left the shop to walk home. He crossed the square, waved at Shirley through the window of the Mermaid café, then made his way slowly up the steep hill of Cross Street. The early evening air was sharp and it sliced through his thin jacket. He paused to catch his breath in the usual spot, leaning against the rail. The coldness of the metal scorched his hand and he wondered if they were in for a late snap of winter. Just because they were on the verge of April, and had recently experienced a few welcome days of spring weather, it didn't mean they were out of the woods. He could recall many an April morning when he'd had to scrape ice off the windscreen. Then he remembered he had left his car at the shop. He had driven to work that morning because he had taken his mother in with him on the pretext of needing her help again. 'I'm knee-deep in stuff that needs cleaning,' he had told her the night before. 'I don't suppose you'd come in for another day and give me a hand with it, would you?'

By the time he had parked the Volvo outside his house, it was almost seven. He'd have to get his skates on now or they'd miss the opening minutes of the film. As he let himself into the house at the back, he called to his mother. It was the moment in the day he dreaded most, other than first thing in the morning when he knocked on Bessie's bedroom door. He told himself repeatedly not to keep imagining the worst, but the memory of finding Bessie on the floor of her own home last year was difficult to shake off.

Hearing voices, and thinking she was in the sitting room watching the television, he pushed open the door and found her rigged up in one of her best dresses – collar and buttons askew – listening attentively to an earnest young man who could be no more than seventeen. He was reading from a copy of the *Watch Tower* and next to him was an older woman pouring tea. All three looked up as he came into the room.

'Hello,' he said, cheerfully enough, but inwardly annoyed. 'What's going on here?'

'Archie,' his mother said, unaware of the tension that his presence had caused, 'this is Rickie and his hummer.'

'I think she means mother,' the woman said, lowering the teapot.

'And I think she may have lost track of the time,' Archie said firmly. 'We're due out shortly, so I think it would be better if we brought this cosy chat to an end.' He was livid now. How dare these people think they could take advantage of a defenceless woman and indoctrinate her with their religious beliefs?

'Another time perhaps?' the woman said smoothly, rising to her feet and pulling on her coat. She had probably been thrown out of more homes than Archie had had hot dinners.

When he had hustled them to the front door, he realised how uncharacteristically rude he was being. 'Look,' he said, 'I'm sorry, it's just that you could have been anyone – robbers, murderers, you name it. She's too sweet-natured for her own good. She thinks well of everyone.'

'A fault with which more people should be blessed,' the woman said, with a smile of such forgiveness that he felt twice as churlish.

Watching them close the wrought-iron gate behind them, Archie noticed that the boy's trousers were too short for his long thin legs and his conscience pricked again. He wished he could replay the scene and deal with it better. It's not your religion or beliefs I have a problem with, he wanted to call after them, it's the world we live in. A dog-eat-dog world that takes advantage of innocent children and old ladies.

Later, as he was driving to the cinema, he thought how heavy-handed he had been. He knew he had hurt his mother's feelings by behaving like a boorish, arrogant bully, taking it upon himself to censor her enjoyment, which was bad enough, but what pained him more, was that he had reminded himself of his father.

Determined not to let this thought put a damper on the evening, and knowing that Bessie was still upset, he said, 'I'm sorry about turfing Rickie and his mother out, but in this day and age you really ought to be more careful who you let into the house.'

What she said next made him feel even worse. 'Lonely, Archie, on my bone.'

Cut to the quick, he drove on in silence. Then he thought of something that might cheer her up, and told her about the call he had had from Clara Costello. 'She's only gone and got herself working for that dreadful man I told you about at the hospital. You know, the one who was so rude to Dr Singh. I hope he doesn't take advantage of her.'

28

'Mr Liberty, please don't think you can take advantage of me. I'm really not that sort of a girl.'

Gabriel scowled. She was merciless in the way she kept twisting his words. But two could play at that game. 'Miss Costello, I may have lost some of my social skills of late, and the use of plain English may have changed since I last made anyone such an offer, but as far as I'm aware I believe I only suggested I'd cook you supper. There's not the slightest chance of me wanting to seduce you. As disappointing as that might be to you.' Hah! Let's see you bat that one back!

They were standing in the dining room, where she had been hard at work all day. She was polishing a pair of silver candlesticks he hadn't seen in a long while. He couldn't even remember where they had come from. She stopped what she was doing, folded the yellow duster in half, then in half again and turned away to place the candlesticks on the stone mantel above the fireplace. Without looking at him, or giving him an answer, she said, 'What are you hiding behind your back?'

He cleared his throat and mentally conceded the point to her. She was good, very good. But now they'd got to the tricky part. This was when he had to apologise. 'Ahem . . . It's a peace-offering.'

She turned slowly and he held out a tightly wrapped bunch of red tulips, their petals still closed. She didn't say anything. Feeling a desperate compulsion to fill the awkward silence with words, he heard himself rambling out of embarrassment: 'You rather rudely asked me the other day when was the last time I had bought anyone flowers – well, I saw these when I was in Deaconsbridge this afternoon and they reminded me of you.'

She made no move to take the tulips from him, but lowered her gaze to them. He could see the curious doubt in her eyes. 'Reminded you of me, eh?' she said. 'Care to explain?'

He cleared his throat again. 'I've always thought of tulips as an efficient-looking flower. Upright and businesslike. They give the impression of not wanting to waste their time frolicking about the flower-beds. In short, they strike me as purposeful. Like . . . like you.'

Her gaze met his. It was softer than it had been. 'Hush now, Mr Liberty, go easy on the schmooze or you'll have me blushing to the tips of my ears. But you mentioned they were an apology. For what exactly?'

'You wouldn't be trying to extract blood from a stone, would you?'

'But of course. That goes without saying. So, come on, let's hear it. And no mumbling. I like apologies to be loud and clear. Then I can be sure they're genuine.'

Corralling what was left of his shaky resolve, he pulled at his nose, scratched his chin, and tried to recall the exact words he had prepared for this moment while driving back from town. He pictured himself as a newsreader, lifting the words from an auto-cue, but trying to add some meaning to them. 'I just want to say that I've been left with a nasty taste in my mouth after that incident with your son. I had no business prying into your affairs and I wanted you to know just how sorry I am.' His mission completed, he clumsily thrust the flowers at her and turned to flee.

He was nearly at the door when she said, 'That was really quite good, Mr Liberty. Full marks for content but running off before taking a final bow loses you valuable points when it comes to artistic expression.'

He didn't risk looking at her, kept his face to the door. 'Please don't make fun of me. Not when I'm—'

'Trying to be nice?' she finished for him. 'Now, why don't you come back here and let me thank you properly? That's if you have the nerve.'

It was a challenge he couldn't refuse. He'd never been short of nerve. Who did she think she was to accuse him of such a thing? But when he stood in front of her again and she raised herself on her toes and softly kissed his cheek, he wondered if he hadn't met his match. 'We'll make a decent human being of you yet, Mr Liberty.' She smiled.

Caught so thoroughly off guard, he couldn't stop himself from lifting a hand to his cheek and touching, with his fingertips, the spot where he could still feel the light pressure of where her lips had been. Then he discovered he hadn't shaved that day. Had he even washed? Burning with self-loathing, he edged away from her.

Still smiling at him, she said, 'I hope you're not going to withdraw your offer of supper.'

With a supreme effort of will, and managing to sound his normal self, he said, 'You should know well enough by now that I'm a man of my word. But don't expect anything other than plain fare. I've got some boil-in-the-bag cod in parsley sauce knocking about in the freezer. Jonah keeps buying it for me and I keep forgetting to eat it. Is that good enough for her ladyship and her son?'

'Quite good enough. Talking of Ned, where is he?'

Glad of the diversion, he led her out of the dining room and along the hall. 'I took the liberty – no pun intended – of buying him a little something while I was in Deaconsbridge.'

In the kitchen, Ned was kneeling on a chair, his head bent over the table. When they came in he looked up. 'Mummy, Mr Liberty bought me a scrapbook and some postcards. I've been drawing a picture of his house. Do you like it?'

Out of the corner of his eye, Gabriel watched the boy's mother anxiously. Had he overstepped the mark? Would she think he was interfering? But he had only done it because the boy had told him during their walk before lunch that she had forgotten to buy them for him. 'We're going to keep a diary of our holiday,' Ned had said, releasing himself from Gabriel's grasp and running on ahead like a giddy spring lamb.

'Don't go too far without me,' he had called after the lad, his voice catching on the wind. 'Your mother said you had to stay close to me. And if I have to go home and tell her I've lost you, she'll have my guts for garters.'

The boy had slowed down until Gabriel caught up with him. 'What are guts and garters?' he had asked.

Prodding at his small belly, he said, 'Guts are inside there, your squelchy innards. And garters are elastic bands that people used to wear years ago to hold up their socks.'

Considering this, the boy had unzipped his anorak and felt his stomach through his clothes. 'But how would Mummy get your guts out?'

'Depending how angry she was, and bearing in mind I'd just told her I'd lost you, she might take a large knife to me and cut my stomach open.' He drew a line from his own chest down to his trouser belt. 'Then she'd take a stick and coil my innards around it.'

'And then?'

'Well, she might hang them up on the washing-line and let them dry before cutting them into the required lengths for the garters.'

'Would she sew you up afterwards?'

'Probably with the biggest, rustiest and bluntest needle she could lay her hands on.'

They continued their walk, the child's small warm hand now locked in his. Gabriel was taking Ned to the copse, where he hoped to show him a badger's sett. As they took the downward slope of the field, their muddy shoes skidding on the wet grass, and a nippy wind hustling them from behind, Ned said, 'I don't believe you, Mr Liberty.'

'Hmm ... what don't you believe?'

'About Mummy and your squelchy bits.'

'You think I'd tell you lies?'

'You were joking, weren't you? Are you frightened of my mummy?'

'Good Lord! Frightened of a slip of girl like your mother? Now it's you who's joking.'

But standing in the kitchen, as Gabriel awaited her verdict on his purchases, which had now been added to the bonanza of coloured pencils and glue that covered the table, he had to admit that part of him *was* scared of her – of stepping on her toes and offending her.

He watched her move in beside the lad. She stroked the top of his head absently and studied his drawing. 'Ned, it's brilliant. How clever of you to draw the tower so well.' She placed the tulips on the table and bent down to his level for a closer inspection. 'But, my goodness, who is that handsome man?'

The boy beamed. 'Mr Liberty.'

Curious, Gabriel drew near to see how he had been depicted. Expecting to see a scowling old man with wild hair, he saw instead an enormous matchstick man who dwarfed the tower of his house – which bore an uncanny resemblance to the leaning one in Pisa. His massive head was wearing a ridiculously large pair of ears, and stretched between them was a crescent-shaped smile. 'You've forgotten my nose,' he said.

The boy reached for a coloured pencil and gave the matchstick man a pastel pink swirl that obliterated one of his eyes.

'Perfect,' his mother praised him. 'And thank you, Mr Liberty. You couldn't have given Ned a better present. It was very kind and thoughtful of you.'

Twirling the pencil in his hand, then trying to balance it on his top lip, the boy said, 'Mr Liberty said he'd help me with some of the writing tomorrow.'

'But only if you're good,' Gabriel said, moving away from the table and crossing the kitchen to the freezer compartment above the fridge. When he had finished rummaging through the bags of frozen peas and sweetcorn, and had found the stockpiled cod in parsley sauce, he realised that Miss Costello was standing behind him. 'What's that smirk on your face for?' he asked.

'You wouldn't be going soft on me, would you?'

'Of course not. I'm feathering my own bed. By keeping the boy out of mischief I'm ensuring that you get more work done. I don't want you having an excuse for slacking.'

'And while I'm not slacking, I'll defrost that for you tomorrow . . . and in case you're wondering, I'm referring to the freezer, not your frosty exterior.'

To round things off, Clara decided that they would eat their supper in the room she had spent all day cleaning. It had proved a lot less trouble to sort out than the kitchen. The dining room had been left to its own devices and it was more a matter of treating neglect to a large dose of tender loving care.

She had started by throwing open the windows and letting in some much-needed fresh air, then vacuuming the parquet floor, the rugs and the curtains. Using a full-height ladder she had found in an outhouse, and putting the vacuum cleaner on to its lowest setting, so as not to shred the brittle fabric damaged by years of exposure to sunlight, she had carefully removed the thick blankets of dust. Balls of fluff the size of walnuts were rounded up from under the mahogany table, chair legs and the corners of the room, and thick-legged spiders found themselves given short shrift and an abrupt change of address.

Next she had dusted the faded wood panelling that went from floor to ceiling, and the framed antique maps of Derbyshire that hung on it. Then she cleared out the contents of the sideboard and the matching pair of glass-fronted cabinets that stood at either side of the fireplace. She immediately wished she hadn't. There was so much of it. Quite apart from the hundreds of crystal wine glasses, brandy balloons and whisky tumblers, all of which needed careful washing, there was a mind-blowing quantity of elegant but tarnished silverware: teapots, coffee-pots, cream jugs, coasters, sugar tongs, snuff boxes, candlesticks, candle snuffers and tea strainers. And every item had a brother or sister. It occurred to Clara, as she spread out the sheets of newspaper and set to with the silver polish, that everything in the house, except its owner, was multiplied by a factor of at least three. It had been the same in the kitchen yesterday: if she found one Kenwood mixer, she unearthed a whole family of them. It made her wonder who had collected such a hoard. Surely not Mr Liberty. His wives probably. Perhaps out of pure devilment he had considered leaving the mess for his children to deal with when he departed, just to teach them one last lesson.

Now, as Clara set the table for supper, with cutlery, mats, glasses, her lovely red tulips and a candelabrum at one end, she thought of the youngest member of the Liberty family she had met last night. He had seemed pleasant enough, which paradoxically had made her dislike him on principle. His slightly hesitant manner had irritated her, had made her want to say, 'How dare you live on the doorstep and do so little to help? Anyone can fetch the weekly shop. How about scrubbing the floor or cleaning the toilet?'

Mr Liberty seemed greatly amused by the splendour of the setting for their simple boil-in-the-bag supper. He had wanted to eat in the kitchen, but Clara had insisted on showing off her efforts, barring anyone entry until she had everything just right.

'*Ta-daa!*' she chorused, when at last she allowed him and Ned to come in.

She watched his face as he stood for a moment, taking in the scene, a large tray of steaming food in his hands. Even to her critical eyes the room looked and smelt magnificent. Darkness was pressing in from outside, so she had drawn the heavy brocade curtains and lit the room with candles, their flickering flames bouncing soft light off the furniture and panelled walls. There was a warm, burnished look of opulence to the room and copious amounts of fresh air and lavender polish had seen off the musty, depressing smell of neglect.

Ned's eyes were wide and luminous. 'It's like Christmas,' he said. 'Only bigger.'

Mr Liberty set down the tray on the table and made a low bow. 'Another day, another miracle for you, Miss Costello. I applaud you once again. A small point, though. Where did all the candles come from? I had no idea I had so many.'

'I found them on a shelf in the laundry room. Some of them are so old they're probably medieval church relics.'

'Well, just so long as we don't go up in flames. Will we be warm enough in here, do you think?' He cast his eyes over to the empty grate in the fireplace, where she had placed a pottery jug of daffodils picked from the garden.

'I wanted to light a fire but thought I wouldn't risk it. As well as antique candles you're probably the proud owner of a ton of antique soot. I'll get hold of a chimney sweep. But for now, I'm starving.'

Despite the blandness of the meal, it was their most convivial so far – the second bottle of Chablis they were roaring through might have had something to do with that. Ned, who was sitting on two cushions and a telephone directory to get him up to the right height, and who was surprisingly perky for one whose bedtime should have been more than an hour ago, was telling her Mr Liberty's gory tale of guts and garters when Clara heard a sound and interrupted. 'What was that?' She cocked her head towards the door.

'What was what?' asked Mr Liberty.

She allowed him to top up her glass. 'I must be spending too much time with you, I'm going mad and hearing things.'

He crashed his glass against hers. 'Here's to you. May you always speak your mind!'

'Just you try and stop me.'

'I suspect I'd need a Panzer tank to stop you doing something you'd put your mind to.'

They were both mid-laugh when Clara noticed the door open slowly at the far end of the room. She froze. Mr Liberty turned to see what she was looking at. A smartly dressed man had come in. Clara would have recognised him anywhere. It was the long-faced rude man from the supermarket with the trolley of bargain-priced champagne.

'Hello, Father,' he said, in a pompously creepy voice. 'Do hope I'm not interrupting anything.'

29

'As a matter of fact you *are* interrupting. What is this? Suddenly everyone's treating my home as if it was Liberty Hall.'

Caspar forced a smile. 'Never underestimate those old jokes, Dad.' He stepped further into the candlelit room, his leather-soled shoes sounding loud in the sudden hush. 'Liberty Hall indeed.' His words were directed at his father, but he was more interested in Gabriel's dining companions, in particular the woman: the scheming Miss Costello. Though she was scruffily dressed in khaki trousers (he'd got that right!) and a loose-fitting T-shirt stained with something he didn't care to think about too deeply, and had the kind of childish, unattractive haircut he never approved of on a grown woman, she didn't match up to the pierced, tattooed New Age scrounger he'd pictured.

But appearances could be deceiving.

It was odd, though: the more he looked at her and the child, the more he felt he had come across them before. But where?

He could see that she was appraising him, and that his presence was not to her liking. Which confirmed his hunch: she was working a number on the old man but now knew that she had been confronted with a spanner in the works. Well, get ready, little lady, you're going to be out of here before you get your feet any further under the table.

'Caspar, are you going to stand there all night gawping at us?' his father barked. 'Or are you going to share with us what's brought you here? Or perhaps you were just passing through and thought you'd check up on your dear old pater. Make sure he hadn't snuffed it in his bed.'

'Passing through' was exactly the cover Caspar had decided to use and he slipped seamlessly into his prepared speech, pulling out a chair beside his father and imposing himself on the cosy scene of candles, flowers and best silver. 'As it happens, I *am* just passing through,' he said. 'I've been to see baby bro Jonah. I had no idea how concerned he is about you.'

Gabriel snorted. 'Hah! That'll be the day, when any of you worry about me.'

Caspar laughed expansively. 'Come on, Dad, there's no need to take that line. You know jolly well that we all care about you. But where are your manners? Aren't you going to introduce me to your dinner guests?' He leaned across the table, hand outstretched. 'Caspar Liberty, your humble servant and eldest custodian of my father's welfare. And you are?'

He had intended his words as a warning shot, but when his hand was ignored and Gabriel said, 'Is there any need to introduce you?' he felt the full force of one of his father's warning shots.

'Sorry, Dad, you've lost me. You know I'm no good at cryptic clues. That's much more your scene, what with all the crosswords you do. Any chance of a glass of that wine?'

'Cut it out, Caspar. I know exactly why you're here. And it won't do.' Gabriel slapped one of his knobbly hands on the table. The cutlery rattled and the small boy with staring dark eyes jumped and leaned in towards his mother.

'Steady on, Dad, you're frightening your guests. An unforgivable breach of etiquette in anyone's book. In some quarters poisoning one's guests is an acceptable mishap, but to scare them to death—'

'Caspar, while I'm familiar with the fact that you listen to nothing but the echo of your own voice, my guests are not so well informed, so will you do them a great kindness and shut up?'

'I think it's time we were going, Mr Liberty.'

The scheming minx was on her feet now and staring pointedly at him. But as she manhandled the child out of his seat and hooked his short legs around her waist, Caspar saw how small she was. Not the glowering Amazon she had appeared while seated. Quite insignificant, really.

'There's no need for you to leave, Miss Costello,' his father said. 'In fact, I would rather you stayed.' The voice was imperious, as Caspar remembered it from his childhood – 'You'll stay right where you are, young man. You'll leave this room on my say-so, and not before.'

'No can do, Mr Liberty. Ned's tired and I need to get him to bed. Same time tomorrow morning?'

'As you wish, Miss Costello. Goodnight.'

What was all this? 'As you wish, Miss Costello' and 'No can do, Mr Liberty'? What kind of game did they think they were playing?

The door closed silently behind her, signalling that Caspar could get down to business. He pushed back his chair and turned to face his father. But Gabriel was ahead of him and gained the advantage by creaking to his feet. 'I hope you're satisfied, Caspar,' he glowered down at him, 'because for the first time in a long while I was enjoying myself, but as usual, you had to spoil everything. Nothing changes with you, does it?'

Caspar's jaw dropped. Good God, it was worse than he'd thought. The old fool had got it bad. He didn't know whether to laugh or jump out of his seat in horror. He played it cool, preferring to extract as much embarrassing detail from his father as possible. 'I'm not sure what you're getting at, Dad. What exactly did I interrupt here this evening?' He cast his eyes meaningfully over the remnants of the candlelit dinner.

Standing by the fireplace, one clenched fist jammed into his side, the other on the mantel, his father stared at him. Then his withered features acquired a firmness that was both vital and tenaciously implacable. Inexplicably, he began to laugh. A nasty sneering laugh that started as a low rumble until it grew into a full-blown body-shaker before climaxing in a fit of wheezy coughing. Sweet Moses! Any more attacks like that and the man would kill himself! Caspar stood up. 'You all right, Dad?'

Gasping for breath, Gabriel swiped Caspar out of the way as if he were a fly. He moved back to the table and took a swig from his wine glass, then another. Just as he was confident that he had his breathing under control, he almost started to laugh again. The situation was hilarious.

Bloody hilarious!

Caspar, poor stupid, greedy Caspar, thought his father had finally lost his marbles and fallen for the charms of a pretty girl! Ha, ha, ha! Well, let the arrogant buffoon think what he wanted.

'Are you going to tell me what you were laughing at, Dad?'

Using all his guile, Gabriel kept his face poker straight and joined Caspar by the fireplace. He put a fatherly arm around his son's shoulder. 'Caspar, I know this may come as a shock to you. To be honest, it's been a seismic shock to me. The thing is, I'm fairly well smitten with the lovely Miss Costello. But you must have grasped that. You've seen what a beautiful woman she is. She's stunning, isn't she? Intelligent. Poised. And utterly charming. Quite a catch for an old thing like me.'

To his delight he felt his son stiffen and it was all he could do to stop himself grinning. He sighed the sigh of a man hopelessly in love and continued to turn the screw. 'And for some reason that is quite beyond my comprehension, she seems besotted with me. So, what I'm trying to say is, and I know she's much too young for an old duffer like me, but how do you feel about a new step-mother? Your approval matters to me, you know.'

30

There was little to be gained from telling Caspar to calm down – Jonah had tried that already only to provoke a louder and more incoherent outburst – so he poured his brother a glass of wine.

Caspar took the glass and tossed back half of its contents in one gulp. To Jonah's relief, it brought him to a standstill, and he repeated, more calmly, what he had said on his arrival at Church Cottage. 'This proves beyond all doubt that the old man is definitely losing it.'

'You still haven't said—'

But Caspar was off again. 'I warned you something like this could happen. But would you listen to me? Oh, no, you had to carry on as you always do with your head buried in the sand. Maybe now you'll take more notice of what I say.'

'I might listen if you started talking sense,' Jonah replied, keeping his voice level. 'What's happened to cause such a rush of blood to your normally temperate head?'

'Oh, please, save the witty sarcasm for your brain-dead pupils. Haven't you heard a word I've said?'

'Every syllable, but I still haven't a clue as to what you're raving on about.'

Caspar's face hardened. 'Look, Jonah, our father is on the verge of marrying for the third time. Do you have any idea where that will leave us? Out in the cold, that's where.'

'Who is he thinking of marrying?'

'The gold-digging Miss Mop.'

'But that can't be right.' Jonah was stunned.

Caspar regarded him pityingly. 'Of course it's not! But I'm pleased to see that I'm finally getting through to you. We've got to put a stop to this nonsense ... Any more of this lighter fuel going?'

Jonah poured the remains of the bottle into Caspar's empty glass. Reaching for the corkscrew, he opened a second, wondering if the joke he had played on his brother had been trumped by a bigger one from their father. He simply could not equate the assured woman he had met yesterday with one who would be interested in marrying a man like Gabriel Liberty. Or was it possible that Caspar was right, that the efficient Miss

Costello was nothing but a scheming gold-digger? He recalled how jealous he had felt in the kitchen at Mermaid House that she had an empathy with Gabriel that few other people had ever had, least of all the members of his family.

But despite this, he couldn't go along with Caspar's theory. There had been nothing in her manner to suggest that she was up to anything so devious as fooling an elderly man into marrying her for financial gain. But then why was she at Mermaid House?

He leaned against the Rayburn. 'Right, Caspar, tell me exactly what Dad said to you. Try to remember his exact words. Don't exaggerate.'

Caspar rolled his eyes. 'Stop treating me like a fool, Jonah. I may have flunked university, which Dad has never let me forget, but credit me with sufficient intelligence to read the signs. And it was you who alerted me to what was going on in the first place. If you hadn't told me on the phone last night—'

'Just tell me what he said.'

'My, how snappy you are these days. He asked me how I felt about having a new step-mother. And I think that even *you* can grasp the significance of that. He also said that he was smitten by the lovely Miss Costello and that she was equally besotted with him. *And* he put his arm round my shoulders.' He shuddered and took a long sip of his wine. 'I can't remember the last time he touched me.'

'Did he say anything else?'

'Plenty, most of which makes me cringe to think of it. Once he got started it was impossible to shut him up. He even asked me for my advice as to where they should honeymoon, and if I thought it might be worth his while to see the quack about some Viagra! He's certifiable if you ask me.' He put down his glass, tugged at the white cuffs of his shirt that poked out from his jacket sleeves, then straightened his cufflinks. 'Do you suppose that's a line we could pursue? Put a stop to the marriage by proving he's not in his right senses?'

Having listened to Caspar, Jonah was doubly suspicious that his brother had been duped. Never in a million years could he see their father seeking advice about Viagra. That put the tin lid on it as far as Jonah was concerned. The more he thought about it the more convinced he was that, just as their father had enjoyed pulling a fast one on Dr Singh with Miss Costello's help, so he had with Caspar. But why couldn't Caspar see that? 'Did the object of Dad's affections have anything to say on the matter?'

'No. This all happened after she'd left us alone. They were in the middle of a romantic candlelit dinner when I arrived.'

'And her son?'

'Oh, he was there too.'

'So, a romantic dinner *à trois*, then?'

Caspar looked at him hard. 'She could hardly have left him sitting on the doorstep with a bottle of pop and a bag of crisps.'

Side-stepping, Jonah said, 'I think our best policy is to stay quiet and see how things progress.'

'Oh, that's bloody typical of you, isn't it? Some tart is planning a move on our inheritance and you want to pretend nothing's going on. Don't you care that if Miss Costello becomes the third Mrs Liberty, we can kiss goodbye to Mermaid House?'

'You speak as though you have a right to it,' Jonah said.

Caspar's expression grew tight, and his nostrils flared just like their father's. 'That's because I do. A share of Mermaid House *is* my birthright. I hardly need point out to you that it's what our mother would have wanted for each of us.'

There was absolutely nothing Jonah could say to this last, dangerously weighted comment, so he kept quiet and waited for his brother to leave.

The next morning Jonah's curiosity had got the better of him, and after calling in at Kwik-Fit to have a new exhaust pipe fitted, he drove out on to Hollow Edge Moor.

Thick banks of clouds were being dragged across the sky and a blustery wind buffeted the car; rain was imminent. Only a few hardy walkers dressed in full-length cagoules with knapsacks were braving the elements up on the ridge, their distant figures leaning into the wind. Black-legged lambs sheltered with their mothers in the lee of a drystone wall, and the recent warm spring weather was now a distant memory. But the dismal nature of the day didn't bother Jonah: he found it invigorating.

As the brooding outline of Mermaid House came into view he felt a stab of doubt. What did he hope to achieve by seeing his father again? 'Two visits in one week, Jonah?' Gabriel would sneer. 'Suddenly I'm the most popular man in the Peak District.'

He supposed that, deep down, he hoped he was right that his father had played a prank on Caspar and might want to let him in on it.

'Sibling rivalry makes fools of us all,' he muttered, as he drove through the archway and parked alongside Miss Costello's camper-van, noting that the large yellow skip was still in residence.

He switched off the engine and felt nothing but contempt for himself. Why hadn't he just told Caspar last night that he thought their father was having a laugh at his expense?

Because they were all so used to fighting one another.

Out of his car, he looked across the courtyard to see the energetic figure of Miss Costello hurling a cardboard box into the skip. Only the other day he had wished he had the courage to clear the decks for his father and now an outsider was doing precisely that. The thought irritated him. He strolled over, uncomfortably aware that he was trying too hard to put on a casual air.

Seeing him, but not stopping what she was doing, she said, 'You've got your exhaust fixed then?'

'And Dad's got you hard at work even on a Sunday.'

She tipped another box into the skip and a gust of wind caught some sheets of newspaper. She pushed them down hard. Wiping her hands on the back of her close-fitting jeans, she said, 'Understand this, Master Liberty, it's me who sets the agenda. I decide the hours I work.'

'I don't doubt that for a minute. Here, let me help you.' He expected her to refuse his offer, but she didn't and between them they added a smelly rolled-up rug to the pile of rubbish. 'Caspar will be furious if he thinks you're chucking away the family heirlooms.' His tone was light, but she didn't say anything, merely reached for a black plastic sack and threw it on top of the rug. 'I believe you had the pleasure of meeting him last night,' he added.

'I'd had that pleasure already.'

'Really?'

'In the supermarket, in Deaconsbridge. I decided then and there that he was the rudest, most self-centred, arrogant man I'd ever set eyes on.'

Jonah tried not to smile. 'And did last night alter your opinion?'

She didn't answer him. Instead she said, 'If you're looking for your father, he's in the library.'

He was clearly being dismissed and, baffled, he wondered what he had done to deserve such frostiness. 'Miss Costello, you don't like me very much, do you?'

She paused, lifted her chin and looked him dead in the eye, her small face stern. 'Does that bother you?'

He took from her a dusty dried flower arrangement, which Val had put together a long time ago, and placed it carefully in the skip. He was used to brutal honesty from his family, but not from someone he hardly knew. He decided to fight back, force her to drop the annoying deadpan manner he was sure she had adopted for his benefit. 'If you're going to be my stepmother,' he said mildly, 'don't you think we ought to make more of an effort to get along?' He watched her closely for her response.

'Well, what can I say?' she said, her manner giving nothing away. 'I suppose you're right. How do you suggest we go about it, young Master Liberty?'

'First you can stop calling me Master Liberty. My name's Jonah. And second, you can be honest with me.'

'Oh, I don't know whether that's a good idea. Families are rarely honest with each other, are they? There's always something we like to keep from each other. By the way, who spilled the beans about your father and me getting hitched?'

'Dad told Caspar last night.'

The conversation wasn't going at all how Jonah had thought it would. Who was bluffing who? But he was determined to get a straight answer to a straight question. 'Miss Costello, please, will you level with me?'

She held up a hand. 'Don't be so formal. Call me Mother. Or would you prefer Mum?'

'Please,' he tried again, 'a straight answer for a straight question. Are you indulging my father by playing along with another of his self-satisfying games?'

'As I always tell Ned, you must believe what you want to believe.'

'In that case, I don't believe a word of what my father has told Caspar. Or that you're a gold-digger on the make as my brother thinks you are.'

She stuck out her chest and placed her hands on her hips provocatively. 'Is that because you don't fancy me in the role of step-mother?'

He knew she was teasing him, but her playful tone and the sight of her breasts showing through her thin T-shirt were an unexpected turn-on. 'I'm afraid that imagining you as my step-mother would take too much suspension of belief.' He lowered his gaze. He had no choice but to accept that he wouldn't get any further with her. Exasperated, he said, 'Where did you say my father was?'

'He's in the library with Ned.'

As Clara watched Jonah go inside, she almost felt sorry for him. What in the world was the incorrigible man up to now? He might have had the decency to warn her that not only was she his stand-in daughter but also his fiancée. How would they explain that to Dr Singh?

31

On his way through the house to the library, Jonah noted the changes and improvements Miss Costello had single-handedly brought about. Whatever his feelings towards her – and he wasn't entirely sure what they were – he couldn't fail to be impressed by the effect she had had on Mermaid House. There was a lightness about it that he hadn't felt in years. No, more than that: it was as though, with each room she had touched, the house was being coaxed out of mourning, something which had been going on for as long as he could remember. He poked his head round the dining-room door, which was ajar. He saw and smelt yet more telltale signs of Miss Costello's refreshing handiwork – polished wood, flowers in the grate and on the table, sparkling glass and silverware on the shelves of the gleaming glass-fronted cabinets. The transformation was incredible.

Hearing a squeal of high-pitched laughter, he carried on towards the library, calling to his father so that he couldn't be accused of turning up unannounced. He pushed open the door and braced himself for another in a long line of difficult encounters. But he had miscalculated his father's mood.

'Jonah? Well, I can't say I'm surprised to see you, not when I'm suddenly flavour of the week, but your timing is perfect. Pull up a chair and help me. This cheeky whippersnapper has me on the run.'

The room hadn't yet received the Miss C treatment, and after shifting a dusty pile of *National Geographic*s from a chair to the floor, Jonah joined them in the bay window where a game of draughts was in progress. The 'cheeky whippersnapper' smiled exuberantly at him. 'I've just taken another of Mr Liberty's pieces,' he said proudly. He waved the grubby ivory disc in front of Jonah. 'And look at all these other pieces I've got.'

'Enough of the boasting, young man. Now; ssh! I need peace and quiet while I think out my next move. What do you advise, Jonah?'

Jonah observed the board, the same board on which he had learned to play both chess and draughts – games his father had always played ruthlessly to win, no matter the age or ability of his opponent. On several occasions Val had told him to give Jonah a fighting chance. 'He's only a child. How will he ever improve if you don't encourage him?' Looking at the board now and its scene of one-sided carnage, Jonah could only conclude that either Ned was a child genius, or Val's advice had finally been heeded: Gabriel was down to just a few pieces. 'Strikes me that you're in real trouble, Dad,' he said. 'Any move open to you looks risky to me.'

'And since when have I ever been afraid of taking a risk?' Licking his mottled lips, Gabriel nudged one of his few remaining pieces forward. 'There now, you little rascal, pick the bones out of that!'

Lost in the depths of the leather chair opposite, and resting his chin on a knee drawn up close to his chest, the boy stared hard at the board, his bright eyes flicking from left to right. The only sound in the room was Gabriel's wheezing – was it louder than it had been? – and the steady ticking of the clock on the mantelpiece. Jonah willed Ned to see for himself that with one simple move he could win. A small hand hovered over the left of the board. Jonah felt disappointed; Ned had missed the obvious. He cleared his throat to attract Ned's attention and looked meaningfully at the other side of the board. A moment passed before Ned took the hint, but then his hand moved towards one of his kings, and with a burst of gleeful realisation he claimed the last of Gabriel's pieces. He was gracious in his victory. He sat back in his chair and smiled. 'Mr Liberty, I think you've lost.'

Gabriel stared at the board and slowly smiled. 'Clearly I've been too good a teacher. Well done, young man.' He brought his hands together and gave him a short round of applause. Jonah noticed that each clap made his father wince.

Leaning forward in his chair and repositioning his triumphant army, Ned said, 'Can we play again?'

Gabriel groaned. 'Not now. Maybe after lunch. My poor old brain needs a rest. You run along and tell your mother what a smart lad you are while I have a chat with my son; I doubt I'll need my brain for that.'

Alone, and expecting his father's mood to change, Jonah started setting out the board ready for another game. He said, 'Do you remember teaching me to play?'

Gabriel pushed himself to his feet, setting off a crackle of dry joints. 'Like it was yesterday. And talking of yesterday, I imagine that's why you're here, isn't it? Come to get the news straight from the horse's mouth about my approaching marriage, I presume.'

The last of the draughtsmen lined up, Jonah said, 'Why are you doing this, Dad?'

'What? Marrying the delectable Miss Costello? Wouldn't you if you had the opportunity?'

Jonah had let one conversation slip out of his grasp and had no intention of this one going the same way. 'We're not talking about me, Dad,' he said firmly. 'We're discussing why you're pretending to Caspar that you're marrying the *delectable* Miss Costello, as you describe her.'

'Who said anything about pretending?'

'I did. It's another of your games, isn't it?'

'I'll say this for you, Jonah, you're verging on the astute.'

'So why taunt Caspar?'

'Because it was fun! You should have seen the feckless little runt. I thought he was going to pass out on me with shock. I haven't enjoyed myself so much in years.'

'But is it right to do so at somebody else's expense?'

Gabriel waved aside the implied criticism. 'What do I care for Caspar's finer feelings? When did he or Damson ever care about mine, eh?'

'Am I not to be included in that condemnation?'

'Carry on with this interrogation and you might well find yourself top of the list!' His father turned abruptly and looked out of the window. 'Damn! It's started raining. I was hoping to take young Ned for a walk later on. Do you want to stay for lunch? Or have you something better to do?'

Jonah stood next to his father and stared through the dirty glass at the heavy downpour that was flattening the daffodils on the sloping lawn. He couldn't remember the last time his father had made an invitation so spontaneously. He didn't know how or why, but it felt as though a small bridge had just been crossed. Prepared to take whatever was on offer, he said, 'Lunch would be great. Thanks. Do you want me to see to it while you prepare yourself for another whipping at the hands of your protégé?'

Upstairs, in what had been Val Liberty's bedroom, Clara was sorting through the dead woman's belongings. She had wondered who had been responsible for the clutter in the house, and now felt sure she had found the culprit: the second Mrs Liberty had been an inveterate hoarder.

Judging from the drawers, cupboards, bedside cabinets and wardrobes, she had never thrown anything away. She had kept all sort of curious things: train tickets to Sheffield and Manchester, dental appointment cards, hairdresser's receipts, shopping lists, bent hairpins, ancient suspender belts, empty scent bottles, hairbrushes, crumbling bath cubes, packs of safety-pins and half-used tubes of hand-cream. There was a collection of hot-water bottles, so old and perished they had become glued together into the kind of rubbery collage the Tate Modern might exhibit. There were several boxes of Carmen heated rollers as well as one of those inflatable hood devices for drying your hair.

Mr Liberty had given her *carte blanche* to get rid of everything. 'None of it's of any use to me, so you might just as well ditch the lot,' he had said. This was after she had arrived for work first thing that morning and told him she wanted a change from scrubbing and polishing.

'Aha! Trying to get out of the heavy-duty work so you can take it easy with the light stuff, are you?'

'Keep the words of love and kindness for your family, Mr Liberty. Did you enjoy your late-night cigar-and-brandy session with your son?'

He had cracked the air with a bellow of laughter. 'Immensely. I'll tell you about it later when I bring you your elevenses. Ned, m'boy, you stay with me. Today's the day you learn to play draughts.'

Folding yet another thick woollen skirt and adding it to the bag of clothes she had already sorted – there were two piles, one destined for a charity shop and the other for the skip – Clara thought how funny it was that the three of them had slipped into such an unlikely but easy-going routine. Ned was perfectly at home with Mr Liberty, whom he probably regarded as a temporary grandfather. Which was fine by her, because, as far as she could see, they were all getting something out of the week. Mr Liberty was getting spring-cleaned, Ned was being entertained and taught to play draughts, and she was getting paid enough to convince herself that she hadn't been mad in taking on such an extraordinary assignment.

Last night, after reading Ned a bedtime story, she had written her first postcard home to Louise and the gang.

I can't believe it's only a week since Ned and I set off in Winnie. It feels like we've been away for ever. Having the most unbelievable time. Not quite what I'd had in mind, but lots of fun all the same. We're doing missionary work (I'll explain later), staying with a crazy man in the Peak District – so far north for you, Louise, you'd need a pocket phrase book! Ned is having the time of his life. He's four going on fourteen now. More news in the next card. Love to everyone, Clara. P.S. Missing work? Get real!

She had deliberately omitted to mention that she had turned herself into a cleaner for a week, because she knew that Louise would despatch David to fetch her home.

With the rails of the first wardrobe empty now, she stood on a chair to clear out the stuff from the top shelf. She found a battered hatbox hidden beneath a pink candlewick bedspread. It was quite heavy, so she took off the lid and found that it contained a bundle of large notebooks.

She climbed down, sat on the bed, and pulled at the frayed satin ribbon that held them together. Picking one at random, she opened it, expecting to find nothing more interesting than a rambling extension of the cluttered woman she had so far glimpsed – a variety of recipes for prize-winning chutney, perhaps.

But she saw straight away that what she had in her hands was a diary.

She knew she shouldn't but she couldn't stop herself reading the erratic writing that covered the lined pages.

Sunday, 16 September

There are times when I hate this dreadful house! I know that sounds overly dramatic, but there it is, that's how I feel today.

I warned Gabriel something like this would happen, that Caspar wasn't above such an appalling act of treachery. But, as usual, the stubborn old fool refused to do anything about it. 'They're grown men, they should be able to deal with this themselves,' he said, when I told him this evening what had been going on. 'No man is ever fully grown,' I said, but he just gave me one of his baleful looks and went off to his wretched library.

The trouble started the moment Caspar and that dim girlfriend of his (whose name escapes me, I doubt we'll ever see her again, so it doesn't really matter) arrived to celebrate Jonah and Emily's engagement. During dinner I could see what Caspar was up to (I've seen him do it countless times before, so I could recognise the signs) and knew that no good would come of the weekend, and that it was my fault – it was me who had insisted on everyone being present. As soon as that silly girl Emily started giggling, I knew she had been taken in. Poor Jonah, he just sat there quietly seething, his head down, his mood darkening by the second. 'Do something!' I wanted to shout at him, but he didn't. He just let his brother walk all over him as he always has. He's frightened of him, I know. Frightened of Damson too. And Damson could see what Caspar was up to, and I think that maybe even she was a little shocked. But she made no attempt to stop him – she's the only one who can rein him in – and in doing nothing, she condoned his behaviour. Though to be fair, she's so caught up in herself she probably doesn't care. Half the time I can't understand what she's talking about. She hasn't got enough to do, of course. That's the real problem. If she had some real direction in her life, she wouldn't be like this. So airy-fairy.

By lunchtime today it was all over. Jonah left without saying a word. I watched him from the kitchen window as he drove out of the courtyard – I don't think I've ever seen anyone so angry and so unable to express themselves.

Minutes later, Caspar's girlfriend came hobbling into the house in my borrowed boots and, glory be, there's a creature who can express herself! Such language! (Calls herself a model too – not a model of decorum, that much is clear!) From what I could gather from her highly colourful language, she and Jonah had seen Caspar kissing Emily, in Jonah's favourite haunt by the rocks, where he likes to go and think. And while she waited for Caspar and Emily to reappear, she phoned for a taxi and packed her bag. When Caspar did deign to show his face, she slapped it hard for him and left. (Can't say I blame her!) Emily, the stupid girl, had the grace to look ashamed of what she had done, but Caspar was his normal arrogant self. 'Well,' he said, in that annoyingly cocky voice of his (I know it's wrong but my hand always itches to slap him when he puts that voice on!), 'there goes a girl with some spirit. I wish her next sparring partner all the luck in the world.' He then had the gall to say to me, 'Val, old love, it looks like lunch is off. Another time perhaps?'

And during all this commotion, where was Gabriel? Where he always is. Hiding in the library, of course. Why won't he deal with his family? Why does he always leave it to me? I'm tired of it, truly I am. I often wonder what would become of them all if I was no longer here.

A flurry of footsteps out on the landing had Clara shoving the books back into the hatbox, slapping the lid on it, and standing guiltily to attention. The door flew open and in came Ned. 'Mummy, guess what? I beat Mr Liberty at draughts.'

'Aren't you the clever one?' She went to him, knelt on the floor and hugged him.

Wriggling out of her grasp, and staring intently into her face, he said, 'It's a real grown-up game, Mummy, and I still won. I did, really I did. No help from anyone. Well, maybe a tiny bit from Mr Liberty's son.'

She kissed the tip of his nose, basking in the shining rays of his euphoria. 'Do you want to help me up here now? Or would that be too boring?'

He looked around the room, eyeing it for the fun factor. His gaze slid over the piles of clothes and he shook his head. 'I'll do my scrapbook downstairs with Mr Liberty.' He was already moving towards the door.

'Okay, then, but don't make a nuisance of yourself, will you?'

'I won't.'

'Oh, and while you're with Mr Liberty, remind him to bring me up some coffee. It's well past eleven.'

As soon as she was alone again, Clara slipped the lid off the hatbox and reached for another diary. Just a couple of pages, she told herself.

Friday, 2 December

Well, he's finally done it. I never thought he would, but he's sold up. And I know he feels terrible about it. He won't say anything, of course, but the whole thing has taken a far greater toll on him than he will ever admit to.

And why did he have to sell to a rival firm of engineers? A firm he's despised for as long as I can remember. A firm that will strip his business for its assets and throw the rest to the dogs. It's as if he's done it deliberately. As though out of spite he wants the whole thing to implode in on itself. He says he doesn't care what happens to it. 'I've washed my hands of it,' he said this afternoon, when he came home after his meeting with the lawyers and accountants and poured himself a large glass of his most expensive malt whisky. But I simply can't believe he meant it. 'What about all those men and women who have worked so loyally for you?' I asked him. 'Don't you care what will happen to them?' He grunted something I couldn't make out and told me I didn't understand. Maybe I don't. But what I do understand is that what Gabriel devoted his life to, and his father before him, has to mean something. I also understand how much it hurts him that none of his children wanted to step into his shoes – he so badly wanted at least one of them to do that. But I can see it from their point of view too: they have their own dreams to follow.

Why does he always have to take things so personally?

Again, the sound of footsteps – less hurried ones this time – had Clara furtively hiding the diary. She stuffed it back into the hatbox and pretended to be folding a matted Fair Isle sweater.

'Dad sent me up with your elevenses and an apology for being late.' It was Jonah with a mug and a plate of ginger nuts. He handed her the mug and put the plate on the dressing-table, clearing a space for it among the mess. 'How's it going?'

'Slowly.'

He looked about the room. 'I guess it's easier if you're detached from it. I know I'd struggle to be objective. I did try to do it for Dad, but it was probably too soon for him.' He settled his gaze on the sweater she had just folded. 'I remember Val knitting that. It was a Christmas present for Dad but it shrank and ended up fitting her better than him. She only ever wore it in the garden. Oh, and if it helps things between us, apparently the engagement's off.'

For a moment she thought he was referring to what she had just been reading in the diary – the engagement between him and Emily – but then she realised he couldn't possibly be talking about that. 'Sorry?'

He shrugged. 'It's okay, you don't have to carry on with the game any more. Dad's told me the truth. It was a wind-up for my brother's benefit last night.'

'Oh, so I don't even get the chance to be jilted at the altar. How disappointing. And to think I was so looking forward to being your wicked step-mother.'

Given the room they were in and its contents, Clara wished she hadn't said that. Her cheeks burned. How could she have been so insensitive?

He spoke before she could apologise. 'Not all step-mothers are wicked, you know.'

'I'm sorry.' Wanting to make good the damage, and intrigued by the entries in the diary, she said, 'What was your step-mother like?'

He hesitated fractionally, then said, 'To put up with us Libertys, Val was two parts saint and one part sergeant-major. On reflection I think we gave her a terrible time. I don't think she was always very happy.'

Though she couldn't comment on its accuracy, she was impressed by the incisiveness of his reply. 'How old were you when she married your father?' she asked.

He moved away from the bed, went over to the window. 'A little younger than Ned, and before you ask, no, I can't remember a time before that.'

'Not even your real mother?'

'Not likely, given that it was my birth that killed her.'

Once more Clara wished she could retract her words. 'Oh dear. I'm sorry. I keep putting my foot in it.'

'"Oh dear", indeed. It's quite the party-stopper, that line, isn't it?' He was moving again, this time towards the door. 'Don't forget your coffee. Lunch is in an hour, so you'd better not scoff too many ginger nuts or you'll upset Chef.'

'And we all know the consequences of annoying your father.'

'Sorry to disappoint you, but it's not my father's culinary delights you're being treated to. Lunch is on me.'

For the next hour, Clara worked doubly fast to make up for the time she had spent reading. But all the while she was sorting through Val Liberty's things she kept thinking what kind of a woman she must have been to take on such a family. What an enormous challenge she had accepted the day she had agreed to marry Mr Liberty – or Gabriel, as she now knew him as – a widower with three young children who between them must have tested her love and patience beyond endurance.

Clara had done many things in her life of which she had later thought better, but this one was perhaps the most unworthy. She knew she had no right to do it, but she was hooked. Having begun to see the Liberty family in a new light, she wanted to know more, understand them better.

She took the diaries from the hatbox and slipped them into a bag with the intention of reading them later. She would return them to Mermaid House tomorrow morning with no one else the wiser.

Where would be the harm in that? She was only borrowing them.

32

In bed that night, long after Ned had fallen asleep, Clara was reading the diaries. As she turned the pages in the soft beam of light, she was conscious that while she might refer to the diaries as 'borrowed', she was actually stealing the private thoughts of a woman who, if she were alive, would have every right to be furious at Clara's intrusion into her honest record of her own failings as well as the shortcomings of others. Clara knew from what she had read that Val had been a fair woman. She had tried hard to see a difficult situation from every angle. Yet there were times when Clara got annoyed with Val's 'understanding'. She longed to shout, 'Stop making excuses for them all!' The tricks that had been played on her by Caspar and his sister were breathtakingly diabolical, and as their father had turned a blind eye to what was going on, he was no better than his scheming brats.

The first diary began a month after Val, in her own words, had 'taken on the job of nanny and housekeeper at Mermaid House'. This bleak description of herself, so soon into her marriage, seemed to have been prompted by a case of good intentions on her part that had gone disastrously wrong.

I cannot believe what happened today! I'm still shaking with anger and indignation. The whole situation is so gruesomely destructive I have to get my thoughts and shock down on paper – hence this journal, something I haven't done in years, not since I was a child with TB and had to spend so much time in the sanatorium and thought I would die of loneliness. N.B. Clearly there is a connection here!! Will think about this in more detail when I have calmed down!

The trouble started last week, and I really could kick myself for not seeing how I was being manipulated – just like the heroine of *Rebecca* at the hands of Mrs Danvers – but in all truth, how was I to know? I suggested to Caspar and Damson that the three of us ought to get our heads together and do something about Jonah's birthday. 'How do you know it's his birthday?' Damson had asked, her closed face watching me slyly from behind her long curtain of hair. 'Why, is it a secret, darling?' I replied (and yes, I do try to call the children something endearing, even if I don't mean it half the time). She didn't

180

say anything and I didn't think it strange that until that moment no one had mentioned the fact that Jonah's fourth birthday was just round the corner. I only found out about it by chance when I had been putting away some papers – just another example of the stuff that Gabriel is for-ever leaving about the house. Putting the letters and documents away in his desk I saw a card that must have come in the post that I hadn't seen. It was from the doctor's surgery in Deaconsbridge recommending that Jonah be brought in for his pre-school booster. It was then that I saw the date of his birth. The only thought that crossed my mind at that point was that it was lucky I had seen the card as otherwise, and knowing Gabriel and his lack of foresight when it came to anything to do with his children, the child's birthday would probably have been and gone without any of us realising.

Still sitting at the table with Caspar and Damson – Jonah was upstairs in bed – I asked them why neither of them had thought to tell me when their brother's birthday was. Damson shrugged and said, 'If you'd wanted to know, you only had to ask.' There was something in her voice that made me want to snap back at her. Cold and patronising, she was treating me no better than a charlady. Restraining myself, I said, 'Why don't we arrange a party for him? You'd like that, wouldn't you? Help me blow up the balloons and make the jellies.' I thought I was doing the right thing, involving them in something by treating them as equals, rather than tiresome children. (Goodness, how weary I am from trying to win them over! When all the time they begrudge me the very air I breathe!)

Eventually it was decided, between Caspar and Damson, that we would organise a surprise party the following Saturday for Jonah, and that it would coincide with the day their father was returning from his three-week trip to Helsinki. I should have smelt a rat when Caspar and Damson insisted I didn't mention what we were doing to Gabriel, but I was so caught up in my own pride and vanity that I was finally forging a link with the twins that I didn't see the warning signs. Oh, if only I had! The pair of them made the invitations – pieces of paper with a cake drawn on (rather crudely in my opinion, given their age), and I wrote out the envelopes with the addresses of Jonah's little friends from his nursery school. These were duly posted – or so I thought – by Caspar and Damson, who even today after all the commotion, swore blind they had walked to the end of the drive and handed them over to the postman, but I just know that if I were to tackle Mr Potts, he would confirm that no such thing occurred.

Meantime, I had forged ahead with the shopping and baking, and last night while the children slept, I worked like a mad thing in the Banqueting Hall, blowing up balloons, setting out the trestle tables, decorating them with colourful paper tablecloths, paper plates and cups. I put a tape-recorder on a table in front of the fireplace so that we could have games of musical chairs and pass the parcel, and before going to bed I iced the cake I'd made that morning, giving it the finishing touch of 'Happy Birthday Jonah' and placing four blue candles, one at each corner.

Then this morning, and on Caspar and Damson's instructions, I wished Jonah a happy birthday but kept quiet about the present we had for him – the twins had claimed that it wouldn't be fair to their father for Jonah to open it without him being there to share the moment. Again, I should have thought something was wrong when Jonah didn't pursue the matter. He just looked at the card I had given him, turned it over and ran his fingers over the embossed picture of a little boy flying along at top speed on a bicycle. So intent was his scrutiny, it was as though he had never seen anything like it before.

Why, oh why, didn't I put two and two together? Why didn't I question the fact that in the run-up to his birthday he never once referred to it? In my defence I shall have to put it down to my ignorance of children and their mores. Jonah's quietness is also a factor. I've never come across anyone with more natural reticence. Rarely does he speak unless spoken to directly, and even then his words are so reluctantly given one can hardly make them out. 'Speak up!' Gabriel yells at him. 'Stop muttering!' But that only makes it worse, as I often tell him. Jonah needs someone in his life with a gentler manner than his father has. Someone with the patience to tease out the words, to give him the confidence he so badly lacks. I can't imagine what kind of nannies these children have had in the past. The twins are practically out of control, little better than savages. In contrast, Jonah has the anxious look of somebody who's lost a shilling and found sixpence.

Just after breakfast, Gabriel phoned to say that his flight was going to be delayed, but he hoped to be home by three, which unbeknown to him, meant he would miss the first hour of the party. But I wasn't deterred. At least he would be there for when it came to blowing out the candles on the cake and singing Happy Birthday to Jonah. By now I was almost as excited as a small child myself, imagining the delight on Gabriel's face when he walked into the middle of his youngest son's party. But by half past three, my excitement left me. Not one child had shown up. Poor Jonah, there he was, standing in the Banqueting Hall wearing a party hat with a long feather poking out from the top that Damson had made him wear, tearful bewilderment all over his face.

'Looks like no one's going to turn up,' Caspar said, helping himself to a cocktail sausage and flicking the stick on to the floor.

Jonah went over to the tables, stared hard at the plates of crisps, sandwiches and jugs of juice. There was such a look on his face. I couldn't fathom it for the life of me. And then we heard the sound of a car. It was Gabriel. The twins rushed to meet him, but Jonah came and stood next to me. If I had known better, I would have realised he was frightened. The next thing to happen was that Gabriel came marching in, knocking a bunch of balloons out of the way that was hanging above the door. 'What the hell's going on here?' he roared. 'Whose idea was this?' Jonah stepped behind me – dear God, he was actually hiding from his own father! I could feel his small body shaking against my legs.

It breaks my heart to say what happened next, but Gabriel continued to shout, oblivious to the harm he was doing to Jonah, and probably has been doing these last four years. In the end I took hold of Jonah who looked as if he was going to be sick with fright and carried him across the courtyard and inside the main part of the house. Gabriel followed, the twins at either side of him, and told me I had had no right to do what I had. 'But why?' I demanded – I was close to tears myself now. And then it all came tumbling out. Jonah's birthday was never celebrated because that was the day his mother – Gabriel's first wife – had died. 'So – so why didn't anybody tell me?' I stammered, my stomach sinking right down to my toes, my head feeling light with shock. 'It's not something I care to mention,' Gabriel snapped back at me. 'And what about Jonah?' I pressed – the poor lad was still burying himself in my skirt. 'Doesn't he deserve better than this?' I got no answer, and after Gabriel had stormed off, the twins trailing in his wake, I was left to explain to Jonah that there had been a terrible mix-up. Oh, my saints! What an understatement! Just as Jonah must have thought he was at last having his very own birthday party, it was snatched away from him. And he never said a word. Just stood there holding back the tears, his chin up, his eyes blinking rapidly. I bent down and hugged him. 'Don't worry, darling, you'll have your party if it's the last thing I do.'

Silently cursing Caspar and Damson's deviousness – my goodness, how that sly pair took me for a fool and manipulated me for their own pleasure! – I knew that from then on I would have my work cut out bringing this family together.

There was a gap of several weeks before Val took up her pen again. It seemed she had won herself, and Jonah, a small but important victory. From the little she had read of the diaries, Clara decided that based on the randomness of the entries, and their heated, exasperated content, Val only wrote when she needed to get something off her chest. It made Clara wonder if the poor woman had had any friends to whom she could turn. And if she hadn't, how awful it must have been for her to be so isolated at Mermaid House where there was so much to contend with.

Never did I think I would have to assume the role of mediating diplomat to the extent I have. An agreement has been reached. Jonah is to be allowed to celebrate his birthday, but on the condition that it's done a week after the official date. According to Gabriel, this will give the memory of his first wife the degree of respect it deserves.

I know very little about the woman I have replaced, other than what her portrait in the library tells me – that she was beautiful and serene, with an edge of fun-loving determination beneath her gentle surface. To my shame, I am now desperate to listen to the snatches of gossip that come my way during my shopping trips into Deaconsbridge, as well as the snippets of information the cleaning lady lets slip. Until now I had forced myself not to dig too deeply into Gabriel's previous marriage, accepting his silence quite readily and acknowledging that the past was best left to deal with itself. But regrettably my shield of common sense has dropped and I'm eager for the smallest of details.

Also to my shame, I'm beginning to wonder if I didn't agree to this marriage a little too hastily. Would it have been so very bad to remain alone and unmarried? Hindsight tells me I should have got to know Gabriel better before I accepted his proposal, but I suppose we both saw the convenient opportunities each could offer the other. But how will I ever manage Caspar and Damson? Of course I understand that they're both hurting from losing their mother at so young and tender an age but, really, at some point in their lives they are going to have to knuckle down and move on. But there I go again, being too hard on them. I must remember that when all is said and done, they are only children.

Clara's eyelids were drooping, so she turned out the light reluctantly, but instead of falling asleep, her thoughts turned to Jonah and lunch that day, when they had been sitting at the table in the kitchen. She had watched him talking to his father as he served him a portion of tuna and pasta salad, and had realised that what she had previously condemned as his irritating casual manner was an act. The relaxed body language was there to cover his uneasiness: the reserve between father and son could not have been greater. And reflecting on his inability to do more than the weekly shop for his father, Clara wondered if this was the only way he felt able to help a man he was scared of. Admittedly, twenty-four hours ago she would have trounced him as a wimp for not standing up to his father, but now she was seeing things differently. She saw not a grown man but a small boy hiding behind the skirts of a woman he scarcely knew while his father ranted at his audacity in wanting to celebrate the day he was born.

And what of Gabriel Liberty? What heartbreak had he buried beneath that gruff exterior? What bitterness did he still harbour over his children's refusal to carry on the family business?

The next morning Clara woke early, made herself a cup of tea – careful not to let the kettle whistle and disturb Ned – then slipped back into bed to carry on where she had left off last night. The diary had moved on to 1973.

Tuesday, 29 August.

Goodness! Gabriel left this morning on another of his big trips – it's Oslo this time, inspecting a pipeline he's supplied something or other for – and I feel like I'm living in a madhouse! Last week Caspar and Damson told the vicar I'd converted the household to Catholicism, which of course I haven't, I merely suggested that something a little more uplifting than the low church service at St Edmund's would suit me better, to which Gabriel had snorted and called me a papist candle-worshipper ... oh dear, I seem to be losing the thread here. What I was trying to say was that on top of that Caspar and Damson have now developed a morbid fascination with death and have been carrying out mock funerals with anything dead they've found on the hills and moors. Added to which, they now dress up like something out of a Gothic romance. I've no idea where or how they've got hold of the outfits, but they spend their days drifting about the house in black velvet cloaks. Damson spends her evenings winding her long hair up with bits of rag – a pillow case is missing from her bed I notice – so that in the morning she has what she thinks is an authentic hairstyle. Most suitable for 1973, I'm sure! She wears an old cotton nightdress under her cloak and seems to be modelling herself on Cathy in *Wuthering Heights*. Caspar, complete with riding boots and a floppy white shirt – drooping cuffs, limp collar – is a latterday Lord Byron. Oh, yes, he even has an absurd hat! Yesterday they spent all day out on the moors. When I asked them what they had been up to, they looked at me as though I had no right to ask such a question. With a vagueness that made me want to take a rolled-up newspaper to them, Caspar waved a book of poetry under my nose and said, 'If you must know, we were reading poetry.' While I applaud anyone for extending their knowledge, I can't help but think I'd prefer them to be more like other teenagers. Normal teenagers. What I wouldn't do to be worried about trivial matters like Damson defacing her bedroom walls with posters of pop stars and sighing from dawn till dusk with the ache of an unrequited crush on some boy or other, and Caspar pestering for a motorbike. I mean, that's what teenagers are about, aren't they? I wonder if it isn't just a little unhealthy the way Caspar and Damson cling to each other. I hardly dare bring myself to write this, but every time I look at them with their arms linked, their eyes fixed on each other, I come over with the most awful feeling. Surely I'm wrong? Oh, please let me be wrong. Please let their bizarre behaviour – this exclusive need to be apart from others, to scorn the rest of the world for its ignorance – be an adolescent phase. Nothing more worrying. Nothing untoward.

Saturday, 18 November.

Just as I thought life was beginning to settle down, the building bricks of normality, which I have been so carefully arranging, have come tumbling down on me yet again. For the fourth time in as many weeks, Jonah has run away from school. But at least now Gabriel will have to do something; he will have to get his stubborn head out of the sand and DO SOMETHING!

Knowing that Jonah has been so unhappy makes me feel negligent and useless. For some time now I had thought perhaps we had turned the corner with him. He was beginning to come out of his shell, talking more. Well, talking more to me – the moment his brother and sister showed their faces (or his father) he clammed up. Reports from school also confirmed that he was making good progress, claiming that he was 'participating' more actively. He had even joined in with a few clubs and was spending less time on his own. It had all sounded so encouraging, as if, at long last, he was through the worst of it. But then the phone call came from school to say that he had tried to run away, but we were not to worry. He had been found by a keen-eyed teacher who had come across him hitching a lift as she drove to school. 'All under control, Mrs Liberty,' the house-master said. 'Most of the little devils try it at some time or other.' His tone was oily and patronising, though he probably thought he was reassuring me.

The third time it happened I suggested to Gabriel that we ought to review the situation, which was a phrase Jonah's house-master had used on the phone when he called to say that Jonah had been found sleeping in a bus shelter: 'Perhaps, Mrs Liberty, it's time for us all to review the situation.' In response to this, Gabriel declared that Jonah was attention-seeking, that he just had to face facts – certain things in life were damned unpleasant but one simply had to square one's shoulders and accept one's lot. No further comment.

No further comment! Honestly, I could have hit him with a frying-pan!!

But instead of confronting Gabriel as I know I should have done, I phoned the house-master and demanded to know what they were doing to Jonah to cause him so much unhappiness. 'What kind of a school are you running, that you allow children in your care to sleep rough in bus shelters?'

'I understand your concern, Mrs Liberty, but let me assure you, we do the best we can. But if a pupil isn't prepared to co-operate, then frankly, it's an uphill struggle and there's not a lot we can do.'

Co-operate!

Uphill struggle!

Where was the love and support these children needed? And, yes, I noticed that not once in the conversation did the thoroughly irksome little man refer to Jonah as a child. He was nothing but a lump to be added to the sausage-meat that would be squeezed through the machine and pushed out the other side as a supposedly mature and responsible member of society.

'He's not happy,' I told Gabriel, when the fourth phone call came. This blatant truth was reinforced by the headmaster (we were obviously above the level of mere house-master now), when he summoned us to school to discuss the matter. Gabriel tried to wriggle out of the appointment, but I was having none of it. 'You will do this one small thing, Gabriel Liberty, or you will live to regret it.' It was the sternest I had ever been with him.

So there we were, in the bone-chilling inner sanctum of the headmaster's study, to discuss Jonah's fate. Gabriel was still of the opinion that Jonah needed to take the rough with the smooth, but I stuck my neck out (I knew I'd never forgive myself if I didn't) and said, 'I have seen and heard nothing here this afternoon to convince me that this is the right environment for a sensitive boy like Jonah.' Once Gabriel had got his furious throat-rattling under control, the headmaster said, 'I'm inclined to agree with you, Mrs Liberty. And let me tell you, rarely do I agree with parents on the issue of what they think is best for their offspring. Not enough objectivity in my opinion. But, in Jonah's case, I wholeheartedly agree that he would benefit from a different school.'

Yes, I thought, as we drove home with Jonah looking ashen-faced in the back of the car, you're washing your hands of a problem child who challenges the whole ethos of your horrible school.

Gabriel can't stomach the notion that he is the father of a problem child. 'There's no shame involved,' I told him, as he gripped the steering-wheel with steam practically coming out of his ears. His face was grim and he made no response, but I saw his eyes flicker to the rear-view mirror to look at his son in disgust.

Poor Jonah, eight years old and the weight and guilt of the world squarely on his young inadequate shoulders.

The sound of creaking from Ned's bed above the cab had Clara snapping the diary shut and sliding it under her mattress. She waited for him to make his way down the short ladder before slipping into bed with her to claim his all-important first hug of the day.

Just in time she remembered what day it was. When he appeared at her side, she said, 'Ooh, Ned, what's that on your nose?'

His hand flew to his face. 'What?' he said, alarmed.

'April Fool!' She laughed. Pulling him into bed with her, she planted a huge kiss on his cheek then blew the fruitiest of raspberries into his warm neck. As he squealed, giggled and wriggled, the strength of her love for him rose up within her and she held him tightly, vowing never to make him unhappy as Jonah Liberty had been. And God forbid that you should ever end up with a sadistic sibling like Caspar or Damson, she thought.

A better person might be prepared to make allowances for people like the Libertys because they had never truly come to terms with the death of Anastasia, who had been such a central figure in their lives, but Clara thought that nothing in the world would ever make her feel sympathetic towards Caspar and his freaky-sounding twin sister.

Still cuddling Ned, she despaired of Machiavellian men like Caspar. Vain men who revelled in their own perceived perfection. Not so much running on testosterone as functioning on super-strength narcissism. She had loathed him in the supermarket, and the second viewing on Saturday night had confirmed her initial reaction.

She hoped that he held the same opinion of her and that while she was still around he wouldn't be in any hurry to grace Mermaid House with his presence again.

33

Archie was relieved to be getting through the morning's workload faster than he'd thought they might. When they had turned up at the cottage in Castleton the woman who had done most of the gabbing in the shop on Saturday took one look at Samson and his battleship-sized body and said, 'You will be careful, won't you? We've only just had the decorators in.'

'We'll be like silk rubbing against velvet, love,' Archie had reassured her. The look she gave him said she didn't appreciate being called 'love'. No chance of a brew, then, he had thought, as he and Samson carried a three-seater sofa over the threshold, taking care not to scrape the twee Victorian-style wallpaper and mahogany-stained dado rail.

Now they had finished and went to settle up with Mrs Hoity-Toity. Like the good tradesmen they were, they humoured her by waiting in the hall while she wrote out the cheque in the kitchen, then beat a hasty retreat back to the shop, picking up sandwiches from the bakery in town for a late lunch.

Comrade Norm had been holding the fort, along with Bessie, who had been doing sterling work on some boxes of crockery. Dressed in an old nylon overall, which she used to wear when she was doing the housework, she seemed happy in the little kitchen with a stack of washed plates, cups and saucers on the draining-board. With slow, deliberate movements, she was drying the china carefully before arranging it on a set of cheap veneer shelves in the front of the shop. Archie pretended not to notice the broken sugar bowl in the bin, half hidden beneath an old newspaper.

Lunch dealt with, he took the van and drove home to check the post. These days, it never came before he left for work, but when he saw what was on the mat in the hall, he wished he hadn't bothered. It was another pompously worded letter from Stella's solicitor wanting to know which firm of solicitors he had instructed to take care of the divorce. It was ironic that today of all days – April Fool's Day – he should receive such a communication. It was the anniversary of the day on which he had proposed to Stella and it had been a long-standing joke between them that she had been a fool to accept.

'Running jump' and 'go stick it' were the words that were ready to leap from Archie's tongue after he had read through the letter. But he swallowed them, knowing that he should have taken on a solicitor by now. He hadn't consciously shied away from the task, it just hadn't figured too highly on his list of jobs to do. One way or another, he never had a minute to himself now. Still staring at the piece of stiff grey paper in his hand, he considered whether it was worth approaching Stella directly: that way they might save a lot of hassle and expense by cutting out the middlemen. But perhaps he was being naïve: in this greedy day and age, the winner took all. Except there could never be an outright winner in divorce. All there could ever be were two disappointed, wounded victims, who had to live with the sad knowledge that they had let each other down.

He sighed and went outside to the van. No time for such maudlin meanderings, he chided himself, not when a pretty young woman was waiting for him at Mermaid House.

It had rained for most of the weekend but today a weak sun was trying to find a crack in the thick blanket of grey cloud. It was still unseasonably cold and Archie was glad of the heater in the van.

Mermaid House was the most extraordinary place he had seen in a long while. 'Well, I'll be blowed,' he said, when he first caught sight of it on the brow of a rise in the landscape. 'What a godforsaken place to live.' He carried on along the bone-shaking drive in awed amazement, the empty van rattling noisily as it splashed through muddy puddles. He pulled in beside Clara Costello's camper-van, and wondered how many times his modest end-of-terrace could fit into this vast old place. He got out and crossed the shiny wet cobbles of the courtyard but came to a stop when he drew level with the skip. He couldn't resist having a quick shufti – after all, one man's rubbish was another's livelihood. His surreptitious foray was brought to an abrupt end by a door being flung open and a none-too-friendly voice saying, 'Who the hell are you and what d'you think you're doing snooping through my belongings?'

Clara had warned Archie what to expect. 'Herr Liberty runs a boot-camp up here on the quiet,' she had told him on the phone, 'but take no notice of his commandant persona. He's a real sweetie when you get to know him.'

Archie stepped forward. 'Archie Merryman's the name. Miss Costello phoned me on Saturday about some odds and ends you wanted to get rid of.'

He was given a disdainful eyeball-frisking, followed by, 'Uh, so you're that rag-and-bone man she got in touch with, are you? I suppose you'd better come in. But be sure to wipe your feet.'

Archie did as instructed, then followed him to a large kitchen. He was allowed no further, though, and after he had been ordered to stay where he was, the cussed old man went over to an open doorway. 'Miss Costello,' he bellowed, 'your disreputable rag-and-bone man's here.'

A door opened and footsteps sounded.

'Mr Liberty, there is no need to shout. And how many times do I have to tell you, Mr Merryman runs a second-hand shop and he's the least disreputable man I know.' Her voice and footsteps grew louder until finally she came into the kitchen. She was dressed in dirty jeans, a grubby T-shirt, and a cobweb decorated her dark hair; she looked younger than Archie had remembered her. The bright eyes and smile were the same, though. 'Hello, Archie,' she said. 'The Commandant treating you as rudely as I said he would?'

'Not so badly. How's that lad of yours? Did he find his mermaid?'

'Oh, yes. It was here just as he said it would be. How's your mother, everything okay with—'

'Great Scott! How much longer have I got to put up with this incessant tea-party chatter? I thought there was some business to be transacted.'

Clara winked at Archie and tutted. 'You leave the business to me, Mr Liberty. But talking of tea parties, bung the kettle on, would you? I'm sure Mr Merryman would appreciate a cup of your finest PG Tips.'

Mr Liberty's nostrils flared and Archie speculated as to who was the real commandant here. He fell in step beside Clara as she led him the length of the house, the rubber soles of her shoes squeaking on the polished wooden floor. 'I'm afraid none of it is of any great worth,' she said, 'but I've tried to organise everything into two piles: stuff you might be able to sell and stuff that's a little more dubious.'

She pushed open a heavy door and showed him into an enormous drawing room that had to be about thirty feet by twenty. Stella would have loved all this, Archie thought suddenly: the grandness of the room, the high ceiling, the massive stone fireplace and the beautiful mullion windows. For years she had been on at him to move. 'We need more space,' she would say, leafing through the local paper and admiring houses way out of their reach. He couldn't understand why she tormented herself looking at them. 'But why do we need more space?' he had argued back. 'There's only the two of us, and this is plenty.' In return, she had given him one of her standard you-don't-understand looks. Well, she'd been right on the button there. He didn't understand her need to stretch their finances just so that she could indulge in a bigger version of playing house. But this place might just about have satisfied her. It would have given her all the room she could have ever wanted. There was sufficient space here to swing a Tyrannosaurus Rex, never mind a cat.

The furniture wasn't up to much though, he reckoned. Most of it was shabby and not much better than the pieces he sold in his shop. The room was home to a hotchpotch of paraphernalia: an elephant's foot that had been turned into a stand for a tatty old Swiss-cheese plant, a bamboo table with a cracked glass top, a leather hand-tooled pouffe with a gaping hole and stuffing oozing out of it, a Chinese silk wall-hanging, a set of African drums, a lacquered chest, and a cabinet chock full of bits of jade, ivory and carved wooden animals. Souvenirs brought home by a man who had travelled, thought Archie, a little enviously.

He began to look at the room more critically, seeing the cracks in the high ceilings, and the gaping holes in the plasterwork above the moulded skirting-boards. Why, it was nothing but a demanding bugbear – and would cost a fortune to heat and keep clean. Other than Stella, who in their right mind would want to take this on?

He felt his mood turning bitter and he thought again of the solicitor's letter he had to deal with when he got home that evening. For the first time since she had left him he felt angry. Until now he had resigned himself to what had happened: he had failed his wife, so what else could he expect? But now he felt the unfairness of Stella's actions, the sting of the implied criticism and blame, the cruel, underhand way in which she had carried on her affair. Then there had been the continuous sniping at him for supposedly holding her back. 'I could have done so much better for myself if I hadn't married you,' she had told him once. She had apologised later for that, but once said, words can never be retracted. He had always thought of himself as a considerate man, who took people at face value, who didn't judge and condemn, because at the end of the day no one is perfect. And that was why he had never confronted Stella about her affair. He had wanted to give her space to resolve whatever she was going through. But now he saw how weak he had been, and that Stella had taken advantage of him and turned him into a fool.

An April Fool for sure.

Realising that Clara was waiting for him to speak, he shook himself out of his despondency. 'Sorry, what were you saying?'

'I was just saying that if any of these things are too awful to contemplate, you must . . . Are you okay, Archie? You look a bit bothered.'

He forced himself to smile. 'I'm tired, that's all. Now, then, let's see about this little lot, shall we? Looks to me like you've got the whole bag of tricks here.' And with a supreme act of will, he focused his attention on the boxes on the floor. Without needing to sift too deeply through them he could see that the assorted junk was mostly saleable – pots, pans, ladles, a china toast rack in the shape of a loaf of bread, a rusting hand whisk, various discoloured and outdated kitchen gadgets, a bedside lamp and an old money-box. It was the usual household stuff he saw every day. What he couldn't get rid of he'd pass on to a fellow dealer up in New Mills whose customers weren't so choosy as his. He reached into his trouser pocket for his roll of money. 'No problem,' he said, 'I'll take the lot, save you the trouble of messing about with any of it. Is that it?'

She pulled a face. 'I'm afraid not. I've got a load more upstairs. Oh, and I should have said, the electrical items all work. I've tested them myself.'

He put his money away for now. 'I'll say this for you, you're doing a thorough job here.'

'A little too thorough at times.' Mr Liberty was lumbering in with two mugs in his hands. 'Having her around is akin to taking laxatives,' he said to Archie, handing him a mug of tea. 'She sweeps you clean, whether you like it or not.'

'Thank you for sharing that delightful analogy with us, Mr Liberty.' Clara smiled. She took her mug. 'Was there anything else?'

Judging from the twist to his mouth, the old boy had taken his dismissal with pleasure. Strange man, thought Archie. He sipped his tea. 'What on earth possessed you to take on this colossal task?' he asked Clara.

She laughed. 'A question I've been asking myself several times a day since I started.'

'And the answer?' he pressed.

'I'd like to say that it's down to pure altruism, but my friends would claim it's due to my perverse desire to take charge and organise everything around me.'

'Now that's just what I could do with.'

'Oh?'

Something in her tone made him want to unburden himself. The thought shocked him: until that moment he had never seen himself as a man who was burdened. He felt crushed. He looked at her enquiring expression and wondered if she would mind being used as a sounding board. Because that was what he needed. Someone objective in whom he could confide. He hadn't turned to his friends for advice. Male pride, he supposed. That, and he didn't want the whole of Deaconsbridge knowing his business. A small town was the devil for gossip. He also hated the idea of people feeling sorry for him, viewing him differently. He'd always been good old Archie, cheerful, dependable. He knew it was irrational, but he felt as if he would let everyone down by being anything else.

Go on, he urged himself, confide in her. She's an outsider. Who would she tell? Say something. Anything. Because if you stand there any longer looking like a prize idiot, she'll think the lights have gone out and you're a meter short of a shilling.

Staring at him over the top of her mug of tea, she said, 'It's none of my business, but is it something to do with your mother?'

Her gentle probing did away with the remnants of his resolve, and he acknowledged the dragging pain that had been with him since Stella had left. 'Yes and no,' he volunteered. 'Bessie is certainly one of my concerns, but . . . the thing is, my wife left me recently and I haven't a clue how to deal with it. I thought I was handling it, but now I'm not so sure.'

'How recently?'

'Just—' He swallowed and hung on grimly to his self-control. 'Just over a week ago.'

'Oh, Archie, I'm so sorry.' She reached out and touched his arm lightly. 'Come and sit down.' She led him across the room, avoiding the oozing pouffe and elephant's foot, to two high-backed armchairs in the bay of a window. 'It must be awful for you. Did you have any idea that this was going to happen?'

'I'd be lying if I said it came as a surprise. Things have been difficult for a while, and what with Bessie's stroke and her moving in with us, well . . . let's just say I haven't helped matters.'

'But it must have been a terrible blow.'

He ran a finger over the fraying fabric on the arm of his chair. 'I think it's only now that it's finally hitting home. I'm ashamed to say I feel angry at what she's done.'

'And what's wrong with that? Why shouldn't you?'

'Because . . .' He gave the chair a light thump: a cloud of dust rose into the air. 'Because I'm not like that. I never get angry.'

'*Never?* What an exceptional man you must be if that's true.'

'Not exceptional. Not by a long chalk.' In his mind's eye he saw his father losing his temper and lashing out at Bessie. Until Archie had been big enough to step in and end the nightmare for her.

'What does your solicitor advise?'

'I haven't got that far.' He told her about the letter that had arrived that morning. 'You're probably thinking I've been stupidly slow and cowardly, aren't you?'

'Not at all. But you have to accept that the problem isn't going to go away on its own. Have you spoken to your wife since she left?'

'No.'

'Do you know where she is?'

'She's in Macclesfield with the man who—' He broke off. An agonising moment passed before he managed to pull himself together. 'Sorry, it's just hearing the words out loud makes it seem all the more real. I suppose that's what I've been doing this last week or so, keeping it to myself so that I don't have to face up to what I'm going to have to do.'

'And do you know what you *want* to do? What choices you need to make?'

He smiled ruefully. 'Oh, aye, I'm double-parked on what's to be done. I'll agree to the divorce, sell the house and move into something smaller and cheaper. I'll keep Second Best going and somehow look after Mum.'

'That takes care of today. What about tomorrow?'

In spite of his flagging spirits, he laughed, and felt better for it. 'That's just the kind of talk I need.' He drained his mug. 'Now, then, let's get back to work or your man Liberty will be after me.' They both rose to their feet. 'Thanks,' he said, 'thanks a million.'

'What for? I haven't helped you resolve anything. More's the pity.'

'No, sweetheart, but you've listened, and maybe that was all I needed.'

34

Before he had even opened his eyes Gabriel knew the day would not be a good one. It was Friday morning, and it was Ned and Miss Costello's final day at Mermaid House. He didn't know how it had happened, but somehow during the last week he had got so used to having them around he was going to miss them when they were gone.

A skew-eyed glance at the alarm clock on the bedside table told him it was a quarter past seven. He pushed back the bedclothes and, with a creak of springs, thumped his feet down on to the floor. He wriggled his buckled old toes, then launched himself stiffly upright. He went over to the window and gave a cautious tug at the curtains. They glided smoothly and soundlessly along the track and he imagined Miss Costello scolding him for not putting more faith in her ability to operate a drill and knowing which rawlplugs to use. She had even filled in the gaping holes left by the chunks of plaster that had fallen out. He stood at the window, breathing in the fresh outdoor smell of the curtains, which had been washed yesterday and left to dry in the blustery wind and sunshine. She had ironed them while they were still slightly damp and a comforting steamy warmth had filled the kitchen. While she had been doing that he had helped Ned with the latest page of his scrapbook – a drawing of a box on wheels (supposedly a camper-van) and three sloping lines of wonky writing. 'How do you spell diesel?' the boy had asked.

'D E I S E L,' Gabriel had answered.

'D *I E*,' Miss Costello had corrected him, from behind a cloud of steam.

'Should have been a school-teacher, your mother.' He winked at Ned.

'Jonah's a teacher, isn't he? Can you write "diesel" for me, please?' A scrap of paper was pushed across the table. 'He must be very clever to be a teacher. You have to know *everything*.'

'That's a matter for dispute.' He passed the piece of paper back. 'Any old fool can stand up in front of a class and tell them what to do. Even I could do it.'

There was a snigger from the direction of the ironing-board. 'Spelling lessons would be interesting.'

'I'll have you know that was a mere slip of the tongue.'

'How do you spell "engine"?'

'Here, let me write it down for you before your mother gets out her stick of chalk. Or, worse, her cane to beat me.'

'Six of the best and a detention would do you the world of good, Mr Liberty.'

'You'd have to catch me first.'

'A ten-minute head start suit you?'

'She's a cruel, heartless woman, your mother.'

The boy looked up from his wobbly writing. 'My mummy isn't cruel. She's nice. And she makes *you* laugh.'

'Pah! Who told you that? It's a shameless lie and one that I shall defend till the cows are blue in the face.'

'Ahem, don't you mean till the cows come home? Fine English teacher you'd be with your metaphors running away with themselves.'

'Yes, but which is more likely to happen? The cows wandering home, or their faces turning blue? I think I have you there, Miss Costello, the point is mine.'

Still standing at his bedroom window, Gabriel sighed heavily. Life was going to be dull without them around.

He washed, shaved and dressed in his pristine bathroom, put his dirty clothes tidily in the laundry basket, as instructed, and went downstairs. The kitchen was beautifully warm – another of Miss Costello's miracles. She had had the Aga serviced by a man who knew what he was talking about: turned out all that had been wrong with it was a faulty thermostat. The treacherous gas heater that had burnt his arm had been banished to the gun room. And talking of treachery, that interfering Dr Singh had been conspicuous by his absence. So much for turning up here on Monday as had been threatened. Not that Gabriel was complaining: as far as he was concerned, the less he saw of the annoying quack the better.

He put the kettle on and went to sit in one of the Windsor chairs placed in front of the Aga. This had been another of Miss Costello's reforms. By moving the table, she had created a space beside the Aga where he could comfortably warm his feet of a morning. The chairs had been brought down from one of the rooms upstairs and she had awarded him and Ned the job of polishing them while she tackled the unenviable task of cleaning the main bathroom.

On day one of her assignment to sort out Mermaid House, Miss Costello had taken him at his word and put together a shopping list of things she considered would make his life easier. Then, the day before yesterday, she had dragged him off to the shops with the intention of making him buy these so-called labour-saving products. 'You have remembered to bring your wallet, haven't you?' she said, as they drove to the other side of Deaconsbridge in her camper-van, to the retail development he had never before visited. The vast range of electrical appliances on sale in the store was bewildering. 'How long will this take?' he asked warily, looking at the shelves of brightly coloured kettles, irons and toasters, which all seemed to resemble toys.

He needn't have worried. She knew exactly what she was looking for and, much to his admiration, badgered the spotty young assistant into giving them a ten per cent discount, plus free delivery for that same evening.

He had watched in further admiration late that night after she had put Ned to bed and had got down on her hands and knees and plumbed in the dishwasher. 'Are you deliberately trying to make me feel completely useless?' he had said, passing her a spanner and wishing he was forty years younger.

'Not at all. You do too good a job of it yourself. Now, let's see if this baby's going to perform. I'll put it on a quick rinse cycle.' She wriggled out from under the work surface, stood up, and rocked the slimline dishwasher into place. She shut the door, turned the dial with a clickety-click and pressed the start button. Water rushed through the pipes and the machine whooshed and whirred. He looked at her doubtfully. 'Should it make that noise?'

'Absolutely. And trust me, it'll transform your life. You'll wonder how you ever managed without it. Shall we sort out the microwave next?'

'What do you do for an encore? Walk on water?'

'Give it time, Mr Liberty. Give it time.'

Eating his breakfast of toast and marmalade and resting the plate on his stomach as he sat by the Aga, Gabriel listened to the news on the radio – or, rather, listened to the news on his new all-in-one, all-singing-and-dancing radio-CD-cassette player. It was another of Miss Costello's fine-tunings. 'Treat yourself, Mr Liberty,' she had said. 'Or do I have to twist your arm up round your shoulder-blades?' The reception and sound quality were certainly better than he was used to from his old radio, but the news was still as tedious. And as from tomorrow, the highlight of his day would be answering back some jumped-up nobody who fancied himself a political smart-arse.

Clara and Ned were having their own breakfast, and as her son dipped his spoon in and out of his bowl of Coco-Pops while he looked at his scrapbook spread across the narrow table, Clara had the feeling that he wasn't looking forward to moving on. He hadn't said anything, but the way he was lingering over each page she knew that leaving Mermaid House was going to be a wrench for him.

But the same was true for her. What was the old song about having become accustomed to somebody or other's face? It was from a musical. Yes, *My Fair Lady*, one of her mother's favourite shows. And while she hadn't fallen in love with the cranky owner of Mermaid House, she had enjoyed seeing him mellow. She'd also enjoyed keeping up the game of formality between them. Despite the shift in their relationship that had taken place, she always made a point of calling him Mr Liberty to his face – and he still referred to her as Miss Costello – but in her mind he had become Gabriel; not exactly archangel material, but a man with a softer side to him than he was used to exposing.

It had been a week of hard slog, though: her aching back and sore hands were proof of that. But she would leave knowing that she had spent a week doing something positive and worthwhile. She wasn't so sure of how long the benefits of her work would last. If left to his own devices Gabriel would probably let things slide back to how they had been. But she couldn't do anything about that. Perhaps she could speak to Jonah before she left and impress upon him that his father needed a cleaner, or maybe a housekeeper.

But he knew that already. What would be the point?

In the back of her mind she heard Louise and the gang telling her to leave well alone: 'Stop trying to control what isn't your concern.'

Sound advice.

Mercifully Caspar had stayed away from Mermaid House, and she hadn't seen Jonah since Sunday. Apparently he had been away on a school history trip to northern France and Belgium. Having read some of Val's diaries she could only marvel that any of the Liberty children had survived their childhood. She had alternated between being furious with Gabriel for ignoring the needs of his family and feeling desperately sorry for him. Clearly the death of his first wife had left him a broken man with no one to turn to. At various times in the week she had been tempted to ask him more about his family and the past, but the moment had never seemed right. Either Ned was around, or he and Gabriel were off on one of their adventures.

During the last few days the weather had picked up again, and while she had been busy clearing out cupboards, polishing neglected furniture, arranging with Archie to pick up yet more junk, supervising the chimney sweep and the collection of the skip, Gabriel had taken Ned down to the river to play. Yesterday they had returned from one of their expeditions smelling of fresh air, their faces red from the wind, announcing that they were starving. 'Lucky I picked up some scones and crumpets from the baker this morning,' she had said, when they were kicking off their mud-caked boots and about to leave them in an untidy heap. One look from her and they were lining them up beneath their neatly hanging jackets.

But whatever Gabriel and his family had suffered in the past, it was really none of Clara's business and she had no right to pry. Just as he had had no right to interrogate Ned about his father. She winced. Where did that leave her with Val's diaries? Guiltily, she made a mental note to return them before she and Ned left.

Looking at Ned as he scraped up the last of his cereal, Clara knew that her priority that day was to keep him cheerful. She didn't want him to be upset about leaving and the only trick she had up her sleeve to soften the blow for him was that once she had finished her work here today, they would be free to visit the Mermaid Cavern.

*

At Gabriel's insistence they were to have lunch in town at the Mermaid café. 'It's one o'clock, and I declare you officially out of contract now,' he said, when she appeared in the kitchen, expecting a sandwich – or a 'shambly', as Ned called them. Presenting her with an envelope, he added, 'It's your wages. You'll find I've been more than generous.'

Without opening it, she slipped it into her pocket. 'Fair enough, but I insist on driving. I'm not going anywhere in that death-trap of a Land Rover. At least two of the tyres are bald and I bet it hasn't been anywhere near a garage for years.'

He put up a show of resistance that got him nowhere, and after she had changed out of her filthy work clothes, they set off.

'Can I have chips, please, Mummy?' Ned called from his rear seat as they turned into the market square. 'And ketchup?'

'It's market day,' Gabriel said. 'You might have trouble parking.'

'Beans would be nice.'

'Of course, if you'd let me drive my death-trap, we'd be able to slip into any old space.'

'Mm . . . and lots of vinegar, please. I like vinegar. I like it when my lips go white because I've had too much.'

'Damn! You'll have to go round again.'

'Can we have a pudding as well?'

'There! There's a space. Quick!'

'For goodness' sake, Mr Liberty, calm down! You'll give yourself a heart-attack at this rate.'

'No chance. I'm saving that pleasure for when I've over-feasted on a coronary lunch-time special.'

They were met by Shirley and a raised eyebrow when she saw who they had with them. 'We missed you last Friday, Mr Liberty,' she said, handing them each a copy of the menu. 'Thought perhaps you'd taken your business elsewhere?'

'You mean you hoped I had.'

She smiled at Clara. 'Shall I get you some drinks while you choose?'

Gabriel took off his cap and thwacked the table with it. 'You make it sound as if you're offering us something decent, like a glass of single malt whisky.'

'Just give my sour friend a pint of your finest malt vinegar and ignore him,' said Clara.

'Don't worry, I always do. So what'll it be? How about a nice strawberry milkshake? We've just had a new machine installed and I'm itching to give it a whirl.' This last remark was directed at Ned, who nodded enthusiastically.

It was Ned who brought up the subject of their leaving. Expertly dipping the end of a chip into the pool of ketchup on his plate, he said, 'Will you miss us when we've gone, Mr Liberty? Will you be sad when you're all alone again?'

Clara willed the old devil to say something nice. But not too nice.

'That depends, doesn't it?' he said evasively, his gaze flickering over Clara.

'Why?' asked Ned.

'If I thought I was never going to hear from you again, that *might* make me sad.'

They both looked at Clara. Expectation was etched over their faces. 'You could send Mr Liberty the occasional postcard, Ned,' she said, thinking fast, while hiding her surprise that Gabriel had said something so refreshingly agreeable and tactful. 'That way he'll know what we're up to.'

Another chip went into the tomato sauce while Ned thought about this. 'But how will we know what Mr Liberty is doing?'

'You won't, lad. No one ever knows what I'm up to. And that's the way I intend to keep it.'

Ned's frown showed that this wasn't the answer he wanted. 'Couldn't we stay longer, Mummy? You could clean a bit more of Mr Liberty's house for him.'

Clara smiled. 'Mr Liberty's house is like the Forth Bridge. I could go on cleaning it for ever and ever.'

Ned's face brightened at the possibility. He turned to Gabriel, a chip dangling from his fork. 'Would you like Mummy to clean your house for ever and ever?'

'I'd like nothing better, but I suspect your mother wouldn't. Now, are you going to eat the rest of those chips or watch them grow?'

Over pudding – the obligatory Bakewell tart and custard – Gabriel said, 'Do you really have to rush off, Miss Costello? We came to an arrangement a week ago, couldn't we do something similar again?'

'And what about the holiday Ned and I are supposed to be enjoying? I told you, I'm making this trip to spend more time with my son, not spend my every waking hour cleaning for you. Or anyone else for that matter.'

'But wouldn't you agree that your son has benefited from his time at Mermaid House?'

She looked at him sternly, kept her voice low. 'Don't play dirty, Mr Liberty, it doesn't become you.'

'In my experience, there's no other way to play.'

Her patience was waning. 'Look, Ned and I have been here for over a week and we still haven't had so much as a glimpse of what we came to see. We want to see the sights. We want to be tourists. We want to laze around eating overpriced locally made fudge, and turn up our noses at tacky souvenirs and buy them all the same. We want to be day-trippers trudging round in the rain. We want to—'

'Then stay on at Mermaid House for a few more days as my guests, and you can do all the day-tripping you want to do in this area.'

She hesitated, and in that instant knew that she had lost the upper hand in the argument. Gabriel leaned in towards her. 'Miss Costello, hear me out.

I would very much like you to stay so that I can repay a little of your kindness.'

'But you've done that already. You've paid me.'

'It's not always about money.'

She smiled. 'Is this the same man who once said everything had a price, that everything was for sale?'

He shifted in his seat. 'Well, maybe I've . . .' His words petered out.

'Maybe you've what?'

He drew his eyebrows together, screwed up his paper napkin, tossed it into his empty pudding bowl. 'Changed,' he mumbled.

It was difficult for her not to laugh at his discomfort. The poor man had come a long way in just one week. 'Well,' she said, 'just so that we're clear on a few points. If, and I say *if*, we were to stay, there would be no more scrubbing and polishing?'

'Agreed.'

'No more—'

'I said *as my guests*. Don't you ever listen?'

'Only if I like the sound of what's being suggested.'

'And do you?'

'In parts. But before I commit myself, I have to mull it over with the boss.' She turned to her son. 'Ned, what do you think we should do?'

His eager face was answer enough.

35

At bedtime that night, Clara knew it was important to put the brakes on Ned's excitement by stressing that they would only be extending their stay by a few days. 'We'll be moving on first thing on Monday morning, Ned,' she told him. 'There's so much more to see and do. Who knows what's round the corner for us?' He nudged the book she was supposed to be reading to him. He hasn't been listening, she thought, when she eventually turned out his light and gave him one last kiss. He thinks two more days will turn into three, then four, then goodness knows how many.

She sat at the narrow table with a glass of wine, a plate of crackers and a gooey wedge of Camembert, enjoying the peace and quiet of her own company, and wondered why she was so reluctant to hang around Mermaid House for much longer. It would still be a holiday for them, so what was the problem?

Because it hadn't been part of her original plan.

She cut into the soft cheese, picked the sticky lump off the knife, slipped it into her mouth, and let its creamy smoothness melt on her tongue. Helping herself to another piece, she thought of her original plan, designed to make her and Ned feel like intrepid explorers. She had wanted to show Ned what an exciting world he lived in, so that he would grow up knowing that there were endless possibilities out there for him. Getting caught up in the lives of a handful of folk – however interesting – had never been a part of it.

Once again, she heard Ron and Eileen extolling the virtues of their easy-come, easy-go lifestyle. 'Oh, yes, we always start out with a plan,' Ron had said, 'we like to tease ourselves with a map of intent, but half the fun in life is changing your mind and abandoning the rule book. Spontaneity is the name of the game.'

That's all very well, thought Clara, getting up and reaching for her writing things from the overhead locker, but sometimes spontaneity had a habit of getting above itself. If it wasn't too much of a paradox, spontaneity needed careful managing.

Putting these thoughts aside, she settled down to write a letter to her parents in Australia, with a separate page enclosed for her brother, Michael, and then she turned to the postcard she had bought in Deaconsbridge that afternoon. It showed a colourful selection of mermaid shop signs.

Dear Louise
On the verge of leaving Deaconsbridge, having completed our
missionary work – the natives are almost civilised now! We're finally
getting to see the local sights this weekend (the mermaids are a clue!)
and then we'll be moving on to who knows where. Further north
probably. I'll give you a ring some time next week just to check all is
well.
Lots of love,
Clara and Ned

Now that she had put down their departure date in writing, it made their leaving on Monday seem more real, which pleased Clara. And, as Louise would be the first to say, seldom did Clara Costello change her mind or go back on her word. U-turns, according to the Clara Costello School of Management, were for back-pedalling wimps.

She tidied away the remains of the cheese and crackers, put her writing things away in their allocated place, and made up her bed. As she pulled her duvet out of the cupboard beneath the seat, and caught sight of her filthy jeans hanging on the hook of the shower door, she remembered that Gabriel had offered her the use of his washing-machine before they left. She also remembered the envelope he had given her, and which she had stuffed into her back pocket. Better remove it now before she forgot about it and threw it into the washing-machine tomorrow morning. Ripping open the envelope she extracted a slip of paper on which was written, 'Don't even think about turning this down!' Paper-clipped to it was a cheque. When she saw the amount – he had doubled the agreed sum – she shook her head, partly with disbelief, but also with affection. 'Silly old fool,' she murmured. A rush of fondness for him brought tears to her eyes. She was deeply touched. 'Silly, silly, *silly* man. I was right all along, more money than sense.'

The next morning Ned woke first. He got dressed without disturbing Clara, and she only realised he was up and about when he slipped under her duvet for a hug.

'Shall we ask Mr Liberty to come with us today?' he asked, when he surfaced from her embrace.

'Do you think he'd want to? He's probably seen the Mermaid Cavern hundreds of times.'

'But not with us.'

'True.'

He smiled and slid out of the bed. 'Shall I go and ask him?'

'How about some breakfast first?' But he was already standing by the door, a hand working at the lock. 'Oh, go on, then.' She gave in. 'But don't be surprised if he shouts at you for disturbing him.'

Yawning, she dragged herself reluctantly out of bed, wiped the condensation from the window above the table and watched Ned scamper across the courtyard. The back door opened before he reached it and she saw Gabriel staring down at his early-morning caller. She strongly approved of Ned's suggestion and she hoped Gabriel would accept the invitation with good grace: it would be her way of thanking him for his more than generous cheque.

Armed with a map and several guide books, Gabriel in the front with Clara, and Ned in the back with Mermy, they embarked on a day's worth of sightseeing.

But first they had to make a stop in town.

'Just let me pop into the bank,' Clara said, switching off the engine and grabbing her bag. 'I need some cash.' She also wanted to offload Gabriel's cheque. Inside the bank, and because it was only open for the morning on a Saturday, she joined a long queue that snaked its way round the small building. Minutes later someone else joined the queue behind her. It was Archie.

'Hello,' she said. 'Didn't think you bothered with banks. I thought you were strictly a cash-only man.'

'Ah well, my mattress gets uncomfortable if I put too much underneath it. It plays havoc with my back. Has the Commandant let you out for an hour or two?'

'I've finished work now. Ned and I are officially on holiday again. We're taking Mr Liberty to see the Mermaid Cavern.'

'Does that mean you'll be leaving us soon?'

'Monday morning.'

He looked disappointed. 'That's a shame. The place won't be the same without you.'

'I expect you'll manage pretty well.'

Someone at the front of the queue moved away and they inched forward.

'By the way,' he said, 'I wanted to thank you for passing all that work in my direction. I really appreciate it. Oh, and you might like to know, I took your advice. I've got myself organised with a solicitor. The ball is definitely rolling, as they say.'

Another person at the head of the queue moved off, and they shuffled forward again.

'I hope it works out for you, Archie. I'm sure it will. Eventually.'

He shrugged. 'You're probably right. Anyway, cheer me up by promising you'll come and say goodbye before you and Ned disappear. Leave town without doing that, and the sheriff and I will have to send a posse after you.'

'It's a promise.'

*

The Mermaid Cavern was only a few miles from the centre of Deacons-bridge. The road climbed out of the town, and in no time the landscape became markedly different: it was softer, greener, more curvaceous. This was limestone country, where the White Peak reigned and the harsher, darker terrain of the High Peak receded into the northern distance.

According to the guidebooks, the Mermaid Cavern was often overlooked in favour of the bigger and more commercialised show caves in nearby Castleton. None the less, they agreed that it was of geological and historical interest and worth a visit.

But the million-dollar question was: did the mermaid rock formation really look like a mermaid?

Parking Winnie between another camper-van, which had a Dutch numberplate, and a people-carrier containing two panting, slobbering Labradors, Clara asked Gabriel if he knew the answer.

'It's so long since I saw it, I can't remember,' he said.

'How long ago? Time for her to have grown taller?'

'It was 1963, if you must know.'

'Oh, well before I was born, then.' She leaned through to Ned. 'Okay, Buster, you can unbuckle yourself now. We're all set.'

'I came here with Anastasia. We went for a picnic afterwards, but it rained. It came down so hard, so suddenly, we had to shelter under a tree. She joked we would get struck by lightning and that we would both die and go to heaven. I told her I was already in heaven.'

Moved by the unexpected tenderness in his voice, and the vivid picture his words had just painted, Clara turned slowly to look at him. 'And you've never been back?'

He gave her an odd look. 'What? To heaven?'

'No.' She smiled. 'Here.'

'Wouldn't have been the same.'

Signposts directed them to a path that ran alongside a row of pretty cottages where yellow daffodils, purple crocuses, and tiny blue scillas brightened small neat gardens. Twists of smoke plumed from chimneys and the crisp morning air was filled with the old-fashioned smell of burning coal.

The entrance to the cave was reached by a series of steps carved into the rock. In places they were slippery from the rain that had fallen overnight. Clara held Ned's hand and was tempted to take Gabriel's, too, but thought better of it: he would have his pride, after all. And pride seemed to have influenced his appearance that day. If she wasn't mistaken, he had spruced himself up, even wearing a tie beneath his V-necked pullover, which didn't have any holes in it.

They paid for their entrance tickets at the wooden booth and were shepherded through to a dimly lit tunnel where they joined a group about to embark on the tour of what had once been an old lead mine.

Fifteen minutes later Clara was glad she had bundled Ned up in his warmest clothes. It was bone-numbingly cold with no escape from the icy damp that had already seeped through the thick soles of her shoes to gnaw at her toes. The tips of her ears and nose were tingling too, and the occasional splash of water from the low roof on her exposed skin made her shiver. As she listened to the guide and watched the direction of his torch, which he used to indicate points of interest – the flowstones, the stalactites and stalagmites – she thought of the harsh conditions in which those early miners had worked.

The guide led them further into the series of caves, warning them to be careful and to hold on to the rail as they took the steep descent down towards the pool.

'Are we going to see the mermaid now?' whispered Ned, squeezing her hand.

'Any minute.'

When they reached the bottom, a boat was waiting for them. They were helped into it and when all was secure, they moved smoothly through the water. It didn't seem very impressive at first: the ceiling of the cave was still quite low, and though a few lights were fixed into the rock-face there wasn't much to see.

But then they turned a corner and there was an *aah!* from everyone in the boat. Even Gabriel, that stalwart of indifference, looked impressed. The vaulted roof of the cave soared above their heads, and shimmering lights gave it a serene, cathedral-like quality. People reached for their cameras, including Clara. After they had taken their pictures, the guide took them on further.

They came to a large rock that jutted out into the pool, steered round it and there before them, raised out of the water and subtly illuminated with softly glowing lamps, was the mermaid. To Clara's surprise and delight, no leap of imagination or suspension of belief was needed to make out what she was. There was her tail, the forked end skimming the surface of the pool, and her curvy body reclined gracefully against another rock.

For the benefit of those who enjoyed a good yarn, the guide told them how she came to be here. The story went that she had been a real live mermaid who had got lost at sea and had somehow found her way to the cavern – that she was so far inland was glossed over. She had liked it so much that she had made it her home, and after wishing that she could stay here for ever, she had been turned to stone to make wishes come true for others. As tales went, it was far-fetched and fanciful, but it satisfied Ned, and as Clara drew him closer to her, she hoped he would never lose the sense of wonder she could see in his eyes. Everything was such a pleasure for him. New, exciting, full of mystery. Heaven forbid that life should ever become a chore for him.

Just as she was thinking this, the guide pointed the beam of light from his torch at the small raised pool behind the mermaid. 'If you want her to grant you a wish,' he said, 'you have to throw a coin into her pool.'

Judging from the number of coins already tossed into the crystal-clear water, there had been plenty of people here before them who had gone along with the lark. Clara reached for her bag. 'Go on, Ned,' she whispered, 'make a wish.'

He took the ten-pence piece from her. 'But what about you, Mummy? Don't you want a go? And, Mr Liberty, you have to make a wish too.'

Gabriel pulled a face. 'I've never heard anything so absurd in all my life. A lot of stuff and nonsense.' But then he smiled – reminding Clara of the big bad wolf in *Little Red Riding Hood* – and produced a pound coin from his pocket. 'Shall we make it a good one, Ned, eh? Come on, Miss Costello, get your money out. After your visit to the bank this morning I know you can afford it.'

They waited for the rest of the group to throw their pennies and make their wishes, and then, at last, it was their turn. 'Don't say it out loud,' Ned informed Clara, 'it won't come true if you do.' Four years old and how well versed he was in these matters. 'And you mustn't tell anyone what you wished for,' he said afterwards, as the guide steered the boat away and they waved goodbye to the mermaid. 'Telling people what you wished for brings you bad luck, and we don't want that, do we, Mummy?'

'No, Ned. We certainly don't.'

Clara's wish had been the same as it always was whenever irrational reliance on omens and charms was called for: she wanted Ned to be happy. But on this occasion she had tagged on an extra request: that the months ahead would be as enjoyable as the last two weeks had been.

She glanced at Gabriel's face in the subdued light. There was no knowing what he had wished for.

36

On Monday morning, as Clara unhooked Winnie from Mermaid House's electrical supply, Ned was anything but happy. He wanted to stay longer. The weekend had passed all too quickly, with most of it spent sightseeing. They had visited Peveril Castle, the plague village at Eyam, Buxton, and even another cave – the Blue John Cavern in Castleton. But now they were preparing to leave.

'There's still more to see,' Ned said, showing her the evidence to support his argument. He was pointing to a picture in one of their guide books that showed a place in Matlock Bath where they had cable-cars to get you up and down the wooded hillside. 'Couldn't we go there today? Oh, please.'

She stopped what she was doing, sat down, and pulled him on to her lap, knowing that if she wasn't careful, she'd have a tearful rebellion on her hands. She flicked through the pages of the book to the next section. 'And look,' she said, 'even more to see.'

He stared at the picture of a traditional steamer crossing Windermere, then at the one showing the Beatrix Potter museum. Clara hoped that the sight of Peter Rabbit in his blue jacket nibbling a carrot would tempt Ned to get back on the road.

Originally the plan had been to use the Peak District as a stepping stone for Yorkshire, before carrying on towards Berwick-upon-Tweed and Scotland, where they would then work their way round the coast, to the top, then drop down the west coast and keep on going till they hit Devon and Cornwall for the summer. But in bed last night Clara had decided to change the route. The Lake District, which was full of all things cute and wonderful, would give her a better chance of luring Ned away from Deaconsbridge.

She wasn't ready for what Ned said next.

'Couldn't we take Mr Liberty with us to see Peter Rabbit? He'd like that, wouldn't he?'

She put an arm round him. 'I'm not sure he's a Beatrix Potter kind of man, Ned. Besides, he has his friends and family here to think of.'

Ned shrugged away her arm and gazed at her intently. 'He doesn't have any friends. He told me. He said most of them are dead.'

'I'm sure that was just another of his exaggerations. He's not that old.'

'He is! He's going to be *eighty* on his next birthday.'

'I'm sorry, Ned, but the answer's still no. Winnie is only big enough for the two of us. Imagine having a great big man like Mr Liberty sharing it with us.' It was such an awesome prospect Clara felt her face twitch with the threat of laughter. Keeping her expression under control, she added, 'And I bet he snores as loud as a giant.'

For the first time since getting out of bed that morning, Ned smiled. 'He'd be just like the giant in *Jack and the Beanstalk*. When he snored it was so loud all the buttons fell off Jack's coat.'

Clara giggled. That colourful little detail had been her father's. He was always contributing his own lines to the stories he read to Ned. 'Pepping it up,' was what he called it. She hugged Ned close. 'Well, we wouldn't want *our* buttons falling off whenever Mr Liberty had a nap. It would be too embarrassing for words.'

With the situation more or less under control, and Ned rounding up his cuddly toy collection, Clara carried on tidying the van. She was almost through with checking for potential rattles in the lockers and cupboards when there was a loud thump at the door. 'Time you were going, isn't it?'

It was Gabriel.

'Always a mistake to outstay your welcome,' he growled, filling the doorway and blocking out the light. 'Remember that, Ned. When it's time to go, you go. No hanging around.'

Clara felt a wave of gratitude towards him for being his usual blunt self, for not making things worse for Ned by giving him a show of treacly affection. 'And a good morning to you, Mr Liberty.'

He stepped inside, looked at his watch. 'It's afternoon, as near as damn it.'

'Mr Liberty, guess where we're going?' Ned chimed in. 'We're going to see Peter Rabbit and some big lakes and mountains. Do you want to see?' He held up the guide book that he and Clara had been reading earlier. 'Mummy says we'll go on a really old boat that has steam coming out of it. And there's a museum where we can see pencils being made. And when we've done—'

'Sounds much too exhausting to me,' Gabriel interrupted, scarcely glancing at what Ned was showing him.

'I think we're about done now,' Clara said, shutting the last cupboard with a clunk. She took the book from Ned and stowed it in the rack with the rest of the maps and guides. 'If you'd like to say goodbye to Mr Liberty you can climb into your seat and strap yourself in.'

But all at once Ned didn't seem able to move from where he was standing. He put his hands behind his back and screwed a shoe into the floor. His eyes lowered to the level of Gabriel's knees, but not before Clara saw them fill. Then a little voice mumbled, 'Goodbye,' and his lower lip wobbled and she knew they were in real trouble. She moved towards him, to put a comforting hand on his shoulder but, with a creak of bones,

Gabriel got there before her. He bent down to Ned, gently picked him up with his big-knuckled old hands and carried him outside.

Staying where she was, Clara watched them go. This was their moment. For something to do she repacked one of the cupboards and tried to ignore the large lump in her throat and the tears that were threatening to do their worst. Damn the man, why and how had he got to them both?

Finally they were in their seats with the engine running, and it really was time to go. Coming round to the driver's side of the van, Gabriel poked his head through the open window. 'You take good care of yourself, won't you, Miss Costello?'

'Is that an order?'

'If needs be, yes.'

'And you'll take care as well, won't you? Don't lose any of those instructions I spent ages writing out for you. The dishwasher will need salt and Rinse-aid adding now and again, and you'll also have to—'

'Yes, yes, yes, Miss Costello. I have your infernal instructions Sellotaped to the inside of the cupboard, just as you insisted. I'll have them tattooed on my chest if it will make you feel any better.'

She revved the engine and knocked the gear-lever into first. 'Well, then, nothing more to be said. Apart from thanking you for having us to stay. Ned and I have had a great time. We won't forget you in a hurry, that's for sure.'

'Pah! You'll forget me so fast you won't even remember to send me a postcard.'

'We will remember,' cried Ned, fiercely. 'We'll send you one every week.'

'Goodbye, Mr Liberty. Despite everything, it's been a pleasure.' His grizzled head was still close to the window and, seizing her chance, she leaned towards him and kissed his bristly cheek.

'What was that for?'

'What do you think, you silly old fool?'

'I never thought I'd say it, Miss Costello, but if I were a younger man—'

She laughed. 'If you were a younger man, I wouldn't have dared to kiss you.'

'Oh, so old age makes me less of a sex object, does it?'

'It makes you more accessible, you whingeing old pain in the proverbial!'

He laughed too, then reached through the window, lifted her right hand off the steering-wheel, raised it to his lips, and very gently kissed it. 'I'm going to miss you, you delectable sharp-tongued girl. You've been a breath of fresh air for me. Goodbye now. Drive safely. And if you're ever passing . . .' but his voice trailed away.

Touched, she said, 'We wouldn't dream of not calling in on you if we were in the area. You can take that as a promise. Or maybe a threat!'

Steering Winnie out of the courtyard and tooting the horn, they gave one last wave to the solitary figure that stood in the shadow of the archway. He didn't linger.

Neither Clara nor Ned spoke until they had reached the midway point down the long drive. Ned looked out of his window and said, 'Shall I wave one more time in case Mr Liberty's watching us from the tower?'

She patted his knee. 'Good idea.'

He kept on waving until the house was almost out of sight. When they were nearly at the end of the drive, they saw a car approaching. It was Jonah.

Clara was glad to see him. She reckoned Gabriel could do with some company right now, even if it was only someone he could bully. She pulled over so that Jonah could come alongside the van. They wound down their windows at the same time.

Clara said, 'How was it on the Western Front with your school trip?'

'All quiet when we left it. Wet and cold too.'

'Too bad. So, not at school today shaping fertile young minds?'

'No, we've broken up for the Easter holidays. I've come to see if Dad wants some shopping fetching. Where are you off to?'

'The Lake District. You'll be pleased to know I've given up trying to marry your father and swindle him out of his vast fortune.'

'You're leaving?'

'Yes, Ned and I are moving on to pastures new, where scheming gold-diggers are given the proper respect they deserve.'

He smiled, not hugely, but enough for her to realise how attractive he was. Yet what struck her most about him in that split second, as she took in the curve of his mouth and the way his hazel eyes caught the light as he looked up at her, was that everything about him was reminiscent of the young woman in the painting in his father's library. The likeness to his mother was unmistakable and she wondered if he was aware of it, and whether or not Gabriel found it a comfort or a painful reminder of what he had lost.

'Caspar will be relieved to hear that,' he said good-humouredly. 'Scaring off a potential step-mother would have been a time-consuming business for him.'

'I bet it would. But do me a favour, will you? Persevere with your father.'

The smile was gone and his face turned awkward and defensive. Annoyed that she seemed to have an uncanny knack for rubbing him up the wrong way, she said, 'I might have misjudged you when I first met you, but . . . well, a week with your father and I think I understand things better now.'

But the smile didn't reappear as she had hoped it might. 'I doubt that,' he said, with feeling. 'Anyway, thanks for everything you've done for Dad. I'll do my best to carry on where you've left off. That's if he'll let me.'

'I find the shotgun approach usually works. You ram it up his nose and lay out your demands. Nothing to it. Goodbye.'

37

Dear Archie,
Apologies for sneaking out of town without saying goodbye. Ned was so upset about leaving Mermaid House I thought it better to keep the farewells to a minimum. As you can see, we're in the Lake District now – weather damp, scenery stunning, people almost as friendly as those in Deaconsbridge.
Thanks for all your help at Mermaid House.
Regards, Clara and Ned
P.S. What happened to the posse?

10 April

Dear Louise and associated rabble,
The hardship continues! Currently languishing beside beautiful Lake Windermere with Mrs Tiggywinkle and chums and getting fat on cream teas. Tomorrow we're going in search of lonely clouds and hosts of golden daffodils. Sorry I still haven't got round to phoning – will try to mend my ways. Do hope you're all behaving yourselves and missing us terribly.
Love from Clara and Ned
P.S. Happy Easter!

11 April

Dear Mr Liberty,
Just to prove we keep our promises, Easter greetings from Dove Cottage, the home of William Wordsworth. Maybe you should pen a few lines of poetry and open Mermaid House to the public, I'm sure you'd love thousands of tourists tramping through your home. Think how rude you could be to them!
   Ned says thank you very much for the money you gave him – that was v. naughty of you (slapped wrists!), but v. kind. He's used some of it to buy himself a pocket-sized Peter Rabbit.
Take care,
Ned and Miss Costello
P.S. Have you advertised for a cleaner yet?

Bateson, Hardy, Willets and Co.,
Chartered Accountants,
Dean Street,
Manchester
M10 9PQ

16 April 2001

Dear Caspar,

Re: Tax Return – C. Liberty

Please find enclosed copy of latest letter received from the Inland Revenue.

In view of the claims made, I suggest we meet and discuss the matter so that we can devise some sort of strategy that will satisfy our friends at the IR.
Kind regards,
Harvey Wilson

2 Canal View,
Manchester

21 April

Dear Damson,
What the hell's going on? Why won't you speak to me?

Five times I've tried to get you on the phone and on each occasion some Guardian-reading, bean-eating beardy type has told me it's not convenient. Since when is it not convenient to speak to your brother? Or is this all part of the brain-washing process that's going on up there?

Damson, surely you can see what's happening. Divide and conquer, it's how these cults operate. They isolate you from those who care about you, telling you it's for your own good.

If I don't hear from you soon, I will personally come up there and beat the **** out of that patronising wimp of a man who won't let me speak to you.
Caspar
P.S. How much money have they stung you for?

Rosewood Manor Healing Centre,
Blydale Village,
Northumberland

Saturday, 26 April

Darling Caspar,
If you really care about me, don't be silly and drive all the way up
here just to take out your frustration on poor Roland – who is
neither vegetarian nor the wearer of a beard, and he certainly doesn't
read the Guardian! *Instead, why don't you write and tell me what's*
wrong. And please don't deny that there is anything bothering you –
as twins, you know I always feel it when something is wrong with
you.
Love and warmest wishes,
Damson

27 April

Dear Louise and everyone,
Here we are north of the border! Glasgow is terrific! Moira, you'd
love it – more designer shops than you can shake a stick at. Wall-to-
wall Rennie Mackintosh stuff as well, tho' not sure Ned shared my
enthusiasm for it! Tomorrow we're setting sail for the bonnie banks
of Loch Lomond – Rob Roy country.
Och aye the noo!
Clara and Ned
P.S. It was great to speak to you on the phone last week, Louise – it
almost made me miss you!

28 April

Dear Mr Liberty,
Saw this wonderful card of a fierce-looking Scotsman playing the
bagpipes and thought of you! Ever thought of dyeing your hair red?
Hope you're taking care of yourself and haven't slipped back into
your bad old ways.
Best wishes,
Ned and Miss Costello

Bateson, Hardy, Willets and Co.,
Chartered Accountants,
Dean Street,
Manchester
M10 9PQ

1 May 2001

Dear Caspar,

Re: Tax Return – C. Liberty

Once again I enclose a copy of the latest communication from the
Inland Revenue. As you can see from the detailed documentation,
they leave us with little choice or room for manoeuvre.
Kind regards,
Harvey Wilson

2 Canal View,
Manchester

5 May

Dear Damson,
I would much rather discuss this over the phone, or even face to face.
Please let me speak to you.
Caspar
P.S. I might have guessed his name was bloody Roland!

Rosewood Manor Healing Centre,
Blydale Village,
Northumberland

Monday, 5 May

Dearest Caspar,
So much anger!
Please, just tell me what's wrong.
Thinking of you, all my love,
Damson

17 Cross Street,
Deaconsbridge

7 May

Dear Stella,
Before the solicitors get too carried away with their expensive games,
why don't we meet and discuss matters in private, just the two of us?
It's the least we owe each other.
Yours hopefully,
Archie
P.S. We don't have to meet in Deaconsbridge if you don't want to.
You choose.

2a Carlisle Terrace,
Macclesfield,
Cheshire

12 May

Dear Archie,
I could meet you a week next Tuesday after work in Buxton, but only for
a short while. I'll see you 6.00 by the bandstand.
Stella

Date: 14/05/01 14.44 GMT Daylight Time
From: ClaraCost@hotmail.com
To: GuyXXX@Phoenix.co.uk

Hope I'm in luck and that you're sitting in the office twiddling your
thumbs as you always used to!
    It had to happen sooner or later; I've found myself in a cyber café in
the middle of Edinburgh e-mailing you silly boys. How goes it? Who and
what is the latest gossip? Don't hold back on the dirt!

Date: 14/05/01 14.49 GMT Daylight Time
From: GuyXXX@aol.co.uk
To: ClaraCost@hotmail.com

Hey, Clarabelle, is that really you? This is like old times. Makes me
realise how much I miss your sharply worded e-mails! I'm working from
home today, so we can gossip quite freely – no chance of the surfing police
earwigging! We have it on good authority (David) that the big chiefs in

Wilmington are dispatching a couple of their smart-alecky types to suss out the takeover – Les Francais Garcons are definitely putting their francs on the table so it's all systems go. Not that anyone is supposed to know this, of course, but I don't need to tell you that it's been common knowledge here for some time that the plant doesn't fit in with the strategic direction of the CEO's thinking. And guess who's coming to see us? None other than the big honcho lawyer himself, Fenton Bexley, and the stellar-rated finance director, Todd Mason Angel. Aren't we the lucky ones?

Fondest etceteras,

Guy

P.S. Didn't you get to know TMA during your stint in Wilmington? What's he like? Is he likely to drive the women on the packing line mad with desire? You know what they were like with the last blue-eyed wonder boy who crossed the water to see us! Sexual harassment didn't come close!

38

It was five weeks since Gabriel had received the first of the postcards from Ned and Miss Costello and he had kept each one they had sent. He had them carefully lined up along the kitchen window-sill and every day, around twelve o'clock, when the postman finally got round to making a delivery at Mermaid House, he hung on to the hope that there would be a new addition for his collection.

It was a mild, sunny morning in May and he bent down to gather the scattering of envelopes that were spread so far and wide that he wondered if the postman made a game of firing the mail through the letterbox to see how far it would go.

Once again, there was no card and he tasted what was now the familiar bitterness of disappointment. Silly old fool, he berated himself. Get a grip, man. But then, hiding beneath a buff-coloured envelope addressèd to 'The Occupier', he glimpsed a flash of blue sky. The pendulum of his emotions swung from disappointment to delight. Without looking at the card – not wanting to spoil his enjoyment of it – he took it through to the kitchen where he dropped the buff-coloured envelope into the bin. Next he scanned his monthly bank statement for any anomalies, threw away a book-club offer and the chance to take out a fifteen-thousand-pound loan, then got down to the card, drawing out the process slowly, wanting to make it last.

The glossy picture showed a busy harbour: there were fishing boats, large and small, steep rows of terraced houses with red pan-tiled roofs and the ruins of an abbey on a distant clifftop. He recognised it instantly. It was Whitby. How well he knew it.

For three years running his father had taken him there when he was a boy. Just the two of them. They had stayed in the same modest boarding-house each time and always in the first week of August. The routine never varied: fishing in the morning, lunch overlooking the quay, and the afternoon spent going for long invigorating walks. Seventy years on he could still hear his father's voice booming above the crashing waves on the rocks below them as they marched along the cliff: 'Come on, Gabriel. Keep up, no lagging behind.' The last time they had made the trip he had fallen over and cut his knee on a rusty tin, but he hadn't cried, hadn't wanted to make a fuss. His father wouldn't have tolerated that. It wasn't until they were at home two days later and he woke in the night with a thrashing fever that had induced nightmares of goblins chasing him over a cliff that he allowed his mother to look at his leg. Straight away she called the doctor: the gash to his knee was infected and his temperature was soaring dangerously.

Gabriel turned over the postcard and smiled. Miss Costello had written it but Ned had added his own name and his topsy-turvy, oversized writing was thrown across the bottom of the card like tumbling building bricks.

Gabriel read it through once more then placed it on the window-sill. But, unlike the rest of the postcards, he positioned it so that the writing faced him. And while he made himself an early lunch, hacking at the remains of a loaf and adding a slab of Wensleydale to the thick hunks of granary bread, he continued to stare at Ned's handiwork, picturing the lad in the camper-van, kneeling up to the narrow table, his fingers gripping the pen, his hair falling into his eyes and his tongue poking out of the corner of his mouth as he concentrated. The thought of Ned's determination and the attachment he seemed to have made to an old man he scarcely knew, caused Gabriel to stop chewing his sandwich.

His *shambly*.

A few moments passed before he could swallow what was in his mouth.

If someone had told him two months ago that he could be so moved, he would have laughed in their face.

But every time he thought of Ned, he experienced a tightening in his chest. And if he pictured that moment in April when the boy had tried to say goodbye to him, he felt overwhelmed by sadness so heavy his breath caught. It happened to him now, made him feel as if his heart had just been torpedoed.

On impulse, that day, he had carried Ned round to the front of the house and together they had sat on the curved stone bench beneath the library window. 'I don't want to go,' the poor blighter had sniffled, rubbing his sleeve across his face, his legs swinging. 'I like it here. Nowhere else will be as nice.' The plaintive note in his voice had cut right through Gabriel.

'Now that's where you're wrong, Mr Smarty Pants,' he had said, putting an arm around him and tucking him into his side – he was so small. 'Do you think your mother would take you anywhere she thought you wouldn't like? No. Of course not. She's much too good a mother to do that to you.'

Ned had wrinkled his nose. 'I wish you could come with us. I asked Mummy if you could but she thinks you'd snore and keep us awake at night.'

Laughing, he had said, 'Your mother's a very wise woman, but Ned, and you must promise to keep this under your hat, it's not something I want everyone to know – I'm too old for travelling.'

'I know you're very old,' he had said, so solemnly it had made Gabriel want to smile, 'but you wouldn't have to drive. Mummy would do all that.'

'And she has enough on her hands without having me along for the ride and getting in her way. Now then, dry your eyes and promise me one more thing, that you'll look after her. When you're older, you'll discover that the people who least appear to need help are those who need it most. Do I get a hug goodbye?'

Ned had squashed himself against Gabriel, burrowed his head into his neck and held on to him tightly.

Even now, all these weeks on, Gabriel could smell the sweet warmth of the boy and the bubbling sense of energy within his little body. It was a happy memory, but at the same time it made him feel low and weary. And so very alone.

The emptiness of the house – the deathly quiet of it – had never seemed so oppressive as it did now, and that was with Jonah constantly making a nuisance of himself. Solitude had never bothered Gabriel in the past, but now he wanted none of it. He craved the sound of a small child's excited voice calling to him, the hurried, purposeful footsteps of a young woman, the crisp humorous taunt, the robust mocking smile. But he knew he could crave those things all he wanted and he would never know them again.

Through the window, beyond the courtyard, he watched a kestrel hovering on the wind, its wings beating the air. Seconds passed, and then it was gone, attracted by something a long way off.

Oh, how he missed that little firecracker and her son.

It was against school policy for a member of staff to visit a pupil at home on his or her own, especially if the pupil was a girl, so Jonah had wisely enlisted the help of Barbara Lander – an experienced, seen-it-all-before geography teacher – to help him get to the bottom of why Sharna Powell was missing from school yet again. He had a pretty good idea of what was going on, and had decided it was time for him to put in a personal appearance. He was taking this slightly unorthodox approach, rather than bringing in the Education Welfare Service, because, rightly or wrongly, he believed he could resolve the problem. In his opinion it was all too easy to pass on the difficult children to a higher authority and wash one's hands of them, but he didn't think that was the way to improve the pastoral system at a school like Dick High.

The Powell family lived on the same estate as Jase O'Dowd, along with the majority of the kids at Dick High, but unlike most of the others, who occasionally stayed away from school for the hell of it, he was certain that Sharna's frequent absences were due to a more worrying influence than mere peer-group pressure to bunk off classes.

Parking outside number twenty-three Capstone Close – predictably, the letter R had been inserted with a black pen into the road sign – Jonah said, 'Thanks, Barbara, for doing this. I appreciate your help.'

'No problem. Just don't be too hopeful that we'll get anywhere. If it is the mother who's deliberately keeping Sharna home, our presence is likely to be inflammatory.'

'I know, but it's worth a try, isn't it?'

Barbara slipped her bag over her shoulder. 'As I said earlier, I'm going to leave you to do all the talking. This is your show and if *you* can't charm this particular birdie down from the tree, I don't know who can.'

He shoved open his door and got out. 'And what's that supposed to mean?'

She looked at him over the top of the car. 'Don't sound so shocked. It's common knowledge in the staff room that your crusading techniques leave the rest of us standing. Must be something to do with that fine-boned face of yours and the disarming boyish smile. It takes the little sods by surprise, makes them want to help you out. The old dragons like me only get results by beating them into submission. I'm just pleased you picked me for this assignment because I'll get to observe you in action, and at close range.'

'I had no idea I was such a focus of attention,' he said drily.

'Come off it, Jonah, surely you know that everyone in the staff room calls you Walker behind your back.'

'Walker?'

'Yes, Walker as in crisps, as in potato chips, as in—'

'Mr Chips,' he finished for her. 'Great! Just what I need, a sobriquet from the Dark Ages.'

She laughed. 'Do you want to know what's also being said about you behind your back?'

'In or out of the staff room?'

She laughed again. 'What the hormonally charged girls say about you is unrepeatable, but it's hotly rumoured in the staff room that you're going to be put in charge of the sixth form in the autumn.'

'You're kidding?'

'Nope. At the rate you're going, you'll be Dick High's very own Moses, parting the water with a flick of your angelic curls. Don't frown like that, Jonah, it spoils the whole effect. You can't be a shiny-eyed enthusiast with stress and worry lines like the rest of us.'

The Powells' semi-detached house was as run-down as the neighbouring properties – the fascia boards needed replacing, the windows were filthy, the net curtains were torn, and the overgrown front garden was a dismal sight: home to a tangle of two dismantled motorbikes, several burst bags of cement and a supermarket trolley minus its wheels.

They picked their way through the debris and knocked at the door. It was ajar and Jonah could hear the sound of a television from somewhere within. He knocked again, louder this time. The volume on the television was turned down and a woman's voice shouted, 'Get that, will you, Shar?'

'Hello, Sharna,' Jonah said, when the door opened fully to reveal an overweight girl with a pasty complexion that flushed ten shades of red and clashed with the skimpy purple halter-neck top she was wearing. The lower part of her was covered, just, by a crotch-hugging skirt, and as if to lessen the effect of so much exposed thigh, she tried to hide one leg behind the other.

'Sir! What're you doing here?'

'I might ask the same of you. Okay if we come in?'

Reluctantly she took them through to the back of the small house, to the kitchen. Next to a steaming kettle there were two full mugs of coffee, an opened jar of Nescafé and a carton of long-life milk. As well as the aroma of instant coffee, there was a less appetising smell that came from a gas cooker where a charred grill-pan contained a blanket of solidified cooking fat. It looked as if it had been used many times: blackened scabs of burnt food poked through its hard, rancid surface.

With some of her fourteen-year-old spirit returning, Sharna said, 'Not expecting lunch, are you, Sir?'

'No, but I am expecting a good reason for why you're not in school. *Again.*'

'It's me asthma. Same as before.' She gave her substantial shoulders a heave and produced a corroborative cough.

'Then perhaps you ought to cut back.' His gaze fell on an overflowing ashtray on the draining-board where two packets of frozen sausages were defrosting.

'I've given up. It's only Mum and me brothers who smoke now.'

'Good for you. Is your mother in?' He saw her hesitate and knew he had put her on the spot.

'Um . . . she's not well, Sir. She's having a lie-down.'

'She's probably thirsty too. Shall we take her coffee through? It seems a shame to keep her waiting.' And before she could stop him, he picked up one of the mugs, went back to the hall, then opened the door of what he assumed was the front room. The air was blue with the fug of cigarette smoke. An enormous television, with a china dray horse on top of it, squatted in the furthest corner of the room – John Leslie was putting a contestant through the rigorous hoops of *Wheel of Fortune*.

'And about time too. How long does it take to boil the kettle and make us a drink? Who was that at the door? Go on, mate! Spin the bloody thing!' The voice was thick and husky and emanated from a woman sitting on the edge of a PVC sofa that crackled with her agitated movements. Sharna's mother was a larger version of her daughter – the pasty complexion and the broad shoulders were the same, as was the shaggy permed hair.

'Mrs Powell?'

She swivelled her head and looked at Jonah with breathtaking hostility. 'Who the hell are you?'

'I'm Mr Liberty, your daughter's form teacher, and this is Mrs Lander, a colleague from school.' He handed her the coffee and, uninvited, sat down beside her. 'If it's not inconvenient,' he said, 'we'd like to discuss why Sharna is absent from school so often. We're very concerned for her. You see, every day she misses puts her at a disadvantage with her GCSEs, and that strikes me as a great shame, given her ability.'

Mrs Powell shifted forward and reached for her cigarettes. She flipped open the packet, took out a Marlboro, hunted for a lighter among the mess on the table in front of her. 'It's her asthma. How many times do I have to tell you lot?' She found the lighter and lit the cigarette. Inhaling deeply, she stared him in the eye, her expression sullen and challenging. 'What's more, I put it in that note last week when she was off.'

'It has nothing to do with this, then?' He picked up a two-inch-square polythene bag of tin-tacks from the coffee table, then poked at a pile waiting to be bagged up. 'Piece-work can take for ever, can't it? An extra pair of hands makes all the difference – really lightens the load.'

She threw down the lighter, scattering tin-tacks on the carpet. 'What're you on about? It's me who does this. *On my own.*' She placed the cigarette between her lips, drew on it hard, then blew a cloud of smoke into his face. 'Coming round here with your bloody fancy posh voice accusing me of friggin' knows what! And why, I'd like to know, aren't you in school doing what you're paid to do?' Her tired, lined face blazed with insolence.

While her manner didn't bother Jonah, it upset Sharna, who hadn't said a word. Now she stepped forward. 'Mum! Don't shout at him like that, you'll get me into even more trouble.'

'Shut up and leave this to me.'

'But Mum—'

'If you can't be quiet, get out.'

'He's only trying to help. It's his job.'

Keeping his voice low and smooth, in contrast to Mrs Powell's bullying screech, Jonah rose to his feet and said, 'I think we've said all we need to, Mrs Powell. You're a busy woman and we have no right to take up any more of your valuable time. Sharna, perhaps you'd show us out.'

Standing at the front door, the volume of the television in the sitting room turned up again, Sharna said, 'Sorry about that, Sir. She loses it now and again.'

He looked at her kindly. 'It's okay. But, Sharna, you do have a choice in this. If you see yourself in years to come earning your living from packing tin-tacks, like your mother,' he paused meaningfully, 'then so be it. But if there's the slightest chance that you might want more out of life, I'd be delighted to see you in school first thing tomorrow morning. Think it over. It's your decision. Nobody else's. The law says you must attend school in one form or another, but nobody has the right to bully you into making the wrong decision. Not me, not your mother, not even Mrs Lander here.'

The girl put a finger to her lower lip, pushed it against her teeth, chewed at it anxiously. 'I'll ... I'll see y' then, Sir.'

'Soon, I hope.'

The door closed slowly behind them, and when they were driving away,

Barbara Lander said, 'Creeping bloody ivy! So it *is* true what they say about you. You were as slick as an oiled eel.'

'Do you think so?'

'Oh you know so! The moment that horrible woman started attacking you, the daughter leaped to your defence, just as you knew she would. Me, I'd have blown it by throwing the letter of the law at the mother and getting both their backs up. But not you, you cunningly got the girl on your side. And if there isn't a tick by her name in the register tomorrow morning, I'll cover your lunch duty for the rest of term.'

'And it's two whole weeks until half-term – how very generous of you. However, the hard part will be ensuring we keep her at school. She'll need a lot of support to stand up to that mother of hers. And we don't want to cause so many waves that the heavy brigade get brought in. That would be totally counter-productive.'

He slowed down to let a car pull out in front of him. It had come from the road where Jase lived, and Jonah was almost tempted to take a detour and see how he was getting on – year eleven was officially on home study leave for their GCSEs. The first of the history papers was set for next Tuesday and Jonah was giving an eleventh-hour revision lesson on Monday after school. Jase had said he would be there, but would he?

Shuffling through his collection of dusty cassettes, and not looking too impressed with his choice of music – Barbara was a country-and-western devotee – she said, 'I'm intrigued, Jonah. Where did you learn to deal so effectively with bullies?'

He smiled wryly. 'It comes from being a coward. I don't like confrontation. I prefer to disarm rather than mobilise the tanks of aggression.'

Of course it had nothing to do with growing up at Mermaid House.

That evening he stayed on at school to do some marking, but instead of going home straight away when he had finished, he drove to Mermaid House. He was concerned about his father. Since the miraculous Miss Costello had moved on, Gabriel had been morose. Only a fool would think that her influence had been restricted to overhauling an uncared-for house: Jonah knew that it had gone much further than that. She had touched Gabriel Liberty in a way that few people ever had. Amazingly, she had made him happy.

But what worried Jonah most, was that his father's trademark fighting spirit had dwindled to nothing. He had mentioned this to Caspar on the phone, but all his brother had said was, 'Well, it was bound to happen at some time or other. He can't go to his grave snapping and snarling – we'd never get the lid down on him.'

'For pity's sake, Caspar, how can you talk like that? He's our father.'

'He's also a miserable old man who won't listen to a word of common sense, and who, I might add, took malicious pleasure in making me look a fool over that Costello woman.'

Jonah had put his brother out of his misery about their father supposedly marrying for the third time. Predictably Caspar's anger had been cataclysmic. 'I thought you might have been relieved,' Jonah had reasoned.

'Relieved he despises me so much that he had to humiliate me in front of a complete stranger? Are you mad? And why do you always have to miss the bloody point?'

Changing tack, and hoping to move on to safer ground, Jonah had said, 'So how's business?'

But the ground had opened up beneath him. 'And what the hell do you care about my business?' Caspar had sniped. 'Since when have you ever cared about anything I do?'

'Hey, I'm only asking.'

'Well, don't! Take your snivelling civility and stick it—'

Jonah had ended the conversation by putting the phone down quietly. There was nothing to be gained from talking with his brother when he was in that kind of mood. He didn't hear from Caspar in the following weeks, which meant that he was no longer under any pressure to do his bidding. There had been no further mention of selling Mermaid House – their father had made it clear that there would be no question of it – but privately Jonah still thought it was the right thing to do.

It was still light when he arrived at Mermaid House, and he found his father in the gun room, locking the glass-fronted cabinet. 'Bloody crows,' he said, pocketing the key. 'They've been at the lambs again. Vermin. Should be wiped off the face of the earth. What brings you here? And what's that smell?'

'It's this.' He held up a paper carrier-bag. 'Indian take-away. Thought you might fancy a change from your usual bean-feast.'

Gabriel eyed the bag suspiciously. 'You did, did you?'

'It'll need heating up in the oven for a short while. Shall I see to it?'

'Feel free.'

A week had passed since Jonah had last called in and he was relieved to see, as he slid the foil packages inside the oven, that his father was still keeping the place relatively clean and tidy. There were no feminine touches of flowers or tablecloths, but the kitchen was still hygienically sound. 'Any luck with finding a cleaner?' he asked, bending down to a cupboard for two plates, then opening the cutlery drawer. He knew that Gabriel had placed an advert in the local paper.

'No. Word's probably gone round the whole of Derbyshire that I'm a no-go area. Drink?'

'Thanks. But only a small one. I'll add some water.' Despite his father's look of disapproval, he took the tumbler of whisky over to the sink. He ran the cold tap for a while then added an inch to the glass. He noticed the postcards lined up along the window-sill and looked at the latest addition.

He picked it up and turned it over to see where it had come from. 'I see the Costellos are in Whitby,' he said, his back still to Gabriel. 'Didn't you go there with your father when you were a boy?'

'How much longer is this meal going to take?'

Acknowledging that prising any information out of his father about the past was as productive as trying to squeeze blood out of a stone, he replaced the card on the sill. 'Another five minutes should do it.' He raised his glass. 'Cheers.'

While they ate, Jonah kept up the conversation as well as he could, but it was hard going. His father was even more uncommunicative and morose than usual. For something to say, he told him about Sharna and her mother.

'Sounds like you're wasting your time there,' Gabriel said, picking at his food uninterestedly. 'If people don't want help, you can't force it on them.'

Jonah looked up from his chicken korma. 'So you think they should be left to dig themselves a deeper hole from which there's no hope of them ever climbing out?'

Gabriel lowered his gaze. 'I didn't say that.'

'So what did you mean?'

'You have to wait until people are ready to accept your help. Or ask for it. Go blundering in as a self-appointed champion of the underdog with scant regard for anyone's feelings and you'll find yourself up against a brick wall.'

'But not everyone knows how to ask for help.'

'True. But maybe in the end they do.' His father pushed away his plate.

Jonah hadn't expected the conversation to take this turn and he steeled himself to ask, 'Dad, who are we really talking about here? Disadvantaged teenagers or . . . or you?'

As soon as the words were out, he regretted them. Gabriel glowered at him, his thick eyebrows drawn together, his mouth set so firmly that his lips had all but disappeared. Oh, God, he recognised that look. He had seen it a million times and felt the consequences. Why couldn't he have kept quiet?

But when his father spoke his voice was anything but firm – anything but recognisable. It shook almost as much as the knobbly hand that reached clumsily for the glass of whisky. 'I . . . I would have thought that was patently obvious, Jonah.'

It was madness to go any further, but with the thought of Miss Costello's parting words echoing in his head – about the shotgun approach and laying out one's demands – he felt compelled to force his father, just once, to be honest with him. 'Are you saying what I think you're saying? That you want my help but don't know how to ask for it?'

The heavily loaded question trapped them in a long, silent pause, and they stared at each other across the table. It was as if they were frozen with fear. Then, to Jonah's horror, his father's eyes were swimming with tears.

'Dad?' Jonah rose from his chair uncertainly. He could cope with irate, booze-sodden parents threatening him and thuggish students disparaging him. That was a breeze. But this? His father crying? Dear God, what had he done? He moved slowly round the table, every step filling him with alarm and confusion. His father's tears were flowing freely now, his body had slumped forward, his head was in his hands, and his breathing was coming in sharp, noisy gulps.

Jonah bent down to him cautiously, and for the first time in his life, he placed a tentative hand on his father's shoulder, expecting it to be pushed away roughly, to be told, 'Don't touch me!'

But there was no rejection. Gabriel turned into him, rested his head against his shoulder, and continued to weep. Words streamed out of him, but Jonah could make no sense of them. It didn't matter, though. Understanding would come later. For now, comforting his father was all that was needed.

39

Gabriel woke with a start. There was someone – *something* – in his room! He sat bolt upright. A shadowy figure was coming towards him.

'Dad, are you all right?'

'Jonah?'

'I've brought you a cup of tea. How are you feeling? Did you sleep okay?'

The painful rush of adrenaline that had coursed through his veins now abandoned him and a heaviness, not unlike a hangover, pushed Gabriel back against the pillows. Through dry, gritty eyes he watched Jonah draw the curtains, letting sunlight spill into the room. He blinked at the brightness. 'Why are you here?' he croaked. His throat felt as if it had been sandblasted and his voice sounded distant, not like it normally did. Nothing made sense, and forcing his brain to battle its way through the lethargy that was consuming him, he wondered if he had been drugged. But who would have done that to him?

Jonah came and sat on the bed. There was an expression on his face that made him look different somehow. Something in the eyes, the mouth too. It was something oddly familiar ... something that made Gabriel's heart miss a beat and made him, inexplicably, want to cry. Overwhelmed, confusion closed in and he felt as weak as a baby. He swallowed hard but his mouth was so parched he couldn't.

Panic-stricken, he was terrified suddenly that something awful had happened to him while he had slept. He sat forward so that he was eye to eye with Jonah. He gripped his son's hands, and drew a deep, shuddering breath. 'Jonah, has something happened to me? Tell me the truth. Have I had a stroke? I feel different. Strange. Not myself. Am I making sense to you?'

'Dad, calm down, you're fine.'

But the frown on Jonah's face only made him think he was being lied to. 'The truth,' he demanded. 'Tell me why I feel so strange and why you're here.'

'Don't you remember last night?'

'What about last night?'

'You were ... you were very upset.'

'Was I? What about?'

The frown deepened. 'We were having supper together, we were talking and . . . Dad, do you really not remember?'

But suddenly Gabriel did have a glimmer of recall. 'You brought an Indian meal . . . we were talking about somebody called Charlene—'

'Sharna. She's one of my pupils.'

He waved aside the interruption. His befuddled brain had started to piece together the bits of the jigsaw and he didn't want it to be put off by unnecessary details. Not when he could feel a new, disturbing emotion growing inside him. Finally, like a wreck being raised out of the water, it surfaced and he recognised it as shame. He groaned, remembering vaguely that something had caused him to lose control in the kitchen. Appalled, he closed his eyes. How had that happened? He concentrated hard, and saw himself bent over the table, heard himself howling. Then he recalled his younger son holding him, and later helping him upstairs to bed. And all the while he was blethering like a lunatic. But even as he felt the debilitating shame of what he had done, and could recall the reasons why, he sensed a closeness to Jonah that he couldn't explain. He knew though that he could never talk to him about it. He would never be able to find the right words. And there was always the danger that if he tried he might lose control again.

He jerked his eyes open, and said, in his firmest voice, 'I think it would be better all round if neither of us referred to last night again.' He saw hesitation in Jonah's face. What was left of his dignity lay in his son's hands and Gabriel willed him to do as he had asked. Do this small thing for me, Jonah, he urged.

'Is that really what you want, Dad?' Jonah asked.

'Yes, it is.'

'But . . .'

'But what?'

'You don't think we ought to talk about what happened?'

'No, I don't!'

'Okay,' he said soothingly. 'If that's what you want, that's fine by me.'

Relieved, Gabriel sank back into the softness of the pillows. He was home and dry. The relief was as potent as the earlier rush of adrenaline had been. Jonah passed him his tea and as their eyes met, his son smiled and suddenly Gabriel wasn't so sure that he *was* home and dry. He knew that smile so well, had loved it. A hot wave of panic flooded him, his heart thudded painfully in his chest and his hands shook so much that he had to put the mug on the bedside table. He wanted to speak, but couldn't. Consumed with the absurd need to weep on his son's shoulder again, he summoned all his strength, heaved himself out of bed and blundered blindly from the room.

His head spinning, frightened he was going to be sick, he locked himself into the bathroom and sat on the edge of the bath. He pressed his clenched fists to his eyes and wept as silently as he could. God in heaven, why had it taken him almost thirty-five years to see just how like his mother Jonah was?

40

The May sunshine had warmed the wooden bench Archie was sitting on, which helped to relax him a little. He wasn't a jumpy man, but today his nerves were shot to pieces. Which was crazy: he was only meeting Stella, for heaven's sake – a woman he'd known for most of his adult life.

But perhaps he hadn't ever *really* known her. If he had, surely he wouldn't be sitting here in Buxton, in the Pavilion Gardens, waiting to meet her so they could discuss their divorce in a civilised and amicable manner.

It had seemed the right thing to do when he had written to Stella earlier in the month, and it had still seemed right when she had penned a hurried note last week to say she couldn't make it that day after all, but would the following Tuesday be okay? He had sent a note back saying it would be fine.

But now it felt anything but fine. What would they say to each other? Would they argue and cause an unpleasant scene that would play right into the solicitors' hands?

The sun and nervous energy were making him sweat – he unbuttoned his cuffs and rolled his sleeves up. He was ten minutes early, and he watched the people around him enjoying themselves. Picnic blankets were laid out on the grass where cool-bags, discarded socks and shoes had been scattered, and groups of tiny children, their lips and clothes stained with ice-lolly juice, squealed and laughed while their mothers chatted. Through the leafy trees, and down by the lake, where ducks were being fed chunks of processed bread, the miniature train rattled along its narrow-gauge track, whistling. In the shade of an oak tree, a girl and a boy were oblivious to the world around them as they kissed.

He sighed. Oh, what a world it was, at one minute so beautiful and full of golden opportunities, and at the next hopelessly confusing and fraught with difficulties.

'Archie?'

He started. 'Stella!' He got to his feet. Was it really her? Surprise must have been stamped all over his face.

Self-consciously she patted her short, flicked-back hair. 'I'm still getting used to it,' she said.

But the dramatic change in hairstyle and colour – from mousy grey to harsh teak – wasn't the only thing that was different. She had lost weight, more than a stone. And since when had she had such long nails? They must be false – she had never been able to get hers to grow. She had always complained they were too brittle. The jewellery was new too, and there was too much of it, he thought. Gifts from the new man in her life, perhaps. The silky overshirt covered a camisole top that was low at the front, and between her breasts an amber pendant he didn't recognise caught the sunlight. She had changed the colour of her lipstick too. It was darker. Too red. It gave her teeth a yellowed appearance. 'You're looking great,' he said.

'You too.'

They sat down and Archie cringed at how easily she could lie. He knew he looked far from well. Only that morning when he had been shaving he had noticed the unhealthy pallor of his skin and the extra lines and shadows around his eyes.

'How's the shop going?'

Pride made him want to say that business was booming, that since she had gone the money had poured in, that he spent every evening counting his new-found booty and devising ways to spend it – a yacht here, a second home there. And that was when he wasn't fighting off the women! Oh, yes, all the gorgeous young women he'd had in his life since he had become a single man – banging on his door they were. 'Oh, same as ever,' was all he said, thinking that this was the answer his circumspect solicitor would expect of him – '*Make the shop sound too profitable, Mr Merryman, and she'll want a cut of that too!*' 'Business is up and down,' he added, further obliging the lawyer in his mind.

'And your mother?'

'A little better.' No thanks to you, he wanted to say, with an uncharacteristic spurt of malice. Oh, this was no good! They wouldn't get anywhere if he carried on like this. What was done was done. Bitterness wouldn't help either of them. 'Do you fancy an ice-cream?' he asked, catching sight of a tot leaning forward in his pushchair, trying to grasp the cornet his mother was keeping at a safe distance.

'I shouldn't, really,' she said, smoothing out a crease in her skirt, then crossing her legs and revealing a shapely calf. 'I'm on a diet.' She made it sound like it was the 'in' thing to be doing, that over in cosmopolitan Macclesfield that's what everyone was up to.

'Oh. Sure I can't tempt you? Not even a small one?'

She shook her head. Not one hair moved, he noticed. 'But don't let me stop you.'

Childishly, he took her words as a challenge and strode off to the nearest ice-cream seller. With a strawberry Cornetto in his hand, he took the return journey more leisurely. Come on, he told himself, drop the pathetic dumped-husband routine and relax or this meeting will be a waste of time.

'So what was it you wanted to discuss?' she asked, when he joined her on the bench again. He saw her sliding two gold bracelets apart on her wrist so that she could look at her watch. Couldn't she have done that while he'd been gone? And how come she was so cool? He was sweating and squirming like a pig.

He moistened his lips and launched into what he wanted to say. 'This isn't easy for me, Stella, but I just wanted you to know that . . . that I'm sorry.'

She looked at him blankly. 'Sorry?'

'Yes. For not being the husband you needed. I let you down and this . . . this awful awkwardness between us seems . . . Oh, Stella, this coldness between us seems a heck of a price to pay, especially when you think how happy we once were.'

She continued to stare at him, and in such a way that he wondered if what he'd said hadn't made sense. He opened his mouth to try to make himself clearer.

'I don't understand,' she said, her tone icy. 'Is this some sly trick of yours to make me feel guilty?'

'Huh?'

'I know what you're doing, Archie, you're clinging to the past. You're trying to—'

'I'm not!' he blurted out. 'I was trying to say that I want you to know I understand. Or, rather, I think I understand. Over the years we both changed without either of us realising it, and—' A high-pitched squeal of laughter distracted him. He turned to see a small child lying on his back waving his legs in the air as his mother tickled his tummy. 'Perhaps if we'd had kiddies, things might have been different,' he said flatly.

'This isn't about us not being able to have children,' she said pointedly. 'It's not even about you forcing your mother on me.'

That really hurt. He tried to respond, but his voice failed him.

'I'm not coming back, Archie. I thought I'd made that perfectly clear. I have a new life now. One that makes me happy. Happier than I've been in a long while. I only came here to make sure you understood that.'

He was stung by her hardness and felt himself shrivel inside. Melting ice-cream trickled down his thumb. 'Stella, I asked you to meet me so that we could try to make things easier between us. To make our divorce less painful. I thought it would give us the chance to go our different ways with a more positive attitude.'

'I don't believe you. You wanted to drag me here to flaunt your forgiveness at me, to make me feel bad about what I did. You always did want to be the good guy – self-righteous Archie Merryman. Well, now you've got what you always wanted. I'm the villain for walking out on you and you're the hard-done-by man everyone feels sorry for.' Her voice was tight with recrimination, her words spilling out as though she had been storing them up specially. Suddenly she leaped to her feet. 'There's nothing to be gained from this. I knew it would be a mistake. And look!' She pointed to his left hand accusingly. 'You're still wearing your wedding ring.

You haven't accepted anything at all.' Without another word, she wheeled round and marched away.

He was dumbfounded. He watched her stride out in the direction of the opera house, her unfamiliar hair bobbing through the strolling holiday-makers. Her arms swinging, she veered off-course only once to avoid bumping into a man with a pushchair. Then at last she disappeared.

Archie thought, if your new life makes you so happy, Stella, why do you look and sound so miserable?

He drove home to Deaconsbridge more confused than when he had set out. What had she meant by him always wanting to be the good guy? Sure, he liked to be liked. Who didn't? It was human nature to want to get on with other people. The belief that there was good in everyone was at his core. Take that Mr Liberty, for instance. He certainly wasn't everyone's cup of tea, but Clara Costello proved his point perfectly: she had seen something worth digging for beneath the layers of prickly rudeness or why else had she put herself out for him?

To his surprise, by the time he reached home and was locking the car, he no longer felt so sorry for himself. It was Stella his heart went out to. Her bitterness seemed so much greater than his own.

He let himself in at the back door and saw that his mother had managed to peel some potatoes for their supper – a hopeful sign. He went through to the sitting room where he could hear *Emmerdale*'s theme playing on the television.

'Hi, Mum,' he said, forcing himself to sound carefree and jolly. He had told her where he was going, that he was trying to smooth things out between him and Stella, and he wanted her to think that the meeting had gone well, that he had it all under control now. He reached for the evening paper, which had slipped on to the floor beside her armchair and passed it to her. It was then, when she made no move to take it from him, that he realised she had had another stroke.

The doctor said there was no need for him to stay. 'You might just as well go home and get a decent night's sleep in your own bed,' she advised.

But Archie said no. 'I wouldn't sleep anyway.'

The doctor, a woman in her early forties with a kindly, understanding smile, nodded. 'I thought you'd say that. But do your best to grab the odd nap. We don't want you conking out on us. You look too useful a chap to lose.'

With the curtain drawn around the bed, screening them off from the rest of the ward, Archie sat alone with his mother while she slept. Except it wasn't a true sleep. She was now in a world where he couldn't reach her.

Dr Singh had warned him that a second stroke was on the cards, that it would probably strike within a year of the first, but when it had happened, he had been taken unawares. 'No use looking for warning signs and symptoms,' Dr Singh had said, 'it'll just make you more anxious, which will make Bessie more anxious.'

He laid a hand on his mother's and hoped she could feel his touch. He wanted to believe that she knew he was there and that she wasn't facing this alone. With her head turned away from him, she looked just as she always did when she slept. But the other side of her face told a different story. The corner of her mouth was open and looked as if it was waiting to have a pipe or a cigar popped into it. Her eyelid looked as if someone had tied a thread to it, then pulled it down towards her cheek. It was a heartbreaking sight.

Still with his hand on hers, he sank back into the chair, tilted his head, closed his eyes and listened to the noises beyond the curtain. Someone was coughing – a dry, tickly cough – another patient was muttering in her sleep, and beyond the ward, voices rose and fell. A phone was ringing and hurried footsteps squeaked on the polished floor.

This last sound dredged up a pleasant memory for Archie, of his first visit to Mermaid House and Clara Costello's confident step as she led him the length of the impressive hallway towards the drawing room.

As sleep claimed him, he wondered where she was now. What wouldn't he give to pack up his troubles and take to the road?

41

That night Clara dreamed she was running. Her legs carried her effortlessly through fields of long, dry, swaying grass. Her feet were bare and a warm breeze blew through her hair – not short as it was now but streaming out behind her – and in her arms she carried Ned. There was no weight to him and together they were almost flying. In the distance, there was a hill, and Ned asked her to take him to the top. Their laughter rang out like birdsong as she ran sure-footed up the steep incline. The higher she climbed, the lighter and freer she felt. From the top, where the sun was brighter, the wind keener, they looked down on to a small town. It was Deaconsbridge. There was the church, the bustling market square, Archie's shop and the Mermaid café. Away from the town, and perched on a hill which he had all to himself was a man. He was waving to them. Standing beside her, Ned clapped his hands. 'Mummy, there's a man waving to us. Is it Mr Liberty? Has he come to see us?' But as she shielded her eyes from the glare of the sun, she caught Ned by the hand and started running again, down the hill, her feet scarcely touching the ground beneath them. 'That's not Mr Liberty,' she cried, the wind tossing her words over her shoulder, 'that's your father.'

She woke violently from the dream, her heart racing. That was twice now she had dreamed of Todd.

Didn't you get to know TMA during your stint in Wilmington?

How innocently Guy had typed those words, never once thinking they would have such an effect on her. How hard it had been to e-mail him back and say casually, *Oh, I met him once or twice. And yes, you'd better keep him safe from the women on the packing line!*

It was stupid of her, really, but she should have guessed that Todd would be assigned to visit the plant and oversee the buy-out. It was part of his job. She wondered if he was anxious about bumping into her.

Probably not.

She was measuring the depth of his response by her own, which couldn't be the same. He didn't know that their brief love-affair had created Ned.

Since she had returned from Wilmington, she had observed his progress within the organisation from company reports and morale-boosting in-house magazines. She had also tuned in discreetly to any snippets of transatlantic gossip that buzzed around the plant. But last year she had been brought up short when she had unexpectedly come across him in the pages of the *Financial Times*. It had been an article about Phoenix's latest rise in profits after the US drug regulator had given the green light to its new anti-depressant drug, but all she had been interested in was the photograph that showed the company finance director. It was clearly an up-to-date picture because he was wearing glasses, which he hadn't needed when she had known him. Two thoughts had occurred to her as she looked at the photograph: (a) the frameless glasses suited Todd, and (b) she would need to check Ned's vision as he grew older.

She straightened the duvet and turned on to her side, knowing that sleep would elude her for a while yet. She wished there was someone in whom she could confide. For more than four years she had kept her own counsel, and convinced herself that she would never have to deal with Todd again. She supposed it said a lot about her controlling nature that she had believed she could wrap things up so tidily.

But now, because she knew Todd would soon be arriving in England, a voice was asking if she had done the right thing in keeping the truth about Ned from him.

Her intentions had been good, though: she hadn't wanted to jeopardise the relationship he needed to rebuild with his wife and daughters. But would it have been fairer to give him the facts and let him decide what to do? And would he be angry, if he were to find out about Ned, that he had been denied the right to know his son?

That was what worried her most.

Even so, part of her was convinced that it would be better to go on keeping Todd in the dark – what the eye didn't see, the heart couldn't miss. But what if he discovered that Clara Costello had jacked in her job to spend more time with her son? She could imagine the conversation all too well. 'She has a son? When did she marry?' An awkward pause. 'Oh, not married. How old is the child?'

When he had done the sums, would he track down those to whom she had been closest at work, and through them seek her out?

And that was where the need to talk to somebody came in. Should she confess to her friends so that Guy and David could be on their guard for any unfortunate slip of the tongue, and prime them to lie about Ned's age?

She knew that to expose them to such a secret wasn't fair.

No. Her only hope was to carry on as before and pray that Todd wouldn't ask after her. He hadn't up till now, had he?

But the next morning Clara was tempted to phone Louise. She thought she would go mad if she didn't confide in someone. The need to be told that she had done the right thing, that no blame could be apportioned to her, was so great she could think of nothing else.

Ironically, it was Ned who provided her with the means to stand firm. With him around, there was no opportunity for her to make such a telephone call. After breakfast, and following a lengthy, fun-filled washing-up session, they left the campsite in Pateley Bridge – which had been home for the last three days while they had toured Ripon, Harrogate and Skipton – and set off for Haworth. This was primarily Clara's choice – she had always wanted to see where the Brontë sisters had lived – but there were plenty of things to interest Ned too. A trip on a steam train run by the Keighley and Worth Valley Railway, and a visit to Eureka!, the Museum for Children in Halifax. They might even drive over to Leeds to see the Armoury. Education as well as entertainment was the order of their trip.

She had been worried that Ned would tire of being a perpetual tourist, but they had yet to encounter boredom. The trick, it seemed, was to provide a wide-ranging variety of places to visit, as well as allow themselves occasional days of doing nothing so they could relax and catch their breath. They did this when they were fortunate enough to find themselves on campsites with plenty of facilities – a swimming-pool (preferably indoor), a play area, a woodland trail, a crazy-golf course. One place they had stopped at in Northumberland, not far from Bamburgh Castle and Holy Island, had had its own ten-pin bowling alley and they had spent a hilarious afternoon trying not to drop cannon balls, as Ned called them, on their toes.

They arrived at the Haworth campsite shortly after twelve. They checked in and hooked up to the electricity supply. As they had already stocked up on groceries, fresh milk, a loaf of wholemeal bread, some Edam for Ned, Stilton for her, and a bag of treats – chocolate fingers, crisps and a bar of Fruit and Nut – they decided to have lunch. It was warm enough to sit outside, and while they ate Ned kept his eye on a family a few pitches away. Two small girls were laughing at their father as he danced around like a gorilla with a rubber mallet in his hands; their mother looked on, amused, as she brushed grass off a large plastic groundsheet.

Clara watched Ned closely. What was going through his mind as he took in this ubiquitous family unit? Did he ever feel he was missing out in some way?

Inevitably Ned had enquired early on in his young life where his father was: the children he mixed with at nursery school seemed to have one, if not two, in their lives – there were plenty of step-fathers on the scene. Clara had been dreading this question, but had believed she would wing it when it surfaced. Ever since Ned had started to talk, Clara's mother had been on at her to devise a reasonable explanation, saying that it wouldn't be fair to Ned to be anything but honest. She had also been concerned that Ned might ask *her* the crucial question, and had needed to know what she should say.

It had crossed Clara's mind, and for no more than a nanosecond, to say that his father was dead, but the consequences of such a lie were too awful to contemplate. As were those of saying she didn't know who his father was. In the end she had told him the truth, or as near to it as she could. She had explained that sometimes adults had to make difficult decisions, and the hardest one she had had to make was to bring him up on her own because his father lived a long way away and wasn't able to be a real father to him. She had waited for him to probe deeper, but the questions didn't come. He seemed satisfied with what he had, and once more, she put his happiness down to the fact that he was blessed with wonderful grandparents and other people who truly cared for him. She didn't fool herself that she could get away so lightly for much longer, though. The older he became, the more enquiring he would grow, and in turn she would have to be more honest with him. As his mother, that was her responsibility.

As her son, it was his right.

Haworth was beautiful. Surrounded by deserted, unspoilt moors, it was easy to conjure up the brooding sense of melancholy conveyed in Emily Brontë's classic novel. Windswept moors, abandoned hope, neglect and decay, it was all here. It was a place of pilgrimage for anyone whose heart had ever been broken. The long walk up to Top Withens, reputedly the ruins of the house that had inspired Emily's *Wuthering Heights*, almost defeated Ned, and Clara had to carry him for a short while, but afterwards they rewarded themselves with tea in a pretty café in the steep main street of Haworth. Fortified by strong tea, with lots of milk in it for Ned, and floury scones, home-made raspberry jam and cream as thick as butter, they joined a guided tour of the parsonage where the Brontë family had lived. Then they dawdled through the leafy graveyard, where they played an impromptu game of hide-and-seek. Ned was easy to find: he always had a foot or an elbow sticking out from the lichen-coated headstone he was giggling behind. They had a leisurely snoop through the gift shops – it was still early in the season and the vast crowds of sightseers were yet to invade – and found some beautiful handcrafted wooden toys. Ned picked out a funny little acrobat who swung his brightly painted body when the sides of the toy were squeezed, and they added to their collection of postcards, as they did in every place they visited. Clara also bought herself a copy of *Wuthering Heights*. It was years since she had read the book, and apart from being a perfect memento of the day, it would be a nostalgic treat.

Ned went to bed early that night, worn out, and while he slept, Clara read. When she had finished the first chapter, she laid it aside and fished out the tapestry kit she had bought in Glasgow. She had never tried tapestry before, condemning it as a time-wasting occupation for those with not enough to do, but she found the repetitive motion of pushing the needle in and out of the canvas oddly relaxing. It was also addictive: the steady process of producing neat rows of orderly stitches had its own appeal for her. She studied what she had done so far, trying to make up her mind which piece of the intricate pattern to do next, and settled for the bottom right-hand corner, where a dusty-skinned Victoria plum had rolled away from the bowl of fruit that made up the majority of the design. She selected a length of wool, threaded it, and thought, as she made the first stitch, how like the plum she was: she, too, had rolled away from what had been the mainstay of her life – her career.

The decision had not been taken lightly, but it made her smile to think how dramatically different her life had become. Here she was, in a second-hand camper-van, surrounded by stunningly picturesque scenery, spending her evening sewing while her son slept. She had never felt so full of energy: the closeness she now had with Ned was truly uplifting. But who was this rejuvenated Clara Costello, who had been so happy to let go of her old life? And where did she see herself in the months ahead when it was time for Ned to embark upon his sixteen-year sentence of scholastic hard labour? Did she really want to slip back into the rat-race she had left behind and become again the frazzled woman she had allowed herself to turn into? Was there something she would rather do?

She rethreaded her needle. What *did* she want to do?

She felt confident that she could resume her career more or less where she had left it, maybe not with Phoenix, but there were plenty of other pharmaceutical companies. The all-important question, though, was: did she want to pick up where she had left off? Perhaps it was time to change direction and do something new.

Not so long ago she would have been annoyed and frustrated that she couldn't find an answer to this but now she was content to take each day as it came; it was enough to be happy with what she had right now. And because she had never been a spendthrift she had sufficient funds to tide them over for some time yet. Come the New Year she would have to get a job and start bringing in a decent salary again, but that was months away. It wasn't even June, and they had the whole of the summer stretching gloriously ahead of them. Three wonderful months of come-what-may. How lucky she was.

It was when she was lying in bed, having just turned out the light, that her thoughts slipped back to where they had been first thing that morning.

Todd.

All at once her anxiety about him returned. It was a warm night and, with several windows open, she tossed and turned for nearly an hour listening to noises from their fellow campers – a dog barking, a car door slamming, a kettle whistling. Before long, the surge of worry turned into a thumping headache and, knowing she would never get a decent night's sleep if she didn't take something, she slipped out of bed and opened the locker above the cooker. It was too high for Ned to reach and she kept in it the first-aid kit and the bottle of paracetamol. It wasn't easy to find in the semi-darkness, not with all the important documents she had stored in there: the vehicle insurance details, her cheque book and building-society pass book and a file of other essential records. She continued to rummage for the paracetamol. She pushed aside a bulging A4 envelope and her mobile phone, then found something large and bulky that she didn't recognise. Then, with a flash of guilt, she realised what it was: the tied-up bundle of Val Liberty's diaries.

She let out a smothered moan of self-reproach – how many times had she made a mental note not to forget to put them back? – and lifted the notebooks down from the locker. Despite herself, she couldn't resist the pull of Val's story-telling. She found the paracetamol, slipped back into bed, switched on the overhead light and flicked through Val's last diary. Scanning the pages for something of interest, her eyes were drawn to the final entry.

The writing was a lot less sure than it had been on previous pages. She must have known she was dying when she wrote this.

To whoever is reading this (and it will probably be Jonah, he is the only one who would be interested), all I ask is that you give my diaries to Gabriel when I am dead and ask him to read them. I know he won't sort through my things (just as he didn't with Anastasia), but I do so badly want him to know that in my own way I did love him. There was so much unsaid in our marriage – so much that needed saying – that this is perhaps the only way I will be able to communicate my feelings to a man who has been too hard on his family, but mostly too hard on himself. He wasn't able to offer his children the love and affection they needed, for the simple fact one can't give what one hasn't got. A broken heart is exactly that – a broken vessel with the love drained out of it.

I've tried to give a fair picture of life at Mermaid House, and though Gabriel might not like what I've said, I want him to know that he has to forgive everyone he thinks has let him down. He needs to forgive himself and be reconciled with the truth that all any of us can ever do is our very inadequate best.

There were tears in Clara's eyes as she closed the book. It wasn't so much the poignancy of the words that touched her but all the blank pages that followed.

She turned out the light and knew that she had no choice but to return the diaries to their owner. And, just as surely, she knew that the task had to be performed in person. There could be no cheating, no sending them anonymously in the post.

She had no idea how she was going to explain to Gabriel why she had 'borrowed' them.

42

It was just as Caspar feared: the bank had pulled the rug out from beneath him. They had turned down his request for another thirty days' grace. And with no one else to turn to, it was financial melt-down time.

He threw the letter on to the pile of bills on his desk with contempt and directed his anger at those who could have helped.

His accountant for not moving fast enough to save him from bankruptcy.

His vindictive father for being such a tight old buzzard and too stubborn to sell Mermaid House.

The bloodsucking man at the Inland Revenue for hounding him so relentlessly.

The European Commission for insisting that the special relationship between car manufacturers and dealers had to be shaken up, and that forecourt prices had to be cut.

He also blamed the hordes of cheapskate cowboys who were ruining decent businesses like his by bringing luxury cars into the country by the back door. He supposed it said a lot about the calibre of his customers who were now taking their money to these fly-by-night Johnnies with their low overheads, fast turn-around, cheaper imports and undercut prices. Never mind the after-sales problems they experienced. Never mind the fake documents with which these cars often came. Never mind that men like Caspar Liberty were forced to rob Paul to pay Peter and go to the wall in the process.

Through the glass panel of his office, which looked out on to the showroom, he watched a young man of no more than twenty-five approach a Jaguar XKR. It was late afternoon and sunlight was shining in through the plate-glass window, showing off to perfection the car's smooth, sleek lines and glossy red finish. The man slipped into the driver's seat, one hand cupping the head of the gear-lever, the other stroking the steering-wheel. With his well-cut suit, open-necked shirt, gold watch, ostentatious bracelet, deep tan and collar-length hair, he bore all the hallmarks of a vulgar young blood: in other words, a genuine punter. He was probably a professional footballer, or big in the world of popular music. God knows, there were enough of them in Manchester. What he couldn't be mistaken for was a member of the anorak crowd; pathetic time-wasters who came in to drool over something they could never afford.

Caspar waited for one of his salesmen to materialise. Minutes passed, and no one appeared. He was about to go and deal with the man himself when the telephone on his desk rang. He hesitated, caught between the two. Then he thought, What the hell? The business was sunk.

He sat at his desk with his head lowered, and let the phone ring until the caller gave up.

In the staff room at Dick High, Jonah put down the phone. He had never rung his brother at work before, but then, he had never been so worried about their father.

It was four days now since he had witnessed the unimaginable: Gabriel Liberty crying. Since then he had called at Mermaid House every day, intending to carry on where Miss Costello had left off, but his father had had other ideas. 'I'd rather you didn't meddle with my things,' he had said, taking from Jonah the roll of plastic sacks for the bin he had just emptied. 'And what, I'd like to know, has got into you all of a sudden? Why have you taken it upon yourself to keep pestering me?'

He had wanted to say, 'Because I'm worried about you,' but his courage had failed him: showing concern was tantamount to showing weakness, and that was something no Liberty was ever allowed to do.

His father's stolid manner and desire to pretend that there had been no breakdown at the kitchen table proved that he was determined the matter should never be referred to again. But Jonah knew he would never forget the night when he had helped his father upstairs and put him to bed. Gabriel had fallen asleep almost immediately his head had touched the pillow, and not wanting to leave him alone, Jonah had found himself a blanket and passed an uncomfortable night in an armchair beside the bed, imagining that the morning would bring a degree of openness between the two of them. His hope had been misplaced. The next day his father had indicated that once more the shutters were down. But his words had been at odds with his actions, for seconds later he had fled the room, locked himself in the bathroom and stayed there for nearly an hour.

Jonah was convinced that his father was depressed, that in his current state he would isolate himself further and his health would suffer. On more than one occasion he had found him standing in the library staring blankly at Anastasia's portrait. He had tried several times to get him out of the house, suggesting they go for a walk while the weather was warm and dry. But anything he put forward was thrown back at him with the same taciturn reply: 'Why can't you just leave me alone?'

Jonah had to face facts. As ever, his presence was adding to his father's discomfort. Or, more accurately, his presence was the cause of his pain. He had considered getting in touch with Dr Singh, but, again, his courage had failed him.

Yet the concern that was uppermost in Jonah's mind, and the reason why he had taken the unprecedented step of phoning Caspar at work, was that he felt their father's mental state might deteriorate to the extent that one day he would go out for a walk with one of his guns and never come back.

Though why he thought Caspar would be of any use, Jonah didn't know. He would probably offer to load the gun. But perhaps turning to his brother reflected the depth of his concern. In desperation, he even wondered if it would be worth his while to get in touch with Damson.

He sighed deeply. Why was it always he who had to sort things out? It had been the same when Val had died. Everyone had expected him to deal with the funeral arrangements. 'But you're so good at these humdrum things,' Damson had said airily, when he'd hinted that maybe she and Caspar might like to give him a hand. 'And anyway,' she'd added, 'you wouldn't want me organising a funeral. I'd feel duty-bound to turn it into a theatrical event.' Jonah hadn't doubted it. His sister's idea of a funeral would probably include a pair of black horses pulling a Victorian glass hearse, with a cortège of professional keeners trailing behind.

In the staff room, standing at the window looking down on to the playground, he saw a familiar figure striding across the tarmac: a lad wearing a Marilyn Manson T-shirt and hugely baggy jeans hanging off his hips. Talking into a mobile phone, Jase O'Dowd was pushing against the tide of shambolic gangs of jostling home-leavers, one of whom was Sharna Powell. It was early days yet, but since Jonah's visit to twenty-three Capstone Close, Sharna's attendance at school had been a hundred per cent.

Checking his watch, Jonah saw that it was four o'clock and time for his eleventh-hour revision lesson for his GCSE history set. Gathering up his briefcase, pleased that Jase had shown up, he set off for his classroom, thinking how easy it was to motivate his pupils but how impossible it was to do the same with his family.

That evening, to the sound of church bells – it was bell-ringing practice night – Jonah cooked himself supper. After he had eaten, and while it was still light, he went outside to work in the garden. He was in just the right frame of mind to deal with the ancient honeysuckle.

He hacked away at the woody growth, thinking how sad it was that the only person who could lift their father's spirits was not a member of the family but the redoubtable Miss Costello.

He stood back from what was left of the mutilated bush and decided to have a bonfire. It was almost dark now, very quiet – the bell-ringers had gone home – and there was little wind, so he bundled up the honeysuckle, took it down to the bottom of the garden, and dropped it on to the blackened remains of a previous fire. He fetched some sheets of newspaper and a box of matches from the shed. Twigs were soon snapping and crackling and tiny flames flickering, and before long, small billowing clouds puffed into the still night air. As Jonah stared into the darkness, at the outlines of the distant hills, spotted here and there with glowing lights, he found himself wishing he could track down his father's fairy godmother. He would drag her back to Deaconsbridge and make her wave her magic wand over Mermaid House once more.

As he absorbed himself in this scenario, he was forced to admit that his altruism was transparently thin. He didn't want Miss Costello back just for his father's benefit: since her departure from Mermaid House, he had thought of her frequently. He wanted to figure out what had attracted him to her. Had it been her challenging manner? Or the sharpness of her mind and the way she always seemed to be one step ahead of him? He smiled wryly. Or perhaps it had been nothing more than the pose she had struck that day in the courtyard? Was he merely the same as the next man, aroused simply by the thought of a woman's body and the potential pleasure and gratification held within?

Disconsolately, he poked the charred end of a long stick into the glowing embers of the fire. What did it matter anyway? She was never coming back.

43

Yorkshire was behind them now. They had left Haworth early that morning in a blaze of sunshine, taken the A629 to Halifax, then on to Huddersfield and Holmfirth – *Last of the Summer Wine* country – before crossing the boundary into Derbyshire. If they kept up their current speed, Clara reckoned they were less than an hour from Deaconsbridge. She had thought of ringing Mermaid House to announce their arrival, but Ned had begged her not to: he was desperate to surprise Mr Liberty.

Just as she had anticipated, Ned had been overjoyed when she had told him that they would be making a return trip to Mermaid House – though, of course, she hadn't told him the reason behind their visit. His eyes wide with excitement, he had burst out that this was what he had wished for when he'd tossed his coin into the mermaid's pool in the cavern. 'You see, Mummy,' he'd said, hopping from one small foot to the other, 'wishes do come true!' He had wanted to pack up there and then, but she had insisted that they finish visiting what they had come to see in Haworth and the surrounding area. But now, and much to Ned's delight, they would shortly be seeing Gabriel Liberty. His excitement gave him an extra bounce and she wished she had half his vitality. As she concentrated on the winding road, she was aware that a nagging headache was developing and that she felt drained.

The cause was anxiety – and guilt: she was nervous about coming clean with Gabriel over Val's diaries. She just hoped he could forgive her for what she had done. She didn't know why, but his forgiveness was important to her.

Gabriel pushed his stockinged feet into his walking boots, and after a brief stab at tying the laces with his useless fingers – they were particularly painful that day – he slipped a shotgun over the crook of his arm and shut the door after him. He crossed the courtyard and skirted round the front of the house, across the sloping lawn where the daffodils had long since gone over, and carried on towards the copse. The rhododendrons were in full flower, splashes of vermilion brilliant against the dark green of glossy leaves. He trudged on, his boots sinking into the soft grass. Sheep scattered at his approach, bleating mournfully, and above him, the sun shone on the back of his neck, making him regret putting on the waxed jacket.

His thoughts, never far from his younger son these days, turned to Jonah and how badly he had treated him – and was continuing to treat him. But it was too late to make amends for the damage he had wreaked. What good would it do to tell Jonah that he was sorry? It wouldn't change anything, not the words, the gestures, the neglect, or the downright cruel way he had excluded and blamed the boy.

If only he had been a better man – a better father – he would have realised that his younger son had never deserved such rough punishment. It hadn't been Jonah who had killed Anastasia: fate had done that. But for all these years, ever since Gabriel had come home in the middle of the night and had been told that his wife was dead, he had needed to lay the blame on someone. And he had done it that night when the young nurse had handed Jonah to him. He had turned his back on her and his baby son, and walked out of the room, out of the house. In the darkness, he had stumbled down to the copse and stayed there until dawn had bruised the sky, tearing it apart with harsh streaks of sunlight. Eventually he went back to the house, but didn't look at that newborn baby, not until after the funeral, and only then for a few seconds. How could he, when he saw him as the cause of his beloved wife's death? It was years before he was able to lay eyes on the child without wishing he had died instead of Anastasia.

For years, tolerance was the best he could manage. A thin veneer of tolerance that was often stripped back to reveal his bitterness, and to let his child know what it was to suffer. Oh, how callous he had been.

And what had woken him to the truth?

It was the shock of recognising Anastasia's face so clearly in Jonah's. Seeing the two of them so inextricably bound together had brought him up short, had made him, for the first time ever, see Jonah for what he really was: his mother's son. He was not, as Gabriel had made him out to be, a malevolent stranger who had walked into his life and wrecked it.

He was the son of the woman Gabriel had never stopped loving.

Now, whenever he looked at his son, he saw Anastasia staring back at him. She was in Jonah's eyes, the turn of his head, the shape of his mouth. The pain of his guilt went so deep inside him that sometimes Gabriel had to sit down and wait for it to pass. But the one thing he couldn't do was face Jonah and confide in him. He was too ashamed. Ashamed to admit that for all this time he had harboured such a monumental and misplaced grudge. That was why he continued to rebuff Jonah. Having him around only added to his grief. Because that was what it felt like. Since that appalling night when he had broken down, it was as if he was being forced to grieve for his darling Anastasia all over again.

Plunged further into misery, he pressed on down to the copse where, in the dense shade of the trees that were in full leaf now, a blanket of bluebells shimmered, their colour brightening the darkness. Though not the darkness by which he felt so consumed. That would never lift. That was *his* punishment. It was no more than he deserved. But he'd had enough of the burden, the strain of knowing that in this life he would never be released from the shame and the guilt. It was too much for him. He wanted to be with Anastasia. He needed her forgiveness for what he had done.

The weight of the gun pressed heavily on his arm. He shifted it to a more comfortable position and entered the wood, feeling at once the welcome cool shade offered by the trees. He paused, making up his mind where he wanted to be. As to the rest, he had thought it all out, had prepared himself so that he could at least get this right.

The triumphant entrance Ned had hoped to make was spoiled by Gabriel not answering the door.

'Shall we go inside and find him?' Ned asked, assuming that the door would be unlocked. He pressed his forehead to the door, peered in through the letterbox.

Clara tried the handle and stepped inside, Ned at her heels. 'But we'll only go as far as the kitchen,' she said. 'We ought not to intrude any further.'

She was surprised to see that her hard work had not been in vain. While the kitchen had gathered a few extraneous piles of paperwork – mostly bills and bank statements – the place was still reasonably clean and orderly. She wondered if Gabriel had found himself a cleaner. Leaving Ned to call him, she noticed the postcards lined up along the window-sill. Touched that he had kept them, she went over to look at them, recalling exactly when and where each had been written.

Still not getting any response to his eager cries, Ned joined her at the sink. 'Do you think he's gone for a walk?' he asked, his elation fizzling into disappointment.

'I think that's precisely what he's done. Shall we see if we can find him?' She had seen the battered old Land Rover in the courtyard, so it was a safe bet that he hadn't gone far. Unless, of course, Jonah had given him a lift somewhere.

They shut the back door and set off towards the copse, which, according to Ned, was where Gabriel liked to go. 'He makes sure the badgers are all right,' he informed Clara.

It was a truly glorious day. The sun shone brightly in a perfect canopy of blue, and the air smelt sweet from the grass beneath their feet. In the distance, the hills were golden with flowering gorse bushes. Nearing the copse, Clara was overcome by the most beautiful sight: bluebells, hundreds of them. She had never seen so many in one spot before. It was breathtaking: a magical infusion of colour. She stood for a moment to take it in. It was so tranquil here. So perfect.

High up in one of the trees, a wood pigeon broke the calm, clattering its wings as it flew out of the copse. It came towards them, and ahead of her,

Ned came to a stop. He tilted his head so far back to watch the bird, she thought he might fall over. She caught up with him, and together they passed from the sunny brightness into the dappled, shadowy gloom. The fresh meadow-sweet fragrance of crushed grass was replaced by the earthy smell of moss, rotting bark and mouldy damp leaves.

'He usually goes this way,' Ned said knowledgeably, pointing towards a leafy path that twisted through the thicket of trees.

They had only taken a few steps into the cool woodland when Clara stood still. She craned her neck. Ned looked up at her. 'What?'

'I thought I heard something.' She smiled. 'It was probably one of Mr Liberty's badgers.'

But within seconds, they had stopped again, and this time she knew she wasn't imagining it. Someone else was in the copse. Remembering that day down by the river when they had first arrived in Deaconsbridge, she held Ned's hand firmly. The sound grew louder and she wasn't sure what it was she could hear. It was a groaning of such guttural rawness it was animal-like. Bravely she carried on, until at last they came to a small clearing and she saw the source of the noise.

It was Gabriel Liberty. He was on his knees, crumpled over the trunk of a fallen beech tree, and beneath his waxed jacket, he was shaking violently.

'Stay here, Ned,' she commanded. Confusion written all over his anxious face, he did as she said, and she moved in closer to Gabriel, who seemed to have no idea that they were there. She reached down to him, placed a hand lightly on his shoulder. He didn't react and the racking groans and rasping breath continued. 'Mr Liberty,' she said, 'it's me, Clara – Miss Costello. Are you hurt?'

He stiffened and turned towards her, his face contorted with abject misery. Disbelieving eyes, brimming with tears, focused on her. It was then that she saw the shotgun cradled in his arms. Her instinct was to step back, to get as much distance as possible between herself and the gun, but instead she prised it out of his shaking hands, and placed it on the other side of the tree-trunk. Then she got down on her knees on the soft cushion of leaves and took him in her arms. She held him tightly, hushed him with soothing words, as if he were Ned, until finally, he gave one last, shuddering sob, slumped against her and gradually became still.

It took all of her strength to pull him on to his feet and sit him on the damp, moss-covered tree trunk. When she had settled him and found a grubby old handkerchief in one of his jacket pockets, she beckoned Ned over.

'Mr Liberty isn't very well, Ned,' she said matter-of-factly. 'Come and sit down and help me make him feel better.'

With one of them sitting on either side of him, the poor man's first coherent words were 'I – I can't bear you to see me like this.'

She took the handkerchief from him and dabbed at his eyes. 'And I can't bear to think of you suffering like this all alone. What's been going on?'

He dropped his chin to his chest. 'It's – it's Jonah . . .'

'Jonah? What's happened to him?' Alarmed, Clara thought of the last time she had seen Jonah. How his expression had transformed when he had dropped his guard. She thought too of all she now knew about him from reading Val's diaries. 'Has . . . has there been an accident?'

Gabriel looked at her, confused. 'No,' he murmured, 'it's me. It's what I've done to him. Terrible things. I'm – I'm so dreadfully ashamed. And there's no going back. I know that.' His voice cracked and she felt a tremor run through him. She took his hands in hers and squeezed them firmly.

'There might not be a pedal for going backwards,' she said, 'but there's always one for going forwards. Do you think with my help you could make it up to the house?'

He raised his red-rimmed eyes to hers. 'Miss Costello, I honestly believe that with your help, I could do almost anything.'

She kissed his stubbly cheek, then helped him to his feet. 'Well, before we take on the world, let's start with the short walk home, shall we?'

44

In Clara's opinion, the best place for Gabriel was bed, but he refused point-blank to do as she said. Just as he had vehemently rejected her suggestion that she ought to ring Jonah or Dr Singh. So she removed his cumbersome jacket, sat him in the chair next to the Aga and sent Ned upstairs to fetch a blanket – the poor man was in shock and shivering despite the warmth of the day.

While Ned was out of the room, Clara knelt in front of him. She rubbed his hands. 'We can't talk now,' she said, 'not really talk, but later tonight, when Ned's asleep, I want you to tell me what's been going on here. But for now, all I can do is dose you with hot, sweet tea and some chocolate cake we brought for you from Haworth.'

He turned his bloodshot eyes on her. 'Dear girl, why are you so good to me? I don't deserve such kindness.'

'Ulterior motive, I'm still hoping to seduce you and get that ring on my finger.'

He laid a hand over hers. 'What made you come back so soon? Did you forget something?'

'In a manner of speaking,' she hedged, 'but we'll talk about that later too.'

Puffing from his exertion, Ned burst into the kitchen. 'Will this do?'

Clara took the heavy, feather-leaking eiderdown from him with a smile. 'Perfect, Ned. Here, help me to wrap up Mr Liberty. We want him as snug as a bug in a rug.'

They sat with their mugs of tea and plates of cake. Clara let Ned do all the talking: sitting on Gabriel's lap, with cake crumbs falling from his fingers as he waved his arms in the air, he told him all about their travels: of the castles they had seen, the mountains, the lakes, and the people they had met. 'We even stayed on a farm,' he said proudly, 'where I learned to milk a goat. And I fed the chickens. And I rode a pony too. I had to wear a hat that kept slipping over my eyes.' Drawing breath, he paused before saying, 'But nowhere was as nice as this. We didn't meet anyone as nice as you, Mr Liberty.'

'I'm delighted to hear it.'

Clara topped up Gabriel's mug with more tea, relieved to hear a glimmer of his old spirit returning.

When the time came for Ned to go to bed, Gabriel said he wanted them to be proper guests and stay the night inside Mermaid House. Apart from his bedroom, Val's old room was the only one Clara had cleaned and sorted, and though she had irrational reservations about using it, she made up the double bed to share with Ned.

When she bent to kiss Ned goodnight, he hooked his hands round her neck and pulled her closer. 'I'm glad we came back,' he said.

'I'm glad too.'

Then, more seriously, he said, 'Is Mr Liberty better now?'

She kissed him and unhooked his hands. 'He'll be fine. He just needs a little tender loving care. He's like a flower that someone has forgotten to water. We need to water him and make him nice and strong again.'

He considered this. 'How long will that take?'

'I don't know. We'll have to see.'

'Two days? Three days?'

She kissed him again, amused that he was subtly negotiating with her. 'Like I say, we'll have to wait and see.' He seemed happy enough with her reply and didn't push her any further. Instead, he yawned; he suddenly looked sleepy. 'Come on,' she said, 'it's late and you need to get some rest or you'll be the one in need of watering. Enjoy your night's sleep in a proper bed. And no kicking me when I join you later.'

He yawned again, turned on to his side, and reached under the pillow for Mermy. 'I promise,' he said drowsily.

Turning out the light, Clara felt the day catching up with her. More tired than she had felt in a long while, she took the stairs slowly, knowing it would be several hours before she would lay her aching head on a pillow. It was now time to get to the bottom of Gabriel's problems. Having read Val's diaries, she had a fair idea that raging guilt would be mostly to blame. Chances were it had finally caught up with him. The question was, why?

She thought of that moment when, just before entering the copse, she had paused to admire the bluebells. She remembered thinking then that she was in the right place at the right time. She wasn't one of those cranky types who believed in synchronistic events shaping collective destinies – making sense of coincidence with the benefit of hindsight was child's play – but there was no avoiding the extraordinary timing of her arrival here today.

Call it luck, call it predetermination, call it what you will, but it was a good thing that someone had been there for Gabriel Liberty when he most needed a friend. Thank goodness for Val's diaries! Thinking of the diaries, Clara decided that it would be better to hang on to them until Gabriel was feeling a lot stronger. In his present state they might upset him too much.

He was waiting for her in the kitchen. He had moved from his chair by the Aga and was clumsily stacking their supper things in the dishwasher. Despite his protests, she shooed him back to the chair. 'Leave that to me.'

'I'm not an invalid,' he argued, a little more of his old spirit shining through the clouds of his melancholy. But he relented anyway.

She tidied up, then poured two glasses of whisky, wondering who needed it more. She felt unaccountably lethargic and headachey, and wondered if she had a cold coming. When they were settled at either side of the Aga, she said, 'So what drove you to think about killing yourself?'

Gabriel flinched. He had known that this straight-talking woman would not couch her questions in polite euphemisms, had known, too, that her candid approach was what he needed and that it would bring him equal measures of pain and relief. But even so, hearing her put into such plain words what he had tried to do filled him with self-loathing. How desperate he had been. And how typically self-centred. Once again, he had put himself first, prepared to leave his family to clear up the mess he had made of his life ... and his death. He was nothing but a coward.

He took a gulp of his drink. 'Failure,' he said, at last. 'I've been a lousy father and it's only just dawned on me the harm I've done.'

She looked at him over the rim of her glass. 'Who do you think you've failed the most?'

'The lot of them. But especially Jonah. I've ... I've also failed Anastasia.'

'Not Val?'

He kept his eyes lowered. 'Her too. I never gave her the credit she deserved. She was a good wife and, against all the odds, a good mother.'

A silence settled on the room. Not rushing to fill the pause, Gabriel took a long sip of his drink.

'Tell me about Anastasia,' Clara said softly. 'She was the true love of your life, wasn't she?'

He took another swig of his whisky. 'That phrase doesn't even come close.'

'How did you meet?'

'At a wedding. And let me tell you, she outshone the bride by a long stretch. She was the most beautiful girl present – the most beautiful I had ever seen.' He cleared his throat, shifted in his seat. 'I was no spring chicken, no innocent, but she dazzled me from the moment she spoke. She was so compassionate, so genuinely warm-hearted. So full of joy. She had this wonderful ability to make me feel special. Corny I know, but the truth. She had that same effect on me even when we were married. We could be at a party, separated by a roomful of tedious people whom I had no desire to talk to, and our eyes would meet, and it would be as if we were alone.'

'You're lucky to have experienced that depth of love. Few people do.'

'It didn't feel lucky to have so much one minute, then have it snatched away the next.' His tone was bitter. 'Sorry, back to wallowing in self-pity again.'

She waved aside his apology. 'Did you ever allow yourself to grieve for Anastasia when she died? And I don't just mean going through the motions of accepting well-meant platitudes and attending a funeral. I mean, did you let yourself howl? Did you give in to the pain and let it render you helpless? Did you put yourself beyond caring what anyone thought of you?'

Fiddling with his glass, he said, 'You know the answer to that, or you wouldn't be asking.'

'But today you did put yourself beyond caring, didn't you? Today you did openly grieve for her, and for everything that has happened since.'

He nodded. 'And I know what you're going to ask me next. You want to know what precipitated all this ghastly baring of the soul and the realisation that I've let Anastasia down, quite apart from what I've done to Jonah—'

She raised a hand to interrupt him. 'Forgive me for splitting hairs, but you've known that all along. It's why you've suddenly acknowledged it that needs explaining.'

Swirling the last of his drink round, then downing it in one, he said, 'I see, as ever, that you have your gloves off and are sparing me nothing.'

'Business as usual. So what was the catalyst?'

'You, my dear.'

'*Me?* But how? Why?'

Until that moment Gabriel hadn't known the answer to that question, which he had asked himself earlier that day. But now he knew with certainty just how important a role this young woman and her son had played in opening his eyes. 'You and Ned made me feel better about life,' he said simply. 'You made me realise what I'd been . . . what I'd been missing out on.' He swallowed, suddenly frightened that his emotions were in danger of sliding out of control again. He was being so honest it hurt. As if understanding, she reached for the bottle of Glenmorangie on the table and refilled his glass. When she had sat down again, he said, 'In a nutshell, you cared.'

Oh, there was so much more he could say, so many truths he now understood. How she had never judged him, never looked at him with eyes that feared or despised him. How she had never hated him because he had neglected his family. How she had amused him with her spirited put-downs. How she had charmed him by not treating him as a decrepit old man. He could have said all this, if only he trusted himself to get the words out without looking and sounding foolishly sentimental.

As ever, she said just the right thing. 'I might have known you'd try and lay the blame on me.'

He managed a small smile. 'How do you think it makes me feel, knowing that in our politically correct society, which as you know I abhor, our roles have been reversed and I've been cast as Sleeping Beauty while you've taken on the role as the Prince who's awakened me with a kiss.'

She laughed. 'Perhaps Beauty and the Beast would be a more comfortable analogy for you. And, in case you're wondering, you're the Beast. So how did you get from seeing life as a more worthwhile proposition to viewing Jonah differently?'

'After you and Ned had left I realised how lonely I was.'

'And you shared this with Jonah?'

'No. Oh, I wanted to, but have you any idea how hard it is to admit that you're lonely?'

'You've just done it with me.'

'That's because you're ... you're different. You're a girl of unique charm and sensibility.'

She raised her glass to him. 'Still up to speed with the schmaltz, I see. But back to Jonah. What changed between the two of you?'

'I ... I stopped blaming him for his mother's death.' Keeping his voice as steady as he could, he explained about the night he had broken down in front of Jonah, how a connection had been made between them, but which he had found impossible to acknowledge or discuss. 'And it was all because I suddenly saw the likeness between Jonah and his mother.'

'And you'd never seen it before?'

'It sounds absurd, doesn't it? But no. Not consciously. What the hell's been going on inside my brain all these years is anybody's guess.' With a deep sigh of regret, he added, 'What does any of it matter? Jonah will never forgive me for what I've done.' He stared at her miserably.

She met his gaze with a shake of her head. 'Be warned, I'm about to split hairs again. You know jolly well, just as I do, that Jonah is one of the most compassionate people alive, and that he'll forgive you at the drop of a hat. What you're scared of is how that will make you feel. That all this time his love and forgiveness were there for the asking, but you were such a heel you chose to ignore it.'

'You don't think it's too late for reparation, then?'

She looked at him sternly. 'No, I don't. And, what's more, the sooner you do it, the better. Because then you'll realise that Jonah was one of the many gifts Anastasia left you. Perhaps the best gift of all.'

'But how will he react when I tell him that all these years I blamed him for her death?'

'You don't think he's always known that? Come on, it's time to be brave. Jonah's a big boy, he can take whatever revelations you throw at him.'

He took a moment to absorb this idea. To let faint hope take root. Finally he said, 'And what about Damson and Caspar? What do I say to them?'

She rubbed her eyes and yawned. 'If you don't mind, I'd rather leave those two until tomorrow. For now I need to go to bed. I'm shattered.'

'Yes, of course. You must be tired after your long drive.'

They both rose to their feet. After they had locked up and turned out the lights, Clara slipped her arm through his. They climbed the stairs together. She said, 'Would you ever consider seeking professional help? I mean, someone qualified to discuss what you've ... Well, it was a close call today, and if I hadn't—'

He squeezed her arm. 'You're professional enough for me, my dear. And don't worry, I've learned my lesson.'

'Which is?'

'That while one is caught in the throes of a low and unhappy mood, it's not the ideal time to distinguish a right course of action.'

When they reached the top of the stairs, Clara said, 'I might not be as old as you, or have gone through as much, but my guess is there's no magic cure or easy way to cope with grief or guilt. You have to plough headlong through it, take whatever it chucks at you, good or bad.'

'You sound as if you're talking from experience.'

'This might come as a shock to you, but you don't have a monopoly on self-reproach. Most of us scourge ourselves from time to time with a little bit of soul-searching.'

'Even you?'

'Oh, yes. Even me.'

He walked her to Val's old room, and as she pushed open the door, causing a shaft of soft light to spill from the landing across the carpet to the bed where the cause of her own soul-searching slept, she suddenly felt emotional and overwrought. She was tired, she told herself firmly. Nothing that a good night's sleep wouldn't cure.

But she slept fitfully, tossing and turning in the large creaking bed, one minute hot, the next freezing cold, all the while crashing from one bizarre dream sequence to another. Next to her, Ned slept on, blissfully unaware of her discomfort. By the time daylight filtered through the gap in the curtains, she had managed to chase away the nightmares and fallen into a deep, more restful sleep.

She woke to find the other side of the bed empty and her head thumping. She was drenched in sweat but icy cold. Her eyes were sore, her throat felt dry, raw and lumpy, and her chest was as tight as a drum. She had only experienced full-blown flu once, but she suspected she was in for a second taste of it. Determined to prove herself wrong, that it was only a cold, she launched herself out of bed. A hot shower was all she needed. That, a cup of tea and a couple of paracetamol. She was half-way across the room when the door opened and Ned came in. He was dressed in the clothes he'd worn yesterday, and a few paces behind him was Gabriel with a breakfast tray. He took one look at her and said, 'Good Lord, what've you been up to? You look dreadful.'

'I feel dreadful,' she croaked.

She was immediately chivvied back into bed. Pillows were shaken and plumped, and the duvet straightened while Ned opened the curtains to brighten the room. Gabriel fetched some paracetamol from the bathroom and she washed them down with the mug of hot strong tea. She couldn't face the toast and marmalade he had so kindly made for her, and within minutes her head and eyelids were drooping and she was faintly aware of a door shutting quietly. Sleep sucked her into a nightmarish maze of hunting for Ned, but never finding him; of driving Winnie up and down a network of narrow lanes and hills that always brought her to where she had started.

She dreamed she was back at work, that she and the boys were conversing in German, even though they were working for French-speaking gnomes who sat crosslegged on their desks with little fishing-rods and on the stroke of each hour burst into Rod Stewart's old song, 'Do You Think I'm Sexy?'

When she surfaced again she needed to go to the loo. Shivering, and squinting against the brightness, she focused on her watch. Heavens! It was four o'clock!

Rallying her aching body, she made her way to the bathroom. When she had traversed the landing – which felt as unsteady as the deck of a ship on the high seas – and had locked the door after her, she had the second shock of her day. Damn! Her period had started. She groaned, recalling that she didn't have any of those wonder items tucked away in Winnie that would enable her to swim, roller-skate and skydive to her heart's desire – she had used them all up during last month's extravaganza of sporting events. She groaned again. There was nothing else for it: she would have to rouse herself and drive into Deaconsbridge. She would need to buy super-strength painkillers too. Something lethal enough to stun a charging rhinoceros. Otherwise she'd be in for several days of rolling around on the floor in agony with a hot-water bottle strapped to her stomach. With chattering teeth, and her head feeling like pulsating cotton wool, she unlocked the door, pulled it open, then jumped back, startled. Looking for all the world like a welcoming committee, Ned and Gabriel were waiting for her.

'We heard a noise and came to check on you,' Gabriel said, making a show of looking anywhere but at the rumpled state of her *déshabille*. 'No need to ask how you're feeling. You look ready to drop. Back to bed with you.'

She wrapped her arms around her shivering body. 'Er . . . actually I need to go into Deaconsbridge.'

'Yes, my dear, and I need to marry Lucrezia Borgia. But before I send out the wedding invitations, you must go back to bed.'

'No, really. You don't understand, I *have* to go shopping.' But even as she was speaking, she was being taken by the arm and steered towards the bedroom. Too weak to disentangle herself from the firm hands that were guiding her, she was in bed before she knew it. Sitting next to her, his legs stretched out alongside hers, Ned said, 'Mummy, are you very sick?'

She forced her dry lips into a smile. 'Just a little. But I'll be fine. Honestly.'

He dipped his head towards her shoulder so that she could put an arm around him. 'I told Mr Liberty about us having to water him to make him big and strong again, and he said it was his turn to water you now.'

Right on cue, Gabriel passed her the mug of tea he had brought up. She took it gratefully, then remembered about her need to go shopping. She knew, though, that in her current state, driving would be a monumental challenge, as well as putting others on the road at risk. Yet the thought of asking Gabriel to buy her such personal items seemed far more daunting.

Down in the kitchen, while Ned organised the draughts board for another game, Gabriel cringed at what he had been asked to do. Though he had been married twice and had raised a daughter, 'intimate womanly matters' had been an accepted no-go area of secrecy and mystery. Nothing had ever been divulged to him, and he had certainly never felt the urge to probe. Now, though, he was expected to walk bold as brass into the chemist in town and hunt through the shelves for ... for ...

He ran his hand through his hair and shuddered. He couldn't bring himself to say the words, not even inside his head. Worse still, he had no idea what the wretched things looked like.

And yet he had to do it. Miss Costello – Clara who had shown him such kindness – was upstairs in bed, relying on him. This was no time to be squeamish and embarrassed. He tried to remember the last time he had been into the chemist. It was when he'd burnt his arm and had needed antibiotics. He saw himself in the shop, waiting for the prescription to be made up. Closing his eyes, he tried to recall where everything was kept. Tissues. Toilet rolls. Shampoo. Nappies. Combs. Brushes. Makeup. Camera films. Plastic rainhoods. Nail-clippers. Pumice stones. Sponges. Sponge bags. Toothpaste. Throat lozenges. Vitamin tablets. Witch hazel. Laxatives.

Oh, it was hopeless! He could practically do a roll-call of everything in the damned shop and still not locate the crucial items Clara required.

Hearing his name called, he opened his eyes and turned round. 'What's that you're saying, Ned?'

'The telephone's ringing, Mr Liberty, can't you hear it?'

He looked about him, confused – his brain was still in the chemist's searching the shelves for the elusive items. 'Oh, so it is.' He crossed the kitchen, went out into the hall to where the phone was ringing. He picked up the receiver, glad of the diversion.

'Hello, Dad, it's me, Jonah. I'm just nipping to the supermarket and I wondered if you needed anything. I noticed you were getting low on cereal the last time I was there. Anything in particular you fancy?'

Thank God for Jonah, thought Gabriel, five minutes later, when he had explained that the Costellos were staying with him again and he had offloaded – after a few false starts – the task that had been thrust upon him.

45

Jonah was still smiling to himself as he worked his way methodically round the supermarket, which was busy with early evening shoppers.

Weaving a path through the stop-start traffic of trolleys, he didn't know what amused him more: his father's excruciating embarrassment as he mumbled into the phone, trying to avoid the unmentionable T and ST words, or the fact that Miss Costello was back, albeit under the weather with flu and 'female malaise'.

Arriving at Mermaid House, and parking alongside the Costello camper-van, he thought of how, only the other night, he had wished for its owner to return to Deaconsbridge so that she could wave her magic wand over his father. Well, amazingly, the first part of that wish had come true. Now it was a matter of getting her back on her feet so that she could fulfil the rest. As to any pleasurable hopes he might have secretly harboured for himself, time would tell on that score.

He opened the boot of his car and lifted out two carrier bags. One contained everyday bits and bobs for his father, and the other everything necessary to get the patient on the road to recovery.

His father met him at the door. He looked anxious. 'Did you get everything?'

'Everything,' Jonah reassured him, and stepped into the kitchen. 'Hi, Ned. Nice to see you again. How're you doing? Hope you're not going to come down with flu. You ought to be careful too, Dad.'

Ned got down from the chair by the Aga where he had been reading a book and came over. 'Have you brought some medicine to make Mummy better?'

'That's right, lots of medicine. We'll soon have her well enough to chase you round the garden.' He passed one of the bags to Gabriel. 'Do you want to take it up?'

His father's face coloured. 'Er . . . no, I was just about to start cooking some supper. You do it.'

'Okay, but why don't you hang fire on the cooking and let me do that for you?'

He realised when he was climbing the stairs that he hadn't asked his father which bedroom had been turned into a sick room. But the sound of coughing directed him towards Val's old room. He knocked on the partially open door. A croaky voice answered, 'It's okay, I'm as decent as I'll ever be, you can come in. Oh, it's you.'

'You sound disappointed.'

She blew her nose. 'I haven't the strength to be disappointed. You can come closer, if you want. I promise not to breathe over you. What have you got there?'

He handed her the plastic bag, hovered awkwardly at her side, then sat in the chair next to the bed. At once he felt history repeating itself: how many times had he sat here in this chair chatting to Val when she was ill? 'I was going shopping anyway and Dad enlisted my help.'

Despite her discomfort, she smiled knowingly. He could see now just how ill she was. Her complexion was flushed, and beneath her eyes, puffy dark arcs bruised the skin. Her breathing was shallow and echoed with a trace of a wheeze that made him want to clear his throat. 'Your poor father,' she said hoarsely, 'I've never seen anyone dissolve into such a heap of toe-curling embarrassment.'

Jonah smiled too. 'Not his scene, I'm afraid. Womanly matters were always taboo in this household. He would much rather you were suffering from something less indelicate, something dignified with backbone. Bubonic plague, for instance.' Lowering his eyes to the plastic bag, he said, 'I've tried to cover every eventuality, but if I've forgotten something or got the wrong thing, just say, and I'll make another trip. The supermarket stays open until eight tonight.'

She rummaged through the bag. He could see the relief in her face. 'Good heavens,' she said hoarsely, 'I'm looking at a small chemist's shop. You're a real life-saver, Master Liberty. You've thought of everything. Super-strength painkillers and a selection of feminine hygiene to suit every occasion. I can even go swimming now.' She coughed, then reached for a tissue and blew her nose. 'That's if the mood takes me, of course. Mind if I make a timely exit?'

He rose quickly to his feet. 'Shall I bring up a drink so you can take the painkillers?'

'Tea would be great. Though don't make it as strong as your father does. With the amount I'm getting through, I don't want to risk sprouting chest hairs.'

She was back in bed when he knocked on the door again. He noticed she had brushed her hair and sprayed on something pleasant. She took the mug from him and said, 'Maybe this is the moment to say that you can call me Clara, seeing as we've been so intimately thrown together.'

'I'll call you Clara if you stop calling me Master Liberty.'

'Agreed. So – and given your stunted upbringing at the hands of a father like yours – where did you pick up such a wonderful understanding of female needs? How come you're not so bashful?'

'No big deal. My last girlfriend suffered badly every month. She found yoga helped. Shall I pop out the pills for you?'

She nodded, then settled back into the pillows and sipped her tea. Suddenly she looked doubly tired, as though just talking to him was taking it out of her. 'You're too much, Jonah, you really are.' She sighed. 'Emily was a fool to let a saint in human form slip through her fingers.'

He put the tablets into her outstretched hand. 'How did you know her name was Emily?'

Her eyes wavered away from his, looked out of the window at the distant crest of Kinder Scout bathed in the soft early evening sunshine. 'Your father must have told me,' she said. 'How else would I have known?'

It seemed unlikely that his father would have discussed something as personal as his younger son's love-life, but Jonah let it go. She started to cough again, her shoulders jerking violently. He took the mug from her and put it on the bedside table next to the box of tissues. From the carrier bag that was now at the end of the bed he pulled out a bottle of cough mixture. He read the instructions on the box. 'You're not pregnant or asthmatic, are you?'

'Not asthmatic, and certainly not pregnant. Not unless this is a contagious bout of immaculate conception I'm suffering from.'

He unscrewed the metal top of the bottle, measured the specified dose into the plastic cap provided, and gave it to her. 'Every four hours, it says.' He checked his watch. 'So the next dose will be at eleven.'

She gave him a limp salute. 'Yes, Doctor.'

'I'm on cooking duty next. Any special requests?'

She shook her head weakly. 'No, I'm not hungry.'

'Not even a boiled egg? Everyone likes a boiled egg when they're not well.' Smiling, he added, 'Perhaps I could rustle up a soldier or two.'

'Sorry, but uniforms have never done it for me.'

He emptied some of the contents of the bag on to the dressing-table behind him, lining up the packets of Lemsip, throat lozenges, vitamin supplements, and the extra soft tissues. He caught her eye in the mirror as she watched what he was doing. Thinking that she had probably had enough of his company, he folded the bag, and said, 'Well, I'll leave you to it then. Shout if you change your mind about something to eat. And don't worry about Ned. Dad and I will take good care of him.'

He was across the room and standing by the door when she said, 'Thank you for the tea, Jonah, and . . .'

'And?'

'And for everything else. Give yourself a gold star and go straight to the top of the class.'

'I guess it's the least I can do, given the amount you did here for Dad.'

A burst of coughing rattled her chest and when she had recovered, she said, in a voice laden with sleep, 'You need to talk to him, Jonah. There's something he wants to say to you, something he *needs* to say. Help him to seize the moment. He's not brave enough to do it on his own.'

Puzzled, Jonah went downstairs. He could hear the animated sound of his father's voice in the kitchen. He stood in the doorway, taking in the scene. By the Aga, sitting on Gabriel's lap, Ned was enthralled with the story that was being read to him with relish and enthusiasm.

How perfect they looked together. It seemed a shame to disturb them.

The vote was carried by a unanimous show of hands that Jonah should cook cheese-and-ham omelettes and Ned's favourite vegetable, sweetcorn. He was a happy and remarkably trusting little boy, who appeared to take everything in his stride – a trait he had probably inherited from his mother, thought Jonah. Though moderately concerned that she should soon be well, he wasn't put out by her absence. It was only when he started to yawn and Gabriel announced that it was his bedtime and that he ought not to share a bed with his mother that night that he became anxious. 'But where will I sleep? In Winnie on my own? What if I have a bad dream?'

Jonah stepped in quickly. 'You could have my old room if you like. It's next door to your mother's. Let's go and have a look at it, shall we?'

It was a dreary sight in the dim light cast by the low-wattage bulb hanging from the ceiling rose. There were several boxes on the double bed, but when these had been removed and the bed made up with a clean sheet and Ned's own pillow and stripy blue and white duvet, he seemed happy enough with the arrangements. Especially when he found a collection of Jonah's long-forgotten books in a chest at the foot of the bed. There were ancient *Rupert Bear* books that Val had given him at Christmas, as well as an old *Blue Peter* annual. Despite their age, they were in pristine condition, but Jonah had always been careful with his things.

'Will you check my teeth for me?' Ned said to Jonah, when he had changed into his pyjamas and stood poised with his toothbrush in the bathroom, his chin level with the basin. 'Mummy always does that. I have to do them first, then she brushes them again to make sure I've done them properly.'

This duty carried out, Ned then asked if he could see if his mother was awake to give him a goodnight kiss.

'Okay, but be sure to be very quiet, just in case she's asleep.' Jonah waited for him outside the door, not wanting to intrude. Seconds later, Ned reappeared, disappointed.

'She is asleep. But I climbed up on to the bed anyway and gave her a kiss.'

As he walked Ned to his bedroom, Jonah was surprised when the youngster slipped a small hand into his and said, 'Will you tell me a bedtime story, please? A made-up one? I like those. They're fun.' A winning toothy smile appeared on his face.

He was hard to resist, so after Ned had settled himself beneath the duvet, Jonah sat on the edge of the bed and started his tale. He soon realised that he was cheating and was giving Ned a jumbled-up version of *The Selfish Giant*. Deciding that there were too many deaths in it for a four-year-old, he improvised and gave the tale a different spin so that everyone lived happily ever after.

His eyes glazed with sleep, Ned said, 'Why didn't the giant like the children who came to play in his garden?'

'Because he thought they were noisy and might spoil his garden.'

'But they didn't, did they? They made it nice for him. The flowers grew and the sun shone.'

'And he was jolly lucky to realise that before it was too late,' said a gruff voice at the door. Ned lifted his head from the pillow and Jonah turned round. How long had his father been standing there? He came into the room. 'Do I get a goodnight kiss from my favourite house guest, then?'

Jonah patted Ned's shoulder affectionately. 'I'll leave you to it. Goodnight.'

'Will you be here tomorrow?'

'I'm at school during the day, but maybe I'll pop in and see you in the evening. Sleep well.'

While he waited for his father to join him in the kitchen, Jonah decided to take Clara at her word. *Help him to seize the moment.* Well, perhaps that moment had come.

But what if the consequences were as devastating as the last time he had tried to talk to his father?

Driving home later that night, Jonah brought his car to a sudden stop. For a long moment he sat and stared at his hands as they gripped the steering wheel in front of him. Then, in a swift, decisive movement, he switched off the engine and got out of the car. Breathing hard, he went and leaned against the drystone wall alongside which he had parked. He gazed across the darkened landscape, back towards Mermaid House. He saw that his hands were shaking. It was shock.

What had just passed between him and his father had gone well beyond anything he had thought might come of a heart-to-heart chat. To hear his father asking him for his forgiveness had been unbearably painful. It had been the culmination of a lifetime of confused guilt and regret. A lifetime of wondering how things might have been for his father, and for his brother and sister, if he had never been born ... if their mother had lived.

Forgive me, Jonah. Please.

He had never thought to hear those words. Never imagined such a moment when his father would lay a hand on his shoulder and say that he was sorry. Almost too choked to speak, he had mumbled something about it being okay, that there was nothing to forgive. That it was all in the past.

'It'll never be in the past,' his father had said, 'not until I know you forgive me.'

They were standing in the library, symbolically beneath the portrait that Jonah had made countless wishes upon as a child: *Make my father happy . . . Make him notice me . . . Make Caspar and Damson like me.* Caspar had once caught him staring up at the painting and had taunted him cruelly. 'You killed her, you know that, don't you? If it hadn't been for you, she'd still be alive.'

'Please, Jonah,' his father had said, 'I know I've done everything wrong, but I want to change all that now. It's not too late, is it?'

A shake of the head was as much as he could manage, and with an unsteady hand, he had taken the glass of whisky his father had just poured for him. He'd downed it in one, willing its warmth to relax his throat so that he could speak. It worked. 'It's okay, Dad. Really. I've never held anything against you. I knew it was all down to circumstances.'

It was then that his father had told him about going down into the copse with one of his shotguns – just as Jonah had feared he might. 'No, Jonah,' he'd said, raising his hand to stop him from interrupting, 'and don't look at me like that. I don't deserve your sympathy. Not one ounce of it. I've been a damned silly fool. I can't promise to change overnight, but I want you to know that I do care about you. I care very much. Another drink? You look like you could do with it.'

'I'd better not, I'm driving.'

'Of course.'

An awkward silence then followed when neither of them spoke. Not until Jonah said, 'It's getting late. I ought to go.'

They parted at the back door, not with a great show of new-found emotion, not with an uncharacteristic hearty embrace, but with a warm handshake, as though they were two people who had just met for the first time and had decided they quite liked each other.

Turning from the drystone wall, Jonah got back into his car and drove home.

46

That same night, in Cross Street, Archie was eating his supper in front of the television. The news was on, but he wasn't listening to it. He was too tired. It was as much as he could do to cut into the chicken and mushroom pie he'd picked up on the way home.

It had been a long, long day, with a house clearance in Whaley Bridge that had taken more effort and time than he'd anticipated. Valuable hours had been wasted because the relatives of the deceased owner of the house couldn't decide who should have what. It should all have been settled before he and Samson had arrived but it hadn't, and they were soon caught up in a classic family dispute with the dead woman's daughters-in-law arguing over who had been promised a pretty little carriage clock from the front room. When things had got ugly, he and Samson had retreated to the kitchen to start on the cupboards, leaving the rapidly dividing family to resolve matters alone. It wasn't as though there was much worth fighting over: the house was small and the possessions meagre. Maybe that was the problem: the fewer the bones to pick over, the more frantic and bitter the feeding frenzy.

Perhaps it was some folk's way of handling grief, letting off steam by bickering among themselves; it distracted them from what was really going on. But this lot had been mean and grasping. They hadn't been interested in sentimental keepsakes: they only wanted the stuff they thought had a bit of value.

It had been left to him and Samson to clear out the rest, which the family plainly regarded as rubbish. Archie always felt he owed it to the person who had spent a lifetime gathering these mementoes to do his best by them. It was the bedside tables that invariably got to him. It was in those little drawers that, often, the most personal and poignant objects had been kept, and which gave the deepest insight into that person's habits and thoughts. Today's bedside table had revealed the usual old tubes of ointment, packets of indigestion tablets, buttons, rusting safety-pins, bent hairpins, and a string of cheap, gaudy beads. There was a tiny-faced watch that didn't work, a money-off voucher for washing powder (dated October 1988), a pair of tweezers, a throat lozenge that had oozed a sticky trail across an envelope of black and white holiday snaps, a crumbling bath cube that had lost its scent, and a small trinket box containing a collection of Christmas cracker jokes, unused party hats, two plastic whistles and a key-ring. There was also a small Bible, its pages thickened with use.

He had got away from the house just in time to nip home, clean himself up, then drive to the hospital. He went every day, hoping for some sign of improvement in his mother. He always came home disappointed. Her condition had remained the same since she had been admitted: unmoving, lost in a world where he couldn't reach her. He talked to her all the time, though, needing to believe that while she couldn't make any movement, not even a flicker of her eyelids, she could still hear him. He couldn't bear the thought that she might be lonely, that she might feel he had abandoned her. So he kept her abreast of everything that was going on around her. He told her about the attractive nurse who had just got engaged and was planning to marry on a far-away Caribbean island, and with his voice deliberately low, he gossiped about her fellow patients – the uppity woman opposite who was always complaining about the food, the woman who was addicted to crossword puzzles, and the woman in a risqué nightdress whose husband was smuggling in a regular supply of illicit hooch for her. He didn't tell her about the woman in the nearest bed, who had died and whose place had been taken by someone new. She had appeared on the ward yesterday, an elderly woman with badly fitting dentures who wouldn't stop interrupting Archie as he talked to Bessie. Maybe she was lonely and didn't have anyone to visit her, but she had tested his patience. 'What did you say your name was?' she had asked him, for the hundredth time.

'Archie,' he replied, for the hundredth time.

'I knew an Archie once. He was a terrible man. Kissed me outside the butcher's for all the world to see.' She laughed loudly, her loose teeth sliding around in her mouth. 'What did you say your name was?'

'Archie.'

'I knew an Archie once. He was a terrible man. He—'

Feeling trapped, and hating himself for his rudeness, he had drawn the curtain around his mother's bed. Looking down at her still body, it was as if her features had been stolen from her face. All the warmth and light had gone from it. The true essence of Bessie Merryman was no longer there.

He ached for her to open her eyes and say something. Anything would do. 'Archie, be a love and fetch me a cup of tea, will you?' Or: 'Archie, where am I? What am I doing here with all these poor old dears?'

Oh, to have one last conversation with her, to say all the things that needed saying. What he'd give to hear just one of her nonsensical words from her creative lexicon.

Forking up the remains of his chicken and mushroom pie, he realised that he'd never hear another word from Bessie, that he was days away, maybe hours, from the end.

When the telephone rang again, Caspar could have knocked whoever it was to the ground. He was sick of the phone ringing constantly. Word had soon gone round that he was on his uppers and the vultures had gathered. Friends, they called themselves, well-wishing friends who were concerned about the rumours they had heard.

To hell with that! They just wanted to gloat.

He poured himself another glass of wine from the second bottle he'd opened that evening, staggered to his feet, and grabbed the cordless phone. 'Whoever you are, why don't you take a one-way trip to hell.'

'Mr Liberty?'

'Sorry, did I make that too complicated for you to understand?'

'Mr Liberty, this is Roland Hall. You might recall that we have spoken before.'

'Too right I remember. You're the patronising wimp who wouldn't let me speak to my sister. What do you want? Are you hoping I might be as stupid as Damson and want to join you?'

'No. I'm calling to say that I think you should come and visit her.'

Though Caspar was very drunk, enough of his brain was functioning for him to hear something in the man's voice to make the hairs on the back of his neck stand on end. 'Why? What's going on? And why isn't Damson saying this to me?'

A pause.

'Damson doesn't know I'm making this call.'

'Is that how you operate, then, sneaking behind your punters' backs, tittle-tattling to friends and relatives?'

'Mr Liberty, our alternative way of life here at Rosewood Manor may not—'

'Look, buddy, I'm all out of rapture and patience, so cut the drivelling waffle about your Arcadian existence and get to the point.'

There was another pause. 'Your sister is ill and I think you should come to see her.'

After drinking copious amounts of head-clearing espresso coffee, Caspar lay in bed cursing the day Damson had ever been introduced to Rosewood Manor Healing Centre. Oh, he knew what had happened up there, all right. They'd fed her some wishy-washy diet of ginseng and cabbage, had made her ill and were now frightened at what they'd done to her.

He punched his fist into the pillow, regretting the amount of wine he had drunk. If he hadn't knocked so much of it back he would have been able to drive straight up there and fetch Damson home. As it was, he had to wait until he was free of the risk of getting done for drink-driving. He already had six points on his licence, and on top of everything else, a year-long ban would be the final straw.

As soon as it was light, Caspar was ready for the journey north. He'd managed a couple of hours' sleep, and with yet another fix of strong black coffee inside him, he gripped the steering-wheel with steely determination.

He had it all worked out. He would arrive at Rosewood Manor, give that Roland Hall a piece of his mind, put Damson in the car and get the hell out of it.

Then he would drive south, stopping somewhere for the night. Harrogate perhaps, somewhere half decent. He had enough cash on him to stump up for a twin-bedded room for him and Damson, but he would have to be careful: credit cards were a no-go area now. He had a bit stashed away that not even his accountant knew about, but that was real rainy-day stuff. And, of course, there was always Damson. Once she knew of the bother he was in, she would tide him over until he got himself sorted and was on his feet again.

Unless, of course, those manipulative, brainwashing weirdos had bled her dry.

This thought had him pressing down on the accelerator and, flashing his lights at the car in front of him, he sped on towards Northumberland.

Clara opened her eyes, wanting to believe that she would feel better today.

But she wasn't. She was worse. Her skin was so flushed and sensitive it felt raw all over, as if someone had taken a cheese-grater to her in the night. Her joints seemed to have tightened while she slept and ached horribly. Her throat was so sore she would have sworn on a stack of Bibles that she had gargled with broken glass. Her chest ached from prolonged bouts of coughing and her head throbbed. Added to this, her stomach was cramping painfully.

She eased herself into a sitting position and reached for the box of tissues, then took a sip from the glass of water someone had thoughtfully left for her and forced down a couple of painkillers.

From downstairs, she could hear voices: one high, one low. She glanced at her watch on the bedside table and saw that it was half past nine. This was no good, she had to get herself moving – she had to get back into the land of the living. She pushed away the duvet and swung her legs out of bed, her mind set on having an invigorating shower – on the other hand, given that the plumbing at Mermaid House was not for the faint-hearted, a bath might be a better option.

But when she reached the bathroom, it was as much as she could do to brush her teeth and use the loo. Then she shuffled back to bed and pulled the duvet over her. A knock at the door interrupted a coughing fit. 'Come in, if you dare,' she rasped.

'How's the patient?' asked Gabriel.

'Are you feeling better, Mummy?'

The look of hope on their faces was enough to make her cry. 'Sorry,' she said, 'but I think I'm worse.'

'I'll send for Dr Singh,' said Gabriel, so resolutely that she knew it would be useless to try to overrule him. 'It's about time Sonny Jim did something worthwhile round here.'

The doctor called later that afternoon. But it wasn't the much maligned Dr Singh, it was a locum, a diminutive young man with the beginnings of a moustache on his top lip and a pair of nervous blue eyes. He checked her over, diagnosed flu, wrote out a prescription, and advised her to drink plenty of fluids.

'As if we hadn't thought of that,' Gabriel growled, when he'd shown the doctor out and Clara told him what he had said.

'Sorry to be such a nuisance,' she said. 'Sorry, too, that I'm not making a speedy recovery.'

He sat on the end of the bed with Ned. 'Can't be helped. Just glad that you're here with me and not stuck on a campsite in the middle of nowhere. Do you feel like eating anything yet? All you've had since yesterday is a bowl of tomato soup.'

She shook her head, then wished she hadn't. She closed her eyes, waited for her brain to stop spinning inside her skull, and at once felt herself drifting on a tide of sleep. In the distance she heard Gabriel say, 'Make haste, young Ned, we need to get your mother's prescription made up before the shops close for the day.'

Rallying herself, she said, or thought she said, 'Make sure you strap yourself in, Ned.'

The room went quiet and sleep claimed her fully. She sank into a dream that held her in an endless loop of knocking nails into the hull of a boat to stop the sea flooding in. Again and again she frantically banged the hammer against the nails.

Bang. Bang. Bang.

Tap. Tap. Tap.

She roused herself out of the dream, only to slip straight into another. She was dreaming of Jonah. He was dressed in a pair of jeans with a loose-fitting pale blue shirt, his sleeves were rolled up to the elbows, and he was carrying a large vase of flowers. 'Put them in the cupboard with the rest,' she told him, 'but don't try eating them. They'll make you shrink.' He raised an eyebrow, tilted his head to one side, and gazed at her quizzically. She giggled, thinking how gorgeously fresh-faced and kissable he looked. 'Well, Master Liberty, I'll wager you've broken a few hearts in your time, you being such a romantic cutie.' That was the nice thing about dreams, you could think and say what you liked with delicious impunity. He came closer, still tilting his head, and still, it had to be said, looking adorable.

A slow smile appeared on his face. 'You're not mixing your medication, are you?' he asked.

She grinned back at him, but then began to feel that something was wrong with the dream. It was too real. Too three-dimensional. She focused on the vase of flowers and realised she could smell them – could even identify the particular scent of carnations. Was that possible? Did things really smell in dreams? She decided not, and raising herself into a sitting position, she dragged her sluggish brain into a more alert state and registered that he was assessing her a little too intently for her liking, as if trying to decide if she was a candidate for Care in the Community. 'Did I just say something silly?' she asked.

'Very silly. But it's my fault, I shouldn't have disturbed you.'

She cringed. 'Sorry about that. I keep having these awful dreams that don't make any sense. I thought I was still dreaming when you came in.'

'Ah, well, that would explain the *romantic cutie* bit,' he said playfully. 'These are for you, by the way. Where would you like them? And no worries about me eating them, I'm not hungry.'

She groaned. 'Oh, go right ahead, why don't you? Make fun of a girl when she's too weak to defend herself. If you put them on the window-ledge, the breeze will waft the scent in my direction. And before you think I've lost my manners completely, thank you, they're beautiful.' She watched him put the vase on the ledge, noting that he did everything with carefully considered movements, just as he had yesterday when he had set out the items from the chemist on the dressing-table: there was nothing slap-dash about him. With his back to her as he looked out of the window, she said, 'School finished for the day?'

He turned, the sunlight shining from behind him and making his hair glow with a coppery warmth. 'Yes. And for the next week. It's half-term now.'

'Goodness, you're always on holiday when we meet.'

'Not quite.' He came back towards the bed. 'Are you up for a chat?'

'Sure.'

He settled in the chair next to her, stretched out his legs in front of him, and smoothed the wrinkles in his jeans with long, straight fingers. 'Where are Dad and Ned?' he asked.

'The last I heard they were going into Deaconsbridge to get my prescription made up.' She checked her watch. 'That was more than two hours ago.'

'You've seen a doctor?'

'Yes. Your father insisted on calling one out. A boy not much older than Ned diagnosed I had flu.'

He smiled. 'He's very fond of you, isn't he?'

'Who? The pubescent doctor or my son?'

'My father.'

'This may surprise you, but I'm quite fond of the old devil myself.' She coughed, then coughed again, and once she'd started, she couldn't stop. She held a tissue to her mouth while her chest crackled and her ribs ached, and as she struggled to catch her breath, he stood up and rubbed her back. Within seconds the spluttering convulsion passed and she flopped exhausted against the pillows. 'Sorry about that,' she wheezed.

'Can I get you anything?'

'A new body would be nice, I'm tired of this one, but I'll make do with some cough mixture and a cup of tea, if it's not too much trouble.'

'Your wish is my command. You see to the cough mixture and I'll organise the tea.'

He soon returned with a tray on which he'd placed two mugs of tea, a segmented orange, and a plate of chocolate biscuits. 'Vitamin C and something to give you energy. If the crumbs are too painful to swallow, you can make do with licking off the chocolate.'

He made himself comfortable in the chair again, and after he had persuaded her to take a biscuit, he said, 'I thought you might like to know that I took your advice last night.'

She dunked the biscuit in her tea. 'I'm having trouble remembering my name, never mind what I said last night. What did you do?'

'I got Dad to talk to me.'

She looked at him blankly. 'Did *I* tell you to do that?'

'Yes. You told me to seize the moment.'

She thought about this. There was a vaguely familiar ring to the words, but she couldn't be sure they had been hers. 'I think I may have been delirious when I said that. Was it good advice?'

He nodded. 'Excellent advice. I have a lot to thank you for.'

It seemed an age since she and Ned had found Gabriel on his knees in the copse, and Clara wondered just how honest he had been with Jonah. 'He's had a lot to come to terms with recently, hasn't he?' she said, prompting Jonah into expanding on what he had just said.

He ran a hand through his thick wavy hair – an elegant movement that momentarily caught and held her attention. 'That's putting it mildly. I just wish he could have opened up years ago.' He raised his eyes to hers. 'Dad told me about you finding him in the copse.' For a long moment his words, and what they implied, hung between them. 'I feel I've let him down,' he continued, 'that he reached such an awful point and—'

'Don't, Jonah. There's been enough self-recrimination going on in this family already. You tried your best with someone who wasn't ready to be helped. Just be glad that the two of you are reconciled. And remember, it wasn't your fault that he kept his feelings under house arrest all that time.'

He smiled that soft hesitant smile of his and passed her another biscuit. 'Yes, ma'am.'

She waved the plate away.

'Feeling tired again?'

'Yes.'

'Anything I can get you before you slip away on another of your hallucinogenic trips?'

She thought about this. 'Actually, yes, there is. I need some clean things to wear. Take Ned with you to the van when he gets back with your father, and he'll show you where everything's kept. The keys are in my handbag.'

'Is that all?'

'Mm ... something to read would be good. Though not the copy of *Wuthering Heights* in the rack above the table. My brain will crash completely if I attempt that. Pick me something else. Something light and comforting.'

'Something romantic?'

She closed her eyes, all her energy now spent. 'No. A nice gory murder would suit me better.'

47

Caspar's day wasn't going as smoothly as he had wanted it to. A snarl-up on the motorway had added an extra hour and a half to his journey, and now it was taking him for ever to find Rosewood Manor. He'd gone round in circles, doubling back on himself again and again along roads that cleaved through windswept moors and all looked the same. It was a wild inhospitable place of craggy bleakness with few houses, and in places it reminded him of Hollow Edge Moor. He had left Manchester in the sun earlier that morning, but up here, in this godforsaken land where the rain was pouring and the wind gusting, it wasn't difficult to picture the tribes of marauding savages from the north that the Romans had been so keen to keep out by building Hadrian's Wall.

Whatever had possessed Damson to settle here?

Eventually he stopped to risk lunch at a pub, where the copper-topped tables were sticky with beer and scarred with cigarette burns; the padded stools were so filthy he thought twice about sitting down. His order was taken by a charmless old hag who was more interested in watching the wide-screen television hanging from the wall at the far end of the overheated room than serving anyone. There were few other punters: a wizened man with his nose dipping into his pint, and a group of youths lolling around a pool table.

He planned to stay just long enough to satisfy his growling stomach and to ask the whereabouts of Rosewood Manor Healing Centre.

Nobody had heard of it, but he was informed that Blydale Village wasn't a village as such. 'Nothing more than a sprawling place that's got above itself,' the hag said, with a disapproving sniff, when he handed over a ten-pound note for a plate of artificially pink microwaved gammon steak and a glass of unspeakably rough brandy.

Just because the Romans had departed aeons ago, it didn't mean the natives had gone soft on tribalism, Caspar observed, as he slipped back into the refined comfort of his Maserati. He knew the sensible thing to do was phone Rosewood Manor and ask for directions, but he'd be damned before he was reduced to doing that. Getting that nerdy wimp Roland Hall on the phone and asking him for help was out of the question.

He drove on determinedly, back towards Blydale. Ten minutes later, luck shone on him when he saw the remains of a wooden sign he hadn't noticed before, although he had driven up and down this stretch of road several times. He stopped the car, got out and, with the rain pelting down on him, poked around in the long, sodden grass with his foot. Flipping the rotten piece of wood over, he saw the words 'Rosewood Manor Healing Centre' carved in a pretentiously curlicued script. Hallelujah! Now, at long last, he was getting somewhere.

Back in the car, he took the next left, as the sign had originally indicated. The road dipped and narrowed, twisted and climbed and all but disappeared up its own access before it brought him to the brow of a hill and a T-junction. There were no helpful signs, but in the distance, submerged in the misty gloom of a verdant coniferous plantation, he saw a large house.

He drove on hopefully. At the approach to the house, a metal gate barred his way. Attached to it was a sign that read, 'Private Property' and 'Keep Out' in red. A brick-built postbox stood to the left of the gate, but there was nothing, other than a strong feeling in his guts, to suggest that this was where he would find Damson. He made a lightning dash to the gate, swung it open, then dived back into the car. Driving on, he left the gate swinging in the wind.

The house was as he had visualised it: Victorian and unrelentingly grim. It had probably been used as a school, or even a remand home, at some time: it had that institutionalised look about it. Ugly and over-extended, it was a solid mass of brickwork with staring windows. With a shudder of revulsion, Caspar thought of the elegant flat in Bath Damson had given up in favour of this remote, heartless monstrosity. What had she been thinking of when she came here this time last year?

He parked the car as near to the front door as he could, bolted across the gravel towards the shelter offered by the porch, and yanked on the metal bell pull. Getting no response, he thumped on the door loudly and waited. Was it his imagination, or could he detect the whiff of institutional cabbage?

Predictably it was some time before someone eventually deigned to open the door. A scrawny barefooted individual with a shiny bald head stood before Caspar, placed his palms together, and bowed from the middle. 'Welcome to Rosewood Manor Healing Centre. My name is Jed, how may I help you?' His gormless face was insufferably beatific and made Caspar want to ram a fist into it.

'Oh, save it for someone who cares. I've had the devil of a day so don't waste any more of my time. I'm Damson's brother, so take me to your leader and then do me the kindness of scarpering.'

Not a flicker passed across the man's face. He bowed again, stepped aside to let Caspar in, then shut the door silently. Suddenly Caspar felt uneasy, as though he had entered a strange, eerie world and the only escape route had been closed off.

He was shown into a large room that had probably been built as an impressive drawing room for some Victorian industrialist. A hundred years on, it was cold and reminded Caspar of Mermaid House, except it was shabbier and a lot less inviting. A circle of assorted chairs dominated the oblong space; the floor was bare, and the walls had been painted an insipid shade of mint-green with the intricately carved cornice and ceiling rose picked out in a darker green. And where, presumably, pictures and mirrors had once adorned the walls, there were now rows of pin-boards. While he waited, he read some of the notices. The first was full of silly mantras:

> Make the renewal of your soul your priority.
> A hardened heart is an impoverished heart.
> Know thyself and be at peace.
> Self-esteem comes from confronting your insecurities.

It was nothing but the crazy psychobabble that every New Age hippie traded in these days, he thought. The next board revealed a series of rotas. There seemed to be one for almost every mundane domestic activity: cooking, cleaning, laundry, shopping, even scrubbing out the toilets. He noted that Damson's name was absent from any of the lists. A separate piece of paper showed another range of activities, from cheese-making and bee-keeping to the construction of wooden toys and hammocks.

'Mr Liberty?'

He turned. 'Yes.'

Caspar recognised good-quality clothes when he saw them, and striding across the room, his hand outstretched, was a man of about his own age and height who clearly took pride in his appearance. He was wearing cream chinos and a Ralph Lauren striped shirt with a navy-blue cashmere sweater draped around his shoulders; a gold watch hung loosely from one of his wrists. With mounting satisfaction, Caspar knew that he was face to face with the devious brain behind this whole scam. 'And you are?'

'Roland Hall. It's good to meet you at last.'

Hiding his surprise, Caspar ignored the outstretched hand and gritted his teeth. It was time to get down to business. 'Damson. Where is she?'

'Yes, of course, I quite understand your eagerness to see her. But perhaps a drink first? How was your journey? The weather must have slowed you considerably.'

The fraudulent act of smooth charm and slickly offered hospitality incensed Caspar. 'My sister's welfare is the only reason I'm here, so let's dispense with the small-talk.'

The man's expression remained impassive. 'As you wish. But I feel it only right that I should warn you that your sister—'

Caspar held up a hand, jabbed a finger at the man's face. 'I'm not interested in what you have to say about Damson. Whatever comes out of your mouth is guaranteed to be one hundred per cent garbage. The half-baked drop-outs you're used to dealing with might be taken in by your cool, calm and collected manner, but I'm not. I know a man on the make when I see one.'

He was almost disappointed that Hall's response was restricted to a noncommittal nod. 'I'll take you upstairs,' was all he said. There was something annoyingly self-possessed about the man. He led the way out to the entrance hall where, at the foot of the stairs, a small group had gathered. There looked to be equal numbers of men and women, and they all turned and smiled when they saw Hall advancing towards them. Caspar detected the look of naked lust in some of the women's faces as they watched their leader climb the stairs. So it wasn't just greed for money that had brought him here: it was the pumping up of his gigantic ego too.

They came to a room at the furthest end of a long, thin corridor and a door that had had many layers of paint added to it over the years; it was chipped in places, particularly around the handle. Hall knocked softly. 'Damson, it's me, Roland. I've brought someone to see you.'

So the weasel hadn't even bothered to tell her he was coming!

As they entered the room, it was impossible to know who was more shocked: Damson at the sight of Caspar, or Caspar because he couldn't believe the devastating change in his sister.

Shock rendered him immobile. He stood staring at the woman sitting in the bay window. For a moment, he almost convinced himself that this was some cheap trick on Hall's part. Where's my sister? he wanted to shout. What have you done with her? Who is this bone-thin woman with hollow cheeks and gruesomely short hair?

But the words that came out were, 'My God, Damson, what have these charlatans done to you?' Then he was across the room, kneeling on the floor in front of her, clasping her cold hands in his.

Caspar wasn't aware of Hall leaving them, but when he raised his eyes to Damson's pale face, he saw that the door was shut and they were alone.

'Oh, darling Caspar, why have you come? I didn't want you to see me like this.' She brushed the hair back from his forehead, and kissed him tenderly.

Still holding her hands, which had no strength in them, he moved to sit in the chair beside her. 'I don't understand what's going on, Damson. I got a call saying you were ill, that I ought to come and see you. Not for one second did I think it was anything serious. That smug crook, Hall, should have said something. Why didn't you ring me yourself?'

She sighed. 'It's complicated.'

'Please don't fob me off. Give me the truth. Do that much for me, tell me what's wrong. I mean, for God's sake, you're ... you're in a wheelchair. Have you been in an accident?'

She shook her head. 'No accident, Caspar. Truth is, I'm dying.'

The shock of her words winded him and he gasped. She reached out and placed a hand on his forearm. 'Too much honesty hurts, doesn't it, darling?'

'But – but you can't be! Not you. Anyone but *you*!' His head spun and a rushing sound filled his ears.

'Oh, Caspar, didn't you know? It happens to the best of us. And who knows, this might be something I get right.'

He simply couldn't accept what he was hearing. She was being much too cavalier and flippant. He stood up, towered over her frail body, spread his arms in an accusing gesture. 'It's this place. They've done something to you. If I get you away, you'll be well again. You're probably not eating properly. You could be anorexic.'

'Please sit down, and please calm down, Caspar. This is just why I didn't want you to see me. Don't you think I would know if I was anorexic? No, my darling, I have ovarian cancer and I'm in the final stages. We're talking a tumour as big as a fist. Conservatively, I have weeks to live rather than months. Though, personally, I think it might be less.'

He collapsed on to the chair. 'No! This can't be happening. Damson, you have to listen to me, you have to fight this. I don't care what you've been brainwashed into believing.'

'No, it's you who has to listen. I've been ill for some time. In fact, that's why I came here. I met Roland in Bath at a party, a month after I was diagnosed with cancer. He told me about Rosewood Manor, which he had just started up, and the more he told me about it, the more I thought it would be the ideal place for me to live out my remaining days. I needed somewhere to rest. Somewhere I could resolve things. And before you say anything else about Roland, he didn't know I was ill when we met. I kept it from him ... from everyone.' She paused to take a small shallow breath. 'You see, Caspar, I knew I wouldn't have the courage to cope with all that chemotherapy – the nausea, the tiredness. Nor did I want to be constantly in and out of hospital, treated like an experiment. So I decided to be a coward and let nature take its course. It's for the best.'

Clutching at straws, and with his voice cracking, Caspar said, 'So if you haven't tried conventional medicine, how – how do you know it won't work for you now?'

She smiled at him wanly. 'Roland made me see a doctor earlier this year when he realised that something was wrong, that I was in pain and had been hiding it from him. After agreeing to see the local man, I saw several specialists who all said the same, that the cancer was so advanced nothing could be done. In a way, I was glad. It meant that I was finally in control of something. You know how flighty and out of control I've always been.' She gave a little laugh, with a brittle, hollow ring.

To his horror, tears filled Caspar's eyes and he knew real despair. 'But Damson, you're not in control, the cancer is. It's – it's killing you and I can't bear it.'

Once again he was on his knees, and with his head in her lap, he began to cry.

Oh, God in heaven, he was losing the only person who had ever meant anything to him.

Damson was the only person he had truly loved.

48

Seldom did Gabriel consciously keep track of the days, but since Clara had been struck down with flu, he was unusually aware of them. It was now Saturday and this was her third day of being confined to quarters. Each morning when he looked in on her he willed her to feel better, but she seemed to be withering before his eyes. Seeing her so incapacitated made him realise that she wasn't invincible after all, and that having her here at Mermaid House, where he could look after her, he was repaying a little of her kindness.

He was glad, though, that he had Jonah to share the load, and in more ways than one. Since Thursday night, when he and Jonah had talked – really talked – he had come to know the truth of Clara's words: Jonah was indeed a gift from Anastasia, and his forgiveness had been instant.

To thank Clara for what she had instigated, Gabriel would go to any lengths. He had told her as much this morning when he and Ned had taken up her breakfast on a tray the lad had decorated with one of his drawings and some flowers picked from the garden. At Jonah's insistence both Gabriel and Ned were under orders to stay at the foot of her bed, as if her germs were too stupid to travel that far, and from there, Gabriel had thanked her for everything she had done and told her that if there was anything she needed, she had only to ask.

The sound of laughter broke into his thoughts and he turned to look out of the library window. Ned and Jonah were in the garden playing football; the little boy was chasing Jonah, who was heading for a pair of makeshift goalposts – two upturned flower-pots.

Suddenly they caught sight of him and waved. Gabriel waved back, then pointed at his watch, indicating that it was time for lunch.

And time was something he had wasted too much of since his retirement and Val's death – he had wantonly frittered it away. Well, not now. What he had left, he would make good use of. What had Clara said when she had agreed to sort out Mermaid House? Oh, yes: 'I'll give you one week of my precious time, Mr Liberty.' She was right, time was precious, and he had squandered so much on living in the past. He had allowed himself to feed off his grief and turn it into a destructive force that had nearly cost him everything.

But to make things completely right there was something else he had to do. He was reconciled with Jonah, and now he had to do the same with Caspar and Damson.

'When were you going to tell me, Damson?' The question had been on Caspar's lips since yesterday afternoon when his sister had told him she was dying, but until now, he hadn't had the nerve to ask it.

They were lying together on her bed, her head turned towards him, and the afternoon sunshine streaming through the windows. It was years since they had lain like this, although as children they had done it all the time, cutting themselves off from the rest of the world.

'I hadn't thought that far,' she said. 'Cowardice, I'm afraid.'

'You were never a coward.'

'We both were, Caspar.'

He raised himself so that he was leaning on his elbow and looking down into her face.

'Don't look at me like that, darling, not when you know I'm speaking the truth. Help me to sit up, and let me tell you what I've learned while I've been here.'

Caspar slid off the bed and went round to his sister's side. He lifted her frail body gently so that her shoulders were against the pillows. He had to force himself not to wince when he touched her because there was nothing to her. The cancer had hollowed out her body until she was just the shell of the beautiful woman she had once been.

Last night, he had listened in horror to her acceptance that her life would soon be over. She had told him that she had everything arranged. When the time came, and she felt it was no longer fair to inflict herself on Rosewood Manor, she planned to go into a hospice: she wanted the minimum of fuss. 'Just this once, Caspar, I shall behave myself. I intend to go gently into the night.' He had wanted to go on talking, but she hadn't had the strength and had fallen asleep. He had tucked a blanket around her, then sat in the growing shadows as night fell, just staring at the face that had captivated so many men in her wildly extravagant life. Always unpredictable, always exhilarating, she had lived each day as it came, as though – as though it would be her last.

When darkness had fallen, he had gone in search of Roland Hall. It was supper time and the rest of the inmates had their noses in the trough in the dining room, their voices bright as they chatted. He had experienced a surge of rage as they stuffed their faces while his sister endured untold pain.

'How is she?' Hall had asked, when Caspar finally tracked him down.

The man's mild tone had infuriated him and he'd turned on him savagely. 'Oh, she's fine! Bloody marvellous for a woman who's dying! Why the hell didn't you tell me?'

'You must believe me when I say it wasn't what I wanted, but she made me promise not to. I had to respect her wishes.'

'So why disrespect her wishes last night and phone me to say I should come?'

'I thought it was time.'

He'd grabbed Hall by the shoulders. 'And who do you think you are making all these decisions? God Almighty?'

Still Hall didn't react. His calmness made Caspar let go of him. He stepped back. 'I'll sue you. I'll sue the shite out of you. You've wilfully let my sister go beyond help. You've as good as murdered her.'

'I can assure you, I've done no such thing. I only ever wanted the best for Damson. Perhaps when you're calmer, we'll talk more. For now, you must be hungry. I'll send something up on a tray for you both.'

Caspar had gone back upstairs to Damson. She was still sleeping. He switched on lamps and drew the curtains, wanting to block out the rest of the world. There was a knock at the door and a red-haired girl with a large tray stepped in. She placed it on the low table in front of Damson's wheelchair then left without a word. Caspar lifted the stainless-steel domes from the plates and saw that the food had been labelled: for Damson there was a bowl of vegetable soup, and for him, poached salmon with a baked potato and a green salad. Pulling out the stops to impress him, no doubt. He woke Damson, and after she had shaken off her drowsiness, and swallowed a handful of tablets, they ate their supper. He tried not to notice how little of the soup she spooned into her mouth. No wonder she was so thin.

'You must stay the night,' she said, when she pushed her tray away. 'I'll get Roland to organise a bed for you. There's a room next door that's free.'

'Can't I sleep in here with you? I could manage in a chair.'

'No, I'd disturb you. I sleep lightly at night and often read to pass the time.'

'I could read to you – like old times.' He nearly choked on his words. She shook her head. 'Not tonight. You need to rest.'

He was too dazed to argue with her. Under no other circumstances could he have imagined spending a night at Rosewood Manor, but the world had found a new axis on which to spin and everything was sliding out of his grasp. Nothing felt real any more.

Now, sitting on the bed with Damson nearly twenty-four hours later, the situation didn't feel any more real to Caspar. But knowing he had no choice, he was beginning to resign himself to it. He had to accept that, before long, his sister would be dead. He listened now to what she had to say.

'I know you think Rosewood Manor is a ghastly place full of the lost and insecure,' she began, 'and you'd be right. People come here suffering from all sorts of problems: executive burn-out, failed marriages, abuse – oh, yes, I've heard heartbreaking life-stories that would bring even you to your knees, Caspar. What Roland has created here is an oasis of—' She held up a hand. 'No, please, don't interrupt, I don't have the energy. I wish you could see Roland for what he is. He's the most honourable and decent man I've ever met. He's helped me so much. There's nothing bogus about him, Caspar. Truly, there isn't. But I've wandered from what I wanted to talk to you about.' Her voice trailed away and she seemed caught up in her own thoughts, a long way from him. Slowly she drifted back. She said, 'We need to discuss your future, Caspar.'

'It's hardly important to me now, Damson.'

She seemed not to hear him. 'Did you know that when there's not much future left, the past magnifies itself and becomes much clearer?' She didn't wait for an answer, but continued. 'We need to talk about Mermaid House, about Dad and Jonah. I want you to promise me something. It won't be easy, but take it as a woman's dying wish.'

He swallowed hard. Didn't she realise how distressing it was for him to hear her speak like this? But then, as if sensing his pain, she touched his cheek. 'No hiding or running, Caspar. We're beyond that now. Remember when we used to say, "It's the two of us against the world"?'

He nodded jerkily, remembering the first time she had ever uttered those words. It had been the night their mother died. He had crept into Damson's room and stood at the side of her bed. 'I can't sleep,' he had whispered. Without a word she had pulled back the bedclothes and let him in. She had cradled him in her arms, already assuming the role of protector to him. 'It's just you and me now, Caspar,' she had said, 'you and me against the world.' They had fallen asleep, and the following morning, with their lives changed irrevocably, and unable to penetrate the wall that had sprung up around their father, they knew they could rely on no one but themselves.

'Caspar, are you listening to me?'

'I'm sorry, what did you say?'

'I was saying we got it wrong. We should never have isolated ourselves as we did, or been so cruel to Jonah and Val. We treated her despicably.'

Caspar felt his body tauten. He didn't want to think about Jonah or Val, the woman who had dared to try to replace their mother.

A knock made them look up. The door opened and Hall poked his head round it. 'Damson, the nurse is here to see you. Okay if I show her up?'

'Of course, Roland. Caspar, would you mind leaving me now, please? These nurses can be very thorough and I don't want you to see more of me than is necessary. Why don't you go for a walk? It's such a lovely day.'

But Caspar didn't go for a walk. He shut himself in the room he had been given last night and wondered how Damson could be aware of what the weather was like. Since his arrival he had been oblivious to what was going on outside Rosewood Manor. Every thought revolved around the appalling knowledge that he would soon be without his beloved Damson.

Now he regretted every bad word he had ever spoken about the way she had recently chosen to live her life. He should have tried harder to understand what she was doing instead of condemning it. He had considered her weak and deluded, and he had never stopped to ask why she was doing this.

It hurt that she hadn't turned to him when she knew she was ill. But it hurt more to know that, although they were together now, it was too late. With painful clarity he realised that most of the derisive comments he had made about Rosewood Manor had been based on jealousy. It had been impossible to accept that his precious Damson had chosen to be with a bunch of misfits rather than with him.

He lay on the bed and stared up at the ceiling rose, tracing the circular pattern of leaves with his eyes. He remembered doing the same as a young child in the summer months when his bedroom was still light and he couldn't sleep. He could recall one particular occasion, before their mother died: Anastasia had come in to kiss him goodnight before going out to a party. Dressed in an elegant evening dress that showed her shoulders – the fabric was silky soft and whispered as she moved – she had kissed his cheek and let him twist her lovely long hair around his fingers. Then Dad had come in and kissed him too. How happy he had felt, lying between them, so loved, so safe.

And as Caspar drifted off to sleep now, he was back in his old bed in Mermaid House. He was covered with a blanket of love . . . It reminded him that Damson hadn't been the only person he had truly loved.

Before everything had gone wrong, he had loved his parents.

Jonah took Clara's supper in to her. She was sitting up in bed reading, which he took to be a positive sign.

'On a scale of one to ten, how are you feeling?' he asked. From where he was standing, she looked a little better, less flushed and feverish.

She lowered the book. 'Around four,' she said, 'bordering on five.'

'That's good. I hope you're well enough to eat this.' He placed the tray on her lap. 'Scrambled eggs with smoked salmon and a glass of freshly squeezed orange juice. I trust everything's to Madam's liking.' He shook out a white linen napkin with a flourish and offered it to her.

She smiled. 'I could get used to this.'

He passed her a knife and fork. 'Eat it while it's hot.'

'Yes, Teacher.'

'That's "Sir" to you. Are you in the mood for some company, or would you rather eat alone?'

'Company would be fine. The house is quiet, where is everyone?'

He positioned a chair in front of the open window and sat down. 'Dad's taken Ned to the stream. They've gone fishing, with the most high-tech equipment they could find: a plastic sieve and a jam-jar. How's the book going? Decided who the murderer is yet?'

She finished what was in her mouth. 'Two chapters to go and I think I have it in the bag.'

He smiled. 'When you've proved yourself right, do you want me to fetch another book for you?'

'Please, if it's not too much trouble. Also, if you could bring me my mobile, I'd be grateful. Though to be honest, I think it's high time I pulled myself together. I feel guilty about you and your father having to amuse Ned.'

'Well, don't. Dad and I are quite happy to look after him. He's a great kid. I'm used to hulking great teenagers, so a four-year-old is a novelty.'

'I'm not sure I like my son being described as a novelty, but I'll let you off if you tell me about the school where you work. Your father says it's full of hooligans.'

He started warily, but when he saw she was genuinely interested, he talked at length about the pupils at Dick High, his frustration with some of the other teachers, and his hopes for the school. He even told her about Jase. 'I just hope the wind was blowing in the right direction for him when he sat the first history paper this week. He's never been given any encouragement before, and I want to prove a point to him, and everyone else.'

She smiled. 'You're a real heart-on-your-sleeve crusader, aren't you?'

Thinking of the conversation he'd had recently with Barbara Lander from school, he recrossed his legs and frowned. 'I don't see it like that. And please don't make me out to be a naïve idealist. I'm not. I'm a determined, hard-working optimist.'

She drank her orange juice and looked at him thoughtfully. 'And would I be right in thinking this isn't the type of school you, Caspar and Damson went to?'

'More or less, but there are comparisons between Dick High and the first boarding-school I attended. The number of demoralised teachers and the degree of bullying were certainly the same. I hated the place and spent most of my time planning my escape.'

'But your brother loved it?'

Surprised at her insight, he laughed. 'It made Caspar the man he is today. So what about you, then? Tell me about the job you gave up to become a happy wanderer.'

It was the first conversation they had shared without his father as the focus, and because Jonah was curious to know more about Clara, he listened attentively to her husky voice, trying to read between the lines of what she was saying. When she had finished, he said, with a touch of irony, 'And you don't miss all that? The money, the power, and the kudos of being a corporate high-flyer?'

'I'd hardly describe myself as a high-flyer, but there are bits I miss, mostly the camaraderie with some of the people I was close to. David and Guy were great colleagues, friends too.'

'It must have been hard to juggle a demanding career with bringing a child up on your own.'

Clara laid her knife and fork together neatly on the plate. She wondered why Jonah was suddenly giving her the third degree. But then she realised she was overreacting: always on her guard to protect the identity of Ned's father, she was too sensitive to any question she thought might lead her to giving the game away. 'I've been extremely fortunate,' she said carefully. 'My parents have been wonderful and helped out selflessly with Ned.'

'And Ned's father, where – where does he fit in?'

She looked up sharply. 'Nowhere.'

'I'm sorry,' he said hurriedly. 'I had no right to ask that.' He got to his feet and took the tray from her. 'Ready for pudding now?'

'No, thank you,' she said stiffly. Then, 'I'm full. That was more than enough. It was delicious too. Thank you.'

'Sure I can't tempt you with a strawberry meringue bought fresh from the baker this morning?'

She hesitated. 'Well . . .'

'One meringue it is. Tea?'

'Need you ask?'

While he was downstairs in the kitchen, Clara relaxed and stared through the window at Kinder Scout. Suddenly she wanted to be out there in the hills, to feel the wind on her skin, to breathe in the peaty smell of the moors. She was tired of being in bed with nothing to do but read or sleep. Which was why Jonah had become such a comfort, she supposed. She was sorry that she had just been so curt with him when she liked him so much. She thought of his enthusiasm for his job and envied him. When had she last felt like that about her work?

He had reminded her of Todd's imminent visit to England, and it occurred to her that Jonah, who was a good listener, might be just the person with whom she could discuss the problem. He was so detached from her life back home that he would be a safe pair of ears. There was the added bonus that he could give her not just an objective opinion but a considered male view.

She waited for him to reappear. When he did, she said, 'Jonah, would you mind me using you as a sounding-board?'

'I've been used for far worse things, believe me.'

She sank her teeth into the meringue he'd just given her. 'Mm . . . heavenly,' she murmured. After another mouthful, she said, 'Now, what I'm about to tell you, you must promise never to discuss with anyone else.'

Leaning against the window-ledge, he raised an eyebrow. 'Sounds intriguing.'

'Do you promise?'

'Hand on heart.'

'You asked me earlier about Ned's father. I'm sorry I was a bit short with you, but back home, people know better than to press me on who he is. I've got rather used to shooting people down in flames if they get too close.'

'Does that make me incredibly brave, or very foolish?'

She smiled. 'Neither.' Then she plunged in, and told him about her relationship with Todd and its consequences, ending with, 'So, what I want to know is, how would you feel if you were in Todd's shoes, if a secret like that had been kept from you?'

Jonah rubbed a hand over his jaw. He had wanted to know more about Clara, but this was way beyond anything he had expected her to share with him. Putting his surprise to one side, he tried to imagine how he would feel if Emily, whom he had loved and wanted to marry, turned up now with a child and announced that it was his. Shock would come first. Then anger. Yes, he would definitely be angry that he had been kept in ignorance of something so important. But next would come acceptance, and delight that he was a father.

Looking steadily at Clara, he said, 'If I were in Todd's shoes I would want to know the truth. No matter how complicated it might make my life.' He pushed his hands into his trouser pockets. 'Does that help?'

She nodded. 'I think it's the conclusion I'd reached too, but I needed someone else to confirm it for me. Thanks.'

Later, when his father and Ned had arrived back from their fishing expedition, Jonah remembered Clara had asked him to fetch her mobile phone. He had the key already in his pocket, so he went out to the camper-van, thinking, as he turned the key in the lock, that when Clara was feeling better, he would invite her to have dinner with him. He had already suggested that he could take her and Ned on a walk to show them some of his favourite haunts, and she had accepted quite readily, but would the idea of dinner – just the two of them – go down so well?

He let himself into the van, and was just acknowledging how much he would enjoy an evening alone with Clara when he realised she hadn't given him any clue where her phone would be. He began hunting through the racks and overhead lockers. He found lots of maps and colouring books that belonged to Ned, and a copy of *Wuthering Heights*, but no phone. There was one last cupboard, the one above the cooker. He opened it and peered inside. Moving aside a first-aid kit and a lot of buff-coloured envelopes, he found the mobile and was about to let the door click shut when something caught his eye. He did a double-take, thinking he must be imagining things.

But he wasn't. He'd know those notebooks anywhere. He had seen Val with them hundreds of times, but had never let on to her that he knew she was keeping a journal. But since her death, and until this moment, he hadn't given the notebooks a thought. But what on earth were they doing here in Clara's camper-van?

He sank down on the bench seat behind him, untied the ribbon, and opened one of the books. He read the first page, the second, the third, and kept going, turning the pages and absorbing every painful word his step-mother had written. But with every instalment he took in, he was conscious that Clara had been there before him.

So that was how she knew about Emily!

Furious, he slapped the diaries together, tied them up, and wondered at her nerve.

49

By the time Clara was feeling better, May had slipped into June and summer had arrived. The weather was glorious, sunny and warm. The yellow gorse bushes scattered over the surrounding hills were ablaze with golden flowers and the sky held wisps of fresh white clouds. Everything seemed sharper, more intense. Although Clara's temperature was normal now, and the racking cough little more than an occasional annoyance, she was still under orders from Gabriel to take it easy.

To her amusement, Gabriel continued to fuss over her, insisting at every opportunity that she rest and build up her strength. He had also stressed there would be no talk of her and Ned moving on until he was convinced she was fully recovered. 'And be warned,' he'd barked at her, 'I'll confiscate your keys if I detect any insubordination in the ranks, young lady. So behave and do as you're told.'

Now she was in the library doing some of her tapestry. Sitting in the bay window, where the sun shone warmly through the glass, she could hear the trill of birdsong with the occasional bass note in the echoing call of a dove. Other than this, there was no other sound to be heard. Gabriel had taken Ned into Deaconsbridge to post some letters and to buy some cheese, and ham and a loaf of bread for lunch. She knew, though, because she'd caught Gabriel whispering to Ned, that they would be gone for a while – they were planning to slip in a don't-tell-your-mother visit to the Mermaid café for a clandestine sticky bun or two. Thick as thieves, the pair of them.

Whatever adventures she had envisaged for Ned during this time away from home, acquiring a second grandfather had not featured. But that was exactly what had happened: Gabriel had won Ned's devotion. Ned had played his part too: he had befriended an old man nobody else had wanted. But that was children for you: they saw things the way they wanted to see them. And now that Gabriel, like her, was feeling so much better, she felt the time had come for her to give him Val's diaries: they contained the final truth he needed to confront and accept.

She knew that when the time came for them to leave, she and Ned would always stay in touch with him, for a connection had been made between them.

Once again, she recalled what had led her to Mermaid House, and it all

288

came down to Mermy. Who would have thought that when her parents gave her that little bit of nonsense, it would lead her and Ned to Gabriel?

It made her wonder if there really might be such a thing as fate.

And if there was, what did it have in store for Ned in the foreseeable future? Was Todd about to make his appearance in his son's life? It seemed likely. From the moment she had received that e-mail from Guy in Edinburgh she had known that events were conspiring against her. Her conversation with Jonah had also flagged up what she had known already: that Todd had a right to know about Ned.

But this didn't take away the fear: she was terrified of losing control of a situation at which she had worked so hard to stay on top. Despite what people thought of her, she did have moments of self-doubt – not often, and not over trivia, but with something as important as this, she needed to know she was doing the right thing, and for the right reasons. Which was why she had confided in Jonah.

To her disappointment, there had been no sign of Jonah for some days now. The last time she had seen him was when she had told him about Ned's father. She missed his company, his thoughtfulness and quiet sense of humour. It had been nice having somebody of her own age to talk to.

She put down her tapestry and looked out of the window. Who did she think she was kidding? Her enjoyment of Jonah's company went deeper than that. She had liked having an attractive man around – she hadn't experienced that in quite a while.

And Jonah was, to use a Louise-ism, borderline gorgeous. He was patient and attentive with a sensitivity that one rarely came across in a man. Beneath it, though, she sensed a strong will and spirit. How else could he have survived his childhood and hung on to his sanity? She thought of the entries she had read in Val's diaries, the fight he had got into at school, and she didn't doubt that, if sufficiently provoked, the mild-mannered Jonah Liberty would come out fighting.

So why had he disappeared? It was so unfair, just as she was feeling better and looking less like a bag-lady, he was nowhere to be seen.

She tidied away her tapestry and reached for *Wuthering Heights*. Perhaps it was reading of such passion and unrequited love that was making her long for Jonah's quiet, responsive company. With this in mind, she decided to test herself. It was a game she and Louise had played late at night, when they were more than a little mellow. You had to close your eyes, picture a man you knew and imagine kissing him. If the image made you cringe and squeal, you could safely assume that he had as much charm and sexual magnetism as a landfill site. But if . . .

Well, the 'if' was obvious.

She sat back in the armchair, closed her eyes, and conjured up the necessary scenario: a backdrop of rugged moorland against which she and Jonah were indulging in a slow, tentative kiss. However, before long it had developed into a wallopingly good, lip-smacking, heart-thumping, knee-buckling snog of monumental proportions.

She snapped her eyes open, faintly embarrassed by such an enjoyably erotic image.

Archie let the door of the estate agent's office close slowly behind him. He had agreed to sell his home, or more correctly, his and Stella's home. It was practically a done deal, with no reason why contracts couldn't be exchanged within two months.

It was all happening so fast.

The For Sale board had only gone up on Friday afternoon, but by Sunday three couples had viewed the house and the first – who were planning to get married in the autumn – had offered him the full asking price. They weren't in a chain and, as the estate agent had just said, they were a safe bet, as eager to buy as he was to sell. Except he wasn't eager to sell. It was his *home* and he was parting with it reluctantly.

He crossed the busy market square to go and view what might well become his new home, albeit a temporary one. It was a small, unfurnished flat above Joe Shelmerdine's antiquarian bookshop, which he let on a strictly short-term basis. 'Nothing worse than to be stuck with a bad tenant,' he had told Archie yesterday afternoon. Archie hadn't been able to view the flat then, because the carpets were being cleaned, but Joe had told him to come back today. 'It's not very big,' he warned Archie now, as he handed him the key, 'and the carpets haven't come up as clean as I'd hoped they would. It needs a lick of paint too.'

The entrance to the flat was via a gloomy alley at the side of the shop, and in the half-light, Archie stepped cautiously round·a wheelie bin and an upturned rusting metal stool. He put the key in the lock and climbed the narrow stairs, determined to like what he found at the top.

A lick of paint was an optimistic understatement. The walls of the sitting room were covered in dirty marks, and there were holes where picture hooks had once been. Chunks of plaster had come away from one wall where there was clearly a damp problem, and the window that overlooked the square had two cracked panes.

However, he told himself, as he stood in the middle of the room, it wasn't a bad size, and there was a working fireplace, which would make it nice and cosy in the winter. But the thought of winter depressed him. He saw himself celebrating Christmas alone here.

The floorboards creaked as he moved through to the tiny kitchenette. It looked big enough to accommodate the cooker and fridge freezer he would bring with him. But there was no room for a table, or for all the crockery and glassware Stella had collected over the years and which they had hardly used. But that wasn't a problem: she would probably take it. If she didn't, he'd sell it.

The bedroom, like the kitchenette, overlooked what had been the backyard: Joe had turned it into an attractive courtyard. There were vines covering the white-painted brick walls, some raised beds with flowers growing in them, and a wooden bench and table. He imagined Joe sitting there during a lull in the day, enjoying a glass of wine.

There was an ominous smell in the bathroom, but the modern suite and shower over the bath appeared new and clean. He located the smell to the stained cork tiles around the toilet and wondered if Joe would object to him replacing them.

It would do, he decided, returning to the sitting room and visualising it with his own furniture, until he had made some real decisions about what he was going to do permanently. Really, when all was said and done, compared to others, he was a lucky man. What's more, Shirley had offered to lend a hand with curtains and the like, stuff he was useless with. She had even offered the decorating services of her son, Robbie. 'Not that I'm saying you can't manage yourself,' she'd said, 'but it's time, isn't it? There's never enough of it.' And when he had a bit more time on his hands, he ought to do something about thanking her for all her kindness.

He stood at the window and stared down at the crowded market square; a car horn tooted, a door slammed. Over the weekend, the council had put up hanging baskets, as they did at this time every year, and the bright splashes of colour gave an added gaiety to the shop fronts. Everywhere he looked the place was buzzing with people, cars and tourist buses. Now that it was June, and visitors were pouring in, the place had a jolly, prosperous air, but by next month it would feel the strain of so many visitors: the roads would be clogged and tempers would fray as people fought over too few parking spaces. He watched a dusty old Land Rover reverse into a space that looked perilously small, but the driver seemed to know what he was doing. Having accomplished the impossible, he got out and walked stiffly to the nearest pay-and-display machine. Archie recognised the tall, slightly stooping figure: it was the Commandant from Mermaid House. He continued to watch the man as he returned to his vehicle. He put the sticker on the dashboard, then went round to the passenger door to let someone out. It was young Ned, Clara Costello's boy.

After taking one last look around the flat, he locked the door and returned the key. 'I'll have it, Joe,' he said. 'Okay if I come back later to tie up the loose ends?'

'Any time you want. By the way, I forgot to mention the floor tiles in the bathroom. I'll see to those for you.'

Out on the street, Archie saw the Commandant with Ned again. They were crossing the road in the direction of the post office. Archie needed some stamps, so he decided to wander over and see if Ned remembered him. He caught up with them as the Commandant was lifting Ned so that he could slip some letters inside the postbox. When Ned saw him, he said, 'Look, Mr Liberty, it's Archie.'

'Archie who?'

Archie smiled to himself. Trust the Commandant not to remember him. 'Hello there, Ned, what are you doing back here?' With a tilt of his head, he added, 'Archie Merryman, Mr Liberty, Miss Costello's disreputable rag-and-bone man.'

'Ah, yes, I remember you now. You came to the house a couple of times, didn't you?'

'That's right.'

'Mummy thinks we're only here to post some letters and buy some bread,' Ned said importantly, 'but we're going to have a cake and a milkshake in the café as well.' He leaned in close to say this last bit, as though it was a big secret.

'Well, aren't you the scallywag? And how is your mother?'

'She's been very ill with flu and Mr Liberty has been looking after her. Do you want to come and have a cake with us?'

Archie laughed. 'I'd love to, but I've got to get back to the shop. Will you give your mother my best wishes when you get home? Tell her I hope she's soon feeling better.'

Ned nodded, then said, 'Have you got any more jigsaws in your shop? Mummy gave me a pound to buy myself something. A jigsaw would be nice. I liked the last one you gave me.'

'As a matter of fact I have got some more. Why don't you come and have a look?'

'Can we, Mr Liberty?' He looked up eagerly at the Commandant, who had been silent throughout this exchange.

He said, 'I should think that could be arranged.'

Ned swivelled his head back to Archie. 'Do you have anything that Mummy might like? I wanted to buy her a present too.'

'I'll have to think about that. You go and see Shirley in the café, and I'll have a fossick and see what I can find for you. How does that sound?'

Archie walked back to Second Best wondering what Clara might like. She had far too much taste and class to want anything from his tatty old shop. But then he remembered the teapot Samson had nearly smashed yesterday morning when he was emptying a box from a house clearance. It was a novelty teapot, with a pair of stumpy legs, an arm for a handle and another for the spout. He could easily get more than a pound for it, but Ned's pennies were good enough for him. Quickening his pace, he hoped no one had bought it while he'd been out.

As he let himself into the shop and saw Samson with his feet up, reading the paper, his mood was lighter than it had been when he'd gone out. He had been miserable at having to go to the estate agent and accept the young couple's offer on his house. Now things didn't seem so bad: he'd found himself a decent flat that was cheap and conveniently handy. Okay, it wasn't anything special, but it would tide him over until he'd sorted himself out. If there was one thing he'd learned recently, it was that you never knew what was around the corner.

Half an hour later the irony of those words was brought home to him. The hospital phoned to say that his mother had just died.

50

With the house still empty, and confident that she would be alone for some time yet, Clara decided to be brave.

Well, brave-ish.

Although she'd had her mobile phone with her since Saturday, and had intended to ring her friends while she was housebound, she had not got around to doing so, for the simple reason that she had lacked the courage to set in motion the sequence of events she knew would unfold once she spoke to Louise.

But now she was determined to grasp the nettle.

To seize the bull by the horns.

To seize—

Oh, get on with it! she reprimanded herself.

She tapped in Louise's work number, muttering that there was to be no more yellow-bellied prevaricating. It was time to see what Louise knew about the latest goings-on at Phoenix – specifically if the corporate wonder-boys were over from the States yet. It made more sense to speak to one of the boys, but she was in the mood for a good old girlie gossip with Louise. But Louise's voice-mail informed her that she was out of the office for the next two days. Clara mentally tossed a coin: Guy or David. Guy won. She tapped in his number and waited for him to pick up.

'Clarabelle!' he said, when he heard her voice. 'How's it going?'

She pictured him leaning back in his chair with his feet up on his desk. 'I'm fine. Well, not that fine, I'm recovering from a nuclear attack of flu.'

'Poor you – but that explains why your voice is husky and sounds so dead sexy. So where are you now? Outer Mongolia?'

'We're back in the Peak District. It's a long story, but do you remember we stayed with an eccentric man in a place called Mermaid House?'

'Yes.'

'Well, we're with him again. He's been fantastic and taken care of Ned while I've been flat on my back with—'

'Clarabelle, please, you're shocking me. I've told you before, your private life is your own.'

'Guy Morrell, the only thing that would shock your delicate ears is if Moira told you she was pregnant.'

'Ooh, as sharp as ever. So how's Ned? Still as cute as a button? Missing us all, I hope.'

'Of course he is. He's grown. He's already gone through two pairs of shoes and is due for another hair-cut. My mother would claim it's all the fresh air he's getting.'

'She might be right. Hey, and before I forget, you were right about that Todd Mason Angel dude, the women on the packing line have been drooling over him ever since he arrived.'

Clara tightened her grip on the small mobile phone, pressed it harder to her ear. 'You always did say I was a good judge of character,' she said lightly.

'What's even more galling is that he's a nice bloke into the bargain.'

'You've met him?'

'Don't sound so surprised, of course we have. David and I took him out for a drink. We discovered he was a keen squash player and the next thing we knew we were being thrashed within an inch of our lives. But to get our own back, David invited him home for a typically English barbecue. The rain never stopped, and the poor bloke thought we were mad when we put the brollies up and carried on as though nothing was wrong.'

Clara couldn't believe what she was hearing. Her friends were socialising with Ned's father! The meddling hand of fate was up to its tricks again.

'Oh, and I mustn't forget,' Guy carried on blithely, 'when he realised you were a close friend of ours, he sent his best wishes. I have to say, it strikes me that you were holding back on us, Clarabelle. We're all getting the impression that you knew him a lot better than you've been letting on.'

He laughed and Clara wondered if he was fishing. But then a more worrying thought occurred to her. 'Guy, is your door shut or are you broadcasting this conversation to the whole of Phoenix?'

'The door's shut, but the phone's on monitor and I'm in the middle of a meeting.' He must have heard her sharp intake of breath. 'Hey, I'm only joking. Clara, what is it? What's wrong?'

She kept her voice level. 'Nothing's wrong, silly. So what else have you been up to with your new-found chum?'

'Not a lot. In a way, we all feel sorry for him. He's obviously homesick. You know what these Yanks are like, no place like the old homestead. He got some photographs out of his wallet during the barbecue, showed us pictures of his wife and daughters, even phoned home while he was with us. A true blue-blooded family man, I guess. A rare breed.'

Clara couldn't take another word. 'Guy, are you sure your door's shut?'

'Yes. I told you it was. Why, what's up?'

She took a deep breath and threw herself into the abyss. 'The thing is, Todd is Ned's father.'

There was a stunned silence. Then, 'Gee whiz, girl, does he know? I mean, does Todd know about Ned?'

'No. I never let on that I was pregnant.'

Another silence. Until: 'But Clara, he's seen pictures of you and Ned!'

It was her turn to fall silent.

Filling the gap in the conversation, Guy said, 'It was late and we'd all had a bit to drink. Well, *we* had, he hadn't, he's practically teetotal, but, oh, Clara, don't be cross, we were in the kitchen and he was looking at the collection of photos David and Louise have on the wall, you know that montage Louise made.'

Clara knew it well. Quite apart from a range of silly pictures of her and the gang, there was a large picture of her with Ned slap-bang in the middle of it – she had an arm around him while he puffed his cheeks with air ready to blow out the four candles on his birthday cake. 'Go on, Guy, tell me the worst. He asked who the boy was, didn't he? And then he counted up the candles, I'll bet?'

'He did.' Guy's voice was miserable.

'Oh, well, that would do it. Did he say anything?'

'I can't remember. It was one of those crazy moments when we were all doing something. Moira was making the coffee, and David and I were sorting out the dish-washer and making our usual hash of it. We weren't taking much notice of him to be honest.'

'So it was Louise who was talking to him?'

'Yes.'

'Then I have to speak to her.'

'I think she's away on a course in London. But she's at home in the evenings.'

'I know. I tried her office before ringing you.'

'Well, I wish she'd been there, then she would have been the one to get the grilling.'

Clara felt awful. 'Guy, I'm sorry. It's not your fault. It's mine.'

'I don't understand why you didn't tell us.'

'I ... I couldn't. I thought the fewer people who knew, the less danger there was of Todd ever finding out.'

'You don't think he had a right to know?'

'Come on, Guy, you said it yourself, he's a family man. I couldn't rock the boat for him.'

'He's not that committed if he had a fling with you.'

'It wasn't a fling.' She explained that when she had met Todd he had thought his marriage was over.

'So what will you do?'

She sighed heavily. 'I think I have to tell him, but I'm frightened of the consequences. I don't want to do anything that might jeopardise his marriage.'

'And what about you?'

'What about me?'

'Do you still have feelings for him?'

'How sweetly put, Guy. But if you're asking am I still in love with him, the answer is no.'

'Are you sure? Or is this why there's been no one since? From the little I know of the man, I'm under the impression he might be a hard act to follow.'

'Don't give up the day job, Guy, you'd make a hopeless agony aunt. You're wrong on all counts. Look, I'm going to have to go, I can hear a car – it must be Ned coming back with Mr Liberty.'

'Okay, but before you go, do I have your permission to tell the others so that we can be on our guard? And what do we do if Todd starts interrogating us? If he's guessed, and let's face it, he must have, he's probably going to want to know where you are and how he can see you.'

'For now, tell him the truth, that I'm in the Peak District, but you don't know where. But don't let on to him that we've had this conversation. Play it as dumb as you can.'

'You mean, play it like a man, don't you?' The wry laughter in his voice lifted Clara and she said a hurried goodbye, then waited for Ned to come rushing in with Gabriel following behind.

But Ned didn't come bursting into the room as she had anticipated. He ambled in, his face downcast. He came over to where she was sitting, climbed up on to her lap and said, 'I wanted to buy you a present but I couldn't because when we went to Archie's shop it was closed. His mummy had died and he wasn't there.'

Hugging Ned to her, she got up from the sofa and went to find Gabriel so that he could elaborate on what Ned had told her.

He was in the kitchen, and while they put some lunch together, he explained how they had met Archie outside the post office and after they had been into the Mermaid café they had popped along to Second Best to find Ned a jigsaw. 'The door was locked,' Gabriel said, as he hacked at a wholemeal loaf and laid out the uneven slabs of bread on a plate, 'but because we knew he was expecting us, we knocked on it to get his attention. Anyway, someone else, a brute of a man with few words at his disposal, came to the door and told us they were shut as a mark of respect. Apparently Archie's mother had just died and he'd left for the hospital.'

Although Clara had met Bessie Merryman only once – and Gabriel not at all – lunch was a sombre affair. They both admitted that the faintest association with death tended to make one re-evaluate what was important.

It made Clara realise that the sooner she talked to Todd about Ned, the happier she would feel. She also sensed that now wasn't the right time to hand over Val's diaries, not when Mr Liberty was so quiet and downcast.

Across the table Gabriel was thinking of what he had done in Deaconsbridge that morning with Ned, when he had posted a letter to Caspar and another to Damson.

He had written late last night, asking his elder children to come and see him: he had something important to discuss with them.

That night, when Ned was fast asleep and Gabriel had also gone to bed,

Clara phoned Louise at home. 'Have you heard the news?' she asked, without preamble. 'Has Guy been beating those tom-toms?'

'He has. But I'd guessed already, Clara.'

'You had?'

'Yes. Whenever your name came up, I noticed that Todd showed a little too much control over his reaction. Then when I saw his face while he was looking at the photos of you and Ned, the penny dropped and I knew for sure. He went so pale I thought he was going to faint. He excused himself and spent ages in the loo. He might even have been sick. He looked very green about the gills when he came back into the kitchen.'

Clara groaned. 'And the boys didn't reach the same conclusion?'

'Oh, come on, you know the boys never reach any kind of a conclusion on their own.'

'So why didn't you put them in the picture?'

'Because, Clara my sweet, I'm not the ditsy blabbermouth you clearly have me down as. You could have confided in me, you know. I feel quite hurt that you didn't trust me.'

'I'm sorry, it's just that once a secret is shared, it has a ripple effect that's impossible to contain. Forgive me, please?'

'Done already. So what happens next? Guy says you're going to come clean with Todd about Ned. Are you really?'

'Yes, I am. I have to.'

'Not that you've asked for my opinion, but I think you're right. The day was always going to come when you would have to be straight with Ned. You might just as well bite the bullet now. And from what I hear, this sell-off that Todd's over here for will soon be wrapped up, so you'd better get your act together. I'm assuming you want to do it face to face and not over the phone.'

'You assume correctly.'

'So, tell me about you and the lovely Todd Mason Angel. I must say, I'm pretty envious – he's very attractive. No wonder Ned turned out to be such a great-looking boy. It also explains why you haven't looked at another man since.'

'Not you too! I had enough of that from Guy this afternoon. And for your information I *have* looked at another man with lustful thoughts – quite recently too.' Immediately Clara regretted saying that. 'Strike that from the record,' she said. 'I never said it.'

'Not on your life. If there's a man up there and you have the hots for him, I need to know all about him. Give.'

Clara squirmed. 'There's absolutely nothing to tell.'

'Thank you, but in view of how close to the chest you play it, I'll be the judge of that. Who is he and what's his name?'

'Louise, this goes no further than you. Not a word to another living soul. Do you hear me?'

'Loud and clear. Come on, I'm all agog. What's he like?'

'Um . . . tall, dark and handsome.'

'Oh, please, spare me the cliché!'

'But it's true. He is tall, he is dark and he is handsome. His name's Jonah and he's a history teacher and he's the same age as me.' She told Louise how sweet he'd been while she'd been ill in bed.

'Hot diggity, the man's a gem!'

'I think you could be right.'

'And talking of *bed*, is he a *lurve* machine between the sheets?'

'Louise, keep it focused!'

'That's exactly what I'm doing. I want you to promise you'll be careful. You got pregnant during your last away match and I don't want a repeat performance.'

'Believe me, there's no danger of that happening again. And if he is a *lurve* machine, I wouldn't know.'

'What, no nooky? None at all?' Louise sounded incredulous.

Clara laughed. 'Certainly not. He doesn't even know I like him.'

'Is he soft in the head? Oh, I get it, he's another married man, isn't he? For crying out loud, Clara, what is it with you?'

'What a blast you are, Louise. Now, stop leaping to conclusions and pay attention. He's not married, he's pleasant to have around and as every good celeb says, Jonah and I are just good friends.'

'Mm . . . but let's not forget those lustful thoughts you have for him, eh?'

Having made the fatal error of getting herself drawn into the conversation, Clara knew it was going to take real effort on her part to end it: Louise would be reluctant to let go of this one. She realised too, having heard herself openly discuss Jonah, that he was the first man, since Todd, who made her feel that he might be worth taking a risk for.

On the landing, just the other side of Clara's door, and having been downstairs to make himself a drink, Gabriel considered what he'd overheard.

Now, who'd have thought it? The lovely Clara carrying a torch for Jonah.

Taking care where he placed his slippered feet on the wooden floorboards, he crept back to his bedroom. By jingo, he hoped that Jonah had the sense to see what was right under his nose.

Sitting at the kitchen table, the last of Val's diaries now read, Jonah stared at his step-mother's final entry and wished that her life had been happier. She had deserved better than she had received from the Liberty family. She had tried so hard to pull them together, to make everything better for them. And what had they given her?

Nothing but trouble, heartache and bitterness.

Caspar had always been particularly brutal. 'Don't think for one minute you can seduce us with a slice of home-made apple pie,' he'd said to her one afternoon, when they were sitting down for tea. 'You'll never replace our mother, so don't bother to try.'

How Val had coped and never lost her temper was a mystery to Jonah. She must have been angry at times, had to have been, but she had never shown it. Not once.

He poured the last of the wine into his glass, then went and stood at the back door that opened on to the garden. Staring into the darkness, he considered the reasons behind his own anger, which had increased with each page he had read of Val's diaries. It was bad enough that Clara had read them, but it was worse that she had kept them from him. From his father too. He did not doubt that his father had no idea what she'd been up to behind his back.

Draining his glass, and feeling he had been taken for a fool – that Clara had derived some kind of perverse pleasure from stringing him along – he decided he would go to Mermaid House tomorrow morning and confront her.

It would be interesting to see how she would justify her actions.

51

While she was hanging out a basket of washing in the warm sunshine, Clara congratulated herself on feeling better than ever that morning. She felt so good she was even humming a little tune, slightly off key. She stopped, though, when she heard a car approaching. She continued to peg a row of Gabriel's shirts on the line, until the car turned into the courtyard and she saw it was Jonah. In view of what she had admitted to Louise on the phone last night, she felt awkward suddenly at the prospect of talking to him.

She watched him shut his car door and walk towards her. He was dressed, as he so often was, in jeans with a loose-fitting cotton shirt, the sleeves rolled up. But there was something unusually purposeful about his step, which was curiously at odds with his appearance: it made Clara think he had come here with a specific task to complete. Or perhaps he was just in a hurry.

'Hi,' she said, 'long time no see. We've missed you.'

'I've been busy. How are you feeling?'

She pegged the last of the washing on the line – Murphy's law dictated it was a pair of her knickers – and said, 'Much better, thanks to you and your father cosseting me and—'

'Good,' he cut in. 'Are you up to a walk?'

Something jarred with her in his unfamiliar clipped tone, and it occurred to her that maybe he was nervous. Was it possible that he had reached the same conclusion about her as she had of him? 'I should think so. I'll go and get Ned.'

'I thought we could go on our own.'

She bent down to pick up the empty washing basket and allowed herself a small smile that had a hint of *Yesss!* tucked into it. It was to be a romantic stroll, just the two of them. 'Okay, then, I'm game if you are. Shall we go inside and see if your father will agree to look after Ned?'

Gabriel greeted the suggestion with such enthusiasm that Clara was prepared to put money on it that he was in on the whole thing. Perhaps, and in view of their new-found relationship, Jonah had confided in his father.

'Quite all right by me,' Gabriel said, putting an arm around Ned and ruffling his hair. 'You go off and enjoy yourselves. Ned and I will be fine, won't we, lad?' And then to Jonah, 'But be careful – mind you don't go too far and tire her out.'

After she had swapped her slip-on shoes for a pair of trainers, they set off in an easterly direction across the fields. They climbed over a wooden stile that had been built into the drystone wall and soon Mermaid House was far behind them. They were alone, surrounded by a patchwork of lush green slopes. Filled with a lightness of heart she hadn't felt in a long while, Clara felt sorry for anyone who didn't have the opportunity to experience such a golden summer's day. It was what her mother would call a Grateful Day – a day to be glad one was alive. In the distance sheep bleated and overhead she heard the call of a bird she didn't recognise.

'What's that, Jonah?' she asked.

'It's a skylark,' he responded, without interest. Puzzled at his terseness, she decided that he was one of those people who preferred to take his nature walks in peace and quiet.

They walked on, the path rising steeply, the sun warm on their backs. She tried not to steal too many sideways glances at him, but found her gaze drawn irresistibly to his face: it was set as if he was deep in thought. There was no sign of a smile, or that he was enjoying himself. They crossed a tumbling stream, and in front of them, Clara saw a gathering of large rocks. She opened her mouth to suggest that they rest awhile, but before she could speak Jonah said, 'I expect you're tired. Let's sit here.'

Glad of the opportunity to catch her breath, and grateful for his intuitive consideration, she chose a comfortable-looking stone on which to sit, one that was large enough to accommodate the two of them. But he remained standing, his back to her, his hands thrust into his trouser pockets as he stared at the view. A soft breeze blew at his hair, rippled his shirt, and Clara had to fight back the urge to reach out and touch him. Irrationally, she wanted him to turn and kiss her. 'I used to come up here on my own when I was a child,' he said, turning slowly to face her. 'In fact, it's one of my favourite places, where I like to come and think.'

His expression was serious and made her want to touch him even more. Kiss me, she willed him. One kiss to make me feel young and wild again. One divinely long-drawn-out kiss and I'll never trouble you again. How about it?

'But you know that, don't you?'

She stared at his sexy mouth, not listening to his words, but taking in the soft curve of his lips and how they might feel pressed against hers.

'Like you know that this is where my brother clinched matters with Emily. Just as you know all about my family.'

Suddenly she saw that the beguiling softness was gone from his mouth, and a feeling of sick dread swept through her.

'Jonah, what is it?' But she knew what was wrong. Knew it with painful and shameful clarity.

He stared down at her, his eyes dark and hard. 'I'm talking about Val's diaries. I found them among your things in your camper-van when I was looking for your mobile.'

There was no point in denying it. 'I – I was going to put them back,' she confessed, accepting that while she had to give him the truth, it would not lessen the seriousness of her crime. She lowered her gaze. She had nearly made a fool of herself. Jonah hadn't brought her up here for a passionate smooch, as she had hoped, but to take her to task. Oh, how stupid and misguided she had been!

'So you admit you took them?' He was towering over her, blocking out the sun and everything around her – everything but his simmering contempt.

She nodded. 'I'm sorry. It was awful of me, I know. But it was when I was sorting through Val's things. I started reading them and was fascinated by what she—'

'You took them and read them,' he said sharply, as though she hadn't spoken. 'Despite their intensely private nature, you felt you had a right to read them. What Val wrote was private. She never intended a stranger to read them. A lying stranger at that. They were meant for my father. No one else.' His voice was cold and stinging, utterly condemning. He was every inch the tough adversary she had imagined him to be if sufficiently provoked. But he hadn't finished. 'What gave you the right to do that?' he persisted.

'It was wrong of me,' she murmured, 'and I'm sorry. But it was why I came back to Mermaid House. I forgot I still had them, and when I'd got to the end, when I read Val's last entry, I knew I had to give them to your father . . . I've been waiting for the right moment.'

He turned away from her. 'Perhaps it would have been better if you hadn't come back.'

She let this last comment sink in, then realised she couldn't let it go, and with her humiliation and meekness subsiding, she said, 'If I hadn't come back when I did, your father might have gone through with what he'd intended to do down in the copse.'

He swung round. 'If you're going to take that line of argument, I could say that if you had never come here in the first place my father would never have got so depressed.'

Clara was getting angry. She didn't like illogical arguments, and this one was heading that way. 'Oh, please, enough of the self-righteous fest, Jonah! If it wasn't for me, you and your father would still be carrying on like a couple of bickering children.' She saw she'd hit home. And, oh boy, he looked as mad as hell now.

'Don't you dare denigrate what my father and I have been through in so offhand a manner!' he thundered.

She leaped to her feet, stood just inches from him. 'Time to bring the truth trolley round! What bothers you most about me reading those diaries? Could it be something to do with the fact that I know more about you than any other living person? That I know your weaknesses as well as your strengths. That you ran away from school all those times because you were so desperately unhappy. That you've never stood up to your brother because, deep down, you're scared of him. Oh, I think it's all of that and more, but what probably irks you most is what we both know, that if you had kicked Caspar into touch years ago, you would have married the woman you loved and be standing with her here. Instead you're stuck with me, a "lying stranger". Which begs the question, who do you despise more? Me or yourself?'

For a moment she thought she had gone too far. His face turned white and his eyes took on a wild, shining darkness that made her step back from him. His body was taut with barely concealed rage. 'I'm sorry,' she said. 'I shouldn't have—' But she got no further. He stepped in close, pulled her to him and kissed her. She resisted at first, unnerved by the rough suddenness of what he was doing, but then the desire she'd felt for him earlier came flooding back and she relaxed into him and let herself be kissed. And before long, the dreamy, knee-buckling kiss she had fantasised about was a thrilling reality. His arms held her tightly and she pressed her hands into his shoulders, wanting to feel the warmth and strength of his body through the soft fabric of his shirt, wanting to absorb every bit of him.

But, annoyingly, the need to cough got the better of her desire. 'I'm sorry,' she said, releasing herself from his embrace. 'I hope I'm no longer infectious.'

He waited for her to finish coughing, then circling her waist with his hands, drew her gently back to him. 'What you said a moment ago about Emily, you're wrong. I'd much rather be standing here with you.' He smiled hesitantly, his handsome face now devoid of all animosity. 'May I kiss you again but this time without the threat of world war breaking out? And when I've done that, it might be a good idea for us to talk.'

52

The mail at Rosewood Manor was delivered by van, usually at around ten o'clock, and after someone had carried it up the long drive from the postbox by the gate, it was sorted and placed in the appropriate pigeonholes in the purpose-built shelving unit in the dining room. Damson's was brought up to her by one of Roland Hall's acolytes, a frumpy earth-mother type in sandals. That morning Caspar decided he would check Damson's pigeonhole himself.

It was Monday and he had been at Rosewood Manor for over a week, and while the place and its creepy inhabitants continued to get on his nerves – had him wanting to nuke all of the brain-dead idiots – its isolated location and day-to-day routine made him focus on what was important. Being with Damson was all that mattered now. The rest of the world could go hang, as far as he was concerned. He didn't know how much longer he would stay, that depended on his sister, but he didn't care. It was a relief to have escaped his problems at home.

When he had arrived, he'd been worried sick about the loss of his business – the money he owed, and the humiliation. Previous business ventures that had gone belly-up on him had involved other partners and backers so the fallout had been shared. This time the buck had stopped with him and there had been no one to bail him out. But stuck here in the middle of nowhere, he was experiencing a strange, unexpected sense of freedom. It was as if he was in exile, buffered from the raging storm the Inland Revenue and his creditors had whipped up, and he felt absurdly safe.

It was weird and he had told Damson about it, just as he had told her everything since his arrival. She had smiled – especially when he confessed to having thrown away his mobile phone so he could be doubly sure that no one would track him down. He had driven into the nearest town for some items of clothing to tide him over – some new shirts, underwear and socks, paid for by Damson – and on the way back he had stopped the car and hurled the phone into the air. Hearing it crack open against a drystone wall and smash to a thousand pieces had been surprisingly satisfying.

Damson had made no comment on what he had just told her, but had asked if he would do something for her. They were sitting in a secluded spot in the garden, the afternoon sun was shining down from a clear sky, but despite its warmth, Damson needed a rug over her legs. On the other side of a wall, they could hear the irritating chatter of a group of inmates who were working on the vegetable plot: they were discussing the most humane way to deal with the army of slugs that, overnight, had invaded their organically grown crops. 'What is it?' he had asked, his heart bursting with the need to make her well again, to have her as she'd once been.

'I want you to accept that what we did as children, and continued to do as adults, was wrong.' Her voice was faint and he had to strain to catch her words. 'We held Jonah responsible for destroying our family, for taking our mother away, and for making Dad so unhappy. But we both know the truth, have known it since the day we first blamed him.' She paused, as if stocking up on air and energy. 'We both held on to that anger in the misguided hope that it would protect us from the pain. But Caspar, it caused us so much more. It still is, for you, isn't it?' Covering his hand with hers, she had held his gaze steadily. 'We turned ourselves into victims, when really we're survivors. Remember that, Caspar. And here's a little Rosewood Manor truism for you, one that will make you shudder with cynicism, but I want you to think about it. For every sixty seconds of anger you experience, you deny yourself a minute of happiness.' From nowhere a smile had appeared on her face, and suddenly the real Damson was there beside him, the beautiful, bright-eyed twin sister who had comforted and empowered him, and meant everything to him.

There was just one letter in Damson's pigeonhole and Caspar instantly recognised the handwriting on the envelope. Climbing the stairs, and ignoring the moronic greetings of passers-by, he gripped it and felt that his haven was under attack. The outside world was never far away, no matter how much he kidded himself.

Damson was sitting in her wheelchair by the window when he tapped on her door and stepped inside. She was combing her cropped hair. When he had asked her why she had had it cut, she had said, 'It seemed frivolous in the circumstances. You don't like it, do you?'

'Not much,' he'd said. He found women with long hair attractive; he had never looked twice at a woman with short hair.

As he looked at Damson now, he saw that she appeared weaker today. He held out the letter to her. She hesitated, then said, 'You open it for me, darling.' It was almost as if she had been expecting it.

'You don't seem surprised. Does he write to you often?'

She put the comb down on the table beside her. 'No, but I was expecting this one. The pieces are all coming together, just as they should. Just at the right time.'

He slit open the envelope. There was just one sheet of paper. The writing was uneven, the lines badly spaced, and there were crossings-out in several places.

Damson sank back into her chair. 'Read it to me. Please.'

'Are you sure?'

She sighed heavily. 'Yes. And read it nicely.'

He caught a hint of a smile as she said this. 'Nicely does it, then,' he said.

Dear Damson,

Just lately I have been forced into thinking a lot about the past and I'm ashamed to say it's been a painful process and made all the worse by knowing that I put you and Caspar through a hell of a time.

I know you will probably regard this letter with cynicism, and I can hardly blame you for that, but please, I would very much like to see you again. Caspar too. I have written to him in the hope that the pair of you might be prepared to forgive a stupid, selfish old man who should have known better. It would mean everything to me if you would get in touch.

Regards,

Your father

Caspar lowered the letter and looked at his sister. Her eyes were shut, her head tilted back against the chair. He was used to seeing her fall asleep without warning, but he had never seen her so still. He cleared his throat. 'Damson?'

She didn't answer.

He bent down to her. 'Damson?' He was frightened. He reached out to her. At his touch, her eyelids opened and relief, like none he had ever known, washed over him. He swallowed his fear.

She took the letter from him and stared at it, tears filling her eyes. 'I said the pieces were coming together, didn't I?'

'I'd rather they didn't if it meant you could be well again.'

'It's the way forward, Caspar. If the future is going to mean anything for you, you must do as he asks.'

'What about you?'

She held the letter to her chest. 'This is enough for my future. He'll understand.'

Understanding only one horrible truth in all of this, that a future without Damson would be worse than any hell his father could imagine, Caspar left her sleeping peacefully. He went downstairs, and sat in the garden where yesterday he and Damson had chatted. It was another warm, sunny day, and as if he were locked in a time loop, he could hear the same people arguing the toss about the best way to deal with the slugs – jars of home-made beer was held up as the ideal solution. 'Take a bloody great spade to them!' he yelled at the brick wall. 'Smash their stupid brainless bodies in!'

The voices went quiet.

'For once I'm in agreement with you.'

Caspar turned his head sharply and saw that Roland Hall had crept up on him.

'Oh, it's you. What do you want?' Though Damson had told him repeatedly that Hall was a good, sincere man, that he had never tried to turn their friendship into anything more, or to inveigle money out of her, Caspar still didn't trust him. But then, other than Damson, whom had he ever trusted?

Hall sat down. 'I want to talk to you about Damson,' he said. 'It's been your sister's intention to move into the local hospice when she felt she couldn't cope with the pain any more. I think that time is drawing near.'

Caspar wanted to take a spade to Hall and smash him to smithereens. To see the man's infuriating face pulped. 'You want to be rid of her now, do you?' he muttered savagely. 'She's become a nuisance, is that it? Frightened that the smell of death will scare the punters off?'

Hall's expression was impassive. 'It's what she wanted, Caspar.'

Exasperated, he dragged a hand over his face. 'Tell me, Hall, what the hell did you do before you took up scamming deluded fools who are more concerned about the finer feelings of slugs than themselves? You're so bloody inscrutable. What were you – an MI5 interrogator?'

'Actually, I was a monk.'

Caspar laughed nastily. 'A monk? Oh, that's a good one. But, don't tell me, the celibate life proved too much of a challenge for you?'

'I had no problem with the vow of chastity. It was the other monks I found difficult to live with. There was no escaping them and their inbuilt prejudice of right and wrong.'

'So what's different about this place?'

Hall sat back, steepled his hands together in front of him, the tips of his fingers just meeting. 'I'm not saying it's perfect here – community life can never be that. Put a group of people together and it's human nature for them to disagree over something or other. Here at Rosewood Manor, in our search to build a caring and sustainable lifestyle, we value autonomy and independent thinking. We try to support one another and support ourselves in any way we can, for instance, by growing and selling organic food.' He canted his head towards the brick wall. 'But even that provides a breeding ground for dispute. It means we have to try harder, to be more self-aware. And while we're striving to achieve all that, no one at Rosewood Manor is forced to be what they're not. So long as one isn't harming another person, one can be oneself here, without fear of being judged. It's why your sister has enjoyed being with us.'

Caspar took this as a criticism of his sister, which he couldn't countenance. 'Damson has never been frightened of anyone, or anything.'

Hall looked at him hard. 'That really isn't true, Caspar, and it's time you realised it. Damson was terrified of herself and what she was capable of inflicting on her mind and body. She came to us crippled by fear and regret. She'd had two abortions by the age of twenty-two and she never forgave herself. It's haunted her for most of her life.'

Caspar's jaw dropped. 'No! That can't be true. I don't believe you. She would have told me.'

'She never wanted you to know. She told me you idolised her and saw her as perfect. She hated knowing that she wasn't, hated knowing that she had let you down.'

'But she didn't!' cried Caspar. 'She hasn't let me down. She could never do that. Not ever.'

Hall's voice was steady. 'Are you sure about that? What about her coming here? Didn't that annoy you? Didn't you berate her for hitching up with a bunch of sad losers whose only interest in her was to relieve her of her worldly goods?'

Caspar had the grace to turn away. He tried to take in what Hall had told him. He was mortified that he had added to Damson's problems. And, worse, that he was perhaps the source of some of them.

'When you're thinking more clearly,' Hall said, 'you'll understand that Damson has spent most of her life searching for something to make her happy, something to take away the guilt. She's told me about the series of unsuitable men who used and abused her, and who, in her own words, she used as a means to inflict yet more punishment on herself.'

'Stop! I don't want to hear any more. Just be quiet, will you?' Caspar pushed the heels of his hands against his eyes. It was too much to take in. Unable to speak, he got to his feet and left Hall sitting on the bench alone. He went back inside the house. He needed to be with Damson. Needed to apologise to her.

She was sitting in the window where he had left her no more than half an hour ago. The sun was shining through the glass and its rays lightened her hair – the same colour as his own. He remembered how she used to dye it during the school holidays, much to Val's and their father's horror. One summer, having already dyed it jet black, she had another go at it and it turned a vivid orange. She didn't care: she just laughed and tied it up on top of her head with a green silk scarf and said, 'How's that for a carrot head?' Nothing bothered her. 'It's just another experience to add to the rest,' she said.

But some things had bothered her and she had not shared them with him.

Why hadn't she? The truth bit into him. Because she had been selfless in her love and support for him and, like a spoiled child, he had greedily accepted her unconditional love. By putting her on a pedestal, he had imposed restrictions on what she could do with her own life. He was allowed to change and make untold mistakes, but she wasn't. She was his sister, but he had treated her as a mother. And everyone knows a mother must be constant in a world of chaos and upheaval.

He crossed the room silently. There was so much he had to say to her. More than anything, he wanted Damson to know that she would always be perfect in his eyes, no matter what.

But when he knelt beside her, took their father's letter that was still on her lap and laid it on the table, he saw that he was too late.

Damson was dead.

He held her in his arms and wept. Wept as he had never wept before. 'Oh, Damson,' he groaned, 'I'm so sorry for what I did to you. I didn't realise.'

Jonah had spent the afternoon on tenterhooks. His GCSE history class was sitting its last paper. Once the exam was under way he had slipped in at the back of the sports hall and had scanned through the questions, reassuring himself that there weren't any horrible surprises in store for his pupils. Or him. But it had been fine. He had covered all the ground in his lessons. He went back to his classroom to share the joys of the 1832 Reform Act with 7B, confident that so long as his students kept their cool they would do well.

When it was all over and the papers had been gathered in, he was waiting outside the sports hall to see how they had survived. He was greeted with a mixture of relief, anxiety and cautious optimism. And an element of cockiness from an unexpected quarter. 'Did you get the eight main points to the Treaty of Versailles?' he asked the group.

Jase grinned at him. 'No sweat, man. It was a breeze.'

Jonah smiled. 'Atta boy. You off home now?'

'Nah. Thought I'd stick around and polish up the candelabras. 'Course I'm off home. Were you offering a lift?'

'I wouldn't inflict that on you again, Jase. I wouldn't want to be held responsible for damaging your image.'

'A word of advice, Sir, you wanna get yourself fitted with a flash set of new wheels or you'll never pull a decent woman.'

'I was wondering where I was going wrong.'

Driving home, Jonah wondered how Clara might have responded to Jase's worldly wisdom. From what he had learned of her lifestyle before she'd upped sticks in favour of taking to the road in a camper-van, she had owned a smart car herself. And, like shoes, he had always believed that a car gave away a lot about its owner. He could easily imagine Clara dressed in a power suit sitting behind the wheel of a sports car, mobile phone ringing, headlamps flashing.

In contrast, his rusting Ford Escort, which would pass its next MOT by the skin of its teeth, shouted from the rooftops that his attitude to life had a more casual slant. Sure, he could splash out on a better car if he wanted, he certainly had the money, but so long as his existing one provided him with a safe, reliable drive, he didn't much care what it looked like.

And, anyway, he *had* managed to pull himself a decent woman. He was seeing Clara that evening.

His father would baby-sit Ned, and instead of taking Clara to a restaurant, Jonah had offered to make dinner at his cottage. 'Having already sampled your cooking and enjoyed it, I'll take the risk,' she had said. What surprised him most about the evening ahead was not that Clara had agreed to see him, but that his father was so keen for them to enjoy themselves. Jonah had anticipated a somewhat less than enthusiastic response to his poaching Clara away from Mermaid House for the evening, but it seemed that the opposite was true. 'No, no, don't you worry about me, Jonah, you go ahead and have a little fun. It's high time you did. Ned and I will have a grand old time of it.'

Jonah was always suspicious when things came to him too easily. Everything he had really wanted in life he had had to fight for.

It was only yesterday that he had behaved like a pompous idiot with Clara over Val's diaries – oh, he'd gone the full nine yards – but it felt like days ago. She had apologised over and over again for what she had done, and each time she said she was sorry he felt a bigger heel. He had tried hard to make her understand why he had been so angry.

'It was reading them and having everything brought back so vividly,' he had said, still with his arms around her. 'It was a shock reliving it, I guess.'

She had looked deep into his eyes and said, 'I'm sorry, Jonah. Truly I am. It wasn't a gratuitous act on my part, I was genuinely interested in you all. I wanted to understand why your father behaved as he did and why you had such a bad relationship with him. I admit it was wrong of me to do it so sneakily, but it just sort of happened. I wish I could apologise more. I feel awful. I should never have said that bit about you and Emily.'

'It's okay, forget it. Though I ought to 'fess up the reason I became so angry and Joe Regular turned into Stormin' Norman. I didn't want you to think I was a spineless wimp.'

'I'd already decided that anyone who enjoyed teaching at a school like Dick High was anything but a wimp.' She'd kissed him, then added, 'I've been lucky, Jonah. I've had what must seem to you a very boring middle-of-the-road but happy upbringing, and it's made me the way I am. Just as your upbringing has made you wary and guarded, not to say perceptive, it's also, I suspect, made you determined to fight for what you want. So don't go selling yourself short.'

'In that case, dare I ask you to have dinner with me?'

'Just the two of us?'

'Is that a problem?'

'Only if your father doesn't want to baby-sit.'

They had walked back to Mermaid House, hand in hand, and as though to underscore what he had already told her, he said, 'I'm not devaluing what Val wrote, but I can think of any number of kids at Dick High who have suffered far worse than any member of my family has. Some of those kids survive levels of violence, abuse, degradation and neglect that make my childhood look like something out of *The Waltons*. I don't want your sympathy.'

She had come to a stop and given him one of her stern but sassy looks. 'Don't worry, it's the last thing you'll get from me.'

*

311

Clara's first impression of Church Cottage was that she liked it. She could see why Jonah had bought it: it was him down to the ground, from the cosy proportions of the rooms to the eclectic taste in décor and furniture. She had plenty of time to poke and pry, as the moment he had opened the door to her the telephone had rung. 'Don't worry about me,' she had told him. 'I'll make myself at home while you see to that.'

Standing in the sitting room, which looked out on to the street where she had parked Winnie, she studied the small, simply framed pictures that had been squeezed in where there was space between overfilled bookcases. In front of the window, there was a mahogany desk and two piles of exercise books along with a collection of wooden puzzles – she pictured Jonah patiently piecing them together. Either side of the fireplace, where there was a wood-burning stove, there were two sagging armchairs and, set out neatly on the mantelpiece, a collection of old clockwork toys: a performing seal with a ball attached to its nose, a marching soldier beating a drum, a laughing policeman and a strutting sausage dog with a bone in its mouth. She wandered over to the largest bookcase and ran her eyes over his taste in reading matter. It was mostly historical, with biographies coming a close second, and the complete works of P. G. Wodehouse, Oscar Wilde and Evelyn Waugh bringing up the rear. An interesting mix, she decided. Scholarly with a dash of whimsy.

And no slacker when it came to matters of the heart, she thought, remembering their embrace on the moors. Their second kiss had been just as intense as the first, but in a completely different way. Slow and gentle, but sublimely erotic, it had held her firmly in a dizzy state of longing. Him too, if she wasn't mistaken.

Through the open door she could hear him winding down the call. Seconds later he was back with her. 'Sorry about that,' he said. 'A neighbour wanting me to keep an eye on their house while they're away.'

'Does everyone rely on you?'

He raised an eyebrow. 'Meaning?'

'Hey, no criticism. I just get the feeling people see you as rock steady, someone they can turn to in their hour of need.'

'A bit like you, then?'

She smiled. '*Touché*. First point of the evening to you.'

He smiled too. 'Well, that's the pleasantries dispensed with. I thought we could eat outside, if it's warm enough for you. Come through to the kitchen and I'll pour you a drink.'

The kitchen smelt heavenly, and she said so.

'Thai fish cakes. Wine?' He held up a bottle of white for her approval.

'That's fine. Anything I can do?'

He passed her a glass. 'No, it's all done. I'm quite organised for a mere man, don't you think?'

'Young Master Liberty, you wouldn't be casting your net in search of a compliment, would you?'

'Credit me with more sense than to do that.' He chinked his glass against hers. 'Cheers.'

They ate on the small terraced area just off the kitchen. It was still light, and just above a pretty lilac tree, a cloud of gnats danced in the warm evening air. The view from where they were sitting was stunning. 'This is lovely,' she said. 'You've created yourself a proper home here, haven't you?'

He leaned back in his chair. 'It's going to take something very special to make me want to leave. Caspar thinks it's a hovel, but it suits me perfectly.'

'And what kind of house does Caspar live in?'

'A clinical wasteland. An airy loft apartment in Manchester. Very grand, and very expensive. What about you? What's *chez* Costello like?'

'Oh, executively smart – four beds, two baths, double garage. Not very imaginative, I'm afraid.'

He smiled. 'But eminently practical, like its owner?'

'Eminently practical. With the demands of my job I had to buy something that would fend for itself and leave me free to enjoy my weekends with Ned. Patching up leaking gutters was the last thing I needed. Though I suppose you're the opposite. I bet after a tough week at school you like nothing more than to get stuck into some house-restoration therapy.'

'Something like that. Between you and me, my next-door neighbours keep dropping hints that they might be putting their house on the market. If so, I'm hoping I might get first refusal. Knocking the two together would make a great conversion. I'd love to get my teeth into a project like that.'

'Here's to knocking through, then.' She raised her glass. 'You're a man of many talents, Jonah.'

'If you say so.'

They continued eating in contemplative silence, until the church bells struck the half-hour and Jonah said, 'Clara, it's none of my business, but have you decided what you're going to do about Ned's father?'

She put down her knife and fork. She had been wondering at what stage in the evening to bring up the subject that had occupied her mind for most of that day. And the decision she had reached after speaking to Louise on the phone again. 'Yes. I'm going home to see him before he returns to America.'

'When will you leave?'

'In a couple of days.'

'Have you told Dad?'

She shook her head. 'Not yet. I only decided this afternoon.'

'He's going to miss you when you've gone.'

'It works both ways. I'll miss him.' She wanted to add, 'and I'll miss you,' but her nerve failed her: her come-hither skills were too rusty to dish out romantic one-liners. Instead, she said, 'And goodness knows how Ned will take it. He loves being here. Mermaid House has become a second home for him.'

Another silence grew between them. Finally, Jonah said, 'Is there any chance you'll come back? You've still got a few months before Ned starts school in the autumn. You know you'll always be welcome.'

She knew what he was really asking and she knew she had to be straight with him. 'Each day as it comes, Jonah. I need to keep the plans to a minimum. That's what I've learned from this trip. Nothing works out quite the way one thinks or hopes it will.'

'Would it be pushing things to ask you to keep in touch? Just as friends, perhaps?'

She stretched out her hand across the table and made contact with his. 'I think I'd like it to be more than that. But first I need to settle things with Todd.'

'I understand,' he said. Turning her hand over so that her palm faced upwards, Jonah laid his on top. Dispirited, he had the feeling that maybe this was the end between them, and not the beginning as he had hoped. He could tell from the way she spoke about this Todd character that he'd meant a lot to her. He was the father of her son, after all. And now, after more than four years of not seeing him, who knew what the outcome might be of their meeting up again?

The shrill ringing of the telephone made them both jump. 'That's probably Dad checking up on me, making sure I'm behaving myself and not besmirching your good name.'

She laughed. 'Tell him we're being very respectable, and that although we're making mad passionate love in full view of the neighbours, I've still got one foot on the floor.'

He answered the phone in the kitchen, but the smile was wiped off his face when he heard Caspar's distraught voice and what he had to say.

53

'How can this be? It's against nature for a parent to outlive his children.'

Gabriel's voice was thick with tiredness and bewildered grief. 'Three women. All gone! Tell me why. Just tell me why.' He thumped his fist on the table, sent an empty coffee mug flying and hung his head. While Clara picked up the shattered pieces from the floor, Jonah went to his father.

It had been a long night with only a few hours of sleep for any of them. After he had received the call from his brother, he and Clara had driven straight over to Mermaid House to break the news. Gabriel had been sitting alone in the library, enjoying a glass of whisky and reading. 'What's this, Miss Costello?' he'd joked, closing the book and putting it aside. 'I didn't expect to see you back so early. Jonah's cooking frightened you off?' But he must have seen from their faces that something was wrong.

Once the words were out, he had looked at Jonah as if he hadn't understood. Within seconds, though, his eyes had filled and his hands had started to shake. He had tried to stand up, but his body had failed him, and he had remained slumped in his chair. Clara had made them all tea, and while she was in the kitchen, Jonah had pulled up a footstool beside his father, taken his trembling hands and held them firmly. Gabriel had suddenly looked old and confused.

Now, at six o'clock in the morning, as Ned slept peacefully upstairs, Jonah and his father were setting out on the journey to Northumberland. Neither knew quite what to expect when they arrived. Caspar had sounded a broken man on the phone, but if his grief had turned to rage, it was anyone's guess what kind of reception awaited them.

Before going to bed last night – Jonah had spent the night at Mermaid House – he had made two telephone calls. One was to a colleague from school to say he wouldn't be in for the next couple of days, and the second was to get more information from Rosewood Manor about his sister's death. He spoke to a helpful man called Roland Hall, who had stressed that he would do all he could to take care of Caspar. He had explained about Damson's illness and how Caspar had been with their sister in the last week of her life. He had also given Jonah directions on how to find Rosewood Manor.

Armed with these and an AA road atlas, he was now helping his father into the front seat of his car. For the first time ever, he regretted the state of his old Escort and just hoped that it would get them up to Northumberland in one piece.

Gabriel was too dazed to say goodbye to Clara, but Jonah stood with her for a moment. Nothing had been said between them, but Jonah knew that she and Ned wouldn't be at Mermaid House when he returned. 'I'm not sure when we'll be back,' he said, 'but when are you going?'

'Tomorrow morning. It feels the right thing to do. If you're bringing Caspar back here, my presence won't help him. We didn't exactly hit it off.'

'I know the feeling. But I have a hunch that Caspar is going to need what's left of his family.'

'You'll take care, won't you?' she said, opening her arms and hugging him.

He squeezed her hard, then pulled away. 'You take care as well. If you want to ring, or drop me a line, you know where I am.'

'I will. And please, explain everything to your father for me. I feel bad that I won't be here to help, but—'

He silenced her with a feather-light kiss, held her gently, pressed his cheek against hers, then walked away.

Clara took Ned to the Mermaid café for breakfast. Shirley greeted them as if they were old friends and gave them a table in the window.

There was a lot Clara had to tell Ned: why Gabriel had gone away with Jonah so unexpectedly, but more importantly why they were leaving. She hated lying to Ned, but she could hardly tell him the truth: that they were going home so she could arrange to meet his father.

Instead, she told Ned that she was feeling homesick and wanted to see her friends.

He listened to what she told him while he munched on a piece of fried bread, holding a corner of it delicately between his thumb and forefinger – he was such a tidy eater. 'Does this mean we're going home for ever?' he said finally. 'No more Winnie?'

She sipped her tea. 'Not at all. We still have two and a half months left before we have to part with Winnie.'

He dipped the fried bread into the yolk of his egg. Stirred it round a little. 'Then I start school?'

'That's right.'

'Will I like it this time?'

'You'll love it. Think of all the tales you'll have to tell the other children. They'll be so envious of what you've been up to.'

He frowned and wrinkled his nose, and Clara knew that if she looked under the table his legs would be swinging. 'I didn't really like St Chad's,' he confided.

'Maybe we'll find a different school. But don't forget, you're older now and it will feel better. Also, you were missing Nanna and Granda.'

His face cheered up at the mention of Nanna and Granda. 'Will they be home from Australia now?'

'No. They're not back until after Christmas.'

Another frown.

'But don't worry. When I've seen Louise and the gang, we'll be off on another adventure.'

'Back here?' The change of expression on his face was so rapid, so telling, that Clara didn't know what to say. There was a danger that if they came back to Deaconsbridge, they might never leave. There was so much about the place she had grown to love, from the beautiful countryside, to the busy market square, so pretty in its summer finery to the friendly people who lived here. Unwittingly, she and Ned had become a part of it, and *it* had become a part of them. It had also caused her to consider abandoning her old life and creating a new one here, where the pace was slower, the people more genuine.

Deaconsbridge aside, there was also the small matter of their involvement with the Liberty family. She would never forget the protective love Gabriel had showered on her and Ned.

And there was Jonah.

With his benign social conscience, his understated charm and thoughtful kindness, he had achieved the impossible: he had tempted her to wonder what it might be like to be in a relationship with him. But where could it lead them? When she and Ned were back in their old routine, what use would a long-distance relationship be? How soon before it fizzled out?

She felt sure, however, that even if it did run out of steam, they would remain friends. And friends, as she had come to know, were what counted.

'You look lost in thought. Where were you? Lying on a tropical beach having coconut oil rubbed in somewhere pleasant?'

Clara smiled and passed her empty plate to Shirley, who had arrived to clear their table. 'Not even close.'

'Oh, well, how about a teacake?'

'Ned? Can you manage anything else?'

Kneeling up on his chair and wobbling from side to side with his bottom balanced on his heels, Ned puffed out his cheeks. 'No, thank you. I'm very full.' He patted his tummy.

Passing him a lollipop from her apron pocket, Shirley said, 'You're the politest little boy I know.' Then, in a more serious tone, she said to Clara, 'Have you heard about Archie's mother?'

'Yes, I have. How's he getting on? They were very close, weren't they?'

'Cut up something rotten but, like he always does, he's putting a brave face on it. It was the same when that stuck-up grabby wife of his left him. It was ages before he let on that she'd gone. If you want my opinion, he's better off without her. It was what everyone told me when my old man left me. Thing is, you don't believe it at the time. But I'll tell you this for nothing, she was a snooty whatsit, always looked down her nose at the rest of us.' She paused to let a customer squeeze past, then continued, 'The funeral's the day after tomorrow. I thought I'd get an hour off and go along. Moral support and all that. Did you know he's sold his house? He's moving into the square, above Joe's bookshop. I thought I'd get him a house-warming present. Something small. Just a token. No point in being flash when discreet will do.'

Goodness, thought Clara, when Shirley left them to serve a middle-aged couple dressed in shorts and walking boots, what a lot Shirley has to say about Archie. And how highly she regards him. She wondered if Archie realised what a devoted friend he had in Shirley.

Clara paid for their meal and they left the café. Standing on the step outside, waiting for a young mother with a pushchair to trundle by, Clara felt a pang of sadness: Ned and she had probably eaten at the Mermaid café for the last time. It was going to be even more of a wrench leaving than she had anticipated. 'Shall we go and see Archie?' she said, forcing brightness into her voice.

The bell tinkled as she pushed the door of Second Best. It was a cheerful sound that had to be at odds with how the owner of the shop was feeling. There was no one about, so she called Archie's name. She heard the scrape of a drawer being pushed in and Archie's head appeared from behind a pine veneer wardrobe. 'Hello there,' he said, 'and what a sight for sore eyes you two are.'

'How's things, Archie? I heard about Bessie.'

He pushed his hands into his pockets, jangled the loose change in them, rocked on his feet. 'Oh. Not brilliant. Funeral's the day after tomorrow.'

She nodded sympathetically. 'I know, Shirley's just told me. I'm so sorry, Archie.' He seemed lost for words, so she said, 'Shirley also said you were moving into the square. It's all change for you, isn't it?'

'It's probably for the best. Nothing like a shake-up. Fancy a brew? I was just about to make one.'

Clara was awash with tea from Shirley's generous ministrations, but she said, 'That would be nice. Thank you.'

Turning to Ned, Archie said, 'Have a good old forage in that box over there. If you're lucky, you might find a couple of jigsaws.'

Clara went through to the back of the shop with Archie, to a tiny kitchen area where there was only just room for the two of them. He filled the kettle at the sink where a bowl of used mugs lay waiting to be washed. 'Sorry about the mess,' he said, catching her glance. 'It's always the same, the moment I leave Samson in charge . . .' His voice trailed off. 'Hang on a minute, that sounds like the door.'

By the time he had joined her again, she had made their tea and given the kitchen a blitz.

'Here, there was no need for that.'

She smiled and flicked the tea-towel at him. 'Drink your tea and be quiet, Archie Merryman.'

Leaning against the sink, he relaxed visibly. 'That's what I like about you, you always cheer me up. So what's new at Mermaid House? Apart from you having had flu. You look as if you've recovered well. Fresh as a daisy, I'd say.'

'And you can save the flattery for the punters.'

'Just speaking as I find. One look at you and I feel made up. Now, did Mr Liberty take good care of you? I bet he terrorised you into getting well, didn't he?'

'I've told you before, he's a poppet.' She went on to explain about his daughter. 'I think her death coming out of the blue has hit him very hard.'

'Oh, God, the poor man. To have lost two wives and now a daughter.' He lowered his eyes and delved into his pocket for a handkerchief. 'Life, eh? If we had any idea how tough it would be we'd give it up as a bad job.'

Clara's heart went out to him. What he needed was a great big hug.

She was still hugging him when a crisp voice said, 'If I'm interrupting, I'll come back later. Or maybe it would be better if I didn't bother.'

Neither of them had heard the shop bell, or the sound of footsteps, and they sprang apart, which made an innocent embrace seem altogether more furtive.

'Stella, what – what are you doing here?' Archie's voice shook with alarm. He fumbled with his handkerchief, pushed it back into his pocket.

'I heard about your mother and came to offer my condolences.' The brittle formality of her words was as flinty as the look she gave Clara, which left no one in any doubt of what she thought had been going on.

Clara decided to make a tactful exit. She didn't like the look of Stella. Too much makeup. Too much jewellery. And way too high and mighty. Shirley had been right. Picking up her bag to go, she said, 'I'll leave you to it, Archie. Excuse me, please,' she added, when Stella made no attempt to let her pass.

'And you are— ?'

'Clara is a friend of mine, Stella,' Archie said gamely, 'but I think you gave up the right to know who I mix with the day you left me. Thanks for the condolences. Was there anything else?'

Good for you, Clara applauded him silently. And, even better, the horrible woman took the hint and departed as quickly as she had arrived, slamming the door behind her and making the bell jangle long after she'd gone.

They watched her through the window as she crossed the road to the square until she became lost in the crowd of shoppers and tourists. Archie looked anxious. 'Do you think I was too hard on her?'

Clara smiled. 'Given the circumstances, you played it just right.'

He laughed. 'And just think, she now imagines that her boring soon-to-be-ex-husband is capable of pulling a woman as young as you.' He laughed so hard the tears rolled down his cheeks. 'What a joke! What a huge joke!'

His mirth didn't ring out with pure happiness though. There was a strained false note to it that Clara knew echoed the emptiness of his new life. Watching him wipe his eyes with the back of his hands, she said, 'Archie, how's your social life these days?'

He shrugged. 'About as good as an agoraphobic hermit's. Why?'

'In that case, I think it's time you did something about it.'

He smiled. 'You asking me out on a date?'

'Oh, dang! You've rumbled me.' She smiled. 'Actually, I had Shirley in mind. Why don't you ask her out? I've a feeling she's quite fond of you. And just think of the great perks on offer. More fry-up breakfasts and Bakewell tart than you can shake a stick at.'

He rubbed his jaw, unconvinced. 'You think she'd say yes? I mean . . . well, we've been friends for a long time, but this . . . this would be different.'

'Oh, come on, Archie, try listening to me. The woman's mad about you.' Clara wasn't sure that this was strictly true but, hey, what the heck? If she was going to start flinging Cupid's arrow about, she might just as well make a proper job of it and aim for a bull's-eye. Besides, Shirley wouldn't have gone on and on about Archie in the way she had, if she wasn't just a little bit sweet on him.

They stayed with Archie until Ned had chosen three boxes of jigsaw puzzles – having tried them all out – and Clara had explained that they would be leaving the next day.

'Is this the last I'll see of you both?'

'Who knows?' she said evasively. 'When the wind changes Ned and I might just roll into town again.'

He gave her a final hug goodbye. 'You're a regular Mary Poppins, you are. Not got a carpet bag and an umbrella with a parrot's head on it, have you?'

She was almost out of the door when she was struck by what she thought was her second great idea of the day. She turned back. 'I know this is a lot to ask of you, Archie, but I don't suppose you'd do me a favour, would you?'

'For you, sweetheart, anything. Just name it.' But when Archie had waved them goodbye and shut the door, he wasn't so sure he would be able to carry out her request.

Unlike Clara Costello, he wasn't a miracle worker.

Before leaving the next day, and with Ned's help, Clara prepared Mermaid House for the days ahead. Intuition told her that Jonah would suggest that Caspar stay with their father while their sister's funeral was organised. Caspar had been adamant on the phone with Jonah the other night that Damson was to be buried in the churchyard in Deaconsbridge, where their mother was buried. Clara had never thought of it before, but Jonah lived next door not just to his mother's grave but his stepmother's. It was a weird thought.

She changed the sheets on the beds and, working on the assumption that Caspar would be staying, made up the bed in his old room. She cleaned the bathroom, and even did her best with the guest bathroom, which hadn't been used in years – the massive iron bath had more than a dozen rust spots scarring its interior and a dripping tap had left an ugly stain. She put some flowers from the garden on the table in the kitchen, and left a note for Gabriel saying that she had been to the supermarket and had stocked up on easy-cook meals for them. She also promised him that she would be in touch soon. Lastly, she added a postscript:

> *This is obviously a time for you and your family to be alone. But I*
> *want you to know that I'll be thinking of you often.*
> *All my love,*
> *Clara*

She wrote a separate note for Jonah, put it into an envelope, and stuck it down. That was definitely not for Gabriel's eyes.

She locked the door, slipped the key through the letterbox, and turned her back on Mermaid House, wondering whether she would ever see it again. She wanted to say that she would. That she would make it happen. But she knew as well as the next person that life was full of unexpected twists and turns.

54

The silence in the car lay over the three of them like a shroud. On the back seat, his father slept, and in the front, next to Jonah, Caspar was sitting with his head resting against the window. His eyes were closed but Jonah knew he wasn't asleep.

Never before had Jonah seen such a change in a person. Normally fastidious about his appearance – to the point of obsession – Caspar was unshaven, his hair unkempt, his clothes rumpled, and his face sallow and ravaged through lack of sleep. He was almost unrecognisable. His grief was so tangible it shocked Jonah almost more than the death of their sister.

When they had arrived at Rosewood Manor, yesterday lunchtime, Roland Hall had been waiting for them. Jonah had approved of him instantly, grateful for his quiet, reflective manner, though his father had been less impressed. He had demanded to know what kind of a healing centre had allowed his daughter to become so ill that she had died without proper medical care. Roland had explained that Damson had chosen the care she wanted and that she had been seen regularly by an excellent doctor.

Next, he had taken them to Caspar. He was in Damson's room, sorting through the few belongings she had brought with her to Rosewood Manor. Quietly shutting the door behind him, Roland had left them alone. For what seemed for ever, they had stood in awkward silence, not knowing what to do. Nothing had prepared them for this moment.

Seeing a framed photograph by the side of the bed, Jonah went over to it. It was of Damson and Caspar when they were teenagers. Dressed in matching velvet flared trousers and cheesecloth shirts, they looked wildly attractive and were undeniably brother and sister: they had the same long straight nose, the challenging flashing eyes and high cheekbones that gave them an air of lofty grandeur.

'Please don't touch it,' Caspar murmured from the other side of the bed, where he stood hunched like an old man sheltering from the rain. In his hands he held a silk scarf, which he was twisting around his fingers. 'Don't touch anything.'

Jonah and Gabriel exchanged glances. 'So what can we do to help?' their father asked gruffly.

Caspar stared at him blankly. 'Nothing. Absolutely nothing. I don't know why you've come. I didn't ask you to.' There was no cruelty to his voice, just painful detachment.

'We're here because we care.'

The blank stare swivelled round to Jonah. 'Well, as you can see, your care has come too late.' There was a trace of blame in his tone.

Gabriel moved slowly across the room, and with his big, rough old hands, he gently removed the scarf from Caspar's whitening fingers. 'I know how you feel, son. Believe me, I do. I lost someone who meant the world to me. But don't make the same mistake that I did. Let people help you.'

Jonah had never admired or loved his father more than he did then. What courage had it taken for him to lay down the past and reach out to Caspar in the way that he had?

Raising his head, Caspar looked his father in the eye, but there was no clue in his face as to how he was going to react. From his back pocket, he slowly pulled out a piece of paper. 'The letter you wrote to her . . . I . . . I . . .' He swallowed. 'I read it to her yesterday morning . . . She said it came just at the right time.'

Gabriel closed his eyes. 'Too late,' he groaned. 'Too bloody late. I should have done it years ago.' His body sagged. Worried, Jonah shot across the room and, with Caspar's help, manoeuvred him into the nearest chair. Gabriel sobbed openly. 'My poor girl,' he wailed. 'What have I done?'

'What have we all done?' murmured Caspar, the colour gone from his face.

There had been a lot to organise, and with Caspar and Gabriel in no fit state to do it, Jonah had dealt with everything. Damson's body had already been taken to a chapel of rest by a local firm of undertakers, who were delivering it to Deaconsbridge for the funeral later that week. There was endless paperwork and phone calls to get through, but with Roland Hall's help, Jonah got it all done. Roland wanted to attend the funeral, so he offered to drive Caspar's car down to Deaconsbridge and catch the train home afterwards.

'It might be better if we did a swap,' Jonah said, thinking of his brother's reaction to anyone else driving his expensive car. 'Caspar might prefer to have his own car when he gets home. Which means, I'm afraid, you'll have my old wreck to cope with.'

'Whatever you think best.'

Jonah and Roland had stayed up late, talking long into the night. Jonah was glad of the opportunity to talk to someone who seemed to have understood his sister better than anyone. 'Does everyone here get such special treatment?' he had asked, conscious that his question sounded disagreeably loaded.

But Roland took it in his stride. 'Damson was special to me.'

'You loved her?'

'Not in the physical sense, if that's what you mean. I didn't exploit her like so many had before. She needed someone to love her for what she was.

Battle scars and all. We were friends. Close spiritual friends.' He looked away, stared into the distance, lost in his own thoughts. Jonah realised that this man, who had taken Damson under his wing and given her unconditional love, which she had had from no one else, was grieving privately for her.

They arrived home to find Mermaid House empty, just as Jonah had known it would be. But there were still some comforting signs of Clara's presence, from the freshly made-up beds to the flowers on the kitchen table and the two letters she had left for them.

Jonah had told his father in the car on the way up to Northumberland that Clara and Ned would be gone when they returned. He had explained the reasons why, and Gabriel had said, 'She once told me that we all scourge ourselves from time to time with a bit of soul-searching. Obviously, she knew what she was talking about. I hope the boy's father behaves decently.'

It was strange being home. Strange because, though it felt familiar and welcoming, it no longer felt like home. Which was an absurd reaction, Clara decided, they hadn't been away for that long.

But it was great to see Louise and the gang again. When she had phoned Louise to ask if she and Ned could stay with her and David, she had been met with, 'Oh, so you're bored with being cooped up in a camper-van, are you? No danger of me being proved right, is there?'

'Rule number one for us travelling folk, we grab the chance of free facilities whenever and however we can.'

'You're nothing but a freeloading parasite,' Louise had laughed.

They had arrived at David and Louise's last night, after a long, tedious journey. Guy and Moira were there too, and they'd stayed up late with several bottles of wine and a Chinese takeaway. Ned had fallen asleep on the sofa and David had carried him upstairs and put him to bed. 'Just like old times,' he said, coming down shortly afterwards, 'except that he's grown and he's heavier. I'll have to get down to the gym and build up my muscles if he's going to keep growing at the same rate.'

It was now Thursday morning and Louise had managed to get the day off work, so that she could indulge in a marathon gossiping session with Clara. She had devised a simple but guaranteed way to keep Ned amused. He had been denied access to a television since March, so he was putty in her hands when she switched on David's latest toy, an enormous wide-screen telly. Sitting cross-legged on the floor with a tube of Pringles and a pile of videos, he was hypnotised.

'I don't approve of you brainwashing my son,' said Clara, when they retreated to the kitchen and Louise put a large cafetière of coffee on the table, with two mugs and a jug of milk.

'Now don't come over the perfect Goody-Two-Shoes mother with me,' said Louise. 'Let me have you all to myself, just this once. And I said it last night, and I'll say it again, you look fantastic. Better than I've seen you in years. You're glowing with so much good health I almost hate you. I love the hair too. Makes you look years younger.'

'You should have seen me two weeks ago when I had flu – I looked like death on legs.'

Louise smiled. 'So bring on the lovely Jonah who took such great care of you. Give me a proper run-down on him.'

'I told you everything last night.'

'No, you didn't. That's what you were prepared to tell us as a group. Now that it's just the two of us, I want the important bits you've held back.'

Clara reached for the cafetière, pushed the plunger down, then poured their coffee. 'Honestly, there really isn't much more to tell.'

'But you think you could go the distance with him?'

'I think I could, but I'm not sure that it's worth the trouble of trying. My life is here, and his is there. Why invest valuable time and effort, not to say emotion, in something that has no future?'

Louise added milk to her coffee and stirred it. 'You don't know that, not for sure. You wouldn't be hedging your bets, by any chance, would you?'

'Meaning?'

'Meaning Mr Todd Mason Angel. Don't forget I've met him. He's knock-out smart and extremely easy on the eye, just your kind of man, I'd say.'

Clara frowned. She straightened the mats on the table, squared them precisely. 'I admit he *was* my kind of man,' she said thoughtfully, 'which is why I fell in love with him in the first place. But I certainly haven't come back here to meet him under the delusion that we'll magically pick up where we left off. I'm not that stupid.'

'But how would you react if he suggested you did do exactly that?'

She was saved from answering the question by the telephone. It was David calling to say that the first part of Clara's plan had been put into place.

Todd had accepted an invitation to meet for a drink after work. Except it wouldn't be a drink with Guy and David as he thought.

Ned didn't bat an eyelid when Clara said she had to go out for a while that evening. He was much too busy to worry about where she was going or what she was doing. He was showing Louise his scrapbook and he was telling her all about Mr Liberty and the amazing house he lived in; about the tower, the secret passageway in the library, and the badgers down in the copse. Clara kissed the top of his head, gave her friend a grateful smile, and slipped away.

Louise had kindly loaned her the use of her BMW, and with the soft top down she drove to the Kingfisher Arms where Todd was expecting to meet Guy and David.

It was a lovely summer's evening, and the car park at the front of the pub was almost full. Though it was mid-week, it seemed that everyone had decided to come out and enjoy the warm weather. David had told her that Todd was driving a hired bronze-coloured Lexus. She saw it straight away and her heart began to pound.

Inside the pub, she scanned the bar, but drew a blank. She ordered a glass of fizzy water and took it out to the garden where she flipped down her sunglasses and surveyed the tables of drinkers. She eliminated them one by one. Then she saw him. He was sideways on to her, dressed in his work clothes – a lightweight suit and pale blue shirt. He had loosened his tie, undone the button on his collar, and there was no denying that he stood out from the crowd. He had that indefinable quality that made it obvious he was from across the Atlantic. Part of it was the confidence in his bearing, the head held high, the neatly cut hair, the firm jaw. He looked well, and just as handsome. Just as she had remembered him. The only thing different about him was the glasses, but they enhanced rather than detracted from his features.

She began the long walk across the garden, shaking so much that she was spilling her drink. She tried to steady her hand, as well as her nerve. She was almost upon him when he turned. For a moment he looked as if he had seen a ghost: his mouth dropped open and he simply stared. Then disbelief propelled him to his feet. 'Clara?'

She raised her sunglasses, as though it might convince him it really was her, that she was no ghost. 'Hello, Todd. Mind if I join you?'

There was so much they had to say but neither knew where to start, other than with a polite exchange.

'I like your hair. It suits you.'

'Thank you. The same goes for you and the glasses.'

'I hear you've been away, travelling.'

'Yes. Life on the open road. How are you getting on with the French?'

'Fine. We should be done by next week. The shares will really hit . . . Oh, hell, Clara, this is no good. Talk to me properly. Tell me how you really are. Tell me about Ned . . . about our son.'

Her mouth clamped itself shut. She repeated his words inside her head. Our son.

Our son.

Suddenly she felt as if all the strength had been ripped out of her. If she hadn't been sitting down, she would have fallen to the ground. All this time Ned had been *her* son. Now, just like that, he was to be shared.

To her horror, she began to cry, but didn't know why. She felt Todd's arms around her and she leaned into him, remembering how good he had always felt. How good it had been between them.

Through blinding tears, she felt him pulling her up, then leading her away. He took her down towards the river, to the shade and privacy of the willow trees that arched their graceful branches over the water.

'I'm sorry.' She gulped and sniffed. 'I had no idea I was going to react like that. It's just—'

He held her tightly. 'How do you think I feel? When I found out about Ned I nearly went crazy. I've been out of my mind, not knowing what I should do. I so badly wanted to turn to your friends, but it was clear they didn't know about us. Oh, Clara, why didn't you tell me?'

She straightened up, pulled away from him. 'You know the answer to that. I didn't want to ruin everything for you. I knew how much your wife and children meant to you, and the day I discovered I was pregnant, you came into my office and told me you and Gayle were getting back together.'

'Oh, my God, you knew then.' He took his glasses off and passed his hand over his eyes. 'If only I'd known.'

'It wouldn't have worked, Todd. Ned and I would have got in the way of what you really wanted. What you already had . . . Gayle and your girls.'

She could tell from the look in his eyes and his silence that she had been right. She had been right all along. Vindicated, at last. She turned away from him, let her gaze fall on a pair of mallard ducks that were kicking up a row further along the river. Composed now, she said, 'Let's go back. I don't know about you, but I'm in need of a real burn-the-back-off-your-throat drink.'

Their table was still free, and after Todd had fetched two glasses of Jack Daniel's, she said, 'It's important that you understand I expect nothing from you. I made the decision to have Ned and he's my responsibility. I'm not about to make any demands of you.'

'Now hold on a minute, Clara. I hear what you're saying, but the situation has changed. I can no more turn my back on Ned than I could disown my children back home. Don't I have a say in anything to do with him?'

Clara felt a knot of panic tighten in her stomach. If Todd wanted to feature in his son's life, she would have to part with him. Todd would want to have him over in the States for prolonged stays. And the more that happened, the more likely it was that Ned would grow away from her. Tears threatened again, but she fought them back and took a gulp of her drink. She was being irrational, she told herself. She looked at Todd warily. 'What are you proposing to do?' she asked. 'Tell your wife?'

He lowered his gaze and played with his glass, turning it round slowly. She knew she'd hit him below the belt, that she had deliberately tried to score a point off him. She felt cheap and unworthy. 'I'm sorry,' she said, 'that was uncalled-for.'

He let out his breath. 'It's a perfectly valid question, though, and one for which I don't have a ready answer. It's what I've thought of ever since I guessed who the boy with the neat smile was in the photographs your friends showed me.'

On firmer ground now, she relaxed a little and said, 'It's your smile.'

He shook his head. 'That's great. Just wonderful. My daughters look like Gayle, but the child I've never seen takes after me.'

'My mother describes his smile as a gift from the angels.'

'Oh, my. And who says we Yanks don't get irony?'

They sipped their drinks. 'You haven't married, then?'

'No, Todd. Probably something to do with not having the time or energy to bag myself a good 'un.'

'But you've managed okay on your own? I mean, financially.'

She bristled. 'Financially I've been fine. Making money hand over fist.'

'I'm sorry. That was rude and patronising of me. But it can't have been too easy bringing up a child on your own.'

'Everyone says that to me, but it's been okay. Mum and Dad have been great. My friends too.'

As if sensing he was treading on thin ice, and thinking a change of subject would be a good idea, he said, 'So what made you trade in Phoenix for a camper? I would never have had you down as doing something as off the chart as that.'

People change, she wanted to say, feeling another frisson of antagonism. 'It was Ned,' she said. 'I wanted to spend more time with him before he starts school in September. It was now or never.'

'So what kind of school have you got in mind for him?'

Again, she felt herself tense with possessive defensiveness. 'A dreadful school, of course.'

He looked at her, puzzled. 'What is it, Clara? I'm getting the feeling I'm saying all the wrong things.'

She drained her glass. 'Forget it. It's me. I can't handle this. I thought I could. But the truth is, I'm not sure I want to share Ned with you. I've done everything for him, made all the decisions, wiped away all the tears, read all the books, sat up all the nights—'

He laid a firm hand on her arm and stopped her. 'You did all that, and much more, because you chose to do it, Clara. Don't sit there throwing hurtful accusations at me. While you were doing all those things, I never even knew Ned existed. So don't try to make me feel guilty.'

She pushed his hand away. 'And if you had known of his existence, what would you have done?' She watched him collect his thoughts before making his measured reply.

'You're angry with me, I can see that. And I can't blame you. But please, don't think I don't care about Ned now. I do. I have no idea how to resolve things, but I promise you, I'll do my best by him. Which doesn't mean I'm about to wade in like an FBI agent and take him from you. You're his mother, and as we all know, it's mothers who make the important decisions when it comes to children. Dads are just hangers-on who need to know their place.' He gave a small smile and said, 'You can put down your weapons now.'

She relented and smiled too. 'So, when do you want to meet your son?'

55

The back door slammed so violently that the windows rattled. Caspar was leaving the house to go for another of his long walks. Since they had arrived back from Northumberland, he had done a lot of walking, always alone and always for hours at a time. It was as if he was trying to walk his grief out of his system. Gabriel knew from bitter experience that it wouldn't work.

They had buried Damson yesterday. It had been an exhausting, emotionally draining day. An unlikely mixture of people had turned up for the funeral.

Jonah and Roland had gone through Damson's address book and had contacted as many people as they could, working on the theory that because Damson was so pragmatic, if she had entered a name in the book, it was because she liked that person: ex-husbands' and boyfriends' names were conspicuously absent.

Not knowing how Caspar was going to survive the day, Gabriel had concentrated on keeping people away from his son: their looks and words of sympathy, no matter how well meant, were not what he needed. Once the service was over, they had walked next door to Jonah's house where he had laid on a modest buffet of sandwiches and drinks. While Jonah and Roland had poured drinks and chatted politely with the guests, Gabriel had grabbed a plate of sandwiches and taken Caspar back to the churchyard. 'Your brother has it all in hand,' he'd said. 'Let's have some time on our own.' They had sat on a wooden bench in the warm sun, just yards away from Damson's grave. The gravediggers had finished their work and the hole was now filled in, decorated with flowers. To the right of this was her mother's grave, and further along, her step-mother's. Gabriel had deliberately avoided coming here since Val's funeral and it surprised him to see how well tended the plots were. There was only one person who could have been caring for them so diligently. And how typical of Jonah that was. There was never any song and dance about him. He never went out of his way to look for thanks and glory. It was a trait that was wholly reminiscent of his mother.

'Is this supposed to help?' asked Caspar, his gaze on his sister's grave.

Putting the plate of sandwiches on the bench between them, Gabriel produced a dented silver hip flask from his suit-jacket pocket. He passed it to Caspar. 'Can it make it any worse?'

Loosening his tie, Caspar took a swig of the brandy, then another. He wiped the back of his hand across his mouth. 'No. You're right. Wherever I am, I'll always feel the awful loss of her.'

'Better to accept the truth of that than spend the rest of your life running from it.'

'Is that what you did with Mum?'

'I never stopped running. It's why I buggered up things with you three children so spectacularly. I turned away from you, left you to cope with something you weren't able to deal with. It's only now that I've come to realise the harm I caused through my selfishness. Heartbreak rots our integrity, Caspar, remember that. And I'm telling you this because I'm being selfish once again. I need you to know why I behaved as I did.' He cleared his throat. 'My biggest regret is that I didn't have a chance to apologise to Damson. Are you going to drink that flask dry?'

Caspar passed it back to him. 'I think Damson was ahead of you, had worked it out for herself.'

'She had?'

'She was always the smarter one of the two of us. More astute than anyone gave her credit for. One of the last things she said to me was that we're survivors, not victims.'

Gabriel pondered on this. 'From what Jonah's told me, Roland Hall played a crucial part in her life towards the end.'

'Are you saying I didn't?'

At once Gabriel felt Caspar's body turn rigid on the seat next to him. 'No, I'm not,' he said emphatically, keen to avoid upsetting his son. There had been enough explosive outbursts from Caspar lately, when he had ranted and raved and thrown things, then left the house to tramp across the moors, returning hours later exhausted, his rage spent. It was just what Gabriel had done when Anastasia had died. 'I'm saying you, me, Jonah, we weren't the people she needed at that time.'

Caspar's chin dropped. 'So what's brought on all this understanding, Dad? Bit of a change of tune, isn't it?'

Gabriel ignored the dismissive tone, and after a swig of brandy, he said, 'I came very close to killing myself last month.' He waited for the words to sink in, then saw the disbelief in his son's face.

'You? But why? How?'

'Yes, me – of all people. But you see, I suddenly understood how much I hated being alone and the reasons why I was alone. Having reached that conclusion, it seemed the perfect moment to take my cue to exit stage left. As to the how, well – picture the scene if you will – I went down to the copse with a shotgun, all ready to blast my stupid head off.'

Caspar looked suitably horror-stricken. 'What happened?'

'You mean, what went wrong? I didn't have it in me when push came to

330

shove. Oh, I meant to do it, I really did. Maybe if I'd taken some Dutch courage with me I would have done it. But there I was, bawling my eyes out, the gun shoved up under my chin, and an angel of mercy appeared from nowhere.' He watched Caspar's expression change to one of time-to-humour-the-old-boy. 'She was an angel of sorts,' he went on, 'although she doesn't have wings.' He smiled. 'It was Miss Costello.'

Caspar looked confused. 'But I thought she'd left weeks ago.'

'She did, but she came back that day. Was it fate, or just good timing?' He shrugged. 'Who knows? Sandwich?'

'No.'

'You need to eat, Caspar.'

'I will. Just not today.'

The sound of knocking jolted Gabriel out of his reverie. He was expecting Jonah – it was the weekend – but Jonah never knocked twice. He knocked once then let himself in.

He opened the back door and was momentarily nonplussed. It was Clara Costello's junk-dealer friend, Archie Merryman.

They stared at one another warily.

'I was sorry to hear about your daughter—'

'I was sorry to hear about your mother—' they said simultaneously, and in a perfect mirror image of each other, they looked down at their feet, not knowing what to say next. Crippled with embarrassment, they were like a pair of schoolboys who had been forced to apologise for fighting in the playground.

Clutching a carrier bag, Archie hoped that he could live up to Clara's expectations of him. She had asked him to visit the Commandant with a view to keeping an eye on the old boy. 'He's going to need someone to cheer him up in the weeks ahead,' she had said, 'and I can't think of anyone better suited to the task.' Personally, Archie thought he was the last person on earth fit for such a task. But still, she had thought him capable of it, so here he was.

'I've brought you this,' he said, dipping his hand into the bag and pulling out a bottle of whisky. 'Just by way of saying I reckon I know what you're going through.'

Gabriel stared at the bottle. He thought of the letter Clara had written for him on his return from Northumberland, in which she had asked him, when he felt able to, to keep an eye on Archie Merryman in her absence. 'I know you like to think of yourself as an unsociable crosspatch,' she had written, 'but underneath it all, I know you're the sweetest man alive who won't think twice about doing this one small thing for me.'

Just for the sheer hell of it, he'd show her what he was made of.

He took the offered bottle and said, 'Mr Merryman, it's a little early, but how do you feel about a pre-lunch snifter?'

'Please, it's Archie, and thank you, a drink would slip down a treat.

Especially after the week I've had. Though yours can't have been much better.'

'You're not wrong there. Not wrong at all.'

'For once it looks as if we'll get through an entire barbecue without a drop of rain.'

Clara passed Guy a glass of wine and agreed with him absently.

'Oh, come on, Clara,' he said, 'lose the long face. It'll be okay. Anyone would think Ned was being put through some kind of test.'

Louise came over from where she and Moira had been setting the table. 'You're not still worrying, are you?' she said to Clara.

'Of course I am! Wouldn't you be, if your child was meeting his father for the first time?' Though Ned was at the bottom of the garden playing football with David and well out of earshot, Clara kept her voice low.

'The important thing is that Ned doesn't have a clue what's going on,' Guy said, equally circumspect. 'As far as he's concerned, Todd is just another of his mother's many friends.'

Clara knew that what Guy was saying was right. But, oh, she just wished this day could be over. It had seemed so reasonable when Louise and David had offered to invite Todd to a lunchtime barbecue so that he could meet Ned in a relaxed setting. But now she was regretting the whole idea. What if Todd suddenly felt the need to blurt out to Ned who he was? Common sense told her that Todd would never do that: he was one of the most rational people she knew.

They had discussed this important day on the phone several times and had even met up again for a drink last night. He was as concerned as she was that Ned was not put through any emotional upset. It helped enormously that he was the same understanding Todd with whom she had fallen in love, and while it seemed a paradox, she frequently found herself thanking her lucky stars that she had had an affair with such a considerate man.

Determined to safeguard Ned, Clara had laid down the ground rules straight away. She had told Todd that until he had decided whether he was going to tell his wife about Ned and therefore offer a real, open commitment, he could not reveal who he was. It was harsh, but it was Ned's feelings that mattered, not hers, not Todd's.

Yet she wasn't without sympathy for Todd. She knew he was up against the worst dilemma he would probably ever have to face. But the cool, efficient and detached woman within her reasoned that it was *his* problem. She had cleared her conscience by telling him about Ned; what happened next was down to him. She could do nothing to help him.

She was a hard-headed realist, if nothing else.

She had said this to Jonah on the phone late last night – she had phoned him several times, always when Louise and David had gone to bed and she could be sure of talking to him without Louise listening in. 'Nothing wrong in being hard-headed or a realist,' he'd said.

'Did I say there was?'

'No, but something in your tone suggested you were defending yourself.'

'Goodness, you're being mighty forward all of a sudden.'

He'd laughed. 'Only because I know I'm out of slapping range.'

After he'd brought her up to date with how his brother and father were getting on, he'd said, 'It's a pity you're not here, it's a beautiful night.' He hadn't said he was missing her, but the implication was there.

'Are you in the garden?'

'On the terrace with a glass of wine and a bag of pistachio nuts.'

'Sounds good. Describe the view for me.'

'Mm ... it's dark and starry.'

'Come on, you can do better than that.'

'Did I mention the moon?'

'No.'

'It's very white and looks like a clipped toenail.'

'Stop! You're spoiling it for me. Where's your romantic, chivalrous soul, Jonah Liberty?'

'It's cowering under the table too scared to show itself.'

'Then tell it to pull itself together.'

'I've tried but it's no good. It said, "What's the point? Who's here for me to sweet-talk?"'

It had been good talking to him, and not just because he took her mind off Todd.

Todd arrived exactly on time, just as Clara had known he would. One look at his face as he stepped out of his car and she knew he was as nervous as she was. It made her feel better, took away some of her edginess.

Which couldn't be said of her friends.

They tried too hard to show that they were relaxed with the situation. Louise and Moira laughed too loudly at Todd's joke about the weather, and Guy took the bottles of Californian wine he'd brought with such expansive gratitude that anyone would have thought he had been presented with the Holy Grail.

And while they tried to hide their awkwardness, a piercing squeal came up from the bottom of the garden. Seconds later, Ned came running towards them, his dark hair shiny in the bright sunlight, bouncing with each step he took. His face was a huge grin of delight. 'Mummy, Mummy, I beat Uncle David. Ten goals to five!' Breathless, he threw himself at her legs and raised his arms for her to scoop him up as she usually did. But on this occasion, she didn't. 'Ned,' she said, 'this is an old friend of mine. He lives in America and his name is Todd. Have you got enough puff to say hello to him?'

Ned looked up at him and smiled confidently. 'Hello, Mr Todd. Do you like playing football?'

It was such an emotionally charged moment that everyone suddenly found something to do – the barbecue coals needed lighting, the salads had to be dressed, and a new bottle of wine opened. Clara watched Todd's face as he hunkered down to be on eye level with Ned. 'Hi,' he said, 'I'm more of a baseball fan, but I'll give football a shot if you'll teach me.'

Ned grinned. 'I'm very good. Jonah taught me when Mummy was ill in bed. He showed me how to tackle. Do you want to see?'

Todd glanced up at Clara and her heart twisted as she saw both sadness and joy in his face. 'Would you mind?' he asked.

She smiled. 'Not at all.'

They were three very important words, she thought later that evening when Todd had left for his hotel, and she was kissing Ned goodnight.

'Todd was nice,' Ned said, snuggling down beneath the duvet and holding Mermy up for her to kiss as well. 'I like the way he talks. Will he come and see us again?'

'I don't know. He's very busy at the moment and then he has to go home to America.'

She pushed the hair out of his eyes, and was about to get up from the bed when he said, 'Mummy?'

'Yes?'

He gave her one of his melting looks. 'What do you think Mr Liberty is doing right now?'

'Probably wondering what you're doing right now.'

He seemed pleased by this thought. 'Do you think so?'

'Absolutely. You're a hard boy to forget, Ned.'

'Can we go back to Mermaid House to see him?'

She had known it would only be a matter of time before he asked her this question.

'Don't you like being here?'

He hesitated, as though not wanting to cause offence. 'Mm . . . it is nice, but I miss Mr Liberty.'

'Well, that's not a bad thing. It means you care about people, and that's good.'

'It doesn't feel good. It feels . . . horrible.' His lower lip wobbled.

'Oh, Ned.' She lifted him out of bed and sat him on her lap. It wasn't often he cried, but when he did, Clara knew it was with good reason. She cuddled his warm body against hers, but the tears had taken hold of him and there seemed no way to comfort him. Hearing the noise, Louise popped her head round the door.

'What's wrong?' she asked, concerned.

'A surfeit of good times, I think.'

Eventually Clara settled him by promising that they would ring Mr Liberty tomorrow morning so that Ned could speak to him. When she joined her friends downstairs, she sensed they had something to say to her: they had formed themselves into what looked suspiciously like a deputation.

Guy patted the seat next to him on the sofa. 'Clarabelle, for once in your life you're going to take the advice of your friends.'

'And please don't take this the wrong way,' Louise said, 'but quite frankly you've outstayed your welcome.'

'Yes,' agreed David, handing round cups of coffee. 'So you can pack up your things and go. We've had enough.'

'More than enough,' said Guy. 'If I have to hear one more word about Ned's superhuman friend, Mr Gabriel Liberty, I think I'll go mad.'

'And as for the wonderful Jonah Liberty,' said Moira, 'well, please, is any man that perfect?'

'Oh yes,' groaned Louise. 'If I have to eavesdrop on another of your midnight phone calls, I'll die of envy.'

Clara stared at them confounded. 'What's going on? What are you up to?'

'Get real, sister,' laughed Guy. 'You and Ned have done nothing but go on about Deaconsbridge. If we've heard it once, what a fantastic time you had, we've heard it till we're ready to go up there and see for ourselves the Utopia you've discovered.'

'But—'

'No buts,' interrupted Louise, with a warning finger. 'If you hadn't come back here to see Todd, you'd still be up there in the Peak District, wouldn't you?'

Clara nodded. 'Possibly.'

'No possibly about it! Now, what's stopping you from taking off tomorrow and seeing how the land lies?'

'But why would I want to do that?'

Nobody answered her. They just stared at her hard. She knew she was being pushed into a corner, and that her friends wouldn't let the matter drop until they were satisfied. She decided to humour them.

'Look, the truth is, it has crossed my mind to do just as you're suggesting, but—'

'We told you, no buts!'

'But, Louise, I'm worried if Ned and I do go back we might not want to leave.'

'I'm sorry, call me a dumb old bloke,' said David, 'but what's the danger in that? You've found somewhere you like, where you've made friends, and where there's even the chance of you getting off with a real live man. Explain the problem.'

'The problem is you lot! What would I do without you all?'

'Oh, so we're just here to be used, are we?'

'Guy, don't you dare try twisting my words. I meant, how would I survive without your friendship permanently on hand?'

Moira shook her head. 'Poor excuse. We're not having that one, are we?'

'Certainly not,' agreed Louise. 'You left us behind in March without so much as a second thought. What's different now?'

'Are you trying to get rid of me?'

'*Yes!*' they all shouted together.

'But this *is* different,' she said, trying not to get carried away with their enthusiasm. 'If Ned and I go back, and we find that we want to stay, what then?'

David sighed as if she was being particularly dense. 'You'll get a job, get Ned into school and find yourself somewhere to live.'

'And if it doesn't work?'

'You come back here,' Guy said. 'But what would be worse, doing that, or knowing you were too much of a coward to try it?'

'You sneaky dog, Guy Morrell. Nobody gets away with accusing me of cowardice.' Smiling, she thumped him with a cushion. 'I'm beginning to think that I *would* be better off living miles away from you lot.'

Louise grinned. 'I think we're getting somewhere. We're wearing her down.'

'Oh, you did that a long time ago. But be serious for a minute. Do you really think I should go back for the rest of the summer and see how it pans out?'

'All you have to do is ask yourself, what have you got to lose?'

Louise's question stayed with Clara as she fell asleep that night. The only answer she could come up with was that she had a resounding nothing to lose – but maybe everything to gain.

With her fondness for having everything organised, and every conceivable contingency catered for, Clara spent the following week planning. At no time did she let on to Ned what she was doing.

There was one important phone call she had to make, to her parents. 'I just wanted to know how you would feel if Ned and I weren't here when you came back from Australia,' she said to her mother.

Her mother went very quiet and said, 'Whatever decision you make, you know we'll go along with it. We always have and there's no reason why we would change now.'

'You're the best, Mum.'

'I know.'

'Wonderfully modest too.'

'You would know, dear – like mother like daughter. Now, explain what you're up to, but quickly, this call must be costing you a small fortune.'

After Clara had outlined her plans, her mother wished her luck and asked if Ned was around for her to speak to.

'I'll go and get him, but don't mention anything I've just told you. I want it to be a surprise for him.'

The night before she planned to drive north with Ned, she met up with

Todd one last time. His work was almost finished at Phoenix and he was due to fly home in two days.

They sat in the garden of the Kingfisher Arms once more, but Clara didn't press him for details about the future. She had no right to do that.

'I want to thank you for being so understanding,' he said, 'and for letting me see Ned. A lot of women wouldn't have acted as generously as you have. I'm more grateful than I can say.'

'But I have so much more to be grateful for,' she said. 'I have Ned. He means the world to me.'

'I know he does. I can also see how much you mean to him. He's a wonderful boy, you've done a fine job of raising him. I'm just envious and shamefaced I haven't been there for you both when I should have been.'

There was an awkward moment when he brought up the question of financial support. 'I'd feel a whole lot better if you'd take this, Clara.' He handed her a cheque. Without looking at it, but knowing instinctively that he would have been generous, she passed it back to him.

'And I'd feel a whole lot worse taking it. When you know exactly what you want to do about Ned, then we'll discuss money. Not before.'

'Fair enough,' he said. Then, looking faintly embarrassed, he added, 'By the way, what . . . what did you put on the birth certificate?'

She smiled and covered his hand with hers. 'What do you think? Your name, of course.'

He swallowed. 'You always did play it dead straight, Clara. Thank you for doing that.'

They exchanged addresses and telephone numbers, and after they'd drunk a toast to Ned's future, Todd took her by surprise.

'So who's this Jonah I kept hearing about from Ned when he was trying to teach me to kick a ball?'

Annoyingly, she felt the colour rise to her face. 'A friend.'

'A special friend?'

'Maybe.'

'Ned seems quite taken with him. What's he like?'

Driving back to Louise and David's, Clara felt sorry for Todd. How complicated his life had suddenly become. He had arrived in England a happily married man with, presumably, few cares in the world, and he was returning home with the knowledge that he had a son. Not only that, he had an unexpected emotion to deal with. One that Clara certainly hadn't anticipated.

Jealousy.

In his brief cross-examination of her about Jonah, he had clearly been troubled by the idea of another man forming a relationship with Ned.

Funny that Guy and David hadn't undergone the same scrutiny.

56

For the last day or so, the weather had alternated between blustery showers and intermittent sunshine, but now it had settled again and the sky was blue save for clouds of fluffy whiteness that bubbled up then drifted away on the light wind that blew in from the west.

Standing in front of the mirror, Gabriel straightened his tie and admired his new blazer. He pushed his shoulders back, turned to the right, then to the left, and decided it wasn't a bad fit. He was glad now that he had asked Caspar to take him shopping for some new clothes, and even more so that he had taken his son's advice and chosen the single-breasted rather than the double. Next he turned his attention to his hair. Again, Caspar had intervened and pushed him to have it cut dramatically shorter than he wanted. Grudgingly Gabriel admitted that it was a great improvement. It made him look younger, distinguished – with a dash of jauntiness, he liked to think. He tilted his chin up, raised an eyebrow like Roger Moore did in all those old Bond movies and mentally declared himself a handsome devil.

Chuckling, he turned his back on the mirror and left his room. Enough of the preening. Time was of the essence. He still had lots to do. Ned and Clara would soon be here. He paused on the landing outside Val's old room, then went in. With Archie's help, he had had it spruced up for Clara. When he had mentioned to Archie that he wanted to have it redecorated, he'd said, 'I know just the chaps you need.' Turned out that Shirley from the Mermaid café had a son who, with a friend, had started up his own painting and decorating business and was looking for work. 'You'd better be cheap,' he'd said to them when they arrived on their motorbikes to give him an estimate. 'Just because I live in a large house, don't imagine my wallet is a bottomless pit.'

The following day they'd shown up in a wreck of a van with a ladder strapped to the roof. Dressed in overalls, they plugged in a large radio that belted out something that could never be described as music and got down to work, stripping off the old flowery wallpaper that had been there for more than twenty years and replacing it with a cheerful yellow paper that brightened the room. Shirley's son, Robbie, had explained to him that there was a range of bed linen to match the paper and border they'd used, so he'd instructed them to get that too. 'Might as well go the whole hog,' he'd said, handing over more money. They had transformed Jonah's old room too, giving it a fresh new look that they swore blind would appeal to a small boy. They had worked quickly and tidily, and Gabriel was so pleased with the results that he thought he might get them to have a go at some of the other rooms. His own, perhaps.

Shirley had been a great help too. Funny, that – he'd only ever talked to her in the café when he was ordering his lunch, but she had been ready to lend a hand when he had mentioned the party he wanted to give. 'You'll be needing food, then,' she'd said. 'Want any help with that?'

'I don't want anything fancy.'

'You mean you don't want anything expensive, you old skinflint.'

She and Archie were somewhere downstairs. It was only a small party he was throwing, but he didn't know how he would have organised everything if they hadn't offered to help. He supposed Archie still needed to be busy. He'd had a tough old time of it recently, what with his wife leaving him and his mother dying, and Gabriel was looking forward to telling Clara that he'd more than risen to her challenge of keeping an eye on him. Under the guise of clearing out yet more junk from the house, he'd seen quite a lot of Archie, had found him an agreeable man, and he was pleased, if not a little amused, that he and Shirley were getting on so well. He knew, from first-hand experience, that it wasn't good to be on one's own too much. Having people around made things bearable.

And that was what he had wished for, that day at the Mermaid Cavern. He had tossed his coin into the pool and wished that he would have the pleasure of seeing Ned and his mother again. Because when they were around, life was infinitely better.

Downstairs, he found the kitchen empty. An appetising smell was coming from the oven, but apart from that, there was no sign of any activity. Like Clara, Shirley was a tidy worker and she put everything away after she had finished with it. She had been coming to Mermaid House for just over a week now to keep the place in order, and the arrangement was working well. She still had her part-time job at the café in town, but as she had said to him after Archie had come up with the idea, 'We'll give each other a trial run for a month. And this is what I'll do for you. For six pounds an hour, I'll keep your home sweet if you promise to keep your temper sweet. How does that sound?'

'It sounds to me as if we ought to spit and shake on it before either of us changes our mind.'

So far she had been as good as her word. The rooms that mattered were as neat as a pin. He had no complaints at all.

The only gripe he had was that Dr Singh wasn't around to see how smoothly he now had his life ticking over. He'd heard through Shirley that he had moved up to Blackburn. Or was it Bury? Anyway, wherever he had beggared off to, doubtless he was poking his nose into some other poor devil's affairs. Though, of course, despite his annoying interference, Gabriel was aware that if Dr Singh hadn't been such a nuisance, he might never have formed the friendship he now had with Ned and Clara. Or be reconciled with Jonah and Caspar. He still had a way to go with Caspar: his elder son had yet to recover from the shock of Damson's death. He was currently dividing his time between Manchester and Mermaid House, and though it was hard work having Caspar around, Gabriel didn't want him to be on his own. The more time they spent together, the more alike Gabriel realised they were. Neither suffered fools gladly, both were as stubborn as hell and they each possessed a temper that could scorch asbestos. And while Caspar's dandified arrogance and assumption that the world revolved around him would always infuriate him, Gabriel could, none the less, appreciate and admire his sharpness of mind. If only he would apply it to something more constructive than he had until now.

In the meantime, Gabriel took it as an encouraging sign that Caspar had agreed to join the party today. He had expected his son to turn down the invitation, denouncing it as in poor taste. Instead, he had said he would try to put in a brief appearance.

Jonah was the only person who didn't know what was going on. He didn't even know that Clara would be here this afternoon – he had been deliberately misled into believing that she was arriving tomorrow. Revelling in all the skulduggery, Gabriel had phoned Jonah and told him to get here when school was finished because there was something important they needed to discuss. Which was partly true, there *were* things he needed to say this afternoon. Things he should have said and done a long time ago.

It was reading Val's diaries that had clinched it for him. Jonah had given the notebooks to him last week, saying Clara had found them when she had been sorting out Val's room. Seeing the anxiety in Jonah's face, Gabriel had guessed that he wouldn't be the first person to see the journals. They had made for difficult reading, and it saddened him to know that Val had felt such an outsider at Mermaid House. What moved him most, though, was her determination to try to understand a family that had, in her words, 'had its heart ripped out of it'. More graphically, she had written, 'I've been brought in as a plaster for this family, but what they really need is a tourniquet to staunch the flow of their misery. I doubt they'll ever know peace of mind. Because, perversely, they don't seem to want it.'

After he had finished arranging the flowers on Damson's grave, Caspar straightened up. He flicked at a hover-fly that had landed on his sleeve and then stood still, his head bowed, his eyes closed. Anyone seeing him would have thought he was praying, but he wasn't. He was remembering Damson as a young girl. Vital and beautiful. Sharp and funny. Wilful and passionate. And dangerous to be with at times. 'I'm just like my namesake,' she would say to anyone meeting her for the first time, and commenting on the uniqueness of her Christian name. 'I have a dark and bitter-sweet soul.'

That darkness of the soul of which she had spoken frequently as a teenager had frightened him. She talked endlessly about death, and what it might feel like when you knew the end was near. Around the time of their twentieth birthday, she had taken to disappearing for weeks at a time. He hadn't liked her doing that, had hated not knowing where she was, who she was with, or what she was up to. Selfishly, he had felt excluded. But when she surfaced again, she was the same old Damson, ready to party and stir up some fun. In view of what Hall had told him at Rosewood Manor, it was possible that these absences had been connected with the abortions.

He opened his eyes and sighed. How was it possible to be so close to someone, and yet so far from them?

Checking his watch, he saw that he would have to leave soon. He wasn't in the mood to be sociable, but he had made his sister a promise, and he would do his damnedest to keep it. He had let her down when she was alive, he would not do the same now she was dead. So a party it was.

He knew exactly why his father had chosen today to throw a party, and he supposed it was about time, but it was a woefully sentimental and symbolic gesture. And what a lot of fuss he was making about it. New clothes. A hair-cut. Not to mention the bedrooms that had been tarted up for the benefit of the shrewish Clara Costello – the angel in the copse – and her son, who were coming to stay for the rest of the summer. Bizarrely, it seemed that his brother had fallen for the woman's sharp-tongued charms, and stranger still, their father was keen to play the part of Cupid and encourage the blossoming romance.

'Oh, Damson,' he murmured softly, 'I wish you were here with me to witness this madness.'

He turned and walked away, back down the gravel path and out on to the road where his car was parked in front of Jonah's house.

He was now the not-so-proud owner of a second-hand Rover. The Maserati had been sold, and his beautiful loft apartment was on the market. The bank, the creditors, the taxman, they were all feasting greedily on his remains, but he didn't give a monkey's. It was gone. Another chapter in his life dealt with.

Bruised and battered he might be, deserted by his so-called friends and treated as a social leper, but he was far from being down and out. Oh, not by a long chalk. It would take more rope than that to hang Caspar Liberty.

Ironically his father, after stubbornly refusing to help him, had changed his mind the other day and offered to bail him out when he discovered the mess he was in, but Caspar had rejected the offer. Pride had made him sensitive to pity. Besides, Damson had left him her pretty little house in Bath with a sizeable amount of money, which she had made from shrewd investments from her two divorce settlements. He planned to move down there and start afresh. A new beginning was what he needed. And, thanks to his sister, he had been given the opportunity to do just that.

Damson's will had been clear on two points in particular, that (a) she had been of sound mind when she had written it, and (b) Caspar was to be the main beneficiary of her estate and that he was to agree to her instructions that Rosewood Manor was to receive a modest annuity from a trust fund she had set up.

He had no problem with this. He might not like Hall and all he stood for, but he would always respect Damson's wishes.

Darling Damson. How dull his world was going to be without her.

Ned was so excited, he was in danger of bouncing out of his seat. If he hadn't been strapped in, he very nearly would have when Clara swerved to avoid a large pothole. They juddered on, and suddenly Mermaid House appeared over the brow of the hill. It was the most welcoming sight, made her heart beat just a little faster. For the coming months it was to be their new home.

Before they had set off first thing that morning, Louise had threatened to come up in the next week so that she could see Mermaid House for herself.

'You're all talk, Louise,' Clara had said, giving her a huge hug goodbye. 'You've never been further north than the Cotswolds.'

'Yes, but I'm prepared to make an exception in this case.'

Guy had moved in for a final hug and produced an envelope from his jacket pocket. 'For you, Clarabelle.'

'What is it?'

He'd smiled. 'A bet's a bet. Open it and see.'

She'd laughed when she'd seen the cheque for two hundred pounds. She'd forgotten all about the bet he'd made with her that she would be crawling home within a month and applying for her old job.

Saying goodbye to her friends this time round had been tough, because in her heart she knew she wanted to give Deaconsbridge her best shot: she wanted to stay there and really make it work. Other than the brief sojourn in the States and her time at college, she had never lived away from where she had grown up, she hadn't felt the need to break away.

But now she did. And tied into this was the realisation that she wanted to give herself the chance to discover what else she was capable of doing. The Clara Costello she knew was – and to paraphrase her friends – smart, unflappable, hard-working and supremely resourceful. Less flattering, and to paraphrase her brother, she was a regular bossy boots. 'Give it time and you'll turn into a formidable old battle-axe,' he'd said to her not so long ago.

Maybe she would, maybe she wouldn't. But unless she allowed herself this chance to find out what other talents she had, she would always regret it. She had never liked the expression 'down-shifter', but in essence that was probably what she was opting for. A simple life that would enable her to spend more time with Ned had to be more enriching than the hectic one she had tried before.

And if it didn't work out? Who was to judge and condemn the path she had taken? And was there really such a thing as a wrong path? Critics were ten a penny. They were people too scared to try it for themselves. Too scared to break with convention and enjoy life to the full.

But she wasn't without a back-up plan. Gabriel Liberty's part in all of this was crucial. In letting her and Ned stay at Mermaid House for the rest of the summer, he was giving her the luxury of time and space to reflect on her next move. For now, she had only vague glimpses of the future. She saw herself living here, having traded in her overpriced executive house for something old with character, and odds on, in need of some work. If she let her imagination break free, she pictured herself running a bed-and-breakfast. Okay, she might be deluding herself that she could scrape a living from it, but it was an idea that refused to budge, despite common sense waving a threatening stick at it. It would take a lot of thought before she committed herself to it, and she might even come up with something else, but the big plus was that she saw herself being happy. Ned, too.

And she would be the biggest liar that had ever walked the planet if she didn't admit to wanting Jonah to be a part of that happiness. Just to see if he fitted into her life. And if she and Ned could fit into his.

She pulled into the courtyard, and before she had yanked on the handbrake, Ned was out of his seat. She watched him hurtle across the cobbles and pound on the door with his small fists.

When Clara caught up with him, it was all noise and laughter in the kitchen. Archie was there, and so was Shirley. Wearing a PVC apron over a tight-fitting black dress, she was sliding a tray of sausage rolls out of the oven, her face flushed from the blast of heat. With Ned held aloft, Gabriel came towards her. He stooped to kiss her cheek. 'Welcome back. You're late.'

'Well, well, well. And who might this handsomely rakish stranger be with the smart hair-cut and snazzy blazer? Where's the scruffy Mr Liberty I know and love?'

'But Mummy, it is Mr Liberty! Look, it's him!'

She smiled. 'I know, Ned. I'm only teasing.'

'Ah, I see the first of the honoured guests have arrived.'

They all turned. It was Caspar. Brandishing a bottle of champagne, he said, 'A contribution towards the merriment.' He put it on the table and held out his hand towards Clara. 'We didn't ever really introduce ourselves properly, did we? Caspar Liberty, the family ne'er-do-well.' He clicked his heels together and bowed elegantly.

Clara shook hands with him, seeing him as other women might: handsome, charming, but above all else, dangerous. For a lot of women that might be his appeal. But he held no attraction for her.

'We need to hide your van,' Gabriel said, some minutes later, when the kerfuffle of their arrival had died down.

'I'll help you bring your stuff in if you like,' offered Archie.

They went outside together, and after Clara had put Winnie out of sight, and was passing Archie Ned's bag, she said, 'How have you been since I last saw you? You look much better, if you don't mind me saying.'

'Thanks, love, I'm feeling great, on top of things again. And you were right about Shirley.'

'No kidding?'

He smiled shyly. 'And I've moved into what she calls my bachelor flat. It's quite comfortable, really. Less to fret over, if you know what I mean. It's been quite liberating throwing off a lifetime of clutter. You'd think I would have sussed that long ago, given the work I do. Funny thing is, I needn't have moved. Bessie left me her house over in Derby and the money it's going to fetch, much more than I'd ever thought, could have been used to pay off Stella.'

She touched his arm. 'For what it's worth, I think you did the right thing in moving. Leave the memories behind.'

'Oh, aye, I don't regret selling up. It was the best thing I could have done. Now I've got a bit of spare cash to enjoy myself. I'm thinking of taking a holiday. Do a bit of travelling.'

'Good for you. Hey, I don't suppose I could interest you in a camper-van, could I? Generous rates for friends.'

He laughed. 'Oh, that sounds dangerous. I might do a Clara Costello – find somewhere I like and never come back.'

She wagged a finger at him. 'Not dangerous, Archie. Adventurous. Living life to the full. That's what you must do from now on. Just think of the fun you and Shirley could have in a camper-van.'

Jonah wondered what his father wanted to see him about. He had sounded serious on the phone and he hoped it wasn't bad news. There'd been enough of that recently.

He drove into the courtyard and parked alongside his father's Land Rover. He knocked on the back door, then entered. 'Dad,' he called, 'it's me, Jonah.'

There was no reply.

Passing the gun room, he caught the smell of cooking. Bit early for his father to be getting his supper ready, wasn't it? He pushed open the kitchen door, but stopped dead in his tracks. 'Clara! What are you doing here? I thought you were arriving tomorrow.'

She put down the tea-towel she'd been using to dry some plates. 'I could go away and come back in the morning if you'd prefer.'

'Don't even think about it!' He moved forward, was all set to put his arms around her and kiss her, when he held back. 'Are we alone?' he asked. He glanced over her shoulder towards the hall. 'Or are we likely to be interrupted by a curious son and a jealous father?'

She smiled. 'We're alone. And you have full permission to make the most of it.'

He did.

Afterwards, he said, 'It's so good to see you again. When did you change your mind about coming?'

'Oh, days ago.'

'But you never said anything. We spoke on the phone last night and—'

'The plot thickens, Master Liberty.' Grinning, she took his hands in hers. 'I think it's time you came with me. But you have to promise to close your eyes.'

Puzzled, he did as she said and allowed her to lead him outside. He knew they were crossing the courtyard, but all too soon he became disorientated and didn't know where they were heading. 'No peeping,' she said, just as he was tempted to open an eye.

He heard a door creak and she told him there were two steps in front of him. He lifted a foot exaggeratedly. Then the other.

'You can open your eyes now.'

He was in the banqueting hall. It had been thoroughly cleaned, was almost unrecognisable. There were candles everywhere, and balloons and streamers. A long, thin table ran the length of the room; it was laden with food. There was a square cake in the middle of it all and it had . . . small blue candles on it.

And then it dawned on him. It was a party. A birthday party.

His father came towards him with a glass of champagne. 'Happy birthday, Jonah.'

'But . . . it's not until next week.'

His father shook his head. 'This is your proper birthday, son. This was the day you were born, and from now on, this is when we celebrate that fact.'

Still recovering from the surprise of seeing Clara, Jonah now had this second shock to deal with. Nothing could have stunned him more. To anyone else it might have seemed an act of madness to accept what his father had laid down all those years ago, but it had never bothered him. All families had their foibles, their unique way of handling difficult situations, and Jonah had simply gone along with Gabriel's wishes. But it touched him deeply to know that his father now cared enough to rewrite the rule book. He took the glass from Gabriel's outstretched hand. 'I don't know what to say,' he murmured. 'I'm overwhelmed.'

Gabriel turned to the rest of the room. 'In that case, how about we all have a crack at it for him?'

With his arm round Shirley's waist, Archie raised his glass. 'Here's to new beginnings and making the most of what time we have.'

'Hear, hear!' said Shirley, chinking her glass against his.

'Or, how about here's to Clara not discovering that Jonah's gay?'

'Caspar!'

'Only joking, Dad. Here's to it, brother, may you always look older and uglier than me. May the heavens always rain on you and the sun shine its rays on me.'

Smiling, Jonah turned to Clara who now had Ned resting on her hip – he was dipping a finger into her glass. 'And do you have any words of wisdom?'

'I think I'm with Archie on this one. It's got to be, "To new beginnings".'

They sat in the gathering darkness on the stone bench beneath the library window. The air was warm and still, and way off in the distance, a dog was barking. Archie and Shirley had gone home, Ned was in bed, and Gabriel and Caspar were in the kitchen tidying up.

Clara leaned into Jonah and he rested an arm around her shoulder. 'A good birthday?' she asked.

'The best.'

'Even if Caspar did try to bring your sexuality into question?'

He tilted his head back and smiled. 'I took that as a reassuring sign that my brother is on the mend. I'd rather have him like that than the shattered mess he's been since we brought him back from Rosewood.'

'How generous of you. I'm not sure I'd be so forgiving.'

'Don't go making me out to be a saint, I haven't always thought so well of him.' He picked up her hand, raised it to his lips and kissed it tenderly. After a companionable silence had passed between them, he said, 'Clara, this might seem a strange question, but why do you and my father still call one another by your surnames?'

'Because it's all part of the act we put on for one another's benefit. It would spoil everything if we ever stopped doing it. It's a sign of affection between us. A code, I suppose. A game that only the two of us are in on. Sorry if that excludes you.'

'Don't apologise. I think it's nice. You realise, don't you, that it's going to be a strange old courtship, trying to win the heart of a woman who lives with my father? Heaven help me if I don't get you home on time.'

She laughed. 'Only you would call it a courtship.'

He laughed too. 'What would you prefer I called it?'

She thought about this. 'Mm . . . after giving it my fullest consideration, I think courtship will do just fine. Despite outward appearances, I'm a straightforward old-fashioned girl, who needs to take things slowly.'

'Just my kind of girl, then.'

'I bet that's not what you thought when you first met me.'

'That's true. If I remember rightly, it was fear at first sight. I thought, Here's a woman who could more than punch her weight.'

'No better basis for a long and lasting relationship.'

Smiling, he turned his head towards her. 'Dare I ask permission for an extremely long and lingering birthday kiss?'

'Permission granted.'

Having said goodnight to Caspar, who had decided to head back to Manchester and not stay the night as he had thought he might, Gabriel stood in the darkness at the library window. With a glass of whisky in his hand, he gazed at the silhouetted figures on the bench outside.

He raised his glass to them both. 'Happy birthday, Jonah. By God, you've earned it. And to you, Miss Clara Costello. I may have lost my daughter, but I have the feeling I might be lucky and have the gift of another.'

He turned and looked up at Anastasia's portrait, conscious that she had waited a long time for this moment. 'We got there in the end, my darling girl. It took a while, but I think we got there.'

Raising his glass once more, he said, 'To you, my dearest Anastasia. To Val, and to Damson ... In my clumsy inadequate way, I loved you all.'

Hidden Talents

To Edward and Samuel,
my multi-talented sons.

Acknowledgements

As ever, countless thanks to everyone at Orion, in particular Helen, Jo, Ian, Linda, Erin, Maggy, Juliet, Jenny, Trevor, Malcolm and Dallas. It wouldn't be the same without you all. (Even you, Mr Taylor!)

Thanks too, to Anthony Keates for my precious paperweight and for the donkey story ... And what would I do for days out were it not for Raymond, Jon, David, Dominic and Graham?

Thank you, Jane, for your continued support and keen editorial eye. And thank you, Susan, for telling me to stop whingeing.

Special hugs and thanks to Mr Lloyd.

Lastly, a whopping great thank you to Helena and Maureen for putting up with me.

1

Dulcie Ballantyne had made a lifelong habit of not making a drama of the unexpected: for sixty-three years silver linings had been her stock in trade. Moreover, she would be a rich woman if she had a pound for every time someone had remarked on her calmness of manner and her continually sunny and optimistic outlook. 'Overreaction serves no purpose other than to make a difficult situation a lot worse,' she would say, whenever anyone remarked on her unflappable nature. It wasn't a happy-go-lucky, trouble-free life that had given her the ability to cope no matter what, it was a wealth of experience. In short, life had taught her to deal with the severest catastrophe.

But as she sat at the kitchen table, waiting for the day to fully form itself, tearful exhaustion was doing away with the last remnants of her self-control and she was seconds away from making a terrible mistake. She had promised herself she wouldn't do it, but desperation was pushing her to ring the hospital to find out how Richard was. As his mistress, though – even a long-standing mistress of three years – she had no right to be at his bedside or have his condition explained to her. 'Are you family?' the nurse had asked her on the telephone late last night, when she had almost begged to know how he was. She should have claimed to be a sister or some other close relative, but shock had wrenched the truth from her and she was informed politely that Mr Richard Cavanagh was still in the coronary care unit in a stable condition.

Stable.

She hung on to this thought, closed her eyes, and willed the man she loved not to leave her.

How often had Richard said that to her? 'Don't leave me, Dulcie. Life would be intolerable without you.'

'I'm not going anywhere,' she had always told him. She had meant it too. Her affair with Richard had been infinitely better than any other relationship she had known since the death of her husband twenty-two years ago. Before she had met Richard, there had been a series of liaisons and one or two men had almost convinced her she was in love, but mostly they had proved to her that she enjoyed living alone too much to want anyone with her on a permanent basis. Commitment phobia was supposed to be the prerogative of men, but as far as she was concerned, commitment was an overrated phenomenon. Much better to let things take their natural course, to do without the restrictive boundary that was frequently the kiss of death to a relationship.

She swallowed hard, ran her fingers through her short, dishevelled hair, and only just kept herself from crying, 'No, no, *no!*' She had changed her mind. She wanted Richard to stay in her life for ever. She would give anything to deepen the commitment between them.

She heaved herself out of the chair where she had been sitting for the last two hours and set about making some breakfast. She hadn't eaten since yesterday afternoon when she and Richard had met at their usual restaurant for lunch – a hotel at a discreet distance from Maywood, where they'd hoped they wouldn't be recognised. It was while they were discussing the creative writers' group she was forming that he had grimaced, dropped his cutlery and clenched his fist against his chest. Horror-struck, she had watched his strong, vigorous body crumple and fall to the floor.

It had been so quick. One minute they were chatting happily, wondering what kind of people would sign up for the group, Richard joking that he would join so that he could spend a legitimate evening with her, and the next they were in an ambulance hurtling to hospital, an oxygen mask clamped to his face. She had behaved immaculately: no hysterical tears; no distraught behaviour that would give rise to the suspicion that they were lovers. She had called Richard's home number on his mobile and left a message on the answerphone for his wife. She hadn't said who she was, just that Mr Cavanagh had been taken ill: a heart-attack. Half an hour later, though it was the hardest thing she had ever done, she had left the hospital before people started to ask awkward questions.

Now she wished she had stayed. Why should she care about the consequences of her presence at his bedside, or worry about anyone else's feelings but her own? Yet that would be so out of character. She *did* care about other people's feelings. Richard had once said to her, as they lay in bed together, 'You care too much sometimes, Dulcie. You're too understanding for your own good.'

'No I'm not,' she'd said, lifting her head from the pillow and gazing into his eyes. 'If I was that saintly I would think more of Angela and call a halt to this affair. It's very wrong what we're doing. It's selfish to be happy at someone else's expense.'

He'd held her tight. 'Don't say that. Don't even think it. Not ever.'

She had always thought that his need for her was greater than her need for him. Now, however, she wasn't so sure. She longed to see Richard. To tell him over and over how much she loved him.

Rousing herself, she cleared away her untouched breakfast and went upstairs to dress. Moping around in her old dressing-gown – not the beautiful silk one Richard had given her, which she wore when he was with her – wouldn't help anyone. It was time to pull herself together and become the cool, composed Dulcie Ballantyne everyone knew her to be.

From overpacked, higgledy-piggledy rails, she chose an outfit that would give her a superficial but necessary lift – a comfortable pair of wool trousers with a cream roll-necked sweater and a pink silk scarf, which she unearthed from the bottom of the wardrobe among her collection of shoes and handbags. She thought of her daughter, and how much she disapproved of Dulcie's untidiness. Kate despaired of her, and had tried since the age of sixteen – she was now twenty-nine – to organise Dulcie's wardrobe. 'Colour co-ordination is the key, Mum,' she would say, riffling through the hangers and shunting them around. Curiously, and for no reason that Dulcie could fathom, it was the only area in the house, and her life for that matter, that she allowed to be muddled, where restful harmony didn't take precedence.

Once she was dressed, she looked down on to the walled garden from her bedroom window. Curved steps led down to the lawn, which was edged with well-stocked borders; some, despite the onset of autumn, were still bright with colour. Leaves had begun to drop from the trees, but the garden remained defiantly cheerful. In the middle of June, Richard had helped her spread several barrowloads of manure over the rose-beds. It had been a Monday afternoon and his family had thought he was away on business. But he had been with her. She'd had him to herself for a whole delicious two days. She smiled at the memory: a rare two days together and they had spent the afternoon shovelling horse droppings. They had laughed about that afterwards. He had claimed that that was what he liked about their relationship, its down-to-earth nature. 'You allow me to be myself,' he said. 'You expect nothing of me, which means I'm free when I'm with you.'

Their love was founded on a strong understanding of each other's needs and a companionship that was both passionate and close, something so many married couples lost sight of. She seldom wanted him to talk about his marriage, but often Richard felt the need to explain, or perhaps justify, why he, an ordinary man (as he called himself), was behaving in the way he was. From what Dulcie knew of his wife, she was an anxious woman who depended on him too much.

Turning from the window, she glanced at herself in the full-length mirror and tried to see beyond the stocky roundness of her body and the burst of lines around her blue eyes, beyond the short fair hair she had dyed every six weeks because she knew it took years off her, and beyond the skin that had lost its firmness. Beyond all this, she saw a woman who was a chameleon. She had played so many different roles in her life, and was destined, she was sure, to play a few more yet.

Downstairs in the kitchen, while she was trying to summon the energy to go out and rake up the leaves, the telephone rang. She snatched up the receiver, her heart pounding. Richard. Darling Richard. He was well enough to call her. Well enough to reassure her that he was all right.

But it wasn't Richard. It was a young girl enquiring about the creative writers' group. She had seen the card Dulcie had placed in the window of the bookshop in town, and wanted to know if there was an age restriction.

2

Jaz Rafferty switched off her mobile and stared up at the sloping ceiling above her bed. It was covered with neat rows of Pre-Raphaelite prints she'd bought during last week's college history-of-art trip to Birmingham's City Art Gallery. Her favourite was *The Last of England* by Ford Madox Brown; the artist had been so dedicated to capturing the coldness of the day – the grey sea and sky, the couple huddled together in their thick winter coats – that he had forced himself to paint much of the picture outdoors, his hands stiff and blue. According to Miss Holmes, her teacher, the picture was all about the young couple and their child embarking on a new and brighter future, but within it there was also a sense of regret at leaving home.

To a large extent Jaz could empathise with the couple, she was all for leaving home as soon as she could, but she doubted she would feel a second's regret when that happy day dawned.

She put her mobile on her bedside table and relished a rare moment of blissful quiet. Added to this was the knowledge that she had a secret. Secrets were great, especially if she could keep them from her brothers and sisters, who were the nosiest, most interfering and irritating bunch on the planet. They were the pain of pains. The wonder was that she hadn't left home years ago. When she was thirteen she had gone through a phase of saying that she was adopted; anything to make people think she wasn't related to four of the most loathsome people alive.

Phin (short for Phineas) was the oldest at twenty-two, then Jimmy, who was twenty. Although they were both earning good money working for Dad's building firm – Rafferty & Sons – they still lived at home. 'And why would we want to live anywhere else?' they would say, whenever she called them mummy's boys for not finding a place of their own. 'Ah, it would break Mum's heart if we moved out.'

They were probably right. Mum loved and spoilt them to bits. Nothing was too much trouble when it came to Phin and Jimmy. 'Oh, go on,' she'd say, the minute Phin looked warily from the iron to the creased shirt he wanted to wear that night.

Pathetic.

And pity the poor girls who would be stupid enough to attach themselves to the Rafferty boys. They'd need to be certifiable to put up with them.

At seventeen, Jaz was next in line in the family pecking order. Every year on her birthday, 5 September, Dad always trotted out the same joke, that he'd had a word with the Almighty before she was conceived. 'Lord, I know how pushed you are, so I'll save you the bother of another boy. We'll make do with a girl this time round.'

Dad wasn't a religious man, not by a long chalk, but he used his Catholic upbringing in the same way he banged on about being so proud of his Irish heritage. 'Dad,' she said to him once, 'you're such a fraud. You wouldn't know a penny whistle if a leprechaun shoved one up your bum. You're as English as the Queen.'

'Yeah,' he'd grinned, 'and she's half German, isn't she?'

His hotline to God backfired on him, though: after a gap of several years, Tamzin (ten) and Lulu (eight) arrived. 'Sweet Moses,' he often complained, 'I'm overrun with women! What have I done to deserve this?'

More to the point, what had *she* ever done to deserve such a family?

From a very young age she'd had a feeling of being displaced. If it weren't for her colouring – so like her mother's – she would have believed that owing to some quirk of nature, or to a mistake made at the hospital where she was born, she had ended up in the wrong family. She could have been no more different from her brothers and sisters, who all took after their father: he described himself as being heartily robust of build and temperament. Jaz would have put money on Tamzin and Lulu having been born with fists clenched, ready to take on the world and destroy it. In contrast, she herself was small and pale with annoying childish freckles across the bridge of her nose. Her hair was long, to her waist, and auburn ('*Not red!*' as she repeatedly informed her brothers, when they called her Gingernut), and she preferred to think rather than yack like the rest of her family. Family legend had it that she had been slow to talk as a toddler, and had been labelled 'a solemn little thing' by her father. Self-reliant from the word go, she had, at the age of six, briefly created her own make-believe friends to play with, but she soon had to lose them: they became as irritating as her brothers, crowding her with their insidious presence.

When the boys were old enough, they were allowed to help their father tinker with his collection of motorbikes. They also started to accompany him on trips to Manchester to watch boxing matches and to the horseracing in Chester and Liverpool. It meant that Jaz had her mother to herself, but not for long. When Tamzin was born, followed quickly by Lulu, Jaz accepted that she was destined to be the odd one out. Everyone but her was one of a pair: her parents, her brothers, and now her sisters. She withdrew and immersed herself in books, reading herself into other people's lives, happily escaping her own. With hindsight it seemed only natural that one day she would discover the joy of writing, that the simple process of putting words on paper – poems, short stories, rhymes, observations – would allow her to escape yet further.

She rolled off the bed, went over to her desk and switched on her computer. She checked that her bedroom door was shut, then opened the file marked 'Italian Renaissance'. She scrolled through the six-page essay she had written on Uccello's *The Hunt in the Forest,* for which she had been awarded an A, and stopped when a block of blank pages had flicked by and she came to the words 'Chapter One'. After months of messing around with poetry she was writing a novel. She had started it last week but, what with all the homework she'd had, there had been little time to devote to it. Being at sixth-form college was great, but the workload was crazy.

Vicki, her closest friend from school, had moved with her to Maywood College last month, and there was no shortage of new students to get to know. There was one in particular Jaz wanted to get to know better. He was a year older than her and was in the upper sixth. His name was Nathan King, and all she knew about him was that he lived near the park in Maywood. He was tall, wore his hair short, but not too short, and was never without his long black leather coat, which flapped and swished behind him as he strode purposefully to wherever he was heading. He looked as if he knew exactly what he was about, as if he had it all sorted. It was his confident manner that had singled him out to her on the first day of term.

Hearing the sound of feet thundering towards her room, she snapped forward in her seat and scrolled back to the start of the history-of-art essay.

The door flew open. 'Who were you talking to?'

Without bothering to turn round, she said, 'Tamzin Rafferty, get out! You too, Lulu. Can't you see I'm working?'

'You weren't a few minutes ago. We heard you talking to someone. Was it a boy? Have you got a boyfriend?'

She twisted her head, gave her sisters her most imperious stare. 'Were you listening in on a private conversation?'

They looked at each other and sniggered. Then they began to giggle in that high-pitched tone that grated on her nerves. She moved calmly across the room to the bookcase and her CD player. She picked up the remote control, switched it on at eardrum-bursting level and watched Tamzin and Lulu take flight. They hated her music, especially the Divine Comedy – they hadn't yet evolved beyond S Club 7.

'Sweet baby Moses on a bike! Turn that racket down.'

Her father, Pat (or Popeye, as her mother and their oldest friends called him), stood in the doorway, his massive body filling the gap. Jaz switched off the music and he came in. 'Jeez, girl, that was loud enough to shake the paint off the walls. How you can work with that rubbish playing, I'll never know.' He looked towards her computer. 'Much to get through this weekend?'

'A fair amount,' she said, sliding past him to sit down. She was worried he might decide to fiddle with the keyboard and accidentally find her novel. Her dad liked to give the impression he understood nothing about computers, but she knew that he had recently had the business kitted out with an expensive new system and had insisted on being shown how to work it. She kept her eyes lowered and waited for him to leave. But he didn't. He drew nearer, stooped slightly, and began to read aloud what was on the screen. "'Uccello was fascinated by perspective and this can be clearly seen in this painting, which is both richly coloured and ingeniously constructed ...'" He straightened up, placed a hand on her shoulder. 'I've said it before, Jasmine, and I'll say it again, you owe it all to your mother. You get your brains from her. Never forget that, will you?'

She turned and smiled affectionately at him. He was always saying that, always making himself out to be the ignorant, silent partner in his marriage. 'Oh, I'm just the brawn in the Rafferty outfit, that's why they call me Popeye,' he'd say. 'It's Moll who knows what's what.' But let anyone make the mistake of taking him at his word and they'd soon regret it.

'You're not going to give me that old I'm-just-a-thick-Paddy spiel, are you?' she asked.

He returned the smile. 'But it's the truth. I couldn't read or write when I met your mother. She wouldn't marry me until I'd mastered *Janet and John*.'

'That's true love for you, Dad.'

He gave her a light cuff around the ear. 'Cheeky madam. Now, get on with your work. I'm expecting great things of you.'

'No pressure, then, Dad?'

He was almost out of the room when he stopped, turned back to her and said, 'So, has my little Jazzie got a boyfriend?'

She rolled her eyes. 'Chance would be a fine thing.'

'Hmm ... best keep it that way until you've got college sorted.'

She watched him go. As dads went, he wasn't bad. Woefully sentimental at times, and scarily volatile but, beneath it all, she knew he was proud of her. He was always boasting to his friends about how clever she was. 'Mark my words,' he'd swagger, with a beer in his hand, 'this is the Rafferty who's going to put our family on the map. Jazzie's like her mother, book-smart.'

What he didn't realise was that his pride put unbearable pressure on her to perform. What if she let him down? How would he cope with the failure of a daughter on whom he'd pinned such high hopes? And did he have any idea how trapped she felt by the restrictions he placed on her in his desire to see her do well? He was happy for her to go out with Vicki, but heaven help any guy who showed the slightest interest in her. Dad would put him through untold tests before he would be satisfied that he was suitable. He never came right out and said it, but she knew her father wouldn't tolerate the distraction of a boyfriend at this stage in her life. But who'd be interested in her anyway?

She dismissed this line of thought and got back to the opening sentence of her novel. But the more she repeated it in her head, the clumsier it sounded. It wasn't long before her thoughts strayed once more. To her wonderful secret.

Next week she would be going to the first meeting of Hidden Talents. Just think, a writers' group where she would be taken seriously. Where she could talk openly about her writing and not be laughed at. Because that's what her family would do if they ever found out what she was up to. She could hear her brothers now. 'Oo-er, little Miss Clever Clogs reckons she's an author, does she?'

She wondered what the other people in the group would be like. The woman she'd just spoken to, Dulcie Ballantyne, had sounded really nice. Hesitant, maybe, as though her mind was elsewhere, but quite friendly. Well, so long as the others were nothing like Phin and Jimmy, Tamzin and Lulu, she would be sure to get on with them.

3

Beth King was often told that she ought to invest in a dishwasher. 'You could easily whip out this cupboard here,' people would say, thinking they were the first to come up with the idea, 'and slip in a dishwasher, no trouble at all. Just think of the hours you'd save yourself. And the wear and tear on your hands.' This last consideration was a favourite of her mother's. 'Hands, more than anything, age a woman,' she would claim. 'You can have any amount of surgery done to your face, but your hands will always give you away.'

They were probably right, these well-meaning friends and family, but the truth was, Beth enjoyed washing-up – not for any strange, puritanical reason, but because the kitchen of the first-floor flat that she and Nathan had lived in for more than ten years overlooked Maywood Park. The view was a constant source of pleasure to her: there was always something different to watch – squirrels scampering across the grass, couples, young and old, strolling arm in arm along the winding paths that led down to the river and the tennis courts, mothers with prams, dogs and children playing on the swings and roundabout – which Nathan had enjoyed when he was little. And then there was the ever-changing look of the park. Now that it was autumn, the trees were losing their coppery leaves, and the fading leggy bedding plants that the council had planted in the summer would soon be replaced with pansies tough enough to survive the rigours of winter.

The last of the lunch dishes rinsed, Beth dried her hands and reached for the tub of luxury hand cream her mother insisted on sending her, along with the rubber gloves Beth always forgot to use. Her parents were wonderfully generous and still went out of their way to make her life easier.

As did her in-laws, Lois and Barnaby King.

But while she was grateful for her parents' generosity, which came from three hundred miles away – they had retired to warmer climes on the south coast – she found it difficult to feel the same enthusiasm for Lois's doorstep offers of help. Lois tried too hard and made Beth feel as if she were a charity case. 'Would you believe it?' Lois had said in April. 'I've stocked up at the supermarket and, without any warning, Barnaby's decided to take me away for the Easter weekend. You'd better have it, you know I hate to see good food go to waste.'

It would have been ungracious to refuse, especially as Beth knew Lois meant well. She always had. Ever since Adam's death, eleven years ago, she had committed herself to taking care of her son's widow and her only grandson. Occasionally Beth privately questioned Lois's motives, but she hated herself for thinking so cynically. What Lois did was kind and honourable and she should think herself lucky that she had such supportive in-laws. Nothing was ever too much trouble for them, and living just a few miles away in the village of Stapeley, they had always been there for her. Many a time Lois had despatched Barnaby to fix a leaking gutter or sort out a rotting window-ledge. 'Heavens! Don't even think of getting a man in to do it – you'll be charged the earth. Let Barnaby take a look for you. You know that's what Adam would have wanted.'

After all these years of living without Adam, it was difficult for Beth to know if Lois was right. Would he have wanted his parents to play such a central part in her life? Or would he have expected her to move on?

'Moving on' had become an irritating cliché to Beth. Everyone had served it up to her: her mother, her friends, the people she worked with – in fact, anyone who thought she should have remarried by now. Or at least found a serious boyfriend. 'You're not getting any younger, Beth,' her closest friend, Simone, had said only last month. 'You're forty-three, not twenty-three, in case it's slipped your notice.'

'Fat chance of that happening,' Beth had retorted, wishing that a sandstorm would engulf her friend's house in Dubai where she was currently living with her husband, Ben.

'Or are you working on the misplaced theory that the choice of eligible men increases with age?'

'No, I'm just being selective. I haven't met anyone who measures up to Adam.'

'Rubbish! You haven't allowed anyone near enough to see how they'd measure up. You're being a coward.'

Simone's words were uncomfortably near the truth. Fear and guilt had played a part in stopping Beth finding a new partner. She had hated the idea of being disloyal to Adam.

In the aftermath of his death, she had thrown herself into taking care of Nathan. He had been only six, too young to feel the pain of loss, but old enough to understand that his and his mother's lives had changed. Within six months of the funeral they had moved from their lovely house in the country, with its pretty garden, to this flat in Maywood. Money had been tight. Without her knowledge, Adam had taken out a second mortgage on their house and had invested what little savings they'd had in a business venture that had gone disastrously wrong. It had taken Beth some time to find work, but perseverance had paid off: she had landed a gem of a job at the recently expanded health centre in town. She had worked there ever since and had been happy; the hours were fairly flexible and the camaraderie had been good for her self-esteem. Her sanity too.

Her social life had not been so fulfilling: on a receptionist's salary she couldn't afford to do much. She was always totting up the pennies – a modest trip to the cinema plus a babysitter amounted almost to the cost of a pair of shoes for Nathan. Funnily enough, as supportive as Lois was, she never offered to babysit so that Beth could go out at night. Nothing was ever said, but Beth strongly suspected her mother-in-law didn't want her to meet anyone. To Lois, it was unthinkable that Beth could replace Adam.

But Beth's friends had had other ideas and before long they were dropping hints that it was time for her to start dating. Invitations materialised for her to meet unattached men at dinner parties. Simone had set her up with several unsuitable candidates – it was still a mystery to Beth where her friend's supply of single men came from. In those early years few got further than a second date. The first man she'd agreed to go out with had taken her for dinner in Chester. Just as she was beginning to think that he was almost 'promising', he had leaned across the table and asked about her favourite sexual fantasy. She hid her shock, and told him that an early night with a good book did it for her. Another man had bored her rigid with endless talk about his high-powered job and interdepartmental politics in the company. She had suppressed a jaw-breaking yawn, then nodded and politely said what she thought he wanted her to say.

When she grew tired of fending off men with whom she had no desire to form any attachment, she started to turn down Simone's invitations, using Nathan as an excuse – 'Sorry, Simone, I have to give Nathan a lift somewhere that night.' Or, 'Sorry, Nathan needs me to help him revise for an exam.'

Simone was no fool, and reminded Beth ad infinitum that time waits for no woman, especially a single one. Eventually she had said, 'How much longer are you going to use your son in this shameful manner? What excuse will you come up with when he leaves home? Or are you going to turn into an eccentric old woman who collects stray cats and makes marmalade that nobody will ever eat?'

'Anything would be preferable to the ear-bashing a so-called friend is subjecting me to. And if you really want to know, I'm putting things off until it's more convenient.'

'And as we all know, Beth, my poor deluded friend, procrastination is the thief of time.'

Beth knew that Simone was right, she *was* hiding behind Nathan. Plenty of parents struggle to come to terms with flying-the-nest syndrome, but she knew that because she and Nathan were so close she would undergo a painful period of adjustment next year when he left for university. She had never suffered from loneliness – mostly because she didn't have time for such an indulgence – but that might alter when Nathan went to college. Common sense told her that she had no choice but to fill the void his absence would create.

In preparation for this change, she had taken an important step this morning, which she hoped would expand her horizons. She was joining a creative writers' group. She had always enjoyed 'scribbling', as she called it. It had started after Adam died: when she couldn't sleep at night, she had written down the thoughts that were keeping her awake. It had been soothingly cathartic and before long she had grown confident enough to turn the random scribblings into short stories. She now had a collection that no one but herself had read. Or ever would. Those clumsily put-together vignettes were about the past. Now she wanted to write something to reflect the new life ahead of her.

This morning she had told Simone about Hidden Talents during their fortnightly phone chat.

'Good for you,' she'd said. 'Any men in the group?'

'I wouldn't know. We have our first meeting next week.'

'What else are you going to do to occupy yourself?'

'Isn't that enough to start with?'

'You tell me.'

'Goodness, you're giving me the choice? What's got into you? Has the sun fried your brain?'

'Crikey, it's time to come home to Cheshire if it has.'

For all Simone's bullying, she was a wonderful friend, and Beth missed her.

She screwed the lid back on to the tub of hand cream and put it on the window-ledge. Looking down into the park, she noticed a fair-haired man sitting on one of the benches; he had two young children with him. For a few moments she watched the smallest and blondest of the two little girls as she tried to catch a leaf that whirled in the wind. She wondered where their mother was, then chided herself for jumping to such a sloppy conclusion. It always annoyed her when people assumed she had a husband.

She was still staring at the man and his children when she remembered that Nathan was out for the rest of the afternoon and that she had promised to go downstairs to see her neighbour.

Adele – Miss Adele Waterman – had moved into the ground-floor flat a year after Beth and Nathan had arrived, which made them not just long-standing neighbours but good friends. To Beth's sadness, the old lady had decided, now that she was eighty-four, to call it a day: she was putting her flat on the market with the intention of moving into a retirement home. 'I'm under no illusion that my nephew wants the burden of me. He can never spare any time to visit so I'm spending his inheritance the fastest way I know how,' she had told Beth, with a chuckle.

Beth picked up a tin of home-made chocolate cake and went out, hoping that when the time came, Nathan would treat her more kindly than Adele's only relative had treated her.

4

Jack Solomon switched off the car radio before Jimmy Ruffin's 'What Becomes Of The Brokenhearted?' could do its worst. The traffic-lights changed to green and he pressed his foot on the accelerator.

It was a typically tedious Monday afternoon. It was also his birthday. He was thirty-six, but felt more like sixty-six, and he certainly wasn't in the mood to celebrate. The girls in the office had surprised him with a card and a CD and he had been touched by their thoughtfulness, but less so by the choice of CD. He had nothing against Britney Spears, but it was too much of a cliché, men of his age listening to music aimed at a much younger generation. There was nothing worse than a middle-aged man trying to be hip. A wry smile twitched at his lips. He could have been describing that bastard Tony.

He felt the sudden tension in his shoulders and loosened his grip on the steering-wheel. He mustn't dwell on Tony, he told himself. But it was a futile instruction. Now that his brain had hooked on to the thought, he'd be stuck with it until he'd worked it out of his system.

Tony Gallagher ... the best friend he'd ever had. Once they'd been inseparable. They'd grown up together, played and learned together. They'd smoked their first cigarette together, drunk their first pint together, and inevitably experienced their first hangover together. They'd shared practically every rite of passage. But Tony had taken 'togetherness' and 'what's yours is mine' too far and too literally.

Almost a year ago Jack had come home early from work one afternoon with a high temperature and found Tony in bed with Maddie. Turned out they'd been having an affair for the last six months and dumb old Jack hadn't had a clue what was going on.

Dumb old Jack Solomon, that was him all right. Too blind to see what was going on under his own nose, in his own home. Too in awe of his old friend to think he'd ever betray him. Other men sank to those levels, but not Tony. Admittedly he'd been a bit of a lad, but he was one of the good guys. Imbued with an easy sense of entitlement and an air of confidence that drew people to him, he was a man you could trust.

But these things happen. Marriages fell apart all the time ... apparently. Jack wished that every time some smug prat said this he could smack them in the face. 'These things happen' was supposed to make him feel better about losing his wife and only seeing his daughters on alternate weekends. Relegated to being a part-time father, he now had to trail his children round theme parks, cinema complexes, bowling alleys and fast-food restaurants. If he never had to order another burger and milkshake, he'd be a happy man. No, that wasn't true. It would take a hell of a lot more than that to make him truly happy.

Amber and Lucy had stayed with him at the weekend and, thankfully, the weather had been warm and sufficiently dry to make going out less of a chore. During the last year he had become a fanatical watcher of weather reports: if rain was forecast he had to plan indoor entertainment; if it was dry, he'd plan a trip outdoors.

On Saturday he'd taken the girls to the park in Maywood. Lucy had enjoyed it but, then, she was only seven and still young enough to feed the ducks and play on the swings. Amber, though, was eleven and fast becoming too grown-up for such childish entertainment. While Lucy had flung bread at the ducks, Amber had sat on the bench with him and watched her sister disdainfully. When Lucy's supply of bread had run out, she had skipped towards them, her face wreathed in smiles.

'Can we go now?' Amber had asked, getting to her feet and folding her arms across her chest. 'I'm cold.'

'But I want to play on the swings,' Lucy had pouted. 'Dad said I could.' She'd looked at him, eyes wide and pleading.

'Five minutes on the swings,' he'd said, 'and then it's Amber's choice what we do next.'

The peace had been kept and Amber's choice had been to walk back into the centre of town to have tea at McDonald's. During the weekend, he'd sensed friction between the girls, and when he was putting the tray loaded with burgers, chips, nuggets and milkshakes on to the table where they were waiting for him, he caught Amber telling Lucy off. 'Hey, what's the problem?' he'd said.

'It's nothing,' Amber said matter-of-factly and, assuming the role of dinner monitor, opened her sister's carton of nuggets and handed it to her.

'It doesn't look like nothing to me,' he persisted, putting his arm round Lucy. 'What's up, Luce?' He noticed Amber flash her a warning look and when Lucy began to cry, he said, 'Okay, that's it. What's going on?'

'I only said I was looking forward to our holiday,' Lucy sniffed.

'What holiday?' he asked, dabbing her eyes with a paper napkin.

She took it from him and blew her nose. 'Tony's taking us to Disney World for half-term. We're going to America.'

'That's nice,' he forced himself to say. He unwrapped his burger, knowing he wouldn't be able to eat it now.

'Well, I'm not going!' Amber announced. She looped a long chip and stuffed it into her mouth. 'I'm going to stay with Dad for half-term. I wouldn't go to America if you paid me.'

Atta girl! he wanted to cheer. But he didn't. Not when Lucy looked as if she was going to cry again. His heart went out to them both, caught as they were in an impossible situation. 'Is it definite?' he asked, playing for time. 'Has Tony booked it?'

Amber shrugged and reached for her milkshake.

Lucy nodded. 'He showed us a picture of the hotel we're going to be staying in. It's huge. And there's a pool with a slide and—'

'Shut up, Lucy.'

'Amber, don't speak to your sister like that.'

She looked at him, hurt.

Damn! He wasn't handling this at all well. Poor Amber, she was only trying to be loyal to him. 'Sorry, sweetheart,' he said, 'I didn't mean to snap at you. How's your meal? Burger up to standard?'

He drove them back to Prestbury the following day, to where Maddie had set up home with Tony. Home for her, these days, was a modern pile of impressive proportions and, with its over-the-top electric gates that positioned it on just the wrong side of good taste, Jack had nicknamed it Southfork. From what the girls had told him, it had six bedrooms, three bathrooms, a sitting room the size of a football pitch and a sauna to sweat away the day's troubles. Well, yippity-do, hadn't Tony Gallagher done well for himself? Always ambitious and always on the lookout for a way to make a quick buck, Tony had come home after a holiday in Thailand and set up his own business importing Oriental rugs, furniture and knick-knacks. This had been in the early nineties, things had taken off for him, and he now had a string of shops throughout the North West. Oh, yes, Tony Gallagher had done very well for himself. Too damned well.

Tony opened the door to him and it took all of Jack's willpower not to shove the smug devil up against his expensive wallpaper and smear his brains right across it.

'I hear you're off to Disney,' he said, with false bonhomie as he passed the girls their weekend bags. Instead of rushing upstairs to their bedrooms as they usually did, they hovered anxiously in the hall.

'Yes,' said Tony. 'I thought it would do Maddie and the girls good. Some sun to cheer us all up.'

'You do surprise me. I thought you had everything you could ever want to make you happy.' His caustic tone rang out discordantly and Maddie materialised. As if sensing trouble, she placed herself between the girls, a hand on each of their shoulders. Even now, despite the bitterness that consumed him, he was reminded of the intense love he'd once felt for her. She was as slim as the day they'd met, and just as pretty. The girls had inherited her delicate bone structure, her clear complexion, and her pale blue eyes. Many a time when they'd holidayed in Greece, she'd been mistaken for a Scandinavian.

'Everything all right?' she asked, her chilly briskness telling him to back off.

'Oh, everything's hunky-dory, Maddie. Nothing for you to worry about. Although it might have been nice for you to inform me about your plans for half-term. But, hey, Amber and Lucy told me, so that's okay, isn't it?' Then, in a less acerbic voice, he said, 'Good night, girls. I'll see you when you get back.'

He moved forward to kiss them goodbye, but Amber wriggled free from her mother and said, 'You can't go yet, Dad. Lucy and I have something for you.' She shot upstairs and was back within seconds. She handed him a present that must have taken ages to wrap, judging by the amount of sellotape and the bulky edges of the paper around it. 'Happy birthday for tomorrow, Dad.' She gave him a fierce hug. When she stepped away, she narrowed her eyes and gave Maddie and Tony a pointed look.

He drove home, close to tears. All he could think of was the harm that had been inflicted on his children by his and Maddie's separation. Poor Lucy, so guilty and upset because she was excited about going to Orlando, and Amber defiantly refusing to go, but knowing she would have to. And how long had she been rehearsing the little scene when she had given him his present in front of Tony and Maddie?

Jack knew he had to come to terms with what had happened. He had to find a way to resolve his anger and bitterness.

He parked outside 10a Maywood Park House, where Miss Waterman lived. A shame it wasn't the whole house he'd been instructed to sell, but a flat in this area would be easy to shift, so long as Miss Waterman was realistic about the selling price. It never paid to go in too high. Fingers crossed that the old lady didn't have any greedy relatives manipulating her behind the scenes. Fingers crossed also that she wasn't too frail to make a cup of tea: he was parched.

He gathered up his clipboard and tape measure from the front passenger seat and locked the car. He examined the small front garden with a professional eye. It was well tended, with laurel bushes and a lilac tree screening the ground-floor window from the road; established shrubs filled the narrow bed to the right of the path. So far so good. He wondered who was responsible for its upkeep. Surely not the elderly owner – a gardener, perhaps? Then he took the three steps up to the front door, which had its original lead-and-stained-glass fanlight. Again this was a good sign. There were two bells – one for 10a and one for 10b. He pressed the former, straightened his tie and tried to imagine Miss Waterman. From her voice on the telephone she had sounded the archetypal sweet old lady. He pictured her in a high-necked frilly blouse with a string of pearls and a pale mauve cardie, an embroidered hanky poking out from a pocket. There would probably be a ball of wool rolling about the flat, and the smell of cat litter, mothballs and throat lozenges.

The door opened. 'Er ... Miss Waterman?' Either his client had undergone thousands of pounds' worth of plastic surgery and had indulged in some super-strength HRT, or this was a relative who had been called in to check out the potentially scurrilous estate agent. She was an attractive woman with wavy fair hair, collar-length and tucked behind her ears: a tousled look that suited her bright, open face and went well with her figure-hugging knitted black suit. She looked vaguely familiar, but he couldn't think where he might have met her before. Perhaps she had been into the office at some time.

'No, I'm not Miss Waterman,' she said, 'I'm a neighbour. I live in the flat upstairs, which is where Miss Waterman is. I'm afraid her boiler's conked out and I insisted she stay in the warm with me. You must be Mr Solomon.'

'I am indeed. I didn't know neighbours like you still existed.'

'It helps that we're such good friends. Luckily I had the afternoon off. Come in.' She closed the door behind him and led the way along a communal hallway to 10a, her shoes clicking on the chequered tiled floor.

Inside the flat he was pleased to see that most of the original features were still intact. He stood for a moment to take in the proportions and features of the sitting room: the bay window, the fireplace, the high ceiling and the intricate cornice.

'I've been instructed to stay with you,' she said, observing him from where she stood next to a baby grand piano, which was home to a collection of framed black and white photographs and a vase of silk flowers.

'Quite right too,' he said. 'I could be anyone, after all.' He slipped a hand into the breast pocket of his suit and pulled out a business card. He gave it to her and noticed that she took it with her left hand and that she wore no rings – this was a skill he'd learned since he'd been on his own: he could spot a wedding ring at fifty paces.

She read the card and said, 'Well, Mr Jack Solomon of Norris and Rowan the Estate Agents' – her voice was playful – 'I've also been instructed to give you some tea when you've finished. Miss Waterman was most insistent on that. I should point out, though, that she'll drive a hard bargain with you over your commission. Be warned.'

And you'll see that she does, he thought, as he started making notes on his clipboard. But instead of feeling hostile towards Miss Waterman's helpful neighbour, he found himself warming to her. Dodging the clutter of antique furniture, and being careful not to knock anything over, he pulled out a length of the tape measure and hooked the metal end into the edge of the carpet against the wall. It was going to be a tricky job, this one: no area of floor or wall space had been wasted. Corner cupboards and glass-fronted cabinets were stuffed with china and glassware. Tables, large and small, displayed silk-shaded lamps and yet more china.

'Do you need any help?' she asked.

'Only if you don't mind.'

'It'll keep me warm, having something to do.'

With the sitting room measured, they moved on to the dining room: it was also jam-packed with furniture, a veritable minefield of bits and bobs just waiting to be smashed. 'And what do you do when you're not looking after your neighbour?' he asked, reeling in the tape.

'I work at the medical centre in town. I'm what people refer to as an old dragon.'

He raised an eyebrow. 'Why's that?'

'I'm a receptionist, and most of the patients think I derive some kind of perverse pleasure in keeping them from seeing their doctor.'

Ah, so that's where he'd seen her.

The job didn't take as long as he'd feared, and he was soon being led upstairs to meet Miss Waterman. When he stood in the hall, inside 10b, he realised how cold he'd become downstairs. The warmth wrapped itself around him, as did his new surroundings. There was a homely smell and feel to this flat, which Miss Waterman's lacked: hers was too formal and prim for his taste. He thought of his own rented modern townhouse and acknowledged what he'd previously tried to ignore: that he didn't much like it. It wasn't a home, merely a stopgap, somewhere to lay his head until he found something better. When Maddie had left him, he'd sold their house almost straight away, finding it too painful to live there alone. She had refused her share of the money, and initially this had infuriated him. It was as if she was deliberately flaunting the wealth and status she had acquired as Tony's Gallagher's partner.

'Is that you, Beth?' called a voice.

'Yes, and I've brought Mr Solomon up.'

When he entered the main room of the flat, L-shaped and clearly used for sitting, dining and cooking, he came face to face with his client. She was sitting opposite a log-burning stove and he almost stopped in his tracks at the sight of her. Unbelievably, he'd pictured her perfectly, right down to the pearls and the colour of her cardigan. How extraordinary! One–nil to his vivid imagination.

'Goodness, Mr Solomon, you look like you've seen a ghost.'

Smiling, he stretched out his hand. 'Not at all, Miss Waterman. It's good to meet you at last.'

'I wanted to show you round myself, but Beth wouldn't hear of it. She's such a dear. I'm going to miss her dreadfully when I leave.'

While he and Miss Waterman discussed the marketing of the flat and the thorny issue of commission, he was conscious of his client's neighbour moving quietly at the other end of the room, where she was making a pot of tea and arranging some cake on a plate. As he warmed himself in front of the log-burning stove, he felt absurdly at ease. There was something calming about his surroundings, although there was nothing special about the way the flat was furnished and decorated – if anything it bordered on shabby: inexpensive pine units in the kitchen area had been painted cream and looked in need of a touch-up; the dresser beside the open brick hearth was chaotically filled with cookery books, photographs, CDs, and china that didn't match; the sofa was worn and lumpy; the rugs on the wooden floor were threadbare, and the blue and white cloth that covered the dining table was splattered with candle wax. For all that, it was one of the most charming homes he'd been in for a long while.

Out of the corner of his eye, he saw Beth pick up the tea-tray. He got to his feet. 'Here, let me do that.' He took it from her and noticed, for the first time, the view from the window. He wondered if she had seen him on Saturday in the park with the girls.

'That was delicious,' he said, after he'd eaten two slices of cake and drunk his tea, 'but I really ought to be going. I wish all my appointments were as convivial.' He meant it.

'Any chance of you knocking a chunk off the extortionate commission you'll be charging in return for our generous hospitality?'

'Beth, my dear, you shouldn't embarrass Mr Solomon like that.'

He smiled. 'Perhaps we'll do something creative with the marketing budget. Free advertising for the first month. What do you say?'

Miss Waterman tilted her head to one side. 'And a reduced rate for the subsequent month?'

The old lady was as sharp as her friend. 'Agreed, Miss Waterman. But I doubt that will be necessary, given the excellent location. We'll have sold your flat long before then.'

He shook hands with the two women, first with his client, then with her neighbour. 'Thank you for the tea and for your help downstairs. I hope you didn't get too cold.'

It was when he was driving back to the office, before going home, that he remembered it was his birthday and Clare, his girlfriend – *girlfriend*: even after five months he wasn't used to that expression – was cooking a special meal for him. He wished now that he hadn't eaten so much cake.

5

From the garden, Dulcie heard the telephone ringing. She threw down the rake and, almost missing her footing on the steps, rushed to the house, hoping it was Richard.

It was Tuesday morning, four days since Richard's heart-attack, and for all she knew the unthinkable might have happened. So many times she had wanted to ring the hospital, but she knew how gossip could spread. Enquiries from an unknown woman about a male patient could mean only one thing and Dulcie could picture, all too easily, the scene of Angela overhearing a couple of nurses discussing her husband and the concerned caller.

Breathless, she snatched up the receiver. Before she could say anything, a man's voice she didn't recognise said, 'Hello? Who am I speaking to?'

'This is Mrs Ballantyne,' she answered, irritated by the pompous voice at the other end of the line. 'And who am *I* speaking to?'

'My name's Victor Blackmore and I'm calling about the writing group. I'd like to know some more details. Is it a serious group, or just an excuse for people to get together and chat over endless cups of coffee?'

'I'm sure there'll be coffee on offer for those who would like it,' she said coolly, instinct telling her that this man would not be an asset to Hidden Talents, 'and doubtless there'll be a lively exchange of views and opinions. After all, that's partly the function of a writers' circle. I would imagine it's safe to say that it will be as serious as its members want it to be.'

'Mm . . . So what can you tell me about the other people who have signed up for it? I don't want to get involved with time-wasting cranks.'

Bristling, Dulcie said, 'I'm not sure that's a fair question, Mr Blackmere. It rather depends on your definition of the word "crank".'

'Black*more*. Victor *Blackmore*. Perhaps I'd better explain. I'm working on a novel and I'm keen to find an expert appraisal. What are your qualifications for running a writing group?'

It was time to get rid of this ghastly man. Under no circumstances did Dulcie want him joining Hidden Talents. 'I have absolutely no qualifications whatsoever, Mr Blackmore. Now, it sounds to me as though our little group wouldn't suit you at all. We're very much on the bottom rung, just starting out, and you're obviously further on. Have you thought of submitting your novel to a publisher for a professional appraisal?'

'Publishers! What do they know?'

So he'd already been down that route and had his work rejected. She decided that her only course of action was to be firm. 'Oh dear, I must go, there's someone at my door. Goodbye, Mr Blackmore, I hope you find what you're looking for. Best of luck with the writing.' She replaced the receiver with a smile. It was the first time she had smiled in days and it felt good. She imagined telling Richard about the dreadful man and saw them laughing together. She loved it when Richard laughed: his face showed the lightness of his spirit.

Back out in the garden, she resumed her leaf-raking. There was rain in the air, but she carried on regardless, soon warm from the exertion. She was picking up the handles of the overflowing wheelbarrow to push it down to the compost heap when she heard the telephone once more.

She was getting too old for this, she thought, as she stood in the kitchen and caught her breath before answering it. She ought to have one of those cordless contraptions that Richard had suggested so many times.

'Mrs Ballantyne? Victor Blackmore again.'

Her heart sank.

'I wanted to go over a couple more points with you.'

'Does this mean you'll be joining us?'

'Let's just say I'll give you a try and see how it works out. Now, then, what will the format be?'

'Format?'

'I presume you've thought of that? If there's no order or structure to the classes, I can't see them working. Take my word for it, it will turn into an unmitigated shambles. I have years of managerial experience behind me so I know what I'm talking about. How much will you be charging?'

'Just a token amount to cover biscuits and coffee. I thought a pound wouldn't be unreasonable.'

Fifteen minutes later, her patience pushed to its limit, Dulcie managed to get rid of him. She wished now that she had never come up with the idea of forming a writers' circle. What had she been thinking of? And what if more people like Victor Blackmore wanted to join? So far he was the third person to make a definite commitment to Hidden Talents – there had been other enquiries, but they had come from people looking for something to do during the day. 'I'm afraid our meetings will be in the evening,' she had told them. 'Otherwise people who work will miss out.' Also, she hadn't wanted to end up with a group consisting only of retired people or young mothers who might have to rush off to collect a small child. Some of the enquirers had been surprised that the group wouldn't be meeting in a public room, and again this had been deliberate on Dulcie's part. The size of the group was important. If it was too large, people wouldn't get a chance to read out their work and would feel excluded. A small gathering would encourage members to relax, and once a bond of trust had been established, they would express themselves more openly – essential if the fragile buds of creativity were to blossom.

It was raining heavily now. Dulcie abandoned her intention to continue gardening, and decided to write instead. Which meant she would need a cup of tea to get her started. A biscuit or two as well.

She carried the tea-tray through to her study – like the kitchen, it overlooked the garden. The previous owners of 18 Bloom Street – a Georgian townhouse in the centre of Maywood – had used this room as their dining room, but Dulcie had known straight away that it would be her study. It was beautifully proportioned, and very elegant. She had painted the walls herself, a creamy buttermilk shade, and had chosen a carpet of royal blue to make a sharp but classic contrast – it was hopelessly impractical, showed every bit of fluff, but she loved it. It gave the room exactly the right feel. She set the tray on her desk, which was positioned in front of the sash window. Then, as the day had turned so gloomy, she switched on the lamps and lit the fire. She had cleared away the ashes earlier that morning, so all she had to do was put a match to the kindling and the scrunched-up newspaper.

Within minutes she had picked up a pen and was reading through what she had written before Richard had suffered his heart-attack. When she had told the boorish Victor Blackmore that she had no qualifications to lead a writing group, she had been a little economical with the truth. For years now she had had modest success with writing short stories for magazines. She had also picked up the occasional prize for her literary endeavours. And a long time ago, before moving to Maywood, she had been a member of a writers' group, although she had never led one. But, of course, none of this would impress Victor Blackmore. Only Salman Rushdie as their tutor would have impressed a pompous twit like him.

She had always written, even as a child, yet had never seen it as anything more than a hobby. She had played with words – like others played squash or tennis to amuse themselves – bouncing them around on the paper until they formed just the right pattern. It was immensely satisfying. However, it had been a sporadic hobby. Marriage and children had been her priority, but once Kate and Andrew had left home, she had been able to devote more time to it. Before then, and while the children were young, she had nursed her husband for almost six years until his death. Parkinson's disease had turned him into a chronic invalid, but he had borne the debilitating illness with great dignity. Sadly for him, he had been a doctor and had known his future better than anyone. She would never forget how brave he had been, or how hard he had tried to lessen the effect his illness had on them as a family. Kate and Andrew had been wonderful and had taken it in their stride. For them he was still plain old Dad and they accepted his limitations. In their eyes, it didn't matter that he couldn't kick a ball around the garden with them: he could read to them instead, help them with their homework, or play chess. When the tremors in his hands became unmanageable, they watched his eyes to see which piece he wanted them to move on his behalf.

But his death was a shattering blow. She and the children had grown so used to the permanency of him being ill that they had somehow convinced themselves they would carry on like that for ever. His departure created a haunting emptiness in their lives, especially hers. Dulcie had known she must do something positive, so she and the children had moved from south Manchester to Maywood to make a fresh start and to be nearer her closest friends, Prue and Maureen. For a while she busied herself with decorating their lovely new home in Bloom Street, but she soon recognised the danger of having too much time on her hands, and decided to form her own business, a relocation company. She had wanted to do this for some time.

It had been many years later, when she had been on the verge of selling the business and retiring, that she had met Richard. A company move from Wiltshire to Cheshire put him and his wife in contact with Home from Home – the name had been Kate's idea. Initially Dulcie dealt with Angela, who made it very clear she was moving north reluctantly. 'My friends and family all live in Wiltshire,' Angela had lamented, over the telephone. 'I don't know what I'm going to do without them.' She flitted rapidly from one line of conversation to another, and Dulcie had to work at keeping her client on track. 'We don't want anything modern, or anything that needs a lot of work doing to it. Oh, and nothing with those awful replacement PVC windows. I saw a programme on television once where a family perished in a house fire because they couldn't smash a window to escape. It was awful. Three children. All dead. A paddock would be nice. We want to be out in the country – did I say that? I'm sure I must have because I can't cope with being confined. I've never lived anywhere but the country. We'll need five bedrooms with at least two en suites. We have two grown-up children living in London and they will be frequent visitors, and we have another two still at home, Christopher and Nicholas. I'll need your help in finding them a suitable school.'

'And your price range?' Dulcie had asked, making notes of all these requirements, at the same time forming a mental picture of her client: she foresaw a long haul. 'I ought to warn you that house prices around Maywood are almost comparable with those in the south of England,' she added tactfully.

'Is that so? Well, my husband will sort that out. In the meantime, perhaps you can send details of what you have available and we'll come up and take a look.'

Two weeks later, with a string of viewings arranged, Dulcie drove to the Maywood Grange Hotel on the outskirts of town to meet her clients. Richard Cavanagh was waiting for her in the hotel lounge. He was doing *The Times* crossword, one leg crossed over the other, fountain pen poised mid-air, his chin tilted upwards as he tussled with a clue. He didn't notice her approaching, and when she said, 'Mr Cavanagh?' he started. 'Sorry,' she apologised, 'I didn't mean to make you jump.' She held out her hand. 'Dulcie Ballantyne.'

He put down his pen and paper, rose to his feet, slipped his tortoiseshell glasses into the breast pocket of his beige linen jacket, and shook hands warmly. 'Please, call me Richard. But how did you know it was me?'

She looked at the coffee table on which an open wallet file revealed a collection of house details. 'They don't call me Miss Marple for nothing.'

He smiled. 'Would you like some coffee before we set off?'

She checked her watch. 'Yes, thank you, though it will have to be quick. Our first appointment's at eleven.'

'Plenty of time for you to sit down, then.' He indicated the sofa, where he'd been sitting, and took a hard upright chair for himself. She felt the warmth from his body in the cushions when she sat down, and watched him attract the attention of a young waitress. He was older than she had expected, but attractive with it. His eyes were blue and his hair silvery grey; it curled boyishly into the nape of his neck, and looked good against the dark blue of his shirt. He passed her a cup of coffee. 'My wife sends her apologies. Our youngest has chicken-pox and she didn't want to leave him with anyone else.'

As the day wore on – and with six houses viewed – Dulcie discovered quite a lot about Richard Cavanagh. He was charming and quick-witted, clear about what he did and did not want in a home, and appeared a thoroughly nice man. To say that he captivated her would have been an exaggeration, but she was certainly attracted to him.

But, and it was a colossal but, he was married, and therefore out of bounds. End of story. Married men were to be avoided at all costs.

Yet she allowed herself to be drawn in. He invited her to join him for dinner that evening. 'Don't let me suffer the ignominy of dining alone,' he said. 'I'll have everyone feeling sorry for me.'

'Nonsense! You'll have all the waitresses rushing to keep you amused.'

'I'd rather *you* kept me amused.'

They were sitting in her car in the hotel car park, and he'd turned to face her as he said this, his gaze as direct as his words.

She didn't answer him, but she didn't need to. He knew she would accept, just as she knew what the consequences would be.

That had been three years ago, and now she was in love with a man who . . . who, for all she knew, might be dead.

She put down the pen she had been holding – a fountain pen Richard had given her on the first anniversary of their meeting – and lowered her head into her hands. It was no good. She couldn't take the not knowing any longer. She removed her reading glasses and went to make the call from the kitchen where she had the number of the hospital pinned to the notice-board beside the phone. She was almost across the room when the telephone on her desk rang. Probably that annoying Victor Blackmore again, wanting to know what type of coffee she would be serving.

But she was wrong. It was Richard. She sank into her chair and, at the wonderful sound of his voice, she burst into tears.

'Dulcie?'

'Oh, Richard, I've been so scared. I'd almost convinced myself you were dead.' Tears of relief were flowing.

'Ssh, my darling, I'm fine. Well, fine for a man who's recovering from his first heart-attack. They've let me use a phone today, which I'm taking as a positive sign. I'm no longer hooked up to the main grid so I must be over the worst. Oh, Dulcie, I'm so sorry to have put you through this. How are you bearing up?'

'Oh, you know, not bad for a mistress whose lover has suffered his first heart-attack.'

'Don't speak like that. You know I hate that word. You're not my mistress, you're the woman I love. Oh, hell, I can't talk any more, I have to undergo yet more tests in a few minutes and I can see a posse of nurses and junior doctors heading in my direction. I'll ring you again as soon as I can. I love you, Dulcie.'

'I love you too. Take care.'

'And you.'

After she had put down the phone, Dulcie went outside and stood in the rain, her face turned up towards the sky. It was the maddest thing she could think to do. She was so unbelievably happy that nothing but an act of sheer lunacy would satisfy her. Only when she was wet through did she go back into the house.

6

By rights Jack should have been looking forward to the evening – he'd had some excellent news during the afternoon, and that, combined with seeing Clare, should have made him feel a whole lot happier.

But last night he and Clare had argued. It wasn't the first time, but the nature of the exchange had made him feel awkward about seeing her again. He would have preferred to get together with her later in the week, but that would only have upset her more: they'd already had to reschedule this evening's dinner, arranged for him to meet Clare's parents.

The cause of their row still rankled. Clare had accused him of being obsessed with Tony or, more specifically, with what Tony had done. 'Just get over it,' she'd said. 'What's done is done. My husband left me for someone else, but do you hear me banging on about it?'

'Banging on?' he'd said in disbelief. 'Is that what you think I'm doing?'

She screwed up her napkin and threw it on to her empty plate. 'Face it, Jack, you've done nothing but moan about him this evening. It's your birthday and I've gone to a lot of trouble to cook you this meal – which you've hardly touched. I'm bored of hearing you complain about your soon-to-be-ex-wife who, allegedly, is stopping you seeing your children. What's more—'

He put down his knife and fork. 'I think you've made your point.'

She got to her feet and started to clear the table, stacking the plates and dishes with noisy haste. 'Have I? And what point exactly do you think I'm making?'

He stood up too, and took the crockery from her. 'That I'm making a mountain out of a molehill.'

In the kitchen, they moved around each other warily and in stifling silence, putting things away, making coffee. 'Jack,' she said, at last, 'we have so much going between us, but I can't compete with Maddie and the girls.'

'I don't want you to.'

'That's how it feels.'

'Then that's your problem.'

She pressed the plunger down on the cafetière, looked at him sharply. 'Surely it's *our* problem?'

Exasperation made him say, 'I have enough problems of my own without taking yours on board. If you can't hack the idea that I have two daughters whom I love and need to see, then that's something you have to deal with. I can't do it for you.'

'Can't or won't?'

'Don't be pedantic.'

'That's right, Jack, run away from the question rather than answer it. Frightened of the truth, are you?'

'What truth would that be?'

'That you haven't moved on. It's time you accepted that Maddie and the girls are making a new life. Okay, it doesn't include you, and that doesn't seem fair, but it's all that's on offer. You have no choice but to make the best of it. Because if you don't, you'll end up lonely and miserable, an embittered man whom Lucy and Amber won't want to see. Is that what you want?'

He hadn't stayed the night, as they'd planned. Instead he drove home, wondering why the hell he was bothering to be in a relationship with Clare.

They had met through mutual friends – the usual scenario for recently separated people who had unexpectedly found themselves back in the singles market. 'Clare's great,' Des had told him, during one of their boys-only curry nights at the beginning of May. 'She's one of Julie's work colleagues, a friend too. She's recently divorced, but prepared to give the male species the benefit of the doubt. You'll hit it off, I'm sure.' Des ran the Holmes Chapel branch of Norris & Rowan, and Jack had accepted the offer of dinner with cautious interest. Much to Des's satisfaction, Jack and Clare had hit it off.

So tonight, five months on, Jack was meeting Clare's parents. 'It's no big deal, Jack,' she'd said, when she'd first put the suggestion to him. But he knew it was. And he didn't feel comfortable with it. It was too soon. It made him feel as if he were living on a fault-line: the ground might crack open beneath his feet at any moment.

He drove in through the gates of the Maywood Grange Hotel, and parked his car in the last remaining space, next to Clare's Audi TT. He switched off the engine, drummed his fingers on the steering-wheel, and wondered why he had allowed himself to be manoeuvred into this situation. 'Come and meet the folks' was tantamount to saying, 'Do you fancy a finger buffet or a sit-down meal at the reception?'

The thought sent a chill through him and he felt a sudden urge to start the car again and head home.

Clare had apologised for what she'd said – she'd phoned him at the office this morning. 'Oh, Jack, I shouldn't have said those things. Of course the break-up of your marriage is a lot harder to come to terms with than mine was for me. I don't have any children to complicate the issue. Are we still on for this evening? Mum and Dad are really looking forward to meeting you.'

'Clare, I'm not sure—'

'I've said I'm sorry, Jack.'

Aware that he was being unfair to her, he'd said, 'Okay, what time do you want me there?'

Clare saw him before he saw her. She came over and kissed him. 'I was getting worried,' she said, wiping lipstick off his cheek. 'Thought perhaps you might have ... Well, it doesn't matter what I thought, you're here now.' She straightened his collar. 'Okay?'

'Fine,' he lied. He took her hand. 'Come on, then, introduce me to your parents.'

Mr and Mrs Gilbert – oh, please call us Terry and Corinne – were trying too hard to be nice, probably at Clare's instruction. Every now and then he caught a knowing wink, even the odd smile of collusion. The unease he had felt outside in the car was now magnified many times over. Their eagerness for their only daughter to remarry – and doubtless provide them with grandchildren – was shockingly obvious. But when they started asking after his own children, suggesting that he and Clare should bring them over for tea one day, he found their manner disturbingly intrusive. He changed the subject abruptly and said, 'Clare, I forgot to tell you, I had some good news today. I've been invited to—'

'Oh, yummy, look at that,' she said, eyeing the sweet trolley as it was pushed past their table and on to the next. 'The tiramisu looks to die for. Sorry, Jack, what were you saying?'

He fixed a smile to his face and said, 'It's okay. I'll tell you later.'

But later didn't come. After the goodbyes, Clare had squeezed his arm and said, 'There, that wasn't so bad, was it?' Then he had driven home alone. Except he didn't go home. He put the car into the garage then went for a walk. The row of townhouses he lived in overlooked the river and, following the path alongside it, he headed towards the centre of town. He was in the mood for a drink.

His timing was awful. The first pub he went into was packed; last orders had been called and a crowd of youngsters had descended on the bar. The next pub he tried was the same: music blared and eye-watering smoke filled the air. Feeling old and curmudgeonly, he gave up on the idea of a drink and decided instead to walk his bad mood out of his system. Anyway, turning up for work tomorrow with a hangover would not be a wise move. It would hardly give the right impression, not now that he had been invited to become a partner.

That was what he had tried to tell Clare during dinner. His reaction to her lack of interest – not to tell her – now seemed more akin to the behaviour of a petulant child than a grown man. Why was he behaving so badly?

If he was honest with himself, he hadn't wanted to share his good fortune with Clare. Which, he supposed, spoke volumes about his feelings for her. He had to end it, he knew. Deep down, he had known it for weeks. He had met her too soon after his split with Maddie, when he was still vulnerable, and had thought her to be the answer to his loneliness and hurt pride. And although she might never admit it, Clare had probably viewed him as the means to get herself back on-line with her plan to be happily married with children. He didn't begrudge her that – after all, a family had been what he and Maddie had most wanted. They had both experienced fragmented family life while growing up – Maddie's parents had divorced when she was twelve, and his had died in a car accident when he was in his late teens. It was important to them to create what they felt they had missed out on. Children would give them security, stability and continuity. And they had, until Tony had intervened.

Tony had never married. 'I'm too busy to settle down,' he had claimed in the past, whenever Jack and Maddie teased him about becoming a disreputable *roué*: as he grew older, his girlfriends became younger. Not so long ago, and in a moment of drunken self-pity, he had confessed that he envied Jack. 'You have everything I've ever wanted. A beautiful wife who adores you and two children who think you're the best thing since sliced bread.'

'But you're the one with the Porsche and a different girlfriend for every night of the week.'

'It means nothing,' Tony had said, putting his arm round Jack, as he always did when he'd had too much to drink. 'Take it from me, it means absolutely nothing unless you feel you can't live without that woman.'

And, if Tony was to be believed, that was what he now felt about Maddie. 'I'm sorry, Jack,' he'd said, after Jack had found them in bed, 'but she means the world to me. I can't live without her.'

'Neither can I!' Jack had roared. And, landing a direct hit on Tony's jaw, he'd knocked him to the floor. 'She's *my* wife and you're not having her!'

If he had thought violence was going to put an end to the affair, he had misjudged Tony. And Maddie. That very night she had taken the girls and moved in with Tony. She instigated divorce proceedings immediately. One minute Jack had been a happily married man, the next he was alone in Dumpsville. Friends had rallied round to bolster his confidence by telling him he was a great catch and that his only problem would be fending off all the gorgeous women who would come his way.

All rubbish, of course, but they had meant well. One or two had even admitted they were jealous, that they wished they were single again and weren't tied down by the Three Ms – marriage, a mortgage and a monastic sex-life. It was all talk. None of them would want their marriage to end in the way his had. Or for their children to suffer as his did.

The streets were busier now: it was chucking-out time and the carefree youngsters who had monopolised the bars were now filling the cold night air with their boisterous laughter. Sidestepping a couple who had fallen into each other's arms for a passionate kiss, he crossed the road and turned into the main street of Maywood. He passed Turner's, an old-fashioned department store that, against all the odds, had kept going, and went on towards Boots, Woolworths and W. H. Smith where the road had been pedestrianised. The shops were smaller here, and more individual. There was a bridal shop, a jeweller's, a florist (all three conveniently placed together), an Aga shop, an excellent delicatessen and, across the road, two shoe shops (side by side), a dry-cleaner's, a pine shop, a hair-dressing salon and Novel Ways, the town's only bookshop. Last year the owner had acquired the next-door premises – Jack had been in charge of the sale – so that he could knock through to provide his customers with a coffee shop.

Before Clare had appeared on the scene, Jack had often browsed the shelves before sitting down to a café latte and a quiet read. Clare wasn't a reader: she was a doer who preferred her time to be action-filled. Nostalgia for those pre-Clare days made him cross the road to look in the window of Novel Ways. He saw that the latest Harry Potter was out and made a mental note to pop back tomorrow and buy it for Amber and Lucy. He and his daughters had read all the previous ones together and the thought of sitting down with them to enjoy this one lifted his spirits. It would be something to look forward to when they returned from America.

But what if Tony bought it for them before Jack could?

He gritted his teeth and was about to walk away when something caught his eye. It was a piece of paper stuck to one of the panes of glass in the door.

Ever thought of writing a book, or penning a few lines of poetry? You have? Then why not join a writing group, where, among new friends, you can discover those hidden talents you never knew existed?

He read it through one more time and thought of all the song lyrics he had written as a teenager. He had given up when he'd met Maddie, dismissing his work as immature ramblings. But writing again might be cathartic. It might be an outlet for all the anger and bitterness he didn't know what to do with.

Without giving himself time to change his mind, he hunted through his pockets for a pen. He found one and wrote down the contact name and phone number on the back of his hand.

7

It was the last lesson of the day – double English with Mr Hunter – and Jaz was impatient for it to be over. It had been a long week for her, but at last it was Thursday and, the way things were going, she wouldn't have much homework to do tonight.

Her parents thought she was going round to Vicki's for the evening, and as long as all went to plan, they would think the same every Thursday night. She didn't like lying to Mum and Dad, and she rarely did, but she knew that the alternative, in this instance, was unthinkable. Better to keep quiet than put up with the teasing from her brothers and sisters.

At three forty-five the bell rang and, as he always did at the end of his lessons, Mr Hunter bowed and said, 'Thank you for your time, ladies and gentlemen. You may now take your leave of me. But remember, I want that Seamus Heaney essay in by Tuesday. That instruction extends to you also, Ross Peters.' Books and files were slapped into bags, and chairs scraped noisily on the tiled floor. Outside in the corridor, Jaz caught up with Vicki, who was getting something from her locker. They usually walked home together, unless one of them had an after-college activity. Vicki had just landed the role of Gwendolen in the drama department's production of *The Importance of Being Earnest*; from next week she would have rehearsals on Mondays and Wednesdays, leaving Jaz to walk home alone. More crucially, Vicki, with her enviably sleek long hair the colour of jet and her flawless skin, which tanned the second the sun shone, would be spending all that time with Nathan King, who was playing Algernon.

From the moment Vicki had told her about the play, Jaz had debated with herself whether to let Vicki know that *she* had her eye on Nathan. Yesterday, after several days of torturing herself, she went against her instinct to keep quiet and confided in her friend.

'Nathan King,' Vicki had said, with a wide grin, 'I like your taste, girl. But you might need to take a ticket and get in line.'

'What? You mean you're interested in him?'

'I'm teasing. But there is something tempting about him. Oh, don't look like that! Billy the Kid is more my style.'

'Billy Kidswell?'

'Yeah. He's playing Ernest.'

If Vicki was considered to be the hottest date in the lower sixth, Billy the Kid was the fittest, most lusted-after guy in the upper sixth. It was rumoured that he kept the underwear of all his conquests. Though why on earth Vicki wanted her knickers to be added to his Lycra trophy collection was a mystery to Jaz. She could think of nothing more demeaning.

Her friend's declared interest in Billy should have put Jaz's mind at rest. But it didn't. Of course Nathan King would fancy Vicki so there was little point in Jaz getting worked up about him. Never in a million years would he look twice in her direction. And if he did, once he knew what kind of a family she came from he'd make himself scarce. She didn't like to think that she was ashamed of her family, but she was. Mum was okay, but her father was embarrassingly larger than life and always had to know what she was up to, and as for her brothers and sisters, well, they were just savages with as much sense between them as a peanut. She seldom invited Vicki home with her, and only when she knew Tamzin and Lulu wouldn't be there.

'So tell me again about this writers' group,' Vicki said, shutting her locker and swinging her bag over her shoulder. 'Won't it be a load of frustrated old women writing about men in bulging riding breeches?'

Jaz laughed. 'It might be, for all I know. I'll find out tonight.'

Vicki stared at her. 'You're a strange girl, Jaz. Way too secretive for your own good.'

'As the middle child of a big family, it's the only way to survive. It's okay for you, you're an only child. You don't have to keep things from pathologically annoying brothers and sisters.'

'And I've told you before, it's not that easy being the centre of your parents' universe. Whoa, hold up! Look who I see.'

Ahead of them, and standing within a group of other students, mostly girls, were Billy the Kid and Nathan King. Billy looked towards them and waved. His fair hair was highlighted with blond streaks and it was cut so that part of the fringe flopped artfully down on to his face, partially covering his trademark sunglasses. 'Yo, my precious Gwendolen, how's it going?'

'Ernest, my love, how sweet of you to enquire. Truth to tell, I'm feeling quite faint and in need of a handsome Adonis to carry my bag home for me.' She tossed her shiny black hair with an exaggerated sigh. 'If only such a man existed.'

Jaz marvelled at her friend. How did she always manage to do and say the right thing?

Billy grinned. 'Then, my sweet, allow me to oblige and give you a lift in my carriage.'

'I didn't know you'd passed your test,' Vicki said, assuming her normal voice and somehow becoming part of the group, leaving Jaz on the edge.

'I passed yesterday, so I'm quite legal.' He pushed a hand through his hair affectedly. 'Fancy a ride ... home?' he drawled.

Vicki ignored the innuendo and said, 'Jaz too?'

Everyone turned and looked at Jaz. Including Nathan. Was it her imagination, or was he staring at her harder than the rest? She shrivelled inside and felt an excruciating flush creep up her neck. No! With her hair and skin tone, blushing was the kiss of death! She wished the ground would open up and swallow her. 'It's okay,' she said, 'I'd rather walk—'

'You haven't got room, Billy,' Nathan interrupted her rudely, 'not with all the other groupies you've offered to drive home.'

She felt the sting of his words. So, she was just another groupie, was she? A silly little groupie for whom Billy the Kid didn't have room. Well, she'd show him. In a gesture that Vicki would have been proud of, she tossed one of her long plaits over her shoulder. 'I'll see you, then, Vicki.' She walked away quickly, her head held high. She kept on walking, out of the college gate and right to the end of the road, where she turned left. Only then did she slow down to catch her breath. Bloody Nathan King! Whatever had she seen in him?

'Do you always walk this fast?'

She spun round. Oh, hell! It was him. 'Yes,' she snapped. 'I find it preferable to hanging round people who don't have any manners!'

He fell into step beside her, his long, languid strides outpacing her short, hurried ones. She waited for him to say something. But he didn't. They walked on in silence, past the supermarket and towards Mill Street. They stopped at the level-crossing, and he said, 'Carry your bag for you?'

She turned and saw there was a faint smile on his face. He was teasing her. 'I doubt you'd manage it,' she said and, seeing a gap in the traffic, she darted across the road.

He followed her. 'Would I be right in thinking I've done something to annoy you?'

'Yes. So leave me alone.'

'Oh,' he replied. 'Well, fair enough.'

With his hands deep in his pockets, the tails of his leather coat flapping rhythmically behind him, he sauntered beside her. She wished he'd get the message and push off.

But at the bottom of Chester Street, he said, 'And does everyone get this treatment, or have I been singled out specially?'

Enough! She stopped dead and gave him the kind of contemptuous look she practised in front of the mirror for Tamzin and Lulu's benefit. 'Don't flatter yourself that I'd single you out for anything.'

He tilted his head. 'Any reason why?'

She shifted the heavy bag on her shoulder and started walking again. 'Figure it out for yourself.'

'Give me a clue. Am I wearing the wrong aftershave, or am I just not your type?'

'My type? That's a joke! You'd never be my type. Not in a million years. Not even if you learned some manners. Not even if you were the last guy on the planet with a pedigree that stretched from here to Uranus.' She paused for breath, regretting her choice of planet. Why couldn't she have picked Pluto? He'd be bound to seize his opportunity for some more fun at her expense.

But he didn't. 'Aha,' he said, 'we're getting somewhere. So it's my behaviour that's rattled you. Something I said? How about we rewind the last fifteen minutes? My first words to you were when Billy offered your friend a lift home. What did I say?'

She shot him a furious look. 'Short-term memory not what it used to be?'

'Evidently not.'

'You told Billy not to give me a lift home with Vicki because he already had a carload of groupies to bolster his ego. Now, you can take this as a first official warning: I am nobody's groupie. Got that?'

'You think I snubbed you? Is that it?'

'Oh, please, give the boy a round of applause!'

'Listen, if you hadn't gone stomping off, you would have heard what I was going to say next.'

'I didn't go stomping off . . .' She hesitated. 'What *were* you going to say next?'

'That rather than let you risk your life in Billy's death-trap of a car, I'd walk you home.'

She looked at him suspiciously, far from convinced. 'And why would you want to do that?'

He thought for a moment, then smiled. 'I guess I must get some sort of perverse pleasure out of girls giving me a hard time.'

8

Beth felt as if she were a child again getting ready for the first day of the school term. She had made so many last-minute checks – A4 writing pad, biros (two, in case she lost one on the way or one failed to work), pencil, and lastly . . . What else did she need to take with her to the first meeting of Hidden Talents?

Nothing, she told herself firmly.

'How about a ruler? Or maybe a dictionary? Better still, a thesaurus.'

She looked across the kitchen to where Nathan was helping himself to an apple from the fruit bowl. 'Don't tease me, Nathan,' she said. 'I'm nervous enough.'

He leaned back against the worktop, a picture of easygoing nonchalance. 'Keep it chilled, Mum, that's what you've got to tell yourself.' He bit into the apple and chomped noisily.

She smiled. 'I'm not sure I like all this role reversal.'

'It's the future. Which reminds me, I'll see to your computer for you tonight while you're out.'

'There's no hurry.'

'Yes, there is. I want you hooked up to the Net and best-friends with it before I leave home. How else will I be able to keep an eye on you?'

'By telephone?'

'Old ground, Mum. We've been there before. Email's much better, a piece of cake to get the hang of. Now I must learn my lines. Oscar's waiting for me in the bedroom.' He swept past her in a flourish of camp theatrical posturing.

It was a fifteen-minute walk to Bloom Street. She could have driven, but since it wasn't raining she decided to walk the nerves out of her system.

It was ridiculous that she was so keyed up. She was only going to a writers' group. Even if it was a departure from the norm, it was a necessary one, she reminded herself. She was on a mission: to convince all those doubters, herself included, that she would be able to cope when Nathan flew the nest. She was a capable woman – as Simone frequently reminded her – she had a comfortable home, a reasonable job and a brain that functioned relatively well. Now she had to learn how to enjoy exploring the unfamiliar.

She wished she could be more like Nathan, who took everything in his stride: exams were a challenge, as was standing up on a stage and performing for an audience. She could never do that. Just the thought of looking out at a sea of expectant faces made her stomach lurch. It was bad enough watching Nathan, because although he was extraordinarily good at learning his lines, she always sat in the audience rigid with worry that he might miss a cue.

His outward self-assurance came from his father. Nothing had seemed to faze Adam, which had made his untimely death all the more shocking. He had hidden his anxiety well. Too well. If only he had been more open she might have been able to help him.

She arrived at number eighteen exactly on time. Bloom Street was considered the prettiest street in Maywood, the most sought-after address in town. Having said that, her own address had become almost as highly prized – if the asking price that the estate agent had put on Adele's flat was anything to go by. There had already been two couples to view it and Beth knew that both were keen to go ahead with the purchase. She hoped for her elderly neighbour's sake that things would go smoothly.

She rang the bell, admiring the creamy white pansies and trailing ivy in the window-boxes at either side of the handsome wooden door. It was painted a deep blue and was finished off with a shiny brass knocker in the shape of a lion's head. Whoever Dulcie Ballantyne was, she had style, Beth decided.

To put everyone at ease, Dulcie had decided to offer a glass of wine before the meeting got under way. They made a small gathering, but an interesting one. That was the thing about writers' groups; they brought together a diverse mix of people who, on the face of it, had little in common. She, for example, wouldn't ordinarily socialise with a man like Victor Blackmore. She doubted that any of the others present would either. He had been in the room for just a few minutes, but it was patently obvious that he was a spanner in the works. She put him in his late fifties; he had thinning, sandy grey hair, and was very pale with beady eyes tinged with pink. He was wearing a pair of seen-better-days trousers that were too short – an inch or two of shiny, hairless white shin was exposed as he nursed a bulky file on his lap – and a selection of pens was clipped to his breast pocket. He looked ill at ease as he sipped his red wine.

Nearest to Victor, and sitting on the sofa, was Beth King. She had been first to arrive and, when Dulcie had opened the door to her, had looked ready to turn tail. She was an attractive, fair-haired woman, somewhere in her early forties. In a navy blue polo-neck sweater with straight-legged jeans, she wore no wedding ring, so was possibly divorced. She had a son at the local college and his name had already been mentioned several times during the conversation. Dulcie wondered how dependent Beth was on him. When Philip had died she had seen how easy it would be to rely on her children, to live her life through them, and she had done everything in her power not to make that mistake.

It was good to see that Victor Blackmore wasn't to be the sole man of the group. With a bit of luck Jack Solomon's presence would keep the dreadful man from thinking he could lord it over the rest of them. He was good-looking, if a little sombre, and cut a striking figure in his dark blue suit and silk tie. But she detected a sag in his shoulders and a tiredness in his eyes. He had apologised when he'd arrived for being so formally dressed, but apparently work had run on. 'Don't worry,' she'd said, taking him through to the sitting room where everyone was gathered. 'You won't be marked down for it. Now, let me you introduce you.' It turned out that he had already met Beth King, and they seemed surprised to see each other. A little awkward, too.

The most interesting member of the group was Jaz Rafferty. Dulcie was delighted that someone so young wanted to be involved. If she could bear to be with a bunch of old fogies, which was probably how she viewed them all, she would add a fresh and exciting dimension to the group. She was a delicate sprite of a girl and probably had no idea how pretty she was, with her striking auburn hair and charmingly freckled complexion. There was a delicious defiance in her manner – heavily booted feet crossed at the ankles, arms clamped across her chest – and she bristled with that beneath-the-surface defensiveness of teenagers. Dulcie thought she was lovely and envied her her youth and tiny body, which looked so endearing in the minuscule black skirt and oversized baggy jumper. She had forgotten how fascinating and intense teenagers could be; how terribly serious life was for them.

It was time to get things started, and Dulcie had an opening exercise in mind; something lighthearted to set the right note and help everyone relax. She offered everyone a top-up of Shiraz, except Jaz, who was sticking to orange juice, and said, 'How would you all feel about playing a little game, just something daft to get us in the right mood?'

Victor was first to speak. 'I haven't come here to play games,' he muttered.

The rest of the group was galvanised.

Jack said good-humouredly, 'Squash or tennis? Either way, I'm afraid I haven't brought my trainers.'

'Sounds okay to me,' smiled Beth, 'so long as it doesn't involve a Trivial Pursuit board.'

'Is it role play?' asked Jaz doubtfully. 'We used to do a lot of that at school in Drama.'

'No, it's not role play,' Dulcie assured her. 'It's basic story-telling, and I'm sure you'll all have played the game before, as adults or as children. We each take it in turns to add a sentence to the story. We'll go clockwise, just to be conventional. Victor, perhaps you'd like to set the ball rolling.'

'Very well.' He leaned back in his seat, closed his eyes, steepled his fingers together and inhaled deeply. He let out his breath and they waited for him to speak.

Nothing.

Complete silence.

Beth looked at Dulcie, who winked at her.

Still nothing.

Someone – Jaz? – cleared their throat.

Victor's eyes remained shut. 'I'm thinking,' he said, in answer to the not-so-subtle prompt.

Another deep inhalation. And then it came. 'It was the best of times, it was the worst of times.' He opened his eyes and looked about him as though expecting a round of applause. Across the room, on the sofa next to Jack, Dulcie was aware of Jaz stifling a snigger. She swallowed to stop one escaping her as well and said, 'Good start, Victor. Beth, your turn now. And perhaps go for a slightly longer sentence, something for the rest of us to play with and get our teeth into.'

'It was the best of times, it was the worst of times,' Beth repeated slowly, her gaze focused on the clock on the mantelpiece, 'but no one could have been prepared for the awful calamity that struck, that wild, windy night, on exactly the stroke of midnight.'

With visible relief, she turned to Jack, who dived in straight away. 'Not even Gibbons, the one-armed gardener, who could never steer a straight course with a wheel-barrow, especially if he'd spent the morning in the potting-shed savouring his favourite tipple of potato gin and absinthe.'

'But despite his strange drinking habits,' said Jaz, 'and the loss of his arm during a fight over his prize-winning marrows, Gibbons was a crack shot, and was quite used to killing trespassers who came on to the master's land.'

It was Dulcie's turn next and she was glad to see that the game was working well and, with the exception of Victor, that the others were enjoying themselves. 'Now, the master was a curious man,' she took up the story, 'and it was generally rumoured within the village that he was not all he claimed to be. Some said he had never been the same since the incident with the pitchfork, while others claimed that his time in Africa had left him with a fever for which there was no known cure.'

After several more rounds, which had them all laughing – the master, Jack told them, was a cross-dressing lap-dancer and Gibbons a Mafia boss on the run from his domineering mother – Dulcie pronounced an end to the game. She had decided that Jack was a quick-witted good sport, an asset to the group.

'And the point of that exercise?' asked Victor, drumming his fingers on his file.

'To relax us,' Dulcie said. 'And to make us see how easy it is to slip into clichés and stereotypes,' she added, more seriously. 'Something we need to avoid, if we're going to write anything of worth and originality.'

'Quite so,' Victor agreed. 'First rule of writing, avoid clichés like the plague.'

Surprised at his ready wit, Dulcie laughed. Then, seeing the dead-pan expression on his face, she stopped short. Oh, Lord, the wretched man wouldn't know a cliché if it whacked him on the bottom. 'Right, then,' she said, careful to avoid Jack's eye – which she knew would betray his amusement at Victor's gaffe – 'now that we know one another a little better, why don't we discuss what we each hope to gain from these sessions? Perhaps we could also be brave enough to share a few details about ourselves and say why we write.' Across the room, she saw Victor lean forward. 'Beth, would you like to leap in first?'

'Oh. Well, it's . . . Oh, goodness. Well, I've been writing for some time, um . . . since my husband died, eleven years ago. I suppose you could say it's been cathartic for me. Oh dear, that sounds terribly like a cliché, doesn't it?'

'Not at all,' Dulcie said encouragingly. 'When my husband died I wrote frantically. Any spare moment I had that might leave me dwelling on Philip, I filled with words. Have you had anything published?'

'Oh, no. I've only ever written for myself. I've never wanted other people to read my thoughts.'

'So what are you doing here?'

They all looked at Victor. Dulcie could have slapped him.

'Surely that's the whole point of writing,' he continued, 'to know that one has a talent and share it.'

'That's a fair enough theory,' said Jack, leaning back in his seat and looking directly at Victor, 'so long as one is sure one has such a gift.'

'Yes,' agreed Jaz, recrossing her legs and bouncing a booted foot in the air. 'No point in shoving a load of opinionated rubbish on people in the mistaken belief you can write. I can't think of anything worse.'

Good for you two, thought Dulcie. 'So, Beth,' she said, 'what would you like to get out of our meetings?'

'Oh, um, basic teaching, I suppose. Someone to show me where I'm going wrong. I know I'm not very good, and I'd like—'

'You can't teach people to write. You're either born a writer or you're not.'

'That's an interesting point that we'll discuss another time, Victor,' said Dulcie smoothly. He was such a textbook case of prejudice and arrogance, she was almost enjoying the verbal tussle with him. It was like dealing with a truculent child; a child of whom she would get the better. Smiling, she said, 'I ought to say at this stage that every time one of us apologises for our writing, or says, "I'm not very good," a fifty-pence piece will have to be put into the Self-belief Box.'

Beth laughed. 'In that case, do you take credit cards?'

'How about having a Know-it-all Box?' muttered Jaz. She was examining a silver ring on her thumb, but no one could have doubted at whom her remark was aimed.

Dulcie was growing ever fonder of the youngest member of the group. 'Jack, how about you tell us a bit about yourself and why you're here?' she asked.

'Not much to tell, really. I'm at a point in my life when I need to have a rethink, try something new, and, well, it was a spur-of-the-moment thing when I saw your card in the bookshop window.'

'And hopefully you're not regretting having responded to it?'

'Not yet,' he said, with a smile.

'Any writing experience?'

'Nothing published, if that's what you mean. I wrote some rather poor song lyrics when I was very young and probably when I was very drunk. More recently I've been thinking of keeping a diary.' He turned to Beth. 'More catharsis for the soul, I guess.'

'And your expectations of the group?' asked Dulcie.

He ran a thumbnail the length of the crease in his trouser-leg. 'I'm not sure I have any. Like I said, I just wanted to try something new.'

Victor clicked his tongue. 'This was what I was afraid of. Unless we're all serious about writing and getting published, this group will be a waste of time.'

Dulcie saw Jack's hand clench. She reminded herself that patience was a virtue. 'I don't think that's a helpful thing to say, Victor. For all we know, Jack may turn out to be the next Tony Parsons.'

'Tony who?'

Jaz rolled her eyes. 'Tony Parsons. He wrote *Man and Boy* and *One For My Baby*.'

'Well, I've never heard of him or his books.'

'I think we may be missing the point,' Dulcie intervened. 'We're not here to judge one another. We're here to offer support and helpful criticism. Jaz, do you want to take a turn?'

'Okay. I've just started writing a novel, so you could say I'm very serious about writing.' She shot Victor a direct glance. 'That's it. Nothing else to say.'

'Was there a particular reason why you decided to write?'

Jaz paused. 'Hmmm . . . I like doing stuff on my own. I suppose I like the power it gives me.'

'Yes,' nodded Dulcie, 'writing does empower you. It's just you and that piece of paper, and when you've filled it, you know no one else had anything to do with it. A nice point, Jaz. And finally, Victor, you're obviously a seasoned writer. We'd love to know more about the book you're working on. Also, how and why did you start writing it?'

He squared his shoulders, ready to take the stage. He'd probably been wondering if he'd ever get a turn. 'It's a thriller set in a fictitious state, somewhere between Macedonia and Albania, and encompasses everything from drug trafficking and prostitution to political intrigue.'

'That's quite a canvas you're working with,' Dulcie said. 'What gave you the idea? A trip to that part of the world?'

'A programme on television, not that I watch much – rubbish, most of it, these days. And no, I haven't been there. But writers should learn to depend more on their imagination than on mere bricks and mortar.' He tapped his forehead. 'It's all in here.'

'How much have you written?' asked Jack.

'Two hundred thousand words,' Victor said proudly. 'And still going strong.' He opened the file on his knees.

Dulcie's heart sank. From what she could see it was an editor's nightmare. There were pages and pages of tightly packed old-fashioned type, smudged ink and Tipp-Ex. 'Don't you use a word-processor?' she asked.

He shook his head so vehemently that she might have asked him if he wrote in blood. 'I wouldn't feel the same creative flow using a computer. I feel more in tune with the spirit of being a real writer when I'm bashing away on my old Remington. Hammering on the anvil of true creativity, that's what I'm doing.'

'Goodness, how do you find time to write so much?' asked Beth, staring in awe at the manuscript.

'I'm very focused,' he replied, crossing his legs and revealing more white shin.

'You'd have to be,' said Jack. 'I couldn't begin to think of writing to that extent after a hard day's work. I take my hat off to you.'

Jack's praise caused Victor to blush with pride, and he gazed at his file lovingly. 'It's all in the focus,' he murmured.

Later, when Dulcie was showing them out, having set a simple exercise to be completed by next week, she knew that as much as Victor had initially harangued the group, he would continue to grace it with his awkward and at times antagonistic presence. Doubtless he was secretly delighted that he had written more than anyone else in the group: it put him above the rest of them. Which meant that deep down, just like everyone else, he was hopelessly insecure about himself.

9

'Mother, I'm shocked! *Who* was that man I saw you with?'

Despite knowing Nathan was teasing her, Beth felt her cheeks colour. She shut the door behind her, removed her jacket, and hung it up on the row of hooks. She decided to play along with him. 'And what man would that be?'

He wagged a finger at her. 'Don't come the innocent with me, my girl. I saw the two of you, bold as brass out there in the road for all the neighbours to see.' He shook his head. 'I don't know, I've tried my best to bring you up properly and this is all the thanks I get. What's a son to do?'

She squeezed past him and planted a kiss on his cheek. 'For starters you can put the kettle on and I'll tell you all about it. You wouldn't believe one man who was there. He was such a bigoted know-it-all. I don't know how we got through the evening without taking a swipe at him.'

They sat at the kitchen table with their mugs of tea. Nathan had kept the log-burning stove alight while she'd been out, and Beth felt herself relax for the first time that evening. She knew she had given a less than impressive performance in Bloom Street, and she didn't like to think too hard about what the rest of the group must have thought of her. Probably had her down as a simpering idiot. She hoped she scored higher in their estimation than Victor Blackmore.

'So, first off, who was the guy in the Beamer?' asked Nathan, his bare feet stretched out towards the stove. 'The bigoted know-it-all?'

Momentarily distracted by Nathan's long legs – she never failed to be surprised by the size of him – she said, 'No, that was Jack Solomon. Coincidentally, he's Adele's estate agent and is really quite nice.'

Over the rim of his mug, Nathan raised an eyebrow. 'How nice?'

She swatted him with one of the cork tablemats. 'Not in that way. He's much too young for a decrepit thing like me.'

'Oh, Ma, give it up! I bet you were easily the best-looking woman there. And the youngest to boot.'

'Wrong again. There was an interesting girl about your age. Goodness knows what she thought of the rest of us. I expect she wrote us off as the local bunch of ageing crazies. You might know her, she goes to Maywood College.'

'Name, rank and number?' He pulled out an imaginary notebook from his pocket and pretended to flick through it, searching for a character match.

'Jaz Rafferty and she lives on—'

He looked up. 'Marbury Road,' he finished for her.

'You know her?'

'I walked home with her after college today. Did she know you were my mother?'

'Why? Are you worried I might have told her the truth about you and put her off?'

'Now, Mum, don't let this fiction business go to your head.'

Beth laughed. She told him about the game the group had played.

'Transvestite lap-dancers? I'm beginning to have reservations about this writing group. Perhaps I ought to come along as your chaperon and keep an eye on you.'

'Spoilsport.'

Later that night, soaking in a scented bath, Beth took stock of the evening. She concluded that it had gone well. She had enjoyed herself more than she'd expected to, and felt a sense of achievement. She put this down to Dulcie Ballantyne: with her quiet, reassuring manner, she had led the group firmly but not autocratically. She had given encouragement without resorting to patronage. It was just a pity they had had to put up with Victor. It was possible that by next week he would have pulled out – and also that new members might join. It was selfish of her, but Beth hoped this wouldn't happen. She wanted the group to stay as small as it was. Excluding Victor, she had liked everyone. Maybe it was because Victor was such a pain that the rest of them had gelled so nicely.

She soaped a leg with a banana-shaped sponge Nathan had given her for her last birthday and recognised she was being a wimp. *Courage, mon brave!* she told herself. It was odds on that no one else from the group was having these pathetic thoughts. Certainly not Jack Solomon. She wondered what he had meant when he had said that writing would be cathartic for him. What did he have to work through? He had seemed relaxed and confident to her. But no one knew better than she did that appearances could deceive.

If any of the patients from the health centre had seen or heard her mumblings this evening, they wouldn't believe she was the same person who had to stand firm when they claimed their sore throat was life-threatening and they just *had* to see the doctor. Often, in such cases, the only life under threat was hers – she was the one who had to deflect the tirade of abuse thrown at her down the telephone line.

Her mind still preoccupied with the group, she thought of Jaz Rafferty. Had she imagined it, or had Nathan shown a little too much restrained interest when she'd mentioned the girl's name? As popular as he was with girls – the phone was always ringing for him – there had never been anyone 'special' for him. He joked that he liked to keep his options open and play the field, but she knew it wasn't in his nature. That was more Billy's style.

While Billy's *raison d'être* was clocking up as many broken hearts as he could, Nathan's was attracting girls as friends.

With an expert nudge of her foot, she turned on the hot tap and wondered why women were so often attracted to the wrong sort of men. Handsome, shallow men who would do them no good.

A knock at the door interrupted her thoughts.

It was Nathan. 'Will you test me on my lines?' He came in and settled himself in the creaking wicker chair beside the bath. It was a familiar routine between them. For years she had tested Nathan like this, whether it was lines for a play or vocabulary for a French test. When he'd hit adolescence she'd assumed he'd stop coming into the bathroom when she was in the bath, having decided he was too old for such openness, but he hadn't. It amused her that it didn't work the other way round: whenever he was in the bath the door was locked.

She turned off the tap. 'Go on, then. Pass me a towel.' After she'd dried her hands she took the script from him.

'If you start at the top of the page, I'll come in from there.'

Assuming her best Edith Evans accent, Beth began to read the part of Lady Bracknell, the high ceiling of the bathroom giving her voice an extra resonance: '"It really makes no matter, Algernon. I had some crumpets with Lady Harbury, who seems to me to be living entirely for pleasure now."'

'"I hear her hair has turned quite—"' Nathan broke off. 'What is it? What's wrong?'

She handed him the text. 'Quick, fetch me a pen and a piece of paper.'

He returned within seconds and watched her scribble in large block capitals the words, LIVING FOR PLEASURE.

'What do you think?' she said. 'Good title for a book?'

'Not bad. But why not give Oscar full credit and go for "Living Entirely for Pleasure"?'

She shook her head. 'No, it's snappier my way.'

Beth went to bed happy that night. The homework Dulcie had set the group had been to think of a suitable title for a novel, and to put together an opening page. 'Key features to get across,' Dulcie had said. 'You need a hook to grab the reader's attention, a sense of time and place, and the general tone of the story.'

Well, she'd stumbled across the title. Now all she had to do was write the necessary three hundred-odd words.

As Nathan might say, a piece of cake – surely?

10

On Sunday morning Jack woke with one of Clare's arms draped over his chest. He lay for a moment without moving, his eyes fixed on the narrow gap in the curtains: rain was pattering against the window. Another wet, miserable day, he thought. Thousands of miles away, Amber and Lucy would be enjoying blue skies and sun-drenched days in Florida.

He looked at the digital alarm clock on the bedside table and saw that it wasn't yet seven. There was no need for him to be up early – it wasn't a work day – but he knew he wouldn't get back to sleep. Not wanting to disturb Clare, he lifted her arm gently and slid out of bed.

He shut himself into the bathroom and stood beneath the shower, letting the powerful jets of water batter him into full consciousness. He wondered if this was such a good idea. In his present mood, it might be easier to get through the day in a state of hazy detachment.

Out of the shower, he wrapped himself in a large towel, wiped away the condensation from the mirror above the basin, and reached for his shaver. When he wasn't working he often liked to skip the tedious monotony of shaving, but Clare was a stickler for a stubble-free chin, especially if they were going out. Today they were meeting Des and Julie for lunch at the Italian in town. It had been Clare's idea to celebrate him becoming a partner, but Jack didn't feel comfortable at the prospect. He knew that Des had expected to be offered the same promotion, but nothing had materialised for him, and this would rub his nose in it. What was worse, a step up the career ladder would have been a welcome break for Des: six months ago his wife had given birth to Desmond Junior. But Clare had arranged it behind Jack's back, then delivered it to him as a *fait accompli* last night. 'I was going to keep it as a surprise,' she'd said, hooking her fingers round his neck and kissing him, 'but you know what I'm like with secrets. Completely hopeless.' She had manoeuvred him down on to the sofa, and before he'd known what he was doing he was undressing her, not slowly and tenderly as he normally did, but roughly, suddenly filled with the need to feel the effect of his own strength. To feel *something*. Afterwards he had fallen asleep with a chilling sense of desolation growing within him.

He had finally got round to telling Clare about his partnership on the day of the writers' group's first meeting. They were speaking on the phone, late afternoon, and she had immediately suggested they go out for dinner. 'Sorry,' he'd said, 'it'll have to be another night, I'm busy this evening.'

'Oh? Got something or some*one* better lined up?' Her words were playful, but beneath them he caught an edge of jealousy.

He hadn't wanted to tell her about Hidden Talents and had said, 'Now I'm a partner there'll be even more late nights I'm afraid, regular meetings I'll be expected to attend.' As soon as he'd said this, he'd realised he'd given himself a plausible alibi for every Thursday evening when he would be attending the group.

'Oh, well,' she'd replied, more happily, 'that's the price of success, I suppose.'

He slipped back into the bedroom, helped himself to some clothes from the wardrobe, and returned to the bathroom. Once he was dressed, he went downstairs. The kitchen was on the middle floor of the house and looked over the river. When he'd viewed the property this had been its one redeeming feature. He didn't like modern houses – an opinion, in his line of work, that he kept to himself. But necessity had quashed any aesthetic preferences: he had needed a place to live that was convenient for work and affordable. Maywood was an established pocket of affluence in Cheshire where, for many years, demand had outstripped supply. If beggars wanted to live in Maywood, they could not be choosy. He could have rented in a cheaper area, but he hadn't wanted to do that. One didn't have to be an estate agent to know that location, location, location was everything. What he wouldn't give to live in Bloom Street. Or Maywood Park Road.

Making himself some toast and a cafetière of coffee, he envied Beth King and Dulcie Ballantyne. He didn't know their circumstances, just that they were both widowed, but they seemed to have coped and got on with life. Perhaps if he got to know them better, he might learn something from them. He had given up looking for help and advice from his immediate circle of friends: all happily married, they had no comprehension of what he was going through. Besides, he sensed that they were tired of that particular conversation. He didn't blame them. What could be worse than another man's obsession? For that was what it seemed like, some days. How long, he wondered, had it been before Beth King had sorted herself out? Dulcie too.

It had been interesting seeing Beth last Thursday evening: she had seemed quite a different woman from the one he had met a few days earlier when she had been determined to make sure that old Miss Waterman wasn't duped. The other night she had been less sure of herself.

Maybe she had thought the same of him. He had told the group he was thinking of writing a diary, and after he'd driven home that night – having given both Beth and Jaz a lift – he had dug out an old notebook and made his first entry. After several lines, he had decided instead to write on his laptop. It was more private – less chance of Clare happening upon his innermost thoughts.

He stood looking at the river: it was as grey as the sky. The rain was coming down harder now. It wasn't the kind of day that induced one to go out. Much as he liked Des and Julie, reading the papers stretched out on the sofa with a bottle of wine would be more the mark for him today. He also wanted to spend some time writing. He had that exercise to do for next Thursday evening. He hadn't had time to make a start on it yet, but he was itching to do so. Trouble was, Clare had stayed over since Friday and he didn't want her to know what he was doing. He wanted to have something that was his, and his alone. He chewed his toast, and reflected that this was why he and Clare had no future together. She wanted too much of him: if they were to be together she would expect him to hand over his life to her lock, stock and barrel, and he wasn't prepared to do that. He couldn't share so much with another person: he wasn't ready, not so soon after Maddie.

Or was he oversimplifying matters, like that pretentious prat Victor Blackmore? He poured himself a second mug of coffee and, in spite of his morose mood, he smiled. Now there was a bloke who needed to be taken down a peg or two. Who in the group would be first to tell him to shove it?

His money was on Jaz. Sitting next to her that evening, he had felt her bristle whenever Victor had opened his mouth. She had reminded him of Amber or, more precisely, had made him think that this was how his elder daughter might be when she reached seventeen. Amber was only eleven but she was already showing signs of becoming a feisty teenager. He hoped she would never become so troubled or distant with him that they couldn't talk. The thought of anything spoiling his relationship with his precious daughters caused him to grip his mug so tightly that he almost snapped off the handle.

Then an even greater fear took hold of him: what if his inability to come to terms with what Tony and Maddie had done jeopardised his relationship with the girls, as Clare had warned him? He set down the mug on the worktop unsteadily. 'That must never happen,' he told himself. 'If you make just one promise for the rest of your days, Jack Solomon, it's to protect Amber and Lucy from the person who can hurt them most. You.'

During lunch, Jack drank too much and found himself drifting in and out of the conversation. Clare had never been interested in Des and Julie's baby son, but today she seemed inordinately keen to know everything about Desmond Junior: had his nappy rash cleared up, was he giving them many sleepless nights with teething problems? Once or twice Jack made eye-contact with her, and in return she rubbed her foot against his leg. He almost wished he could make it work between them. It would be so easy. So convenient. She was intelligent – her job as a solicitor was proof of that – attractive, and eminently capable of making someone a good wife. Any number of men in his shoes would leap at the chance to have her. Why couldn't he?

Because he didn't love her. And never would. It was as simple as that, and she deserved better. The sooner he ended it, the better off they'd all be. He decided that when and how he told her would be crucial. He wouldn't rush it; he would take his time to ensure an amicable split. He took another thirsty gulp of his wine, suddenly annoyed that he was treating his brief relationship with Clare as if it were a marriage. Five months, that was all it had been.

'Hey up, Jack? What's thee dreamin' of?'

He shook himself out of his reverie. 'Nowt you'd understand, Des, my lad.'

Julie groaned. 'Oh, they're off again, Clare, speaking int' northern tongues.'

It was a joke between the four of them: Clare and Julie had grown up in leafy Cheshire, as they called it, while Jack and Des both hailed from hardier climes – Lancashire and Greater Manchester respectively. When sufficient alcohol had been consumed, Jack and Des would slip into their Monty Python routine of *lookshree* living in a soggy paper bag.

'Oh, let's leave them to it and go to the loo,' Clare said, folding her napkin and rising from the table. 'We can talk about them behind their backs,' she added, with a smile.

When they were alone, Des topped up their glasses – the girls had offered to drive. Jack had drunk more than he would normally, and could feel that it was making him lightheaded and belligerent, but even so he allowed Des to fill his glass to the top.

'You okay, Jack? You're very quiet. Everything all right *chez* Solomon?'

As he looked at Des's concerned face, Jack was tempted to confide in him. Maybe that was all he needed to do. Perhaps it was nothing more than a case of cold feet that was making him back away from Clare. He hadn't known Des very long – just two years – but he was a good and loyal friend, someone he trusted, in and out of the office.

Someone he trusted.

The words played themselves over inside his head.

Someone he trusted.

Someone like Tony.

He raised the full glass to his lips and downed it in one. 'Nothing's wrong,' he said, holding out his glass for another refill. 'What the hell could be wrong with my life? Eh? I've got it made, haven't I? A fantastic girlfriend who I'd be nuts to lose, and a partnership thrown in for good measure. What the hell could be wrong with that?' His voice was sharp and much too loud. People at a nearby table looked in their direction.

Still holding the bottle of Valpolicella, Des stared at him. Then, 'You tell me, Jack.'

11

Marsh House was one of the coldest houses Nathan knew, and whenever he and his mother visited Grandma Lois and Grandpa Barnaby they always made sure they wore something warm. Today he was in jeans with his thickest sweater over a long-sleeved shirt and a T-shirt and Mum was wearing her Marsh Twinset, as she called it: a seriously uncool piece of expensive fluffy knitwear that Grandma had given her one Christmas. She only pulled it out of the wardrobe for a Marsh House visit. Usually, and at Mum's contrivance, his grandparents came to the flat, where Grandpa, unused to warmth, would doze by the fire. It wasn't that they were too mean to heat their large house properly, it was just that, according to Mum, they were of a generation that had been brought up to believe that the cold was good for you.

'Watch out for the cyclist, Nathan.'

'Relax, Mum, I saw it way back.' He indicated, overtook the cyclist and turned to smile at his mother.

'Eyes on the road!'

'Mum, I know the road. Pop another Prozac, then sit back and relax.'

He drove on in silence, ignoring his mother's right foot, which twitched on an invisible pedal. He knew it was difficult for a parent to be a passenger, everyone at college said they got grief from their parents, but at least Mum let him drive as often as she could. Whenever they went anywhere together, she always passed him the keys and said, 'You drive.' It would be great to have his own car, like Billy, but they couldn't afford it. He didn't mind: one day he would earn enough money not to worry about how expensive things were. When he'd got his law degree and was in London, things would be different. It would be a hard slog to get there, and he'd probably get a part-time job while he was at college, but he'd do it.

Unlike Billy and most of the others at Maywood College, who saw university as a means to extending their childhood, Nathan had the next five years of his life carefully worked out – as long as he got the right grades next summer he hoped to go to Nottingham – and he was determined that nothing would spoil his plans.

Billy was planning on a gap year in which he would travel at his parents' expense. Nathan wasn't envious. But, then, he'd never been envious of Billy.

That was why their friendship worked. Billy, who couldn't be serious if his last pot of hair wax depended on it, had a simple outlook: he wanted nothing more than to enjoy himself with the least amount of effort. Nathan, however, knew that hard work paid off.

There was no rivalry between them, because Billy was Billy and Nathan was Nathan. They rarely argued, and while Nathan thought Billy was an idiot when it came to girls, and told him so, they never fell out. 'They know the score,' Billy once said, when Nathan had chastised him for the cruel way he had treated one particular girl. From what Nathan could see of the relationships that went on at college, the aftermath, when a couple split up, was invariably a minefield of who was no longer speaking to whom. He preferred to be friends with everyone; it kept things from getting messy or complicated. Anything else would blur the edges of the bigger picture he had drawn for himself.

Even so, he couldn't deny his interest in Jaz Rafferty. There was a spiky independence about her that appealed to him. He'd noticed her around college since the start of term and liked the distinctive way she dressed and spoke; she clearly wasn't a girl who would dumbly follow the crowd. But he suspected that her huffy manner, when he'd walked home with her on Thursday, had had nothing to do with his apparent snub, but everything to do with her fancying Billy. It was always the same: the girls who didn't receive a second glance from Billy always claimed they couldn't understand what anyone saw in him.

He drove through the gates of Marsh House and tried not to give in to the temptation that always seized him when they arrived: to increase his speed and spin the wheels recklessly before screeching to an abrupt stop at the front door, gravel flying.

Grandpa Barnaby opened the door to them. He was wearing an apron and a wide smile. 'Good-oh,' he said. 'Now that you're here Lois will let me have a drink. I was so worried you'd be late.' He shook hands with Nathan, which he had always done, even when Nathan had been knee high, and kissed Beth, who almost got lost in the enthusiasm of his embrace.

When she emerged, salvaging a crushed bunch of flowers, she said, 'You sound as if you're in dire need of one, Barnaby.'

He grinned and stroked his moustache, tilting his head towards the inside of the house. 'When am I not? Anyway, come on in. Lois is beavering away in the kitchen. Got all manner of delights in store for you. She's had me on spud duty for the last hour. You know there's no holding her back when she gets the bit between her teeth. I hope you brought healthy appetites with you.'

They followed him through the house, their shoes clattering noisily on the polished wood floor. As well as being cold, Marsh House was as silent as the grave. Rarely was there any music playing, or Radio 4 on in the background, like there was at home. As a young child the quiet stillness of Marsh House had unnerved Nathan and he had tiptoed round the place warily, half expecting someone, or something, to leap out at him. He could remember staying here when he was about five, when his parents had been away, and being terrified of going to bed alone. Grandpa Barnaby had sat with him for ages, reading book after book, until finally he had fallen asleep with his head wedged under the pillow.

Now, at a standstill in the kitchen doorway, Grandpa Barnaby said, 'Look who I've found, Lois! A charming couple bearing gifts of the horticultural variety.'

This was a variation on one of the many lines Grandpa came out with when they visited. It had started as a joke for Nathan's benefit when he'd been little but had become part of the ritual of their every arrival. *Look, Lois, two of the finest people in the county have come calling.* Or: *Lois, did you know we had royalty visiting today?*

But Grandma Lois never played along. She usually made a face at her husband and tutted. Now, with rubber-gloved hands held aloft, she turned from the sink where she was washing a large cauliflower. 'Ah, Beth dear, there you are. Oh, and how lovely you look. That really was such a good buy, that angora twinset I gave you, wasn't it? I can't believe you get so much wear out of it. And, Nathan, look at you in your smart leather coat. Very dashing. What a fine young man you've become. So tall.' She sighed and Nathan knew what was coming next. 'The spitting image of your father.' They'd been in the house less than two minutes and already the first comparison had been made.

Although he had promised himself he wouldn't react, Nathan clenched his jaw. Out of the corner of his eye, he saw his mother glance at him. She was trying to reassure him, but it didn't stop him wishing they weren't here. He hated having to keep quiet for his mother's sake, and keeping up the pretence that had become an absurd reality for Grandma Lois. This whole day – his father's birthday – was a mockery, and he no longer wanted to be part of it.

Why were children punished for telling the most innocent lies, when adults could go to extraordinary lengths to conceal the truth and never once be accused of deceit?

'Nathan, you've been jolly quiet. What have you been up to recently? More apple sauce?'

'No thanks, Grandma.' His grandmother was a great cook, but she always overdid it: there was enough food on the table to get them through the entire winter. They were in the dining room, possibly the coldest room in the house with its north-facing windows. The walls were painted an acidic yellow which, rather than brightening the drab room, accentuated its chill.

At the head of the table, opposite Nathan, Grandpa Barnaby chuckled and gave him a conspiratorial wink. 'Careful, Lois, he's a good-looking young man, there's bound to be any number of things he'd rather keep private.'

She clicked her tongue. 'What nonsense! What could he possibly want to keep from his grandparents? Another roast potato, Nathan? Perhaps a parsnip?'

Knowing that there would be a choice of at least three puddings, he refused politely. This was one of those occasions when several brothers and sisters to share the burden of grandparental spoiling would have come in handy. To deflect his grandmother, whose eyes were roaming the table for something else to offer him, he said, 'Did Mum tell you I'm in the college play?'

'Ooh, are you? How exciting. Which one?'

'*The Importance of Being Earnest.* I'm Algernon.'

She turned to her husband, then to Beth. 'The best part, of course. Adam was the same. He could always land the lead in a school production.'

Irritated, Nathan said, 'It's essentially an ensemble piece. I think you'll find Lady Bracknell steals the show once or twice.'

But Lois seemed not to hear him. 'Barnaby, do you remember the time Adam played Puck in *A Midsummer Night's Dream,* and afterwards everyone kept coming up to us saying what a natural he was and that he ought to consider a career on the stage?'

Nathan stood up abruptly, knocking his plate askew. He caught his knife before it fell to the floor. 'Shall I clear away for you, Grandma?'

She turned from her husband and beamed at him. 'How kind of you, Nathan. But there's no need, I'll see to it.'

From the other side of the table, Beth also got to her feet. 'That's okay, Lois, you sit down and rest. Nathan and I will tidy up. It's the least we can do.'

'Sorry, Mum,' he whispered, when they were alone in the kitchen, 'but I can't stand it when she goes on and on about him.'

His mother put the pile of plates on the draining-board and rested a hand on his arm. 'I know, Nathan, but it's only for today. It's her way of coping with it.'

'But she's *not* coping with it. She's simply denying everything that really happened. Is that what Dad would have wanted?' He turned and stared out of the window, his resentment growing. 'And it's not as if it's just for today. She's doing it more and more. I can't tell her anything without her comparing me to him. Sometimes I just want to shout at her, "I'm *me*, *Nathan* King! Not Adam King, the deceased golden boy of Lois and Barnaby King."' He lowered his head, vaguely ashamed of his childish outburst.

His mother's hand moved from his arm to his shoulder. 'Look,' she said softly, 'this isn't the moment to talk about it. For now, let Lois remember her son the way she needs to. Okay?'

A brief silence passed between them. The rage inside him began to subside. He felt leaden. 'We're trapped ... defined by what happened to Dad. You'll always be the widow and I'll always be the orphaned grandson.'

She frowned. 'Excuse me, but you're not an orphan. You have a mother who loves you very much. And if you weren't so keen to drive us home, she'd suggest you had a drink.'

He made an effort to smile. 'It's come to something when my own mother's encouraging me to hit the bottle.'

'How do you think Barnaby gets through the day?'

They went to investigate the pantry, where Lois had told them she had put the desserts. On the highest shelf, alongside jars of home-made jam, pickles and chutney, were two old-fashioned china basins. Tied with string, they each bore a lid of greaseproof paper and a flowery label that read, 'Christmas Pudding'. 'I see Grandma's ahead of the game as usual,' Nathan remarked. Neither of them commented on the assumption Lois made every year, that they would spend Christmas together at Marsh House.

On the lowest shelf they found what they'd been instructed to uncover, and removed the tea-towels, clingfilm and aluminium foil to reveal a pavlova, a chocolate mousse, and a large trifle, which, as he was repeatedly told by his grandmother, had been one of his father's favourite puddings. 'He couldn't get enough of it,' she would say. 'I made it for him every Sunday.' Nathan wondered, as he so often did when he was at Marsh House, how his father had survived, growing up with a mother like Lois.

His father's death seldom got to him, these days. It was only when he was forced into a position of recalling a time before it had been just him and his mum, like today, that he thought of what it meant to lose a parent. He had been six when his mother had told him his father was dead. She hadn't been as brutal as that, of course, she had softened the words – he couldn't remember how, exactly – and she had held on to him so tightly that he had said, 'Mummy, you're hurting me.' Funny, he could remember that part of the conversation, but not what had come before. There had been tears. Lots of them. Once he'd realised that she was crying, he'd been scared and started to cry with her.

And then Grandma Lois had appeared in his room. He hadn't known that she was in the house. She had one of her cardigans draped around her shoulders and seemed sort of hunched. Older suddenly. She had stepped on one of his Lego animals, but didn't seem to notice it sticking out from beneath her shoe. In a chilling voice he had never heard her use before, not even when he'd tripped over a light flex and broken one of her expensive Chinese lamps, she said, 'Beth, stop this at once! You're frightening Nathan. That isn't what Adam would have wanted.' What Lois didn't know was that, in that moment, she had scared him more than his mother's tears had. He could remember vividly how his mother had tensed, how she had looked as though she had just been slapped. But, then, that had been his grandmother's intention, to bring his mother to her senses. In Lois's world you didn't admit to sadness or loss. You gritted your worn-down teeth and got on with it. As a result, his father's death was never referred to directly at Marsh House. Instead, he was revered and held up as the perfect son.

The perfect husband.

The perfect father.

Just once, Nathan would have liked someone at Marsh House to tell the truth so that his remaining memories – the honest ones – of his father could be treasured, not tainted with Lois's deluded portrayal of a man who had only ever existed in her mind. No one could have been *that* perfect.

When Nathan and his mother went back into the dining room, and Grandpa Barnaby saw the quantity of desserts on offer, he groaned and clutched his stomach. 'Oh, Lois,' he said, 'you'll be the death of us all.'

Nathan winced. In any other household a remark like that would have meant nothing, but Lois shot her husband a look of total horror.

'It was a joke,' Barnaby back-pedalled. 'A slip of the tongue.'

But the damage was done. Lois's face was drawn, her lips a thin line, and when she spoke, her voice was tight and brittle. 'I really don't think it's appropriate, today of all days, for you to use me as the butt of your stupid schoolboy jokes.' She pushed back her chair, stood up and walked out of the room.

'Oh, Lord,' muttered Barnaby. 'Do you think I ought to go after her?'

Already on her feet, Beth said, 'How about I go and talk to her?'

'Would you? I'd be eternally grateful. You girls always manage to smooth ruffled feathers better than us chaps.'

Nathan watched his mother leave the room. 'Sorry about this,' his grandfather said to him. 'You'd think I'd know better at my age.'

Nathan nodded, then realised that for once he and his grandfather were alone. Normally Lois was with them, which meant she dominated the conversation. He didn't mean that unkindly: she just had a habit of taking over, leading people in the direction she wanted them to go. She did it particularly with his mother. It used to annoy him that his mother became a different person when Lois was around. The Beth King he knew was strong-willed, determined and fun to be with. When Lois was on the scene, she withdrew into herself. She lost some of her confidence, became diminished. Sometimes Lois went too far and trampled over his mother's feelings. On the few occasions when there had been a hint of a man in Beth's life, Lois had been quick to stamp on it. On one occasion he had overheard her say, 'Really, Beth, what are you thinking of? The man's clearly only after one thing. And what kind of a stepfather would he make for Nathan?'

Her voice hesitant, his mother had said, 'But, Lois, we've been out for dinner twice, that's all. Marriage is as far from my mind as it could possibly be.'

'You must be careful, Beth. Nathan's at an impressionable age. You don't want him getting the wrong idea about you. Mothers have to be above reproach. Surely I don't need to spell it out for you.'

Oh, yes, thought Nathan. Lois could be cruelly manipulative. But she could also be extremely generous – yet even that was not without its own agenda. While she was paying for things – driving lessons, school trips – she had a hold over them. His mother would never admit it, but he knew she didn't like the situation. That was why, when he had passed his GCSEs, he had insisted on leaving the private school Lois and Barnaby had paid for since he was seven. Instead, he'd opted to go to Maywood sixth-form college. 'I need to spread my wings,' he'd said, when his mother had asked him why. They both knew the truth of his decision, though: it was his way of releasing the vice-like grip Lois had on them.

It wasn't like this with his mother's parents. They never interfered. When they'd offered him the money to buy his leather coat for his birthday, he had accepted with grateful thanks. If Lois had made the same offer, he would have turned it down flat.

The ugly truth of this gave him a prickle of misgiving. He was being too hard on his grandmother. She meant well, he knew that. She and Grandpa had been very good to him and his mother. It was just that, like her Sunday lunches, she went too far and overdid it.

Beth found Lois upstairs in her bedroom. She was sitting on the bed, crying. When she saw Beth, she gave her eyes one last stoic dab then pushed the handkerchief inside her sleeve. 'Silly of me, I know,' she said, her voice frayed with edgy cheerfulness. 'Barnaby's such a fool, I shouldn't let him get to me.'

Beth stepped further into the room, the heels of her shoes sinking into the soft peach carpet that had only been fitted last week: it still had that slightly oily smell. 'He didn't mean anything by it,' she said, with a shiver, and noticed that one of the windows was open. 'He was just showing off for Nathan's benefit.'

Lois said nothing. She stood up, smoothed out the pleats in her skirt.

'He probably thought he was helping to make light of the day,' Beth added.

The pleats were now dealt with. As was Beth's attempt at offering sympathy. 'Well, he failed badly,' Lois said, and moved away from the bed. 'I don't suppose he's thought to put the coffee on, has he?'

She was past Beth now and standing at the door, a hand raised to it. The moment to talk, really talk, about Adam and how Lois still felt about him was gone. Perhaps a stronger woman would have taken her by the scruff of her neck and made her confess, but Beth would never be able to do that. When the two of them were together, she became a coward. She despised herself for it, but doubted she would find the courage to change. Her own mother said repeatedly that it was folly to play along with Lois. That if anyone should make a stand, it was Beth. But how, after all these years, could she make Lois understand that living the lie only made it worse for them all?

She followed her mother-in-law down the wide staircase, and once more the curtain went up on another Lois King performance. Like Norma

Desmond, Lois was an expert on putting on the face she thought the world wanted to see.

They had their coffee in the sitting room, and just as she and Nathan had known would happen, Barnaby was assigned the task of setting up the old projector and screen. For the next hour they sat in semi-darkness watching jumpy images of a skinny, dark-haired boy grow into a handsome teenager. Last year Barnaby had suggested they should have their old cine films transferred on to modern videotape, but Lois had vetoed the idea. She had been terrified that the precious canisters of film might get lost or damaged – like her son, they were irreplaceable. From the scratched and faded reels of 8mm film, they progressed to turning the pages of Lois's photo albums. Beth knew that Nathan was finding this annual ritual more of an ordeal than ever, and her heart went out to him. Years ago he had taken a more active role in flicking through his father's past, asking his grandmother questions that helped her relive Adam's life, but today he was quiet and showed little interest. In response, she found herself compensating for him, drawing Lois on the names of other people in the photographs, or deliberately misremembering a crucial detail so that Lois could correct her.

It was dark and raining when they left Marsh House. Nathan was driving faster than Beth would have liked and she told him so.

'Worried I might put us out of our misery by killing us both?' he said savagely.

Horrified, she did not reply. How could he have said that? What terrible anger had fuelled such words?

'I'm sorry,' he said, some minutes later when he'd dropped his speed. 'That was a shitty thing for me to say.'

'Yes, it was.' Then, with false brightness, she said, 'And, anyway, an accident would result in a dreadful mess in the boot.'

He groaned. 'How much stuff did she offload on to you this time?'

'Oh, just the usual amount. Two puddings, the remains of the joint of pork and half a cauliflower.'

'What it is to be poor!'

'We're not poor,' she said crossly. 'Compared to some people, we live in the lap of luxury. Remember that, Nathan.'

'Doesn't it ever get to you, this constant supply of leftovers and hand-me-downs?'

She looked straight ahead of her. 'I think I'm beyond caring.'

He changed into fourth gear with a clumsy jerk. 'Doesn't pride make you want to say no occasionally?'

'Of course it does, but I also recall how grateful I was in the early years when keeping you in socks and shoes was a constant worry. You've no idea how fast you grew then, or what an expensive liability your feet were.'

The rain came down harder and Nathan flicked at the switch to make the wipers go faster. After a few minutes, he said, 'I know it hasn't been easy for you, Mum, but I do want you to know that – that my enormous feet and I are very grateful for all you've done.'

In the light cast by the street-lamps she could see that there was now a softness to his face. 'I'm glad to hear it. And maybe you'll think more of me when you know that I did refuse one of Lois's kind offers today. A carpet.'

'You're joking!'

'Her and Barnaby's old bedroom carpet. Apparently she thought it might replace the tatty one in your room, with a piece left over for the hall. You see what I saved you from? A flowery nightmare of the worst order.'

'You're a star, Ma!'

'I know. It's a knack I have. Watch your speed, there's a camera just up here.'

Nathan smiled. 'And there was me thinking I'd steal a Kodak moment to record the day.'

As if they'd ever need one, Beth thought miserably.

Back at the flat, in the warmth once more, their mood picked up. There was a pretty card from Adele Waterman inviting Beth to have a drink with her tomorrow evening, and a message on the answerphone from Simone in Dubai. 'Just thought I'd give you a ring and see how you got on today,' her friend's cheerful voice rang out. 'Was lunch as awful as it always is? I'll ring again tomorrow.'

In bed that night, Beth thought of Nathan's anger in the car. Never had he spoken with such bitterness before, and it scared her. She wished he didn't know the truth about his father's death. If he hadn't overheard her conversation with Simone all those years ago, he would have believed it was a tragic accident. A terrible twist of fate. But he knew the truth. That his father had gone out that night and deliberately killed himself. He had stopped off at the local off-licence, bought a bottle of cheap whisky, drunk half of it then driven into a tree. He had died instantly.

And that was what Lois had spent eleven years refusing to accept. She simply would not admit that Adam had been so depressed he had taken his own life as a way out of his problems. Despite all the evidence to the contrary, she wanted to believe it had been an accident.

Beth had always believed that the reason behind Lois's denial was her inability to forgive her son for being less of a man than she had thought him.

Poor Adam.

And poor Lois.

But there would be hell to pay if Lois ever discovered that Nathan knew the truth.

12

Des couldn't sleep. And if Jack knew what he knew, he doubted his friend could either. From the look of Jack at lunch, it wasn't likely that he was getting much sleep anyway. Des had never seen him put away so much booze and he hoped it wasn't becoming a regular thing.

He turned over and gazed at his wife in the semi-darkness. A thick lock of hair lay across her cheek. He pushed it away carefully, his fingers light on her warm skin. She stirred, but not enough to wake. I'm a lucky man, he thought. If he hadn't felt so troubled, he might have kissed her and woken her so that he could make love to her. But he wasn't in the mood.

All he could think of, and be grateful for, was that he wasn't in Jack's shoes. What a mess Jack's life had become. He didn't know what he would do if he came home one day and found Julie in bed with Paul, his oldest and closest friend. For starters he'd beat the hell out of Paul, and then he'd do it again.

He ran a hand over his face, then slipped out of bed. He went into the room next door and stared at his tiny son as he slept in his cot. It was only now as a father that he knew he would do anything to protect and preserve what he had. Love made you vulnerable, but it also made you strong; tough enough to fight to the death, if it ever came to it.

Outside, rain lashed against the window and a gust of wind rumbled in the blocked-off fireplace behind him. He thought of what Jack had said at the restaurant while the girls had been in the ladies'. How he knew he had to break it off with Clare but that he was scared of hurting her.

'But I thought it was going so well between the two of you.'

'It was, but then . . . Oh, it's just getting too heavy. Too serious.'

'You'll hurt Clare even more if you carry on deceiving her,' Des had said, matter-of-factly. He had accepted that there was no point in trying to change his friend's mind: it was clear from his face that it was made up.

'I know, but it makes me feel such a bastard. She keeps dropping hints about getting married. We hardly know each other but I bet she's even drawn up a guest list in her head.'

'Jack, you have to talk to her. Tell her what you've told me. She'll understand. She'll be upset to begin with, but then see it just wasn't meant to be.' Then he'd tried to lighten the tone of the conversation: 'And she'll realise what a lucky escape she had.'

But Jack hadn't laughed. He didn't seem able to, these days.

In the car afterwards, when they were driving away from the restaurant, Julie had said, 'You must promise not to say anything, especially to Jack, but guess what Clare told me in the loo during lunch.' Without giving him a chance to open his mouth, she'd pressed on eagerly: 'She's not a hundred per cent sure, but she reckons she might be pregnant.'

'You're kidding!'

'Do I look like I'm doing a stand-up comic routine?'

'I wish you were,' he'd muttered.

Coming to a stop at the traffic-lights in the town square, she'd regarded him thoughtfully. 'Something you're not telling me, Des?'

'Only that I don't think Jack's ready to be a father again. Not after everything with Maddie and the girls. It's too soon and, besides, technically he's still married.' He didn't like lying to Julie, but if things were going to get sticky between their friends, it would be better all round if they stepped back from it, tried to remain impartial.

Julie had shrugged. 'Then perhaps he ought to have been more careful in bed with Clare.'

He kept the thought to himself that maybe Clare had deliberately 'allowed' the situation to develop. She wouldn't be the first woman to do that, and she certainly wouldn't be the last.

Des pulled up the covers over his son and wondered who would confess first – Jack, that he wanted to end things with Clare, or Clare, that she was pregnant.

Either way, they were both in for one heck of a shock.

13

It had rained all day on Monday and for most of Tuesday, but this morning the sun was shining and the sky was a brilliant blue, the kind of fresh, clear sky that Dulcie associated with autumn. She had gone to Scotland once at this time of year and had fallen in love with the clarity of the wide open skies and vastness of the beautiful landscape. Now, as she pedalled her bicycle along Bloom Street and turned into Jameson Street, she was filled with that same *joie de vivre*. The older she became, the more she believed that it was the simple things in life that provided the most pleasure: the sun on one's face and a happy heart. It wasn't much to ask for, was it? She pedalled faster, feeling that nothing could take the shine off her day.

Richard had been discharged from hospital yesterday and he had phoned her earlier this morning to give her the good news. 'I can't talk for long,' he'd whispered. 'Angela's in the shower, so five minutes is all I have.'

Five wonderful minutes of hearing his voice had been enough, and to know he had made such a good recovery that he was now at home. 'The bad news is that I'm still confined to bed,' he'd complained.

'And you must stay there until your doctor thinks you're well enough to be up and about.'

'Goodness knows when I'll be allowed to leave the house. Alone.'

She'd heard the wistful longing in his voice and knew he was saying he wouldn't be able to see her for some time. She said, 'Richard, I want you to promise me something.'

'Anything, my darling. You know I'd do anything for you.'

'You mustn't be silly and think you know better than the doctor. You mustn't convince yourself that you're well enough to sneak out of the house behind Angela's back to come and see me.'

There was a pause, during which Dulcie knew that that was exactly what had gone through his head.

He said, 'You're not very good with numbers, are you, Dulcie?'

'I beg your pardon?'

'That's two promises by my reckoning.'

'And you're too sharp for your own good.'

'I love it when you tell me off. Look, I can hear Angela coming out of the shower. I'll ring you when I can. Love you.'

Despite the brightness of the sun, the day was cold, but Dulcie glowed with an inner warmth. She pedalled across Bridge Street warily, staying as close to the kerb as she could, then turned into the relative quiet of Crown Street. She waved to Mr Colroyd, who was selecting flowers for a customer from his galvanised buckets at the front of his shop. She pedalled on further, towards the town square, and hopped off her bicycle at Churchgate; she was slightly out of breath. Gardening and cycling were her only forms of exercise, and the latter she only did when the weather tempted her to blow the dust off her daughter's old Raleigh. She locked it to the railings of St Cecilia's, unclipped her basket from the handlebars and went back to Crown Street where she had some shopping to do before meeting Prue and Maureen for lunch.

Every three weeks she and her friends got together for lunch and a gossip. Although they were close and had known each other for many years – they had children of roughly the same age – she was selective in what she shared with them about her personal life. She had never confided in them about Richard, believing that the fewer people who knew about her affair, the less chance there was of it becoming known to Angela. She liked to think that Prue and Maureen had their own secrets.

She called in at the delicatessen for some cheese for supper that evening and a couple of her favourite rolls, one baked with caraway, the other sprinkled with poppy seeds. She also bought a large tub of black olives, shiny with oil and flavoured with garlic. With these purchases carefully stowed in her shopping basket, and knowing she had a bottle of excellent red wine at home, she looked forward to the evening ahead.

It was one of the nicest things about living alone: she could eat what she wanted without having to consider anyone else. Just occasionally she wondered if she wasn't in danger of becoming self-absorbed, but whenever this thought surfaced, she reminded herself that she had devoted most of her life to others – Philip and the children. Now it was time to pamper herself a little. It was too easy to slip into the habit of justifying one's happiness. If she allowed that to happen too often, she might forget to relish the joyful simplicity of her life.

She never took her happiness for granted. She knew all too well how fortunate she was, that financially she was better placed than a lot of people she knew. She had used the money paid to her from Philip's life-insurance policy to buy the house in Bloom Street and knew it was the best investment she could have made. When the time came for her to sell up, it would provide her with the means to live out her old age in relative comfort.

She would never have dreamed that she would be so suited to living alone. She had turned into a most self-contained person. Not for her the frantic need to be constantly occupied or entertained: a good book, a glass of wine and she was content. And it was only now, at sixty-three, that she had discovered that if she demanded nothing of another person no demands were made of her.

It was this philosophy that was at the heart of her relationship with Richard; it was why it worked between them. Given the immovable parameters of their affair, neither could be possessive of the other. Few people would understand, and fewer condone, what she was doing, but she had come to know that there was no such thing as a one-size-fits-all dream. It suited her to have an affair with a married man: it meant that she could retain her singleness yet feel as if she were part of a couple.

Next she called in at Novel Ways to see if the book she'd ordered last week had arrived. It had and she handed a ten-pound note to the girl on the till. While she was waiting for her change, she heard a voice behind her: 'Come on, Nicholas, do hurry up and choose what you want.' There was something disturbingly familiar about the thin, careworn voice. She turned her head, cautiously, and her suspicions were confirmed: it was Angela. She looked just as she had the last time Dulcie had seen her – harassed, hair tied back in a childish, unflattering ponytail, tall, spare body swamped by a tatty waxed jacket. She was hovering over an angular boy with a sensitive face – currently buried in a rock-star biography – and in her hands was a pile of paperbacks; the latest Ian Rankin, a Robert Harris thriller, and two John Grishams. Books to occupy Richard while he was convalescing? Dulcie thought of the sweet little book of poetry he had given her – a collection of love poems from which he often read to her.

With a trembling hand, she took her change from the girl behind the counter, pocketed it and fled.

By the time she slowed her pace, she was standing outside St Cecilia's, her heart thudding painfully, her legs shaking. She felt sick, panicky and guilty. And weepy. She glanced over her shoulder; it was a long while since she and Angela had met but she was convinced Angela would have recognised her and come after her. It was nothing short of extraordinary that until today she had never bumped into the woman. This was partly because Richard and Angela lived in a village on the outskirts of Chester, rather than in or around Maywood. Richard had often said that Chester satisfied all of Angela's shopping needs: why, then, had she chosen to come into Maywood all of a sudden?

It was an irrational thought and one with which Dulcie quickly dispensed: Angela had the right to shop wherever she chose.

Relieved that there was no sign of her now, Dulcie walked slowly to the side of the church. It was still too early to meet Prue and Maureen for lunch in the café opposite, so she pushed open the door of St Cecilia's, and went inside. She had what she called a 'religious temperament' but rarely attended a Church of England service: she found the atmosphere too chaotic – modern vicars were inclined to allow unruly youngsters to run up and down the aisles. In a secular sense, she was a frequent visitor to St

Cecilia's because of the many concerts it hosted – Maywood boasted a fine choir, of which both Prue and Maureen were members.

The gift shop was on her right and two elderly ladies were browsing through the racks of books and postcards and other assorted Christian paraphernalia of tea-towels and monogrammed teaspoons. No one else was about, and after walking the length of the nave, Dulcie turned to her left to sit in the small side chapel where an exquisite stained-glass window caught the bright autumnal sunshine. St Cecilia – famous since the sixteenth century as the patron of musicians – looked down benignly at her from the colourful window: in one hand she held a lute, and with the other she indicated an intricately decorated organ.

Dulcie closed her eyes. She didn't feel she deserved such a look of kindness. Sitting on the hard pew she felt horribly unworthy, and strangely isolated, as though she were being punished for loving Richard. The happiness that had filled her only a short time ago had gone. Now her heart was heavy.

Still with her eyes shut, she considered how an affair was generally acknowledged to be a roller-coaster ride of out-of-control emotions: at one minute its participants would be wallowing in insecurity and doubt; at the next, they'd be euphorically high on the exhilaration of sexual fulfilment. But it hadn't been like that between her and Richard; she had never put herself through the he-loves-me-he-loves-me-not game. Nor, until recently, had she spent hours waiting for the phone to ring, or wasted time wondering where he was, or what he was doing. Grounded in her own sense of who she was, and the fulfilling life she led, she had been perfectly content with what they had. 'I will not be a demanding and possessive lover,' she had promised him at the outset. 'I will never disgrace myself by doing that.'

'Not even a little bit?' he'd teased. 'It might flatter me if you were.'

'Then you've picked the wrong woman to have an affair with.'

They were having lunch in the hotel that would soon become the scene of many such occasions. He had reached across the table, taken her hands and said, 'I've picked the *only* woman I would have an affair with. Betraying my wife and my marriage vows is not something I make a habit of.'

She had never harboured the hope that he would leave Angela: he had made it very clear that he wouldn't. 'I couldn't leave her,' he confessed. 'It would destroy her.' Also, there were the two younger children to consider – they had been eleven and nine at the start of the affair, and Dulcie knew that Richard was a devoted father and loved them dearly. To leave his wife would be to leave his sons, and it was out of the question. He simply wasn't that kind of man.

There were four children in all, the older two – Henry and Victoria – were grown-up and living in London, but Christopher and Nicholas had come along late in the marriage. Angela had just turned forty-one when she discovered she was pregnant with Christopher: Richard had been forty-seven. As with so many parents who find themselves with an unexpected addition to what they had imagined was a complete family, they decided to have another so that Christopher would have company.

Dulcie respected Richard for his devotion to his family, but questioned his belief that Angela would be destroyed if he left. From the dealings she had had with Angela when she'd helped them to find a house, she had formed the impression that Angela was an inefficient woman, who, like a clockwork toy, rushed around in ever-decreasing circles before winding down having achieved nothing. But she also had a streak of stubbornness. From what Richard had told her, Dulcie concluded that what Angela wanted, Angela invariably got. This didn't mean that Richard was weak. It was just that finding the middle ground through compromise came more naturally to him than all-out confrontation.

When he'd told Dulcie that he had never been unfaithful to Angela before, she believed him. In the early stages of their affair, he had been overwhelmed by guilt. One evening, she had told him that perhaps it would be better if they called a halt to it: she couldn't bear to see him so miserable. He had looked at her, sadly. 'Is that what you want?'

'No,' she'd said truthfully. 'But I don't want to be the cause of your unhappiness.'

They hadn't stopped seeing each other, but after that their relationship slipped into another gear and they became more at ease with the situation.

Right from the day they had met, in the lounge of the Maywood Grange Hotel, there had been a spark between them, and the first time they had kissed, Dulcie had known it was only a matter of time before they slept together.

After she had had dinner with him, he had walked her to her car. Several awkward moments had passed before he had asked if he could kiss her goodnight. Mute with longing, she had nodded, and he'd raised a hand to her hair and stroked it gently, then her cheek and her neck. Lost in the intensity of his gaze, all she could think was that it had been years since she'd felt like this. When their lips had touched, they had held each other with quiet, loving relief. It was as if they had both waited a very long time for the moment.

Prue and Maureen were on fine form, which was just what Dulcie needed to lift her spirits. Where would we be without our friends? she thought, as they ordered their lunch and got down to discussing Maureen's impending holiday in the Algarve and how she was going to avoid playing golf morning, noon and night with her husband, Geoff.

'Just tell him you can't see the point in hitting small white balls for hours at a time,' Dulcie said.

'Oh, that's easy for you to say,' Maureen remonstrated. 'You've lived alone for so long you've forgotten what husbands are like. They sulk if they don't get their own way.'

'Yes,' agreed Prue. 'Count yourself lucky that you can go on holiday without the impediment of a husband. You have no idea how envious we are of you. I can't think of anything better than a week all to myself.'

It was a measure of their close friendship that Prue and Maureen were able to refer to Dulcie's single status so offhandedly. Others tiptoed around it, either in fear that it might be contagious or that it was still a sore subject. It had taken years for them to reach their current level of candour and Dulcie loved them for it.

'Then why not do exactly that?' Dulcie said to Prue. 'If you want some time alone, tell Robert.'

Prue shook her head. 'Don't be silly, Dulcie, you know it doesn't work like that. Robert would immediately put on the spoilt-little-boy act – pouting lip and silences. Husbands hate the idea of their wives enjoying themselves without them.'

'Then you have to box clever. Choose to do something Robert would think was a hardship. Go on an activity holiday like I have in the past. I had a wonderful week in Provence learning to paint.'

Frowning, Prue said, 'I'm not sure that's really my scene.'

Dulcie laughed. 'Then stop whingeing and make do with what you've got.'

They ordered their meal, and while the waitress organised their cramped table to accommodate the basket of bread and carafe of house wine, Dulcie thought of the last trip she'd made: a touring holiday to Florence and Rome. She had had a wonderful time, and had met so many interesting people. Next summer she was hoping to go to the Italian lakes and she already had a couple of brochures to browse through. She loved Italy and always felt at home there. Richard said it suited her carefree temperament and that he could easily picture her sitting on a balcony sipping a dry Martini and watching the world go by from beneath the brim of a large hat. 'And, of course, you'll be inundated with advances from countless unsuitable men,' he'd elaborated, 'but you'll handle them in a demure and politely English manner.'

'Goodness, you make me sound like a character out of an Anita Brookner novel.' She'd laughed.

He had kissed her, and said, 'No, you're much too passionate for that.'

At her age it was nice to be described as passionate. She glanced at her two friends and wondered if Geoff or Robert ever thought of them in that way.

Just as the waitress appeared with their plates of quiche and salad, Dulcie caught sight of someone else approaching their table. For the second time that day, she felt wrongfooted and panicky.

It was Angela. From the expression on her face, it was clear that she had just recognised Dulcie and was coming over to say hello.

14

It was at mealtimes that Jaz most envied Vicki. Her friend had no idea how lucky she was to be an only child. If she were here now to witness the racket, she'd soon count her blessings.

It was a typical night around the Rafferty supper table and, with a book resting on her lap, Jaz was speculating as to what a visiting alien would make of it. His report home would make interesting reading:

> It would appear that the sole purpose of these sessions is to shout louder than the earthling sitting next to you. Nor does it seem to matter that the yelling goes unheeded. There would also appear to be some kind of ritual contest taking place: the more food these primitive life forms can grab and shovel inside themselves, the more unpopular they become with each other, which in turn provokes yet more yelling and shouting, particularly among the smaller and uglier female members. It is a spectacle that requires much rational thought to discern any point in the proceedings.

'Hello, Jazzie's got that faraway look in her eyes again. Either that or she's stopped taking the medication.'

Jaz looked up from her book and pulled a face at her brother. 'I was imagining myself a million miles away from you, Phin, if you must know.'

'Oo-*er*! How about I make your dreams come true and help you pack?'

'You wouldn't know how. When was the last time you managed to fold your own arms, never mind cope with something as tricky as a bag of clothes?'

'Snappy, snappy,' mocked Jimmy. He helped himself to the last of the mashed potato, then elbowed his brother in the ribs. 'Probably that time of the month again. I'd go careful if I were you. You know what a Rottweiler she turns into.'

'Oh, that's *so* original. A girl outsmarts a man and she's accused of being hormonally unbalanced. Well, for your information I'm not pre-menstrual.'

Lulu and Tamzin leaned into each other and sniggered. They were still of an age to laugh at the mention of bodily parts or functions.

'Hey, hey, *hey*! Less of the dirty talk, if you don't mind.'

'Dad, menstruation isn't a dirty word.'

Popeye Rafferty dropped his knife and fork and reached for his beer. 'It is when I'm trying to eat. Cut it out. And how many times have I told you it's rude to read at the table?'

Jaz turned to her mother for support, but Molly Rafferty seemed preoccupied and oblivious to the commotion going on around her. She was absently spooning an extra portion of peas on to Phin's dinner plate.

'Helpless baby,' Jaz muttered under her breath, scowling at her brother. Ignoring her father's reprimand, she returned her attention to the book on her lap and reminded herself that she would have the last word. And in a way her brothers and sisters could never imagine. The novel she was writing was based on them, and the more she wrote, the more empowered she felt. She didn't think she was a vindictive person, but every jibe they made about her, every put-down they laughed over, was a point they scored against themselves. Oh, revenge would be sweet!

Later, upstairs in her room, Jaz switched on the computer. She wanted to read through what she would be taking to the writers' group tomorrow evening. When she'd finished checking it, had changed a couple of lines, then put them back to how she'd written them originally, she decided to leave it well alone. All Dulcie had asked them to do was produce the opening page of a novel (with title), which, of course, she'd already written, so she hadn't had much to do. She clicked on SAVE and PRINT, and wondered how the others had got on with the assignment.

Being with a group of adults had been more fun than she had thought it would be. Maybe it was because they had treated her as one of them, not as a child. They'd all been really nice to her and, apart from Victor, hadn't patronised her. Victor was a right pain, though. Nobody had said anything during the meeting but she'd reckoned, from looking at their faces, that they'd all thought as she had about him. She was proved right in the car on the way home, when Jack had remarked, 'I shouldn't say this, and don't either of you quote me on it, but where on earth was Victor dug up?'

Beth had laughed and said, 'I don't know, but he should be put back straight away.'

'Oh, please! Let's start digging a hole for him right now.'

'First-rate idea, Jaz,' Jack had said. 'And we'll give you the honour of pushing him into it.'

Jack and Beth were a laugh, and it had been kind of Jack to drive her home. Both she and Beth had said they'd walk when he'd asked if anyone needed a lift. Then Dulcie had opened the front door, they'd seen the rain coming down and changed their minds. Victor, she'd noticed, hadn't offered to take anyone home. He hadn't even bothered to say goodbye, just dashed rudely to his car further up the road and driven off.

So that she didn't give the game away with her family, about where she'd spent the evening, she'd asked Jack to drop her on the corner of Marbury

Road. 'It's a dead end,' she'd said, already undoing her seatbelt, 'so it'll be easier for you if you let me get out here. Save you having to turn round.'

'It's no trouble,' he'd said.

But she'd insisted, said goodnight to them both and got out. Hurrying home, she hoped he hadn't thought her ungrateful. She also thought how weird it was that she had spent the evening with Nathan King's mother when she'd talked to him for the first time that afternoon. How spooky was that?

She had thought a lot about Nathan since that day, but couldn't decide what to make of him. Why had he walked home with her? To report back to Billy and tell him what a klutz she was, so they could laugh at her behind her back? Or had he been genuine? But why would he want to spend time with her? And, more importantly, why was she wasting her valuable time and energy thinking about him? He was a whole load of trouble she could do without. She had been attracted to him from afar, and had decided that, close up, he was even better-looking and would be no more interested in a girl like her than Billy would.

She would have to be careful when half-term was over and she was back at college. Not for a minute must she let him think she had ever been interested in him. He had hinted, but he might have been joking, that maybe he would walk home with her again some time. Whichever way she looked at it, worse things could happen to her than being seen in the company of a good-looking bloke from the upper sixth. Perhaps he'd tag along again when Vicki was busy. Immediately she saw the flaw in this: she'd be walking home alone on the days when Vicki, Billy and Nathan would be rehearsing the college play.

A knock at the door had her clicking on CLOSE.

'Okay if we come in?' said a voice.

Her mother was the only person who respected the sign on her bedroom door that read, 'Private – Please Knock Before Entering.' Everyone else ignored it and burst in, but Mum was different. She was eight years younger than Dad, and Jaz had always thought her beautiful. Dad joked that when he'd first set eyes on her his legs had turned to overcooked spaghetti. 'That was because you were so drunk,' Molly would say, a soft smile brightening her face.

'A touch mellow,' he'd acknowledge, 'but the truth of the matter is that it was love at first sight.' Dad was such a screaming sentimentalist.

Nothing was too much trouble for Mum. She could always be relied upon. But not so much, these last few weeks. Most of the time she seemed lost in a world of her own. Jaz had been talking to her last night, telling her something about a parents' evening at college, only to realise that her mother hadn't heard a word she'd said. She was practically nodding off.

'What's wrong?' she asked, when both of her parents came in. They only ever put in a double appearance if they had something important to say.

Like that time they'd sat either side of her on the bed and told her Granddad had died.

'Nothing's wrong, Jazzie,' her father said. 'Now, why would you think that?'

She shrugged. 'Dunno. Something to do with your serious faces? Hey, you're not getting divorced, are you? Because if you are, I want it understood that I'll go with whoever doesn't want custody of Tamzin and Lulu.'

Her mother, who looked exhausted, tutted and cleared a space on the bed to sit down. 'You know you don't mean that.'

'Don't you believe it.' Oh, hell, if her mother was sitting down, this *was* a serious newsflash. Had they found out that she'd lied about being at Vicki's last week?

She pushed away the thought. 'So what's up, then?' she asked. Her money was on some nosy neighbour having filed a report to her parents claiming she'd been seen with Nathan.

Suddenly a huge grin appeared on her father's face and, after exchanging a look with her mother, he said, 'Jaz, we've got brilliant news, and your mother wanted you to be first to know. She's pregnant.'

Nothing could have surprised Jaz more. She fumbled for a response. 'You're ... you're joking, right?'

They were both grinning at her now. Oh, this was terrible. 'You're kidding,' she repeated. *Oh, please, say you're having me on. I couldn't stand another brother or sister.*

'And what's more,' her father said, putting a hand on her mother's shoulder, 'we've hit the jackpot. It's twins.'

15

It was Thursday evening and once again the group was assembled in Dulcie's sitting room. They were listening to Victor, who had just summed up his magnum opus – *Star City* – and was now giving an over-the-top reading of his opening page. Predictably he'd elected to go first and was intent on getting across the dramatic content of his writing. Dulcie would have liked to ask him to start again and read it with a little less theatrical conviction, but she didn't think it would be fair on the group to have to hear it twice.

'Thank you, Victor,' she said, when at last he paused. 'What a lot you squeezed into one page.' She wanted to add, 'Are you sure it was only three hundred words?' but she knew there was no point. They all knew he'd read out at least twice the specified amount.

He nodded and leaned back into his seat. 'That, of course, is my objective,' he said. 'I want to hit the reader right between the eyes with as much action as possible. Grab them by the throat.'

A shame if it all ends up sticking there, thought Dulcie. She said, 'An ambitious opening such as that requires skilful handling to pull it off. Anyone else want to make a comment? Jack? What was your reaction?'

Dressed in jeans and an open-necked shirt, Jack was looking less formal than he had last week, but he didn't appear to be any more relaxed. He looked tired and drawn, like a man with the weight of the world on his shoulders.

'Ah,' he said carefully. 'To be honest, I got confused. There seemed to be a great number of characters thrown at us. It was difficult to keep up with what was happening.'

'I thought that too,' agreed Jaz. 'And they all had foreign names ending in *avinski.*'

'That's because they *are* foreign,' Victor said waspishly.

'I think the point they're making,' Dulcie said, picking her way cautiously, 'is that you gave a tad too much information. Remember what we discussed last week? To create the all-important hook to draw the reader in, you need to offer some tantalising details, but you must treat them as magic ingredients and use them sparingly. Perhaps you could cut back on some of the characters. Ideally, just have one or two. And was that second explosion really necessary?'

Victor cleared his throat. 'Essential.'

'You don't think it weakened the effect of the first?' suggested Beth.

Before Victor exploded, Dulcie said quickly, 'Good point, Beth, and one we should all bear in mind. Less is frequently more when it comes to writing. But well done, Victor, for sharing that with us.' Trying to encourage him, she said, 'Victor's given us a hard act to follow, but who's going to be brave enough to go next? Any takers? Jaz, how about you?'

'Okay. So long as I'm not queue-jumping.' She glanced at Jack and Beth, who shook their heads.

'No, you go ahead,' Jack said.

'It's called *Having the Last Laugh*,' she said, then launched into reading her work in a clear, confident voice. When she'd finished, she looked at Dulcie for her verdict. 'What do you think?' she asked. 'Was it okay?'

Dulcie smiled. 'Jaz, that was more than okay. It was brilliant. My only quibble is that you stopped when you did. I wanted more.'

'Me too.'

'And me.'

Blushing, Jaz smiled at Jack and Beth. 'Really? You're not just saying that?'

The only person not supporting Jaz was Victor. Dulcie had noticed that while she had been reading, he'd been making notes on his A4 pad. 'I have a couple of quibbles,' he said, clicking his biro. 'What's a head-mash? And don't you think it's risky using modern-day parlance? I was under the impression that it limits your audience and dates the book before it's even published.'

A protective motherly instinct made Dulcie want to come to Jaz's aid, but she needn't have worried.

'A head-mash is when you've scrambled your brains trying to work something out,' Jaz said levelly. 'I expect you get that a lot, Victor, don't you?' He looked at her uncertainly and she smiled sweetly at him. 'I know I do after a long day at college and then three hours of homework. As for worrying about writing a book that's unpublishable, I don't give a monkey's. I'm writing for my own satisfaction. No one else's.'

A case of putting that in one's pipe and smoking it, thought Dulcie happily. Goodness, youngsters today could easily hold their own. At the same age, she wouldn't have said boo to a day-old gosling, never mind a grumpy old gander like Victor.

Dulcie went next, and then Beth took her turn, a little nervously, but with an amusing central character called Libby, an insecure self-confessed self-help junkie. It was titled *Living For Pleasure* and, like Jaz, Beth had written the piece in the first person. Unlike Jaz, she made the mistake of apologising for what she'd written. Dulcie waved the Self-belief Box under her nose. 'I warned you.'

Beth laughed and reached for her bag to pay her fine.

And then it was Jack's turn.

'I'm afraid it's still a bit rough,' he confessed. Dulcie rattled the box at him, and he smiled and added a coin to Beth's. 'But here goes anyway. It's called *Friends and Family*.' He cleared his throat and fiddled with the neck of his shirt. '"By their friends shall ye know them. That's what I'd been brought up to believe, and believe it I did. Until now. Now I know differently. Friends are rarely what they seem. Friends come and go. Like chameleons they change their colours to suit the moment. I once had such a friend. But, there again, I once had a wife."' He swallowed, straightened the papers on his lap, then continued, his voice low.

Dulcie listened intently. She saw the profound sadness in Jack's face as his eyes moved across the page. Poor man, she thought. But how brave to put it down on paper and share it with the group. When he'd finished, the room fell quiet. Nobody rushed to speak. Not even Victor.

'Sorry,' Jack murmured, 'was that a bit too much of the Misery Joe's?'

Both Jaz and Beth reached for the Self-belief Box at the same time and rattled it in front of him. It broke the tension in the room and Dulcie, feeling faintly troubled, suggested they discuss his opening page over a cup of coffee.

'Would you like some help?' asked Beth.

'No need, I've got everything ready. All I need to do is put the kettle on.'

Out in the kitchen, while she waited for it to boil, Dulcie listened to Victor telling Jack that what he needed to do with his opening page was lose some of the introspection and liven it up with a bit more action. Dulcie sighed. What with? A couple of car crashes? The man didn't know the words 'subtlety' and 'sensitivity'. With him it was wham, bang, wallop. Horribly patronising too.

Not dissimilar from how Angela had treated Dulcie yesterday lunchtime.

'I thought it was you,' Angela had said, her voice so loud that everyone in the café had turned to look. 'I said to Nicholas, "Isn't that the woman who helped us move house?" But, of course, he couldn't remember. How are you? Still running your little business?'

Dulcie had bristled to hear her livelihood dismissed as no more than a hobby. 'No,' she'd said. 'These days I'm a fully fledged lady of leisure.'

'Oh, good for you. I wish I could say the same, but with Christopher and Nicholas to chase after, my leisure time is non-existent. And now I have Richard at home.'

'Oh?' Dulcie had tried to make her voice neutral, as though she didn't know what Angela was referring to. 'Is he working from home, these days?'

'Dear me, no, he won't be working for some time yet. He's just recovering from a heart-attack. He gave us all a dreadful scare. I've been on at him for years to slow down, but you know what men are like, they never listen and always think they know best, and the next thing you know, you're a widow passing round the sherry at a funeral.'

Dulcie had cringed at Angela's overly jolly manner. Or was she simply trying to hide her concern for a husband who had nearly died? And might well have done so, if he had been alone.

'You must give him my best wishes,' Dulcie had said.

'Thank you, I will. But I doubt he'll remember you. He has the most shocking memory. Anyway, I must press on. I've left Christopher to keep an eye on Richard and I promised we wouldn't be long. What a coincidence meeting you like this, after all this time. I seldom bother coming into Maywood, such a funny old-fashioned little town. I usually go to Chester, but I thought this would be quicker.' She rolled her eyes. 'But it's proving otherwise. I can't find half the things I need.'

And then she was gone, hurrying back to her son who was sitting at a corner table, absorbed in one of the novels they'd bought for Richard.

As perceptive as ever, Maureen had said, 'Whoever that woman was, you didn't much care for her, did you, Dulcie?'

'Oh,' she'd said airily, hoping her face wouldn't give her away, 'she was one of those clients who tend to be a thorn in one's side. Nothing was ever right for her. She had very high expectations.'

'Doesn't look like anything's changed,' observed Prue. Both Dulcie and Maureen had followed her gaze to where Angela was ticking off her son for having his elbows on the table. He frowned with a trace of petulance and retreated further behind his book.

It was a frown Dulcie recognised: she had seen Richard look just the same. He didn't often frown, or behave petulantly, but when he did, it made her laugh. She wondered how long it would be before she saw him again, how many weeks or months before he was well enough to drive. It was tempting to speak to her son, a doctor, about Richard, but even to discuss him in vague terms – 'Andrew, I know someone who's recently suffered a heart-attack, how long do you think it will be before he makes a full recovery?' – broke the rules of being a mistress. She must never allude to Richard. Not even as a friend or one-time client. There was always the chance that a casual reference could give them away.

After talking to Angela, she might have expected to feel guiltier about her affair with Richard but, perversely, the reverse had happened: Angela's offhand manner – as if his heart-attack had resulted from his own carelessness – had irritated her, and she strongly believed that Richard deserved the love and happiness she could offer him. Any pangs she had experienced while sitting in St Cecilia's had vanished.

Now, pouring boiling water into the mugs, she thought of Jack. There was no doubt in her mind that what he had written and read out to the group was autobiographical. How would she feel if she was in his position?

Or, more to the point, in Angela's shoes?

Stop it, she told herself. Life can't be so neatly pigeonholed. People make mistakes. They fall in love with the wrong people. They don't mean to, but it goes on all the time.

Yet as resolute as she tried to be, when she took the coffee into the sitting room and passed round the mugs, she found herself unable to meet Jack's eye.

It was raining again, and after dropping off Jaz at the end of her road, then Beth, Jack drove home. It was just after ten thirty when he let himself in. He helped himself to a beer from the fridge, then checked his answerphone. There were two messages: one from Des suggesting a boys' night out, and another from Clare.

'Jack, if it's not too late when you get in, give me a ring. There's something I need to talk to you about.'

He took a long swig of his beer and erased the message, as though it had never existed.

16

After a relatively wet but mild October – the warmest on record – the back end of November was making up for the earlier discrepancy. Winter had arrived, with icy mornings and bitter winds that shook the last remaining leaves off the trees.

Maywood Health Centre was always busier when the weather turned cold, and on this particular Monday morning, it was teeming with what Beth called winter-sickies. She had a theory that the first note of a piped Christmas carol was the harbinger of medical doom and gloom. She also believed that if sufficient people banged on about the threat of a flu epidemic there would be one. And now that they were only a week away from December, and a short step from the onslaught of Christmas, everyone was convinced they were suffering from the most virulent strain ever endured.

The waiting room was packed this morning, and as she listened to the endless coughs and sniffles, Beth knew, without any medical training, that most of the patients weren't as critically ill as they claimed. Beth felt sorry for the elderly, those who suffered in silence, who would not dream of troubling their overworked doctor.

Only a couple of days ago, she had called on Adele Waterman and found her in a terrible state. She had immediately called out the old lady's doctor – Rose Millward from the health centre – who diagnosed pneumonia. 'Lucky we caught it when we did,' Dr Millward told her patient. 'Otherwise we'd probably have had to whisk you into hospital.'

Beth and Nathan were taking it in turns to keep an eye on her, ferrying down food and drink at regular intervals. Before leaving for work this morning, Beth had given Adele a flask of hot vegetable soup for her lunch and hoped she would eat it. Nathan had promised to call in as soon as he was home from school, and Beth knew Adele would benefit from his company. The old lady had said that if she was feeling up to it she would help Nathan with his lines for the play: it was curtain up in two weeks' time.

Beth would miss Adele when she moved. According to Jack, if all went well with the sale, she would be leaving in the New Year. Just as he'd predicted, there had been no shortage of people interested in the flat and the full asking price had been offered. 'You see,' he'd joked with her over coffee one night at Dulcie's, 'I'm not the shark you thought I was.'

'I never said you were,' she'd responded.

'You didn't need to. It was in your eyes.'

'Oh, surely not?'

'That and a look that said, "Mess with my neighbour and you're a dead duck."'

'Sharks and ducks – goodness! What a mix of metaphors. Are we allowed to be so careless?'

Thursday nights had become part of her routine, and Beth looked forward to seeing the group each week. Apart from Victor, who never spoke of his life outside Hidden Talents, they were learning about each other. It had occurred to Beth that, without exception, they all had a raw spot, or an area that was strictly out of bounds. As open as Jaz was, she refused to speak about her family, even the fact that her mother was pregnant – Beth only knew this from seeing Mrs Rafferty at the health centre for an antenatal check-up – but she wrote amusingly, perhaps tellingly, about a fictional family from hell. Jack, clearly going through a painful divorce, wrote in poignant detail about the break-up of a marriage, and only last week had hinted to her in the car on the way home that he'd got himself into a mess with a subsequent relationship. Surprisingly, Dulcie was the most reserved of them all, though unlike Victor, who was breathtakingly rude when any of them enquired how his week had gone, she always answered questions but somehow managed never to tell them what she'd really been up to. Perhaps she didn't get up to anything. Maybe that was why she had started Hidden Talents. As plausible as this sounded, Beth didn't think it was the whole truth.

But the really good thing, as far as Beth was concerned, was that she was gaining in confidence with regard to her writing. *Living For Pleasure* was growing fast, and almost had the feel of a novel. Well, all five chapters of it. She didn't think she would ever be as good as the others – Jaz and Jack undoubtedly had a natural flair for it, Dulcie too (the less said about Victor, the better), but she got a lot out of their evenings together and that was what counted. Dulcie had encouraged them to have a go at entering a short-story competition, which none of them had considered before. It had been advertised in *Writing News* – a magazine to which Dulcie subscribed – and it was the group's latest piece of homework: they had two weeks to complete the task.

'Thank heaven for that,' said Wendy, when the last of the patients had been seen and the waiting room was clear.

Magazines and healthy-eating leaflets lay strewn about, toys, books and puzzles were scattered everywhere, and a wastepaper bin had been upturned. It was twelve thirty. Lunchtime. 'You put the kettle on,' Beth said, 'and I'll put this little lot straight.'

There were three receptionists: Wendy and Beth worked full-time, while

Karen came in for the afternoons and early-evening surgeries; she also covered when Beth and Wendy were on holiday. They made a good team, so going to work was a pleasure rather than a chore. As they relaxed in the staff kitchen over their lunch, Wendy said, 'You know, we ought to start thinking about where we're going to have our Christmas beano this year. If we leave it too late we'll miss out.'

'What's wrong with Bellagio's? I thought everyone enjoyed that last year.'

Wendy groaned. 'Same place, same faces, same everything. I fancy somewhere new. We don't have to stay in Maywood, we could go further afield. We could live dangerously and go into Chester. Any chance of you bringing a *friend* along this year?'

Beth smiled. 'No.'

'Isn't there anyone from your writing group you could ask?'

'No again.'

Wendy dipped a spoon into her blueberry yoghurt. 'You know, I reckon I could write a book. It'd be a raunchy bestseller. I'd give it so much of the sizzle factor I'd become the Jackie Collins of Maywood.'

'Well, they say there's a book in all of us,' Beth told her.

'At the last count, I've got three or four. But before I put pen to paper and make myself a million, how about I find you someone for our Christmas bash?'

'I'm repeating myself, I know, but no. And I certainly don't want one of your cast-offs.'

A big jolly divorcee, Wendy was a thirty-eight-year-old party girl. She had been single for three years now and always had a smile on her face, even when she was dealing with a particularly irritating patient. A horrid man had once called her a power-crazed fat bitch because she told him he would have to wait more than an hour to see a doctor. 'Save your breath, Mr Austin. You'll not get to see the doctor any faster by flattering me,' she had replied. She had no children, but she did have a hectic social life and never seemed short of men to go out with. Beth teased her that she must be suffering from RSI – repetitive strain injury – from all the first dates she went on. 'Can I help it that I get bored easily?' was Wendy's favourite retaliation. She probably wanted to hold their Christmas dinner out of town because she'd exhausted Maywood's supply of eligible men.

Stirring her yoghurt, Wendy gave her a hard stare. 'How long before Nathan goes off to college?'

In exchange for all the times Adele had babysat Nathan, Beth did the heavier work in her neighbour's garden and took her to the local supermarket each week. It was a delicate balance, which Beth was careful to respect. She would never dream of interfering with the old lady's independence. Didn't she suffer enough of that herself? And not just from Lois.

But today Beth had carried out an extra errand for Adele – a trip to the library to stock up on her reading matter. With her coat buttoned, her head bent into the biting wind as she carried the heavy load of books, she walked home in the dark, disconsolate. All that afternoon she had thought of what Wendy had said, and been thoroughly annoyed by it. Why did people think they had a right to try to organise her life for her? Why did they keep implying that she lived it through Nathan?

She didn't.

She absolutely did not!

As his mother, she had simply put Nathan's needs before her own. And what was wrong with that?

She let herself in to the flat and called, 'Hi, it's me, I'm back.'

No answer.

She hung up her coat, put the pile of historical romances on the hall table, and was struck by the emptiness of the flat. Before long, this was how it would feel every day when she came home from work. She shrugged off the disagreeable thought and went through to the kitchen to put the kettle on and think about supper. It was then that she remembered where Nathan was.

'He's been such delightful company,' Adele said to Beth, when she went into the flat below.

'He hasn't been wearing you out, has he?' she asked, placing the library books on the ottoman at the foot of the bed. She noticed the play script on Adele's bedside table and a chair pulled up close: Nathan was making tea.

'Of course he hasn't. He's cheered me up wonderfully. And he's word perfect with his lines. He's going to make an excellent Algernon. I do hope I'll be well enough to come along and watch. How was your day?'

'Oh, the usual, Wendy and I playing good cop, bad cop with the more tiresome patients.'

Nathan came in with a tray. 'Okay if I leave you to it? I have an essay I need to make a start on.'

When he'd gone, Adele said, 'He's a real credit to you, Beth, but how on earth will you manage without him?'

She sighed inwardly. 'Oh, I expect I'll find a way.'

Late that night, and long after Nathan had gone to bed, Beth poured herself a glass of wine and switched on the computer. It had belonged to Nathan, but when her parents had offered to buy him a more up-to-date model, it had been passed on to her. Although she had used the computer at work for some time, and readily enough, she had never been a fan until Nathan had bullied her out of her technophobia. He had given her several evenings of instruction, and now she was hooked and did all her writing on it. The best part was that she was in daily contact with Simone by email, just as Nathan had said she would be once she'd got the hang of it.

By shifting the furniture around, she had created her own little bit of 'personal space' where she could write in the kitchen, beneath one of the windows with a perfect view of the park. Now, she checked to see if there was an email from Simone. There was. She spent more than twenty minutes replying, then hesitated before she switched off the machine. Last night, she had done the craziest thing: she had visited a chat room. She blamed Simone: it had been her suggestion. At first Beth had been dubious about doing it. 'What if I get chatting to some pervy anorak type?'

'Not everyone using the Internet is a raging weirdo,' Simone had emailed back. 'Of course, if you're not sure how to go about it, you could always ask Nathan to help you ...'

There had been something in Simone's tone that had made Beth want to explore a chat room on her own. Just to prove to her friend, and herself, that she could do it. It was all about motivation, and scoring a point off her old friend was motivation enough. To her surprise, not only had it been straightforward but there were several chat rooms specifically for writers. She had picked one at random and was soon reading a selection of messages in the 'meetings' room. It all seemed innocent enough: critiques wanted, word-processor services offered, listings of poetry workshops and crime-writing events advertised. Someone wanted to know how to go about writing for children, and another was seeking advice, tongue-in-cheek, on how to get even with a publisher who had just rejected his novel.

She hadn't plucked up the nerve to respond to any of the messages, but tonight she thought she might give it a go. She accessed the chat room she'd been in last night. One message in particular caught her eye:

I'm new to this, and as someone once wrote, 'One should always be a little improbable,' so I'm giving it a whirl. I've had one of those days, and to quote again from the same source, 'I am sick to death of cleverness.' Anyone on the same wavelength? Mr Outta Laffs.

After a brief tussle with the warning voice in her head, Beth typed:

I know just what you mean, Mr Outta Laffs. 'Everybody is clever nowadays. You can't go anywhere without meeting clever people.'

She signed herself BK.
A few seconds passed. Then another message appeared.

'The thing has become an absolute public nuisance.'

Her brain working overtime, her fingers flicking at the keys, she wrote,

'I wish to goodness we had a few fools left.'

'We have.' And how refreshing to find someone who knows

their Oscar Wilde so well. Bravo! Are you a fan?

My son is currently rehearsing The Imp of Earnest. He's playing Algernon.

Professionally?

No, it's for his sixth-form college.

As soon as she clicked on SEND, she regretted it. Even in a chat room she had resorted to mentioning Nathan.

I'm a parent too [came the reply]. My daughter once played Gwendolen and after spending weeks helping her learn her lines, I became hooked on Oscar Wilde. By the way, if I may be so bold, you sound like you're a woman. Am I right?

She hesitated before answering, suddenly picturing the pervy in the anorak hunched up over his keyboard. Too much information, perhaps? Quoting Oscar Wilde again, but this time from *An Ideal Husband* – she and Nathan had only recently hired the video – she typed:

'Questions are never indiscreet. Answers sometimes are.'

Point taken. But let me assure you, I'm no cyber Peeping Tom!! I'm a very respectable man, whose only vice, thus far, is to have come on-line (for the first time) to chat, instead of getting on with my novel. I seem to be stuck. Any advice?

I find a glass of wine helps.

Way ahead of you. On to my second. What's your preferred drug of choice? In terms of writing, that is! Which genre?

I'm very much a novice. A history of unpublished (and unpublishable) short stories behind me, but now I'm trying my hand at a novel. And you?

Oh, this and that. Novels primarily. Occasionally the odd short story. And I mean odd. But odd as in quirky!

How long have you been writing?

Years. What's your book about?

A self-help junkie.

Autobiographical?

NO!

I'll take that as a yes. Title?

Living For Pleasure.

Aha, do I detect more overtones of Mr W?

Guilty as charged. Time for me to go now. Goodnight, Mr
Outta Laffs. It's been . . . interesting.

Well, thought Beth, as she stood in the bathroom brushing her teeth, whoever Mr Laffs was, he had taught her that chatting on-line was as easy as pie. That was one in the eye for Simone.

She went to bed wondering what he was like. For all she knew she had just spent fifteen minutes in the presence of a nerdy type who believed in crop circles and aliens.

Or, worse, a dead ringer for Victor.

As was her habit before giving in to sleep, she read for a quarter of an hour. Beside her bed was her inspiration for writing *Living For Pleasure*: a stack of self-help books Simone had given her over the years. There was *The Road Less Travelled*, a selection of *Chicken Soup* paperbacks and her current favourite, *Feel the Fear and Do It Anyway*.

She'd certainly done that tonight. She awarded herself a gold star and a wide, smug smile.

17

For obvious reasons, people preferred not to move house during the winter and estate agents often had to resign themselves to a period of quiet tedium. It was now, during the predicted lull, and despite feeling terminally exhausted, that Jack chose to overhaul the office filing system. It wasn't going as well as he would have liked. The back of the office, the part the public didn't see, was a scene of paper carnage. He was a tidy man by nature and found himself growing steadily more irritated each day when he came into work and found the mess no better. If anything, it appeared to be getting worse.

Just like his life.

When Clare had told him she was pregnant, he had been poleaxed, as though the world had crashed in on him. 'Are you sure?' he'd asked, once he could think straight enough to string a sentence together. They were having a drink at her place – he'd wondered why she was drinking bitter lemon, not her usual vodka and tonic.

'Yes,' she'd said, 'I've done a test.' And then she'd smiled, a smile that told him just how she felt about the situation. He thought he would never forget that look on her face. Or the sense of being trapped by it.

'But I thought you were on the pill, that that was all taken care of.'

'All taken care of?' she'd repeated. 'What a funny way to describe something so important.' She suddenly sounded every inch the legal adversary she was.

He put his glass down on the coffee-table and turned to face her, moving slightly away. He needed space. 'I notice you haven't answered me,' he said, barely able to keep his voice level.

Her gaze didn't quite meet his. 'I'd been having trouble with the pill,' she murmured, 'so I was using something else.'

'What? Ignorance? Hope? Faith?' He was getting angry now, could feel his head throbbing. She'd done this deliberately, he knew it. This was her way of making sure that she got what she wanted.

She stood up. 'What's got into you, Jack? I don't understand why you're taking this line. I thought you'd be pleased. You love children, you told me that.'

He went and stood as far away from her as he could. He stared out of the window, on to the small fenced garden of her modern estate house. He had never felt so confined before. He pushed a hand through his hair. 'I was talking specifically about my own children, Amber and Lucy. Not every Tom, Dick and Harry's children.'

Now it was she who sounded angry. 'This child is yours, Jack, not Tom's, not Dick's or anyone else's. It's yours. *Ours.*'

He made no response, and they were quiet for a long, threatening moment. Until Clare said, 'Thank you for making your feelings so clear. At least I know exactly where I stand. I think you'd better leave.'

He turned from the window, suddenly ashamed. 'Look, Clare, it's the shock. I never expected this to happen. I had—'

She raised a hand to stop him. 'No, Jack. You can't unsay what you've said.' He could see that she was trying to tough it out, but there were tears in her eyes.

'We need to talk about this,' he said, more gently, his anger and resolve faltering.

'I don't think I want to hear anything you've got to say right now. Please, just go.'

He didn't move. 'Clare, don't try to twist the situation. It's bad enough without you doing that.'

'Bad enough?' Her voice was low. 'Bad enough? Oh, that's good. You should try viewing it from where I'm standing.' She started to cry. He went to her and put his arms around her, then led her back to the sofa, where she clung to him. 'Oh, Jack,' she cried, her tears warm, then cold, against his neck. 'I know what you're thinking. That I was deliberately careless. I wasn't. Please believe me. And please don't go. Don't leave me. I love you.'

He held her tightly, moved by the strength of her need for him. But as he tried to comfort her, he knew he was caught. It was too late now to walk away from her. From her and the baby.

No matter how much he wanted to.

The phone rang on his desk, making him start. He picked it up and was told that Mr Mitchell was on the line for him. The news wasn't good. The sale of the man's property in Altrincham had fallen through and consequently he was withdrawing his offer on Miss Waterman's flat. They were back to square one again. Damn. He was more than usually upset that a vital link in the chain had been broken. Miss Waterman was one of their nicer clients and he had wanted everything to go through smoothly for her. She was also Beth's friend, which made it more personal. He went over to the chaos of the filing cabinets, riffled through a drawer, found Miss Waterman's file and was about to sit down again to telephone her when he changed his mind. He decided to deliver the bad news in person. Just once, he'd leave early.

He slipped on his jacket, then his coat and scarf, and went through to the front office where Janine and Nicky were sitting at their desks discussing when to put up the Christmas decorations. 'I'm off for the day,' he said.

'Can you put 10a Maywood Park House back in the window, please? Mr Mitchell's sale has bitten the dust. Oh, and not a single decoration up for at least a fortnight,' he added, with a smile.

He drove out of the small car park at the rear of the office, and joined the stream of early-evening traffic. It was almost dark and the shop fronts along Bridge Street were brightly lit. By next week he wouldn't be able to move for twinkling lights and sprayed-on snow.

The thought of Christmas depressed him. Maddie still hadn't got round to letting him know when he would see the girls – apparently Tony had some grand notion about taking them skiing during the festive season. Jack had only just got over hearing about their half-term holiday. Lucy had raved about it and shown him all the clothes and cuddly toys Tony had bought her while they'd been away. Amber had been less enthusiastic to talk about the trip, but he'd done his best to be ambivalent and tried to coax out of her what she'd enjoyed most. Gradually, she'd lowered her guard and shown off an expensive pair of trainers Tony had given her. Judging from her expression, they were the latest word in high-tech footwear and he'd made all the right noises about how cool they made her look and how well they went with the cropped jeans – another Uncle Sam export, of course.

Good old generous Tony.

He parked outside Maywood Park House and saw there were lights on in both flats. Perhaps he'd call on Beth when he'd talked to Miss Waterman.

But when he rang the bell for 10a, it was Beth who answered the door. 'Hello,' she said, stepping back to let him in from the cold. 'Is Adele expecting you? She hasn't mentioned your visit.'

'No. I've called on the off-chance, with bad news, I'm afraid, which I thought I'd impart face to face.'

'Oh dear, that's the last thing she needs right now. She's in bed with pneumonia.'

'I'm sorry to hear that. And I certainly don't want to add to her troubles. I could always ring tomorrow. Or leave a message with you to pass on.'

She hesitated, as if weighing up the options. 'Hang on. I'll go and have a quick word with her. Why don't you go through to the sitting room?' She reached past him and switched on the light.

While he waited, he prowled round Miss Waterman's antique furniture. The flat was a lot warmer than it had been on his last visit and he found himself liking it more. He felt awkward for intruding, though. A phone call would have sufficed. He was standing with his back to the room and looking at his haggard reflection in the blank window when Beth returned.

'Adele says you're welcome to see her, as long as you behave like the perfect gentleman and don't look too closely at her. Cup of tea?'

'That would be great.'

Miss Waterman was propped up with several pillows behind her, the bedclothes decorously drawn up to her chin. He could see straight away that she wasn't at all well and he apologised for barging in. 'I should have telephoned,' he said. 'Please forgive me.'

She waved aside his words and indicated a chair. 'Nothing to forgive. Now, then, why don't you give me your news. It's bad, I presume.'

He took off his coat and laid it across his lap as he sat down. He told her about Mr Mitchell withdrawing his offer. 'Of course, as soon as you're feeling better,' he continued, 'we'll get people viewing again. It's a pain, I know, especially with Christmas just round the corner, but I'm sure we'll find another buyer in no time.'

'What about the others who viewed and who were so keen?' asked Beth, coming in with a tray of delicate cups and saucers.

'I'll chase them first thing in the morning, but they've probably found somewhere else by now.' He took the cup offered to him and watched her sit on the bed with Miss Waterman.

'You look tired, Mr Solomon,' Miss Waterman said. 'Are you working too hard?'

He smiled. 'Please, it's Jack. And, no, I can't admit to working too hard.'

Beth laughed. 'That's not what your client wants to hear.'

He saw the funny side. 'Oops, bit of a slip-up, that.'

'You two may be joking,' Miss Waterman remarked, and eased herself into a more comfortable position, 'but I'm being serious. You look nearly as bad as I feel, Mr Solomon – Jack.'

If anyone else had been as frank, he might have felt insulted, but coming from this sweet old lady, he took the words in the spirit in which they had been voiced. 'A few personal problems at the moment,' he said lightly. 'Nothing that will get in the way of me selling your flat, I assure you.'

'The flat be damned,' she said, with surprising feeling. 'You look as if you need a good hearty meal to build you up. Beth, as Nathan's out this evening, why don't you invite Jack for supper?'

It was difficult to know who looked more astonished, Beth or Jack.

'I think Adele might have been trying her hand at a little matchmaking,' Beth said to Jack, later that evening when he was helping her to lay the table. 'I hope you weren't embarrassed.'

'Not in the least.'

She gave him a handful of cutlery. 'Well, just so long as you don't think I put her up to it. If I didn't know better, I'd say she's been overdosing on romantic novels. It's time for me to change her prescription for library books.' She went back to the cooker and stirred a pan of ratatouille. 'But she's dead right, Jack, about you looking tired.'

'Do I really look that awful?'

Still stirring, she turned her head to look at him. 'To be brutally honest, and speaking as a friend, yes.'

'Then I must do something about changing my friends. I'm not sure I can handle such honesty.'

While Beth took a small plate of supper downstairs to Adele, leaving him to open a bottle of wine and put on a CD, Jack was struck again by how comfortable he felt in Beth's flat. It had an almost magical ability to make the rest of the world and its troubles disappear. He wished his own home had the same effect on him.

He had nearly turned down Beth's offer of supper – knowing that the idea hadn't entered her head until Miss Waterman had put it there – but he was glad now that he had said yes. He liked the idea of spending an evening with someone who was straightforward and easy to talk to. He didn't even feel guilty that he was in the company of a woman Clare had no knowledge of. And, anyway, there was nothing going on between him and Beth. It was a platonic friendship, nothing more. But he had the feeling that Clare would need convincing on that score. Since she had told him about the baby, she had become increasingly possessive. She had wanted to move in with him, but he had held off. 'Let's just take it slowly,' he'd said, 'one step at a time.' He had used Amber and Lucy as an excuse to preserve what little privacy he still had, claiming that he didn't want to unsettle or alarm them. He had also asked her not to tell anyone just yet that she was pregnant. She had been disappointed by this. 'What about Mum and Dad?' she'd asked. Especially not them, he'd wanted to say. He was being a coward, he knew. As if keeping it a secret would somehow make it seem less real. Less of a mess. She had later confessed that she had confided in Julie. Which meant Des knew. Funny he hadn't said anything.

Clare's possessiveness also stretched to her badgering him about his regular absences on Thursday evenings. He still hadn't let on about the writers' group, determined more than ever to keep that secret from her. Sometimes he thought it was only his new-found passion for writing that kept him sane. Whenever he sat down in front of his laptop to write his diary or his novel, the words tumbled out of him, an unstoppable outpouring from the heart.

He was just switching on the CD player when Beth came back. 'I'm under orders to feed you till you burst,' she said brightly, 'and to get to the bottom of what's troubling you.'

'I could always fob you off.'

'You could. But how productive would that be?'

They sat down to eat, and before long he found he was telling her everything. About Maddie and the girls, Tony and Clare, and now the baby.

'Oh, Jack, what a load you've been carrying. I'd sort of guessed about Maddie and Tony from what you've read to us at the group, but I had no idea that you were so unhappy with Clare.'

He sighed heavily. 'I've only myself to blame. I shouldn't have rushed into things with her as I did. At the time I thought she was the answer. Now I know differently. I've been bloody stupid.'

'Don't be too hard on yourself. You haven't said, but presumably Clare wants the baby?'

'Very much so. And I wouldn't want her to do anything ... well, you know, anything drastic like get rid of it.'

'I'm probably letting the sisterhood down, but you don't have to marry her.'

He looked grim. 'I feel as if it's inevitable. But that's a long way off. For now I'm still married to Maddie.'

'But you mustn't marry Clare if it means the pair of you will end up hating each other. You have to be sensible. Look long-term, Jack. You have a duty to the child, but also to be true to yourself. And there's Amber and Lucy to consider. If you're unhappy, think what that will do to them.'

He was no nearer to solving his problems, but the evening spent with Beth had cheered him, and the first thing he did when he got home was not to pour himself a large drink, as he'd got into the habit of doing, but go to bed. It had been good sharing so much with Beth, even the painful stuff. He knew now that he'd deliberately not confided in Des because of Julie. He'd wager the last coin in his pocket that those two kept few secrets from each other, and therefore whatever Jack shared with Des about his current situation would go to Julie, then straight to Clare. It was a risk he couldn't take.

But thank goodness for Beth.

He slept well that night. The best sleep he'd had for what seemed like for ever.

18

Richard Cavanagh knew he was taking a risk – to himself and others. Driving a car so soon after a heart-attack wasn't advisable. The medical view was that he should wait for at least another month, but he simply had to see Dulcie. He missed her so much it hurt. This evening, while Angela was out with the boys at a school function, he was seizing his opportunity.

He reversed his beloved old Aston Martin out of the garage: he hadn't driven it for nearly six weeks and the controls felt unfamiliar. At one time his beautiful classic car had meant the world to him. He had lavished untold care and devotion on it, had polished it lovingly, restored it, even tinkered with the engine, convinced that no one understood it better than he did. Now he knew it was nothing but a stylish and extravagant piece of machinery. With nothing to do while he'd been recovering from his heart-attack, he'd thought a lot about his life: what was important to him, and what wasn't. And before it was too late, he had to make the most of what was left to him. His near-death experience had taught him a lot. It was a wake-up call he could not ignore.

It was dark and he flicked on the lights, then closed the garage door with the remote control, turned the car on the gravel and drove away slowly. He didn't have much time, but he knew better than to hurry. If he only got to be with Dulcie for half an hour, it would be better than nothing. The possibility that she might be out had crossed his mind, but there had been no question of telephoning, not when he knew she would be furious at the risk he was taking and try to stop him.

Gaining confidence, he squeezed the accelerator, enjoying his moment of freedom. With Angela taking his convalescence so seriously, fending off calls from work and insisting he mustn't be exposed to stressful situations, he had been kept a virtual prisoner in his own home. He lowered the window, just to feel the cold evening air on his face. It made him feel truly alive. And so very glad to be so. When he'd been lying in that hospital bed, he'd had plenty of time to count his blessings and grasp just how fragile life was. How easy it was to take it for granted, to imagine that one was immortal. He had thought of his children often – Christopher and Nicholas in particular – and had hated the idea that he might not see them grow to adulthood.

The doctors had put down his heart-attack to an unaccountable change in his blood pressure. It was all they could come up with, because in all other areas he had a clean bill of health: he'd never smoked, had never had a problem with cholesterol, and hadn't worked himself into the ground as so many of his colleagues did. He had been unlucky, was their conclusion. At least at the time Dulcie had been with him. Her prompt action had ensured that within the hour he was in the coronary-care unit. It meant that the severity of the attack had been reduced and any permanent damage limited. That morning he had told Angela before leaving for work that he would be taking an extended lunch break to drive down to the classic-car garage on the Whitchurch road – something he often did when he needed a replacement part for the Aston Martin; it was only half a mile from the Belfry Hotel where he and Dulcie met occasionally. When Angela had asked who had come to his aid, he had lied. He had told her that because he'd been feeling unwell he'd stopped off at a hotel for a drink, and had got talking to a woman in the bar. 'What a pity we don't know her name or where she lives,' Angela had said. 'It would have been a nice gesture to write and thank her for what she did. She probably saved your life.'

He could have told a partial truth, he thought later. Would there have been anything so odd about a chance encounter with the woman who'd helped them move house?

Angela's innocent reference to the supposed stranger who had saved his life might have caused him to flinch a short while before, but now it didn't. Ever since she had told him how she and Nicholas had bumped into Dulcie, his heart had hardened towards her. 'I expect you can't remember what she looks like, but I don't recall her looking so old,' Angela had gloated. 'And I'd bet a pound to a penny she's put on weight.' Angela had never had to worry about her weight. She had been in her coat, fresh from her shopping trip in Maywood, and was bustling absentmindedly around the bedroom, a carrier-bag in her hand. 'It would explain why she's still a widow,' she'd added, further annoying him.

With his hands forming fists under the duvet, he'd said, 'How do you know she hasn't married again?'

'Oh, Richard, you men are so hopelessly unobservant. She wasn't wearing a ring, of course.'

He rushed to defend the woman he loved – and also decided to buy Dulcie a ring at the earliest opportunity. 'That doesn't mean a thing in this day and age. She might live with a loving partner who cares passionately about the woman within, not the superficial exterior of size and looks.'

She had stared at him as if he were mad, then switched her glance to the plastic bag in her hand. 'Oh, I bought you some books.' She held the bag out to him and he took it without a word of thanks.

He couldn't say with any certainty when or why he had stopped loving Angela but, like middle age or a change in season, it had crept up on him, a gradual dawning that they had run their course as husband and wife and had become more like brother and sister – older brother and little sister. At times he felt choked by her neediness, stifled by her inability to stand on her own two feet. Ironically, it was this very trait that had attracted him when they first met. In those days she had been painfully shy and he had got a kick out of being able to make her smile, to make her happy, to give her the strength and confidence she so badly lacked. Being needed – *wanted* – was powerfully seductive.

How arrogant that made him sound. Years later it had been an independent spirit and a quiet sense of self-containment that had attracted him.

Often it was the silly things that got to him about Angela, like her haphazard approach to housework, the way she could never keep on top of the ironing and left the kitchen to tidy itself. He tried hard not to show his disapproval but, being obsessively tidy himself, he frequently stepped in and did the job for her.

Angela had her good points. She was a wonderful mother: she gave her all to the children, ensuring that she was always there for every play, every parents' evening, every concert. It was him who was at fault. He had forced too much upon her. He had chased a good promotion at work to satisfy his own needs – more money, greater status, bigger challenges. He had justified uprooting Angela and the younger children by saying it would get them out of a rut, that it would give them an exciting new start. It hadn't worked. Angela had never settled: she missed her friends and family, particularly her old schoolfriend, Rowena. She felt isolated, cut off from all that she knew, became more dependent on him.

Looking back on that time, when he had realised he no longer loved his wife – long before they'd moved to Cheshire – he often wondered if she ever sensed he was drifting away from her: as he'd retreated, she had advanced on him, becoming more affectionate and loving. Then she had told him she was pregnant and the future he had begun to imagine was snatched from him. He had no way of knowing, but he had always suspected that Angela had deliberately become pregnant with Christopher. Oh, she'd done an excellent job of pretending she was as shocked as he was, but something in her manner – her readiness later to provide Christopher with a younger brother or sister – told him that this was all part of the plan to bond them together for a long time yet. She had probably told herself she had given their marriage a new lease of life.

And in much the same way, his heart-attack had done the same for him.

He didn't mind admitting that being in hospital had terrified him. Even now, when the expert opinion was that he was well on the road to recovery, he often went to bed at night frightened that he might not wake up. Every time he had the slightest twinge of pain, or a change in the rhythm of his heartbeat, he worried that he might be dying.

It took him almost thirty minutes to reach Maywood. As he turned into Bloom Street his heart pounded at the thought of seeing Dulcie. He forced himself to breathe slowly and deeply, and stopped the car a short distance from her house: there were lights on and it was all he could do to resist the urge to quicken his step towards the door.

Dulcie heard the front-door bell and stopped mid-sentence. She had been absorbed in what she was writing. Annoyed at the interruption, she took off her reading glasses and reluctantly went to see who it was. If it was another of those young men with holdalls of dusters and ironing-board covers, she would give him short shrift.

'Richard!'

'Hello, Dulcie. It's not a bad time to call, is it?'

They held each other tightly, kissed, and cried with the sheer joy of being together again. It was a while before either of them could speak.

'You've no idea how much I've missed you,' Richard said, when they'd calmed down and were in the sitting room.

'Oh, I do. It's been the same for me.' Then, more seriously, she said, 'But you broke the promise you made. You risked too much by doing this. What if—'

He took her hand and pressed it to his lips. 'I'm sorry but I had to see you. I thought I'd go crazy if I didn't. Don't be cross.' He put his arm round her and drew her close. 'I can't stay long, though.'

'I know. I understand.'

'But one day I will. If you'll agree, I'd like to stay for ever.'

She looked deep into his eyes and saw the conviction in them, and the love. But still she doubted what he'd said. He was speaking from his heart, not his head, and when the emotional trauma of what he'd been through had settled, he would know that his place was with his family. They both knew it. For now, though, none of that mattered. They were together for a few precious moments and she didn't want anything to spoil it, least of all let the dull thud of reality impinge on their happiness.

He took her face in his hands and kissed her. 'I don't suppose you'd take pity on a sick man and make love to me, would you?' he whispered.

Smiling, but gently chiding him, she said, 'I'd like nothing better, but I'd rather not have your demise on my conscience or have it take place in my bed. I'm squeamish like that.'

He hushed her with another kiss. 'But what a way to go.'

19

'William Kidswell, you're such a tart!'

Billy slid into the passenger seat of the car, lowered his sunglasses and gave Nathan one of his classic lazy-eyed looks, the kind that he knew was such a turn-on for girls. He smoothed down his suit and flicked at the absurdly floppy points of his enormous collar. 'Takes one to know one, darling.'

Nathan laughed. 'I can't make up my mind if you're playing the camp dandy or the seventies game-show host.'

'Either way, it's Friday night and I'm in the mood for *lurve*.' He reached inside his jacket pocket and pulled out a small bottle of tequila. 'Something to help the party along.'

Nathan wound down his window. 'But did you have to smother yourself in so much CK? I'm dying of passive aftershave poisoning here.'

'Do you mind? It's Paul Smith. But drink it in, boy, it might just do the trick and give you the necessary to pull tonight.'

'Yeah, right, like I need your help in that department. The king of dump 'em and run.'

Billy grinned. 'So what's the score between you and that cute little redhead, *Jasmina* Rafferty? And give me the real score – I don't want you holding back on me.'

Keeping his expression inscrutable and concentrating on the road, all Nathan said was, 'Her name's Jasmine. Jaz.'

It turned out that Nathan had got it wrong about Jaz being interested in Billy. She'd been horrified when he'd suggested as much. Scornful, too. 'Oh, please,' she'd said, 'credit me with more sense. Billy's so into himself he's in danger of vanishing up his own bum.'

'Vicki seems to think differently,' Nathan had ventured.

She'd laughed. 'I think you'll find Billy may have met his match there.'

He was glad that she was smart enough to see through Billy. He and Jaz only saw each other at college; occasionally they walked home together. They talked about the kind of books and films they enjoyed and her writing. She was different from most other girls he knew, more serious and intense. Occasionally she gave him a contemplative smile, but more often than not her manner was defensive and prickly. It made for some great exchanges between them. Once or twice he had wondered if it wasn't an act she put on for his benefit. If so, why?

And why did he feel he was surrounded by people putting on an act? Jaz.

Billy.

And, of course, the greatest of them all, his grandmother.

Lois had phoned last night. 'Sorry, Gran,' he'd said, 'Mum's not in. Can I pass on a message? Or get her to ring you when she comes back?'

'Oh, is she working late?'

'No, she's at her writers' group.'

'Her what?'

He'd seen his mistake immediately, but had known there was no way to wriggle out of the situation. Lois was a determined inquisitor when she wanted to be. He tried to play dumb, but everything he said seemed to rouse his grandmother's curiosity further. 'It's just an evening out for her,' he said.

'And what goes on at this group?'

'Writing, I suppose.'

'But why?'

'Why what?'

'Why does your mother want to do something so peculiar? Is this another of Simone's harebrained schemes? I've never known anyone so faddish. It was her who passed on all those absurd self-help books to your mother. As if she needed that kind of thing when she had us.'

Nathan had always known that his grandmother disapproved of Simone, but it was only recently that he had realised the extent of it. Hack away the veneer of Lois's attempts at humour and it was patently clear that she saw Simone as a threat.

When his mother arrived home, humming to herself in the hall as she removed her coat and hung it up, he told her that he'd dumped her in it with Lois.

'Oh, Lord,' she'd said, after he'd explained and apologised. 'Now I'll be cross-examined on the dubious company I'm keeping. Not to worry, it was bound to happen sooner or later. Lois has a nose for sniffing out a secret.'

Humming again, she went through to the kitchen and put her writing file on the small desk where her computer was. He was surprised that she didn't seem bothered by what he'd told her. Only a short time ago, she would have tried to justify her right to have a life that Lois knew nothing about. Things were changing for the better, he decided.

Was it possible that her mood had been influenced by a certain man from the writers' group – Adele's estate agent, Jack Solomon? Hadn't they had supper together the other night?

Nathan and Billy arrived at the party to find the usual suspects present from the upper sixth, as well as several cast members from the play who were in the lower sixth. It was Kirsten Dempsey's eighteenth birthday – she was playing Cecily Cardew – and because she was friendly with Vicki, Nathan had hoped secretly that Jaz would be there.

He left Billy to his admiring fans, including Vicki, and went in search of a soft drink – he'd drawn the short straw and was the designated driver that night, which meant he'd stay stone-cold sober. Billy would probably need to be put into the recovery position on the back seat of the car.

There was no sign of Jaz. Disappointed, he stared round the sitting room, which the Dempseys had wisely stripped of most of its contents, and wondered where she was and what she was doing.

He hoped she was enjoying herself more than he was.

Jaz was furious. How could her parents do this to her? It was so unfair. And why was it always she who had to babysit Tamzin and Lulu? Why did they never ask Phin or Jimmy? And it wasn't just for tonight: they were away for a long weekend staying at the apartment in Tenerife. 'My Molly-doll deserves a bit of pampering,' Dad had announced at breakfast, 'and a blast of sun too. So long as we can get on a flight, we'll be off this afternoon.'

Jaz hated it when Dad used his pet-name for her mother: it was so childish. And what did they think they were doing at their age by having more children? Why couldn't they just accept that they were past their sex-by date?

Every time she thought of her mother being pregnant, she felt sick. She had been eight when Lulu was born and had never forgotten that dreadful night. Tamzin had been two (for a change she had been fast asleep in her cot and not trying to climb out of it), and apart from Jaz and her mother, no one else was at home. It was St Patrick's Day and her father had taken the boys to Dublin to expose them to their Rafferty roots. To be fair to her father, he had dithered about going – the baby was due in three weeks – but Mum had insisted she'd be okay and he'd headed out of town. That night she had gone into labour. The first Jaz knew of this was when her mother woke her and said, 'Jaz, I need your help. The baby's decided to come early.'

Instantly bolt upright, Jaz had said, 'What do you want me to do?' Her mother's face was covered with a sheen of perspiration. She looked awful.

'Don't look so worried. I've phoned for an ambulance and until Mrs Dalton can get here, I want you to take care of Tamzin while I'm at the hospital.'

'Why can't Mrs Dalton come sooner? She's only next door.'

'I can't get hold of her – she must be out for the evening.' Her mother's face twisted and she gasped. Frightened, Jaz threw her arms round her. She wanted to cry, but somehow knew it wasn't the time. 'It's okay, Jaz,' her mother said, moments later, 'everything will be fine.'

But it wasn't fine. Mrs Dalton didn't come back from wherever she was and the ambulance took for ever to arrive. Within minutes of it showing up, Lulu was born, but not before Jaz had heard her poor mother cry out with a pain she swore she would never experience.

'I thought it was supposed to get easier the more you had,' her mother said to Dad, after he and the boys had got home – they had caught the night ferry.

'Maybe after the tenth it does.' He'd laughed. 'We'll have to carry on and find out.'

From the foot of the bed, Jaz had watched her father cradle the scrawny baby, which was squirming like a horrible worm in his large hands. She had prayed for all she was worth that he had been joking.

And now her mother was going to go through all that again. With twins. Jaz had a sneaky feeling that her father viewed babies as a badge of honour: the more who bore the name of Rafferty the better.

With her head in her hands as she sat at her desk, Jaz shuddered. She had long since grown out of believing in the Catechism and the Catholic God of her upbringing, but she offered up a new prayer: 'Please, God, don't ever let me be stupid enough to get pregnant.' She couldn't think of anything worse: all that screaming and disgusting mess. She tried to block the nightmarish thought from her mind, but was distracted by an almighty racket from downstairs. She gritted her teeth, ready to read the Riot Act to Tamzin and Lulu. She took the stairs slowly, planning a suitably satisfying punishment for her sisters.

She found them in the sitting room, the television blaring and a sweating Robbie Williams strutting his half-naked, tattooed body across the screen. There were crisps, Cheerios, peanuts, and feathers all over the carpet. A small table lay on its back and one of Mum's china ornaments lay broken among the chaos. From where they were standing on the sofa – feather-leaking cushions in hand – Tamzin and Lulu stared at her. Both were out of breath with hysterical laughter and both had covered their faces in what Jaz could only hope, from the empty pot on the floor, was chocolate mousse.

It was the most surreal moment, and when her scream came, she gave it full vent. Once she had started, it was difficult to stop, especially when she saw the effect it was having on her sisters. They jumped off the sofa and managed to look almost contrite. She was still yelling at them when she heard the doorbell ring.

'That'll be the police,' she said, blurting out the first thought that came into her head. 'I called them from upstairs and they said they'd get here as soon as they could to take you away. I hope you enjoy spending the night in a cell.'

Lulu was young enough to be taken in and she looked horror-struck. But Tamzin wasn't so convinced. 'I don't believe you,' she said, sticking out her chocolaty chin. She had probably watched sufficient police dramas to know that they never arrived quite so quickly.

Jaz went to answer the door. She did a double-take when she saw who it was.

Nathan stood hesitantly on the doorstep. He'd heard the commotion and was now confronted with an expression so hostile he wished he'd remained at the party. When Vicki had told him Jaz had had to babysit her sisters, he'd come up with what he'd thought was a brilliant idea to surprise her and see if she fancied some company. But from the drawn brows and the arms pinned across her chest, she plainly didn't want him here. He was all set to leave when she seemed to change her mind: 'Look, you can come in, if you like, but you'll have to put up with my awful sisters. They're a right pair of savages, evil personified. Riff-raff. Trash. You name it. Collectively, they're Public Enemy Number One.'

He smiled. 'Every family should have one.'

'So why did mine end up with two?' She stepped back to let him in. 'Hey, I don't suppose you'd do me a favour, would you?'

'What? Adopt them?'

'What a spectacularly wonderful idea, but no. Could you pretend you're a policeman and that you've come to arrest them? You'll understand why when you see what they've done.'

He laughed. He was already having more fun than he'd had at the party. 'Anything to oblige, miss.'

With the collar of his leather coat pulled up and an authoritative swagger, Nathan walked into the middle of the sitting room and tried to look every inch the plain-clothes detective inspector as he surveyed the damage. It was awesome.

He shook his head.

He tutted.

He inhaled deeply.

He exhaled deeply.

He shook his head again.

Most of all, he tried not to laugh. He'd never seen anything like it. Even the Dempseys wouldn't be confronted with a sight on this scale after Kirsten's party. How could two kids create such a scene of devastation? And what the hell was that muck they'd smeared over their faces?

'I told you it was bad, Officer,' Jaz said, switching off the television. She put down the remote control, folded her arms again and looked fierce.

'Strikes me that I came in the nick of time.' He stepped towards the pair. 'What do you have to say for yourselves, then? And I must caution you, anything you say will be taken down and used as evidence.'

The smaller of the two girls took a step behind her sister, but the bigger one held her ground. 'How do we know you're a real policeman? Where's your badge? You could be a piddyfile for all we know.'

Nathan was taken aback. When he was their age, he'd never heard the word 'paedophile'. He ignored her request to see his badge and said, 'You must be the ringleader, eh? Would I be right? Name, please.'

Her eyes darted nervously from him to Jaz, then back to him. 'I know my rights,' she said, rebelliously. 'I'm allowed to make a phone call. I'm going to ring Mum and Dad.'

'Yes,' said Jaz. 'You do that and I'll tell them what you've done here, broken ornament and all.'

Nathan was beginning to feel that they'd carried the joke as far as they could. 'Seeing as it's a first offence,' he said, 'how about you tidy up the place and we'll say no more about it? But I'm warning you, you've committed several serious offences here tonight.' He held up his hands and counted off their crimes on his fingers. 'Breach of the peace, aiding and abetting, unlawful conduct, and violation of section 16a and 22b of the Law and Order Act.' Gratified to see their jaws drop, he added sternly, 'Now, don't do it again. Do you hear?'

They nodded and began to clear up. Except they made it worse. Their hands were covered in the same stuff as their faces and everything they touched stuck to their fingers. They tried to shake off the feathers and Cheerios, but began to giggle when a feather landed on the end of Lulu's nose. 'Oh, for heaven's sake,' Jaz shouted, 'go upstairs, have a bath and then go straight to bed. I'll sort this out. Go on, *scram!*'

When she and Nathan were alone, she closed the door, leaned against it and groaned. 'You see what I have to put up with? It's like that twenty-four hours a day. Please don't judge me by their awfulness.'

He had taken off his coat and was crouched on the floor picking up the broken china. 'Hey, it's okay, I'm on board with the gruesome-sister act. No comparison made.'

'I can't wait to leave home. University can't come quick enough.' Then, registering what he was doing, she went over to him. 'There's no need for you to do that. I'll see to it.'

'It's okay, I don't mind helping. I think we're going to need a cloth, a bin-liner and a vacuum-cleaner. I doubt that this china can be glued back together.'

They worked together, binning, scrubbing and hoovering, until at last the place looked as it should. After she'd been upstairs and checked on her sisters – making sure they were in bed, not flooding the bathroom – she said, 'The least I can do is offer you a drink. Or would you like something to eat?'

Out in the kitchen, she made some hot chocolate and two fried-egg sandwiches. They kept their voices low, so as not to bring her nosy-parker sisters down again. She was glad now that she'd invited him in. Her initial reaction at seeing him had been acute embarrassment. But this was great, sitting here in the kitchen: it was as if they were proper friends. Since that first time, they'd walked home together quite often, and occasionally they chatted during their lunch breaks in the college cafeteria. Usually there were others at the table with them, but once or twice they'd had a moment to themselves. Those were the times she'd liked best. She was relieved that he didn't fancy her: it meant they stood a chance of developing a friendship that might last – he was good company. And now that Vicki and Billy were hitting the smooch button, Jaz spent less time with Vicki, and more with

Nathan. She was still wary of him, though, reluctant to show too much of her real self in case he didn't like it.

'So, how was the party?' she asked.

'You didn't miss anything, believe me.'

'I guarantee it would have been better than my evening here. What made you leave?'

'Oh, you know, I'd heard that there was a better gig going on in this upwardly mobile neighbourhood.' He looked about him, assessing the large and expensively kitted-out kitchen. Jaz knew where Nathan lived and that he and his mum had just a small flat. She was suddenly aware of how others might perceive her – spoiled little rich kid. 'What does your dad do for a living?' he asked, confirming her thoughts.

'Don't be so sexist. My mum might have been the one to fund all this.'

He raised his hands in mock surrender. 'Okay, okay, I'll keep my big mouth shut.'

'Actually, you were right.' She relented. 'Dad runs a building firm. My brothers work for him now.' She gave a short laugh. 'That's because no one else would be stupid enough to take them on.' She took a bite of her sandwich, then ran her tongue over her lips to catch a dribble of melted butter and egg yolk. She noticed he was staring at her. Self-conscious, she said, 'What? Have I missed a bit?'

He shook his head slowly, his gaze still on her lips.

She didn't believe him, so got up and went over to the cupboard where her mother kept the kitchen roll. She ripped off a piece, wiped her mouth, then went back to the table, taking another square with her in case she made any more mess. He was still staring at her. 'You're beginning to spook me. What is it?'

He brushed some breadcrumbs off his fingers and cleared his throat. 'I was just thinking how much I'd like to kiss you.'

Stunned, she wiped her mouth again. But instead of thinking how much she might enjoy him kissing her, she was suspicious of his motives. Suppose he was trying it on? Suppose Vicki had told him at the party that her parents were away and he had come here with the express intention of taking advantage of her being alone ... of trying to get her into bed? She had a horrible vision of Billy, and everyone else at the party, urging him to do exactly that. Then a far worse picture came into her head: what if she succumbed and got pregnant? Vivid flashes of her mother in labour swam before her. She drew back from the table sharply. 'I think you should know there's absolutely no chance of you getting me into bed. Got that?'

He frowned, looked genuinely perplexed. 'Well, I'm glad we've got that sorted out.'

She was saved from having to respond by the sound of a door slamming upstairs. Grateful for the distraction, she excused herself. She took the stairs two at a time, wishing, as the distance grew between her and Nathan, that she could turn back the clock on the last five minutes.

What had just happened?

How could she have made such a fool of herself?

Of course he hadn't been trying to jump her. All he'd asked her for was a kiss. It was no big deal.

When she'd taken out her embarrassment on Tamzin and Lulu, she went back to the kitchen and found Nathan waiting for her. He was in his coat, ready to go.

She watched him drive away, knowing she'd blown it.

Now they wouldn't even be friends.

20

There was a very different atmosphere among the group that evening: they were relaxed and enjoying themselves – and they had Victor to thank for that. He hadn't turned up.

Until now, no one had missed a meeting and Beth was surprised that Victor had the first black mark against his name. She almost wished that his absence would not be a one-off and that he had decided Hidden Talents wasn't for him.

At Dulcie's suggestion last week, they were trying something new. From now on they were taking it in turns to lead the group. The reason behind this, according to Dulcie, was to induce a greater level of participation. Beth had dreaded being picked first, but all credit to Jack: he had risen to the challenge and volunteered. He was now explaining what they had to do.

'I'll come clean,' he said, 'I pinched the idea from a how-to-write book, so it's not original. It's an exercise to teach us the importance of fair-minded characterisation. To kick off with we have to create a character in no more than fifty words that no one in their right mind would like. Don't hold back, make him or her as nasty as you want. Okay?' He pointed to the clock on the mantelpiece. 'We have precisely ten minutes to do that.'

After a few moments of rustling paper and cranking up their brains, they fell quiet and concentrated on the task in hand. Minutes passed before Beth wrote anything. Then, with the pressure on, she panicked and scribbled the first thing that came into her head. To her shame, she found herself caricaturing Lois – the archetypal interfering mother-in-law.

She had nearly lost her temper with Lois at the weekend and the memory of what the other woman had said still hurt. Lois had shown up unexpectedly at the flat – usually she phoned in advance to check that they would be in – and had gone round the houses before she got to the real purpose of her visit. She wanted to know all about the writers' group. 'What kind of people would go to something so extraordinary?' she'd asked. 'I could scarcely believe it when Nathan told me what you'd been up to. You're turning into quite a dark horse, Beth. How many more little secrets are you keeping from us?' Her light, tinkling tone barely disguised the brittle hardness of her words and Beth regretted that she hadn't got this over and done with sooner. She should have returned Lois's call, as Nathan had said she would. She looked across the kitchen table to where Lois was unashamedly reading an electricity bill and said, 'Hardly a dark horse, Lois. I've joined a creative-writing group, not the Ku Klux Klan.'

'But what on earth for? I wouldn't have thought you'd have time, what with Nathan so busy in his final year at Maywood College.'

A flutter of anger released itself inside Beth. She knew she had to take a stand, had to put an end to Lois's insidious need to control her. It was outrageous that Lois should use Nathan to manipulate her like this.

'Lois, Nathan is quite capable of taking care of himself while I treat myself to the odd night out.'

'But it's such an important time for him. And it's not the odd night, is it? It's every week, so I understand from Nathan. You know, if he fails to get the grades he needs, you'll never forgive yourself. I was always there for Adam. I always put him first.'

Beth stared at Lois and wondered if she had any idea how cruel and absurd she sounded. 'I think you're exaggerating,' she said, more calmly than she felt. She got up from the table, suddenly confronted with the shocking discovery that she was on the verge of hating Lois. She didn't want to hate anyone, least of all Adam's mother. She went and stood at the window, stared down on to the park. A strong wind was scattering the clouds and a father was teaching his young son to ride a bicycle without stabilisers. For a moment she was disoriented as she recalled Adam doing the same with Nathan. Finally she spoke. 'Lois, I don't think you have any idea how offensive or hurtful you've just been to me. I've always put Nathan first.' She turned slowly from the window. 'But that's not what's really behind this, is it?' They were dangerously close to a point of no return and, more than anything, Beth wanted to clear the air. It was time to confront the lies and pretence. They couldn't go on as they were.

Lois's normally composed face twitched. A hand went to her throat and fiddled with a beaded necklace. 'I'm not sure what you mean. I'm ... I'm sorry if I've offended you in some way, but I was merely showing concern. Taking too much on is never a good idea. I should know, I've done it myself countless times.' She gave a shrill laugh, fanned her reddening face and looked at the fire reproachfully. 'Goodness, it's warm in here. Oh, did I tell you about Barnaby cutting his hand on a broken pane in the greenhouse? I don't know how often I've warned him to get it fixed. What he thought he was doing out there at this time of year is anybody's guess.'

And that was it. In one of her classic manoeuvres, Lois had made her point then moved the conversation on so that it would appear churlish to retaliate or pursue the argument further. She went on to discuss Christmas and what they would all be doing. 'I thought I'd do us a nice goose this year. What do you think?'

As if Lois cared what Beth thought.

Beth was about to put a line through what she had written when Jack called time.

'Right,' he said, 'now fold up your pieces of paper and hand them to the person on your left. Don't read them until I say so.'

Beth handed hers to Dulcie, hoping that Dulcie wouldn't guess at the extent of her unkindness.

'We now have twenty minutes to create a believable scenario in which we can turn round our neighbour's character,' Jack said. 'We have to make him or her not just likeable but redeemable.'

Dulcie nodded approvingly, but Jaz said, 'Flipping heck, Jack, you're not asking much, are you?'

Jack smiled. 'For a smart girl like you, Jaz, it'll be a breeze. Oh, and I forgot to say, we have to write this in the third person.' He looked at the clock again, and said, 'Okay, you may now turn over your exam papers.'

A collective groan went round the room. Beth read through the paragraph Jack had given her, and her heart sank. From what she knew of his circumstances, she could see that he had described the man who had once been his closest friend and was now living with his wife, Maddie.

It was interesting, but with the exception of Victor and Dulcie, who was the most experienced member of the group, everything they wrote was in the first person, which was probably why Jack had specified the third person now. No one had mentioned it before, but it was glaringly obvious to Beth that she, Jack and Jaz were writing about themselves. Apparently most writers did this when they embarked on their first novel. Other than Victor, they seldom spoke about getting published: they were all writing for the fun and challenge.

And, more importantly perhaps, for the escapism it offered.

Over coffee last week, Dulcie had said that while she was absorbed in writing, she didn't brood over things she couldn't control. It was a rare confidence that took Beth unawares, as Dulcie, so self-assured and congenial, didn't seem the anxious type. After this, and curling one of her long plaits around her finger, Jaz had said that she loved writing because it took her away from her brothers and sisters, who never gave her a minute's peace. 'I guess it's a power thing,' she said. She'd then admitted that her fictitious family, the Clacketts, was based on her own (not that they had needed to be told that) and Beth wondered if they were as riotous as Jaz painted them. But, then, wasn't it always the case that truth was stranger than fiction? Neither Victor nor Jack had contributed to this part of the conversation, but Jack had already told her, the night she'd cooked for him, that there were times when he thought he was writing his way out of the black hole he'd been sucked into.

She still cringed when she remembered Adele's attempt at matchmaking. 'You're not to do that again,' she had told the old lady the next day, when she'd popped in to see her before going to work, 'or I shan't fetch any more books from the library for you. It was mortifying for the poor man.'

'Nonsense,' Adele had said. 'He was charmed by the idea.'

'You mean he was struck dumb with shock.'

'But you had a good evening, didn't you? It was hours before he left.'

'Adele Waterman, you're the sneakiest neighbour I've ever had the misfortune to know. If you weren't so ill, I'd give you a proper ticking off. Now, behave yourself and take your medicine. And don't forget to have some of the soup I've made for you.'

Adele had looked at the Thermos beside the bed and smiled. 'It's not poisoned, is it?'

'Not on this occasion, but if you try to set me up again with Jack, I might just consider it. Anyway, he's seriously involved with someone else so you were wasting your time.'

Settling back into the pillows, which Beth had rearranged for her, Adele had said, 'Then he should look happier.'

Beth didn't tell Adele what was bothering Jack. What he had shared with her had been extremely personal, and she knew that he wouldn't want one of his clients to be privy to such information. To gossip about him behind his back would also be disloyal.

That was another aspect of the group that had surprised her. They hadn't known each other for long, yet a bond was forming between them. At the outset, Dulcie had said that the aim of the group was for them to support and encourage each other, not to criticise and demoralise. Maybe it was because they were writing about such personal things, and being brave enough to share them, that trust was developing. It was as if, without meaning to, they'd formed their own self-help group. She made a mental note to explore this thought more deeply: it might come in handy for Libby, her self-help junkie in *Living For Pleasure*.

She dragged her thoughts back to the here and now and wondered why Victor hadn't come. Perhaps he'd gone down with one of the many pre-Christmas bugs doing the rounds. For the first time it struck her how little they knew about him. Was he married? Or did he live alone? If so, and he was ill, did he have anyone he could call on for help?

Later that night, when she had tidied the kitchen, taken a load of washing out of the machine and put it to dry in front of the fire, Beth settled at the computer and tried to get on with Chapter Eight. It had been annoyingly obstinate in its unwillingness to play ball with her, but now she was determined to get the better of it. She had set herself a goal of a thousand words a day, and the more she wrote, the more convinced she became that an author often had little say over a character's input to a story. At first she had thought that this was because she was inept, but apparently the most experienced writers suffered from this phenomenon.

Mr Outta Laffs had told her this. Since their introductory chat on-line, they had slipped into a nightly habit of emailing each other. She wasn't a secretive person, but she had decided to keep quiet about Mr Outta Laffs. She knew what people would say if they were aware of what she was doing: that he could be anyone – at best a saddo with a dandruffy centre parting who wore white socks and grey shoes and still lived at home with Mother, or at worst a serial murderer who would track her down and add her to the scores of bodies he had buried under his patio.

But instinct – or was it misplaced hope of delusional proportions? – told her that Mr Outta Laffs fitted into neither category. He seemed as sane as she was, which, admittedly, didn't say much about him, and was just as concerned for his own safety as she was for hers.

How do I know you're the full shilling? [he'd asked in one of their early chats, after she'd admitted she was a woman].

What made you think I was?

Clever reply, a bona fide madwoman would have gone to great lengths to convince me she was firing on all cylinders.

I could be double-bluffing you.

Shucks, I hadn't thought of that. So where does that leave us?

Watching our backs, I guess.

Would that be before or after one of us has revealed themselves to be the psycho? No, don't answer that, I like a bit of suspense in my life. Tell me about your book. How's it going?

She liked the way he showed an interest in what she was doing, and that he understood how frustrating it could be. So far they had discussed little of a personal nature and had only broached the subject of their real names last night. Mr Outta Laffs had said,

In the spirit of you show me yours and I'll show you mine, my real name is Ewan. Yours?

Beth.

Short for Elizabeth?

No. Bethany.

Nice. Does anyone ever call you Bethany?

Not since I was a child.

Then I shall distance myself from the crowd and from time to time address you by your proper name. That's if you don't object.

She hadn't minded. Quite the reverse, in fact. It added an element of intimacy to their correspondence – not even Adam had called her by her full name. As Simone would say, the whole thing was straight out of the Tom Hanks and Meg Ryan movie, *You've Got Mail.*

At midnight, and after Nathan had announced he was going to bed, Beth logged on to the Internet. She was looking forward to chatting with Mr Outta Laffs – or, rather, Ewan.

But there was no message waiting for her as there usually was. She left one for him, rearranged the washing in front of the fire, wrote a few Christmas cards, then checked to see if there was a reply.

Nothing.

Disappointed, she switched off the computer. She felt almost as though she'd been stood up.

Ewan Jones gave the keyboard one last thump of frustration. But it was no use: no amount of coaxing was going to get the machine working again. The damn thing had crashed. For good. To his disgust, he knew he was looking at a complete overhaul. He'd had his faithful Hewlett Packard for almost six years, and he viewed the prospect of change with annoyance. He would have to summon help first thing in the morning. While he was about it, he ought to do the sensible thing and buy a laptop too. If nothing else, it would provide him with some decent back-up. For a borderline technophobe, this was pioneering stuff.

He turned out the light in his office and made his way to the kitchen, where he filled the kettle and plugged it in. While he waited for it to boil, he read the letter he'd left on the table earlier that evening after he'd got in from a hectic day in London. It was from a publisher who had read the first three chapters of his novel, *Emily and Albert.* It was a love story set in the fifties and based, loosely, on the illicit relationship between his parents, a young schoolteacher who taught at the local village school and a GP who was married to a well-heeled woman ten years his senior. They had never married but, after causing much scandal in their strait-laced Welsh mining community, they had fled across the border to take up residence in Shropshire where they produced a child: Ewan. For all sorts of reasons, his book was a secret project – only his daughter knew about it – and to his delight the publishers were interested and wanted to see the rest of the manuscript. All he had to do was finish it, along with everything else that needed doing yesterday. Which was why it was so irritating that his computer had chosen to give up the ghost. Still, as Alice would be the first to say, 'Stop moaning, Dad. Just bite the bullet and replace it.'

How easy life was for a twenty-year-old girl who possessed sufficient self-confidence to reduce Anne Robinson to a quivering jelly. Everything was achievable for Alice. She was resourceful and resilient, and since she'd left home for university, he'd missed her. The frequency and length of her visits were shrinking, and he was looking forward to her coming home for Christmas.

They had always been close, but when Alice had turned nine her mother had left him for a man in deepest Devon – a tofu-eating Buddhist – and father and daughter had become inseparable. Now and again Alice received a letter from her mother, but she had never gone to see her, although Ewan often suggested that she should. Over the years, he'd discovered when not to push things with a headstrong daughter.

He looked at the clock on the kitchen wall and thought about ringing her to share his good news, but as it was just after midnight, he decided it was too early. Alice had an active social life in Leeds, and she wouldn't be available to chat until the clubs had closed. Lord, how did she do it? He was no slouch when it came to late nights – invariably he burned the midnight oil to write – but that was different: the only energy he was exerting was brainpower. At the age of forty-six, that seemed to be all the heavy-duty excitement on offer to him.

He was continually told by friends and Alice – especially Alice – that he didn't have enough going on in his life. That he had to do something about his long-term single status. He sipped his tea thoughtfully, and wondered if an on-line friendship counted.

21

It was a freezing Saturday afternoon. A misty blanket of fog shrouded the whitened banks of the river and elegant willow branches drooped with brittle stiffness; here and there, gossamer cobwebs hung petrified with a dusting of sparkling frost.

In the warm, and to the sound of 'Walking In the Air' playing on the radio, Amber and Lucy were decorating the Christmas tree. Jack was regretting his choice – an artificial one from Taiwan that smelt of the polystyrene chips in which it had been packed, which now lay scattered over the living-room floor. He should have chosen a richly scented pine tree from the outdoor display at the garden centre, but it had been so cold that it had seemed a better idea to rush inside for a boxed one. He had given the girls free rein on choosing the ornaments and they had shown scant restraint for taste or expense. Consequently he was going to spend Christmas with the most kitsch tree this side of *It's A Wonderful Life*. There were strings of twinkling multi-coloured fairy lights, gaudy baubles of every shape, size and colour, swathes of tinsel and beads. These were now being draped over already heavily laden branches, and there was a strong possibility that the tree might collapse under the strain.

But Jack was happy to let the girls go wild: to watch their eager faces as they worked together so industriously was reward enough. Amber had complained earlier that they hadn't been allowed to touch the tree Tony had put up last night: he'd told them that he and Maddie would be decorating it when the girls had gone to bed. According to Lucy, the Norwegian blue spruce was so tall it had had to stay in the high-ceilinged hall. Doubtless Tony had gone into the forest, hacked it down with his bare hands, then carried it home over his heroic shoulder.

Down, boy! Jack told himself. Remember, this is the season of goodwill to all men.

And that includes Tony.

When he'd shown up first thing that morning to fetch the girls, Maddie had been at the hairdresser's getting ready for the party they were giving that evening – that was why he had been allowed to have the girls for two weekends on the trot. Tony had offered him a drink, but he'd refused, just as he always did, and had stationed himself in the hall, his hands shoved deep in his trouser pockets. He was there for one purpose only, to collect his daughters. Polite chit-chat wasn't on the agenda. Never would be.

'What do you think, Daddy?' Lucy was looking at him expectantly. 'Do you like it?'

He studied their handiwork, then scooped up his younger daughter so that she was eye to eye with the angel on top. 'It's the best I've ever seen. We'll be the envy of everyone in Maywood. Once word gets round, they'll be queuing up for a look.'

Giggling, Lucy pushed her face into his neck and kissed him. He lowered her to the floor, smiled at Amber and gave her a high five. 'Great work, partner! How about a drink and a mince pie?'

Lucy, always hungry and pin-thin, set off towards the kitchen. 'Are they home-made like Mummy's?' she called over her shoulder.

'But of course.'

Amber looked at him doubtfully.

'Okay,' he admitted. 'A hard-working chef at Marks and Spencer made them for me.'

The kitchen was too small to eat in, so they took their drinks and plates into the living room to admire the tree. It had a worryingly drunken tilt to it, but neither Amber nor Lucy noticed this defect. 'We'll need to put some presents around it,' Lucy said, sitting on the floor and surrounding herself with squeaking polystyrene chips. 'It looks too bare at the bottom. Have you got any?'

'Only yours.'

Lucy's eyes lit up.

Amber came and sat on the sofa next to Jack. 'Don't be stupid, Lucy, you can't have them yet. It's too soon. Christmas isn't for another two weeks.'

Lucy's face dropped and her chin disappeared into the neck of her sweater.

'Well,' said Jack slowly, 'you could have them this weekend if you want, seeing as I shan't be with you over Christmas.'

Lucy perked up again, but Amber, who was becoming more grown-up each time he saw her, shook her head decisively. 'No. I want to keep mine until the day. I want Dad's present to be special.' She snuggled close to him.

'So do I,' added Lucy, but her voice lacked conviction.

'And don't forget,' he said, 'you'll have lots of presents from Father Christmas too.' He knew Amber was too old to go along with such things, but he hoped Lucy was still a happy believer. She had been forced to cope so young with so much harsh reality and he wanted her to enjoy what innocence was left in her childhood.

With her legs stretched out in front of her, knees and ankles together, she looked at him thoughtfully. 'Do you think he'll be able to find us in France?'

'Of course he will. And, what's more, he'll deliver the presents to you before all the children here in England.'

'Why?'

'Because France is an hour ahead of us,' said Amber. 'Honestly, don't you know anything?'

'I know lots of things,' Lucy rallied. 'Like I know it's about to snow.' She picked up a handful of polystyrene chips and threw them at Amber. Laughing, Amber got down on the floor and started to tickle her sister. They rolled around together like a couple of puppies and Jack thought how good it was to see Amber relax: these days, she hardly ever let herself go.

Maddie had finally informed him last week of the arrangements for Christmas and New Year, and it was just as he'd feared: the girls were going to France for a two-week skiing holiday. 'Good of you to keep me up to date,' he'd said drily.

'Please don't be like that, Jack,' she'd said, impatiently. 'We've only just decided what we're doing.'

'And I don't suppose it crossed your mind that I might like to make plans for Christmas?'

'Look,' she sighed, 'I'm sorry. It's not as easy as you think.'

'What's so damned difficult? Tony looks at his calendar, reaches for his chequebook and that's it, you're off skiing. I should be so lucky to have that much choice.'

'If you can't be civil, Jack, I'd rather not speak to you.'

'Oh, believe me, the feeling's mutual.'

'I would have thought, if only for the sake of the children, you would make more of an effort.'

That had hurt and he'd lost his temper. 'And if you'd cared more for the children in the first place, you wouldn't have been carrying on with Tony behind my back!'

It had been another disastrous conversation, and once again he had told himself that it would be their last angry exchange. He would keep a lid on his anger. He would swallow his pride. And his bitterness. Except he didn't seem able to.

'Who's for another mince pie?' he asked, when the squeals of laughter died down.

'Me, please!' panted Lucy.

Jack smiled at her. 'Go on, Luce, help yourself. Amber?'

'No, thanks.'

'You sure?'

She pulled her ponytail back into shape. 'I'm on a diet.'

Convinced he'd misheard, Jack said, 'Come again?'

'It's no big deal, Dad, I just don't want to get fat.'

'There's about as much chance of that happening as there is of me becoming prime minister. What's brought this on?'

She shrugged.

'Does your mother know?'

Another shrug.

Appalled, he reached out to her and pulled her on to his lap. 'Listen to me carefully, Amber. You're perfect as you are. Girls of your age don't need to diet.'

She leaned away from him so that she could look him in the eye. 'But, Dad, all the girls at school are doing it.'

He stroked her cheek lovingly. 'Maybe that's because they're not as beautiful as you.'

She didn't say anything, but she leaned back into his embrace and he was reminded of all the times he'd held her as a baby and a toddler. She had been such a tactile little girl. Nowadays the hugs were rarer, but no less precious. He suddenly thought of the baby Clare was carrying and, to his sickening shame and dismay, he couldn't imagine feeling the same strength of love for this new child as he'd always felt for Amber and Lucy.

The next day, Jack drove the girls to have Sunday lunch with Clare. They were meeting her for the first time. He was on edge, as were they. He'd told them about Clare last night while they were eating a Chinese takeaway supper. He had tried to describe Clare as a friend, someone he'd got to know since he'd been on his own. It was the truth, but a little economical. He hadn't wanted to give Amber and Lucy any reason to think they weren't his number-one priority. 'If she's just a friend, why are *we* meeting her?' Amber had asked, her eyes weighing him up shrewdly. Lucy had stopped chewing on a spare-rib and was staring at him too.

'Well, I suppose she's a special friend and I'd like you to meet her.'

There was a pause.

'Are you going to marry her?' asked Lucy. The spare-rib was on her plate now and she was looking at him intently. He leaned across and wiped her chin with his paper napkin. 'There's a chance I might one day. But that's a long way off.'

'But you can't marry her! You're – you're still married to Mum.'

He switched his gaze to Amber. She looked as surprised by her outburst as he was. 'I know that,' he said soothingly, 'but one day I won't be.'

'But why?'

'Why what, Luce?'

'Why do you want to get married again? Don't you love us?'

'Love you? I'm mad about you. You mean the world to me. And nothing's ever going to change that. You'll always come first with me.'

He could tell they weren't buying it. They spent the rest of the evening bickering between themselves and went to bed tired and fractious. At breakfast Amber had refused to eat anything and Lucy had cried when her sister had knocked over her favourite mug, breaking the handle off and spilling juice over the floor.

It was not the start to the day he might have wished for, and as Jack parked in front of Clare's house, he had a feeling that things were about to get worse.

463

Straight away Jack could see Clare was tired. It was also clear that she had put a lot of effort into creating the perfect lunch for Amber and Lucy, food that she was sure would appeal to them – spaghetti Bolognese, then apple crumble and Häagen Dazs ice-cream. More than that, he sensed she was uptight, probably because she knew she was facing the two most critical judges she would ever encounter.

As the four of them sat at the table – decorated with Santa-shaped candles and red and gold crackers – the conversation grew ever more limited. Slumped in their seats, Amber and Lucy were picking uninterestedly at their food.

'Come on, you two, eat up before it gets cold,' he told them.

'But there are bits in the sauce,' Lucy complained, prodding her meal with her fork.

'Bits?' Clare repeated. She looked at the offending item on the plate and laughed. 'That's a mushroom.'

Lucy pulled a face. '*Ugh!* I don't like mushrooms. Mummy never gives them to us. They're slimy – and they might be toadstools. Toadstools are poisonous, aren't they? I saw it on television.'

'I promise you they're harmless, from the fruit and veg counter in Tesco's. Why don't you cover them up with some Parmesan and see if they taste any better?' Clare passed her the dish.

But Lucy didn't take it. 'Can I have some proper cheese, please?'

'Lucy, I don't think—'

'It's okay, Jack,' Clare interrupted. 'There's plenty of Cheddar in the fridge. It won't take me two seconds to grate some.'

He watched her leave the dining room, then turned to his daughters. 'Eat as much as you can, girls,' he said quietly. 'Clare's gone to a lot of trouble for you.'

Neither of them said anything, and when Clare came back into the room, he noticed she was frowning. 'You okay?' he asked, taking the dish of cheese from her. 'You look tired.'

She smiled unconvincingly. 'Knowing my luck I've got that bug that's doing the rounds at work.' She sat down heavily and drank some orange juice.

Ten minutes later, when it was apparent that Amber and Lucy weren't going to eat any more, Clare said, 'You can leave that if you want. I'm sorry I made something you don't like. Next time I'll check with you first, shall I? Perhaps the two of you could put a list together of your favourite meals. We'll call it your Yummy List. What do you think?'

An indifferent shrug was all she got in answer. Embarrassed by his daughters' behaviour, Jack was about to reprimand them when Clare stepped in before him. 'Hasn't anyone told you it's bad manners not to answer a question?'

Amber looked up sharply. 'And hasn't anyone ever told you to shut up?'

In the silence that followed, Clare stared at her across the table, then at

Jack, who was as shocked by Amber's rudeness as Clare had been. 'Amber, what on earth's got into you?' he said. 'Apologise this instant.'

'No!'

'Amber, I'm warning you. Say you're sorry.'

'Why should I when I'm not? I didn't want to come here and I certainly didn't want to eat this!' She raised her hand to point at her unfinished lunch, misjudged the distance and the plate, plus its contents, flipped over. Amber began to cry. 'I hate you,' she cried, looking straight at Clare, 'and I wish you'd drop down dead and leave my daddy alone.'

Jack got up abruptly and knocked his glass: red wine bled into the tablecloth. 'Amber, please, that's no way to speak to Clare, not when she's tried so hard to – Clare, are you all right? *Clare?*'

He watched her try to stand, but she swayed towards him. He grabbed hold of her and held her firmly. 'What is it, Clare? What's wrong?'

'Bathroom,' she whispered. 'You'll have to help me.'

Before they'd got as far as the stairs she was out cold. Keeping as calm as he could, Jack carried her through to the sitting room and laid her on the sofa. Lucy and Amber hovered behind him anxiously. 'Is she all right?' Lucy asked.

'She'll be fine,' Jack said, willing Clare to open her eyes. 'Don't worry. She'll be fine in a minute.'

'Is she going to die?' asked Amber.

His daughter's voice was so faint that Jack had to strain to catch it. He held her hand and squeezed it. 'Of course not,' he replied, keeping to himself that for most of the hair-raising journey to the hospital he had been terrified by the same thought. This is all my fault, he'd thought, driving as fast as he dared. What if she dies? How will I live with the guilt? And why didn't I call an ambulance? All the while, Clare had been dipping in and out of consciousness, alternating between gasps of pain, and frightening silences. Everything told him that she was losing the baby, but that this was no ordinary miscarriage. Des and Julie had lived through that nightmare twice, and he knew from them that what was happening to Clare was different.

'I didn't mean it when I said I wished she'd die,' Amber murmured. 'I'm sorry, Daddy. And I'm sorry about the spaghetti too.' Tears filled her eyes.

Jack hugged his daughter. 'None of that matters, sweetheart. Everything's going to be all right. Clare knew you didn't mean it.'

On his other side, Lucy was swinging her legs and flicking through a tattered comic. She said, 'But what's wrong with Clare, Daddy? What made her suddenly be so ill? Do you think it was those mushrooms? Maybe they *were* toadstools.'

'I don't know,' he lied, unable to meet her gaze. 'Let's wait and see what the doctor says, shall we?'

22

It was the day before Christmas Eve and Dulcie stared in disgust at the amount of food she had just lugged in from the car. It hadn't seemed such a mountain of greed when it had been in the supermarket trolley, but here, in her kitchen, it looked obscene. She began the tedious task of putting everything away in the cupboards, the fridge and the freezer.

If it weren't for her children's nostalgic fondness for a traditional Christmas with all the trimmings, Dulcie would have been happy to kiss goodbye to the whole wretched business and stay in a cottage somewhere remote and beautiful. Even being at home on her own had its appeal: she would be perfectly content with some simple but tasty food in the larder and a few bottles of wine. She never felt the need to live life at a hundred miles an hour, like Prue and Maureen who, if they didn't have a full diary of events, became bored and miserable and longed for the phone to ring. Or invented some reason to ring someone else. Prue had done exactly that yesterday morning, interrupting Dulcie's train of thought when she was trying to finish the short story she was submitting for a competition. She had admitted to the group only last Thursday that writing competitions were her weakness: 'They're addictive,' she had told them, 'so be warned.' With all the festive commitments, they had decided to take a couple of weeks off for Christmas and wouldn't be meeting now until the New Year. She would miss the group over the holiday period.

The last of the food put away, Dulcie stuffed the bundle of plastic carrier-bags into the bin and made a pot of tea. She rewarded her efforts with a glance at the newspaper, ignoring the beds she still had to make up and the towels that needed putting into the guest bathroom. There was plenty of time yet. Kate and Andrew – plus an unknown friend – wouldn't be arriving for another three hours. She had offered to drive across to Crewe to meet them off the London train, but they'd insisted they would catch the connecting train to Maywood – it would only add another forty-five minutes to their journey.

Andrew had been curiously secretive about his friend, saying only that he was bringing someone he was keen for her to meet. Which, naturally, added to Dulcie's speculation that she might soon be on the verge of a new role, that of mother-in-law. She liked the idea. She had asked Kate on the telephone what she knew, but Kate had replied, in what Dulcie recognised as evasive tones, 'Hardly anything, Mum, only that the pair of them seem ideally suited to each other. I don't think I've ever seen Andrew so happy.'

'So it's serious, then?'

'Depends what you call serious,' Kate said. 'Now, stop interrogating me, Mum, it's not fair. Have you put the tree up yet?'

'Yes.'

'The lights working?'

'You want lights?'

'Oh, Mum, don't say you haven't ... Oh, you're kidding, aren't you?'

'I might be. And before you ask, yes, I've bought chocolate money for you and several kilos of Brazil nuts, which will still be here for Easter.'

'But you can't have Christmas without Brazil nuts. It wouldn't be the same.'

'I know, darling – but just once, I'd like someone to eat them.'

At half past four, just as he'd promised he would, Richard telephoned. He was back at work now, part-time and under strict orders to take it easy – only two and a half days a week. That meant he was able to call Dulcie more regularly. They had even met for lunch. He was looking much better, and Dulcie grew more confident that he would soon be his old self.

But his opening remark had her clutching the receiver in panic. 'Dulcie,' he said, 'you don't have to agree to this, but we're throwing one of our usual Christmas drinks parties and Angela wants to invite you.'

'*Me?* Why? Oh, my goodness, does she know? Perhaps she wants to test us, observe us at close quarters as we try to avoid each other. Is that it, do you think?'

'Darling, calm down. It's nothing of the sort. Ever since you met that day in Maywood she's wanted to show off the house to you.'

'I don't care if she's turned it into a version of Graceland with Elvis singing "Love Me Tender" at the door, I don't want to see it.'

He laughed. 'But if it means we can be together for a few hours, wouldn't it be worth it?'

Dulcie couldn't believe what she was hearing. 'Are you saying *you* want me to come?'

'Yes, I do.'

'You're crazy!'

He laughed again. 'Only for you.'

'Richard Cavanagh, these dreadful clichés are going to have to stop.'

'There speaks the writer. So, you'll come?'

'I haven't decided. And you haven't told me when the party is being held?'

'Boxing Day.'

'But Kate and Andrew will be here.'

'Then bring them. The more the merrier. Besides, I'd like to meet them.'

She hesitated. 'I don't know, Richard. What if we give ourselves away?'

'Then so be it, I'm tired of the—'

'Richard,' she interrupted, 'you can't be serious.'

'I've never been more serious. I want to be with you, you know that. Oh, hell, my other phone's ringing, I'm going to have to go. Listen, Angela will probably call you later this evening, so do your best to sound surprised.'

'That won't be difficult.'

It was dark and raining hard when Dulcie drove to the station, but her spirits were high. On reflection, and despite the risk she was taking, she was pleased that she would see Richard over the Christmas period, which she never had before. A mistress was invariably denied such a pleasure.

When she drew up outside the station she saw that the London train must have arrived: the entrance was crowded with people sheltering under umbrellas waiting to be met. She spotted Kate and Andrew before they saw her, and she pipped the horn to attract their attention. Kate saw her first and Dulcie was just wondering where Andrew's girlfriend was when she caught sight of a dark-haired young man. He stood out from the crowd, tall and elegantly dressed in a thick overcoat with the collar turned up. He was strikingly handsome.

I don't think I've ever seen Andrew so happy.

Dulcie drew in her breath and hated herself for feeling shocked. Why had Andrew never told her? Had he thought her so narrow-minded?

These thoughts hurtled through her head in the time it took Kate to lead the way to where Dulcie was parked. Ordinarily she wouldn't get out of the car, would leave the children to throw their luggage into the boot, but on this occasion she felt she should act differently. She had to make it clear from the outset that she was delighted to meet her son's friend. Her son's *boyfriend*? Or was *partner* the more politically correct term? She went round to the other side of the car to hug and reassure Andrew: he looked strung out.

Miles proved the perfect houseguest and Dulcie liked him enormously – not just because he had presented her with a large box of her favourite *pâtes de fruits*. Throughout supper he had been amusing and helpful, and had further endeared himself to her by insisting that he and Kate would tidy the kitchen so that she and Andrew could have a quiet chat. 'Here you are,' he said, pulling a bottle of port out of a bag Dulcie hadn't noticed before. 'Take it with you to the sitting room. Oh, and perhaps you might enjoy this.' A Fortnum and Mason's ceramic pot of Stilton magically appeared.

She watched her son move nervously about the room, picking up a card from the mantelpiece, straightening a candle on the bookcase, even rearranging a bauble on the Christmas tree. She poured two glasses of port and waited for him to speak. She knew Andrew didn't like to be hurried: as a small boy he had always taken his time, whether it was in tying his shoelaces or spooning up the last drops of milk from his cereal. It had been a habit that had driven his sister mad. 'Hurry up!' she would yell at him, as she stamped her feet on the kitchen floor, terrified that she would be late for school. He never had made Kate late, but his placidity inflamed his hot-headed, volatile sister. Mothers instinctively know their children's strengths and weaknesses, and Dulcie had never doubted Kate's ability to cope with whatever life threw at her, but she had worried that Andrew, who had always been a gentle, thoughtful boy, would be taken advantage of. So far, her fears had been unfounded and Andrew had shown himself to be as tough as his sister. If not tougher. He worked ridiculously long hours in a London teaching hospital in a busy ear, nose and throat department. He'd always wanted to be a doctor, and his father would have been so proud that he had achieved his dream.

'I'm sorry, Mum,' he said at last, with his back to her as he examined another Christmas card. 'I should have told you, but the time never seemed right.' He put the card back into its place, turned slowly and met her eye. 'Are you okay about this, or are you putting on one of your famously brave faces?'

'Oh, Andrew, how well you know me, but how little too. Of course I'm all right about it. I'm just disappointed you thought you had to pick your moment to tell me. Surely you never doubted my reaction?'

He smiled. 'Telling your mother that you're gay – even as a supposedly intelligent grown man – isn't easy.'

'How long have you known?'

'Most people say they've known, deep down, for ever, but I wasn't sure until I left home. And before you ask and start to lose sleep over it, I haven't been promiscuous.'

She tried not to look too relieved. But he swooped in on her expression. 'I've always been selective, Mum. And careful.'

'And Miles?'

'Him too.'

'Good.' She kicked off her shoes and tucked her feet under her. Would Philip have handled this so well, she wondered. She liked to think so, but men could be funny about these things. After taking a sip of port, she said, 'How long has Kate known?'

'I told her – or, rather, she guessed – last year. Until then I'd done an excellent job of covering my tracks. Which was stupid and pointless.'

Disappointed that Kate, not normally known for her observational skills, had been more perceptive than she had, Dulcie said, 'I like Miles a lot. Kate told me she'd never seen you so happy. Is that true?'

He nodded and sank into the soft cushions on the sofa opposite her. 'It feels right with Miles.'

Thinking of Richard, she gazed into the flickering flames of the fire. 'I know exactly what you mean.'

'Is that what it was like between you and Dad?'

Dulcie was about to agree, when she changed her mind and decided to share her own secret life with her son. 'This might come as a surprise, Andrew, but I've been having an affair with a married man for the last three years. We're very much in love and I can't ever see the relationship coming to an end.' It was remarkably satisfying to see the shock on his handsome young face.

Especially when he smiled.

23

Lois sighed for the second time. 'Barnaby, do we have to have the television on?' she asked irritably. 'It's so antisocial. We ought to be playing a game. Anyone for Scrabble? Nathan, you'd like that, wouldn't you? Beth?'

It was Christmas Eve and they were in the sitting room at Marsh House. Seconds after setting foot over the threshold earlier that afternoon they had been under attack from a steady bombardment of food – ham and mustard sandwiches, mince pies, dates, a chocolate Yule log. Supper had followed, salmon *en croûte* with boiled or mashed potatoes, and a medley of vegetables. They'd got off lightly with dessert – there was only one: pear and almond tart with custard. The waistband of Beth's trousers already felt tight and she dreaded tomorrow when Lois would be up at the crack of dawn to prepare a mammoth lunch that would have brought a team of Sumo wrestlers to their knees. Beth had tried to limit their stay to one night, but Lois had insisted, 'Oh, Beth, you must stay a minimum of three. We see so little of you.'

Once Lois had decided on something, it was futile to resist. Over the years, Beth had tried several times to wriggle out of this annual duty, saying her parents wanted her and Nathan to spend Christmas with them. But Lois had no hesitation about playing her trump card: 'Since we lost Adam,' she'd say, in a small, wavering voice, 'you're all we have. If it weren't for you and Nathan we wouldn't bother with Christmas. There'd be no point.'

Other than wilfully upsetting her, Beth could see no way to change the situation. She supposed that the time would soon come when Nathan would make up his own mind how he would celebrate Christmas. Before long he would be armed with a variety of excuses: newly made friends to visit, work commitments to honour. Oh, how she envied him. Meanwhile, she would still be undergoing this ordeal.

Barnaby had switched off the television, bringing an abrupt end to a Christmas special of *Jonathan Creek*, which Beth had been enjoying, and was now back from his foray in the cupboard under the stairs where Lois kept their collection of ancient board games. 'Scrabble it is,' he announced, with a flourish. He began to set out the board on the coffee table and shook the bag of plastic tiles vigorously.

'There's no need to be quite so rough,' Lois reprimanded him. 'You'll rub

471

off the letters. Nathan, you can go first. Now, then, where are the pencils and the pad of paper I always keep in the box? Barnaby?'

'Clueless on that score, I'm afraid. Drink, anyone?'

As usual they let Lois win – the trick was to give her access to a triple-word score – and as usual they went to bed with strict instructions not to mind Lois getting up early on Christmas morning. 'No, no, Beth, there's no need for you to help. You make the most of a well-deserved lie-in.' Beth had taken her at her word one year and poor Barnaby had spent most of Christmas Day being subjected to mutterings that no one had offered to help.

After a whispered conversation with Nathan, who was in the room next to hers, Beth got ready for bed, slipping quickly into her thickest fleecy pyjamas. She had put a hot-water bottle into the bed earlier: now she shifted it down to her icy toes and pulled up the duvet around her neck.

An hour later she was still wide awake. If she'd been at home she would have got up and made herself a drink, but nothing would entice her to do the same at Marsh House. Instead, she switched on the bedside lamp and reached for the book she was reading. Ewan had recommended it and she was enjoying it immensely. Every time she opened it she felt as if she were connected to him in some way. Their correspondence, which was always a lively and entertaining exchange of views and opinions, had moved on considerably. Their favourite topic was the pros and cons of being a single fortysomething.

> Would you agree that people in their forties are at their most reflective and have become more aware of their age and appearance? [she had asked Ewan.]

> Only those who are single. The married ones are too busy for such navel gazing. They have their hands full pretending to their divorced friends that couples have a much better time.

> So that's why my married friends are obsessed with trying to fix me up. They want me to be in the same boat as them.

> Got it in one!

She knew now that Ewan was forty-six, that he was divorced and had a daughter called Alice, who was two years older than Nathan. In his own words he had 'reluctantly' let his only child fly the nest to go to university:

> It was the worst day of my life driving her to Leeds and leaving her there. I was tempted many times during the journey home to turn around and go back for her. I'm afraid that makes me sound a hopeless case.

But I shall be far worse when the same thing happens to me next year. I shall behave very badly, I know. I'll worry all the time about the state of his diet and underpants.

But that's the prerogative of being a mother: you're allowed to behave badly. It's we fathers who are supposed to wear the stiff upper lip.

She had also discovered where Ewan lived: in Suffolk, on the coast. It sounded idyllic: a writer's paradise with views out to sea. She had told him a little about where she lived and that her view when she wrote was of the park. She was itching to know what he looked like, but couldn't pluck up the courage to ask for fear of . . . well, appearing shallow. Or, worse, pushy, as if she was angling to turn their correspondence into something it clearly wasn't. All the same, it would be nice to have an image of him rather than the mugshot she had created in her mind. She'd decided that he had short dark hair with just a hint of grey and that he was tall, perhaps a little overweight – he'd mentioned he was allergic to strenuous exercise, but that he liked to take a daily constitutional along the beach, either first thing in the morning before work, or in the evening. When she'd asked what he did for a living, he'd told her he ran his own public-relations business:

My job is to make people suspend their disbelief and accept what they wouldn't ordinarily go along with. It's all in the spin, as they say.

She still hadn't told anyone about the mystery man in her life, as she now thought of Ewan, and she knew that it was dangerous to become fond of someone she had never met. It would be so easy, in view of how little she knew about Ewan, to turn him into something he wasn't, to attach feelings to him that, in reality, were misplaced. It was all very well having a few things in common, such as single parenthood and writing, but what did they *really* know of each other? For all she knew he was a foaming-at-the-mouth racist. And, of course, there was still a chance that he was a serial killer.

But why should any of this matter? she asked herself, as she turned over, still waiting for sleep. Because, as naïve as it sounded, she liked her mystery man, and was convinced that if they met they would get on. She had missed him when he hadn't emailed her for some days – it turned out that his computer had gone wrong and he'd had to replace it. When he'd reappeared on her screen, she'd been so pleased that she'd had to acknowledge how disappointed she'd be if their e-correspondence ended.

She had also forced herself to accept that part of the attraction for her was that Ewan was safe. He was a man with whom she could chat quite openly and not feel threatened. Or, more importantly, because he wasn't 'real' – he was a virtual man floating around in cyberspace – she could allow herself to like him and not feel disloyal to Adam. No one needed to tell her that this was absurd, that after all these years of widowhood she was at liberty to have a relationship with another man, but with Lois's determination to keep Adam's memory alive it was often an uphill struggle to believe it.

At least it was progress. She was now thinking in terms of climbing the hill. And, if she was honest with herself, she got a thrill out of having a secret man in her life. She could let her imagination run wild and conjure up any number of lovely scenarios. It was easy to be in love with someone you hardly knew – you could fill in the rest to your own liking and have the best of all worlds. At the end of the day, romantic love was only a projection of one's thoughts, and why shouldn't she indulge in a little of that?

Nathan woke to the sound of his grandmother singing along to 'Once in Royal David's City', which was playing on the radio downstairs. It was still dark but the noise in the kitchen beneath his room told him that Lois had been up for a while. He buried his head under the pillow. 'Happy Christmas, one and all,' he muttered.

He thought of Billy – lucky Billy – who was spending Christmas in Barbados with his family. His friend had invited him to join him, but even if his mum had been able to afford the air fare he wouldn't have left her to cope alone at Marsh House. To torture himself, he pictured Billy sitting in the shade of a palm tree downing a beer. He held the picture in his mind's eye for some time, telling himself that, one day, that would be him.

But at least he was having a break from college. It had been a busy term, what with *The Importance of Being Earnest* and applying for a place at university. Exeter had made him an offer, as had Sheffield and Hull; he was still waiting to hear from his first choice, Nottingham. He would have to be patient.

The play had gone well and he'd been the only one in the cast not to dry. Even Billy had messed up on the opening night and had had to rely on Nathan to carry him until he'd recovered and got back on track. Lois and Barnaby had had front-row seats on the last night; afterwards, Lois had said how like his father he was on stage. 'Nathan has such a very real presence when he performs,' she'd said to his mother, 'and we all know from whom he gets that.' Nathan had wanted to ask why his mother could never be allowed to take her share of the credit.

That night Jaz had been in the audience, too. He'd hoped she might come to the end-of-show party, but she hadn't.

They hadn't spoken since the night he'd gone round to her place and he'd stupidly asked if he could kiss her. She couldn't have made it any more obvious that she didn't fancy him – not that he'd had any intention of getting her into bed. The memory still made him flinch.

*

Christmas Day wore on slowly and tediously. Vast quantities of food were pressed upon them, paper hats were worn, terrible jokes were read out. After the Queen's speech, they were given the go-ahead to exchange presents.

As a child it had always been Nathan's job to gather up the parcels from beneath the tree and hand them round. Now, at eighteen, it was still his job: Grandma never saw the point in doing away with a tradition of her own devising. She'd probably get him to act the part of Marsh House Santa when he was a father. In her eyes, he would always be a small boy, the image of her own small boy. Just as his mother would never be anything but Lois's daughter-in-law. Her possession, in other words. He gave his mother a present from Lois. Neither of them needed to unwrap it to know that it was a tea-towel. They had a kitchen drawer stuffed full of them. Next he handed Barnaby a small book-shaped gift with a tag on it bearing Lois's handwriting. Again, no surprises here. It would be a pocket-sized Lett's diary.

'Nathan, dear, before you give me anything, I want you to find a present for yourself. There's a special one for you.'

He did as his grandmother said and reached for a large, flat object, which he knew would be yet another wildlife calendar. He'd been mad about animals when he was six, but now he couldn't give a toss if every panda or red-arsed monkey disappeared off the face of the earth. 'No, not that one,' Lois said. 'The small one to the left of it.'

He held up a long, thin package. 'This one?'

She smiled. 'Take care how you open it – you'll see why.'

He was suddenly the focus of the room. Dreading what he'd find, and preparing himself to look pleased, he sat next to his mother. The wrapping paper dispensed with, he held an old velvet jewellery box. He sensed his mother stiffen beside him, but Lois was leaning forward in her seat. He opened the case and saw a watch inside. It was a Rolex, old and scratched, but he knew its significance. He took it out of the box and looked at it closely. He had no recollection of it.

'It belonged to your father,' Lois said unnecessarily. 'I was keeping it for when you were twenty-one, but I thought that since you've grown into such a sensible young man, you'd be careful enough to have it now. Go on, put it on. Let me see how it looks on you.'

But he couldn't do as she asked. Burning from within, he felt an uncontrollable desire to throw the watch on to the carpet and grind it under the heel of his shoe.

'Nathan?'

He looked up, saw the expectation on his grandmother's face. He was confronted with a choice: he could either do as she said and allow her to bully and manipulate him and his mother for ever, or he could take a stand. He swallowed and made his choice. Very carefully, he put the watch back into its box and snapped the lid shut. He stood up and gave it to his grandmother. 'Thank you,' he said, 'but I don't want it.'

She stared at him, as if not understanding what he'd said. 'But, Nathan, it was your father's. We bought it for him for his twenty-first birthday. He wore it every day. He—'

'Didn't you hear me? I said I don't want it. And if you make me take it, I'll throw it away. I want nothing from my father. Absolutely nothing. I'm sick to death of hearing his bloody name.' He was almost shouting, and out of the corner of his eye he could see that his mother was pale and shocked. Across the room Barnaby's jaw had gone slack. Nathan could see that he was hurting everyone, but he didn't care. This had been waiting to happen for a long time. Wanting to hurt Lois some more, he said, 'And if Adam King was such a fine man, as you keep saying, why the hell didn't he sort out the mess he'd created? Why did he have to dump us in it by killing himself? He was nothing but a pathetic coward and I hate him for what he did to Mum.'

He heard his grandmother start to cry, but he didn't hang around. He grabbed his coat from the hook in the hall, the keys in the pocket, and slammed the door after him. He threw himself into his mother's car, started it and hit the accelerator. Gravel flew into the air as he took off down the drive. He didn't know where he was going, or what he would do when he got there, but he had to get as far away from his grandmother as he could.

Beth stood on the doorstep and watched her son narrowly miss colliding with one of the gateposts. Near to tears, her arms locked around herself, fear flooded her.

What if history repeated itself?

Consumed by a frightening anger she had never known before, Beth went back into Marsh House. Lois was going to pay for this. Because of her selfish, blind stupidity she had made Nathan act dangerously out of character. If anything happened to him – God forbid that it did – she would see to it that Lois carried the guilt of this day to her grave.

24

After checking that the oven was at the right temperature, Richard slid a tray of vol-au-vents on to the top shelf. Behind him, Henry and Victoria, home for Christmas, were slicing oranges to go into the mulled wine. The three of them were chatting and laughing together. They didn't notice Angela come into the kitchen. 'You all seem very cheerful,' she said. Her brisk voice instantly quietened them.

Closing the oven door, Richard said, 'How about a drink, Angela? A quick gin and tonic before everyone descends on us?'

'Thanks,' she said. 'I think I will.' She reached for her apron to protect the new blouse and skirt she was wearing and tied it round her waist. Her decisive movements suggested she was making the effort to take charge. She picked the wooden spoon out of the pan of mulled wine, put it on the draining-board and found a ladle. 'Don't you think you ought to go and change, Henry?' she said.

'Plenty of time yet.' He shambled across the kitchen towards his father and added a splash more gin to his own glass. It was nearly twelve o'clock, and Henry was still in his pyjamas and dressing-gown; his hair was sticking up in clumps on top of his head. As a small boy he'd hated getting dressed and had gone to extraordinary lengths to avoid it – he still did. But it was a trait at odds with the ambitious and hard-working thirty-four-year-old man he had become. He worked in the City as a broker for an American bank, drove a Porsche, and had recently bought a flat in Canary Wharf. By his own admission, he was filthy stinking rotten rich. Richard always found it difficult to equate the confident Henry of today with the bungling little boy he and Angela had frequently taken to hospital because, yet again, he had tripped and bumped his head.

He handed Angela her drink and joined his daughter, who was clearing up the mess around the chopping-board, fastidiously wiping and tidying: a habit she had picked up from him. Out of the four children Victoria was the quietest and, perhaps, the most intuitive. She kept her opinions to herself, and only expressed them if pushed. When she did, they were always worth listening to. She rarely judged others and could always be relied upon to defuse an inflammatory situation. In many ways, she reminded Richard of Dulcie: they were both easy to be around.

*

Nervously drumming her fingers on the steering-wheel while she waited for the traffic-lights on Bridge Street to change, Dulcie wondered if it wasn't too late to back out. She must have been mad to accept Angela's invitation. She had even tried to use her children as an excuse to stay away.

'Oh, bring them too,' Angela had said.

'But Andrew's got a friend with him. We couldn't possibly impose—'

'Nonsense. She's perfectly welcome too.' Like Dulcie, Angela had assumed that Andrew's friend was a girl.

'I'm not sure.'

'Henry and Victoria will be here so there'll be other young people for them. They won't have to stick with us old codgers.'

Dulcie had taken umbrage at that: Angela might see herself as past it, but Dulcie certainly didn't.

'Wakey, wakey, Mum, the lights have changed.'

She looked at her daughter. 'What? Oh, silly me.' She drove on. 'I hope you won't be too bored at this party,' she said. 'You could have stayed at home and amused yourselves.'

'It's always good to broaden one's horizons,' Kate said. 'And, anyway, didn't you say an eligible man's going to be there? I need to cast my net wherever I can – I'm not getting any younger.'

In the back of the car, Miles laughed. 'Oh, Kate, don't sell yourself too cheap.'

'It's all right for you two soul-mates,' she retaliated, with good humour. 'You've joined the ranks of the happily hitched. I'm almost thirty – only five months to go – and if I'm not careful I'm going to turn into a bitter old spinster. So, Mum, tell me again about the eligible bachelor.'

'I never said he was eligible, or that he was a bachelor,' Dulcie said, disconcerted. 'He'll probably turn out to be thoroughly obnoxious with bulging eyes and buck teeth.'

Kate tutted and Dulcie exchanged a look of concern with Andrew in the rear-view mirror. Having shared her secret with him, she had made him promise not to tell anyone about her affair with Richard, and she knew from his expression that he was thinking as she was – that it would be disastrous for Kate to form an attachment with Richard's son, Henry. She considered telling Kate now about her and Richard, to warn her off, but she decided against it. Andrew could be relied upon to be discreet – hadn't he proved that with his relationship with Miles? – but Kate could not. As a child, Kate's face had always given her away. Philip used to say that she was as honest and open as a book. With Fiery Kate, as he called her, you always knew where you stood. But despite her apparent toughness, she was easily hurt and capable of holding a grudge for as long as it took the guilty party to make amends. She had tremendous staying power, which Dulcie presumed was an asset in the dog-eat-dog world of advertising where Kate worked.

But perhaps she was being unfair to her daughter, pigeonholing her too rigidly. Hadn't she kept quiet about Andrew's relationship with Miles? For a split second Dulcie was seriously tempted to tell her daughter about Richard, but the moment was lost when Kate leaned forward and switched on the radio, then tutted at her mother's choice of music station. 'How can you listen to that bland trivia?' she said, fiddling with the buttons until the authoritative tones of Radio 4 filled the car.

Richard had almost given up hope of Dulcie coming. All the other guests had long since arrived, even those who made a habit of being late. With several drinks inside them, they were happily swapping Christmas Day gripes: of turkeys that hadn't tasted of anything, pullovers that would have to be returned to M&S, of livers and waistlines that would never be the same again. As well as friends and neighbours from the village, and the odd parent from school, they had invited some of his colleagues from the office, and if he hadn't been on such tenterhooks waiting for Dulcie to appear, he would have considered the party a success.

He was on his way to the kitchen to make sure that plenty of wine and soft drinks were available when he heard the doorbell ring. His heart leaped. Dulcie? 'I'll get it,' he called to Angela, who was in the sitting room instructing Christopher and Nicholas to pass round the canapés.

He opened the door and saw, to his delight, that he'd been right. He smiled the smile of a congenial host and shook hands with Dulcie. 'Mrs Ballantyne, how lovely to see you again, and after all this time. How are you? Come on in.' Her reply was lost in the moment of closing the door behind them, and he switched his attention to her family. He introduced himself, recognised Kate and Andrew at once from the numerous photographs Dulcie had of them around her house. Her son, he noted, took after her: he had the same wide cheekbones and the broad forehead that Dulcie covered with a wispy fringe. The daughter was pretty, with dark eyes and an expression that was alert and friendly. She had her mother's wide smile. Lastly, he shook hands with a good-looking man whom he suspected might be of interest to Victoria. 'Hi,' he said. 'You must be Andrew's friend up from London.'

'That's right. Miles. That's the name, not the distance. Sorry, it's a shocking joke and I really ought to know better by now.'

Richard smiled, grateful that someone was helping the conversation along. 'Let me take your coats and get you a drink.' He ushered them in the direction of the kitchen, weaving a path through the crush of guests. He hoped he appeared to anyone observing him as good old Richard getting drinks for a group of new arrivals, not a man who was cheating on his wife and had had the audacity to bring 'the other woman' into the family home. Some would be appalled by what he was doing. 'Who'd have thought Richard Cavanagh capable of such duplicity?' he could hear his critics say. 'And we thought he was such a decent man. But you know what they say, it's always the quiet ones. The ones you'd least suspect.'

Yet as contemptible as his behaviour might seem to others, it didn't feel so awful to him. What's more, he wanted to put an arm round Dulcie's shoulders and declare to everyone that this was the woman he loved, that he had never felt so strongly for anyone as he did for her. He wanted to share his good fortune, to say, 'Look, happiness is a choice. Leave it too late, and you'll regret it.'

Much as he was tempted to devote his time to Dulcie and her family, he couldn't: there were other guests to see to, drinks and food to organise. Moreover, he ought to find Angela and tell her that Dulcie had arrived. But before he did that, he stood back to observe Dulcie as she chatted with Juliette, a young legal executive who'd recently joined his department at work. Seeing how relaxed and fully composed Dulcie was, and loving her for it, he knew with certainty that this was the woman with whom he wanted to spend the rest of his days.

He was so sure of what he wanted that he knew the time had come to tell Angela. He would go quietly. He would do everything in his power to make their parting bearable. He would give her the house, most of their savings, and whatever percentage of his pension she was entitled to. More, if necessary. And the boys, Christopher and Nicholas, they mustn't suffer. He would do whatever it took to keep the pain, the confusion and upheaval to a minimum.

From across the room, Dulcie caught him looking at her. She gave him one of her half-smiles and his heart swelled. He raised his glass to her and wandered off to the conservatory to find Angela. She was nowhere to be seen, but he discovered that this was where the 'young people', as Angela called them, were hiding. They seemed to be getting along well enough. 'Sorry to barge in,' he said. 'You all okay for drinks?'

'Fine, thanks, Dad, though some food wouldn't go amiss.'

He smiled at Henry. 'Give me a hand, then, and we'll get you sorted with some supplies.'

Back in the kitchen, loading up a tray of dips, crudités, canapés and anything else that was going, Richard said, 'How's your sister getting on with Miles?'

Henry shook his head. 'Definitely not her type.'

'You surprise me. I would have thought he was exactly her type. Smartly dressed and very good-looking.'

Henry lowered his voice. 'And very *gay*, Dad.'

'Oh. *Oh*, I see.'

'He's Andrew's partner.'

'Really? Dulcie never . . . I mean Mrs Ballantyne never said anything.'

'Don't sound so middle-class and shocked. Why should she say anything? It's no one else's business. But, between you and me, I'm rather taken with the lovely Kate.'

'Kate?'

'Your memory going, Dad? Mrs Ballantyne's daughter. I think if I play my cards right, we'll be seeing each other in London. Often, if I have anything to do with it.'

Richard slowly absorbed what his son was saying. He pushed the tray of food at Henry. 'I've just remembered something I was supposed to do.' He hurried back to the sitting room to find Dulcie. He had to tell her that under no circumstances could *his* son and *her* daughter become involved with each other.

25

Intolerable: insufferable, impossible, from hell, insupportable, unendurable, unbearable.

Jaz closed the thesaurus with a weighty slap. None of those words came close to what she had to put up with. If Dr Roget and his pals had had first-hand experience of a Christmas with the Raffertys, they'd have thought of something far more explicit and appropriate. But, try as she might, she couldn't think of any one word that expressed the horror of living with her family. Finally, she admitted defeat and picked an adjective at random: *insufferable*. It would do for now, until she could think of something better.

The more she wrote, the more she found that sometimes words were inadequate: they just didn't supply the right meaning. It was as if they turned into a strait-jacket that wrapped itself round her brain. She knew how she felt, right enough, but couldn't convey it on paper. The thought depressed her: now even the secret world in which she lost herself was mocking her. Maybe she wasn't cut out to be a writer: she had been fooling herself all along.

She switched off the computer, and went to lie on the bed and stare up at the sloping ceiling. It was proving the longest, most boring Christmas known to mankind. They'd trailed round all the relatives, or had had them here, and if Tamzin and Lulu asked her one more time to play Twister with them she'd have to hit the booze cupboard big-time. To make it worse, there was no one to hang out with or chat to on the phone – Vicki was away, visiting her grandparents. Never before had Jaz longed so much for a holiday to be over. She'd done all her homework and was all revised-out in readiness for her mock exams the first week of the new term. There was nothing else to do.

She'd hoped that her mother might take her clothes-shopping when the sales started, but it looked like it wouldn't happen now. Not with Mum being pregnant. Dad was worse than a hen these days, fussing over his Molly-doll as if she was a piece of china. And Mum had gone all airy-fairy. She hadn't been the slightest bit cross when she came home from Tenerife with Dad and found her favourite ornament broken and a stain on the carpet. The only good thing to come out of that incident was that her sisters had kept quiet about the policeman who had reprimanded them. To this day, they still thought Nathan had been a real plain-clothes officer, and every now and then, when they really got on her nerves, she would remind them quietly that if they didn't leave her alone she would tell Mum and Dad they'd behaved so badly that she'd had to call the police.

She thought again of what a good job Nathan had done in putting the wind up her sisters, and smiled. Anyone who could do that was a true hero. But the smile soon disappeared when she thought of what an idiot she'd been. She had overreacted and now she had lost Nathan as a friend. And she would give anything, right now, to have his company.

She flipped over on the bed and buried her face in the pillow. Oh, she'd made such a mess of it. Hundreds of times she had wanted to pluck up the courage and apologise to him, put things back to how they'd been, but she hadn't been able to face him. She had watched him in the play and thought him brilliant – far better than Billy, who everyone always raved about. She hadn't gone with Vicki to the party after the last-night performance: her pride wouldn't let her. She couldn't bear the thought that he might throw her apology back in her face, in front of everyone.

Once, at the writers' group before Christmas, when Jack was talking to Dulcie, she had almost asked Beth how Nathan was, just to see if he had mentioned her to his mother. But, again, her nerves and pride had got the better of her.

If she thought of Nathan too much, and how he must despise her for her immaturity, she felt sick with shame, so it was better to push him out of her mind.

It was a pity the writers' group wasn't meeting during the holiday – at least that would have given her something worthwhile to focus on. She missed her secret Thursday nights out.

Bored, and restless with frustration, she decided to go for a walk. She hunted for her favourite baggy jumper among the pile of clothes on the end of her bed. On her way downstairs she met Phin coming up. From the look of him he was just back from a night out. There was a massive love bite on his neck and he stank of booze and fags. He yawned hugely and messed up her hair. 'Hey there, little sis, how's it going?'

'Fine until you appeared stinking like a brewery. I see you've had some old bat chewing at your neck again.' She tried to slip past him, but he didn't move, just stood there grinning at her. 'Phin, can you figure on your own how to shift yourself, or do you want me to help?' She dodged round him and made her escape. Her mother was in the kitchen, listening to the radio while she stripped the turkey carcass – it would be turkey curry that evening, it always was the day after Boxing Day. She noticed how tired she looked, and felt sorry for her. 'Need a hand, Mum?' she asked.

Molly looked up. 'That's okay, Jaz, I'm just pottering. Where are you off to?'

'I need to fill my lungs with some of that stuff they call fresh air. Are you sure you don't need any help?'

'No. Off you go and enjoy yourself.'

Disappointed, Jaz shut the back door behind her. She hadn't wanted to do anything as gross as pick over turkey bones, but part of her would have liked her mother to want to include her in something. They never did anything together, these days. She frowned. When had she become an outsider in her own home, so out of step with everyone else?

The day was cold, almost freezing, and the sky was grey and heavy with the promise of snow. There was that lovely quiet muffled feeling in the air that she'd loved as a young child. She had always known when it was going to snow. She pulled down the long sleeves of her jumper, covered her hands to keep them warm and headed towards the park.

At a loose end, Nathan was standing at the kitchen window. The park was busy with young families: small children wearing helmets were trying out new bikes, and others were showing off their skills on shiny new scooters. But there was no mistaking the solitary figure in black jeans and knee-length baggy sweater that came into his field of vision from the right of the park. It was Jaz.

He watched her play with one of her long plaits as she settled on a wooden bench, and thought how much he missed her company. Missed her as a good friend, someone with whom he could talk. It still annoyed him that he had botched things so spectacularly. Perhaps he should apologise. He decided that there was no time like the present, slipped on his coat, locked the door after him, and went downstairs to tell his mother – who was knocking back mince pies and dry sherry with Miss Waterman – that he was going out.

He took the short-cut route to the park, through the gate at the end of Miss Waterman's garden. He made his way over to where Jaz was still sitting on the bench. 'Hi,' he said casually, when he was almost upon her.

She looked up, startled. She must have been deep in thought. 'Oh. Hi.'

'Okay if I join you?'

She slid along the wooden seat to make room for him. 'Good Christmas?' she asked.

'You don't want to know.'

'It must have been better than mine. You've met Tamzin and Lulu. Need I say more?'

'Yeah, well, while you were having a picnic with them, I stirred up World War Three.'

'Who with? Not your mum, surely?'

He shook his head. There were many things in his life that he would always remember, but the look on his mother's face when he'd arrived home late on Christmas night – he'd known she would be at the flat, just as she'd known he wouldn't go back to Marsh House – was one that would stay with him for ever. She had been crying, and he'd known why: he had put her through seven hours of hell. She had been convinced that he was lying dead in the wreckage of their car. But she hadn't lost her temper, as he'd expected her to. 'I was too relieved that you were alive to be cross with you,' she'd admitted later. 'Besides, I took out my anger on Lois.'

'Really?'

'I'm afraid that, between us, we've blotted our copybook at Marsh House. We won't be welcome there for a long time.'

'I didn't mean that to happen.'

'I know. But until your grandmother sees sense and understands why you lost it with her, I think we have to accept that she will not be "at home" to either of us in the foreseeable future.'

'You're making light of this, aren't you?'

'I'm not sure I can do it any other way.'

He didn't ask for the details of what had been said in his absence, but before going to bed, she said, 'Nathan, promise me that you'll never drive again when you're not fully in control of your emotions. Driving while out of your mind with anger is as dangerous as being drunk behind the wheel.'

It was only in the morning, in the cold light of day, that he realised how selfish he had been. He hadn't thought about anyone's feelings but his own. He had never known such rage, and it had been directed solely at his grandmother. He had hated her with all his being. Hated her for pretending she could make his father live through him.

Aware that a silence had settled on them, and that he hadn't given Jaz a proper answer to her question, Nathan turned and saw that she was looking at him intently, but when his gaze met hers, she lowered her eyes. He couldn't work her out, couldn't decide whether she liked him or not. 'You look cold,' he said. 'Do you want to walk?'

She was on her feet almost before he'd got the words out. 'It looks like it's going to snow,' she said.

They wandered down towards the pond where a family with two young children were feeding the ducks. They continued along the path, and when a boy riding a bike much too big for him came careering in their direction, Nathan instinctively pulled Jaz out of harm's way. When the boy had passed, he let go of her, embarrassed. 'Sorry,' he said. 'That's an even blacker mark against my name, isn't it? Rough-handling in the name of safety probably goes down as well as asking for a kiss.'

She stared at him, her brows drawn together. For a nasty moment she looked so furious that he thought she was about to thump him. But then, just as he noticed a snowflake land on top of her head, her face broke into a tentative smile. Once again, just as he had on the night of Kirsten's party, he had the urge to kiss her. This time, though, he didn't ask permission, simply leaned in close and pressed his mouth gently to hers. Her lips were icy cold, the same as his, but he sensed no coolness in her. He wrapped his coat around her shivering body and looked down into her pale, lightly freckled face. 'Just for the record,' he murmured, 'I have no immediate plans to drag you off into the bushes for a mindless shag.'

She stiffened within his arms. 'Please don't tease me.'

He held her firmly, understanding, now, the real reason why she had brushed him off before: she had thought he would treat her like Billy would. 'I'm not,' he said. 'I'm trying to put your mind at rest.' He felt her relax and kissed her again. And, as the snow fell slowly around them, he felt strangely at peace. Being with Jaz made him happy. Holding her made the rest of the world disappear.

No more Lois.

And no more Adam King.

26

For five consecutive years Des and Julie had thrown a New Year's Eve party, but this year, now that they had Desmond Junior, they had agreed to give tradition a miss and settle for a low-key evening with a bottle of bubbly and Angus Deayton on the telly.

But, to Des's disappointment, even those simple plans had been thwarted.

After he had given in to Julie's last-minute insistence that her friend couldn't possibly spend New Year's Eve alone – 'Not after all she's gone through' – Clare had arrived yesterday afternoon to stay the night. When she wasn't berating Jack for being such a bastard, she was begging them, as the wine flowed, to make him see sense. 'I'm sure he's terrified of being hurt again,' she'd said weepily, clutching at the finest of straws. 'That's why he's done this. He cares for me, really. I know he does.'

It didn't matter what he or Julie said, Clare wouldn't listen: it wasn't advice she wanted but the opportunity to vent her feelings. She was wretchedly unhappy and, in Des's opinion, given her weakened state after what had happened, she shouldn't have been drinking so much. If at all. In the end, so that they could go to bed and get some much-needed sleep – it was nearly four in the morning – Des had promised to talk to Jack.

Now, at five past seven, while he was giving a perky little Desmond his breakfast, Des knew it wouldn't do any good. Jack had made his decision and, for what it was worth, Des was right behind him. Okay, maybe his timing might have been better – telling Clare it was over while she was still recovering from an ectopic pregnancy hadn't been the smartest or most sensitive way to handle it – but the upshot was that Clare had to accept she and Jack were finished.

Spooning mushy Weetabix into his son's open mouth, then scraping off the excess goo, Des hoped that his friendship with Jack hadn't been damaged. Friends were often expected to take sides in these situations and currently Julie had little sympathy for Jack. What she refused to acknowledge was that while Clare had been carrying his child Jack had been prepared to do the decent thing and stick by her, even though he had admitted to Des that he didn't love her and didn't think he ever would.

Lost in his thoughts, he didn't hear footsteps coming into the kitchen.

Clare was standing right next to Desmond Junior's high chair before he noticed her. 'Hi,' he said. 'How're you feeling?' He didn't need to ask: still in her nightclothes with traces of yesterday's makeup – what had survived the tears of last night – smudged around her eyes, she looked hollowed out.

'In need of a cup of coffee,' she murmured.

Desmond Junior whipped his head round at the sound of her words and the spoonful of Weetabix that Des had been about to slip into his mouth smeared across his cheek. He put up a small chubby hand, grinned, then rubbed it into his hair. Des put the bowl of cereal prudently out of reach and fetched a cloth from the sink. 'Sit down and I'll put the kettle on for you,' he said. 'Breakfast will be a while yet. If you and Julie are good, I might do us one of my famous fry-ups. Gotta start the year as we mean to go on.'

She dropped into the chair opposite the one he'd vacated. 'Sorry, Des, I'll have to pass.'

'Nonsense,' he said cheerily. 'You need building up, and there's nothing like a plate of eggs, bacon and devilled kidneys to put the colour back into your cheeks—'

He didn't get any further. Clare's complexion had turned green – not quite the colour he'd had in mind – and she rushed from the kitchen to the downstairs loo. Poor girl. A hangover as well as a broken heart. Hardly the best way to start the New Year. He wondered how Jack was feeling this morning.

Jack had been up since six-thirty and was on his fourth cup of coffee. He was in the spare room doing the one thing that kept him from dwelling on Clare. So long as he focused on the troubles and dilemmas of his characters, he could block out the events of the last few weeks.

But not entirely. He would always feel responsible for putting Clare through such a painful ordeal. The guilt he'd felt while she had been undergoing the emergency operation to remove the tiny foetus that had caused one of her Fallopian tubes to rupture had been unlike any he had ever known. And while it was far from ideal that Amber and Lucy had witnessed the frightening scene of Clare's collapse, he had been glad they were with him at the hospital: they gave him something to think of other than his own culpability. When he had been told that the operation had been a success and that Clare was going to be all right, he had almost wept with relief.

Shortly afterwards, and he knew it had been unthinkably selfish, he remembered that he'd had a lucky escape, and that he had to act on it . . . as soon as Clare was over the worst. But decisive action came sooner than he'd intended.

With her parents staying while she convalesced at home, Clare started talking in earnest about how much she wanted Jack to move in with her. He couldn't lie to her or give her false hope and, as her mother loaded the washing-machine downstairs and her father fixed a wonky cupboard in the kitchen, he'd found himself telling her it was over between them, that if she were honest, she would admit that she had known this for some weeks too. He'd held her hands and looked her straight in the eye as he'd spoken, knowing he would never have been able to forgive himself if he'd done it any other way.

'You bastard!' she'd murmured, withdrawing her hands from his. 'Couldn't you at least have waited until after Christmas?'

The irrationality of her question hadn't struck him till he was driving home. Of all the things she could have accused him of, it was his poor timing that had mattered most. It struck him then that it more or less summed up how superficially Clare viewed him. She expressed her love for him readily enough, but the reality, he was sure, was that she had been in love with the fantasy of a happy ending.

He hoped that there would come a day, soon, when she would accept that they were never meant to be more than friends. But when he'd voiced this thought, she hadn't been ready to hear it. 'Don't you dare suggest that that's what we should now become. I never want to set eyes on you again. Because of you, I'll probably never be able to have children.'

He hadn't argued with her, although the surgeon who had operated on her had said it was still possible for her to have a normal pregnancy in the future. 'I'd advise against rushing things,' he had said, 'but essentially you're still in with a good chance of producing a healthy baby.'

For Clare's sake, Jack had to believe this was true.

At half past nine he finished the chapter he'd been working on since yesterday morning. He set the printer running and took his empty coffee cup to the kitchen. He was ravenous. He opened the fridge and helped himself to a packet of sausages, some bacon, two eggs and a tomato. Within half an hour he was back in the spare bedroom eating his breakfast and reading through the printed pages. Anything he wasn't quite happy with, he marked with a pencilled comment in the margin. On the whole, he was pleasantly surprised by how well the chapter had come together. He didn't kid himself that what he had written would put him on the shortlist for the Booker Prize, but it struck him as eminently readable. According to Dulcie, *Friends and Family* could be categorised as 'bloke lit', which sounded disparaging, but as this was the term used to describe the books of Tony Parsons, Nick Hornby and Mike Gayle, he considered himself in excellent company. In the last month he'd read all the books by these authors and had quickly noticed that he was writing from the same perspective – guess what, guys have feelings too!

His breakfast eaten, he leaned back in his chair, his hands clasped behind his head. It wasn't just having written another chapter that pleased him, it was knowing that he was starting the year on a positive note. He had made an important decision on the stroke of midnight last night, a New Year's resolution, you could say, which seemed to have been staring him in the face for some weeks. He intended to make an offer on Miss Waterman's flat.

The idea had come to him out of the blue, but perhaps it had been there subconsciously for a while. A new start in a new home was just what he needed. Admittedly he hadn't been all that taken with the flat when he'd first seen it, but it had grown on him. Probably because he'd seen what Beth had done with hers. She had made it into a real home – and that, more than anything, was what he wanted. If he closed his eyes he could picture himself living there, could even visualise knocking through from the kitchen to the sitting room to make one large comfortable room – again, as Beth had done upstairs. The flat also had the added advantage of the park being right on the doorstep: the girls would be able to let off steam there. Okay, Amber was getting too old for swings and slides, but the tennis courts might appeal to her. If she fancied it, he could find a coach and she could have lessons.

Now that he had resolved matters with Clare, he could plan for the future.

At what he considered an appropriate time to call, bearing in mind that it was New Year's Day, Jack phoned Beth to enquire after Miss Waterman. 'She's well on the mend,' Beth said, 'much more her old self. Why? Have you got good news for her about the flat?'

'I might have,' he said carefully. He didn't want to say anything to Beth before he spoke to his client. 'So, you think she won't mind if I give her a quick call?'

'I have a much better idea. Why don't you come here for lunch? Adele's joining us. As is a friend of Nathan's. Someone you might know.' There was a hint of laughter in her voice.

'Are you sure? I don't want to intrude.'

'If that were the case I wouldn't have invited you. It'll be very informal. No need to get dressed up.'

He spent the next hour showering, shaving and dressing, not because he wanted to impress Beth but because he was in dire need of smartening himself up. While he'd been off work – four days at home alone – he'd adopted some distinctly slovenly habits: he wrote all day in his scruffiest clothes and didn't bother to shave. If it hadn't been for his writing, he didn't know how he would have survived Christmas and New Year. By absorbing himself in the world of *Friends and Family*, he had escaped the mess of the one in which he lived. It wasn't only the guilt of what he'd done to Clare that had weighed so heavily on him: it was also being apart from the girls. This was the first Christmas when he hadn't been with Amber and Lucy and he missed them like hell. On Christmas morning he had unwrapped their present and had spent the next hour deciding which photograph to put in the frame they'd given him. He finally settled on a photo he'd snapped of the two of them in the summer when they'd gone on holiday to Devon – hair bleached by the sun, faces freckled, and smiles widened by the good time they were having.

The streets were empty as he walked to Maywood Park Road, his footsteps echoing along the deserted pavements. A hard frost had left gardens and grass verges cloaked in a whiteness that sparkled in the sunlight. But there was no warmth in the sun and his breath hung in the cold, sharp air. At bang on one o'clock, he rang Beth's doorbell. Minutes passed before she appeared. 'Happy New Year,' he said, and passed her the bottle of champagne he'd had in the fridge but hadn't felt inclined to open last night.

She took it from him with a smile. 'How very kind of you. *Brr* . . . come on in! It's freezing out there.'

He followed her upstairs and through to the sitting room, where Miss Waterman was resplendent in what had to be a 'special occasion frock'. She looked regal and a lot better than when he'd last seen her. He told her as much when they shook hands. 'It's the sherry Beth keeps giving me,' she said, pointing to a small glass on the table beside her chair. 'That and the delicious food she's spoiling me with. I've decided I should be ill more often.'

'I'm not sure that's such a good idea, Miss Waterman,' Jack said.

'Please, don't be so formal. Call me Adele.'

From behind him, he heard a familiar laugh. He turned to see Jaz coming through the front door – so this was the someone he might know whom Beth had mentioned on the phone. Following hot on Jaz's heels was a tall lad whom Jack took to be Beth's son.

It was during lunch that Jack brought up the reason for his visit. 'I've found you a buyer, Adele,' he said, 'and one I have every reason to believe will be a dead cert. There's no chain involved at his end so it would be a straightforward sale.'

'Really?' she said. 'How wonderful. This *is* good news.'

'Hang on a moment,' Beth said, pausing with a dish of roast potatoes she was passing to Jaz. 'No one's been round to view Adele's flat for ages. Who's made an offer?'

'Ah,' he said, amused by her sharpness, and her continued protectiveness of the old lady. 'Time to come clean. It's me. I'm making an offer.'

'Is that ethical?' asked Adele.

'It is if he's divvying up the full asking price,' said Beth.

'Everything will be done above board and correctly,' said Jack. 'Have no fear on that score. And, yes, I'm offering the full asking price. What's more, so that you can be sure there's no funny business going on, I'll pay for you to have the property independently valued. That way you'll know I've priced it correctly.'

'Well,' Adele beamed, 'I'm delighted with the news. I can't think of anyone I'd rather have moving into my flat.' She raised her glass. 'To you, Jack. I hope you'll be very happy living here in Maywood Park Road.'

'Thank you. I'll be instructing my solicitor first thing tomorrow morning. So long as no one has any objections.' He looked directly at Beth.

'And what possible objections could I have?'

'I'm just making certain that I meet with the approval of the chief custodian of my client's business affairs.'

'It goes without saying that there'll be a detailed questionnaire for you to complete before your offer is accepted. One can never be too careful.' Then, looking round the table, she said, 'If everyone's finished, I'll clear away.'

'That's okay, Beth,' said Jaz. 'Nathan and I'll see to this. Won't we, Nathan?'

'Will we?'

'Yes, so on your feet and be quick about it.'

Adele winked at Jack, and when Jaz and Nathan were stacking dishes over by the sink and making a noisy job of it, she said, 'Don't they make a lovely couple?'

'Stop it, Adele, or I shall have to send you home. Without your party bag. More wine, Jack?'

'Please.'

Beth topped up Jack's glass, then her own – Adele was sticking with sherry – and while Nathan and Jaz larked around at the other end of the room, she let Jack talk business with his client. Surprised though she was by his announcement, she welcomed the prospect of having him as her new neighbour. She had dreaded neighbours from hell moving in. The only downside to the arrangement would be that she would now have her work cut out convincing the mischievous Adele, and the sceptical Nathan, that there was nothing going on between her and Jack. She had seen the look on Adele's face earlier and knew all too well what the old lady was thinking.

But her neighbour's misplaced determination to bring about a romantic union for Beth was the least of her worries. She hadn't seen or spoken to Lois since Christmas Day, and not for lack of trying. Each time she had telephoned Lois had cut her dead. 'I have no wish to talk to you, Beth,' she had said. 'You've treated me abominably. And after all I've done for you and Nathan. What really hurts is that I believe you've deliberately turned my only grandson against me by filling his head with lies about my poor Adam. I shall never forgive you for that.' Her voice had been shrill and she was evidently on the verge of tears.

'But, Lois, you know as well as I do that Adam committed suicide. Every report that was made on his death reached the same conclusion. The coroner's verdict was—' She got no further. Lois slammed down the phone.

There had been many moments when Beth had regretted her outburst at Marsh House after Nathan's dramatic departure on Christmas Day. She had turned on Lois with a viciousness she hadn't known she was capable of. 'You stupid bitch!' she had yelled at her mother-in-law. 'You stupid, unthinking bitch! Have you any *idea* what you've done to my son? And do you even care?' Backed against the bookcase, Lois had stared at her, her mouth open, her eyes wide. But she didn't answer Beth.

Barnaby had tried to intervene and cool things down. 'Come on, Beth,' he said, patting her arm. 'Shouting won't help anyone. Let me get you a drink and we'll discuss this—'

She shrugged him off. 'You're wrong, Barnaby. On this occasion, shouting is exactly what's needed. I just wish I'd done it years ago.' Her gaze was back on Lois. 'The truth is, you don't give a damn, do you? You're so obsessed with keeping a pathetic myth going, a myth nobody else believes, that you've lost sight of what's going on around you. Nathan despises you because you've refused to accept that his father was anything but perfect. He was a normal human being, Lois. A man who, when the chips were down, couldn't go on.'

It was then that Lois spoke, and she attacked Beth the only way she knew how. 'If you had been a better wife, Adam would never have been so depressed!'

'You don't think his upbringing was responsible? It was you who brought him up to believe that no member of the King family was allowed to fail. Poor Adam, you taught him that there was only one rule by which he had to live, and that was to win. But when it came down to it, he wasn't the tough fighter you wanted him to be. And when he realised that, it was too late. He was set on a course from which there was no escape other than to end his life.' She pointed her finger at Lois. 'You made him do it, Lois. You made Adam so ashamed of failing that you might just as well have handed him the bottle of whisky and car keys yourself.'

Lois swallowed hard, and held her head high. 'I want you to leave, Beth. I want you out of my house. Now.'

Barnaby had offered to drive Beth home and she had accepted. 'I'm sorry, Barnaby,' she said, once Marsh House was behind them. 'I've put you in a bloody awful situation. But right now, this very minute, I'm not sorry for what I said. That will probably come tomorrow and I'll feel terrible.'

Barnaby didn't say anything. He just nodded, his face sad and tired. He helped her into the flat with her bags, Nathan's too, and stood awkwardly in the hall. 'I'd better not stop,' he said, staring miserably at his shoes. 'Lois will be needing me.' He reached out to open the door, then hesitated. 'He was my son as well, you know. I think people forget that sometimes.' His eyes misted over, but before Beth could say anything, he had pulled the door shut and was gone.

Beth had kept all this from Nathan, not wanting to burden him any more than he already was. She blamed herself for not having seen the signs, for not having realised just how deeply affected Nathan was by Lois's constant comparisons between him and his father. Both Simone and her mother had been right: they had warned her to put a stop to Lois's make-believe version of Adam's death. And life. Her only hope now was that time would heal the rift. An outside hope was that Barnaby might find the courage to talk to his wife. But that was unlikely. Barnaby might tease Lois, but he would never go behind her back. He was the most loyal of husbands.

She had waited hours for Nathan to come home that night, despairing of ever seeing him alive again. It was the longest wait of her life, and when she'd heard his key in the lock, she had rushed to meet him. They were both too wrung out to talk properly about what had happened, but in the morning they went for a long walk to clear their heads, and the awkwardness between them. 'How did you know I'd come home?' he asked.

'I didn't think you'd show your face at Marsh House so soon and, anyway, I was asked to leave. I'll tell you about that later. For now, talk to me about your father. You don't really hate him, do you?'

'Sometimes.'

'He doesn't deserve that.'

Nathan kicked at a stone on the path and frowned. 'You speak as if he's still alive.'

'I meant his memory. What's left behind of him doesn't deserve to be treated that way.'

'But I have so little memory of him. And what I do have has been spoiled by Lois.'

'Then we have to work on that. I don't know how, but we'll do it. I promise.'

Meanwhile, Beth was left with myriad feelings of guilt, anger and confusion. Not so long ago, if faced with a crisis, she would have looked automatically to Simone for advice and support, but she hadn't this time. Instead she had turned to Ewan, telling him everything that had happened, recounting all the ghastly details as if she was writing it out of her system.

By sharing the problem with an outsider, she felt less disloyal to Lois. When she had mentioned this to Ewan, he'd said,

It's loyalty to Lois that's helped to create this mess. How about a bit of loyalty to your own self-respect? Sounds to me as if Lois has tried systematically to diminish you, Bethany.

That sounds harsh.

It was meant to be. No point in dressing up what you already know to be true.

Ouch. And double ouch. Are you always this blunt?

Only with . . . those who I care about.

Flummoxed by his comment, she hadn't known how to respond. A further message appeared on her screen.

Strike that disclosure from the record if you'd prefer. My fingers are getting above themselves.

No [she'd typed, after another brief hesitation]. It was nice. It took me by surprise, that's all.

An okay-ish surprise?

Yes.

In that case, I have a favour to ask. But first, do you have a scanner?

Nathan has one. I could use that. Why?

How do you feel about exchanging pictures of ourselves?

Smiling, she'd replied,

Only if you promise not to cheat.

What? Like do some sneaky cutting and pasting to enhance my naturally cute features?

Something like that, yes.

Hand on heart, I'll play it as straight as you do.

This had taken place last night and they'd agreed to do the exchange this evening. The photograph Beth was going to use was one that Nathan had taken of her at Ben and Simone's farewell party last year before they'd left for Dubai. She hoped it showed her at her best.

She was shaken out of her thoughts by Jaz and Nathan clattering dessert plates and cutlery on to the table. She glanced up and noted how relaxed her son was as Jaz flapped a napkin at him. Before yesterday, when Nathan had asked if it was all right for him to invite Jaz to lunch, she'd had no idea that they were such good friends. Or, rather, such *close* friends.

With the horror of Christmas Day still hanging over them, it was good to see him so happy.

27

Whenever Ewan was anxious, frustrated or under pressure, he had a fail-safe method for taking his mind off what was bothering him: he opened a bottle of wine and made bread. At the time of his divorce, when he had been struggling to hold down a job and look after Alice, he had stumbled by accident upon this little-known form of therapy.

One afternoon, when Alice hadn't been feeling well, he'd offered to cheer her up by making one of her favourite treats: gingerbread. The tray of gingerbread men – stumpy fellows with misshapen legs and arms – had been such a success (they were edible!) that he had felt compelled to flick through the cookery book to see what else he could turn his hand to. Bread looked easy enough and, working on the theory that the end result of throwing grains of yeast into warm water and sugar was no more mysterious than basic chemistry, he had taken on a white loaf and found the task immensely absorbing. And relaxing.

His début baking days were long behind him, and now his repertoire included pizza bases, wholemeal plaited loaves, potato bread, garlic and herb bread cooked in terracotta pots, and cheese and chilli flatbread. Tonight he was making a poppy-seed loaf and as he sank his fingers deep into the soft dough he felt the soothing effect almost instantly.

It was usually when his brain went into overload that he turned to the flour bin for solace, but on this occasion the reason was that he was having second thoughts about exchanging photographs with Beth. They had agreed to do the deed at midnight, and as the time grew nearer – it was eleven thirty-six – he couldn't shake off his rising doubts.

Would it be a mistake?

And wasn't this just what he'd wanted to avoid?

What annoyed him most was that he had no one to blame but himself. He had sent himself down this particular route, so if anything bad happened as a consequence it would serve him right.

The stupid thing was that he was genuinely bothered by what Beth might think of him. He'd never considered himself a looker: in his opinion, he was just an ordinary middle-aged man with lines fast developing around his eyes, grey hairs aplenty and the kind of filling-out face that was as average as it was unmemorable. Even he sometimes had trouble in the morning recognising himself. Who the hell are you? he'd think, when he looked in the mirror to shave. Where's that energetic young man I used to be? Alice said he was getting too hung up on his age, that he should stop being such a vain old slapper.

While his daughter had been at home for Christmas, he'd confided in her about Beth. 'Are you out of your mind, Dad?' she'd cried. 'What was it you used to lecture me about? Oh, yeah, I remember. I wasn't to talk to strangers.'

'This is different,' he'd said defensively, all too aware of the truth of what she was saying. If the boot had been on the other foot and Alice had struck up an on-line relationship with a man she didn't know, he'd be waving the parental big stick at her.

'Different?' she'd said. 'Like hell it is! For all you know this "Beth" could be a man getting off on some weird sexually perverted game he's playing with you.'

'Credit me with a modicum of savvy,' he'd replied.

With her hands on her hips – a typical Alice stance – she'd argued, 'Show me an ounce of evidence that you know who or what she really is.'

It wasn't the first time their roles had been reversed – and certainly wouldn't be the last. As he stared into her stormy face, all he could say was, 'Sometimes one has to take a chance in life. Some risks are worth taking.'

'I'll remember that when I'm hitching a lift home at two in the morning, shall I?'

'Oh, Alice, it's not the same.'

'Seems to me that it's a case of don't do as I do, do as I say.'

There was no arguing with his headstrong daughter so he'd agreed to disagree. 'Whatever does it for you, Dad,' she'd said, helping herself to a slice of cold turkey from the fridge. 'I would have thought there were easier ways for an eligible man like you to pull.'

'I'm not on the pull!'

'Then perhaps you should be. You have a lot to offer, Dad. You're a better catch than you think you are. You're intelligent, funny, and not bad-looking. The only downer is that you're as rich as Midas. But, hey, nobody's perfect.' She opened the fridge again and helped herself to more turkey.

'Why don't you get the whole thing out and make a sandwich?' he suggested.

'Too much effort.' She shrugged. 'Mm . . . these chipolatas are great. Any cranberry sauce left?'

'Second shelf down.'

After another rummage in the fridge, she turned to him and said, 'Oh, and something I have to ask, as the only responsible adult round here. Are you indulging in regular cyber-sex? Because if you are, I hope you're taking precautions.'

'What? Like wearing a spellchecker at all times?'

She smiled. 'Just be careful, Dad. I know you think you're a great sage with all the answers, but really you're just an innocent. You haven't had enough experience with women.'

'Oh, go right ahead and build a man's confidence up, why don't you?'

She pointed at him with the stubby remains of a sausage. 'Okay, then. How many women have there been since Mum?'

He scowled. 'A few.'

'Too few. And it's not as if you don't get plenty of offers.'

'Yes, but they're not from anyone I'd be interested in.'

'But this Beth character does interest you?'

He hesitated. 'As a friend, yes. And ... and if it so pleases the prosecution, may I be excused any further interrogation? I have some mail to see to. Of the snail variety, I might add.'

A glance at the kitchen clock told Ewan that it was now eleven forty-five. He kneaded the dough some more and pondered over his feelings for Beth. Despite all of Alice's warnings, innuendoes and jokes, he really did view Beth as a friend – and a friend he wanted to get to know better. It was obvious that their correspondence meant a lot to both of them; certainly Beth had shared some pretty personal stuff with him. But by taking this step of seeing what the other person looked like, were they running the risk of spoiling what they had? Odds on, and he reckoned he was a fair judge of human nature, if Beth didn't like the look of him, she would 'run out of things to write about' and the correspondence would grind to a halt. And, of course, it worked the other way too. If Beth had a smile on her like a snarling pit-bull terrier, he'd think twice about continuing.

It was inexcusably shallow, but it was the way the world worked. Always had. Always would.

He thought of the photograph he'd already scanned into his computer. It was slightly out of focus and lopsided, but he'd chosen it because, for once, he appeared as he actually saw himself. He had any number of better photographs to choose from, but they all tended to distort who he really was.

At eleven fifty-two he covered the dough with a damp tea-towel, put the bowl on the shelf above the radiator, washed his hands, poured himself another glass of wine, and approached his office.

'Okay,' he said aloud. 'It's Checkpoint Charlie time.'

Beth clicked on OPEN, closed her eyes, held her breath and waited for Ewan's picture to materialise, knowing that he would be doing the same in Suffolk.

It was the most excruciating moment. Would Ewan turn out to be the greasy-haired, bespectacled, nerdy anorak she'd always hoped he wasn't?

She opened a cautious eye and saw that the electronic wizardry had done its stuff. More bravely now, she stared at the screen and saw a face that ... that she liked the look of. Reflected in his relaxed expression was the humorous warmth she had come to know through her exchanges with him.

His smiling mouth was framed by two deep lines at either side, which gave the impression that he was holding back a laugh. She couldn't be sure what colour his eyes were, the picture quality wasn't that good, but she had a feeling they were blue. His hair, short and grey – no hint of a centre parting! – was receding. She hoped that her photograph was being equally well received in Suffolk.

Ewan's first thought was that Beth was just the kind of woman he would look twice at. It wasn't only the fair hair or the slim body that appealed to him, but the brightness of her smile.

His second thought was that he wanted very much to meet her. It was in his head for no more than a nanosecond before he squashed it flat. It was the dumbest thing he'd ever come up with.

Or was it?

28

It was the first Thursday of the year and the first time the group would be together since half-way through December. There had been no word from Victor – not even a Christmas card in return for the one she'd sent him – and Dulcie decided to give him a call, to see if he was going to join them.

Using the phone in the kitchen, she tapped in Victor's number from her address book and waited for him to answer. She supposed that if he had left the group for good she should re-advertise Hidden Talents, although she would have to check with the others first. Dulcie sensed that Beth, for one, would prefer to keep things as they were. The doorbell interrupted her thoughts and she replaced the receiver with a feeling of relief, more than happy to put off the task of encouraging Victor back into the fold.

Richard was standing on the doorstep. 'What a lovely surprise,' she said. But straight away she could see that something was wrong. His arms didn't linger around her as they usually did when they embraced, and the kiss was on her cheek, not her mouth. 'Come through,' she said, keeping her voice light to disguise her concern. While she filled the kettle to make some coffee, she watched him prowl uneasily round the kitchen.

'What is it, Richard?' she asked, his behaviour making her anxious. 'Is it Angela? Does she know? I knew it was a mistake to accept her invitation to your party.'

He came over to her, put his arms round her shoulders and held her to him. 'You're jumping to conclusions, and that's so unlike you.'

She slipped out of his grasp, looked into his face. 'Then what is it? Have you been overdoing it and made yourself unwell again?'

He shook his head. 'No, I'm fine. But it's what we dreaded. Henry and Kate are seeing each other.'

'No!'

'I'm afraid it's true. Henry phoned last night. They've met up regularly since they got back to London. Oh, Dulcie, there was something so ... so upbeat in his voice. And I know it's only a couple of weeks, but my guess is that this is more than a passing fancy. Henry has fallen hook, line and sinker for Kate. He's mad about her.'

Dulcie tried to think straight. This couldn't be happening. She and Richard had been scrupulously determined to keep their affair secret so as not to hurt his family, and now this. When Richard had first warned her at the party that Henry had hinted he was taken with Kate, she had been as shocked as he was. But what could they do? She had driven home reminding herself that Kate might joke about casting her net to catch a boyfriend, but the reality was – as Kate had often said – she was too engrossed in establishing herself at work to want to be sidetracked by a serious relationship. Thus Dulcie had reassured herself that there was no need for them to warn Kate off Henry. She had always agreed with Mark Twain when he wrote, 'I have spent most of my life worrying about things that have never happened.'

'Maybe it's one-sided,' she said finally. 'Kate hasn't mentioned anything to me.'

'When did you last speak to her?'

Dulcie tried to think straight. 'When she rang to thank me for Christmas. More than a week ago.'

Richard frowned. 'A lot could have happened in that time.'

'Well, it certainly seems to have,' Dulcie said stiffly. She made the coffee and they went into the sitting room. 'So what's to be done?' she asked, when they were settled on the sofa.

He stared across the room, through the french windows and out on to the terrace where a robin was pecking at the frozen water in the stone bird bath. 'I'm damned if I know,' he said.

She reached for his hand, and as her fingers touched his skin, she saw how things stood. 'You want me to warn Kate off, don't you? I have to tell her about *us* and the inappropriateness of there ever being a Kate-and-Henry?'

Slowly he faced her. 'You do see that it's the only way, don't you? I can't possibly tell Henry. I'd have to tell him why.'

An unexpected niggle of resentment rose in Dulcie. That, and the motherly need to fight for her daughter's freedom to go out with whom she chose. What right did she or Richard have to interfere with her life? 'I thought you no longer cared what others thought,' she said, her voice flat. 'I thought you were on the verge of telling Angela about us.'

If he caught the pointed bluntness in her words, he chose to ignore it. He passed a hand over his face. Suddenly he looked very tired. 'But not like this. This . . . this would be too brutal. I couldn't do it to her. Surely you understand that?'

Dulcie understood only too well. The world was full of women who had to carry out other people's dirty work.

The college library was packed with students doing what they weren't allowed to do: eating, drinking and chucking things about. A rubber landed on the A4 pad on which Jaz was making revision notes. Without looking up – she knew that the culprit was a greasy-haired, cretinous oik from the upper sixth – she placed it on the desk in front of her, wishing that Mrs

Barr, the librarian, would come back. With so much noise going on, she gave up on her Seamus Heaney notes and allowed herself to think of something more interesting: Nathan.

It was official. Jaz Rafferty and Nathan King were an item. It was also official that they would not be one of those awful couples who slobbered over each other in the lunch queue or held hands in the corridor – like Billy and Vicki. One reason behind this was that Jaz didn't want to attract attention to herself or have people discussing how soon it would be before Nathan tired of her. Since Billy and Vicki had got it together, supposed friends were openly betting on who would dump whom first. It was all so sordid and shallow. Also, she didn't want anyone in her family to find out about Nathan. The thought of her sisters pestering her, her brothers teasing her and, worse, her father interrogating her had made her extract a promise from Nathan that he wouldn't call for her at home. 'And only ring me on my mobile,' she'd insisted.

'Are you embarrassed about me?' he'd asked.

'No. I just like to keep certain areas of my life private,' she'd said, not admitting that it was the rest of the Raffertys who embarrassed her. 'I don't want everyone knowing what I do. Least of all my family.' To her shame, she was lying even more to her parents, telling them she was at Vicki's whenever she was with Nathan.

They saw each other most days. Usually they went back to his place after college. She liked where he lived: it was so quiet. When Beth was out at work, and it was just the two of them in the flat, they would lie on the sofa in silence. The first time they'd done this he had wanted to put on a CD for them to listen to, but she'd said, 'Please don't.'

'Why? Don't you like my choice of music?'

'It's not that.'

'What, then?'

She'd tried to explain how good it was to hear nothing but the beat of your own heart. That all she got at home was constant mayhem: doors banging, voices shouting, music blaring. 'If you had to put up with that you'd understand.'

He'd wound a lock of her hair around his finger and smiled. 'You're not like other girls, are you?'

She wasn't offended by his comment. She knew she was different and was destined never to fit in. People would always refer to her as strange, a loner. Often, as if peeping through the crack in a doorway, she caught glimpses of herself when she was older: she was always alone.

At the far end of the room, the door flew open and an instant hush fell on the library. It was Mrs Barr. Thank goodness for that, thought Jaz. Now she'd be able to get some work done.

When college was over Jaz walked home with Nathan. He wanted to call in at Novel Ways, and when he'd found the book he needed for some background reading on Virginia Woolf they decided to have a drink in the coffee shop. 'We'd better not stay too long,' she said, after they'd paid for their café latte and had found themselves a table. 'It's my writers' group tonight and I've still got some revision to do for my exam tomorrow.'

'No sweat, I know the score. Mum was on at me this morning not to be too late either.'

She smiled. 'How awful for you – two women nagging you.'

'Could be worse. I could make the mistake of listening to them. Hey, who's so interesting you can't tear your eyes off him?'

'Sorry. I've just noticed someone from the writers' group.' She lowered her voice. 'His name's Victor. Your mum must have told you about him. He's the biggest pain going.'

He followed her gaze across the coffee shop to where Victor, trousers half-way up his legs, pens stuffed into his jacket pocket, was tussling with a small sachet. When he managed to rip it open, sugar scattered over the table and several sheets of handwritten notes. Jaz could see exactly what was going to happen next and, sure enough, Victor waved a hand impatiently at the mess and promptly knocked over his cup. A puddle of brown liquid flooded the papers and dripped on to his trousers. There was something so pathetically hopeless about the silly man that Jaz felt sorry for him. She scooped up a handful of napkins and went over to help. 'Hi,' she said. 'I thought these might come in handy.'

He seemed not to recognise her. 'A cloth might be of more use,' he said ungraciously, on his feet now, shaking the papers so that the coffee dripped on to the wooden floor. Amused that he appeared to be holding her responsible for his own ineptitude, Jaz went to the woman behind the counter and asked if she had something with which to clear up the mess. The woman gave her a handful of paper towels. 'He's one we could do without. Every day he sits there scribbling away, and he's as tight as they come. He makes a cup of coffee last more than an hour. I hate skinflints.'

On her way back to Victor, Jaz raised her eyebrows at Nathan, who was smiling at her. 'There you go, Victor,' she said. 'Are your papers okay? Are they from *Star City*?'

He narrowed his eyes at her, and finally she saw recognition dawn. 'Oh, it's *you*,' he said.

'Well, it certainly was the last time I looked in the mirror. Are you coming to the group tonight? It's our first meeting since the Christmas break.'

Making a poor job of mopping up the puddle of coffee, he muttered something unintelligible. Jaz left him to it.

'Was that your good deed for the day?' asked Nathan, when she was sitting down again.

'For the entire month, more like. Honestly, he's such an ungrateful weirdo. I bet the words "thank you" don't appear in his vocabulary.'

She was still thinking this when, later that evening, she rang Dulcie's doorbell and recalled what the woman who worked in the coffee shop had said about Victor always being there. If that was true, why wasn't he at work? The obvious answer, she decided, was that he was on holiday.

29

From as early as Victor could remember, life had dealt him a rotten hand. As a child his hard work was never rewarded as it should have been. It didn't matter how hard he tried at school, his reports rarely reflected the true worth of his endeavours. He'd been surrounded by idiots, show-offs and bullies who boasted of never doing a stroke of work but somehow always got straight As for the end-of-term exams. He, who had diligently applied himself week in week out, was denied the grades he deserved. He knew it was because the teachers didn't like him. He'd once corrected the English teacher on a point of grammar – 'Sir, I think you meant to say, if I *were*, not if I *was*' – and was ridiculed for the rest of the term. Thereafter, and because of the flak to which he was continually subjected, he was known as Victor Flakmore.

It was no better when he left school at sixteen and started work as a junior clerk in the local council offices. From day one he was expected to be the general dogsbody and the butt of everyone's jokes. 'Oh, Victor, be a love and open a window for us,' the girls in the typing pool said to him on his first day, causing him to blush and fumble with the stack of papers he'd been sent to deliver. Fanning themselves with their long-nailed hands and undoing the buttons on their tight-fitting blouses, they'd sighed and swivelled on their typist's chairs, showing off their legs. The windows had been similar to the ones at school, high and narrow, the kind that required a long pole with a hook at the end to open them. A tall, busty girl from the front row of desks had risen from her seat and approached him with it. 'Just shout if you need any help, Victor,' she'd said, towering over him and thrusting her massive bosom into his face. Nearly suffocating from the smell of her cheap scent, he'd started to shake, stammered that he had to be somewhere else, dropped the pole and bolted. Their laughter had followed him the length of the corridor and up the stairs to the third floor, where he shared an office with half a dozen other men, all of whom were coarse and of below-average intelligence. They had sniggered at him when he burst in, and he'd realised that he'd been set up.

Just as he had at work before Christmas. He'd worked for J. B. Reeves and Company for almost twenty years. He'd started as a rep, driving round the North West of England with a bootload of office-supply equipment, but selling had never been his strong suit and after six months he was offered a job in the accounts department. Initially it meant a drop in salary and no car, but he didn't mind because at last he'd found his niche. He was a great believer in dotting Is and crossing Ts. There was also something satisfying about keeping an eye on the firm's money. He had a keen nose for sniffing out irregularities on expense claims and he had no qualms in summoning a miscreant to his office to explain himself. He knew that behind his back he was called Penny-pinching Blackmore, but he didn't care: his word was final. Ultimately they had to toe the line or not get paid. It made him unpopular, but his duty was to the company. It was his job to stamp out the cheats who thought they could steal from their employers, whether it was claiming for petrol that hadn't been used for business purposes or sneaking toilet rolls home in shopping-bags.

He had always done exactly what he was paid to do and a lot more besides. He had been a loyal, trustworthy employee who had given his all. He'd been punctual, consistently hard-working, seldom took his full holiday entitlement and had only once missed a day – and that had been to attend his mother's funeral. Which was why he felt so aggrieved by what had happened, just before Christmas, when he was called into the senior manager's office. He had been expecting news of the bonuses that came at that time of year, but instead he was informed that he had been made redundant. 'You're not alone,' Steve Cartwright had said, as if it would help. 'Cuts are being made across the board. People younger than you are being given their terms. It's them I feel sorry for, guys with families and mortgages to keep afloat. From your point of view, at least you only had six years to go before retirement. If I were you, I'd treat this as a lucky break, an excuse to go off and enjoy yourself with Mrs Blackmore.'

'There is no Mrs Blackmore.'

'Oh, I'm sorry to hear that. When did – when did she pass away?'

'She didn't. I've never been married.'

He'd returned to his desk, furious. Steve Cartwright had worked at J. B. Reeves for five years and hadn't known the first thing about one of the firm's longest-serving employees.

'Streamlining' was what head office was calling the loss of jobs. Indiscriminate bullying was what it amounted to, picking on those unable to fight back. Oh, it had been ever thus. But he'd show them. By God, he'd show them. Now that he had time on his hands, he'd finish his novel, get it published and revel in its success. He'd prove to the whole damn lot of them that while they thought of him as no more than Penny-pinching Blackmore – an expendable employee – he was a true winner.

Yes. Victor Blackmore was a winner.

He had programmed himself to say this, aloud (if he were alone), every half-hour, and as his digital wristwatch pipped the hour – eight o'clock – he put down his pen, closed his eyes and said, clearly, 'Victor Blackmore, you are a winner.' He repeated the words several times, visualising the glory of

Star City displayed in the window of Novel Ways. He also pictured a long line of people queuing patiently to buy a signed copy.

Several years ago the company had brought in a supposed expert on team-leadership skills and one of the pieces of advice the woman had given was that self-affirmation was the key to fostering a strong belief in oneself. She had suggested they start their day with a mantra that would help them to feel more positive about themselves. Until he was made redundant he had ignored such preposterous psychobabble, but now he was writing in earnest, he was prepared to do anything to secure his future success as one of Britain's leading authors. It was this belief that got him out of bed every morning, stopped him losing faith. He reminded himself regularly that redundancy was the best thing that could have happened to him: hadn't it given him the chance to concentrate all his energy on his book?

What he disliked most about losing his job was the look on people's faces when they asked him why he wasn't at work. Only the other morning, as he put the rubbish out, his neighbour – a young man with a Vauxhall Astra that he washed and polished every weekend and parked in front of Victor's house – had asked him about his job. 'Working flexi-hours, are you now, Mr Blackmore? You're a lucky bloke, wish I could. What wouldn't I give for a lie-in?'

And what wouldn't he give for people to mind their own business? Like that girl this afternoon in the coffee shop. Poking her nose in where it wasn't wanted. Why couldn't people just leave him alone? Of course he wasn't going to bother with that absurd excuse for a writers' group. He had more talent in his big toe than the rest of those amateurs between them. He'd known it would be a mistake to join them and, once again, he'd been proved right. He really ought to trust his instinct. Hadn't his mother always said that the only person one could trust was oneself?

His love of books had come from his mother. She had read to him from as early as he could remember, and every Saturday morning they had gone to the library together. While she searched the shelves for a crime novel she hadn't yet read, he knelt on the dusty wooden floor to make his choice from the limited selection of children's books. Before long he was writing his own stories, tales of escape and heroic adventure, of good guys who would save the world from notoriously evil villains. He wrote and wrote, always in private, and always to blank out the daily grind of school and the bullying he had to endure.

He swallowed at the painful memory of there being no one to whom he could turn and, recalling that it was Thursday, he pictured the writers' group sitting in that smug woman's front room doing nothing more constructive than playing silly word games. What was the point in that?

Writing. That's what it was all about. Solid writing. Head down, words on the page, nothing to distract the focus.

He used to write downstairs in the dining room, but he'd found there were too many distractions – the noise of the children playing next door, the fussy pattern of the wallpaper, the creak of the table, the tick of the clock, the smell of burning dust from the electric fire. Now he worked upstairs in the smallest bedroom at the back of his terraced house. He'd emptied it of all clutter, removed the bed, the chest of drawers, the pictures on the walls, the carpet, the curtains, even the lightbulb from the overhead fitting. In place of these extraneous objects, he now had nothing but a desk and a chair, which he'd placed in front of the window. During the day, when he wasn't writing in the coffee shop, he worked there, and at night he lit the room with candles. He allowed himself no form of heating, other than a small Calor Gas burner on which he boiled water for mugs of tea and heated cans of baked beans or tomato soup. If he felt the cold while he was typing, he wrapped a blanket around his shoulders. And there was no danger of being interrupted by the telephone: he'd had it disconnected.

He had made a proper artist's garret to work in, and by depriving himself of any comforts he hoped to dig deep into his creative soul and produce his best work.

The thought that he might be taking things too far never crossed his mind.

30

Dulcie woke with what was now a familiar sense of foreboding.

It had been the same every morning since Richard had told her about Kate and Henry. That had been more than two weeks ago and, as she'd promised Richard, she had called her daughter some nights later, prepared to explain the situation. But on hearing the happiness in Kate's voice as she had talked so enthusiastically about Henry – she couldn't believe how well they got on, how ideally suited they were, and how much they had in common – Dulcie had lost her nerve: she couldn't bring herself to burst the bubble of her daughter's euphoria. All she could hope for was that whatever was going on between Kate and Henry would fizzle out within a month or two. Kate bored easily and boyfriends never lasted long.

She had told Richard this over lunch the day before yesterday. Sitting in the kitchen, with the low January sun streaming brightly through the french windows giving the illusion of a warm spring day, there had been a tension between them that she had never known before. 'I disagree,' he'd said, when she'd explained how she felt. 'I'm convinced that Henry wants something to come of this relationship with Kate. He'll pursue her until he gets what he wants. He was like that as a child. He might not look the determined go-getter but, believe me, beneath the affable exterior is a will of iron.'

'Have you spoken to him again?' she'd asked.

He shook his head. 'No, but Angela has. He phoned last night while I was out. When I got home she was full of what he'd had to say. She seems to find it enormously amusing that life should be taking this particular turn. "We could end up being related to Dulcie Ballantyne."'

'What did you say?'

'I said I thought it highly unlikely, and that she was jumping the gun somewhat.'

'But you don't believe that, do you?'

'No. There just seems something horribly inevitable about the situation.'

She'd reached across the table and touched his hand lightly. 'This isn't like you, Richard. I've never known you so fatalistic.'

'I can't help it.' He sighed wearily. 'It's how I've felt right from the start when Henry first mentioned Kate at the party. It's as if we're destined not to be together.'

'Nonsense,' she'd said robustly. But she couldn't think what else to say to reassure him.

Out of bed now, she poured a few drops of the aromatherapy oil Andrew and Miles had given her for Christmas into her bath water, and went downstairs to see what the postman had brought that Saturday morning. Her heart gave a tiny jolt when she saw a large, buff-coloured envelope with her own handwriting on the front. She left the rest of the mail on the hall table but took this upstairs to read in the bath.

Once she was settled in the warm scented water, she dried her hands on the towel beside the bath and opened the letter. She let her eyes skim over the first few words. This time there was no rejection. No 'Sorry, better luck next time.'

> *Dear Dulcie Ballantyne,*
>
> *I am delighted to inform you that your short story 'Young At Heart' has won first prize in our annual creative-writing competition. We had a record number of entries this year, of an extremely high standard, but the judges were particularly impressed with your clear use of narrative and full understanding of your central character.*
>
> *You might like to know that all winning entries are to be published in our quarterly magazine, which we will, of course, be forwarding to you when it is to hand.*
>
> *Please find enclosed your prize money. May it encourage you to go on to bigger and better things.*
>
> *Yours sincerely,*
> *M. Cadogan*
> *(Competition Secretary)*

Paper-clipped to the back of the letter was a cheque for fifteen hundred pounds.

Her earlier mood was immediately replaced with a burst of pure happiness. Elated, she sank back into the water and allowed herself to gloat with satisfaction. At her age she had experienced the full gamut of highs and lows that life could offer, but nothing matched the thrill of having one's writing accepted. She had won prizes before, admittedly not as large as this one, and she'd had nearly a dozen short stories published, but the thrill never diminished.

Her happy mood stayed with her for the rest of the day. Until the phone rang early that evening.

'Hello, Kate. How are you?'

'I'm fine, Mum. Well, better than fine. Lots better, in fact.' Girlish laughter – which Dulcie rarely heard from her daughter – echoed down the line. 'The thing is, I'm ringing to let you know that I'm moving in with Henry. We only decided this afternoon, but as of tomorrow I'll be living in—'

'Kate, slow down! When did you decide to take such an important step?' Even to Dulcie's ears, her question sounded heavy-handed.

'Oh, come on, Mum. You must have guessed this would happen sooner or later.'

'You don't think you're hurrying things a little?' Dulcie struggled to keep her voice level.

Kate was quick to go on the attack. 'Did you say that to Andrew and Miles?'

'No, but that was different. They'd known each other a lot longer before they—'

'Don't you like Henry? Is that it?'

'How can I answer that when I hardly know him?' She was stalling. Hopelessly so.

'Then you'll just have to take my word for it. I wouldn't be moving in with him if I didn't love him. He's everything I want in a partner. Oh, Mum, I really think he's The One.' There was more girlish laughter and Kate went on to list Henry's finest qualities. Only half listening, Dulcie closed her eyes. It was just as Richard had feared.

'Mum, are you listening to me? Honestly, here I am, baring my soul, and you're not even—'

Rallying herself, Dulcie said, 'I heard every word. And I'm very pleased for you.'

'Good. So tell me what you've been up to since we last spoke. No chance of there being a man in your life, I suppose?'

Dulcie forced a laugh. 'Heavens, what made you ask such a question?'

'I don't know. Maybe it has something to do with being so happy myself. I sort of feel I'd like the same for you.'

The irony was not lost on Dulcie. 'I'm touched,' she murmured.

'You shouldn't leave it too late, Mum. I know you won't believe me but you're still a good catch. There's bound to be a man out there who'd be interested in you.'

'Thank you, darling. I'll try to remember that when I'm at a low ebb.'

'Rubbish! You've never been at a low ebb in your entire life. You're the most positive and upbeat woman I know.'

It was dark by the time she got off the phone and, sitting in the study in a pool of soft light cast from the lamp on her desk, Dulcie lowered her head. As a mother, she could not deny her daughter the chance to be happy, which meant she had to sacrifice her own happiness.

If there was to be a Kate-and-Henry, there could not be a Richard-and-Dulcie. The mix was too volatile. The pressure on Kate and Henry would be intolerable. The natural way of things was that sons gravitated towards their mothers, but if Henry wanted to be with Kate – whose mother had broken up his parents' marriage – how would he ever be able to look Angela in the eye? And how would Angela view Kate?

No. She had no choice but to end her affair with Richard.

31

It had snowed heavily during the night, just as the weather forecasters had said it would. As Jack pulled back the bedroom curtains, he squinted at the brightness that met his eyes. Everything was covered in a blanket of sculpted whiteness. Along the riverbank, branches drooped under the weight of the snow and, from a crystal blue sky, the sun shone down on the intense beauty of the day. Lou Reed's 'Perfect Day' came into Jack's mind. He had the whole weekend off, the girls were with him until Sunday evening, and this afternoon he was taking them to see what would soon be his new home. Theirs too, albeit it on a part-time basis.

Almost a month had passed since he'd made his offer on Adele Waterman's flat and so far the purchase was going through without any delay. Owing to the efficiency of both solicitors involved, contracts had been exchanged and, if his luck held, he'd move in during the second week of February. As an estate agent, he had seen it all when it came to the best-made plans going awry, but he had every confidence that his own move would be accomplished without any hitches. He was looking forward to it: the purchase of a home was a step in the right direction. He knew how important it was for his daughters to believe that he was happy, and he had talked a lot about the new flat last night when he'd collected them from Prestbury. As they tucked into the takeaway pizzas they'd picked up on the way home, he'd stressed how great it would be once he'd made it his own. To do that, he told them, he needed their help. 'I want you to choose the wallpaper for your bedroom and all that kind of thing,' he'd said. 'You'll be much better at it than me.' Lucy had jumped at the opportunity, but Amber had been less enthusiastic. Unnervingly, she had looked at him as though she suspected him of manipulating her. Which, of course, he was.

'What's wrong, Amber?' he'd asked.

She'd shrugged her shoulders and poked a fork at her pizza.

He wasn't taking that from her. 'Come on, Amber, you can do better than that for an answer. Don't you want to decide how your bedroom will look? Leave it to me and you could end up with something totally naff, like . . . like Walt Disney.'

She scowled and put down her fork. 'Will you really let us choose?'

'Sure. That's what I've just said.'

She didn't seem convinced. And then he understood why: she said, 'Mum and Tony said we could choose how to decorate our rooms, but every time I told them what I wanted Mum said I couldn't have it. She kept saying it wouldn't go with the rest of the house.'

'Well, never mind what goes on in Prestbury. So long as you and Lucy can agree on what you'd both like, you can have whatever you want. And that's a promise. A gold-plated one.'

They arrived at 10a Maywood Park Road slightly late and out of breath. They had left the car beneath its duvet of snow and walked across town. Except that it was a case of two steps forward and one back. In common with most children, Amber and Lucy treated the snow as something they'd never seen before, although they'd played out in it for most of the morning. If they weren't throwing snowballs at each other, or at him, they were shrieking at the top of their voices. Their enjoyment was infectious: he couldn't remember the last time he'd felt so happy and relaxed.

He rang the doorbell and in the following minutes, while he waited for Adele to appear, he checked out the girls: they were standing on either side of him gazing up at the house. He tried to see the property through their eyes so that he could gauge their reaction. It was important to him that they liked it. As if she was reading his mind, Lucy said, 'It looks old, Daddy.'

He interpreted this as a negative comment, and said, 'Oh, not very. Only about a hundred years.'

'It's quite dark,' she added, standing back from the covered porch and staring up at the brick walls, which contrasted sharply with the whiteness all around them. 'Do you think it might be haunted?'

He laughed. 'Not a hope.'

'I think it's nice.'

This was from Amber.

'Really?'

She nodded. 'Yes. It looks ... sort of cosy. And friendly.'

Before he could respond, the door opened and there was Adele, dressed in a pleated skirt and lace-frilled blouse with a pale lilac cardigan. Suddenly he realised that he and the girls – boisterously red-faced and damp from snowball-throwing – weren't fit to cross this elegant lady's threshold. If she thought so, she didn't let on, but welcomed them in and asked if they would like to take off their wet shoes and boots. Then she offered to take the girls' coats and wet gloves and put them on the radiator in the kitchen. 'Let's see if we can have them dry by the time you leave,' she said.

Always more forward than her sister, Lucy said, 'My socks are wet too.'

'Are they? In that case we'd better dry them as well. What about yours, Amber?'

'Sorry to impose on you like this,' Jack said, when they were standing in the high-ceilinged kitchen, divested of anything wet. It was then that he noticed the tea-things set out on the small table in the corner of the room. There were dainty cups and saucers, plates of biscuits and crustless sandwiches covered with clingfilm. There was also a tiered cake-stand bearing an assortment of jam tarts and fairy-cakes, which had caught Lucy's eager eye. Exchanging a look with the old lady, he said, 'We won't keep you long, Adele, I can see you're expecting company.'

She looked at him, puzzled. 'Oh, I see.' She laughed. 'How silly of me. Of course, I should have said. I thought that when you'd shown your daughters round the flat you'd like to join me for some tea. Unless you have something else to do.' She switched her gaze from Jack to Amber and Lucy.

'I'd like to stay, Miss Waterman. And my sister would too.'

To Jack's surprise it was Amber who had spoken. How grown-up and polite she sounded.

'Excellent,' Adele said. 'Now, off you go with your father while I put the kettle on. Would you prefer juice? Or milk, perhaps? I'm afraid I don't have any fizzy drinks.'

'Tea's fine, thank you,' replied Amber, not giving Lucy a chance to speak and already moving towards the door.

It didn't take them long to explore the flat, and Jack brought their tour to an end in what was to be their bedroom. Like all the other rooms, it was crammed with treasured possessions: a large wardrobe that took up an entire wall, a high chest of drawers, shelves of china figures, a full-length mirror on a mahogany stand, a double bed with an ornate wooden headboard, a waist-high bookcase packed with rows of faded hardbacks and a pair of bedside tables.

'So what do you think, girls? Will it do?'

'Will all this furniture be here when you move in?' asked Lucy, her tone unsure as she lifted the lid on a large sewing basket and peered inside.

'No. It belongs to Miss Waterman and she'll be taking it with her.'

Lucy moved her attention from the sewing basket to the chest of drawers and a selection of framed photographs. 'Where's she going to live? Will it be as nice as this?'

'She's moving into a retirement home, where she'll have lots of people to keep her company.'

Amber turned from the window where she had been looking down on to the garden and the park. 'I think she'd be happier staying here. This is her home. It doesn't seem right that you're pushing her out.'

'Your father is doing no such thing,' said a firm but kindly voice at the door. Adele came into the room and stood next to Amber by the window. In a gesture that Jack expected Amber to shrink away from, the old lady rested a hand on his daughter's shoulder. 'But you're right. This has been my home and I've been very happy here. Now it's time to let someone else enjoy it. And that's where you come in. I need to know that the three of you will like being here and that you'll take good care of it for me.'

They had their tea in the sitting room, in front of the old-fashioned gas fire that hissed and fascinated the girls. It was when he was watching Amber and

Lucy warm to Adele that Jack realised how sad it was that they had no grandparents. Given the tension between himself and Maddie, some neutral adult company was probably just what they needed.

When Lucy started to fidget, Adele asked if they would like to go outside and play. 'You could build a snowman for me,' she said, making it sound as if they would be doing her an enormous favour. 'I haven't had one of those in my garden for many years. I think the birds would like it too. Something new for them to look at. I might have a carrot I could spare for a nose, but you'll have to think of something outside to use for his eyes.'

After the girls had bundled themselves up in their warmed coats and gloves and had slipped on their boots, Adele let them out and made a fresh pot of tea. When she and Jack were back in the sitting room, watching Amber and Lucy through the window, Adele said, 'They're lovely girls, Jack, you must be so proud of them.'

'I am,' he said simply. 'They mean the world to me.'

'I can see that. And you're a very special man to understand how important they are. It isn't every father who makes that connection with his children.'

'I've always felt this way about them, but . . . but nearly losing them when Maddie took off, well, let's just say the experience has sharpened my focus.'

She handed him his cup. 'You sound bitter, Jack.'

He swallowed. 'I am. Sorry if that sounds petty.'

'Certainly not petty. Just a great shame. Sugar?'

He raised his hand to the proffered bowl and silver sugar tongs.

'And Maddie, your wife, she's now with your oldest and closest friend – Tony, if my memory serves me correctly from one of our earlier conversations.'

Bristling slightly, he said, 'Your memory serves you very well.' But what she said next had him even more on edge.

'I fully understand your sense of betrayal and hurt, Jack, especially towards Tony, and please forgive an old lady's impertinence, but may I offer you a piece of advice? Or, rather, ask you something extremely personal?'

He shifted uncomfortably in his seat. 'I probably don't have much choice in the matter, do I?'

She smiled and took a sip of her tea. 'Think back to before Maddie left you when, for all those years, Tony was your best friend. If anything had happened to you, who would you have wanted to help Maddie take care of Amber and Lucy?'

Unable to meet her piercing stare, he looked beyond her, to the garden where his two precious daughters were playing in the snow. He didn't know if the old lady was psychic, but years ago he and Maddie had had it written into their wills that if anything happened to both of them, Tony would not only be the executor of their wills but would become Amber and Lucy's legal guardian.

Minutes passed before he spoke. 'I don't think that's a fair question. The circumstances have changed.'

'Indeed they have . . . and for all concerned. But I would imagine that Tony would want only the best for those two delightful girls. Give him the credit for that much, at least. You might be surprised by how much peace of mind that thought could give you. Now, then, tell me about your writing. Beth says you're quite the rising star of the group.'

32

It was rare for Beth to have an entire day to herself, but on this particular Sunday, early in February, she was entirely alone.

With January behind them, which meant Nathan's mock A levels were over – no more study leave and late-night revision sessions – an air of calm routine had returned to their lives. To reward himself, Nathan had borrowed the car and driven Jaz to Nottingham University for the day to show her where he hoped to be studying, come the autumn. He had been delighted when the letter from Nottingham had arrived last week and he'd been offered a place. Beth had wanted to caution him on the perils of counting chickens before they'd hatched – he had yet to sit the all-important summer exams and acquire the necessary grades – but she'd held her tongue and told him instead to drive carefully.

She sighed. Would he ever take her concern seriously? And would she ever learn to trust his judgement? How did a parent make that enormous leap of faith?

The only person she knew who had made and coped with this transition was Ewan – most of her friends either had much younger children or none at all, like Wendy, and Simone and Ben. But she and Ewan had had frequent conversations on the subject.

> Ah, the eternal question [he'd said once], how to locate the on/off button for being a parent. Let me know if you find it, won't you?

The only on/off button she could locate with any certainty was the one on her computer. Having spent the morning blitzing the flat after a chaotic week of late nights at the surgery – she had been covering for Wendy, who was basking in some winter sun in the Canary Islands – it was time to treat herself to an afternoon of uninterrupted writing. Armed with a mug of tea and a ham and tomato sandwich, she settled herself at her small desk and switched on the computer. Before losing herself in her novel – she was in the middle of a chapter that was proving particularly enjoyable to write – she would check her emails. There was nothing from Simone, which was disappointing, but understandable – her friend's parents were staying with her – but there was one from Ewan. She smiled and clicked on OPEN.

Hello Beth,

How about this? I'm all wired up with the latest in mobile phone and laptop technology. Yes, I know I've always been proud of my technophobe status, but this baby's a real cutie to play with. More importantly it means I can keep in touch while I'm away from home.

I'm currently down in deepest Cornwall, showing my face at a conference. Supposedly I'm here to work, but in reality I'm doing nothing more vital than shoring up the local economy by sampling the excellent seafood on offer. The local beverage isn't bad either. I'm here until Tuesday, and while I'm hanging out at an undisclosed address I feel brave enough to ask you something important.

I'm only too aware that I've taken enough liberties with you already, that I've pushed the envelope as far as is decent, that I've thrown my undeserving self upon your gentle nature once too often, that I've squandered your precious time in forcing reply upon reply to my inadequate electronic meanderings. And, oh, that an ill-favoured wretch such as I should even . . . 'Stop!' I hear you plead. So with a hey, and a ho, and a hey nonny no, I shall cry, 'Havoc!' and let slip the dogs and get to the point.

Bethany, p-p-please . . . (huge intake of breath here, maybe even a drum roll) . . . p-p-please, if it so pleases your ladyship . . . (clears throat in attempt to cover up excruciating nervousness) . . . c-c-can we meet?

Your stuttering with nerves, humblest of lowly humble servants,

Ewan Barefaced-Cheek Jones

Beth laughed, and was all set to reply when the doorbell rang. What timing! She clicked on SAVE, hurriedly shut down the machine and rushed downstairs. Out of breath, she opened the front door to find Barnaby on the step.

'Am I welcome?' he asked.

It was almost six weeks since she had last seen Barnaby and the sight of him standing hesitantly at her door moved her to tears. They embraced each other tightly, and when he released her, she wiped her eyes with the backs of her hands. 'I'm sorry,' she said, 'it's just so good to see you.'

His eyes were moist too. 'I would have come sooner, only I didn't know how I'd be received. Didn't want to walk into hostile territory. You know what a shocking coward I am.'

It was on the tip of Beth's tongue, as she led the way upstairs, to say that anyone who lived with Lois was anything but a coward, but she refrained from making such an inappropriate remark. She took his scarf and overcoat and offered to make him his favourite drink.

They sat at the table with mugs of hot chocolate and the biscuit tin between them. Beth got up to put a couple of logs on the fire. 'How are things at Marsh House?' she asked. 'How's Lois?'

'Oh, don't you go worrying about Lois. She's keeping her spirits up by rapping me over the knuckles when the mood takes her.'

'That doesn't make me feel any better. Worse, if anything. It's hardly your fault she and I have had a falling out.'

'I'm more than used to a daily dose of admonishment. My day wouldn't be complete without a good scolding.'

She admired Barnaby for his apparent indifference, but Beth knew that he wouldn't be there unless he was upset about the situation in which they found themselves. 'Barnaby,' she said, adopting a firmer tone, 'we can't let this go on. There has to be a way. Lois has to understand that while I'm genuinely sorry for what happened there was a lot of truth in what I said. Does she know you're here?'

He dunked a chocolate digestive in his mug. 'Er . . . no. Thought it best to keep my visit under wraps. She thinks I'm at B&Q pricing Black and Decker Workmates.'

If the situation weren't so serious, Beth would have laughed at his subversive behaviour. 'Oh, Barnaby, if I didn't know better I'd say you were enjoying yourself. But what's to be done? Between us we have to make Lois see sense.'

He finished his biscuit and leaned forward in his seat. 'I have a plan. It's risky, but it might just work. I'll need your help. Nathan's too.'

Nottingham was busy with rush-hour traffic and it wasn't until they were heading towards the A50 that the congestion on the roads eased. Even so, Nathan wasn't taking any chances. It was dark, and with sleety rain obscuring his vision, he was keeping a healthy distance between himself and the car in front. He had no intention of arriving home with a crumpled bonnet. His mother had enough to cope with already without him adding to her worries.

Lately, though, he had noticed that his mother's confidence was growing. He'd put it down to the writers' group she had joined. Since she'd taken up with Hidden Talents she had changed. For the better. She was smiling more these days. Several times he had caught her staring out of the window, looking as if she was on the verge of laughter. 'Something amusing you, Mum?' he'd asked yesterday at breakfast.

'Oh, not especially,' she'd replied, her face inscrutable, as she waited for their toast to pop up. If he didn't know better, he'd suspect she was keeping something from him.

He stopped for a bus to pull out in front of them, and turned this thought over in his head: he was surprised by how much it bothered him. He supposed that, because he and his mother had always been so close, they had seldom kept things from each other. It made him wonder how he would react if that was to change. He explored this thought further, and a troubling feeling crept up on him. It was the disturbing realisation that he understood the root cause of his grandmother's problem. Perhaps her overbearing and sometimes bizarre behaviour stemmed from a basic need to be close to him and his mother. By trying to stop things changing, by denying the truth, she had hoped to preserve the safe little world she had invented for them all to live in.

A world that he had nuked ruthlessly on Christmas Day.

For the first time, he felt a wave of shame and regret. He had gone too far, he saw that now.

'You're looking very serious.'

He turned his head towards Jaz. 'Just thinking.'

A wry smile flickered across her face. 'Whoa, check out the man trying to do two things at once.'

He brightened instantly. 'Hey, I'm the one driving, so watch the attempts at biting wit.'

'Any chance of Michael Schumacher finding the brake pedal? I need the loo.'

A short time later they stopped at a Little Chef and, leaving Nathan to join the queue for a table so that they could have a drink and something to eat, Jaz went in search of the toilets. In the cubicle next to her she could hear a woman talking: 'Stop it, darling, Mummy doesn't like it when you do that. That's better. Now, stand straight and Mummy will see to your buttons.'

She stood at the row of basins, washing her hands, listening to the stream of gibberish still coming from the cubicle. Before long, when the latest batch of Raffertys arrived, her mother would be speaking the same nonsense. She switched off the hot tap, grabbed a couple of paper towels and dried her hands. And who would be called upon to babysit? Good old Jaz. After all, she was the only sensible one who could be trusted with such a job. That's what her father had said last night when he'd come up to her room to tell her it was time she turned out her light. 'It's gone midnight, Jaz,' he'd said. 'Do you think I'm made of money and can afford to keep this many lightbulbs going?'

'Jimmy and Phin's lights are still on,' she'd countered, while surreptitiously closing down her computer.

'Yeah, but theirs aren't as bright as yours.'

'Like their brains, then.'

He came further into the room, laughing. 'Don't I always feed you the best lines? We could become a double act, you and me.'

'Let's not be hasty, Dad. I don't fancy being anyone's stooge. Was there something you wanted? Other than to keep me informed of your fiscal policies.'

He laughed again. 'You're a true Rafferty, Jaz, make no mistake. An answer for everything.' He sat on the end of her bed. 'Actually, I wanted to have a quiet word with you. I'm worried about your mother.'

Jaz gave her father her full attention. 'What is it? She's not ill, is she? The pregnancy isn't—'

He raised his hands, palms facing her. 'Calm down. It's nothing serious. But you must have noticed how tired she is.'

Jaz had. Most days now her mother looked washed out. She was sick a lot in the mornings too, usually after Jaz's father and brothers had left for work. While her mother was suffering in the bathroom, Jaz saw to her sisters' breakfast and got them ready for school – no mean feat, given the inherently cussed nature of Tamzin and Lulu. By the time Jaz arrived at college she was frazzled and in no mood to concentrate on her work. Several times she had found herself nodding off.

'So what I'm saying, Jaz,' her father had continued, 'is that I want you to help your mother as much as you can. I want to know that I can rely on you.'

'But what about the others?'

He chuckled. 'You mean your sisters? I think we can safely say they're as useful as a pair of chocolate candlesticks. Unlike you, they're not blessed with an ounce of common sense or reliability.'

She knew she was clutching at straws, but said anyway, 'There's Phin and Jimmy. They could do something.'

His expression turned stern. 'Are you saying you don't want to help?'

'No. It's not that, it's just—'

'Then stop making such a fuss.' He got up. 'Anyone would think I'd asked you to repaint the Vatican. Which reminds me, I want us all to go to Mass tomorrow. We've let it slip.'

'But I can't go. Not this Sunday.'

'Oh? Can't or *won't?*'

'I told you I was spending the day with Vicki.' The lie had tripped off her tongue, as they did so easily, these days. Her family still didn't know about Nathan and she intended to keep it that way for as long as she could.

33

'Dulcie, please, I beg you to reconsider. Don't do this to me ... to us.'

'I don't have any choice.'

'But you do. Of course you do.'

'My mind's made up, Richard. Please don't make this any more difficult than it already is for me.'

Hearing the terrible finality in Dulcie's voice, Richard passed a shaking hand across his face. He had never felt more shocked. When he had arrived to have lunch with Dulcie there had been nothing in her manner to hint at the devastation she was about to wreak. He had just opened the sandwiches he'd bought from the sandwich bar near his office and put them on to their plates, when from nowhere she was telling him it was over between them.

He hauled himself to his feet, ready to try again. He had to make Dulcie see that she couldn't expect him to walk away from her. That he was never to see her again. His life would be over if that happened. He moved silently across the kitchen, went and joined her at the french windows where she had her back to him, arms folded across her chest, gazing at the rain that lashed against the glass. He placed a hand on her shoulder and turned her gently towards him. Tears filled her eyes and he saw his own pain mirrored in them. 'Dulcie, this is madness. We can't inflict so much pain on ourselves.' He took her in his arms and held her close. He feared she might resist, but she didn't, and burying his face in her neck, he kissed her soft, warm skin. He felt her quiver in his embrace, worked his mouth along the line of her jaw and kissed her deeply, wanting desperately to forget the pain of the last few minutes. He held her tightly against him, his body tense with the need to be reassured that everything would be all right. 'Let's go upstairs,' he whispered, his hand pressing on the nape of her neck.

But that was when he knew he couldn't change her mind. Tears were streaming down her cheeks. She pulled away from him. 'Please, Richard, I love you, and probably always will, but it's over between us. It has to be.'

He let go of her, bewildered. Angry too. Angry with Kate and Henry.

And Angela. It had been Angela's idea to invite Dulcie and her family to their wretched Boxing Day drinks party. If she hadn't come up with such a stupid suggestion Kate and Henry wouldn't have met and he wouldn't be facing the worst moment of his life.

The irrationality of this thought slammed into him. His head pounding, despair welled up inside him. He took hold of Dulcie's arm. 'Explain to me one more time why and how you can justify what you're doing.'

She looked at him sadly, her face still wet with tears. 'I'm not thinking of us. I'm thinking of your son. If you ever leave Angela for me, you put Henry in an impossible situation with his mother.'

'He'll get over it. So will she.'

She shook her head. 'No. Angela would feel doubly betrayed. By her husband *and* her son. What could be worse for her?'

'Then I won't leave Angela. We'll carry on as before.'

'You might be capable of doing that, but I'm not. I wouldn't be able to face Kate. The deceit would build and build. I just know I couldn't live with it.'

Her cool reasoning was too much for Richard. 'But, Dulcie, what they feel for each other is nothing compared to what we have. Our love is worth infinitely more than theirs.'

'How can you say that?'

'They're young. They're—'

'They're not that young, Richard. And if you loved your son as much as I love Kate, you'd want to give him the benefit of the doubt. After all, it was you who said you believed their attraction was more than a passing fancy.'

He drew in his breath sharply, felt as if she'd dealt him a physical blow. 'That's unfair, Dulcie. I wouldn't have thought you capable of such a cheap shot. You know how I feel about my children. How important they are to me.' His voice shook. 'And who, I'd like to know, gave you the monopoly on familial love?'

In response, Dulcie's shoulders sagged and she wrapped her arms around herself as if she were cold. 'This isn't doing either of us any good,' she said. 'Please, let's finish it by being civil. We owe each other that, if nothing else.'

She was asking too much of him. 'No!' he argued wildly. 'I can't. I can't be civil. I won't give you up. I love you, Dulcie, and stupidly I thought you loved me. Perhaps ...' he went on, more slowly, knowing he was being cruel, but wanting her to understand what she was doing to him '... perhaps I've been wrong all this time. You were never really committed to me, were you? Maybe that's why you didn't warn Kate off before it was too late.'

She turned on him, eyes blazing. 'I don't think you're in any position to speak of commitment. You're a married man who's been sneaking around having an adulterous affair behind his wife's back. How's that for commitment?'

He knew when he was beaten and he slumped into the nearest chair. Resting his elbows on the table, he covered his face with his hands and wept. For a while he was aware of nothing but the sound of his own choking sobs. Then gradually he sensed Dulcie moving towards him and felt the slight pressure of her hand on his shoulder. 'I'm so sorry,' he mumbled. 'I shouldn't have accused you like that. Forgive me, please.'

She stroked his hair, a gesture that was so evocative of their being in bed together. He shuddered, knowing, and now accepting, that he would never experience that pleasure again.

Dulcie marched through the park gates. The moment Richard had gone, she had left the house, grabbing her filthy old waxed jacket from the back of the kitchen door, the one she only ever wore for gardening. But she didn't care how awful she looked: she needed to be outside, away from any physical reminders of Richard – her house contained too many memories of him.

The rain had eased off, but the biting February wind was gusting, sending leaves and a rogue crisp packet skittering as she strode past the swings and slides. She followed the path towards the duck pond. Already breathless, she increased her speed, as if to convince herself that her heart wasn't breaking.

But it was futile.

She had just made the ultimate sacrifice, had given up the man she loved for her daughter's happiness. She felt no virtuous gain for what she had done, only the deep ache of loss.

She wished that there had been a better way to end it with Richard, a way that wouldn't have hurt him so much. Would she ever forget the anguish in his face when they had held each other and kissed for the last time?

The park was almost deserted – just a couple walking their floppy-eared springer spaniel – and with the pick of the park benches overlooking the pond, she chose one directly beneath a large oak tree, so that, should it start to rain again, she would have a degree of shelter.

She recalled Kate's words – *You've never been at a low ebb in your entire life. You're the most positive and upbeat woman I know.*

Oh, Kate, if only you could see me now, thought Dulcie, as she stared through swollen, tear-filled eyes at the ripples caused by the wind on the surface of the pond. How had she found the strength to walk away from the man who had meant the world to her? Only a short while ago, when Richard had suffered his heart-attack and she had thought she'd lost him for ever, she had woken up to the extent of her love for him. And now, when she had never been surer of his love for her, she had thrown it away. What was the sense in that?

She lowered her head, and let the tears flow. What did it matter if anyone saw her?

But she changed her mind when, coming towards her in the distance, she recognised Victor Blackmore. Strangely, though, he wasn't walking in a straight line along the path. He was zigzagging between the trees in a bizarre fashion, glancing over his shoulder every now and then or stopping to tie a shoelace.

How very odd.

34

Victor was in character. With his hood up, his anorak zipped to his chin, his hands thrust deep into his pockets and dark glasses covering his eyes, he was Irving Hunter, special-ops agent, the protagonist of his novel *Star City*. Peering furtively over his shoulder, he was checking the trees, bushes and litter-bins for CIA agents secretly drafted in by NATO to take out Macedonian subversives.

He had started work on Chapter Ninety-six at five o'clock that morning, but the hours had slipped by and the words failed to flow. Something jarred. And then he'd got it. The situation hadn't felt real to him, and without further delay he'd left the house and thrown himself into acting the part of Irving Hunter. Prowling the streets, dodging in and out of shop doorways, following suspects, he was finally getting the feel of Irving's day-to-day routine. He'd found the experience both exhilarating and exhausting. His feet ached and were wet from the rain, but a little discomfort was a small price to pay. All the great writers had suffered for their art, and he was to be no exception. It was what put him above all the wannabe writers out there. What those fools didn't understand was that the noble craft of novel-writing was like scaling Everest – the harder and higher the climb, and the more one struggled, the more worthwhile the task and the finished result. If only he could find a publisher who had half a brain and the wit to take on his book, he knew *Star City* would be a huge success. In his opinion, it was written to a far higher standard than most of the rubbish on the shelves. It had pace, tension, and plenty of action. What more could a publisher want? It had blockbuster stamped all over it! And there was always the chance that it would be turned into a film. He was out of touch with actors these days, but a young Michael Caine would have done justice to the role of Irving Hunter.

He caught a blast of icy wind in his face, and was suddenly annoyed with himself. He'd got sidetracked, had slipped out of character and forgotten that he was Irving Hunter scouring the deserted streets of Skopje for Albanian rebels and ruthless terrorists.

He took in his surroundings, not sure how he'd got there. This was happening to him more and more: he would go out for a carton of milk and come back two hours later with a loaf of bread. He put it down to his absorption in his writing. Since his redundancy, *Star City* had become his *raison d'être*: nothing else mattered to him.

A swivel of his head informed him that he was in Maywood Park. And there, a few yards in front of him, sitting on a bench, was someone he recognised. It was Dulcie Ballantyne from the writers' group. He debated what to do. Should he walk past her and risk being recognised then be forced to make polite conversation, or turn and retrace his steps?

He hesitated. How would Irving Hunter react in this situation?

He would brazen it out. That's what he'd do. He'd stroll by and nonchalantly wish the woman a good day, while all the time never slowing his step.

The decision made, he picked up his pace and pushed on, acknowledging why he didn't like Dulcie Ballantyne. As self-elected leader of the writers' group, she had assumed she was better than the rest of them. With her posh house and fancy furniture, she had looked down on them. Him in particular.

He was almost level with the woman when a voice inside his head said, 'Why not stop and show her what you're really made of? Isn't that what Irving Hunter would do? Remember, you're a winner. *A winner.*'

Dulcie braced herself. 'Hello, Victor,' she said, rising quickly to her feet to give the impression she didn't have time to hang around. 'How's the writing going? We've missed seeing you on a Thursday evening.'

He lifted his sunglasses. 'I'm very well, Mrs Ballantyne. Thank you for enquiring. And, yes, the writing is going well. Never better. And yours?'

'Oh, you know, muddling along.' She thought it better not to mention anything about the short-story competition she'd won recently: with his rampant insecurity he would only think she was boasting. A gust of wind rattled a swirl of leaves around their ankles and for a moment she forgot her own problems and took in the shock of Victor's appearance. He'd lost weight and his bloodshot eyes had a strained, slightly manic look. Perhaps he was working too hard and wasn't getting enough sleep. But who was she to talk? With her tatty old jacket, hair all over the place, and face blotchy with crying, he was probably thinking what a mess she looked. The silence continued between them, until Dulcie's compassionate nature got the better of her and she said, 'Victor, I've been sitting here for some time and now I'm chilled to the bone. I don't suppose you'd like to join me in a cup of coffee at Novel Ways, would you?'

A downpour of sleety rain hastened their departure from the park. Dulcie didn't know what surprised her more – that she had made such an invitation, or that Victor had accepted it.

35

Jack was running late. After work he'd met up with Des for a drink. It was ages since they'd done that and he suspected it had something to do with Julie. She was still cross over the way he'd left Clare although, according to Des, she was coming round slowly. 'Best not to rush things,' Des had advised. 'You know what women are like. Once they get something into their heads, it's there carved in stone until time weathers it.' He'd asked after Clare and Des had told him she was much more her old self. 'Getting over you by swearing allegiance to the school of thought that denounces all men as Neanderthal numbskulls.'

'I still feel guilty about what happened,' Jack admitted.

'Good. That means there's hope for you.'

'Do you think it would be okay for me to get in touch to try to make my peace with her?'

Des had shaken his head vehemently. 'Take my advice and leave well alone for a few more months.'

It was raining hard when Jack drew up outside Dulcie's house. He checked his watch. Ten to eight. He should have been there twenty minutes ago. He reached for his file from the passenger seat, locked the car and hurried up the steps to number eighteen, the rain hammering on the road and pavement.

Beth answered the door to him. 'We'd almost given up on you, Jack.' Then, as he shrugged off his coat and draped it over the newel post at the foot of the stairs, she said softly, 'You'll never guess who's here – Victor.'

'Really?'

'Apparently Dulcie ran into him this afternoon and persuaded him to join us again.'

He rolled his eyes. 'Is she feeling okay?'

Still with her voice scarcely more than a whisper, she said, 'Between you and me, I don't think she is.'

'Any idea what's wrong?'

'No. But I'll try to get her alone in the kitchen at coffee time and see if there's anything we can do.'

Following Beth, Jack realised that he knew practically nothing about Dulcie. She had shared little with them about her family or friends. He couldn't even say for sure how many children she had. Or had he been so wrapped up in his own problems that he hadn't listened properly?

In the sitting room, Jack saw that Victor was occupying the chair he'd always sat in. 'Hi, Victor,' he said cheerily. 'Long time no see. How's it going?' Not good, he thought. The man looked wrecked. Dishevelled and ready to drop. And flakier than Jack remembered. He was dressed in his usual jacket, but the shirt beneath it was rumpled and his tie was marked with a greasy stain.

'I'm very well,' replied Victor, eyes darting. He crossed his legs and fidgeted with the A4 pad on his lap.

In response to the man's curt reply, Jack decided to be equally blunt. 'So, what brings you back to the group?'

Victor picked at one of his fingernails. 'It was Mrs Ballantyne. She insisted I came. She seems to think I have something unique to offer to you all.'

Jack was saved from making a reply to this extraordinary comment when from the kitchen, he heard Jaz talking to Dulcie. He turned to greet them. Instantly he saw what Beth had meant: there was an agitated air about Dulcie that was at odds with the calm woman he knew – and, if he wasn't mistaken, she'd cried recently.

Everyone was getting on with the exercise she had set them and, in the silence of their intense concentration, Dulcie was regretting her decision to go ahead with tonight's meeting. She should have been sensible and cancelled it. But she hadn't been thinking straight today. Why else would she have encouraged Victor to join the group again? Had it only been pity that had driven her to take him to Novel Ways for a coffee then sit with him for more than an hour while he regaled her with an in-depth, blow-by-blow account of where he was up to with *Star City*? If she was to believe half of what he said, his manuscript was on the verge of becoming the hottest property the publishing world had ever got its hands on.

It was all too easy to laugh at people like Victor, but her own vulnerability that day had given her an empathy towards him and she had felt an inexplicable urge to offer her protection. It was clear to her, even in her dazed state, that he was sick. Depressed, probably. She hadn't been able to turn her back on someone so obviously in need, who very likely didn't have many friends he could approach for help. As irritating as he was, she hoped the rest of the group would forgive her for foisting Victor on them again. Perhaps tomorrow she should ring them individually and explain the situation.

Across the room she could hear a distracting clicking sound. Victor was fiddling with his biro. He was breathing heavily too. My, how he filled a small space. It was pure madness what she was taking on, but rescuing Victor from himself would stop her agonising over Richard.

With fifteen minutes left in which to complete the writing exercise,

Dulcie focused her thoughts. The group was writing a thousand words about a box. 'It can be any kind of box,' she'd informed them, 'and you can do anything with it.' At first Victor had declined to take part, but after gentle persuasion, he had relented, and she'd set the stopwatch. Her own piece of writing wasn't going well. It was chock full of clichés and embarrassingly sentimental. But how could she even think of writing when all she wanted to do was crawl upstairs and hide under the duvet for the rest of her life?

'Time's up!' declared Victor, so loudly that Dulcie jumped.

'How did we all get on?' she asked.

Jaz let out her breath. 'I think I may have gone on longer than a thousand words.'

'Show-off,' teased Jack.

'Beth, how about you?'

'It's not quite what I thought it would turn out to be, but I did finish it.'

'Good for you. And, Victor, how did you get on?'

'It was straightforward enough. I can rattle off a thousand words in my sleep.'

'That's excellent,' she said. 'Jack, would you care to be first off the blocks to read to us?'

The evening progressed with everyone taking a turn to read out their work. All except Dulcie. 'Sorry, everyone,' she apologised. 'I wouldn't inflict my attempt on my worst enemy. A very poor effort, I'm afraid.' And before anyone could argue with her, or shake the Self-belief Box, she put down her pen and suggested it was time for coffee.

'I'll give you a hand,' offered Beth, quick to get to her feet.

No sooner were they in the kitchen, Dulcie filling the kettle and Beth putting milk into a jug, than the telephone rang. Dulcie picked up the receiver, gesturing to Beth where the sugar was kept. The kettle almost slipped out of her hand when she heard who it was.

'Dulcie, please don't put the phone down on me. Just listen to what I have to say.'

'I'm . . . I'm afraid I'm rather busy at present.' Her voice sounded cold and stilted. She saw Beth shoot her a curious glance.

'Dulcie, I can't do this. I can't accept that I'll never see you again.'

'Perhaps we could discuss it later.' Again, the same toneless voice.

'You've got someone there?'

'My writing group.'

'*Dammit!* What time do they leave?'

She was about to answer his question when she realised that she wasn't brave enough to speak to Richard later, when she would be alone. Instead, she said, 'Goodbye, then.' Hating herself, she dropped the receiver on to its cradle with a clumsy clatter.

Then she burst into tears.

Beth was instantly at her side, a hand on her shoulder. 'Dulcie, whatever is the matter? What can I do to help? Shall I get rid of the group?'

Unable to speak, Dulcie leaned into her and sobbed. But there was no relief, the physical contact of another person made her cry all the more. Minutes passed, and to make things worse, Jack appeared in the doorway. 'Don't suppose I can hide out here with you two—' He stopped short. 'Anything I can do to help?'

'Yes,' said Beth, taking command of the situation. 'Tell the others Dulcie isn't feeling well.'

'There's no need for that,' Dulcie muttered, fumbling for a tissue but not finding one. She felt such a fool for breaking down.

'Yes, there is,' asserted Beth, briefly leaving her side to fetch a box of Kleenex from a shelf above the fridge. Dulcie took a handful and blew her nose hard.

'Maybe Beth's right,' she said. 'Would you mind, Jack? Please say how sorry I am.'

'Of course. Leave it to me. I'll run Jaz home. Do you have anything stronger than coffee in the house? You look like you could do with a stiff drink.'

'There's nothing seriously wrong with her, is there?' asked Jaz, as Jack pulled away from Dulcie's house.

'I hope not.' And, making light of the situation, 'Maybe it was the shock of having Victor back in the group.'

Jaz smiled. 'That would be it, then. Did you know he was going to be there?'

'No. All Beth had time to tell me when I arrived was that Dulcie had bumped into him this afternoon.'

She cringed. 'I can think of any number of people I'd sooner bump into. He looked like a walking freak-show, didn't he?'

'He certainly wasn't at his best.'

'You don't think it's catching, do you? I mean, perhaps he and Dulcie have got some awful bug.'

'Here's a promise. If you start looking anywhere near as bad as Victor, I'll cart you off to Maywood Health Centre.'

'Cheers.'

He turned into Jaz's road and stopped the car on the corner. 'See you next week. And fingers crossed everyone's feeling better.'

She was just unbuckling her seatbelt, when a P-registered Rav-4 came towards them, its headlamps shining straight into their faces. It stopped at the junction, just yards from where they were parked, music booming. Two men in their twenties sat in the front. At the same moment, they turned and looked down at Jack, then at his passenger.

'Oh, hell!' Jaz cursed.

'What? What's wrong?'

'Everything.' To his astonishment, she flung open the door and marched away down the road in the pouring rain. Puzzled, he watched her go. Then, realising that the car was still alongside him, he turned his head. The driver scowled at him with such menace that Jack had to look away. And then they were gone, tyres squealing.

The evening was getting weirder by the minute.

He decided he'd better stay to check that Jaz got in safely and watched her disappear up the drive of a large modern house. Then he sat for a moment to consider what he'd just witnessed. Perhaps the two men in the car were loony neighbours. He was certain Jaz knew them, and even more certain that she wasn't fond of them. Once more that evening he was shamed into admitting that he knew hardly anything about a member of the writers' group.

He turned the car and drove back the way he'd just come to Bloom Street. Again, Beth opened the door to him.

'Did you forget something?' she asked.

'No. I just thought I'd see if there was anything I could do to help. I also thought you'd need a lift home at some point.'

'Oh, that was thoughtful of you.'

'How's Dulcie?'

'Come and see for yourself.' Dropping her voice, she added, 'She hasn't let on what's troubling her.'

Dulcie was where he'd left her half an hour ago in the kitchen. He was pleased to see that she looked less agitated. On the table in front of her stood a bottle of whisky, a pot of tea, some mugs and a large plate of toast and honey. 'Comfort food,' she said, with an attempt at a smile. 'Beth's idea.'

'And an excellent one at that. Okay if I join you?'

'Of course. And I can't apologise enough for my loss of control. Very melodramatic of me. You can always trust a writer to go to pieces. It's the drama, I suppose.'

He pulled out a chair and sat down. 'If you apologise any more I'll have to fetch the Self-belief Box.' This elicited a proper smile from her. 'You would say if there was anything I,' he glanced at Beth, 'or we, could do, wouldn't you? I'm sure I read somewhere that it's *de rigueur* for writers to show a brothers-in-arms solidarity to each other.'

She patted his hand. 'That's very sweet of you, Jack, but I shall be fine. A long soak in a hot bath followed by an early night should do the trick. Now, then, who's going to help me polish off all this tea and toast?'

Her tone was brisk and hearty, and Jack had to accept that he had done as much as he could for her. 'Honey and toast, how could a man resist? Count me in.'

The three of them sat round the table talking about anything that was safely neutral: his imminent house move and how Amber and Lucy had taken such a shine to Adele Waterman, then Beth's son, Nathan, and how he and Jaz were such a cosy item. It prompted Jack to describe the incident when he had dropped Jaz at home.

'Goodness, how peculiar,' said Beth.

'Did Jaz give any clue that she knew these men?' asked Dulcie.

'She didn't say anything, but I'd put money on her knowing exactly who they were. She was off like a rocket when she saw them.'

Beth looked thoughtful. 'They must have been her brothers.'

'I didn't know she had any,' Jack said. 'She's never mentioned them.'

'Oh, yes, she has,' Beth corrected him. 'The novel she's writing is about the family from hell, the Clacketts. It's probably based on her own family. What's more, I'm sure Nathan once said something about a couple of brothers and how she can't stand them. She also has two younger sisters.'

'Well, that's that mystery cleared up,' Dulcie said.

But Jack wasn't satisfied. If the two men had been Jaz's brothers, why had they looked at him so threateningly?

They had moved on to Victor, when the shrill ring of the phone made them all start. Jack saw the frozen expression on Dulcie's face and registered also that she made no move to answer it. It rang three more times. He slid a glance in Beth's direction.

Another excruciating ring.

Still Dulcie stayed where she was.

'Erm . . . shall I answer that for you?' he offered.

She opened her mouth to speak, but nothing came out.

He sat through two more rings, his nerves jarring. 'Whoever it is, shall I tell them you're busy?'

'No,' she murmured, tight-lipped, 'let it ring. He'll give up.'

So that was it. The poor woman was being plagued by a nuisance-caller. No wonder she was so upset. When at last the kitchen was quiet again, Jack said, 'Dulcie, how long has this been going on?'

Her eyebrows came together in an uncharacteristic frown. 'I'm not sure that's any of your business,' she said primly.

'If someone I know is receiving obscene phone calls,' he said, 'I think it is my business. How long?'

'He's right, Dulcie,' said Beth. 'There's no need for you to put up with it. BT can do all sorts of things nowadays to track down these people.'

To their combined amazement, Dulcie smiled. 'Oh, you two wonderfully concerned people. If all I had to worry about was a heavy breather I'd consider myself most fortunate.' She drained her glass of whisky and seemed to come to a decision. 'I suppose it won't do any harm to tell you. Today I told the man I love that I couldn't see him any more.' She pursed her lips until they were almost white. 'That was him, probably. As it was earlier this evening.'

'But if you still love him, why stop seeing him?'

Jack and Beth spoke at the same time.

'Because—' Her voice cracked and she blinked hard. 'Because we've been living a secret life. He's married, and now my daughter's fallen head over heels in love with his son. A tangled web, wouldn't you say? Sounds like a novel.'

Jack could only nod in stunned agreement.

36

The second Jaz walked into the kitchen, she knew she was in trouble.

The radio wasn't on, as it was normally during breakfast, and the silence – so rare – was awesome. It told her that her sleepless night worrying about whether her brothers would say anything to their father had not been in vain.

Thanks to Jimmy and Phin, who were sitting on either side of their father, it was obvious they all knew. There was no sign of her mother – she must be feeling unwell again.

Jaz took a long, deep breath and sat down next to Tamzin. She poured milk over her muesli and stirred it, willing herself to eat at least one mouthful. But she knew she couldn't. Her stomach was draining away from her. It was currently on a level with the tops of her knees. In the silence that continued, she thought, miserably, Oh, just get on with it. Do your worst. 'How's Mum?' she asked.

'And what would you care?'

She lifted her chin, gave her brother a sharp, challenging look. 'A darn sight more than you, Phin. When was the last time you did anything round the house to help Mum?'

'Watch your tongue, young lady.'

She squared her shoulders, indignation overruling her earlier decision to toe the line. 'Why, Dad? Why shouldn't I speak the truth?' *No!* Not the right thing to say. Her father seized the opportunity she'd handed to him.

'Well, I'd like to hear you speaking the truth some time. Wouldn't that be a great thing?'

'Please get to the point, Dad. If you're going to accuse me of something, spit the words out and have done with it.' So much for meekness.

Her father seemed to grow in his seat; taller, broader. 'Let's get this clear, Jasmine Rafferty, I'll spit my words out when I'm good and ready. Not when you tell me to.'

A dangerous bubble of mirth rose in Jaz as the image of a gobbing camel popped into her mind. She gritted her teeth and swallowed hard. This was no time to laugh: she was about to be grounded for the rest of eternity. She'd be in solitary confinement for ever, all privileges withheld. She'd be lucky to go to college, never mind attend her writers' group. A worse thought came to her. What if she had to show her father what she'd been writing? Suddenly the Clacketts didn't seem such a great move on her part. 'Sorry, Dad,' she said, trying hard to sound as if she meant it, but failing hopelessly: it came out too loud, as if she was being sarcastic.

Her father asked Lulu to pass him the marmalade, and leaned back in his chair. 'Now, the problem I have, Jaz, is that on the one hand I'm led to believe you were at Vicki's for the evening, and the next I'm hearing from your brothers that last night they saw you getting out of some man's car. Either Phin and Jimmy need to get down to Vision Express pretty damn quick, or you've got a *doppelgänger* wandering about town. Or maybe there's a third option. Any theories of your own?'

Everyone looked at her.

'It's no big deal—' she began.

'You're on dangerous ground, girl, so don't go giving me any of that old malarkey! You can't make an eejit out of me, your brothers saw you good and proper. I don't know how long you've been sneaking off behind our backs seeing this – this man, but let me tell you, when I get a hold of him, he'll wish he'd never set eyes on you. If he's so much as laid a finger on you, I'll – I'll bloody kill him!'

Jaz gasped. When she'd been lying in bed last night unable to sleep, she'd been so concerned about her father finding out about the writers' group that she hadn't considered he'd make such a mind-blowing assumption. Jack was old! Okay, he made her laugh and could write like a dream, but he was *old*! 'Dad, you've got it all wrong. It's not what you think.'

'Yeah, well, you would say that.'

'Phin, just butt out, will you? Dad, you've got to listen to me. Jack's a friend. He gave me a lift home.'

Her father banged his fist on the table; her sisters jumped. 'Oh,' he mimicked, in a mocking falsetto, 'Jack's a friend, is he? So maybe it's time he started hanging out with *friends* of his own age, instead of preying on a girl young enough to be his daughter! What is he? Some kind of pervert? Have I got to be careful with these two as well?'

Tamzin and Lulu giggled.

'Look, Dad—'

'Don't give me any of that "look, Dad" stuff, you lied to your mother and me. You told us you were seeing Vicki when all along you've been seeing this man. And if you weren't seeing him, why the lies?'

Jaz stared at her father, knew it was pointless to argue with him. She knew also that if she told him about her writing and how important it was to her he'd want proof. Only trouble was, that proof would send him into orbit. The contents of her novel, *Having the Last Laugh*, would make everything worse. If he read a word about the Clacketts and sussed that she had been making fun of her family behind their backs, he would go ballistic. He would bring an end to the world as she currently knew it.

Beneath the table her knees shook. She was in serious trouble. Weighing up the odds – which all seemed unfairly stacked against her – she decided she'd be better off keeping quiet. If she said nothing, her precious writing would be safe. So what if they thought she'd been having secret assignations with a bloke as old as Jack? They didn't know who he was, or where he lived. It was bite-her-tongue time.

37

At first Jack thought he was imagining it, but after several miles of driving along country lanes to and from meeting a new client and measuring up her charming thatched cottage in Bunbury, he had to admit that his imagination wasn't playing tricks on him. A car was following him.

He couldn't be sure but he thought the black Golf had been with him since he'd stopped for petrol a short distance out of Maywood. It was currently positioned one car behind his, and he couldn't see the face of either the driver or the passenger. He decided to flush them out. He lowered his speed to twenty-five miles an hour, which he knew would infuriate the driver of the Fiesta immediately behind, and sure enough, when they came to an appropriate stretch of road, the Fiesta accelerated past, leaving Jack with a clear view in his mirror of his pursuers.

To his amazement, it was the two men he'd encountered in the Rav-4 last night when he'd dropped Jaz off – the two men who might or might not be her brothers. But what in hell's name were they up to?

The Golf shot in front of him, then slammed on its brakes. His heart in his mouth, Jack jammed his foot on the brake pedal and skidded to a halt, inches short of the ditch at the side of the road. He made a grab for his mobile phone.

It was the wrong thing to do. He should have locked the door. The next thing he knew he was being hauled from his car and bundled into the Golf. They pushed him into the rear seat, sandwiching him between them. He was more shocked than scared. 'What's this all about?' he asked.

The young man on his right, the bigger of the two who was chewing gum, spoke first. 'We're gonna make this as simple as we can, mate. So listen up. You so much as set eyes on our Jaz one more time and we'll tear you apart. Got that?' He sounded like he'd watched one too many gangland movies.

Jack stared, open-mouthed. 'Does this mean you *are* Jaz's brothers?'

Now it was the turn of the man on his left. 'Don't play dumb, Jack. We saw you last night so we know exactly what you've been up to. And just so you know, we don't like it.'

'But I'm not up to anything.'

'Oh, yes, you are.' Jack turned back to the first man. 'We know all about you. It's amazing what you can find out about a person once you've got their car registration. The Internet's a wonderful thing. I expect you use it a lot, don't you? Men like you do. Perverts who can't keep their hands off girls half their age. Can't get yourself a real woman so you make do with jail-bait. But we're here to let you know that nobody messes with our little sister.'

Men like you ... Perverts ... Nobody messes with our little sister. What they were accusing him of was preposterous. Disgusting. 'Look,' he said, trying hard to sound reasonable, like an upright citizen – anything but a child molester! 'You've got this all wrong. There's nothing going on between Jaz and me. Honestly. You have to believe me. I was giving her a lift home from our writers' group. As I do every week.'

There was a pause.

'Writers' group?'

It was the brother on his left. 'Yes,' said Jack.

'What d'you mean, as you do *every* week?'

'There's five of us in the group and we meet on Thursday nights. But surely you must have known that. We've been meeting since October last year.'

At this, the two men exchanged looks. He saw doubt on their faces and, keen to seize the advantage, he said, 'If you don't believe me, ring the woman who runs the group. She'll back me up on everything I've told you.'

'Outside,' the first man instructed his brother. 'You stay where you are,' he said to Jack. Both doors were slammed shut so he wasn't able to hear what was being said, but the gist was plain. They had realised they'd cocked up and were now reviewing matters. Jack knew he was within his rights to threaten them with police action but, bizarrely, he respected them. Who was he to hold a grudge when they'd only been looking out for their sister? As a father, he knew all too well how far he would go to protect Amber and Lucy.

The door was yanked open. 'Seems like we ... Well, how about a drink, mate?'

'Is that your way of apologising?' Jack asked, when a hand was thrust towards him and he was helped out of the car.

'We could throw in some lunch, if you want.'

Jack laughed. 'I wouldn't want to put you to all that trouble.'

'So, a drink to put matters straight?'

He smoothed down his suit jacket, amused at their front. 'I'd love to, gentlemen, but I have lunch planned already. Something a little less physical.'

'No hard feelings, then? Oh, and we'd appreciate it if you kept schtum. Don't tell Jaz, she wouldn't understand.'

He put a hand in the air, started to walk away, straightening his collar and tie.

538

'Hang on a minute. Before you go, tell us about this writers' group. What exactly do you do?'

'We write,' Jack said, over his shoulder.

'What about?'

'Life, fellas. You ought to try it some time.'

Perhaps he should have been more shocked by what had happened to him, but the more Jack thought about it, the more absurd and bungled the whole thing appeared. Why hadn't Jaz told her brothers about the group? But there again *he* hadn't let on about it to Clare, or even to Des and Julie, and for the simple reason he hadn't wanted to face a barrage of questions or be mocked for considering himself a writer.

Gradually, the more he thought about it, the less surprised he was that Jaz had kept Hidden Talents from her brothers. He might be doing them a disservice, but they didn't strike him as being on the same wavelength as their sister. However, what they lacked in sensitivity they made up for in their eagerness to keep her safe. He had a feeling, though, that Jaz wouldn't see it in quite the same way.

When he had told her brothers that he already had a lunch appointment, he hadn't been lying: he'd arranged to meet Maddie. He had arrived at the office early that morning, and had called her on her mobile knowing that she'd be driving the girls to school. 'What a coincidence,' she'd said. 'I was going to give you a ring today.'

'Oh?'

'You first.'

'What?'

'I said . . . Oh, never mind. What do you want?'

'I wondered if you'd meet me for lunch. There's something I want to discuss with you.'

They'd agreed to meet in Maywood at Casa Bellagio and now, as Jack ordered himself a glass of orange juice, he thought how uncomfortable he felt about meeting Maddie like this, just the two of them. Which, after the experience he'd just gone through, was laughable. Having lunch with his soon-to-be-ex-wife should be a cinch in comparison with abduction.

Ex-wife. It still didn't seem possible. He and Maddie had been so convinced of their love for each other, but at some point it had gone wrong. When did she stop loving him? Had it been a Road-to-Damascus revelation when she had seen that their lives didn't fit together any more? Or had it been a gradual process, each day building on the disappointment of the one that had gone before? She had never given him a straight answer as to why she had felt the need to have an affair, and he'd been left to scrutinise his own input to their marriage. Certainly he'd often spent more time at the office than he had at home, but they'd known that that would happen. If they were to have the lifestyle they both craved – holidays abroad, his-and-hers BMWs on the drive – then he'd had to prove himself partnership material. It had seemed justification enough, but now he knew better. The choice had been there, he just hadn't picked the right one.

It had been talking to Adele Waterman that had set him on this line of thought, and it was why he was here today to meet Maddie. For the sake of the children, he wanted to put things right between them.

Maddie was coming across the restaurant towards him, hips swaying in that unconscious way he'd always loved, hair immaculately cut and perfectly framing a face that was still faintly tanned from the Christmas skiing holiday. He noted the cream leather trousers, the pale pink cashmere sweater, and the pashmina slung stylishly around her shoulders. Designer from head to toe, he reckoned, while he was in his Next suit and Principles shirt and tie.

'I'm glad you came,' he said, pushing back his chair and rising to his feet. For an awkward moment, neither knew how to greet the other.

A kiss on the cheek?

Out of the question.

A handshake?

Too formal.

They settled for a wary smile and a bob of the head.

They ordered just one course because Maddie said she couldn't stay long.

'So what was it you were going to call me about?' he asked, when their plates of pasta and salad had been delivered by a diminutive girl who didn't look much older than Amber.

'Oh, it'll keep,' she said airily, and pointed out to the young waitress that she'd forgotten the mineral water.

Jack smiled at the girl when she reappeared with it. Maddie took the glass without a word of thanks and said, 'In America you never get such sloppy service.'

'I wouldn't know. I've never been to the land of plenty where fries and doughnuts rain down from a sky of maple syrup.'

She looked at him sharply. 'Don't goad me, Jack.'

'I'm not.' He sprinkled extra Parmesan over his pasta and tried to relate to the irritable woman sitting opposite him. Where had the happy-go-lucky girl gone? In fairness they had all changed: Jack, Maddie and Tony. He forked up some pasta and thought of Adele's words, that Tony would have the girls' best interests at heart. It focused his mind on what he needed to say. He put down his fork. 'Maddie,' he said, 'I want to talk seriously. About you and Tony. But mostly about the children and their future.'

Her expression changed. Gone was the sharp defensiveness, and in its place a softening. A softening he knew so well. His heart ached that she could still have that effect on him. He watched her dab the corners of her mouth with her napkin. She said, 'And that's what I wanted to discuss with you.'

The waitress materialised beside their table. 'Everything all right?' she asked, a little breathlessly.

Jack smiled and said everything was perfect.

'Another drink?'

He shook his head. 'Maddie?'

'No.'

'I think we're fine,' he said, and she left them alone.

'Jack, I've got something important to tell you,' Maddie said.

His emotions went from nought to sixty in two seconds and all at once he was on full alert. Well, she wasn't about to tell him she and Tony were getting married – that couldn't happen until the divorce had gone through. Perhaps she was pregnant. But what did that have to do with him? 'Go on,' he said.

She looked him dead in the eye. 'Tony's got a new business venture that's really taking off in the States.' She paused. 'Nothing's definite, but we're considering going to live in California. It would be great for the girls. They'd have the time of their lives. It would be a fantastic opportunity for them.'

Her words knocked the breath right out of him. Along with all his good intentions. He sat back in his chair. 'Over my dead body. That bastard is not taking my children anywhere.'

38

More than once during the day Jaz had considered the coward's way out, running away. Her father's parting words that morning had been 'I'm too angry right now to decide how to punish you, but by tonight I'll have cooled off enough to think straight. And make no mistake, Jasmine Rafferty, you'll not get off lightly this time.'

This time. He'd spoken as if she was always in trouble. As if he'd lumped her in with Tamzin or Lulu. If only Mum hadn't been upstairs feeling so rotten Jaz might have had an ally but, as it was, she had no idea what was going on. And, worse, Dad had warned her not to involve Mum. 'Do that, young lady, and you'll regret it. Your mother's suffering enough as it is without having this lot to worry about as well.'

Several times during the morning Vicki had asked her what was wrong and at first she'd pretended everything was fine. By lunchtime she'd relented and confided in her friend. Vicki lapped up every word. 'So your family reckons you're seeing some old guy on the quiet? How awesome is that? You're not, are you?'

'*No!*'

She looked almost disappointed. 'What does Nathan say?'

'He doesn't know. And . . . and I don't want him to know. You mustn't say anything. And not to Billy either, he'd go straight to Nathan with it.'

'Suit yourself. But this might not be a bad time to tell your parents about Nathan. I mean, your dad'll be so relieved you're going out with someone your own age, he'll think Nathan's an answer to a prayer. Which, let's face it, he is.'

Now, during last break, as Jaz waited by her locker for Nathan to tell him he'd have to walk home alone, she thought over what Vicki had said. Would it be such a bad idea to do as she suggested?

Yes, it would. She could picture the scene perfectly: her father demanding to meet Nathan so that he could interrogate him and her gloating brothers preparing to embarrass him. And what would Nathan think of them and, as a consequence, of her? Oh, it was so unfair!

'Hi, Jaz. You look serious, what's wrong?'

It was Nathan.

'Nothing's wrong,' she said. The sight of him made her want to fall into his arms, to be hugged and reassured that maybe the day wasn't going to end as badly as she knew it would.

'You sure?'

'Hey, what is this?' she joked, in an effort to convince him she was okay. 'Dr King making school visits, these days? Now listen up, I can't walk home with you as I'm staying on for a bit.'

'I'll stay as well, if you like. What are you doing?'

'There's no need. Anyway, I don't know how long I'll be.' And before he could ask any more questions, the bell rang for the end of break, she grabbed her rucksack and scooted off.

She found that her instinct to walk home on her own had been good. No sooner had she set foot out of the college gates than Jimmy's black Golf appeared: it crawled along the kerb beside her, its tweaked engine rumbling and making her feel like a gazelle being stalked by a hungry panther. This was the reason she hadn't wanted to walk home with Nathan. She'd known her brothers would come for her, checking that she wasn't slipping off for another assignation with her middle-aged lover.

Jimmy lowered the driver's window. 'Get in, little sis.'

'Push off. I'd rather walk.'

'Looks like rain to me,' said Phin.

'I don't care if a typhoon's heading this way, I'm not going anywhere with you two.' She walked faster, but Jimmy kept the car level with her, its engine growling.

'We met a friend of yours this morning,' he said. 'What was his name, Phin? It's slipped my memory. Was it John?'

'Nah. It was Jack.'

'Ah, that's right. Jack. Jack Solomon.'

Jaz froze. She stared after the car as Jimmy drove slowly down the road, her stomach churned and her mouth went dry. Her brothers had spoken to *Jack*? But how had they found out who he was? And what had they said? She chewed her lip. As teenagers Phin and Jimmy had both learned to box and once, as adults, much to Mum's horror, they'd been involved in a late-night brawl in Manchester. Someone like Jack – a man to whom they were determined to teach a lesson – wouldn't stand a chance. 'Wait!' she yelled after the car. 'Wait for me!' She sprinted after them, her heavy rucksack banging against her back. Phin got out of the front passenger seat and let her in.

'What have you done to Jack?' she asked, when she'd caught her breath. 'If you've hurt him, I swear I'll make sure he goes to the police and has you put away.'

Jimmy grinned at her in the rear-view mirror. 'Cool it. Jack's fine. We left him in more or less one piece, but why don't you tell us what you've really been up to? We know you haven't been putting it about with some dodgy old bloke.'

She hesitated. Did this mean what she thought it did? Were they on to her writing? Or did they know about Nathan? Perhaps they were only bluffing. 'I don't know what you're on about,' she muttered. Then, trying to deflect them, she said, 'How did you find Jack?'

'Easy as pie,' crowed Jimmy.

'Yeah, even for a pair of oiks like us,' added Phin. 'Which is how we know you view us, you being such an intellectual and all. But it looks like we might have outsmarted you for once.'

She leaned forward. 'So tell me how, then.'

'One word,' said Jimmy. 'Numberplate.'

Jaz's heart sank. 'You're nothing but a pair of loathsome yobs,' she said. But what had Jack told them?

Her father was home early, his Jaguar parked on the drive alongside Phin's Rav-4. Jimmy snatched on the handbrake. Jaz told herself to keep calm, to say nothing until she knew exactly what she was accused of. Against all hope, she wanted to believe that she wouldn't have to own up to everything she had been doing since October. The thought of being ridiculed for her writing was bad enough, but the fallout, if her father got wind of the Clacketts, didn't bear thinking about – she'd decided during the day that she would have to delete *Having the Last Laugh* from her computer, as well as ditch the paper copy. She hated the idea of losing her hard work, but she had no choice.

She was greeted by her mother, who was cooking tea while listening to the radio and humming along with it. The comforting smell of roast chicken with sage and onion stuffing reminded Jaz that she hadn't eaten that day: she'd been too sick with nerves. Now, hunger and apprehension made her want to hurl herself across the kitchen and cling to her mother. 'I'm sorry,' she wanted to say. 'I'm sorry I've lied to you all. Please forgive me.' And maybe, if her brothers hadn't been standing behind her raiding the fridge for a drink, she would have done exactly that.

'Hello, Jaz,' her mother said, turning to see her. 'I see the boys found you. We wondered where you were. You didn't say you'd be late.'

'Sorry,' she murmured. 'It was a last-minute thing.' Conscious that she'd just lied again, she shook off her jacket and said, 'How're you feeling? Anything I can do to help?'

'I'm fine. Supper's nearly ready, so go and get yourself washed.'

She moved uncertainly towards the door. 'Where's Dad?'

'In his snug. Perhaps you could poke your head round the door and give him the five-minute warning that we'll be eating soon. Oh, now I come to think of it, he did say he wanted a word with you when you came home.'

Avoiding her brothers' eyes, she went to find her father.

'Ah, there you are, Jaz,' he said, as she stepped into the room he called his snug. It had its own bar in the corner, a couple of reclining leather armchairs, an enormous flat-screen telly – the largest in the house – and a display shelving unit that was home to rows of old car-racing magazines, as well as photographs of the various racehorses he'd had a share in over the years. He had made it his private hide-away ever since Tamzin and Lulu had declared themselves too old for a playroom. 'Close the door after you,' her father added ominously.

He waved the remote control at the telly, then turned to give her a long, hard stare. 'Come and sit with me, Jaz.' He indicated the other chair.

She did as he said, sensing that his mood was different from the one he'd aired at breakfast that morning. There was something like kindness in his voice. Absurdly it made her want to cry. She loved her father and didn't want him to be angry with her. And she didn't want to go through another day like today. But she steeled her resolve, reminding herself that it could be a ruse to make her confess more than she wanted to.

'Jaz,' he began, 'out of all our children, your mother and I always had you down as the most sensible. The one with the brains we could trust. But now,' he shook his head, and she could see the disappointment in his eyes, 'well, now I'm not so sure. You've turned everything arse over tit. I don't know what to make of you. You've let me down. I think that's what hurts the most, finding out that you had it in you to deceive us all these months.'

He stood up, as if to give himself the advantage. It worked. Jaz felt small and unworthy as he towered over her. 'You probably know by now,' he carried on, standing in front of the television, his hands placed in the small of his back, 'that your brothers have spoken with your so-called friend, Jack Solomon, and if we're to believe him, and Phin and Jimmy reckoned he was kosher, apparently you've been sneaking off to some kind of group where you sit around writing.' He paused. 'Is that true?'

So, he and her brothers knew that much. 'You make it sound like a subversive activity, Dad.'

He widened his eyes. 'Well pardon me, Miss Hoity-Toity, but in my book, not telling us about it in the first place immediately makes it subversive. Why lie to us about it if it was so innocent? Unless, of course, it isn't. Well? I'm waiting.'

'Tamzin and Lulu are always lying,' she said, buying herself some time. 'You never go on at them like this.'

He dismissed her comment instantly. 'They tell childish fibs that are as transparent as water. Whereas you've wilfully misled us week after week. You looked us right in the eye and took pleasure in making fools of us.' His expression hardened. 'You should know by now, Jaz, that nobody makes a fool out of me and gets away with it. And what, I want to know, is the effect of this group on your college work?'

'I've always put college first, Dad.'

'And you'd better be telling the truth over that.' He let out his breath, and just as Jaz was beginning to think she might be off the hook, he said, 'But you still haven't explained why you acted the way you did.'

She swallowed. Her father wasn't going to let it drop. The truth, she decided, was the only way to satisfy him. 'Dad, I kept it from you and Mum because I couldn't face the backlash.'

'Backlash?' he repeated. 'What's that supposed to mean?'

'Phin and Jimmy would have gone on and on about me kidding myself I was a writer, and as for Tamzin and Lulu, they would have been forever nosing around in my room trying to find what I'd written. You know what they're like, always poking their noses into my stuff.'

He looked at her as if he hadn't understood.

'Dad, you don't get it, do you? I have no privacy in this family. None at all.' Her voice wavered: the strain of the day was catching up with her. 'Everything I do is made fun of. I can't even yawn without someone accusing me of yawning differently from everyone else. I don't fit in. I know I don't. Is it any wonder I keep things to myself?' She lurched to her feet, tears welling in her eyes. 'I'm sorry I lied to you, and that you're disappointed in me. But you'd better prepare yourself for more disappointment because I'll probably fail my exams next year and never be the brilliant success of the family you expect me to be. Why don't you save that honour for the next load of babies Mum's having?'

Shaking, she fled the room. She heard her father call after her, but she stumbled up the stairs to her room, threw herself on her bed and sobbed.

39

Richard stalked back into the centre of the village, where he'd just been, knowing that his behaviour had been unforgivable. He should never have shouted at Angela like that. It wasn't her fault. It was his: the slightest thing set him off. 'Can't you do anything to keep them quiet?' he'd snapped at her yesterday, when Christopher's music had thumped overhead while he'd been trying to read a report. Just now, after he had collected the Sunday papers, he'd let rip at her over the state of the kitchen – piles of laundry waiting to be ironed, last night's grill pan in the sink, a row of bulging carrier-bags she kept meaning to take to the Oxfam shop, and the wreckage of breakfast still on the table. 'Look at this mess!' he'd shouted. 'It's nearly lunchtime and nothing's been done.' He'd thrown the newspapers on to a chair and started to roll up his sleeves.

'Good gracious, Richard, whatever is the matter?' she'd said, looking up from the button she was sewing on to one of the boys' shirts.

'How can you sit there and say that? Even by your standards the place is a tip. I've had enough of it, and if you won't put some order back into it, I will.'

Except he hadn't. He'd clenched his teeth, turned on his heel and stormed out of the kitchen.

Poor Angela. She really didn't deserve to be on the receiving end of his ill-humour.

Ill-humour! Could going half crazy really be described so simply?

It was three agonising days since Dulcie had ended their relationship. He couldn't sleep, couldn't eat, couldn't concentrate. His mind was always on Dulcie. He'd nearly screwed up with a potential client on Friday. When a brash Yorkshireman, clearly used to getting his own way, had asked him a question too many, he'd said the first thing that had come into his head: 'Take it or leave it. Either way I don't give a damn. If you're looking for cheap, where safety is a secondary consideration, I suggest you go elsewhere. Find yourself a tin-pot outfit to match your own.' A shockwave of paper-shuffling and throat-clearing had gone round the table, and everyone had lowered their eyes, but not before Richard had read the look in them. Cavanagh's past it . . . Cavanagh's losing it . . . Cavanagh's on his way out.

But to their disbelief, and disappointment perhaps, the Yorkshireman had reached for the water jug and laughed. 'Now there's summat we don't often hear, a bit of plain speaking from a lawyer. Maybe we can do business, after all.'

He might have pulled off the deal by the skin of his teeth, but it meant nothing.

If he didn't see Dulcie again, he wasn't sure he could continue living. Every day was torture. The thought that she was able to carry on her life without him made the pain more excruciating.

How could she?

And how could she have destroyed what they had, when it had been so special and had meant the world to them?

He would give anything to turn back the clock, for Henry and Kate never to have met. He wouldn't have thought it possible that he could wish any of his children a moment's pain, but now he wanted Henry to know just a fraction of the misery he was experiencing.

He wasn't even ashamed of it. He didn't care that it was selfish of him to want something for himself at the expense of another. Dulcie had accused him of not loving Henry as much as she loved Kate – well, perhaps she was right. All he knew was that he loved Dulcie more than he'd loved anyone.

He passed the post office, then the newsagent, and continued through the village, towards the church and the footpath he had often used during his convalescence. He took the steep incline slowly, becoming aware of the warmth of the sun on his back. He glanced up, and saw that the sky was the clearest of blues, marred only by a scattering of billowing white clouds in the west towards Shropshire and the distant swell of the Welsh hills. He paused to catch his breath; anger alone wouldn't propel him up the slope – it might even kill him.

But who would miss him if he had another heart-attack and died?

Angela would miss him as a provider and the rock upon which she'd built her life, but not as a husband or a lover. As for the children, Nicholas and Christopher would mourn his passing, but the older ones were sufficiently established to get on perfectly well without him.

Despite the mildness of the day, he shuddered, chilled to think that he might die up here on this deserted hill and no one would truly grieve for him.

Not even Dulcie. She had cast him out of her life so easily, fobbed him off on the phone when he'd tried to speak to her, proving that she could not have felt the same for him as he did for her.

A frightening weight of depression cast its insidious black shadow over him and he flung back his head, wanting to berate whoever it was up there who was playing so cruelly with his life.

Then, filled with a desperate urge towards self-destruction he began to walk again, rage and despair quickening his step, his breath coming fast, his chest aching.

40

Beth was glad it was time to go home. It had been a long day and several of their more tiresome patients had appeared. Some people never grasped that the medical centre was where sick people came to get better, not an annexe of the Citizen's Advice Bureau, or an extension of the local pub where malicious gossip and bitchy complaints could be directed at the staff. She buttoned her coat, said goodbye to Wendy and braced herself for the cold walk home.

When she let herself in, Nathan was in his bedroom, head bent over several open books on his desk. 'Good day?' she asked, from the doorway of his room as she surveyed the mess. He'd always been untidy – clothes littered the floor, the back of his chair and the end of his bed, and a welter of papers, files and books filled the remaining spaces on the floor and the window-sill. For one as clear-sighted and analytical as he was, and so concerned about his appearance, it amazed Beth that he was content to live in such a muddle. She wondered what Jaz made of it.

He swivelled in his chair, the light from his Anglepoise lamp illuminating his handsome face, accentuating the strong line of his jaw and emphasising his dark eyes: how like his father he was. 'A *tour de force* of a day,' he said. 'Oh, before I forget, Barnaby called. He said he'd try again later.'

'Did he say what it was about?'

'Nope. But I should think it's to do with Grandma. Otherwise he'd have said something.'

'How astute of you, Nathan. Don't suppose your brilliance stretches to making a cup of tea for your old ma while she slips into something more comfortable, does it?'

While she exchanged her work clothes for a pair of jeans and a polo-neck sweater, Beth considered returning Barnaby's call. But what if Lois answered the phone? She really wasn't in the mood to speak to her mother-in-law. Better to leave it to Barnaby to ring when the coast was clear.

Beth was full of admiration for Barnaby. His plan to get Lois back on speaking terms with Beth and Nathan was to whisk his wife away on a luxury cruise. He hoped that after three weeks on the high seas she would feel like a new woman and would be receptive to an extended olive branch. While the two of them were exploring the Caribbean, Beth and Nathan would look after Marsh House. 'If we came home to find there'd been a cold snap and the pipes had burst, I'd be in no end of trouble. For the chop, good and proper.'

'Presumably you won't be telling Lois who'll be taking care of things?' Beth had asked, anxiously.

'Good Lord, no! I shall tell her I've got an agency involved and there's nothing for her to worry about. I've planned surprise weekends away before, and I'm confident I can pull this off too.'

'When do you plan to tell her the truth?'

'I don't. She'll be presented with a *fait accompli* on our return.'

It was a risky plan and Beth didn't think there were many husbands in the world who would go to such lengths. She gave Barnaby full credit for being so brave: railroading Lois was not for the faint-hearted.

After supper, leaving Nathan to continue with his homework, Beth went downstairs to see Adele. She was moving out the day after tomorrow – Jack was moving in on Friday – and Beth had promised to help with some of the more personal items of her packing.

Adele looked tired and flustered when she opened the door and, for the first time since the move had been planned, Beth wondered if the old lady was doing the right thing. Was it all proving too much of a strain for her? When she stepped into the hall, she soon realised the cause of Adele's discomfort. A balding man in a suit that didn't fit his squat chunky body and a thin woman in an unflattering short black leather skirt were unhooking a pretty Victorian watercolour from the wall above the radiator. Beth knew that it was a particular favourite of Adele's and she couldn't imagine her friend wanting to part with it. 'I'm sorry, Adele,' she said, 'I didn't know you had visitors. Shall I call back later?' She had no intention of leaving, but she had to make a show of courtesy.

'No, please, don't go.' A hand was placed insistently on her forearm. 'This is my nephew, Vernon, and his friend Sheila.'

'*Sylvia*,' the bald man corrected her. He held out his hand to Beth; there was a sheen of sweat on his top lip. 'And you might be?'

'Oh, Vernon, don't be so pompous. Beth is my neighbour from upstairs, and quite possibly the nicest person you'll have the pleasure of meeting. She's always looked after me so well.'

Beth smiled at Adele, but she saw Vernon's grey eyes grow sharper and the proffered hand fell to his side. She didn't much care for the look of him. Or his skinny friend. To her knowledge, this was the first time in ages he had called on his aunt, and he was manhandling one of Adele's favourite paintings. His showing up like this smacked of opportunism, and Beth was having none of it.

The telephone rang and while Adele went to answer it in the sitting room, Beth said, in her most commanding receptionist voice, 'I should be careful with that picture. It's extremely valuable.'

'Do you really think so?' Vernon took it from Sylvia, and held it up to the light for closer inspection.

'Yes,' said Beth. 'I'd go so far as to say it's practically priceless . . . to your aunt. So why don't I put it back where it belongs before it gets damaged?'

The grey eyes gleamed, and bored into her. But Beth held her ground and took the picture. 'Are you staying to help Adele pack, or do you have to rush away?'

Vernon looked as mad as a hornet. He opened his mouth to speak, but was cut short by Adele reappearing in the hall. 'That was Jack,' she said to Beth. 'Just wanting to reassure me that everything's going like clockwork. Oh, not stopping, Vernon?'

Still looking furious, Vernon had dug his car keys out of his jacket pocket and was jingling them agitatedly. 'No,' he said briskly. 'We'd better be making tracks. You obviously have it all sorted here.' He threw Beth a hostile glance and jingled the keys again. 'Well, good luck with the move. Call if you need anything.'

'Thank you, Vernon. It was nice of you to drop in.' Adele had relaxed and was acting the part of perfect hostess. 'You must come and see me in my new home. You too, Shirley.'

'It's *Sylvia*.'

'Of course it is, Vernon. Whatever was I thinking? It must be my age.'

They stood on the doorstep waving off the scavengers. Out of the corner of her mouth, Beth said, 'You wicked woman. You knew perfectly well what her name was, didn't you?'

One last wave and they closed the door.

'Beth, how could you think such a thing? Oh, but I'm so glad to see the back of them. For a moment I was quite unnerved. Now, where shall we start?'

Beth suggested the bedroom. 'If you're anything like me, that's where you keep your most personal possessions.'

Beth insisted that Adele direct operations from a chair, and took on the lion's share of the wrapping and packing. Before long they had cleared the contents of one chest of drawers and a bedside table and felt justified in awarding themselves a coffee break.

'What brought the dutiful nephew out of the woodwork?' Beth asked, handing Adele her cup. 'Apart from the opportunity to pick over the spoils.'

'Heavens, Beth, am I to take it that you didn't fall for my dear Vernon?'

'You assume correctly. And I didn't like his motives either. Sorry if that's too brutally honest.'

Adele smiled. 'I appreciate your honesty and your timely coming to my rescue. I've never seen myself as a dithery old lady before, but seeing Vernon sizing up my possessions so blatantly brought it home to me that I'm on borrowed time and the vultures are circling.'

'You're not dithery and you're certainly not on borrowed time, not by a good many years. Plenty of deviousness left in you yet.'

'I'd like to believe you, my dear, but sadly your kind words will not keep the bell from tolling for me.'

Later that night, Beth felt weary of spirit. Before the move business had taken root, Adele would never have spoken like that. It grieved her profoundly that her friend seemed to be giving in without a fight. And who would chivvy her along when she moved into the retirement home?

To cheer herself up, Beth switched on her computer. There were two emails. The first was from Simone, complaining about how hot it was and that if she wasn't careful she'd soon be able to get a job as a Mother Teresa lookalike.

The second was from Ewan.

She clicked on OPEN, her heart stepping up a gear or two, as it always did when she heard from him. It had taken a lot of courage on her part to agree to meet him. 'Let's not rush things,' she'd said, in response to his suggestion, 'but I'd like to meet you. Although you know what they say, curiosity killed the cat.'

Miaow! What are you saying, my feline friend? [he'd responded.] That you think I'm going to bump you off?!!!

No, but we might kill off our friendship with a dose of nasty reality.

Mmm . . . it's certainly a possibility, but sometimes you have to take a risk. I promise I won't press you. I'll leave you to decide when, how and if. If it makes you feel any better, my daughter thinks I'm off my head. She reckons I'm the one in danger, and that you could be a man – a crazed psychotic man – pretending to be a woman. You're not, are you?

She'd told him she was definitely a woman and that the only psychotic episodes she experienced were when she was suffering from PMT.

On the computer screen Ewan's latest email was before her.

BAD NEWS, I'VE BEEN REJECTED!
    Tossed aside on the scrap-heap of failure. Not me personally (though it feels that way), my manuscript. The publisher, who seemed so keen, has now read the whole caboodle and thinks, and here I quote, 'Blah, blah, blah . . . not quite what we're looking for in the current climate . . . more blah, blah, and . . . therefore sadly not suitable for our list.'
    Oh, to have one's fragile spirits soaring one minute only to have them dashed upon the rocks of one's shattered hopes and dreams! Don't worry, I'm not going purple-prosey on you.

But I will admit to feeling a tad crushed. In fact, very crushed. Stupid, I know. But there we have it, a man felled by his own hurt pride.

Are you getting the hint that I'm feeling sorry for myself? No? Well, believe me, there's plenty more self-pity at my disposal, but I shall manfully resist the urge to come across as a big girl's blouse.

But something good did come my way today – the opportunity to attend a writers' conference. It's a week-long residential course near Harrogate where wannabe writers get the chance to meet agents and editors and attend talks and workshops.

The thought has occurred to me, that maybe – just possibly, at a pinch . . . erm . . . that you might like to . . . erm . . . attend said course as well.

A shocking suggestion, I know. But if you think about it, you'd be completely safe, surrounded, as it were, by so many other people. Granted I can't vouch for their sanity, and let's face it, writers are not the sanest lunatics in the asylum, but at least you'd have plenty of folk to protect you, should a full moon appear and I turn into a madman, or a howling wolf.

Hang on a tick, moonlight is streaming through the curtains and I can feel . . . oh, my saints, I can feel a tickling sensation working its way down my back and arms. Oh, no! Shaggy hairs are sprouting all over my . . . Ah-whoo-oo! Ah-whoo-oo!

Write back post haste and tell me something to cheer me up.

Ewan X

Beth smiled and began typing.

You're mad, Ewan Jones! Totally mad! As barking as the werewolf you pretend to be.

Glory be, one little rejection and you go to pieces. Get a grip, man! Pull yourself together.

Seriously, though, I'm sorry to hear you've had such a horrible knock-back. But you're a big boy and I'm sure you'll pick yourself up, dust yourself down, and try again. At least the publisher didn't tell you that you'd written a load of old rubbish – as I'm sure they'd tell me if ever I had the nerve to submit anything I'd written. As rejections go, that must rate as quite a nice one. Remind yourself that you haven't written a bad book, your only mistake was to send your manuscript to the wrong publisher.

Now then, and don't fall off your chair with shock, I think the writers' conference sounds a good idea. But you'll have to give me more information before I commit myself . . .

Forever cautious,
Beth X

She still couldn't believe she was conducting such an enjoyable relationship via the Internet. She was utterly charmed by Ewan's ability to poke fun at himself, even when he must have been feeling low. He was a refreshing change from all the men who took themselves so seriously.

If meeting him was a risk, she was more than happy to take it.

41

With the three removal men now gone, Jack surveyed the mess they'd left behind them. Although he and they had worked hard at emptying boxes and placing furniture, there was still a lot to put straight. An hour ago his new home hadn't looked too bad, but now there didn't seem enough space for all his belongings.

First, before he unpacked anything else, he needed a drink. Luckily, he knew where to locate his limited drinks cupboard – it was in the dining room, lined up on the mantelpiece. He poured himself a large glass of single malt whisky, stood with his back to the door and faced the fireplace. When the original house had been divided into two flats, this room had suffered: space had been taken from it to provide a kitchen. As soon as he had the flat organised, but before he got too comfortable, he would get a builder in to open up the rooms. The work would cause massive disruption, but the end result would be worth it. He'd put a lot of thought into how he wanted the room to look. The old gas fire would be ripped out and the chimney opened up so that he could have a real fire, and in front of it a new sofa. There would be floor-to-ceiling shelves along the main wall, and he'd have two waist-high cupboards built either side of the fireplace and more shelves above for CDs and books. He'd have to do something about the lighting – spotlights and lamps, probably. The kitchen needed a complete revamp, new units and a new layout. He'd also buy a proper-sized table so that he and the girls could eat in comfort, instead of perching on stools at a breakfast bar as they had at his last house. He wanted to create a stylish room that would be the focus of the flat, somewhere Amber and Lucy would feel at home.

If they didn't go to America.

His throat clenched and he tightened his grip on the glass. Maddie's words from last Friday came back to taunt him. *It would be a fantastic opportunity for them.*

'And what about the fantastic opportunity of seeing their father?' he'd thrown at her, once he was able to speak without resorting to swearing.

'Keep your voice down, Jack,' Maddie had hissed. 'People are staring.'

'Let them!' He'd tossed his napkin on to his half-finished plate of pasta, his appetite gone. 'But it's good to see that you're more concerned about what people think of you in public than the welfare of our children. And talking of that, what the hell are you doing about Amber not eating?'

'It's just a phase,' she said dismissively. 'All girls go through it.'

'That's right, throw it into the okay bin along with everything else. Oh, it's okay that Amber's self-esteem is so low she's starving herself because every girl her age is doing it. Just as it's okay to cheat on your husband because everyone's doing that too!'

'Oh, for heaven's sake, stop it! Why do you always have to turn everything into a drama? You never used to be so bloody melodramatic.'

'You just don't get it, do you? You don't understand that there's nothing worse you could do to me. You sleep with my best friend, you leave me for him, and you limit the amount of time I can see our children. Then, and this is the best bit, you expect me to sit back and keep my voice down while you inform me that I'll be lucky to see them again. Well, pardon me if I don't play along with how you think I should behave.'

'I didn't say you couldn't see the girls again.'

'As good as,' he flung at her. 'So, come on, then, what's the big plan you and Tony have hatched? Do I get to see the girls every other summer holiday? Is that it?'

She picked up her handbag and plonked it on to her lap. 'If you're not going to talk reasonably, there's no point in continuing this conversation. There's nothing to be gained.' She retrieved her car keys from the bag and stood up. 'I feel sorry for you, Jack. You've allowed yourself to be blinded by your bitterness. Perhaps it would be better if Amber and Lucy did see less of you. I'd hate the girls to see you like this. It would harm them far more than anything Tony or I could do to them.'

Too angry and upset to follow her, he stayed where he was, weighed down with impotent fury. He was appalled by her vile accusation that he could ever hurt his children.

The unfamiliar ring of his doorbell interrupted his thoughts. He climbed over a coffee table and, sidestepping boxes, cushions and a stack of lampshades teetering on a pile of paperbacks, he made it to the front door, hoping that whoever it was wouldn't depress him even more. So long as he didn't think about Maddie and Tony, he was okay.

When he opened the door he was pleased to see that his first caller was Beth.

'Hi,' she said. 'I've just got in from work and wanted to make sure you hadn't forgotten you were having supper with us tonight.'

Smiling, he said, 'It's only been the thought of a decent meal to look forward to that's got me through the day.'

She peered round the door, to the war zone of the hall. 'Has it been awful?'

'Not really. If you're brave enough, come in and see for yourself.'

They stood in the middle of the hall, the perfect vantage-point from which to see into every room.

'Doesn't look too good, does it?' he said gloomily, overwhelmed by the enormity of the task ahead.

'It'll be fine,' she said. 'Every move is the same – you'll soon have it together. I could give you a hand tomorrow if you like. I'm not at the surgery in the morning. It's my weekend off.'

Touched, he said, 'That's really kind of you, but I'd hate to be accused of taking advantage.'

'Nonsense. Anyway, we're friends too. Comrades of the written word, as I think you once said. Now, I'd better get my skates on or there'll be no supper tonight. Eight o'clock suit you?'

As it turned out, Beth had time to set the table and grab a quick soak in the bath. Afterwards, while she was slipping a pair of pearl studs into her earlobes, she heard Nathan talking on the phone in the kitchen.

It was half-term, and to Beth's knowledge he hadn't spoken to Jaz all week. She had wanted to ask him if everything was all right between them but, respecting her son's privacy, she had held off probing. After all, she had her own need for concealment. She was beginning to feel guilty that she was behaving so furtively over Ewan. But her reluctance to tell anyone about him was based partly on embarrassment – how could she admit that she had grown fond of someone in such a way? – and partly on her enjoyment of the secrecy. It was fun to have a mystery man in her life. And exciting.

One day at work Wendy had commented that there was something different about her. 'I can't put my finger on it, but if I didn't know better, Beth King,' she'd said, 'I'd say you were indulging in more than a good night's sleep before coming into work. You're not seeing someone on the sly, are you?'

Smiling, Beth had said, 'Wendy, I can categorically tell you that I'm definitely not *seeing* someone on the sly. If I were, you'd be the first to know.'

Jack arrived promptly at eight o'clock, bottle of wine in hand. Beth thought he looked more cheerful than he had earlier, and was glad she'd invited him to dinner. During the meal she told him about Adele's ghastly nephew, Vernon, and he offered to accompany Beth when she visited the old lady in her new home next week. 'Why don't you bring Amber and Lucy as well,' Beth said, knowing how Adele had loved entertaining them some weeks ago.

'It wouldn't be too much for her?'

'I think she'd be tickled pink.'

They were clearing away the main-course plates when Jack asked Nathan, who was about to go out for the evening with Billy, if he'd ever met Jaz's brothers.

'No, but I get the feeling she isn't too keen on them. Why do you ask?'

'Oh, no reason.'

'Jack?'

He refilled his and Beth's glasses and looked at Beth, with a strange half-smile. 'Well, okay, I'll tell you, but I don't want this to get back to Jaz. She'd hit the roof if she knew what happened. Her brothers followed me last Friday and when they got the opportunity they bundled me into the back of their car and threatened me. They'd seen her in my car the night before and they thought I was carrying on with their little sister. Very laudable behaviour on their part, you could say.' He glanced at Nathan. 'And for the record, just in case you were preparing to swing a right hook in my direction, I'm *not* up to anything with Jaz.'

'That doesn't make sense,' said Nathan, with a frown. 'Her family know that Thursday night is her writers' group night. Why didn't they assume you were her legit ride home?'

'Ah, well, for reasons best known only to Jaz, it appears that she's kept her family in ignorance of that one important fact.'

Nathan looked thoughtful. 'Do you suppose that means she's been lying to them?'

'Almost certainly,' said Jack.

'Which would mean,' Nathan said slowly, 'that if she's been caught lying, she's probably been grounded.' Suddenly he smiled. 'Thanks, Jack, you've cleared up a mystery for me. Well, folks, I'm off out now. Don't wait up.' He left the flat whistling, the jaunty spring back in his step, which Beth now realised had been missing all week. She saw the puzzled expression on Jack's face, and said, 'I think you've just solved what's been bugging him. There hasn't been a peep from Jaz. No visits. No phone calls. Now he knows why. And it's nothing to do with him.'

'Well, if I were Nathan I'd be careful. If Jaz's brothers take a dislike to him, he'd better have some nifty self-defence manoeuvres up his sleeve. Do you think she's told her parents about him?'

Beth pondered this as she unwrapped the selection of cheeses she'd bought at lunchtime and arranged them on a plate. She decided Jaz hadn't. As far as she was aware Nathan had never been invited to the Raffertys' house. It was always the same arrangement: either Jaz came here or she met Nathan in town. She sat down. 'Dulcie told me yesterday that she'd given up trying to contact Jaz to tell her she was cancelling last night's meeting. She couldn't get a response from her mobile and the Raffertys' telephone number is ex-directory. At the time I'd thought that perhaps Jaz and her family had gone away for the week to their apartment in Tenerife. But if she's in trouble with her parents, perhaps they've punished her by taking away her phone.'

'How did she seem when you spoke to her?'

'Jaz?'

'No. Dulcie.'

'Oh. No better, really. Tired and subdued, feeling guilty too for letting the group down.'

'I would never have thought her capable of something like that.'

'Like what?'

'Deliberately moving in on a married man to break up his marriage.'

Beth knew how sensitive Jack was about the break-up of his own marriage, and chose her words with care. 'I don't think these things are ever deliberate. Besides, she hasn't broken the marriage up, has she?'

He helped himself to a cracker from the plate in the middle of the table and snapped it in two. 'She certainly wasn't strengthening it.'

A silence fell on them, until Beth said, 'You okay?'

'Since you ask, no.'

'Want to talk about it, or would you rather I minded my own business? By the way, do you want some cheese with those crumbs?'

He looked down at his plate rufully. 'I'm turning into a wreck, Beth.' He sighed. 'Just as I think I'm getting my act together, another load of crap falls into my lap. The latest news from Maddie and Wonderboy Tony is that they want to go and live in California. It would mean I'd never see the girls. I'll – I'll lose them for sure.' His voice broke and he turned away, his jaw set hard.

For an awkward moment Beth didn't know what to do. Instinct told her that he needed physical reassurance, a gently placed hand, or a hug. But years of hiding her own emotions and keeping herself to herself held her back from showing physically how deeply she cared for his pain. She resorted to words. 'Oh, Jack, I'm so sorry. That's awful. Is there anything you can do to stop it?'

He swallowed, but kept his eyes from hers. She could see that he was close to the edge and her heart went out to him.

'I've spoken to my solicitor and he says all I can do is appeal to their mother's better nature.' His cynicism rang out in the quiet of the kitchen and he turned to face her. 'And I stand as much chance of doing that as I do of winning the Booker Prize.'

Beth gave him a small, tentative smile. 'Stranger things have happened,' she said softly. She poured the last of the wine into his glass. Why couldn't she just give him a hug? She hadn't always been like this. Before Adam had died she had never been afraid of physical contact with a man. It was as if the woman inside her had withered and died too. Inexplicably she felt like crying. But more inexplicable was the anger she suddenly felt towards Adam. How dare he still have the power to do this to her?

She got up abruptly to fetch another bottle of wine. While she opened it, she asked Jack about the plans he had for Adele's flat – it would be some time yet before she saw it as his.

Plainly relieved to talk about something else, he apologised for the inconvenience he would soon be causing. 'I hope you won't be disturbed too much when the builders arrive,' he said.

'I'm sure it will be fine. And, anyway, I'll be out at work when they're here, unless you plan to have them hard at it during the night. Then I might have something to say.'

'Along with the rest of the neighbourhood, I shouldn't wonder.'

It wasn't long before Beth had drunk too much and she knew that she would pay for her recklessness in the morning with an almighty hangover. But she didn't care. And it didn't stop her switching from wine to spirits. Her anger had now given way to giggling mellowness. Jack, too, was laughing and smiling more than usual and together they sat on the sofa, finding whatever the other said absurdly witty and amusing. When she offered to make them some coffee, Jack pulled her back with a clumsy tug. 'Coffee's for wimps,' he said. 'How about another glass of that excellent single malt?'

'Sorry,' she said. 'Clean out now. I've got some inferior blended whisky if you like?'

He shook his head. 'I never touch the cheap stuff. It's guaranteed to bring on a hangover.'

'Adam used to like whisky,' she said, mournfully. 'He drank half a bottle of it the night he died. You mustn't tell anyone I said that.'

'Why?'

'Because it would be very, very, *very* disloyal to Adam.'

He leaned back on the sofa, put his arm around her. 'And you're a very loyal person, aren't you, Beth? Is that why you haven't remarried?'

'In part.'

'Which part in particular?'

She was enjoying the feel of his arm resting on her shoulder. 'The part other beers cannot reach.'

He joined in with her laughter. 'Oh, Beth, what a pair we make. But have you really never been tempted to get married again? You must have had offers – you're a very attractive woman.'

'Nobody's asked me.'

'Is that because you've had the drawbridge up?'

'It's not a crime to be discerning,' she said, with a hint of defensiveness.

'It *would* be a crime if you ended up depriving yourself of a happier life. But, then, who am I to talk? Look at the mess I made of things when I rushed into the arms of the first woman I came across.'

Hearing a maudlin tone creep into his voice again, Beth said, 'I have a secret. A whopping great secret no one knows anything about.'

His face broke into a wide smile. 'So what precisely are you hiding up your sleeve?'

'A man.'

'A man?' he repeated. 'Let me see.' He pulled her arm towards him and peered up her sleeve. 'I see no man.'

'That's because he's not there. He's—' She broke off and laughed. 'He's . . . he's a cyberman.'

He cocked an eyebrow at her. 'You sure about that? There's no chance you're muddling him up with the Dalek I saw in town the other week?'

Still laughing, she said, 'His name's Ewan Jones.'

'And?'

'And what?'

'Well, you'll have to fill me in on the details. All I've got so far is that he's a cyberman called Ewan Jones. Does that make him a Welsh enemy of the Time Lords?'

She shook her head, then waited for the room to stop spinning. 'He's a little older than me and has a great talent for making me laugh. He's also a fellow writer. Not published, but hopeful.'

'So where did you meet him? At a *Doctor Who* convention?'

She hesitated. 'Um . . . we haven't actually met.' She told him how they'd 'met' on-line and how their friendship had developed. 'I suppose it all sounds a bit silly to you, doesn't it?' she said, when she'd told Jack everything, even the possibility of meeting Ewan at the writers' conference.

He squeezed her close to him. 'I think it's bloody brilliant. How else should a writer meet his or her ideal partner but through the written word? Perhaps I should give it a go.'

'But what do you think about me meeting him in the way he's suggested? Tell me honestly.'

'Go for it, Beth. You know deep down you want to. So why not?'

'We might not like each other in the flesh. For instance, he might wear the most awful shoes – grey slip-ons – with white towelling socks.' She pulled a face. 'It might be disastrous. Stop laughing, Jack, these things matter. More seriously, he might turn out to be—'

'A roaring nutcase,' he interrupted her. 'In which case you need a chaperon.' He paused. 'Hey, and I know I'm almost as drunk as you, but I've just had the best idea of the night. Why don't we all go?'

'All who?'

'Hidden Talents – Dulcie, Jaz, Victor, you and me. We could go as a group. It'd be great. Just the thing to spur us on with our writing and at the same time we'd be checking out your bloke for you. What do you think?'

'I think, and I know I'm going to feel lousy in the morning, but we should both get drunk more often. You're a genius, Jack Solomon.'

'And to prove my brilliant idea isn't a one-off, here's another. Let's email your cyberspace boyfriend right now and give him the good news.'

'Now?'

'No time like the present. Then you won't back out. What's more, let's spice up the message and give him a taste of the real Beth King.'

She looked at him doubtfully, but he laughed and pulled her to her feet. 'Don't come over all wimpish on me, Beth. We're going to make him even keener to meet you in the flesh. You're always saying how good with words I am, well, tonight we'll put that to the test. I plan to have the man drooling at the thought of you.'

It was a mark of how drunk she was that she allowed Jack to drag her across the room to her computer. 'I hope you're not going to make me do something I'll regret,' she said.

42

The following morning, in Suffolk, Ewan went for a brisk walk along the beach. A blustery wind blew off the North Sea, sending waves crashing in. It was an invigorating start to the day, and he felt better for it. One way or another, he'd had a lousy week. The rejection of *Emily and Albert* had hit him harder than he'd thought it would. He'd taken it personally. Put simply, the story mattered to him and he'd wanted to share it with others.

He bent down and picked up a stone and hurled it far into the churning sea. 'I must be turning into a sentimental old fool,' he said aloud, his words catching on the wind. He threw another stone, then another. He never tired of the sea, could never imagine himself living anywhere else. At last, he turned his back on the shore, and tramped up the shingle incline towards the brightly coloured beach huts, one of which, so the local paper claimed last week, had been sold recently for a staggering ten thousand pounds. The world was a crazy place. The shelter of the dunes came as a welcome relief from the ravages of the shore, and he enjoyed the relative quiet and warmth before heading for the main street, where he stopped off at the handy open-all-hours shop for a newspaper and a packet of bacon.

While he was cooking his breakfast, cracking two eggs into the frying-pan alongside the bread and sizzling rashers, he thought of the dinner party he would be going to that evening. It was yet another attempt by some of his well-meaning friends to partner him off. That was the trouble with the happily married: they hated having a single person loitering untidily about the place. He hoped the woman he'd be seated next to tonight would have something interesting to say. The last woman at one of Phil and Susannah's dateline parties had been an intensely bitter divorcee – an English lecturer and a foaming-at-the-mouth feminist to boot. She'd had only one topic of social chit-chat when she'd drunk too much wine: that all men were feeble and devious, and, come the revolution, deserved everything and more that they had coming to them. Hardly the type of engaging conversation to inspire any man to volunteer for active service. 'What in God's name did you think we'd have in common?' he'd asked Phil the next morning, when he'd called to thank his friends for their hospitality.

'Susannah thought you'd enjoy the intellectual challenge,' Phil had said. 'Not forgetting the literary connection.'

'Oh, yes. What was it she said about popular fiction? It should be strangled at birth. Phil, if she had her way, bookshops up and down the country would be cleansed of all gold-embossed jackets.'

He tipped his breakfast on to a plate and sat at the table, where he'd laid out the arts pages of the *Daily Telegraph*. After he'd read the book reviews he tidied the kitchen, and went through to his office, pretending, as he always did, that he wasn't eager to see if there was a message from Beth.

There was.

He read it twice, and hoped she wouldn't regret having sent it. It was a gem. Written, he presumed, while she was under the influence of something a little more intoxicating than a mug of bedtime Ovaltine.

Beth knew that something was terribly wrong even before she opened her eyes and found that the light penetrating the gap in the curtains was burning the back of her eyeballs. She turned on to her side and tried to sleep again. To pretend that her hangover was nothing more than a nasty dream.

But she knew it wasn't, and as she recalled the events of the night before, she drew her knees up to her chest, assuming the foetal position, as though it would protect her from the shame of her behaviour.

Drunk.

Oh, horribly drunk.

She remembered Jack kissing her goodbye and leaving, and Nathan arriving home to find her bent over the toilet. 'I don't think I'm very well,' she'd whimpered, thinking of the countless lectures she had given him on the evils of alcohol. 'It must have been something I ate.'

'Yeah, that would be it, Mum,' he'd said, helping her into bed. She'd bet a pound to a penny he'd been laughing at her.

Then she remembered something even more shameful: the email she and Jack had sent Ewan.

She groaned, and sank further beneath the duvet.

'Oh, let the world end now,' she murmured.

43

Dulcie had thought she was covering up remarkably well, but it was clear from Prue and Maureen's expressions that she had failed miserably. Under the full glare of her friends' gaze, the last of her defences crumbled.

'I'm not going to beat about the bush,' Prue said, with her customary directness, after their waitress had brought them their baked potatoes and salads, 'but what on earth is the matter with you, Dulcie? Are you ill?'

It took all her strength to inject a light-hearted quip into her response. 'Of course I'm not ill. What's more, I'll see the pair of you out.'

'Nonsense!' declared Prue, grinding a shower of salt over her lunch. 'I've never seen you looking so down in the mouth.'

In a less acerbic tone, Maureen said, 'She's right, Dulcie. You don't look your normal self. It's not Andrew or Kate, is it?'

'No, they're both fine. But thanks for asking.' She forced a cube of cucumber into her mouth.

It had been a mistake to agree to meet up with her dear friends. Why hadn't she cried off, with some plausible excuse? How had she thought she could ever convince them that all was well when she knew she looked a mess and that her demeanour told the world that she had undergone a dramatic transformation for the worse? Everything was slipping away from her. She'd had to cancel the writers' group last week and didn't think she'd be able to cope with it tomorrow evening either. Writing was the last thing on her mind.

And all because of Richard. Of what she had denied herself. Oh, how she missed him! With each day that passed, the pain grew worse. He phoned her every morning on his mobile, trying to make her see sense. He'd broken down this morning and she'd heard him sobbing, 'Don't do this to me, Dulcie. I'd rather be dead than not see you again.' Hating herself, she'd gently replaced the receiver with a trembling hand. The pain of hearing his anguish, knowing that she was the cause of it, was too much.

She had loved Philip, and had gone on loving him long after he'd died, but losing him hadn't been as painful as this. She could only conclude that it was because she had played no part in causing her loss and the heartbreaking devastation that followed. There had been no guilt to deal with. Only the purity of grief.

She looked up suddenly and saw that both Prue and Maureen were hunting through their handbags. She wondered what they were looking for. When Maureen handed her a small packet of tissues, she understood that the game was up, that there was no hiding from them now. She wiped her eyes, blew her nose and said, 'Would you mind very much if we ...' She blew her nose again and cleared her throat. 'I think I ought to go home.'

While Maureen sat with Dulcie on the sofa, Prue pushed down the plunger on the cafetière and poured three cups of coffee. When they were all seated, Dulcie told them the whole story. She started at the beginning, with the day she had met Richard – the day he had changed her life. She told them how easily she and Richard had fallen in love, and even, with a degree of pride, what a wonderful lover he was: tender, considerate and infinitely passionate. 'He really was the most perfect man,' she murmured, knowing that her revelations were being received with more than a little envy.

'Except for being married,' muttered Prue.

'Yes. Except for being married,' echoed Dulcie. Then she told her friends about Kate and Henry. Which shocked them. They hadn't seen it coming. Who would?

'Is that why you've ended it with him?' asked Maureen.

Dulcie nodded. 'You understand, don't you? I had no choice. If there's a chance of those two young people being happy, I couldn't stand in their way.'

Prue put down her coffee cup. 'All I can say is, I hope they bloody well appreciate what you've done for them.'

'That's just the point, Prue,' said Maureen. 'They mustn't ever know. If they did it would ruin everything. Then no one would be happy.'

Prue looked at Dulcie in admiration. 'If I were in your shoes, I'm not sure I could be so selfless.'

Dulcie drained her cup and placed it carefully on its saucer. 'Anyway, it's all over now. And it's time I pulled myself together. I need to remind myself that I had a perfectly good life before Richard popped into it.'

Her friends looked at her doubtfully. Prue said, 'Dulcie, you need a break. You should get right away from Maywood. Why don't you go to London and stay with Kate or Andrew? You could treat yourself to leisurely trips to the galleries, lunches in smart restaurants, and no end of shopping sprees.'

Maureen warmed to the idea. 'And the theatre. Don't forget all those plays and musicals you could take in. Concerts too. It would be perfect.'

'It would also be exhausting.'

'Yes, but you wouldn't have time to dwell on ... well, you know what I mean.'

Dulcie smiled at Maureen, loving her for her sensitivity. 'It's all right, you can say his name. I shan't faint at the sound of it.'

That evening, while she was listening to *The Archers*, Dulcie's mind kept wandering. What her friends had suggested wasn't so silly. But London didn't appeal. If she went there, she would inevitably end up seeing Kate and, very likely, Henry.

No. London was out of the question.

But now that the idea had been planted in her mind, she couldn't let it go. Prue and Maureen were right: time away from Maywood would do her good. It would also mean that Richard wouldn't be able to ring her.

Leaving Ambridge to its own devices, she went upstairs to the cupboard on the landing where she kept a stock of holiday brochures. The one on the top of the pile caught her eye – *Italian Escapes*. She took it downstairs to the kitchen, put it on the table, and made herself a sandwich, most of which she knew she wouldn't eat. But she needed something to occupy her while she let the thought of going to Italy take root. What would best suit her current frame of mind? The dramatic scenery of the Amalfi coast? The lakes? Como? Garda? Maggiore? Or should she venture inland to the hills and valleys of Umbria? Tuscany was a possibility too, although she had been there before.

Her sandwich made, she poured herself a glass of wine – Italian, as it turned out. An omen? She sat at the table and opened the brochure. Already she had dismissed the lakes: she wanted to keep them for a summer trip, as she'd previously planned. She flicked through the glossy pages, seeing images of Byzantine and Renaissance art, of rustic hotels nestling in rural idylls and snow-capped mountains, of piazzas, palazzos and stunning waterfronts, of perfectly ripened tomatoes, basil and creamy white mozzarella sprinkled with black pepper and drenched in olive oil.

For the first time in days, Dulcie felt hungry, and she bit into her sandwich – the bread was past its best, and the lettuce had lost its crispness. Delving further into the brochure, she stopped at the section for city breaks. A photograph of St Mark's Square and the majestic domes of the basilica stared back at her.

Venice?

Oh, surely not. Venice was for couples strolling romantically hand in hand through the maze of narrow streets, or taking magical moonlit gondola rides along the Grand Canal.

It was a terrible idea. How could she consider rubbing salt into such a raw wound?

But how long was she going to allow herself to wallow in self-pity? Life had to go on.

She read on, scanning the range of hotels, looking for one that appealed. The Hotel Isabella was described as a hidden jewel, an oasis of tranquillity and refined charm reminiscent of a bygone era. Five minutes' walk from St Mark's Square, it was ideally situated and wouldn't inflict too large a dent in the bank balance, the brochure claimed. It sounded perfect. She bent back the corner of the page to mark the place, then realised that she'd finished her sandwich. It was the first meal that she had managed to eat in days. She took it as a good sign. Her friends would be pleased. 'You must eat,' they'd told her. 'How can you expect to think straight if you're not taking care of your body's needs?' They had left her with hugs of sympathy and repeated instructions that if she needed them she must ring, no matter what time of day or night. 'We're here for you, Dulcie,' Prue had said. 'I just wish you'd told us before.'

There had been no criticism of her affair with Richard, which was what she had feared. She had been convinced her behaviour would meet with their disapproval – people who were married, happily or otherwise, tended to take a dim view of others who appeared to ride roughshod over the sanctity of marriage.

How long, she wondered, before she would rid herself of the guilt? Not just for being party to Richard's betrayal of his marriage vows but for the pain she was now causing him.

Eventually she dragged her weary body upstairs to bed, telling herself that Richard was as culpable as she was, and that he had to take his share of the responsibility for what they had done. But men were different. Guilt slid off their consciences so easily.

She slipped her nightdress over her head, and tried to remember something Jaz had once said. Something clever about men and women and their response to guilt. It came to her while she was brushing her teeth. 'Show me a woman who feels no guilt and I'll show you a man.' Jack had taken issue with this, but Dulcie and Beth had laughed heartily.

How extraordinarily mature and perceptive Jaz was, despite her age.

44

With a terrible feeling of *déjà vu*, Jaz listened intently to what her mother was saying.

'Now, Jaz, there's plenty of food in the freezer so you won't need to worry too much, not for a couple of days anyway. But if you could keep an eye on the girls, make sure they do their homework, it would be a great weight off my mind. I expect I'll be home by the weekend, so everything will be back to normal then.'

It was Thursday, almost two weeks since her father had found out about Hidden Talents. With no lesson after last break, Jaz had come home early from college to find her mother upstairs packing an overnight bag. 'What's going on, Mum?' she'd asked.

'Oh, nothing to worry about. My blood pressure's sky high so the doctor's ordered me to have a few days' bed-rest in hospital.'

Jaz's heart had plummeted. 'If there's nothing to worry about, why do you have to go into hospital?'

'Oh, I suppose they want some of those young trainee doctors to have a geriatric mother to practise on. Who am I to argue? Cheer up, Jaz, it'll be fine.'

But Jaz didn't think so. She watched her mother close her overnight bag. 'Where's Dad?' she asked.

'He's on his way with Phin and Jimmy. They'll be here any minute and then your father will take me to the hospital.'

'But if there's nothing wrong, Mum,' Jaz persisted, 'why the rush?'

She didn't get an answer because just then they heard the back door nearly crashing off its hinges, followed by the noisy entrance of Tamzin and Lulu, bags thrown on the floor, fridge door pulled open and war breaking out over who was entitled to the last of the Sunny Delight.

'You will be patient with them, won't you?' her mother said.

Jaz took the bag from her, and walked with her to the bedroom door. 'I'll try, Mum, but they act up even more when you're not around.'

Her mother stroked her hair. 'We have to make allowances for them,' she said good-humouredly. 'They're throwbacks to the Rafferty side of the family, unlike you. You take after mine.' Out on the landing, she paused, and with one of the soft smiles that reminded Jaz of how much she loved her mother said, 'I'm sorry how things seem to fall your way, Jaz. That's the trouble with large families. There's always one who attracts more than their fair share of responsibility.' Her expression turned serious. 'Now, I don't know what's going on between you and your father because he won't tell me. All he says is that he's got it in hand and that there's nothing for me to lose any sleep over, but if there is anything I should know about, you would—'

A loud crash from the kitchen made them both start. Jaz didn't want her mother to pursue this line of conversation any further so she said, 'Dad's right, Mum, there's nothing for you to worry about.'

Her mother smiled again and laid a gentle hand on Jaz's shoulder. 'He can be bombastic and sometimes irritatingly stubborn, but underneath it all he means well. I just want you to know that if you need anyone to talk to, please don't think I haven't got time for you.'

How tempted Jaz was to spill it all out there and then in the hope that her mother would take her side.

Her father's punishment hadn't been as bad as she'd thought it would be. She was allowed out now, but he'd banned her from Hidden Talents. It was this that hurt most. 'It's for your own good, Jaz,' he'd said. 'You've got a lot on your plate at college and the last thing you need is a distraction. Besides, you should be mixing with people your own age, not hanging around a bunch of arty navel-gazers.' She could have argued with him, defended the group – her friends – but she hadn't. Keeping quiet, she had learned, was the best way to handle her father. If she could win him round by doing as he said, that's what she would do.

It had been great when half-term had ended and she'd been able to see Nathan at college again. Explaining what had happened and admitting that she was being treated like a child had been mortifying, but Nathan was fantastic about it. 'And there was me thinking you'd got bored of my amusing company,' he'd said, during lunch in the cafeteria.

She was so grateful to him for his understanding and for not laughing at her. He said it was because he knew better than most that families could be weird. She'd even confessed to him that she'd switched off her mobile so that he couldn't get in touch with her. 'I was feeling so sorry for myself, I knew if I spoke to you I'd burst into tears.'

Vicki and Billy had said she should stand up to her father.

'You're seventeen, you don't need to take this crap,' Billy had said. 'Stopping you going to a writers' group must be against some kind of human-rights law. Hey, you sure your father isn't a member of the Taliban? Any sign of him growing a beard and wearing a tea-towel on his head?'

'Shut up, Billy!' warned Nathan. 'Haven't you sussed yet that not everything in life is a big joke?'

'Why not talk to your mum?' Vicki had asked. 'Mine's great for getting round my dad and making him do what we want.'

But Jaz knew, as she stood on the landing, looking at her mother's tired face, that she couldn't confide in her. Not with her going into hospital. 'I'm okay, Mum, really. You mustn't worry about me.' She peered over the banister towards the front door. 'Sounds like Dad's back.'

She was right. Her father burst through the front door like a member of the SAS. He flung down his jacket and called, 'Moll, where are you?'

'Up here, Popeye.'

For such a large, heavy-set man, he flew up the stairs, taking them two at a time. 'You okay, Moll?' he said breathlessly; he folded her into his enormous arms. 'Holy Mother of God, I've probably been caught on camera that many bloody times I'll be facing a lifelong ban. Are you sure you're okay?'

At their mother's insistence, no one but their father was to go with her to the hospital, and waving them off, with Phin, Jimmy, Tamzin and Lulu, Jaz realised that her father loved her mother very much and would do anything to keep her safe. How many husbands, after so many years of marriage, felt so strongly for their wives?

But that evening as she cooked supper, at the same time reading through some history-of-art notes she'd made for an essay, a worrying thought occurred to her. What would Dad do, if the unthinkable happened and something happened to Mum? How would he cope without his beloved Moll?

She buried the thought deep. Nothing was going to happen to her mother. She was pregnant, not ill. She wasn't suffering from an incurable disease. Just as soon as the doctors had her blood pressure back to normal, her mother would be home.

45

Never in the history of Most Embarrassing Moments had Beth experienced such head-hanging shame. What had she been thinking when she'd sent Ewan that email? And what must he have thought of her when he'd read it?

Oh, he'd been pleasant enough about it in his response, had only teased her mildly, but deep down, he must have been quietly reviewing his opinion of her. What else could he have done in view of what she'd suggested she might like to do with him and a bar of chocolate?

Top tip, Beth [he'd emailed back]. Be sure to melt the chocolate first. But for the sake of clarity, would that be Galaxy or Cadbury's? I'm rather partial to a bar of Fruit and Nut, if my personal preferences ever need to be taken into account.

It was now March, and nearly two and half weeks since the night she and Jack had got so thoroughly plastered. The embarrassment should have passed by now, but it hadn't.

The next day Jack had apologised to her when she'd summoned the energy to go downstairs and help him with his unpacking.

'I'm struggling to piece together the exact details of last night,' he'd said, 'but I'm pretty sure I didn't behave too well. I can't remember the last time I woke up feeling so ropy. I didn't let the side down too much, did I?'

'I don't think so,' she'd murmured, 'but if you could lower your voice, I'd be eternally grateful.'

Smiling – obviously not feeling quite so ill as she was – he'd offered her a cup of coffee.

'When I'm convinced I'll be able to keep it down, that would be great.'

They didn't get much done in the first hour, but after Jack had forced her to drink several glasses of water, building up slowly to her eating a whole Rich Tea biscuit, they made some headway on the boxes in the kitchen. 'For a single man, you have a surprising amount of stuff,' she'd said, when the last of the boxes was empty.

'That's because Maddie didn't want any of it. I think she fancied the idea of taking Tony by the scruff of the neck and starting from scratch with him. Women like to do that, don't they?'

'I wouldn't know.'

He closed the door on the cupboard they'd just filled with a set of glass fruit dishes and a cut-glass punch bowl complete with cups – classic wedding-gift stuff that rarely, she guessed, saw the light of day. 'Okay, point made,' he said, 'I'm guilty of condemning the whole of womankind based on the actions of one particular woman. I retract the statement.'

And that's what Beth wished she could do with Ewan – retract that drunken email. Despite his reply, she hadn't had the nerve to correspond with him again, and wondered if she ever would. During the week, when Jack had given her a lift into work – this was now a regular occurrence – he'd asked her about Ewan and how things were going.

'Things aren't going anywhere. I blew it with that email we sent.'

He'd frowned. 'I can remember us writing it, Beth, but I can't recall precisely what we said. Remind me.'

Shame and disappointment – disappointment that she'd ruined things between her and Ewan – made her turn on Jack. 'But it was all your idea! You dictated it to me.'

'Did I?'

'Well, not all of it.' She had to accept her part in the sorry tale. She told him what they'd written.

He looked appalled. 'Oh, Beth, I'm really sorry. Did he take offence?'

'It's hard to tell, but perhaps not.'

'So what's the problem?'

'I'm the problem. I can't shake off the embarrassment of what we – I – said.'

When he dropped her off in the health-centre car park, Jack had said, 'If he's half the man you think he is, he'll treat the whole thing as a joke. Especially if you explain to him that you were drunk and aided and abetted by your new neighbour, who was in a far worse state than you.'

Since Jack's BMW had become a regular feature in the car park the tongues had been wagging furiously at work, and Wendy was in danger of wearing herself out with all the nudging and winking she was doing. 'I knew all along that you were seeing someone on the sly,' she declared triumphantly, the first morning she caught sight of Jack. 'He's a looker too. How much younger than you is he?'

'Wendy, how many times do I have to tell you? He's just a friend from the writers' group.'

'Who just so happens to have moved into the flat below yours. The man's got it bad for you, if he's gone to all that trouble.'

It didn't matter how often or how vehemently she denied the charges, Wendy would have none of it. But it made Beth register a happy truth: Jack was a friend, a good *platonic* friend with whom she felt quite at home. Maybe because she knew he felt the same about her. The age difference between them wasn't that great, but it provided a natural barrier over which neither of them had any intention of climbing.

But now there was this barrier between her and Ewan, which she didn't want. Yet how was she to dismantle it? What could she say to convince Ewan that she wasn't the wanton woman she'd made herself appear?

After work that evening, Beth drove to Marsh House to help Barnaby pack. Lois was at her South Cheshire Women's Group, listening to a guest speaker talking about her midwifery work in Calcutta. Barnaby had told Beth on the telephone that if there was any sign of Lois's car she was to drive on and come back later.

But the coast was clear, and Beth rang the doorbell to join in Barnaby's act of skulduggery. First thing tomorrow morning Lois, unknown to her, was being whisked off to Manchester airport to fly to Miami where she and Barnaby would embark upon their cruise.

Upstairs on their double bed was a large open suitcase: every wardrobe door and drawer was open. 'I've put a list together of the type of clothes I think Lois will need,' Barnaby said, 'but I want you to choose shoes and jewellery, and . . .' he lowered his eyes '. . . those all-important undergarments. You being a woman, I thought you'd know how these things work better than me. I'll be downstairs making us a drink if you need anything.'

It was a strange experience to sort through Lois's clothes, especially when it came to selecting her underwear. It was doing this that caused Beth to see her prim mother-in-law in a different light. Here was a woman who indulged herself in exquisite lingerie – M&S didn't get a look-in. La Perla – she'd heard Simone talk about it in tones of hushed reverence – featured heavily, as did another make she'd never heard of, and Beth was astonished by the amount of silk and delicate lace that took up three entire drawers. Every item was carefully folded and laid out like a shop display; she hesitated to disrupt its pretty order. In comparison, her limited range of worn-out chain-store bras and knickers would never pass muster. I've lived on my own too long, she thought. I've let things slide.

She looked at her reflection in Lois's dressing-table mirror. Her hair needed cutting, but otherwise she didn't think she was beyond redemption. There were a few too many lines around her eyes, a shadow or two, but with a lick of paint here and there, she'd almost get away with it. Whatever *it* was. Thank goodness she'd never been able to afford expensive holidays in the sun so hadn't ruined her skin. Her figure wasn't too awful either: she was still a size twelve and could wear the same clothes from years back. It was a boast she shouldn't be proud of, she realised. Those old clothes should have been thrown away a long time ago.

She held one of Lois's black lacy suspender-belts against her – she'd never worn stockings – and decided that one day she would like to spoil herself with something as frivolous and pretty.

'Here we are then, coffee. Oh . . .'

She whipped round from the mirror to see Barnaby looking almost as embarrassed as she was. She added the suspender-belt to the case on the bed and took the proffered mug. She smiled awkwardly. 'I – I was just thinking how lovely all these things are. Lois has exceptionally good taste. I'm ten shades of green with envy.'

For a moment Barnaby looked as if he didn't know what to say. Then he chuckled. 'Between ourselves, it's a little weakness of hers, and one I'm rather fond of.'

'You sweet man.'

They stood in silence, staring at the open suitcase. Then: 'I've never said this before, Beth, but you're a very attractive woman, who . . . who ought to have remarried by now.'

She blew on her coffee. 'To be honest, Barnaby, it's not as if I've had much choice in the matter.'

'But it's not right. I don't like the way things have worked out for you. You deserve better. A nice man, to make you feel . . .'

'To make me feel what?' she prompted.

'Complete.'

She laughed. 'There are women beyond these four walls who'd pluck out your nose-hairs for saying that.'

He squared his shoulders. 'Yes, and they doubtless live alone and will never know the joy another person can bring into their lives. I know Lois and I don't always give the impression of being in accord, but for the most part we've been happy. I suspect you and Adam would have been the same.'

'Maybe,' she demurred. 'Who knows?'

He looked at her. 'You *were* happy, weren't you?'

Smiling, she said, 'Oh, yes, extremely so. If we hadn't been, then perhaps I *would* have met someone else.'

Another silence grew between them.

'You won't leave it too late, Beth, will you? Even I know it gets harder for women to find a partner as they grow older. Stupidly, men think a woman half their age is the answer.'

'Gracious, Barnaby, I didn't know you were so clued-up on these things.'

'I take in more than most people give me credit for. I also understand the pressure you've been under from Lois. She's never fully recovered from Adam's death, and I doubt she ever will, but one day I pray that she'll accept you have every right to move on and fall in love again.' With his free hand, he put his arm around her. 'You've always been more than just a daughter-in-law to me, Beth. You're the daughter I never had. And I'll move heaven and earth to see you happy. Hence the drastic measures.' He indicated the bed with its half-packed suitcase.

Unable to express her gratitude in words alone, she leaned into him and buried her face in the warm softness of his woollen sweater so that he couldn't see her tears.

It was almost nine o'clock when Jack came off the telephone. He'd just been talking to Dulcie, who, after much apologising for letting down the group again, had told him she was going away for a brief holiday. 'I feel awful for bailing out like this, but I need a break,' she said. 'I'm hoping the change of scenery will do me good. You've seen for yourself what a state I'm in, so I've decided to do something positive, to shake me out of the doldrums.'

'Good for you,' he'd told her, marvelling at the human capacity for understatement. Dulcie had given up the man she loved, was clearly suffering for it, yet was prepared to make light of her pain. Although he hadn't changed his stance on what she'd done – adultery would always be unacceptable to him, and he didn't give a damn how judgemental or holier-than-thou it sounded – he liked Dulcie and didn't want her to be unhappy. 'Going anywhere nice?' he'd asked. 'Somewhere hot and exotic?'

'Somewhere pleasantly warm and extraordinarily beautiful. Venice. I've never been before.'

'That sounds great. Anything you need doing in your absence?'

'Yes. That's why I'm calling. Jack, I know this is a terrible imposition, given that you've just moved house and must be very busy, but I'd feel inordinately better if you could keep the group going while I'm away. I've failed you all, these last couple of weeks, and I want to make amends somehow.'

'Is it worth it, with so few of us able to attend?' he asked. 'Jaz still can't join us and Victor doesn't seem keen.'

'Even if it's just you and Beth who get together, I'd feel better about it.'

'Okay, then,' he conceded. 'But how long are you going to be away?'

'I'm keeping my plans flexible. A week, maybe two. Perhaps longer. I'll see how the mood takes me. And how well the money lasts. Now, tell me about your new flat. How's it going?'

'I'm gradually getting it sorted. Which is stupid because I'm going to mess it all up next week – I've got the builders coming in on Monday. They're knocking through from the kitchen to the dining room.'

'Oh, I wish you luck in that enterprise. The dust will be horrendous.'

He was just about to ask her what type of exercises she wanted the group to do while she was away when she said, 'If it all gets too bad for you, Jack, you're more than welcome to stay here. In fact, you'd be doing me yet another favour, house-sitting for me. Shall I let you have a set of keys, just in case?'

While he heated up a microwave meal for one, Jack wondered why Dulcie had asked him to lead the group. Why not Beth? She was just as capable as he was. It might have something to do with Victor, he concluded. Perhaps Dulcie had thought Beth would find it difficult to stop Victor dominating what was left of the group. He was a real oddity, that man, the sort who'd never fitted in anywhere.

But Jack was more concerned about Jaz than he was about Victor. It wasn't his place to interfere in the affairs of another family, but he felt that Jaz's father had overreacted. Dulcie had thought the same. 'Do you think it would help if I spoke to her parents?' she'd asked, on the phone. 'I could explain to them that we're a perfectly respectable group of people, not a cabal of local nutters.'

'I don't think our sanity or standing in the community is at the root of the problem,' he'd said. 'It's that she lied to her parents to hide what she was up to.'

'What a silly girl. And what a waste of all that talent. I do hope her father relents and lets her join us again. She's a bright girl and he should be proud of her. He ought to take a long, hard look at the situation and understand why she felt compelled to lie.'

Dulcie had hit the nail on the head, he thought, as he ate his supper in the sitting room and channel-hopped through a selection of make-over programmes and medical dramas. There was nothing worthwhile to watch so he admitted defeat and switched it off. Anyway he didn't have time to waste: there was plenty to do before the night was through. He wanted to do some writing as well as get the girls' bedroom ready. He was picking them up tomorrow morning and he wanted the flat to look its best for their first proper stay. They'd only seen it when it had belonged to Adele Waterman and secretly he wanted them to be impressed at the transformation. And that was before the builders moved in.

There had been no more talk from Maddie about California, but he didn't think that was because the threat had gone away. His fear was so great that the girls might go away that he didn't trust himself to raise the subject with Maddie or Tony. It was all he could do to contain his anger, some of which he used in his writing, venting it late at night in controlled bursts of passion. On a more practical level, he had instructed his solicitor to write to Maddie's, asking her to think what would be most beneficial to Amber and Lucy, stressing that they had to come first, and that an obvious basic need for them was to see their father regularly. He'd insisted on seeing a copy of the letter before it was sent – he didn't want it to inflame an already volatile situation – and he could only hope Maddie would take it in the spirit it was meant and respond accordingly. But the bottom line was, if he had to go to court to settle the matter, he would.

On the other side of town, Victor tried to ignore the person who was knocking on his front door. Why couldn't people leave him alone? He could keep himself to himself so why couldn't they?

Bent over his typewriter, his skull throbbing with the headache he'd had since he woke that morning, he closed his eyes and covered his ears with his hands. Go away, he willed whoever it was. Leave me be.

At last the knocking stopped. But the intrusion wasn't over. He heard the sound of metal on metal: the letterbox was being opened.

He pushed himself to his feet unsteadily, feeling lightheaded. He took the stairs slowly, wondering why he couldn't move faster.

There was no one at the door when he reached it, but on the floor was a single white envelope. With shaking hands he ripped it open. It was a handwritten note from Dulcie Ballantyne. What did she want *now*?

He read the few lines she'd written, then tore it up in disgust, letting the shreds of paper fall at his feet. She was going away: in her absence that jumped-up estate agent would be in charge of Hidden Talents and they'd be meeting at his new flat in Maywood Park Road.

What did Jack Solomon have that Victor Blackmore didn't? Why hadn't she thought to ask him if he'd lead the group? He was more experienced than any of them. He was the one with the most complete manuscript.

He dragged himself back upstairs, the thumping inside his head almost unbearable, as if all his blood had surged to his brain and was threatening to burst out through his eye-sockets. He yanked the page he'd been writing from his typewriter, laid it on the desk and inserted a fresh piece. Then he hunted for the notes he'd made earlier, remembering, ten minutes later, that he'd written them on the wall behind him. This was a new technique he'd adopted, using the walls as four large noticeboards: it was a foolproof method to keep his notes safe. He was rather proud of himself for coming up with such a simple, clever idea.

Shivering, he rewound the scarf around his neck and rubbed his hands. He went over to the Calor Gas burner to make himself a drink. But when he tried to light the gas, it spluttered, hissed, and the flame slowly died: the cylinder was empty.

Silently, and not knowing why, he crouched on the bare floorboards, covered his unshaven face with his hands and wept.

46

Dulcie was glad she had taken Prue and Maureen's advice: without question, Venice was a wonderful distraction, the perfect tonic.

From the moment the water taxi had dropped her off in the Castello district, and despite being tired from a day's travelling, she had felt at peace. Walking the short distance to her hotel, she had become absorbed in her surroundings and had marvelled at the early-evening sky, a glorious infusion of fading blue and subtle shades of pearly pink: it was simply the most beautiful sight she had seen and for a minute it had held her motionless. Tourists had buzzed around her, probably annoyed with the obstruction she was causing, but she had ignored them, continuing to drink in the still, magical atmosphere of the lagoon as day surrendered itself to the dusky mist of twilight.

Enchanted, she had reluctantly torn herself away and, armed with her map, had wheeled her suitcase in the direction of the family-run three-star Hotel Isabella. It had taken her ten minutes to locate it and, within the blink of an eye, she had fallen in love with its unmistakable Venetian charm and hospitality. The sixteenth-century building didn't offer a view of the lagoon or any of the waterways but, at the end of a narrow alleyway, it lived up to the brochure's claim that it was an oasis of tranquillity. She had at once felt perfectly at home.

This had been two days ago, and her love of the city was growing with each hour. 'Today,' she told herself, 'I will not walk too far.' She made the promise as she helped herself to a sweet pastry and a bowl of fresh fruit from the breakfast buffet in the small hotel dining room. She exchanged a smile and a 'good morning' or a '*buon giorno*' with her fellow guests – they were mostly American with one or two Italians – then sat down, knowing that her promise would be almost impossible to keep. Such was the temptation to explore every square inch of Venice, lest she miss some unrivalled gem of architecture, yet another Tintoretto or a spectacular reflection of light on water, that she was in danger of wearing herself out.

She laid her napkin on her lap and smiled at the young waiter who appeared silently at her elbow to pour her tea. '*Grazie*,' she said, loving the special treatment she was receiving. One of the joys of travelling alone as a single woman, even an ageing one, was the preferential treatment she received. She was all too aware that she was an object of curiosity to the staff at the hotel, as well as to the other guests, but she didn't mind: it worked to her advantage. Alberto, the impeccably well-mannered concierge, about the same age as Andrew, fussed over her at every opportunity: 'Signora Ballantyne, you know where you are going? You have a map?' The waiters saw to it that each morning at breakfast she had a table looking out on to the pretty courtyard where shade-loving shrubs grew in terracotta pots and the walls were covered in creepers so rampant there was hardly any discernible brickwork.

Wearing her most comfortable shoes, she set out for another day of adventure. She left the narrow alleyway, Calle Lorenzo, behind her when she turned into Calle della Pietà and stopped in front of the church of Santa Maria della Pietà. There was a board outside the *chiesa* advertising a concert for that evening. Alberto had told her that there were many concerts to enjoy in Venice and, making a snap decision, she climbed the steps and went inside. There was a small ticket booth at the entrance and, the transaction quickly made, she left the church to walk the length of the Riva degli Schiavoni looking forward to an evening of Vivaldi.

It was a beautifully warm March day and, arms swinging, she walked through the crowds of tourists, past the world-renowned Hotel Danielli, which, according to her guidebook, had once been a haunt for nineteenth-century writers and artists; Ruskin, Balzac and Dickens, to name but a few. Perhaps one day she would write a bestseller and be able to afford to stay there herself. The thought made her smile.

Until now she hadn't thought of her writing, but Venice was a place of unique inspiration and she knew it wouldn't be long before she would be itching to get back to it. Maybe she could buy herself a notebook and write here in Venice. She could find an open-air café and sit in the warm sun to let her convalescing mind take on the challenge of a blank page. Excited by the prospect, she knew she was recovering. 'I'm on the mend,' she said aloud, causing the striking young woman walking alongside her – so obviously Italian in her stylish black trouser suit and chic sunglasses – to glance at her and hurry on ahead.

She passed the colourful souvenir stalls on her left, which lined the busy waterfront, and came to the Ponte della Paglia, more commonly known as the Bridge of Sighs. Hordes of tourists were congregated here to photograph each other in front of the bridge but, considering herself practically a local now, Dulcie barely slowed her step to admire the view – she had snapped a selection of pictures yesterday.

The Doges' Palace was the next point of interest, followed by the two soaring columns of San Marco and San Teodoro. For several centuries the granite pillars, one topped with a marble statue of St Theodore and the other a bronze of the Lion of St Mark, had framed a place of execution; now they were the focal point for the flocks of pigeons and tourists alike. From what Dulcie had read in her trusty guidebook during dinner last night, even in these enlightened times superstitious Venetians eschewed walking between the two columns for fear of bringing bad luck on themselves.

Leaving behind her the hubbub of the *piazzetta*, she headed for the *vaporetto* stop for the water-bus that would take her to the Dorsoduro district and the Guggenheim. Yesterday she had covered the major sites, such as the basilica, the campanile, and the Doges' Palace; now she was giving her attention to what she called her B list. Peggy Guggenheim, an accomplished art collector and a woman who had certainly lived life to the full – if a little recklessly – struck Dulcie as an interesting role model. Just recently there had been an article in *The Times* about the fabulous collection of modern art housed in Venice and Dulcie was keen to see it.

The *vaporetto* was packed and, not for the first time, Dulcie wondered how the rickety diesel-run motorboat kept afloat with so many crammed on to it. Ahead of her, at the entrance to the Grand Canal and bathed in brilliant sunlight from a sky of powder blue, was the magnificent Baroque church of Santa Maria della Salute. It was true, Dulcie thought, as a man beside her pointed his video camera at the church, that every way you turned in Venice there was a view of breathtaking beauty. Who needed physical love, when the senses could be touched so satisfyingly with this heaven-like perfection?

The same thought struck her again that evening. She had had dinner in a nearby trattoria – her appetite had fully returned – and she was now being seduced by a string quartet. It was irrelevant that the Four Seasons had become such a cliché: to hear it played in a church where the great composer himself had written and directed performances of his own work was a joyful experience, which she hoped she would never forget. The music sounded so fresh, so vital, that it was as if she was hearing it for the first time.

During the interval, when there wasn't anything to do but go outside for some fresh air or wander around the church, she stayed where she was, avoiding the crush of a large audience on the move. When the initial rush had passed, she looked across the nave and recognised an American couple from the hotel. The woman, a tiny slim thing in her mid-forties, stylishly dressed, with large brown eyes, waved at her. Dulcie returned the greeting and wasn't surprised when they came over and introduced themselves. They were an engaging couple, who were quite at ease talking to strangers. Dulcie took an instant liking to them. Their names were Cathe, pronounced Cathy, and Randy Morris. 'Oh, I know what you're thinking.' The woman laughed. 'My husband's name is such a joke where you come from.'

'Well, only—'

'No, it's okay, we can laugh as well as the next person. Isn't that right, Randy?'

He nodded and smiled. 'How're you enjoying the concert? The acoustics are great, aren't they?'

'I'm loving it. It's the perfect end to a perfect day. Have you visited Venice before?'

'We sure have. We came here for our honeymoon. We're doing a kind of re-enactment twenty-two years on, you could say.' The man put his arm around his tiny wife's shoulder and looked deep into her eyes, which Dulcie could see now were skilfully enhanced by carefully applied makeup. But the man's gesture was so loving that Dulcie was reminded of Richard. She caught her breath.

'Are you okay?'

Dulcie dropped her programme to give herself time to restore her equilibrium, and made a great play of fumbling for it at her feet. 'Goodness, what a butterfingers I am,' she said, when the fear of crying had passed and she was able once more to meet their gaze.

Other members of the audience were making their way back to their seats and she was relieved when her new friends said they ought to return to their own chairs, but not before they had invited her to join them for a drink afterwards.

She spent the rest of the concert trying not to allow memories of Richard to intrude, forcing herself to focus on Venice and how much better she was feeling and what she had planned for tomorrow. But, remembering that today was Thursday, her thoughts strayed homeward. Would Mr and Mrs Rafferty have forgiven their daughter for deceiving them? Would Jack have been successful in getting the group together? She wasn't a fanciful woman, but Dulcie had a gut feeling about Jack. She was convinced that he would become a published author. There was an incisive honesty about his writing that she was sure would have huge appeal. That was why she had asked him to keep the group going while she was away: she had wanted to be sure that he would keep his own novel flowing.

Jaz perched on the edge of her mother's bed. For once she was glad that her father believed in throwing his money around: Mum had a private room and could have visitors more or less whenever she liked.

'So how's everything at home?' her mother asked. 'The girls behaving themselves?'

'Oh, I've got them well under my thumb,' Jaz said breezily. It was a lie, but she felt justified in telling it. She didn't want her mother to worry. She'd been in hospital for a week now, and her blood pressure was still too high for her to come home. Her ankles had ballooned and Jaz doubted they would ever go back to how they'd been before. There were other complications with her pregnancy too, something to do with too much amniotic fluid. There was even the threat that the babies might be born too soon. So, no, she could not tell her mother that Tamzin and Lulu were as out of control as they had ever been. More so, perhaps. They played up at the slightest provocation because they knew they could get away with it. Dad was so preoccupied with work and worrying about Mum that he didn't seem to notice what was going on right under his nose. Phin and Jimmy were doing their usual double-act of Dumb and Dumber, so no change there.

But the good news was that, at Mum's insistence, Dad had got in touch with an agency and now Mrs Warner came in every day to cook, clean and do the ironing. She was a godsend and Dad was thinking of keeping her on when the babies arrived. 'But, Popeye, I've always done my own housework in the past,' her mother had complained.

'And you never had twins to deal with in the past,' he'd argued back. 'A bit of help round the house will give you a much-needed break.'

They had visited Mum every day, and Dad usually came twice, but this evening he, Phin and Jimmy were out on the town in Liverpool: it was St Patrick's Day and they probably wouldn't be home until the early hours. Dad had made a few unconvincing noises last night about not bothering this year – 'Oh, Moll, it wouldn't be worth it. How could I go, knowing you were stuck here in this blasted hospital?' – but he hadn't needed much encouragement from Mum to go off and enjoy himself.

'Popeye, there's no point in both of us being miserable. Go and have some fun. But to make me feel better, fix up a babysitter for Tamzin and Lulu so that Jaz can come and visit me on her own. These days, we never have a chance to natter, just the two of us.'

As it turned out, they didn't need to arrange for anyone to keep an eye on Tamzin and Lulu: friends, whose parents presumably hadn't met them, had invited them both for a sleep-over. Her father had given Jaz the money for a taxi to and from the hospital so, for one fantastic night, it was just her and Mum.

'Is anything bothering you, Jaz?'

Her mother's question made Jaz look up from the pattern on the blanket, which she had been tracing with a finger. 'No. Why would you think that?'

'It must be the serious expression I keep seeing on your face. How's college? You hardly mention it these days.'

'It's great.'

'Really?'

'Really.'

'So what *is* troubling you? Come on, Jaz, talk to me. Why do you think I made the trade-off with your father? He gets to go to Liverpool to be with his old friends, and I get the chance to talk to you alone.'

'I didn't know you were so sneaky, Mum.'

She smiled. 'I play by my own rules. Now, then, spill it all out. I want to know what's been going on behind my back.'

Jaz was dying to share everything and knew she would feel better for it, but she couldn't forget why her mother was stuck here in bed. She held her tongue.

As though reading her thoughts, her mother said, 'If you're worrying about upsetting me and sending my blood pressure off the chart, don't. Think about it – there's no better place I could be for receiving bad news.'

Worn down by her mother's gentle insistence, and the need to talk to her, Jaz said, 'You won't like it, Mum.'

'I'll be the judge of that. Now, come on, do us both a favour. Let's get this over and done with and I guarantee you'll feel better for it.'

Jaz told her everything. About Hidden Talents, and how she'd been going to the group most Thursday evenings while pretending she was at Vicki's. She explained her reasons for her secrecy. Also about Dad's ban on her attending the group for the foreseeable future. 'They're a really nice bunch of people, Mum. There's nothing weird about them, like Dad seems to think there is. Dulcie lives in a lovely house in Bloom Street where we meet, and she's the one who's in charge, though she tries to make out that she isn't and—'

'A bit like me, then,' her mother interrupted, with a twinkling smile.

Jaz smiled back at her, gaining confidence now in the telling of the story. 'And then there's Beth ...' She hesitated, thinking of Nathan. 'Um ... I'll tell you about her in a minute. Jack's great, he's an estate agent in town and a really cool writer. Only trouble is, Phin and Jimmy jumped to the conclusion that something was going on between us.'

Her mother's eyes widened.

'There isn't, Mum, honestly. It was because Jack always gave me a lift home and they saw me in his car. How're you doing? Blood pressure okay?'

'Go on. I'm fine. Tell me more about the group.'

'Well, the only other person is Victor, and he's seriously cranky.'

'I thought you said there weren't any weirdos?'

'He's the exception. Delusional too. He reckons he's writing the book of the century. God, Mum, he couldn't write a shopping list, never mind a novel.'

Her mother laughed, reached out to Jaz and hugged her.

'What's that for?' Jaz asked, when her mother released her.

'For making me laugh. For taking my mind off being pregnant. I'm sick of mother-and-baby talk.'

'You're not angry, then?'

'I'm cross with your father for overreacting. So typical of him. In his daft way, he thinks he's protecting you. He hasn't learned to trust you yet. Trouble is, he judges others by his own standards and mistakes: he was a terrible tearaway before he met me. You've only got to look at Phin and Jimmy to get a glimpse of what he was like in his old wildcat days.' She leaned back against the pillows and sighed. 'But if that's the height of it, I'm sure I can sort it with your father. Leave it to me.'

But Jaz wanted to have everything out in the open: no more secrets or lies. 'Um ... actually, Mum, there is something else. Something I haven't told Dad.'

'Oh?'

'I've been seeing this really nice guy from the upper sixth. His name's Nathan King and his mother is the woman I mentioned earlier, Beth.'

'So what's wrong with him? Why keep him hidden from us? Is he covered from head to foot in tattoos and body piercings?'

'No! Nothing like that. He's great. But ... but I didn't want anyone to know about him. I thought Phin and Jimmy would scare him off.'

Her mother gave her one of her soft, knowing looks. 'He wouldn't be much of a boyfriend if he was that easily put off. It's you he's interested in, not your brothers. And presumably he's intelligent enough to reason that you're as sane as you're pretty. A bit silly at times, but nothing that a dose of self-belief and common sense wouldn't cure.'

Jaz took a moment to consider what her mother had said. She was right. Jaz had told countless lies because she had been convinced that the slightest thing would frighten Nathan away. But it wasn't just her insecurity that was to blame: pride had clouded her vision and caused just about the entire mess she now found herself in. She felt a hand on hers.

'Did you hear what I said, Jaz?'

'I'm sorry, Mum. I was thinking. But, yes, you're right.'

'Good. Now, when do I get to meet Nathan? Don't look so horrified. If we're to get round your father, I ought to meet the young man so I can put Popeye's mind at rest. Perhaps we could pretend that you've only just got to know him. That way we can avoid a lot of unnecessary trouble.'

Jaz flung her arms round her mother. 'Oh, Mum, you're the best.'

'A pity you didn't think that some months back and confide in me. Think of the hassle-free life you could have been enjoying.'

Jaz rode home in the back of the taxi happier than she'd been in a long time. Mum had been brilliant. And, even better, she was interested in her writing. She'd asked to see some of it. 'I could do with something good to read,' she'd said.

Jaz hadn't had the heart to tell her she'd wiped her novel off her computer and thrown away the only paper copy.

At home, she paid the taxi driver, let herself into the house, and stood in the hall in the darkness.

Instinctively she knew something was wrong. The burglar alarm wasn't on: the little red light above the window wasn't winking as it should have been. Her mouth went dry and her heartbeat quickened. She walked nervously towards the sitting room, her footsteps slow, her knees trembling. Holding her breath, she pushed open the door and switched on the light.

It was difficult to be certain, but it looked as if anything that had been worth taking was gone: hi-fi, telly, video-player, silver ornaments, pictures. Worse, the place was trashed: sofas turned over, cushions ripped open, curtains pulled down, lamps and the glass-topped table smashed, walls and carpets smeared with God knew what.

47

'Don't worry, I'll be there in seconds. Just hang on.'

Nathan switched off his mobile and looked at Jack and his mother's concerned face. 'Sorry to break into your two-man writing group, but it's Jaz. She's just got back from visiting her mum and found they've been burgled. I'm going round to make sure she's okay.'

'Is she on her own?'

He was already out in the hall pulling on his coat. 'Yes.'

'In that case,' his mother glanced briefly at Jack, who nodded, 'we're coming with you. She's called the police, I take it?'

'I didn't ask, but I expect so.'

Jack drove, and when they got there they found a police car on the drive and lights blazing from every window of the house. Nathan was glad the police had arrived so quickly. He hadn't said anything to Jaz on the phone, but his primary concern had been the possibility that the burglar – or burglars – was still in the house.

A WPC opened the door to them, and after they'd explained who they were, they were shown through to the kitchen, where Jaz was pacing the floor wringing her hands. Nathan went straight to her. 'Dad'll kill me when he finds out,' she cried, holding him tight. 'He'll say I didn't put the alarm on. But I did.' She stifled a sob. 'He'll blame me, I know he will. Oh, *why* did this have to happen?'

'Of course your dad won't blame you,' he reassured her.

'Your friend's right.' Another police officer joined them in the kitchen. He held a pair of wire cutters. 'The alarm's been tampered with. They knew what they were doing and broke in through the french windows in the dining room. Same as the house broken into last night. Place trashed, no room untouched. Looks like we're in for a run of it. Little sods.'

It wasn't until the two police officers had gone, just after midnight, that Jaz managed to get an answer from her father on his mobile. Nathan could tell when she held the phone away from her ear what his reaction was.

'It's okay, Dad,' she said, when he allowed her to speak. 'I'm fine. I've got some friends here with me. Dad, you'll have to speak up, I can hardly hear you . . . Well, tell them all to shut up! Look, the place has been trashed. It's awful . . . every room . . . Oh, Dad, they've written on the walls . . . ruined the carpets . . . There's . . .' She gulped. 'Mum must never know. We'll have to get it sorted before she comes home from hospital. She'll be devastated.' When Jaz started to cry, Beth stepped in and took over the conversation.

'Hello, Mr Rafferty. You don't know me, but I'm a friend of your daughter's from the writers' group . . . Yes, that's right, Hidden Talents. I'm here with my son and Jack, who's also from the group . . . Oh . . . Thank you, but there's no need. We came as soon as Jaz called. She's shaken but, on the whole, I'd say she's doing pretty well . . . No, there's nothing more to be done. The police have been and gone and Jack's boarded up the broken pane of glass in the dining room where they got in. What I was going to suggest was, rather than you come rushing home, Jaz could stay the night with Nathan and me . . . Okay, I'll hand you over to Jaz and she'll give you our address.'

'Thanks, Mum,' Nathan said, when they were back at the flat. Jack had gone downstairs and Jaz was in the bathroom, getting ready for bed.

'What for?'

'Being so nice.'

'Nice doesn't come into it. I wouldn't have dreamed of leaving the poor girl on her own. And if you'd spoken to her father, you would have known there was no way he could drive home. He and everyone he was with sounded as drunk as skunks. A shame we had to spoil the party for him. I hope he remembers our address in the morning.'

He helped his mother to make up a bed on the sofa for Jaz, and just as they were hunting for a spare pillow, Jaz appeared self-consciously in a pair of oversized Winnie the Pooh pyjamas. 'Don't you dare laugh,' she warned him.

'It never crossed my mind.'

'And if it does, you have my full permission to pinch him hard,' his mother said. 'Anyone for a drink before we turn in for the night? No? In that case, I'll wish you both sweet dreams.'

'I'm sorry I was a bit of a headcase earlier,' Jaz said, when they were alone and she was curled up beneath the duvet on the sofa.

'When was that? I must have missed it.'

She nudged him with her foot. 'Don't patronise me.'

'I wasn't.' He stroked her face, then tugged one of her plaits. 'Anyway, how could I do that to someone wearing such a colossally cute pair of pyjamas.'

Her face reddened. 'My mum bought them for me years ago, thinking I'd grow into them. I never did.'

'I'm glad you didn't – otherwise you'd be huge.'

She laughed, and he moved in to kiss her. But she frowned and pushed him away. 'It's okay,' he said, 'I'm not going to do anything silly.' He smiled. 'Certainly not with my mother in the next room.' The frown vanished and she put her arms round him.

He lay down next to her and closed his eyes. Before long they were both asleep.

In the morning, Beth found them lying on the sofa, her son fully dressed and wrapped in Jaz's arms. Who was protecting whom?

For a man who had to be nursing a monumental hangover, Jaz's father was hiding it well. As were her brothers, Beth suspected.

The flat didn't seem big enough to accommodate these three large, imposing men and, given what she knew of Mr Rafferty and his sons, Beth was relieved that they'd arrived long after Jaz and Nathan had woken. Any evidence that the two had slept together, albeit quite innocently, had been tidied away, and Beth was now handing round cups of coffee as if she was perfectly used to entertaining at this time of day: it was five to eight with college and work to get to. 'You must have been up early,' she said to Mr Rafferty. 'Sugar?'

He helped himself to three spoonfuls. 'I couldn't sleep for worrying. The boys and I hit the road at seven.'

'Have you been to the house yet, Dad?'

The big man turned to his daughter. 'No. I wanted to make sure you were okay first.'

'I'm fine.'

Her voice sounded tight and edgy and Beth could see that Jaz's main concern this morning had nothing to do with the burglary, but everything to do with Nathan being in the same room as her father and brothers. She hadn't so much as glanced at Nathan since her father's arrival when he'd swamped her in a massive hug.

Stirring his sugar-laden coffee, Mr Rafferty returned his attention to Beth. 'Look, Mrs King—'

'Please, it's Beth.'

'Well, Beth, I just want to say how grateful I am for what you and your son did last night, leaping into the thick of it and taking care of my Jasmine at such short notice.'

Jaz cringed. 'No one calls me that, Dad.'

He pointed at her with his spoon. 'They do if they really care about you, sweetheart. And this Jack bloke, I need to thank him as well. Holy Mother of God, what the sweet Fanny Adams is that?'

From beneath them came the noise that Beth and Nathan had grown used to. It was Jack's builders starting work. From what he had said, they were a shambles. They arrived inconveniently early and left shortly after lunch – Jack knew this because he'd seen their van driving past his office on Tuesday. When he had confronted them, they had admitted they were double-booked and had another job on the go.

Beth explained about Jack living downstairs and the work he was having done.

'Who's he got in to do it?' Mr Rafferty shouted, above the racket. 'Someone reputable, I hope.'

'I'm sorry,' she yelled back, just as the noise stopped, 'I don't know their name. They're a small outfit, I think.' She told him how unreliable they were.

All three Rafferty men rolled their eyes. 'Bloody cowboys. Here today, gone tomorrow. If he needs someone decent, tell him to get in touch. I owe him.' Mr Rafferty drained his cup, put it down carefully on the table and pulled out his wallet. He handed Beth a business card. 'Right, then, are we set?' This was to Jaz.

She reached for the bag she'd brought with her last night. 'It's okay, Dad, I've got all my stuff for college. I'll walk with Nathan.'

'Don't be an eejit, Nathan can have a lift too. There's plenty of room in the Jag. That okay with you, lad?'

Nathan nodded. 'Thank you. I'll just get my things.'

While he was gone and Beth was clearing away the cups and saucers, she heard Jaz's father whisper, 'Nice boy that, Jaz. You could do a lot worse.'

Turning on the tap and filling the sink, Beth smiled to herself. Funny how things worked out.

48

With his impressive track record for cocking things up, Jack should have known better than to court disaster by getting any building work done. Given the opportunity, he would have sacked the builders: they'd been as good as useless. As it was, they'd done a runner, leaving the job half done and his flat practically uninhabitable, brick dust and rubble everywhere – they hadn't bothered to organise a skip – and bare wires dangling. Was he depressed? Was he downhearted? Yes. Yes. And bloody *yes*!

But it wasn't all bad, as Beth had been quick to point out. She'd handed him a business card and told him to get in touch with Jaz's father. 'I got the feeling he'd do it for a good price as a favour to you. He was very grateful to us for helping Jaz on the night of the burglary. I received a gorgeous bouquet of flowers from him and, from what Nathan says, he's had a change of heart regarding Jaz and Hidden Talents. Having met me, and seen for himself how normal I am, he's decided she can come back.'

That had been yesterday morning, Saturday, and since then things had moved apace. Jack had spoken to Mr Rafferty, feeling slightly guilty for bothering him at the weekend, especially as he had his own problems to deal with, and had arranged for one of his men to visit on Monday – tomorrow. Then he'd moved out of the flat to take up Dulcie's offer. 'She wouldn't have suggested it if she hadn't been serious,' Beth assured him. 'Dulcie's not that kind of a woman.'

So that was where he was now. He'd moved in this morning, having rung Dulcie in Venice to check that it really was okay for him to set up temporary camp. 'Of course it's all right, Jack. Though I'm sorry to hear the reason why you've resorted to making use of my house. Still, at least my mind is at rest to know you're there.' Stupidly he'd told her about the Raffertys' burglary, although not the possibility that Maywood was in for a spate of them. He hoped the news wouldn't spoil her holiday. She'd asked if he'd managed to get the group together on Thursday evening, but he'd had to admit that only he and Beth had met, and that was before they'd had to abort and go to Jaz's aid. 'It was a very informal evening,' he'd confessed, 'but it was quite useful in as much as I bored Beth to tears with a chapter I'd just finished writing.'

'I doubt that you bored her,' Dulcie had admonished him. 'You're an extremely able writer, Jack, and I have high hopes for you. You have a real talent for telling a good story. Now, what about Victor? What's the latest on him?'

'I tried ringing him as you asked, but the number doesn't work. If I have time during the week, I'll call on him one evening.'

He'd also told her that Jaz might be allowed to join the group again.

'Goodness, Jack, I turn my back for a few minutes and everything happens. Perhaps I should leave you in charge more often.'

'And that's not all.' He told Dulcie about the writers' conference. He omitted to say how Beth had come to hear of it, or that there was now a chance that she might not want to go. 'What do you think, Dulcie? Should we go as a group?'

'I think it's an excellent idea. These conferences can be so encouraging. Where's it being held?'

'Somewhere near Harrogate, so not too far away.' He'd then gone through a few domestic details with her about the central-heating system and which bedroom he should use. Finally he said goodbye, conscious that she had a holiday to get on with.

He'd brought a selection of work suits with him, some shirts, two pairs of jeans and a sweater, plus basic provisions, some ready-made meals for one and, most importantly, his laptop and printer. He wanted to make the most of any spare time he had. There hadn't been much so far: today he'd taken the girls swimming, then on to McDonald's and the cinema before driving them back to Prestbury. The original plan had been for Amber and Lucy to stay the weekend with him but, given the chaos of the flat, it had seemed sensible to cut short their visit. He had hated doing this and Amber had taken him to task. 'It's not fair, Daddy.' She'd pouted. 'I wanted to see you for the whole weekend. It doesn't matter to me how messy the flat is.'

'It would matter to me if bricks started falling on top of you,' he'd said.

'I bet you're exaggerating. It can't be that bad.'

'Believe me, Amber, it is.'

It was now eight o'clock and an age away from the Double Mac and fries he'd had for lunch. He opened a bottle of Budweiser and started to fix himself some supper with the intention of getting down to Chapter Thirty-five afterwards. He reckoned he only had another five to do before *Friends and Family* – his first book – was finished. He liked the sound of that: *his first book*. It implied there would be more. He had a feeling that, now he had started, nothing would stop him. Writing was addictive.

He grilled some sausages and buttered some slices of soft white bread, adding a squirt of ketchup – which he had been surprised to find in Dulcie's kitchen – then sat down to eat his culinary masterpiece. In front of him was his laptop, plugged in and ready to go. But a ring at the bell stopped him mid-bite. With a mouth full of sausage, he answered the door. He stared at the grey-haired man on the step, not recognising him – it was hardly likely that he would: this was Dulcie's house, after all. Sensing that it would be imprudent to admit to this stranger that the owner was away, he waited for the man to speak first.

'Is . . . is Dulcie in?' the man asked awkwardly.

Jack hedged: 'Um . . . not just at the moment.'

Suspicion passed across the man's face. 'Can you tell me when she'll be back?' His voice was scarcely polite now.

Finishing what was in his mouth, Jack said, 'Sorry but I can't.' His words came out more belligerently than he'd intended.

They pushed the man over the edge of politeness and into hostility. 'Look, I don't know who you are but, please, go and find Dulcie and say that Richard wants to speak to her. Please, do that much for me.'

Jack hadn't considered that while he was in Bloom Street the man from whom Dulcie had run away might turn up. There was something so desperate about him as he stood on the step pleading to see Dulcie that Jack stood back from the door and said, 'I think you'd better come in.'

Richard's hopes soared.

At long last he was going to talk to Dulcie face to face. Suddenly he no longer cared who the unknown man was who had deigned to allow him across the threshold, and who was now walking through Dulcie's house as if he owned it.

He had tried so hard to get her out of his mind, but he couldn't. She had torn his life apart. Finally, he had the chance to repair it. But when the stranger led him into the kitchen and he saw no sign of Dulcie, hope drained out of him. He took in the sandwich on the table, the laptop, the open bottle of beer. 'What's going on?' he demanded. 'Where's Dulcie? And who are you?'

'I'm a friend of hers,' the man said calmly. He held out his hand. 'Jack Solomon, a member of the writers' group.'

'And Dulcie?' Richard prompted, ignoring Jack's hand. 'Where is she?'

'She's away, and I'm house-sitting for her.'

'Away? Where? With Kate and Andrew?'

'Why don't you sit down? Beer?'

Richard shook his head, irritated that someone other than him was acting host in Dulcie's house. He repeated his question: 'Where exactly is Dulcie?'

'On holiday.'

Exasperated, Richard began to pace the floor. 'Look,' he exclaimed, 'I'm getting the feeling that you're playing games with me. Do you know who I am?'

'I know exactly who you are. You're Richard Cavanagh, Dulcie's ex-lover. Now, before you get any more uptight, why don't you just accept that until Dulcie returns from her holiday you won't be able to speak to her? Perhaps you should go home to your wife and children.'

The directness of the man's words brought Richard up short. 'How dare you?'

'A bit of straight talking too much for you?'

'Who the hell are you to judge me?'

Jack reached for the bottle of beer on the table. 'I'm a man who knows what it feels like to wake up one morning and find that his wife has been sleeping with someone else.' He drank deeply from the bottle, eyeing Richard as he did so.

Richard winced. He passed a hand across his face. Oh, hell. What could he say? 'I don't suppose that offer of a beer is still on, is it?'

They sat at the table, the laptop shut down, and a barely touched sausage sandwich between them. 'Don't let me stop you eating,' Richard said.

'Would you like half?'

'No, thank you ... Oh, go on, then. I'll get another plate.'

They ate and drank in an awkward silence.

'This feels very peculiar,' Richard admitted.

'I know what you mean. And I'm sorry for coming on so strong. It's really none of my business what you and Dulcie have been up to.'

'Neither of us planned it.'

'Maybe not, but the result's the same. People get hurt.'

'I'm not making excuses, but I've never loved anyone the way I love Dulcie. I don't expect someone as young as you to appreciate that love is just as exhilarating and wonderful at my age as it is at yours.' He paused. This was the first time he had spoken to another person about his relationship with Dulcie. It felt strange, but it was also a welcome relief to speak openly about her. 'Dulcie means everything to me,' he said simply.

'Still? Even though she's finished with you?'

'I'll go on loving her for ever. It's the rightness of our love I can't turn away from. Where's she staying, Jack? Is she in London visiting her children?'

'No. And I'm not sure she wants you to know where she is. That's the whole point of her going away. She needed to put some distance between the two of you.'

'Do you have any idea how long she'll be away?'

'A week. Perhaps two. She was very unhappy before she went.'

Richard nodded. 'I understand. But she's got it wrong if she thinks a holiday will solve anything. I'll still be here when she comes home.'

'And your wife and family? Where will they be?'

He felt the stab of Jack's question, pushed away his plate and leaned back in his chair. 'I've told Dulcie that if she wants to make a go of it, I'm prepared to make my choice ... and bear the full brunt of the consequences.'

Jack fixed him with a disdainful stare. 'I have two young daughters who are currently bearing the full brunt of their mother's choice, so I know what I'm talking about when I say it's never the straightforward business you think it will be. Being a part-time father is an emotional minefield. You want to do your best, because you feel so damned guilty, so you pack too much into too small a chunk of time. And every little disagreement you have with your children gets magnified by your guilt, reminds you, yet again, that you've failed. You even begin to wonder if you should cut your losses because maybe, just maybe, they might be better off forgetting all about you. How old are your children?'

Richard swallowed. This wasn't what he'd come here for. This critical directness was too much. 'Please, if you don't mind, I'd rather not discuss my children.'

'No, I guess not. Another beer?'

'No, thanks.' Richard watched Jack help himself from Dulcie's fridge. He caught a glimpse of the kind of stuff he'd never seen in Dulcie's kitchen before: processed meals for one – a curry, a cottage pie, and a packet of haddock in cheese and broccoli sauce. Bachelor food. Or, more accurately, separated-man food.

He was about to try once more to get out of Jack where Dulcie was when the phone rang. It was the faint tone of a mobile. 'Excuse me a minute,' Jack said. 'Hi, Des, how's it going?' He wandered out of the kitchen, into the hall.

Left on his own, Richard relaxed. Dulcie's house-sitter was a nice enough man, but there was something disturbingly judgemental about him. He saw things only in black and white. Life wasn't like that. He got to his feet, and put the empty plates into the sink, then went back to the table for his beer bottle and glanced at Dulcie's noticeboard. Pinned to it were the familiar photographs of Kate and Andrew, plus one of Dulcie wearing a large straw hat. It was a particular favourite of his: he'd taken it in the garden last summer. It was a picture he would dearly love to have on his desk at work or in his wallet so that he always felt she was close to him. He was tempted to slip it into his pocket, but his attention was diverted by a piece of paper. On it, in Dulcie's expressive handwriting, was the name and address of a hotel in Venice. He looked out to the hall and, seeing that Jack was still deep in conversation, he grabbed a pen and a square of paper from the pad Dulcie kept by the phone. He scribbled down the details and, just in time, pocketed the scrap of paper as Jack came back into the kitchen.

'Sorry about that,' he said.

Richard waved aside his apology with a smile. 'No, it's me who should apologise. I shouldn't have come here and ruined your evening, not to mention scrounge half your supper. Which was great, by the way. It's a long time since I've had a sausage sandwich. Anyway, I'll leave you in peace now.' He held out his hand. 'No hard feelings, then?'

49

Jaz and Nathan both had a free period so they were able to leave college early that Tuesday afternoon to drive to the hospital.

When Jaz had asked Nathan if he'd like to meet her mother – 'the sanest and nicest member of my family' – he'd agreed and said he'd see if he could borrow his mum's car.

To Jaz's horror, her father was now encouraging her to go out with Nathan. 'He looks a regular decent boy to me,' he'd said, at breakfast only that morning. 'Smart, too.' As he tucked into his plate of bacon, black pudding and scrambled eggs, he'd added, 'I could do with a tame lawyer in the family. Think of the fees I'd save.'

'Dad!' she'd remonstrated. 'I'm only seventeen. I'm not thinking of marrying anyone, let alone Nathan King.'

'Aw, get away with you, girl. I'm looking to the future.'

Blushing to the ends of her toenails, and seeing her brothers sauntering into the hotel restaurant for their breakfast with her sisters tumbling in behind, she'd finished her toast and made a hasty exit. It was difficult to decide which was worse: her father taking a hard line with her or being too interested in fixing her up with Nathan. But as he'd given her the go-ahead to rejoin Hidden Talents, she was happy to let him think whatever he wanted.

It had been Beth and Jack's kindness after the break-in that had won him round. 'Anyone who takes that kind of care of a child of mine is okay in my book. That Beth struck me as a sensible woman. Nice with it.'

Jaz was so happy she'd given him a huge hug. 'Thanks, Dad.'

Trying to look stern, he'd said, 'Just you see it doesn't get in the way of your studies. And no more lying to your mum and me.'

She'd told her mother that there was no need for her to have a word with Dad, that it had all been sorted. Of course, she couldn't tell her why he'd had this change of heart – 'He must be in a particularly good mood,' was all she could come up with. 'Maybe the thought of being a father all over again is mellowing him.'

'Well, to make sure there's no misunderstanding, I'm going to tell him that I know all about Hidden Talents,' her mother had said. 'It's best that we're straight with him, Jaz.'

But her father had much more to think about than Hidden Talents.

On seeing the house, he had taken one look at the mess and moved them lock, stock and barrel into the Maywood Grange Hotel. 'If I ever get my hands on those bastards, I'll bloody staple them by their friggin' ears to the walls of their own homes and leave them there to rot!' He was incandescent with rage that this had happened to him of all people.

Jaz had never seen her father so angry, or so upset. Unable to take out his anger on the burglars – who had struck again, he had learned from the police – he had vented some of it on the police officers in charge, accusing them of incompetence and wasting tax-payers' money. Apart from Mum's jewellery, he wasn't bothered about the stuff that had been taken: 'That can all be replaced,' he'd said matter-of-factly. 'That's what insurance is for.' It was the damage that had been done to the house that incensed him. 'I built that house for your mother,' he'd said. 'It was her dream home. Now it's a friggin' nightmare.' High on impotent fury, he'd threatened to wash his hands of it and put it on the market. Jaz was surprised by how sad this had made her. It made her realise how attached to her home she really was. Her own bedroom had been trashed, like all the others: clothes pulled off hangers and randomly ripped, her mattress hacked to pieces, files and important college work thrown around the room. Her CD player and all her CDs had been taken, as had her computer. She was glad now that she'd wiped her novel. For a stranger to have had access to something so personal would have left her feeling even more violated.

It had been a crazy few weeks, what with worrying about her mother being in hospital and the burglary, but the experience had forced her to get things into perspective. As a result, she had come to see that *Having the Last Laugh* had been a cruel parody of her family. It had had its funny moments but, overall, it had been childishly spiteful. Where had been the depth and integrity she so admired in other writers?

Once her father had overcome his anger, he had decided not to sell the house. 'I'll not let the buggers get the better of me,' he'd cursed. And so, after Phin and Jimmy had arranged to have everything removed that had been ruined, he had pulled out all the stops to get the house put right. An army of professional cleaners had worked round the clock, and now the decorators were doing their bit. When they had finished, every carpet was to be replaced and Jaz couldn't begin to calculate how much money her father was throwing at the problem to resolve it. And all so that Mum would never know the worst of it. 'This is the last thing she needs to worry about,' he'd said to her, her brothers and sisters. 'You're all sworn to secrecy,' he'd added, looking pointedly at Tamzin and Lulu, who hadn't been allowed to see the state of the house – another instance of his desire to protect his family. 'If you breathe a single word of this to your mother, you'll regret it. Got it?' For the first time in their lives her sisters seemed to understand that a serious response was expected of them. Coincidentally, from that moment on, their behaviour in the hotel improved: they stopped mucking about in the lifts, raiding the ice machine or ringing Room Service for a midnight feast.

Breaking into her thoughts and, as if reading them, Nathan said, 'Jaz, how does your father expect to pull off such an elaborate stunt? I mean, your mother will know that something's gone on. The smell of fresh paint, new wallpaper, new carpets, new everything – it'll be a dead giveaway, won't it?'

'Of course he plans to tell her, but he wants everything to be as normal as he can make it before she comes home. He wants to lessen the shock.'

'He must really care about her.'

Jaz noted the thoughtful expression on his face. 'He does. Funny thing is, I'm only just seeing how much. I always knew he was mad about Mum, but I'd put it down to exactly that – madness. You don't think about your parents actually being in love with each other, do you?' She immediately regretted what she'd said. 'Sorry, that was insensitive of me.'

'It's okay. But I know what you mean. I think my parents probably loved each other a lot too.'

In the quiet that followed, Jaz's thoughts turned to her father again. As a small child she had grown up listening to people telling her what a great man Popeye Rafferty was. If a friend or relative of the family was in need, he was always the first to offer help. She could remember being so proud of him. When had she become so critical?

At the hospital, Jaz reminded Nathan not to say a word about the burglary to her mother.

He took her hand. 'This might come as something of a shock to you, Jaz, but there's nothing wrong with my attention span. I'm fully on board with the scam. And do you really think I want to incur the mighty wrath of your father, and just as he's taken such a shine to me?'

'Don't push it. One word from me and you'll be history!'

They were both smiling when Jaz poked her head round her mother's door. She was relieved to see that her mother was looking better than she had in days. She was sitting up in bed, wearing her best nightdress. She had applied some makeup and her lovely auburn hair had been washed and nicely blow-dried. Jaz ushered Nathan inside and said, 'Hello, Mum, how are you?'

'All the better for seeing you.' She put down the magazine she'd been reading. 'Ah, now you must be Nathan. Close the door and come on in.'

They drew up two chairs and Nathan handed over a prettily wrapped box of chocolates. 'I thought you might like these,' he said. 'That's if they're allowed.' He glanced at the large basket of fruit on the other side of the bed.

'They'll make a welcome change from the healthy stuff I'm being forced to eat. Last night I dreamed I was cooking Jaz's father's favourite meal, a large suet-crust steak and kidney pudding. I woke up starving.' She took the box from Nathan and thanked him. 'We'll have one right now, shall we?'

Jaz was touched that Nathan had gone to so much trouble for her mother, but she was equally pleased to see how well received the gift had been. Mum was good like that. Jaz supposed it was one of the reasons why Dad showered her with so many: he received much more in return, in terms of love and affection. A distant memory surfaced, something she once heard her mother say to her father: that it was easy to love the lovable, the child who always smiled and raised its arms for a cuddle, but it meant so much more to get a hug from the quiet, withdrawn one. Only now did she understood that her mother had been talking about her.

Jack could think of any number of ways he would rather spend his evening, but he'd promised Dulcie he would call on Victor. After locking up the office, he drove out of the car park and turned on to Bridge Street where he joined the queue of busy rush-hour traffic waiting to negotiate the town's main roundabout. He inched his way forward, and finally reached the head of the queue, then turned towards Station Road. He passed the large pay-and-display car park on his left, then Maywood College, and watched the house numbers on his right. He knew Station Road well – Norris & Rowan currently had three properties for sale along this stretch of terraced houses; they had always changed hands regularly.

He parked between a shiny Astra and a less than well-maintained Peugeot, which he recognised as Victor's. He knocked at the door.

Knocked again.

And knocked again.

Nothing. From what Dulcie had told him on the phone, it had been the same when she'd tried to call on Victor. 'But I felt sure he was in,' she'd said. 'Don't ask me how, I just felt it.'

Jack felt it too. Standing back from the house, he looked up at the windows, which were thick with grime. Was it his imagination or was there a flicker of light coming from one of the upstairs windows? It was so faint he thought it might be a reflection from the street-lamp behind him, which had just come on with a pale orange glow. But no: the more he looked up at the window, the more convinced he became that a light was on inside. He decided to walk to the end of the row of houses and see if he could get round to the back.

He walked along the cinder path to the rear of the properties until he drew level with Victor's. It was then, when he looked up at the back of the house, that he realised that what he'd thought to be a softly glowing light was a fire. Victor's house was on fire.

Quick as a flash he phoned for the emergency services on his mobile, then tried the gate. It was locked. He threw his weight against the rotting timber, burst through it and stumbled into the small backyard. The door into the house was locked, but he seized a wooden broom that was propped against the wall and swung it at the kitchen window.

Once inside, he called to Victor as he peered into the dining room, then the sitting room. He got no response so he went back to the kitchen, grabbed a tea-towel and shoved it under the cold tap. When it was soaking, he took a deep breath and made for the stairs. On the smoke-filled landing, with the wet cloth pressed to his face, he braved the room where the source of the fire was. Thick smoke stung his eyes and made them water. He forced them to stay open, and saw a body on the floor: flames were licking over and around it. He pushed himself forward, grasped Victor under his armpits, and dragged him from the room. Out on the landing, he took off his jacket, wrapped it around Victor's apparently lifeless body to snuff out his smouldering clothes. Then he heaved him down the stairs, to the hall, where he laid Victor on the floor, and allowed himself to catch his breath. Just as the shock hit him of what he'd done, and what might happen if he didn't get out of the house fast, he heard the high-pitched wail of a siren. Jack fumbled with the front-door lock and carried Victor to safety. Within seconds a team of firemen was on the scene, a crowd of onlookers too: neighbours who claimed to have smelt smoke but had put it down to a bonfire.

Jack rode in the ambulance with Victor to the hospital. His own injuries were superficial – a raw soreness in his throat and chest, some cuts from when he'd climbed through the window and a few burns – nothing that wouldn't heal within a week or two. But Victor looked like he'd be damned lucky to live.

50

With the curtains drawn back, Dulcie lay in bed looking at the surrounding jumble of rooftops and chimneys. She was listening to the church bells clanging softly and thinking what a perfect way it was to start the day.

She had been in Venice for over a week now, and she had never felt so settled in a foreign place as she did here. Perhaps it was the compact size of the city that made it feel so homely. And so safe. In all the times she had wandered the maze of narrow streets, night or day, she had never felt she was in any danger. Recently, though, her solitary nocturnal strolls had dwindled. Her American friends, Cathe and Randy, had seen to that by discreetly taking her under their wing. 'We can't have you on your own too much,' her petite protector had declared, and once or twice Dulcie had allowed them to have their way. It would have been churlish to do otherwise. Besides, she enjoyed their company – they were refreshingly honest and direct: qualities Dulcie admired.

The past two evenings they had enjoyed an exorbitantly priced nightcap at Florian's in the Piazza San Marco. The atmosphere was enchanting, and listening to the small orchestra as it attempted to outplay the competition from the bar across the square was an added delight. Last night, when they had finished their drinks, they had browsed the display of pictures on sale around the square, the artists vying enthusiastically for their attention. Dulcie had fallen in love with a beautiful etching of the island of San Giorgio Maggiore – it was the view she saw every morning when she left the hotel and stood for a moment on the Riva degli Schiavoni to admire the lagoon and all its activity. She had purchased it from a young girl with jet black hair, and looked forward to taking it home and having it professionally framed. She knew exactly where she would hang it: in her study above her desk so that she could lose herself in it when her writing wasn't going well.

But for now, and since she had bought herself a notebook, her writing was flowing effortlessly. She had written two short stories so far, and was eager to start another. The muse was definitely performing for her and its reappearance was a sign that she was almost back to normal. It meant that she could think of the future and getting on with her life without Richard.

She had thought hard about the writers' conference Jack had mentioned on the phone, and had concluded that the group should go. Having attended similar courses in the past, she knew it would be a marvellous opportunity for them all. If it was well run there would be interesting guest speakers to learn from, tutors on hand to give advice, and possibly one or two agents and editors to talk to. She hadn't said anything to Jack, but she harboured a real hope that he might be 'discovered'. It was a long shot, but these things happened. He wrote so compellingly that she was convinced *Friends and Family* was publishable, that a professional eye would see it as a potential hit. What she liked most about Jack was that he had no inkling of the extent of his talent. Too often would-be writers had an overly inflated view of themselves and their work.

Would-be writers such as poor old Victor.

Any dislike or critical views she had once held for Victor had now been subdued by her concern that something was terribly wrong with the man. She sensed that the group had only half a picture of him, as if he were a character in a book who had been badly sketched in. She hoped that Jack had found the time to call on him. 'I know it's asking a lot,' she'd said to Jack, on the phone, 'but I'm worried about Victor. Didn't you think he'd lost an awful lot of weight when we last saw him?' She trusted Jack to do the right thing: he was a good man.

A glance at her travel clock on the bedside table told her it was time to get up. She was having breakfast with Cathe then going on a trip to the islands in the northern lagoon. Randy had opted to forgo the excursion, saying he had some important phone calls to make.

As they set off for the waterfront, where Alberto had told them to pick up the boat, Cathe linked arms with Dulcie and said, 'Randy is the sweetest man alive. His phone calls aren't that important, he just thought we'd prefer to have a girls' day out.'

Dulcie smiled understandingly. 'I can't think of many men who would want to spend a day looking at glass or lace.'

They paid for their tickets and joined the chattering group of tourists who had already climbed aboard the vessel and taken their seats. Last to get on was their guide for the day, a tanned Italian man of about the same age as Dulcie. With his distinctive Roman nose, his swept-back grey hair and lightweight cotton sweater draped around his shoulders, she thought him exceedingly handsome. As the boat pulled away from the jetty, he smiled at her and slipped on a pair of fashionable wraparound sunglasses. After he'd turned away, Cathe nudged Dulcie. 'Cute, wouldn't you say?'

'And some,' Dulcie whispered back. 'But he knows it.'

Murano was their first stop, and after the group had disembarked, their guide, Antonio, filled them in with some background information about the island. His English, though heavily accented, was excellent and he explained how Murano had been the centre of the glassmaking industry since the thirteenth century. 'Here, on this little cluster of islands that make up

Murano,' he told them, 'mirrors were made a long time before anyone else thought of it.'

'Trust the vain Italians to be the first to spot that niche market,' murmured Cathe.

'And spectacles too,' Antonio continued. 'It is thought that they were also invented here. It was truly a marvellous and creative place. During the sixteenth century, Murano glass became the must-have accessory all over Europe. Every palazzo had to have its share of exquisite crystal, and today you, too, can be a part of the rich history left to us by those early-glass artisans. Come, I take you now to see some glass-blowers at work. And then I invite you to join me in the showroom to see the many splendours on offer for you to purchase and take home.'

Following Antonio, as he strode ahead of the group, Cathe said, 'Don't you just love the understated way they try to relieve us of our dollars?'

Dulcie laughed. 'Shame on you for being such a cynic.'

Most of what was for sale – stunning handmade chandeliers and exquisite sets of wine glasses – was wildly expensive and would require shipping home, but both Dulcie and Cathe settled for some modestly priced scent bottles. Next the tour moved on to the island of Burano. 'This is the prettiest of the islands in the lagoon,' boasted Antonio, handing out roughly drawn maps. 'Nowhere else will you find such a collection of colourful houses, a rainbow of colour that will delight your senses. *Si, si*, it is the truth I tell you, no exaggeration. And wait till you see the lace. Ah, the lace, you will fall over yourselves for this. Here you will see local Buranese women hard at work with the stitching. But before all that excitement, we stop for lunch.' He smiled broadly. 'Where I promise you will taste the best fish in the best trattoria Burano has to offer.'

Everyone laughed, by now used to Antonio's effusive gilding of the lily.

'*Si*,' he exclaimed, 'I know this restaurant to be the best because it is my youngest son Giorgio who runs it. It is the one marked on the map I have just given you. If you follow the directions, I will meet you there in . . .' he looked at his watch '. . . in precisely thirty minutes. Do not worry about getting lost, it is impossible. Burano is a very easy place to be.'

'And is Giorgio as handsome as his father?' asked Cathe, as Antonio helped her out of the boat and on to the jetty.

'Oh, he is even better-looking. He is the image of your Tom Cruise.'

He offered his hand to Dulcie, who was last to get off, and said, 'You permit me to invite you to join me for a drink before lunch perhaps?'

Dulcie was so taken aback that she nearly lost her footing. He held her firmly. 'Was that such a dreadful shock to you?'

'Yes,' she said, flustered. She straightened her sun hat, which had become dislodged.

He smiled. 'In that case I will have to make amends by insisting you accept my invitation. It is a deal? *Si?*'

Not one to be bamboozled, even by a man as attractive as Antonio,

Dulcie said, 'I'm afraid it isn't possible. I'm here with a friend and it would be rude of me to abandon her.'

But when she looked for Cathe to corroborate this, there was no sign of her on the jetty: she'd gone on ahead with the rest of the group and was waving at Dulcie, a sly grin on her small elegant face.

'It looks to me as if you are the one who has been abandoned,' he observed, with a smile.

He took her to a bar in a small, shady square where he was greeted by a number of elderly men who obviously knew him well. She wondered how many times a week they witnessed this very scene – Antonio with yet another woman from one of his tour groups. He removed his sunglasses, placed them carefully in the breast pocket of his shirt, and, without asking her what she would like to drink, called through to a man behind the bar and ordered two Bellini cocktails.

'You look surprised,' he commented, when the waiter brought them their drinks.

'Frankly I am,' she said. 'It doesn't look the kind of place that would serve a cocktail. Or do they keep a bottle of Prosecco here specially for you?'

He laughed and raised his glass. 'Here is to many more surprises for you during your stay in Venice.' He took a slow sip, then lowered his glass. 'How long are you here for? But wait, before you answer that, tell me your name. After all, you have the advantage, you know mine.'

She swallowed a refreshing mouthful of sparkling wine and fresh white peach juice. 'It's Dulcie,' she said, 'and I've been here for just over a week.'

'And you leave when?'

'I haven't decided.'

'Oh. So you are a flexible lady?'

She laughed. 'Perhaps not in the way you might be thinking.'

He slapped his forehead and laughed too. 'Oh, my English, it is not always so good. Please, forgive me.'

A wiry dog came over to their table and sniffed at their legs. Finding nothing of any interest it soon wandered off.

'Dulcie, that is an unusual name, is it not?'

'I suppose it is. It comes from the Latin *dulcis*, meaning—'

'Meaning sweet,' he finished for her. 'Yes, I am a man of education too. The name suits you. And is there a husband for the sweet-natured English lady?'

'No.'

'Divorced?'

'Widowed.'

'Ah. I am sorry. Did your husband die recently?'

'No.'

He drained his glass. 'One-word answers, they tell me to mind my own business. You are here on holiday to enjoy yourself, not to be interrogated by an Italian man with too much curiosity. Come, it is time for us to join the rest of the group and your American friend, who will want to know exactly what you have been up to. The friend who thinks that we Venetians are only after one thing ... your bucks and pounds.'

Disappointed to be leaving so soon, Dulcie hurriedly finished her Bellini and gathered up her bag. 'Thank you for the drink,' she said. 'I enjoyed it.'

'*Prego.* I almost believe you.' He slipped his sunglasses back on, making her feel as if he'd pulled down the shutters on their conversation.

'Look,' she said, feeling as if she owed him an explanation, 'it isn't anything personal, I'm just quite a private person.'

He put a hand under her elbow and led her across the square. 'And do such private people ever risk having dinner with men they hardly know?'

Again taken aback, she thought of Richard and how easily she had accepted his invitation to have dinner with him that first day they met. 'They do if the situation feels right.'

'It's only dinner,' Dulcie had to keep reminding herself later that evening when she was relaxing in a hot bath at the hotel.

Then why did she feel so guilty, and that she was being disloyal to Richard?

Oh, it was ridiculous. Richard was a married man whom she'd sensibly shooed off back to his wife, where he belonged. Now she could do as she pleased. She was a free agent.

So long as she didn't hurt anyone, a faint voice whispered to her.

She chased it away. 'The only person likely to get hurt is me,' she said aloud, while reaching for a towel and stepping over the edge of the bath.

She chose her clothes with care – nothing too dressy, she didn't want Antonio imagining that she'd gone to extra trouble for his benefit, and equally nothing too casual – she suspected that Antonio, like most Italian men, would be smartly turned out. She opted for a pair of loose-fitting black silk trousers and a cream overshirt. Then she applied some strategic touches of makeup and appraised her reflection in the dressing-table mirror. She was particularly pleased with her eyes. They were a toned-down version of Cathe's and she was impressed with the subtle transformation. Not too old to learn a few tricks, then. She picked up her hotel pass key, hooked her bag over her shoulder, and went downstairs to wait for Antonio in the hotel foyer, as arranged.

From behind his desk, where he was on the telephone, Alberto greeted her with a smile and a wave. She didn't have to wait long: Antonio appeared through the revolving door almost at once. She'd guessed correctly: he was wearing a jacket and tie and the confident air of a man who knew he could still turn the head of a woman half his age. Once again, and after he'd politely told her how nice she looked, he placed a hand under her elbow and steered her out of the hotel, much to the amusement of Alberto – who, Dulcie knew, had been watching them keenly.

'Would you like to walk or take the *vaporetto*?' he asked, when they were facing the waterfront.

'It depends where we're going,' she answered.

'I have booked a table at my favourite restaurant near the Rialto Bridge. It is not far.'

She smiled. 'But a *vaporetto* ride is so pretty at night.'

He smiled too. 'In that case I would be a heartless man to deny you such a pleasure.'

Dulcie soon discovered that Antonio was known to nearly every local they came across – the woman from whom they purchased their tickets addressed him by name, the man who drove the boat waved to him, and the waiters at the restaurant all smiled and joked with him, one even slapping him on the back. 'I have lived in Venice all my life,' he explained, when they were sitting down with a ringside view of the brightly illuminated Grand Canal with all its passing traffic, 'apart from a brief time in London when I was a student.'

'What were you doing there?'

'Studying, of course.'

She caught the playfulness in his voice. 'I meant, what were you studying?'

He straightened the cuffs on his shirt, lining them up an inch beyond the cuffs of his jacket, then said, 'I was a medical student, training to be a doctor.'

'Really?'

'Aha, once again I have surprised you! Yes, the simple guide turns out to be more than you thought.'

'That's not fair,' she said defensively. 'My husband was a doctor. And so is my son. I was merely thinking of the coincidence.' She took the menu their waiter handed to her, wondering why on earth she was here being goaded by this monstrously egotistical Italian.

'I'm sorry,' he said, when he had taken it upon himself to order aperitifs without asking her what she would like, 'I have upset you with my twisted sense of humour. To make amends I shall bore you with my life story. But, fear not, it is not long. You won't be in need of resuscitation at the end of it, though to give you the kiss of life might be rather pleasant. Aha, that is better, now you are smiling again. Well, as I said earlier, I have always lived in Venice. My wife, too, was a local girl and we had five children.' He laughed. 'They say that doctors always have large families, and I am proud to say that I did my part in upholding this belief.'

'So what kind of doctor were you?'

'An excellent one!'

'You're impossible.'

Their drinks arrived, and after she'd taken a cautious sip and found it to her liking, he said, 'I was an eye surgeon at the local hospital here in Venice, but I retired two years ago, not long after my wife passed away. It was time for me to lay down the tools of my trade, my hammer and chisel, and try something new.'

She winced at his joke and said, 'So you became a tourist guide?'

He shook his head vehemently. 'No, no. I became an *excellent* tourist guide. I do everything with great skill.'

He was incorrigible, had no understanding of the concept of modesty. But he was amusing company, she decided, and felt herself relax into the evening. They ordered their meal along with a bottle of wine, and the spotlight was turned away from Antonio and on to her. He wanted to know where she was from in England and why she was travelling alone. In the end she told him much more than she had intended, probably because of the quantity of wine she was drinking.

'So this Richard from whom you are running, you still love him?'

'Yes.' The admission was out before she could stop it.

He topped up her glass. 'I do not understand this need you have to punish your heart so cruelly.'

'It's for the best. For Kate and Henry, for Richard's wife and his young sons.'

'But not the best for Dulcie. Or Richard, I would dare to suggest. To have pestered you so intensely before you came away shows the strength of his love for you.' Suddenly he leaned forward in his seat, his face barely inches from hers – it made her wonder how many of his patients had been dazzled by him when he'd been examining their eyes. 'Dulcie,' he said, 'permit me to be straight with you. I believe you have made a terrible mistake. To be blunt, at our age we have to grab the chances that come our way. No, no, do not argue with me. A stranger sees these things more clearly. Let the young people, Kate and Henry, sort themselves out. If they truly love each other they will find a way to continue their relationship.' He held up a hand to stop her interrupting him. 'Please, I know what you are going to say, but you are wasting your time protecting Richard's wife. Do her the kindness of letting her live a happier and more fulfilling life. Oh, yes, it will be difficult in the beginning, I do not dispute that, but by being honest about your love for Richard, you will give his wife the opportunity to find her own happiness and she will stop clinging desperately to a man who loves another. There, I have finished. It is now your turn to speak.'

But Dulcie couldn't. She was literally struck dumb by the man's audacity ... and maybe by the sense of what he'd said.

51

Dear Beth,

I have the distinct impression that you are hiding from me. Is it something I said? Did I push you too hard over the writers' conference? Just because I'm a writer, (a recently rejected writer at that!), it doesn't mean I'm any good at subplots and subtexts. I'm just an idiot who blurts out the first thing that comes into his head. Some of which – most of which – he instantly regrets. (There are those who hold the view that my ramblings should come with a government health warning.) If I've done anything to offend you, please don't hesitate to show me the error of my ways.

Yours, confused-and-disappointed-of-Suffolk,

Ewan

PS I can take constructive advice and criticism as well as the next thick-skinned man, though I do tend to bottle out sometimes and wear a hard hat when the brickbats really start to fly. I can even take rejection, as recently demonstrated. But what I'm not so hot on is seeing a blank screen every night when I log on to see if there's a message from my favourite correspondent from Maywood . . .

PPS For all I know you might have been away for the last few weeks, or have had such a busy time of it you haven't had a spare minute to keep in touch. If so, disregard all of the above and accept the apologies of a pathetic man whose only excuse is that he's turning into the whingeing sad old fool he promised his daughter he'd never become.

Beth finished reading Ewan's email, then scrolled back up to the beginning, and read it through once more. Without giving herself a chance to change her mind, she clicked on REPLY and started typing fast.

Dear Ewan,

Please, please, PLEASE don't berate yourself. My silence had nothing to do with you, but everything to do with me. Or, rather, everything to do with being so embarrassed. I'm ashamed to say that when I last emailed you I was disgustingly drunk. I half hoped you'd realise this and therefore make an enormous allowance for me, but I didn't want you thinking that I made it a regular feature of my evenings to get off my head – as Nathan would probably describe the state I was in. Truly, I am the most temperate of souls. And please believe me when I say I wouldn't dream of sending such an outrageous message in a more sober state. I've been hanging my head in shame ever since, wanting very much to put the episode behind me.

And to change the subject completely (I'm reddening like the proverbial beetroot as I sit here making my excuses and apologies), I'll fill you in on what's been going on. You won't believe the half of it!

She told him about the Raffertys' house being broken into and of Jack staying at Dulcie's while she was away in Venice recovering from the end of her affair with Richard.

But more dramatic than any of this [she wrote] was that Jack called round to see Victor (he was the peculiar man from the group who wouldn't take any advice), at Dulcie's request, only to find his house on fire. Jack had to smash a window to get in and rescue Victor, who is now in hospital recovering from the most awful burns. It looks as if the fire was started by a candle falling on to a pile of papers. According to the hospital, Victor must have collapsed before the fire got going. He was incredibly lucky to survive. Lucky, too, that Jack called on him when he did. I feel really sorry for Victor, especially as he's lost what was most precious to him. When Jack and I visited him, we had to break the news to him that his manuscript had perished in the fire – it was probably what fuelled the flames in the first place. And because he wrote it on a typewriter, he doesn't have a copy of it. It was heartbreaking to see him cry, Ewan. Poor man, he was utterly devastated. He doesn't seem to have any friends or family, and from what the nurses tell us, we're his only visitors, so Jack and I are trying to see him as often as we can – Jaz has also said she'll call in on him tomorrow after she's been to see her mother.

Well, that's about the height of it this end. Oh, only to add that my in-laws are away on their cruise and Barnaby emailed me from the ship (such technology!) to say that all was going very well. To his great relief (and mine) Lois was thrilled with the surprise he'd pulled on her. She didn't even mind him packing her clothes behind her back – she doesn't know yet that he asked me to do it for him. Barnaby is hoping that, on their return, Lois will be more receptive to the idea of calling a truce to our big bust-up over Christmas. Fingers crossed!

I've also been to see my old neighbour, Adele (who used to live in the downstairs flat). I'm so relieved that she's enjoying the retirement home she's moved into. She's made lots of friends and joins in with the occasional outing to a National Trust property or the theatre. It's the future, Ewan. It's what awaits us all . . . if we're fortunate enough.

That really is all the news from Maywood. Nathan is at the cinema with Jaz, which leaves me with a nice quiet evening and a chance to do some writing, which has taken a bit of a back seat this last week, what with the many hospital visits to see Victor.

Best wishes,
Beth

PS I've decided to take the plunge and go to the writers' conference. Jack's coming too, to act as my chaperon . . .

PPS I don't think there's anything remotely whingeing or sad about you. The old is yet to be verified!

Conscious that her message was overly factual and not in the least witty like Ewan's, she clicked on SEND, then logged off. There, she'd done it. She'd put the humiliating incident behind her and committed herself to meeting Ewan. Anticipation outweighed any last remnants of her embarrassment, and happiness swelled inside her.

It was a long time since she had experienced the butterfly sensation in her stomach at the prospect of meeting a man, but there was no denying that she felt it now as she left her computer to make herself a cup of tea. The conference wasn't until next month, which meant she either had plenty of time to change her mind, or weeks of distracted thoughts to endure.

At work today Wendy had caught her tapping a pencil absently against her teeth while staring into mid-air and daydreaming about Ewan. 'Thinking of that gorgeous man again, are you?' her friend had teased.

Flustered that Wendy had read her thoughts so clearly, she dropped the pencil. Then came to her senses and realised that Wendy was referring to Jack. 'Oh, don't be so ridiculous,' she'd responded – the jokes about him were wearing thin. 'Jack is the last person I'd be daydreaming about. I've told you before that I don't go for younger men.'

But it would have to stop. Daydreaming was for the young. A grown woman of forty-three ought to know better. Yet more and more she was finding that being a sensible adult was such a chore. Why shouldn't she indulge herself in a little harmless frivolity?

Having decided to go to Harrogate, her next hurdle was telling Nathan about Ewan. She didn't have to, but she felt she should. Trouble was, she knew what his reaction would be: 'Let me get this straight, Mum. After all those lectures you gave me about not talking to strange men in public loos, you've struck up an email relationship with an unknown man?'

It was gone eleven when she finished writing and, knowing that Nathan would be back soon, she logged on to see if, on the off-chance, Ewan had responded to her email.

There was a message awaiting her: she clicked on READ.

Do my eyes deceive me? Or is this really an email I see before me from my sweet maiden in Maywood?

Gadzooks, it is!

And what an extraordinary time you've been having. I'm surprised CNN isn't covering the events going on in your little town and beaming them around the world. Just think of the book it would make!

Seriously, though, that poor guy Victor has my full sympathy. Was his house badly damaged in the fire? And, if so, where will he go when he's well enough to be discharged from hospital? As for losing his precious manuscript, there are worse things that could happen, but not many for a writer. On the other hand, perhaps this will give him the chance to start afresh. After such a harrowing ordeal, he's bound to want to explore a whole new area in his writing. Or does that sound too glib? For what it's worth, I think that's the approach I would take. Would have to take.

But to move on to less grim matters. I'm polishing my shoes in readiness for meeting you at the conference. I know all too well that women judge men by their shoes, and I'll have you know you won't find me wanting in that oh-so-crucial department. Hands and nails are important too, so nearer the time I shall be booking myself into the nearest beauty parlour and arranging a full-buff manicure. From there the hair will have to be groomed to within an inch of its life and the best suit dry-cleaned. As you can tell, I aim to make an excellent impression. If I have a nervous breakdown in the interim period, then so be it: the cause will have been a good and noble one.

Now to a slightly tricky problem. Since your last email, I've been stockpiling bars of chocolate, but now it appears I won't have a use for them. Any ideas what I should do with two dozen catering packs of Fruit and Nut?

Time to dash for the bunker. I feel a Scud missile heading this way from Maywood.

Yours, so-very-glad-to-hear-from-you,

Ewan X

PS Please don't waste any more vital energy worrying about THAT email. It will be wiped from the memory banks, as of now.

PPS Hey, what's with all the Jack references? Do I have a rival for your affections? If so, you'd better warn him that it will be quills at dawn the first day of the conference.

Hearing Nathan's key in the lock, Beth logged off hurriedly and decided that now was the time to tell him about Ewan.

52

The pleasing rhythm of Dulcie's stay in Venice had changed subtly.

Cathe and Randy had left for Paris first thing in the morning – before Dulcie had made it downstairs – and already she felt their absence. She had become accustomed to starting the day by seeing the couple at breakfast, then catching up with them in the evening in the hotel bar before they went their separate ways for dinner, maybe getting together later for a nightcap. They had been easy to grow fond of, had never overstepped the mark or imposed themselves on her, just offered simple friendship, expecting nothing in return. Last night they had exchanged addresses and Cathe had impressed upon Dulcie that she was welcome to stay with them any time she wanted. They lived in Maine, and the thought of visiting them during the autumn – the fall – was tempting. Likewise, Dulcie had said her home was always open to them.

And home was somewhere she would have to return soon. Perhaps prompted by Cathe and Randy's departure, her thoughts were increasingly of Maywood and everything she'd left behind. Antonio's words during dinner, two nights ago, had also had an effect on her. Was there a chance he had been right? If so, could she really put her own happiness above anyone else's?

'Trust me, these things resolve themselves, Dulcie,' Antonio had said, as he walked her back to her hotel that night. 'If only we let them.' He had kissed her lightly on the cheek and wished her luck. 'It is time to stop being a coward, Dulcie. Go home to the man you love. *Arrivederci.*'

Now it was just gone two o'clock and she had been wandering the labyrinth of alleyways in the San Marco district, after a visit across the Grand Canal to the Accademia. Finding herself in the Campo San Stefano, she decided to stop for a late lunch. Her legs were tired after several hours of walking and she was thirsty. In honour of Antonio she ordered a glass of Prosecco and selected a sandwich from the *tramezzini* menu. While she ate, she took out her notepad and pen and continued with the short story she had started yesterday – appropriately it was set in Venice. Before she knew it, and after she'd ordered a second glass of Prosecco, two hours had sped by and the sun had moved round the square. Feeling it on the back of her neck, she paid her bill and set off for the hotel. She had another concert planned for the evening, and if she was going to avoid falling asleep during it, a siesta was in order. Drinking at lunchtime was invariably a mistake and, holding tight to the rail on the *vaporetto* as it bumped against the San Marco Giardinetti stop, she yawned hugely. People clambered off, their places on the boat immediately filled by more passengers. Then they were chugging away, the smell of diesel filling the air.

As they drew level with the stately granite columns that marked the entrance to the *piazzetta*, Dulcie shaded her eyes from the glare of the afternoon sun. For the craziest moment, she thought she saw Richard among the blur of tourists. She strained her eyes, telling herself it couldn't be him, that she was imagining things – the result of too much sparkling wine. But, yes, unbelievably it *was* him.

Her heart thumped wildly and she was seized with the urge to wave madly and call his name, as she willed the boat on to the next landing-stage. It seemed to take for ever, but at last she was off and pushing through the queue of people waiting to board. On the waterfront, she almost broke into a run, rushing past the Hotel Danielli, over the Ponte della Paglia and on alongside the Doges' Palace. She was out of breath when she reached the *piazzetta*: the stitch in her side was so painful she had to stop to recover. She feared now she would lose track of Richard, that he would be lost in the crowds, or vanish into one of the many alleyways. But, amazingly, she caught sight of him again. He was side on to her, his gaze fixed rigidly on the rows of gondolas gleaming in the sunshine, water lapping at their sides. He didn't hear her approach or know that she was now standing next to him until she said, 'It's a stunning view, isn't it?'

He turned, did a double-take, then flung his arms around her. The strength of his embrace was so great it nearly knocked her off her feet. They were both in tears when they released each other. Around them, people were giving them odd looks, and a wide berth.

'Oh, Dulcie, don't be cross with me,' he said, clasping her hands in his. 'Don't be angry that I followed you here. Just let me talk to you. Hear what I've got to say, then I'll go ... if you want me to.'

She took him back to the Hotel Isabella. Smiling broadly, Alberto handed over her key. 'And, Signor Cavanagh, *your key?*'

Dulcie glanced at Richard as he took it. He looked shamefaced. In the small mirrored lift, and in answer to her unasked question, he said, 'It's a long story, and I'm all too aware of how devious I must seem. Forgive me, please?'

'Nothing to forgive,' she said, still dazed with shock that he was here. She let them into her room. The chambermaid had been: the bed was made, and sunlight streamed across it. She stood for a moment at the foot of the bed, acknowledging that words could wait: now she wanted to feel Richard close to her. She wanted to lie beside him and feel the tender warmth of his hands on her body. But if she allowed that to happen, as she knew she would, she would never let him go. She couldn't live as she had in the past.

Selfishly, she wanted him for herself. All of him. There would be no more half-measures. She wanted to live her life to the full. The hiding had to stop.

Behind her, she heard him moving. She closed her eyes, anticipating what he would do next. She felt his breath on her neck as he gently pressed his lips to her skin: oh, he'd always known the effect it had on her. He turned her round and kissed her. They made love in silence, with an intensity that left them both exhausted.

They fell asleep, Richard's arm wrapped protectively around Dulcie's shoulders. His last words before he drifted away from her were 'I love you, Dulcie. Be with me . . . always.'

Dulcie hadn't been asleep for long when a flash of memory jolted her awake. She recalled the moment, on the *vaporetto*, when she'd seen Richard in the *piazzetta*. Something was wrong. Something jarred. But what?

She was almost asleep again when the answer came to her. Richard had been standing between the two granite columns where . . . where superstitious Venetians never set foot.

It was irrational, but in her drowsy state she lifted her head from the pillow to check that Richard was all right. His breathing was steady, and when she laid a hand on his chest she felt the reassuring rhythmic beat of his heart.

She closed her eyes and chided herself for her stupidity.

All thoughts of a concert that evening were abandoned, and as Dulcie and Richard lay in bed, he explained how he'd found her. 'You mustn't blame Jack. He played no part in this.'

'Jack? You've spoken to him?'

'Yes. I went to see you, to throw myself on your mercy one more time, and found myself confronted with a strange man who was giving nothing away. I have to confess that initially I was far from polite to him. To give him his due, he was the model of guardianship, and refused point-blank to tell me where you were staying. He made it clear he didn't approve of me.'

She told Richard about the break-up of Jack's marriage, that it was still painfully raw for him. 'So how did you find out where I was?'

'It was on your noticeboard in the kitchen. You're too organised for your own good, Dulcie, not that I'm complaining. I wanted to book the first flight available, but I had to wait for things to calm down at work. I couldn't believe it. We've had a relatively quiet spell for some weeks, then suddenly a large contract I thought we'd sewn up started to unravel. I was convinced, the way my luck was going, that I'd arrive too late, that you'd already have flown home.'

'And Angela? Where does she think you are?'

The mention of his wife's name was the first hint of reality to cloud their happiness, to remind them that, beyond the walls of the Hotel Isabella, the real world awaited them.

He rolled on to his back and stared up at the ceiling. 'In Bristol, at a corporate ra-ra. You know, the usual kind of thing, wall-to-wall team building and effective management training. Dawn-till-dusk bonding.'

His words hung heavily in the silence between them. She ran her fingers over his chest and said, 'What happens when we go home, Richard?'

He took her hand and raised it to his lips. 'I do what I should have done a long time ago. I tell Angela the truth. I've been a coward and I'm not prepared to go on hurting either of you the way I have till now.'

Over dinner that evening, in a trattoria only a short walk from their hotel, where Dulcie had eaten on several occasions, he asked her what had changed her mind. She told him about Antonio. 'I know it sounds far-fetched, but he made it seem, oh, I don't know, reasonable somehow. I've come to the conclusion that Kate and Henry will have to decide for themselves what to do. And Angela, well, I feel this terrible weight of guilt every time I think about her, but maybe she really will be better off without you. Who knows? Learning to stand on her own two feet might be the making of her.' She reached across the table and placed her hand over his. 'Are you sure you want to do this, Richard? The ramifications will go on for the rest of our lives.'

'I know, but believe me, I've never been surer about anything. I love you, Dulcie, and while I won't be able to offer you all that I'd like to in the way of financial security—'

She removed her hand from his, stopping him short. 'Richard, I don't care what money you may or may not have. It's you I love, not your bank balance.'

'Which will be seriously depleted by the time I've squared things with—'

She stopped him again. 'Put your wretched male pride back into its box, and listen to me. It's *you* I want in my life. I'm not in the least interested in your worldly goods and chattels. All I expect you to bring to our relationship is commitment and honesty.'

He looked serious. 'Some might say, in view of how I've treated Angela, that I'm incapable of either of those things.'

After dinner, arm in arm – something they had never been able to do back in England – they went for a stroll: it was a perfect night wrapped in moonlight and gently lapping water. Richard hadn't been to Venice before, and Dulcie found herself wanting to share her love of this romantic place with him. To her delight he was equally taken with Venice's unique charm and beauty. I shall always remember this night, she thought, as beneath a starry sky they lingered on a tiny bridge overlooking a narrow waterway of shimmering inky blue. It was a peaceful backwater of neglected buildings and crumbling brickwork; humble, magical and stunningly beautiful. How could a city of such faded grandeur touch the hearts of so many? But answering that was like trying to dissect the very essence of love – like trying to catch hold of quicksilver.

Standing behind her, his arms around her, chin resting on the top of her head, Richard said, 'One day, when we're married, we'll come back here and stand on this same spot and I shall tell you that you've made me the happiest man alive.'

'Not before then?'

'No.' He turned her round to face him. 'I want us to be married as soon as we can. I wish it could be tomorrow, but I'm afraid we'll have to be patient.'

She shushed him with a kiss. 'One step at a time.'

They took the *vaporetto* back to the hotel, and went straight to bed. But they couldn't sleep. There was too much to think about. The days ahead, when they returned to Maywood, were going to be fraught with pain, particularly for Richard and Angela. Dulcie hoped they were all strong enough to survive the ordeal.

Victor was sick of people telling him how lucky he was to have survived the fire. Would any of those infuriating nurses feel lucky if they were going through this pain? It was worse during the night when he was alone and all he had to think about was the agony he was in. The painkillers and sleeping-pills never seemed strong enough, and by four in the morning he was wide awake and wishing he'd never been rescued.

He didn't remember a thing about the fire. His last memory was of sitting in front of his typewriter, feeling dizzy. Jack had explained that he'd found him on the floor and had carried him downstairs. He'd also told him that there was no sign of his manuscript in the room where the fire had started. To his everlasting shame he had cried when he'd heard this. That Beth woman had looked near to tears too. He'd asked them to leave him alone. They'd gone, but had returned the following day. And the day after that. He'd lost track of how long he'd been stuck here in the burns unit – it felt like for ever. No one would give him a straight answer when he asked when he'd be able to go home. The worst of his burns were around his neck, chest, right shoulder, arm and hand, and the doctors spoke of the risk of infection, that there would have to be skin grafts. He was hooked up to an intravenous drip, which fed in antibiotics and God knew what else. His throat and lungs were still suffering from the effect of smoke inhalation, and he could only speak in a hoarse whisper.

If he was honest, he didn't want to go home. Both Jack and the policeman who had come to talk to him about the fire had said the damage to his house was confined to just two rooms. Again, he had been lucky. But were they telling him the truth or merely sparing his feelings? What they didn't know was that the insurance company wouldn't pay up. Because of his redundancy, he'd let the monthly payments slip. If his throat hadn't hurt so much, he would have cried out his frustration. But all he could do was lie in this wretched bed as helpless as a baby. Sometimes just opening his eyes was all he could manage.

The next morning brought a troupe of trainee doctors to gawp at him.

Lunchtime came and went, followed by a bossy nurse who spent an age fiddling with his dressings and made him cry with the pain. When at last she left him alone, he lay back exhausted, pitying the man in the bed alongside him who was in for the same treatment.

Hours later he woke up from a deep sleep to find a girl staring down at him. Through the crack in his eyelids she looked vaguely familiar, but indistinguishable from the hundreds of young nurses he saw every day.

'Hello, Victor, how's it going?'

He closed his eyes. 'Go away,' he croaked.

'Charmed, I'm sure.'

Still with his eyes shut, he said, 'I'm tired. I just want to sleep.'

'That's okay. I'll sit here and eat my way through this bunch of grapes I've brought for you.'

He forced his eyes open and focused on the girl sitting beside the bed. 'It's you,' he said, in disbelief. 'You're that lippy girl from the writing group.'

She grinned. 'Nice one, Victor. You sound like my father. How are you?'

'How do you think I am?'

'Well, for a man who's gone through what you've been through, I reckon you don't look so bad. The husky voice is an improvement. Almost sexy.'

'If you've come here to mock me, have your fun, then go.'

'Now why do you think I'd do a thing like that?'

'Why else would you be here?'

'To see how you are. Jack and Beth told me you didn't have any visitors other than them, so I thought you'd appreciate a friendly face. Oh, and I brought you these.' She delved into a small black-leather rucksack, pulled out a newspaper and a box of chocolates and put them on his bedside locker. 'They're contraband,' she said, her voice lowered. 'Liqueurs. I thought you might be in need of the alcohol.'

'And the paper?'

'There's an article in it about you.'

'Me?'

'You and Jack. Because of you, he's a hero.'

'I thought you said something about grapes.'

'I was kidding. Of course, if you'd rather have the vitamin C, I could take the choccies away and bring you something healthy instead.'

'No,' he said. 'I'll make do with those.'

She laughed. 'Good to see you've not lost your touch, Victor. You're still a miserable old goat.'

He stared at her, incensed. 'How dare you talk to me like that?'

'I dare because you're stuck there in bed unable to do anything about it. Now, when are you going to start writing again?'

'That's none of your business.'

'Yes, it is. We're members of a writers' group. We're supposed to support and encourage each other.'

He sighed. His voice was growing weaker and the pain in his throat was getting worse. 'I doubt I'll be able to hold a pen for months.'

She looked at him solemnly, her gaze taking in the wreck of his body. 'Is it very bad?'

He swallowed, and to his horror tears filled his eyes. With an effort that sent waves of unbearable pain shooting through him, he turned his head. 'I'd like you to go now.'

To his immense relief, he heard her get to her feet. But the relief was short-lived. 'I'll see you tomorrow, Victor. Take care, won't you?'

53

Jack had said he would visit Victor during the afternoon, between clients, and with Beth working late, Jaz had said she would do the evening slot. It fitted in well with seeing her mother first, who was still under orders to stay in bed – her blood pressure was showing no sign of coming down.

Jaz had been warned by Beth that Victor looked awful, but on her first visit nothing had prepared her for the sight of him. He was straight out of a horror movie. She'd done her best yesterday to hide her shock and had chatted to him as though nothing was wrong, even being rude to convince him she wasn't there out of pity. When he'd started to cry, she hadn't known what to do or say – other than to go, as he'd requested.

But she was back to see him today, as she'd said she would be. She'd asked Mum how she ought to handle things, and had been advised to be herself. 'If you do anything else, he'll know you're uncomfortable with the situation, which in turn will make him feel worse. Just be your usual self, Jaz. And if he starts to cry again, don't be embarrassed, find him a tissue.'

It was great being able to talk so openly with her mother. It was like it used to be between them.

The house was looking better now, too: the decorators had almost finished and the carpets were being fitted next week. But they'd nearly been found out. Tamzin and Lulu had been arguing at the end of Mum's bed and Dad had told them to keep the noise down. When Lulu had pushed Tamzin off the bed, Dad had roared, 'Just you wait till I get you monkeys home! I'll knock your stupid heads together!'

'Don't you mean when you get us back to the hotel?' Tamzin had said.

Jaz had thought her father would explode and throttle her sister on the spot, so she stepped in and said, 'Will you listen to the girl? She treats the house like a hotel and now even *calls* it a hotel.' With much tutting and rolling of eyes, she'd dragged her sisters out of the room, saying their sugar levels were probably at an all-time low and she'd get them a can of Coke. Later that night her father had thanked her for her fast thinking. He'd even apologised for having punished her so harshly over Hidden Talents. 'Your mother's taken me to task,' he admitted. 'She says I've got to treat you more like the adult you are. Thing is, Jaz, I still want to keep you in my pocket where I'll know you'll be safe.'

'Oh, Dad, less of the cheesy routine.'

'It's true. You're the special one in our family and I don't want you to come to harm. Tamzin and Lulu are natural-born fighters, like the boys, but you're so small. Nothing but a waif of a girl who needs someone to look out for her.'

'Dad, I'm more than capable of taking care of myself. I've been doing it for years. You've taught me all you know.'

He'd laughed and left her to get on with her homework while he went to check on Tamzin and Lulu in the room next door.

Now Jaz stepped out of the lift on the third floor of the hospital and followed the signs for the burns unit. Victor was lying in exactly the same position as he'd been in yesterday, flat on his back, staring up at the ceiling.

'Hi, Victor,' she said. 'I threatened you with another visit, and here I am. Don't ever accuse me of short-changing you. So, what's new? I'm afraid I've come empty-handed this time.' She noticed that the box of chocolates she'd given him yesterday was open on his bedside locker and that three barrel-shaped chocolates were missing.

'Nothing's new,' he whispered morosely.

She repositioned the chair next to his bed and sat down. 'I've just been to see my mother – did I tell you she was here? No? Well, she's been stuck in bed for much longer than you. She's expecting twins, and she's been told that if she doesn't do as the doctors say she might lose the babies. Pretty serious, eh? Hey, you know what we ought to do? Fix the pair of you up with walkie-talkies and you can moan to each other about how awful it is in here.'

She rambled on, chattering nineteen to the dozen, only occasionally eliciting a response from Victor – a roll of his eyes or a disapproving croak. She told him about the burglary and the house being wrecked. 'They messed up all my college work, but I've managed to sort it out.'

A flicker of something, possibly understanding, passed across his face and he said, 'What about your writing?'

'Ah. Long story. I had to ditch it. It was rubbish, anyway. I'm waiting for inspiration to hit me so I can start something new. What will you do next?' Jaz saw his lips move, but she didn't catch what he said. She leaned towards him. 'Sorry, Victor, I didn't hear you. What did you say?'

'I said, I'll give up.'

She was shocked, and poignantly nostalgic for the old Victor: the pompous, ego-inflated Victor. 'You'll do no such thing,' she said. 'If I can start again, so can you.'

'I think we can safely say our circumstances are very different.'

'And that's where you're wrong. We have one very important quality in common with each other: we're writers. And once a writer, always a writer. You just need to get going again. It would be great therapy for you. Once you start using your brain again, you'll soon be feeling less sorry for yourself.'

'Sorry for myself?' he echoed, in a hoarse whisper. 'Next you'll be telling me to pull myself together.'

She smiled. 'I hadn't thought of that. It's not a bad idea, is it?' She waited for his response, to see if she'd gone too far. For what it was worth she thought she had. But something about his beaten manner made her want to shake him up, to make him believe in himself again. She didn't have to be a brain surgeon to know that if he didn't believe his body would heal he'd never get better inside. What spurred her to carry on talking to him in this no-nonsense way was the hope that, while she had his attention, he wasn't thinking about his appalling injuries. At least there was no sign of him crying as he'd done yesterday.

He'd made no response to her comment, so she said, 'Did you know that the writers' group hasn't met for a while?'

'No, I didn't,' he murmured. 'I've had more important things to occupy me.'

'That's right, so you have. Anyway, Jack and Beth thought that while Dulcie was still away on holiday, and you were stuck here, there wouldn't be any meetings.'

'I'm overwhelmed by the group's consideration, as I'm sure Dulcie will be.'

'Okay, that's me done here. I've got a stack of homework to get through this evening.' She stood up. 'Shall I come again tomorrow?'

She had to hide a smile of satisfaction when, in a tired, strained voice, he said, 'If it isn't too much trouble, perhaps you could bring me a book to read.'

'Consider it done.'

As she waited for the lift to take her down to her mother's ward, where her father would be waiting to give her a lift back to the hotel, she had the weirdest thought: *Consider it done.* It might have been Popeye Rafferty speaking.

Now, there was a scary thought. Was it possible she was more of a chip off the old block than she'd ever given herself credit for?

Despite knowing what he would have to face when he and Dulcie returned home, Richard had never enjoyed a day more. Or maybe it was because he knew they had to make the most of it that it had passed so happily. For a brief period he and Dulcie had been an ordinary couple. There had been no hiding, no fear of a chance encounter with someone who knew either of them. And this was how the rest of their lives would be, once the initial horror of telling Angela that he wanted a divorce had passed. They were returning home tomorrow. Returning, paradoxically, to the future. *Their* future.

While Dulcie was in the bath, he checked his mobile to see if there were any messages for him – he'd deliberately left it in the hotel room, not wanting a second of their day to be ruined. There was only one message, from Juliette at the office. The first time he listened to it, he frowned at its cryptic content. When he pressed the button to play it again, the frown deepened and he sat down on the edge of the bed.

'Sorry to do this, Richard, but I needed to get hold of you. I thought you ought to know that I've just spoken to your wife and, well, I must have got my wires in a tangle because I had no idea you were on a course in Bristol. I thought you were on holiday. Lucky you'd briefed your wife so thoroughly on that point or I would have looked very silly. Anyway, sorry again, hope I haven't caused any problems. Oh, and we've got a bit of a crisis here, but that can go on hold until you're back. We'll muddle through without you. Speak to you soon. 'Bye.'

Oh, hell. It had started.

54

It was raining when they landed at Manchester airport. The dirty grey sky and the strong gusting wind that met them were a far cry from the beautiful weather they'd enjoyed in Venice. For most of the flight, they had sat in silence, nervous of what lay ahead.

As she held Richard's hand, Dulcie's heart went out to him. Shortly after he'd listened to Juliette's message, Angela had phoned: most of the conversation was audible in the small hotel room. 'Exactly where are you?' she'd asked. 'Because I know you're not in Bristol. I've phoned round, and no one knows anything about the course you told me about.'

'Angela, please, I'll be home tomorrow. We can discuss it then.'

'I want to discuss it *now*. You're . . . you're having an affair, aren't you?'

'Angela—'

'Please tell me it isn't true,' she had cried. 'Tell me I've got it wrong.'

'I'm sorry, but it is true.'

'Are you . . . are you with her now?'

'Yes.'

She had ended the call. Ten minutes later Richard had tried ringing her back, but the line was engaged: either she was speaking to someone else or she had taken the phone off the hook.

Dulcie hadn't wasted her breath on reassuring Richard that it didn't matter how Angela had found out, that he had been going to tell her the truth anyway. She knew it made all the difference to him. He had wanted to spare his wife's feelings as far as he could, to break it to her gently and help her over the worst of the shock. To let her know that he would stand by her and the children, and do everything in his power to make the situation more bearable.

Richard had left his car at the airport and he drove them to Maywood. Dulcie had telephoned Jack late last night to warn him that she would be arriving home today, and when they let themselves into her house, she saw that he had been as good as his word: everything was just as she'd left it, with the bonus of a well-stocked fridge and the mail left in an orderly pile on the kitchen table. There was also a vase of daffodils with a note attached: 'Thanks for letting me stay. See you soon. Jack. P.S. Hope Venice did the trick.'

Richard didn't want to stay long. He prowled anxiously around the kitchen, refused the offer of lunch, drank half a cup of coffee and said, 'I ought to go. The sooner I get this over with the better – and before the boys come home from school.'

She stood on the doorstep and reluctantly let him leave, then rushed after him to give him one last hug, no longer concerned if any of her neighbours saw them. 'I wish I could be there with you,' she said, 'to give you moral support.'

He held her tightly. 'This is definitely something I have to do alone, Dulcie.'

'I know.' She stepped back from him. 'I love you, Richard. Remember that, won't you? Call me when you can. It doesn't matter how late. Or how early. I'll be here.'

It was raining hard as Richard drove out of Maywood. With the wipers swishing back and forth, he was on auto-pilot, passing familiar buildings, road signs, hedges and swathes of open farmland but not seeing any of it. He was thinking of the day he'd first met Dulcie. It had been the most extraordinary and glorious moment of his life. Until then he had never believed in anything as rhapsodic as love at first sight. But it had happened. And to a middle-aged sceptic such as he.

He had been sitting in the lounge of Maywood Grange Hotel when he had heard someone say his name. The voice was distinctively low and, to his ears, incredibly seductive. He'd looked up from the crossword he'd been doing in *The Times*, and had literally felt his heart jolt. He could still remember her exact words: 'Sorry, I didn't mean to make you jump.' If he had started, it was not because she had taken him unawares, it was because she had rocked his world.

They had slipped into an easy rapport and he had spent the rest of the day in bewildered astonishment, trying to conceal his attraction to her as she showed him round the selection of houses she had arranged for him to view. But that evening he had lowered his guard and invited her to join him for dinner. It was then that he had sensed the attraction was mutual.

And what of his wife and family while all this was going on?

Out of sight, out of mind.

He wasn't proud of it, but that was the truth. In the course of that one day the rest of his life had been changed. He hadn't intended it to happen, he had always dismissed men who embarked upon affairs, but he'd been unable to withstand the force of his attraction to this unusual woman. With her sense of fun and independence, her uncomplicated love of life, she made the world seem a better place. She was strong and refreshingly direct.

It was unfair to compare her with Angela, but she was everything his wife wasn't. She was both restful and exciting to be with, and if he had to sum up the effect she had on him in a single phrase, it was that she allowed him to be himself. Once, when he had felt lousy and knew that he looked far from his best, he'd apologised to Dulcie for it. She had given him one of her level stares and said, 'It's okay, Richard, off-days are permissible. You're not on parade with me.'

Oh, if only they had met in their twenties. What a rich and fulfilling life they would have had together.

He swung through the gates and came to a stop in front of the garage, next to Angela's mud-splattered Range Rover. He switched off the engine and looked up at the house through the pouring rain – the house Dulcie had found for him and his family. Could he really put the boys through such an ordeal? Would they ever forgive him? And how would he feel if they refused to see him again? It happened. Children caught in the crossfire of divorcing parents often saw things in black and white and clung protectively to the parent they considered to be in the right. Henry and Victoria would probably do that, initially. Although Henry might have reason never to speak to him again.

He groaned and lowered his head to the steering-wheel.

He roused himself and went inside. The house was eerily quiet. He put down his case at the foot of the stairs and called to Angela.

No reply.

Without removing his raincoat, he went through to the kitchen. No sign of her there either. But, on stopping to look out of the window, he saw her sheltering beneath an umbrella at the bottom of the garden. His heart thudded.

It must have rained solidly for some time, for when he walked over the lawn his shoes sank into the sodden grass. He didn't want to startle her, so he called softly, 'Angela, what are you doing out here?'

She turned, slowly, as if she had been waiting for him. He could see that she'd been crying. Inside his chest, his heart thudded again, painfully.

'Oh, Richard . . . why? Why have you done this to us?'

'I'm sorry,' he said, 'more sorry than I'll ever be able to say.'

'I don't understand. I thought we were happy. I know I'm not the easiest of wives, that I irritate you with my silly—'

He stopped her. 'It's not you, Angela. You must never think that. It's me. I . . . I changed. I became someone different. I didn't mean to.'

The rain was coming down harder now and he was drenched, but he made no move to seek refuge beneath her umbrella. She didn't offer it. Tears flowed down her cheeks. She said, 'I suppose it's some young girl from the office. A pretty bit of ego-boosting fluff half my age.'

'Don't do this, Angela.'

She sniffed defiantly. 'Why not? Why shouldn't I be allowed to know who you've been with? Is she very pretty? Is she—' Her voice faltered and she began to cry in earnest, her sobs loud and choking. 'Oh, God. Why, Richard? Why did you have to do this?'

He stepped forward, took the handle of the umbrella and walked her back to the house. He sat her in the kitchen and knelt on the floor at her side. And still she cried. He hated himself for doing this to her. She didn't deserve such pain. 'I'm sorry,' he said. 'I never meant to hurt you.'

She lifted her tear-soaked face to his. 'Tell me about – about this other woman. Don't shake your head as if I'm a child to be protected. I want to know. I *need* to know.'

He stood up and went to the window. 'It's not what you think. It isn't someone from the office.'

'Do I know her? Is it someone from the village?'

'No. It's Dulcie. Dulcie Ballantyne.' He heard her sudden intake of breath. And then, unbelievably, he heard her laugh.

'But she's *old*!'

He swung round. 'No, she isn't.'

'But she's old,' Angela repeated. She threw back her head and laughed. It was a cruel, mocking laugh, which he'd never heard from her before. But as suddenly as it had started, it stopped. 'She's not even remotely beautiful,' Angela said. 'And she's certainly not slim. Dumpy isn't far off the mark, I'd say. My God, Richard, is that the best you can do? What on earth is the attraction?'

He clenched his teeth. He understood that Angela needed to vent her fury, but he wouldn't countenance a disparaging word about Dulcie. 'You don't have to resort to being spiteful,' he said.

'Oh, that's wonderful. That woman can wreck my marriage but I'm not allowed to say a word about her age or her crabby old looks. Now I've heard everything.'

Richard kept his face impassive. 'I know you're upset and angry, Angela, but if we're going to sort this mess out, we need to remain calm and level-headed.'

She cleared her throat. 'You're right,' she said. 'I'm being my usual stupid self. I need to—'

'You're not being stupid,' he interrupted impatiently. Then, in a more placatory tone, 'Please don't keep saying that. Shall I make us some tea?'

They sat at either end of the table, divided by a pile of laundry that was waiting to be ironed and several days' worth of newspapers destined for the recycling collection point in the village.

'Right,' Angela said, after a sip of tea, 'what happens now? Do I make you promise never to see her again and we carry on as if nothing has happened?'

His heart slammed against his ribs. Angela had no idea of what was coming next. She thought he had stepped out of line and assumed that, because he'd been caught, he would get back where he belonged, his 'misdemeanour' discreetly tucked away.

'Or do I,' she continued, 'for the sake of the boys, have to accept that there'll always be this . . . this third person in our marriage?'

He closed his eyes briefly. When he opened them, he said, 'I'm afraid neither of those options will work, Angela.' He swallowed. 'I want a divorce. But I want you to know that nothing here,' he glanced around the kitchen, 'will change. This will always be your home, yours and the children's. You won't have to worry about money. I'll see to all that. I promise I'll take care of everything.' But as he tried to fill the yawning gap between them with words, wanting to reassure her, he knew she wasn't listening.

'A divorce? You can't be serious.'

'I'm sorry, but I am. I – I want to marry Dulcie.'

She shook her head. 'No. No you don't. You're having a silly mid-life crisis.' Her voice had reached a high hysterical pitch. 'Oh, why couldn't you have just made do with growing your hair and buying a motorbike?'

'I think you'd agree that I'm too old for either of those choices,' he replied.

'Well, you're too old to have an affair,' she retorted. Then, more calmly, she said, 'It's because you had a heart-attack, isn't it? It's made you realise you're getting older. That time is running out. But it'll pass. You'll soon be your old self.' She was pleading with him.

He said nothing.

'So, when did the affair start? After our Boxing Day party?'

He knew the truth would hurt, but there had been enough deceit. If he lied to her now, they would get nowhere: she would carry on believing that it was just a phase he was going through. She had to know he was serious about Dulcie. 'Since I first met her, when we were house-hunting to move up here.'

Angela's mouth dropped open, a small cry escaped her, and then she fled from the room, crashing the door after her.

With his elbows on the table, he leaned forward and hung his head. The worst, or so he hoped, was over.

55

The flat was looking less like a bombsite now and more like the airy, comfortable home Jack had envisaged. He had Rafferty & Sons to thank for that. Because of his connection with Jaz, he knew he'd been treated as a priority. However, it had occurred to him that maybe the real reason he was getting such gold-star treatment was because of what her brothers had done to him, that this was the Rafferty way of settling the account. But he'd soon dismissed the idea: he couldn't imagine Patrick Rafferty conducting business that way. He didn't strike Jack as a man who would condone what his hot-headed sons had done. Odds on, they had acted without his approval. And hadn't they told him to keep schtum? Especially where Jaz was concerned.

The men Patrick Rafferty had organised to do the job had been one hundred per cent reliable. Most days, and during his lunch break, Jack had called in to see how they were getting on, but his supervision wasn't required. They knew what they were doing and planned to finish the job next week, when they would return to see to the odds and ends. One had a mate who was a joiner and specialised in fitting kitchens. 'I could give you his number, if you like, so you can get him round here to give you a quote. I'm not saying he's cheap, but he'll do you a quality job for a reasonable price. He did the boss's kitchen, so that tells you all you need to know. Assuming, that is, you're planning on losing those old units. A right seventies nightmare, aren't they? Floor's not much cop either. You wanna rip up them old lino tiles and get some laminated wood down.'

Jack had formed no lasting relationship with the antiquated kitchen – fake teak-fronted units with the obligatory aluminium edging – and was only too pleased to be given the name and phone number of someone who came so highly recommended. He lost no time in ringing the joiner and arranging for him to come and see what the job would entail.

Now, as Jack stood in the soon-to-be demolished kitchen beneath the harsh glare of a fluorescent strip-light, he went through his mail. The only envelope of any interest had been addressed by hand: it was from the organisers of the writers' conference in Harrogate. In reply to his phone call they had sent him several copies of the programme with some application

627

forms. He slipped the pieces of paper back into the envelope and took it upstairs with him.

Yet again Beth was bestowing more neighbourly generosity on him: he was looking forward to the day when he would be able to return her kindness by inviting her and Nathan to eat *chez* Solomon.

Nathan opened the door. 'Hi, Jack. Mum's just getting changed, she won't be long. Jaz and I have nearly got supper ready. Don't look so worried, we washed our hands before we started.'

'That's not worry on my face, Nathan, it's awe. Hello, Jaz. What's cooking?'

'Chilli con carne.'

'And pudding?'

'Banoffee pie.'

'Now I *am* impressed. Anything I can do to help?'

'Absolutely not,' said Nathan. 'We promised Mum a night off, and we're not going to be accused of being incapable because we've taken on extra help.'

Beth joined them in the sitting room. 'Aren't they sweet, Jack? I'm racking my brains as to what they're after. More use of the car, perhaps? Or more money?'

During the meal they caught up with each other's news. Anyone observing them, thought Jack, as they laughed and joked, would think they were a regular family going about its evening business. The thought made him sad: he wished Amber and Lucy were there too. He still didn't know if Maddie and Tony were going to up sticks and move to the States. His solicitor's letter had prompted a guarded reply, informing Jack that no decision had been made as yet, but that his concerns regarding the children had been duly noted. Meanwhile, all he could do was hope and pray that the move wouldn't come off. He didn't know how he would handle being so permanently apart from the girls. He saw them little enough now, but just once or twice a year would be intolerable.

'More chilli, Jack?'

Shaking off his morose thoughts, he helped himself from the dish Jaz was offering him, and said, 'How was Victor when you saw him yesterday?'

Nathan laughed. 'Ah, yes, the other man in Jaz's life.'

Jaz elbowed him. 'You leave poor Victor alone. Actually, Jack, he's being almost polite to me.'

'And she's being too modest to sing her own praises,' said Beth. 'Against all the odds, Jaz has done the impossible. She's got Victor writing again.'

'No? How?'

'She was downright rude to him, from what I can gather,' said Nathan. 'Shook him by his singed shoulders and told him to stop whingeing.'

'I did no such thing!'

'So what words of encouragement did you offer him?'

'I merely suggested that having something else to think about would give him less time to feel sorry for himself.'

Jack smiled. 'That's my girl.'

'She's thinking of joining the UN next,' teased Nathan. 'I can't think how they've managed till now without her obvious skills in diplomacy.'

'You're all making too big an issue of it,' said Jaz. 'He asked me to take in a book for him, so I gave him a notepad and pen as well, just in case anything came to him in the middle of the night.'

Beth passed her the basket of garlic bread. 'I think you've been brilliant. You've done more for Victor than the rest of us ever could. You even got him to admit that he'd been made redundant.'

'I just gave him the opportunity to talk. It must have been hard on him, losing his job like that, after so many years.' She bit into a piece of garlic bread. 'Do you want to know what my latest plan for Victor is?'

'Go on,' urged Jack. 'Let's have it.'

'Now that Dulcie's back, I think we ought to start up the group again and hold our meetings at the hospital so that he can join in.'

Jack looked at Beth. 'Can we do that? Will the hospital allow so many of us to visit at the same time?'

'I don't see why not. I've seen quite large families gathered round patients' beds. So long as we don't make too much noise and only stay for the specified time, what harm would we do?'

'And who'd have thought we cared enough about him?'

Beth glanced at the burns that had almost healed on Jack's hands. 'And there speaks the hero who risked his own life to rescue Victor.'

'But it's true, isn't it?' persisted Jaz. 'He's the biggest pain going, but you can't help feeling sorry for him.'

Nathan put his arm around her shoulders. 'I had no idea you were such a sentimental softie.'

'I'm not,' she warned. 'Tough as old boots, me, so watch your step.'

The banoffee pie was a triumph and, after accepting their praise, Jaz confessed that the chef at the Maywood Grange Hotel had made it for her. 'It turns out that he and Dad know one another from way back and now we're getting whatever Dad fancies to eat,' she explained. 'It's so embarrassing – the other guests must hate us.'

'Oh, let them,' said Jack. 'Your father's a top man. The flat's coming on a treat.'

'I'm surprised you've come back to this lowly neighbourhood,' said Beth, handing him a bottle of wine. 'After whooping it up in Bloom Street, Maywood Park Road must be something of a drop in standards for you.'

'Oh, I'm making do,' he said, with an exaggerated shrug. 'I'm sure I'll get used to being back in such a rough area.'

'And talking of Dulcie, how do you think she's faring? I did ask her to join us tonight, but she said she wasn't in the mood for company.'

It was four days since Dulcie had returned from Venice and, from the limited conversations he and Beth had had with her, they'd learned that her affair with Richard was now back on and out in the open. As for what would happen next, Dulcie had refused to comment. Perhaps she didn't know.

'I haven't a clue,' Jack said, in answer to Beth's question. 'She doesn't give much away, but when I called round last night to thank her properly for letting me use her house, she seemed okay-ish. I think she's dreading Richard's wife turning up on her doorstep wanting an all-out confrontation.'

'I still can't believe that Dulcie's been having an affair,' said Jaz, scraping up the last of her dessert. 'She just doesn't seem the sort.'

'Why's that?' asked Beth, with a wry smile. 'You wouldn't be casting aspersions on her age, would you?'

Jaz missed the implied criticism. 'There is that. But, well, she seems so nice and normal, not the man-eater type. The opposite, in fact.'

'I didn't know adulterers had a certain look. What would it be? A lascivious leer?'

Jaz rolled her eyes. 'Don't be obtuse, Nathan. All I meant was, she doesn't fit the profile.'

'And which profile would that be?'

While Beth made the coffee, Jack pondered this thought. Had he demonised Maddie and Tony because of their actions? Weren't they really just two people who had fallen in love? And if Maddie had been any other woman, wouldn't he have wished his old friend all the luck in the world?

From across the kitchen, while she waited for the kettle to boil, Beth watched Jack's face growing ever more solemn. She could guess what he was thinking of. How long, she wondered, would it be before he could think of Maddie and Tony without it hurting? A year? Two? A decade? Maybe never. Perhaps something like that stayed with you for a lifetime.

To lighten the mood for his benefit, she said, 'You wouldn't believe what I've had to put up with these last few days, Jack. I told Nathan about Ewan and it's been non-stop innuendoes, warnings and advice. It's got to the stage where I'm thinking of running away from home. Only I know he'd come looking for me, wagging his finger.'

'Too right. Honestly, I teach her how to use the Internet and the next thing I know she's cosying up with some bloke. Irresponsible or what?'

'Oh, give your mother a break, Nathan. I think it's cool what she's done. And, ooh, *so* romantic.'

Beth blushed. 'It's not like that, Jaz. We're just friends. How could it be anything else when we haven't met?'

'But that's about to change,' said Jack. He got up, went over to the sofa where he'd been sitting earlier and came back with a thick envelope. '*Voilà!* Application forms for the writers' conference. What's more, Beth, you and I are going to sit here this evening and fill them in, ready for posting tomorrow morning. And, Nathan, I promise I'll give this Ewan chap a thorough vetting when I meet him. Your mother will be in safe hands.'

Late that night, after Nathan had driven Jaz back to the Maywood Grange Hotel and Jack had left, Beth switched on her computer hoping there would be a message from Ewan. There was.

Dear Madly Teased of Maywood,

Oh, how I feel for you! There's nothing like the brutal teasing of one's offspring to make one squirm. I'm convinced Alice has switched courses and has abandoned her degree in politics for one in how-to-humiliate-one's-ageing-father. At the rate she's going she'll get a first, no problem!

Why do children turn themselves into boringly mature adults? Or, in our case, fussy carers? Lord help us when we're so infirm we genuinely need their assistance. I hope I die before Alice shows an unhealthy interest in stair-lifts and incontinence pads.

I wish I could reassure your son that my intentions are perfectly honourable, that he shouldn't lose any sleep worrying that your reputation might be sullied by meeting me. But I fear I'll be whistling in the wind. If he's anything like Alice he'll have made up his mind that you're incapable of making a reasoned decision for yourself. It's called love, Bethany. Don't be too hard on him. Because of your circumstances, he's had to grow up very quickly (as Alice did) and has assumed responsibility for you.

And don't worry that you suspect his comments contain a more serious undertone beneath the surface of the lighthearted joshing. They probably do. It's his way of protecting you. He needs to put thoughts into your head that he thinks you're too naïve to come up with on your own – as if! Alice's comments vary from making you out to be a man who gets off on pretending to be a woman or a potential Fatal Attraction bunny-boiler. Her favourite put-down is, 'Oh, ple-ease, you're not still corresponding with Ms Loony-Tune are you?' (Sorry if any of this causes offence, but by giving you the picture of what I'm up against, I hope you'll understand that you're not the only one being put through the mill!)

Anyway, I must away now and do some writing. I haven't been able to do much recently owing to a hundred and one other commitments. If you don't hear from me over the next couple of days, worry not, it'll be a hectic schedule that's kept me from getting in touch, not a moody turn.

All the best,
Ewan X

PS How very rude of me, I haven't enquired how your writing
is progressing. Do you ever hit a wall when a blank screen
cruelly mocks you? It happens to me now and then. I find
the only solution is to brew up some hot Ribena and switch
on the telly for some daytime revelry. There's nothing like a
shout at Trisha or Kilroy to stir up the juices first thing in
the morning. Though my preferred choice, later in the day,
is a languish on the sofa with Watercolour Challenge.

But what am I saying? This giving away of my innermost
secrets has to stop. I dread to think what kind of an
impression you are forming of me. Be assured I am ALL
man, there's not a wimpish bone in my body. Well, none
that I'm prepared to own up to.

(Oh, hell, now I come to think of it, on top of the
appointments I've made for the beauty parlour and hair
salon, I will now have to firm up my wilting pecs at the gym
before we meet! I said PECS, Beth!)

As ever, Ewan's self-effacing humour made Beth laugh. Behind her,
Nathan said, 'I do hope he's keeping it clean, Mum. We don't want the Vice
Squad hammering on the door in the middle of the night with allegations of
improper use of the Net.'

Beth turned round. 'You'll be relieved to know that every word he writes
is squeaky clean.'

Nathan came and stood next to her. She sensed he wanted to say
something important.

'Mum?'

'Yes?'

'You will be careful, won't you?'

'I know what you're saying, but do you have any idea how *careful* I've
been all these years? I'm tired of being so circumspect. Everyone else is
allowed to have some fun and take the occasional risk. Why can't I?' She
switched off the computer and sighed. 'The truth is, Nathan, I don't want to
end up boring myself to death.'

He smiled. 'You'll never do that, Mum.'

'Can we call a truce, then? No more lectures?'

'Maybe just the odd one. To counter the hundreds of warnings you give
me every time I go out in the car.'

She reached up and, just as he often did to her, ruffled his immaculate
hair. '*Touché.*'

56

Fourteen days after they'd flown home from Venice, Richard moved in with Dulcie. He brought with him clothes, a selection of his favourite books, a small album of photographs, some files, and a heavy heart. Seeing him so downcast, so worn down and wretched, Dulcie had doubts about what they had done. 'You don't have to do this,' she told him, as she watched him hang his clothes in the wardrobe she'd cleared for him. 'It's not too late to change your mind.'

He stopped what he was doing. 'Is that what you think is going through my head?'

'You wouldn't be the man I love if you weren't wondering whether you were doing the right thing.'

He tossed the remaining clothes on to the bed and came to stand with her in front of the window. He stroked her cheek. 'Thank you,' he said.

'For what?'

'For always allowing me to be me. For giving me the space to doubt and yet not be doubted.'

She turned her face into his hand and kissed it.

Leaving him to finish his unpacking, she went downstairs. For once the house was quiet. Was it too much to hope that a restful calm had been reinstated?

In the days immediately after Richard had told Angela the truth, the phone seemed never to stop ringing. She had been tempted to wrench the wires out of the wall sockets, but the thought of Richard being unable to talk to her prevented her succumbing to such an action. The first person to ring her had been Richard, to say that Angela now knew everything: with whom he'd been having an affair and his intentions.

'How is she?' Dulcie had asked, wishing that he wasn't speaking to her on his hands-free mobile as he drove to his sons' school to bring them home: the reception was so poor she had to strain to hear his voice.

'Devastated. As I expected. The worst part was she thought that we'd put it behind us and carry on as normal.'

'That was brave of her. It's not every woman who would be prepared to forgive so easily. And how are you?'

'I think my feelings are irrelevant.'

For a moment the line fizzed and crackled and she missed what he said.

'I said it's going to take a while, Dulcie. She's going to need a lot of help to recover from the shock. I can't just walk away immediately.'

'I understand. Believe me, I do. However long it takes, Richard.'

The connection had broken then, and she'd spent the next few minutes standing by the phone willing it to ring again. But it didn't.

Not until the following morning when Kate phoned her. It was the call Dulcie had dreaded most, knowing that it would only be a matter of time before either Angela, with a need to turn to her elder children, or Richard, wanting to explain it all to them, made Henry aware of the difficult situation he was now in regarding his relationship with Kate.

Disbelief, anger and horror were at the top of Kate's agenda and Dulcie could say nothing to appease her daughter.

'Oh, Mum, you of all people! How could you?'

'I don't see what makes me any different from anyone else,' Dulcie had countered.

'But with a married man! And young children are involved.' Kate's voice was shrill with condemnation and righteous disgust.

'I'm well aware of the situation, Kate. Are you sure your view of me isn't coloured by the delicate position in which you now find yourself?' Dulcie enquired, with an edge to her voice.

It was then that she felt the full force of Kate's wrath. 'I'm in no such position, Mum. For your information, and because of your sordid goings-on, Henry's dumped me. I'm back in my flat now. How does that make you feel?'

'How very short-sighted of him,' Dulcie said drily, recalling Antonio's advice in Venice: if Kate and Henry loved each other they would find a way round the problem.

A four-letter expletive she'd never heard Kate use hurtled down the line followed by, 'How can you be so bloody insensitive?'

Dulcie tried to interject, but the question had been rhetorical: Kate was in full flow. 'You've wrecked two relationships in one go, quite a feat, wouldn't you say? I don't know how you can justify what you've done. It's the most appallingly selfish thing I've ever heard of. And I can't believe you've been seeing Henry's father for so long. Why didn't you say anything? No, don't answer that. Deep down you were ashamed of what you were doing. Well, I sincerely hope you feel even more ashamed now.' She drew breath, but not for long enough to give Dulcie time to speak. 'And what was going through your mind when Henry and I started seeing each other? Why didn't you stop me? You could have saved me all this – all this pain.' She started to cry, and at once Dulcie's animosity towards her daughter vanished: she longed to take Kate in her arms and make everything right for her.

'I'm sorry, Kate,' she said, 'but there's nothing I can say or do to make amends, I know that. I just hope that one day you'll forgive me.'

The phone went dead and Dulcie replaced the receiver.

An hour later Andrew phoned. Without preamble, he said, 'I've just had Kate ranting and raving on the phone, Mum. How're you doing?'

'Coping. Just.'

'Anything I can do?'

'Yes. Make it all go away.'

'It'll sort itself out in the end,' he said pragmatically.

He sounded so like his father, so optimistic – even when he was dying Philip had remained upbeat – that Dulcie had to swallow against the tightness in her throat. She said, 'I wish I had half your certainty.'

'She'll be okay, Mum. Trust me. I might be the gay one in the family, but we both know that Kate's the real drama queen.' He paused. 'That was an attempt at a joke, by the way. You were supposed to laugh and feel better for it.'

'Oh, Andrew, what would I do without you?'

'Shall I see if I can get some time off and come up?'

'That's sweet of you, but there's no need. I'm just reeling from the shock of Kate's anger.'

'Look, I can't speak for long now. Shall I call again this evening?'

'That would be nice.'

And so the days had progressed, with Kate phoning regularly to take out her anger on Dulcie and Andrew to pick up the pieces. Poor Andrew, he was also on the receiving end of his sister's fury because he had known since Christmas about the affair and not told her.

Then one day, around lunchtime, Angela phoned. There was reproach in her voice, but skittish desperation too. 'Why can't you leave him alone?' she cried. 'He's my husband, the father of our children.'

'I don't think this conversation is a good idea,' Dulcie had said. 'I can't say anything that will help – other than that I'm sorry.'

Her apology had been flung back at her. 'Don't patronise me with your smug sympathy. I don't need it. Perhaps it will be you who'll need the words of pity when you find that Richard won't leave us. He loves his children and would never do anything to hurt them.'

Dulcie went out into the garden, thinking of Richard and what he was doing upstairs – transferring his life from one home to another – and felt an even bigger weight of guilt and sorrow towards Richard's wife. If Angela had thought their two young sons would be her trump card in keeping her husband, she was now facing the agonising truth that it had failed her.

Richard was sitting on the edge of Dulcie's bed – *their bed* – talking to his eldest son. Henry had phoned because he'd just heard from Angela that his father had moved in with Dulcie.

'Henry, there's no point in going over the same ground again and again. At some stage you have to accept that this is the decision I've made and I'm sticking with it. And, no, it isn't a spur-of-the-moment thing. It has nothing to do with having a heart-attack and wondering what the hell I've done with my life.'

'But, Dad, it's so not you.'

'What? Being happy?'

'No. Being such a bastard to Mum.'

Richard flinched. 'That's exactly what I'm trying to avoid, Henry.'

'Yeah, it really looks like it. Next you'll be spouting crap like you have to break eggs to make an omelette. Do you have any idea what you've done? Mum says Christopher and Nicholas won't stop fighting, they're turning into a pair of hooligans. And all because of you.'

'Credit me with sufficient—'

Henry cut him dead. 'Right now, Dad, I can't credit you with anything but gross stupidity. For God's sake, all marriages go through a rocky period, but most couples pull through and get on with it. Especially couples who've been married as long as you and Mum. Security is more important than a momentary fling of passion that stands bugger-all chance of lasting.'

Losing patience, Richard said, 'And what would you know about marriage? You, whose idea of commitment is to remember a girl's name after you've bedded her!' He heard his son gasp. 'I'm sorry,' he said hastily. 'That was out of order. I shouldn't have said it.'

'Why not, if that's how you feel about me? It's good to get these things into the open and know where we stand with each other. But I'd like you to know that Kate – yeah, how about that? I can remember her name! – well, Kate and I thought we had a future. But you've put paid to that.'

'It needn't be so.'

'Get real, Dad. How can I possibly go on living with her when you, to use your own choice expression, are *bedding* her mother? You might not have any principles, but I do. I wouldn't hurt Mum in so vile a manner.'

Richard sagged beneath the vicious onslaught. 'We're not getting anywhere, Henry, so I suggest we say goodbye.'

'Suits me. I only called to let you know that Victoria and I will be up at the weekend to stay with Mum. I thought it might matter to you.'

No, thought Richard, when he'd rung off. You called, Henry, because you still can't accept that your boring old father has dared to do this dreadful thing. He's chosen love over staid security. One day you'll understand that you only get one chance. And, yes, there was some truth in what his family was throwing at him: his heart-attack had had an effect on him. It had opened his eyes to what was important to him.

He got up and went to the window. Dulcie was in the garden, sitting on the wooden bench in her favourite spot, surrounded by clumps of daffodils. With her face tilted towards the pale spring sun, she looked so content. He felt a rush of love and knew that, between them, they would get through this mess. The strength of their love would ease his conscience and eventually he wouldn't feel as bad as he did now. Already he missed Christopher and Nicholas and he was scared of the terrible division that would come between him and them. Victoria had spoken to him only twice, and although she hadn't been as forthright as Henry, her disdain had been evident.

Initially Angela had insisted that they keep the younger children in ignorance of his affair with Dulcie: he would soon come to his senses and they should avoid putting the boys through any unnecessary upset. But he had been insistent. 'Angela, please don't make this worse by pretending it's not happening.' In the end, he had to move out to make her understand that he was serious. It was brutal, but she had left him with no choice.

By far the hardest part had been telling Christopher and Nicholas. Christopher had stared at him, sullen and tight-lipped, while Nicholas had kicked the wall and said, 'That makes five of us.'

'Five what?' Richard had asked.

His youngest son had given the wall another kick, denting the plaster. 'Five of us in my class at school whose parents have split up.'

Still staring out of the window at Dulcie he made a promise to work hard to repair the damage he'd inflicted on his family. With Dulcie's support, he would do it.

'Family,' announced Popeye, beaming round at his, 'that's what it's all about. You can't beat it.' His eyes moist, he bent down and kissed his wife, then the tiny bundles in her arms. Even Jaz was moved by his speech, and by the sight of the wizened little faces blinking in the light.

Five hours ago her mother had unexpectedly gone into labour and given birth to two healthy babies, a girl and a boy, as yet unnamed. Although premature they were a good weight, according to the midwife, and Jaz was relieved that her mother's difficult pregnancy was over.

'Shall I take some photographs now?' she asked.

'Yes,' her father answered. 'Come on, Tamzin and Lulu, get yourselves lined up here, you too, Phin and Jimmy. Right, then, everyone smile.'

'Hang on,' said her mother, 'that's not right. Jaz has to be in the picture as well. Someone go and fetch a nurse to take it.'

Phin obliged and returned with the prettiest he could find. As they all posed for the camera, Jaz allowed her eldest brother to put his arm around her, which she had never done before. If he or anyone else noticed, they didn't comment on it.

When they were driving back to the hotel, leaving her mother to rest, Jaz reflected on how weird it was that they had all started to get on better with each other since Mum had gone into hospital. In a funny kind of way the break-in had also brought them together.

The latest news about the house was good. The decorators had finished and so had the carpet-fitters. Dad was planning for them to move back in tomorrow. Which was perfect timing because if Mum and the babies were okay they would be allowed home at the weekend. Between now and then he was going to come clean with Mum. Jaz had the feeling that her mother would be so preoccupied with feeds and nappies she wouldn't have time to worry about how bad the damage had been to their home.

As Dad had said, it was family that counted. And as none of them had come to any harm, what did they have to complain about? When she thought about Victor, alone and in pain, the Rafferty troubles paled into insignificance. In fact, as her father was in such a good mood she was going to ask him an important favour: she wanted to see if he'd help sort out Victor's house. 'It's only small,' she intended saying to him, 'so it wouldn't take long.' She just hoped she was right – because if they didn't help Victor, she didn't know how he'd get things put straight. When he'd told her he'd lost his job, he'd admitted that he hadn't kept up his insurance. 'I was looking for ways to save money,' he'd said.

'You idiot, Victor. Even I know that's a short-cut not worth taking.'

She was also going to ask her father if she could go up to Harrogate with Dulcie, Jack and Beth for the writers' conference during the Easter holidays. She had exams to do after the break, which her father would probably use as a reason for her not to go, but now that she had her mother's support, she was quietly confident that any objections he made would be overruled.

57

It was the weekend and Richard was driving home. Or, as he corrected himself, to his former home.

Last night he had decided to accept Angela's invitation to join them all for Sunday lunch – Henry and Victoria were up from London, and for once the boys didn't have a sporting fixture to fulfil. His reluctance to give an unequivocal yes straight away, when Angela had called him at work, had prompted her to say, 'We need to put on a united front for the sake of the children. But, of course, if you can't tear yourself away from *that woman* for a couple of hours, I'm sure Christopher and Nicholas will understand.'

'Angela, please don't use the boys to manipulate me.'

'I'm not! I'm merely stating the obvious. Your sons would be disappointed to know that *she* comes before them. But I suppose you've proved that to them already.'

'She's understandably upset and needs you to know it,' Dulcie had said, when he told her of the conversation.

'But does she have to be so bitter?'

'Wouldn't you be?'

That was the thing about Dulcie: she could be uncomfortably honest, unfailingly fair-handed, and was disposed to see a situation from every viewpoint.

Instead of parking in his usual space, next to Angela's Range Rover in front of the double garage, he came to a stop beneath the dining-room window. It was a symbolic gesture he needed to make: there was no point in thinking, or letting others think, that nothing had changed. Respecting his new status, that of a guest, he rang the bell.

Victoria opened the door. She looked at him for a moment or two, as if sizing him up as friend or foe.

'Okay if I come in?' he asked.

She stepped back. 'Don't be stupid, Dad. You don't have to ask permission to come into your own house. Why didn't you use your key?'

'It didn't seem appropriate.'

She brought her eyebrows together in a frown of intense disapproval – she had done it so often as a young child, usually when confronting food that was green and described as good for growing children. The memory made him put out his arms. 'How about a hug?'

The frown vanished and she slipped into his embrace, burying herself inside his coat. 'Oh, Dad, why have you left us?'

He held her tight. Finding it difficult to speak, he breathed in the sweet smell of her freshly washed hair. 'I haven't left you,' he murmured. 'I'll always be there for you, you know that.'

'Ah, so it was you I heard.'

It was Angela, and to Richard's consternation, Victoria almost leaped out of his arms: she stood with her hands behind her back against the radiator. To hide his awkwardness, he took off his coat and hung it in the cupboard under the stairs. 'What can I do to help?' he asked Angela.

'Oh, nothing,' she said airily. 'It's all done. Henry's opened the wine and, with Victoria's help, the boys have set the table.'

Disappointed that he had nothing with which to occupy himself, and getting the message that Angela was making a point, he said, 'I'll go and have a word with the boys, then.'

He found them upstairs in Christopher's bedroom. Their eyes fixed on the small television on the desk, they were playing a rowdy shoot-'em-up game, blasts of gunfire preceding animal-like cries of death and destruction. He placed himself in their line of vision. 'Hi, boys, how's it going?'

They switched off the game and the room was instantly quiet: neither seemed to know how to answer him. And how could he ask them so glibly how it was going when very likely all they wanted to do was hit him? Angela was right: as far as they were concerned, he had given them an uncompromisingly clear message. But he had to convince his young sons that, when it came to his love for them, nothing had changed: they still meant the world to him.

He heard Angela calling. 'Sounds like lunch is ready. We'd better go.'

Downstairs in the dining room they threw themselves on to their seats, one either side of Richard at the head of the table. 'I've sharpened the knife for you,' Angela said. He felt her watch him as he made a start on carving the pork. In silent concentration, he sliced it with slow, deftly precise movements, each piece the same thickness as the last. He wondered how he could appear so calm before his family after all that he'd done to them. At the other end of the table Angela blew her nose, then excused herself.

Victoria asked Christopher to pass the plates round, and by the time Angela reappeared, with a jug of apple sauce, a stilted conversation had sprung up. 'One of these fine days,' she interrupted them, 'I'll produce a meal and won't leave half of it in the kitchen.' The conversation ground to a halt.

Lunch with his family was proving as great a strain as Richard had feared it would. Henry looked as if he wanted to kill him, Victoria was quiet, and the boys were more interested in a noisy contest over whose jaws could accommodate the largest roast potato than in answering any of his enquiries about school or their friends. Their fidgety kindergarten antics annoyed him, but he felt in no position to reprimand them – he was learning fast what it was to be an errant father. Opposite him, Angela was firing off random statements that bore no relation to the reality of the situation. Twice now she had referred to the change in the weather and how unseasonably warm it was. 'More like June than the beginning of April,' she had enthused.

His being here was a mistake. It was too soon. He should have said no, waited until they were all feeling calmer about his leaving.

'So, Dad, when are you going to stop this nonsense and come home?'

Everyone stopped eating and turned to look at him. He put down his knife and fork and steadied his nerve with a sip of wine. 'Henry, I don't think this is the time or place to—'

'I would have thought it was exactly the time and place.'

'Henry—'

'No, Mum, this has to be said. One of us has to drill some common sense into Dad's befuddled head. He's made his point, and now he has to grasp that enough is enough. What he's doing to you, to *us*, is wrong, and it has to stop.'

'It's not a matter of making a point,' Richard said calmly, conscious that Christopher was banging a foot against the table leg and Nicholas was biting his nails, which he'd never done before. 'And I really don't want to discuss it now.'

'More apple sauce, Victoria?' asked Angela.

'When, then?' Henry's voice was querulous and demanding.

'No thanks, Mum.'

'I said, when, Dad?'

'I heard you, Henry, and I'm not prepared to answer you when you're behaving with scant regard for anyone's feelings but your own.'

'Nicholas? Any more to eat? Another potato?'

'I've had enough, thanks.' Nicholas dropped his cutlery on to his plate with a deafening crash.

'Me behaving with scant regard for other people's feelings? Oh, that's good. And where does that leave you, I wonder?'

'Please, Henry, don't spoil what's been a perfectly pleasant lunch. Simmer down and pass me the gravy.'

Henry switched his gaze from Richard to his mother. 'Are you completely mad, Mum? No one in their right mind would describe the last hour as having been pleasant. Wake up and smell the divorce papers!'

'Don't you dare speak to your mother like that.'

'It's all right, Richard, Henry doesn't mean it. Do you, darling? He's just upset. Nicholas, stop biting your nails and, Christopher, please don't keep kicking the leg of the table. How would you like it if—'

'I don't give a shit about the table.' Christopher lashed out with a vicious, well-aimed kick. 'And if you'd cared more about Dad, he wouldn't have needed to go off with some other woman. It's all your fault.'

Angela's face turned white. 'Christopher!'

'Oh, shut up, all of you!' cried Victoria. 'Can't you see that none of this is helping? The simple truth is that Dad no longer loves Mum, and no matter how much she or we pretend otherwise, he's not coming back. He loves someone else and all we can do is accept that and get on with it.' Her voice wavered, and she added, 'Painful as it may be.'

'Nice one, Victoria, that really hit the spot,' muttered Henry when Angela had slowly risen from her chair and walked out of the room. 'I suppose, and as I'm the only one here with a sensible and sympathetic thought in his head, I'd better go and make sure Mum's all right.'

'Stay where you are,' instructed Richard, scarcely able to keep his fists from pounding the table. '*I* will go and see how your mother is, but not before I've said this.' He folded his napkin, placed it neatly on his side-plate. 'While I have to take full responsibility for what I've done to your mother, I will not,' he looked around the table, 'I repeat, I *will not* tolerate any one of you speaking to her like that. None of this is her fault. Do you understand that? Christopher?'

Christopher chewed on his lip and nodded.

'What's more,' Richard continued, his voice still low and severe, 'Victoria was correct when she described the situation I've created as being painful. It is, and will remain so for some time yet. We need to help each other, not argue and dish out blame that isn't deserved.' He rose to his feet. 'Now, while I go to your mother, I suggest you do your part by clearing away the lunch things.'

He found Angela upstairs in what had been their bedroom. She was on the bed, sobbing, her face turned into the pillow, her knees drawn up to her chest. 'Leave me alone,' she said. 'Go back to the woman who means so much to you.'

He bent down and offered her a tissue from the box on the bedside table. She ignored it, kept her face turned away from him.

'Shall I bring you up a cup of tea?'

'No.'

'What can I do to help?'

'Please, just leave me alone.'

'There must be something I can do.'

She turned over and looked at him through swollen, tear-filled eyes. 'There's nothing. Can't you see you're doing more harm than good by being here? Haven't you humiliated me enough? Go, Richard. *Go!*'

He was so upset that he had to stop the car on the way back to Dulcie's. He sat motionless for a full ten minutes, overwhelmed by the icy chill of being cut off from his children.

58

While Nathan checked Ceefax to see if Lois and Barnaby's flight was still on time, Beth fiddled with the vase of tulips she'd spent the last ten minutes arranging. She was convinced that their presence at Marsh House when Lois and Barnaby arrived home would not be met with the forgiving acceptance Barnaby was hoping for. She hated the thought that Lois might turn on him after all he'd done: 'How could you be so devious? I told you I never wanted to speak to them again.'

Originally Barnaby had wanted Beth and Nathan to meet them at the airport but – imagining the drive home with a poker-faced Lois sitting in the back of the car – Beth had suggested that it might be better for them to come home in a taxi and be greeted with a warm house, a cup of tea and a piece of cake. 'Just as you think best,' Barnaby had conceded. 'I'll trust your judgement in the matter. Women usually know what's what.'

Smiling at this typically old-fashioned remark of Barnaby's, Beth thought that if she really knew what was best, she would have taken hold of Lois a long time ago and shaken her out of her refusal to leave them all, Adam included, in peace.

When they heard the sound of a car at the front of the house, Beth gripped Nathan's hand. 'Now, remember, we're doing this for Barnaby.'

'No, Mum, we're doing this for *all* of us.'

They stood in the hall, listened to car doors being opened and shut and luggage hauled out of the boot. Only when they heard the taxi driving away did Beth steel herself to open the door. Smile fixed firmly in place, she said, 'Hello there, you two, welcome home.'

To her relief there was no hostility in Lois's face, just confusion, followed swiftly by alarm. 'Beth, what are you doing here? And you too, Nathan? There's nothing wrong with the house, is there? Oh, please don't say we've been broken into.'

Barnaby cleared his throat. 'Beth and Nathan have been keeping an eye on things, Lois, while we've been away. At my instruction, I might add.'

Frightened of what Lois's next words might be, Beth reached for one of her bags, and handed it to Nathan. 'Everything's absolutely fine with the house. The kettle's on and I've taken the liberty of turning up the heating for you. After the lovely hot weather you've been enjoying, I thought you'd need to acclimatise slowly. The weather has been quite warm just recently, but the evenings are still on the chilly side.' Beth could hear herself talking too much and too fast but, unable to stop the nervous flow, she carried on while she ushered Lois and Barnaby inside, telling them where she'd put the enormous pile of mail, that the milkman was due to come first thing in the morning and that they'd missed nothing on television. 'Only repeats,' she informed them, 'and an excess of cookery and gardening programmes.' On catching a bemused look from Nathan that told her to calm down, she finally drew breath. 'Tell you what, I'll stop fussing, make the tea and let you settle in.'

She beetled off to the kitchen. She was just pouring boiling water into the teapot when she heard footsteps behind her.

Lois.

She put the lid on the pot and turned round. 'You look fantastic, Lois,' she said, speaking the truth. 'I've never seen you so tanned. And you've had your hair done. Did you have it cut on the ship? It looks great. Very elegant.' When Lois still didn't say anything, Beth gave in, her heart sinking fast. 'Please don't be cross with Barnaby. He thought he was doing the right thing, that this would help. If you'd rather we left, just say the word.' Beyond the kitchen, and out in the hall, Beth could hear Nathan offering to carry the heavy luggage upstairs. Oh, how she wished she could change places with her son, and not be here, face to face with Lois, who, as she stood with her hands clasped in front of her, was giving no indication as to how she was going to retaliate to the supreme act of meddling that had gone on behind her back.

Beth was just about to apologise again, when Lois raised a hand. 'It's all right, Beth. It's me who should be making the apologies. I'm sorry, so very sorry. I don't deserve your forgiveness, not when I've behaved so badly, but please, if you could find it in your heart to . . .' She trailed off.

'Oh, Lois, there's nothing to forgive. Really there isn't.'

But Lois disagreed and, with great stoicism, she met Beth's eye. 'I've given the matter a lot of thought these last few weeks and I'm left with the conclusion that I could have treated you and Nathan a lot better. And I'm not just talking about my refusal to see or speak to you since Christmas. It . . . it goes a long way back.'

Beth knew that this conversation was costing Lois dear and, acting on impulse, she put her arms round her. It was only a brief embrace for Lois was not a demonstrative woman – she considered hugs an emotional extravagance. She patted Beth's shoulder. 'Perhaps we could have a proper talk some time.'

The next day Lois came to the flat. It was Saturday: Nathan was out with Jaz, Billy and Vicki, and Beth had a good feeling about the outcome of her mother-in-law's visit.

They sat at the kitchen table, sunshine streaming in through the windows, catching on the jug of daffodils on the sill and lighting the room with a golden warmth. The preliminaries had been dealt with – a pot of tea stood between them, as well as a plate of expensive all-butter cookies that Lois had brought with her: she never had been able to turn up empty-handed, it simply wasn't in her nature.

'Beth,' she began, 'you've been a part of my life for more than twenty years, and yet, in all that time, I've seldom been truly honest with you.'

This didn't come as a shock to Beth: she knew that when Adam had first introduced her to his parents, Lois had not been overwhelmed by her son's choice of girlfriend. Beth had always suspected that she had wanted someone a little more top-drawer as a daughter-in-law; a younger version of Lois, perhaps. In those far-off days, Beth had been a carefree and independent young woman who regularly threw caution to the wind, who had lived her life as she wanted to. As students, she and Simone had thought nothing of throwing a handful of clothes into their backpacks to go island-hopping round Greece for an entire summer.

'You see, Beth,' Lois pressed on, a finger playing with the biscuit crumbs in front of her, 'I'm not one of those people who would survive on their own. You might find this hard to believe, but I've always admired you. You coped so well with Adam's death. Alone, and with a young son to bring up, you stood there as solid as a rock. While I floundered hopelessly. I almost hated you for that. I even tried to convince myself that you couldn't have loved Adam, or how else could you have managed without him?'

'It always felt the other way around to me,' murmured Beth. 'You seemed so strong. So in charge.'

'I shut down, Beth. I closed off my emotions. Whereas you, you didn't hide your grief. To me, that showed real strength. And I'm sorry to say I despised you for it.'

'But I only kept the show going because of Nathan. And because of your and Barnaby's help. I felt I owed it to the three of you. And, of course, there was Adam. It was as if I had to keep going for his sake.'

Lois looked up. 'Yes, there was always Adam, wasn't there?'

'That's been the problem, Lois. He's haunted us all these years. For too long. We can't go on living in the past. It's not fair to any of us. Especially not Nathan.'

'I know, and I'm truly sorry that poor Nathan has suffered as he has. I had no idea of the harm I was doing to him. But, please, let me finish saying why I admired you so much for coping on your own. You see, I'm frightened of being alone, of losing those I care for most. If anything happened to Barnaby, or if he left me, I don't know what I'd do. And I know what you're thinking: why do I give him such a hard time if that's the case? It's my way of trying to prove to myself that I don't need him as much as I do.'

'So when you lost Adam ... when he killed himself,' Beth said gently, 'you were confronted with one of your worst fears?'

'Yes. I couldn't accept the way he'd died. How could he have taken his own life when he was surrounded by people who loved him? How could he possibly want to leave you and Nathan? And his own mother. I don't think I'll ever understand why he did that.'

'For what it's worth, I don't think I will either. I've made myself accept that he simply wasn't the Adam we all knew and loved on the night he died. Perhaps the plain truth is that we never truly know another person. He hid his unhappiness well ... just as we all do,' she added.

'But, Beth, it was only money he'd lost. A stupid investment that had gone wrong.'

'It was pride he lost too. He'd borrowed extensively to make that investment and he couldn't face the fallout.'

Lois's shoulders sagged. 'He could have come to us. We would have helped. He only had to say. We would have done what we could.'

'He chose not to.'

Lois frowned. 'Doesn't that ever make you angry? That he deliberately made the wrong choice?'

'It used to. Now I'm more concerned with making the right choices for myself. And for Nathan. Of course, these days, he's making his own.'

They both fell silent, until Lois said, 'Aren't you frightened of being alone when Nathan leaves home?'

'I was. But now I'm just beginning to discover the wonderful opportunities that await me. What's more, I've come to the conclusion that I deserve a little fun.'

Lois sighed. 'I wish I had half your pluck.'

'But you do, Lois. You just haven't got round to using it.'

'Maybe you're right. All I'm sure of now is that I've lived in a state of fear for too long. When Adam died I was terrified I'd lose you and Nathan as well. That's why I tried to keep things as they were, making sure you stayed close to me. I did everything I could to make you believe you didn't need anyone else.'

'Oh, Lois, a caged bird thinks of nothing but flying away.'

Lois nodded. 'I dreaded the day you'd fall in love with another man and not need Barnaby and me any more. I was terrified of losing our only grandson. Watching Nathan grow up was almost like having Adam all over again. The most precious gift I had been given.' She wiped away a tear and Beth reached out a hand to her.

After a minute's silence, Lois said, 'Goodness, you must be wondering what's brought this on.'

As she topped up their cups, Beth said, 'I'm assuming it has something to do with Barnaby.'

For the first time since she had arrived, Lois's expression relaxed. 'When he wants to be, Barnaby can be quite an adversary. Beneath that gentlemanly exterior he can be as cunning as a wily old fox.' For a moment, staring down at her wedding ring, she was lost in her thoughts. Then: 'One night when we were away, we were sitting on the veranda of our cabin watching the sun go down and I suddenly realised I was happy. And happier than I could remember being in a long time.' She smiled unexpectedly, the tightness gone from her face. She looked almost young. 'And that was when Barnaby took advantage of me.' She laughed. 'As a result of too much of the high-life in its liquid form, I might add. He told me in no uncertain terms that if I didn't apologise to you and Nathan when we arrived home, I would lose you both for ever. He also said he would never forgive me if that were to happen. He didn't say as much but it was implicit in his tone, that if I didn't do as he wanted, I might lose him too.'

Beth was shocked. Who would have thought he had the nerve? Three cheers for good old Barnaby.

That evening, when Nathan came home, Beth told him about her conversation with Lois. 'I don't think we should hold out for a miraculous change in your grandmother,' she concluded, 'not right away, but let's do all we can to help this dramatic change of heart. By the way, I've invited them to spend Easter Sunday with us. Is that okay with you?'

'Fine. But won't you be busy preparing yourself to meet the Chosen One?'

She blushed – and it wasn't a faint glow in her cheeks, but a full unexpurgated redness that covered her, or so it felt, from head to toe.

He laughed. 'It's okay, Ma, you're allowed to slap me for my impudence, but only if you can catch me.' Grinning, he dodged out of her reach and went chortling off to his bedroom, leaving her to squirm alone.

The Chosen One, indeed!

That was how Nathan now referred to Ewan, and as the day of the writers' conference drew near, her son had upped the pace of his teasing. 'How long till D-Day?' he'd joked at breakfast that morning. D-Day, to give it its full title, as dubbed by Nathan, was Dénouement Day – the final outcome – the day on which she would meet Ewan.

'I think you might be getting carried away, Nathan,' she'd responded mildly, hiding her face behind the packet of Special K. 'Perhaps your own budding romance with Jaz is getting the better of you.'

Never missing a beat, he'd pulled aside the cereal packet and said, 'In your dreams, Ma.'

The writers' conference was the day after Easter Monday, hence Nathan's comment about her being too busy to cook for Lois and Barnaby. Apart from Victor, who was still in hospital but making a surprisingly good recovery, everyone in the group was going, although only for the first three days of the week-long course – Jaz couldn't spare any more time away from home as she had exams to face at the start of the summer term, and Jack hadn't wanted to use up too much of his valuable holiday entitlement. He'd kindly offered to drive, which had come as a relief to Beth – her car had been playing up recently and she hadn't relished the idea of it breaking down. The only aspect of going away that she didn't like was that Nathan would be on his own. It was silly, but she hadn't left him alone for any length of time before, and while she trusted him she felt guilty leaving him on his own to revise for his exams. 'It's fine, Mum,' he'd said, when she'd started backing out of the trip, 'I'll get far more done without you here.' He'd also accused her of trying to find an escape route. 'It's too late now to use guilt as a means to avoid the Chosen One.'

He was right, of course. She *was* suffering momentary attacks of cold feet. What if she didn't like Ewan? What if he had bad breath? What if he smoked – a habit she abhorred? She had confessed to Dulcie about him – after last week's group meeting, which they'd held at Victor's bedside. Dulcie had said, 'If you don't like him, that's an end to it. But if there's more chance of the opposite happening, then it would be a lost opportunity, wouldn't it? You'd always wonder how things might have turned out if you'd only had the courage to meet him.'

Now that Richard had moved in with Dulcie, Beth was inclined to think that her advice came straight from the heart.

Victor was looking forward to something, which he couldn't remember having done in a long, long time. The last time it had happened was when he'd sent some chapters of *Star City* to a publisher in London. He had walked home from the post office as if on air. It had been one of the most exciting moments of his life, knowing that soon his dream would come true: he would be a published author.

But once more his moment of acceptance had been denied him. He'd waited days, then weeks without hearing anything, until finally he couldn't stand another day of not knowing. During his lunch break at work he had telephoned the publisher, only to be told that his manuscript had not yet been read. Another month came and went, and finally a letter arrived telling him that the editor wished him luck elsewhere with his manuscript. Luck! It wasn't luck he required, it was recognition, acknowledgement of his talent. But it was perhaps what he should have expected. Life had never played fair with him.

However, that was behind him now. As were the days of mourning his manuscript. Now he was really on to something. That extraordinary girl, Jaz, had set him on this track. 'I've brought you something else to read,' she'd said. 'I thought it would cheer you up.'

He'd taken the book from her reluctantly and read its title. 'But it's for children,' he'd said.

'Get real, Victor. Harry Potter's for everyone – he cuts across all boundaries. That's half his charm. I bet you a shiny pound that when I see you next you'll have finished the book, and if you're really nice to me, I'll bring in the next in the series.'

To his astonishment she'd been right. He'd read *Harry Potter and the Philosopher's Stone* in a day, finding it both gripping and strangely comforting. He'd scrounged a pound from one of the nurses and put it on his bedside locker next to the book ready for when she next visited.

Smiling, she'd handed over the next instalment.

'Of course, it's nothing but money for old rope,' he'd said. 'Simple enough idea that anyone could have dreamed up.'

She'd nodded and agreed. 'It's always the simplest ideas that are the best. Now, I can't stop long today, I promised Mum I'd take care of the twins so that she can run Tamzin and Lulu to their gymnastics class.'

'Oh,' he'd said, trying not to show his disappointment. He never told her as much but he looked forward to her visits and her bulletins on the world outside the walls of the hospital. 'How is your mother?'

'Pretty good, considering she's recently given birth and then discovered Dad tried to cover up the burglary and that everything worth stealing had gone. But she's forgiven him, and that's cool.'

The day after that he'd had the surprise of being visited by Hidden Talents *en masse*. 'We thought we'd hold the meeting here with you tonight,' Jaz had told him.

'Is that allowed?' he'd asked doubtfully, casting his eyes in the direction of a nearby nurse – she was the bossy one and he was sure she took pleasure in making him cry out when she changed his dressings.

'We checked with the top brass,' said Jack, 'and were told that, so long as we keep the noise down, nobody will mind.'

'A pity you didn't think to check with me first,' he'd said peevishly. He didn't like it when people got above themselves and started organising him.

'Quit whingeing, Victor,' snapped Jaz, 'or I'll cut off your Harry Potter supply, and where will you be then? Trawling the streets for a new dealer.'

As it turned out, he'd enjoyed the group being with him. Not that he'd said anything, of course. Give that Dulcie woman too much praise and it would go straight to her head. The only downside to their visit was that they told him about the writers' conference they were all attending. He'd felt left out.

Jaz had promised to bring in the third Potter book for him, and he'd decided to tell her this evening when she visited that his next novel was going to be something along similar lines. Obviously his would be better, and with less emphasis on the gimmickry and clever names, but it would appeal to children and adults. To get started, he needed Jaz to buy him a new A4 pad and a proper fountain pen. He was able now to sit up for longer periods and writing would kill the hours of boredom he had to endure.

But as the clock in the ward ticked away that evening's visiting session and there was no sign of Jaz, all the anticipatory excitement he'd been experiencing slowly drained away. She wasn't coming. She'd let him down. Looking about the ward, he saw that everyone else had a visitor. He was the only one with an empty chair beside his bed. Feeling depressed and very alone, he closed his eyes, pretending to anyone who might glance his way that he was asleep and in no need of a visitor.

Minutes passed.

'Sleeping on the job again, Victor?'

He recognised the voice instantly. He opened his eyes. 'You're late.'

'And you're a miserable old devil, but I try not to let that get in the way of our special time together.'

He smiled. 'Have you brought me the next book?'

'Would I ever let you down, Victor?'

'Everyone else has. Why should you be any different?'

'First, I *am* different. That's why I go to all the trouble to visit you and deny myself an evening with my gorgeous boyfriend. And second, you can switch off the self-pity tap. Any more of that and I'll spill the beans about what happens in *The Prisoner of Azkaban* and spoil the ending for you. Deal?'

Later, when she was leaving, he asked her why she kept coming to see him.

She slung her small leather knapsack over her shoulder. 'Didn't I tell you? It's my care-in-the-community work. I'll get a nice gold badge to wear when I've got you back on your feet. See you.'

He watched her go. What *was* in it for her? Certainly not a gold badge.

59

The Rafferty builders had finished work on Jack's flat, and now that it was just how he'd wanted it, he felt a growing desire to tidy up the loose ends of his life. This Easter Sunday was destined to be a turning point, and if Christ's Resurrection was to be taken as a symbol of new life, then it was apposite that today he should do his damnedest to put the past behind him.

An excited cry from Lucy, who had her nose pressed to the window, made him look up from the garlic he was crushing. 'Dad, they're here!'

He washed his hands quickly and called through to Amber, who was in the bedroom listening to a CD by a bunch of teenage boys he'd never heard of – that was before she had first started playing it at eight o'clock last night. Sixteen hours on he was practically word perfect on the title track, which had been given full-volume treatment every time it came round. Upstairs, Beth and Nathan, who had their own guests coming for Sunday lunch, were probably singing along too.

First to arrive was Julie with Desmond Junior who, on seeing Jack, grinned from his car seat, reached for a foot and proudly pulled off his sock. He stuffed it into his gummy mouth and gurgled, as if to say, '*Ta-daa!* And my next trick will be to swallow my Osh Kosh dungarees.'

Des brought up the rear with what looked like enough survival gear to aid a party of ten to the top of Mount Kilimanjaro. 'It's his travel cot and duvet, and a small collection of toys,' Des explained, when the door had been closed. 'Oh, yes, and his high chair.'

'Don't say you've forgotten his changing mat and bag,' complained Julie.

Des checked out the contents of his arms, his back and his shoulders. 'No, my sweet, I think that's here somewhere. Hello, girls, long time no see.'

In the crowded hall, Amber and Lucy stepped forward, their interest not in Des and Julie but in the smiling Desmond Junior, whom they'd not met before. 'Look, Dad.' Lucy had been waiting particularly anxiously for his arrival and was itching to play with a real baby. 'He's eating his sock.'

Julie clicked her tongue. 'Anyone would think we didn't feed him, the way he carries on. Do you want to help me take him through to the sitting room, Lucy?'

'Hey,' said Des, standing in the middle of the large room and giving it a professional once-over, 'this is great. Must make the hassle with those cowboy builders seem almost worth it.'

'Oh, don't remind me. Bodge It and Run will be marked on my psyche for the rest of my life.' He helped relieve Des of his load. 'Now who's for a drink?'

'I drew the short straw today, so I'll have some orange juice, please,' said Julie.

'Des?'

'Any beer on offer?'

'Need you ask?'

Leaving Amber and Lucy to watch over Desmond Junior, Des and Julie followed Jack to the far end of the L-shaped room and into the kitchen. 'Now, this I do approve of,' observed Julie. She ran her hand over the polished granite work surface, then opened one of the cream-painted cupboards to inspect the racks and shelves. 'I hope you're taking note, Des, because when we get round to gutting our pathetic excuse for a kitchen, this is just the kind of design I'd like.'

'Damn you, Jack,' Des smiled, 'why do you have to have such good taste? More to the point, how in hell did you manage to get it done so quickly? I thought these jobs dragged on for months.'

'You know the old maxim,' Jack said, as he poured their drinks, 'it's not what you know, it's *who* you know. Rafferty and Sons were excellent, and the kitchen fitter they recommended rated this as a piddling little job, compared to the large-scale kitchens he usually works on. I guess I was lucky.' He almost added, 'For once,' but didn't. During the last week, he'd come to the conclusion that he was luckier than he'd ever realised. He had two beautiful daughters, a relatively secure job, a great roof over his head, and a circle of friends that now included those who shared his passion for writing. The members of Hidden Talents were of varied ages and backgrounds, with little else apparently in common, but the bond that held them together was strong, and one way or another they had all been looking out for each other this last month or so. He handed round the drinks. 'If it doesn't sound too corny or pretentious,' he said, 'I'd like to propose a toast.'

Des raised his eyebrows. 'Oh, yes? That sounds ominous.'

'I finished *Friends and Family* last night.'

'Come again?'

He smiled, enjoying the look on his friends' faces. No one outside Hidden Talents knew about his writing. 'I've written a book.'

Des looked incredulous. '*A book?*'

'Yes, one of those strange objects with rows of letters covering the pages. I know you're not the most literate of men, Des, but you must have come across one at some time.'

'Ha, ha, *ha*. How long has this been going on?'

'Since last October.'

'But you never said anything.'

'Sorry, Julie. Don't be offended, it wasn't personal.' He frowned. 'Or maybe that's the point. I've found the whole exercise extremely personal, and I couldn't bring myself to tell anyone who might think I was crazy for doing it. I mean, whoever heard of an estate agent having the wit to write a book?'

Julie laughed. 'Certainly I couldn't imagine the one I'm married to having the wit.'

'Hey, what is this? Gang Up On Poor Old Des Day?'

'Ah, is diddums feeling got at?' She pressed a kiss on his cheek, and got one in return.

'No more than usual.' Then Des turned back to Jack and, with an arm round his wife, he said, 'So, what's the book about? Is it a saucy exposé of the world of estate agents? Any car chases in it?'

'Ignore him, Jack, he's a Philistine. Who's it aimed at? You must have an audience in mind.'

He thought about this. At length he said, 'People like us,' then added, 'With the exception of Des, perhaps,' and grinned.

'On what grounds am I being excluded?'

Both Jack and Julie laughed. 'Being a nincompoop,' said Julie.

He tipped his nose in the air. 'In that case I'm taking my beer and going to mix with more congenial company.'

They watched him join the children, getting down on the floor and letting his small son out of his seat. A moment passed and Jack said, 'Thanks for burying the hatchet, Julie. I really appreciate it.'

She gave him a hard stare. 'There wasn't ever a hatchet. It would never have come to anything half so drastic.'

'But I upset you over Clare, and I'm sorry for that.'

'That's water under the bridge now. Clare is only too happy with the way things are currently shaping up.'

'Yes, I'm intrigued to meet the new man in her life.'

Less than five minutes later, his curiosity was satisfied when the sound of the doorbell heralded the arrival of Clare and Colin. Inviting Clare for lunch had been, he liked to think, the first step on the road to his very own *glasnost*. He had expected her to turn down his offer, and he would never know if she had accepted just so that she could flaunt Colin – *See, now I'm with a man who really cares about me.* But whatever her motive for coming, he knew that he had done the right thing in contacting her. 'Of course you can bring him,' he'd said, when she'd mentioned a new boyfriend. 'The more the merrier.'

Colin, an accountant, had a good sense of humour, and before long they were having a classic battle of estate agents' versus accountants' jokes. 'Right, then,' said Des, rolling up his sleeves and getting into the swing of it. 'Why were estate agents invented?'

'Don't know. Why?'

'To give accountants someone to look up to!'

They all laughed, except Lucy, who said, 'I don't understand any of your jokes. I think Desmond is much funnier than any of you.'

'Would that be Desmond Junior or his brilliant father?' asked Des.

'Don't ask the question if you don't want the honest answer,' warned Jack. 'Now, who's for dessert? We have a choice of M&S's finest crème brûlée or their equally fine lemon tart.' He started to gather the plates and dishes from his end of the table, noting that Amber had eaten more than she had of late. He took it as an encouraging sign.

Clare passed him her plate. 'Need a hand?'

He sensed that she wanted to be alone with him and, knowing that this would be their only opportunity, he said yes. Between them they cleared the table and took everything through to the kitchen. 'I love the flat, Jack,' she said. 'You've put a lot of thought into it.'

He stopped what he was doing. 'Perhaps if I'd put as much thought into what I was doing with you, I wouldn't have hurt you so badly.'

'It works both ways. If I hadn't been in such a hurry I wouldn't have scared you off so effectively. I think we can safely say it was too much too soon for both of us.'

'Does that make us friends now?'

'I'd like to think so.'

'That's good. I'm pleased.' He carried on stacking the dishwasher. 'Colin seems a really nice bloke. If it's what you want, I hope it lasts between the two of you.'

From where she was standing, by the fridge, she looked towards the table, to where Colin was chatting to Amber and making a rabbit out of a paper napkin for her. 'He is. He's a lovely man. More importantly, he's not divorced.'

'So, no baggage?'

'Travelling light, you could say.'

'Even better.' He wanted to offer her a word of caution – 'Don't rush him, Clare, let things take their natural course' – but he knew it wasn't his place. Only a very close friend like Julie could offer such advice.

That evening, a few hours after the lunch party eventually broke up, Jack drove the girls home to Prestbury. 'That was nice today, Daddy,' Lucy said, from the back of the car. 'Can we see Des and Julie again?'

'I don't see why not.'

'When I was a baby, did I dribble like Desmond and blow bubbles with it?'

'Oh, all the time.'

Sitting in the front seat, Amber wrinkled her nose. 'That's disgusting.'

'But it's nothing compared to what you did as a baby.'

She shuddered. 'I don't want to know.'

'Oh, go on Daddy, tell us. How horrible was Amber when she was little?'
Jack laughed. 'I didn't say your sister was horrible.'
'I bet she was.'
'Bet I wasn't.'
'You were both as cute as buttons, and that's an end to it.'
They drove on, Lucy humming to herself and Amber perfectly still, her
eyes closed.
'Have you really written a book, Dad?'
He looked at Lucy in the rear-view mirror. 'Yes, Luce, I have.'
'Is it for children?'
'No. Grown-ups.'
'Is it good?'
He smiled. 'I don't know. I'm not really the right person to ask.'
'Yes, you are, you wrote it.' This was from Amber: her eyes were open
now.
'It doesn't work like that, sweetheart.'
She didn't look as if she agreed with him. 'What's it about?'
'A family,' he said, hoping to leave it at that. He didn't feel entirely
comfortable about telling the girls any more. But children have an in-built
knack for knowing when a parent is hedging.
'And?' prompted Amber.
Keeping his eyes on the road, he said, 'It's about a family who, one
minute, is happy, but then everything starts to go wrong and . . . and the
parents split up because—'
'Is it about us?' interrupted Lucy.
'In some ways, yes, but in other ways, no.'
'What happens in the end?' Amber's voice was cool. 'Do the parents get
back together?'
'No. But they promise each other never to do anything that would hurt
their children.'
'And do they keep their promises?'
'In the end, yes.'

60

'There's no need for you all to see me off,' Jaz said, coming down the stairs with a heavy bag.

When she reached the bottom step her father took it from her and plonked it by the front door. 'I agree,' he said, 'absolutely no need to do anything half so daft, but we'll do it all the same, if that's okay with you, you silly eejit.'

She smiled, first at him, then at her mother, who asked, 'You've got everything you need, haven't you? Did you find your favourite black jeans? I put them on your bed.'

'Yes, Mum. Thanks.'

'And you have enough money?'

'Plenty. Dad's seen to that. Now, will you all stop fussing? I'm only away for a few days.'

Phin gave her a punch on the shoulder. 'Yeah, but who will we spat with while you're gone?'

She gave him a playful kick in return. 'You won't have time for that, now that you're occupied with the lovely Nurse Della. How long have you been going out with her? If it's more than a week, it must be a record. In fact, if you're still seeing her when I come home, I'll know that it's serious and I'll have to help Mum find a mother-of-the-groom outfit.'

Phin rolled his eyes at her and was about to offer a suitable riposte when they heard a car pull into the drive.

'Okay, stand aside, everyone, that's my ride out of here.'

If she had thought she would be able to sneak off without any further embarrassment, she had miscalculated the new mood of family-together-ness her father had been so keen to foster since the arrival of the twins – they had been named Declan (Tamzin and Lulu were delighted with that as they were mad about Ant and Dec) and Amelia Jane. 'How come the boys get the Irish names and we girls don't?' Jaz had asked her father.

'Because that's the way the cookie has crumbled,' he'd replied. 'Any complaints?'

'None at all,' she'd said. 'I'm just relieved I didn't end up as Bernadette or with something I couldn't pronounce or spell.'

Jack, Beth and Dulcie were coming towards the house when Jaz broke free of her father's hug and escaped outside. While she added her bag to the luggage already in the boot of Jack's car, a round of hand-shaking ensued.

'Don't worry, Mr and Mrs Rafferty,' Beth was saying, 'we'll take good care of your daughter.' Jaz noticed that her brothers were talking to Jack, a little apart from the rest of the group. She wouldn't put it past them to bribe him to keep an eye on her. She crept up behind them, pretending to listen to Dulcie as she congratulated her mother on the twins' birth, and tuned into what her brothers were saying. None of it made any sense: Jack was laughing and saying something about treating the whole thing as a joke, that maybe one day he would immortalise the incident in a book. 'All the same,' muttered Phin, his face oddly serious, 'fair play to you for taking it so well. The flat okay?'

'It's great. I wish I'd come to Rafferty's in the first place.'

'You'll know another time. And if we hadn't been tied up with a job in Crewe, we'd have done the work ourselves. Anything else you need doing, just give us a bell. It's the least we could do.'

... the least we could do. Jaz took this as positive proof that something was going on. And what on earth had Jack taken so well? Over the coming days in Harrogate she planned to get to the bottom of it.

The mood in the car as they headed towards Harrogate reminded Dulcie of long-ago school trips. The excitement and anticipation were the same, and as she twisted round to offer a bag of Murray Mints to Beth and Jaz in the back, she felt that all that was missing from their excursion was a hearty rendition of 'One Man Went to Mow'.

The traffic on the M62 was light, and Jack was an able driver who drove smoothly and confidently; he wasn't one of those aggressive types who swoop in close to the car in front and jab at the brakes every twenty seconds. Feeling relaxed, and enjoying the music that was playing on the radio, she closed her eyes and gave in to her tiredness.

Richard had been tense all last night, and at half past three they had given up trying to sleep and had gone downstairs for some tea. With his head in his hands, he had sat at the kitchen table and groaned. 'My children hate me,' he said, despairingly, 'and I can't see them ever changing their minds.'

'Give it time,' she had said soothingly, hating to see him so wretched. 'It's too soon to make judgements like that. You mustn't be so hard on yourself. Be patient with them. Let them be angry for a while, and eventually it'll pass. They'll come round when they're ready. They just need time to adjust.'

And wasn't that exactly what she was doing with her own daughter? The angry telephone calls had stopped, and instead there was now a stony silence: Kate was refusing to speak to her, and it hurt. Andrew had tried talking to Kate, but she was almost as angry with him as she was with Dulcie.

Half an hour before Jack had come for her that morning, Richard had left for work, his face ashen from lack of sleep and worry. 'Why don't you take the day off?' she'd said, concerned how drained he looked.

'I can't,' he said. 'I have two important meetings to chair.'

She had kissed him goodbye and warned him not to overdo it while she was away.

'Early to bed every night,' he'd said, with an attempt at a smile. 'You will ring me this evening, won't you?'

'Of course.'

'And you have the mobile I gave you?'

'Yes. I might even remember how to work it.'

She had watched his car move slowly down the road, already missing him. But she cheered herself with the thought that when she came home she would be greeted not by an empty house, as she was used to, but by the man she loved.

Unlike Dulcie, who was now asleep, Beth was wide awake and fidgety, her mind racing. She couldn't settle with the book she'd brought for the journey and she certainly couldn't sleep. The prospect of meeting Ewan was tipping her over the edge of reason. She had fully intended to go to bed early last night but she'd been up until nearly two, dithering over what clothes to pack. Nathan, usually so helpful, had made things worse by appearing in her bedroom with a silly smirk on his face as she refolded – for the umpteenth time – her smartest pair of jeans. 'Make one single remark about the Chosen One and D-Day,' she'd warned him, 'and I'll never let you use the car again.'

'Cool it, Ma. I only came to see if there was anything I could do to help. Do you think that top's a good idea?'

She looked at the top she'd been about to add to the bag. It was one of her favourites: a rare item in her wardrobe that she thought flattered her figure – it was a hug-tight fit. 'What's wrong with it?' she asked, holding it up for closer inspection.

He sucked in his breath. 'You don't think it's a touch risqué for a first date? You don't want to give the wrong signals by wearing something too revealing.'

'*Out!*' she cried. He was having her on. 'Go to bed, you tiresome boy.'

When she had called a halt to the dithering and the last item of clothing was neatly folded inside the bag, she sneaked back to the kitchen – she didn't want Nathan to know what she was doing – and quietly switched on her computer. Ewan had promised to send her one last message before they met in Yorkshire. She had checked earlier, before the ten o'clock news, but there hadn't been a word from him.

Now there was.

Hi Beth,
    No time to chat for long – so much to do, so little time,

blah-de-blah.

Glad to hear things have been resolved between you and the in-laws. Barnaby sounds like a veritable saint on wheels. Thank goodness he's so fond of you and Nathan. And you mustn't worry about leaving Nathan on his own to do his revision – from what you've told me of him, he sounds motivated enough to get the work done.

And here's me telling you not to worry, when I'm down to the very beds of my nails at the thought of meeting you.

What if she doesn't like the colour of the anorak I've bought specially for the occasion?

What if she susses I'm wearing a syrup fig?

And, oh, I hardly dare write this for fear of instant rejection, but what if she doesn't go for a man who likes to keep his small change in a handy little purse?

These questions, and many more, have kept me awake at night over Easter. All I ask of you, Bethany, is to be gentle with me. I'm a sensitive soul who cries every time the Andrex puppy on the telly is replaced with a new one. Where do all those cute superfluous puppies end up? Are they flushed away with all that loo paper? Ah, 'tis a cruel world out there.

But I digress. Tomorrow dawns. I aim to arrive at Norton Hall around supper-time – save me a scrap or two of stale bread and gruel, won't you?

Looking forward (it goes without saying, but feel it would be an appalling omission if I didn't) to meeting you. Travel safely.

All best,

Ewan X

PS You'll recognise me by the aforementioned anorak.

PPS On the other hand, it might be better if I look out for you – an attractive blonde woman trying to avoid the furtive gaze of a man playing nervously with the snap-fastener on his faux leather purse . . .

Apart from a brief hitch near Cambridge, where a lorry had jack-knifed, Ewan had had a good run across the A14 to join the M1, and so far the traffic had moved at a steady pace. He was now skirting Leeds and reckoned he'd arrive at Norton Hall earlier than he'd anticipated.

According to the programme of events, Norton Hall had once been a private residence, but since the mid-seventies it had been extended and converted into a conference centre. He'd stayed in many such places over the years, but this one was new to him. He hoped there would be a few basic necessities, such as a decent supply of hot water, edible meals and an electrical system that didn't fail. During the last conference he'd attended there had been a complete power failure and at bedtime everyone had been guided to their rooms by torchlight. Just before they'd been despatched to their rooms, he'd needed to visit the loo. Fumbling in the dark to find the urinal was not an experience he was in a hurry to repeat.

The organisers of the Harrogate conference boasted that Norton Hall had a swimming-pool, a croquet lawn and two tennis courts as well as a large canteen, a bar, a central conference hall that seated four hundred, a library, and a small computer room. There were half a dozen rooms for discussion groups and workshops, two lounge areas, and even the ruins of a small chapel in the grounds, which, so the author of the programme declared, were 'of an extensive nature and worthy of a constitutional stroll'. The accommodation was situated in a modern two-storey block adjacent to the original house and, while basic (in the author's opinion), was warm and clean, and came with tea- and coffee-making facilities.

What more could anyone want?

An *en suite* bathroom would be nice, thought Ewan, as he overtook a people-carrier. A power shower and a mini-bar bursting with salted cashew nuts wouldn't go amiss either.

He cruised along at a blistering speed for the next mile or two, then eased off the accelerator when he spotted a police car in the inside lane further up the motorway. All around him the traffic slowed as they played Grandma's Footsteps, trying to slip past the police car without being seen.

The games we play, he thought.

And the game he was playing with Beth, he reminded himself, had every chance of backfiring on him. While he hadn't actually lied to Beth, he had been less than straight with her. He hadn't meant to mislead her for as long as he had, but before he knew it, he had been caught up in a mire of his own making and unable to admit the truth. It seemed easier to wait until they met and she could take the facts at first hand, then decide for herself what she thought of him. And his reasons for his deviousness.

Alice had expressed her opinion in her customary blunt fashion: 'I can't believe you're going through with this crackpot idea,' she'd exploded, when he'd got round to confessing. He'd had her on the phone for nearly an hour last night, listening to her last-ditch attempt to make him see sense.

'Look, Alice,' he'd said, as patiently as he could when she finally allowed him to speak, 'I'm not the innocent schmuck you think I am.'

'Then which schmuck are you?'

'Ho, ho! Now, stop being so bossy and cut your decrepit father a bit of slack.'

'But, Dad, if I don't look out for you, who will?'

He sighed, exasperated. 'Where did I go wrong with you? Did I love you too much when you were growing up? Is that it?'

'Don't try to sidetrack me by getting mushy or I'll think you've really lost it. Now, promise you'll ring me, and if she starts wanting to check your credit rating, get the hell out of there.'

'Yes, Alice. No, Alice. Anything else, Alice?'

'That's it for now, but if something else occurs to me I'll give you a ring.'

'Oh, no, you won't. I'm switching off my mobile, as of now. Goodbye, Alice.'

'But, Dad, that's not fair!'

'Yes, it is. 'Byee.'

He almost missed the sign for Millingthwaite, the village where Norton Hall was, and he had to brake sharply to make the turning. He slowed his speed as he took the narrow lane – it was so tight the hedges almost brushed the sides of his car. He silently chastised the author of the programme of events for not warning conference delegates of this potential hazard.

But a scratched car would probably be the least of his concerns after Beth knew how he'd deceived her.

61

With conference participants having to share bathroom facilities, the accommodation was appropriately segregated: girls at one end of the block, and boys at the other. Wedged between them were two dozen rooms for couples and committee members, along with visiting guest speakers and anyone deemed important enough to warrant their own bathroom. Unless you were a VIP, there was an extra charge for this luxury, as the conference administrator had informed Jack when they arrived to register at the designated meeting point. They were given name badges – 'It's for security,' they were advised. 'We've had problems in the past with strangers wandering in and helping themselves. Make sure you lock your rooms.' It wasn't the most auspicious start, but perhaps a sensible one, and as Jack unpacked his bag, putting the few clothes he'd brought with him into the rickety old wardrobe, which smelt faintly of vanilla, he looked out on to the grounds of Norton Hall.

Some early arrivals were already sitting on the benches dotted around the croquet lawn, others were sprawled on the grass enjoying the afternoon sunshine, and in the shade of a large oak tree, a woman dressed in what looked like a kaftan was sitting cross-legged with her palms extended, as if checking for rain. Dulcie had warned them during the journey that writing courses had a tendency to attract a rich and varied mix. It looked as if she was right.

A knock at the door made him start. He opened it and was confronted with yet more proof of Dulcie's theory. A gangly man in sagging jogging trousers and a T-shirt stood before him. His hair was very grey and tied back into a bushy ponytail. He wore copper bangles on both wrists and around his neck hung a golf-ball-sized crystal on a leather thong. The crowning glory of his attire was a pair of scruffy green slippers; through a hole at the front of one poked a yellowing big-toe nail.

'Hi,' he said. 'Just thought I'd make myself known to you.' He pointed to his name badge, which Jack hadn't noticed until now – it was lost in the Celtic knot design of his T-shirt. 'Zed Wane. I'm in the room next door. This your first time?'

Jack nodded.

'Aha, a Norton Hall virgin. I thought I didn't recognise you. I came last year, and the year before that, so I'm what you might call an old hand. I could show you round, if you like. They'll be serving afternoon tea any minute. But a word to the wise, get there quick or there'll be nothing left. You could come with me now, if you want.'

'Er . . . I'll be along shortly,' Jack said, judging it prudent not to become Zed's best new buddy too soon. 'I want to finish unpacking first. I'll catch up with you later.'

'I'll keep an eye out for you.' His neighbour shuffled away, shoulders hunched, slippers slapping at his heels.

Jack closed the door and wondered if he was going to regret coming.

At three o'clock, as arranged, he knocked on Beth's door. Dulcie and Jaz had got there ahead of him, and after they'd swapped notes on the quality of their accommodation – Dulcie's window wouldn't open and Jaz's bed creaked – they set off for a cup of tea and a slice of cake. It was being served in one of the lounge areas in the main part of the house, and this was reached by a covered walkway that joined the two buildings. They tagged on to the end of a small queue and Jack noticed that Zed was at the front of it: he was loading slabs of fruit cake on to his plate. 'Someone to watch out for,' Jack told the others, in a low voice. He explained about his friendly neighbour.

Beth laughed, but Jaz said, 'You're sure he said his name was Zed? It wasn't Ewan, by any chance, was it?'

'Hey, now you come to mention it, he did say something about a pseudonym.'

'Jack,' warned Dulcie, with a smile, 'Beth's going through enough turmoil as it is. Behave yourself. You too, Jaz.'

A hubbub of voices filled the high-ceilinged room, and it was obvious that many of the delegates knew each other from previous conferences. But unlike Zed, if their dress sense was anything to go by, they gave the impression of being relatively normal. There was a wide range of ages, but Jack reckoned Jaz would win the prize for the youngest participant.

Zed wasn't alone in his eccentricity: grouped around a sofa in the far corner of the room was a noisy crowd of men and women sporting identical black T-shirts with the name Jared Winter emblazoned across them. Jack knew him to be a well-known science-fiction writer. Or was he a fantasy writer? The distinction had always been lost on Jack. He'd never been interested in either genre, especially fantasy – those wacky book covers showing women with unfeasibly large breasts and powerful thighs put him off. Jared Winter was one of the guest speakers at the conference, and Jack decided, from the look of his devotees, that the man was in for some serious hero-worshipping.

He turned to Beth. 'I think I've found Ewan for you.'

'Oh, Lord, have you? Where?'

He inclined his head towards the far corner of the room. 'See the big fella with the mane of black hair and purple-tinted sunglasses? It has to be him.'

Beth dug at him with one of her elbows. 'Not funny, Jack. That's a woman.'

'Good God! Is it?'

At four o'clock they made their way to the main conference hall and listened to the formal introductions made by several committee members. Beth craned her neck to see if she could spot a half-decent-looking man with the name Ewan Jones pinned to his chest. In the end she gave up and concentrated on what she'd come to Norton Hall for. Once the introductions were over, they were given the dos and don'ts of the conference: smoking was allowed out of doors, voices were to be kept down after midnight, high jinks kept to a courteous minimum, and no pestering of guest speakers, editors and agents would be tolerated. Then they were dismissed and the conference got under way.

With her file, borrowed from Nathan, clutched to her chest, Beth set off with the others for a workshop on characterisation. They took their seats – in the back row, as dictated by Jaz – and Beth saw that the session was to be led by a formidable woman with a face plastered in makeup; chunky rings adorned all but one of her fingers. Her name was Dorothy Kendall and she reminded Beth of Fanny Craddock. She was about to whisper this to Jaz, when she realised that the observation would be wasted on someone so young.

The first half of the session flew by, and Nathan's file of A4 paper now contained several pages of useful notes. 'Just goes to show,' she said to Dulcie, when they were given a five-minute break, 'never judge a book by its cover.'

'I know what you mean,' Dulcie said. 'She gave the impression she might horsewhip us if we didn't pay sufficient attention.'

In the second half of the workshop they were paired off and after a ten-minute conversation they had to write a hundred-word description of the other person. 'And don't any of you insult me by going for the obvious,' Dorothy Kendall barked at them, 'such as the colour of hair and eyes. I want you to look out for interesting mannerisms, turns of phrase, and use them to give a fresh, cliché-free character sketch. The writer who comes up with the worst offering has to buy me a drink in the bar tonight.'

Beth concentrated hard, as if her life depended on it: she didn't fancy spending any time alone with the awesome Dorothy Kendall. Later, and relieved to survive the workshop without being humiliated as the class dunce, she slipped out of the room before their teacher changed her mind and hauled her back in for an extra session. 'I had no idea it would be as scary as this,' she said to Jack – Dulcie and Jaz had gone on ahead of them. 'I hope the rest of the course tutors aren't like her.'

'But she got us working, didn't she?'

'But at what cost? I'm exhausted. Thank goodness we're only here for three days.'

'Come on, I'll see if I can rustle up a strengthening cup of hot sweet tea for you.'

'Bugger that! I need something stronger. Lead me to the bar!'

He laughed. 'Beth King, hush your mouth! Whatever would Nathan say? Less than twelve hours away from home and you've turned into a fishwife.'

The bar area was packed. Jack left his file and pen with Beth, and joined the crush of thirsty writers. He eventually surfaced and gave her a tall glass clinking with ice. 'Vodka and tonic,' he said, 'as the lady requested. Any sign of Jaz and Dulcie?'

'No, we seem to have lost them.'

'And there's still no sign of the elusive Ewan Jones?'

'I told you before, he said he wouldn't be here until supper-time.'

Jack glanced at his watch. 'Which is served in just over an hour and a half.'

'Stop it, you're making me nervous.'

The bar was even busier now, and as they were unable to hear each other, Beth suggested they find somewhere quieter. They squeezed through the throng, heading in the direction of the glass-roofed extension and some comfortable chairs. When they were almost there, Jack said, 'You go ahead, I need to make a trip to the little boys' room.' She tucked their files under her arm, took his drink from him and made a beeline for the last unoccupied squashy sofa. She settled into the cushions and waited for Jack. It was a full ten minutes before he returned, and when he did, he was grinning from ear to ear. 'I hardly dare ask what you've been up to in the gents' loo to make you smile like that,' she said.

He sat down next to her, still grinning. 'I've just had the pleasure, as it were, of standing side by side with Felix McCallum.'

'Who?'

'You know – the editor I have an appointment to see tomorrow.'

'The one who's giving you a critique on the chapters of *Friends and Family*?'

'The very man.'

'And?'

'He saw my badge and asked if I was the one who'd sent him the stuff last week about a bloke whose marriage goes belly up.'

'Good with words, is he?'

'Don't nitpick. It's what he said next that's important. He said he hoped I'd brought the rest of the manuscript with me because he was very keen to read it.'

'Jack, that's brilliant. Well done, you!'

Jaz was starving so she was stuffing herself with one of the Mars bars her mother had given her – typical Mum, she'd packed her a supply of goodies just in case the food wasn't up to much. Home seemed a long way away, and it was just as well it was. Jaz was furious with Phin and Jimmy. During the car journey up here, she had asked Jack what he and her brothers had been discussing before they'd set off for Yorkshire. He'd refused to tell her at first, but had then relented, concluding that it didn't matter now.

But it did! She felt so ashamed. How could her brothers have done that to him? She was so furious that she had nearly phoned home from the car, but Jack, Dulcie and Beth had persuaded her not to. 'They were only looking out for you,' Jack had said. 'Leave it be. Besides, you don't want to let anything spoil the next few days.'

She threw the empty Mars bar wrapper into the bin, licked her lips and smiled: her dim-wit brothers had inadvertently given her the means to get Victor's house sorted for him. When she got home she would blackmail them into doing the job; they wouldn't have any choice in the matter. As they had tried to hush up the incident, she knew they didn't want Mum and Dad to find out what they'd done. And rightly so. Dad would be livid that his name had been associated with such low-life behaviour, and Mum, well, if anyone upset her they would have Popeye Rafferty to answer to. Thank you, boys!

She locked her door and went to meet the others in Jack's room. Amazingly, and after a chance meeting in the men's loos, Jack had handed over the manuscript of *Friends and Family* to an editor called Felix McCallum, and they were having a glass of fizzy wine (the best Norton Hall could come up with) before dinner to celebrate.

When they joined the queue for dinner, and were scanning the conference noticeboard for information about tomorrow's activities, Jaz found she had something of her own to celebrate. As a result of Dulcie's encouragement to take advantage of whatever competitions were on offer, she had submitted a short story. To her delight, it had been shortlisted for a prize and the winner was to be announced later in the week – when, unfortunately, they wouldn't be around.

Dinner was surprisingly good – pork in green peppercorn sauce with glazed carrots and creamed potatoes, then lemon cheesecake. When coffee had been served they were told that there would be a fifteen-minute break before the guest speaker took the floor in the main conference hall. The title of Jared Winter's talk, they were told by the committee chairman, was 'The Perception of Honesty in Novel Writing – What You Can and Cannot Get Away With'. From across the dining hall a loud cheer went up from his fans and, as one, they scraped back their chairs and made a noisy exit. 'Wow,' said Jaz, 'they're eager to get front-row seats, aren't they?'

The rest of the audience trickled into the hall more sedately, and once again Jaz insisted they sit in the back row. 'Last thing we want is to be associated with a bunch of crazies. Polo mint, anyone?' She passed the tube to Jack, who passed it to Beth – but just as Beth moved to take it from him, the lights went out, a hush fell on the audience, and the tube dropped to the floor. Beth leaned forward to retrieve it, but the mints had rolled under the seat in front of her. When she had rescued them and had straightened up, everyone was clapping the guest speaker who was making his entrance into the hall. 'Sorry about that,' Beth said to Jack, whose leg she had knocked several times during her scrabbling. She was just about to join in with the applause when she froze. Up on the podium, taking his seat beside the conference chairman, she could see a man wearing a navy blue anorak holding, of all things ... a small purse.

Ewan?

62

'You lied.'

'I'm sorry.'

'But you *lied*. And you did it all the time. Every exchange we had was a sham. You conned me.'

'Are you going to let me try to explain?'

'Why? So you can fool me with yet more lies?'

'Please, Beth. I owe you an explanation and I want you to try to understand why I lied. Which, if I wanted to be pedantic, I'm not guilty of doing, not in the true sense. What I *am* guilty of is keeping things from you, but not of lying to you. If you don't believe me, it's all there in the emails I wrote.'

Enraged, she said, 'So now you're saying I should have been more clued-up and read between the lines?'

He shook his head. 'No.' A group of delegates was approaching, including the conference chairman. 'Look,' he said, 'I can't talk now. I've got to sign some books. Will you meet me later? In the bar?'

'I don't know.'

'Please, Beth. It's important.'

She gave in with bad grace. 'Oh, all right. But don't expect me to be falling over you like all those adoring fans of yours.'

For the first time in their conversation, he smiled. 'That's exactly the point, Beth.'

She joined the others – when Ewan (Jared?) and she had left the hall, they had followed then withdrawn to a discreet distance.

'You look like you could do with an extremely large drink,' Jack said.

'Make it several,' she answered grimly.

The bar wasn't as busy as they'd expected, and the lad who served them said it was always the same when a popular author was signing copies of his latest book. 'I'm hoping to nip along in a minute myself.'

'So just how popular is he?' asked Jaz.

The lad gave her a pitying look. 'Don't tell me you've not heard of him.'

'I'm not into science fiction.'

'Strictly speaking, he's fantasy.'

Beth snorted. 'I'll say he is.'

They took their drinks to a nearby table and sat down. Beth still couldn't get over how shocked she had been when she'd recognised Ewan. Amid the applause, he'd stared out at the audience, his eyes sweeping the rows of faces. Frightened he'd spot her, she'd sunk down in her chair. Jack had asked her if she was okay. 'It's him,' she'd hissed. 'It's Ewan.' Jack had glanced at the people around them.

'No, up there. Jared Winter is Ewan.' She'd only ever seen the one photograph of him, but she knew she wasn't mistaken – the hair was the same, and the smile.

'You're kidding?' exclaimed Jaz, who'd overheard.

'I wish I were.'

Jaz had passed the news to Dulcie, on the other side of her, but there was no time to say any more: the chairman of the organising committee was on his feet introducing the speaker and telling them how honoured and fortunate they were to have Jared Winter with them. 'These days, he rarely has time to make such a commitment, but what some of you may not know is that Jared got his lucky break on a writers' conference just like this one, and he feels it's important to put something back into the system. Ladies and gentlemen, I give you Jared Winter.'

More applause followed and Jared – Ewan – rose to his feet and adjusted the microphone. 'You might be wondering why I'm dressed like this,' he began, as he put the purse into his anorak pocket, 'and the answer is twofold. The theme of my talk this evening is honesty, or its perception as carefully orchestrated by the author. The way I'm dressed is to prove how easy it is to manipulate and mislead the reader into believing what you, as the writer, want them to believe. Put a character into an anorak and show him sorting through his loose change in a purse, and you've created a shy mummy's boy. More sinisterly, he might be a shy mummy's boy by day, but a potential serial killer by night. According to convention, what he isn't – based on those two simple details – is a red-blooded Adonis with a taste for fast cars and even faster women. Or is he?' He waited for the laughter to die down. Then, scanning the rows of faces, he said, 'And the other reason for my turning up like this is that I'm sharing a private joke with a friend in the audience.'

At this, Beth had sunk even lower into her chair. How could he have said that?

'But if no one objects, I think I'll dispense with the theatrics.' He unzipped the anorak, creating a stir among the women in the front two rows – several wolf-whistled – and tossed it onto the chair behind him. His talk was self-effacing, entertaining and informative, and had it been delivered by anyone else Beth would have enjoyed it, but she sat motionless for the next forty-five minutes, stunned by the depth of his deviousness.

'Well?' said Dulcie, as they sipped their drinks, while around them the numbers swelled at the bar: it was impossible not to notice that a good many paperbacks bearing Jared Winter's name were now in circulation. 'I think it's obvious why he lied to you, Beth.'

'Yes,' agreed Jack. 'He was seeking anonymity.'

'It doesn't help,' Beth said. 'I feel as if he's made a fool of me. If I'd known who he was I'd never have kept up the correspondence.'

'And he probably knew that,' said Jaz.

Three pairs of unblinking eyes stared at Beth.

It was another hour before Ewan reappeared. Beth saw him searching the bar for her. 'He's here,' she said to the others.

'In that case, we should go,' said Dulcie.

'No,' said Beth anxiously. 'Please stay.'

'Absolutely not. If there are apologies to be made, he deserves the right to make them in private. Goodnight, Beth. Breakfast is at eight, I'll knock on your door at ten to. Come on, Jaz. You too, Jack.'

Ewan looked tired as he came over to Beth. 'Have I scared your friends away?'

'No. They're being diplomatic and giving you the benefit of the doubt.'

'Am I allowed to sit down?'

She nodded.

'And how about you? Are you prepared to give me the benefit of the doubt?'

'That depends on how convincing you are.'

He leaned forward, but just as he was about to speak, a woman in tight black leather trousers tapped his shoulder. Beth couldn't catch what she said, but the gist was plain: she wanted him to sign a book. He obliged politely, but Beth could see that he was frowning as he reached for a pen from the inside pocket of his jacket. No sooner had she thanked him and turned to go than another appeared wearing a pair of dangly earrings made of pink feathers.

'Could we go somewhere else?' Ewan asked, when they were alone again. 'Somewhere quieter?'

They ventured outside. He said, 'Did you know the grounds were extensive—'

'And worthy of a constitutional stroll,' she finished for him.

'You've read the programme, then.'

'From cover to cover.'

In the darkness, he pointed to a bench across the lawn and led the way. The wooden seat was conveniently private, shielded from view by a rhododendron bush. 'Are you warm enough?' he asked.

She nodded.

'Sitting comfortably?'

Another nod.

'Okay, then, time to start the grovelling. But you must have sussed now why I did what I did.'

She nodded again.

'In which case, you must have also sussed that I'm the most extraordinarily attractive man you've ever set eyes on.'

She turned and looked at him incredulously.

'Aha! At least that elicited more than a passing nod.'

'Don't play games with me. You've done enough of that already.'

'Okay, I admit I kept things from you because I'm sick of meeting people, women in particular, who think of me as Jared Winter.' He inclined his head towards the house. 'Believe it or not, that bunch in there is pretty typical.'

'And how many other women have you conned in this way?'

'None. I swear it. You're the first.' He groaned. 'That didn't come out right. What I meant was, I've never chatted with anyone on the Internet before. The night I met you was the first time I'd tried it. And, you have to admit, we hit it off. If we hadn't, we wouldn't be sitting here now.'

'But I feel as if I wasn't chatting to the man I thought I was. Who are you, really? Jared Winter or Ewan Jones?'

'I'm Ewan Jones. JW, as I think of him, is a pseudonym. He's not even an alter ego.'

'Why didn't you tell me before now? All right, not at the start, I can see that. But why not tell me the truth once we'd got to know each other? Why wait to spring the surprise on me here?'

'I had to be sure.'

'Of what?'

'That it was me, boring old Ewan Jones, you wanted to get to know better, not JW, the zany fantasy writer. You should see some of the mail I get from my female readers.'

'Fond of you, are they?'

'I don't think fondness comes into it. Some of the things they say they'd like to do to me . . . Well, let's just say it's reading those letters that's turned my hair grey.'

She laughed, but stopped short when she remembered her drunken email and what she'd suggested she might do with several bars of chocolate.

'It's not funny,' he said.

'I'm sorry. But just for a minute, you sounded like the Ewan I know.'

He leaned back on the seat. 'Thank goodness for that. Here, you're shivering, have my jacket.'

'You should have hung on to that ghastly anorak.'

'I suppose that joke fell flat, didn't it?'

'As a pancake.'

'When I first saw you in the audience, I thought perhaps you'd lied about your height.'

She looked at him, puzzled.

'But then I realised you were trying to hide from me and weren't vertically challenged after all.'

She blushed. 'You spoke very well. You had the audience hanging on your every word.'

'But not you, I suspect.'

'I was in shock.'

'And now?'

'Mm ... coming round, slowly.'

'Excellent. So tell me what you've done today. Which workshop did you attend?'

'"Characterisation" with Dorothy Kendall.'

He whistled. 'And you survived? You're made of stronger stuff than I thought. Did she threaten the group with having to buy her a drink if you didn't perform well enough?'

'Yes, and it put the fear of God into me. Is she always so fierce?'

'Legendary for it.' He lowered his voice, although there was no one within eavesdropping distance. 'I met her years ago at a similar writers' conference and I was so struck by her I used her in my next novel. Trouble was, the readers loved her as she strutted about in her red leather basque and shiny thigh-high boots. She had to become a regular turn in all the subsequent books.' He smiled. 'I owe it all to that woman.'

'I'm afraid I haven't read any of your books,' Beth admitted.

'I was hoping that might be the case.'

She turned to him, remembering something important. 'You *did* lie to me. You said your book was rejected.'

He shook his head. 'Sorry, but that was true.'

'But how? If you're so successful, why—'

'I wanted to write a novel that was totally different.'

'Wouldn't the Jared Winter name sell it anyway?'

'I wanted it to be accepted in its own right, so I submitted it under another name.' He smiled ruefully. 'And I experienced a healthy dose of rejection, just as I did before I started writing as JW.'

'I'm sorry. That must be hard for an established writer to come to terms with.'

'In some ways, yes, but occasionally it's good to be reminded of one's strengths and weaknesses.' He paused. 'Any chance that I've been forgiven yet?'

'I'll let you know in the morning.' She slipped off his jacket and handed it to him. 'I ought to be turning in.'

'Am I allowed to show how gallant I am by walking you to your room?'

She got to her feet. 'I doubt you'll make it past the security guards. But thanks for the offer.'

'Of course – I was forgetting the single-sex accommodation. I'll walk with you as far as the cross-border checkpoint, then.'

Ewan's room was on the first floor, overlooking the croquet lawn. Unusually, given the rattles, creaks and clunks that a strange room invariably yielded, he'd slept well. At the last conference he'd attended, the one when there had been a power failure, the room had been unbearably hot. The central-heating pipes had run along the length of his bed and he'd ended up throwing open the window, only to wake at three and find that a downpour of rain had soaked the notes for his talk, which he'd left on the desk under the window. Immediately after breakfast he'd had to address a three-hundred-strong audience feeling as if he'd passed the night shovelling coal into the furnaces of hell.

But this morning, drawing back the curtains and seeing that the warm spring weather was holding, he felt refreshed. He was looking forward to the workshop he was leading.

And to seeing Beth again.

He'd known all too well the risk he'd taken with her, and had anticipated her reaction right to the last accusation. All he could hope for was that she had calmed down since last night and was prepared to carry on as before. The plus side of it was that while he had been explaining himself and apologising, they had been spared the awkwardness of sizing each other up. But, then, that was only his take on the events of last night. For all he knew, Beth might have been disappointed with him in the flesh – hair too grey, waistline too full, wrinkles too many. And that was on top of discovering that he was your bog-standard, no-good devious man with a score of ulterior motives.

But there hadn't been any disappointment on his part: Beth was just as attractive as her photograph had led him to believe. He'd had no trouble spotting her in the audience – the look of horror had helped. When he'd left her last night, he'd apologised again for misleading her. She hadn't said he was off the hook, but he was hopeful that, after a good night's sleep and maybe a chat with her friends, she would have forgiven him.

Washed, shaved and dressed, he locked his room and took the staircase down to the ground floor. With luck an enthusiastic fan wouldn't waylay him, or an overly efficient conference organiser insist that he had breakfast with the committee members.

He entered the dining hall. Many of the tables were already occupied by conference participants tucking into plates of eggs and bacon, and taking care to avoid eye-contact with anyone, he sought out Beth and her friends. Eventually he located them and went over to their table.

In for a penny, in for a pound. If she'd decided he was *persona non grata*, he was about to find out.

The afternoon was going slowly for Jack. The workshop he'd signed up to do on the importance of dialogue was interesting, but his mind kept straying to his manuscript, which had been with Felix McCallum since yesterday evening. How much of *Friends and Family* had he managed to read? And had he liked it? Jack knew he would have to wait until after dinner, when he had an appointment with Felix, to find out.

At last the workshop was over. He had arranged to meet up with the others in the garden before they went back to their rooms to change for dinner, so he headed in that direction. Dulcie, Beth and Jaz had all opted for a talk entitled 'Women on Top'. It was led by an author called Jessica Lloyd, a romantic novelist from their own neck of the woods in Cheshire. Amusingly, they had gone to great lengths to assure him that it wasn't a gender-bashing session, but an in-depth study of the changing image of romantic fiction.

Jack saw that all the benches had been taken, so he tested the grass. On finding it quite dry, he sat down. Too late, he saw Zed approaching. From the look of him, he hadn't changed since yesterday: same baggy jogging trousers, same T-shirt, same slippers. He sat heavily on the grass next to Jack, his knees drawn up to his chin. 'I'm glad I found you, I wanted to ask you something.'

Warily, Jack said, 'Oh, yes?'

'Yeah, I'd really appreciate you having a squint at my novel. I've almost finished it and I'm getting a good vibe off it. I think you might too.'

Jack was reminded of Victor. Perhaps he was getting soft in his old age, but he felt sorry for Zed, so he said, 'I'm no expert, but I'll have a look at it if you like.' That opened the floodgates and for the next ten minutes he was subjected to a detailed account of a book that sounded as quirky as its creator. He had never felt so relieved as he did when he spotted Dulcie, Beth and Jaz coming across the lawn towards him. Give me women on top any day, he thought, as they apologised to Zed for dragging him away.

'Can you believe we're nearly half-way through our time here?' said Jaz, during dinner.

'I know what you mean,' replied Dulcie. 'The time is flying by. Are you glad you came?'

'Oh, yes. I'm having a fantastic time. I thought Jessica Lloyd was brilliant and incredibly encouraging. I'm going to read all her books when I get home. How about you, Beth?'

Caught with her thoughts elsewhere, Beth said, 'Mm . . . sorry? What did you say?'

It was Jack who was brave enough to ask, 'So, how're you getting on with Ewan? Have you forgiven him for wanting you to like him for *who* he is not *what* he is?'

She had been thinking of the conversation she'd had with Ewan after lunch, when once again her friends had left them discreetly alone. 'I think we've reached an understanding.'

'And?'

'And nothing, Jack.'

As the conversation returned to the afternoon's talks and workshops, and then more importantly to what Felix McCallum would make of Jack's novel, Beth's thoughts wandered again. Ewan had invited her to go for a drive tomorrow. 'I don't know this area of the country,' he'd said, 'and I'd like to explore. I wondered if you'd consider taking some time out of the conference to come with me.'

'Only if you promise not to wear that appalling anorak or bring your purse with you.'

'I think I could agree to those terms.'

They had both seemed relieved by the ease with which the deal had been struck, and had chatted happily while they finished their coffee. When they left the dining hall together, Beth had the feeling they were being watched. She had assumed Ewan was the focus of attention, but she was almost through the doorway when she saw two of Jared Winter's groupies looking daggers at her.

She held her head high. 'Look all you like, girls,' she felt like saying. 'The name's Beth King, and I'm licensed to make you green with envy.'

63

Dulcie was bursting with pride and happiness: Felix McCallum had read Jack's novel, liked it, and wanted to make an offer for it.

Late last night, while they'd been celebrating in the bar, Ewan had advised Jack to find himself an agent. 'You shouldn't agree to anything until you have someone to act on your behalf, someone who understands how the business works.' Ewan had offered to ring his own agent in London and put him in touch with Jack.

'I'm so proud of you,' she'd said to Jack, when they'd finally called it a night. 'But didn't I say all along that you had that magic touch publishers are on the lookout for?'

'Search me if I know what it is,' he'd said.

'It's called talent,' Beth and Jaz had said together.

In an uncharacteristic display of emotion, he'd thrown his arms around all three of them, and said, 'But I couldn't have done it without you. If you hadn't been so encouraging and supportive I might never have finished writing the book.'

'And just you remember that when you're filthy rich and famous,' Jaz said.

Dulcie had wanted to share the good news with Richard, but decided not to bother him so late. Now, with a few spare minutes before breakfast, she tapped in his number on the tiny phone he'd given her. He answered straight away and she could tell from the background noise that he was in his car using his hands-free mobile. He sounded pleased to hear from her, which gave her a lovely warm feeling inside and reminded her how much she missed him.

'Sorry I didn't call you last night,' she said, 'but it was very late when I got back to my room.'

'Ah, so you were out partying all hours, were you?'

'And with good reason. Jack has a publisher interested in his novel.'

'That's marvellous! He must be cock-a-hoop. Give him my best wishes.'

'I will, darling. And how are you?'

'Oh, okay. Missing you.'

'I miss you too. But I'll be home tomorrow and we'll be able to make up for lost time.'

She heard him laugh. 'Is that a promise?'

'A dead cert.'

The line crackled noisily. 'Are you still there, Dulcie?'

'Yes. The line's awful. Where are you?'

'On the M6 heading for Worcester. The traffic's horrendous.'

'Well, just you make sure you drive carefully. I'd better go now, the others will be waiting for me. Take care.'

'You too. And remember to pass on my congratulations to the star of your writers' group.'

She rang off, inordinately happy. Happy for Jack, and for herself, for the deep sense of commitment that existed now between her and Richard.

Although Beth had been hopping mad that Ewan had hidden his true identity from her, she could now see the situation from his point of view. Much to her surprise, the conversations she'd had with her son had also helped her to accept that Ewan wasn't the monstrous liar she had at first thought him to be. 'Nathan, I feel so stupid,' she told him, when she called to make sure he was all right.

'Why, because for a moment you thought you might have to admit your cocky son was right? Now you see what I was trying to protect you from? People who use the Net aren't always what they make themselves out to be.'

'I know. Please don't make me feel any worse than I already do.'

'But look on the bright side. This guy, Ewan, Jared, whatever his name is, felt he had more to lose than you. So I guess that makes him okay.'

'Really?'

'Yeah, he has a profile he needs to protect. He must have decided you were worth the risk. Any chance you can get me a signed copy of one of his books?'

'Is that approval I hear in your voice? Are you giving me the go ahead?'

'Do you need it?'

Beth was glad she had agreed to take time out from the conference to see some of the local countryside. The first surprise of her expedition was Ewan's car: a slinky black Porsche.

'I make no apology for being a big kid who likes a flashy motor,' he said, opening the door for her.

She slid into the low-slung seat and thought of Nathan and what a kick he would get from driving such a beauty. 'You're not going to terrify me by showing what this is capable of, are you?'

'Certainly not. But if it reassures you, the button for the ejector seat is right here.' He pointed to a small red button on the dash. 'Or maybe that's the cigarette lighter, I forget. You any good with a map?'

'Since you ask, yes; I have a PhD in navigation.'

'Good, you can do the honours, then.' He passed her an OS map, already folded to the appropriate section.

'Where are we heading first?'

'I fancied going up to Brimham Rocks.' He leaned in towards her, and pointed to what had been marked on the map as a place of interest. 'It's only a short drive, so we should be there in no time at all. Depending, of course, on your skill as a navigator.' This was said with a smile and, being so close to her, when he looked up she noticed the colour of his eyes for the first time. Blue.

She lowered her gaze back to the map. 'I think you'll find my map-reading ability will more than make up for any inadequacy on the driver's part.'

Laughing, he started the engine and carefully reversed out of the space. He proved to be a man of his word and didn't frighten her once. The rock formation was enormous, much larger than either of them had expected. Leaving the car, they set out on foot to explore. The view was spectacular and, beneath a cloudless blue sky, they could see for miles.

'It's beautiful,' she said. 'Stunning.' When he didn't respond, she turned and was surprised to find that he wasn't looking at the view. 'Ewan?'

'Sorry, I allowed myself to be distracted by a far more interesting sight.' He groaned and covered his face with his hands. 'Tell me I didn't say that! Tell me I didn't say something so clichéd. Dorothy Kendall would flay me alive!'

She laughed. 'You did, and you should be ashamed of yourself.'

'Oh, I am. Believe me, I am.'

When he suggested they walk on, it seemed perfectly natural that he should take her hand. Quite at ease in his company, Beth said how much she was enjoying herself.

'Good,' he said, 'because I am too. Thank you for coming.'

'Thank you for the invitation.'

'And thank *you* for being so polite.'

'Are you making fun of me?'

'Just a little.'

'Well, don't.'

'Not ever?'

'Only if you don't object to me getting my own back.'

'How will you do that?'

'I shall tell on you to La Kendall. About the basque-wearing character in your books and the gratuitous clichés.'

He burst out laughing. 'Ooh, go straight to my Achilles heel, why don't you?'

From Brimham Rocks they followed the road back towards Norton Hall, then took the route to Harrogate.

'We can't possibly come to this part of the world and not experience afternoon tea at Betty's,' he told her. 'I hope you're a cream tea person, Beth, or there'll be no hope for us.'

'I'll have you know I can eat my own weight in scones and clotted cream.'

They had only a ten-minute wait before a waitress in traditional black skirt, white blouse and pinny showed them to a table. They ordered a selection of sandwiches, cakes and scones, and sat back to observe their surroundings and the other customers. When their food arrived, Beth looked at Ewan in horror. 'Did we really order so much?'

He shrugged. 'That's just yours, mine will be along in a minute.'

They tucked in. 'I hate to be so picky,' Beth said, 'but I've just thought of a whopping great lie you told me in one of your emails. You said you ran your own public relations business.'

'And you think I don't?'

She frowned. 'But you're a writer.'

'Correct. And to be a writer who sells well these days, you have to get out there on the road and do your share of PR work. I've been doing it for years, showing my face at writers' conferences, signings, interviews, meeting booksellers. You name it, I've done it.'

'That's cheating.'

He smiled. 'I also recall telling you that my job is to make people suspend their disbelief, that it's all in the spin.'

'You mean, it's the way you tell 'em?'

'Exactly.'

She poured out more tea, passed him his cup and said, 'Tell me about the book you had rejected. The other night you said it was very different to a Jared Winter novel. In what way?'

He finished the sandwich he'd been eating, wiped his mouth with his napkin. 'Confession time. You see before you a man who is trapped by his own success. I've written twelve fantasy books now and I've reached the point when I'd like nothing better than to switch horses mid race.'

'You mean try a different genre?'

'Yes. I wrote a love story; about my parents. Back in the righteous fifties, they caused a heck of a rumpus when they scandalously fell in love. Dad was already married but they persevered and despite the stigma of living in sin, which really meant something then, especially as they had a child, me, they were immensely happy. Until sadly my father died.'

'What an interesting story. Will you try again with it?'

He smiled. 'Eventually, when my bruised ego has recovered. You can't keep a good man down. It's what I tell every rejected would-be writer I meet at these conferences. Get back into the saddle and give it another go.'

'So what's wrong with the books you're so successful with?'

'I'm bored with them. I need to do something different. If it doesn't sound too pretentious, I feel confined. I want to spread my creative wings. But all is not lost. I have a plan. I write phenomenally fast and currently I can produce two books a year. I'm hoping to stockpile a few then take a break from JW and write something else.' He helped himself to another egg and cress sandwich. 'Well, does that satisfy you? Are you convinced now that I haven't lied to you?'

Respecting him for his honesty, she said, 'You did lie to me, about something else.'

'Go on?'

'You played down how nice you are.'

She could see from his expression that for a split second she'd wrongfooted him. But then a slow smile worked itself across his face. 'Got you on a technicality again. That wasn't an untruth, that was an omission. The same one you made.'

All in all it had been a good day. The meeting Richard had driven to Worcester for had gone well, and the mood of everyone around the table had turned from weary pessimism to optimistic determination to wrap the job up. The turning point came when the lawyers of the customer they were dealing with, a large retail organisation, finally accepted the newly offered terms: this was after weeks of frustration, when draft after draft of the logistics contract had been written and summarily rejected. Motivating a large team during such delicate negotiations took time and effort, but when the result was good, it made the job all the more worthwhile.

He'd left his jubilant team in the Worcester office to celebrate and driven home. He was now on the M6, not far from Maywood, but the traffic was heavy and slow. Knowing that he was bone tired, and probably not concentrating as he ought, he wound down the window and decided to stop at the next service station for some strong black coffee.

He pulled into the car park, found himself a space, and switched off the engine, tempted to take a short nap. As he turned the key, a pain shot through his left arm. He let out a cry, drew his fist to his chest and clutched his shoulder, waiting for the pain to subside. But it didn't. Light-headed, suddenly covered in sweat and feeling as if he were being crushed, he fought for breath. He tried to keep calm, knowing that he was having another heart-attack, that possibly a worse agony was inevitable. He fumbled for his mobile – just inches away – but another spasm of pain shot through him and he jerked his head back against the head-rest.

'Oh, God,' he gasped, 'this is it . . .'

His last conscious thought was of Dulcie. Of never seeing her again.

64

Dulcie was worried. It was unlike Richard not to answer the messages she'd left on both his mobile and the telephone at home in Bloom Street – her own voice informed her each time she tried that she was unable to come to the phone. During breakfast, while Beth and Jaz had been chatting with Ewan, Dulcie had shared her concern with Jack. His advice was to call Richard at work. It was the obvious solution, but it had been one of her many golden rules throughout their relationship that she never rang him at his office. But, as Jack rightly pointed out, the nature of their relationship had changed; he was openly living with her.

She put off phoning until lunchtime, two hours before they would be leaving Norton Hall. The weather was so warm and bright that she went outside to make the call. She wandered in the grounds until she came to the chapel ruins. No one was about so she sat on a bench and tapped in Richard's work number. The telephone in Cheshire was answered by a young girl with a sing-song voice, whose tone changed immediately when Dulcie asked to speak to Mr Richard Cavanagh.

'Oh – I'll – I'll just put you through to someone who can help you. What did you say your name was?'

'I didn't. It's Mrs Ballantyne.'

Dulcie had expected to be put through to Richard's secretary, and was taken aback when she heard the resonant timbre of a man's voice. For no real reason, anxiety twisted into the piercing stab of certainty. Something *was* wrong. 'Is Richard there, please?' she asked.

'I'm afraid not,' the man said. 'May I ask who's calling?'

She noted his cautious tone. 'My name is Dulcie Ballantyne and I'm – I'm a close friend of his. I've tried ringing him on his mobile but I can't get an answer.'

'I see.' He cleared his throat. 'I'm sorry to be the one to tell you but Richard died yesterday.'

Her hand flew to her mouth, held back a cry of disbelief. *No! Oh, no! Not dead. Not Richard. He can't be.*

'Hello? Are you still there?'

She uncovered her mouth and tried to speak. But she couldn't. As her eyes filled with tears, she swallowed hard and forced the words out. 'Yes, I'm

still here. When did Richard . . .' Her voice broke. She tried again. 'How did
. . .' But it was no good: her throat was clenched and nothing would come
out.

The man came to her rescue. 'At the moment the only information we
have is that it was another heart-attack. He was on his own, driving back
from Worcester yesterday afternoon, and—'

This time she couldn't stop the cry escaping. 'No! Not on his own!' She
ended the call and held the phone to her chest. She sobbed aloud, her entire
body shuddering with the shock. Above her, a cloud passed over the sun
and she felt as if the whole world had just gone dark.

While Jaz and Jack finished their packing before lunch, Beth volunteered to
look for Dulcie. There was no sign of her anywhere and, on the verge of
giving up, thinking Dulcie might have gone ahead to the dining hall, Beth
decided to widen her search to the chapel ruins. It was there that she found
Dulcie. Her head was bowed and she was weeping silently. She didn't notice
Beth until she had joined her on the bench and put her arms around her.
Instinctively, Beth knew what had happened. She let Dulcie cry some more,
and then almost in a whisper, she said, 'Is it Richard? Has something
happened to him?'

It seemed an age before Dulcie raised her head from Beth's shoulder.
'He's dead, Beth. Another heart-attack. I – I should have been with him.'

Beth held her tightly again. 'Oh, Dulcie, I'm so sorry. So very sorry.'

Shivering, Dulcie pulled away from her. She stared up at the sky, her
mouth and chin trembling. 'I can't believe I'll never see him again. And just
as we'd begun to plan a real future for ourselves. It was really going to
happen.'

Reminded of her own grief when she had been told Adam was dead, Beth
blinked away the tears that were pricking the backs of her eyes. She held
Dulcie's hand: it was icy cold. 'Come on, Dulcie, let's get you back to your
room. I'll ask Jack to rustle up something for you to eat.'

'No. I want to go home. I want to be nearer Richard.'

Dulcie could remember little of the journey home. She must have dozed at
some time because when she next opened her eyes they were back in
Maywood and turning into Bloom Street. Beth helped her out of the car
and Jack carried her bag. Seeing the look of concern on Jaz's face, Dulcie felt
a wave of pity for her – death wasn't for the young, they weren't equipped
to cope with it. As if she had been thinking the same, Beth suggested that
Jack took Jaz home. While he was gone, Dulcie watched Beth move about
the kitchen as she made them some coffee. There was no milk, but Dulcie
didn't care. She wasn't going to drink it. Instead she warmed her hands on
the mug.

When Jack reappeared the three sat at the table, which reminded Dulcie
of the night she had first told them about Richard and how she had just

ended their relationship. She thought how cruel she had been and how desperate she had made him. The memory was too much and she buried her face in her hands and wept for the man she had lost, for what she had done to him and the effect it must have had on him. 'This is all my fault. I made this happen. If only I hadn't fallen in love with Richard he would still be alive, his heart wouldn't have—'

'You're not to think like that,' Beth said firmly. She placed a hand on her arm. 'The weakness must always have been there – it had nothing to do with you.'

'But if it wasn't for me causing the stress in his life, the weakness might never have shown itself.'

'You can't know that. And that way madness lies, so clear it from your mind. Now.'

She had never heard Jack speak so severely and it helped. She stopped crying.

They sat with her for the rest of the afternoon and late into the evening. Beth had suggested she stay the night to keep her company, but Dulcie wanted to be alone.

Except she wasn't alone. In the silence of the night as she lay in bed, she felt Richard's presence. The smell of him was still on the pillow and sheets and the book he'd been reading was at his side of the bed. Next to it stood a silver-framed photograph of the two of them in Venice – it had been taken by a tourist, a man who had slipped briefly into and out of their lives and unwittingly provided Dulcie with a keepsake she would always treasure.

She fell asleep lying on her side, her hand resting on the space where Richard had once been.

65

Since they had returned from Yorkshire, Beth and Ewan's email correspondence had tailed off. It was more common now for them to phone each other: they had swapped telephone numbers and addresses during Beth's last night at the conference.

'I don't suppose there's any chance that I've convinced you I'm not a serial killer with a penchant for bumping off fellow writers, is there?' he had asked, as they took a late-night stroll through the grounds of Norton Hall.

'You might have. Why?'

'Oh, no reason.'

When she didn't push it, he said, 'You're not playing the game properly. You should have pressed for the reason.'

'Is that so?'

'Yes. So go on. Press away.'

'Do I have to? I'm quite happy walking along in the dark minding my own business.'

'You're making this very difficult for me, Bethany King.'

She tried not to smile. It was ages since she'd played the flirting game: she was rather enjoying it. 'If I knew what I was making so difficult for you, I might do something about it.'

Coming to a stop, he said, 'Okay. I'd like to ask you two questions. The first is this. Can we stay in touch, and not just by email but by that antiquated device known as the telephone?'

She had no hesitation in agreeing. 'Yes. I'd like that very much. And your second question?'

'Crikey, not so fast, Beth, it took all my courage to get that one out. I need to psych myself up for question number two.'

'Is it that bad?'

'You might think so.'

'Oh, well, when you're ready.'

He started walking again, but this time with his arm around her shoulders. He wasn't wearing his jacket tonight and she could feel the warmth of his skin through the soft cotton of his shirt. She could smell his aftershave, a fresh citrus fragrance that she knew would always remind her of this moment. And how attracted she felt to him. She had hoped he might want to kiss her, and had to acknowledge that if he didn't she would go home disappointed.

Plenty of other people were taking advantage of the mild night, and after several women – diehard Jared Winter fans – had stared openly at Beth, she had suggested he might like to remove his arm. 'Your book sales are going to plummet if you don't,' she added.

He surprised her by leading her towards the middle of the floodlit croquet lawn. And there, for all to see, he said, 'This is my last night with you, and even if I have to spend the rest of my life dodging looks that could kill, it's a price I'm prepared to pay.' He took both of her hands in his. 'Prepare yourself, Bethany King, here comes question number two.' He coughed. 'Would it be too much of a liberty to ask if a lowly wretch such as I, a simple soul who is scarcely worthy of your attention—' He took a breath. 'Well, would he be allowed one small kiss? And to hell with the book sales!'

She had laughed. 'For that, I'll grant you a colossal kiss.'

And she had. A kiss that was so perfect that even now when she recalled it – thought of his arms around her and his lips moving slowly against hers – her legs went weak. Suddenly a loud cheer had gone up behind them. They hadn't noticed the crowd of onlookers who had spilled out of the bar.

'Okay,' he called. 'Show's over. Nothing more to see. Go about your business.'

Then, laughing, Beth and Ewan had slipped away to a less visible spot in the garden, and after he'd apologised for sullying her good name, he held her close and kissed her again, tenderly, lovingly. 'Thank goodness our children aren't here to witness such appalling behaviour,' he joked, as he stroked her cheek, his eyes never leaving hers. 'I'd be grounded for at least a month if Alice knew what I was up to.'

That was what she liked so much about Ewan: his sense of humour. He could make her laugh and was sexy too – it was a winning combination in her book!

But it didn't feel right to be so happy when she knew how sad Dulcie was. Poor Dulcie was torn apart with grief. It was heartbreaking to see. Especially as Beth knew just how it felt and that the painful memory would never leave her entirely. As she'd told Ewan on the phone, to experience that depth of loss once is bad enough, but twice, as in Dulcie's case, with her husband and now Richard, was unthinkable.

She had been touched that Ewan had sent Dulcie a card of sympathy: he was as sincere as he was generous. He'd kept his word about speaking to his agent on Jack's behalf, and as a result Jack had sent a copy of *Friends and Family* to London and was now waiting to hear what kind of offer Felix McCallum would make. It was all very exciting. She was glad that Jack had been the one from Hidden Talents to find success with his writing; he richly deserved it. She had no illusions about her own scribblings – in comparison with what Jack could do, she was still in kindergarten. But getting published had not been her *raison d'être* for joining Hidden Talents.

Back in October, when she had plucked up the courage to respond to the card in the window of Novel Ways, she had hoped it would provide her with an opportunity to meet new people and explore a shared interest. To her delight, it had given her a whole new lease of life far beyond anything she could have imagined: with a new circle of friends and revitalised self-confidence, Nathan's leaving home in the autumn didn't look half so daunting now.

On top of that, and to her amazement, there was also the potential for romance. She and Ewan had arranged to meet again in a couple of weeks' time. She was going to stay with him in Suffolk and secretly, like a child waiting for Christmas, she was ticking off the days on the calendar.

The other day Simone had phoned, and howled with laughter when Beth had told her what she'd been up to all these months. Her reaction was partly based on the coincidence that Ben had recently discovered Jared Winter's books and had taken to reading them in bed at night. 'And you know what an infuriating laugh Ben has – he's like a pressure cooker about to explode. Tell your new friend to stop writing such off-the-wall books or I'll be citing him in my divorce petition. By the way, is he as quirky as Ben says the books are?'

Since coming home Beth had read several of Ewan's novels, so she could answer her friend's question from an informed standpoint. 'Not really. He's funny, but never at the expense of anyone else.'

'Does he remind you of Adam?'

'No.'

'Good. Adam took life too seriously. That was why he killed himself. Now, go and have some fun, Beth. Don't, whatever you do, talk yourself out of this one – it sounds as if the two of you have really hit it off. Maybe it's because you've taken the time and effort to get to know one another as friends.'

As a consequence of her improved relationship with Lois, and wanting to continue the new sense of understanding between them, Beth had decided to tell her and Barnaby about Ewan. She chose to confess when she and Nathan were at Marsh House, having been invited to look through the holiday snaps and watch an hour-long video recording of cruise highlights. While Nathan was out of the room answering a call on his mobile, she made her announcement. 'I thought you ought to know, not that there's much to tell, that I've met a man I'm quite fond of. He lives in Suffolk, so there's no danger of . . .' She lost her nerve.

'No danger of what?' prompted Lois, a hand playing with a tiny pearl button on the cuff of her blouse, her faded blue eyes blinking behind her reading glasses.

She summoned her courage by reminding herself how Ewan had made her feel when he'd kissed her so publicly; she quickly found the right words. 'Of making a fool of myself or getting too involved too soon.'

Barnaby picked up the remote control for the video-player and said, 'I would have thought it was high time you threw caution to the wind and got involved with a man, Beth. Wouldn't you agree, Lois?'

'Does he make you happy when you're with him?'

The question was so unlike any other Lois had asked her that Beth responded with equal candour. 'We haven't had the opportunity to spend much time together yet, but yes, he does.'

'Well, then, what else is there to say? Does he have a name?'

'Ewan Jones.'

'And what does he do?'

'He's a writer.'

For a moment Beth waited to hear Lois exclaim, 'I knew all along that you had an ulterior motive for joining that writing group!' But she didn't. She smiled stiffly and said, 'That's nice. At least you have something in common. Something on which to build.'

'He also has a twenty-year-old daughter who he's brought up on his own, so he understands how important Nathan is to me and the special relationship we have.'

At that point Nathan had come back into the room and, hearing his name, had said, 'Talking about me behind my back, Ma?' But before Beth could reply, his grandmother had tactfully changed the subject. Certain things would never change: Lois would always be a firm believer in the not-in-front-of-the-children school of thought.

Jaz stood back to admire their handiwork. Not bad.

For the last week she and her brothers, with help from Nathan, and even, occasionally, from Billy and Vicki, had been secretly working on Victor's house. Her brothers had seen fire-damaged houses before and said that Victor's was only singed in comparison. As it was, the work was restricted to the bedroom in which the fire had started and the room immediately below, because the ceiling had given way under the deluge of water the firemen had used to put out the flames.

She had seen the house for the first time when Victor had asked her to have a look at it, then report back to him. 'Why me?' she'd said. 'Why not Beth?'

'Because I know you won't lie to me. I want to know just how bad it is.'

So, using the key he had entrusted to her, of which she had a copy made, she had let herself in. She had been relieved to see that things weren't as bad as she'd thought they would be. It was the smell that really got to her: the acrid stench of smoke filled the small house. What also came home to her, as she stood at the top of the stairs, was that if Jack hadn't been the kind of man he was, Victor would be dead. And as far as she knew, only she, Jack, Beth and Dulcie would have been upset by his death. She thought of Dulcie and the state she'd been in since they got back from Harrogate, and hurriedly pushed away the thought of death. Victor was very much alive and would soon be home.

What she hadn't anticipated when she'd enlisted her brothers' help was that Dad would be so impressed by their apparent enthusiasm to help a man they'd never met – and in their free time – that he wanted to pitch in too by supplying the materials and tools. 'Don't think I'm going soft, though,' he'd said, when Jaz thanked him. 'I'm after the publicity. When your friend comes out of hospital, we'll get the local rag round to do a feature.' Jaz wasn't fooled: she knew her father couldn't resist a good cause.

And now, a week on, with only the replastered walls in the bedroom to be painted when they'd dried out, the small terraced house was habitable again. She couldn't wait to see Victor's face.

It would be almost as interesting as her brothers' faces had been when she'd impressed upon them the reasons why they had to help her. 'Boys,' she'd said, not long after her return from Norton Hall, 'I have a job for you.'

'Oh, yeah, little sis,' said Phin. 'What's that? You need a hand counting your winnings?'

Everyone at home had been amazed when she'd received the letter from the organising committee of the writers' conference telling her she'd come second in the short-story competition and had won fifty pounds. Tamzin and Lulu were now scribbling stories of their own in the hope that they, too, would earn money so easily. Dad had been particularly chuffed and had slipped another twenty pounds into her hand, saying, 'Well done, Jazzy, I'm dead proud of you.'

'No, I don't need any help with that, Phin,' she'd said, 'but I'd like your assistance with something I know you can do.' She'd explained about Victor's house and they'd laughed at her. Until, that was, she'd said, 'Do you think Mum and Dad will laugh when they hear what you did to Jack?'

They'd looked at each other in silence, then back at her. 'What're you saying?'

'Oh, Jimmy, did I not make it simple enough for you? Well, here's the thing. You help me put Victor's house in order and I shan't spill the beans about what second-rate villains you are. You know how Mum thinks the sun shines out of your bums; it would be a shame for her to discover that her boys used undue force to push a respectable pillar of the community into the back of their car and threaten him.'

'She wouldn't believe you.'

'Prepared to take that chance, are you? And think how mad Dad would be if he found out what you did. *And* that you'd upset Mum.'

They gave in. The only irritation was that now Dad was holding up her brothers as paragons of charitable good will. 'If only everyone had a social conscience like Phin and Jimmy,' he kept saying. It was all Jaz could do to hold her tongue. Reluctantly, she came to the conclusion that her brothers would always come up smelling of roses.

Standing alongside Phin and Nathan in Victor's hall, she clapped her hands. 'We've done it, boys. Well done.'

Already stripping off his overalls, Phin said, 'And now we're quits, right?'

'Absolutely. No question.'

Jimmy came out of the dining room, a pair of stepladders over his shoulder. 'We'll leave you two to lock up, then.'

When they were alone, Nathan said, 'Happy now?'

'I will be when Victor comes out of hospital next week and sees what we've done.'

'You're sure he'll approve? You don't think he'll accuse you of interfering?'

'Nah. He'll be beside himself with joy.'

'You reckon?'

'No. He'll be as ungracious as he always is, but inside he'll be okay about it. He just won't know how to express his gratitude. I get the feeling he hasn't had much experience in that area. Anyway, what's the worst he can do? Shout at me for poking my nose in?'

Wiping his hands on an old cloth, Nathan smiled. 'And I can tell him right now he'd be wasting his time.'

'You guess right. I switch off when Victor starts moaning, and he knows it.'

'I almost feel sorry for the man.'

Nathan took Jaz home, then drove to the health centre to pick up his mother. It was Adele Waterman's birthday today and they were treating her to dinner. It seemed ages now since she had moved out and Jack had arrived, but that was the funny thing about change, he supposed; once it had happened, the new became the old. The same would be true once he left home for college – before long both he and his mother would have adjusted to the changes in their lives. Last year he'd been worried how she would cope on her own, but not now. With Jack living in the flat downstairs, he knew help would be on hand, should his mother need it, and with Ewan on the scene, he was sure she would soon start to live her life quite differently from the way she had since his father had died.

Thinking of his father, he was glad that things had been resolved with his grandparents, and happier still to know that he no longer had to compete with the distorted memory of a man he could scarcely remember.

Change, he'd come to realise, happened all the time. Whether they wanted it or not.

66

Once again Victor was being told how lucky he was, and he was almost tempted to believe it. He was being allowed home next week and, compared to the man who had come in yesterday afternoon with burns far worse than Victor's had ever been, he had a lot to be grateful for.

It was the endlessly chatty WRVS woman who brought round the trolley of papers and magazines every day who was currently telling him how fortunate he was. She had only started the job last week and he'd noticed that since Monday she'd developed the habit of hovering around his bed as if she had nothing better to do. 'We'll miss you when you've gone, Mr Blackmore,' she was saying, 'but all good things must come to an end. You're a lucky man to have recovered so quickly. It must be the combination of the excellent nursing care here and your devoted little girlfriend who visits you so regularly.'

He looked up from his A4 pad, horrified. 'My devoted what?'

She smiled. 'The pretty redhead.'

'For your information Jaz doesn't have red hair, she has *auburn* hair.' For a split second he wondered why he'd said this. Then he remembered Jaz telling him that she hated anyone describing her hair as red.

The woman's smile broadened. 'The two of you are the talk of the ward – you're the envy of every man here.'

'But I'm old enough to be her father – her grandfather!'

'For most of them here,' she threw a glance at the rest of the patients, 'that's what's driving them mad. They want to know what your secret is and if they can adopt her as their special visitor when you've gone.'

'That's disgusting! There's absolutely nothing between Jaz and me. We're . . .' He sought to find the right word. Acquaintances? No. They were more than that. Writing associates? Again, it didn't sound adequate. 'Friends,' he said, surprising himself with the admission. 'And I take great exception that you should think otherwise. You can tell this perverted lot that—'

'Calm down, Mr Blackmore, I'm only teasing you.' The woman, who was about the same age as Victor, clicked her tongue. Then, just as he thought she was moving away, she said, 'Oh, I hope you don't mind me saying, but I really like what you're writing.'

He eyed her suspiciously. 'And what would you know about that?'

'I've read it. It's very good.'

'When have you read a single word of what I've written?' he demanded, outraged.

'Ssh – don't get so worked up.' She gave a faintly embarrassed shrug. 'Perhaps I shouldn't have done it, but, well, there we are, I did.'

'But *when?*'

'Oh, here and there. When you were paying a call of nature, or were busy with—'

'You went behind my back? Is that what you're saying?'

'You left your notebook on your bed. I thought you wouldn't mind. I mean, why would you? If you're hoping to get published one day you've got to get used to people reading what you've written.'

'But it's private! It's at a raw, unstructured stage. It's not fit to be read, least of all by a woman I hardly know. It's an invasion of my privacy, that's what it is, and I'm going to report you.'

She looked alarmed. 'Oh, please, Mr Blackmore, don't do that. I didn't mean any harm. I was curious. And the trouble was, once I'd read the first couple of pages I couldn't stop. I wanted to know what would happen next. I felt so sorry for the poor little boy, I just had to know if he'd get his own back on those rotten bullies.'

The heat of his anger began to cool. 'You wanted to know what would happen next?' he asked. 'Really?'

'Oh, yes. I was hooked.' She lowered her gaze, shamefaced. 'I don't suppose you'd let me read the rest when you've finished it, would you?'

Victor's annoyance disappeared. 'I'll think about it,' he said. He watched her trundle her trolley along the row of beds and returned her wave as she left the ward. He made a note to find out her name. An objective opinion from someone with such a refreshing view of his writing might prove invaluable. The thought occurred to him that she might also help him after he had been discharged next week. He would need the odd errand running for him, and she seemed pleasant enough.

All the members of Hidden Talents had said they'd lend a hand when he went home, but it was Jaz's offers of help that had surprised him most. She had always been rude to him, but he liked her because she was so remorselessly plainspoken with him. That was why he'd trusted her to look at his house. Anyone else would have tried to put a gloss on the state of it to spare his feelings. Jaz hadn't done that. 'Well, Victor,' she'd said, after she'd taken a look at it, 'it's not as bad as you'd think it would be. Sure, there's a mess, but I reckon you've been lucky. Tell you what, why don't you leave it to me to get it sorted for you?'

'But it must be worse than that? It has to be.'

'Victor, would I lie to you?'

'Mm . . . maybe not. How will you get it sorted, though? You can't do it alone. And I told you about the insurance—'

She'd interrupted him again and tapped her nose with a finger. 'I have contacts. Don't forget, I come from a family of builders. If you want, you can settle the money side of things when you're back on your feet. Meanwhile, stop twittering and give a girl a break. I'm trying to do something nice for you and you're being boringly negative. Just give thanks that luck, at long last, is shining on you.'

Victor closed his eyes and thought over the last six months of his life. The shame of being made redundant seemed lost in the mists of time, as did those depressing days and nights of sitting, cold and alone, in the spare room writing *Star City*. He knew now that he'd made himself ill doing that, had very nearly lost his life. But how could he ever have believed he would produce his best work by writing in that stifling vacuum? Nowadays, and because he was used to having company twenty-four hours a day, he felt a hundred times more creative. As soon as he was well enough, he would start looking for a new job and attend Hidden Talents more regularly. And he'd go on a course like the one everyone else from the group had gone on.

Jack was finding it difficult to concentrate at work. His mind was constantly elsewhere, his fingers metaphorically crossed every second of the day as he waited to hear the latest news from London.

Other than Des, who had been sworn to secrecy, no one at work knew that Jack had been spending his spare time writing a novel, and while he had wanted to share what had happened at Norton Hall with Des and Julie, he was keeping quiet until he had something concrete to tell them. He'd last heard from Nick Ellis – Ewan's agent in London who had read *Friends and Family* – two days ago. 'Leave it with me, Jack,' he'd said, on the phone, 'but I think we can safely say you should get in a bottle of your favourite drink. You're going to need it. I don't suppose you've started on the next book, have you?'

'Are you joking?'

'Get to it, Jack. Publishers like to know there's more of the same in the offing. I'll tell Felix you're well on your way with book number two.'

Jack had the feeling that literary agents could knock spots off estate agents when it came to wholesale flannel and brass-necked cheek.

At five thirty, he left his staff to lock up the office and drove to Prestbury to fetch the girls, his thoughts switching from the outcome of Nick Ellis's negotiations with Felix McCallum to the rehearsing of the script he'd put together for tonight. If only he knew that the others concerned would stick to the lines he'd written for them, he'd feel a whole lot happier. As it was, he knew only one thing: he was about to leap into the unknown and he wasn't sure he had it in him to be as magnanimous as he needed to be.

He'd mentioned to the girls on the phone last night that he wanted to talk to Mummy and Tony when he came to pick them up. 'Do you think you could be really good and stay upstairs while we have our chat?'

'You're not going to argue again, are you?' Amber had asked.

'No,' he'd said, ashamed that she'd witnessed such scenes before.

Maddie answered the door. She looked anxious, probably wondering what it was he wanted to discuss.

'Is it okay if we talk in the kitchen?' she said. 'Tony's in the middle of cooking supper.'

'That's fine by me,' Jack said, amused by such a notion. But, sure enough, there was Tony, the one-time dedicated bachelor who had sworn never to learn to cook, standing at the Aga stirring a large pan. 'I'm experimenting with vegetarian cuisine,' Tony said. 'Lentils. It's a Jamie Oliver recipe that he claims is foolproof. Glass of wine?' He replaced the lid on the pan and reached for an opened bottle of Merlot that was warming at the back of the Aga.

'Just a small one,' Jack said.

The wine was poured and glasses were handed round. They each took several sips before anyone spoke.

'Look,' said Jack, needing to clear the air, and put them at their ease, 'I haven't come here to fight or make a point. I just want to talk to you.' He took a sip of his wine. And another. 'The thing is, I doubt I'll ever feel totally happy seeing the pair of you together but, for Amber and Lucy's sake, I have to learn to appear that way. To achieve that, you two have to help me.'

'How? Every time I try to discuss anything with you, you fire off at me,' Maddie said defensively.

'I know. But sometimes . . . sometimes it's as if you deliberately fail to see things from where I'm standing.'

'That's what you always say. What you don't realise is—'

'No, Maddie,' Tony intervened gently. 'There have been occasions when Jack's been right and we've been wrong.' She looked at him as though he'd slapped her. He touched her arm lightly. 'We're only human,' he said, 'it's inevitable that we'd make mistakes.' He turned to Jack again. 'What do you want us to do?'

Jack put his glass on the table in front of him, pushed his hands into his trouser pockets. 'I don't know.'

'Would saying sorry help?'

The unexpectedness of Tony's suggestion, its sheer simplicity, brought Jack up short. He crossed the kitchen to look out of the window, giving himself time and space to think.

'Jack?'

He turned his head, and saw before him . . . not the man he'd come to hate, whom he'd vilified for everything wrong in his life, but his exuberant boyhood friend. Memories of their glory days flashed before him. Until this moment he had thought that writing *Friends and Family* would be the last word in catharsis, but now he knew differently. He had to hear that Maddie and Tony were genuinely sorry for what they'd done.

'Would it help, Jack?' his old friend pressed.

'Yes, Tony,' he murmured, his voice shaky. 'I can't explain why, but I think it would.'

Tony put down his nearly empty wine glass and passed a hand through his hair. He glanced briefly at Maddie. 'I've known you nearly all my life, Jack. I've loved you as a brother. To all intents and purposes, you *were* my brother and what I did to you was wrong. I was a shit for falling in love with Maddie, but I did and I can't change that. All I can say, and I'll say it for the rest of my life if it helps, is that I'm sorry. I'm sorry for wrecking everything between us, and to prove it there'll be no more talk of California. I just couldn't do that to you and the girls.' He glanced again at Maddie, who was standing next to him now. 'Sorry if you're disappointed.'

She shook her head. 'Far from it.'

'But I thought you wanted to go?'

'I only went along with it because I thought you wanted it so badly.'

Tony groaned. 'Oh, the great unsaid. It must be responsible for nearly all the world's troubles.' He put his arms around Maddie and held her.

Jack stiffened, then forced himself to relax. Maddie caught his eye and slipped self-consciously out of Tony's embrace. 'I suppose it's my turn to apologise now,' she said. She moved towards Jack and, in an elegant gesture that reminded him of when they used to dance together, she held out her hands and waited for him to take them. When he did, she said, with tears welling in her eyes, 'I'm sorry, Jack. Truly I am. Please don't hate me for what I did. I couldn't bear it.'

'I don't hate you,' he murmured. 'I never have. And never will.' Then, unbelievably, he took her in his arms, something he hadn't thought he'd ever do again.

The phone was ringing when he let Amber and Lucy into the flat and the answerphone kicked in before he could get to it. He let the caller leave her message – he would deal with it later after the girls had gone to bed. He played back the only other message that had been left for him. It was from Nick Ellis. 'Give me a call, Jack, I've got great news for you. I'm in the office till late, so you'll catch me here until about eight thirty.'

While the girls helped themselves to a drink, Jack dialled Nick's number in London. The phone was answered instantly.

'Oh, hi, Jack. How are you?'

'Fine. Actually, better than fine. I'm over the moon. I've just had some excellent news.'

'It must be your lucky day. How does a two-book contract for a six-figure sum sound to you?'

His heart racing, Jack gestured to Amber and Lucy not to switch on the television. 'Depends what the six figures are. What have you in mind?'

'I was thinking of a cool one hundred and fifty thousand pounds.'

Jack swallowed. 'Did I hear right?'

'You did. Felix loved the book, he said it was amusing and poignant and straight from the hip. Or did he mean heart? Whatever. I've told him I had to okay the offer with you, but if I were you I'd take it, Jack. It's a good one.'

Laughing, Jack said, 'You don't have a clue how good.'

'I do, actually. It's my business to sift the wheat from the chaff, and this is definitely a wheat situation. Shall I say yes to Felix?'

'Affirmative. You might like to add on a thank-you from me.'

'Steady on! Let's not give him ideas above his station. And don't be surprised if he wants you to change the odd thing here and there. From what you've told me, you wrote the book at lightning speed, so there's bound to be some rewrites on the cards. But it'll be a breeze. Now, go and do the sensible thing and celebrate.'

'Do you fancy going out for supper?' Jack asked the girls, when he came off the phone.

'McDonald's?'

'I was thinking of something a little more up-market, Luce. How about Chinese?'

'Spare-ribs and lemon chicken?'

'The whole shebang! Whatever you want. Our objective tonight is to celebrate a double-whammy.'

'A double-what?' asked Amber.

He hugged them both. 'We're celebrating two mega-fantastic events in my life. One, you're not moving to America, which is pretty fantastic, and two, against all the odds, I'm suddenly the happiest man in Cheshire. Hey, scrub that. I'm the happiest man in the whole wide world!'

Amber squirmed in his arms. 'You okay, Dad?'

'You know what? I think I am.'

Dulcie was driving to Maywood station to meet Andrew and Miles. They had insisted they would grab a taxi from the rank outside the station, but she'd told Andrew, 'I might have lost the man I love, but as yet I've not lost the ability to drive a car.' They had wanted to come up sooner so that they could make a fuss of her, as Miles had put it so sweetly, but work commitments had dictated otherwise and this was the earliest they had been able to get away. She was looking forward to their company – not that she'd spent much time on her own. Prue and Maureen, Beth, and Jack had seen to that. With their kindness, which was sometimes gentle, sometimes firm, depending on her state of mind, they had ensured she wasn't left to her own devices for long.

It was a fortnight since Richard had died, and initially she had thought that keeping her mind on anything other than him would be the answer, that blocking him out would get her through the lonely days and nights. It had been a vain hope. Nothing could keep her thoughts from him. She had wanted to spend her every waking moment recalling their happy times together. And there were so many of them. Their time in Venice would always be special to her. She would never forget the beauty of the moment when they had stood on the small bridge in the twinkling darkness of the night and he'd said that one day they would return as man and wife, that he would be the happiest man alive.

Occasionally she tortured herself by questioning whether she had made Richard happy. If they'd never met he would not have had to endure the pain of choosing between his wife and her. She still couldn't rid herself of the thought that it was her fault he'd died.

She wasn't alone in thinking that: Angela had written to her, a letter of vengeful cruelty blaming Dulcie for Richard's death. 'You caused the stress that ultimately tore his heart apart,' Angela had written. 'I just hope you never know a moment's peace for what you did.'

Jack and Beth had been firm with Dulcie when she'd shown them the letter. 'You're not to believe a single word of what she's written,' Beth had said.

Jack had been more forthright. He'd taken the letter from Dulcie and ripped it up. 'We all understand why she felt the need to write it, but it helps no one. Least of all her.'

Even now the letter, though it was long gone, still hurt Dulcie. But it didn't hurt as much as not being able to attend Richard's funeral. She had accepted that she had no right to be there and had only found out when and where the funeral would take place the day before it happened. Juliette Simpson had phoned to explain that she still felt badly about what she'd done. 'Richard never held you responsible,' Dulcie said. 'He was on the verge of telling his wife anyway, so please don't feel guilty. It's quite unnecessary.'

'I know, he told me about . . . about the two of you when you came back from Venice.'

Dulcie was surprised by this admission. 'Richard confided in you?'

'Yes. He wanted me to have your telephone number in case I ever needed to contact him out of work hours and I couldn't reach him on his mobile. He said he was going to tell more people in the office when you returned from Harrogate. He wanted to be honest with everyone. I don't suppose you'll be at the funeral tomorrow, will you? Everyone from his department will be going. Richard was very popular. He was a good man to work for. One of the best.'

'No, I shan't be there,' Dulcie had said, 'but perhaps you should tell his wife what you've just told me, that he was so well liked.'

Another woman might have sent an anonymous wreath to the funeral, but Dulcie planted a climbing rose against the back of the house where she and Richard had often sat. Patting down the soil, she spoke aloud as if Richard was there with her: 'I once promised you I would never play the part of a possessive lover, my darling, and now I'll make you another promise. I will do my best to grieve for you quietly and lovingly. I will think only of the good times we shared. Just as you'd want me to.'

The following day she had a surprise visitor.

Richard's daughter, Victoria.

'I haven't come here to make a scene,' she said. 'I just want to talk to you. But I'll go away if you'd rather.'

'No. Come in. Please.'

She took her through to the sitting room, then regretted it. The kitchen would have been better: it would have been less formal and helped them to relax. She waited for Victoria to sit down. 'I suppose you've come for his things,' Dulcie said, sitting opposite from her.

Victoria frowned. 'What things?'

'All the things he brought with him.' She was thinking of his clothes and books upstairs, and more importantly, his papers and documents. 'I was going to post some of it, but ... but somehow I haven't got round to it.'

The frown was still on Victoria's face – reminding Dulcie of Richard – and she said, 'That's not why I've come.'

'Why, then?'

'I need to understand why you meant so much to him. It was so out of character what he did. I still can't accept how he could do it.'

'You probably won't believe me, but we felt the same ourselves. Neither of us felt proud to be deceiving so many.'

'But you still went on doing it?'

Dulcie nodded. 'Yes. I don't expect you to condone what we did, but we loved each other. I didn't throw myself at him, didn't trick him into an affair. It was love. I'm sorry if that hurts, but it's the truth.'

Dulcie watched Victoria chew her lower lip, and then, to her horror, the poor girl started to cry. Dulcie went to her. 'I'm sorry,' she said, 'perhaps I shouldn't have said that.'

'No, it's okay. In a way it's what I came to hear. I wanted to know that Dad was happy before he died. The last time I saw him he looked so sad. I hated seeing him like that. Henry was bullying him into coming home, back to Mum. He caused an awful scene. I knew then that Dad would never come back. I felt as if we'd lost him. As if *we* were lost to him.'

'Oh, no. That wasn't the case. He loved you. You four children meant the world to him. He was terrified you'd stop loving him. It was why he stayed as long as he did. He was a good man, Victoria. A devoted father. You must never doubt that.'

She left an hour later, after Dulcie had given her the documents she felt belonged to his family rather than to her. 'What will you do with his clothes?' Victoria had asked when she was at the door, ready to go.

'Give them to charity when I can bear to part with them,' she said. 'The books I shall keep. Unless you want them?'

'No. You have them.'

They had parted with a handshake, which was more than Dulcie felt she deserved. But, that night, she had slept peacefully for the first time in days. She had woken in the morning with a sense of calm. She might have found herself thrust into yet another new role – that of a grieving mistress – but she knew she would cope. Her love for Richard would see to that.

She had been waiting for no more than five minutes when a stream of people emerging from the station caught her attention. She twisted her head round to look out for Andrew and Miles. But when they appeared, she saw they weren't alone.

Kate was with them, a tentative smile on her lips. Dulcie's heart soared. To be reconciled with Kate so soon was more than she could have hoped for.

Dear Beth,

I've just heard the news from my agent about Jack's book offer. Please pass on my best wishes. I know exactly how he'll be feeling, as if he's won the Lottery ten times over.

Now, while I have your attention, and knowing what a worrier you are, I'd like to put your mind at rest. I want you to know that when you come to stay here next weekend, there won't be a trace of the bars of chocolate I'd stockpiled in the garage apropos an earlier suggestion on your part. I'd hate to think of you having sleepless nights fretting over this and just wanted to reassure you that I will be the epitome of the perfect gentleman during your visit. Only trouble is, I've eaten the aforementioned chocolate and have ballooned into the size of a humpback whale. Hope this won't put you off coming to stay.

Lots of love,

Ewan X

PS Alice will be putting in a brief appearance while you're here, so be warned, Attila the Hun will be on the prowl to give you the once-over!

PPS How about I nip out and buy us the one bar of Fruit and Nut? Just in case . . .

Dear Ewan,

I have a sweet tooth, better make it two . . .

Love Beth

Paradise House

To Edward and Samuel,
with love and respect

Acknowledgements

I'm indebted to many people who helped with the writing of this book, but any errors are all down to me!

Thanks to everyone at the Dyslexia Institute in Wilmslow and to Caroline Aspin for being kind enough to share her experiences.

Thanks to everyone at the Deaf Centre in Northwich, especially Linda Gill who was so generous with her time.

Thanks to all those in Pembrokeshire who unwittingly helped by allowing me to strike up conversation with them. And I apologise for fiddling with the geography and making room for Angel Sands.

Thanks to John and Celia Lea for the guided tour – sorry I missed the bluebells.

Thanks to Val and Barry of Congleton Farm for the helpful insight.

Thanks to Paul and Amanda for allowing me to pinch Paradise House.

Thanks to my ol' mate Welsh John for his insider knowledge.

Thanks to the real Christian May who, of course, bears no relation to the fictional character – just in case he's thinking of suing!

Thanks to my Cranage Buddies – Sheila and Kath – for their warmth and friendliness and for not laughing (too much) at my fake tan!

And lastly grateful thanks to Jonathan Lloyd and everyone at Orion.

Part One

1

When Genevieve Baxter was eleven years old, her family played a trick on her father; they organised a surprise fortieth birthday party for him. Nineteen years later, Genevieve and her sisters were planning to surprise him again.

The plan, once they'd given him his cards and presents after breakfast, was to make him think that they were all far too busy to spend the day with him (or be up to anything behind his back) and to hint that perhaps he ought to take himself off for a long walk. To underline this, Genevieve had told him that she had a thrilling day of ironing and bookkeeping ahead, Polly had said that she had lessons to teach in St David's, and Nattie had kicked up a fuss that she would have to put in an appearance at the wine bar where, reputedly, she worked. This was perhaps the least convincing fib as Nattie rarely worked if she could help it. She claimed a job wasn't compatible with being a single mother. Truth was, despite being all of twenty-eight, she still believed that money grew on trees. The rest of the family lived in hope that one day Lily-Rose, a sweet-natured four-year-old, would teach her mother the ways of the world. No one else had managed to.

Genevieve carried her tea and toast to her favourite spot in the garden (the private area, away from their guests) and thought of the one person who might give the game away: Granny Baxter, Daddy Dean's mother. The name Daddy Dean had been Gran's invention. She had started calling him this when Genevieve was born. The name had stuck and his daughters had subsequently followed their grandmother's example, as had Lily-Rose. Gran had always been a one-off, but these days she alternated between blithe confusion and sparkling lucidity, which made her as unpredictable as the weather.

Yesterday had been a typical example of the fickleness of the Pembrokeshire weather, an area known for having its own climate. The morning had started out pleasantly enough but by the afternoon the wind had gusted in from the Atlantic and rattled the windows of Paradise House. Driving rain had sent all but the hardiest of coastal walkers fleeing for cover – straight into the teashops of Angel Sands and the only public house, the Salvation Arms. This morning, though, the wind and rain had passed and a golden sun shone in a sky of misty apricot: it was a beautiful May morning.

At eight o'clock, in an hour's time, Genevieve would be cooking and serving breakfast. Three couples and a single man were staying with them – all first-timers, which was unusual; a lot of their bed and breakfast guests had been coming for years.

Before moving to Angel Sands, Genevieve and her family had been regular visitors to this part of Pembrokeshire, spending every summer holiday in a cottage a mile out of the village. It had become a second home to them, somewhere Genevieve longed to be the moment she was back at school for the start of the autumn term. But there again, whenever she was at school she longed to be anywhere else. Then their father had decided to sell their home, Brook House Farm, a 450-acre dairy farm that had belonged to his father and his father before him. Genevieve knew that he had never forgiven himself for this bold step. 'It's a new beginning,' he'd told the family, when he finally accepted an offer that was too good to turn down from the builder who had pestered him to sell up for more than three years. It was an offer that would give them financial security.

The New Beginning had been Mum's idea. Serena Baxter had never really taken to the role of farmer's wife. 'Whoever came up with the design for a cow deserves to be one,' she used to say. 'Anyone with an ounce of sense can see those legs at the back aren't made right. That's why they walk in that peculiarly stiff way.'

Genevieve's parents had met at a church barn dance. It had been love at first sight when Serena had tripped over a bale of hay and fallen into the arms of an anxious-looking man five years older than her. The spirited youngest daughter of the local vicar was an unlikely match for the stolid only son of a farmer, but they were wed within the year and settled into married life without a backward glance.

The years passed. Genevieve arrived, her sisters following shortly after, and their father took on the running of Brook House Farm, his own parents deciding it was time to take it easy. He threw himself into updating the milking parlour for greater efficiency and acquiring extra land from neighbouring farms to grow more of his own animal feed, while Serena began to dream of another life – a life that didn't include five o'clock milking or smelly overalls that needed washing every day. She imagined an idyll by the sea, a picturesque guest house with breeze-filled bedrooms decorated in pastel shades, with borders of stencilled flowers; bowls of pot-pourri placed on polished antique furniture that she and Daddy Dean had lovingly restored together; scented bags of lavender tucked under guests' pillows; linen as white and fresh as snow. And because their father was crazy about Serena, her dream became his.

The day they heard that a sizeable property with ten bedrooms in Angel Sands had come onto the market, he made an offer for it. They knew exactly which house it was, didn't need to view it to know that it was just what they wanted. Paradise House, with its whitewashed walls and pantiled roof, was well known to anyone who had ever visited Angel Sands – it even featured on local postcards. It stood imposingly alone on the hillside with magnificent views of the pretty bay and out to sea. The previous owners had let the Edwardian house go. Water poured in through missing roof tiles, broken windows were boarded up and gutters hanging off, and the lantern roof of the original conservatory leaked like a sieve. It was going for a song, and was just the opportunity her parents needed. Although more than ten years had passed, Genevieve could still recall the family's excitement the day they moved in. She suspected the removal men could remember it, too. The drive to the house was too steep and narrow for the large van to negotiate and the men had nearly killed themselves lugging furniture up to the house in the sweltering heat of an August afternoon.

And so The Dream became reality and they all lived happily ever after. Except it didn't quite work out that way.

Selling Brook House Farm had been the hardest thing their father had ever done, and his conscience told him he'd sold out. Not that he said as much – he was a man of few words and rarely expressed himself – but as the years went by and Serena eventually guessed what was on his mind, she too fell victim to a guilty conscience, for hadn't she been the one to instigate the change in their lives? Yet instead of sitting down to discuss it – talking things through wasn't a Baxter trait, as Genevieve knew better than anyone – Serena turned the problem into an even bigger drama by running away from it. Literally.

'We need some time apart,' she told their father, as the taxi waited at the front door to take her to the station. 'I still love you, but I can't bear to see what I've done to you. Forgive me, please, and let me go.'

Unbelievably, he did just that, and Serena went to stay with her sister in Lincoln. 'I had to do as she said,' he told Genevieve and her sisters. 'She'll be home soon. When she's ready. I know she will.' This apparent benign acceptance of the situation was so typical of their father. Many times Genevieve had seen him wrong-footed by the complexities of life, but rarely had she witnessed him lose his temper or act impetuously. He was a stoic to the last. Genevieve was frequently maddened and frustrated by his behaviour, but she was too much like him to hope that he would ever change. Neither could cope well with confrontation.

Serena had been gone six months now and he was still patiently waiting for her to come home. Initially she phoned every other week and chatted about nothing in particular, but the calls petered out and were replaced by letters. At the end of March, Genevieve and her sisters, plus little Lily-Rose, went to see Serena in secret, to try to persuade her to come back. Lily-Rose was their trump card, or so they thought. But no. Serena had Plans.

An old school friend, living in New Zealand, had invited her to stay. The so-called friend ran a winery in Hawkes Bay and was, of all things . . . a *man!* She swore blind that there was nothing to read into the situation, but Genevieve and her sisters had been so appalled that they left early, Nattie driving like a lunatic and swearing she would never speak to their mother again. To leave their father temporarily to go off and find herself was excusable, but to travel to the other side of the world and take up with some New World man was unthinkable! Until then, they had been patient and believed that their mother was just going through another of her phases. Like the time she had insisted there was no need for them to wash their hair, that once their scalps were allowed to behave as nature had intended their hair would adapt and acquire a healthy sheen. The phase came to an abrupt end when Polly caught nits from the girl she sat next to on the school bus; consequently every known chemical was vigorously applied to their heads.

They never told their father about the visit, nor said anything when Serena wrote to him with the news that she was going to New Zealand to visit a friend. They pretended it was the first they'd heard of it and, by way of distraction, Genevieve suggested that he threw himself into getting Paradise House into better shape. Things had been allowed to slip – the bags of lavender had certainly lost their scent – and some of the comments in the Visitor's Book were less than kind.

Another father in another family might have been able to rely upon his grown-up children for practical help, but sadly this was not to be. Polly, the baby of the family and the only one still living at home, was undeniably the cleverest and the prettiest, but she was dreamily vague and languid. She went in for what Genevieve called a 'vintage' look, wearing long Forties style flowery dresses she picked up from charity shops or jumble sales, and it wasn't unheard of for her to be seen leaving the house in shoes that didn't match. She was a brilliant musician, though. She could play the flute, violin and piano, and could have played in any number of orchestras if she'd put her mind to it, but she opted to work as a peripatetic music teacher. She loved her subject and she loved children, probably because, though twenty-six, she still possessed a wide-eyed innocence and an endearing ability to think well of others. The boys she taught, big or small, were always having crushes on her.

But her practical skills rated a big zero. Only the other day Genevieve had asked her to keep an eye on the bacon while she went to take another breakfast order: when Genevieve returned from the dining room, smoke was billowing from the grill. Glancing up from the book she was reading – *Charlotte's Web* – she had looked at Genevieve with an expression of mild curiosity, as if wondering why her sister was throwing open the back door and hurling the smoking grill pan through it. She was exasperating, but Genevieve knew it was pointless getting angry with Polly, she meant no harm. You just had to grit your teeth and accept that she inhabited a different world from the one in which everyone else lived.

As for Nattie, well, it was difficult to know where to start. She was the middle sister and lived in Tenby in a grotty bedsit in a house of giro-claiming slackers. There was a tenuous boyfriend on the scene, but he wasn't Lily-Rose's father. Which was just as well because he was totally unsuitable, a feckless beach bum who spent his every waking moment riding the breaking waves at nearby Manorbier, thinking he could surf his way through life with nothing more to his name than a pair of baggy shorts and flip-flops.

If Nattie excelled at picking appalling boyfriends, she also excelled at being rebellious and stubborn. As a child she had driven their parents mad with her constant tantrums – nobody, even now, could slam a door quite like Nattie. She was a loving mother to Lily-Rose, but perhaps wasn't as consistent as she ought to be. She thought nothing of arriving at Paradise House and expecting someone to take care of Lily-Rose while she went off on some crusade or other. Life for Nattie was one long fight against those who would abuse or exploit others. It never occurred to her that she did her own share of exploiting. No one at Paradise House rebuked her for her lack of consideration, for luckily they enjoyed looking after Lily-Rose. Blue-eyed and strikingly blonde with corkscrew curls, Lily was adorable and a delight to have around.

It was partly because her sisters were so impractical that Genevieve had, over the Easter break, made the decision to come home to Paradise House during her mother's absence. She'd held off from doing so, knowing that like her mother she was running away, but it would only be for a while, until life had steadied for her and she knew what she wanted to do next. It wasn't just Paradise House that needed a firm hand to steer its course; she did too.

Top of Genevieve's list of Things To Be Done at Paradise House had been to advertise for a cleaner – the last woman had left shortly before Serena departed and no one had thought to replace her. But finding a replacement hadn't been straightforward. The only applicants were drifters, male and female, wanting to fund their surfing habits – did she have any idea how expensive decent boards and wet suits were? Well, yes actually, she did; Nattie's boyfriend constantly bored them all to death on the subject.

She advertised again. The only candidate to come forward this time was Donna Morgan, a cousin of Debs who ran Debonhair, the local hair salon. Donna had recently moved from Caerphilly to Angel Sands to escape her bully of an ex husband. She was in her mid-fifties with a touch of the Bonnie Tyler about her – lots of back-combed dyed blonde hair, husky voice, faded denim and high heels, and a heavy hand when it came to eye make-up. Donna worked part-time behind the bar at the Salvation Arms and had already made a name for herself on karaoke night with her rendition of 'Lost in France'. She had only been in Angel Sands for three weeks, but was already a fixture.

Genevieve had offered her the job but couldn't deny how uneasy she felt. Had it been her imagination, or had Donna looked at her father with more than passing friendliness when they had discussed the work involved? Since Serena had gone and tongues had begun to wag, there had been a surprising number of female callers at Paradise House. They came bearing offers of help – did her father want his ironing done? Or maybe a casserole or two cooked? It would be no trouble. It was difficult for Genevieve to view Daddy Dean as a sexual being, but there was clearly something about him that was drawing attention from the widowed and divorced. Gran said it was a biological fact that once a single woman got a whiff of a helpless and bewildered man, there was no stopping her. 'Heaven help him, but they'll keep banging on that door until Serena comes home.'

Helpless and bewildered described her father perfectly. Like so many men who have lost their partner, he'd suddenly become inept at the simplest tasks. Just finding his socks and underpants required all his attention.

But any female attention lavished on him was in vain and invariably had him running in the opposite direction, usually to his workshop in the garden. If things got really bad, he shimmied up a conveniently placed ladder and hid on the roof, claiming the lead flashing or a broken tile needed fixing. Essentially he was a shy man who hated to be the focus of attention, but he was also a man who loved his wife as much as the day she'd tripped and fallen into his arms more than thirty years ago. Genevieve knew he had built an exclusion zone around himself so he could go on living in the hope that Serena would simply turn up one day and say, 'Surprise! I'm back!' If Genevieve was honest, she thought this was exactly what her annoyingly, capriciously inconsiderate mother would do. It would be typical of Mum, to behave as though there were no consequences to her actions.

Her tea and toast finished, Genevieve walked back up to the house. She had seven breakfasts to cook, a birthday cake to ice and a surprise party to arrange. Donna would also be arriving for her first day at Paradise House, which meant her father would make himself conveniently scarce and perhaps go for that long walk she had suggested.

2

Genevieve rang Granny Baxter's doorbell. Waited. Then rang it several more times. Not because her grandmother was hard of hearing, but because the television would be on and the volume turned up. Ten minutes to three wasn't the best time to come – Dick Van Dyke would be in the final stages of uncovering the guilty party in Diagnosis Murder. Gran was an avid follower of daytime telly. She was no slouch when it came to late-night viewing either. At eighty-two years old, she was embarrassingly up to date with all the latest trends. She drew the line at Graham Norton though, saying he was too saucy by half.

There had never been any question of leaving Gran behind in Cheshire when the family moved to Angel Sands. But she had surprised everyone by insisting that she didn't want to live with them at Paradise House. 'I want my own little place,' she'd said, 'like I have here.' For years Gran (and Grandad before he'd died) had lived in a specially built bungalow on the farm: she had kept herself to herself and expected others to do the same. As luck would have it, a month after they'd moved into Paradise House a cottage had become available. Perfectly situated in the main street of the village, it was fifty yards from the nearest shops and, in Gran's own words, within shouting distance of the rest of the Baxters up on the hill. It meant she still had her independence, but help would be on hand should she need it.

Genevieve had a key to let herself in at Angel Cottage, but she had promised her grandmother to use it only in an emergency. 'And what constitutes an emergency?' the old lady had demanded.

'Knowing what a telly addict you are, Gran, losing the remote control for the TV.'

At last the duck-egg blue door was opened. 'I knew all along who the murderer was,' Gran said. 'It was that smart piece of work with the shoulder pads. She had spurned lover stamped all over her face. You'd think they'd make it harder, wouldn't you?'

Genevieve followed her through to the sitting room. It was low-ceilinged and appeared even smaller than it was due to the quantity of furniture and ornaments squeezed into it. Hundreds of framed photographs adorned every surface – faded ones of long-dead relatives; any number of her father growing up; myriad ones of Genevieve and her sisters doing the same and, of course, snaps of Lily-Rose repeating the process. In pride of place on the television was a black and white picture of Gran and Grandad on their wedding day, the pair of them staring poker-faced into the camera. But for all the clutter in the room, it was spotless. Gran, an early riser, was usually dusting, polishing and running her ancient Ewbank over the carpets before most people were up. Invariably she was snoozing in the armchair by nine but was awake in time for elevenses and then *Bargain Hunt*.

In the last year Dad had banned her from washing the windows and the outside paintwork. But after a neighbour told him she had spotted her polishing the windows with a ball of scrunched up newspaper, he confiscated the small pair of stepladders she kept in the under-stairs cupboard. Outraged, she'd said, 'Daddy Dean, I'll thank you to keep your nose out of my affairs!'

'I will when I can trust you to do as you're told,' he'd said quietly but firmly. He rarely raised his voice.

'You always were a cussed little boy, Dean Baxter!'

From then on, Dad had cleaned Gran's windows. Of course, they never shone as brightly as when Gran did them.

'I was about to make myself a snack,' Gran said to Genevieve. 'Do you want anything?'

'No thanks. You haven't forgotten the party, have you? There'll be plenty to eat then.'

Her grandmother clicked her tongue. 'Of course I haven't forgotten!' She moved a cushion on the sofa and revealed a carefully wrapped present. 'I hid it there in case your father popped in.' She repositioned the cushion and said, 'If we're going to be drinking this afternoon, we ought to line our stomachs. I'll make us a quick sandwich.'

'Really, it's okay. I don't need anything.'

The tiny kitchen was just as cluttered as the sitting room. Genevieve's hands always itched to tidy it. The ironing board was out and the iron was hissing gently, sending little puffs of steam into the air. Goodness knows how long it had been left there.

'Shall I put this away for you, Gran?'

'Better still, finish those odds and ends for me.' With a flash of steel that made Genevieve step back, Gran used the bread knife to point to a pile of undergarments and dishcloths. Granny Baxter was famous for ironing absolutely everything. 'The day she stops ironing her knickers, we'll know it's time to worry,' Nattie often said.

While Gran hacked at the wholemeal loaf, Genevieve pushed the nose of the iron into places other irons dare not go. She was conscious that if she didn't keep an eye on the time, and the reason she was here – to fetch Gran and take her up to Paradise House – her father's party would never happen. Being with Granny Baxter wasn't dissimilar to being sucked into a black hole.

The sandwich made (Genevieve having taken a surreptitious glance at the best-before date on the pot of crab paste), Gran sat at the postage-stamp-sized table the other side of the ironing board. 'So how are you, Genevieve?'

Genevieve had wondered how long it would be before Gran seized her opportunity. She kept her eyes on the iron. 'I'm fine,' she said.

'Sleeping?'

'Better.'

'Still taking the pills?'

'No.'

'That's good. Any more nightmares?'

'A few.'

'Eating properly?'

'Of course.'

'Mm . . .'

Seconds passed.

'You should talk about it more, Genevieve. Bottling's for fruit, not people.'

Obviously Gran was in one of her more lucid frames of mind. 'Coming from a Baxter, that's nothing short of pioneering stuff,' Genevieve said.

'We should learn from our mistakes. It's time you and your parents did the same. You're not depressed, are you?'

'No. I told you, I'm fine.'

Gran went to change for the party, her sandwich scarcely touched. Genevieve knew the last fifteen minutes had been nothing but a ruse to ensure some time alone. Listening to her grandmother moving about upstairs, Genevieve tidied the kitchen, or tidied what she could without incurring Gran's fury at being interfered with. She put the loaf back in the bread bin, butter in the fridge, knife, plate and empty paste pot in the sink. She knew better than to throw it away. Glass bottles of any size were always washed and stored in the pantry, ready for jam-making, pickling and bottling.

The interrogation hadn't been as bad as it could have been. Considering her grandmother's nickname of Gestapo Gran, she had let Genevieve off lightly. She was right, though; Genevieve *should* talk about it more. But each time she did, she ended up reliving the experience and for days afterwards felt anxious and unable to sleep at night. She had been told that she would have to be patient with herself, that it would be two steps forward and one back.

Telling herself that today wasn't a day for taking a step backwards – there was her father's party to enjoy – she pushed the memories away and put the iron on the window sill to cool. She went through to the sitting room to wait for Gran.

The local paper was on the coffee table. She picked it up and read the lead story slowly. It wasn't until she was twelve that she had been diagnosed as dyslexic. Up until then, while she'd been at primary school, she had learned to keep quiet during lessons, to blend into the background and hope the teacher wouldn't ask her to read anything out – by this time she'd realised that she couldn't read as fast as everyone else. By the age of twelve it was getting harder to cover up her embarrassment at never being able to copy correctly from the blackboard. Embarrassment then turned to shame as she was classed as a 'slow learner'. Finally, an English teacher, long exasperated with the muddled mess of her homework, suggested to her parents that Genevieve be professionally tested for dyslexia. Tests showed that while the language part of her brain didn't work properly, her IQ was surprisingly high. This, Genevieve and her parents were told, explained why she'd managed to cover her tracks so successfully. If her coping strategies had been less effective, the disorder might have been picked up sooner.

No matter how sympathetically she and her disorder were treated from then on, the harm had been done: the label of 'lazy and thick' had been applied to her for so many years, subconsciously it would never leave her. Even now, at the age of thirty, she felt the need to prove she wasn't stupid.

One of her biggest regrets was that when she was seventeen, due to what became known as That Time When She Wasn't Well, she'd dropped out of school and taken a variety of jobs – cinema usherette, shop assistant, even a stint as a kennel maid. Then from nowhere she got the idea to become a cook, and found a part-time job in a restaurant as little more than a skivvy – washing, chopping and stirring. Before long, by attending the local technical college twice a week, she proved herself both competent and quick to learn. But just as things seemed to be coming together for her, her father sold the farm in Cheshire and they moved down to Pembrokeshire. For the next nine months she helped her parents run Paradise House, but inevitably she soon felt the need to widen her horizons. She applied for a post at a hotel in Cardiff, where Nattie was doing a Media Arts degree at the university. The two of them shared a poky one-bedroomed flat.

It was a disaster. Genevieve would stagger home from a twelve-hour day on her feet in a sweltering understaffed kitchen, while Nattie, not long out of bed, would be in party mode. Genevieve seldom had the energy to do more than collapse exhausted on the sofa. She lasted ten months working in the kitchen from hell, putting up with ridiculous hours and a foul-mouthed, hard-drinking chef who knew less than she did, before she decided enough was enough. She found another job in an upmarket restaurant specialising in overpriced nouvelle cuisine, but soon realised she was out of the frying pan and into the fire. Her new boss was an arrogant Gallic chef from Marseille. He had a fiery temper – euphemistically referred to as an artistic temperament – and clammy, groping hands. She gave in her notice after three months. When the owner of the restaurant, the groping Gallic's wife, asked her why she was leaving, Genevieve told her. 'Because your sleazy husband can't keep his hands to himself. If I had the energy, I'd have him for sexual harassment. Oh, and you might like to check the cold store; I locked him in there five minutes ago.' That had been Nattie's inspired idea.

She walked out of the restaurant, head held high, in search of a change of direction. She was only twenty-two, but felt more like ninety-two. Trainee chefs, she had come to realise, were treated as little more than cannon fodder, to be used and abused by egotistical maniacs in a male-dominated environment. It wasn't for her.

A spate of jobs followed, as diverse as the ones she'd tried on leaving school. Then clever old Gran came up with a novel career move for her. 'Why don't you keep house for some la-di-da family? I bet there's plenty of folk willing to pay through the nose for someone who can cook as well as you do and keep them organised.'

As daft as it sounded, Genevieve pursued the suggestion and found to her astonishment that there was quite a market for housekeepers – and not the scary fictional ones dressed in black with keys hanging from a belt! So long as she was prepared to be flexible and take anything on, plenty of opportunities were on offer.

Having been bitten before, she started as she meant to go on and chose her employers with care: no more egotistical maniacs, and no potential gropers. The work was varied and not badly paid. It also came with live-in accommodation and occasionally the opportunity to travel, when the families took her on holiday with them, claiming it wouldn't be the same without her. The only downside was that she had so little time off, it was difficult to make friends outside the family. And sometimes she grew too fond of the people she worked for, and they of her, so when the time came to move on, the wrench was hard.

The sweetest of all the people she'd worked for had been George and Cecily Randolph, an elderly couple who had treated her more as a granddaughter than an employee. But just thinking of them brought on a stab of pain, and she was glad to hear Gran coming down the stairs singing 'Mine Eyes Have Seen the Glory'.

Good old Gran. She could always be relied upon to chase away a maudlin thought.

3

To Genevieve's relief, everything had gone according to plan and the surprise party was well into its stride. A quick glance round the garden told her that the guests were having a good time and mixing happily. Even her father looked as though he was enjoying himself. It was good to see him smiling.

Their friends were mostly what the born-and-bred locals referred to as Newcomers, but when it came down to it, there were very few in the village who could lay claim to being a true local. Stan and Gwen Norman, who'd taken over the mini-market in the village five years ago, were laughing and chatting with Huw and Jane Davies who, a short while after the Baxters had moved to Angel Sands, had given up the rat race in Cardiff, bought the former blacksmith's cottage and workshop and converted it into a pottery and art gallery. Jane was a noted artist in the area and Huw (a former Inland Revenue inspector) produced whimsical mugs, jugs and teapots in the shape of dragons. Clichéd stuff, he'd be the first to admit, but it was instant bread and butter on the table. As a sideline, he helped them all with their tax returns.

Over by the conservatory and sitting in the shade, Ruth Llewellyn was nodding her head to whatever Gran was saying. Ruth and her husband ran Angel Crafts, a gift shop in the centre of the village – William was currently holding the fort with their two teenage daughters. They were recent arrivals in the village, having bought the shop last year when it had been a ramshackle angling supplier.

One of the facts of life in Angel Sands was that running any business off the back of tourism was harder than people thought, and shop premises changed hands almost as regularly as the tide came and went. The Lloyd-Morris brothers, on the other hand, had stood the test of time. Roy and David had been butchers in Angel Sands for as long as anyone could remember and, once tasted, their Welsh spring lamb and homemade sausages could never be forgotten. There was talk that with the help of their wives, Ann and Megan, they might set up a mail order side to the business. Sadly only Roy and Ann had been able to come to the party as David had drawn the short straw and was back at the shop.

Genevieve had thought about holding the party in the evening, but then Huw and Jane wouldn't have been able to make it, along with Tubby Evans – his real name was Robert. So late afternoon it had to be. The only other guest was Adam Kellar. Everyone knew that Adam had an enormous crush on Nattie, and predictably the object of his desire was ignoring him. She stood barefoot, wearing a pair of enormous dungarees rolled up to her knees, nothing underneath, and was lecturing Tubby on the perils of pesticides, flinging her hands about to emphasise the seriousness of her message. Genevieve suspected that Tubby was only letting her rant on because there was every likelihood that a small pink breast would peep out from behind the bib of her dungarees.

Tubby – so called because of his short legs and rotund shape – drove the local mobile fruit and veg van and was very much the man in the know. He had access to anything newsworthy in the area; houses had been bought and sold via him in a single afternoon. It was Tubby who had nicknamed Genevieve and her sisters the Sisters of Whimsy. He claimed they were the strangest collection of girls he'd ever come across. But as their father commented wryly, Tubby had never had a family and experienced the hair-raising roller coaster of bringing up three daughters.

A flash of white across the lawn caught Genevieve's attention. It was Polly, dressed in an ankle-length white cotton dress that was practically see-through, and looking like a girl from a Timotei shampoo advert. She was drifting absently through the orchard in the dappled sunlight, clutching a bunch of bluebells. Lily-Rose was following closely in her footsteps, quite a feat in the long grass, given that she was wearing her mother's multi-coloured clogs. She trailed behind her a cardboard box containing a collection of favourite dolls and teddy bears.

Seeing that Adam was standing on his own, Genevieve carried a tray of canapés over to him. 'How's it going?' she asked. She was fond of Adam and couldn't help but feel sorry for him. Ever since he'd arrived in Angel Sands, he'd been hopelessly smitten with Nattie. But Nattie refused steadfastly to have anything to do with him. Genevieve thought her sister was a fool. Adam was warm-hearted and endlessly generous. Endlessly forgiving, too, especially with Nattie.

'But how could I consider him as a potential date?' she would say. 'I mean, for pity's sake, he wears a gold bracelet! And worse, he holds a knife like a pencil!'

As children, the Baxter girls had been repeatedly warned by their mother of this heinous crime. 'The way you eat says a lot about the person you are,' she would tell them. That Nattie should ever think her manners were better than anyone else's was, of course, laughable.

Adam helped himself to a miniature Yorkshire pudding topped with a sliver of rare beef and horseradish sauce, the movement causing the offending piece of jewellery to slide down his tanned forearm. 'Everything's just cracking,' he said. 'Couldn't be better.' Adam was always upbeat. 'I've bought another caravan park. At Nolton Haven. I signed the contract yesterday.'

'So I hear.' Genevieve had already heard the news, from Tubby, of course.

'I got it cheap as buttons. It needs wads of cash throwing at it, but by the time I've finished, I'll have turned it into another of my premier sites.'

This was how Adam had made his money, buying run-down caravan parks and turning them around. He owned five in Pembrokeshire, three in Devon, five in Cornwall and another two near Blackpool. He was thirty-five but had been a bona fide millionaire since the age of twenty-six, after selling everything he had and borrowing heavily to buy his first site in Tenby. He'd cashed in on a changing market, he'd once explained to Genevieve. He'd seen how caravan sites were being remarketed – nowadays no one referred to static caravans; they were called Executive Holiday Homes and their owners included football players, retired bookies and well-off car dealers as well as ordinary holiday-makers wanting a bolt-hole by the sea. According to Adam, some of these people were so image-conscious they competed with each other over who had the biggest balconied decking, the best exterior lighting, or the best boat. 'What's a man to do,' Adam would say, 'but pander to them shamelessly?' He did this by providing excellent on-site facilities in the form of clubhouses, swimming pools, play areas, gyms, spa centres and evening entertainment.

Genevieve admired him for his enterprise and sheer hard work. He'd left school in Wolverhampton when he was sixteen and had worked tirelessly ever since, although these days he reckoned he'd earned the right to work the hours he chose. 'What's the point in slogging my guts out,' he'd say, 'if I can't sit back and enjoy it occasionally?' He had a lot to enjoy: a beautiful house in Angel Sands he'd had built eighteen months ago, a choice of flashy cars to drive, and an apartment in Barbados. All that was missing was the right person to share it. The only one he wanted was Nattie but, sadly, she despised him.

'He represents everything wrong in this world,' she complained. 'He's slowly destroying the natural beauty of where we live with his bloody awful shack parks. If he ever tries to build one near here, I'll personally burn it down.'

She would, too.

'Your sister's looking well,' Adam said. His gaze was fixed on Nattie across the lawn, where Tubby was still allowing her to berate him.

Genevieve offered Adam another canapé. 'She's not worth it, Adam. You're better off without her.'

He smiled and for a split second looked almost handsome. He had what Genevieve thought of as a solid, dependable face, the sort that wouldn't get him noticed, but would slowly grow on a person. 'I'm no oil-painting,' he once joked, 'but you should have seen me before I had the surgery!' He also joked that it was okay for Tom Cruise to be a short-arse, but for an ugly devil like him, it was no laughing matter.

Still staring at Nattie, he said, 'She's unique, Gen, and I'm a patient man.'

Genevieve knew this wasn't arrogance, it was his unshakeable belief that if you wanted something badly enough, it would eventually be yours. He chewed on the miniature Yorkshire pudding. 'You know, these aren't bad. Ever thought of setting up your own catering business? You could do really well; small business functions, wedding parties, anniversaries, you know the kind of thing. People today can't be arsed to cook like they used to. Sure, they all watch the cookery programmes on telly, but that's *all* they do. They watch someone else cook then say they haven't got the time to do it themselves.'

She laughed. 'You hate anyone to be idle, don't you, Adam?'

'Not true. I want people to be idle. That's how I make my living. You should try it.'

'What? Sit twiddling my thumbs? I don't think so.'

'No. Start your own catering business. That's if you're going to stick around Angel Sands.'

'On top of running Paradise House for Dad?'

'You can do it, Gen. You know you can. It's a matter of organisation, which I know you're good at. All you have to do is decide what you want, then go for it.'

'Is that what keeps you from giving up on Nattie?'

He ignored her question. 'If capital's a problem, I could fund you initially. You know, just to get you up and running. You'd need a small van. I could probably find you a second-hand one. I know a bloke who—'

'Adam Kellar, you are the sweetest man alive. But I'm okay for money. For the time being, anyway.'

The theme tune from *The Great Escape* had him reaching into his jacket pocket for his mobile phone. Leaving him to answer his call, Genevieve wandered over to Polly. She was sitting on the old rope swing in the orchard, her bunch of bluebells carefully laid to one side. She was humming softly and looking out to sea, her long, baby-fine blonde hair lifting on the warm breeze.

'Everything okay, Poll?'

Her sister turned; her face both beautiful and sad. 'I was just thinking of Mum. She should be here.'

Genevieve sat on the grass beside the swing and gazed at the turquoise sea glittering in the bright sunshine. A lone seagull wheeled overhead, its cry adding a poignant echo to the moment.

She should be here.

It was a simple but true statement. Their mother's absence was the only thing wrong with the party. Serena hadn't forgotten their father's birthday – she had sent a card and a small present all the way from New Zealand – but she was very much the missing guest.

It was when they had finished singing 'Happy Birthday' and Daddy Dean was holding Lily-Rose aloft so she could help him blow out the candles on the cake, all fifty-nine of them, and Tubby had teased him for being a whole two and a half years older than him, that a surprise guest appeared.

'I hope it's not too late for me to wish you a happy birthday,' said a vision in faded denim and sparkly rhinestone gems.

4

Donna Morgan looked very much as though she'd turned up at the wrong party, in her phenomenally tight jeans, fringed and bejewelled jacket and white cowboy boots.

'I don't want to intrude, but I wanted to give you a little something,' she said. With her strong Caerphilly accent and husky voice, the words directed at Daddy Dean came out loaded with sing-songy innuendo.

You had to admire the woman's cheek, thought Genevieve. She had only mentioned in passing, while Donna was helping her clean the guests' rooms that morning, that it was her father's birthday, and here she was dressed for action as the Rhinestone Cowgirl, ready to lasso her man. Genevieve watched her father's reaction as Donna advanced towards him. Holding Lily-Rose as though she were a human shield, he took a step backwards.

Right onto Gran's foot. She let out a yelp and spilled her glass of Madeira down the front of her dress. Adam was instantly on hand with a paper napkin, but Gran was more worried about her empty glass. 'I hadn't even had a sip of it!' she muttered. Once it was refilled and Donna had apologised, calm and order were restored. Donna looked around for the intended recipient of her present, but there was no sign of him. He had fled.

Genevieve had to bite back a smile. 'I'll go and see if I can find him,' she said, picturing her father locked in the loo, refusing to come out. Thank goodness he had Lily-Rose with him and couldn't hide on the roof.

Nattie caught up with her in the conservatory. 'The bloody nerve of that woman! Just who does she think she is, coming on to Dad like that? Tell me you didn't invite her, Gen.'

'Of course I didn't.'

'So how did she know it was his birthday?'

'I let it slip this morning.'

'Well, she'll have to go.'

Annoyed, Genevieve said, 'Perhaps you'd like to pull your weight around here and take her place.'

Nattie dismissed the comment. 'Don't be stupid, you know I can't do that. Not with Lily-Rose. But did you see how tight her jeans were?' She tutted. 'Women of a certain age. They should know better.'

'This from the girl who's been flashing her nipples at Tubby all afternoon?'

'Yeah, but for a good cause. I'm trying to convert him. A bit more persuasion and I'll have him stocking only organic produce on his van.'

'And there was me convinced you were only doing it to wind up poor Adam.'

Her sister feigned innocence. 'Oh, is he here?'

'You really are awful. One of these days you're going to regret treating him so badly. He's a great guy.'

Nattie gave her a withering look. 'Then why don't you go out with Mr Wonderful?'

'Because a, he's never asked me, and b, he's mad about *you*.'

They found their father upstairs in his and Mum's bedroom. He was sitting in the rocking chair he'd bought and restored for their mother when Polly was born. Lily-Rose was bouncing on the bed, beaming happily because no one was stopping her, but Dad was staring wretchedly at the card in his hands; it was the one Serena had sent him.

Genevieve and Nattie knelt on the floor, one either side of the chair. Neither spoke. What could they say? Every time a woman showed the slightest interest in him, it made him think of Serena and how much he longed for her to come home.

'I'm sorry,' he said, his words catching in his throat. 'Silly of me, I know.'

'Not silly at all,' said Genevieve, stroking his hand.

'Absolutely not,' agreed Nattie. She took his other hand. 'I'd be the same if that woman turned up at my party. Do you want me to get rid of her?'

He shook his head miserably. He was about to speak when Lily-Rose, breathless from all the bouncing, came to a wobbly stop and said, 'Don't be sad on your birthday. Come and bounce on the bed with me. Look!' She continued to demonstrate.

Their father's face instantly brightened. He got up from the chair and went to his granddaughter. He was just swinging her off the bed when they heard the sound of a car, its exhaust pipe blowing loudly. Nattie went to the window.

'Damn! It's Rupe with his brother Jules. I told them not to come till later.'

Genevieve joined her sister at the window. She didn't think she'd ever get over the fact that Nattie was going out with someone called Rupert Axworthy-Smythe. Worse, he was a useless waste of space, not yet old enough to shave on a regular basis – attached to his chin was a straggly tassel that would have looked more at home on Donna's denim jacket. All he talked about was surfing and catching the wave. His greatest responsibility in life was to own a Volkswagen camper van that was more than twice his age. When he wasn't posing on the beach with his brother and pals – more over-privileged refugees from Gloucestershire – he was painting naked women onto the psychedelic bodywork of his precious van. What Nattie saw in him was beyond Genevieve.

But then Nattie had never had much taste in boyfriends. Lily-Rose's father had been another example of her poor judgement. The moment he'd learned Nattie was pregnant he'd vanished faster than a ten-pound note during happy hour at the wine bar he worked in. There had been no question of Nattie not having the baby or giving it up for adoption. Neither of those options would have sat comfortably with her crusading instinct.

By the time they made it down to the garden, their father having recovered himself and promised not to do a runner again, Rupert and Jules had helped themselves to a drink and were eyeing up the untouched birthday cake. The other guests were keeping their distance, watching them suspiciously, especially Adam, who looked ready to grab Rupert by his goatee and toss him out to sea.

Genevieve soon realised why. Rupert was drunk.

Catching sight of Nattie, he smiled lopsidedly. 'Hiya, Nat.' He staggered towards her, came to a stop and looked her up and down. 'Ah, so that's where my dungarees went. I wondered why I couldn't find them.' He leaned in for a kiss, but she pushed him away.

'Rupe, are you drunk again?' She sounded bored more than cross, as though it was a question she'd asked him once too often.

'And what if I am? What's it to you? You, who didn't want me to come to your dad's party.'

She folded her arms across her chest. 'You're pathetic, Rupe. I don't know why I bother with you.'

'And I don't know why I bother with *you*.' He jabbed a threatening finger at her shoulder.

Genevieve sensed the other men draw themselves up to their full height, including her father. He said, 'How about something to eat, Rupert?' He'd had years of experience with Nattie's unsuitable boyfriends.

The threatening manner gave way instantly, and was replaced by the boyish grin that Genevieve suspected usually got Rupert exactly what he wanted. 'Yeah, some cake would be nice. Cheers.'

But Nattie wasn't having it. 'No, Dad,' she snapped. 'He's drunk and I don't want him here.' She looked Rupert straight in the eye. 'Please leave, Rupe. I'll see you tomorrow, when you're sober.' She turned to his brother, who had the grace to look sheepish. 'Take him home, Jules.' She walked away, her resolute manner telling them that as far as she was concerned, the matter was dealt with.

It wasn't, though. Rupert swayed on his feet, then moved after her. 'Hey! Nobody speaks to me like that. I'm not a child.'

'Then perhaps you should stop acting like one.' This was from Donna. And any trace of sing-songy innuendo was gone from her voice. In its place was a low, full-throated, assertive tone that brooked no argument. Everyone stared at her, including Rupert.

He looked her over and sneered, 'You're that tart from the pub, aren't you? The one who thinks she can sing.'

'That's enough, young man! You've gone too far now.' Dad's voice was as firm as Genevieve had ever heard it. 'I suggest you apologise to Mrs Morgan and go. You're not welcome here in this state.'

'It's okay, Mr Baxter,' said Donna. 'I can handle myself. I'm more than used to boys still wet behind the ears who can't hold their drink.'

Rupert laughed. 'I'm not apologising to anyone, least of all an old tart from the valleys. What d'yer think, Jules, should we ask her to sing just to give us a good laugh?'

Rupert was so full of himself, he didn't see the punch coming: it landed square on his nose with a squish of bone, followed by a spurt of blood. There was a collective gasp. He reeled backwards, a hand clamped to his face. Then he realised who had thumped him and that she was coming at him again. He took a swing at Nattie. It was his biggest mistake of the day.

Adam grabbed his arm, swung him round and headbutted him. His legs crumpled and he would have fallen to the ground if Adam hadn't had his hands gripped around his throat.

'Now, why don't you put your Home Counties vowels to good use and apologise to everyone here? And when you've done that, get your scrawny body out of my sight before I really lose my temper.'

The apology never came. But Jules did the decent thing and dragged his brother away. 'I never liked that boy,' Gran told Nattie, who now had her hand jammed in a bucket of ice. 'Eyes too close together. Shifty as a cockroach.'

'His eyes won't feel so close when that nose swells up,' laughed Stan Norman. 'When did you learn to box, Nattie?'

'Kick-boxing classes last year,' she said, removing her hand from the bucket and checking it over. 'I'm a firm believer in women learning self-defence. In my opinion it should be taught as a matter of course in schools. Far more useful than freezing to death on a hockey pitch.'

They were sitting on the terrace, plates of birthday cake on their laps. Genevieve knew that while her sister was making light of what had happened, she would be furious that Rupert's appalling behaviour had been witnessed by Adam. She hoped he would have the sense not to try to capitalise on it.

'How's your head, Adam?' she asked him, her voice lowered so her sister wouldn't hear. It was a miracle that Nattie hadn't castigated him for stepping in to help, when she'd thought she had the situation under control.

'It's fine,' he muttered, touching the red patch on his forehead. 'It'd take more than a prat like that to do any real damage. Honestly, Gen, what does she see in him? What's he got that I haven't?'

'I don't have a clue, Adam. And I'm not sure she knows either.'

From across the terrace came the sound of husky laughter – Donna was deep in conversation with Tubby. Funny how things had changed in the last hour, thought Genevieve. One minute Donna Morgan was the enemy and had their father running for cover, and the next he was defending her honour. Not that she'd given the impression of needing it. Like Nattie, she appeared more than capable of taking care of herself.

Genevieve wanted to believe it was progress, her father doing the gentlemanly thing, but something told her it might make matters worse. What if it gave Donna the green light to make further overtures?

5

'But would it really be so bad if Donna did fancy Daddy?' asked Polly later that night.

They were alone in her bedroom at the top of the house where they'd always slept in what had been the attic rooms, while their parents and guests slept on the floor below. Nattie and Lily-Rose were stopping over. Genevieve and her sisters were sitting cross-legged on Polly's double bed with a tray of leftovers between them. An empty bottle of wine stood on the bedside table. Polly's question had taken Genevieve by surprise. Surely it mattered. He was their father.

Nattie said, 'Poll, I'm warning you, don't you dare go all Pollyanna on me, imagining good in everyone. Donna Morgan is bad news.'

'But how do we know that?'

'Because it's obvious. She just is.'

Polly tilted her head and frowned. 'So why did you rush to her defence when Rupert was so rude to her?'

'It's no big deal. He was annoying me and I felt like laying one on him.'

Polly let it go, but Genevieve said, 'You're such a liar, Nattie. You lashed out at Rupert because what he said was unspeakably vile and for a split second you saw Donna as a victim and not a threat.'

Nattie grunted and stuffed a piece of pizza into her mouth.

'It's true,' Genevieve said, 'and what really upsets me is that we've acted no better than Rupert. We took one look at the way Donna dresses and decided against her.'

'And with good reason! The woman is clearly after husband number two and sees Dad as a sitting target. She'd have him for breakfast.'

'You have no way of knowing that,' persisted Genevieve. 'But it strikes me the only crime she's committed so far is to overdress and wear too much make-up. Who are we to talk? We're hardly the epitome of sartorial elegance, are we?'

They looked at each other – Polly in their father's old paisley pyjamas, Nattie in a vest top and a pair of boxer shorts that had belonged to some long-forgotten boyfriend, and Genevieve in her knickers and a faded tee-shirt that seemed to grow each time it was washed.

They fell silent until Nattie said, 'But what you're both losing sight of is that Dad won't ever be interested in her. Or any other woman for that matter. It's Mum he wants.'

'In that case, what are we worrying about?' Genevieve said. 'Donna will soon get the message and leave him alone.'

Not even Nattie disagreed with this piece of logic.

'What are you going to do about Rupert, Nattie?' Genevieve said, 'You're surely not going to carry on seeing him, are you?'

'Oh, don't you worry, I know exactly what I'm going to do. Axworthy-Smythe is for the chop good and proper.' She laughed. 'Get it? Axworthy. Chop. Oh, never mind. Anyway, I was beginning to get bored of him. I reckon it's time for a change.'

'You could try abstinence.'

Nattie looked at Polly and laughed again. 'You two might want to take a vow of chastity, but this girl doesn't. I don't know how you do it.'

Polly blushed. Being so pretty, she was never short of offers, but she was a very particular girl. 'I've told you before,' she murmured, 'I'm more interested in a meeting of minds than meaningless sex.'

'And I've told you before, don't criticise what you haven't tried.'

'We could say the same to you,' said Genevieve. 'Why don't you try a new kind of relationship, one that might lead to love? Or are you afraid to?'

Nattie groaned. 'Oh, please!'

'You think love doesn't exist, then?'

'It's a myth, Polly. You know that, I know that. Deep down, everyone in the whole wide world knows it too, except they're too busy buying into the hype.'

Polly got off the bed and went to stand by the open window. She let out a long, wistful sigh. Even in Daddy Dean's tatty old pyjamas, she still managed to look like a princess worth rescuing from the castle tower. She turned from the window. 'Have you *never* been in love, Nats?' she asked.

Nattie frowned. 'Of course I have. I love you and Gen, Mum, Dad, Gran and Lily-Rose. Most of all Lily-Rose.'

'That's not what I asked. I'm talking about being *in* love. Like Dad still is with Mum.' She came and sat on the bed again. 'When I fall in love I want it to be the real thing. And by that, I mean even if the relationship came to an end, I'd still want the best for him. I'd hate to unravel all that had been good in the relationship.'

Nattie looked sceptically at Polly. 'Cloud cuckoo land, that's where you are, girl.'

Later, lying in her own bed and listening to the sound of the sea lapping on the rocks in the bay, Genevieve thought of what Polly had said. And what Nattie had scorned.

She couldn't claim a wealth of experience on the subject, but the few relationships she'd been in had taught her that love, *real* love, was infinitely better than the inferior version one usually made do with.

She was just nodding off when there was a soft tap at the door.

'It's me, Gen, can I come in?' Polly closed the door quietly behind her and slipped into bed with Genevieve.

'What is it, Poll? Can't you sleep?'

'I've been thinking. About Dad.'

'And?'

'We need to find him a girlfriend.'

'Uh?'

'Only a temporary one. I don't think he deliberately neglected Mum, but he might have overlooked her needs. You know, her emotional needs.'

'Are you talking about romance?'

'Yes. He has to learn how to make her feel special again. And to do that he needs to practise with another woman. Maybe more than one.'

Genevieve put her arms round her sister. Suppressing a yawn and conscious that she was tired and only humouring her, Genevieve said, 'So, how do you suggest we go about finding a suitable woman he can learn from? Assuming, of course, that Donna doesn't fit the bill?'

'We advertise. I've been checking out the Lost and Found pages in the local paper.'

Genevieve hugged her sister. Just as you began to worry that she was behaving too rationally, she put you right. 'I think you mean the Kindred Spirits pages.'

'Is there a difference?'

And there she went again. Absent-minded romantic to incisive genius in one small step.

6

A week had passed since her father's birthday. After hanging out the washing – sheets, pillowcases, duvet covers, towels and bath mats – and leaving a bowl of bread dough to rise, Genevieve decided to go for a walk. Dad was down at Gran's fixing a leaky tap and Polly was playing the piano in the guest sitting room as she waited for the piano tuner to arrive.

Not wanting to disturb her sister, Genevieve wrote a brief note saying when she would be back. If she'd been writing a note for anyone else she would have laboured over it, but as it was for her family, who knew how to interpret her unorthodox spellings, she dashed it off in seconds flat. She propped the piece of paper against the jug of wild flowers on the table and listened to her sister belting out a piece of explosive music. To look at Polly you'd never expect her to play with such energy. Hidden depths, thought Genevieve as she shut the door behind her and stepped outside into the sunshine.

Instead of going round to the front of the house, then down the hill into the village, the way she often went, she walked the length of the garden and climbed over the low wall to join the coastal path in an easterly direction. The path was steep and narrow to begin with, lined either side with golden yellow gorse bushes, but after a while it levelled out and widened. She paused to catch her breath and looked back the way she had come, to Angel Sands, where the houses looked as though any minute they would tumble down the hillside and slide into the water.

It was a funny little community, close-knit and traditional with its roots in limestone quarrying. But the quarrying had stopped a long time ago; nowadays tourism was the staple. When she and her family first started coming here, people called Pembrokeshire the poor man's Cornwall, and for no good reason she could think of, it was still overlooked in favour of Devon and Cornwall. But once discovered, it was a gem of a place that drew one back again and again. Visitors relished the peace and quiet and beauty of the coastline, as well as the genuine warmth of those who welcomed them here. Considered as Little England Beyond Wales, South Pembroke-shire had a reputation for being a happy melting pot of all things Welsh and English. In some of the neighbouring villages and towns, Welsh was often spoken. Genevieve particularly enjoyed hearing it, but despite Tubby's efforts to teach her – he'd been brought up in Llanelli and had the most marvellous 'Valley's Welsh' accent – she had never mastered more than a few basic words. But then for a dyslexic, one language was more than enough.

But it would always be the rhythmic ebb and flow of the sea and the invigorating walks that Genevieve loved most about being here. There were plenty of stories, some even true, about the rugged coastline; many a tale of ships that had run aground and of locals descending upon the beach to gather in the booty washed up on the shore. One tale told that the timber used in the building of some of the older cottages in Angel Sands had come from a ship that had been smashed on the rocks in the neighbouring bay, aptly named Hell's Gate.

Angel Sands had acquired its name because of these treacherous rocks. Centuries ago, if a storm blew up and an unfortunate ship found itself being pushed towards the mouth of Hell's Gate, the sailors knew their only chance of escape was to hold fast against the wind and hope to sail into the calmer waters of the bay around the headland. Unsurprisingly, given the superstitious nature of sailors, a myth was soon established, that the bay was guarded by an angel and it would only come to your aid if you prayed hard enough and loud enough. There were a few fanciful people in the village who believed that if you listened carefully on a wild and stormy night you could hear, rising up from the swelling waters, the agonised cries of those whose prayers hadn't been answered.

Genevieve started walking again, enjoying the warm, salty breeze against her face: it was good to be out in the fresh air. It had been a hectic morning. The guests had been down early for breakfast, eager to make the most of the glorious weather. They were keen walkers and she'd made packed lunches for them all, something she often did. She liked to think that running a successful bed and breakfast was down to being flexible and offering the guests these little extras.

If she stayed – and she might have to if her mother didn't come back – she would want to make some changes at Paradise House. It would be nice to offer an evening meal to those guests who couldn't be bothered to make the short walk down into the village where the Salvation Arms provided basic, unimaginative food. Only yesterday, Donna had been less than flattering about the meals there and had suggested that Genevieve could easily outclass the pub's kitchen staff. Genevieve loved to cook, and the daily round of egg and bacon hardly satisfied her creative flair. Something else she'd thought of doing was setting out tables and chairs in the garden and providing cream teas. But she would have to go carefully. There were already two teashops in Angel Sands and she wouldn't like to step on anyone's toes.

It was working well, having Donna helping with the cleaning. Better than Genevieve could have hoped for. She wasn't one of those sloppy cleaners who rushed through the job, missing hairs in basins and only hoovering the bits of the carpets and rugs that showed. But for all her efficiency, there was still the problem of her and Dad. Whenever she was around, he would instantly make himself scarce. Gran was seeing a lot more of him these days, much to her irritation – with every visit, he claimed to find something else wrong with her little house, something that required his immediate attention.

'What's got into him?' Gran had asked Genevieve and her sisters. 'Just as I'm settling down to watch the telly, he knocks on the door wanting to fiddle with my plumbing.'

'I bet that's the best offer you've had in years, Gran,' Nattie had smirked.

They hadn't told Gran what was going on, that Dad was hiding from Donna, because the last thing they needed was her involvement. It was possible that she'd stir things up just to spite Serena. No, that wasn't true. Gran wasn't spiteful, but she might like to teach her irresponsible daughter-in-law (which was how she currently viewed Serena) a lesson she wouldn't forget.

At two o'clock in the morning, Polly's idea to find their father a woman on whom he could hone his courting technique hadn't seemed too daft, but in the light of day, it had been revealed as the ill-thought out plan it was. 'A typical Polly plan,' Nattie had said, 'okay on paper, but not in practice. That's what comes of being too smart up top. Just how would we have ever got him to go along with it? And how about the small matter of him being married? He would have come across as a right nasty bastard trying to pass himself off as a single man.'

In fairness to Donna, she was showing no sign of intensifying her attack on their father. Maybe she was smarter than they'd given her credit for and knew when she was backing a loser. Nattie wasn't convinced, though, and was sure she was just changing her tactics. 'When we're least prepared for it, she'll strike,' was her opinion.

'Perhaps it's Donna we should be finding a partner for,' Polly had suggested.

'Now why didn't I think of that?' Genevieve had said. 'We could run a dating agency as well as a bed and breakfast.'

But no matter how negative Nattie was, Genevieve wasn't prepared to lose Donna. Especially if she was going to start cooking evening meals. Then, of course, there was Adam's suggestion that she start a catering business.

Goodness, so many options.

So many decisions.

It was good having so much to think about. It gave her less time to dwell on the real reason she had come back home, to the place where she had always felt safe. In all the times she had walked this path, even alone as she was today, she had never once felt in danger. Perhaps it was because death out here wouldn't seem so bad. A small push off the cliff and it would be all over.

Despite the warmth of the day, she shivered at the thought and walked faster. It wasn't good to be gloomy. No one knew better than she did that it was the easiest thing in the world to slip into a downward spiral. But real fear was difficult to shake off, and since that dreadful night when two masked men had broken into George and Cecily's home, she had known exactly what fear was.

It had been a perfectly ordinary evening. She had cooked George and Cecily their supper, and after she'd cleared away, they had all settled down to watch the television together. She didn't always do this, but the elderly couple often invited her to join them. 'We don't like the thought of you upstairs on your own,' they had said when she first went to work for them as their housekeeper. 'Please sit with us. Unless, of course, you'd rather not.' She had agreed all too readily. They had travelled the world and were a fascinating couple to talk to. Right away she felt at home with them and nothing she did was out of a sense of duty. It was a happy time. They lived in a beautiful sixteenth century manor house in Surrey. It was far too big for them, but it had been their home for nearly forty years and they couldn't imagine living anywhere else. They had other help, besides Genevieve; a gardener-cum-handyman and a cleaner, both of whom only came once a week.

The two masked men had got in through a French door in the library and crept into the drawing room while Genevieve was making George and Cecily a cup of tea during an advert break. It was only when she was carrying the tray back to the drawing room that she realised something was wrong. In the short time she had been out of the room, the robbers had tied up the couple and were threatening George with what looked like a hunting knife, its jagged edge pressed against his throat.

Genevieve dropped the tray and tried to make a run for the door, to lock it and call the police from the telephone in the hallway. But the men were too fast for her. They grabbed her by the hair and dragged her back into the room, the knife now pressed against the side of her neck. As they had with George and Cecily, they pushed her to the floor, covered her mouth with tape, strapped her hands behind her back and then tied her ankles. While the men ransacked the house, she willed her employers to cooperate with the men – she knew instinctively that they wouldn't survive unless they did. When the robbers demanded George give them the code to open the safe in the main bedroom upstairs, and he refused, they went mad and seized Cecily . . .

Genevieve sat down on the grass; she was shaking and her heart was pounding. It was too much. The memory of the terror in Cecily's eyes would never leave her. Or the look on George's face when he realised what he'd allowed the men to do to his beloved wife. Never had Genevieve felt so helpless. Or so frightened.

The robbers were never caught. If they had been, they'd be charged with murder; both George and Cecily died as a result of the attack. Three months later, Genevieve was still having nightmares and couldn't face being on her own at night. That was why she'd come home to Paradise House and her family. She knew that once she was back, she would feel safe again and recovery would kick in. So far it was working. The nightmares were fewer and further between and her nerves were less strung-out.

Only Gran had an inkling of what she'd gone through – she'd deliberately underplayed it with the rest of her family, especially her parents, not wanting them to overreact. But Gran had a nose for these things.

There was one inescapable truth about life at Paradise House. Nothing stood still; the moment your back was turned, things happened. When Genevieve returned home after her walk, she found that Nattie and Lily-Rose had moved in, bringing with them a wealth of clutter that filled the hall and stairs. They'd also brought a donkey, and it was tethered to a wooden stake on the front lawn. While the donkey honked and brayed and Lily-Rose went berserk with delight at the prospect of riding him as soon as she'd had lunch, Tubby's van rolled up the drive. Genevieve could tell from the cursory glance he gave the donkey – but there again, he was used to odd goings-on at Paradise House – that he had important news to deliver and nothing was going to stop him.

'Well, look you see, you'll never guess what,' he said, stepping down from the van, his Llanelli accent as bright and jolly as his face. 'At long last, Ralph Griffiths's got planning permission for that dilapidated old barn of his and has agreed to sell it.'

This *was* Big News. The sale of any property in the area caused ears to flap and tongues to wag.

'Who, what, when and how? And name your source,' demanded Nattie.

Tubby wiped his hands on the front of his apron. 'Well, *cariad,* I just heard it down at Debonhair, so it's got to be on the button.'

Both Nattie and Genevieve nodded. The gospel according to St Debs was always to be believed.

'But the bit you girls are going to like is who Ralph's selling to. He's selling to an eligible young man.'

'Anyone we know?' asked Genevieve.

Nattie scowled at her. 'Get real, Gen, how many eligible young men do we know round here?'

'He's not from round here,' Tubby informed them. 'He lives in Buckinghamshire and the barn's to be a holiday home for him. Debs says his name's Jonjo Fitzwilliam and he's only thirty-three but has made a bundle of money out of health and fitness centres. He runs a sort of franchise from what I can gather. So just think, girls. Available totty with cash to flash! How lucky are you three?' He grinned. 'Question is; who would he be brave enough to choose out of the Sisters of Whimsy? Hey, I know! How about you fight for him, and he wins the victor? A mud wrestling session at The Arms would go down a treat.'

While Nattie looked ready to give him the same treatment she'd given Rupert last week, Genevieve said, 'So why's he coming here? If he's got money, why isn't he buying a holiday home somewhere more glamorous?'

'Perhaps he's a man of discernment. Debs also said he's bringing his own architect to turn the barn into something really special.'

Nattie tutted and put her hands on her hips. 'Some fancy architect from London, who's going to turn the barn into a hideous eyesore, no doubt. Well, I certainly hope no one's going to turn a blind eye to the fact that the barn's probably a listed building.'

Tubby smiled. 'Apparently this young architect boyo spent part of his childhood here. His parents owned a house nearby. So with a bit of luck, he'll do a sympathetic job of the conversion.' Then, rubbing his hands on his apron again and bringing the gossip session to an end, he said, 'Now then girls, what can I get you from the van?' He chuckled and glanced over towards the donkey. 'How about some carrots for your hairy friend?'

'Are they organic?'

But Genevieve wasn't listening. She walked away, back into the house, up the two flights of stairs to her bedroom. Only when she had closed the door behind her and leant against it, did she let her brain receive the information her heart had registered the moment Tubby had described the man who would be coming to Angel Sands with Jonjo Fitzwilliam ... *this young architect boyo spent part of his childhood here ... His parents owned a house nearby ...*

It had to be Christian.

7

There were questions that needed answering.

Why had a donkey taken up residence at Paradise House? Why had Nattie and Lily-Rose upped sticks from Tenby? And more importantly, how was Genevieve going to find out if Jonjo Fitzwilliam's architect was indeed who she thought he was?

Although it was this last question that dominated her thoughts, it seemed the donkey was destined to be the focus of conversation while she prepared lunch for everyone, including Gran, whom Dad had brought back with him after fixing a loose stair rod – a stair rod that Gran said had been perfectly secure until he'd got his wretched hands on it.

'In case you were wondering,' announced Nattie as she put Lily-Rose onto her booster seat, 'his name's Henry.'

'That's a nice name,' said Gran. 'Very solid and reliable. What does he do?'

'The usual kind of thing, I guess, if he's given the chance; a romp in the sun, plenty of juicy green stuff to nibble on and a regular supply of carrots. That's why I had to rescue him. I just had to give him the opportunity of a better life.'

'I should think you did. Vegetarianism is all very well, but he won't last two minutes with a girl like you unless he gets some good red meat down him.'

Everyone stared at Gran and laughed.

Genevieve said, 'Gran, Henry's a donkey.'

Realizing her mistake, but utterly unfazed, Gran said, 'Well, I still think Henry's a good name. Even for a donkey. After all, they're solid and reliable, aren't they? Certainly more reliable than any of the young men you've dallied with in the past, Natalie.'

'So how did you come by him?' asked Genevieve. She had a sudden picture of Jack and the Beanstalk in reverse – Nattie going out with a handful of precious magic beans and coming home with the pathetic-looking animal currently grazing in the orchard.

'Huw and Jane told me about him. He'd been horribly neglected by a miserable old bloke who died at the weekend. And good riddance I say. He had poor Henry in a filthy back yard with nothing but a bucket of dirty water and a bag of mouldy hay.'

Dad glanced up from his paper, an eyebrow raised. 'And where's he going to stay, love?'

Nattie turned on the charm. 'Well, I was rather hoping you might like to have him here. He wouldn't be any trouble.'

'Isn't there a proper donkey sanctuary somewhere he could go to?'

'But Daddy, you'd love having him at Paradise House. Just think, you wouldn't have to bother mowing the grass any more. And there'd be an endless supply of organic fertilizer for the garden. Go on, what do you say? Please can Henry stay?'

Her father folded his newspaper and put it down. He helped himself to some chicken and two slabs of Genevieve's homemade bread, and after he'd made himself an enormous sandwich, mayonnaise leaking out through the crusts, he said, 'I suppose there's a chance he might redress the balance around here. It'll be two males to five females if he stays.'

Nattie jumped up from her chair and went to hug him.

Genevieve smiled. As if there'd be any doubt of Henry staying. Their father was incapable of turning anyone or anything away. 'So what about you and Lily-Rose?' she asked, sounding worryingly like the only responsible adult at the table. 'Why have you decided to move back?'

'Call it a run of bad luck. They don't want me at the wine bar any more and the tenancy on the bedsit's come to an end, leaving your wee niece and penniless sister without a home.'

'What will you do?' Again the boring, responsible adult.

'Do?' echoed Nattie, with just a hint of sarcasm, 'Why, stay here of course. Home sweet home. There's nothing like it.' She paused, as if sensing there had been more to Genevieve's question than at first appeared. Which there was. Genevieve knew her sister of old – Nattie wouldn't lift a finger to help at Paradise House. She would actually make more work for everyone. 'If coming home's good enough for you, Gen,' Nattie added, 'it's certainly good enough for me.'

Genevieve wasn't averse to taking Nattie on, but she knew when to back off. She wasn't in the mood for an argument over her sister's legendary slothfulness.

Daddy Dean took up his paper again and Polly, who hadn't yet uttered a word, chewed slowly on a piece of bread and cheese, her attention absorbed by the book she was reading: *Little Women*. Every now and then, Polly reread all her favourite classic children's novels. Very likely it would be *The Secret Garden* next week, followed by her namesake, *Pollyanna*.

All three Baxter girls had been named by their mother and it had been no random affair. Serena had chosen the name Genevieve because of the movie starring Kenneth More, who had reminded Serena of her father; Natalie had been named after Natalie Wood for the simple reason she was the luckiest woman alive being married to Robert Wagner; and Polly was so named because when she was born, Gran said she looked like an angel who would never see bad in another person.

While Polly continued to turn the pages of her book, Nattie and Gran egged on Lily-Rose's noisy farmyard impressions. But a dispute broke out when

Gran started encouraging her to hiss like a snake. Challenged by Natalie about the likelihood of such a species being found in a farmyard, Gran retaliated, 'It's well known that there were adders in Pembrokeshire. Everyone knows that.'

'Okay,' conceded Nattie. 'Now I come to think of it, there are plenty of snakes in the grass hereabouts. Adam and Rupert to name but two.'

Dad rattled his throat from behind his paper, registering his disapproval. He had a soft spot for Adam and wouldn't have a word said against him.

'And I bet any money you like,' Nattie went on, 'that this Jonjo Fitzwilliam will turn out to be just as awful. More money than sense and with terrible taste. He'll ruin Ralph's barn, make it chocolate-box twee with poxy coach lamps and a rusting old plough posing on the front lawn. Or worse, he'll try and turn it into a pseudo loft apartment with—'

Looking up from her book, Polly interrupted, 'Gen, have you thought who the architect might be?'

All eyes suddenly turned on Genevieve, apart from Lily-Rose's – she was carefully unwrapping a triangle of Dairylea and mooing.

'It's crossed my mind that it could be Christian,' said Genevieve.

No one said anything.

'It's only a wild guess,' she said, in the awkward hush. 'I could be wrong, of course. I probably am. After all, there have to be any number of architects who holidayed here when they were children. What's more, we don't know for sure he went on to become an architect.'

Daddy Dean looked at her, concerned. 'And if it is him?'

'Then . . . then I'll look forward to meeting him again. Think how much we'll have to catch up on.'

Nattie leant back in her seat and snorted. 'Yeah, I can picture the two of you. "How are you, Genevieve?" "Oh, not so bad. How about you, broken anyone else's heart recently?" '

'For goodness' sake, all that's in the dim and distant past. I put it behind me years ago. I suggest you do the same.'

Nice try, she told herself later that afternoon as she walked Gran home.

'Come in for a cup of tea,' Gran said, putting her key in the lock and pushing against the door. It had begun to swell in the warmer weather.

Genevieve edged away, afraid to cross the threshold. It wasn't PG Tips Gran was offering, but another of her open-heart-surgery-minus-the-anaesthetic sessions.

'I ought to be getting back,' Genevieve murmured. 'You know what it's like, new guests arriving. A pile of paperwork to do as well.'

Granny Baxter reached out to touch her arm. 'Just a quick cup. I want to show you something.'

Liar, liar, pants on fire! Run for it Genevieve!

'Sorry, Gran, another time.'

It was rude and cowardly of her, but she kissed the old lady's cheek and turned to leave. Instead of going back up the hill to Paradise House – the new guests wouldn't be arriving for another two hours – she headed for the small beach where families with young children were making sandcastles before the tide came in. A frisky dog with a deflated ball in its mouth danced briefly around her ankles, but she ignored it and carried on, taking the footpath that led up the hillside and out west along the coastal path towards the next headland.

Her destination was Tawelfan beach. Tawelfan was Welsh for quiet place, and it was where she and Christian had met. It was also where they had done a lot of other things.

They say you never forget your first kiss. Well, amen to that! She could still remember hers quite vividly – it was nothing like the sweaty disco fumble that Nattie could lay claim to – and as the path dropped down the grassy slope towards the sandy bay where Christian had first kissed her, she pictured the scene. She had been fifteen (laughably old by Nattie's standards) and Christian seventeen. They had been sitting in the shelter of the sand dunes, warming themselves after a swim and eating hamburgers from the kiosk in the car park at the back of the beach. There was a smear of ketchup on her lip, so he later claimed, and he'd tilted his head towards hers and kissed it away.

He was from Ludlow in Shropshire and his family had been coming on holiday to Pembrokeshire for years. But whereas her family stayed in the same rented cottage in Angel Sands every summer, his owned a pretty, stone-built house in the next village. She'd met him when she was twelve. She'd been standing at the water's edge, letting the waves swoosh and swirl around her feet, enjoying the sensation of the pebbles and sand shifting beneath her. She was just thinking how funny it would be if the sand gave way and she fell deep into the centre of the earth, when a voice cut through the squeals of other children playing nearby in the rock pools.

'You're not afraid to go in, are you?' The voice had a strange, almost unconnected tone. She turned to see who had spoken, thinking that perhaps he was foreign. A tall, angular boy in cut-off denim shorts was smiling at her. Or was he taunting her? His question had implied as much.

'I'm not afraid of anything,' she retorted, turning away and running into the shallow water, trying not to gasp at its numbing coldness. She kept going until it was deep enough to fling herself in and swim. There, that would show him! She looked back to the shore to see if he was watching. She was surprised to see him no more than a couple of yards behind her.

'You're a good swimmer,' he said, coming alongside. Again, that peculiar awkward tone to his voice. Definitely foreign.

'I've got badges,' she said. Immediately she was annoyed with herself; it was such a childish boast, the type of thing her best friend, Rachel, would never say. 'I also swim for my school,' she said, not meeting his gaze.

He frowned. 'What did you say?'

'I said I swim for my school.'

The frown was replaced with a wide smile. 'Me too.'

It was the first thing they found they had in common and it set the tone of their friendship.

But the kiss, coming several years later, changed all that.

8

A light, drizzly rain was falling and the churning sea was as grey as the sky. It was a chilly and inhospitable day for the end of May. Inside the cosy kitchen at Paradise House, Genevieve was doing what she liked best, spending the afternoon baking. The comforting smell of syrup and allspice filled the kitchen – a fruitcake was in the oven, a treacle tart cooling on the wire rack – and now she was trying out a new recipe for meringues, carefully whisking glossy egg whites and icing sugar over a pan of simmering water.

When the mixture was the right texture, she switched off the electric whisk and turned to check on her niece, who earlier had been sitting at the table playing with some leftover pastry. The circle of leathery pastry had been abandoned and Lily-Rose was now under the table, her face daubed with flour as she 'read' to her collection of dolls and teddies. They were neatly lined up, legs extended at ninety degrees, and were being told to listen carefully. This was a favourite game. She couldn't read yet, but she had a wonderful memory and a scary fondness for being in charge. With a book of Bible stories on her lap and a floury finger pointing to the words that didn't match her spoken words, she began.

'So the king told his men to throw Daniel into the den with the lions.' She glanced up from the book and growled for extra effect, then said to the attentive toys, 'And what do you think happened next? Don't you know? Then I'll tell you. In the morning, the king ran to the den and called to Daniel, and Daniel shouted back that God had sent a special angel to stop the lions hurting him.' She shut the book slowly. 'And they all lived happily ever after. Except for the bad men. The king threw them into the den and their bones were crushed.' Unaware that she was being watched, she asked the toys if they'd like to hear another story.

Genevieve smiled and left her to it. If you discounted the tantrums brought on by tiredness and the daily arguments over what she wanted to wear, her niece was easy to look after; a confident little girl who enjoyed her own company and was quite happy devising games to keep herself amused. She had never attended a playgroup or nursery school on a regular basis – getting her there each day would have proved too much of a commitment on her mother's part. But at Gran's insistence, Lily-Rose often went to church with her in Angel Sands and was a keen member of Sunday School. The vicar's wife at St Non's, where Polly occasionally played the organ, was in charge of entertaining the handful of children who attended, and she had instilled in Lily-Rose an active interest in the Lord Jesus. The Christmas before last had been Lily-Rose's first acquaintance with Christ and, for months afterwards, whenever she saw a baby, she would smile and say, 'Ah, look, baby Jesus.'

Nattie was far from pleased. 'People will think I'm some kind of religious crank,' she complained. But perversely she never stopped Lily-Rose from attending church with Gran. 'I'm not going to be one of those censorious parents,' she would say. 'She'll learn for herself soon enough what to believe in.'

Back with her meringues, Genevieve removed the bowl from the pan of water, placed it on a tea towel and whisked the mixture some more. According to the recipe, which as usual she'd rewritten to get it firmly into her head, she should keep doing this until it cooled. When it had, she reached for the piping bag.

'It's time to do the piping now,' she told Lily-Rose. 'Do you still want to help me?'

Lily-Rose shot out from under the table. 'Where's my pinny?'

'Here. But first we'd better wash your hands.' Lily-Rose was in the process of dragging a chair across to the sink when there was a knock at the back door.

It was Adam, and by the look of him he'd recently had his hair cut. He was smartly dressed in a dark blue suit with a cream shirt. He would have looked great if it hadn't been for the novelty tie. One day, thought Genevieve, someone would have to tell him to keep the comedy away from his wardrobe.

'If it's Dad or Nattie you're looking for, you're out of luck. They're not here. It's just Lily-Rose and me.'

'That's okay. It was you I wanted to see anyway.'

'I'll be with you in a minute, when I've done this. Sit down and make yourself at home.' Looking at the amount of flour her niece had got everywhere, she said, 'You'd better be careful where you put yourself. I don't want you ruining that classy suit. Where've you been, dressed like the cat's whiskers?'

Instead of answering her, he closed his eyes and breathed in deeply.

'You haven't taken up some weird form of meditation have you?' she asked him.

He opened his eyes and laughed. 'No. For a moment there, I was a small boy. My mum was a great cook just like you. There was always something cooking. Something to look forward to.'

Adam freely admitted that part of his success was attributable to his upbringing. His father left home when he was a baby and when he was sixteen his mother was killed in a car crash: he learned from an early age to stand on his own two feet. After leaving school he went to work in a garage as a trainee mechanic. His employers soon realised that he was a natural salesman, so they took him out of his overalls and put him in a suit. In no time he was easily outperforming the other salesman. From cars he turned to caravans, and then to caravan parks. What would come next for him? Genevieve wondered.

'Genvy, will you help me wash my hands?' Lily-Rose was standing on the chair at the sink, her arms outstretched towards the taps.

'Of course, darling.'

Lily-Rose smiled shyly at Adam. 'You could help us make the cakes.'

'I don't think he's wearing the right kind of clothes,' Genevieve said.

'If you gave him a pinny he'd stay clean.'

'That's all right, Rosy-Posy, I'm just fine watching you two.'

While Lily-Rose giggled at the pet name he used for her behind Nattie's back, he removed his jacket, hung it on the cleanest chair and made himself at home by putting the kettle on. Genevieve liked that about him; he was easy to have around. There was never any standing on ceremony. By the time he'd made a pot of tea and found some juice for Lily, she had two trays of bite-sized meringues ready for the oven, along with a special one of Lily-Rose's oddly shaped efforts. She took out the fruitcake, lowered the oven temperature and slid in the trays.

'So what did you want to see me about?'

But her question went unanswered. From the garden came an unearthly groaning.

'What the dickens is that noise?' Adam joined them at the window above the sink, where Genevieve was once again helping Lily-Rose to wash her hands.

Genevieve pointed towards the orchard and explained about Henry. 'He's been with us for two weeks now, another of Nattie's crusades. Recently he's started braying like a thing possessed. Once he gets going, nothing will stop him.'

'He's lonely,' Adam said knowledgeably.

'How do you know?'

He went back to the teapot and poured out their tea. 'When I was little, the local neighbourhood nutter kept a pair. Then when one of them died we were kept awake all night. The din was horrendous. But as soon as a replacement was found, the lovesick donkey perked up.'

Genevieve groaned. 'As if I didn't have enough to do. Now I have to find Henry a soulmate.' Since being back at Paradise House it seemed each day brought her yet another responsibility.

He passed her a mug. 'I could help you if you like. I know a bloke over in Saundersfoot—'

She interrupted him with a laugh. 'Just how many *blokes* do you know, Adam? You seem to have one for every occasion.'

He shrugged. 'I'm just a fixer. A go-between. Which leads me nicely on to the reason I'm here.'

'Oh? And there was me thinking it was my irresistible company, that you were seeing me behind Nattie's back to make her jealous.'

A faint hue of red appeared on Adam's face. He could take any amount of teasing about his professional life, or the trace of his Brummie accent that crept in now and then, or even his gold bracelet, but Genevieve knew his feelings for Nattie were not to be made fun of. Hiding his discomfort by helping Lily-Rose off the chair, he said, 'I've got a proposition for you. A business proposition,' he added hastily, letting Lily-Rose climb onto his lap as he sat down.

Genevieve took a chair opposite him. 'Go on, I'm listening.'

'I've just had lunch with my accountant and his daughter's getting married next weekend. The thing is, they've been let down by the hotel where they were going to have the reception. Well, actually the hotel's been closed by Health and Safety; mice were found in the kitchen and a dead rat in one of the water tanks.'

Genevieve cringed. 'And you want to know if we've any spare rooms that weekend.' She went to fetch the bookings diary she kept by the phone.

'No. Accommodation isn't the problem; everyone's more or less local. It's the buffet that's giving Gareth and his wife palpitations. And no doubt their daughter, too.'

She sat down again. 'Oh, I get it; I've just become one of your magical *blokes*, haven't I?'

'All I said was that I'd have a word with you. Nothing more than that.'

'And how many would I be cooking for? Twenty? Twenty-five?'

He looked down at Lily-Rose, whose large blue eyes were fixed intently on his tie. 'Um ... the guest list is quite big.'

'How big?'

'Eighty-odd.'

'*What!*'

'You can do it, Gen. I know you can. It'll be nothing but a loaves and fishes exercise for you.'

'Yeah, a flipping miracle! Feeding eighty hungry people, that's a lot of cooking. And a lot of stuff to ferry about.'

'That's where the second part of my proposition comes in. Is there any chance the reception could be held at Paradise House? You have to admit, if the weather's good, it's a great spot. The views are the best in the area. Great backdrop for the photos.'

She had to admire his gall. 'And if the weather is like it is today?'

They both turned and looked out at the garden; the drizzle had become a downpour.

'To be on the safe side, I'll tell Gareth and Gwenda to organise a marquee and tables and chairs. That way all bases will be covered and you won't have to worry about transporting food back and forth.'

'You've put an awful lot of thought into this,' she said, amused he'd taken her consent as a foregone conclusion.

'No more than any problem I'm confronted with.'

'Okay,' she conceded. 'I'll do it. Although I'll have to check with Dad. It's his house, after all.'

Again Adam lowered his gaze to the top of Lily-Rose's curly blonde hair. 'Don't be cross, but I've already done that. He said it was your decision.'

Genevieve rolled her eyes. 'I've been stitched up good and proper, haven't I?'

'Not a bit of it. I merely saved time by having a quick word with your father earlier on.' He smiled. 'Your dad's getting the hang of using that mobile now, isn't he? He answered straight off. No sweat.'

After years of saying he didn't need one, and that the local reception was too variable, Adam had finally persuaded her father that a mobile phone would come in handy. Genevieve was now the only member of her family to buck the trend.

'Don't push it, Adam Kellar,' she warned, 'or I might change my mind about feeding the five thousand.'

Sliding off Adam's lap, Lily-Rose said, 'Can I have another drink, please?'

Adam reached for the carton before Genevieve had put down her mug of tea.

'If you're not careful, you're going to make yourself indispensable where that girl's concerned,' she joked. The look on his face told her he wished the same could be said of the child's mother. Regretting her clumsiness, she said, 'So how much am I going to be paid for stepping into the breach?'

From his jacket pocket, he produced a phone number and a cheque. 'Gareth hoped you'd say yes, so he wrote this out in advance. When the job's done, there'll be that much again coming to you.'

'Trust an accountant to be so organised.' Genevieve said absently. But when she took the cheque, she did a double-take. 'Good grief, what's he expecting me to serve? Truffles and pâté de foie gras?'

'I couldn't say, but I suggest you ring Gwenda asap and get the lowdown on what she has in mind.'

Genevieve looked at him doubtfully. 'You haven't billed me too high, have you? Made out I'm better than I am.'

'All I've done is tell Gareth the truth. I reckon if you do exactly what you did for your father's birthday party, you'll be a huge success. And once word goes round, I guarantee you'll have more offers of work.'

Genevieve turned from tucking the cheque into her bag. 'Adam,' she said slowly, 'it sounds suspiciously like you've engineered this. Are you trying to organise me?' He was the only person outside the family who knew the reasons behind her return, but the last thing she wanted was him thinking she couldn't cope by herself.

He put a hand to his chest. 'Hand on heart, there's been no skulduggery; this has fallen right into your lap. So, if I were you, I'd grab the opportunity.' Then switching his attention from her to Lily-Rose, he said, 'Your auntie isn't very trusting, is she? I wonder why that is, Rosy-Posy.'

Lily-Rose giggled, put down her plastic mug and wandered out of the kitchen. As Genevieve eased the fruitcake out of its tin and onto a wire cooling rack, she reflected how every inch of her trust had been turned to cold-hearted suspicion a long time ago. As a result her instinct was always to question, even if it meant doubting the kindest of people, like Adam.

Her thoughts were interrupted by Adam saying, 'Gen, there's talk down in the village.'

'There's always talk down in the village.' She was only half-listening as she peeled away the greaseproof paper from the base of the cake.

'But this time it's about . . . well, and you know I never listen to gossip—'

She laughed. 'That's because quite often you're the focus of it. You're much too interesting and successful to go unnoticed. So who's the latest victim?'

He hesitated. 'It's you, Gen,' he said. 'And I heard it from Debs while she was doing my hair this morning.'

He had her fullest attention now. 'But what on earth has anyone to say about boring old me?'

'Quite a lot, actually. It's about this Jonjo Fitzwilliam character who's bought Ralph's barn. Or more precisely, about the architect who'll be doing the conversion work. Is it true you used to be childhood sweethearts?'

Thwack! There it was. Exactly what she'd known all along. She plonked herself with a heavy thump in the chair opposite. 'What else are the good folk of Angel Sands saying?'

'That he broke your heart. That you've never got over it. That you've decided to die a spinster of this parish having loved only the one man.'

She stared open-mouthed at him. 'You're kidding!'

He shook his head.

'But that's rubbish. Why, I've . . . I've had plenty of boyfriends. And it's nonsense that I've decided to live out my life as a lonely old spinster.'

'They didn't say lonely. And if it makes you feel any better, there are plenty of men in the village of the opinion they could put you on the road to sexual fulfilment.'

'Put me on the road straight out of here, you mean!' Shock had now turned to anger. How dare people talk about her like that! What right did they have to say such things?

'You can always tell me to mind my own business, but did he really break your heart?'

She nodded. 'And some.'

'Does it bother you to talk about it?'

'I don't know. It's not a subject that crops up much these days.'

'But now that it has, do you want to discuss it?'

'So that I can satisfy your curiosity?'

'No,' he said firmly. 'To put us on an equal footing. You know everything there is to know about me, but you're unusually guarded about yourself. I figured out a while ago that you operate on a need-to-know basis. Much like your father.'

He was right, of course. She *was* guarded, and preferred to keep things to herself. But how to tell Adam what had gone on? Where should she start?

She decided to go right back to the beginning, to that first day, when she met Christian and wanted to prove she wasn't scared of anything. Least of all a taunting boy with a strange voice.

Part Two

9

They swam in silence, away from the splashing and squealing children who were all much younger than them. The tide was going out and Genevieve knew they had to be careful. Her father had lectured her many times on the dangers of being swept out to sea, of children, even grown-ups, drifting away on flimsy lilos and having to be rescued by the air-sea rescue helicopter.

'We better not go too far,' she said. She didn't add that she was supposed to stay within eyeshot of her parents, who were on the beach with her younger sisters.

He nodded and pointed to the nearest rocks, which formed the right-hand spur of the bay. For a few seconds he swam on ahead, his arms cutting through the water cleanly, effortlessly, his body tilting to the side as he came up for air. Most boys she knew made a clumsy hash of front crawl – hands slapping the water, feet thrashing wildly – but this one did it properly, even the breathing. She followed suit and was soon level with him. Neither was out of breath when they climbed up onto the smooth, flat rocks that were warm from the sun. For a moment they both stood and stared at the sea, shading their eyes from the dazzling glare.

'I love it here,' she said, 'it's the best place in the world.'

When he didn't respond she wished she hadn't said anything. He probably thought it was a silly thing to say. Childish and gushing. She squeezed the water from her ponytail and sat down.

He sat down too, and looked directly at her. 'It's great here, isn't it? It's my favourite place,' he said, in his strange, off-key voice.

She frowned, wondering why he'd as good as repeated what she'd just said. 'Yes,' she agreed. 'My family and I come here every year. How about you?'

There was a pause before he answered, during which she realised he was making her feel uncomfortable.

'We've been coming since I was eight,' he said. 'How old are you?'

'Twelve. And you?'

Another gap in the conversation, followed by the same feeling of discomfort.

'Fourteen,' he replied.

And then she understood why he was making her feel so weird. He was staring at her too closely, his gaze too penetrating. She shifted away from him and turned her head to look back towards the beach and her parents. Dad was scanning the water's edge looking for her while her mother was helping Nattie perform the Towel Dance. This entailed a lot of self-conscious wriggling behind a towel before finally emerging – *ta-daa!* – dressed in a swimsuit.

Genevieve stood up and waved to her father. When eventually he caught sight of her and waved back, she sat down again, although part of her didn't want to. This strange boy might be an excellent swimmer, but he wasn't the easiest person to talk to. She'd have to be careful. This was only the first day of the holiday and she didn't want to get saddled with him for the rest of the time they were here, not if he was always going to be so odd. She dangled her feet into the water and felt the tickly touch of the swaying fronds of seaweed attached to the rocks. 'Do you have any brothers or sisters?' she said.

Once again he ignored her question. That's it, she thought. I'm not having anything more to do with him. She turned her head. 'Don't you know it's bad manners to ignore people?' She was about to slip back into the water and swim away when he laid a hand on her forearm.

'You have to look straight at me when you speak. If you don't, I can't read your lips. I'm deaf.'

Never had Genevieve felt so rude or cruel. Or so ignorant. Why hadn't she realised that that was why he spoke in that odd way? And that he had looked at her so intently because he was trying to read her lips. Mortified, she thought in an instant of all the things he was denied: music, television, laughter, birdsong. How awful for him. Head down, she murmured an apology.

He tapped her on the leg. 'What did you say?'

'I'm sorry,' she repeated, this time looking straight at him and stupidly raising her voice.

His mouth curved into a soft smile. 'Why are you sorry I'm deaf?'

'I'm not. I mean . . . well, I *am* sorry you're deaf, but what I meant was, I'm . . . I'm sorry I was so horrible to you.'

'And if I could hear properly, would you be so apologetic?'

He was twisting her words, just like Nattie did sometimes. Holding her ground, she said, 'If you weren't deaf I wouldn't have needed to apologise because I wouldn't have been so nasty.'

He paused, as though he wasn't sure what she'd said.

'I said—'

He stopped her with a hand. 'It's okay. I got it. So what you're saying is that you make a special case of being rude to the deaf. Or do blind people get the same treatment?'

Shocked that he could accuse her of something so awful, she opened her mouth to defend herself but then saw he was laughing at her. He'd been making fun of her all the time! Annoyed, she shoved him hard. She caught him off balance and with great satisfaction, watched him topple into the water.

When he surfaced, he slicked back his wet hair and rubbed his face. 'What was that for?'

'For being a pig and teasing me!' she shouted.

'You'll have to speak up,' he yelled with a grin, 'I can't hear you.'

His name was Christian May and they arranged to meet for a swim the following day, same place, same time. But the weather wasn't so nice, so they went for a walk along the coastal path instead. Her parents were happy for her to go off with her new friend, having met him briefly the day before and concluded that he was 'a well brought up young man who could be trusted to take good care of her'.

They walked for nearly an hour, stopping only to refer to the map and compass he'd brought. This was a new phenomenon to Genevieve; she wasn't used to being with someone so organised. No one in her family would have thought of bringing a map. Mum was always saying life should be a spontaneous adventure, which was her way of covering up for her oversights, like not making a note of dental appointments, losing her keys, going out and leaving the oven switched on or, one afternoon, forgetting to collect Polly from nursery school. 'I wondered where she was,' Serena said when Polly's teacher phoned.

But it was obvious from looking at the contents of Christian's tidily packed rucksack – map, compass, cagoule, camera, can of Coke and Mars bars – that he was as thorough as he was talkative. Now that she'd got the hang of remembering to look at him when she spoke, and to give him time to take in the shapes her mouth made, there was no stopping the flow of chatter between them. He told terrible jokes too. 'What do you call a crab when he's in a bad mood? . . . Crabby! And what was Hitler's first name? . . . Heil!'

To her surprise, she shared things with him that she wouldn't ordinarily discuss. She told him she had recently been diagnosed as dyslexic, something she preferred to keep quiet for fear of people automatically classing her as stupid.

'Does that mean you have fits?'

Thinking he must have misread her lips, she exaggerated her pronunciation to help him. 'Dyslexic, not epileptic.' The slight twist to his own lips told her that once again he'd caught her out. 'You're too sharp for your own good,' she muttered.

'At least you're cottoning on to the fact that just because I can't hear properly it doesn't necessarily mean I'm thick.'

And that was the bond between them. In their different ways, they were both striving to convince the world they were as capable as the next person.

'I hate it when people talk down to me,' Christian told her. 'I get it all the time. Once they realise I have a hearing problem, they halve my age. What they don't realise is that when you have one sense taken away, the others take up the slack.'

'Do you ever wear a hearing aid?'

'Sometimes, but I don't like to. What little I can hear gets drowned out or distorted by background noise being over-amplified.'

'And what about sign language? Can you do all that complicated hand stuff?'

'A bit, but I prefer lip-reading.'

'Could you teach me?'

'I could, but it's not easy. It's not something you can teach exactly; you have to practise it over and over. Like with most things, some make better learners than others.'

She soon realised just how difficult it was when he explained how certain letters looked the same when spoken. 'P, b and m are pretty tricky,' he said. He showed her how hard it was to tell the difference between pat and bat.

'So how do you tell the difference?' she asked, beginning to think he was some kind of genius.

He shrugged. 'You just have to fit the pieces of the jigsaw together by figuring out the context. It's the same with learning any new language. And remember, I've been doing this for years.'

'How many years?'

'Since for ever.'

'You were born deaf?'

'Partially. But I'll tell you about that another time. It's all very boring.'

But there was nothing boring about him or anything he said, and three days into the summer holiday they were inseparable.

And insufferable, if Nattie was to be believed. 'You never want to do anything with me any more,' she complained bitterly at breakfast one morning when Genevieve reminded her mother that she was spending the day with Christian again and would need a packed lunch. 'You're always off with that *boy*.' Nattie spat out the word 'boy' with as much disgust as she could muster. At ten years of age, she was of the opinion that boys, weedy and inferior beings, were like doing the washing up or anything else helpful around the house; to be avoided at all costs.

'But you've got Polly to play with,' Genevieve said, hurriedly buttering her toast and deciding to make her own sandwiches – Mum was miles away, drinking her cup of tea and staring out of the window. 'It's not as if you'll be on your own.'

'As good as. Polly's no fun. All she wants to do is read. Just look at her!'

Though only eight years old, Polly was never without a book. She was reading now at the breakfast table, her cereal bowl untouched, completely oblivious to the conversation going on around her.

Genevieve felt a pang of guilt. Maybe she was being selfish by going off with Christian yet again. 'I suppose you could come with us,' she offered. 'I'm sure Christian wouldn't mind.'

But the invitation was thrown back at her. 'I'd rather eat a plate of maggoty cabbage.'

'Who wants a plate of maggots?' asked Daddy Dean, glancing up from the newspaper he'd fetched at the crack of dawn that morning. Newspapers were his holiday treat. At home the farm kept him so busy he rarely had time for such a luxury. It was a wonder he could spare the time to come away at all. But that was Mum's doing. She insisted every summer that he left Grandad and the relief milkers in charge and took the family on holiday. She claimed she'd put itching powder in his underpants if he didn't do as she said. And they all knew she was sufficiently batty to do just that.

'Nobody's eating maggots, Dad,' Genevieve reassured him. 'It's only Nattie being silly.'

Across the table Nattie stuck out her tongue. Genevieve returned the gesture and got up to make herself a cheese and pickle sandwich. She no longer felt guilty for deserting her sister.

When it was time to go home to Cheshire, Genevieve left her packing to the last minute, more reluctant than usual to return to Brook House Farm and the start of the autumn term. She was going to miss more than just the happy sense of freedom she always enjoyed in Angel Sands; she was going to miss Christian. They had swapped addresses with the intention of staying in touch. But she knew that wouldn't happen. They would go home, pick up the lives they'd left behind, and forget each other.

She was proved right. Every morning for three whole weeks she watched for the postman, but there was no letter for her. And although she enjoyed telling her best friend at school, Rachel, all about the good-looking boy she'd met on holiday – conscious that she was boasting, and, to her shame, omitting to say he was deaf – she couldn't bring herself to write to Christian. Not when there was the risk he might not write back. How humiliating would that be? There was also the small matter of her appalling handwriting and embarrassing spelling to consider.

No. It was better all round to put him completely out of her mind.

10

The following summer, Genevieve and her family arrived in Angel Sands on a chilly, wet evening, to find that it hadn't stopped raining for over a week and the roof of their rented cottage had sprung a leak. Either the previous occupants of Thrift Cottage had turned a blind eye to the problem or they hadn't used this particular room. The sloping ceiling in Genevieve's bedroom, with its pretty eaves and dormer window overlooking the cornfields, was bulging ominously and dripping onto the sodden carpet. Always at his best when confronted with a DIY challenge, their father threw himself with gusto into the project, instructing them to fetch buckets and pans. 'Quick as you can,' he commanded from his frontline position, where he could keep an eye on the ceiling that threatened to give way any second. 'Some towels to mop up the carpet wouldn't go amiss,' he called after them as they stampeded downstairs to raid the kitchen cupboards.

Mercifully the ceiling didn't give way, but that night Genevieve lay awake listening to the steady plop, plop, plop of rainwater filling the circle of pots and pans on the floor. Her parents had wanted her to sleep with Nattie and Polly, but she'd said she'd be okay where she was. She wanted to be on her own. Was even grateful for the plop, plop, plop that kept her awake. It meant she had a full night ahead of her to prepare herself for the possibility of seeing Christian tomorrow.

If he was staying in Tawelfan again, and *if* she saw him, she was going to play it very differently from last summer. She was thirteen, a whole twelve months wiser than the silly girl who'd hoped he'd write. Her disappointment had been short-lived, but it still rankled that his words had been so empty. And hadn't he promised to send her some photographs that he'd taken of her?

The worst of it had been putting up with Nattie's teasing. 'What else did you expect?' she'd crowed. 'Boys always lie.' During the long journey down, in the back of the car, squeezed in with all the suitcases and boxes of food and toilet rolls, Nattie hadn't been able to resist a sly goad every now and then. 'I bet you he's found some other girl to hang around with,' she muttered. 'He won't even remember you.'

Her sister was probably right, but Genevieve was quick to remind herself that it didn't matter. Hadn't she spent the last ten months hardly giving him a thought? And hadn't she only started to think of him again because there was the chance of bumping into him?

All true. But equally true was the hope that they *would* bump into each other so she could show him how changed she was. She'd got rid of her childish ponytail and had her hair cut shorter, to look more grown-up. It had been Rachel's idea and they'd gone to the hairdresser's together. Like her best friend, she was now allowed to wear a bit of make-up. Except she couldn't really be bothered; she'd much rather help her father on the farm, or flick through her mother's cookery books, her mouth watering at the pictures. But Rachel could sit for hours in front of a mirror, happily messing about with her collection of lipsticks, eyeshadow compacts and wands of mascara. As for nail varnish, her best friend had hundreds of little bottles, all lined up along the window ledge. The colours ranged from glittery baby-pink to the deepest shade of purple, so dark it was almost black and made Rachel's hands look as though they were rotting at the ends. Occasionally Genevieve applied some varnish to her own nails, but try as she might she could never get them to grow as long as Rachel's.

'You need to eat more jelly,' her friend would advise, 'that's the way to strengthen your nails. And put Vaseline on them before you go to bed.' Rachel was an expert on most matters these days; she read all the magazines and kept some of the more explicit ones hidden from her mother.

Genevieve had been friends with Rachel Harmony since they'd both started at the local high school. Genevieve had moved up from the nearby primary school, but Rachel was new to the area and hadn't known a soul. Their teacher, Mr McKenzie, a fierce Scot with a purple birthmark on his neck, had assigned to Genevieve the task of taking Rachel under her wing. Before the end of that first week, they were best friends, although their roles had reversed. Whereas Rachel knew all the right things to wear, could sing all the latest pop songs and knew exactly which bands were in and which were out, Genevieve was not so well-informed. She had been brought up on a nostalgic diet of Judy Garland and Broadway musicals. Thanks to her mother's sentimental taste in music, she knew all the words to 'Some Enchanted Evening', 'Meet Me in St Louis' and 'Zing! Went the Strings of My Heart', but didn't have a clue about hits by Duran Duran or Spandau Ballet. Rachel was mad about Simon le Bon and Tony Hadley and had pictures of them on her bedroom walls. The only pictures Genevieve had were embarrassing pieces of artwork she'd done in primary school which her mother had framed and insisted on keeping. And although her bedroom was large, it was, as she'd come to realise, shamefully old-fashioned in comparison to Rachel's.

Beneath a threadbare rug were floorboards that creaked if you so much as looked at them, and gaps between the boards wide enough to let the draughts in. Its furniture included a bed with a rattly old brass bedstead, a chest of drawers her mother had haggled for at a second-hand shop and painted white, and a mahogany wardrobe the size of a small house, which was always used as a hiding place when they played sardines at Christmas. The wallpaper, coming away in places, was ancient and flowery and had been chosen by Gran when she and Grandad had run the farm and lived in the two-hundred-year-old farmhouse.

In contrast, Rachel lived on a recently built development of houses and her bedroom, though smaller than Genevieve's, was a vision of colour coordination and honey-gold pine. The walls, what you could see of them through the posters, were decorated with a smart, modern striped paper. The duvet was made of the same fabric as the curtains. The carpet was cream – Gran and Mum would have scoffed at the folly of this – and went right to the four corners of the room. Fitted cupboards housed Rachel's many clothes, most of them from Miss Selfridge and Top Shop, or from America, and in front of the window stood a proper dressing table with a three-way mirror and padded stool. There were shelves for her magazines, record player and growing collection of records, and the room was always perfectly tidy, not a thing out of place. It was as far removed from any room at Brook House Farm as it could be.

Rachel said her parents were boring and obsessed with keeping the house straight. Genevieve knew she wasn't exaggerating. She had once dropped an ice-lolly on the patio at a barbecue given by Mr and Mrs Harmony. When Rachel's father had seen the raspberry-coloured puddle, all hell broke loose, with him acting as though she'd dropped an atom bomb. Serena, on the other hand, had a much more relaxed attitude and expected Genevieve and her sisters to keep their own rooms tidy. 'If you want to live like pigs, it's entirely up to you,' she'd say. 'Just make sure you keep the mess inside and the door closed.'

If Genevieve had to name one thing of Rachel's that she truly envied, it would be the television in her friend's bedroom. Two years ago Serena had declared the box that stood in the corner of the sitting room was one of the great evils of the modern age, and had banished it to the loft. But the wonderful thing about Mum was that she was never afraid to do a U-turn, and on Valentine's Day last year she got their father to dig out the television set so she could watch Torvill and Dean win the gold medal at the winter Olympics in Sarajevo. With a deadpan face she justified her actions by saying it was a one-off event, a moment in sporting history that she didn't want her children to miss.

But Genevieve knew it wasn't sport or history her mother was interested in; she was an incurable romantic and wanted to see for herself the are-they-aren't-they? chemistry between the two skaters. 'Of course they're madly in love with each other,' she sniffled when the couple got up from the ice and the audience went berserk, throwing flowers and applauding wildly. 'Only love could produce something as magical as that.' She reached out to Daddy Dean and gave him a soppy look. He squeezed her hand in unspoken agreement.

The next day Serena insisted the television was returned to the loft, and

Genevieve hungered for it. She couldn't even turn to Gran and Grandad to satisfy her hunger, for they hadn't got around to replacing their broken black and white set with the coat-hanger sticking out of it. In those days, Gran wasn't the addict she was later to become. So whenever she stayed at Rachel's house, she binged on what her mother would have condemned as mind-rotting trash. It could have been worse, of course. She could have been hanging about on street corners with a gang of boys, as Nattie was now itching to do. Instead, with guilty greed, she feasted on episodes of *Dynasty* and *Dallas* and *Emmerdale Farm*.

Often she watched the telly while lying on Rachel's bed, as her friend, indifferent to what was on since she was never denied it, flicked through her magazine collection.

Genevieve was sometimes glad she was dyslexic; some of the articles in Rachel's magazines were too embarrassing for words, page after page of mushy relationship stuff. And sex. But Rachel lapped it up and relished reading the articles out aloud.

'Listen to this,' she'd say, swinging round from her dressing table. 'It says here, "Think of the happiest and most incredibly satisfying moment of your life and times it by a thousand and that's how good an orgasm feels." '

Genevieve had tried to imagine sinking her teeth into a jam doughnut, tasting the dusty crust of sugar, feeling the sweet swell of soft dough roll around her mouth, jam oozing from the corner of her lips: a perfect explosion of heavenly sweetness. She then tried to imagine the experience increased by a factor of a thousand, as instructed, but could only imagine feeling sick. Would sex make her feel sick too?

The next morning, the first proper day of the holiday, she awoke to brilliant sunshine and a roof that had stopped leaking. Before breakfast was over, her father had borrowed a ladder from the neighbours and was investigating the damage.

'Nothing to it,' he announced, coming back into the kitchen to finish off his mug of cold tea, 'a couple of slates. I'll ring Mrs Jones and tell her I'll fix it myself.' Mrs Jones was the owner of Thrift Cottage and lived in Cardiff. 'Now then, let me fetch my tool kit from the car.' Their father never went anywhere without his red plastic tool box.

'You think more of that tool box than you do of me,' Mum would say. 'If the house was on fire and you had to choose between me and that wretched box, I wouldn't come out alive.'

'Nonsense, darling,' he'd argue good-humouredly. 'You're such a slip of a thing I'd sling you over my shoulder and carry the box in my other hand.'

'You see! I get *slung* over your shoulder and the box is lovingly carried.'

Their arguments were playful, never vindictive.

'Okay if I go for a walk?' ventured Genevieve.

Everyone looked at her. This was a major event in her family, catching everyone's attention at the same time. Even Polly took time out from *Charlie and the Chocolate Factory* to glance in her direction.

'What?' Genevieve asked. 'What did I say?'

Nattie sneered – she had sneering down to a fine art these days. Genevieve was sure her sister practised in front of the mirror, devoting hours to the curling of her lip and the letting out of just the right amount of condescension in her breath.

'I suppose you could run a few errands at the shop for us,' her father said. 'Some sausages for breakfast tomorrow morning would be nice.'

'Um . . . I wasn't thinking of going in that direction.'

'I bet you weren't.'

'Oh, don't be so cruel to your sister, Nattie. You too, Dean.' Her mother put down the frying pan she was washing at the sink and turned to Genevieve. 'If you want to go and catch up with that young man, then off you go. Be back for lunch at one, though. I'm doing macaroni cheese.'

'Thanks, Mum!' She escaped before she could be forced to endure another of her sister's jibes.

The day was fresh and bright, the deepening blue of the sky a welcome sight after the rain. A warm, salty wind raced across the cornfields, rippling it like the sea in the distance. She walked happily down the lane towards the village. Either side of her, quaint little cottages, trim and whitewashed, stood to attention, their doors and window frames painted cheerful colours, their small gardens pretty and well-tended. Some of them had window boxes full of tumbling flowers; vivid scarlet geraniums mixed with blue and white lobelia and orange nasturtiums. She came to a small junction where one road twisted down to the centre of the village, and the other led up the steep hill out of Angel Sands, towards Tawelfan beach. She took the latter and began the climb.

Reluctantly she tugged off her sweatshirt. It was brand new, like her trainers, and chosen especially because it hid her chest, which to her increasing horror seemed much too big.

'Wow,' Rachel had said before the end of term, when they'd been changing for PE. 'When did your breasts get so big? I wish mine would get a move on like yours.' So typical of Rachel to come right out and use the word 'breasts'. Boobs, or bosoomers as Gran called them, would have seemed less graphic. Perhaps smaller too.

But her friend was right. Overnight her breasts had suddenly decided to grow. For ages they'd been hinting at appearing, just little bumps, and then the next moment, *wham*! There they were, tender and ballooning.

'Oh, that's quite normal,' her mother had said, when Genevieve had plucked up the courage to tell her. 'Any sign of your period yet?'

'Um . . . I don't think so.'

'Well, you'll know it for sure when it does start. Meanwhile, we'd better get you sorted with your first bra.'

Genevieve draped the sweatshirt around her shoulders, using the sleeves to hide the cause of her embarrassment.

Thirty minutes later she was looking down onto Tawelfan beach and could see that only a handful of people had staked a claim to the curving stretch of sand. There was no direct access by car, which meant it was never very crowded, the main reason she loved coming here. It was also why Christian's parents, so he had told her, had bought Pendine Cottage, less than a mile away.

The path down to the beach dipped sharply and she had to watch her footing on the rocks, worn smooth and shiny by years of constant use.

Her father had nicknamed them 'the Pembrokeshire Pilgrims' when they first set out from Angel Sands to spend a day at Tawelfan – Dad carrying the deckchairs and cold box, Mum a few steps behind with the travel rug and windbreaker, and Genevieve and her sisters following, with a fishing net and rolled-up towel under one arm, and a bucket and spade dangling from the other. 'We're following in the footsteps of countless other pilgrims,' he'd say, 'pilgrims en route for St David's.'

Genevieve made for her favourite spot in the sand dunes that backed the beach, with the broad expanse of heath behind. It was sheltered and even warmer here. Removing her sweatshirt from her shoulders, she folded it into a makeshift pillow and lay back, her eyes closed against the sun. Perfect. Like wrapping herself in her favourite dressing gown and sitting in front of the fire, drinking a cup of hot chocolate with whipped cream melting on the top of it.

Listening to the sound of the sea, then the plaintive call of a distant bird – a curlew, perhaps? – she thought of the bird-spotting book Grandad had given her on her thirteenth birthday. It had belonged to him when he was a boy and now it was hers. Rachel had thought it an odd sort of present to give anyone, a tatty old book (especially for a dyslexic), but Genevieve treasured it. Grandad had written on the front page: 'To my bonnie Genevieve, may this give you as much pleasure as it has me.'

Lost in thought, she felt a shadow pass over the sun. She snapped open her eyes. At first she didn't recognise him, not with the sun directly behind him, reducing his face and body to little more than a silhouette. It was his voice, though, that clinched it.

'Hello, Genevieve, I hoped I might find you here.'

Oh, that was casual of him. He'd lied through his teeth about staying in touch, and now he was expecting her to believe that he hoped she'd be here. She sat up. 'Really? Why's that?'

He frowned, then sat down beside her, his long legs stretched out in front of him. 'Because I've been looking forward to seeing you again.'

She noticed his voice was deeper than last year, and its pitch was better, less up and down. He looked thinner in the face, which made him seem more grown-up, and just visible through his wavy brown hair, longer and thicker than last summer, was a hearing aid tucked behind his left ear. She didn't know why exactly, but the sight of this quelled her antagonism towards him.

When she didn't say anything, he said, 'How are you, Genevieve?'

'Fine. I'm fine.'

He touched her lightly on the arm and said, 'I can't see what you're saying.'

She felt herself colour and apologised, looking him self-consciously in the eye. 'Sorry, I forgot about that.'

'The same way you forgot to write to me?'

No way was she going to let him get away with that. 'It was *you* who never wrote to *me.*'

He shook his head. 'I couldn't. I lost your address. I waited for you to write so I could send the photographs I promised you.'

He was lying, just as Nattie said all boys did. 'I don't believe you – ' But seeing the earnest expression on his face, she faltered. Deep down she wanted to believe him. 'Did you really lose my address?'

'Yes. I threw it away by accident. And when I didn't hear from you I assumed you didn't want to stay in touch, so I had no choice but to let it go. Why didn't you write to me?'

She thought of fibbing, of saying, 'Hey! What a coincidence! I lost your address, too.' But she was hopeless at telling bare-faced lies. She told a half-truth instead. 'I decided to wait for your letter to come first. And when it didn't . . . well, I thought the same as you, that you hadn't meant to write, that it was just a polite thing to say.' She omitted to mention anything about the fear of him judging her by her inability to spell.

When he'd taken in her words, his face broke into a slow smile. 'So now we've got that straightened out, does that make us friends again?'

'I think it does,' Genevieve said shyly. She scooped up a handful of sand, let it trickle through her fingers and wondered why her stomach felt so odd.

11

It was proving to be Genevieve's best holiday ever. Each morning a patchy sky would greet her when she drew back the curtains, but very soon a warm breeze would chase the clouds away and the sun would burst through. She met up with Christian almost every day and together they followed the same routine: a swim at Tawelfan beach (including a performance of the Towel Dance), followed by a walk along the cliff top until they found a suitable spot for a late picnic lunch.

Today they had climbed down onto a sheltered ledge where spongy cushions of thrift, pink and bright, grew in the cracks of the rocks. They were eating egg and cress sandwiches that Christian's mother had made for them.

'Other people's sandwiches always taste better than your own,' Genevieve said, helping herself to another.

'I know what you mean. Your mother's sandwiches are . . .' he hesitated, as if seeking the right word, 'unique,' he said, with a smile.

'Now you're just being polite.'

Serena's sandwiches were a challenge and not for the timid. Ever since Band Aid's 'Do They Know It's Christmas?' Mum had decided there was too much waste in the world and had taken to making sandwiches using the previous night's supper leftovers. Yesterday, unbeknown to Genevieve, her mother had made them a stack of spaghetti bolognese sandwiches.

'Not bad,' Christian had said, after a tentative bite, then a bigger and more adventurous mouthful. 'Better than you'd think.' Once again he was politeness personified, something Mum loved about him.

'That boy is the most polite young man I've ever come across,' she sighed, after Christian's first visit to Thrift Cottage, when all he'd said was, 'Thank you, Mrs Baxter, but I can't stay for tea, my parents are expecting me back.' From then on, Christian could do no wrong in Serena's eyes. Especially when she learned how he'd lost his hearing.

His mother had contracted German measles when she was pregnant and he'd been born with a partial loss of hearing in one ear, which, his parents had been told, would gradually get worse. But then at the age of four he was diagnosed as having a brain tumour. It was benign, but needed to be operated on immediately; if not, he'd die. However, the operation meant he would lose the hearing in his good ear. It was fortunate, the doctors told his parents, that he'd already learned the necessary speech skills to carry him through life.

'Oh, the poor boy!' Serena had cried, when Genevieve told her the story. 'And what must his poor parents have gone through? If it had been me I would have been beside myself with worry.' It was typical Mum, to put herself firmly in another person's shoes and relive every moment of the drama.

When they'd finished lunch, they both leaned against the rock and closed their eyes. When they were silent like this, Genevieve sometimes made the mistake of thinking that Christian was listening, as she was, to the sounds around them; the waves crashing on the jagged rocks below, the cries of the gulls wheeling above, and the occasional bleat of distant sheep. Earlier in the week, while they'd been sunbathing in the sand dunes, she had patted his arm and pointed out a skylark. 'Its trill sounds just like a telephone ringing, doesn't it?' she'd said.

'I'll take your word for it,' he'd replied.

He never seemed to mind her clumsiness, but she cared deeply. It was important to her that she didn't offend him. It meant that at times she was over-careful, wanting to ask something, to understand the world he lived in, but holding back for fear he'd think her rude. One mistake she'd made was to assume that he heard nothing at all, that his world was silent. But it wasn't. He'd told her that sometimes his head literally roared with the distortion of sounds around him.

Sitting companionably in the bright sun, she touched his arm lightly and said, 'When you found me on Tawelfan beach last week, you were wearing a hearing aid. Why haven't I seen you using it since?'

He shrugged – he did a lot of that. It was another of the changes she'd noticed. Just as she'd grown taller and changed her hair, so had he. He was still thin, didn't quite fill out his clothes, and his shoulders, broad and angular, reminded Genevieve of a coat-hanger. He was quieter too, told fewer silly jokes than he had last summer. In answer to her question, he said, 'It's new. Some piece of state-of-the-art technology that's supposed to help.'

'And does it?'

Another shrug. 'A bit. Depends on the situation. But I still instinctively rely on lip-reading.'

Before she could ask what kind of situation, he added, 'I'm so used to being without a hearing aid, I feel kind of weird with one. As if I'm trying to be someone I'm not.'

'How long have you had it?'

'Just a few weeks.'

'Then maybe you need to persevere and get the hang of it.'

'You sound like my parents. Next you'll be telling me to get my hair cut.'

She surveyed his thick hair that had a hint of New Romantics about it. She knew he never wore it too short because of the scar from his operation. 'Looks fine to me. I like it.'

Sensing that this was as personal as they'd ever got, she turned away and brushed her hand over a cushion of thrift that was as springy as his hair looked. She was suddenly shy. Almost as shy as she'd felt the first day they'd gone swimming together last week. Revealing her new shape – short of wearing a sweatshirt, there was simply no way to hide what was trying to appear over the top of her swimsuit – she had plunged into the chilly water, hoping against hope that Christian hadn't noticed anything different about her. Perhaps if she had gone to a mixed school she might have been less embarrassed, would have held her head up high and been proud of what Rachel envied so much. She never caught him looking directly at the cause of her discomfort, but who knew where his gaze roamed when she was looking the other way. Gradually she relaxed and the need for concealment became less of a priority. She was happy to lie down on the sand beside him in nothing but her swimsuit and not worry what he might be thinking.

'Boys think of sex every ninety-five seconds,' Rachel had once told her. It had occurred to Genevieve that maybe her friend thought of it more often. Rachel's encyclopaedic knowledge on the subject of sex included the dos and don'ts of flirting. 'Forget all that old-fashioned stuff about fluttering your eyelashes,' she'd told Genevieve. 'All you need to do is comment on a bloke's appearance and he'll know you're interested.'

Flirting had been the last thing on Genevieve's mind just now when she'd remarked on Christian's hair, and she hoped he wouldn't read anything into her words.

'By the way,' he said suddenly, 'I meant to say how much I liked your hair. It suits you. What made you get it cut?'

Help! Was he flirting with her?

They had walked further than usual, so it took them longer to get home. They always parted at Tawelfan beach, he to go inland to Pendine Cottage, she to follow the coastal path to Angel Sands. On this occasion, while they were arranging to meet the following morning, he took her by surprise; he held her hand for the last few yards. Nervously, she let her hand rest in his.

A big smile accompanied her back to Thrift Cottage, but when she let herself in, the smile was instantly wiped from her face. At home, at Brook House Farm, Grandad had suffered a heart attack. He was in intensive care and they were driving home at once. Genevieve's first thought wasn't that she might not see her grandfather alive again, but that she wouldn't see Christian tomorrow. The shameful selfishness of this thought haunted her for a long time afterwards.

Genevieve had always thought of Granny Baxter as a big, strong woman.

But seeing her stooped over the cooker as she attended to the ancient jam pan, she revised her opinion. Granny Baxter had shrunk.

Four weeks had passed since Grandad's funeral, the first Genevieve had attended. When their mother's parents had died the girls had been too young to attend. But they'd all been there this time round, neatly lined up in the front pew of the church where they came for Sunday School. Genevieve had been instructed to sit between her sisters; Polly on her left, Nattie on her right. Polly had sat perfectly still throughout the service, her head lowered as she searched through a Bible for something interesting to read, and Nattie, fidgeting and chewing the inside of her lower lip, played with a hanky she'd screwed into a grubby ball. Before setting off for St Augustine's – or St Rattle Bag's as Grandad had called it – their mother had given each of them one of their father's freshly laundered handkerchiefs. 'Just in case,' she'd murmured.

When they were outside in the hot August sunshine – so hot that it made the dark top Serena had forced Genevieve to wear itch against her clammy skin – the time came to lower the coffin into the ground. Clutching her father's hanky, and trying to keep herself from thinking of Grandad's dead body just feet away, Genevieve applied herself to making a list of all the 'just in case' uses for which the handkerchief might come in handy. Just in case she tripped over and cut her knee . . . just in case she needed a lift home and had to flag down a passing car . . . just in case she spilled a drink and needed to mop it up.

She kept the list going, right on until they were back at Brook House Farm and her mother asked her if she was okay. 'I'm fine,' she'd lied, knowing it was the required answer with so many guests to see to.

Four weeks on and Genevieve still had her father's handkerchief, carefully folded just as it had been the morning of the funeral. Now it was in her jeans pocket as she sat at the kitchen table, thinking how frail Granny Baxter looked as she stirred the damson jam. She felt for the 'just in case' handkerchief, just in case she might cry.

Everyone except her had cried when Grandad died. Even her father. That had shocked her, but not enough to bring on her own tears. You're nothing but a selfish cow, she'd told herself, willing the tears to appear. But they wouldn't come, despite the harsh words she scourged herself with: *How could you think of Christian when Grandad was dying in agony? What kind of a granddaughter are you? The worst kind! That's what you are. Selfish and stupid!*

She didn't know for sure if Grandad had died in agony, but she needed to believe he had, to worsen the crime she'd committed. Now all she had to do was find a suitable punishment to fit it.

She dabbed at the crumbs and smear of butter icing on her plate and licked her finger clean. She looked at the remains of Gran's homemade Victoria sponge cake in the middle of the table, and was tempted to ask for another slice. She couldn't recall a day when there wasn't something 'fresh out' of the oven when she called on Gran – ginger biscuits, vanilla cream slices (Gran made the best puff pastry), exquisite choux buns, melt-in-the-mouth shortbread, creamy egg custard tart, and rock cakes sweet and fragrant with allspice.

Egg custard tart had been Grandad's favourite, and it had been a longstanding joke in the family that nobody had a sweet tooth like he did, or the same appetite.

'I'm famished,' he'd say, after spending a day out on the farm with Daddy Dean. 'I could eat a horse between two mattresses and still have room for a double helping of suet pud.' He was a big man, but not what you'd call fat; big-boned was how people described him. To Genevieve, when she was little, he'd been a giant of a man, and wonderfully warm-hearted. 'Come on my Bonnie girl,' he'd say to her, 'climb up here on my lap and I'll read you a story. We'll have a bun too, shall we? And maybe a mug of hot chocolate.' There was a twinkle of mischief in his eyes when he said this, as though the two of them were being naughty and breaking a rule together.

Since his death, Genevieve had expected her grandmother to stop baking completely. But, if anything, she was cooking twice as much and the pantry was filling up fast. 'It's to keep her busy,' Mum said. 'To stop her dwelling on Grandad.'

'Damn and blast!'

Granny Baxter's cursing made Genevieve start. 'What is it, Gran? Have you burnt yourself?' Genevieve went to see.

'It's nothing,' her grandmother said. 'Nothing that a bit of cold water won't put right. Stir this while I run the tap.'

Genevieve did as she was told, keeping a wary eye on the spluttering pan of damsons and the other on her grandmother as she held the inside of her forearm under the tap. 'Jam's the very devil for burns,' Gran said. 'Instead of pouring hot oil on the marauding hordes in the middle ages, they should have used boiling jam.'

Looking up from the pan, Genevieve said, 'I think this is about done now, Gran.' She had helped Granny Baxter so many times in the past, picking the fruit, cleaning it, topping and tailing it, and stirring in the sugar and lemon juice, she knew to the second when it was on the verge of setting.

They filled the jars that had been drying in the warm oven, and Genevieve was given the job of sealing them with circles of waxed paper, cellophane and rubber bands on top, while Gran wrote out the stick-on labels. When the last one had been labelled, sealed and carried through to the pantry, Genevieve said, 'It doesn't seem right that all this goes on without Grandad. He should be here.' She swallowed, not quite sure what had made her say such a thing. When her grandmother didn't respond, she looked at her unsteadily and saw something like confusion on her face. 'I'm sorry, Gran. I shouldn't have said anything.'

'Nonsense, if that's how you feel, then that's just what you should have said.'

'But does it make it worse for you? Hearing people talk about him?'

Gran put down the pan she'd been about to carry to the sink. 'Genevieve, I'd much rather hear you talk about your grandfather than hear nothing from you at all. In fact, I'd go so far as to say you've been much too quiet these last four weeks.'

Genevieve knew it had been a mistake to start the conversation. She could feel the backs of her eyes prickle. Needing something to provide a diversion, she said, 'Here, let me wash that pan for you. Then I'd better be going.'

'No,' Gran said. 'I have a much better idea. Why don't I cut you another slice of cake and make us some mugs of hot chocolate.'

The comforting reminder of her grandfather was too strong for Genevieve, and she fought hard to hold back the stinging tears. But it wasn't working. She yanked the 'just in case' handkerchief from her pocket and pressed it to her eyes. She cried and cried, for what felt like for ever, her head resting on her grandmother's shoulder. She sobbed for all those times she'd curled up on grandad's lap and had been made to feel so special. But mostly she cried because she had thought of herself and not him when she'd been told he'd had a heart attack.

If she had thought the stream of tears would bring her some relief, she was wrong. The world still felt black to her. Horribly black and empty, with nowhere for her to hide her shame.

12

Gran told Genevieve that the worst of the pain would pass. She didn't believe her, but gradually Genevieve found she could think of her grandfather without being overcome by a rush of painful guilt. She had been tempted to share with Gran what was really troubling her in the kitchen that day, but had let the opportunity slip by. Ironically, as autumn gave way to winter and the days turned colder and darker, the blackness that had eclipsed her world lightened, and life didn't seem so bad.

But Grandad's absence from the family on Christmas day was hard for them to bear.

'It's like celebrating Christmas without Father Christmas,' Nattie said, in a moment of rare insight as they set off in the bitter wind to St Rattle Bag's for the traditional morning service. Later, to everyone's surprise, Polly sat at the piano and sang a song she had secretly written for Grandad. She had a beautiful voice and the words were so poignant they brought a stunned silence to the room. Gran was the first to cry, then the rest of them joined in. Even Genevieve. And because she cried so openly she knew she was over the worst.

On New Year's Eve she made a resolution to do better at school. Last term her school work had taken a downward slide. Her teachers had made allowances because of Grandad, but now she wanted to work harder and to concentrate more during lessons. In fact, she'd been told that concentration wasn't the problem, that there was even a danger of over-concentrating, which explained why she had so many headaches. She'd also been told that people who suffered from dyslexia had a thought process many times faster than those who didn't. This was because dyslexics had so much more to contend with – they were constantly trying to break the secret codes everyone else had cracked within the blink of an eye. No wonder she felt so tired most of the time!

But thank goodness she had Rachel to cheer her up. Rachel's latest craze was a quest to find the perfect everlasting lipstick. 'I've given up on flavoured lipgloss,' she announced in Boots one Saturday morning, after they'd taken the bus into Macclesfield. 'I've tried them all and they're a waste of money. Gloss looks great for five minutes, but it either turns into a gummy mess or disappears altogether. Honestly, they've put countless men on the moon; you'd think the least they could do was invent a lipstick that does what it claims, sticks to your lips. It's not asking too much, is it?' Genevieve envied her friend for having so little to worry about.

Easter was early that year and brought with it a letter from Christian.

There had been others. The first, with its Pembrokeshire postmark, had arrived the day before the funeral, and had told her how sorry he was to hear of her grandfather's death. They had left Angel Sands so hurriedly there had been no opportunity for her to explain. But word had soon gone round the village – everyone knew the Baxters who stayed at Thrift Cottage – and by lunchtime the following day, after he'd given up waiting for her on Tawelfan beach, he had knocked on the door of Thrift Cottage. A neighbour told him they'd gone, and why. Genevieve had read the letter again and again, until it gave her a headache, and concluded that he was genuine in his need to let her know he was thinking of her.

But she had thrown the letter away. She didn't want him to think of her. And she certainly didn't want to think of him. Not when it reminded her of her selfishness.

A week after the funeral she relented and sat cross-legged on her bedroom floor, pen in hand. An hour later, the rug was covered in screwed-up balls of paper. The harder she tried, the more the words and letters slipped away from her. In the end, deciding it didn't matter what he thought of her, she scribbled a few lines and slipped the piece of paper into an envelope. She'd thanked him for his sympathy and hoped he'd enjoy being back at school when term started. There was no mention how much she'd enjoyed seeing him again, no hint that she expected another letter in return. She didn't.

A month passed and another letter did arrive. It contained some carefully wrapped photographs, two of her alone, and one of the pair of them. She thought how stupid she looked – all eyes and silly grins – and threw the letter and pictures in the bin. Then a Christmas card came, asking if she'd received his last letter with the photographs. She sent one in return, his name at the top of the card, hers at the bottom. She wanted to deny all knowledge of receiving the photos but she didn't want to lie, so she wrote a few words of thanks, adding that it was a shame she looked so awful in them.

Now, five months later, a third letter had arrived. She sat in the garden beneath her favourite cherry tree, blossom drifting down in the soft breeze, and caught the sound of her father driving the tractor across the top field. She opened the envelope, her mind made up. This time she would write a proper letter back to Christian. She understood now what she'd done; she'd used him to punish herself. She'd been a fool. A misguided fool who had deliberately hurt someone who'd gone out of his way to be nice to her.

This new-found knowledge had been slow to dawn on her, but the truth was plain and it was time to do the right thing. It wouldn't be long before summer was upon them and she didn't want to turn up in Angel Sands with things unsaid. Christian deserved a sincere apology from her.

She opened his letter, her heart racing a little as she anticipated his words, that he was looking forward to seeing her again in Angel Sands.

But her happy anticipation skittered away. She read the letter through several times, hoping she'd misunderstood something. He hoped she and her family were well and that she would spare a thought for him next term when he had to sit his exams, after which he was going on a student exchange trip to Spain for the whole of the summer holiday. He didn't know how he was going to manage lip-reading in another language – a language he couldn't even speak – but his parents had decided it would broaden his horizons. He would send her a card from Madrid, where he'd be staying. If that was okay with her.

No! It wasn't fair. She didn't want him to go to Spain. Not when she'd just got used to thinking of him again. She suddenly remembered the way he'd held her hand, and wished she could turn back the clock. She'd give anything still to be on the beach at Tawelfan and for her grandfather to be fit and well and asking Gran to make him one of her creamy egg custard tarts.

She folded the letter, slipped it into the envelope and went inside. She needed something to eat. Something sweet and comforting.

13

Almost a year later, Rachel suggested to Genevieve that she needed to lose weight.

Genevieve had been thinking she ought to do something ever since she'd given up competitive swimming, but somehow she could never raise the enthusiasm. Her friend's exact words were, 'Don't think I'm being rude, Gen, and I'm only saying this for your own good, but I've heard some of the girls at school calling you names behind your back.'

They were in Genevieve's bedroom, Rachel lying on her front on the bed with her legs in the air, Genevieve sitting on the ledge by the open window. Her friend's words caused a coldness to grip Genevieve and her insides drained away.

'What names?' she asked, turning from the window.

'Oh, you know, the usual kind of unimaginative drivel: Fatso Baxter and wobble wobble, here comes jelly Gen.' Rachel's voice was matter of fact.

Genevieve's heart slammed. The coldness became a burning heat that seemed to swallow her up whole.

'Tell you what,' Rachel continued, 'I'd been thinking of going on a diet myself. We could do it together if you want.'

The offer was absurd. Rachel was stick thin; never in a million years would anyone call her Fatso Harmony. She had the kind of graceful body Genevieve could only dream of. The only trouble she had in buying clothes was finding a pair of jeans tight enough for her minuscule bum. But in that moment Genevieve loved her friend for her thoughtfulness. 'You'd do that for me?' she said, her voice small and croaky.

'Of course. Why wouldn't I?'

'Because you don't need to. You're . . . you're perfect as you are.' She had wanted to say 'beautiful', but thought it might sound a bit weird.

Rachel turned over and sat up, her back as straight and poised as a ballerina's. 'You must be blind, Gen. Look at me!' She lifted the blouse of her school uniform and revealed a stomach that was enviably smooth and taut. She pinched the skin – what she could get hold of – and said, 'That can go for starters.'

Genevieve wasn't convinced. Yet aware that her friend was trying to help and encourage her, she said, 'What sort of diet shall we go on?' She knew nothing about dieting, but was confident Rachel would know all there was to know.

Rachel was on her feet now, standing in front of the full-length mirror on the wardrobe door. She smoothed down her school skirt that was three inches shorter than the regulation length and showed off her slender Barbie doll legs. Genevieve thought hers were more like Cabbage Patch doll stumps. 'We'll cut out all carbohydrates,' Rachel said.

Well, that sounded easy enough. No potatoes or pasta. Or rice.

'That means no cakes or biscuits,' Rachel said with stern authority, hitching up her skirt another inch.

No cakes or biscuits. That wasn't so easy. Especially as for a special treat, Gran had invited the two of them for tea that afternoon.

They took the shortcut to Gran's bungalow, along the footpath that circled the field known as Solomon's Meadow, where the newborn lambs were put because it was so sheltered. It was late afternoon and clouds of dizzy gnats danced in the warm May air. Normally Genevieve would have enjoyed the walk; she would have ambled along spotting birds' nests in the hedgerow or hoping for the first sighting of a particular wild flower. Today, having been told by Rachel that exercise and dieting went hand in hand, she set off at a cracking pace, hardly noticing her surroundings. All she could think of was the humiliation she felt at what the girls at school were calling her behind her back. Had Rachel not been with her, she would surely have been in tears. She was lucky to have such a good friend. And knowing Rachel, she'd probably spared her the cruellest names.

It wasn't the first time she had been made fun of. When she was twelve, Katie Kirby and Lucinda Atkins, the brightest and most popular girls in the class, were always teasing her because she came bottom in almost every test. But when their sniggering turned to outright bitching in front of the whole class, Genevieve's normally stoic indifference caved in and she burst into tears that evening at home.

Genevieve had recently been officially declared dyslexic, and her mother marched into the headmistress's office the following morning and insisted that the two girls were made to apologise and had the facts – the ABC of dyslexia, as Serena had clumsily put it – explained to them.

'Dyslexia is a rare and special gift,' she told the headmistress, 'unlike ignorance. Be sure to make that clear to them. Their parents too.'

When Serena Baxter was provoked, she became frighteningly self-possessed and fiercely to the point. Nothing angered her more than bullying. She was as protective of Genevieve and her sisters as any lioness guarding her cubs. But because she allowed them more freedom than most other children, she didn't always know if they did need her protection. Rachel was in awe of this.

'Your Mum's great. She just lets you get on with your own thing. Wish mine was more like her.'

Now, marching on ahead of Rachel, Genevieve wondered if so much freedom was a good thing. Another mother might have noticed her daughter piling on the pounds and done something about it.

But that wasn't fair. It was no one's fault but her own that she'd got so fat. Besides, her mother didn't know the half of what she ate in secret. She couldn't name the day or place when she started eating too much, but she suspected it began some time after last summer.

Angel Sands hadn't felt the same without Christian. She had missed their swims together, and their long walks. But most of all she'd missed what might have been between them. More holding hands. Maybe even a kiss. She was plagued with visions of him meeting an attractive Spanish girl in Madrid. At night she had tossed and turned, picturing this imaginary girl, whom she eventually named Rosa. She was olive-skinned, dark-haired, dark-eyed and stunningly beautiful. And of course, she was as skinny as Rachel and wore one of those fantastic Flamenco dresses. She had only to stamp her feet, click her fingers and Christian would be hers for ever.

What hope for a plain girl such as Genevieve Baxter? How could she ever compete?

She never told anyone what was going through her mind, not even Rachel. And whenever Nattie teased her about pining for her long-lost boyfriend, she'd pretend not to hear.

Three weeks after driving home from Angel Sands, a postcard had arrived from Madrid – it was the only communication she'd had from Christian since the spring when he'd written to say he'd be spending the summer in Spain. She'd taken it upstairs to read in her bedroom, away from Nattie's prying eyes. She'd unwrapped a Twix, hidden inside an old shoe box at the bottom of her wardrobe. Perched on the window ledge – and only when she'd eaten the two sticks of chocolate – she ventured to read the card. She took it slowly.

> Hi Genevieve,
>   As you can imagine, Madrid is very different from Angel Sands. It's much hotter, for a start. The family I'm staying with are nice, but it's a nightmare trying to understand them! I have to rely on my phrase book and gesture a lot.
>   Miss you,
>   Christian.

She rummaged around inside the shoe box again and pulled out a packet of Rolos, then returned to her seat to read the card again. There wasn't much to go on, but the connection, small as it was, gave her a tingly feeling, a tiny glow of happiness.

Miss you.

She put a Rolo in her mouth, sucked it for a moment, then rolled it gently round her teeth and tongue until the chocolate melted. Then came the taste of softening toffee; its smooth sweetness spreading through her mouth like the golden warmth of the sun. All too soon it was gone.

Miss you.

Had he written that because he genuinely missed her? Or was it just one of those meaningless signing-off things you said, like, 'See you soon' or, 'Lots of love'? Rachel always signed her cards with 'Luv Rachel' followed by a full stop with a heart drawn around it. It didn't mean anything.

By the time she'd finished the packet of Rolos Genevieve had convinced herself that *Miss you* meant nothing more than a polite 'Best wishes'. Even so, to be equally polite, she composed a brief letter in return so that it would be waiting for Christian when he came home. It took her more than an hour to write, not because she kept getting the letters and words in the wrong order, but because she badly wanted to say the right thing.

As the months passed, the number of letters exchanged between them increased, as did her weight. Her jeans no longer fitted, but it didn't matter; jogging suits were the thing to wear anyway. She didn't dare weigh herself, but she reckoned she'd put on a stone and a half. Perhaps more.

Granny Baxter was waiting for them. Ushering the girls inside, she pointed in the direction of the sink and told them to wash their hands. Genevieve knew this would annoy Rachel – they were both fifteen, after all – but Gran treated everyone as though they were five years old, even Mum and Dad.

'I've done your favourite, Genevieve,' the old lady said. 'Egg, sausage, beans and chips. And there's treacle tart and custard for afters. Or ice-cream if you'd rather.'

Rachel threw Genevieve a look of eye-rolling horror. Their backs were to Gran as they stood at the sink. 'There are enough calories in that lot to kill us. Tell her you're not hungry,' she hissed.

'But I *am* hungry.' Actually, she was starving and the thought of Gran's delicious homemade chips sprinkled with salt made her mouth water.

'We're on a diet, Gen. Remember?'

'What are you two whispering about over there?'

'Nothing, Gran.'

But Genevieve couldn't do as Rachel said. She couldn't hurt Gran's feelings by refusing to eat what she'd gone to so much trouble to cook. So she ate everything, even made up for what her friend left on her plate by having seconds. Later that night, when everyone had gone to bed, she thought of what Rachel had told her as they'd walked back through Solomon's Meadow, that all the famous models threw up to keep slim. She crept along to the bathroom and made herself sick. It was the most revolting thing she had ever done. But it was also strangely consoling.

14

In their last exchange of letters, Genevieve and Christian had arranged to meet on Tawelfan beach, even if it was raining.

It was. As Genevieve waited for Christian to appear – in her eagerness, she'd got there far too early – heavy rain pattered noisily against the hood of her cagoule, making her feel as though she were inside a tent. She pressed herself into the hollow of the rocks, glad that the tide was out and had provided her with a place of relative refuge. The beach was deserted and a strong wind was gusting, whipping up the sea and adding a salty taste to the rain. Doubt seized hold of her. Maybe Christian wouldn't show up. He'd have to be nuts to do so.

There had been much made of her meeting Christian again. Nattie, now thirteen going on twenty-three, had discovered horses and boys (in that order) and seldom talked about anything else. She was of the opinion that Christian definitely had the hots for Genevieve. 'Why else would he have kept writing to you?' she'd said.

'Because he likes me as a friend?'

'Because he fancies you!'

Genevieve would have given anything to have Nattie's confidence and certainty. Admitting this to herself, she knew it spoke volumes about her feelings for Christian. She was desperate for him to view her as more than a friend.

She hadn't seen Christian for two years, which, as Gran said, was a long time in which to recreate a person, to turn him into something he probably wasn't. But Gran was old and couldn't have a clue what it was like to be young, to know the joy of lying awake in bed just happy to think of being with Christian again.

But at least Gran listened and didn't make fun of Genevieve when she told her how her feelings for Christian had changed. She had confided in her grandmother while helping to pick the first crop of raspberries from the canes Grandad had planted long ago. In response, Gran had said, 'You know, your grandfather wasn't the first man I fell in love with.'

This was news to Genevieve, a revelation on the scale of Gran suddenly confessing that she used to be a stripper. 'Really?'

'Oh yes. There was Hugh before him. And John, and of course, there was Igor too.'

'Oh Gran, surely you never went out with someone called Igor?'

'I did, as a matter of fact. And we called it courting in those days.'

Genevieve did the sums. 'You must have been very young when you went out – sorry, when you were *courting* with those men. You were twenty when you married Grandad, weren't you?'

'A little bit of experience never did anyone any harm, my girl. Remember that. Too many eggs in the one basket is rarely a good idea. Some get broken. Some tip out.'

'Are you referring to Christian?'

She patted Genevieve's hand. 'Let's just say that Christian is all very well for the here and now, but there's a whole world out there for you to explore and enjoy. What's more, there are many different kinds of love. For instance, there's love that hurts and love that heals. You need to experience both to know the one from the other.'

Genevieve knew what Gran was getting at, but her grandmother was wrong. What she felt for Christian really was love. Okay, she was only fifteen – sixteen in September – but she knew, as she stood waiting for him with the rain dripping off her hood and splashing onto her face, that it was the real thing.

Her biggest fear was that he'd met someone else, but wouldn't he have told her that in one of his letters? 'Oh, by the way, I've met this really great girl. You'd love her, she's funny, intelligent and so very slim.'

Just over two months had passed since she'd first made herself sick, and though she hated herself for doing something so disgusting, the weight had dropped off. She'd lost a stone already and intended to lose another. But rather than show off her slimmer self, she kept her clothes baggy, not wanting to attract attention to what she was doing. She'd stopped swimming competitively ages ago, but now she wouldn't go near a pool – gross as she was, there was no way she could let people see her in a swimsuit. She told her mother she didn't want the chlorine from the pool wrecking her hair, and was told she was old enough to make her own decisions. Three cheers for such a liberal, easy-going mother!

But she knew Mum would go ballistic if she discovered the truth and she had to be careful that she was seen to be eating normally. It was easy to miss meals, though. There were plenty of times when she was able to get out of tea, usually just saying she was in a hurry to get to Rachel's, or that she'd already eaten at Rachel's, was enough. Occasionally, when she was feeling low, if she'd had a bad day at school, she would binge on a comforting boost of crisps and chocolate bars in her room. And of course, there was always something to eat at Gran's. But so long as she had her secret weapon, she could do what she'd previously thought was impossible: she could eat *and* make herself slimmer and more attractive. For the first time she could remember, she felt in control of her life.

Rachel had said they needed to give themselves a reason to lose weight, something that would spur them on. Rachel's goal was to become a wafer-thin model, but Genevieve's target was more modest: she wanted to get into size ten jeans. But she had another incentive. She wanted to look good for Christian. She knew in her heart she wouldn't stand a chance with him if she was anything but slim. And thanks to her friend's encouragement, and occasional bullying, she was back in size twelve jeans and feeling more confident – and hopeful.

What with the noise of the wind and rain, and being deep in thought, she didn't hear footsteps approach. Not until he was standing right next to her did she look up and see Christian.

'Hi there,' he said.

Like her, he was dressed for the awful weather, and all she could see of him was his smiling face peering through the porthole of his hood. But it was enough to tell her that he'd grown even more good-looking in the two years that had passed. She still hadn't returned his greeting when he said, 'It's great to see you Genevieve.'

Then, unbelievably, he threw his arms round her and actually hugged her. And it didn't stop there. He kissed her on each wet cheek. How grown-up he seemed! Or was that a continental souvenir from Spain, perhaps?

'Come on,' he said, 'let's walk. You don't mind the rain, do you?'

Her head spinning, she nodded. She didn't care what they did. He could ask her to paddle across the Atlantic in a cardboard box and she'd do it. He helped her clamber over the rocks, and they headed across the beach, to the other side of the bay and the steeply wooded path that would take them up towards the cliff top. When they reached the grassy headland they stopped to catch their breath. Miraculously – as if she needed any further evidence that there was a God – the rain stopped. They flung back their hoods and simultaneously took a moment to see how changed they were.

'You've grown your hair,' he said.

Immediately she put a hand to her head, self-conscious of the mess it must be with all the wind. Despite being enveloped in the unflattering cagoule, she pulled in her stomach for good measure. 'And you're —' And what? What was Christian, other than perfect? He'd definitely grown more handsome. Had filled out too and easily looked older than seventeen. He was a man now. A man who most certainly would be looked at twice. With her mousy brown hair and nondescript features, she felt incredibly plain beside him, the kind of girl no one would look at twice. She noticed that he wore no hearing aid and realised that there had been little trace of that characteristic 'hollowness' in his voice. No one meeting him for the first time would realise he had such a severe hearing problem. He stared at her, his gaze fixed intently on her mouth as he waited for her to finish what she'd started. She'd forgotten how focused he had to be. 'And you're taller than ever,' she managed.

He laughed. 'I was warned it would happen. That if I ate my greens I'd grow.'

They walked on, the strong wind tearing the clouds apart until at last the sun broke through. They stripped down to their tee-shirts and tied the unwanted clothing around their waists. Genevieve could see how muscular Christian had become; his angular, coat-hanger shoulders were no more. Where was the skinny boy she'd met three years ago? *Bet he looks a real hunk in his swimming shorts*, she imagined Rachel whispering in her ear. Then, noticing the pair of scruffy old walking boots he was wearing, Rachel's whisper turned scornful. *What a turn-off!* It had to be Reebok or Nike trainers as far as Rachel was concerned.

Christian had caught the direction of her glance. 'I know what you're thinking,' he said, 'that I ought to give them a good clean, but what's the point? I spend most weekends tramping the hills.'

'Alone?' The question was out before she registered why she'd asked it. Was he tramping the hills with a pretty girlfriend?

'Usually with Dad, though more often on my own. He's away a lot these days. I was hoping you and I would get the chance to do some really long walks together.'

Her heart swelled. 'I'd like that,' she said.

He eyed her trainers doubtfully. 'Do you have any proper boots?'

'I'll get some.' To hell with Rachel's scorn. Her friend would never see her in them anyway.

Now there was no Grandad to help on the farm, Dad couldn't get away for as long as he'd like. But Mum, being Mum, insisted that it was no reason for her and the girls to lose out.

'We only go on one holiday a year,' she complained. 'I don't see why we should have to forgo it.'

So Dad came for just one week, leaving 'his girls' plus Gran to enjoy a further two weeks without him. It was strange having Gran on holiday with them – made it feel more like home. A home from home, in fact. After their father had set off for Cheshire that time, Mum started to talk about how nice it would be to live in Angel Sands permanently.

'It's not so daft,' Christian said when Genevieve told him of Serena's latest lunatic plan, to sell up the farm and buy a house to run as a bed and breakfast. 'You can pick up property relatively cheaply round here.'

On their way to St Govan's Chapel, they were having lunch at a café in Stackpole Quay, a pretty little harbour which, until today, Genevieve hadn't given much thought to. Certainly she'd never considered its history or geography. But Christian made it come alive. He told her how the quay had been constructed in the eighteenth century to land cargoes of coal, which was then taken to Stackpole Court. Instead of the boats going away empty, they were then filled up with limestone. He knew all about Stackpole Court, a huge house built in 1735 but demolished in the Sixties by its then owner, the fifth Earl of Cawdor. All those years of history, gone. Poomph! He wasn't lecturing her, or showing off that he knew so much about the area.

'If I'd had a history teacher half as good as you, I might have carried on with it,' she said, stirring her glass of Coke with a straw and wondering if she dare eat the rest of her bacon bap. Her stomach was longing for it, but the slim, attractive girl inside her was telling her it was poison.

'It's a difficult subject to teach well,' he said. 'I've been lucky, I've had some brilliant teachers. Really inspiring. Are you going to leave that?'

Saved! 'I'm full. You have it.' She pushed the plate across the wooden bench table, wanting to please her constant companion, the slim, attractive girl. 'So how come you know so much about property prices round here? Thinking of becoming an estate agent?'

'No. But I am interested in houses. Or more particularly, their design. I'm going to study architecture at university next year. Or maybe do a gap year first then go to college.'

She was impressed. Doubly impressed because, against all the odds, he'd made it through mainstream education. He'd told her once how his parents had been determined he wouldn't go to a special school for the deaf, that there would be no half-measure, he was to be a part of the hearing world whether he wanted it or not.

'You've got it all worked out,' she said.

He smiled. 'You once said that I was the most organised person you knew. Remember how you made fun of my perfectly packed rucksack?'

'I never made fun of you.'

'You did.'

'Didn't!'

'Did!'

They were still arguing and laughing when they left the café and continued with their walk on to Govan's Chapel. As they climbed the steep steps up the hill and looked back onto the tiny harbour, Christian rested his arm on her shoulder. Just like the time he'd held her hand two years ago, it seemed the most natural thing in the world.

And that, she decided, was what she liked – *loved* – about Christian. There was no artifice to him. No pretence to be anything other than he was.

Why can't my life be as perfect as this all the time? she thought that night, lying in bed, for once not thinking guiltily about how much she'd eaten, and whether or not she should creep along to the bathroom.

The first time Gran met Christian, she made the mistake of forgetting he was deaf – or had 'impaired hearing' as he now preferred to call it. It was an easy mistake to make. He was so good at lip-reading, even Genevieve forgot sometimes. And Nattie, being Nattie, had decided that maybe he wasn't as deaf as he said and had tried several times to catch him out. But no matter how many times she tried to creep up behind him and see if he jumped when she clapped her hands, he remained completely unaware of her, or that he was being tested.

To her shame, Genevieve still hadn't told Rachel about him being deaf; she was afraid of her friend's reaction. Rachel had very rigid ideas about what was acceptable. Only a Simon le Bon or Tony Hadley look-alike would do.

'There's nothing wrong in being choosy,' she would say, usually at some school disco or other. Every other term they were allowed to socialise with the local boys' school and Rachel was invariably one of the girls the boys most wanted to dance with. She had perfected the art of looking bored, as though a school disco was beneath her, but at the same time appearing interested enough to be an all-important part of it.

Once Gran had realised her gaffe, she made the further mistake of talking to Christian with her voice raised to the rafters. 'Genevieve tells me you want to be an architect,' she bellowed across the sitting room at Pendine Cottage, where the entire Baxter family (minus their father) had been invited for tea. Genevieve wanted to die. Trust Gran to choose today to do her impression of a dotty old lady. While Gran listened to Christian's reply, Genevieve tried subtly to attract her grandmother's attention by clearing her throat several times, in the hope that she might realise her mistake and lower her voice. But Gran wasn't looking her way; she was listening attentively to Christian's every word. Mrs May – Ella – passed Genevieve a plate and a napkin and whispered, 'Don't worry, we're quite used to it. A ham sandwich?'

Genevieve took the offered sandwich, dainty and crustless. Hardly any calories at all, she told herself happily. *Don't you believe it*, Constant Companion warned her. She cleared her throat; this was not the time or place.

Gran threw her a sharp look. 'Genevieve, whatever is the matter with you? I'm trying to talk to Christian and all I can hear is rattle, rattle. Are you ill?'

Genevieve didn't know what to say. But Nattie did. 'She's not ill, Gran, but unless you keep your voice down, we'll all end up deaf. Talk to him normally. He's not some subspecies.'

After an excruciating moment when no one seemed to know what to say, everyone laughed politely and busied themselves with sandwiches and cups of tea, but Genevieve could see from the expression on Christian's face that he hadn't managed to lip-read what Nattie had said. He turned to Genevieve and gave her a questioning look. She shook her head and mouthed, 'I'll tell you later.'

When tea was over, at Philip May's suggestion they all went out to the garden to play croquet.

'You don't know what you're taking on,' she told Christian. 'We Baxters are experts at this game.'

'Yes, but we Mays cheat to win.'

'And you think we don't?'

Gran and her mother were notorious for cheating at croquet. For that matter, they were a rule unto themselves with any game: Snap, Ludo, Scrabble, Monopoly, Rummy. You name it, they'd cheat at it. There was almost a competition between them to see who could get away with the most.

It wasn't long before the game disintegrated into a raucous shambles. Leaving Nattie and Polly to supervise the adults, Genevieve and Christian found themselves a quiet spot elsewhere in the garden. Unlike Thrift Cottage, the Mays' holiday home had an enormous garden. Christian had once told her that his mother was a fanatical gardener. There was no view of the sea, but it was beautiful, sheltered by beech and oak trees with deep borders full of pretty flowers and shrubs, all carefully chosen to withstand the extremes of a seaside climate.

They lay on a tartan blanket on the soft grass and stared up at the cloudless blue sky through a lace-work of tree branches. Genevieve couldn't remember ever feeling so happy. In the distance she could hear Gran and Serena bickering, and closing her eyes, she thought that Christian was lucky not to be able to hear the cacophony of noise her family was generating.

The warmth of the sun on her face was making her drowsy. Floating between that state of not quite awake, yet not fully asleep, she pictured herself drifting away on a magic carpet with Christian. As she was floating high above the roof tops, she felt something tickling her cheek. An annoying fly. She flicked it away, but it came back. Irritated, she opened her eyes, and saw that Christian, raised up on one elbow, was leaning over her with a blade of grass in his hand.

'Caught red-handed,' he said with a smile. Then, very gently, he stroked her cheek some more.

She didn't stop him.

15

Genevieve was frequently told by her family that she felt things too deeply. Where others could let problems and worries slide off their backs as easily as winking, she could not. Nattie, that well-known psychology expert, said she turned everything into a colossal big deal and that one day she would worry herself to death. However, once more according to Nattie, two weeks spent in the company of Christian was having a positive effect on her. 'You're not half so gloomy when you're with him.'

'It must be love,' declared Serena with embarrassing enthusiasm from the front of the car as they set off to Tenby to have a look round the shops. 'That's why you're not eating.'

Defences up, Genevieve was instantly on the alert. Squeezed in between Gran and Nattie – it was Polly's turn to sit in the front passenger seat – she leaned forward. 'What do you mean, I'm not eating?' Too late she realised she shouldn't have reacted so quickly. Or seized on the eating reference. Anyone else's first thought would have been to deny they were in love.

'Don't look so serious, darling, I was just the same at your age. The weight simply dropped off me. It's called love-sickness. You can't eat, sleep, concentrate or sit still for thinking of the object of your desire.' Serena sighed. 'I remember the day I met your father . . .'

Genevieve almost sighed with relief too. She was off the hook. For the rest of the journey, with the windows down and the wind blowing at their hair, Serena told them the story of how she and Daddy Dean had fallen in love. It was a story they knew by heart, but never tired of. They loved hearing how Serena had arrived at the barn dance late because the heel of her favourite pair of shoes had dropped off just as she'd been leaving the house, how when she'd arrived at the church hall, wearing a pair of her mother's shoes, she had caught sight of a handsome man fiddling nervously with his tie and had made a beeline for him. By the time they were in Tenby hunting for a parking space, Serena had reached the punchline of the story, the bit when she'd tripped over, and all of them, including Gran, chorused together 'and Zing! Went the strings of my heart; that was the moment I knew Dean Baxter was the man for me!'

It was one of those barmy moments that the Baxters did best. With an ache in her heart, Genevieve realised that since Grandad had died, these moments had been fewer and further between.

They were allowed to split up and go their separate ways in Tenby. Polly had run out of books to read, so Mum said she'd take her to the bookshop. Nattie wanted to go to the amusement arcade and took Gran by the arm, sure in the knowledge that their grandmother, equally addicted to slot machines, especially those ones that slid in and out, would step in with a purse full of pennies and, later, would probably treat Nattie to a stick of rock, or maybe some candyfloss.

Which left Genevieve happy to wander the narrow streets and cobbled alleyways on her own. It being August, the town was packed with holidaymakers. Genevieve liked it here. She enjoyed the hustle and bustle, the pretty shops and cafés decked out with colourful flower boxes and hanging baskets, and the nearby beaches with their sand so golden and inviting. Rachel wouldn't approve of it, though; the shops weren't big enough or fashionable enough for her. Rachel and her family went to America for their summer holiday, as well as at half-term in the autumn; she always came back with tons of new clothes.

It was funny, but it was as though there were two Genevieves: the cautious, uptight one who lived at Brook House Farm, and who was best friends with Rachel Harmony, and the other one who was relaxed and carefree at Thrift Cottage, and was best friends with Christian May. When she thought about it, the two were incompatible. While Rachel was obsessed with not just her own appearance but everyone else's, Christian didn't give a hoot about what people thought of him. He wore exactly what he wanted, and did exactly what he wanted. A bit like Nattie, really. He set no limitations for himself or those around him. But Rachel, for all her rigidity, was the best friend ever.

Buoyed up with a sense of well-being, Genevieve paused for a moment on the crowded pavement to look at the display of clothes in a shop window. Her gaze was distracted by a girl staring back at her. She was smiling, her long hair tucked behind her ears, her cheekbones forming a heart-shaped face. She was dressed in a tee-shirt that was drab and too big for her, but there was no mistaking the curvy outline of the body beneath it.

Genevieve noted all this in less than a split-second, then she was brought up short by the realisation that the girl was *her*. Despite the number of people – some with pushchairs and young children carrying beach balls and fishing nets – all trying to get past her, she continued to stare at herself, mesmerised. She knew she wasn't anywhere near as slim as Rachel but, and this took her breath away, she wasn't the Incredible Hulk she'd believed herself to be. Elated by this discovery, she felt like hugging the nearest person. 'Look at me,' she wanted to cry, 'I'm not fat any more!'

To celebrate, she shoved open the shop door. Mentally counting out her holiday money – five pounds that she'd saved, five pounds from Mum and Dad and another two pounds fifty from Gran – she scanned the racks of clothes. A top, perhaps? It wasn't the kind of place where Rachel would buy anything; there was no loud music and no surly girls wearing too much make-up and giving Genevieve the kind of stare that said the outsize shop was down the road. She started sliding a row of garments along the rail. A woman about the same age as her mother appeared at her side.

'Can I help you?'

'Um ... I'd like to try one of these, please.' She pointed to the rail.

The woman hesitated. She looked at Genevieve, then back at the row of tee-shirts. 'I'm not sure we have any of your size left.'

Genevieve's heart sank. She should have known the reflection in the window had been a cruel illusion.

'Everything on this rail is much too large for you,' the woman carried on. 'How about these over here? I know we have your size in those tops. Do you see anything you like?'

Clutching her carrier bag and its size ten strappy top – *size ten!* – Genevieve left the shop in a giddy state of euphoria. Nothing in the whole wide world could make her feel any happier.

But she was wrong.

If Christian had thought it odd that she hadn't wanted to go swimming before now, he never said anything. He'd probably put it down to a 'girl thing', though why it had extended over two weeks may have given him cause to wonder. But today, twenty-four hours after the outing to Tenby, with her confidence at an all-time high, Genevieve suggested they went for a swim.

There weren't any full-length mirrors at Thrift Cottage, but last night, after stripping down to her underwear and standing on the edge of the bath, holding her breath to help her balance, she had studied her body in the mirror above the basin. This was something she hadn't dared do since she had started trying to lose weight. Seeing the truth of her naked body would be more than she could bear. But she had been pleasantly surprised. Okay, she still had a way to go, but all in all she was in better shape than she'd thought possible. Perhaps she'd risk a swim with Christian after all.

A loud thump on the door, followed by Nattie demanding to know if she was going to be in there all night had her wobbling backwards and crashing into the empty bath.

'Gen! What the hell are you doing in there?'

'Nothing.'

Now, on Tawelfan beach, as she and Christian stripped down to their swimwear, the taunting voice of Constant Companion whispered in her ear. *Are you sure you want to do this? And just as it was going so well.*

She banished the voice and nervously wriggled out of her jeans. Ever the gentleman, Christian turned from her and unzipped his trousers. While his back was to her, she ripped off the rest of her clothes. Instinct made her want to reach for a towel, but she steeled herself, picturing the girl in the shop window yesterday, and the new strappy top she planned to put on after their swim.

But she wasn't prepared for the sight of Christian in his swimming shorts. He was all muscle; his legs looked firm and toned, presumably from all that walking. He looked so good she had to turn away and catch her breath. When she'd recovered, and risked a glance back at him, she saw his eyes on her. She flinched when his gaze settled on the back of her thigh. Constant Companion whispered, I *warned you!*

'That looks painful,' he said. 'How'd you get that?'

She twisted to see what he was referring to – a mound of wobbling flesh? – and saw an ugly, purplish bruise the shape and size of a pork chop. Ah, a legacy from last night's bathroom antics. 'Too embarrassing to say,' she replied. 'Ready for that swim?'

They picked their way through the sunbathers, playing children and windbreakers, and dipped their toes in the water.

'It's freezing!' she gasped.

He smiled. 'It's the Atlantic. What did you expect? Race you in!'

Suddenly she was that twelve-year-old girl again, the one who had met Christian on the beach and had defiantly risen to his challenge. And before she could think of a reason not to, she was in the water. He came in after her, dived beneath the waves when it was deep enough, then surfaced beside her, his shaggy hair plastered to his head and neck. He stood up – the water came to his chest – and pushed his hair back into place.

'The tide's coming in,' he said, 'so it'll be safe to swim round the headland. Do you fancy doing that?'

She did. It was so long since she'd swum properly she'd forgotten how free and energised it made her feel. By the time they'd swum all the way into the next bay, then returned to Tawelfan beach, they were starving.

'How about a burger?' he asked, towelling his hair dry, then draping the towel around his shoulders.

Constant Companion materialised in a flash. *Oh, that's a good one! A burger. One hundred per cent pure unadulterated poison. Still, there's always the head down the toilet routine to fall back on.*

'Maybe a sandwich,' she compromised.

But as they joined the queue at the kiosk, the temptation of a sizzling, big, fat, juicy burger was too much for her. She told herself that she had just swum nearly a mile, so she'd earned it. She could always pass on tea that evening.

They took their burgers and cans of Coke back to the dunes and found themselves a sheltered spot. It was there, quite unexpectedly, that Christian kissed her. She had imagined this moment for so long, had spent hours daydreaming of The Perfect Kiss, but nothing could have prepared her for the real thing. The softness of his mouth against hers, so light and fleeting, lasted for no more than a few seconds, but it was enough to make the world stop spinning, for a fluttering warmth to spread through her and for her senses to become aware of everything that was going on around them. Music was playing close by on a radio, Elvis Presley singing one of her mother's many favourite songs, 'The Wonder of You'. Looking into Christian's eyes – soft brown flecked with green and gold – she could only think, with painful poignancy, how appropriate the lyrics were: 'When no one else can understand me, when everything I do is wrong, you give me hope and consolation, you give me strength to carry on.'

'What are you thinking?' Christian asked her.

She pointed to the radio. 'There's a song playing and it's . . .' Her voice trailed away.

'And it's what?'

She lost her nerve, unable to share with him that the lyrics summed up how he made her feel.

Later, when they still hadn't moved from the dunes and he was kissing her again, she knew that there would never be anyone else for her. So full of happiness she thought she might burst, she smiled to herself. Just as her parents had 'Zing! Went the Strings of My Heart' as their song, she and Christian would have 'The Wonder of You'.

16

Genevieve didn't know why, but Rachel was in a strange mood; nothing she said or did seemed to help. She decided to keep quiet and ignore her friend's sullen silence. It was probably that time of the month. But Genevieve didn't care; she had a letter from Christian in her blazer pocket.

They were on the school bus, and with another ten minutes to go before they'd be at school, Genevieve's hands itched to pull out the letter and read it through one more time: Christian had invited her to stay with him in Shropshire for the autumn half-term. 'If the weather's nice,' he'd written, 'Dad says we might drive down to Angel Sands for a few days.' Half-term was only three weeks away and Genevieve was fidgety with excitement. She wanted to show Rachel the letter, then run up and down the packed bus telling everyone the brilliant news. She found herself smiling broadly at the thought of seeing Christian again.

'Oh, for crying out loud, Gen, give it a rest, won't you!'

'What? What have I done?'

Rachel shifted in her seat and looked out of the window at the passing shops and houses, her shoulder to Genevieve. 'You know jolly well,' she muttered.

Genevieve frowned. 'Have I done something to annoy you?'

Silence.

'Rachel?'

The shoulder turned a few degrees. 'If you must know, yes. Yes you have. You're always going on about bloody Christian this, and bloody Christian that. Ever since the summer holidays you've been a real pain. I thought I was supposed to be your best friend.'

Genevieve was stung. 'But you *are* my best friend. And always will be.'

'Yeah. That's why you're running off down to some godforsaken place in Shropshire for the whole of half-term. What about me? What am I supposed to do while you're away?'

'But I thought you were going to Florida, like you always do.'

The shoulder was back in place, the face turned even more to the glass. 'We're not going. Mum and Dad have changed their minds.'

'But you always go.'

Rachel whipped round. 'Don't you think I know that, you big fat moron!'

Appalled at the strength of her friend's attack, Genevieve stared straight ahead, concentrating on the neatly plaited hair of the girl in front. They completed the rest of the journey without another word. At school they avoided each other, and during the bus ride home at the end of the day, they sat together, but in tight-lipped silence.

Genevieve got off the bus and walked home with her sisters. They were all at the same school now, but there was an unspoken agreement between them: they were never to sit near each other. Genevieve and Nattie sat upstairs – Nattie on the back row with her rowdy friends and Genevieve in the middle with Rachel – and Polly downstairs, usually at the front, predictably lost in whatever book she was reading. Nattie and Genevieve frequently had to drag her off the bus before she missed their stop. Occasionally, if she didn't have anything to read, she would sit with her eyes closed and hum to herself, causing those around her to smile and point. Nobody ever bullied her for it, though. Not if they didn't want to face the music with Nattie, who wouldn't think twice about lashing out in her twelve-year-old sister's defence.

'So what's up with you, Gen?' asked Nattie, stopping to roll down the waistband of her skirt so Mum wouldn't know how short she wore it for school. 'You've got a face on you like a dog's bum.'

'Thanks.'

'I mean it. You look as miserable as—'

'Enough of the compliments. I've had a horrible day, so please don't make it any worse.'

'Suit yourself. Only I'd have thought you would have been deliriously happy, what with going to see Christian at half term.'

'Have you had a fight with Rachel?' This was from Polly.

'What makes you say that?' Genevieve said warily.

'I noticed you didn't sit next to her during lunch. She was with Katie Kirby and Lucinda Atkins.'

Nattie whistled. 'You must have had a bust-up if that's the case. So what did you argue about?'

'We didn't argue.'

'Liar! Why else would she set up camp with the school she-devils? Hey, interesting point; I thought it was only the real hardened bitches who were allowed to hang out with the Queens of Spite. So come on, what's been going on between you two?'

Genevieve gave in. There was no point in prevaricating with Nattie when she was in full flow. She told her sisters about Rachel's behaviour on the bus that morning, although she couldn't bring herself to repeat her friend's exact words. *You ... big ... fat ... moron!*

'She's jealous,' Nattie said. 'Jealous as hell.'

More kindly, Polly said, 'Perhaps she's frightened of losing you as a friend.'

This wasn't exactly the revelation her sisters thought it was. Genevieve had worked out as much for herself. Question was, why? As far as she was concerned, nothing had changed between her and Rachel.

Gran had the answer when Genevieve called in to see her after finishing her homework and told her grandmother what had happened. 'What's annoyed that girl most is you've done something without her approval.'

'Oh, that's just silly, Gran.'

'All I'll say, Genevieve, is this. Rachel's not as clever or as confident as she makes out. I suspect that she needs you as a friend more than you need her. And because of that, she'll soon make it up with you. Now then, how about a piece of cake?'

'No, thank you.'

'A slice of treacle tart perhaps? I could pop it in the oven for a few minutes and make some custard for you. Or would you prefer some whipped cream?'

After feeling so low as a result of Rachel's hurtful outburst, nothing would have suited Genevieve more than to gorge herself on several slices of Gran's butter-rich treacle tart. But she fought hard to resist the temptation, picturing not Constant Companion tapping her foot and wagging her finger at her, but Christian's letter, now under her pillow ready to read one more time before switching off the light. In three weeks she would be seeing him, and she had no intention of arriving in Shropshire looking as big as The Wrekin.

You ... big ... fat ... moron!

How could Rachel have said that? When she, of all people, knew how hard Genevieve had worked to lose weight?

After returning from Angel Sands, back in the summer, Genevieve had rushed to see her friend; the first thing she had done was to take off her jacket and show Rachel the top she'd bought in Tenby. 'Look,' she'd laughed. 'It's size ten. Can you believe it?'

Rachel looked up from her magazine. 'Really?'

'Yes! Isn't it amazing? I must have lost at least a stone.'

'Haven't you weighed yourself to check?'

'No. I can't bring myself to do it, just in case I haven't lost as much as I think I have.'

Sliding off her bed, Rachel said, 'Well, let's do it now.' She pulled some scales out from under the bed and said, 'On you get. The needle of doom never lies.'

This was what Genevieve had nicknamed the black marker that decided her fate. 'Do I have to?'

'Don't be a chicken, Gen.'

Still Genevieve held back.

'Oh all right,' Rachel said. 'I'll go first. I bet I haven't lost as much as you.'

No, thought Genevieve, but you didn't need to in the first place.

'Bang on seven stone,' said Rachel in a satisfied voice. 'Your turn.'

'Can I take off my jeans?'

'I kept mine on.'

Genevieve stepped onto the scales. 'You read it for me.'

'Eight stone and eight pounds,' Rachel announced, almost straight away.

'But I wasn't ready!'

'What do you mean, you weren't ready?'

'I was still moving. I hadn't got into position.'

'Then hurry up and get into position!'

She did, but this time she watched the needle herself, saw it wobble, then hover into place. 'Eight stone and . . . and six pounds. And that's with my jeans on.' She smiled and hopped off the scales. 'I was right, I've lost a whole stone. Isn't that great?'

'It is. Well done. Now you don't have to bother any more, do you?'

'Oh, no, this is just the start. Now I know I can do it, I want to lose another stone at least.'

Rachel went back to lying on the bed. 'Believe me, Gen, you've lost all the weight you need to. If you get any thinner you'll look stupid.' She twirled a lock of hair between her fingers. 'And if you want my honest opinion, I think you ought to put a bit back on. Your face looks too thin to me.'

Genevieve couldn't believe what she was hearing. Rachel had to be joking. She went and stood in front of the dressing table mirror. But before she could say anything, Rachel said, 'So what's your secret? How did you lose the weight? Before you went on holiday, I swear you'd never have been able to get into that top. Not in a million years. Have you started smoking like those models I told you about?'

It was then that Genevieve told Rachel all about her and Christian. 'Mum keeps going on about me losing weight because I'm in love. I know it sounds silly, but I think she might be right.'

Rachel rolled her eyes.

Now, as Genevieve waved goodbye to her grandmother and walked home through Solomon's Meadow in the dusky twilight, listening to the noisy blackbirds chirruping before settling in their nests, she thought of Rachel's reaction when she'd told her that Christian was officially her boyfriend. With hindsight she could see that Rachel had been distinctly cool about the news.

'But you're not really going out with him, are you?' she'd said. 'It's not like it's a proper relationship.'

'Yes, it is. We've kissed and everything!'

Rachel had laughed. 'That means nothing. He's probably just using you as a holiday fling. What's more, he might be lying to you. I bet there's a girlfriend at home he's not telling you about.'

'There isn't. I know there isn't. Besides, he isn't that sort of boy. He wouldn't lie to me.'

'Yeah, well, you might be right. But you didn't throw yourself at him, did you?'

'Certainly not!'

'Good. Otherwise you'll just end up feeling cheap when he dumps you.'

But Christian never made Genevieve feel cheap. Special was how she felt. Uniquely special. He'd even told her he thought she was beautiful. He said it when they'd been lying on the beach one hot, sunny day. Opening her eyes, she'd found him staring down at her.

'What are you thinking?' she'd asked.

'I'm thinking how beautiful you are,' he'd said simply. For days and weeks afterwards, she spent long, dreamy moments recalling his words.

Saying goodbye at the end of the holiday had been horrible, though. He'd come to Thrift Cottage to wave them off and while no one was looking they had sneaked a final kiss and promised to write straight away.

'I'll miss you,' she'd said, still in his arms, but pulling back so that he could see her lips.

'And I'll miss you too. Let's try and meet up some time soon.'

'I'd like that.'

'Go on, you'd better go. Your mother's trying to pretend she hasn't noticed what we're up to.'

Without fail they wrote every week. On her sixteenth birthday he sent her the most romantic present ever; a bunch of red roses. It seemed so grown-up. And because she'd plucked up the courage to tell him about the song that had been playing on the radio when he'd first kissed her, he also gave her a CD of Elvis songs, including 'The Wonder of You'. She hadn't the heart to tell him she couldn't play the CD because they didn't have a CD player at Brook House Farm – with her prized collection of Broadway musicals, Mum was refusing to believe that vinyl would soon be a thing of the past. Rachel had a CD player, but Genevieve hadn't wanted to play it in front of her friend.

Thinking about it now, perhaps she *had* treated Rachel badly. She shouldn't have talked about Christian so much, or been so ridiculously happy whenever a letter arrived. It had been insensitive of her. Hearing the cows stomping their hooves in the cowshed as she turned into the farmyard, she realised that from where Rachel was sitting, she must have become a real bore, with her Christian this and Christian that. She knew then what she had to do, and after she'd waited for Nattie to come off the phone, she called Rachel to say she was sorry, that she wanted to be friends again.

She apologised again on the bus in the morning, and any trace of coolness that had remained on the phone last night was gone. Rachel accepted her apology with good grace. She even managed to say sorry herself.

'I shouldn't have called you what I did. I don't ever want you to think that I'm jealous of you having a boyfriend, Gen,' she added. 'I'm not. You haven't slept with him, have you?'

'No!'

'Good. And even if he says he loves you, don't believe him. They all say that just so they can get you into bed. It's all they ever want to do. The longer you hold out, the better.'

Keen to please her friend, Genevieve nodded and changed the subject. She asked how Rachel had got on with the English essay they had to hand in that morning.

But perversely Rachel seemed eager to discuss Christian. 'What I don't get is why he never rings you. Why does he only write?'

Genevieve had never considered the possibility that Christian would be able to use a phone, but this summer he'd told her that up until last year, he had in fact been able to use a special telephone, a specially amplified one. But then he'd found that what residual hearing he had had diminished to the point that even with the extra amplification, he couldn't make out more than a blur of sounds. His parents had said they might buy him a textphone, but as he said, what use was that unless the person he was talking to also had a textphone? And he certainly didn't want to talk with her through a third person.

But Genevieve still hadn't got around to telling Rachel about Christian's deafness – her friend could be cruel sometimes and she couldn't bear the thought of Rachel belittling Christian, or worse, making fun of him. Deciding to answer her friend's question, and to hell with what she might think or say, Genevieve said, 'I would have thought it was obvious why he doesn't ring me.'

'Obvious? In what way?'

'He's deaf. Don't you remember me telling you?' She stared out of the window and hoped she wouldn't be struck down for such a blatant lie.

'*Deaf!* You mean, deaf as a post?'

'Yes.'

Rachel poked Genevieve with her elbow, to make her look at her. 'You never told me he was deaf. I'd have remembered a thing like that.'

Genevieve met her friend's gaze, ready to defend Christian should she have to. 'Maybe I forgot to tell you. Either way, it's no big deal.'

'But *deaf*, Gen. Now that's what I call weird. I mean, how do you communicate with him? Hand signals?'

'We talk as normally as you and I are doing right now.'

'How?'

'He reads my lips.'

'Pardon?'

'I said, he reads my—'

Rachel burst out laughing. 'Got you!'

'That's not funny.'

But Rachel was still laughing to herself when they got off the bus, and for the rest of the day Genevieve was subjected to countless I-beg-your-pardon-you'd-better-speak-up jokes. By the end of it, Genevieve was ready to slap her friend's face.

17

'I'm afraid we all have to make allowances for Rachel,' Mum said through a cloud of steam as she thumped the iron down. 'She's going through a tough time. It's not easy for her.'

Over by the sink, Gran looked up from the new potatoes she was scrubbing and said, 'If Genevieve were to bend any further backwards for that girl, she'd be a contortionist!'

'I agree with Gran: Rachel's a complete pain in the backside. Just because her parents have split up, it doesn't give her the right to be such a bloody awful bitch.'

'Natalie Baxter, I've told you before about swearing!'

'Mum, I'm nearly fifteen. I'm a mass of hormonal angst; swearing is a vital outlet for my pent-up emotion.'

'Then I'll thank you to do it elsewhere. Now put your angst on hold and pass me your father's shirt to iron.'

Genevieve listened to her family discussing her friend, who was upstairs using the last of the hot water. Again.

It was five months since Rachel's mother had discovered her husband had been living a double life; turned out he'd been having an affair for years. All the times he'd said he was away chasing deals for his construction business, he'd been down in Kent seeing the other woman in his life. He'd even taken her on holiday. That was what had given him away. He'd been spotted by one of his wife's closest friends in a hotel in Paris. Mrs Harmony had kicked him out, sworn vengeance on his wallet and refused to let him see Rachel, until he hit back with the law on his side and claimed his right to see his daughter. It was horrible for Rachel, Genevieve could see that, caught between her parents and expected to take sides. She could never imagine doing that if her parents were ever to split up.

'Mum's using me to punish Dad,' Rachel told Genevieve on the bus one morning, 'and I hate her for that, almost as much as I hate him for what he's done.'

Overnight, Rachel's behaviour at school changed. She became moody, rude and surly, even to the teachers. She disregarded all the rules, dyed her lovely blonde hair a dirty shade of black and teased it about a foot high, then hardened it with gel and hairspray. She had several more holes pierced in her ears, and was constantly late with handing in her homework, if she bothered to do it at all. She also started smoking, and then began to skip school altogether. Her parents were 'invited' to discuss the matter with the headmistress, as they were only weeks away from sitting their GCSEs. 'Boring!' was Rachel's only comment. Things picked up a bit as a result of the meeting and she got through her exams – the last one for them both had been two weeks ago. Then, at the weekend, she had arrived at Brook House Farm with yet more shocking news.

Sitting on the fence behind the Dutch barn where no one would see them, she had lit up the first of many cigarettes after knocking back a large mouthful of vodka from the bottle in her bag. She told Genevieve she never wanted to see her father again.

'He's a lying cheating bastard and I hope he rots in hell for what he's done.'

'What's he done now?'

'I don't want to talk about it. Can I doss down here with you for a while?' Taking a long drag on the cigarette, she flicked the glowing stub of it into the air. It landed several yards away in the sun-dried grass.

Genevieve leapt down from the fence and stamped it out. 'You mustn't do that, Rachel, you could start a fire.'

Rachel shrugged and raised the vodka to her mouth. 'Lay off, Gen, I get enough nagging from Mum at home. If she isn't screaming at Dad on the phone, she's having a go at me. So can I stay?' She held out the bottle.

Genevieve took it but didn't drink any. In her friend's current mood she wasn't sure she wanted her around full-time. Pushing this selfish thought aside, she said, 'I'll ask Mum.'

Minutes passed as they sat in the gathering dusk. After striking a match for another cigarette, Rachel said, 'Apparently I have a sister.'

'A what?'

She snatched the vodka out of Genevieve's hands. 'You heard. My father has another child, with that woman.'

Imagining this was a recent event, Genevieve said, 'When was it born?'

'That's the good bit. Five years ago.'

'*Five years!* You're kidding?'

'Oh, yeah, like I'd go round joking about a thing like that.'

'And he's kept it a secret all this time? But that's incredible.'

'That's one way of putting it.'

Another silence fell between them.

'Her name's Christine,' Rachel said bitterly, 'and if we can believe a single word my father says, she looks just like me.' She slipped down from the fence and swayed unsteadily. 'How can he say that? How can he even compare the two of us? He always said I was special. That I was his –' Her voice trailed away and she slumped over the fence, her shoulders heaving with angry sobs.

Genevieve put her arm around her friend. She knew exactly what Rachel had been going to say, that her father had always called her his Special Little Princess.

Poor Rachel, her crown had been taken from her a long time ago and she'd never even known it.

But remaining sympathetic towards Rachel wasn't easy. She had been staying with them for five days now and so far she'd argued with Nattie at least once a day, almost coming to blows over whose turn it was to have a bath; she'd been rude to Mum about her cooking; she'd broken one of Dad's fishing rods; and, in Genevieve's eyes, had committed the cardinal sin of laughing at Gran behind her back when Gran had reprimanded her for smoking.

'Ever thought of taking a shotgun to your crazy Gran's head and putting her out of her misery?' Rachel said. 'I hope I die long before I get like her.'

'Keep smoking at that rate and your wish might be granted,' Genevieve told her sharply. Another remark like that and Rachel would get more than she bargained for.

When Genevieve heard the bath water running away, she went upstairs. It was time for some plain speaking. Rachel needed to be told she'd outstayed her welcome.

'Hi, Gen,' Rachel said, appearing on the landing just as Genevieve reached the top of the stairs. She was wearing Genevieve's brand new dressing gown and a towel fashioned into a turban on her head. 'I've just had this great idea. Why don't I come on holiday with you? I can't face Dad this summer, and Mum's turned into a right psycho. What do you say?'

There were any number of reasons why Rachel shouldn't come to Angel Sands. To name but two, she'd drive them all mad, and there really wasn't room at Thrift Cottage. But Genevieve's main concern was that she didn't want Rachel to ruin what had always been special to her. It was selfish, but Angel Sands was like a precious old toy that no one but Genevieve was allowed to play with.

There was also Christian to consider. Having Rachel around would spoil everything: she and Christian wouldn't be able to see as much of each other as they'd planned to. His last letter had been full of all the things he hoped they'd be able to do. Now that he could drive, they'd been looking forward to going further afield.

But all that was about to be wrecked and it was as much as Genevieve could do to be polite to Rachel as they sat in the very back of the family Volvo – in the dickey seat. She answered her friend's annoying questions about Angel Sands. How many pubs were there? What were the locals like? Should she – ha, ha, ha! – have brought her passport? And was it true what they said about the Welsh and sheep?

Eventually Genevieve feigned sleep and wished her parents weren't so generous. Despite Genevieve saying she didn't think it would be a good idea, Rachel went behind her back and asked her parents if she could join them on holiday. And because Mum and Dad both felt sorry for her, they'd said she was more than welcome to join them, but warned her that it would be a bit of a squash.

After the longest and hottest journey Genevieve had ever known, they'd arrived and were unpacking. There were four bedrooms – one for Gran, one for her parents, one for Nattie and Polly, and the smallest, the room that had always been Genevieve's, was home for her and her friend for two weeks.

'When your mum and dad said it would be small, I didn't think they meant dolls house small,' Rachel said rudely, still with half a case to unpack. 'The place is tiny. Where on earth shall I put all my clothes?'

'I told you not to bring so many. Here, put them in the cupboard. I'll use the shelves.'

Genevieve wasn't at all sure she'd survive the holiday. Or that her happy memories of the place would remain intact.

Driving through the centre of the village, passing the shops with their supply of seaside bric-a-brac – the colourful buckets and spades, the inflatable beach toys, the gaudy sticks of rock and racks of flip-flops – she had tried to look at it through Rachel's eyes. But what she'd seen before as quaint and relaxed, now seemed backward and old-fashioned. Where were the High Street stores that her friend would crave? The only saving grace was that the hot weather had brought out the holidaymakers and the beer garden in front of the Salvation Arms was packed, as was the beach. A deserted, rain-sodden Angel Sands would never have survived Rachel's scorn and ridicule.

Their father was keen to try out the new barbecue the owners of the cottage had supplied, and after they'd finished their unpacking, Nattie and Polly were sent down to the village to buy some chops and sausages. 'And you two,' their father said, looking at Genevieve and Rachel, 'can go over to Pendine Cottage, and see if Christian and his parents would like to join us.'

This then, was the moment of truth. And as they set off in the late afternoon sun, Rachel taking the opportunity to smoke, Genevieve knew that if Rachel said one disparaging word about Christian she would never speak to her again. In fact, she'd insist that her parents made her go home.

She had written to Christian to let him know that she would be bringing her friend with her, and warned him to ignore anything rude Rachel might say when they met. Last year, in October, when Genevieve had spent half-term with Christian, she had kept from him the falling-out that she and Rachel had had. But later, during the February half-term when she was invited to go down to Shropshire again, she told him that Rachel had been jealous of her having a boyfriend. Putting an arm round her, he'd said, 'Then she ought to find one of her own and stop worrying about yours.'

It was only then that Genevieve wondered why Rachel didn't have a boyfriend. All those magazines teaching her how to have the perfect relationship and she hadn't even come close to one.

'You never said it would be so pretty,' Rachel said, as they looked down onto Tawelfan beach, where the sea glistened in the sunlight and the golden sand looked as though it had been washed and dried specially for their benefit.

Genevieve checked her friend's face for signs of sarcasm – she was, after all, used to the glamorous beaches of Florida. To her surprise she saw that Rachel was smiling. For the first time in a long while, she looked happy. Perhaps Mum and Dad had been right to bring her with them, and a relaxing no-frills holiday away from her warring parents was just what she needed. Ashamed of her selfishness, Genevieve turned and walked on.

As it turned out, Christian and his parents couldn't come to Thrift Cottage that evening as they were going to meet some friends staying in St David's.

'So at last I meet Genevieve's mystery boyfriend,' Rachel said, when Mr and Mrs May left them alone in the garden to talk. 'Mind if I smoke?'

'I'd prefer it if you didn't,' Christian said.

Unsure how her friend would react to such directness, Genevieve watched Rachel put the packet of cigarettes back inside her bag. She was relieved when Rachel's lips curled into a smile and she said, 'I like a man who speaks his mind. Shows he knows what he wants in life.'

Sitting on the grass and looking up to where Genevieve and Rachel were sitting on the wooden bench, Christian smiled too. Genevieve's heart gave a sudden lurch; she thought she'd never seen him look more attractive. He was dressed in an open-necked checked shirt and jeans, his feet bare and very tanned. His hair, still thick and springy, was wet from having just come out of the shower and was pushed back from his forehead giving him a sexy pop-star kind of look. Just the sight of him made her want to leap up from the wooden seat and throw herself at him.

'So what's this about me being Genevieve's mystery boyfriend?' he said. 'I don't think there's anything remotely mysterious about me.'

Rachel turned to Genevieve and laughed. 'Shall I tell him or will you?'

Frowning, Genevieve said, 'I would if I knew what you were talking about.' She glanced at Christian as if to say, please, just humour her.

'Well, the mystery to me is why Genevieve kept your disability such a big secret.'

Genevieve froze. She felt the colour drain from her face.

Christian's face altered too. Gone was the smile. 'And what disability would that be?'

Rachel switched her gaze from Christian to Genevieve. She slapped a hand over her mouth. 'Oh God, Gen! Have I said the wrong thing?' Then looking back to Christian, 'I'm so sorry. All I meant was; it was only recently that Gen told me you were deaf and I don't know why she did that.

Kept it a secret, I mean. 'Cos, there's nothing wrong in being deaf, is there? Who cares about that kind of thing these days? Certainly not me.'

When neither Christian nor Genevieve spoke, Rachel puffed out her cheeks and said, 'I'm going for a walk. I need a fag.'

They watched her go. When she was out of earshot, Genevieve spoke. 'I'm sorry for what she said.'

He got up and joined her on the bench. 'It's okay. You did warn me.'

'But she shouldn't have said that. You're not disabled. It was an awful thing to say.'

'Clumsy maybe, but not awful.' He put his arms around her. 'Technically I am disabled. So let's leave it at that. Don't suppose you'd like to get your lips a bit nearer so I can read them better?'

Seeing that he was smiling again, she moved so that her face was just inches from his. 'Close enough?'

He shook his head. 'Closer please.'

She pressed her mouth against his. His lips parted, and with her eyes closed, her heart thumping in her chest, she opened her mouth and welcomed the soft, slow movement of his tongue against hers. The feel of his hands around her neck made her skin tingle and a dizzying warmth flooded through her. But there was something new, a burning heat deep within that made her want him to undress her and touch her all over. She knew for sure then, that if there was an opportunity during the holiday, and he asked her to, she would go all the way with him.

They were still kissing when Rachel returned. Neither of them noticed her until she was almost upon them.

'Bloody hell, you two! It's a good thing I'm here or the pair of you would be at it.'

On their way back to Angel Sands, Rachel slipped her arm through Genevieve's. She had started doing this recently and Genevieve wished she wouldn't; people often stared at them.

'Sorry about putting my huge foot in it,' Rachel said. 'Am I forgiven?'

Still high on kissing Christian, Genevieve said, 'Of course. Although it was pretty awful what you said. You must never use that word again in front of him.'

'What word?'

'The D word: disability.'

'Oh, that. He was fine about it. Especially once you got your tongue down his throat.'

Trying to hide her embarrassment, she said, 'You shouldn't have been watching.'

'What else could I do? You were in full view of me. But I'll say this. Your taste isn't bad. He's totally dee-luscious. He looks much older than eighteen. More like twenty-two. And that deaf thing really isn't a problem, is it? I love the way his eyes flickered over my mouth whenever I said anything. Very sexy. I could even fancy him myself.'

Genevieve's heart swelled, any earlier misgivings over her friend's blunder now gone from her mind. 'You really thought he was nice?'

'Get real! He's a drool object! A heartbreaker too, I shouldn't wonder.'

'Oh, no,' Genevieve said, 'you've got him all wrong. Christian's not like that.'

'Gen, you sweet little innocent. Haven't you realised yet that *all* men are like that?'

Thinking of Rachel's father, Genevieve didn't argue the point. Instead, she took pleasure in her friend's approval of something so important to her.

She also felt a sense of relief that Christian hadn't questioned her on why she had waited so long to tell Rachel he was deaf.

Several days after their father had left them to return home to the farm, Genevieve overheard her grandmother say, 'Serena, I wouldn't trust that little minx as far as I could throw her.'

Wondering who she and her mother were discussing – Nattie perhaps – Genevieve hovered outside the kitchen door.

'Oh, she's harmless enough. She's just a little mixed up these days. It'll pass.'

That ruled out Nattie: she'd been mixed up all her life.

'Well, don't say I didn't warn you. But if you take my advice, you'll do something about it.'

'But they're young, they have a lifetime of lessons to be learned, some harder than others.'

'I don't care how young they are, these things stay with you, and if Genevieve gets hurt, I'll never forgive myself for keeping quiet.'

Genevieve's heart pounded. Hurt? Who would deliberately hurt her? Agonising seconds passed as she waited for her mother to say something. She tried to make herself go back upstairs, where only minutes ago she had been lying in bed unable to sleep. Just turn and go, she told herself. But she didn't, and regretting the thirst that had made her come downstairs for a glass of water, she inched a little closer to the door, taking care not to breathe too loudly or step on anything that might creak and give her away. The blood pulsing in her head, she heard Gran say, 'You're making a big mistake, Serena. Mark my words, she's a viper in our midst.'

'Oh, now you're being melodramatic.'

'I'm not. She's a girl who wouldn't think twice about making a play for her best friend's boyfriend. She's wicked and cunning, and the sooner this holiday is over, the better.'

Genevieve felt sick as slowly she climbed the stairs. Staring down at the bed next to hers, where her friend lay sleeping soundly, Rachel's words came back to taunt her. *Gen, you sweet little innocent. Haven't you realised yet that all men are like that?*

Yes, she thought, but only because there are girls out there like you, Rachel Harmony.

Instead of confronting her friend, or confiding in her grandmother, Genevieve took the coward's way out and for the remaining days of the holiday, she watched Rachel with a constancy that bordered on paranoia.

She watched Christian too.

But while it was true that Rachel paid Christian an inordinate amount of attention, asking him endless questions and forever touching him to make sure he could see what she was saying, for his part, he was always polite and answered her questions with humour and patience.

Goodness! Genevieve had never seen her friend show so much interest in another person. But his manner towards her was no more attentive than it was towards Nattie or Polly: in other words, he was his normal friendly self. If doubt crept up on her, Genevieve reminded herself that it was her hand he held, her lips he kissed, her shoulder he put an arm round, and it was for her benefit alone that he would mouth some private joke or comment.

She could hardly believe it when they reached the end of the holiday, the luggage was stowed and Christian was still her boyfriend.

Was it wrong of her to feel victorious?

18

September was a month of enormous change that year. Genevieve and Rachel were settling into the sixth form, Christian was preparing to go to university at the end of the month, and his parents were selling Pendine Cottage to buy a place in the Dordogne to do up. It set Serena off again about them doing a similar thing, finding a house in Pembrokeshire and running it as a bed and breakfast. She spoke of little else, and very soon their father was caught up in the idea too, and began seriously to consider the offer made by a large building firm for Brook House Farm and its lucrative land.

Despite finding her A-level work even harder than she'd anticipated, Genevieve's confidence was rock steady. At last everything seemed to be going well for her. She had never raised the conversation she'd overheard between her mother and Gran, and certainly she'd never broached the subject with Rachel, which meant she would never know if Gran had been right to be worried. But with a resolve that surprised her, she put the episode firmly in the past, concluding that Rachel had probably been doing nothing more cunning than practising her flirting technique. And – *hurrah!* – it had been wasted on Christian.

The weekend before Christian was due to take up his place at Exeter, it was Genevieve's seventeenth birthday and her parents suggested he came to stay, and they'd throw a little party. Everyone knew that there was no such thing as a 'little' party when Serena was involved. She loved arranging them, and when Genevieve and her sisters had been younger she had, once or twice, gone too far. A Halloween party she was particularly proud of had been so lavish and scary – lights suddenly switched off and homemade skeletons popped out of cupboards – terrified children had wet themselves and begged to be taken home early.

Christian arrived on the afternoon of the party. To have some time alone together, Genevieve took him for a guided tour of the farm. She showed him the milking parlour, explained how the machinery worked, and how her father would have to computerise it if he was going to make it more economical.

'That's if we stay,' she added, as she led him outside and across the yard to the old hay barn.

'You think you won't?' Christian asked, taking hold of her hand.

'Mum's become obsessed with us moving down to Pembrokeshire.'

He smiled. 'It would be nearer Exeter.'

'It would, wouldn't it?'

Looking back towards the house, where Nattie was pulling a face at them through the kitchen window and pretending to gag, he said, 'Is there somewhere we can be alone?'

From having the sun on it all day, the barn was warm and stuffy, the air heavy with the sweet smell of hay. Climbing the ladder up to the loft, where Genevieve and her sisters had often played as children, they sat on the dusty floor. 'This would make a fantastic house,' Christian said, taking off his sweatshirt and glancing round at the space. 'I'd love to do that kind of work when I'm qualified as an architect. Converting old buildings into houses would be such a great thing to do.'

But for once Genevieve wasn't interested in what Christian had to say. Since the moment he'd arrived she'd wanted to kiss him and suddenly feeling light-headed and breathless, she pushed him onto his back. She kissed him slowly on the lips, wanting so much for him to know what he meant to her. He returned her kiss, his mouth deliciously soft and tender. And feeling strangely weak, yet fantastically strong at the same time, she slipped a hand under his tee-shirt, wanting to touch the smooth hardness of his stomach. His hands, too, began to work at her clothes and when she sat up and took off her top, he stared at her, his eyes shining, his breath huskily audible in the stillness. She had never felt more sure of a thing, but when she put her hands behind her back to undo her bra, he suddenly looked nervous.

'Gen, don't. Please don't.'

'It's okay. I want to.'

He put out his hands to stop her. 'I want to as well. But . . . but not here. Not now.'

Her heart slammed in her chest. 'Don't you love me?'

'It's not that. It's . . .' His voice broke off.

'You don't fancy me? Is that it?' She could feel everything fall away from her, everything she had believed about him, about the strength of his feelings.

He smiled and put his arms around her neck. 'Oh, I fancy you all right. But I don't want to take any chances. You know, doing it without protection. I don't have any condoms.'

Condoms! Of course. How stupid she'd been. Relief flowed through her. She tilted her head back so that he could see her face. 'Another time, perhaps?'

He stroked her cheek. 'You better believe it.'

Rachel was the last guest to arrive, and she was fabulously over-dressed in a slinky white dress that showed off her perfect figure and, if Genevieve's suspicions were right, the lack of a pair of knickers. On her head was a pink baseball cap with the words 'Spoiled Rotten' written in sparkly fake diamonds.

'A present from my father,' she said, catching Genevieve's glance. 'The dress too. It's his way of saying sorry and I'm quite prepared to take advantage of him.' She handed over an expensively wrapped package. 'For you. Happy seventeenth birthday, Gen.'

'Thanks, Rachel. It looks gorgeous before I've even unwrapped it.'

'Think nothing of it; it's more guilt money extracted from my father. The well is deep and given the chance, I'm going to run it dry.' She took in the other guests. 'There are a lot of people here. Who are they all?'

'Mostly our farming friends.'

'Ah, yes, you told me once that farming blood is thicker than anyone else's and you all stick together like treacle. So where's Christian?'

'He's helping Dad with the barbecue.'

Serena breezed through just then, carrying a large bowl of salad, the smell of spring onions and peppers filling the air. She looked at Rachel. 'Hello dear, I do hope you'll be warm enough. That dress is gossamer-thin.'

Rachel laughed. 'Oh, I expect I'll find some way to keep warm. Gen could always lend me something if I get desperate.'

'She might even lend you some knickers if you're nice. Now, if you'll excuse me, I must get this salad on the table. Have fun!'

When they were getting ready to cut the cake – the Baxters liked nothing better than a good drum-rolling, cake-cutting moment – Genevieve went to look for Christian.

'Have you seen Christian?' she asked Nattie. 'Mum wants to take some photographs of us all together.'

Her sister, who'd been drinking cider for most of the evening, shrugged. 'No, but I'm seeing two of you if it's any help?'

When Genevieve couldn't find Rachel either, a chilling fear crept into her heart.

'I saw Rachel talking to Christian earlier,' Polly said. 'Do you want me to help you find them?'

'No. It's okay. You tell Mum and Dad to hold back the cake for a few minutes more. I won't be long.'

I'm being irrational, she told herself, but despite her firm words, the chill took a stronger hold on her. Determined to find them both, to know the worst, she checked the house.

No sign of them there.

She tried the hay barn and, almost inevitably, that was where she found them. She didn't need to climb the ladder up to the loft, where only hours ago she and Christian had lain – where she'd been rejected – to know what they were doing. It was obvious. Rachel was gasping loudly and Christian was breathing hard, the floorboards creaking rhythmically.

Genevieve wanted to run, to run right out of the barn, but mesmerised by the trickles of dust falling through the gaps in the wooden floor above her head, she moved slowly towards the ladder. She had to see for herself. Had to know she hadn't imagined it. Her hands trembling, she reached for the ladder and began the nightmare climb upwards. But before she'd stepped onto the second rung, the growing pain inside her exploded and she let out a cry of sickening anguish and dropped to the ground.

Only Rachel could have heard the cry, but probably her expression would have alerted Christian and made him realise something was wrong. The rhythmic creaking stopped. Knowing what was about to happen – that Rachel and Christian would peer down at her – Genevieve picked herself up and fled.

She stumbled outside and ran, blinded by tears, across the yard to the house. She didn't stop running until she was upstairs and had thrown herself onto her bed. How could he? How could he betray her like that, and with Rachel of all people?

She was sobbing so hard into her pillow, she only realised Gran was in the room when she felt the mattress dip. She opened her eyes, plunged her head into her grandmother's lap and sobbed even harder.

'Oh, Gran,' she gulped, 'I . . . I saw them . . . they were together . . . in the barn . . . and they were . . . he was . . . I hate them both!'

'It's all right, sweetheart,' her grandmother soothed. 'You cry. You cry for as long as you need.' She rocked her gently. The moment was so reminiscent of that day in Gran's kitchen when finally Genevieve had cried for her grandfather, that the tears flowed as though they would never stop. The ache, already burying itself deep inside her heart, was so profound, she knew it would never leave her.

Part Three

19

'I bet your father wanted to beat the little sod to a pulp! I hope he did.'

Genevieve smiled at Adam. 'You should know Dad better than that. Nattie, on the other hand, didn't waste any time in giving him a piece of her mind. Just as he was getting into his car to drive home, she slapped his face so hard, she knocked him clean off his feet.'

'That's my girl!' Adam laughed heartily, jiggling Lily-Rose on his lap. She was back in the kitchen again, quietly helping herself from the packet of raisins on the table. 'So what happened next?'

'Heavens! Haven't you heard enough? Surely you must be bored to death with all this memory lane stuff?'

'Sorry, am I being insensitive?'

'No. Not at all. But I guess the straight answer is, I recovered from a broken heart and grew up.'

'And the complicated answer?'

'Ah, well. I made myself ill, dropped out of school and drifted aimlessly until I finally got my act together.'

He looked thoughtful. 'How ill, Gen?'

'Oh, you know; the full works. Depression. Anxiety. And starving myself in the belief that Christian had betrayed me because I was a big, fat, unlovable moron. All I could think of was making myself slowly disappear, taking all my problems with me. It became a way of life. Towards the end I was living off peas and toothpaste; the only things I'd allow myself to eat.'

Adam reached across the table and laid his hand on top of hers. He didn't say anything, just shook his head. Lily-Rose, thinking it was a game, added her small hand to the pile. Giggling, she got back to the packet of raisins, eating them steadily, one by one.

'Why have you never mentioned any of this before?' Adam asked quietly. 'Or for that matter, why haven't your parents or sisters ever spoken of it?'

'It's called shame. Plus that well-known Baxter trait, an inability to talk about anything really important. Let's face it, it's why Mum's currently swanning around some winery in New Zealand and Dad refuses to get his head out of the sand.'

'But there's nothing to be ashamed about.'

Genevieve shook her head. 'Look at it from Mum and Dad's point of view. In their eyes they allowed me to slip through the net. What with Nattie's wildness to control and Polly's musical gifts to nurture, I was the easy-going daughter they didn't need to worry about. Okay, there was my dyslexia, but all in all, I was the one they didn't need to lose any sleep over.'

'But they can't still feel guilty, surely?'

'I think they do. The first thing I remember Mum saying when I was taken into hospital, was, "Where did we go wrong?" You see, with nothing tangible to blame, they blamed themselves. They thought they should have been better parents. Then when I recovered, we all started to push my illness under the carpet, and before long it became known as *That Time When She Wasn't Well.* A tidy euphemism for something we wanted to put behind us.'

Adam frowned. 'I'd never have guessed you'd gone through so much.'

'That's because we Baxters are adept at covering our tracks and keeping schtum.'

'So what happened to Rachel? After you'd torn her limb from limb.'

'She stayed on at school, though I never spoke to her again after that night. Other than to tell her what I thought of her the next day.'

'Strikes me that was something you should have done a long time before. Your Gran was right about her.'

'Hindsight's a wonderful thing, but you know, I think Gran was also right about Rachel not being as clever or confident as she made out. I just couldn't see it at the time.'

Adam scoffed. 'Don't start making excuses for her, Gen. She knew exactly what she was doing. She deliberately manipulated you, filled your head with a lot of dangerous nonsense to plump up her own ego. Do you know what she went on to do?'

'The last I heard – this was years ago – was that she went to live with her father.'

'And Christian. Did he ever say he was sorry?'

'I didn't give him much of a chance to apologise. He wrote to me, but I returned all his letters unopened. After his parents sold Pendine Cottage, he never showed up in Angel Sands again.'

'And now the dirty love-rat is about to appear on the scene again. How do you feel about that?'

She got to her feet to make some fresh tea. 'For a start, I don't view him as a dirty love-rat. Don't forget, we were little more than children. Teenage love isn't designed to last. My mistake was to take it too seriously. But then, that's the prerogative of the young. And as my mother said, there were important lessons to be learned.'

'A very pretty speech, Gen. How about you answer my question?'

With her back to him, staring out of the window, the rain still coming down, Genevieve tried, as she had so many times, to think what her answer really was. How she felt about the memory acquiring its final chapter.

'I'm curious,' she said at last, turning to face Adam. 'Curious to see if I still think he's as perfect as I once thought he was.'

Adam left Lily-Rose to her raisins, and came over to Genevieve, his expression serious. 'I'd have thought he settled that matter in the barn that night.'

She smiled. 'Are you protecting me? Worried I might still be carrying a torch for him?'

'And aren't you?'

'I told you, I'm intrigued. Nothing more.'

From outside came the sound of Henry kicking up an almighty row again. Adam switched his gaze from her to the garden. 'The sooner you find that donkey a pal, the better. Now then, I'd better get going. You won't forget to give Gareth and Gwenda a call about the wedding buffet, will you?'

20

Genevieve was aware some people would say that as a teenager she'd been a pathetic wimp. That she'd let Rachel walk all over her, had allowed her to have her way over the slightest thing. And worse, she had willingly let Rachel manipulate her like a puppet. No two ways about it, she had only herself to blame for being so feeble.

Well, there was never any point in preaching to the converted – Genevieve knew better than anyone that she should have been more assertive. But ultimately it had been the axis of her friendship with Rachel that had been at fault. Their relationship had been based on too much mutual neediness. As she'd told Adam, hindsight was a wonderful thing, but at that young age she had been ill-equipped to deal with the complex circumstances in which she'd found herself.

She didn't need to be a psychiatrist to know that her low self-esteem in those days, a direct result of being dyslexic, had made her subconsciously pick out a dominant friend to hide behind, and Rachel, with her desperate need to feel superior, had carefully nurtured Genevieve to play the necessary supporting role. So in that respect, neither of them was to blame.

But what Rachel had done with Christian was another matter altogether. Genevieve would always view that as a malicious and calculating act. Rachel had known exactly what she was doing that night and had deliberately gone all-out to destroy what was most precious to Genevieve.

Genevieve could only surmise that it stemmed from Rachel's parents splitting up. Just as Genevieve had been set on a particular course when her grandfather died, so too had Rachel when she realised she was no longer her Daddy's Little Girl, his Special Princess.

Cause and effect.

But that was then.

Now, today, with the wedding buffet to oversee, she had enough to think about without wasting any more time dwelling on the past. She could change none of it, and perhaps, if she was honest, she didn't want to change it. The experience had taught her two invaluable lessons: to take responsibility for herself, and never to allow anyone to manipulate or bully her. Though perhaps a more important lesson would have been to learn the trick of being more open about her feelings. That was a concept she and her family had yet to get the hang of.

Making her final round of checks, she looked in on the marquee in the garden, seeing if the florist had arranged the flowers on the tables as she'd asked. Yes. They were all there, beautifully displayed; baskets of yellow roses and creamy white irises.

Going back outside into the blazing June sunshine, such a contrast to the rain of last week, she pondered why Adam was going to such lengths to organise her. He seemed determined to make her start up her own catering business, having engineered what she was doing today – providing a buffet for eighty-five wedding guests who would be arriving in less than an hour. Since last week, when he'd asked her to rescue Gareth and Gwenda's daughter's wedding party, he'd been on at her almost daily to consider his offer to back her. In the end, just to silence him, she'd told him about George and Cecily Randolph and the money George had left her in his will. It wasn't an enormous sum, but it was enough to help set herself up in business, should she so wish. It had been almost the last conversation she and George had had when he was dying in hospital.

'You've been so good to me,' he'd said, his voice so low she had to bend down next to him to hear, 'and I'm sure Cecily would have wanted you to have the money. It's such a small amount, so please don't refuse it.'

'So you see,' she'd told Adam, 'you don't have to take pity on me.'

'I wasn't doing anything of the kind.'

'Good. Now please don't mention the money to anyone. I don't want people knowing about it. They'll only ask questions that I shan't want to answer.'

'Mr Discreet, that's me. But one more thing. If you have the wherewithal, why don't you get stuck in to something?'

'Because if I'm going to do it, I'll do it when I'm good and ready. I won't be bullied by anyone, not even you, Adam.'

He'd looked hurt at that. 'I've never bullied anyone in my life, Gen. I'm the least manipulative person in the world.'

'You're a dear friend,' she said, giving him a hug.

Inside the house, the sound of laughter was coming from the kitchen. Nattie, who was helping to serve along with Donna, had decided to dress for the part and was wearing a French maid's outfit. Gran, resplendent in one of her best party frocks, said, 'I think she looks great. How I wish I had those legs.'

But Daddy Dean was wearing his disapproving father's hat. 'You don't think you ought to change into something a little less indecent, Nattie? You do realise the vicar's been invited, don't you?'

Nattie grinned wickedly and hitched up her skirt to reveal stocking tops and suspenders. 'Hey, great idea, we could make it a Tarts and Vicars party.'

Genevieve wondered what Adam would make of his beloved parading herself so provocatively.

At their father's insistence, the welcome party was changed. Instead of Nattie and him standing at the entrance to the marquee to offer arriving guests glasses of champagne, as originally planned, Donna was assigned the task in her place. He judged it prudent to wait until the guests had downed a mellowing drink or two before Nattie was let loose on them.

The bride and groom, plus parents, were the first to arrive. The four of them looked with relief at the marquee and pretty garden with its dramatic backdrop of sparkling blue sea; they were clearly impressed. But having thought they'd be reduced to raiding the local supermarket for its limited selection of mass-produced canapés, and putting on a DIY do at home, Genevieve guessed that anything would have been a welcome sight. Polly was playing her part too. She was providing background music. Last night Adam had helped Dad move the piano from the guest sitting room to the conservatory, so that music would flow out into the garden. Now, as the guests began to arrive, Polly struck up with the first of her popular music pieces, 'Love Changes Everything'. On the cliché scale, it was joint first with 'Lady in Red', but as with most clichés, it was entirely appropriate. Catching her eye from across the lawn, Gareth and Gwenda gave Genevieve the thumbs-up.

So far so good.

Back in the kitchen, there was no sign of Gran or Lily-Rose. But with a foot on a chair, cursing loudly, Nattie was adjusting one of her suspenders.

'Bloody thing, it won't stay put. Ah, that's got it.' She lowered her black stilettoed foot to the floor and straightened up. 'How the hell do women manage in these things?'

'I haven't a clue. Are you sure you're going to cope in those shoes? They look lethal.'

'They are, but they'll do wonders for Dad's precious lawn. I'll aerate the grass as I go. Any sign of the vicar yet? I'm dying to see his face. Adam's too.'

With so much to do, Genevieve let Nattie's remark go. 'If you could put your Ann Summers outfit to one side for a moment, you could help me get these trays in the oven.'

After setting the timer and leaving Nattie in charge to remove the canapés when they were cooked – please God, let her perform that simple task! – she went outside to make sure everyone had a drink. Donna and Dad had done their job, and the guests, glasses in hand, were circulating well. Some of them were openly admiring the garden. This would please her father; he'd worked hard all week bringing it up to scratch. The lavender-blue spikes of the neatly formed bushes of hebe contrasted prettily with the silvery-grey leaves of the senecio with its profusion of yellow, daisy-like flowers. Sheltered by the escallonia hedge were beds of hardy fuchsias, santolina, sea holly and cat mint. Pots of begonias and geraniums lined the terrace, and against the south-facing wall of the house, Dad's treasured palms were bathed in golden sunlight.

Genevieve felt a satisfying glow of pride that she had pulled it off. She hadn't seriously considered she would fail, but it was gratifying to see just how well, with help from her family and Donna, she had arranged everything.

Echoing her thoughts, a voice said, 'You've done a fantastic job, Gen. Just like I said you would.'

It was Adam, dressed immaculately in a lightweight suit, its effect sadly marred by a tie depicting a pink flamingo.

'Thanks,' she said. 'But I didn't do it alone.'

He shook his head. 'Just take the credit and have done with it, will you?'

She laughed. 'Okay, if you say so.' More seriously, she said, 'Have you seen Nattie yet?'

'No. Why do you ask?'

'Oh, no reason.' Changing the subject, she said, 'By the way, I had a word with that man you recommended over in Saundersfoot.'

'And?'

She pointed towards the far end of the orchard. 'See, or rather, listen. It's worked. Henry's been as good as gold, not a peep out of him. He hasn't left Morwenna's side since Nattie and Dad fetched her first thing this morning.'

'Morwenna?'

'Nattie's choice. It's Welsh for maiden. But she's cute, isn't she, with that light sandy face and chocolate body?'

'I can't honestly say that donkeys do it for me, Gen, but – *Sweet Moses on a bicycle made for two!* What the hell does she think she's doing?'

Adam's gaze, no longer directed towards the orchard, had swung round to the middle of the lawn and was fixed on the object of his desire. Carrying a large tray of canapés, Nattie had finally made her appearance.

He wasn't the only one to stare. 'Why?' he said simply. 'Why does she do it?'

'Because she loves to stand out. It's why you're mad about her, Adam. Remember the first time you set eyes on her; she was on a table doing her Madonna "Like a Virgin" impersonation. Now if you'll excuse me, you're here as a guest, but I'm not. I still have a hundred and one things to do.' She hurried away, leaving him to try to comprehend the impossible – what in the world made Nattie Baxter tick?

Before heading back to the kitchen, Genevieve popped into the conservatory to see how Polly was getting on. She had moved on to playing Elton John's 'Your Song'. But she had company. Lily-Rose was sitting on the floor under the piano, stirring a bowl of melting ice-cream.

'I thought Gran was supposed to be looking after Lily,' Genevieve said.

Her fingers still moving expertly over the keys, Polly replied, 'I think she may have got the wrong end of the stick.' She inclined her head towards the marquee.

There was Gran, a glass of champagne in one hand and a canapé in the other. She looked every inch the wedding guest, and not the handy baby-sitter she had offered to be.

'It's okay,' Polly said, 'I can manage. Lily's not a distraction.' But she spoke too soon. Suddenly aware of the piano pedals her aunt was working, Lily-Rose leaned forward to take a closer look. She grinned and tapped one of Polly's bare feet with her spoon; a blob of ice-cream landed on Polly's big toe. Professional to the end, Polly played on.

Genevieve bent down and held out her arms to her niece. 'Okay little missey. Out you come.'

Lily-Rose frowned and backed away. With a quickness of hand a magician would have been proud of, she dolloped another blob of ice-cream onto Polly's other foot. Before she got it into her head to tip the bowl over both her aunt's feet, Genevieve grabbed her around the waist and slid her out on her bottom. Still brandishing the spoon, the little girl used it to try and stop Genevieve spoiling her game, bopping her on the forehead with it and then the nose. Snatching it out of her hand, Genevieve slipped the spoon into her pocket. 'You're becoming more like your mother every day. Now behave or I'll be forced to put you in a lobster pot and throw you out to sea.'

Her words had no impact at all on Lily-Rose and, wriggling out of Genevieve's hands, she suddenly pointed through the open conservatory door and let out a cry of delight. '*Adam!*'

The man in question heard her squeal and turned round. She ran helter-skelter towards him and headbutted his kneecaps.

'Hello, Rosey-Posey,' he laughed, 'how's my best little girl?'

'We've got a new donkey. Do you want to come and see her? Her name's Morwenna.'

'In a moment maybe.'

'I know it's a cheek, Adam,' said Genevieve, when she'd caught up with her niece, 'but I don't suppose you'd like to keep an eye on her, would you? Gran's decided she'd rather be guzzling champagne than helping out.'

'No problem.' He bent down to Lily-Rose and lifted her onto his shoulders. 'Let's go and see if we can find something to eat, shall we?'

'But what about Morwenna?'

'Food first. Then Morwenna.'

Wide-eyed with delight, Lily-Rose beamed and grabbed hold of his ears. 'Giddy up, giddy up!'

'Thanks, Adam,' Genevieve said. 'What would we do without you?' She touched his arm lightly and leaned in to kiss him. But the sight of two men appearing round the side of the house caught her eye, and she froze.

She had a pretty good idea who the taller and darker of the two was, but the other ... the other, without doubt, was Christian.

21

Genevieve would never have thought it possible to take in so much in so short a time. As though a spell had been cast, everything around her became a muffled blur while, across the lawn, Christian was picked out in sharp focus.

He'd changed, of course. As much as anyone would in the thirteen years since she'd last seen him. He'd filled out more and his hair – cut shorter than she'd ever seen it – looked as though, finally, it had been tamed. His eyes were hidden behind sunglasses, but she could tell from his stance, hands pushed into the pockets of his loose-fitting trousers, head slowly turning, that he was scanning the garden, searching for someone.

Question was, who?

His gaze fell on her. His body stiffened and his hand reached for his sunglasses. It was obvious he was as stunned as she was. He turned to his companion, said something, then started to walk towards her. The spell grew stronger and the moment became heart-stoppingly surreal. Behind her, in the conservatory, Polly was playing 'Fly Me to the Moon' – something Genevieve would have paid good money to do right there and then. Everyone else, oblivious, continued to chat and laugh; they had no idea she had become a convert to the school of thought that time really could stand still.

Then the spell was broken. Next to her, Adam said, 'Gen, what's wrong? You look like you've seen a ghost.'

She moved closer to him, as if seeking his protection. 'I have,' she whispered. 'It's Christian.'

'*What?* Where?'

For a second it was tempting to raise an accusing hand and shout, 'There! That's the bastard who broke my heart!' Instead she murmured, 'He's heading this way. Don't leave me, whatever you do.'

'Anything you say.' Adam lowered Lily-Rose from his shoulders and, holding her hand, set her on the grass. 'We'll get something to eat in a minute, sweetheart.'

It felt as though an eternity passed before Christian was standing in front of her.

'Genevieve.'

That was it. That was all he said.

'Hello, Christian.' She forced herself to look him dead in the eye. 'I was wondering when you'd show up.'

He looked puzzled. 'You were? I don't understand.' His voice still had that characteristic flat, hollow timbre to it. The absence of any real inflection.

Over the years she had imagined bumping into Christian, showing him she harboured no ill feelings, that she was a superior being who had always had better things to do with her emotions than waste them on bitterness. She had pictured them catching up on old times, perhaps even becoming friends again. But now, as she stood face to face with the past, she felt a weight of hostility towards him, wanted very much to let him know just how badly he had hurt her.

A childish response? Yes. Proud of it? She didn't care. She even took a twisted, cruel delight in knowing that he appeared more uncomfortable than she did.

'I live here, Christian,' she said, in answer to his question. 'At the moment we all do, Mum, Dad, Gran, Nattie, Polly and me.'

'Really? Where?'

'Here.' She glanced around the garden, up at the house. 'This is our home.'

'Paradise House?' If it were possible he seemed more awkward than ever.

'We run it as a bed and breakfast ... just as Mum always wanted. Remember her dream?'

'I didn't know. Really I didn't.'

'Why would you?' Her voice was sharp. 'Why are you here, Christian? I don't mean, in the area, everyone knows about Ralph's barn being sold and some architect doing it up – we soon realised it was you. But why are you here at Paradise House?'

He turned away, stared at some distant point out to sea, shifted his feet, then looked back at her. 'You're not going to believe this, but we came here hoping there might be a couple of rooms available. We've just discovered the hotel we'd booked into has been closed down. We were pointed in this direction and told that Paradise House was the best place to stay these days.' He paused. 'But given the circumstances—' He paused again. Shifted his feet once more. 'Honestly, Genevieve, I didn't know you were living here. I swear I had no idea. I'm sorry. I'll tell Jonjo we'll try somewhere else.'

Then, as though only just noticing them, he glanced at Adam and Lily-Rose. His gaze rested on the little girl and something almost like a smile passed across his face; it took away some of the awkwardness from his expression. Genevieve was almost struck with pity for him – but not quite.

'She looks just like Nattie,' he said.

Realising his mistake, Genevieve said, 'That's because she's Nattie's daughter.'

He raised his glance back to her. 'What's her name?'

'Lily-Rose.'

'Look,' he said, more to Adam than to Genevieve, 'I'm sorry for barging in. You're obviously in the middle of a party. I'd better go.' He turned to leave, but hesitated, and just stood there staring at her. 'It's . . . it's good to see you again, Genevieve. You're looking well.' His eyes flickering briefly over Adam and Lily-Rose, he turned and went.

She watched him walk away, back to find his companion, presumably their neighbour-to-be, Jonjo Fitzwilliam. She felt a hand on her shoulder.

'You okay, Gen?'

Still watching Christian's retreating figure, she nodded. 'I'm fine, Adam. Thanks.'

It soon became clear that Christian had lost his friend amongst the wedding guests. Soon he was approaching Genevieve once more.

'Sorry about this,' he said, 'but I can't find Jonjo. It's so typical of him. He has the attention span of a goldfish.'

'Do you always speak so highly of your friends?'

Adam's comment went unnoticed by Christian – he'd been looking at Genevieve for a response. Sensing that her friend's hostility towards Christian was more palpable than her own, she said, 'I'll help you find him.'

'Thanks,' he said. 'Then I promise we'll get out of your way.'

They didn't have far to go before they found Jonjo. He was in the conservatory with Polly. They looked like a pair of Jane Austen characters: he was leaning attentively over the piano, watching her, and Polly, probably assuming he was one of the guests, concentrated on playing 'Strangers in the Night'. But Genevieve recognised all too well the spellbound expression on Jonjo's face. She had seen it countless times before; men slain by Polly's bewitching charms. Even Christian stood for a moment to stare at Polly. The last time he'd seen her she'd been a child.

As if the moment couldn't get any more unreal, a strident voice burst into the conservatory.

'Is it only Donna and me feeding this lot? I'll tell you this for free, if one more bloke asks me to bend down for his napkin, I'll poke a cocktail stick up his bum. *Bloody hell!* What're you doing here?'

Not even Polly could maintain her professionalism in the face of so many distractions. She caught sight of Christian and abruptly stopped playing.

In the silence that followed, Jonjo said, 'Christian, you never told me what my neighbours would be like in Angel Sands. Not a word did you say about musical angels or even fallen angels.' He eyed Nattie's outfit.

Genevieve saw that Nattie was dangerously armed with a plate of used cocktail sticks. 'Seeing as you're here, Christian, perhaps you and your friend would like a drink?' she said.

'Are you completely off your head, Gen?' demanded Nattie. 'How can you even *think* of allowing him to stay?'

They were in the kitchen, grabbing more food to take outside to the guests.

'It's called acting civilly. Something you should try.'

'I'd rather take up growing bamboo shoots through my toes than be polite to that pig of a man. What he did to you was beyond—'

'Oh, shut up, will you! Now pass me that chilli and garlic dip for the prawns. Okay, that's it. Out we go. Go on. Get a move on! People are waiting.'

Jonjo had eagerly accepted the offer of a drink, blind to Christian's discomfort. As Genevieve passed round a tray of canapés, she observed the two men sitting on the stone steps outside the conservatory. She had the feeling that neither was much interested in listening to the other. Jonjo, who she would bet a king's ransom didn't know the history between his friend and the Baxters, was being pulled like a magnet to stare at Polly, who was churning out another schmaltzy love song. Christian was picking absently at the moss on the steps, his glass of wine untouched. Perhaps she hadn't done the right thing suggesting they stay for a drink. He looked like he'd rather be anywhere but here.

Served him right.

Having attended to the guests, and with only a few canapés left on her tray, she went over to Christian and his friend. 'Any takers for asparagus tips wrapped in smoked salmon, and Thai prawns with chilli and garlic?'

Christian was instantly on his feet. 'Genevieve?'

'Yes?'

'I don't think this is a good idea.'

'Oh. Well, why don't you try one first?'

He brought his eyebrows together then looked at the tray. 'No, I didn't mean that. I meant me being here.'

Jonjo was now on his feet too, brushing away any dust that might have been clinging to the back of his linen trousers. He'd taken off his jacket, hooked it over the handle of the conservatory door, and Genevieve could see just how finely toned his body was. His black tee-shirt clung to his broad chest and shoulders, the perfect advertisement for the health and fitness centres he ran. She suspected, though, that he might be as vain as he was attractive. He seemed an unlikely choice of friend for Christian. Or for the Christian she used to know.

'But we can't go yet, Christian,' Jonjo said. 'I haven't had a chance to talk to the future Mrs Fitzwilliam. May I?' He helped himself to a couple of canapés.

Christian rolled his eyes. 'Just zip up your brain, will you?'

'I will, the day you channel that sarcasm into something called humour.'

'Take no notice of him, Genevieve. He's only allowed out at weekends.'

For the first time since the two men had appeared, she smiled.

'But seriously,' he said, 'I don't think your family want me here. Nattie's made that very clear.'

'My sister doesn't speak for all the Baxters.'

He glanced about him. 'I don't see any others queuing up to chat. Your father and grandmother keep giving me blood-curdling looks.'

'I'm talking to you, aren't I?'

'Only out of politeness.'

'True.'

'Mm . . . these are great. Any more going? Now tell me, Genevieve, when does your enchanting sister get time off? How can I propose to her if she's chained to the ivories until the end of time?'

'I told you, Jonjo, give it a rest. This is one family you really don't want to mess with.'

'What the hell have you done to upset the natives?'

Seeing that Christian didn't know how to answer or silence his friend, Genevieve said, 'It's okay, you can stay if you like. I'll have a word with Dad to go easy on the dirty looks.'

'There's no need. Come on, Jonjo, we're going. Before you make a complete arse of yourself.'

Jonjo reached for his jacket and threw Polly one last dazzling smile through the open door. 'I hate to pull the plug on a fine idea, Christian, but where exactly are we going? As far as I'm aware, we still don't have a place to rest our weary heads tonight.' He turned the full force of his magnetic smile on Genevieve. 'I don't suppose your sister would take pity on me and make room for a little one, would she?'

'You could try the Salvation Arms,' Genevieve said, trying not to laugh. 'Although the rooms are a bit on the small side, I believe.'

He pulled a face. 'Is that as bad as it sounds? A flea-ridden doss house for the down-and-outs?'

'It's the local pub, you idiot,' snapped Christian. 'And if you want to set off on the right foot with your new neighbours, I suggest you put some thought into showing them some respect.' He turned to Genevieve. 'Thanks for the recommendation. We'll try there next.'

'Good luck. And . . .'

'Yes?'

'If you're really stuck, you could sleep in the marquee tonight, after the guests have all gone home.'

He smiled, a little stiffly. 'You never know, we might just have to take you up on that offer. A night closely confined with Godzilla here holds few attractions for me.'

22

The following morning, Genevieve was up early. She didn't have a wedding reception to prepare for, but she still had ten breakfasts to cook. It was also Sunday, which was often a complete changeover day – every room vacated and re-occupied within a matter of hours. As a consequence, it was often the busiest day of the week. Today was such a day. The last of the clearing up from yesterday remained to be done: the marquee would be taken down by the firm who supplied it, the chairs and tables collected, along with the hired crockery, cutlery and glasses. Once all that was out of the way, she would feel that Paradise House was back to normal and she was in control again.

Routine had become important to her when she realised she had to stop viewing food as a weapon, something with which to punish herself. Structure and order replaced the chaos of what had gone before, and very soon they had become an integral part of her life. Her bedroom went from a ramshackle mess to the tidiest area in the house. She took to keeping a wipe-board by the side of her bed so that if a thought or worry came to her as she was drifting off to sleep, she could switch the light on and jot down the concern before her brain turned it into a major anxiety. She'd been told by the psychotherapist during her stay in hospital, and afterwards, that she should be aware that there was a danger of swapping one addictive habit for another. So she policed her thoughts and actions, watching for anything that had the potential to get out of hand and become a compulsion or obsession.

She still kept the wipe-board by the side of her bed and used it most nights, not as she used to, to offload, but to help her marshal her thoughts for the following day. Her Things To Do list. Ironically, her behaviour scored her a double whammy, because the need to keep her life carefully ordered, to be in control, was a trait often displayed by both dyslexics and anorexics. In short, control was 'her thing'. Remove it, and panic would rise inside her like a soufflé.

Another irony, perhaps one that her family would never understand, was why, since she'd made a full recovery, she now spent her days surrounded by food. She'd read an article once that said this wasn't uncommon, that it helped some sufferers to regain a natural sense of control by cooking for others, proving they were in control, not just to themselves, but to those around them.

'You're not trying to punish yourself some more, are you?' Gran had asked, afterwards confessing that it was Daddy Dean who had put her up to the question. Poor Dad, the world in which he'd found himself was too alien for him to comprehend. Both he and Mum had attended sessions with a therapist to help them understand that it wasn't just a simple matter of their daughter gaining weight, that the weight gain was only the beginning.

Dad had made the mistake one day of saying how well he thought Genevieve looked. 'You've put on a few pounds, haven't you? Well done!'

Just those few words undid weeks of uphill struggle. Panic and self-loathing kicked in – weight gain equalled ugliness – and she was almost back to square one. From then on Dad crept around her, terrified of saying the wrong thing. He and Mum were told that she needed to feel safe to eat, but it was a concept beyond his understanding.

'How can she not feel safe?' Genevieve overheard him saying to her mother. 'We're her family. We love her, for God's sake! How much safer can we make it for her? Tell me and I'll do it. Whatever it is, I'll do it.'

But he'd got the wrong end of the stick. It wasn't her surroundings, or the love of her family that were in question; it was her fear of food itself that needed changing.

With her usual breakfast of tea and a slice of toast and marmalade, Genevieve wandered out to the garden. It was going to be another beautiful day, like yesterday. She settled herself on the wooden bench that overlooked the bay and sipped her tea. She was exhausted. Mentally as well as physically. Not surprisingly, sleep had eluded her for most of the night. Turbulent dreams of Christian staying at Paradise House had merged with nightmares of the robbery. In the most violent of the dreams, she'd viciously beaten one of the robbers with a poker, but after she removed his mask, she'd found it was Christian.

What had shocked her most about Christian's reappearance yesterday was not her reaction to him, but her family's. They were protecting her, she knew, but even so, it annoyed her that they thought she was so fragile she couldn't cope with meeting Christian again. All things considered, she thought she'd handled the situation pretty well. Better than Christian had. He seemed much more uptight than she did. But then, as Adam had pointed out as he was helping to clear up after the revelry, Christian had unwittingly found himself slap bang in the middle of the lion's den.

'I suppose it's to his credit that he did feel so uncomfortable being here,' Adam had said. 'He did at least have the savvy to make a hasty exit.'

'Hardly surprising, given that everyone was giving him such a hard time.'

'I barely said a word to him.'

'Exactly!'

'Oh, for heaven's sake,' Nattie had interrupted, 'what did you expect us to do? Kill the fatted calf and put out the bunting?' She had exchanged her French maid's outfit for her pyjamas – vest top and shorts – and was sitting on the worktop, pouring herself a large glass of milk. She was quite happy to watch Adam and Genevieve stack the dishwasher. Just the three of them were in the kitchen. Lily-Rose had gone to bed hours ago, Polly was in the shower, and their father was walking Gran home. All of them had had their say on the matter, but it was, as always, Nattie who was the most vociferous. Genevieve suspected this was because Nattie had grown fond of Christian all those years ago, and had felt almost as betrayed as Genevieve had. She was firmly of the opinion that anyone who messed with a member of the Baxter family had her to answer to.

Such fierce protectiveness should have been a comfort, but it wasn't. They were making too much of it, and Genevieve hoped they'd get it out of their systems. Especially if Christian was going to be around over the coming months, or however long it took to turn Ralph's barn into a holiday home for his friend.

And what a character that Jonjo was! All that absurd talk of Polly being the future Mrs Fitzwilliam. How many times a week did he say that? Genevieve wondered, as she chewed her toast and watched a speck of a figure in the distance walking the cliff top. She remembered Christian's words: '*I told you, Jonjo, give it a rest. This is one family you really don't want to mess with.*' The terse reprimand certainly implied he'd heard the routine, or something similar, more than once before.

It had been odd, hearing Christian speak like that, so curt and out of sorts. It was only when they were leaving that he'd sounded more like his old self, or the person she knew from thirteen years ago, the easy-going boy with a warm sense of humour.

Soft footsteps behind her made her turn. 'Mind if I join you?' her father asked, a mug in his hand.

She made room for him on the bench. 'You're up early.'

'Not as early as you. Things on your mind?'

'A few.' She knew exactly what was on *his* mind. Knew also that he wouldn't come right out and say it. 'It went well yesterday,' she hedged. 'Thanks for your help. I couldn't have done it without you all.'

He slurped his tea. 'Every commander in chief needs his foot soldiers.'

'I'd hardly describe myself as a commander in chief.'

'Then you should. Adam says you should do more of this specialised catering lark.'

'Adam says a lot of things.'

'Most of which make a good deal of sense.'

Watching the distant figure on the cliff – he or she was getting closer – Genevieve thought of Adam's parting question last night. 'So has your curiosity been satisfied?' he'd asked. 'Does he seem as perfect as you once thought he was?'

'I'll let you know when I'm in a position to think straight. For now it's as much as I can do to wish you goodnight.'

As though picking up on her thoughts, her father said, 'Was it very much of a shock seeing him again?' She noticed he couldn't bring himself to say Christian's name.

'At first, yes. But then I began to feel almost sorry for him. He seemed so awkward, and everyone was making him feel unwelcome.'

'Your mother would have given him what-for, had she been here. I was tempted myself.'

Genevieve smiled. 'Liar. You're the biggest pacifist going, Dad.'

'And perhaps that isn't something I should be proud of. But I'll tell you what I am proud of, Gen, and that's you.'

She shrugged off the compliment with a shake of her head. 'Now you're being silly.'

He placed his mug on the arm-rest. 'It's true. I'm more proud of you than I can say. You know how I dry up when it comes to putting things into words.'

'But words aren't always necessary, Dad,' she said. She thought of all the occasions at school prize givings, when he'd give each of his daughters a single red rose, whether they'd gone up on the stage to collect a prize or not. Polly was forever out of her chair collecting another accolade; a merit certificate here, a highly commended certificate there, or as she did for three years running, the overall Year Achiever cup. But no matter how badly Nattie and Genevieve trailed behind her, their father was always on hand to give them his own special award and gesture of congratulations. It had meant a lot to Genevieve.

'I disagree,' he said. 'Words stay with a person. If they didn't, why would there be all that poetry?'

'So is there something special you want to say to me?' Genevieve asked, almost dreading what he might say.

He cleared his throat. 'Yes. Your Gran told me about the robbery.'

For the first time in the conversation, she turned and faced him. 'But *I* told you about it.'

'No, Genevieve. You told me what you wanted to tell me. That's not the same. Why did you tell your grandmother the robbery had been so brutal, but not me?'

She sighed, glad she hadn't told Gran everything. 'Because I didn't want to worry you. You had enough to think about with Mum going.'

'I don't understand. I'm your father. I'm supposed to worry about you.'

'Perhaps I feel I've given you sufficient worry over the years.'

She could see he wasn't buying it, but he let it go. 'You're all right, though, aren't you? I mean . . .'

She switched on the reassuring smile she knew he needed to see. 'Dad, I'm fine. Really. I get the occasional bad dream, but that will go with time.' She said nothing of the flashbacks she'd experienced in the days and weeks after the break-in. Of the fear of being alone. And of the sleeping pills she'd taken to try and ward off the nightmares. She kept all this to herself, determined to put it behind her. As indeed it was. Apart from last night's glitch, she had started to sleep better, and the fear of being alone had passed. What point would there be in telling her father any of this? He'd only feel guilty that he hadn't been able to do more to help.

Turning the spotlight onto him, she said, 'You didn't seem so nervous around Donna yesterday. If I'm not mistaken, I think I caught you chatting with her, and not just when you were on welcoming duty handing out drinks.'

A ghost of a smile passed across his face and he picked up his mug of tea. 'That's because I think I'm off the hook.'

'Really? How's that?'

'Donna's switched horses, you could say. I pointed her in Tubby's direction. I mentioned several times during the day that he'd been on his own for too long and that, though he'd never admit it, what he needed was someone to take care of him.'

'You sneaky old matchmaker, Dad! So is that why Tubby turned up towards the end of the party?'

'Yes. I invited him for a drink, then got them together. Next thing, just as I hoped he would, he's offering to walk Donna home. I think they'll make an excellent couple.'

'I'm impressed.'

She truly was. In his own quiet way, her father had resolved matters better than she and her sisters could have done. The combination of Donna and Tubby seemed so perfect, Genevieve wondered why they hadn't thought of it before. And hadn't Polly said they ought to find Donna a boyfriend?

Noticing the time, Genevieve said, 'I'd better go inside and make a start on breakfast.'

Her father got to his feet with her. 'I'll help you.'

'There's no need. I can manage.'

'But I'd like to.'

'You never helped Mum.'

His face dropped. 'Maybe I should have.'

Trying to undo the harm she'd done, Genevieve said, 'Oh, you know what Mum was like, she had some daft notion that the kitchen was no place for a man.'

'*Is*, Gen. What Mum *is* like. Please don't put her in the past tense.'

Genevieve could have kicked herself. That was twice now, in as many breaths, that she'd said the wrong thing. What was the matter with her?

He led the way back up to the house and she followed behind. But not before she noticed that the person who had been walking the coastal path was staring across the bay towards Paradise House. Despite the distance, she knew who it was – Christian.

Perhaps he'd had things on his mind and hadn't been able to sleep, either.

Gran appeared after lunch, just as the men finished loading the dismantled marquee onto their van. She swooped on Genevieve and offered to help peg out the third load of that day's washing.

'That's okay, Gran. Why don't you sit down and enjoy the sun. There should be some newspapers somewhere, unless the guests have taken them.' She hid behind a large duvet cover, anxious not to be left alone with her grandmother who, ominously, was wearing her Gestapo Gran face. Genevieve had wondered how long it would be before she showed up. Although, of course, she could go on the attack and ask Gran why she'd broken her promise and gone tittle-tattling to Dad.

Ignoring her, Gran stooped to pick out a pillow case from the laundry basket. She pegged it alongside the duvet cover that was flapping in the breeze. 'I saw him this morning,' she said.

'Saw who?'

Her lips compressed, Gran looked at her for a long, uncomfortable moment. 'Don't be obtuse with me, Genevieve Baxter. You know jolly well who I'm talking about. Now stop fiddling with that washing and come and talk to me.'

'I'd love to, Gran, only I have a lot to get done today.' With a loud flap she shook out a small hand-towel and pegged it to the line. Feeling Gran's eyes burning into her back, she reached for what was left in the basket, a double sheet, and concentrated on finding its corners. But Gran could be as patient as she was determined, and she kept quiet until Genevieve knew she couldn't put her off any longer. 'Okay,' she said, picking up the basket and bag of pegs, 'I give in. What do you want to talk to me about?'

'You.'

No surprise there, then.

Rather than go inside the house, where Nattie was in the kitchen mixing up a cocktail of henna to redo her roots and Polly was teaching Lily-Rose to play the piano, Genevieve tried to gain the upper hand by suggesting they sit on the terrace, away from prying ears and any acerbic opinions Nattie might feel inclined to offer.

'In the absence of your mother,' Gran began, 'I'm taking it upon myself to look out for you.'

'Gran, I'm thirty years old! I don't need looking out for.'

'Age doesn't come into it. Do you think I've ever stopped worrying about your father? I just don't think I would ever forgive myself if I stood back and allowed you to make yourself ill again.'

'Oh, Gran—'

Rattling on like a runaway train, her grandmother didn't give Genevieve the chance to finish what she was saying. 'No, don't interrupt me. I've come here to say my piece, and I'm not leaving until I have. You mean the world to me, Gen, and there's nothing I wouldn't do to ensure your happiness. I added to your problems all those years ago, so it's my duty now to make amends in any way I can.' She paused to draw breath.

Genevieve seized her opportunity. 'Gran, I've told you before, you didn't have anything to do with my problems then; it was me. It was my way of coping.'

'But what if it starts again?'

'You really think that because Christian's here in Angel Sands I'm going to revert to being a confused teenager?'

'It's possible, isn't it?'

Poor Gran. So caring, so concerned. And so wrong. But Genevieve could understand her anxiety, for it had been Gran who had found Genevieve unconscious on the bathroom floor, Gran who'd called for an ambulance, convinced that her eldest granddaughter was dying. At the hospital the old lady and her parents were told that despite months of punishing her body by starving it, Genevieve was far from death's door. Even then her grandmother had difficulty believing that she'd live.

'Gran, I'm touched, but really, there's no need for you to worry. I'm fine.'

'But seeing him again might stir up all those old memories ... remind you of things you thought you'd put behind you.'

Genevieve took hold of her grandmother's hands and squeezed them gently, forcing her to look her in the eye. 'I'm stronger than you think, really. I know you see Christian as a trigger, but he isn't. I'm not that precariously balanced, Gran. Honestly. A relapse is about as likely as me becoming Poet Laureate. Or Nattie winning the Nobel Peace Prize.'

Withdrawing her hands, Gran said, 'Good. So you won't be cross when I tell you I've arranged for you to meet Christian properly.'

'*What!*'

'You heard. That's what he and I were discussing.'

'When?'

'Do try and keep up, Genevieve. I told you I saw him early this morning. In the newsagent's, as a matter of fact. He said he'd just been for a long walk, reacquainting himself with the area.'

So it *had* been him she'd seen. 'So why the change of heart, Gran? Yesterday you were giving him death-threat looks.'

'He said there were things he wanted to say to you. He mentioned the word apologise.'

'He said that of his own accord? You didn't push him up against the shop window and force it out of him?'

Gran looked aggrieved. 'There were witnesses present if you don't believe me. Tubby heard every word.'

'Oh, great, just what I need. Everyone for miles around knowing my business.' She had a sudden mental picture of Gran shouting at Christian like she used to, thinking it would help him to hear. 'But I still don't understand why you've changed your stance. For years you wouldn't even call him by his name.'

'It's called disclosure, Genevieve. They were talking about it on *Kilroy* the other day.'

Genevieve frowned. Then smiled. 'I think you mean closure.'

Gran shrugged. 'Any which way, I told him to come here at four o'clock.'

'Out of the question. I have far too much to do. There are guests arriving around that time.'

'That won't be a problem. Your father and Nattie can deal with them.'

'But I said I'd make them tea.'

'And how difficult is that? Come on, Gen, you're making excuses, and that's not like you.'

Christian arrived exactly on time, just as he always had. In those days he blamed it on his school, saying the teachers were sticklers for punctuality and would beat it into the pupils. Today, though, she could see it was nervousness that had him ringing the door bell on precisely the stroke of four.

A walk seemed appropriate.

They set off in silence, the way he'd just come, to the centre of the village, and up the hill towards ... where else, but Tawelfan beach?

When they'd emerged from the steep path through the woods and were looking back down onto Angel Sands, she touched his arm to attract his attention. 'So what was it you wanted to talk to me about?'

'Do you mind if we sit down? We'll be able to talk better that way.'

'Here? Or at Tawelfan?'

'Here will do. If that's okay with you?'

She nodded.

They wandered away from the main path and found a patch of soft, dry grass to sit on. For a moment they both kept their gaze on Angel Sands and Paradise House. This was where he was standing this morning, she thought. Had he been watching her?

'When did you and your family move here?' he asked, removing his sunglasses and slipping them into his shirt pocket.

Noticing the scar on his head for the first time, she acknowledged that there had to be a degree of small talk, and gave him a brief potted history.

'And the wedding party yesterday, is that a regular thing?'

'No. That was a one-off, Adam's idea. He's a terrible bully sometimes. But his heart's in the right place. He's the son my father never had and gets away with more than he should.'

'From the little I saw of him yesterday, he looks like he fits in well.'

'So how about you? You obviously became the architect you always wanted to be. Where are you living these days?'

'I've moved around a bit, but now I live in a little place you've probably never heard of. Stony Stratford, it's in—'

'Northamptonshire.'

He bowed his head. 'I stand corrected.'

'It's okay. A long time ago I had a boyfriend who was a compulsive obsessive when it came to Formula One. He took me to Silverstone once. And do you live in an amazing house you've designed yourself?'

'No. I'm still waiting to find the time. Clients keep getting in the way of any dreams I might have.'

'Clients like Jonjo?'

'He keeps me pretty busy with the fitness centres, and now there's this barn to do as a personal project for him. So yes, he's currently the most time-consuming client, for sure. But he's also a good friend. And as we all know, friends take the most enormous liberties. They rob us blind.'

He lowered his gaze as they both took in his blunder. 'Well, that's as good a way as any to broach the subject,' he said.

Genevieve suddenly wished he wouldn't say any more. It had been quite pleasant just sitting here, catching up with each other. Like two old friends. She was more than happy to settle for a filling-in-the-blanks session.

But his solemn face told her she would have to endure what he'd come here to do.

23

'Genevieve, I know it's been a long time, but did you ever . . . did Nattie ever tell you about the letter she sent me?'

'Nattie? When?'

He swallowed and stared intently at the grass between his legs. 'When you were unwell.' His eyes slid back to her face.

'You knew I was ill? But how?' Then very slowly the penny dropped. Nattie had written to him behind her back. Annoyed, the colour rose in her face. 'What exactly did my sister tell you?'

'That it was my fault for making you so ill you very nearly died.'

'And you believed her?'

'What was I supposed to think? She said you were rushed into hospital, that you were there for several weeks, that you'd lost so much weight it was touch and—'

She stopped him from going on by raising a hand. 'Okay, okay,' she said, 'I get the drift. And before you ask, yes, I did end up in hospital with a tube down my throat, and yes, I was a fully fledged anorexic who had to be taught again how to eat properly as well as trust people when they said a mouthful of mashed potato wouldn't kill me.'

She watched him piece together her words, then saw him wince. 'I had no idea,' he said, 'I didn't . . . Oh, Genevieve, I'm sorry. I'm sorry I did that to you.'

'You didn't.' Her voice was firm. '*I* did it. Everything that happened to me was a direct result of my own decisions and actions. What I did was like taking drugs. It made me feel strong and invincible, whereas the reality was I was making myself weaker and weaker. I did that to myself, not you. Or anyone else for that matter.'

'But if—'

'No. No ifs and buts. Do you blame your mother for you being deaf? No, of course you don't. So I don't blame anyone for my anorexic days. And just for the record, I had my bulimic moments as well.' She paused, realising that she had raised her voice, was practically lecturing him. 'Look, it all started well before my seventeenth birthday,' she continued, and less heatedly, 'not long after my grandfather died. So you see, you have no cause to blame yourself. My problems were exactly that: mine.'

Again she could see him piecing together what she'd said. When he'd caught up, he didn't look like he believed her. 'I'm still sorry about ... about that night in your father's barn.'

Her tone softened. 'It's okay, you can say her name. Rachel.'

But he didn't register what she'd said. 'To this day, I don't know what the hell I thought I was doing.'

Genevieve raised an eyebrow. 'Don't insult me, Christian. From where I was standing, you gave the impression of knowing exactly what you were doing.'

'No, what I meant was, it shouldn't have been her. It should have been you.'

For the first time in the conversation, Genevieve floundered, unable to find the right response. A wave of nostalgic longing for Christian swept over her. She thought of all those times as a naïve girl when she'd lain in bed and dreamt of furthering their kisses and tentative touches. There had been days when she'd literally ached with desire for him, had itched and burned to feel his hands and mouth explore her body, the whole of it. Some days it had been all she could think of.

Ordinarily, when confronted with an unpleasant conversation, Genevieve could turn away and give a muttered response, but with Christian she couldn't do that. There was no hiding from him. To talk to him, she had to look him full in the face. She did so now. 'Did you stay in touch with Rachel, afterwards?'

'No!' The vehemence rang out in his voice.

'Why not?'

'Why do you think?'

'The last thing she ever said to me was that you'd invited her to stay with you at university.'

'Another of her lies.'

'She'd lied before?'

He picked at the grass between his legs. 'At the time I didn't realise it was a lie, but the night of your party, she told me you'd been seeing someone else, that you had been stringing me along for over a year.'

Genevieve was horrified. Rachel had told her Christian had made all the running, that he hadn't been able to take his eyes – or hands – off her all evening. Instinctively Genevieve knew who to believe now. But she couldn't let him off the hook entirely. 'So you thought you'd get your own back and shag my best friend? Is that it? Asking for my side of the story was out of the question, I suppose.'

'I was angry and wanted to hurt you.'

'Trust me, it worked.'

They fell silent, the cry of a gull filling the space between them as they both stared out at the sea. In the dazzling sunshine, the horizon was an indistinguishable blur of sky and water. As indistinguishable as the truth. Or what they'd both thought had been the truth.

She touched him lightly on the arm. He turned. 'Why did you believe her, Christian? Why did you think I'd be capable of doing that to you?'

He fiddled with his watch, running his finger back and forth under the steel strap as if it was irritating his skin. At length, he said, 'Put it down to too much to drink and ... and colossal insecurity.'

'You! Insecure? Never.'

He tilted his head and frowned. 'You always thought I was so confident, didn't you? But think about it. I was an outcast, a swotty deaf kid totally lacking in any street cred.' He smiled ruefully. 'I'd be called a nerdy geek today. An anorak. You were the nearest thing I had to a best friend in those days, the one person I felt totally at ease with. You accepted me without question. And you never made allowances for me. From the moment you pushed me into the water, the day we met, I knew we were on the level.'

Picturing the scene, and the grin on his face when he yelled at her to speak up, she said, 'I didn't ever see it that way. Compared to me, you had confidence coming out of your—' She hesitated at the inappropriateness of what she was about to say.

'Ears?' he finished for her. 'Don't go all coy and PC on me, Genevieve. Anything but that.'

She smiled and relaxed a little. 'I was just trying to say that I used to wish I had your confidence. Nothing ever got you down. It sounds over the top, but I was in awe of you. Do you remember that day when we were in the sand dunes and—' But once more she held her tongue, on the verge of going a reminiscence too far.

'Go on.'

'No. I was going to say something silly. Something I'd regret.'

'You were thinking of that day on the beach when we first kissed, weren't you?'

She nodded.

'And later you told me about the song that was playing on the radio at the time – "The Wonder of You".'

She cringed. 'Please don't make me squirm.'

' "When no one else can understand me, when everything I do is wrong, you give me hope and consolation, you give me strength to carry on." '

She looked at him. 'You remember the words?'

'Course I do. They came to mean as much to me as they did to you. Why do you think I gave you that CD?'

There didn't seem anything Genevieve could add. 'It's getting late; I ought to be making tracks. There are guests arriving soon.'

She was almost up on her feet, when he put out a hand. 'Please, can we stay a little longer? I feel we still have so much to say.'

But she'd had enough. More than enough. 'No harm in keeping it for another day,' she said lightly.

As they retraced their steps, he said, 'Genevieve, you haven't asked why I didn't try to get in touch with you again after Nattie wrote to me.'

'I imagine it would have something to do with the nature of her message. Nattie, as you probably recall, can be very assertive when she wants to be.'

'It wasn't that I was being a coward,' he said, once again putting out a hand to stop her.

They were standing on the beach at Angel Sands, surrounded by holidaymakers making the most of the late-afternoon sun. The tide was out and several four-wheel-drive vehicles were parked in the shallow water; jet skis and power boats were being winched onto trailers. Distracted by a shout from one of the men rudely yelling at a woman, presumably his wife, to help with the boat, Genevieve glanced away from Christian. It was the only thing about Angel Sands that she, and everyone else in the village, didn't like. The PBP – Power Boat People – were brash and always noisier than anyone else. They strutted about the beach with their flash cars and smelly boats as if they owned it. She felt Christian's hand move from her arm, and looked back at him.

'Sorry,' she said, 'I was just thinking how much better the beach would be without all the noise.'

'Ah, the upside of being deaf.'

Seeing that he was smiling, Genevieve smiled too. 'I've never thought of you as being a coward,' she said, 'if that's what you're worried about.'

It was a while before he answered, as though he'd had trouble understanding her. 'I wrote back to Nattie,' he said finally, 'asking her to pass on a message to you, but she returned the letter, just as you'd done with all the others. She said I was never to get in touch with you, that any contact might make you ill again. I felt so responsible for what had happened, but had no way of helping you. So I did what Nattie told me to do. I kept away in the hope you'd get better, telling myself it was the right thing, the only thing I could do. I've never felt so guilty in all my life.'

Genevieve didn't know whether to be furious with Nattie for meddling or touched that she'd been so concerned. 'Well, all's well that ends well, I guess. Come on, I really need to get home.'

When they were standing outside the Salvation Arms, Christian said, 'Genevieve, while I'm down here with Jonjo, can I see you again?'

'Okay. If that's what you want.'

She could tell from his face that it wasn't quite the reaction he'd hoped for. What did he expect? High-five enthusiasm?

'Would you like to come and see Jonjo's barn tomorrow?' he said. 'If the weather's nice, and you have the time, we could walk and take a picnic. I'd appreciate your comments on some of the ideas I have.'

She hesitated, trying to remember what she had to do tomorrow, convinced that there was something. She visualised her wipe-board by the side of her bed and remembered what it was. 'I'm sorry, but it'll have to be another time. I've promised Lily-Rose I'll do something special with her tomorrow.'

'Oh.' He looked disappointed. But then his face brightened. 'Why don't you bring her? If you think she'd enjoy it.'

After saying goodbye, Genevieve returned to Paradise House alone. She had set out cursing her grandmother for interfering; now she was returning home to exchange some stern words with Nattie. It was nothing new, but that girl had definitely overstepped the mark.

When she walked round to the side of the house, all thoughts of Gran and Nattie's meddling were forgotten. Sitting in the garden with Polly, his arm creeping along the back of the wooden bench they were sharing, was Jonjo. A dangerous mixture of adoration and sparkling mischief lit up his handsome face. But there was no denying what a striking couple they made. Polly's delicate fairness seemed all the more ethereal next to Jonjo's dark good looks. As to whether they were any kind of a match, it was too soon to tell. She wasn't being cruel, but the little she had seen of Jonjo made her suspect that they were poles apart.

'I didn't think you'd be back until after six,' she said to Polly.

'Oh, hello, Genevieve. My last lesson in Milford Haven was cancelled so I came home early.'

'And just as well she did,' said Jonjo, 'or I'd have had a wasted journey.'

In contrast to the charming shade of pink that Polly had turned on seeing Genevieve, there was no awkwardness to Jonjo, no jumping to attention and removal of his arm, just the relaxed air of a man behaving as though he was an old and trusted friend of the family.

'How was your walk with Christian?' he asked. 'I hope you left him buried in the sand up to his neck. He's been such an edgy devil since yesterday afternoon. No chance of you shedding some light on what's giving him the hump?'

Genevieve got the feeling that Jonjo seldom expected an answer to any of his questions. She was about to ask if he or Polly would like a drink, when he pre-empted her.

'I've been trying to persuade your lovely sister to see my new home tomorrow. Do you think you could help me twist her arm? I know, why don't you come too?'

She explained about Christian's invitation. And that Lily-Rose was also included in the outing.

He turned to Polly, like a small boy who'd just been told he could stay up late. 'There! It's as good as settled. Now you'll have to come.'

'I thought you were never going to put the poor man out of his misery,' Genevieve said, when they'd waved Jonjo goodbye and were checking on Henry and Morwenna.

'I wasn't teasing him, if that's what you think.'

'I didn't say you were. But you do realise he's going to keep chasing you until he gets what he wants?'

'Well, that rather depends on what he wants and if I have it. How was your walk with Christian?'

'Um ... interesting.'

If Nattie had been there she would have pounced on Genevieve. 'Interesting?' She would have barked. 'What's that supposed to mean?' But Polly was no interrogator. It wasn't that she didn't care, she just believed in letting people do things their own way.

They strolled back through the orchard and up to the house where Polly was bound for the guest sitting room to put in an hour's piano practice. Some of their regular guests would hang around at this time of day in the hope that Polly would play for them. Today, though, the sitting room was empty and Genevieve left her sister to it.

'Interesting' really was the best description she could come up with to describe the hour she'd spent with Christian. Because there were no overlaps in their lives – no mutual friends who would pass on snippets of gossip – it hadn't occurred to her that he might have found out how ill she'd been. Not even Rachel could have told him, because she'd moved away long before Genevieve had been rushed into hospital.

But trust Nattie to take things into her own hands.

The opportunity to plan what she was going to say to her sister was put on hold when she pushed open the kitchen door and saw the mess. Nattie had agreed to provide afternoon tea for the arriving guests, and as though to prove she'd been true to her word, the crockery had been left to find its own way into the dishwasher. A pair of large bluebottles were feasting on the remains of a ginger cake Genevieve had made that morning. 'Whatever isn't eaten,' she'd told her sister, 'be sure to put away in the cake tin. Don't leave it out, otherwise the flies will think they've died and gone to heaven.'

She was so furious with Nattie she felt like throwing the ginger cake, plate and all, hard against the wall. And she might well have done, had it not meant more for her to tidy up.

24

For Genevieve, picnics were synonymous with sandy beaches and temperamental summers, and as she added salt and white pepper to the egg mayonnaise rolls (never black – it turned the filling a dirty grey colour), she thought how Christian and her eating disorder would always be inextricably bound: she would never be able to think of one without the other. But she had meant what she'd said yesterday; Christian hadn't caused her problems. Low self-esteem had been the culprit. He'd merely been caught up in the chaos of her adolescence. Getting herself straight had been slow and painful, but once she'd made the break from her old self, had killed off Constant Companion, she'd begun to enjoy life in a way she never had before. She discovered the incredible freedom of letting up, of not giving herself a hard time.

Tearing off pieces of cling film, she began wrapping the rolls and putting them in the hamper, with a storage box of potato salad, a tub of cherry tomatoes, and the salmon and broccoli quiche she'd made last night. Next she added a foil-wrapped tray of chocolate brownies, a selection of Lily-Rose's favourite cartons of juice, and lastly some crisps, plates and glasses, and knives and forks. Christian had said he'd see to wine and anything else he thought they'd need to drink. Which was just as well; she could barely lift the hamper off the table as it was.

From upstairs she could hear the sound of Donna vacuuming. The guests had conveniently departed several hours ago, leaving Donna and Genevieve free to blitz the bedrooms and bathrooms. With the picnic now ready, and Jonjo and Christian arriving in less than ten minutes, Genevieve went to look for Polly and Lily-Rose. The last time she had seen Lily, the little girl was having a bad hair day – literally. Her blonde curls had blossomed like a ball of candyfloss overnight, and she was screaming at her mother to sort it out before she and Daddy Dean met up with Tubby to go to a furniture auction in Pembroke.

Genevieve found her youngest sister and niece – hair now tamed – on the top landing. Dressed in a bright orange ra-ra skirt, purple T-shirt, red sandals and yellow sunglasses, Lily-Rose was squeezing a cuddly toy into her small rucksack: it bulged as though she had packed for a fortnight's holiday.

'I suggested that just the one teddy would suffice,' Polly said, helping to get the zip done up, 'but she couldn't choose which one to take. So she's bringing them all.'

Swinging the bag over her shoulder – it was in the shape of a butterfly, and two large wings now appeared to grow out of her back – Lily-Rose adjusted her sunglasses and stuck out her chest with a wide, beaming smile. 'Ready now,' she said.

They were halfway down the stairs when the doorbell sounded. Genevieve's heart gave a little jolt, just as it always had when Christian called for her.

Jonjo had overruled any plans for them to walk to Ralph's barn, as it would always be known to everyone in Angel Sands.

'I don't mind carrying Lily-Rose if she gets tired,' he said, 'but a weakling like Christian won't last two seconds with that hamper. What have you got in it, Genevieve? A microwave?' Again he seemed not to expect an answer. He threw open the boot of his Land Rover Discovery and stowed the hamper inside. 'Now then,' he instructed them, 'Polly in the front with me, and the rest of you, sort yourselves out in the back.'

Seeing a new side to Jonjo, Genevieve exchanged a look with Christian. 'What's brought on the bossy sergeant major act?' she mouthed.

'He gets like this now and then. Just pretend he doesn't exist.'

'I've told you before, Christian, not everyone's deaf, so keep the insults to yourself. Right then, let's be on our way.'

Ignoring his friend, Christian said, 'He's excited about showing off his new house. He's always like this with a new project. Here, do you want some help?'

'It's okay,' Genevieve said as she struggled with the buckle of Lily-Rose's seat belt. She had refused to remove her rucksack and her wings were getting squashed. 'There, that's got it.'

Ralph's barn was situated half a mile inland from Tawelfan beach, a stone's throw from Pendine Cottage. As they drove down the bumpy track, Genevieve asked Christian if he'd ever been back to see the house.

'No. Never.'

'What about when you came here with Jonjo to view the barn?'

'He came alone. I saw the place for the first time the day before yesterday.'

'What's that you're saying in the cheap seats?'

When Christian didn't answer – presumably he didn't realise his friend had spoken – Genevieve said, 'I was just asking Christian why he didn't view the barn with you when you were buying it.'

'A good question, Genevieve. It was as much as I could do to get him to take on the job. You should have seen his face when I showed him the details and where it was on the map. He even tried to talk me out of it, said why didn't I look for something in Cornwall or Devon. But I told him this was exactly where I wanted my rustic bolt hole, if you'll pardon the expression. I came here once as a young boy and always knew I'd come back.'

Christian hadn't caught any of this conversation; he was staring out of the window. Genevieve was left to ponder why he'd been so reluctant to revisit the past.

When they arrived, a pair of crows, startled by the sound of doors slamming, clattered their wings and launched themselves off the roof. The derelict barn didn't look like much, but Genevieve knew that with careful design, and a great deal of money, it could be turned into an amazing house. Especially given the views from the rear. And although she had never seen anything Christian had designed, she felt instinctively that he would do an excellent job. Nattie would be disappointed not to have a crusading save-the-environment fight on her hands.

Jonjo led the way. It was fortunate that the weather had been as dry for as long as it had, as otherwise the ground would have been a skidpan of mud. Where there wasn't bare earth, they had to negotiate rampant nettles and brambles.

'There,' said Jonjo, when he'd moved an old milk churn and swung open one half of the wide double doors. 'What do you think?'

His question was clearly aimed at Polly. Genevieve went and stood in the middle of the gloomy barn. Beams of sunlight filtered through the holes in the roof and the mixture of damp, dust and mouldy hay made her nose twitch. In amongst the cobwebs and shadows there was a graveyard of rusting old farm implements, rubber tyres and ripped tarpaulins. It was far from inspiring.

Christian came and stood next to her. His face was caught in a beam of sunlight and she noticed the flecks of green and gold in his brown eyes. She'd forgotten that his eyes were such a mixture of colour. She waited for him to speak. When he didn't, she said, 'I remember you saying this was just the kind of work you'd like to do; converting barns into houses.'

He stared at her hard. 'I remember it too. I said it the afternoon of your birthday.'

Recalling the scene in her father's hay barn, she turned away, embarrassed. She was glad when Jonjo suggested they explore outside.

The view from the rear was as perfect as she'd known it would be. All that separated them from the sea was a sloping, narrow stretch of heath and the sand dunes that backed the unspoilt beach. It was beautiful. She turned to Christian and saw from his expression that he thought the same.

'I'm going to design it with the living area of the house upstairs,' he said, looking back at the barn. 'Each of the bedrooms will have a door leading out onto the garden. The main bedroom will catch the rising sun and the sitting room will have a fantastic view of the setting sun.'

'It sounds good.'

'Thanks. It'll mostly be open plan. I want to take full advantage of the natural light as well as bring the landscape inside. I don't like houses that shut people out. That's the trouble with a lot of buildings; the doors and walls limit the space available.' 'Do you wish you were designing it for yourself?' she asked, when they were returning to the car to fetch the picnic. Jonjo and Polly were walking on ahead, while Lily-Rose, who'd been unusually quiet since leaving home, was holding Genevieve's hand and sliding occasional sideways glances in Christian's direction.

He came to a stop and looked the way they'd come. 'Yes. It's pretty much what I'd like for myself.'

'And will that affect your judgement when working on it?'

'It might do. But my job is to remain objective, to take into account the client's taste more than my own.'

'And does this particular client have good taste?'

He laughed, which made her realise how solemn he'd been till now. 'Believe it or not, Jonjo does. Look how taken he is with Polly.'

The flippancy of his remark made her say, 'You have told him that he'll have Nattie and me to answer to if he does anything ... anything silly.'

The laughter vanished from his face. But he didn't answer her.

They carried on walking and glancing at her sister, who seemed quite at ease in Jonjo's larger-than-life company. Genevieve touched Christian's arm lightly to make him turn. 'I get the feeling that Jonjo doesn't know our history? Am I right?'

'Yes.'

'Why's that?'

He pushed his hands into his trouser pockets and frowned. 'Because it's none of his business.'

It wasn't a very satisfactory answer, but she didn't pursue it, not with Lily-Rose pulling at her hand so they could catch up with the others.

They had their picnic in the dunes, in a quiet, sheltered spot where a gentle breeze rustled the marram grass. Any wariness Lily-Rose had shown previously towards Jonjo and Christian was now gone. She sat cross-legged between them, slyly adding more crisps to her plate when she thought no one was watching. Even Christian seemed to be relaxing now and was telling Polly how he and Jonjo had got to know each other.

'It was love at first sight,' he joked, 'our eyes met across a crowded gym—'

'Hey,' interrupted Jonjo, 'not any old gym, I'll have you know. It was the first one I set up, my pride and joy. This arrogant bastard told me it was a mess, that he knew a man who could have made a far better job of it.'

'Watch your language,' said Christian, eyeing Lily-Rose. 'What you have to know about this guy is that anyone who disagrees with him, or knows more about a subject than he does, is automatically classed as a bigoted know-it-all.'

Jonjo grinned. 'Can I help being such a good judge of character?'

'Is that why you commissioned me to design your second gym?'

'Call it a moment of weakness.'

'And the subsequent six fitness centres?'

Genevieve smiled at Polly and, while Lily-Rose wasn't looking, removed half the crisps from her plate. 'So is this something you specialise in,' she said, turning to Christian, 'designing commercial properties?'

'It wasn't my original intention, but the work's plentiful and varied.'

'What he means is that it's lucrative, stinging hard-working blokes like me.'

'And do you run your own practice?' asked Polly.

'No, more's the pity. I keep thinking about it, but the time never seems quite right to take the plunge. For now I'm tied into a medium-sized set up, with the prospect of one day becoming a partner.'

Jonjo tutted. 'I keep telling him to get on and go it alone, like I did, but he's too cautious for his own good. Now Polly, how about another glass of bubbly and then we go for a walk?'

'I want to go for a walk,' piped up Lily-Rose. She tossed aside her plate and leapt to her feet.

'Not so fast, sweetheart,' said Genevieve. 'Have something more to eat. All you've had so far is a few crisps.'

She shook her head and rested her hands on her hips, a classic Nattie pose.

'It's okay, Gen,' said Polly, 'I'm sure Jonjo won't mind the extra company.'

Smart move, thought Genevieve, as she watched her sister, dressed in one of her particularly pretty jumble sale dresses, take her eager little chaperone by the hand. If Jonjo was at all disappointed to be denied a romantic stroll along the beach, he didn't show it. Instead, he took hold of Lily-Rose's other hand and said, 'Christian, make sure you behave yourself while we're gone.'

'You must be very proud of her,' Christian said, when they were alone.

Thinking he was referring to Polly's out-manoeuvring of Jonjo, she said, 'I am. Polly may be the quietest and least worldlywise Baxter, but she's no push over.'

He frowned. 'I didn't mean Polly. I meant your daughter. She's really cute. How old is she?'

It was Genevieve's turn to frown. 'Oh, no! No, you've got it wrong, I'm not her mother. Nattie is.'

'Nattie? But you . . . at the party . . . you and Adam, and Lily-Rose.'

Seeing his confusion, she tried to recall the exact moment in the garden at Paradise House when he'd commented on Lily. All she could think was that he must have misread her lips. Of course, that was it! He'd been looking at Lily and had missed her explaining that Nattie was her mother. Before she could say anything, he said, 'But you and Adam . . . you are married, right?'

She laughed. 'Absolutely not.' She told him about Adam being hopelessly in love with her sister. 'He's mad, of course. As I keep reminding him.'

'But you seemed,' he paused, as if conjuring up the right words, 'such a couple. I was convinced you were married.'

'As cheesy as it sounds, we're just good friends. Nattie gives him a hard time and I'm the sympathetic shoulder he's come to rely upon.'

'And you're not ... remotely interested in him?'

'What is this? Are you trying to fix me up?'

He laughed now, and at last seemed relaxed. 'I wouldn't dream of it. How about some more of Jonjo's champagne while he isn't looking?'

She held out her wine glass. 'This is very decadent, isn't it, drinking champagne on the beach? Quite a step up from swigging back cans of coke like we used to.'

'You can always depend on Jonjo for the grand gesture. I had a bottle of wine ready to bring but he wouldn't listen. He said, "I'm not drinking that rubbish to toast my new home." '

'Well, here's to many more of his grand gestures.'

He chinked his wine glass against hers, 'And ... to old friends.'

His words hung in the air as they both stared out to sea and sipped their drinks.

Christian said, 'Jonjo and I are leaving tomorrow evening.'

'Oh.'

'But we'll be back.'

'That sounds worryingly like a threat.'

He tilted his head and looked puzzled. 'It wasn't meant to be.'

Realising he'd missed the joke, she said, 'Any idea when you'll return?'

'I'm not sure. But soon.'

Another silence followed. And then, 'Genevieve, you won't hold the past against me, will you? I'd hate to be forever defined by a mistake I once made.'

Unable to answer him, she turned away.

25

Some guests were more troublesome and ungrateful than others, and Genevieve was checking in one such couple now, who, so far, had complained about almost everything. According to them, the roads were too narrow and winding; the weather was too hot; the beach was too small and pebbly; and lastly, and for future reference for other unwary guests, Angel Sands needed to be better signposted. Thank God they were only stopping the two nights; any longer and she might run out of patience. From experience she knew they were the type to hunt out all that was wrong with their room – the window that rattled; the toilet that didn't flush properly; the plumbing that gurgled; the floorboards that creaked, and of course, the lumpy bed that kept them awake all night.

Bracing herself for the first of the criticisms about their accommodation, she led the way upstairs, offering to carry the woman's luggage, but leaving the man to carry his own; he looked quite strong enough to manage the small case and suit-carrier. She unlocked the bedroom door and stepped back to let them in. All the rooms at Paradise House were large and airy and had been named by Serena, her inspiration coming from songs made famous by Judy Garland; the most obvious being the Rainbow suite. Most guests, when entering the April Showers suite, commented on its size. It was the largest bedroom in the house and the most impressive, with a four-poster bed and chintzy décor straight out of *House and Garden*. The next comment, invariably, would be to admire the south-facing view over the garden and the sea beyond.

But not Mr and Mrs Grumpy. They gave the room a cursory glance, pushed open the door to the en suite bathroom and asked where the bathrobes were kept.

Bathrobes! Where did they think they were staying, the Ritz?

'I'm sorry, but we don't supply them.' She watched the couple mentally chalk up a point against her and added, 'If I could just draw your attention to the sign on the back of the door, you'll see what to do in case of a fire. Oh, and there's no smoking in any of the rooms. When you've settled in, perhaps you'd like a cup of tea. Or coffee? Maybe a scone or some shortbread?'

'We'll have tea and scones,' Mr Grumpy said, without consulting his stony-faced wife.

'Excellent. I'll see you downstairs in the sitting room. Better still, shall I look for you in the garden? There are plenty of tables in the shade,' she said, remembering the complaint about the heat.

In the kitchen Genevieve loaded up a tray, making doubly sure the crockery was squeaky clean and not chipped. People like the Grumpys didn't intimidate her; she viewed them as a challenge, to be humoured. All the same, she would make sure Nattie didn't get anywhere near them, or they really would find something to complain about. Even after all these years of their home being a guest house, Nattie still had a tendency to treat visitors as unwelcome intruders.

Hearing footsteps on the stairs, then voices in the hall, she poured boiling water into the china teapot – one that she knew never dripped – and added it to the tray, giving the tea things one last glance to make sure there was nothing she had forgotten.

She found Mr and Mrs Grumpy in the shade, as she'd recommended. She set down the tray on the wooden table and left them to it. Tubby would be here later and she wanted to go through her shopping list before he arrived. Sometimes she wrote down things that even she couldn't make sense of. Grpefroot, apel, letise, avodaco were typical misspellings, but once, when in a hurry, she'd written witbadge and couldn't for the life of her work out what it was. Days later, when she wanted to make some coleslaw, she realised it was white cabbage. Loyalty was important in a close-knit community, so as her mother had, Genevieve always got their fruit and veg from Tubby. Basic everyday staples like bread, tea and eggs came from the mini market in the village, and bacon, sausages and black pudding from the Lloyd-Morris brothers with whom they had a regular order placed. Every fortnight, armed with a computer-generated list, her father would head off to the supermarket in Pembroke to stock up on the bulkier items, such as breakfast cereals, fruit juice, toilet rolls, cleaning products and washing powder.

After checking her list for Tubby, she gave some thought to what she was going to say in answer to Christian's letter.

It was a week and a half since the day of the picnic. This morning, after their father had intercepted the postman, he had handed her a letter with a Northampton postmark. He'd made no comment, just sorted through the rest of the mail and left her alone. It was so reminiscent of years gone by that she had taken the letter outside to the garden to read. But unlike those childhood handwritten letters, this one had been done on a computer, and the typeface was bold and clear, as though he'd remembered her dyslexia and was trying to help. What he didn't know was that these days, she wore specially tinted glasses to help her read more easily. Nattie called them her rose-tinted spectacles. Rarely did she wear them in front of people who didn't know her well because, vainly, she thought they gave her a strange unflattering look, like a pink-eyed rabbit.

The gist of Christian's letter was that once he'd recovered from the shock and unease of their meeting, he had really enjoyed catching up with her. Would she, he wondered, like to go for a proper walk the next time he was down?

In contrast to the one brief communication she'd had from Christian, Polly had been the subject of numerous calls from Jonjo. Often Polly wasn't around when he phoned and Genevieve ended up chatting with him instead.

'By the way,' he said during one conversation, 'Christian's told me everything. And what a piece of work he turns out to be! Hardly the saint I had him down as. But it's not too late to exact revenge. I'd willingly do it myself on your behalf. What do you think? A hate campaign? Letters of abuse and unspeakable things shoved through his letterbox? Personally, I'm all in favour of publicly naming and shaming.'

'Or we could be very dull and just let sleeping dogs lie.'

'Spoilsport!'

The biggest and most ostentatious bouquet of flowers that had ever been delivered to Paradise House arrived at the weekend. It was for Polly, and the accompanying card said:

> There was a sweet maiden called Polly,
> As tasty as a strawberry ice lolly,
> Call me a poet but wouldn't you know it,
> I'd sooner lick her lips, by golly.

'The man's a fool,' declared Nattie when she read out the limerick to see who the flowers were from. Polly was absorbed in playing a piece of Mozart. 'And an inept one at that. Those last two lines are cringingly awful.'

And not the rest? thought Genevieve with amusement.

Polly stopped mid-chord and gave the flowers a measured glance. She then returned her attention to the pages of music in front of her and began playing again. But not before Genevieve saw a small smile illuminate her face.

Since then there had been numerous phone calls and a further bunch of flowers. The man was certainly persistent, and if Genevieve was honest, not as dangerous as she'd first thought. More importantly, Polly appeared quite capable of taking him in her stride.

Hearing the sound of Tubby's van coming to a stop at the front of the house, Genevieve roused herself and went outside.

As a result of her father's intervention, romance was very much in the air. Tubby was positively glowing with it, bursting to share his happiness. It didn't come as a surprise, though. Donna had not been shy in sharing her own new-found happiness with Genevieve during their coffee breaks. It was funny, but Donna and Tubby were so wrapped up in each other, it was impossible to imagine there was ever a time when Daddy Dean had been under threat.

'Donna cooked me supper last night,' Tubby announced, before Genevieve had even had a chance to inspect his tomatoes. 'And not just some trifling little snack. It was the full works. Prawn cocktail, braised steak with mushrooms and mash, and bread and butter pudding to finish. A feast fit for a king!'

'Well,' said Genevieve with a smile. 'Who'd have thought it? Old Tubby Evans falling in love.'

He blushed and reached for a paper bag, then shook it open. 'I tell you what, *cariad*, a man could get used to it.'

Helping herself to some tomatoes – firm but on the verge of softening – and passing them to him, she said, 'So how come you've been on your lonesome for so long, Tubby?'

There had always been faint mutterings about Tubby in Angel Sands. Some said that he'd never got over the death of his first wife in his mid-twenties, the one true love of his life. And some said that his second wife divorcing him ten years ago had put him off women altogether. What were those gossipers saying now? Genevieve wondered.

'Let's just say I've been biding my time,' Tubby said. 'Waiting for the right woman. A woman with a bit of spirit.'

'Well, I think it's great. You deserve some fun.'

An hour later, after Mr and Mrs Grumpy decided they might risk the late afternoon sun and go for a walk, her father appeared in the kitchen where Genevieve was taking advantage of the peace and quiet to get on with some bookkeeping. Fortunately it was a task that came relatively easily to her – for some reason she'd never truly understood, her brain could handle basic arithmetic; it was something to do with order, sequence and time – and she'd readily taken on the job in her mother's absence, knowing her father hated anything that didn't involve a spirit level or some Black & Decker accessory.

'All alone, Genevieve?' he asked, despite the obviously empty kitchen.

'Looks like it,' she said. 'Nattie and Lily-Rose are still down at Gran's and Polly's not due back until after seven.'

'Oh.'

She took in his shuffling awkwardness as he moved round the table where she was totting up a column of figures. Watching him fill the kettle then plug it in, she sensed there was something he wanted to say, that finding her alone had perhaps been fortuitous.

'Coffee?' he asked.

'Tea please. And there's some bara brith in the cupboard, if you're interested. And some of Tubby's special butter in the larder.'

Watching him as he rounded up mugs, plates and slices of Welsh tea bread, she wondered what was on his mind, and hoped he wasn't still worrying about her. At last he sat down in the chair opposite her. 'Have you got a minute, love?'

She took off her glasses. 'Of course I have. What's up? Nattie hasn't gone and rescued another donkey, has she?' Her tone was deliberately light, but she could see from her father's expression that they were heading into the choppy waters of A Serious Chat.

'No, it's nothing to do with Nattie. It's your mother.' He pulled out a letter from his back pocket and placed it on the table between them. 'It came this morning.'

'You never said anything.'

'You had other things on your mind.' A tiny stab of guilt pricked at her conscience. If she hadn't taken herself off to the garden to read Christian's letter, her father might have ... She let the thought go.

They hadn't heard from Serena since their father's birthday and, with each day that passed, it seemed to Genevieve that the gap their mother's absence had initially created at Paradise House was slowly closing. She hated the thought that they would all eventually get so used to Serena not being around, that one day they'd get on with their lives as though she'd never existed. She hadn't said anything to anyone, but Genevieve was beginning to feel angry towards their mother. How could she do this to them, to Dad in particular? She felt the anger rise in her now as she looked at the letter on the table. Or was it fear she felt? Had Mum finally made her decision? Had she written to say that she was never coming home?

'What does Mum say?' she asked.

'You can read it if you like.'

She put on her glasses again.

My dearest Dean,

I know it's unforgivable of me to have left it so long before writing again, but goodness, I just don't know where the time goes. As you know, it's winter here and Pete and I have been spending time away from the winery and staying in Wellington, visiting old friends of his who used to be neighbours. It was fun staying in The Big City. Wellington is such a sophisticated place – so many art galleries, coffee houses and trendy bars. Don't laugh, but I've developed quite a taste for vodka martinis! There's this bar Pete took me to, where they mixed, or rather, shook them to perfection. You must try them yourself, but I doubt if anyone down at The Arms has a clue how to make a cocktail.

I miss you and the girls and often think of you. Give my love to your mother (although I doubt she'll want it) and a special hug and a kiss to little Lily-Rose (if she hasn't already forgotten who I am). All my love,
Serena.

PS. I expect you've become quite used to me not being there.
Sometimes it feels as though Paradise House was where someone else
– not the real me – used to live.

Giving herself time to think, Genevieve pretended she was reading the letter again. She wanted to think carefully about what her mother had written. On the face of it, it looked like Serena was rubbing their noses in it, telling them what a thoroughly enjoyable time she was having, living this new and exciting life of cruising bars and knocking back cocktails. But maybe there was a more important message hidden behind her words.

Was it possible that Serena was trying to make Dad jealous? Until now the name and sex of the friend in New Zealand had never been divulged. Previous letters had referred obliquely to 'we' or 'us', but now, without a word of explanation, Serena had deliberately slipped in a bombshell guaranteed to make their father sit up and take notice. If Genevieve was right, and she had a gut feeling she was – her mother wouldn't be so cruel as to flaunt a real lover so openly – it meant that Serena wanted to provoke her husband into doing something. Question was, what? And if Genevieve's guesswork was correct, it meant she would have to play her part. It was down to her to reinforce the message that if her father didn't act promptly he would lose Serena. But how to do it without hurting him more than he already was?

She removed her glasses, refolded the letter and pushed it across the table. She met her father's gaze, which was as searching as she knew it would be.

'Who's this Pete character?' he asked. 'Where's he sprung from all of a sudden?'

'He's the old school friend you were supposed to think was a woman,' she answered truthfully.

His eyes widened. 'You knew? You knew all along?'

She tried not to flinch at the pained disbelief in his voice.

'I'm sorry,' she murmured. 'But we thought it would hurt you too much to know the truth.'

'We? Your sisters knew as well?'

She nodded. 'We kept it from you because we never thought there'd be anything in it.' He bent over the table and raked his hands through his hair. 'I've lost her,' he groaned. 'I lost her months ago, and never realised it. What an idiot I've been.'

Genevieve wasn't her grandmother's granddaughter for nothing. 'Dad,' she said, summoning up her most authoritative voice, 'look at me. And listen hard. You haven't lost Mum. But you will if you don't do something to get her back. You can't go on pretending this isn't happening, or kid yourself that she'll come back when she's ready. Whoever this old friend is, you have to prove to Mum that he's nothing compared to you. You know, and I know, there's only one man for Mum and his name isn't Pete. It's time for action. Right?'

He blinked back tears and managed a nod. 'Right,' he repeated, but with a lot less conviction than Genevieve would have liked.

In bed that night, Genevieve began to doubt what she'd been so sure of earlier. What if she was wrong about her mother's letter, and Pete genuinely meant more to Serena than she'd thought? What then?

26

She wasn't entirely sure she was doing the right thing, but Genevieve decided to talk to Gran. Other than Serena, Gran was the only person who could make their father do something he didn't want to.

After lunch, while Dad was mending a faulty shower head – thank goodness there were so many DIY jobs to keep him occupied – Genevieve set off for Gran's. Yesterday's heat had been cooled overnight by a strong, chilly wind and the air was fresh and tangy. Predictably, Mr and Mrs Grumpy had complained at breakfast that they'd been woken in the early hours by a rattling window. Save for a few hearty souls, the beach was almost deserted. A brief spell of cooler weather – better still, wet weather – was good news for Huw and Jane up at the Smithy and also for Ruth and William at Angel Crafts; their takings were always boosted by inclement weather. Passing the first of Angel Sands' teashops, she saw that it was packed. Next door was Debonhair. Scissors and comb poised, Debs smiled at Genevieve through the window. Genevieve gave her a small wave and continued on her way as briskly as the wind that tugged at her hair. She was still annoyed that Debs had been openly gossiping about her.

Two doors up from Debonhair was Angel Crafts. She waved to Ruth, then stopped at the Post Office. She slipped a cream-coloured envelope into the box and stupidly looked over her shoulder to see if anyone was watching her. She half-expected to see Debs craning her neck round the salon door, making a note of her movements. Two thirty-five: Genevieve Baxter posts a letter, recipient as yet unknown. Possible recipient: childhood sweetheart, Christian May.

Had the letter been addressed to anyone else, Genevieve wouldn't have felt so paranoid, but as it was, she felt the whole of Angel Sands would be putting two and two together. But there again, they had plenty to go on, what with Gran broadcasting to the nation the day she bumped into Christian in the newsagent, and the two subsequent occasions Genevieve had been seen with him – their walk and then the picnic. One thing you could be sure of in Angel Sands: nothing was private. Under the guise of taking an interest in one's neighbours, gossip was a fact of life. And let's face it; she couldn't be holier than thou about it. She and her sisters liked nothing better than a tasty titbit coming their way. Just so long as it wasn't about them, of course.

Gran opened the door to Genevieve, and immediately turned her back on her.

'Put the kettle on, dear, I'm watching *Murder, She Wrote*.' Nothing new in that, Genevieve thought with a smile. But what was new was the state of Gran's kitchen. It was several weeks since Genevieve had been inside Angel Cottage, and she wondered what was going on. Was her grandmother having a spring clean? As far as Genevieve could see, Gran must have emptied every cupboard and drawer and stacked the tins and packets of food, crockery, pans and cutlery wherever she could find space on the small table and work surfaces. Opening one of the cupboards where the tea caddy was normally kept, and then another, Genevieve found that she was right. The cupboards were empty.

She unearthed the kettle, filled it, then hunted through the toppling mess on the table for some tea bags. Once she'd located them, she joined her grandmother in the sitting room. 'What's going on in the kitchen, Gran?'

'Ssh!'

Genevieve looked at the television screen and saw that Jessica Fletcher was in the final throes of showing the confused cop how the crime was committed. When the credits rolled, Gran said, 'I've seen it before but I was hoping someone else would have done it this time.'

Genevieve was used to her grandmother's unfathomable logic. 'Are you having a major spring clean, Gran?' she said.

Her grandmother looked at her as though she were mad. 'Now why would I be doing that in the middle of June?' She rose from her chair. 'I thought you were making some tea.'

'I am. The kettle's on.'

'Good. I'm parched. Now come with me; I need your help.'

Thinking Gran wanted a hand with putting everything away, Genevieve followed her back into the kitchen. The kettle was boiling, producing its customary rumbling noise, but the sound was amplified by the emptiness of the cupboard beneath it.

Gran suddenly grabbed hold of her arm, making her jump. 'There! Did you hear it?'

'What?'

'There it is again!'

But all Genevieve could hear was the kettle clicking off. Puzzled, she made the tea and watched Gran. It struck her that her grandmother had a tendency to appear 'odder' when she was within her own four walls. Or was it because when she was at Paradise House, her eccentric behaviour blended in with that of the rest of the family?

'Are you sure you can't hear it, Gen?' On her knees now, the old lady was peering into the cupboard beneath the sink.

Genevieve got down on the floor with her. 'What does it sound like?'

Gran backed out from the cupboard. 'What a silly girl you are sometimes. Since when has a mouse sounded like anything other than a mouse?'

Ah. Now things were beginning to make sense.

'Have you got any traps?' Genevieve asked. 'I could set them for you, if you want.'

Gran shook her head vehemently. 'I don't approve of setting traps. It's too sneaky.'

This, coming from a farmer's wife, was bordering on the ridiculous.

'So how are you hoping to get rid of them? Shake them by the paw and ask them to set up home elsewhere?'

A withering glance told her to be quiet and pour the tea. She wondered when the mouse problem had started. Dad hadn't said anything when he'd come back after visiting Gran the day before yesterday.

'How long's this been going on, Gran?' she asked, at the same time inspecting the sugar bowl for mouse droppings.

'Since last night. I couldn't sleep and came down to warm some milk, and I heard the little blighters. But they're cunning so-and-sos, they wait till I'm not looking, then start to squeak and patter about the place.'

Genevieve was just passing Gran her mug when the old woman whipped round and nearly knocked it out of Genevieve's hand. 'Look, it's coming from there!' Once more on her hands and knees, Gran peered round the back of the cooker. She let out a curse. 'I'm just not fast enough!'

'Are you sure you've got mice, Gran? I didn't hear anything.'

Gran stood up with a creak of joints. 'I hope you're not insinuating that I'm becoming vague and dotty, young lady.'

Genevieve laughed. 'You've been vague and dotty all your life. Now drink your tea and let me talk to you. I need your advice.'

Back in the sitting room, the television switched off in order to have Gran's full attention, Genevieve filled her in on Serena's letter.

Gran was furious. 'The little madam. I'll give her cocktails! Who does she think she is?'

'What Mum's drinking or who she thinks she is, isn't the point,' Genevieve said firmly. 'It's what she's trying to make Dad do that we have to focus on. I'm convinced she wants him to nail his colours to the mast.'

Gran narrowed her eyes and pursed her lips. 'I know who I'd like to nail to the mast.'

'Stop it, Gran. You know you're not supposed to bad-mouth Mum.'

Her grandmother sat back in her chair and sniffed. 'You may not have noticed, Gen, but we're in my house, which means my rules apply; so I'll say exactly what I want.'

Exasperated, Genevieve said, 'But only if it's relevant. Now what do you think is the best way to tackle Dad? We have to make him realise he's the one to change things. He keeps saying Serena has to make her choice. That he can't *make* her come home. But I don't think that's what Mum wants. If she's the woman I think she is, she wants some old-fashioned Judy Garland drama. A husband to sweep her off her feet. A husband worth coming home to.'

Gran stirred her tea, her back ramrod straight with obstinate reproach. 'If it's drama she's after, I know just the thing. It's been on my mind for a while that they're both behaving like a couple of idiotic children. What they need is their bottoms spanking. That would bring them to their senses and give them some drama they wouldn't forget in a hurry.'

Genevieve gave up. Gran wasn't in the best of moods to offer constructive advice. She walked home, disappointed, taking care to keep her gaze on the pavement as she passed Debonhair, just in case Debs was ready to pounce on her.

A shout from the other side of the road, outside Roy and David's butcher shop, made her look up.

'Gen, it's me!' With a bulging carrier bag in each hand, Adam waited for a car to pass, then crossed the road. 'I was calling and calling to you, but you must have been in another world.'

She smiled. 'I was. A very strange place; my head.'

'Ooh, scary. How about you recover from the ordeal by having dinner with me tonight? My treat.' He indicated the bags of shopping. 'Roast lamb's on the menu.'

Nattie was full of scorn when Genevieve said where she would be eating that evening. 'Bloody hell!' she crowed. 'You're letting him cook for you? I'd sooner lick out the loo.'

'Thank you, Nats, for sharing that. Let's hope Dad and Polly don't think the same when they sit down to eat what you've cooked for them this evening.'

'You're expecting *me* to toil away in the kitchen? I don't think so.'

'Honestly! How that daughter of yours has survived, I'll never know. There's a lasagne in the fridge. I'm sure even you can manage to put that in the oven. Throwing a salad together can't be beyond your capabilities either. I'm going for a bath now.'

'He's using you,' Nattie called after her. 'He's trying to get to me through you. Any fool can see that.'

Something in Genevieve snapped. She whirled round and came back to where her sister was feeding carrots to Henry and Morwenna. 'Don't you dare say that about Adam! He's the last person to use anyone. And you know what? If I didn't know better, I'd say you were jealous. You don't want Adam for yourself, but you can't bear the thought of him being my friend.'

She marched away in a state of high dudgeon, arms swinging, teeth gritted. Sometimes Nattie just went too far! If she wasn't careful she was going to feel the full force of her anger. It was years since she and Nattie had had an all-out fight, but the way things were shaping up, Genevieve knew she was inches away from losing control where her sister was concerned.

*

Adam was on the phone when she rang his doorbell. He ushered her in, pointed at the open bottle of wine in the kitchen and disappeared to finish his call.

Whereas Paradise House was Edwardian and possessed a comfortable faded charm, Cliff View was all-singing, all-dancing, brand spanking new. Adam had employed the services of an interior designer from Cardiff, much to the derision of the regulars down at The Arms, and had spent a fortune on kitting out the eighteen-month-old house with up-to-the-minute furniture and soft furnishings; black leather sofas, subdued oatmeal carpets, glass and marble units, remote controlled lighting, several wall-mounted plasma screens, and every electronic gadget a boy could wish for. The kitchen was a high-gloss black and chrome affair with gleaming granite surfaces. There was a huge built-in American fridge the size of a small terraced house, and a range of appliances that you had to play hide and seek to find. If it wasn't for the delicious smell of roast lamb coming from the oven, the kitchen might easily have been nothing more than a film set, it was so pristine and immaculate. To her knowledge, Adam rarely entertained; he always claimed he preferred to eat out. Certainly this was the first time she'd been invited to sample anything created by his own hand.

French doors led out onto a neat patio edged with hardy oriental grasses and pots of spiky palms, tall and erect. The wind had dropped and Genevieve went outside to enjoy the view, very different from the view she was used to seeing from across the bay. She wondered if Adam ever had to pinch himself: he'd come a long way from his roots as a car mechanic in Wolverhampton.

Adam was in casual mode – a striped rugby shirt tucked into belted jeans. Watching him carve the lamb, Genevieve itched to pull out the shirt and loosen him up. No two ways about it, he needed taking in hand.

'Just goes to show that you can have all the money in the world and still have lousy taste,' Nattie had said of him. The annoying thing was, there was an element of truth in that.

'I know what you're thinking,' Adam said, adding another slice of meat to one of the plates.

'You do?'

'Yes, that I'm making a mess of this carving. You being the expert and all.'

She didn't disagree with him, and after they'd taken their plates through to the smaller of the sitting rooms, the one Adam usually used, he set up the DVD for them to watch on the enormous screen on the wall.

'You're sure you don't mind a tray supper?' he said.

'Not at all. This is fine. Much more relaxing.'

The film was the much-hyped sequel to *The Matrix*, which Adam assured her was a classic. If she'd seen it she might have stood a chance of understanding the impenetrable plot of the one they were now watching. It seemed to be nothing but head-spinning effects and incomprehensible dialogue.

'Is it me, or are they muttering?' she asked.

Adam smiled and picked up the remote control. 'You're not enjoying this, are you?'

'It must be too deep for me.'

He laughed and zapped the film. 'I'm sorry, you should have said something.' He refilled their glasses of wine. 'Now tell me what you've been up to. It seems ages since I last saw you.'

'It is. It was the day of the wedding reception.'

'You have been paid, haven't you?'

'Oh, yes, the money's been banked.'

'Good. So what's next? Have you another job lined up yet?'

'If your ulterior motive for inviting me here was to bully me again, think on.'

He chewed what was in his mouth and looked thoughtful. 'Actually,' he said, 'I do have an ulterior motive.'

'Aha, we're getting to it now.'

'It's a bit awkward, but I want to talk to you about something.'

'I don't ever recall a conversation between us being awkward.'

'Well, this is different.' He took a sip of his wine. 'It's about your sister.'

'Oh, in that case, awkward doesn't come close. I hope you're not expecting me to be nice about her. She's far from being my favourite person just now.'

'Don't worry, I'm not expecting anything from you, other than a friendly ear. The thing is, I've come to an important decision. I can't go on as I am. I have to get her out of my head, or she'll drive me nuts. Do you understand what I'm saying?'

Genevieve put her finished plate on the glass-topped table in front of them. 'You're asking *me*? The girl who nearly starved herself to death over a boy? The girl who for years afterwards measured any boyfriend by that one example and found them all wanting?'

It was difficult to know who was more surprised by what she'd said and, for a moment, neither of them seemed to know what to say next. Adam looked away and Genevieve took a moment to reflect on what she'd always taken for granted: she had been wary of committing herself to any boyfriends in the past because she'd found it difficult to trust them. But now she realised it went further than that. It was not a comforting thought.

'Sorry,' Adam muttered, 'that was clumsy of me. It was a stupid question.'

'Forget it,' she said lightly, reminding herself that it was Adam's problems they were discussing, not hers. 'So what's brought all this on? About you and Nattie.'

He sighed. 'Months and months of frustration. And I don't mean sexually,' he added with a smile. 'I've reached a crossroads, you could say. I want to settle down, to share my life with someone special. It doesn't seem much to ask, does it, but I don't seem to be making much headway in that department.'

'Adam, you're only thirty-three, there's plenty of time yet for you to meet the right girl.'

He smiled again. 'You know me. Always in a hurry. I hate to let the grass grow under my feet. Everything done yesterday.'

'Well, now that you've decided to untangle yourself from Nattie, the opportunity to meet the right person will probably arise of its own accord.'

He reached for the bottle of wine and topped up their glasses. 'Now you're just being kind. You may not have noticed but I'm butt-ugly, and odds on the only reason a girl's ever going to be interested in me is because I've got a buck or two.' He swirled his wine round and stared into the glass. 'Maybe that's why I hung on, hoping for Nattie to give me a break. I knew the money wasn't an issue for her. I'd probably have stood more of a chance if I'd been dirt poor. She'd have treated me as a rescue case then.' He sighed and stretched out his legs. 'Maybe I just have to face it, I don't have an abundance of shag-appeal.'

Genevieve leaned forward in her seat. It was time for some straight talking. 'First thing,' she said, 'you're not butt-ugly, and second, there's nothing wrong with your shag-appeal, although it could benefit from some –' Her voice broke off. Could she tell him? Could she really suggest that if he spruced up his wardrobe he might attract the right sort of girl?

'Go on,' he said, 'finish what you were going to say.'

She cleared her throat. 'I don't mean this unkindly, Adam, but I think you might do better if you . . . if you took a closer look at what you wear. Your clothes are a little . . .' The baffled expression on his face stopped her from continuing. She wished she'd never started.

'A little what?' He prompted.

She took a large gulp of wine and steeled herself. 'Confusing,' she said. 'Your clothes give out the wrong sort of messages.'

He stared at her, dumbfounded. 'What's wrong with them?' He glanced down at his jeans. 'These weren't cheap you know, they're Armani. Not market stall tat.'

'I didn't think for one moment that they were. But have you ever thought maybe you try too hard?'

He pushed his plate away and seemed to contemplate what she'd said. She hoped she hadn't gone too far.

'Okay,' he said slowly, 'if that's what you really think, why don't we go upstairs and you can explain where I'm going wrong.'

She laughed. 'If that's one of your chat-up lines, you might like to work on it.'

He laughed too and pulled her to her feet. 'I was referring to my clothes, not my mind-blowing skills in bed. Though, who knows, maybe that's my real problem.'

They stood in his bedroom, which was directly above the main sitting room and looked over the sea. After drawing the curtains, blocking out the moon that shone brilliantly in the night sky, Adam switched on the lights and flung open the doors on the bank of wardrobes.

She whistled. 'Look at all those suits! And so many shirts! I've never seen so many.'

He smiled, proudly. 'And a different tie for each one of them.' He pulled open a drawer and revealed rows and rows of neatly laid out ties.

This was when she knew she had to be cruel to be kind. She held up a particularly awful specimen – Goofy blowing smoke from the barrel of a gun – and said, 'Now there's no gentle way to break this to you, Adam, but believe me when I say that novelty ties are a huge turn-off.'

'But I thought they were supposed to show the warm, funny side of a man's nature. Isn't that the guaranteed ticket to a girl's heart?'

'It can be if you go about it the right way.'

'But women are always saying they want a man with a sense of humour. GSOH, it's there in the ads. Not that I read them. Well, not much.'

She smiled at his embarrassment. 'We all read them, Adam, there's no shame in it. But back to the ties.' She picked out another one, a toothy mouse nibbling on a wedge of cheese. 'This shouts from the rooftops that you haven't grown up yet, that you're as sexy and sophisticated as Donald Duck. Which anyone who knows you properly, knows isn't true. But to a potential date, well, let's just say, it's going to have her running in the opposite direction.'

He took the ties from her and threw them on the bed. 'Anything else? Any more tricks I need to learn?'

'Yes. Let your personality show you're warm and funny, not your clothes.' She caught sight of his gold bracelet on the bedside table. 'And you need to lose some of the flash, be more understated.'

'You mean dull?'

'No. Understated equals classy. Trust me.'

He smiled. 'I do. Completely.' To her surprise, he came over and hugged her. 'You know what? You're the perfect friend.'

When he'd released her, she said, 'And talking of friends, haven't any of them ever told you what I just have?'

'No way! Blokes don't discuss clothes. Cars, sport and gadgets, that's what we talk about. Oh, and money.'

'Well, that would be the problem, then.' Seeing as he'd taken his medicine so painlessly, she went for one last piece of advice. 'Right, this is going to hurt you a lot more than me, but raise your arms to your sides.'

Puzzled, he did as she said, and she untucked his rugby shirt. 'There, that's better. Don't you agree?' She turned him round to look at his reflection in the full-length mirror.

With a doubtful frown, he said, 'It looks untidy sticking out like that.'

'It looks *better*,' she replied. 'Now get used to it.'

'I feel like I've been through the wringer several times over,' he said later, when they were downstairs in the kitchen and he was playing with an expensive coffee machine. 'I had no idea you could be so tough.'

'A mistake other people keep making,' she said.

'Anyone in particular?'

'Not really. It's just that ever since Christian showed up, I get the feeling I'm being watched, in case I have a bad reaction to him.'

He passed her a large cup of frothy cappuccino. 'I did hear you'd been to see Ralph's barn with him.'

'Yes, but did you also hear that Jonjo, Polly and Lily-Rose were with us?'

'No. That minor detail was conveniently omitted.'

She rolled her eyes. 'Great! Why spoil a good story by including the facts?'

'So how did it feel, seeing him again?'

She dipped her finger into the creamy froth of her coffee, then licked it. 'In the end it was fine. I've agreed to see him again when he makes a return trip to look at the barn.'

'And are you doing that to prove to everyone, including yourself, that he doesn't mean anything to you any more?'

'Certainly not. I've agreed to see him because he's good company, just as he always was.' Changing the subject, she raised her cup and took a sip. 'Mm ... this is delicious. Ten out of ten for the perfect cup of coffee.'

He put down his own drink, moved in close, and with his thumb, gently stroked her top lip. 'I like you better without the moustache.'

She lowered her gaze. But when he didn't step back, she suddenly found it difficult to look up at him again. Something weird had just happened and she wasn't sure she understood it. What she was sure of, though, was the overwhelming need to feel Adam touch her again. Just acknowledging this extraordinary thought seemed to open the floodgates and a tremor of pure lust ran through her. Fearing the wobbling cup in its saucer would give her away, she put it down on the counter with a clumsy bang.

A body starved of touch for too long does the craziest of things, she told herself. Trying to keep calm – *remember this is Adam, your old pal and friend* – she forced herself to look up. When she did, she found he was staring at her in a way she'd never seen before. The blueness of his eyes had darkened and they were fixed intently on her own. She cleared her throat and said, 'It's getting late, I ought to be—'

But she got no further. As though the very air between them had imploded and sucked them in, they were suddenly in each other's arms. His mouth was deliciously warm, and when he pushed her against the counter top and pressed his body against hers a thrill of excitement shot through her. Old friend or not, it didn't matter. She wanted him and he wanted her.

27

The next morning, breakfast was a shambles. Toast was burned, eggs were dropped, orders were mixed, and tempers lost. And it was all Genevieve's fault. She couldn't even blame Nattie, who, in contrast to her as she blundered from one mistake to another, was waiting on the tables in the dining room with polished professionalism.

'What the hell's the matter with you?' Nattie demanded, bursting through the kitchen door with a tray of rejected food. 'Table four ordered poached eggs, not scrambled!'

Daddy Dean was hot on Nattie's heels, a plate in his hands. 'You've forgotten the beans,' he said, more reasonably.

When at last the guests had left the dining room, her father asked if she was okay.

'I'm fine,' she lied.

'The hell you are!' said Nattie. 'I've never seen you so disorganised.' She ripped off her apron and threw it on the table. 'Right then, that's me done for the day. Do you think Polly would mind looking after Lily-Rose a bit longer? Only there's something I need—'

'Oh, why bother asking?' Genevieve rounded on her. 'Do what you always do, just leave us to take care of your daughter!'

'Oo-er. Listen to who got out of bed the wrong side this morning.'

Her sister's blithe tone incensed her. 'Save the sarky attitude for someone who gives a toss. I've had enough of it. You're nothing but a selfish cow. I knew it would be a mistake, you moving back here. That you'd make more work for everyone else, me especially.'

Eyes blazing, Nattie opened her mouth to speak, but their father stepped in between them. 'Steady on, you two.'

The telephone prevented the row from developing further. Glad of the diversion, Genevieve pushed past her sister and snatched up the receiver.

It was Adam.

Her face and body burned with shame.

All Genevieve could think to do was go for a walk. The longer the better. A thick sea-mist had rolled in during the night, and it had yet to clear. The muted gloom of the morning had a calming effect on her, and gradually she slowed her pace sufficiently to notice that the grass was glistening with droplets of water and the path was slippery.

No one else was about on the cliff top. Standing in the spot where she and Christian had sat not so long ago, she paused to catch her breath – she'd taken the steep climb so fast, she'd given herself a stitch.

Oh, but what had she done? What had possessed her to act in such a way? And now Adam wanted to see her, to talk it through. How could she face him when she couldn't even face herself in the mirror? She had told him she'd ring back when she had a free moment. Now all she had to do was contrive to be busy for the rest of time.

Poor Adam.

Wrapping her arms around herself, she recalled how they'd scrambled upstairs to his bedroom, ripped off the last of their clothes and fallen onto the bed, crushing the ties and shirts she'd earlier discarded from his wardrobe. Desperate to get on with it, Adam had reached for his bedside drawer. 'Better play safe,' he'd said. But the moment she heard him rip open the small packet, the reality of what they were doing crashed in on her. She pulled away from him, sat up straight.

'Gen?' he'd said.

But she couldn't speak. She lowered her head and reached for one of his rejected and much prized Hawaiian shirts. He sat up too, put his arm around her.

'Gen?' he repeated. 'What is it?'

Still she said nothing.

He must have realised then what the problem was. He slid off the bed, and disappeared to the bathroom, leaving her to get dressed. No easy task, given that her clothes were scattered to the four corners of his house. She threw on what she could find – her knickers were nowhere to be seen – and silently vanished into the night before Adam could follow her downstairs.

She had behaved badly, she knew. Atrociously. And to a dear friend. A better person would have stuck around to apologise, but she'd proved that she could be as cruel and uncaring as Nattie. Perhaps that was why she'd blasted off at her sister in the kitchen just now: she'd seen herself looking back at her, and it was not a pretty sight.

The dampness was seeping through her clothes. Shivering with cold, she started walking again. She had a vision of herself walking for the rest of eternity so she didn't have to face Adam again.

For as long as she could remember, she'd hated confrontation. She knew it was cowardly, but avoidance always seemed a better option. Sometimes, though, not having the courage to speak her mind served only to make a bad situation worse. Ending things with boyfriends had always been tricky for her. With the last one, Mike, she'd hoped he'd realise for himself that their six-month relationship had run its course. But annoyingly, he'd seemed quite happy with the status quo; the occasional disagreements over staying in or going out (he always wanted to stay in and watch the football), and the lack of things they had in common. Rather than offend him by saying she'd had enough (if she was really honest she'd have told him she found him boring), she had fallen back on the old standby of dropping hints of settling down, of making their relationship more permanent. It worked. He was gone within days, panicked by the mere thought of commitment. But more importantly, she'd allowed him to leave with his pride and dignity intact. She would never deliberately take that away from another person, not when she knew how humiliating it could be.

The thought brought her back to Adam. Rejected now by two of the Baxter girls, he must be feeling horribly humiliated. However, unlike Nattie, she would make amends. Just as soon as she felt able to look him in the eye, she would apologise. Would their friendship ever be the same again? For a crazy moment she wondered if it might have been better to have gone through with what they'd started, because at least then she wouldn't have hurt Adam's feelings.

And what of her own? Didn't her feelings count as much as his? Before she had a chance to answer her own question, another formed itself. What would have happened had it been Christian in that bed with her last night?

Shocked at such a thought, she quickened her pace. She certainly wasn't going to dignify the question by answering it. But she couldn't help herself, and started to wonder what it would be like now, as a grown woman, to go to bed with Christian. To experience what she'd been cheated of when Rachel had got there first.

No! She would not go down that route.

The mist was clearing at last and a faint orb of whiteness had appeared in the overcast sky. The cries from a flock of gulls added a mournful note to the eerie gloom. Ahead of her, with a clear view of the headland and Tawelfan beach beyond, she could see a figure in a bulky waxed jacket coming towards her. He had to be someone local because, unless you were an idiot, you only walked the cliff path in this kind of weather if you knew it like the back of your hand. As the figure drew nearer, after a double-take she realised she was wrong. It was Christian.

What was he doing here? He waved to her. Something made her want to run to him, like in one of those old films her mother loved so much, but she forced herself to walk slowly. Casually.

When he was close enough to read her lips, she said, 'You're the last person I expected to see out here.'

'And there was me thinking I was the only one mad enough to be out walking.'

'The mist's taking ages to clear. There isn't enough wind to blow it away. Did you get my letter?' She was glad he couldn't hear the nervous awkwardness in her voice.

He shook his head. 'What letter?'

Then she remembered. 'Of course, I only posted it yesterday. When did you arrive?'

'Eight o'clock this morning, having got up at the crack of dawn. I had a free day and thought I'd do a lightning visit. I needed to take some more photographs of the barn.'

'But I thought you'd taken loads when you were down last.'

'I did, but stupidly I lost the roll of film.' He produced a smart little camera from his jacket pocket. 'I'm using a digital one this time. Not taking any chances.'

'So what brings you out on the cliff path?'

He returned the camera to his pocket. 'I couldn't help myself. I also thought, if I was brave enough, I'd walk as far as Angel Sands, knock on your door and invite you for a cream tea.'

'And do you think you might have been brave enough?'

'That would have depended on who opened the door. If it was Nattie I would have high-tailed it out of there.'

'After the words she and I have exchanged in the last twenty-four hours, she would have been just ready for you.'

'Oh? You two been fighting?'

'It's nothing. Just me flying off the handle.'

'Want to talk about it over that cream tea?'

She was tempted, but the thought of going back to Angel Sands, where all and sundry would observe them, made her say, 'You know what, I'd prefer to walk on to Tawelfan and grab a hot dog at the kiosk.'

After feeling so wretched, it was a relief to sit with Christian and enjoy his steady company. A breeze had sprung up, the mist had gone, and patches of delicate blue had broken through the clouds. They'd taken off their jackets and were using them to sit on as they tucked into two enormous hot dogs – onions, mustard and tomato sauce oozing from both ends.

'We'll need to go for a swim to wash this lot off,' Genevieve said, when she'd finished eating.

'Freezing cold swims are all right when you're too young to know any better, but you won't catch me doing it these days.' He picked up one of the polystyrene cups of tea they'd bought at the kiosk, removed the lid and handed it to her. 'This feels good,' he said. 'It's great seeing you again.'

'Likewise.'

There was no need to say it, but it was just like old times. They drank their tea companionably, watching the amusing antics of a family nearby as they set up a windbreaker, the father issuing instructions to his wife while the children, three of them, fought over the contents of a large cool bag.

'I'm surprised Jonjo isn't with you,' she said, turning her head.

'He doesn't know I've come. I wanted to look at the barn alone, to get the feel of it unhindered. By the way, is he still pestering Polly?'

'Almost continually.'

'Does she mind?'

'No. She's the most tolerant person in the world. She makes up for Nattie and me.'

He smiled. 'You mentioned earlier about words being exchanged between you and Nattie. What was that about?'

'If you don't mind, I'd rather not say.'

'Fair enough.'

An argument had broken out amongst the nearby family about whose sandwiches were whose. Following her gaze, Christian said, 'Having made the mistake of marrying you off to Adam with a child into the bargain, would I be making another mistake to assume you aren't, or haven't been married to anyone else?'

She faced him. 'I haven't even come close to it. Oh, there have been one or two men I thought had potential, but when push came to shove, they got a hearty shove.' She explained the technique she'd employed over the years to end things 'nicely'.

'How very considerate of you.'

'I like to think so.'

'Although, of course, there's always the risk that one day your bluff might be called.'

She scooped up a handful of sand and let it trickle slowly through her fingers. 'Now that would be a disaster. But not the end of the world. I'd then have Plan B to resort to.'

'Which is?'

'I'd force him to spend a week in the bosom of my family. That would have him backtracking at the speed of sound.'

Laughing, he said, 'I've been meaning to ask you, I haven't seen your mother. How is she?'

'For a woman going through a mid-life crisis, she's having a ball.' Genevieve told him about Serena needing time out, and about the most recent letter from New Zealand.

'How's your father coping?'

'Up and down. He's basically paralysed by fear and denial. Part of him wants to believe she'll come home when she's ready and the other part is terrified he's lost her already to this old friend, Pete.'

'What do your sisters say?'

'They don't know about the letter. Dad hasn't shown it to them and as yet I haven't had an opportunity to discuss it with either of them. Polly's busy helping with some music festival in St David's and Nattie, well, Nattie will just hit the rant and rave button. I don't know why, but out of all of us, she's the most furious with Mum.'

Seconds passed before he replied. As it had years ago, it still amazed her how good Christian was at lip-reading: rarely did he misread what was said.

'And if your father doesn't do anything,' he said at last, 'what do you think your mother will do?'

'I wish I knew. Anyway, enough of my family, tell me about yours. How are your parents? Did they ever buy that house in France?'

'They did, but Mum sold it when Dad died three years ago from cancer. Mum's health has gone downhill ever since. She's had one thing after another.'

Recalling he'd always been close to his parents, Genevieve said, 'I'm sorry about your Dad. How often do you get to see your mother?'

'Not as often as I should. I've been trying to convince her to move somewhere smaller that needs less work, especially in the garden, but she won't hear of it. You remember how she loved nothing better than to spend entire back-breaking days in the garden?'

She nodded. 'I do. Will you give her my best wishes, when you see her next?'

'I will.' He checked his watch and said, 'I ought to be going.'

'Really?'

'Yes.'

She walked to Ralph's barn with him, where his car, a Volvo estate, was parked. He threw in his jacket and exchanged his walking boots for a pair of dusty Timberlands.

'Hop in and I'll give you a lift home.'

She had a sudden mental picture of Debs and the coven of gossipers peering out of the salon window as they drove past. 'There's no need,' she said.

'I know there's no need, but I'd like to.'

She held her ground. 'The walk back will do me good.'

He tilted his head. 'What are you scared of, Genevieve?'

Perturbed at his sharpness, she laughed a little too shrilly. 'You forget,' she said, 'I'm a Baxter and we're scared of nothing.'

'Then get in the car and stop worrying about what other people will think.'

She squared her shoulders. 'I don't know what you're talking about.'

He held the door open. 'Yes you do. Now get in.'

She said nothing until they'd dropped down the hill into Angel Sands, whereupon sod's law prevailed. A queue of traffic had built up behind a car towing a caravan, which had acquired a flat tyre and was partially blocking the road. People were out of their cars lending a hand. If she'd wanted an audience, she'd got the biggest one going. Debs, Stan and Gwen, Ruth and the Lloyd-Morris brothers were all standing in their shop doorways observing the commotion.

Slumping into her seat, Genevieve glanced sideways at Christian and saw he was smiling. She slapped him on the arm. 'How did you know?' she asked.

'That you didn't want to be seen with me? Oh, just a hunch. That and the length of time, a whole nanosecond, it took you to reject my invitation for a cream tea on your doorstep.'

'You must think me very silly.'

'Not at all. I'm just sorry you feel like that. As though any of it matters.'

'You're right. I shouldn't worry, but some old habits are harder to shake off than others.'

With his elbow resting on the sill of the open window, he twisted round further and gave her a penetrating stare. It was so intense, she felt herself back away from it. Then, to her horror, the question she had asked herself earlier – what if it had been Christian in the bed last night and not Adam? – surfaced again. She tried to wrench her gaze from his, but couldn't. She waited for him to say something, anything, but he didn't. He just kept on staring at her. Then, hearing a car horn blare from behind them, she said, 'It looks like we can squeeze past now.'

He nodded, put the car into gear and drove on, carefully mounting the kerb to bypass the caravan. It was then that Debs, along with everyone else, saw Genevieve. They all smiled and waved. Debs even had the nerve to bend down to gawp in through the car window to get a better look at Christian.

'Don't ignore your friends, Genevieve,' he said. 'Wave back or I'll stop the car and kiss you, just to give them something worthwhile to talk about.'

'You wouldn't dare!'

'Care to risk it?'

For the rest of the short journey up to Paradise House, neither of them said anything. He switched off the engine and turned to face her. For a moment she thought he was going to carry out his threat and kiss her. When he leaned towards her, raised a hand and pushed her hair away from her cheek, she said, 'Do you think that would be a good idea?'

His hand stayed where it was, pressing gently into the hollow of her neck, until slowly he lowered it. 'You're right,' he said. 'It would be a mistake, and not just because of our history.'

'What other reason could there be?'

'A very good one. Her name's Caroline.'

28

'Seeing someone?' repeated Nattie. 'Now who the hell would be crazy enough to go out with that lying, cheating excuse of a man?'

As ever, Nattie's views on the subject of Christian were implacable. Once she had decided a person's character was flawed, there was no changing her opinion. Genevieve suspected that if Christian were to bring about world peace, then discover a cure for cancer, Nattie would still find a way to condemn him.

Busying herself with pulling on the tangle of towels jammed inside the washing machine, she wished that the house had been empty when Christian had dropped her off. Externally she had been all politeness, appearing hardly to have noticed that Very-Nearly-A-Kiss moment when they'd said goodbye, but internally she was experiencing a tumultuous wave of confusion. Why on earth had he even hinted at wanting to kiss her if he was involved with someone? It was difficult not to think in terms of leopards and spots.

Nattie had been in the kitchen with Lily-Rose when she'd come in from waving Christian off. Perhaps because she needed to confide in someone – even her hostile sister, who was still bristling from Genevieve's earlier loss of temper – she had stupidly blurted out what he had just shared with her.

'And if he has a girlfriend,' Nattie continued now, in the utility room, 'why has he been down here sniffing round you?'

Genevieve dropped the heavy bundle of untangled towels into the basket in front of the machine and stood up to take it outside. But Nattie was barring her way, standing in the doorway, a shoulder resting on the frame, one ankle crossed over the other. Behind her, Lily-Rose was sitting at the kitchen table waggling a paintbrush in a jam-jar of cloudy water.

'You have such a way with words, don't you?' Genevieve said, her voice low so that her niece couldn't hear their conversation. 'All we've been doing is catching up with one another. Nothing more.'

'He hurt you once before, Gen, I'd hate to see it happen again.'

'You make him out to be some kind of serial heartbreaker.'

'What can I say? His actions speak for themselves. But I notice you haven't answered my question. If he has a girlfriend, why would he want to be so pally with you?'

Genevieve shifted the laundry basket to rest it on her hip. 'Oh, don't be ridiculous. The days of having only same-sex friendships are long gone. Just look at Adam and me. Honestly, sometimes I think you live in a totally different world from the rest of us. Now, I have things to do, like putting these towels on the line. Unless you'd like to do it.'

She was almost through the door, wishing the reference to Adam hadn't proved her sister's point exactly, when Nattie said, 'By the way, Adam called for you. Twice in fact. I told him to lay off, that the last thing you needed was a nuisance caller.'

Outside in the garden, Genevieve considered what was going on. In less than twenty-four hours she had very nearly gone to bed with a man for whom she'd never harboured a single amorous thought, and then, unbelievably, she had come close to being kissed by a man she had once hoped never to set eyes on again.

But the immediate problem she had to sort out was Adam. Hiding from him indefinitely wasn't the answer. In a place as small as Angel Sands, she would soon run out of hiding places. She had no choice but to speak to him and plead a moment of insanity. But would that upset him further? *Sorry, Adam, but I only stripped off all my clothes with such eagerness because of a wild mental aberration. It goes without saying that in a sane and level-headed mood I wouldn't dream of doing such a thing.*

Oh, yes, that would really make him feel better.

Eleven o'clock the next morning, following breakfast, Genevieve was tidying the dining room with Donna's help. One of the guests had spilled a bowl of muesli on the floor. Scooping up the soggy mess, Genevieve was listening to Donna's latest news bulletin on her romance with Tubby.

'I came here looking for a new life,' Donna said, gathering the pots of homemade jam and marmalade and adding them to her tray, 'but I never thought I'd fall in love. Not at my age. Well, you don't expect it, do you?'

'You're not old, Donna.'

Donna gave one of her husky laughs, the sexy, full-throated one that only weeks ago had had Dad running for cover. 'I'm hardly in my first flush, though, am I? Although at fifty-four, I reckon I cook better than a lot of women.' She wiggled her tightly wrapped hips and struck a pose like a woman destined never to grow old gracefully.

Getting up from the floor, Genevieve said, 'So it's love, then, is it? You and Tubby?'

'Either that or we're both in lust!' She let rip with another husky laugh.

Whatever misgivings Genevieve might have had about Donna working at Paradise House had long since been replaced with a real fondness. Donna's life hadn't always been happy. 'Let me tell you, living with a vicious drunk was no picnic,' she'd told Genevieve one day. But she was always cheerful and positive.

Later, while they were sorting out the cleaning things for upstairs, Donna took Genevieve by surprise.

'I know it's none of my business,' she said, 'but do you think it would help your Dad if Tubby and I had a word with him?'

'What about?'

Hoisting the vacuum hose over her shoulder as though it were an enormous handbag, Donna said, 'About your mother, of course.'

Genevieve was taken aback. This was a conversation she'd never touched on with Donna. 'Oh, I don't know if that would be a good idea. Dad's very private, he doesn't—'

'He's also very lonely and miserable,' Donna cut in. 'Anyone can see that. And they're two things, in my opinion, which should never be allowed to fester in a man. It can turn them into things they weren't ever meant to be – drunks, like my ex, or prowling womanisers.'

Smiling uneasily, Genevieve said, 'I think that's a bit simplistic. I can't quite see Dad turning into either of those things.'

'Oh, well, like I say, it was just a thought. Knowing how well your father and Tubby get on, I thought it might help.'

'Was it Tubby's idea?'

'Lord help us, no! He's as dim-witted as the next man when it comes to discussing his feelings. Still, we wouldn't have them any other way, would we, love?'

They were halfway through making the beds and cleaning the bathrooms when Genevieve heard the doorbell. She went to answer it. Once again it was the florist, Rhys Williams, who had twice now delivered flowers for Polly. He greeted Genevieve warmly, while handing over a bouquet of beautiful pale pink roses.

'Seems like I'm always here. Whoever the admirers are, keep them coming; I'll be able to retire early at this rate.'

Genevieve took the flowers through to the guest sitting room and put them on the piano. They had to be for Polly. But she couldn't resist a peek at the label.

Dear Genevieve, sorry for what I very nearly did.
Please forgive an old friend ... if you can.

Well, that did it! Now she had to apologise to Adam. If he could be so sweet and thoughtful and ask for her forgiveness, it was only right to summon every miserable scrap of her courage and face him.

That evening, when she could see the lights on in Adam's house across the bay and knew he was at home, Genevieve told her father she was slipping out for a few minutes.

'I shan't be long,' she said, leaving him to watch the television in peace. The guests were all out, Lily-Rose was in bed, Nattie was having a bath and

Polly was at a concert in Milford Haven where one of her pupils was playing.

She took with her a gift of her own making; a lemon meringue pie, which she knew was one of Adam's favourite desserts. He looked as awkward as she felt when he opened the door to her. She thrust the foil package towards him.

'It should be humble pie, but I thought you'd prefer lemon meringue laced with a double helping of whipped apologies.'

He closed the door after her. 'Come on through to the kitchen and I'll make us some coffee.'

'Not if it's going to lead us into temptation again,' she said with a nervous laugh.

'Tea, then? Would that be safer?'

'Actually, a large glass of wine would be better.'

It was warm enough to sit outside. The sky had grown darker, insects hovered in the air and the sea surged below in the bay.

'I'm glad you felt able to see me, Gen. I'd hate for anything to come between us.'

'I know; I feel exactly the same.'

He shook his head. 'I bet you don't. I bet you feel used. As though I tried to take advantage of you the other night.' He looked away into the gathering darkness. 'You probably hate me.'

Appalled, she said, 'No, Adam. That's not true at all. I never once thought you were using me. In fact, I think it was me who started it.'

He turned his head. 'You don't have to spare my feelings, Gen. But you must believe me when I say it wasn't Nattie I imagined I was in bed with.'

Of all the thoughts that had careered through her head, this one hadn't featured. She'd been so wrapped up in her own guilt and embarrassment, she hadn't once thought what might have been going through Adam's mind.

When she didn't respond, he said, 'Look, Gen, I'll be straight with you. I've been guilty of it before, with other girls. I'd take them to bed and make love to them, all the while thinking of Nattie. I'm not proud of that, but it wasn't the same with you. I swear.' He took a large gulp of wine. 'It . . . it's difficult to explain, but it sort of felt right with you. It made me realise how good it must be to have sex with someone you really care about. You know, to experience the whole package. Something I haven't done before.' He suddenly banged his fist down on the arm of his chair. 'Shit! What the hell do I sound like?'

She reached over to him and touched his arm lightly. 'Oh, Adam. I'm sorry. Sorry that it turned out the way it did.'

'And you know what? I wish I could say I don't know what came over me, but I can't. I knew exactly what I was doing.'

'The same goes for me. But for the sake of our friendship, we have to put it behind us.'

He looked up. 'I can, if you can.'

'Good,' she said resolutely. 'So no more embarrassment?'

'And no more hiding from me?'

'It's a deal.' Relieved they'd dealt with the problem so easily, she said, 'By the way, you're looking good this evening. Have you been shopping?'

'I took your advice. I had to go to Swansea this afternoon, so I scooped up a load of new shirts and trousers. You don't think this blue shirt looks a bit boring, do you?'

'No. It looks great. Casual but stylish. The colour matches your eyes.'

He drained his glass and looked glum. 'And for what? Or rather, for whose benefit?'

'Hey, that doesn't sound like the Adam I know and love.'

'Yeah well, it's been a strange couple of days, one way or another. Anyway, no more feeling sorry for myself.' A welcome smile appeared on his face. 'I reckon I might never be allowed the opportunity again, so I'm going to say it now, Gen. You've got a great body, you know. *Very* sexy. I had no idea you had such good legs, either. I can't recall an occasion when I've had so much as a peep at anything higher than your ankles. Perhaps that's why I found the whole thing such a turn-on.'

She blushed and sat back in her chair, arms folded.

'Don't scowl at me, Gen. It's true. You have a fantastic figure. I don't think you have any idea just how attractive you are.'

'That's enough. You can stop right there!'

'No! You had your say with me, about my tacky shirts and ties, now you can have a taste of your own medicine. Polly may be the brightest and prettiest Baxter girl and Nattie the most spirited, but you're the best of the bunch. And you know why? It's because you're not only kind and generous, but you connect with people. You're also damned sexy into the bargain. I can quite understand why your old boyfriend couldn't keep his eyes off you when he was down here. And why he's been back so soon.'

Genevieve snapped forward. 'He's done no such thing!'

'You sure about that? So how come I saw the pair of you on the cliff path yesterday morning, after I'd tried speaking to you on the phone?'

'Adam Kellar, have you nothing better to do than spy on your neighbours? Why weren't you hard at work earning an honest crust?'

He grinned. 'I was. I was working from home.'

'Mm ... clearly not hard enough, or you wouldn't have had time to watch my movements. And what about all that mist? You couldn't possibly have seen us.'

'Binoculars are a wonderful invention. You should try them.' Then leaning forward to top up her wine, he said, 'So how's it going between the two of you? The old magic still there?'

'I think I preferred it when you were miserable and contrite,' she muttered. 'At least you didn't poke and pry.'

'Answer the question, Miss Huffy-Pants. Which reminds me, you left a pair here the other night. They're washed and ready for you to take home. Unless you want me to keep them as a souvenir?'

She blushed again. 'You realise, don't you, that you're being quite intolerable?'

'Another few glasses of this Merlot and I might show just how intolerable I can be. Now tell me, has he made a move on you? You know, just for old time's sake?'

Genevieve pictured the scene in Christian's car. Was that what it had been? A split-second when he had idly wondered what it would be like to turn back the clock and rekindle a time when their days together had been so innocently intimate and uncomplicated? She decided to be honest with Adam.

'I think it did occur to him to try to kiss me, just to see what it would be like, but fortunately he thought better of it.' She explained about the girlfriend back home.

'And how did you feel when he said that? Were you disappointed? Relieved? Hurt? Or maybe plain old angry?'

'A bit of all those things,' she said, after taking a long sip of wine. 'And your point?'

'Well, if you'd been indifferent, you'd be immune from his charms. As it is, you risk—'

'Yeah, I know, being hurt again. In her own inimitable fashion, Nattie's already gone to great lengths to warn me of that peril. But what you're forgetting is that I'm a big girl now and with there being a girlfriend on the scene, he's out of bounds.'

'And if the girlfriend becomes history? Does that bring him within range?'

'As I said, I'm a big girl. I can handle the likes of an old flame curious to take a trip down memory lane. Something I'm not in the least bit interested in pursuing myself.' It was time to change the subject. 'Now then,' she said, 'before I skedaddle out of here and forget why I came, I must thank you for the lovely flowers. There was no need to send them. If anyone needed to ask for forgiveness, it was me. I shouldn't have snuck away like that, but I didn't know what to say.'

He gave her a blank look. 'Sorry, I'm not with you. What flowers?'

'You know, the roses. They came this morning.'

The blank expression was replaced with a slow smile. 'Remind me what the card said.'

Annoyed that he was playing games with her, she said, 'The wording went something like, "Dear Genevieve, sorry for what I very nearly did. Please forgive an old friend ... if you can." '

Adam looked at her steadily. 'Like I said, the guy couldn't keep his eyes off you.'

29

Even at the best of times, Granny Baxter wasn't the most reliable of people. Her memory, so she claimed, was in perfect working order; it was others who confused her by deliberately playing tricks, like hiding her glasses. Exchanges such as, 'But Gran, you're wearing them!' 'Well, who put them there? Was it you?' were frequent. As was wondering why Genevieve or some other member of the family had arrived in the car to take her shopping in Pembroke or Haverfordwest. 'But Gran, it was your idea!' 'What nonsense. But seeing as you're here, you can take me anyway. I could do with a change of scene.'

Over the years, Genevieve and her sisters had witnessed many a scene when their grandmother had turned a perfectly logical situation completely on its head. Today, though, she seemed intent on turning Angel Cottage on its head and giving it a good shake. Convinced that the mice plaguing her kitchen had now taken up residence in the dusty confines of the understairs cupboard, she was issuing orders to Genevieve and her father.

'Careful where you stand, you might step on one!' And, 'Try not to make too much noise; we need to take them by surprise.'

The Mice Thing, as it had become known, was close to being an obsession with Gran. Every conversation anyone had with her was punctuated with some new complaint. The mice were either keeping her awake at night with their squeaky cacophony in the chimney breast, or they were shredding her nerves with their prolonged silences. Either way, their presence was driving Gran mad. Yet it was difficult to use the word 'presence' because, as yet, no one had had an actual sighting. Other than Gran, no one had even heard so much as a squeak.

But now, because Gran was so insistent that the mice had moved from the kitchen to the understairs cupboard, the small hallway of her cottage was strewn with what looked like museum pieces – two ancient vacuum cleaners, boxes of chipped crockery and jam jars, bundles of faded newspapers, cracked old shoes without laces, and one solitary, fur-lined ankle boot.

'What's the point in keeping this, Gran?' asked Genevieve. She held up the boot for her grandmother to see.

The old lady took it from her and turned it over as though trying to place it. 'Well, I'll be darned,' she said at length. 'I was wondering where it had got to. Clever you for finding it. Here, give me a hand.' Leaning against Genevieve, she kicked off her slipper, pushed her stockinged foot into the boot and was just about to pull up the zip when she let out an ear-splitting yelp. 'There's something in it!'

She put all her weight against Genevieve, making her stagger, and tried to shake off the boot. Meanwhile, still digging around in the cupboard for more lost family heirlooms, Daddy Dean emerged to see what all the fuss was about and promptly banged his head on the low door frame.

'Bugger!' he yelled above the noise of Gran's shouts, while rubbing the top of his head. 'What the hell's going on?'

But Gran was beyond answering questions.

'She thinks there's something in it,' Genevieve shouted. 'Get it off before she has a heart attack!'

It was some minutes before Gran was in a calm enough state to drink the tea Genevieve had made. The three of them were in the sitting room, squashed on the sofa, Gran between Genevieve and her father.

'It was a mouse, I tell you,' Gran muttered, more to herself than them. 'It was there, right at the end of the boot. I felt it wriggle under my big toe.' She shuddered and spilled some of the tea from the mug in her hands.

Daddy Dean took the mug from her and put it on the coffee table. 'Mum, it wasn't a mouse,' he said very firmly. 'It was a small ball of wool. Look.' For the third time he showed her the flattened remnant.

But seeing wasn't believing, and Gran turned her weepy eyes on him. 'I know what I felt. It was a *mouse.*'

He put his arm around her. 'It only felt like a mouse because that's what's on your mind at the moment.'

Her expression turned stern. 'Don't treat me like a child. I'm not a simpleton. Don't think you can bully or patronise me.'

'I wouldn't ever think of patronising you,' he soothed. 'Now drink up your tea.'

She took it from him with a look of such fierce petulance, Genevieve was reminded of Nattie. She held back a smile. But deep down, Genevieve was concerned. The Mouse Thing was getting to Gran and she wondered if she ought to suggest to her father that they get Gran checked out by a doctor. Senile dementia or Alzheimer's were not words she wanted to start bandying around, but if Gran was beginning to imagine things, then perhaps it was their responsibility to find out why. Right now Genevieve would give anything to see a family of mice trotting across the sitting room carpet.

She was just wondering which one of them would be brave enough to broach the subject, when her grandmother said, 'And while we're on the subject of bullying, I hope you're going to do exactly what Genevieve thinks you should.'

Uncertain which way the conversation was about to go, Genevieve looked anxiously at her father. 'And what would that be?' he said.

'Doing something about you and Serena, of course.'

It should have been a relief to see Gran revert so quickly to her normal self, but Genevieve flinched on her father's behalf. This was a conversation her father was going to have to face. But watching him remove his arm from his mother's shoulder, she could see him withdrawing already.

'And if you leave it much later, Daddy Dean, you'll go to rack and ruin and no woman in her right senses would be interested in you. No, don't look like that. I'm only speaking the truth. Which reminds me, you're beginning to bear an uncanny resemblance to that silly man on the television.'

'And which silly man would that be?' Dad's voice was tight.

'Oh, you know. The one who waves his arms about a lot.' Gran screwed up her eyes to assist her concentration. 'No, don't rush me, I'm thinking. Oh, dear, whatever is his name? My brain's turned to quince jelly. It sounds like dog. Something dog. Dog. Dog. Ken Dodd! That's who you remind me of.'

Genevieve stifled a laugh but her father looked offended.

'You do!' Gran persisted. 'When was the last time you had your hair cut? Look at it; it's sticking up all over your head. You need to make an appointment with Debs and get yourself tidied up, my boy. Or what will Serena think when you fly to Australia to sweep her off her feet?'

'Serena's in New Zealand, Mum. And I don't know where you've got this notion that I'm setting foot on any kind of an aeroplane.' He got to his feet and looked at his reflection in the mirror above the fireplace. 'I don't look anything like Ken Dodd.'

Gran made a small grunting sound. 'If you don't go and see her, it might well turn out to be the biggest mistake of your life. It's time you brought that wife of yours home where she belongs. It's not just you who misses her.'

Taking her cue, Genevieve said, 'Gran's right, Dad. You can't go on as you are. I really think you should go and see Mum. If you don't, she might start to think you don't want her back.'

In a gesture of despair, he raked his hands wildly through his hair. 'But how can I compete with this old friend who's giving her such a new and exciting time? What have I got to offer?'

'There!' cried Gran, 'now you really do look like Ken Dodd.'

Her father refused to speak another word on the subject for the rest of the day, and it was with a weary heart that Genevieve sat alone in the small office that night. She ignored the pile of paperwork that needed filing, and instead switched on the computer to check her emails.

It was three weeks since she had written to thank Christian for the roses. But even as she penned the note, she half-expected to receive a reply from him that said, 'What roses? *I* didn't send any.' But he'd replied a week later asking if she had a computer and was online. 'Emails are so much more convenient,' he'd written. He'd given her his email address and she'd replied with the message: 'Bet you thought we Baxters were too primitive for such hi-tech equipment, didn't you?' She pointed out that for years now she'd preferred to use a PC when writing letters. 'Spellchecker is the mother of all godsends for me.' He, in turn, pointed out that emailing and texting were easily the most useful forms of communication available to him.

Since then, there had been no more than a couple of brief exchanges, mostly news bulletins about Ralph's barn. Then silence. Perhaps, in view of Caroline, he'd felt it was inappropriate to correspond too often. This had a strange effect on Genevieve: it made her feel guilty, as though somehow she had become the Other Woman in his life.

Of course, nothing could have been further from the truth, despite what Adam wanted to believe. And even if Christian was tempted to turn back the clock, she wasn't. While she had forgiven him for what had happened, she had no intention of getting romantically involved with him. Not because she didn't find him attractive – she most certainly did – but because for once in her life, her head was ruling her heart. And her head was very clear on one crucial point of survival: she would never, ever, ever, allow anyone, herself included, to hurt her again.

The flashing white envelope on her screen showed that she had just one email waiting for her: it was from Christian. She clicked on OPEN and realised straight away why she hadn't heard from him. His mother was in hospital. Cancer. She'd had surgery to remove a lymph node from under her arm, but, from what Christian said, it seemed it had come too late. The cancer had spread.

Genevieve responded immediately, offering what few words of encouragement she could in the circumstances.

Having recently had many nights of relatively peaceful, nightmare-free sleep, she went to bed only to be kept awake by the day's events tumbling through her head: Gran's hysterical turn, her father refusing to see sense, and now Christian's mother, who was probably dying. Listening to the wind blowing in from the sea, she lay staring up at the ceiling. She was troubled by how helpless she felt. It was so frustrating that she couldn't do more to put her grandmother's mind at rest over the Mice Thing, and that she couldn't galvanise Dad into doing more to bring Mum home. She decided, though, to let this last worry go. Her father had resolved the Donna issue without anyone's help, so maybe he would do the same with Serena. Perhaps all that was needed on her part was patience. Something she seemed to be in short supply of these days.

30

By the middle of July, no one needed a weather forecaster to tell them they were experiencing a heatwave. It had started last week, and Angel Sands was tripping over itself with visitors. The usual complaints were heard, that it was too hot and the gardens could do with a drop of rain, but all in all, anyone running a business off the sunburnt backs of holidaymakers was rubbing his or her hands and praying on bended knee that the weather would hold for the rest of the season.

In the garden at Paradise House, Genevieve stood for a moment in the breathless heat to look down onto the beach. It was packed. The tide was in, leaving only a small amount of sand and pebbly surface to sit on, but every square inch was occupied. Rarely had she seen it so busy. 'Who needs to go abroad when the weather's like this?' all their guests were saying.

She had now started cooking evening meals for those who wanted them and, after a two-week trial period, it was proving to be a success.

Predictably, Nattie was muttering that it was more work for the rest of them. 'I'm not spending all my evenings dishing out food,' she said, 'and then tidying up afterwards. Not when I've been on the go all day with Lily-Rose.'

This was too much for Genevieve. 'And I suppose I haven't been on the go all day!'

'Yeah, but that's your choice. You've decided to make all this extra work. Why should I be lumbered with it?'

'Because it's a family business. We're all in this together.'

'I notice you don't go on at Polly like you do with me.'

'And for a very good reason. She's not an idle beggar like you. She's out teaching most days, but during the school holidays she always does her bit. Honestly, Nattie, it's time you grew up.'

'And became a boring adult like you? Not bloody likely!'

As ever, Adam had come up trumps and recommended the niece of a friend of a friend who was spending the summer in the village and would appreciate the unexpected pocket money. Her name was Kelly Winward, a seventeen-year-old student from Bolton, and she was far more helpful than Nattie would ever be.

Now that things were back to normal with Adam, he had been on at

Genevieve again about putting her supposed skills to better use. 'I hate to see good talent go to waste,' he said, when she asked him why he was so concerned about her.

'But if I take on too much, I won't be able to run Paradise House. Now that I'm doing evening meals, I have even less time for anything else.'

'And is that what you want to do for the rest of your life?' he'd asked.

Christian had asked her much the same question during one of their email exchanges. Her answer had been vague. Sometimes she thought she would like nothing better than to stay in Angel Sands for ever, continuing to do exactly what she was doing. But as someone had once told her – probably Gran in one of her wise old lady moments – everyone should have their own dream, and Paradise House had been her parents' dream or, more specifically, her mother's. For the time being, she was happy to be the caretaker of someone else's dream, but sometime soon she would have to chase her own. She did have something in mind, but until the right opportunity arose, she didn't want to tell anyone about it. For now it was a tentative plan with a small p. But given time, it would become her Plan with a capital P.

Meanwhile, she had plenty to do. Thanks to Adam and the wedding party, she now had two party bookings, one for August and another for September. Donna and Kelly would waitress for her, but come the autumn when Kelly was back in Bolton, Genevieve would have to think again.

News from Christian about his mother went from bad to worse. The emails he sent were sporadic; some were just a couple of lines, while others were over a page long. Genevieve sensed he needed someone to talk to. She hoped Caroline, whom he never mentioned, was a good listener. The latest email said, 'Mum's having all the treatment, but I know her heart's not in it. Mentally she's given up the fight and it makes me so angry. Not cross with her, but impotent and furious that I can't do anything to stop the pain or the inevitable.'

Genevieve wished she was better with words and could say something incisive and helpful. But the best she could do was reassure him he was doing all he could by being with his mother as much as possible.

Walking back up the garden to the house, Genevieve thought how wrong Adam was. Other than that Very-Nearly-A-Kiss moment, Christian hadn't given her any cause to worry that he might want more than just friendship. It was a relief, one thing less for her to worry about.

The house was empty so, switching on the answerphone, she walked down the hill to call on Gran, to see if there was any shopping she needed doing. The air was drenched in the smell of suntan oil and the area of parched grass in front of the Salvation Arms was carnival-like, awash with reddening bodies swigging back beer and soft drinks. The shops were also busy, and across the road, outside the mini-market, Stan looked like he was wrestling with a killer whale – he was actually restocking his display of inflatable beach toys. Waving to him, Genevieve carried on up to Angel Cottage.

Since the Mouse-In-The-Boot incident, their father had insisted on getting a pest man in. Reluctantly Gran had agreed and even when her house was declared a pest-free zone, she wasn't convinced. 'Modern mice are more cunning than they used to be,' she said.

The very next day she claimed to have been woken in the night by squeaking, but the funny thing was, she was no longer irritated by the noise. It was as though the enemy had become her ally. Heroes, even. They had beaten the pest man and won her respect.

To Genevieve's astonishment, her father had broached the subject of Gran seeing a doctor. Her reaction, unsurprisingly, was to hit the roof and tell anyone who would listen that there was nothing wrong with her. She told Stan and Gwen in the mini-market, she told Ruth and William in church, and, of course, she told Tubby – because, as everyone knew, if you wanted important news relayed, Tubby was your man.

'It's so embarrassing,' Nattie complained. 'She's making out that we're trying to have her put away.'

'But no one would believe it,' said Polly. 'Everyone knows that's the last thing we'd do.'

'Don't you be so sure,' their father muttered from behind his newspaper. 'The way I feel, I might just lock her up myself.' He was still smarting from the Ken Dodd comparison.

Genevieve knocked on Gran's front door.

She knocked again. And again. And still Gran didn't appear. Genevieve moved to the window where she cupped her hands around her eyes and peered in. The television wasn't on, and there was no sign of Gran. Perhaps she was in the kitchen at the back of the house.

Nothing for it, Genevieve thought, and took the unprecedented step of using the key she'd been entrusted with.

'Gran?' she called out anxiously, shutting the door behind her. 'It's me, Genevieve.'

The house was refreshingly cool and still after the heat outside. It was also unnaturally quiet. She poked her head round the sitting room door, then went through to the kitchen. Still no sign of Gran. She investigated further, calling out all the while – better not give Gran a heart attack by creeping up on her.

When she stood on the small landing, she thought she heard something. 'Gran?' She strained to hear the noise again.

Yes. There it was. It was coming from the bathroom. A faint moaning noise. She pushed open the door.

Her first thought was that subconsciously this was what she'd always dreaded ... finding Gran dead.

31

The doctor saw himself out, leaving them to hover around the bed like actors in a second-rate television drama.

'If you're trying to annoy me,' Gran grumbled, 'you're doing a good job of it. You look like a bunch of greedy mourners who've been called to the bed once too often. Any minute now you'll start squabbling over who's going to inherit the most from my vast fortune.'

'Good, I'm glad we're annoying you,' said Nattie, 'because you scared the hell out of us! If you're planning another dizzy do, let me know so I can make arrangements to be some place else.'

'That's enough, Natalie,' her father murmured. Pale-faced and anxious, he dropped into the chair nearest Gran's bed. He rubbed his hands over his face. 'You're sure you're okay?' he said. 'You're not pretending, are you? I know what you're capable of.'

The old lady drew her eyebrows together. 'Please, I wish you'd all stop fussing. I'm as fit as a fiddle.'

'No you're not! What's more, you're under doctor's orders to stay in bed for the next two days.'

Gran raised her head off the pillow. 'I clearly heard Doctor Shepherd say that all I needed to do was take things slowly. He didn't mention anything about staying in bed gathering bedsores. Now is there any chance of a cup of tea, or am I denied that basic human right too?'

Genevieve and Polly volunteered for the job. In the kitchen, while they put together a tray of tea things, Genevieve said, 'She's at her most imperious when she's hiding from the truth, isn't she?'

'You're right. Beneath it all, she must be as shocked as the rest of us. But how are *you* feeling? It must have been awful finding her like that.'

'I'm fine,' Genevieve said, conscious that she was lying in the same glib way her grandmother just had. When she'd found Gran slumped in a heap on the bathroom floor – her hand still clutching a J-cloth and a puddle of pine-fresh cleaner on the carpet – her brain had registered the obvious, that Gran was moving and therefore alive, but her heart had been several paces behind, causing panic to thump in her chest. She'd turned the old lady over, seen the gash where she must have cracked the side of her head on the basin as she fell, and was about to rush downstairs to phone for an ambulance, when Gran had opened her eyes.

'Gran! Can you hear me? Are you okay? Is it your heart?'

Her grandmother had winced and raised a hand to her head. 'Why are you shouting, Genevieve?' Then, looking about her, 'What are we doing here? Why are we on the bathroom floor?'

The calmness to her voice told Genevieve an ambulance wasn't necessary, but a doctor was. After she'd helped her grandmother to her feet and got her to sit on the edge of the bed – lying *in* bed was out of the question: 'Don't be absurd, Genevieve, you're making such a drama of it!' – she phoned the local surgery. Then, remembering she'd put the answerphone on, she called her father on his mobile. All the while, Gran kept grumbling at the fuss.

'I've only bumped my head. Anyone would think I'd severed a major artery the way you're carrying on.'

'And maybe that's your next party trick,' Genevieve had answered back. 'That really would frighten me to death.'

'Oh, well, if it's death you're fretting about, save yourself the worry. There's nothing you or I can do to stop it happening.'

'Oh, be quiet, Gran. At least have the decency to act like you've had a narrow escape.'

Dad arrived within minutes, followed hotly by Polly and Nattie with Lily-Rose. Finally Dr Shepherd joined the throng and, after a few minutes alone with Gran, he pronounced his patient shaken but in reasonably good health.

'From what she says, it seems she had a blackout,' he told them. 'Her blood pressure's a little higher than I'd like, but I don't see any point in causing alarm by whisking her into hospital for exhaustive tests that will probably tell us no more than we already know. I suggest we leave things be and see how she gets on over the coming days. Don't hesitate to ring the surgery if you have any concerns.'

Part of Genevieve had wanted to disagree with the doctor and demand that the exhaustive tests he dismissed so lightly were carried out. But now, pouring boiling water into Gran's old brown Betty teapot, she saw the sense in what Dr Shepherd had said. Gran's blood pressure would soar if she was forced to lie in a strange hospital bed and subjected to endless prods and pokes. It would be better to keep an eye on her at home.

Polly went ahead of her to open the bedroom door, while Genevieve carried the tea upstairs and considered the best way to take care of Gran over the next few days. The simplest thing would be for her to move in with them at Paradise House, except there wasn't really room. The Rainbow Suite would be free at the weekend, but until then, unless Genevieve moved in with Polly and gave Gran her bedroom, she didn't see how to do it.

As she set the tray on Gran's bedside table her father said, 'Despite a difference of opinion, your grandmother will be having a guest to stay. Me.'

Ignoring Gran's scowl, he added, 'It seems the easiest way, so long as you can handle things on your own, Genevieve?'

Relieved that a solution had been found so quickly, she said, 'I'll manage perfectly.'

As usual she had imagined that it would be she who had to sort things out. It struck her then that she was beginning to behave as though she didn't trust anyone else to get things done. When had that started? When had she begun to be so controlling of others? Was it because she thought she had her own life so tightly controlled that she imagined she could do the same with other people? Maybe Nattie had been right to criticise her for lumbering her with extra work because she wanted to cook something more challenging than bacon and eggs. Could it be that, deep down, she was as bossy and selfish as Nattie?

During breakfast the following morning, Genevieve had to give Nattie her due; without their father around, she was definitely trying to be more helpful. Nothing had been said, but a truce seemed to be in place. Prepared to bite her tongue if there was any lapse on her sister's part, Genevieve was relieved that Nattie hadn't once taken umbrage at being asked to do anything, and that she had even greeted the guests with something that resembled a welcoming smile as she took their orders. Her first negative comment of the day came now as she stood by the open back door trying to escape the sweltering heat of the kitchen.

'It beats me how that lot can still tuck away a fry-up in this weather. You'd think they'd want nothing more than a chilled glass of orange juice and half a grapefruit.' Then turning to Lily-Rose, who was sitting at the table and eating paper-thin slices of apple, she said, 'Pumpkin-Pie, how about a little paddle down at the beach when your Auntie Genvy's finished with me?'

Poking her finger through one of the slices of apple, Lily-Rose looked at Genevieve. 'Will you come as well?'

'I'd love to,' Genevieve said, spooning hot oil over the eggs in the spitting pan, 'but while Daddy Dean is keeping an eye on Gran, I need to go to the supermarket to do a big shop.'

'Mummy could help you.'

Genevieve laughed. 'An important rule, Lily-Rose: never push your luck. Especially not with a sister.'

The little girl looked thoughtful and proceeded to poke at another slice of apple. 'Mummy?'

'Yes.'

'When am I going to have a sister?'

Expecting Nattie to mutter something like, 'When hell freezes over,' Genevieve was surprised to hear her say, 'When I find one as gorgeous as you sleeping with the fairies at the end of the garden.'

Smiling, Genevieve slipped the cooked eggs onto the warmed plates of bacon, black pudding, sausage and tomatoes, and handed them to her sister to take through to the dining room.

When Nattie had gone, Lily-Rose said, 'How often does Mummy look at the end of the garden?'

Before Genevieve could think of a suitable reply, the phone rang. She switched off the radio and lifted the receiver.

'Genevieve, is that you?'

She hadn't spoken to him in a while, but she recognised Jonjo's voice at once. 'Hello, Jonjo. If you're hoping to speak to Polly, she's not here. She left for work over an hour ago.'

'I know; I've just spoken to her on her mobile. She said I needed to speak to you. The thing is; you're my last hope. I know it's last-minute stuff, but is there any chance of a couple of rooms being available this coming weekend? Christian and I are planning to meet with the builders and it's the only time we can both make it, assuming of course that Christian's mother doesn't get any worse. We've tried the pub in the village and they're fully booked. Like just about everything else. So, any room at the inn?'

Genevieve checked the diary to make sure no one else had taken a booking without letting her know. 'If you don't mind sharing, we've just had a cancellation, but I'm afraid it's—'

'That's brilliant! But tell me it's not a double bed. The thought of sleeping with Mr May doesn't appeal.'

'No it isn't. You're quite safe, it's a twin-bedded room, so people won't gossip too much.'

'Better and better. Now, depending on the traffic, we aim to be with you around lunchtime, is that okay?'

'Yes. One of us should be here to meet you. Probably me.'

'Oh, and before I forget, Christian says "Hi" '

'How's he doing, Jonjo? He was always so close to his parents.'

'He's coping pretty well, but I think the change at the weekend will do him good. Splitting up from his girlfriend probably hasn't helped either.'

This was news to Genevieve. 'When did that happen? He never mentioned anything in his emails.'

There was a silence and for a second Genevieve thought they'd been cut off. 'Are you still there, Jonjo?'

'Er . . . yes. Look, forget I said anything. If Christian hasn't mentioned it to you, it's certainly not my place to talk about it behind his back. I'd better go, my other phone's ringing. See you on Saturday. Thanks so much, Genevieve. Don't forget to give your cruets an extra polish for me, will you?'

Putting the receiver down, Genevieve was left with Adam's words echoing in her ears: *And if the girlfriend becomes history? Does that bring him within range?*

It might do, her treacherous heart whispered.

But her head had other ideas. No! She told herself firmly. Not again. She would not allow it to happen. She would not fall in love with Christian all over again.

That afternoon, she took a quiche and some ready-made salad she'd bought at the supermarket down to Gran's so that her father wouldn't have to worry about cooking an evening meal.

'How's she behaving?' Genevieve asked when he let her in at Angel Cottage.

'Like a badly behaved child. I'm nearly out of patience. I've threatened her with another visit from Dr Shepherd if she doesn't do as she's told and stay in bed.'

'Poor you. I don't envy you one little bit. She's not overdoing it with the Baxter Bell, is she?' The Baxter Bell was a small, brass hand-bell that came out from the bathroom cabinet whenever anyone was ill in bed.

'I'm surprised she hasn't broken it, but it's no more than you'd expect from her. Any news from up the hill? Anything I should know about?'

She told him about Lily-Rose wanting a sister, which she knew would amuse him, and then the conversation she'd had with Jonjo, about him and Christian booking in.

'And you're happy with that, for . . . for Christian to stay under the same roof?'

She was touched her father still had difficulty saying Christian's name. 'Christian and I have moved on. Life's too short to harbour grudges, Dad.'

'I know, Gen, but the moment he steps out of line, he'll have me to answer to.'

She smiled and, mimicking her grandmother, said, 'Goodness, Daddy Dean, you're becoming so brutish these days, I hardly know you!'

'Good! Because I've been doing some thinking and have reached an important decision. As soon as I think your Gran can be trusted to be on her own again, I'm going to New Zealand to see your mother.'

'You are? Really?'

'Yes, I'm going to do what I should have done weeks ago. I'm going to try and make her come home.'

Genevieve hugged him fiercely. 'So what's brought on this change of heart?'

'It was your grandmother's fall. It shook me up, made me realise we have no way of knowing what's around the corner, and maybe not everything should be left to resolve itself. Plus, your grandmother has just made a bargain with me; she promised to behave if I stopped being a coward and went and faced Serena.'

'Oh, Dad, you mustn't be too hard on yourself. We're all cowards sometimes.'

'I've buried my head deeper than most. I've let things go on and get worse because I couldn't bear the thought of losing your mother altogether. But it's a risk I have to take. I see that now. Some people say we only have one chance to get things right. Well, I disagree. I think if we're lucky, we get two. Either way, if we let those chances slip through our hands we have only ourselves to blame.'

This was nothing short of radical stuff coming from her father. She never dreamed she'd hear him talk so openly. Her hunch that he might resolve matters himself had been right, after all.

Above their heads, as if to add a musical flourish to his words, came a noise followed by the tinkling of the Baxter Bell.

'Let me go to her,' Genevieve said. 'You've earned a break.'

Genevieve had an ulterior motive; she was keen to thank her grandmother for shaking up Dad. But when she stood in the doorway of Gran's bedroom, she saw that the old lady, head slumped to one side on the pillows, was asleep – the sound had been the bell falling out of her hand and landing on the floor. Genevieve crept into the room and was just placing the bell on the bedside table when her grandmother stirred.

'Sorry, Gran, I didn't mean to disturb you.'

Gran straightened her neck and looked at Genevieve through sleepy eyes. 'It's a bit late to be sorry, Serena. But I suppose it's better late than never. I hope you've apologised to Daddy Dean and the girls. You've caused them no end of heartache.'

'Gran, it's me, Genevieve.'

'Genevieve? Oh, I've no idea where she is. She's always so busy these days. But now you're home, she won't have to work so hard.' The old lady suddenly yawned and, closing her eyes, she leaned back against the pillows. 'Would you mind closing the door after you, Serena? I think I'll snatch a quick forty winks. I can't think why I'm so tired.'

Genevieve knew it was common for old people to muddle up members of their family, even imagining they were talking to a relative who'd died years ago, but Gran confusing her with Serena upset Genevieve more than she could say. But when she joined her father down in the kitchen and saw the look on his face – the upbeat look of a man who had, at last, decided to act – she knew she couldn't tell him of the conversation she'd just had with Gran. He would put off going to see Serena.

Later, as she walked home in the bright sunshine, threading her way through the crowds of trippers, she consoled herself with the thought that Gran was just tired. It was perfectly understandable that she could be confused, especially as Genevieve did bear quite a strong resemblance to her mother.

32

The next morning, in a hurry to get all the chores done, Genevieve found herself thwarted at every turn. The telephone kept ringing and Donna was in one of her turbo-charged chatty moods. And it didn't matter which direction the conversation went – the weather, the ever-lowering interest rates, the mess in one of the bathrooms – she managed somehow to bring Tubby into it. On any other morning, Genevieve would have been amused by Donna's tales of what she and Tubby had got up to, but today she was tired and all she wanted to do was get down to Angel Cottage and put her mind at rest.

She'd lain awake in bed for hours last night worrying about her grandmother. Listening to the sounds of the seashore through the open window, then knowing she would never get to sleep, she'd crept downstairs to make herself a drink. She'd sat in the conservatory, watching the moonlight dancing across the water, wishing she didn't feel so anxious about Gran. For years they'd joked about her not being the full shilling, but Genevieve couldn't bear the thought that her beloved grandmother might really be losing her marbles. And what a silly expression that was, to describe an elderly person's heartbreaking decline into a world where they could no longer be reached.

She had eventually gone back to bed and snatched an hour's sleep before her alarm clock went off.

'So what do you think, Genevieve? Is it a good idea that will go down well in the village? If we make a reasonable fist of it, Tubby reckons it might become an annual event. A tradition.'

Realising she hadn't been paying attention to Donna, Genevieve looked up from the pillow she was knocking into shape. 'I'm sorry, Donna, what were you saying?'

'You okay? You seem sort of distracted. Still worried about your Gran?'

'A bit,' she said non-committally. 'But tell me what you were saying. What does Tubby think might become an annual event?'

'We've had this idea of putting on a charity talent contest at The Arms. You know the kind of thing, *Stars In Your Eyes*, people dressing up and belting out tunes we all know and love. There'd be an entrance fee and an extra charge if you want to take part, and any money we raise, after giving out some prizes, will go to a local charity. What do you think? Will people go for it?'

'Oh, I should think there are any number of people in Angel Sands who'd go for it like a shot. Look how they all enjoy karaoke nights.'

'So what about you? Will you take part?'

'Me? Good Lord, no! I can't hold a note to save my life.'

Donna laughed. 'That's the point. People would pay good money to hear you try.'

'No way! Absolutely not.'

'Is that your final word?'

'Yes. But I'll help in any other way you want. I'm better at the backstage stuff.'

Unlike Donna, she thought, when she walked down into the village an hour later. 'Who do you think I should have a crack at?' Donna had asked Genevieve. 'Bonnie Tyler or Tina Turner? Or there again, I can do a mean Shirley Bassey popping her cork and all.'

But Genevieve couldn't conceive of anything worse than performing in front of an audience. No matter how friendly or mellowed by alcohol they were.

She was doing her usual eyes-fixed-on-the-pavement routine as she passed Debonhair when a loud tap-tap-tap on the glass forced her to glance up. Brandishing her scissors and comb, Debs was standing over a petrified-looking man sitting in the chair nearest the window. It was a moment before Genevieve recognised her father. She went inside. The tiled floor around him was covered with a mat of thick grey hair.

He said, 'I only asked for a trim and look what she's done!'

'Get on with you!' Debs laughed. 'I'm giving him a makeover, just what he needs.' She swivelled his chair to face the mirror and began snipping at the nape of his neck, which was bone-white compared to the rest of his neck and face.

'Not too much off the back,' her father said, raising his head to speak, but Debs pushed it down again. From the depths of his chest, he mumbled, 'I thought I'd be in and out, Gen. I told your grandmother I'd just be a few—'

'You'll be out when I've finished with you,' Debs interrupted sternly. 'Just remember, I'm the one with the scissors in my hand.' Then to Genevieve, she said, 'Has Donna told you about the talent contest she and Tubby want to put on? I've offered to do everyone's hair, and if they want wigs, I can get hold of them, no problem. I'm trying to get your father to do a turn, but he won't have it. How about you, Gen? Are you going to loosen your stays and show us the real you?'

'Oh, I think you all know the real me,' Genevieve said.

Debs winked. 'A bit of letting go never hurt anyone.' Her voice was silky smooth. 'By the way, how's that young man of yours? I hear he's coming here again at the weekend. Staying at your place, too. That'll be cosy for you, won't it?'

Daddy Dean jerked his head up. 'Please,' he begged, 'I only came in for a trim. And that was nearly an hour ago.'

When finally Genevieve could get away – it really was breathtaking how much Debs knew about everyone – she left her father with the promise that she would send out a search party if he wasn't back by dusk.

A large herring gull was standing guard on Gran's gate. It eyed Genevieve suspiciously with its enormous beady eyes, and made no attempt to move until she clapped her hands loudly. It squawked, flapped its wings and flew off.

She let herself in. The sound of the television told her that Gran wasn't where she ought to be.

'I thought you were supposed to be in bed,' she chastised her grandmother, at the same time glad to see that there was plenty of colour back in her face. 'I've just spoken to Dad, and he said you'd promised to be good while he was having his hair done.'

'Your father, baloney! That man is getting above himself and if he doesn't watch his step – oh, be quiet a minute, it's *Bargain Hunt* and the auction's about to start. Come and sit down with me, Genevieve. Then I'll make us a nice cup of tea.'

Genevieve. Not Serena! So it had only been a once-off memory lapse. All the anxiety of last night instantly faded, and Genevieve sat on the sofa with her grandmother. She put her arm around the old lady and kissed her.

'What's that for?'

'For being your usual self.'

'And who else would I be?'

'Ssh! We're missing the programme. Yuck! What's that when it's home?'

'The Victorians used it for syringing out their ears and the Red Team stupidly paid twenty-five pounds for it. Your father could do with cleaning out his ears. I've told him till I'm blue in the face that I don't need him here, that right now he's got more important things to be doing, like bringing Serena home. There! I knew it wouldn't make any money. I'm always right.'

In that moment, Genevieve had never been keener to believe her grandmother.

33

The strain of cooking an evening meal and then getting up early to cook breakfast was taking its toll on Genevieve. It was a misconception that running a B & B was an easy option. The hours were long, practically twenty-four, and the pace relentless: to maintain the word-of-mouth recommendations and repeat bookings, which were essential, you couldn't afford a momentary drop in standards. And of course, during peak season, there was no chance of a lie-in, something Genevieve felt she badly needed right now. But given the choice, she'd rather be working long hours in Angel Sands than anywhere else.

She was making the most of a short lull, relaxing on the steps outside the guest sitting room, watching Nattie read to Lily-Rose on the lawn. Polly was playing the piano. It was a beautifully restful and harmonious piece she'd heard her sister play before. She had no idea what it was, or who the composer was, but it matched perfectly both the weather – there was a gentle breeze rippling the sea and cooling the intense heat – and Genevieve's mood. Despite being so tired, she felt calm: Gran was back to normal, bossing them all about with renewed vigour, and Dad, sporting his dramatic new haircut, was making arrangements to go and see Mum.

And on top of that, she was looking forward to seeing Christian and Jonjo. They wouldn't be arriving for another two hours, but she had everything ready. If they hadn't eaten on the way, there was plenty in the fridge.

Stretching her legs in front of her and lifting her long skirt above her knees, she thought of what Adam had said about her having great legs. Silly man! Okay, they weren't the worst legs in the world, but they were hardly a match for Kylie's or Nicole Kidman's. As a girl she had badly wanted to be a ballerina, and at their mother's instigation all three sisters had attended Miss Marian White's School of Dancing, but only Polly had stayed the course. Nattie had said she'd rather shoot herself than prance about like a prissy idiot (this was after her one and only lesson) and, by the age of eleven, Genevieve had grown too tall. Standing head and shoulders above all the other girls made her feel cloddish and clumsy. That was when she'd taken up swimming. Even today, if she heard the opening bars of *Swan Lake*, she instinctively closed her eyes and pictured herself as a sylph-like ballerina en pointe: she was always dressed in pale blue chiffon and was as light on her feet as Polly.

For years she had envied Polly her long, graceful legs and delicate features, and Nattie her straight up-and-down, tomboy shape. Now, eventually, she had come to terms with the way she looked. She took after her mother, with what Serena called a golden-age Hollywood hour-glass figure. 'Where would Rita Hayworth, Jane Russell, Marilyn Monroe, or Betty Grable have been without their sashaying hips and luscious cleavages?' she had often told Genevieve.

Adam had also described her as attractive and sexy. She liked being called sexy, even if there was no one to share her sexiness with. Anyone eavesdropping on that rather odd conversation might have leapt to the conclusion that there was a danger of Adam transferring his affections from one sister to another. But Genevieve knew Adam was much too sensible to make that mistake. Strangely though, she knew that from now on things would be different between them, now he wasn't trying to win over Nattie. It was going to take some getting used to not being the sympathetic shoulder. She wondered, though, if he could really do it – give up on Nattie. There again, he was one of the most decisive men she knew. So perhaps he could.

Behind her in the sitting room, Polly had started playing something else, something brisk and robust. She closed her eyes and wondered whether it might be fun to organise a picnic tomorrow, like the last time Jonjo and Christian had come down. It would depend on how busy they were, and if they would be around long enough after their meeting with the builder.

Before long, the piano music and Nattie's voice as she read to Lily-Rose, became as distant and muffled as the cries of happy children playing on the beach below, and she slept. She dreamed she was floating on her back in the sea, the waves lapping around her, caressing her lightly, but best of all, her mother was there too, at her side. It was a lovely dream and when the sound of an approaching car shooed it away, she opened her eyes reluctantly. Assuming the car belonged to a guest – they all had a key to let themselves in – she stayed where she was. Then she heard footsteps and a familiar voice.

'Hel-*lo!* Anyone at home?'

Jonjo and Christian? Already? She checked her watch. It was almost twelve. She stood up and straightened her skirt in time to see them coming round the corner of the house.

'You're very early. Was there less traffic than you expected?'

'We decided to set off earlier than planned,' said Jonjo, 'in case the roads ground to a halt or the tarmac melted in the midday sun.' He cocked his ear and smiled. 'Is that the light of my life serenading my arrival?' Without giving Genevieve a chance to respond, he walked the length of the terrace and stepped inside the house to the guest sitting room: the music stopped abruptly. 'If I start apologising for him now,' Christian said with a weary shrug, 'I could spend the entire weekend doing it. Can you just accept that he's a lunatic and humour him?'

'Come off it, Christian, he fits in perfectly with us Baxters. Anyway, officially you're both guests so I have to humour the pair of you.' Then taking in how tired he looked, she said, 'How are you?'

'Completely knackered. Any chance you can find me a quiet spot in the garden where I can sleep for the next twenty-four hours?'

'You're in luck. Dad's rigged up a hammock in the orchard.'

'Lead me to it!'

While Polly showed Christian and Jonjo their room, Genevieve prepared lunch, a choice of mini baguettes filled with smoked mackerel pâté and fresh crab. As she buttered the baguettes, she reflected on Christian's appearance. He hadn't been exaggerating when he'd said he was knackered. Fatigue was etched around his eyes; he looked burdened. She doubted whether he'd slept or eaten properly since his mother had gone into hospital. More than once she'd had to repeat something she'd said, and there was a difference in his voice – some of the sounds seemed to get caught in the back of his throat. She remembered how, as a teenager, whenever he'd been tired, it had been more of an effort for him to keep the timbre of his voice evenly pitched and to keep up with the conversation. The strain of his mother's illness was clearly affecting him deeply.

'I thought we'd eat in the garden,' Genevieve said, when Polly came into the kitchen. She looked flushed, Genevieve noticed. 'How are our guests settling in?'

'Jonjo loved the view.'

'I bet he did! Right, I think I've got everything ready for lunch. Will you give me a hand taking it outside? Oh, by the way, where's Nattie and Lily-Rose?'

'They've gone down to see Gran.'

'And Dad?'

'Helping Tubby to creosote his garden fence.'

Genevieve wrinkled her nose. 'What a revolting job for a day like today. Okay, you take the plates and cutlery and I'll manage the tray.'

They ate their lunch in the private area of garden in the shade. Jonjo did most of the talking. He raved about Christian's designs for his new home and boasted that it would be the best house in the area. Occasionally Christian would roll his eyes and exchange a smile with Genevieve, but his input to the conversation was minimal. When they'd finished eating, he offered to help Genevieve clear away.

'There's no need, there's hardly anything to do,' she said.

'But if I don't move, I'll nod off. Besides, I'm under orders from the Boss to make myself scarce.' He nodded in Jonjo's direction.

Leaving Polly and Jonjo alone, they went inside the house. They worked in silence at first, then she asked him again about his mother. She'd asked him in the garden, but he'd avoided going into any detail.

'She's had a run of good days,' he said, 'which is why I agreed to come down. But it won't last, the doctor says. The prognosis is weeks rather than months. What I can't handle is the suddenness of it. One minute the doctor is saying she's anaemic and the next she's in hospital having lumps cut out of her.'

'Oh, Christian, I'm so sorry. I don't know how I'd cope if I were in your shoes.' She told him about Gran and how worried she'd been over her fall. 'I know it's nothing compared to what you're going through.'

He disagreed. 'You're probably as close to her as you are to your parents. She's always been there for you. You know, I always envied you your family.'

'And I always envied you your quiet, self-contained little unit of three.'

He turned and looked out of the window. She heard him say, 'And then there was one.'

At six o'clock Christian and Jonjo returned from Ralph's barn after a lengthy, but according to Christian successful, meeting with the builder, a man from Haverfordwest who had been chosen because he'd worked on barn conversions before. But with six evening meals to prepare, there was no time for Genevieve to sit and chat, or to admire the intricate model Christian had made of the house-to-be. Christian said he and Jonjo wouldn't add to her workload and would eat out. 'We'll try the Salvation Arms,' he said.

'I don't mind cooking for you.'

'But it doesn't feel right, you waiting on us hand and foot.'

'But it's my job. It's what you're paying me to do.'

In the end, a compromise was reached. Jonjo asked Polly to go out with him for the evening and Christian said he'd eat whatever Genevieve wanted to cook, on the condition he ate in the kitchen with her.

'Not a good idea,' she said, 'Nattie will be around. Tell you what; we'll eat after everyone else, in the garden. Agreed?'

Smiling, he said, 'I don't remember you driving such a hard bargain.'

She cooked him sea bass with polenta and a salad with a sweet balsamic dressing. At midnight, they were still sitting in the garden. The night air was heavy and soft, a faint breeze skimmed her bare arms, and the incoming tide, slowly creeping up the moon-washed shore, rattled the loose pebbles in the sand. The calming sound was lost on Christian, but Genevieve could tell from his face, through the flickering candlelight on the table, that he was more relaxed than when he'd arrived. The tense lines had gone from his brow, and his voice was more evenly pitched. She wondered if now was the right time to ask him about Caroline. Perhaps not. It was none of her business, after all.

'This is so good,' he said simply, gazing out at the moon trailing its silvery reflection across the flat sea. He turned to look at her, his eyes dark and intense.

'It's one of the reasons I came back,' she replied.

'What were the others?'

'You don't want to know.'

'A boyfriend?'

She laughed. 'You're obsessed! Always trying to dig around in my patchy romantic past.'

'I think obsessed is stretching it a bit. Interested is nearer the mark.'

'Well, it didn't have anything to do with a failed relationship.' She could have told him about the robbery, about George and Cecily, but decided against it. She didn't want to think of anything that would spoil the moment.

By the time Christian and Jonjo made it down to the dining room for breakfast the next morning – Jonjo boasting that he'd already been for a jog – the rest of the guests had either left for the day or were in the garden reading the papers before deciding what to do.

'Where's Polly?' enquired Jonjo, when Genevieve asked them what they'd like to eat.

'At church with Gran and Lily-Rose. She plays the organ when the local man is off sick or on holiday.'

His disappointment showing, he said, 'What time will she be back?'

Genevieve checked her watch. 'In about an hour.'

His face brightened. 'So time for me to grab a slimline poached egg on a slice of wholemeal toast and a glass of orange juice before I surprise her and God? Is the church far?'

'Ten minutes' walk.' She told him where St Non's was, then turned to Christian. 'A healthy breakfast for you too?'

'No chance. Give me the works. Whatever you've got, please. I slept like a log and now I could eat a hog!'

'In that case, I'll do you a Paradise Special. Tea or coffee?'

'Tea, please. And if it's no trouble, see to Jonjo's breakfast before mine. I don't want him hanging about making derogatory comments about my fat intake.'

Jonjo was off as soon as he'd finished his breakfast, and Genevieve sat with Christian while he ate the Paradise Special – eggs, bacon, sausage, black pudding, fried bread, tomatoes, mushrooms and waffles to finish.

'I feel very rude eating in front of you,' Christian said. 'Why don't you have something to keep me company? Even though I was famished, I'll never get through all this.'

'If it makes you feel better, I'll pinch one of your waffles.'

'Is that all? How about a sausage? Or some bacon?'

'No. You need building up.'

'I do?'

'Yes. You've lost weight, haven't you? Remember, I know all about weight loss. I know a shrinking body when I see one.'

'It's not been deliberate, I just haven't had time. I've been working all day, then spending every evening with Mum.'

'But you mustn't make yourself ill. That isn't what your mother would want. Have you been in touch with her since you arrived?'

'Yes, by text.'

Genevieve was impressed. 'She's quite a techno-whizz, then? I can't imagine either of my parents getting their heads round text messages. Come to think of it, I'm not that hot myself. I don't even own a mobile. I'd probably lose it or forget how to work the wretched thing.'

He smiled. 'Mum's always been at the forefront of anything new. But there again, texting has been a part of our lives for years. We've arranged for the hospital to call me if ... if there's an emergency.'

'So how is she?'

'She says she's okay. But we both know that's a lie. She tells me what she thinks I want to hear.'

'That might well be true. But you have to bear in mind that people who are ill need rules to play by.'

He stirred his tea. 'You're right. But I'm lousy at pretence. It doesn't come naturally to me.'

'You should be more like us Baxters. We've mastered the art of denial.'

'Is that what you did when you were ...' He stopped stirring his tea and looked awkward.

'It's okay, Christian, you can refer to my starve, binge or bust days without embarrassing me.' Then, changing the subject, she said, 'Presumably we're still on for the picnic?'

'Absolutely.'

The guest list for the picnic kept growing.

When Polly arrived back from St Non's with Lily-Rose and Jonjo, she said they had invited Gran to join them. Or more particularly, Jonjo had invited their grandmother.

'You're sure it won't be too much for her?' asked Genevieve.

'She seemed her sprightly old self in church,' Polly said, 'so I don't see why not. Anyway, Jonjo can always take her home if she gets tired, since it was his bright idea. She seems very taken with him.'

'And why wouldn't she be?' interrupted Jonjo. He put his arm round Polly's waist. 'All in all, I think I made quite an impression on the old ladies at St Non's. My only disappointment was that Polly hardly batted an eyelid when I slipped into the front pew while everyone was praying and blew her a kiss. And there was me thinking she'd fall off her stool straight into my arms. I had plans to carry her up to the altar and ask the vicar to marry us there and then.'

Something in Polly's smile told Genevieve that had Jonjo carried her up to the altar, she wouldn't have protested. She thought back to that night when they'd all been in Polly's room and her sister had been standing at the window dressed in a pair of their father's old pyjamas, but had still managed to look like the proverbial princess waiting for her prince. So was Jonjo her prince? Certainly he was charming, but was he a stayer? Or would he, once he'd had his wicked way – to extend the fairy tale analogy – be off, leaving Polly with a broken heart? Only time would tell.

Meanwhile, Nattie, back early from seeing a friend, announced that she and Lily-Rose would be joining the picnic. She said she'd enjoy the chance to grill Jonjo and Christian on what they would be doing to Ralph's barn. Then, of course, it would have been heartless to leave Daddy Dean at home on his own, so he too was added to their number.

Eventually they set off, picking up Gran on the way, and drove in two cars to Tawelfan beach, chosen above Angel Sands by Gran, who insisted that Jonjo show her where he'd be living, even though she was perfectly well acquainted with Ralph's barn. Polly's comment that Gran was quite taken with him was a massive understatement; she was utterly enamoured.

'Such a delightful young man,' she whispered in Genevieve's ear, after they'd bounced along the rutted, sun-dried track towards the barn and were unloading the boot of Jonjo's Discovery. 'So handsome. If Polly has any sense she'll hang on to this one. They'd have the most beautiful children.'

Apart from Gran, they all carried something – lightweight chairs, the hamper, the cool bag of drinks, towels, two parasols, a fishing net, a bucket and spade and an inflatable dolphin, which Lily-Rose carried like an enormous baby in her arms. As they made the trek through the sand dunes to the beach, Genevieve was reminded of long-ago picnics with their father leading the way. On this occasion he was at the rear of the group, walking slowly with Gran, a supporting hand discreetly resting under her elbow. Genevieve had yet to hear her father exchange more than two gruff words with Christian.

As they'd expected, the beach was busy. They found themselves a suitable plot and began setting up camp. Quick as a flash, Lily-Rose stripped down to her fluorescent pink bikini bottoms and said she was going for a paddle.

'Oh, not yet,' yawned Nattie. 'Can't you wait ten minutes?'

'That's okay,' Genevieve said, 'I'll take her. Where's the suncream?'

Her sister tossed her the bottle. 'Thanks, Gen. I owe you.'

'Anyone else fancy a paddle?' asked Genevieve, rubbing factor thirty-five into Lily-Rose's smooth skin. 'Gran?'

'No thanks, love, I've just got settled.' She was already installed in her deckchair. 'Oh,' she said, as though suddenly remembering something vitally important. 'You did pack a thermos of tea, didn't you?'

'Of course I did, Gran.'

'And my favourite almond shortbread?'

'Need you ask? Lily-Rose, we won't be going anywhere unless you stop fidgeting and let me finish putting this cream on you. There now, that's you done.'

Slipping off his deck shoes and pulling his tee-shirt over his head, Christian said, 'Mind if I come along as well?'

Lily-Rose grabbed hold of his hand. 'Do you want Genvy to rub some suncream on your shoulders?'

He didn't catch what the little girl said. He turned to Genevieve for help, and she felt herself unaccountably blush at the thought of touching his bare skin. 'Lily was just asking if you were ready to go.'

'Ooh, you little liar!' smirked Nattie from behind Christian's back. Genevieve glared at her.

Christian left his mobile with Jonjo, and they set off for the distant water's edge – the tide was out. Lily-Rose scampered on ahead, a castle-shaped plastic bucket swinging like a handbag from her wrist. Genevieve was again reminded of the past, of herself and Christian, hand in hand, walking this very same stretch of beach. She wondered if he was thinking the same. They soon caught up with Lily-Rose and, holding her wrap-around skirt above her knees, Genevieve ventured into the first rush of shallow water.

Christian, beside her, glanced back up the beach. 'They all rely on you heavily, don't they?'

Genevieve shrugged. 'Do they? I've never thought of it quite that way.'

'They'd find it hard to manage without you.'

'They did before I came back.'

'But that was when your mother was here.'

'Look! *Look!*'

Both Genevieve and Christian bent down to see what Lily-Rose was pointing at: it was a starfish, about the size of Lily's hand. 'Can I have it? Can I put it in my bucket to take home?'

It was obviously dead. 'I don't see why not,' Genevieve said.

The little girl picked it up and carefully put it into her bucket. 'I'm going to show Mummy my lucky starfish,' she said proudly. She ran off excitedly, hopping skilfully around the pebbles and other people on the beach. They watched her until she was safely with the family.

'Shall we walk to the rocks?' Christian said.

They walked along the shore. As they approached the rocks, a group of teenage girls, who had been using them to sunbathe on, swam off. Dangling their legs over the side of the sun-warmed rocks, Genevieve touched his arm lightly. He turned to face her.

'This is where I pushed you into the water, isn't it, the day we met?'

'It's also where I thought you were the nicest and prettiest girl I'd ever met.'

'Your memory must be playing tricks on you. I was never a pretty child.'

He shook his head. 'I'm not going to argue with you, Genevieve, so be quiet and accept the compliment.'

His words, said so forcibly, amused her. She swirled the water round with her feet, enjoying the sensation of her toes being gently pushed apart.

'Genevieve?'

She turned back to him. 'Yes?'

'Do you remember me saying at breakfast that I like to be honest and play it straight?'

'I do. But if this is a complaint about the standard of your accommodation, or that you're suffering from indigestion, forget it; you're not getting a discount on your bill.'

He smiled, but somehow still managed to look serious. 'No, it has nothing to do with that. It's something I want you to know. Several weeks ago I stupidly tried to kiss you; at the time you wisely pointed out that it wasn't a good idea. As we both know, you were right, and for two reasons: one, our complicated past, and two, because I was in a relationship.' He paused, just long enough for her to see how hard this was for him. And for her to feel guilty that she already knew what he was about to say. 'The thing is,' he continued, 'I'm not in a relationship any more. Caroline and I . . . well, I've ended things with her. I just wanted you to know that.'

Genevieve didn't bother to feign surprise. Instead, she said, 'And the reason?'

'Do you really need to ask that?'

'I think I do.'

He took a deep breath. 'It wouldn't have been fair to go on seeing her, not when – ' He broke off and swallowed. 'Genevieve, you must have realised that ever since our paths crossed again, I haven't been able to get you out of my head.' He turned away. 'I promised myself I wouldn't say anything, but I guess I'm being selfish. I want you to know how I feel. More than that, I want to know how you feel, too.'

She touched his leg to make him look at her. 'Perhaps it's nothing more than curiosity you're feeling? A desire to relive the past.'

He blinked. 'All I know is that I can't think of you and not wonder what it might have been like between us. It's always there.'

'Some might call it unfinished business.'

'No. It's more than that. There's something between us. Something that will always link us.'

She was surprised by his vehemence. Surprised too by her calm reaction.

'So where does that leave us?' he said. He looked and sounded wretched.

'Precariously placed, I'd say.'

He frowned and stared hard at her lips. 'What placed?'

'Precariously,' she repeated, trying to speak more distinctly, even though she knew it annoyed him and didn't really help. 'We either do nothing and go on wondering for the rest of our lives what might have been, or we throw caution to the wind and you try kissing me.' So much for her head ruling her heart!

His solemn face softened instantly. 'I think I favour the second choice.'

'Me too.'

He had just raised his hand to her neck, and tilted his head to lean into her, when he hesitated and drew back. Following his gaze, over her shoulder, she turned to see Jonjo hurrying towards them, waving Christian's mobile. The look on Jonjo's face made her reach out for Christian's hand.

'I'm sorry, Christian,' he said, 'but it's your mother. The hospital's just been in touch. We need to get going.'

Part Four

34

Christian's mother died three days later. She spent the last thirty-six hours of her life in a coma with Christian at her side. Saddened by his loss, Genevieve was touched when Jonjo phoned to say that Christian wanted her to be at the funeral. Polly too, to keep her company.

Now, as Genevieve turned off the A44 and joined the B4361 heading towards Ludlow, happy memories of staying with Christian all those years ago, came flooding back. Along with some fond memories of his mother. Ella May had been a kind, straightforward woman with a sense of humour, not averse to teasing her husband or her son. Genevieve had always been struck by how supportive she was of Christian, without overprotecting him. A lot of mothers might have wrapped him in cotton wool. Not Ella; she had always encouraged him to go one step further than he thought he was capable of.

Ella had been a considerate host as well, and had always made Genevieve feel part of the family, whether it was at Pendine Cottage or here in Shropshire. During one of Genevieve's visits to Pendine Cottage, in a light-hearted moment after they'd been playing cards, Ella had told Genevieve that she would have liked more children, especially a daughter. Certainly, in Christian's current situation, a brother or sister would help to share the load with him. Though Polly was impractical, and Nattie a pain on occasion, Genevieve knew that in a crisis they would be there for each other. From what Jonjo had told her, Christian had no close family members to turn to.

'There are plenty of ageing rellies he hardly knows,' Jonjo had said on the phone, 'but no one who really matters to him.'

Following the directions Christian had emailed, Genevieve turned into a winding country lane lined either side with verdant hawthorn and wilting cow parsley. It was instantly familiar. She recalled a time when Christian had chased her down it. The rain had recently stopped and, wearing a pair of his too-large Wellington boots, she'd tripped and pitched, almost headfirst, into a squelchy ditch. He'd been so concerned that he didn't realise, until he was pulling her out, that she was laughing and not crying. Catching him unawares, to get her own back, she'd pushed him into the muddy ditch. They'd returned home wet and filthy. After they'd washed and changed, Mrs May had laid out an old-fashioned tea of hot buttered crumpets in front of the fire.

The house was just as Genevieve remembered it: a pretty, half-timbered, thatched cottage (originally it had been two) with an off-centre porch swamped in honeysuckle. Sunshine bounced off the polished, leaded windows, and Genevieve felt heartened that the house hadn't been allowed to slide into decline. She parked the car next to Christian's Volvo and nudged Polly.

'We're here, Polly. Wakey, wakey.' Having been up since five, Genevieve would have liked the opportunity to doze as well. Determined in some small way to help Christian, she had offered to take care of feeding the funeral guests and had put together a modest buffet. It was in the boot and she hoped it had survived the journey.

Leaving Polly to stir herself, Genevieve got out of the car and went round to the boot, but before she'd got it open, she heard footsteps. Christian was coming towards her, dressed in a dark suit with a white shirt, open at the neck. She had never seen him in a suit before and at once thought how dazzlingly handsome he looked. Her heart fluttered and she felt a tightening in her chest. But his face, pale and sombre, showed her the inappropriateness of her reaction. Without a word passing between them, they embraced. Held within his firm grasp, she could feel the tension in his body.

The funeral was to be held in a small local church that would take them no more than ten minutes to reach. The procession of cars moved sedately along the narrow country lanes. Following behind in Jonjo's Discovery, Genevieve sat in the back and stared out at the flowering hedgerows; she left Polly and Jonjo to their murmured conversation in front. Christian had wanted her to sit in the lead car with him, but there hadn't been room: a surprising number of distant relatives had turned up. They had appeared *en masse* for a pre-service glass of sherry. Confirming what Jonjo had told Genevieve, Christian admitted they were practically unknown to him.

By the time Jonjo had found somewhere to park, they were the last to arrive. They slipped in at the back of the crowded church – friends and neighbours had shown up in force – but within seconds Christian appeared and said he'd saved them a seat at the front with him.

'Please,' he said, taking hold of Genevieve's hand, 'I don't want to be alone.'

The service was much the same as any other funeral she had been to: hymns were sung, prayers were spoken, emotions were strained. But then the vicar, looking straight at Christian, asked him to step forward to say a few words about his mother. Letting go of Genevieve's hand, which he'd been holding during most of the service, he walked towards the lectern. From the pocket of his jacket, he pulled out a piece of paper and unfolded it slowly, the microphone in front of him picking up the noise, amplifying it to a crackling roar. Oblivious, he stared at his audience and visibly composed himself.

'All mothers have an extraordinary capacity to love and to encourage,' he began, 'and mine was no exception. She taught me to love and respect others as I would want to be loved and respected. It's a tall order sometimes, and I know I've fallen short more times than I care to admit, but my mother never did. She—' His voice cracked and he briefly closed his eyes. Genevieve's throat clenched and she willed him to carry on. 'She was unfailingly constant,' he continued, his tone less clear, 'a constant beacon of love and hope. Someone we could all aspire to be. I shall miss her more than I can say.' He bowed his head, folded the piece of paper and stepped away.

Around her Genevieve could hear people, including Polly and Jonjo, clearing their throats and blowing their noses. She blinked hard and kept her gaze on the flower arrangements either side of the coffin. She felt, rather than saw, Christian take his seat beside her. She turned to face him and mouthed the words, 'Well done. That was beautiful.'

He nodded and squeezed her hand. 'Thank you.'

He thanked her again when they were back at the house and the last of the guests were leaving. Jonjo and Polly were at the door, waving them off.

'You've been such a help,' Christian said as she moved round the sitting room with a tray, gathering plates and glasses.

'It's nothing,' she said. 'Canapés aren't difficult to make, just a bit fiddly and time-consuming.'

He took the tray from her. 'But you must have been up so early to make them.'

'I was. But I shall sleep well tonight.'

'You are staying, aren't you?'

'If the offer's still on. Yes.'

Jonjo and Polly came back into the room. Jonjo said, 'I blame you, Genevieve. If the food hadn't been so good, we would have been shot of that lot hours ago.'

Christian smiled – the first time he had that day – and said, 'I don't know about the rest of you, but I've had enough. I vote we leave the rest of the tidying up till later. Let's go and sit in the garden with a bottle of wine.'

It was only ten o'clock when Genevieve started to yawn. 'It's no good,' she apologised, stifling yet another yawn, 'I have to go to bed.'

Everyone else agreed that they were tired too, that it had been a long day. After locking up and turning out the lights, they went upstairs. Just as Genevieve remembered, there was a long, L-shaped landing with five bedrooms and two bathrooms leading off. Christian opened the door of the first room and told Polly that it was hers. Next door was Jonjo's room, and going further along the landing, missing out his parents' room, he said, 'I thought you'd like to sleep in the room you stayed in before. If you need anything, I'm in the room the other side of the bathroom.'

It felt slightly comical as they all stood on the landing and said goodnight to each other. Typically it was Jonjo who summed up the moment. 'Anyone for a bedroom farce?' he asked, with a mischievous grin. He kissed Polly on the cheek, and after watching them disappear to their respective rooms, Christian said, 'Well, then, I'll say goodnight. Remember, anything you need, I'm—'

'I know; you're just the other side of the bathroom.'

She had only been in bed a short while when she heard footsteps, followed by the sound of a door creaking open, then shutting. Jonjo and Polly, no doubt. She smiled sleepily to herself. The bedroom farce had begun.

She didn't know how long she'd been asleep, but she awoke with a start. Footsteps. She could hear footsteps. Someone was in the house. A burglar! Her mouth went dry and fear bubbled up inside her. She tried hard to keep calm. To think logically. To put the night of the robbery out of her mind. It's probably Christian, she told herself. Or maybe Jonjo and Polly. But what if it wasn't?

Her heart began to beat faster. She pushed back the duvet. She couldn't just lie here. She had to check. She hadn't acted fast enough once before, but not this time. She crept onto the landing and stood for a moment to make out where the noise was coming from and to orientate herself.

She took the stairs slowly, grasping the balustrade and holding her breath. For a second she wondered what the hell she was doing. If it was a burglar, what was she going to do?

Go back upstairs, her head told her. Knock on Christian's door. Get help.

But he wouldn't hear, would he?

Knock on Jonjo's door, then.

No. He was in with Polly.

Not knowing quite how she'd got there, she found herself at the bottom of the stairs. Where was the noise now? But she couldn't hear anything other than her pulse banging like an enormous drum inside her head. This is madness, she thought. I shouldn't be doing this. Yet still her body betrayed her and she reached for a heavy vase on the hall table as her feet carried her forward.

To the sitting room.

Burglars always made for the sitting room first. For the hi-fi. The video. Antique knick-knacks. Stuff they could easily sell on with no questions asked. She pushed open the door and stepped in. The french doors were open, the curtains billowing. She was right! A gust of cool air rushed at her and she knew what she had to do. She had to fetch help. She couldn't do this alone.

She turned to retrace her steps, but the sight of a shadowy figure coming into the room rooted her to the spot. The vase slipped from her hands and she screamed.

But no sound came out of her mouth. *Oh God, it couldn't happen again!* The blood drained from her, her legs buckled and she fell to the ground.

She came to with a painful jolt of panicky fear and let out a small cry.

Arms held her and a voice said, 'Genevieve, it's okay. It's me, Christian.'

Confused and light-headed, she tried to focus. Christian's face became clear. As did the reason she'd come downstairs. *The burglar!* Where was he? Agitated, she looked around, took in that she was lying on the sofa, that there was a lamp on, and that Christian was kneeling in front of her. Beside him, on the carpet, was a broken vase, and behind him, the french doors were open and the curtains still moving. Her agitation grew and she sat up with a jerk.

'Have you called the police? Did he get away?'

'No, Gen. There's no need. It was me you saw. I'm so sorry I frightened you. I couldn't sleep and—'

'No. I would have recognised you. Of course I would. It wasn't you. It was . . .'

He took her hands in his and rubbed them gently. 'It was dark, Gen. There were no lights on. You couldn't see properly.'

She forced herself to listen to him, to believe what he was saying. Looking at the broken bits of china, she slowly realised that the only intruder had been the one inside her head. She covered her face with her hands. 'Oh, God. I'm so sorry. I feel so—' Stupidly she began to tremble. When he took her in his arms she started to cry.

'It's okay,' he murmured. 'It's my fault, I shouldn't have scared you.' He held her close, and she cried all the more.

She had had to tell the policemen all about that dreadful night with George and Cecily, but she'd told no one else exactly what had gone on. She'd told Gran the most, but each time she had been tempted to unburden herself fully, the thought of reliving the robbery was too much and she was almost physically sick.

But now she knew that the time had come to tell someone. She didn't want to be haunted by the memories any longer. Wrapped in Christian's arms, she felt safe enough to relive the trauma.

When the two masked men had demanded the code for the safe and George had refused, the robbery had turned into something altogether more terrifying. One of the men had seized hold of Cecily and beaten her savagely, kicking and punching her frail body, his boots smashing into her in a terrifying frenzy of mindless violence. It was only the other man pulling him off that made him stop. The terror and pain in Cecily's eyes, as the two men then argued and yelled at each other, was too much to bear, and both

Genevieve and George had tried to shuffle over to her so they could comfort her. But the men, seeing what they were doing, stepped in and the more violent of the two struck out and viciously kicked George. He then turned on Genevieve, catching the side of her head with such a ferocious blow she was knocked back against the wall, to feel a further thud of pain. The sickening look of pure sadistic pleasure on his face had frightened her most and it haunted her still. He ripped the tape from George's mouth, just long enough for him to give them the code for the safe. After they'd taken the jewellery and whatever else they wanted, they left.

As soon as Genevieve was sure they were alone, she wriggled to slide her wrists, which were tied behind her back, under her body and brought them up to her mouth to remove the tape, using her teeth she slowly released her hands. She then shuffled across the room to George and Cecily and uncovered their mouths. Almost as though opening her mouth and breathing in a gulp of oxygen was too much for her, the old lady grimaced and cried out.

By the time the ambulance arrived, Cecily was already dead: her heart – weakened by an earlier heart attack – had failed. Poor George never recovered from the shock. He died a month later in hospital following a massive stroke. Although desperate to go home to her family, Genevieve had stayed on in the house on her own and visited George every day; she'd held his hand, helped him to eat, and read to him, albeit very badly. He and his wife had no children. They'd both been nearly ninety and most of their friends had already died, so Genevieve was his only regular visitor, other than his solicitor and accountant.

At last she fell quiet.

Christian said nothing, just held her hand and stroked her hair.

The relief at having finally unburdened herself was so great that Genevieve began to cry silent tears.

Christian continued to hold her close. 'It's okay, Genevieve, you're safe now.'

It was light when Genevieve awoke. She turned over and saw that Christian had been true to his word. There he was, asleep in the chair in the corner of her bedroom, a blanket sliding off his legs. She had been so shaken that he had refused to leave her alone. He'd been so very kind and loving. He'd sat with her for more than an hour, passing her tissue after tissue, holding her, reassuring her, then making her a drink and bringing her upstairs to bed. It was a miracle they hadn't disturbed the others.

Feeling groggy from all the crying, she remembered how brave people thought she'd been during and after the robbery; how well she'd coped. But she hadn't coped in the right way. Just as she'd bottled up her feelings about her grandfather when he'd died, she'd tried to suppress the horror of that night. During the robbery, when they'd had their mouths taped, they'd been unable to cry out or scream. She realised now that was why she hadn't been able to scream last night in the sitting room. Her brain had played some kind of sick trick on her. Yet reliving her terror had released something inside her. Christian had suggested that maybe now, after shedding so many tears, she would let the memories go.

'You need to be able to remember what happened without reliving it,' he'd said. 'Once you can do that, you'll know you're over it.'

She looked across the room to Christian and hoped he was right. He was still sleeping soundly. The blanket had slipped off his legs now but she resisted the urge to get out of bed and cover him again. Instead she studied his face, the face she'd memorised as a teenager, the face she'd idolised and looked up to, the face she'd thought she'd always love. Was it possible to love him again? Was that what he wanted? More to the point, was it what *she* wanted?

She sighed and thought how unfair it was that while she was asleep she undoubtedly looked awful – mouth open, hair to hell – but Christian managed to look even more attractive than usual. Younger, too. The temptation to wake him with a kiss was so strong she had to remind herself why she was here. They had buried his mother yesterday; it wasn't the moment.

There had been no opportunity since that day on the beach, when they'd so very nearly kissed, to talk about what they'd discussed or what the consequences might be if they really did resurrect their old relationship. In the circumstances she sensed that, for now, all Christian needed was a friend.

35

Genevieve had thought for a long time that the most momentous events in her life had all taken place during the summer months.

She thought this now as she and Polly were driving home to Paradise House. Polly hadn't said anything but, judging from the radiant look of her, Genevieve didn't have to be a genius to work out that her sister had spent the night with Jonjo and had loved every moment of it. There had been no sign of the two of them at breakfast. After Genevieve and Christian had given up waiting for them, Christian had suggested they make the most of the early morning sun.

'What will you do with the house?' Genevieve had asked when they were settled in the garden.

'The sensible thing would be to sell it, but I can't think of doing that yet. It's too soon.'

'Of course. I didn't mean to sound insensitive.'

'You couldn't be insensitive if you tried, Genevieve.'

Frowning, she said, 'You really mustn't make the mistake of thinking too well of me.'

A plump woodpigeon landed heavily on a branch of the chestnut tree at the end of the garden, and they both watched it for a while as it tried to steady itself on the flimsy, wobbling branch.

Christian said, 'I know you might not want to talk about what happened last night, Genevieve, but if you do—'

'It's okay,' she interrupted, 'I think I'm all talked out on that particular subject.'

He smiled ruefully. 'Are you sure? Or are you telling me to back off?'

'A bit of both. I think I need time to recover from how stupid I've been.'

'You haven't been stupid. Far from it. You've been incredibly brave.'

'It doesn't feel that way.'

'That's because you're always so hard on yourself.'

'There you go again, thinking too well of me.'

He shook his head, but he was smiling. 'I give up. You just won't take a compliment, will you?'

'Not without a reasonable fight,' she laughed.

Up in the chestnut tree, the woodpigeon flapped its wings and flew off clumsily.

Christian stood abruptly. 'Come with me,' he said. 'There's something I want to show you.'

He led her to the bottom of the garden, to the summer house, the roof of which was almost entirely hidden beneath a fairy-tale drift of pastel-pink climbing roses. Swollen flowers tumbled gloriously, their fragrance sweet on the morning air; bees hummed drunkenly from flower to flower. When Christian opened the door of the summer house, a further fusion of smells greeted them – sun-warmed cedar wood, mildewed canvas seats, musty old garden tools. Genevieve couldn't spot anything especially worth looking at in amongst the clutter – badminton racquets, a trug and an assortment of plastic seed trays and clay flowerpots – but when he closed the door and came towards her, she realised exactly why he'd brought her here.

At long, long last, his face inches from hers, his hands placed either side of her face, he kissed her. It was thirteen years since they'd kissed, but his mouth was so recognisable against hers that the intervening years fell away. Everything about the soft warmth of his lips, the gentle pressure of his fingers on her skin, the feel of his body pressing into hers, was the same. How could a body remember that? How was it possible? But it was, and she kissed him back with a desire that made him strengthen his hold on her.

'You have no idea how much I've been longing to do that,' he said, when he released her. 'And how many times I very nearly did but always lost my nerve, or someone or something got in the way.'

'Is that why we're hiding in here?'

He smiled. 'Yes. To be sure of not being interrupted.'

'I think Polly and Jonjo have got other things on their minds.'

'In that case, I'd say we owe it to ourselves to make the most of their preoccupation with each other.'

They kissed and kissed, and would have gone on doing so if the summer house hadn't been so hot and airless, and if Genevieve hadn't promised her father she'd get back to Paradise House that afternoon.

The first person Genevieve and Polly saw as they drove into Angel Sands was Adam. He was driving out of the village. There was no other traffic about, and Genevieve flashed her lights. They pulled alongside each other.

'Hi there, you two. How was the funeral?'

'How did you know we'd been to one?' asked Genevieve.

He tapped his nose. 'Usual sources. Either of you fancy a drink in The Arms this evening? It's quiz night.'

Polly nodded her agreement, and Genevieve, having spoken to her father before setting off, and knowing there were no bookings for dinner that evening, said, 'You're on. What time?'

'The quiz starts at eight, so I'll call for you at twenty to. See you.' With a loud pip-pip of his horn, he drove off.

All was quiet at home. The guests were out, as was Lily-Rose, who was down at Gran's.

'I told you we could manage without you,' her father said, as he helped them in with their overnight bags and the cool boxes Genevieve had used to transport the food.

'We haven't had one single emergency,' joined in Nattie, when they went through to the kitchen.

'I never said you wouldn't be able to cope,' Genevieve said.

'Yeah, but the way you carry on, you'd think you'd need to be a brain surgeon to keep this place going.'

'Not a bit of it. I always knew if you pulled your finger out you could do it.'

Nattie laughed. 'Hey, you're on top form, girl. Funerals must bring out the best in you. So how was it?'

Polly answered for her. 'You should have been there, Nattie. Christian spoke so movingly of his mother during the service. He had us all in tears.'

'Even your crazy fella, Jonjo Fitz?'

Polly blushed. 'He's really quite serious when you get him alone.'

Nattie narrowed her eyes. 'You've slept with him, haven't you?'

Polly's colour deepened.

Nattie was triumphant. '*Yes!* I can always tell. Was he any good? With a fit body like his, I bet he was stupendous. Wow, Polly, I'm almost envious.'

It was all too much for Dad. 'For heaven's sake, girls! I'm your father, I don't need to hear about your sex lives. In fact, I'd prefer to believe you didn't *have* sex lives! If anyone wants me, I'll be down at your grandmother's, fetching Lily.' With that, he marched out of the kitchen.

Nattie closed the door and leant against it so there was no escape. 'So come on, Polly, divvy up the details on your sweet little duet.'

'Nattie! Leave the poor girl alone.'

'Be quiet, Gen, we'll get to you in a minute. And don't look so horrified. You didn't honestly expect me to believe you'd stay the night with Christian and not take advantage of him while he was in a vulnerable state, did you? Okay, Poll, while Gen's finding something to hit me with, fire away. Let's have it.'

Polly sighed and sat down. She looked as happy as they'd ever seen her. 'He's asked me to go to Hong Kong with him.'

'*Hong Kong?* Whatever for?'

'Never mind travel plans, what was the nookie like?'

'Natalie Baxter, will you, just once in your life, shut up!' Genevieve turned to Polly. 'So why Hong Kong?'

'It's a business trip. He's branching out. He wants to sell his own brand of leisure and sportswear and he's meeting with some potential suppliers. He wants me to go with him.'

'When?'

'Friday. It's the end of term for all my schools, so I'll be free. But I haven't said I'll go. Not yet.'

This latest piece of news which, typically, Polly had kept to herself throughout the journey home from Ludlow, so dominated the conversation for the rest of the afternoon and evening that Genevieve and Polly forgot all about the quiz night Adam had invited them to. It was only seeing his face at the back door that reminded them.

To their surprise, Nattie said, 'I'm not doing anything tonight. I could come with you. Dad? Do you mind babysitting Lily-Rose for me?'

Adam looked awkward. 'Actually, I was going to invite your father to join us.'

Nattie looked as though she'd just been slapped. She turned to their father.

'That's all right, Nattie,' he said. 'You go and enjoy yourself. Another time, Adam. Thanks for the offer.'

They walked down the hill to the village, Nattie and Polly in front, Adam and Genevieve behind. It was a beautiful summer's evening, and the air was drowsy with a still warmth. Plenty of people were still on the beach. The Power Boat People were winching their boats and jet skis out of the water, making their usual unsociable din and getting in the way of a large group of people playing a makeshift game of French cricket.

Genevieve told Adam about Polly going to Hong Kong with Jonjo.

'I thought there was an extra twinkle in her eye when I saw you in the car this afternoon,' he said. 'If it's love, it suits her. So what about you and lover-boy? How's it going?'

'Oh, you know, so, so.'

'Still kidding yourselves you're just good friends?'

When she didn't answer him, he said, 'So things have moved on, have they?'

She gave him what she was hoped was an enigmatic smile and changed the subject. 'By the way, nice handling of Nats earlier. The look on her face was a treat. She looked well and truly wrong-footed.'

He slowed his step. 'Are you accusing me of something, Gen?'

'No. But you have to admit, the result was very satisfying. She's so used to taking people for granted.'

There was a good turnout for the quiz. Participants were grouped into teams of five and the atmosphere was fiercely competitive. The teams all had names and, as team captain, Adam had called theirs Adam's Angels, much to Nattie's disgust. She was further annoyed when she asked the adjudicator for some upfront points, claiming they were at a disadvantage, only being four – Adam, Genevieve, Polly and herself – but the landlord overruled her and said if anything, they had an advantage. 'You've got

Polly,' he said, 'and she has more brains than the rest of everyone else put together.'

Polly soon proved her worth and was probably the only one in the entire pub who knew the answer to question five: according to John's Gospel in the New Testament, what was the name of the servant who had his ear cut off by Simon Peter? Mutterings of 'unfair' and 'fetch the bloody parson' were heard. Taking the pencil from Adam, Polly wrote down the answer – 'Malchus'.

'You sure about that?' asked Nattie.

'Don't be stupid,' said Adam. 'Polly's never wrong.'

The next question gave Genevieve the chance to shine.

'What is the middle name of J.B. Fletcher, the crime-writing sleuth from *Murder, She Wrote?*'

She grabbed the pencil and wrote the answer: 'Beetris.'

'How the hell do you know that?' asked Nattie, crossing it out and spelling it correctly – Beatrice.

'From watching too much telly with Gran.'

'Ssh, you two, we're on a roll.'

'Ssh yourself, Adam Kellar!'

He gave her sister such a stern look, Genevieve witnessed a miracle right before her eyes: Nattie looked offended.

It may have been the effect of too much wine and the excitement of Adam's Angels winning the quiz, along with a whole twenty-five pounds and a bottle of Cava, but Genevieve wasn't in the mood to go straight home afterwards. 'I fancy sitting on the beach for a while,' she said. 'Any takers?'

Nattie pointed out that it was pitch black and Polly said she wanted an early night.

'More like you want to rush back and indulge in some hot phone sex with Jonjo Fitz,' Nattie teased.

'That just leaves you and me, Adam. How about it?'

After waving the others off, they went and sat on the pebbles.

'How about we open our prize?' Genevieve said.

He pulled a face. 'You're on your own, there, kid. My Cava drinking days are a thing of the past. But if it's something special you want to celebrate, I'm willing to make an exception.'

She laughed. 'You're fishing again, aren't you?'

'Well?'

'Okay, he kissed me.'

Adam didn't miss a beat. 'I should think he did. An attractive girl like you. And did you kiss him back? Oh, Gen, you did, didn't you?' He tutted. 'What a tart you've become! I do hope you're not going to shock me with any further revelations. You know what a chaste, innocent boy I am.'

'No, I was very well-behaved,' she said primly. 'Mouth to mouth contact only.'

Laughing, he put his arm round her. 'Keeping him keen, eh?'

'It wasn't like that.'

'So what was it like?'

She sighed and rested her head on his shoulder and stared up at the velvety night sky. 'It was beautiful. Just like I remembered it.'

His voice low, Adam said, 'You will be careful, won't you, Gen? This guy obviously has quite an effect on you.'

But she didn't answer him. It was too late to think about being careful. Her heart had well and truly won the battle over her head.

36

In the days that followed, Genevieve was filled with longing to be with Christian. In the same way that as a teenager she'd devoted hours to daydreaming of him, she was constantly distracted by thoughts of the two of them in the summer house. How pleased she was that he'd seized the moment! Occasionally, though, slivers of doubt found their way into her thoughts. Were they doing the right thing? Would getting involved again turn out to be a terrible mistake?

Despite Nattie's best efforts to extract the story from her – had she or had she not been stupid enough to sleep with Christian? – Genevieve had told no one, other than Adam, how she felt about Christian. Perhaps it was because she didn't dare put her emotions into words. It might be asking for trouble, tempting fate, and the past, to crush what was still so fragile.

She kept all this to herself, as she did the happy realisation that since the night of Ella May's funeral, when she'd been so terrified, she had begun to put the robbery behind her. She would never forget the savage cruelty she'd witnessed and experienced but, as she wrote in one of her emails to Christian, she was sure it had less of a hold on her now.

She knew from Christian's emails that there was no chance of seeing him for the foreseeable future; he was snowed under with work as well as sorting through his mother's things.

'I wish you were here to help me deal with her personal stuff,' he wrote. 'The clothes I can handle, but I simply don't know what to do with the letters and keepsakes. There are boxes of letters she and Dad wrote to each other before they were married. What on earth do I do with them?'

His question made Genevieve think of all the letters she and Christian had exchanged as teenagers, especially the ones of his she had burned after a particularly gruesome bingeing session, when her anger and self-hate was at its zenith.

He had asked if there was any way she could get away from Paradise House so they could spend some time together, but frustratingly it was impossible. It was peak season and everything was happening at once. The big news was that Dad was leaving this morning for New Zealand. Polly was travelling to Heathrow with him – unsurprisingly, she had agreed to go to Hong Kong with Jonjo – and their flights were only an hour apart.

Nattie, not to be left out, had received an invitation to a school reunion and was going away for a couple of days. As usual she was expecting Genevieve to step into the breach and not only hold the fort single-handedly, but take care of Lily-Rose as well. When Genevieve had hinted that looking after Lily-Rose on this occasion might be the straw that broke the camel's back, Nattie wheedled, 'Oh, please, Gen, I can hardly take Lily-Rose with me, can I? Please say you'll have her? Pretty please with cherries on top? And don't forget, now that Gran's back to normal, she could always help you.'

Genevieve had given in to her sister, on the condition that when Nattie returned, she'd cover for Genevieve so she could have the day off.

Now, since time was getting on and there was a full house for breakfast, she drained her mug of tea, brushed the toast crumbs off her plate for the birds, and told herself not to worry. She'd cope. But as she walked up to the house, she couldn't shake off the feeling that she was being taken advantage of. Reminded of what Christian had said on the beach – *they all rely on you so heavily* – she wondered if this was how her mother had felt. If so, was that why she had upped sticks and run?

Till now, because Serena had left without any warning or apparent contrition, Genevieve's sympathy had lain mostly with her father, but now she wasn't so sure. What if their mother had grown tired of always being the glue that held things together? For that was what she'd been; Genevieve could see that clearly now. Cut through her mother's irrepressible romantic notions, the lapses of memory and cock-eyed way of looking at life, and what did you have? You had Serena always there for them.

After kissing Polly goodbye and hugging her father, Genevieve watched him climb into his Land Rover; he looked like a man on a mission, jaw set firm, shoulders squared. After weeks of dithering, he was at last embarking on what had to be the most important journey he would ever make. Though at times Genevieve had considered him a coward for not acting sooner, in her heart she knew he wasn't. He was just human, as emotionally frail as the next person. She hoped his nerve would hold out. But thank goodness he had Polly with him for the journey to the airport. Nattie, standing beside Genevieve, was even now giving him last-minute instructions guaranteed to make matters worse. Comments such as, 'Tell her to stop being so selfish,' and 'Drag her back by the hair if you have to,' were not only a case of pots and kettles, but highly unhelpful.

Not long after they'd left, Nattie took Lily-Rose down to the beach and Tubby stopped by with a delivery of fruit and veg and an update on the Talent Contest. To his delight, tickets were flying out the door for participants and audience alike; it was going to be a night to remember. Genevieve would have liked to talk more with him about her own contribution to the event, but she didn't have time. She had plans, and in particular a Plan with a capital P.

An hour later she was in Tenby. It took a while to find somewhere to park. After locking the car, she set off on foot for the centre of the walled town. The day was hot – the heat-wave was showing no sign of cooling. She wove a purposeful path through the hordes of dawdling, sun-tanned holidaymakers, and on past the imposing church of St Mary's with its elegant spire. She was tempted to go inside and get down on bended knee to do a bit of negotiating – a sinner's soul in return for a generous act of benevolence – but pressed on ahead until she was standing outside the bank.

Loans, so Adam had told her when they'd been sitting on the beach following the quiz, were two a penny. She was about to discover if that was true.

She pushed against the door and went inside. The air conditioning was cool and made her realise how hot and clammy she was, a combination of weather, nerves and the fact that she was wearing a jacket. She had deliberately made an appointment at this particular branch, not the one in Pembroke that the rest of her family used, because she wanted to keep her affairs private. She didn't want anyone in her family knowing what she was up to, not until she was sure of it herself.

She was shown through to a small office where Mrs Hughes, the Loans Manager, would see her. Unlike the outer office, Mrs Hughes' office didn't have the benefit of air conditioning; the stuffy heat hit her at once. A crisp-haired woman in a lightweight suit rose from the other side of the desk.

'Sorry about the stifling temperature,' she said, 'but there's nothing we can do. We've been waiting for the engineer to show up, but apparently he's inundated. Please, sit down. Now then, what can I do to help you, Miss Baxter?'

The woman seemed friendly enough. Genevieve opened her folder and leaned forward in her seat. She spent the next ten minutes setting out her plans in as businesslike a manner as she could manage, remembering all that Adam had told her.

As she let the bank door close slowly behind her, she stood on the pavement and awarded herself a small pat on the back. It wasn't exactly in the bag, but things looked promising. Her next stop was just off St Julian's Street, where she had arranged to see a solicitor, Mr Saunders. She emerged not long after and stood once more on the pavement in the bright sunshine. She was just thinking she ought to give herself some kind of treat to mark the occasion when she saw a familiar smiling face across the busy street. She waited for a break in the traffic and crossed the road.

'Adam Kellar, are you stalking me?'

'I prefer to see myself as your guardian angel. So come on, future

Businesswoman of the Year, shall I take you for a celebratory drink and you tell me how it went?'

'Oh, I think we can do better than that. Let's have an ice-cream down on the beach.'

He looked doubtfully at his suit. 'No chance. Not even for you.'

'Okay then, we'll find a nice clean bench for you to sit on.'

Genevieve led the way. They pushed through the crowds along St Julian's Street, with its pretty hanging flower baskets, past the Hope and Anchor pub and the stately houses of Lexden Terrace. They got stuck behind a family with a pushchair and a panting dog. When they reached the harbour, they bought two 99s with all the trimmings. In the gardens that overlooked the Prince Albert Memorial and St Catherine's Island they spotted one free seat and quickly claimed it. Genevieve held Adam's ice-cream while he took off his jacket and laid it carefully on the back of the bench. She noticed with approval the muted tie that he was now loosening and the absence of his faithful gold bracelet. He was buffing up a treat these days.

'Why, in the name of all that's wonderful are you wearing a suit on a day like this, Adam?'

'The same reason you're dressed to impress in your cute little power number.' He indicated the skirt and jacket, an outfit that only saw the light of day for special occasions – she'd worn it for Christian's mother's funeral. 'Only difference is, my business was conducted over lunch.'

'So what are you up to now? Another caravan park?'

'No.' There was something oddly evasive in his tone.

'What, then?'

His expression serious, he said, 'Look, this is strictly between you and me. I don't want anyone knowing yet, but I'm thinking of selling up.'

Genevieve was shocked. 'You're kidding! But why? And what will you do? You're much too young to retire.'

He licked his ice-cream. 'Who said anything about retiring? No, the truth is, I'm getting itchy palms, which is always a sign I need a new challenge.'

'What do you have in mind?'

'Mm ... too soon to say. Anyway, tell me how you got on. But first off, how about your dad and Polly? Did they get away on time?'

'They did. Dad promised he'd give me a call from the airport before his flight at seven.'

'And what time's Polly's flight?'

'Ten to six. Jonjo said he'd meet her at the check-in desk at four.'

'Well, fingers crossed all goes to plan. Now, tell me about *your* plans.'

It was good having Adam to confide in, especially as he'd been in on it right from the start, since that night on the beach when she'd first broached the subject.

She recounted her visit to the bank and then her brief meeting with Mr Saunders. 'Nothing's definite, but I've set the wheels in motion. It's a matter of wait and see now.'

'A done deal, I'd say. No question. And as I've said before, if you want any help, just give me a shout.'

When Genevieve was driving home, trying to keep up with Adam's Porsche, it hit her how very upset she'd be if Adam's plans for his future didn't include Angel Sands. If he moved somewhere new to satisfy those itchy palms of his, she would lose her closest friend.

Back at Paradise House, after hurriedly changing out of her dressed-to-impress jacket and skirt so that Nattie didn't catch her in it and start asking questions, Genevieve pushed the excitement of her visit to Tenby from her mind: there were new arrivals to check in, and dinner for two couples to prepare.

She was hulling some strawberries for a Pavlova when the phone rang. It was her father. She could tell straight away from his voice that something was wrong.

'What is it, Dad?' she asked.

'Nothing, Gen. Nothing's wrong.'

'There is. I can tell.' She glanced at the clock above the dresser. 'Has Jonjo turned up to meet Polly?'

'Yes, he was here before us. I've already waved them off.'

'So everything's okay? Dad? You're sure of that?'

The silence told her she was right to worry. More patiently she said, 'What is it, Dad?'

'Oh, Gen, I'm getting cold feet. I am doing the right thing, aren't I? What if I arrive and find there's more going on between your mother and this Pete character than we'd thought?'

Genevieve decided to be firm. 'Either way, Dad, you have to know. But my guess is there really isn't anything going on between them. Mum wouldn't do that to you.' And to boost her father's confidence, she added, 'Mum will get such a kick when you knock on the door and she sees it's you. She'll—'

'I still think I should have spoken to her,' he cut in. 'Surprises are all very well, but if she's not there, if she's gone off somewhere else, what then?'

'Let's worry about that if we have to. For now, just concentrate on boarding that plane and staying positive.'

'You don't think I ought to phone ahead and speak to—'

'Don't you dare! We've been through this before. Mum wants drama and romance from you, not a bloody appointment. Now stop being so feeble!'

'Genevieve, I'm doing my best—'

'No you're not!' she snapped, suddenly filled with fury. 'If you'd done that Mum would never have gone off in the first place.'

Genevieve heard a sharp intake of breath down the line. Mortified at what she'd said, she apologised. 'I'm sorry, Dad, I shouldn't have said that.'

'No, Gen, you're absolutely right.' He spoke firmly. 'I'd better go now. I'll speak to you soon, hopefully with good news.' He rang off.

Genevieve put the phone down. How could she have said such a thing to her father? And where had that anger come from?

But she knew exactly what had made her do it. Picturing herself in Mrs Hughes' office discussing her Plans, she acknowledged the true source of her frustration and anger. If her father couldn't persuade Serena to come home, Genevieve would feel beholden to stay with him at Paradise House. Her own tentative plans would come to nothing.

37

The next morning, as soon as Genevieve had cooked the last plate of bacon and eggs and Nattie had served it, her sister was upstairs throwing a bag together for her school reunion in Cheshire. She was leaving just as soon as she'd fetched Gran to help look after Lily-Rose.

As she scrubbed the grill pan at the sink, feeling distinctly like Cinderella, the phone rang.

'Get that will you?' Genevieve called out to anyone who might hear. Then remembering Polly and her father were somewhere on the other side of the world, she peeled off her rubber gloves and grumbled her way across the kitchen.

It was Donna, to say she was sorry but she wouldn't be making it into work that morning. 'I've been up all night with the trots,' she elaborated. 'I must have lost half a stone. If this carries on my clothes will be hanging off me.'

Genevieve made all the requisite noises of sympathy and went back to the grill pan, muttering under her breath some more. Now she'd have all the rooms to clean on her own, as well as everything else. A cursory knock at the back door announced the arrival of Gran, who, as well-meaning as she was in offering to help out while Dad, Nattie and Polly were away, would very likely add to Genevieve's workload. You're being unfair, she told herself, as Gran came in and at once complained about the heat.

'Mark my words,' she said, flopping into the nearest chair, 'we're in for an almighty storm. Probably tonight. I can feel it in my bones.' Fanning herself with one hand and wiping her forehead with the other, she added, 'I'm not exaggerating, but there's not a breath of air out there.'

'Gran, Nattie was going to fetch you in the car. You shouldn't be rushing around in this weather, it's much too hot.'

'I'm not completely daft, Genevieve. I got a lift from . . . oh, you know, what's-his-name?' She stopped fanning herself and stared into the middle distance. 'Oh, never mind. It'll come to me later. Now then, what can I do to help. Where's Lily-Rose?'

'She's upstairs with Nattie, helping her to pack. And talking of packing, where are your overnight things? You are staying the night, aren't you? If you can manage the stairs, I thought you could have Nattie's room.'

Gran gave her a withering look. 'Of course I can manage the stairs. Really, Genevieve, I'm growing tired of being treated like an old dear. Ever since I bumped my head you've done nothing but—'

'So where's your bag?' Genevieve interjected.

Cut off mid-flow, Gran looked vaguely about her. Her expression suddenly brightened. 'Adam! That's who it was who gave me a lift. I must have left my bag in his porch.'

'And what were you doing in Adam's porch?'

Her grandmother shot her another withering glance. 'I told you, Gen. He gave me a lift here in that fancy car of his.'

Genevieve smiled. 'Adam's car is a *Porsche*, Gran. Not a porch.'

Gran pursed her lips. 'Well, whatever it is, you can take that silly smirk off your face, young lady.'

Making a noisy entrance, Nattie came into the kitchen with Lily-Rose on her back and a large holdall in her hand. 'Hello, Gran. I thought I was supposed to be fetching you.'

'Adam gave me a lift. As I've just been telling your foolish sister.' She looked reproachfully at Genevieve.

Nattie dropped her holdall with a thump, then leaning to one side, carefully manoeuvred her daughter to the floor. 'You'd better be careful, Gran. That man is determined to have one of us Baxter girls.'

Gran chortled. 'Did you hear that, Lily-Rose? I'm going to be Adam's new girlfriend. Wouldn't that be the funniest thing?'

Wrinkling her nose, the little girl came towards her grandmother. Burying her elbows in the old lady's lap, she stared up into her face. 'Mummy says I have to look after the donkeys while she's away. Do you want to help me feed them?'

Gran cupped Lily's face in her hands. 'I will, just as soon as Mummy's gone. We need to give her a proper wave goodbye, don't we?'

Nattie left shortly afterwards, annoyingly taking Genevieve's car because, at the last minute, she discovered her own had a flat battery. Just as well she wasn't thinking of going anywhere, Genevieve thought as she helped Lily-Rose find some carrots for the donkeys.

Genevieve made a beeline for the rooms of those guests who had already left the house. By the time she'd cleaned, vacuumed, emptied the wastepaper bins and made the beds, the other rooms were empty. The last one to clean was the April Showers suite – the room Christian and Jonjo had stayed in. For the second night running there had been no message from Christian last night, and she was halfway to convincing herself he was regretting what they had done and, having satisfied his curiosity, he had gone back to Caroline.

In the bathroom her Cinderella mood intensified as she scrubbed the enamel bath and wished that *she* was swanning off to some school reunion and not Nattie. Bloody hell, she must be fed up! The very thought of making polite chit-chat with her old classmates made her stomach churn. Here she was, thirty years old, yet the taunting memory of being laughed at for spelling like a five-year-old would always be there. Condemned as a slow learner. Nicknamed 'retard'. She scrubbed harder at the tide mark on the bath. Two years ago she had received an invitation to attend a reunion, written by a girl who had been particularly vicious when it came to name-calling, and she had thrown the letter straight in the bin, almost afraid that touching it would transport her back to that humiliating period in her life.

The telephone was ringing. Struggling down the stairs with the vacuum cleaner under one arm and a bucket of cleaning fluids and cloths under the other, thinking it might be her father, she dropped what she was carrying and raced to the kitchen

'Hi, Gen. It's me, Polly.'

Genevieve leaned against the wall. 'Oh, hello, Poll, everything okay? How's Hong Kong?'

'It's amazing. Very beautiful, even if it is raining. And raining like you've never seen. And, Gen, it's so busy. I've never seen so many people squeezed into one small space.'

'You've been out and about already?'

'Hardly at all. We only arrived this afternoon; it's evening for us now. Jonjo and I are going to have dinner and then we're going to bed early. To sleep, that is. We're both exhausted.'

Genevieve could feel hard-done-by Cinders holding back an envious sniffle. Why couldn't she be somewhere exotic, being wined and dined and taken to bed by a gorgeous man, with sleep the furthest thing from his mind?

'Gen? Are you still there? Can you hear me?'

'Sorry, Polly, I ... I was just listening for Lily-Rose. Nattie left earlier.'

'You sound tired. Are you managing all right without us there?'

'Oh, I'm fine. Just a little pushed. Donna's gone down with a stomach bug so I've been tearing round the place on my own. Look, this must be costing a fortune. Give my love to Jonjo. Tell him to take good care of you.'

'He does that already, Gen. I can't believe how lovely he is sometimes. Where do you think he sprang from?'

Genevieve laughed. 'Who cares? Just enjoy yourselves.'

'Have you heard from Christian?' The question brought an instant change of tempo to the conversation.

'Um ... not for a couple of days.'

'I expect he's busy.'

'That'll be it. Anyway, love you.' 'Love you too, Gen. Give Lily a kiss from me. Bye.'

Going back out to the hall to retrieve the vacuum cleaner and bucket of cleaning stuff, Genevieve was suddenly overcome by a desperate weariness, and for no good reason she could think of, a great weight of sadness filled her. She plonked herself on the bottom step of the stairs and sighed. It must be the weather, she thought. It's melting my brain.

As predicted by Gran, the weather broke that night. Lightning lit up the sky with a brilliant luminosity that woke Genevieve with a start. For a second she thought someone had switched on the light in her bedroom. But when the loudest clap of thunder she'd ever heard cracked overhead and rattled the windows, she got out of bed to draw back the curtains and shut the window. Rain was splattering heavily against the glass. She wasn't the least bit afraid of storms, but worried that Lily-Rose might be, she went and checked on her. She was fast asleep, a small foot and an arm hanging over the side of the bed. Genevieve then looked in on Gran, who was also sleeping soundly, outdoing the thunder with the volume of her snoring. On the way back to her room, she heard the murmur of voices from some of the guests downstairs. She sat up in bed so she could watch the diamond-bright lightning ravage the sky. She had often done this as a young child, baffling her mother and father that she could enjoy something so violent.

Eventually she fell asleep. Her last thought was to wonder why her father hadn't phoned. Surely he must have arrived in New Zealand by now.

38

Genevieve stood yawning at the back door, taking in the storm-damaged garden. The lawns and flower beds were untidy with a confetti of crushed petals; fuchsias were toppled, lavatera branches had been snapped off by the weight of drenched foliage, and flower heads on the hydrangea bushes looked weary and sodden. It was a far cry from the glorious sight of yesterday, when it had been bathed in hot late-July sunshine. Initially, the rain must have bounced off the parched, rock-hard lawns, but the continuous downpour had eventually reduced them to a soggy mess that would take days to dry out. And only then, if the rain kept away. It was raining now, just a light drizzle, but it was enough to put a damper on the day, to bring out the waterproofs and umbrellas. At least the air was fresh and clear.

As she suspected it would, breakfast took longer to get through that morning. Guests were in no hurry to embrace the day – these weren't the hardy year-round variety who walked the coastal path no matter what the weather. They trickled slowly down to the dining room, having treated themselves to a lie-in and a prolonged soak in the bath or shower. They took an age over their breakfasts and eventually left the dining room clutching a selection of tourist leaflets. Should they visit Picton Castle, then drive up to St David's, or stay closer to home and see the Bosherton Lily Ponds?

Genevieve would have chosen to go up to St David's, a place she'd always loved, never more so than when she'd gone there as a teenager with Christian. He'd borrowed his father's car and after a walk around the city – the smallest in Britain – they'd wandered down to the cathedral and the Bishop's Palace. The day had been warm and sunny, and they'd eaten a picnic on the grassy slope, surrounded by other holidaymakers. Except they'd felt entirely alone, as they always did when they were together. But that was teenage love for you; the intensity of it precluded anything, or anyone, else. It was years before Genevieve understood that relationships should never isolate you from others. Her relationship with Rachel had done that, too. It was easy to see now that Rachel's actions had been based on jealousy. If she couldn't have Genevieve to herself, then she'd make sure her only friend would have no one. At the time, though, Genevieve had been so wrapped up in her own insecurity and need for approval that she hadn't seen Rachel's destructive influence for what it was.

After an apologetic call from Donna to say she still wasn't well enough to work, Genevieve made a start on cleaning the guest rooms. Gran had offered to help, but Genevieve suggested she read to Lily-Rose instead. 'If you can keep her entertained for as long as you can, I'd be really grateful,' Genevieve told her grandmother.

'But what about Henry and Morwenna?' Lily-Rose asked. 'I haven't fed them. Mummy said I had to.'

'Just as soon as the rain stops you can go and see them,' Genevieve said firmly. 'I'll be upstairs if you need me, Gran.'

She attacked her morning's work with determined energy despite feeling so tired, and was soon back downstairs filling the washing machine with towels and tablecloths. The sky, much to her surprise, was showing signs of brightening. With a bit of luck she'd get the washing on the line. If not, there was always the tumble dryer. With no sign of Gran or Lily-Rose in the kitchen, she made herself a cup of tea and sat down. Five minutes, she told herself, and then she'd tackle the ironing. After that, she'd have a shower. A long, revitalising shower to wash away her lethargy. She couldn't remember the last time she'd felt so bone-tired. She was edgy too, worried that Dad still hadn't been in touch. And then there was Christian. Still no word from him. The longer his silence went on, the more she began to worry she would never be able to trust him.

She yawned, and to taunt herself some more, she pictured herself in the summer house with Christian, in particular that moment when she knew he was going to kiss her. Within seconds, she had lowered her head to the kitchen table and dozed off. She dreamt she really was in the summer house with Christian. That he was standing behind her, kissing the nape of her neck, his hands massaging the tension from her shoulders. The next thing she knew, she was being jolted awake by the jangling ring of the telephone. *Why did that phone never stop ringing!*

Except it wasn't the phone. It was someone at the front door. She shook herself out of her disappointment, feeling cheated that there was no Christian planting warm kisses on her skin, and went to see who it was. She hoped it wasn't anyone she knew. Dressed in a grubby T-shirt, her tattiest jeans with holes in the knees and her hair tied back with a rubber band, she looked and felt a mess.

She pulled open the door.

Christian!

For what felt like for ever, she held onto the door and stared at him. Was she still dreaming? Without speaking, he stepped over the threshold, kissed her politely on the cheek and then a lot less politely on the mouth. She breathed in the fresh, clean smell of him and felt her body go limp with longing. Still kissing her, holding her tight, his hands pressing into her shoulders, he somehow shut the door with his foot. She wanted to ask what he was doing here, but she couldn't. She daren't stop kissing him for fear she would wake up and he'd be gone as magically as he'd appeared. He manoeuvred her up against the wall and, tilting his head back, said, 'Please tell me there's no one else in the house?'

'I don't know. There might be some guests around.'

He kissed her again, his hands warm and firm around her neck. Frightened that any second someone – a guest, or Gran, or Lily-Rose – might appear in the hall, she pulled away. 'I've heard of doorstepping, but I don't suppose you'd like to go somewhere more private, would you?'

She could tell from his expression he hadn't understood her, so she took him by the hand and led him upstairs. Once they were in her bedroom, with the door shut and their bodies pressed against each other, all her earlier tiredness and doubts flew from her mind. 'Why didn't you let me know you were coming?'

'I wanted to surprise you.'

'Well, you certainly achieved that. But what made you do it?'

He tipped her chin up. 'I got a text message from Jonjo and Polly. They said you were a bit down. I would have come sooner, but I couldn't get away before now.'

Genevieve was touched. He had done that for her? She opened her mouth to speak, to say how glad she was to see him, when, very gently, he put a finger to her lips. 'Do you think we could leave the talking till later?'

She couldn't have agreed more. When his hands circled her waist, then slid under her T-shirt and brushed against her breasts, she steered him towards the bed, at the same time unbuttoning his shirt. He slipped her top over her head and trailed his mouth along her shoulder, then down her arm. He was just about to do the same to her other shoulder when she froze. She cocked her ear towards the door. 'What was that?'

Her gave her a half-smile. 'I didn't hear a thing.'

'There! There it is again. Oh, God, it's probably Gran and Lily-Rose.'

He groaned and held her close. 'I suppose it's pointless trying to pretend we're not here?'

'We could try.'

Smiling, he said, 'No, the thought of your grandmother bursting in on us is hardly the erotic scenario I imagined when I drove down here this morning.'

She feigned indignation. 'You knew all along you were going to get me into bed!'

He kissed her lightly on the neck. 'Are you saying it hasn't been on your mind?'

He looked so sexy, his shirt hanging open and his chest just waiting to be kissed all over, she longed to push him onto the bed and show him exactly how much it had been on her mind. 'I'll leave you to figure that one out for yourself,' she said.

'Perhaps you'd better give me a clue; you know how slow I am.'

She pulled his head down to hers and kissed him passionately. 'Does that help?'

'Oh, yes. It makes me want you all the more. Go on, I'm a desperate man. Lock the door; I promise you, this won't take long.' He started to undo her jeans.

Though it was the hardest thing to do, she pulled away from him. 'As tempting as you make it sound, I think we'd better make ourselves decent.'

She was straightening her hair while watching Christian do up the buttons of his shirt, when she heard the thumpty-thump-thump of small feet approaching. The bedroom door flew open and Lily-Rose burst in. Breathless and crying, tears streaming down her cheeks, she threw herself at Genevieve.

'Genvy, Henry and Morwenna have gone!'

Gran greeted Christian as though him showing up out of the blue at Paradise House was an everyday occurrence. Immediately they got down to the business of finding the missing donkeys.

'First off, we ought to speak to your neighbours,' Christian said, 'to see if they've seen them.'

He was perhaps the only one thinking logically. Genevieve was trying to calm a bawling Lily-Rose, who was taking her mother's instruction to take care of Henry and Morwenna too much to heart, and Gran was shuffling about the kitchen looking for the teapot. Plainly she deemed the situation a hot-sweet-tea emergency.

'They must have been frightened by the storm,' Genevieve said, when at last Lily-Rose was calm enough to sit on her lap, producing an occasional full-body shudder and an accompanying sniff.

'But weren't they tethered?' Christian asked.

'No. The orchard had its own natural boundaries, and they've never strayed before.'

'They could have gone anywhere,' Gran said. 'Along the clifftop path in the dark and taken a tumble down into the—'

'Very unlikely,' Genevieve interrupted. She didn't want Lily-Rose dwelling on such a disturbing thought. 'They've probably just wandered down to the beach and are giving rides to all the children in return for ice-cream.' She bounced her knees as though she were giving Lily-Rose a donkey ride. Anything to distract her from what Gran had just suggested.

Leaving Lily-Rose with Gran, Genevieve and Christian set off on foot to knock on doors. They went all round the village, but no one had seen or heard so much as an ee-aw. Gran's vision of Henry and Morwenna wandering the cliff path began to seem horribly likely.

They stood in front of the Salvation Arms, figuring out what to do next. The sun had broken through the thick bank of clouds, but a stiff wind rippled the bunting outside the pub, making the day seem cold and bleak. Down on the beach, a handful of youngsters were playing in the rock pools while the parents, wrapped in fleeces, looked on indulgently.

'Should we go further afield?' Christian asked. 'We could drive along the coast.'

'But Nattie's got my car, and hers isn't working.'

'You're forgetting mine. Let's go back up to the house.'

Genevieve fell in step with him. 'I bet you're wishing you'd never come down here. This is the last thing you expected to be doing – a wild donkey chase.'

He put his arm round her shoulder. 'I wouldn't have missed it for the world. At least I can say I got as far as your bedroom on this visit. Who knows, next time I might actually get you into bed.'

She leaned into him happily.

The house was unnaturally quiet when they let themselves in the back door.

'That's odd,' Genevieve said, after she'd called to Gran and Lily-Rose and got no answer. 'I wonder where they've gone.'

'To your gran's, perhaps?'

'Mm ... maybe.' She was suddenly annoyed. 'Why does my family do this to me? I spend all my time keeping an eye on them. If it's not them I'm worrying about, it's their personal crusades. These are Nattie's donkeys, she should be here to find them. Sometimes I wish I'd never come home.'

He looked at her hard, then took her in his arm. 'I'm glad you did, or we might never have met again.'

She rested her head against his chest, and could feel the thud of his heart. For a few seconds she allowed herself to be soothed by it. But then, tilting her head back to look up at him, she said, 'Do you really mean that?'

He looked offended. 'Genevieve, you have to stop doubting me.'

They spent the next hour trawling the coast road, stopping every now and then to ask if anyone had seen a pair of roaming donkeys. When it started to rain, they drove home. The house was still empty, save for two guests who were reading in the conservatory. Genevieve had just served them tea when the phone rang.

'Hi there, Genevieve.' Tubby's jolly voice boomed down the line. 'Have you lost anything recently? Like a couple of absconding donkeys?'

'Tubby! Do you know where they are?'

He chuckled. 'Yes, and I'm keeping them as hostage until I receive five thousand pounds in used bank notes in the post. Oh, and you can throw in a Ferrari as well.'

'I'll throw in Nattie too, if you're not careful. Where did you find them?'

'I was down at that new pottery and tea room near Stackpole, dropping off some strawberries, when I saw the pair of them grazing in a field. I knew it was them; they had on those ridiculous scarves Nattie makes them wear.'

'But that's miles away.'

'Not really. Anyway, I tethered them up, so they're safe for now. I can get hold of a horsebox and trailer if you like.'

'Thanks, Tubby, but we'll leave them there until Nattie gets back. She can damn well deal with it herself!'

Genevieve rang off and told Christian the good news.

'So, panic over? We can call off the air-sea rescue team?'

She laughed. 'For the time being, yes. But who knows with this family?' She glanced at her watch. 'I've just realised, you haven't had anything to eat since you arrived. You must be starving. What would you like?'

'Some of those scones would be good.' He indicated the open tin on the table, the pot of homemade jam and dish of whipped cream.

'Tell you what, help yourself while I give Gran a ring and see how she's getting on with Lily-Rose. I don't want her wearing herself out.'

But there was no answer from her grandmother's telephone.

'Maybe she's nipped to the shops with Lily-Rose,' Christian suggested.

She shrugged. 'I know it seems silly, but something's not right. And why didn't she leave a note saying where she was going?'

'Does she always let you know what she's up to?'

'No. But—'

He put down his half-eaten scone. 'Okay, then. Let's go.'

'Let's go where?'

'To your gran's, of course.'

'But she's not there, is she? If she was, she'd have answered the phone.' He started leading her towards the back door. 'Christian, what are you doing?'

'I know you well enough to understand that if we don't check on your grandmother, you'll just sit here worrying. Go on. Out you go.'

It was raining again, so they drove the short distance and parked directly in front of Angel Cottage. Genevieve knocked on the door, then knocked again. As she'd done before, she peered in at the window, her hands cupped around her eyes. Gran was on the sofa, her face turned towards the television. But she wasn't watching it; with her eyes closed and her head leaning to one side, she was fast asleep. Genevieve tapped on the window, but got no response. She was just berating herself for forgetting her key when Christian joined her. 'Is there a way in at the back?' he asked.

They went round the side of the house to the back garden and found the kitchen door open. Genevieve went on ahead to the sitting room.

'Gran,' she said softly, not wanting to make her start. The memory of finding her grandmother on the bathroom floor was still fresh in her mind and her heart was beginning to pound. 'Gran, wake up!'

Her grandmother stirred. By the time she was fully awake and asking if Genevieve would put the kettle on, Christian had joined them.

'Genevieve,' he said, taking her aside, 'I've searched the house and garden, but there's no sign of Lily-Rose. She's not here.'

The enormity of his words hit her like a blow. Cold panic took hold of her. Lily-Rose. Where was she?

39

'You're sure she's not here?' The question was futile, but Genevieve had to ask it.

'I double-checked,' Christian said. 'Where do you think she could have gone?'

'I've no idea. She's never wandered off before. She's so young. Four-year-olds don't have regular haunts of their own. Oh, God, Christian, suppose someone's taken her?'

'Let's get out there and start looking.'

Hauling herself to her feet, Gran said, 'What are you two muttering about?'

Genevieve broke the news to her grandmother as gently as she could, not wanting her overly alarmed. But Gran *was* alarmed. She clutched hold of Genevieve.

'It's all my fault,' she cried frantically. 'Lily kept wanting to look for Henry and Morwenna, and to distract her I brought her down here. I said if she was a good girl and played quietly so I could have a short nap, I'd take her to buy some sweets afterwards.'

'Then that's where she must be,' Genevieve said decisively, trying to allay her grandmother's distress – the old lady was now pacing the floor fretfully. 'You stay here, Gran. Christian and I will go round the shops.'

It didn't sound like something Lily-Rose would do. Nattie might not be the best mother in the world but she had brought her daughter up to know that she must go nowhere without an adult.

But their enquiries, as they once again dashed from shop to shop in the pouring rain, got them nowhere. No one had seen the little girl. Everyone promised to keep a lookout and told Genevieve not to worry, that Lily-Rose would show up any minute. In the mini-market, Stan and Gwen said they'd ask anyone who came into the shop if they'd seen a small girl on her own, and Ruth and William in Angel Crafts said if there was anything they could do, Genevieve only had to ask. In the salon, Debs asked how long Lily-Rose had been missing.

When exactly *had* Lily-Rose wandered off? They didn't know how long Gran had been asleep.

'Don't mess about, Genevieve,' Debs said. She was the first person not to pull her punches. 'Call the police. Do it now. Use my phone.'

'Perhaps I should just go and check Paradise House. She might have gone back there.'

'Okay, but meanwhile I'll ring a few people and alert them.'

Alone, Genevieve ran all the way up the hill. Christian had offered to return to Angel Cottage to check on Gran. After frantically searching every room at Paradise House, she drew yet another blank. Drenched to the skin, she stood in the kitchen and phoned the police. She gave the duty officer all the details she could, desperately trying to remember what Lily-Rose had been wearing. Then she made a second call; the one she was dreading. She had to tell Nattie her daughter was missing. But there was no answer from Nattie's mobile. She must have switched it off.

Grabbing a coat, she dashed back down the hill to Gran's, scanning the now-deserted beach for any sign of a child, praying like mad that when she reached Angel Cottage, Christian would tell her that Lily-Rose, all smiles and laughter, had just shown up. Passing the salon, Debs came out to her. Donna was with her. They both looked anxious.

'Any sign of Lily?' Debs asked.

Genevieve shook her head. 'No. But I've called the police. They're on their way.'

Christian opened the door to her, but his concerned expression, together with Gran still pacing the floor, flustered and muttering to herself, told her that Lily-Rose hadn't appeared. Shrugging off her wet coat, Genevieve told Christian she'd phoned the police. 'They said they'd send someone as soon as they could.'

'Good. I'll get my coat from the car.' He stopped for a moment and took her by the shoulders. 'Genevieve, we'll find her. I know we will.'

While he went to fetch his coat, Genevieve led Gran into the sitting room. Her concern for her grandmother was almost as strong as it was for her niece: the old lady was breathless and trembling. She sat with her on the sofa.

'Gran, you mustn't upset yourself.'

'How can you say that when it's no one's fault but my own that Lily's missing? I shouldn't have fallen asleep. I'll never know a moment's peace if something's happened to that poor little girl. Oh, and whatever will Nattie say?' Distraught, her eyes brimmed with tears. She looked very frail and old.

Trying not to let her apprehension show, Genevieve said, 'Gran, I need you to be rock steady. I can't get hold of Nattie, but I'm going to leave you her mobile number so you can keep trying it. You must tell her what's happened.' From her jeans pocket, she pulled out a piece of paper with the number clearly written on it; she handed it to her grandmother. 'Can you do that for me?'

With shaking hands, Gran took the piece of paper.

Joining Christian back out in the hall, where he was rummaging through a small rucksack, Genevieve pulled on her jacket. A knock at the door made her jump.

'What is it?' asked Christian.

'The door,' she said. 'It'll be the police.'

But it wasn't. A crowd of people stood outside: Tubby and Donna, Debs, Stan, Huw and Jane from the pottery, William and Ruth, the Lloyd-Morris brothers, Adam, and some of the regulars from the Salvation Arms. They were all dressed in boots and waterproofs.

'We're here to help,' Adam said, his face grim. 'Where do you want us to start looking?'

Their kindness was almost too much. Genevieve swallowed hard and took a deep, optimistic breath. With so much help, she told herself, they were bound to find Lily-Rose.

It was decided that one of them should go up to Paradise House in case Lily-Rose appeared there – Donna, still not quite recovered from her gippy tummy, volunteered to do that – and then they split into pairs with a mobile between them. Christian produced an OS map from his rucksack and the immediate area was divided and distributed accordingly. Anything over a four-mile distance was ruled out, as there was no way a child of four could have walked so far. No one voiced the thought that if she had been taken by someone in a car, she could be forty miles away by now. The other unspoken fear Genevieve had was that Lily-Rose might have fallen into the sea. She told everyone how upset Lily-Rose had been when Henry and Morwenna had gone missing and how Gran might have put the idea in her head that they could have strayed along the coastal path in the dark during the storm and plummeted to their deaths in the sea.

'It's possible,' she said, forcing herself to voice the unthinkable, 'that Lily went to look for them and got too close to the edge.'

An uneasy murmur went round the group. They exchanged mobile phone numbers and dispersed. Genevieve checked on her grandmother one last time, explaining to her that the police would probably want a photograph of Lily-Rose. She left her to choose one from the selection on the mantelpiece. It might have been kinder to Gran if Genevieve had waited for the police herself, but she couldn't bear the waiting. She had to be out there doing something. Lily-Rose had been left in her care, and *she* had to find her. How could she ever face Nattie again if she didn't?

There was an odd number of people, so Genevieve and Christian teamed up with Adam. The three of them set off to Paradise House, skirted the headland and followed the coastal path in an easterly direction. The rain was coming down harder, making the ground slippery, and the wind, which had grown wild, whipped at the hoods on their jackets. The thought of Lily-Rose out in this weather, wet, cold and alone, sent a chill through Genevieve and she quickened her step. She soon realised the folly of this when Christian pulled at her arm.

'Slow down, Genevieve, or we might miss her.'

'He's right,' Adam said, 'we have to take it slowly.'

They continued in silence, stopping occasionally to peer down the side of the cliff. The sound of the wind roaring in her ears and the sea battering the rocks was beginning to have a mesmerising effect on Genevieve and, disorientated, she felt herself drawn ever closer to the edge of the rocks. She felt a sudden yank from behind as Christian pulled her back.

She wanted to thank him, but couldn't. Desperation was kicking in. She was beginning to fear the worst. But how could a small child disappear off the face of the earth? With a much older child, all sorts of credible scenarios presented themselves – a hitched lift into Tenby or Pembroke, a visit to friends, even a lovers' tryst. But a four-year-old? None of these things were possible.

They had walked as far as Hell's Gate. After pausing to look at Christian's map, the wind almost ripping it out of his hands, the three of them stood looking out at the rough, churning sea. The horizon was lost in the murky rain. The weather was getting worse.

'We'll never find her,' Genevieve murmured dismally. 'Or if we do, it'll be too late.' Only Adam heard her.

'We'll find her, Gen. No question.'

Christian refolded the map, stuffed it back into his rucksack and walked away from them, towards the edge of the path. Genevieve watched him anxiously. Above him, a pair of jackdaws circled, once, twice, and then flew off. Hell's Gate had always been out of bounds to Genevieve and her sisters as children; even now, seldom did they come this far. She wanted to call out to Christian to tell him to be careful, that the rocks below were treacherous, but she knew it was useless; he wouldn't hear her. She waited for Christian to stop moving, but he didn't. He carried on, getting perilously near the edge. He bent down, put a hand on a rock to take his weight and suddenly was gone. Genevieve rushed after him, Adam following behind. They came to what was very nearly a sheer drop, where Adam put a protective hand out to stop her from slipping. Below them, they could see Christian carefully picking his way over the jagged rocks towards a narrow ledge, where gulls were sheltering from the wind and spray. He stooped to pick something up. He turned, looked back to where they were standing and waved a small, bright yellow Wellington boot. Genevieve gasped and grabbed hold of Adam.

'It's Lily's,' she cried. At once she and Adam were scrambling down the rock-face. But the first signs of hope were tinged with fear. If Lily-Rose had been down here, had lost one of her boots, she must almost certainly have met with an accident. How could she have survived if she'd fallen?

Standing on the ledge together, they scanned the area beneath them, staring down into what was effectively a deep bowl cut into the rocks. The tide was coming in, and as the waves slapped and swirled, the wind roared with an animal-like baleful cry. Adam motioned for them to stay where they were, and pushed forward to a shallow cutting in the rock-face. He had to wade into the menacing water. And for what? Could they really be sure Lily-Rose was here? But it was a hope, perhaps their only hope.

Genevieve chewed on her lower lip as she watched Adam. Then, to her horror, she realised there was a lethal undercurrent where the water rushed into the bowl and couldn't get out. The next moment, Adam was sucked under. Genevieve screamed. Pulling off his bulky jacket and his shoes, Christian threw himself into the water. She watched in an agony of suspense for him to bob to the surface again. He did, but then dived back down again. When he surfaced, he was holding Adam. He dragged him over the side of the bowl and the two of them clung onto the rocks, Adam, coughing and spluttering. Genevieve could see he had knocked his head; blood was flowing from his temple. She shouted to them to be careful. After they'd caught their breath, they swam across the bowl to the shallow cutting that, when the tide was out, would have seemed to an inquisitive child like an interesting cave to play in. But with the tide coming in, it was a death-trap.

Holding the yellow boot Christian had found, she watched Adam hunker down and disappear inside the dark hole. She willed their search to be over, that somehow, miraculously, Lily-Rose was safe inside the cave. She stared hard at the opening, and suddenly she saw Adam emerge, and . . . and he had Lily-Rose in his arms. Wet through and shivering, she was clinging to Adam as he carried her to safety. But to get to the ledge where Genevieve was standing, Adam and Christian had to make it back across the bowl. Genevieve suddenly wished it was Christian who was carrying Lily-Rose; he was clearly the stronger swimmer. Then, as if reading her mind, Christian exchanged a word with Adam and took the little girl from him.

Very slowly, they lowered themselves into the dangerous vortex of water. As a huge, swelling wave reared up and almost covered them, Lily-Rose screamed and thrashed her arms and legs about. Christian had to work hard to keep his footing. More agonising minutes passed, until finally he and Adam made it to the ledge. Genevieve reached down, scooped up Lily-Rose and, wrapping the petrified little girl in her coat, gave thanks that the day hadn't ended in tragedy.

40

Once they'd climbed back up to the path and were heading for home, Adam took Christian's mobile – his own had been in his jacket pocket and was now useless – and phoned Donna at Paradise House with the good news. He also asked her to phone the doctor's surgery so that Lily-Rose could be thoroughly checked over.

'Ask whoever's on duty to meet us at the house,' Adam said, 'it'll be better for Lily that way. One less ordeal.'

Dr Shepherd was waiting for them when they crashed, exhausted but triumphant, through the kitchen door.

To Genevieve's enormous relief, while Donna poured them all shots of brandy and fussed for them to get out of their wet clothes – her father's wardrobe was raided for Adam and Christian – Dr Shepherd gave Lily-Rose a clean bill of health.

'She's had an amazingly lucky escape,' he said. 'Best to get her into a nice warm bath and then bed. She'll be as right as rain come the morning.' Switching his attention from Lily-Rose to Adam and the cut to his head, he said, 'Looks like a few stitches wouldn't go amiss there. Sit down and I'll see to it now.'

When he'd finished with Adam, and Genevieve was seeing the doctor out, she thanked him for coming so promptly and joked that, hopefully, it would be a while before they saw him again.

Back in the kitchen, dressed in her pyjamas and wrapped in a blanket, Lily-Rose was sitting on Adam's lap, telling him and Christian what had happened. While Gran was sleeping she'd decided, as Genevieve had suspected, to go and look for Henry and Morwenna.

'Mummy told me I had to make sure they were all right,' she said, 'and I promised her I would.' She explained how she had quietly opened Gran's back door, slipped through the gate at the end of the garden and gone down on to the cliff path. 'It was very windy. I could see the seagulls and I went to sit with them. But they were horrible and pecked at my boots. There was a funny noise, like Henry and Morwenna calling to me.'

The rest was easy to imagine. She'd mistaken the strange-sounding wind for braying and had gone to explore. She'd found the cave and discovered somewhere to play for a while. But then the tide had started to come in, cutting her off. Another half-hour and the cave would probably have been completely under water, and she'd have drowned.

'She's her mother's child through and through,' Adam muttered. 'Intrepid to the point of stupidity.'

'Will Mummy be cross with me?' Lily-Rose asked anxiously.

It was then that Genevieve remembered Gran was supposed to be getting hold of Nattie.

'Donna,' she said, 'when you called the search off, did you ring Gran?'

'Oh, Gen, I'm sorry, I forgot all about that, what with the excitement. Shall I ring her now?'

'No, that's okay, I'll go down and see her.'

Adam shifted Lily-Rose off his lap and stood up. 'I'll walk down with you. I need to go home and change.' He glanced at Christian, also wearing Daddy Dean's cast-offs. 'I could lend you something if you like? Not that any of it will fit you properly.'

'Thanks,' Christian said.

Lily-Rose was happy enough to be left with Donna, so the three of them walked down the hill. Outside the Salvation Arms, Adam suggested Christian went with him up to his house to shower and change.

'Shall I meet you at your Gran's?' Christian suggested.

'If you like. I'll probably be there a while. I ought to ring round everyone and thank them for joining in with the search. I'll leave the door on the latch for you.'

It was becoming a habit, Genevieve thought, as once again she was knocking on Gran's door and getting no answer. After another rap, Genevieve gave up and let herself in with her key, which she'd remembered this time.

'Gran, it's me,' she called out. She closed the door and went through to the sitting room, bursting to share the good news with her grandmother, wanting to be the one to put her mind at rest. 'Get the kettle on, Gran, we found Lily-Rose and a celebratory cuppa's just what we need.'

Genevieve stood very still in the echoing silence. In an instant she knew that her grandmother couldn't hear. Her head leaning back against the sofa cushion, lips dried and slightly parted, she was completely motionless. There was no fall and rise to her chest. No little throaty grunt Gran often made when she was napping. Very slowly, almost reverently, Genevieve bent down and knelt beside the old lady. 'Oh, Gran,' she murmured. 'You never even said goodbye.' Tears filled her eyes and, letting them stream down her cheeks, she held her grandmother's cool, still hand. Never had that knotty, age-spotted hand been more precious to her.

The day had ended in tragedy, after all. But the real tragedy was that Gran's last moments before she died would have been so tormented. She would have left this world not knowing that Lily-Rose was safe. It broke Genevieve's heart that her grandmother had died thinking she'd let them down.

She didn't know how long she'd been kneeling on the floor sobbing, but she was suddenly conscious that Christian was beside her. She felt the steady pressure of his hand on her shoulder and, turning her tear-stained face to his, she said, 'How will we all manage without her? She was always there for us.'

He lifted her to her feet, took her through to the kitchen and cradled her, stroking her back. Eventually, she was able to think straight. There were things she had to do. Dr Shepherd would have to be sent for. Yet again. Then there was her family to notify – her parents in New Zealand and Polly in Hong Kong. And, of course, Nattie. Had Gran managed to ring her? She almost turned to go to the sitting room to ask Gran if she had, when . . . when she remembered.

The pain slapped at her. Never again would she be able to talk to her beloved grandmother. She reached for another tissue and blew her nose.

'This is when I feel so bloody useless,' Christian said.

Not understanding, she said, 'How do you mean?' Then realising she had her mouth partially covered with the tissue, she repeated what she'd said.

'I can't ring anyone for you. Do you want me to fetch Adam?'

Her first instinct was to say no, that she could manage. But the thought of Adam, decisive and always reassuring, made her say yes. 'But before you do that,' she said, 'could you send a text to Jonjo? I think I'd prefer it if Jonjo was the one to tell Polly about Gran. At least then she'll be told face to face by someone who cares about her.'

After everything had been done, including the formality of Gran's death certificate, they returned to Paradise House. Dr Shepherd had told Genevieve that the probable cause of Gran's death was that her heart had simply given out. He wouldn't commit himself to say that it was in any way a direct result of her distress at Lily-Rose's disappearance, but it haunted Genevieve to think that her grandmother had died blaming herself for what had happened. There was also the poignant similarity between Gran and Cecily: both women had died because their hearts had been put under unbearable pressure.

Donna had put a comfortable armchair from the sitting room into the kitchen for Lily-Rose, and the little girl was fast asleep in it, the head of a pink, long-eared rabbit sticking out from the blanket. Keeping her voice low, Genevieve thanked Donna for all her help and told her there was nothing else to be done just now. 'Go home, Donna,' she said, 'you've been wonderful, but I'm sure you'd rather be spending the evening with Tubby.'

'A nice thought, but unfortunately I'm working behind the bar tonight.' She gave Genevieve a hug. 'I'm really sorry about your Gran, Gen. I didn't know her for long, but it was long enough to appreciate what a great woman she was. I'll see myself out.'

Thinking guiltily that she felt better for there being one less person around, and that she wouldn't mind being alone, Genevieve looked at

Christian and wondered if this was how he'd felt immediately after his mother had died. Fond as she was both him and Adam, and deeply grateful for everything they'd done, she wished they'd go. It was a selfish, unworthy thought, because if it weren't for them Lily-Rose would be dead.

Dead.

Her thoughts immediately returned to Gran. But the sound of hurried footsteps, followed by the back door flying open, put a stop to them. It was Nattie, her face as white as chalk. She took one look at her daughter, safely curled up in the armchair, and burst into tears. She cried so hard that Lily-Rose stirred, and when she saw her mother, she too started to cry.

Genevieve signalled to Christian and Adam to give her sister some privacy, and led them to the conservatory.

'What else can we do to help?' Adam asked, his hand resting on her arm.

Genevieve shook her head. 'Adam, you've done so much already.' She turned to Christian. 'And you too, Christian. Besides, don't you think you two life-saving heroes have done enough for one day?'

They shrugged off her praise. Adam, perhaps sensing her mood and that it was time to leave, said, 'You know where I am, Gen, just give me a ring if you need anything. Promise?'

She kissed him gratefully.

After he'd gone, Christian said, 'Do you want me to go as well?'

'Don't be offended, but yes. I think Nattie and I need some time alone.' She saw the disappointment in his face and felt a prickle of misgiving. It had been a long day for him and now he had a lengthy journey ahead of him. He couldn't have picked a worse day to surprise her.

'Are you sure you'll be all right?' he said.

'We'll be fine.'

But they weren't fine. Not really. Nattie was as devastated about Gran as she was. 'I know it's ridiculous,' her sister said late that night, 'but a part of me always believed Gran would live for ever.'

They were in Genevieve's room, sitting on her bed, and all they wanted to do was talk about Gran. To remember her.

'I want to be just like her when I'm old,' Nattie said. 'She was the perfect role model. Dotty as hell, a one-off.'

'She was that all right. And some.'

Nattie was silent for a while, then said, 'Gen, do you believe there's such a thing as an afterlife?'

Genevieve thought back to when their grandfather had died. 'I used to like picturing Grandad running a heavenly farm. I'd see him ploughing fields in a shiny red tractor, providing endless churns of creamy milk for the thirsty angels. A combination of Enid Blyton and the Bible.'

'Was there any ginger beer?'

It was the first light-hearted comment either of them had made. When they were little, Gran had kept them amused for hours reading Blyton adventure stories, and the memory had them both reaching for the tissue box. A collection of used ones lay on the floor around the waste-paper bin.

'I wish Mum and Dad were here,' Nattie said. 'When did Dad say his flight would arrive?'

'He wasn't really making a lot of sense when I spoke to him the second time, but I checked online, and it looks like he should get to Heathrow at breakfast time the day after tomorrow.'

'And you're sure Mum isn't coming back with him? I mean, she wouldn't deliberately miss the funeral, would she? I swear I'll never speak to her again if she does.'

'He said they couldn't get another ticket. The flight was full. He got the last remaining seat. He was lucky to get that.'

Staring into the middle distance, Nattie said, 'He wasn't the only one who was lucky today.' Then, hugging herself, she looked back at Genevieve. 'I was in such a state earlier I didn't thank Adam and Christian for what they did. You too.'

'I'm sure they understood. Anyway, you can go and thank Adam tomorrow.' She thought how brave Adam had been. He could easily have drowned if it hadn't been for Christian. 'Nattie,' she said, 'just for once, try to be nice to him. He'd never say it himself, he's far too modest, but he risked his life trying to rescue Lily.'

Nattie reached for another tissue, her eyes filling with tears. 'Don't you think I realise that?' she said gruffly. 'Here I am practically suicidal with guilt and you're lecturing me on being nice to a man who saved Lily's life. Get real, Gen!'

41

Old habits die hard, and in times of crisis, Genevieve still turned to food. She had been up earlier than usual, and instead of making herself some toast and taking it to eat outside, she'd thrown open the fridge and cupboards to see what was available. It was to be a sweet fest, she decided. A satisfying, irresistible mammoth indulgence: Welshcakes rich with allspice plus the ultimate in gooey comfort food, American pancakes, fluffy and as light as air but glossy with maple syrup. She weighed the flour for the Welshcakes then added butter and rubbed it gently between her fingers. It had been Gran who had taught her the secret of good baking. 'Keep your arms relaxed and your fingers full of kindness,' she'd say. 'Imagine you're handling a newborn baby. The more love you put into the food, the better it will taste.'

But thinking of Gran made Genevieve feel choked and breathless. The sorrow of not saying goodbye seemed too painful to bear. More than anything she wanted to keep her grandmother's memory vivid and alive. But it was too late. Already she was slipping away from Genevieve, and for a panicky moment she couldn't picture the old lady. She fought to overcome the fear and at last Gran's face popped into her head. A happy, smiling Gran.

Two hours later the guests, along with Lily-Rose, were enjoying the fruits of Genevieve's labours; she'd made sure there would be one waffle left for herself when breakfast was over. Her early morning baking session had left her feeling soothed and less tearful.

Sitting at the table, a dribble of maple syrup running down her chin, Lily-Rose was her normal happy self. Genevieve added crispy ribbons of streaky bacon to a plate of pancakes for one of the guests and listened to the little girl pestering her mother as to when Henry and Morwenna would be coming home. Nattie, pale and distracted, clearly wasn't interested in rushing to fetch the donkeys. As though suffering from delayed shock at so very nearly losing her daughter, she kept touching her. And to compound the shock, there was Gran's death to come to terms with. Lily-Rose still knew nothing about it. There hadn't seemed an appropriate moment yesterday to tell her about Gran. Last night, Nattie had said that she would be the one to break the news.

'But I don't want her to know too soon,' she'd said. 'There's a danger that she might connect the two events, and think that her wandering off in some way caused Gran's death.'

Genevieve could see the logic in this, but thought the sooner her sister got it over and done with, the better. As it was, Lily-Rose had already asked twice if they could go and see Gran after they'd brought Henry and Morwenna home. She looked at her niece, standing on a chair washing her hands at the sink. Tilting her head from side to side, she was humming to herself just like a young Polly.

How Genevieve wished Polly was here with them. Earlier, in the middle of making the pancake batter, the telephone had rung. It had been Polly calling to say that Jonjo had got her on a flight home and she was at the airport waiting to board the plane.

'Is Jonjo coming back with you?' Genevieve had asked.

'He wanted to,' Polly said, 'but I wouldn't let him. He came here because of work; he really ought to stay. How are you all coping?'

'Pretty well.'

'Oh, Gen, I still can't believe Gran's dead. I wish we didn't have to have a funeral. They're so morbid. It makes it too final.'

It was a typical Polly remark; sufficiently off-key to resonate with a note of perfectly pitched clarity. Why should there be this need to tie up the loose ends, to put a loved one in a closed box, literally, and then carry on without them? Some would argue it was the only way to accept that a life was over, but Genevieve wasn't so sure she wanted to accept that Gran would no longer be around. As Gran herself might say, 'It'll take more than death to get rid of me!'

They were in the garden having a picnic lunch on the lawn, despite the grass still being damp. The sun was shining again and it felt good to be outside, to feel the uplifting warmth on their faces. Lily-Rose had wanted the picnic. 'A proper picnic,' she'd said, 'with a blanket and a basket.' Neither Genevieve nor Nattie felt inclined to refuse her. And it was now that Nattie chose to tell her daughter about her great grandmother.

In response to her mother's explanation why they couldn't go and see Gran, and breaking off from trying to fit a Hula Hoop onto each of her fingers, Lily-Rose looked solemnly at Nattie. She didn't say anything.

'But you mustn't be sad about it,' Nattie said hurriedly, 'Gran wouldn't have wanted that. She'd want us all to be happy. For us to sit here, just as we are, having a lovely picnic in the sunshine and thinking about her.'

Lily-Rose's hands drooped; a Hula Hoop slipped off one of her fingers. Until she spoke, it was difficult to know what else either Genevieve or Nattie could say to reassure her. But from the blank look on her face, it was evident she had no idea how to react. A timely cry from a gull sitting high up on the chimney pot filled the silence and provided the distraction they needed.

'Do you remember how Gran was always putting bread out for the birds,' Genevieve said to Lily-Rose, 'but she'd chase the big gulls away?'

Lily-Rose nodded. 'She shook her broom at them.'

Nattie smiled. 'When I was little, she shook her broom at me sometimes.'

'Because you were naughty?'

'Oh, Lily, I was the naughtiest girl in the whole world.'

Lily-Rose turned to Genevieve. 'Was she?'

'Well, not all the time. There were occasions when she behaved herself. But not often.'

Removing the remaining Hula Hoops from her fingers, scattering them on the blanket, Lily-Rose stood up. She put her arms around her mother's neck and kissed her smack on the lips. Nattie hugged her tight and pressed a noisy kiss on Lily-Rose's cheek; it made her squeal and wriggle. As though the conversation about Gran had never taken place, she said, 'When can Henry and Morwenna come home?'

Genevieve was about to suggest they take up Tubby's offer of help, when she heard a noise coming from the front of the house. 'Look who's here, Lily,' she said.

Lily-Rose's face lit up. 'Henry! Morwenna!' Before anyone could tell her to slow down, she was off, dashing across the lawn to where Adam and Tubby were leading the donkeys out of a ramshackle horse box.

'They look pleased as punch to be home,' Adam said, when the animals had been led to the orchard and were grazing contentedly on familiar grass. 'And before you accuse us of interfering, Nattie, we thought you and Gen had enough on your plates without worrying about these two.'

Genevieve went inside to fetch two ice-cold beers. When she rejoined them in the garden, they, with Nattie, were watching Lily-Rose feed handfuls of grass to the donkeys.

'If she carries on spoiling them like that,' Tubby said, 'they'll forget how to graze altogether. They'll be tapping on the window waiting to be invited inside.'

They went and sat at the table on the terrace, the mood suddenly politely awkward between them. Nobody was looking anyone in the eye. That was the trouble with death, thought Genevieve; it made people act out of character, made them too deferential. Not so long ago Nattie would have been sitting here being rude and antagonistic, saying anything to wind up Adam and taking Tubby to task over whatever took her fancy.

Tubby left when he'd finished his beer, but at Nattie's invitation, Adam remained where he was. Genevieve took it as her cue to leave them alone. She joined Lily-Rose in the orchard, and suggested they walk down to the shops. 'Let's buy some sweets to cheer us up, shall we?'

Down in the village, Lily-Rose was greeted with a five-star VIP welcome. She lapped up the attention, particularly in the mini-market when Stan gave her a big bag of sweets for free. She offered one to Debs when they called in at the salon so that Genevieve could thank Debs again for putting the search party together yesterday.

'It was the least we could do,' Debs said. 'We're all just so pleased the day ended so well.' Realising her blunder, she lowered her voice so that Lily-Rose couldn't hear. 'It was a dreadful shame about your Gran. We'll miss her. You know, she had the most wonderful hair. Strong and springy, more like a fifty-year-old's.'

Regretting every bad thought she'd ever harboured about Debs, Genevieve said goodbye. They'd only gone a few yards when they saw Adam coming towards them. Lily-Rose slipped her hand out of Genevieve's and ran to him.

He picked her up and swung her round. 'And what have you got there, little Rosy-Posy?'

'Flying Saucers. They're my favourite. Would you like one?'

'No thanks. You keep them for yourself.'

Curious to know how Nattie's attempt to be nice to Adam had gone, Genevieve probed unashamedly. 'Nattie say anything pleasant to you?'

He put Lily-Rose back on the ground. 'As a matter of fact, she did. And you know what? I reckon it was the hardest thing she's ever had to do.'

'You didn't deliberately make it harder for her, did you?'

He looked hurt. 'Gen! What do you take me for?'

'I'm sorry. That was out of order.'

'Forget it. Now look, if there's anything you need a hand with, you will say, won't you? Your grandmother was a popular woman, and people will want to help if they can. You only have to say the word.'

She nodded. 'I know, but until Dad comes home tomorrow morning we're in limbo.'

'And if you want anyone to talk to, you know ... about your Gran, my shoulder's at your disposal.' Smiling, he added, 'I've used yours often enough, it seems only right you should have the use of mine.'

His words were so sincere, she didn't trust herself to thank him. 'Come on, Lily,' she mumbled, 'we ought to be getting home. Your mother will be wondering where you've got to.'

Back at Paradise House, Nattie was sitting on the terrace where Genevieve had left her earlier. Her head was in her arms on the table and it was obvious she was crying.

Lily-Rose put a hand on her mother's arm. 'Mummy, why are you crying? Would you like a sweet?'

Nattie raised her head and sniffed loudly. She tried to speak, but couldn't. She put her arms around Lily-Rose and held her tightly, as if she'd never let her go.

'Sorry about all that in the garden.' Nattie was helping Genevieve get dinner ready that evening. All but two guests had opted to eat in and, on reflection, a busy evening was just what they needed. Kelly had come in to help, and they were carrying on as normal, while Lily-Rose watched a Disney video on the television in the corner of the kitchen. Genevieve was arranging plates of vegetable tempura with aubergine pickle.

'Don't be stupid, Nats, there's no need to apologise for crying.'

Kelly appeared in the kitchen. 'Table two's order,' she said, handing the slip of paper to Nattie. 'Shall I take those through?' she asked Genevieve.

When they were alone again, Nattie said, 'It was Adam's fault, of course.'

Genevieve, her head in the oven as she checked on a main course of braised lamb shank in a Madeira sauce, stopped what she was doing. She looked at her sister sharply. 'How did you reach that conclusion?'

Nattie fiddled with the stubby remains of a root of ginger. 'If you must know, he—' she glanced over to Lily-Rose, and lowered her voice, 'he told me he would have done anything to save Lily-Rose. That she really matters to him.'

'And you have a problem with that?'

'It made me realise what a—' again she glanced over to Lily-Rose – 'what a bitch I've been to him. He really cares, doesn't he? All this time I thought he'd been using her to get round me.'

Genevieve closed the oven. 'You idiot. I've been telling you for ages what a genuine guy he is.'

'You know he's selling up, don't you?'

'He did mention it.'

'You never said.'

'He told me not to tell anyone. Besides, since when have you been interested in what he does?'

'I'm interested now. He says he's moving out of the area. He told me there's nothing to keep him here.'

Saddened by her sister's last remark, Genevieve felt they'd let Adam down in some way.

'And what am I going to tell Lily?' Nattie continued. 'She adores Adam. She's lost her great grandmother, and to all intents and purposes her grandmother, and now Adam is deserting her. I've a good mind to make him tell Lily himself.'

'Oh, for goodness sake, Nats, stop being so selfish and always thinking of number one. Ask yourself the obvious question: why does Adam think there's nothing to keep him here?'

The opportunity for Nattie to respond was snatched from her by Kelly coming back into the kitchen with a stack of empty plates. When they were able to talk freely again, instead of picking up where they'd left off, Nattie changed tack.

'I didn't tell you about the school reunion, did I?'

Genevieve was half-tempted to say she couldn't give a damn about the school reunion. 'Was it worth the effort of going all that way?'

'Yes and no. The food was lousy, what Gran would call a pork pie and pickled onion event.'

'Isn't it the people you're supposed to be more interested in?'

'I'm coming to them. And one in particular. Remember Lucinda Atkins from your year?'

'How could I forget her? She was one of the Queens of Spite.'

'And do you remember her sister, Vivienne, in my year? Well, it doesn't matter if you do or not, but guess who she bumped into six months ago in Edinburgh?'

'Go on, I can see you're itching to tell me.'

'None other than Rachel Harmony! Except now she's Rachel White, married with three children and living in Scotland. Her husband's an accountant, twelve years older than her, and they've just celebrated their sixth wedding anniversary. Who'd have thought it? I'd have put money on her ending up as some designer clothes addict living in London and milking dry her third husband.'

For the first time in years, Genevieve smiled as she thought of her old friend. 'Good for Rachel,' was all she said.

It was almost midnight when Polly arrived home. She was exhausted, having hardly slept during the long flight and then driven herself from Heathrow in a hire car that Jonjo had arranged. Seeing how shattered she was, Genevieve made her get ready for bed straight away and took her up a mug of tea. She and Nattie sat with her for a while, Nattie plaiting Polly's hair like she used to when they were little. They wanted to ask what Hong Kong had been like, but in the circumstances, it didn't seem right. As they were about to say goodnight and close the door, Polly yawned and said, 'Oh, I nearly forgot, Jonjo's asked me to marry him.'

They came back into the room, almost tripping over each other.

'But you hardly know each other,' said Nattie.

'What was your answer?' asked Genevieve, amused at Nattie for sounding so sensible for once, and at Polly for dropping the news so casually into the conversation.

'I said I'd think about it.'

'But you hardly know him,' repeated Nattie, clearly too stunned to think of anything else to say.

'That's what makes the prospect of marrying him so exciting. Who wants to marry someone they know completely? Where's the fun in that?' Yawning hugely, Polly pulled the covers up and closed her eyes. 'Goodnight.'

Shutting the door behind them, Genevieve thought how wonderfully simple and straightforward Polly made life seem. It was good having her home again.

The morning brought a sky of brilliant blue and a sea that was as still and shiny as glass. After breakfast had been served and tidied away, Genevieve took a short break before helping Donna – now fully recovered – clean the bedrooms. All their guests were staying on, so it was a comparatively easy day with no change-overs. Taking the post with her, she went outside to her bench. There was the usual rubbish amongst the mail, which she put aside to go straight in the bin, plus a handful of With Deepest Sympathy cards from neighbours and friends. It struck Genevieve that Gran would have loved all the attention. The thought made her smile, and her smile widened when she opened the next envelope. It was from Christian; a brief note to say that he was thinking of her and hoped she and her sisters were managing. His last comment was to say how much he wished he could be with her.

'Me too,' she sighed.

She opened the rest of the mail, including a formal-looking envelope from the bank in Tenby. She held her breath as she ripped it open. Slowly she read the letter twice to be sure of its content, to be convinced that she'd understood it properly. She then put the letter back inside the envelope and wondered if she really dare go ahead. From nowhere she heard Gran's voice, so clear she could have been sitting on the bench with her.

'You can do it, Gen. You know you can.'

She stood up to go back inside and help Donna. As she was crossing the lawn, she heard a car. She checked her watch. Could it be Dad? Still clutching the pile of mail, she went round to the front of the house and found her father stepping down from the driver's side of his Land Rover and rubbing his lower back. Happy relief swept through her and she quickened her step to greet him.

She was almost upon him when she realised he wasn't alone. Pushing open the door on the passenger's side was Serena Baxter.

42

'But we thought you couldn't get a seat on the flight with Dad?'

'So did we. But they put me on standby at the airport. At the very last minute there was a cancellation.'

'Why didn't you tell us you were coming?' This was from Nattie and there was a distinct accusatory tone to her words.

'Oh, darling, there wasn't time. It's been such a mad, crazy rush. We just wanted to get back as soon as possible, to be with you all.'

'Does this mean you're home for good?' Again the question was from Nattie and it was suitably loaded. She had always been the least forgiving of them and her face was uncomfortably hostile. Genevieve hoped her mother was too jetlagged to take it to heart.

'Goodness,' said Serena, with a spirited show of blithe cheeriness. 'All these questions and I haven't had so much as a chance to draw breath. I'd love a cup of tea. You can't imagine how desperate I am for a decent cup of Typhoo. Where's Polly?'

They were standing in the kitchen, Daddy Dean, Serena, Nattie, Lily-Rose and Genevieve. 'She's still in bed,' Genevieve said, conscious that it was glaringly obvious to everyone that Serena had deliberately not answered Nattie.

'Actually, I'm right here. Hello Daddy. Hello Mum! What a brilliant surprise! I thought I could hear your voices.' Rubbing the sleep from her eyes and still dressed in her nightclothes, Polly stepped into the room. Her sunny presence instantly took the edge off the hostile atmosphere Nattie had generated. She kissed their father first, who had Lily-Rose in his arms, plus a fluffy Kiwi bird, then their mother. 'You look different, Mum. Have you lost weight?'

Serena smiled. 'A little. I've taken up yoga. But I'll tell you about it later. I've so much to share with you. Now then, shall I make us a drink? The kitchen looks very tidy. Better than it used to. That must be your doing, Genevieve.'

'That's okay, Mum. Why don't I put the kettle on while you and Dad freshen up?'

When she was alone with her sisters – Lily-Rose had gone upstairs with her grandparents – Genevieve filled the kettle. 'Nattie, I think you should drop the belligerent act. It's really not the time or the place.'

Nattie picked at a nail and scowled. 'I would have thought it's exactly the time and place. How can she just waltz in here as though it's the most normal thing in the world for a wife and mother to bugger off and then come back like nothing has happened? It'll take more than a toy kiwi bird to get round me. And did you catch the way she didn't say if she was home for good?'

'Yes, I did. But for now, and for Dad's sake, let's just play it her way. Perhaps we'll have to wait until after the funeral before she'll open up to us.'

But Genevieve was wrong. After lunch, while their father, who had scarcely uttered a word since arriving home, got on the phone and started organising the funeral, Serena asked Genevieve and her sisters to go for a walk with her. She said she wanted to talk to them. Genevieve had a sudden fear that Serena was preparing them for the inevitable: divorce. Nattie armed herself with Lily-Rose, counting on their mother's better nature not to say anything unpleasant with her granddaughter around.

They didn't walk far, just down to the beach, where they picked their way through the stretched-out bodies and playing children till they found themselves a place to sit on the pebbles. After kicking off her sandals, Lily-Rose took her fishing net and went to play in a nearby rock pool. Anyone looking at their long faces as they watched her would have thought how conspicuously they stood out from the crowd. Even Polly seemed muted and anxious.

Serena had changed out of her travelling clothes and was now wearing an outfit Genevieve didn't recognise. It was a simple, sleeveless, olive-coloured shift dress that suited her new shape. Her hair was cropped short, and where before it had been shot through with dowdy grey, it was now highlighted with a flattering mixture of copper and nut-brown. She'd had her ears pierced, something she'd always claimed she was too squeamish to have done, and wore a pair of star-shaped earrings with a matching necklace and bracelet. On her feet she wore a pair of smooth leather thong sandals. All in all, she looked great and glowed with a healthy radiance that couldn't be caused by sun alone. And anyway, she had just left New Zealand in the grip of winter. It was hard to admit, but Genevieve could see that the change had done her mother good. But what if it wasn't just the change of scene that was responsible for the new Serena? What if this old friend Pete was the cause?

'I've missed this so much,' Serena said, her arms embracing the shore and looking up to Paradise House.

Genevieve shot Nattie a warning glance, knowing it was probably on her tongue to say, 'Then why did you leave it so long before coming home?'

'I felt exactly the same when I came back,' Genevieve said, taking on the familiar role of mediator. 'I kept thinking I had to make the most of it in case it disappeared.'

'Oh, please,' cut in Nattie, not for a second put off by Genevieve's warning look, 'let's cut the deep and meaningful crap and get to the point. Mum, are you, or are you not, home for good?'

Serena placed a hand on Nattie's arm. 'Still the same old Natalie, then? Looking for a clear-cut answer to every question?' For a moment their mother looked and sounded as quietly composed as Polly.

But Nattie was having none of it. 'There you go again,' she said angrily, 'avoiding the question. Is that what you've been learning to do while we've been consoling Dad? I don't think you have any idea how much you hurt him. What's more, I don't think you even care.'

'Oh, but Nattie, I do. I care deeply. And not just about your father. About you, too. All of you. But did any of you stop and think about me? About why I went?'

Nattie picked up a stone and brought it down hard on another. 'As far as I can see, you went because, selfishly, you wanted to indulge yourself in a stupid mid-life crisis.'

Serena smiled. 'And is there anything wrong with that?'

'Yes, there is! You're a middle-aged woman with . . . with responsibilities. You're not supposed to go off when the whim takes you.'

Quietly, Serena said, 'Maybe I'm wrong, Nattie, but I think the reason you're so angry with me is that you're jealous. What would you give, right now, to be able to go off on your own? To go this very minute without a backward glance for any responsibilities you have? No, don't look so indignant. I know you love Lily-Rose, but I bet there's a part of you that would love to be able to do what I've done.'

Nattie gave their mother a ferocious stare. 'That's not true! And how can you say that after what nearly happened to Lily? God, Mum, how can you be so bloody insensitive?' She got to her feet and marched off, her shoes grinding the stones underfoot as she went over to the rock pools to be with her daughter.

Serena sighed. 'I knew this would happen. It's one of the reasons I dreaded coming home.' She turned to Genevieve and Polly. 'Anything you two want to accuse me of? If so, best we get it all over and done with. Who wants to go first?'

Polly shook her head and Genevieve said, 'Nattie will be okay, Mum. Don't worry. You know what she's like. She doesn't accept change unless she's at the epicentre of it.'

Her mother smiled faintly, then suddenly looked tired. 'I did miss you all, you know. I badly wanted to see you again, but as the weeks and then the months passed by I began to worry if you'd want me home.'

'But our letters! We told you how much we wanted you here.'

'Yes, but why did you? For my sake? Your father's? Or your own?'

Genevieve couldn't meet Serena's eyes. 'A mixture of all three,' she said truthfully.

'What about you, Polly?'

'I just wanted you to be happy, Mum. And if that meant you had to stay away, then sooner or later we would have come to terms with it. Are you going to divorce Dad?'

'Perhaps that's a question you should be asking your father. After all, I've given him every reason to want to divorce me.'

'Oh, Mum,' said Genevieve, 'how could you even think that? He's mad about you. Why do you think he flew to New Zealand to see you? Haven't you had a chance to talk things through yet?'

'Not really. Your Gran's death has put us on hold for the time being. It's very important we make the right decision when we're both thinking straight. Your father has to want me home for all the right reasons.'

'What about Pete?' Genevieve asked. The question came out more snappily than she'd intended. 'Where does he fit in?'

'He doesn't.'

'Come off it, Mum. You've been living with him all these months. Of course he fits in.'

'I've been *staying* with Pete, not living with him, Genevieve. There's a big difference. There's also the small matter of him being gay.'

'*Gay?*' Genevieve had to repeat the word, to make sure she'd heard right. 'But why didn't you say? Why did you leave us to suspect the worst?'

'Because . . . because I needed to. I needed to shake your father up. To see how badly he wanted me. And not just as cook, cleaner and general dogsbody at Paradise House.' It was as Genevieve had suspected. Her mother had grown tired of always being there for everyone. She couldn't blame her for that. Being taken for granted, as she'd come to know, was soul-destroying.

'And do you know what makes it worse?' Serena said. 'It's knowing that it was all my own fault. I encouraged your father to sell the farm and live out my dream; the idyllic dream of running a cosy B and B by the sea. But in the end it turned into something I didn't want any more. Can you imagine how guilty that made me feel?'

'Mum, there's nothing wrong in waking up on Christmas morning and being disappointed by the present you'd always wanted. But have you asked Dad if it's what he still wants?'

'Oh, Polly, you know what your father's like. He always wants to please other people. He's just so infuriatingly considerate.'

'But you still love him, Mum, don't you?'

Serena turned back to Genevieve. 'As you grow older, Gen, you come to realise that it's not just love that keeps a marriage alive.'

'What, then?' But before her mother got the words out, Genevieve knew exactly what she was going to say.

'The unexpected. The thrill of not knowing what's going to happen next. Being stuck in a rut is what kills most marriages. I suppose what I'd come to realise was that without a zing in my heart, I felt dead.'

'You need to talk to Dad,' Genevieve said.

Serena nodded. 'I will. When your grandmother's funeral is over.'

43

It was a beautiful day.

'Your Gran will have ordered the sun especially,' Tubby said to Genevieve as he put his arm round Donna, steering her out of the church and into the sunshine. 'I bet she's looking down and wishing she was here with us.'

Almost everyone from the village had shown up at St Non's for Gran's funeral, and Genevieve was conscious that each and every one of them had something cheerful to say about Granny Baxter. But the best comment had been made by the vicar during the service. He'd said that Gran, who had never been slow in chiding him for the length of his sermons, was sure to be up there in heaven getting along like a house on fire with all the other saints.

In the graveyard, grouped around the hole in the ground where Gran's coffin was now lying, Genevieve thought of the instructions her grand-mother had given them some time ago on how she wanted her remains to be dealt with. She'd made them all laugh by saying, 'Cremation? Over my dead body!' And just so that there could be no confusion on the matter, she'd left them a letter.

I've let you off lightly while I've been alive, but in death I'm determined to be a burden to you all. You'll have to tend my grave regularly and keep it nice with fresh flowers. None of those cheap plastic ones I've seen in graveyards these days. And I want an angel fixed to the stone, something with a bit of class. I've put some money by especially, so you'll not have to worry about the cost.

As if they'd have worried about the price of an angel, thought Genevieve, as she watched her father throw a handful of earth onto the coffin. His face was solemn, beaded with sweat from the warmth of the midday sun – he was wearing his only suit, a thick wool one. Her mother went next, then Nattie, helped by Lily-Rose, who was wearing her butterfly wing rucksack and looking appropriately angel-like. Then it was Genevieve's turn. She threw a sprinkling of dusty earth and willed her grandmother, wherever she was, to know how much she was loved and missed. Silently, eyes closed, she said, 'Life will never be the same without you, Gran. You were the one true constant in our lives.'

When the service was over, people began milling around, murmuring discreetly and admiring the many wreaths and bouquets. Some were blatantly inspecting the cards – who had given what? Had the florist got their order right? It seemed wrong, this undisguised act of curiosity, like snooping through someone's private letters. The scent of so many flowers filled the air and Genevieve was glad her grandmother hadn't specified there were to be none. As she used to say, 'You can't beat a bit of pomp and circumstance.'

A painful lump of grief rose in her throat. She wandered away from the main group of mourners and went to stand in the shade of a large yew tree that was supported on one side by a pair of sturdy oak props. She and Christian had sheltered here once from a sudden downpour. Disappointed that he hadn't been able to make it for the funeral – he'd emailed yesterday to say he was inundated with work – she thought how little contact there had been between them since Gran had died. She sensed something had changed between them, but couldn't put her finger on what it was. A distance had opened up, and not just a geographical one.

Standing under the tree, picking out the members of her family amongst the crowd of mourners, she had never felt so alone or isolated. She hadn't just lost a grandmother, she'd lost an irreplaceable life-long friend. And now, according to Nattie, Adam was thinking of moving away.

From across the graveyard, where he was standing on his own, Adam turned and caught her eye. He smiled and raised his eyebrows, as if to say, 'You okay?' She nodded, then stepped out of the shadows and into the sunlight to join him.

It was just as Gran would have wanted. Everyone, now that they had made a start on Genevieve's buffet, had loosened up and the wine was flowing freely. Not everyone who'd been in church had been invited, but those who had were pleased to see Serena back within the fold and were all making the assumption that she was here to stay. As she brushed Daddy Dean's collar – he'd managed to run a dirty finger round it at the graveside after throwing his handful of earth – she looked very much back for good. But from the way she'd spoken on the beach the day before yesterday, and the fact that she was insisting on sleeping at Angel Cottage, there was no knowing what the future held.

Genevieve had been desperate to talk to her father, to give him some kind of hint of what was expected of him, but her mother had made her promise, along with Polly, that they were not to say anything.

'It has to come from him,' Serena said. 'If there's to be any chance of us staying together, your father has to work things out for himself.'

But was it fair to test him in this way?

Most people were now retreating to the tables placed in the shade, but

Genevieve was sitting on the steps of the conservatory, enjoying the sun. She was now onto her third glass of wine and prepared to drink a whole lot more before the day was out. She didn't normally drink so much – it was a control thing, like keeping everything tidy and in its place – but today was an exception.

'Room for a friend down there?' It was Adam, with a bottle of wine in his hand.

She moved along the step to make room for him.

'You look knackered,' he said, giving her glass a top-up.

'I'm fine.'

'You always say that.'

'Do I? Do I really?'

'Yes, and one day I might go the extra mile and believe you. But not today.' He put his arm round her. 'You need a holiday, Gen.'

She let her head rest on his shoulder. 'You might be right. Where shall I go? I hear New Zealand is particularly good for putting the spring back into one's step.'

'Wherever you want. Alaska or the Antipodes, you name it and I'll take you there.'

She lifted her head. 'Adam?'

'Yes?'

'You're always looking out for me, aren't you? Why?'

'Because I like you. In fact, I like you a lot.'

'How much a lot?'

He smiled. 'Is that a proper sentence?'

'You ... you don't fancy me, do you?'

He laughed. 'Now what the hell made you ask a daft question like that?'

Sober enough to blush, she hid her face in his shoulder and mumbled something about being emotionally unstable just now. When she'd recovered, she said, 'So what's this I hear from Nattie about you abandoning us?'

'Ah. She told you.'

'Of course she did.'

'Do you Baxter girls tell each other everything?'

'Very little. That's half the problem with our family. Anyway, answer my question. I'm sick of people being so evasive.'

'Ooh, scary. Genevieve gets tough!'

She dug him in the ribs with her elbow, spilling some of her wine onto the step, but he just fastened his hold on her and pulled her closer, making her laugh.

'For heaven's sake, you two! Do you really think that's appropriate behaviour on a day like this?' Standing in front of them, hands on her hips, was Nattie, and she looked like thunder.

But all Genevieve could do was laugh even harder. How good it felt to let the tension of the last few days flow out of her.

44

Gran's will was very precise and, in the letter she'd written to accompany it, she was insistent that her wishes were to be respected. Money was not a subject she'd ever dwelt on, but everyone in the family was amazed at how much she'd squirreled away over the years. It was by no means a fortune, but it was more than they'd expected. She'd never been stingy, but she'd lived carefully and from what they could understand, had hardly touched the capital of what Grandad had left her in his will.

Instead of leaving everything to Daddy Dean, as they'd thought she would, she'd left it to Genevieve and her sisters. But whereas Genevieve and Polly were bequeathed an equal share of money, Nattie had been given Angel Cottage. The old lady had written:

This is to provide my granddaughter and great granddaughter with a home. And to ensure that it can never be got hold of by some feckless man Nattie gets involved with, the house is to be put in Lily-Rose's name until her eighteenth birthday. Only then will it legally belong to Natalie, by which time she might have achieved the unthinkable and settled down with a reliable man she can trust.

Nattie's response was not to be outraged that Gran thought so little of her ability to pick a decent boyfriend, but to laugh out loud. 'Good on you, canny Gran!'

Later in the day, though, Genevieve found her in the orchard with Henry and Morwenna, tears streaming down her cheeks.

'Oh, Gen,' she sobbed, 'I don't deserve Gran's little house. She should have left it to you or Polly. You're both so much more deserving.'

'Nonsense. You have Lily-Rose to take care of. Angel Cottage gives the pair of you stability and security. Gran did exactly the right thing.'

Rubbing the heels of her hands into her eyes to stem the flow of tears, Nattie said, 'I wish she was here for me to thank her properly. I miss her so much.'

That had been a week ago and since then Nattie had undergone a dramatic change: she was talking about getting a job. It seemed that canny

Gran had been exactly that. Now that she had a proper home of her own, Nattie was suddenly viewing life differently.

'It's like she's growing up at last,' Genevieve said to Adam. They were having a drink in the beer garden at the Salvation Arms. Mum and Dad were holding the fort together and she was enjoying a rare night off. She never did get the free day she'd bargained for with Nattie. Life had been too eventful since.

'You mean she's going to get off her bum and do a decent day's work?'

'She says she'll take the first job offer that comes her way, so long as it pays enough for a childminder for Lily-Rose, and then when Lily goes to school, she might go back to school herself and complete the degree she dipped out of.'

Adam nodded approvingly. 'Good for her. But I guess finding a reliable childminder for Lily won't be easy, or cheap.'

'It won't, but I'm sure I'll be able to help out now and again.'

Adam turned his beer glass round on the wooden table. 'And what about *your* plans?'

'You mean, how are they going?'

'I mean, how do you think you'll have the time to take care of Lily-Rose if your own plans take off?'

She shrugged. 'Oh, these things have a way of sorting themselves out.'

He didn't look convinced, and after they'd finished their drinks, he went up to the bar for another round. She watched him chatting with Donna and thought about what he'd said. He was right, of course: babysitting Lily-Rose would be difficult, if not impossible. But as things stood, there was no knowing what was going to happen. She'd heard nothing back from the solicitors in Tenby who were handling the sale, despite ringing them several times, and was now concerned that something was wrong. Well, what else did she expect? These things seldom ran a straight course. They might for the likes of Adam, but not for her. She gave herself a mental rap on the knuckles. Adam had probably started out in business with exactly the same chance of making it as she did. And she wasn't doing anything as ambitious as buying acres and acres of run-down caravan park. All she wanted to do, with the help of a loan and the money George had left her, was buy a modest-sized property to convert into a teashop-cum-restaurant.

It had been Tubby who had unwittingly alerted her to the possibility, and the property stood right here in the village, two doors up from Angel Crafts. He had only told her about it in passing, as he did with any snatch of gossip. But she'd pounced on the opportunity at once, before anyone else could get there before her. For years the pretty little end of terrace house had been owned by a family in Cardiff who rented it out all year round, but now they wanted to sell up with the minimum of fuss and expense. Before they'd bought the house, it had been the village bakery, and one of the original bread ovens was still in place in what was now the kitchen. Planning permission to return the property to commercial use was a mere formality, so her solicitor had told her, but now Genevieve wasn't so sure. Perhaps this was proving to be the inevitable stumbling block.

Only two people knew about her plans, Adam and Christian, and they both kept telling her that she was worrying unnecessarily. Deep down she knew what was bothering her: irrationally she didn't believe she could be on the end of such good fortune. Just as Nattie had said she didn't deserve Angel Cottage, Genevieve thought she hadn't earned the right to this lucky break.

'You look glum,' Adam said, when he returned with their drinks. 'What's up? I leave you for five minutes and come back to a face like a mullet.'

She grinned inanely. 'That better?'

'Marginally.'

'So what's the latest news from the bar?'

He took a long sip of his beer. 'According to Donna, the talent contest next Saturday night is a total sell-out.'

'I know, she told me this morning. She also told me she's trying to persuade you to participate. Has she won you over? Adam?'

'Err . . . no comment.'

'She has, hasn't she? You're going to sing! Oh, now this I have to see. What will you sing? Or rather, who will you be?'

He winked. 'Again, no comment. But what about you? Are you going to throw your inhibitions to the wind and give us a song?'

'You must be joking. Polly's the only musical one in our family.'

'Who mentioned anything about me being musical? I'm just going to get up there and make an idiot of myself.' After another mouthful of beer, he said, 'How's everyone at Paradise House? What's the latest on your parents?'

'As you might expect, nothing's been decided.'

He frowned. 'I don't get it. Your mother seems genuinely glad to be back. I can't imagine her leaving again.'

'It's not as simple as that.' She told him what Serena had told her and Polly on the beach. 'It could only happen in my family,' she sighed. 'We just don't seem capable of acting normally. Mum's been home for nearly two weeks and as far as I know, she and Dad still haven't talked properly. They talk about everything else, like sorting out Gran's things, and the wallpaper that needs replacing in the guest sitting room, but they pussyfoot around the really important issue.'

'You'd think they'd both be desperate to clear the air and see how they stand. Especially your father.'

'I think Gran's death has taken precedence. And maybe they're both hiding behind it a little. Particularly Dad. He seems to be avoiding being alone with Mum. I think he's frightened she'll use the moment to destroy any hope he has.'

'It wouldn't do any harm to give your father a nudge in the right direction. Your mother need never know.'

'I could, but in a way I agree with her. She needs to know that Dad wants her home for the right reasons, not just because he can't function properly without her. She also wants to be sure that things are going to change.'

'If I know your Dad, he probably thinks by flying out to New Zealand he's already made the grand gesture to woo her back.'

'You could be right. Anyway, I know he's really upset about Gran, so we shouldn't be too hard on him. The sad thing is, Gran would have knocked their heads together by now and got them to see how committed to each other they really are.'

Adam gave a short, loud laugh. 'Commitment! Now that's a concept you and Nattie could do with familiarising yourselves with.'

'What do you mean? Nattie and I don't have a problem with commitment.'

'Sure you do. Look at Nattie. She deliberately chooses all the wrong boyfriends so she doesn't have to connect with them and get seriously involved. She's either terrified of being tied down or of being hurt.'

Genevieve had never thought of Nattie as vulnerable, but perhaps Adam had a point. And hadn't Serena more or less made the same observation? 'Okay,' she said, 'I'll give you that one. But how about this? Maybe you deliberately wanted Nattie because it saved *you* from having to make a commitment to a long-term girlfriend.'

'And why would I do that? Why wouldn't I want a proper relationship?'

'Mm . . . I don't know. You've got me there. Hey, perhaps you're gay and in denial?'

He nearly choked on his beer. He looked about him. 'A little louder, Gen. That way everyone in Angel Sands will know by the *Ten O'Clock News* that I'm a closet homosexual.'

She laughed and decided to wind him up. 'I notice you didn't answer me. So are you?'

'Am I what?'

'Gay?'

'*No!*'

'You could tell me if you were. It wouldn't make any difference. In fact, I think I'd like a gay friend. Mum seems to have benefited from having one.'

'Sorry to disappoint you, but I'm boringly straight. I wish now I'd proved it to you that night I had you in my bed.'

Now it was Genevieve's turn to see if anyone had overheard their conversation. 'Okay, now we're quits you can keep your voice down.'

He grinned. 'You started it. But before I let you off the hook, what made you ask if I fancied you, the day of your Gran's funeral?'

She raised her glass of wine and did a poor job of hiding behind it. 'Trust you to remind me of that.'

'Well?'

'If you must know, in my drunken state, I was worried you might have transferred your affections from one loony Baxter to another.'

'And what gave you cause to think that?'

She squirmed in her seat, realising how silly she was about to sound. 'Because you're always being so nice to me,' she murmured.

He laughed. 'Nothing else for it, then. I'd better start being nasty to you. Now tell me about you and lover-boy. How's it going? I can't remember the last time you mentioned him.'

She sank back into her seat. 'Difficult to say.'

'In what way?'

'Something's changed between us. Maybe it's because he's there and I'm here.'

'Are you saying it's fizzling out between the two of you?'

'I don't know. I really don't. Perhaps if we could actually speak to each other it would help. The written word isn't my favourite form of communication; I can never say what I feel.' She drained her glass. 'Maybe long-distance relationships just aren't my thing,' she added gloomily. 'It doesn't seem to be enough for me.' She raised her eyes and looked at Adam. 'I sound selfish and greedy, don't I?'

'Not at all. There's nothing selfish in wanting to be with someone.'

Holding the stem of her empty wine glass, she twirled it round on her lap and thought of Polly and her long-distance relationship. Since coming back from Hong Kong, Jonjo had upped the ante in his bid to win Polly's heart. He called at least three times a day and continued to keep Rhys Williams, the florist, as busy as ever. Polly hadn't told their parents that Jonjo had proposed to her, and she'd asked Genevieve and Nattie to keep quiet about it until she'd made up her mind whether or not to accept. Genevieve had confided in Adam, but had made him promise not to breathe a word to anyone else.

'I wish I had what Polly's got,' she said suddenly. 'I don't mean I want Jonjo, nothing like that. I'd just like a bit more romance. Oh, God! I'm beginning to sound like my mother.'

He smiled. 'Do you think Polly will marry Jonjo?'

'You know, I have a feeling she just might. But in her own time. I've never known Polly to make a decision she's regretted, and I think it's because she won't be hurried into anything.'

'Or does she make the most of what happens as a result of simply making a decision, rather than wasting time and energy on procrastinating? It's what I've always guarded against in business. If you procrastinate it stops you from moving forward. You're always looking over your shoulder at what you can't change.'

After last orders had been called, Adam walked her home. Genevieve wondered if that's what she did too often: looked back. Then remembering what Adam had said about her and Nattie being afraid of commitment, she asked him what she was supposed to be too scared to connect with.

'That's easy. You're afraid to connect with yourself, Gen. And until you do, no one else will be able to get really close to you.'

She came to a stop. After he'd walked a few paces on his own, he turned round. 'Oh, Genevieve, don't tell me I've stunned you with my powers of deductive reasoning?'

'Just when did you get to be so smart, Adam Kellar?'

He slipped his arm through hers and made her walk on. 'I didn't make my first million by the age of twenty-six without being smart. People forget that about me sometimes.'

45

With the last of the breakfast guests gone, Nattie was helping Genevieve to clean the dining room. Two young boys – veritable demons from hell – had been allowed by their drippy, shoulder-shrugging, boys-will-be-boys parents to run amok during breakfast. They had left the area around their table a scene of war-torn devastation. The tablecloth was askew and covered in damp patches of milk and orange juice and revolting bits of half-chewed sausages dipped in ketchup; there was a smear of egg yolk on one of the chairs and some soggy Cheerios had found their way into the dish of raspberry jam. Everything Genevieve touched was sticky, including the carpet, which would need a thorough scrubbing in places. She felt sorry for the other guests, two of whom were year-in, year-out regulars: this was not what they came to Paradise House for. She would have to apologise to them later.

Mum had offered to stay and help, instead of going down to Angel Cottage with their father to carry on with the task of sorting through Gran's things, but Genevieve, eager to make her parents spend time alone together, had told her she and Nattie would soon have the dining room shipshape. Annoyingly, Dad had suggested, as he did every morning, that they take Lily-Rose with them. The little girl had jumped at the chance to play with Gran's old musical jewellery box again, so bang went another opportunity to resolve matters.

Maybe Adam was right, and someone would have to have a word in her father's ear. If he went on avoiding being alone with Mum for much longer, he'd lose her for sure. Genevieve had hinted as much to him last night before going to bed, but he'd said, 'Genevieve, I know you think you're helping, but please, your mother and I need to take this gently. This isn't something we can rush. Slow and steady wins the race.' Exasperated, she'd given up and left him to his head-in-the-sand delusion. But she had then reminded herself that once again she was trying too hard to control what was going on around her.

Across the hall, where Polly and Donna were tidying the guest sitting room, Genevieve could hear Donna trying to press-gang her sister into lending a hand with the talent show; apparently the services of a musical director were now required.

'Everyone seems to be taking the talent show very seriously,' Genevieve remarked to Nattie as she shook out a clean white cloth and laid it over a table. 'I hope it's the success Donna and Tubby want it to be. They've put so much effort into it.'

'That's typical of you,' said Nattie. 'Always anxious on everyone else's behalf.'

'I just like things to go well. Anything wrong in that?'

'And if it's a disaster? What then?'

'Nothing, I suppose. But I don't like people to be disappointed.'

'But, Gen, it's *their* disappointment. Not yours. Oh, and talking of disappointments, Adam phoned to say he wanted to call in for a quick chat before going on to Tenby.'

'Did he say what he wanted?'

'No. And if you ask me he sounded distinctly furtive.'

Genevieve laughed and shook out another tablecloth. 'That's probably the nicest thing you've ever said about him.'

Nattie looked affronted. 'Hey, Adam and I are like this these days.' She held up a hand, the first two fingers crossed. 'A closer pair of buddies you couldn't hope to find.'

'So why did you just refer to him as a disappointment?'

Nattie laughed. 'Because he's taking all the fun out of my life. What's he done to his clothes? They're so normal. And have you noticed he doesn't wear that tacky bracelet any more?'

Genevieve kept her face straight. 'Really? I can't say I've noticed. And frankly, I'm surprised you have. What's got into you?'

Nattie ignored the question and, clumsily folding a napkin, said, 'I reckon there's some new girl on the scene we don't know about. Whoever she is, she's obviously taking him in hand. Do you suppose we ought to keep an eye on him?'

'Whatever for?'

'Oh, come on, Gen. Adam's just ripe for the plucking. All that money's bound to attract the wrong sort of girlfriend.'

'And you care?'

'Now look, Gen, I'm getting sick of your cynicism. He saved Lily's life, so in my book, I owe him. Bottom line, I'm always going to be in his debt. Which means the least I can do is save him from some money-grabbing, high-maintenance madam who's going to take him for all she can get.'

Genevieve flicked a soggy Cheerio at her sister. 'Wow! He'll sleep easy from now on, knowing you're on the case.'

Nattie was out in the garden tidying up after Henry and Morwenna when Adam arrived. He was in full suit mode.

'Another business lunch in Tenby?' Genevieve asked.

'Another lunch, another dime.'

'Well, come on through to the kitchen and you can fill me in on what it is you want to talk about. Nattie said you were acting distinctly furtive on the phone. But then she'd say that about a newborn baby with wind. Sit yourself down. Coffee?'

'Actually it was Nattie I wanted to speak to. I thought I'd made that clear on the phone to her.'

'Oh. Oh, right. I'll go and find her. She's knee-deep in donkey doos, as Lily calls it.'

Adam smiled. 'I'll go and find her myself if you're busy.'

It had rained overnight and Genevieve looked at his expensive shoes. 'Dressed like that? I don't think so. Put the kettle on and I'll give her a shout.'

Nattie threw down the shovel and muttered crossly when Genevieve told her that it was her Adam wanted to talk to. 'Don't you dare leave me alone with him,' she said as she stomped back up to the house. 'I don't want him taking advantage of our newfound relationship.'

She kicked off her dirty boots on the doorstep, and went to the sink in the utility room to wash her hands. Seconds later she was in the kitchen with Genevieve and Adam, drying her hands on a towel, which she then slung over her shoulder.

'So what's this about, Adam? You've not come here to propose, have you? Because I must warn you, you should speak to my father first. It's a courtesy thing.'

Adam laughed good-humouredly. 'No, it's not a proposal of marriage, but it is a proposal of sorts.'

Putting their drinks down on the table, Genevieve said, 'You probably don't need me hanging round, I'll just go—'

'It's all right, Gen, there's no need to make yourself scarce. Unless, of course, Nattie would prefer it?' He turned to look at her.

Nattie shrugged. 'Always good to have a witness. Spit it out, then.'

'Right,' he said, 'first off, I hear you're looking for a job?'

She nodded.

'One that will provide you with the means to pay for a good childminder?'

'Spot on.'

'Excellent. Because *I* have a job for you.'

Nattie took the towel from her shoulder and straightened the straps of her dungarees. 'What kind of a job?'

'A nine-to-five kind of a job, working in the office of one of my caravan parks.'

She stopped what she was doing. 'In one of your caravan parks? You must be bloody joking! I'd rather shovel donkey shit all day than set foot in one of your tacky parks!'

He raised his eyebrows. 'I have it on good authority that you said you'd take the first job offer that came your way.'

Nattie threw Genevieve a look of disgust. 'Traitor,' she hissed. She turned back to Adam. 'There was a proviso attached. It has to pay enough for me to afford a reliable childminder for Lily-Rose.'

Reaching for his mug of coffee, his voice casual, Adam said, 'You're in luck. This job comes with a ready-made crèche for Lily; the one the holiday guests put their own children in. I only employ fully qualified girls, so you'd know Lily was being well looked after. What's more, it's free.'

Genevieve smiled to herself. He'd had his trump card up his sleeve all along. It was good to see Nattie being out-manoeuvred for a change.

Nattie chewed on the inside of her lip, then switched her gaze from Adam to Genevieve. 'Did you cook this up between the two of you at the pub last night?'

'No! This is the first I heard of it.'

'She's right,' said Adam. 'I only thought of it when I was having breakfast this morning.'

'I don't believe you.'

'Well, get over your disbelief and give me an answer.'

'How can I? I don't even know what sort of job it is.'

'I need someone to answer the phones and deal with guests' queries. It'd be a challenge for you, Nattie, because you'll have to be pleasant.' This last comment was said with a smile.

'Watch it mate, you push your luck at your peril. Anyway, I thought you were selling the parks?'

'I am, but these things take for ever. Meanwhile, I need someone to do the job for the rest of the season, or however long it takes. The girl who's been doing it for the last two years has just handed in her notice.'

'Why? Didn't she like the boss?'

'This might come as a surprise to you, but people generally like me. I'm a pretty fair employer, too.'

Nattie grunted. 'Okay then, when do you want me to start? But I'm warning you, one wisecrack about a perk of the job being that I get to sleep with the boss and I'll have you for sexual harassment.'

A smile twitched at his mouth. 'Don't flatter yourself, Nattie. Moreover, I never mix business with pleasure.'

Genevieve had to cough and clear her throat several times before she could speak without laughing. 'Adam, are you sure you know what you're doing? You're not worried she might sabotage your business?' She was thinking of the time Nattie had threatened to set fire to one of his caravan parks.

'Don't worry, I know exactly what I'm doing.' He finished his coffee and got to his feet. 'I'll be in touch with all the relevant details, Nattie. Presumably you have a P45?'

'The man's insufferable,' said Nattie, minutes later when Adam had left them.

'How can you say that when he's being so helpful?'

She smirked. 'I was going to add, he's insufferably generous. He'll be handing out blankets to the homeless next.'

Two days later Genevieve received bad news. The estate agent in Tenby who had been handling the sale of the property in Angel Sands wrote to say that the owners had received and accepted a higher offer. There was no hint that, were she to come in with a higher offer, she would be successful. Anyway, she didn't want to play that game. Though the letter knocked her back, she kept its contents to herself. Besides, everyone was preoccupied with their own affairs. Adam was away checking out his parks down in Cornwall, Polly was on a visit to Buckingham to stay with Jonjo and to meet his parents, and with Mum and Dad's help, Nattie was preparing to move in to Angel Cottage before taking up Adam's job offer.

Angel Cottage was almost unrecognisable. The bulky furniture Gran had squeezed into the little house had either been sold or moved up to Paradise House. The biggest transformation, so far, was the smallest bedroom at the back of the house, the one Gran had used as an apple store. Every year she would take the apples from the orchard at Paradise House and spend hours wrapping them in tissue paper, putting them to bed in the enormous mahogany chest of drawers that had dominated the little room. The chest had been put into one of the guest rooms at Paradise House and the apple room, as Lily-Rose called it, was now hers. Mum and Dad had completely redecorated it and had replaced the ancient swirly, head-spinning patterned carpet with a plain one. 'It's like the colour of the sea on a sunny day,' Lily-Rose told everyone, repeating Serena. She was thrilled with her new room, the pale blue gingham curtains Serena had made and the pretty seashells she had stencilled above the window. She was particularly excited about the desk and shelving unit that her grandfather had built for her at lightning speed.

But it was while Mum was up late one night, finishing off the stencilling in Lily-Rose's room, that she discovered what had made Gran think she had mice living with her.

'My first thought,' she told them the next morning, 'was that it sounded just like a mouse squeaking. I went all round the house looking for it, but when I listened closely, it sounded more like a gate in need of oil.'

It turned out not to be a gate, or indeed a mouse, but her neighbour Olwen Jenkins' rusting old weather vane that needed oiling, which Dad had since seen to. And the reason the noise had been intermittent was that it only squeaked when the wind blew from a certain direction. Poor Gran, driven to distraction because her neighbour's hearing wasn't as good as it used to be and she hadn't noticed what was going on up on her chimney pot.

It might have seemed that they were acting with in-decent haste, doing up Angel Cottage so soon after Gran's death, but Genevieve felt sure her grandmother would approve. It did mean that while her parents were spending so much time down at Angel Cottage, they were continually in each other's company, which had to be a good thing. Watching their animated faces as they discussed the planned improvements, Genevieve began to have more confidence in her father, that slow and steady would win the race.

She had mentioned this to Christian in an email and he'd replied that maybe what her parents needed was a new project to interest them. 'It sounds like they've grown bored of Paradise House and not of each other,' he wrote.

It was the last message she'd had from Christian and in the following days she'd steeled herself for what she now realised was inevitable; neither of them was suited to a long-distance relationship. She felt no regret that they'd tried to resurrect what they'd once felt for each other, and she knew she would always treasure the happy memories of this summer. Looking back, it now seemed an omen that they hadn't managed to sleep together. She recalled the scene of the two of them upstairs in her bedroom, and in particular the look on Christian's face when she'd said she could hear someone in the house. The memory made her smile. She would like it if they could remain friends.

Washing the mud from the potatoes she'd dug up from her father's vegetable patch, she thought how much better she was with friendships than love affairs. She thought of Adam and what he'd said about her being afraid to connect with herself. Until then, she hadn't realised that that was what she did. But it was true: time and time again she had withdrawn from a relationship not just because she wasn't able to trust the person, or because they didn't measure up in some way, but because, subconsciously, she didn't want that person to see the real her, the old Genevieve who had never gone away. The fat, ugly Genevieve who had convinced herself she didn't deserve a boyfriend like Christian.

Was she doing it all over again, then? Deliberately talking herself out of a chance of happiness in yet another act of self-destruction? Staring at the garden – it was raining again – and wondering if she would ever change, her attention was caught by a familiar song on the radio. It was Judy Garland singing 'Over the Rainbow'. Genevieve hoped that her parents had the radio on down at Angel Cottage – they were emulsioning the kitchen today. She pictured her mother on the stepladder, brush in hand, streaks of paint in her hair as she sang along, maybe even using the brush as a microphone, like she used to when they were little and she'd had one too many glasses of wine. Then very slowly a different picture appeared in Genevieve's head. It was a picture of her father. Holding her breath, frightened the faint glimmer of inspiration would fade, she held on to the image, right until the very last poignant note of the song.

Was it the answer?

Yes it was. It was the perfect answer.

But if so, would her father have the nerve to carry off her idea? And who would be the best person to persuade him?

Once again, Adam came to mind.

46

It was the afternoon of the talent contest and very nearly everyone in the village was participating in the event or helping with its organisation, including Genevieve. Overnight, though, the extent of her input had grown dramatically. Two members of the kitchen staff at the Salvation Arms had gone down with a nasty cold, so instead of just lending a hand in the kitchen, she was now in charge of cooking and serving a massive lamb and ham carvery with trifle and fresh strawberries to follow. If the menu had been left to her, she would have come up with something a little less traditional. As it was, she decided to throw in a vegetarian option just in case, a mushroom and aubergine lasagne.

In the kitchen at Paradise House, with Donna's help she was now getting to grips with the amount of food she had to prepare. The Lloyd-Morris brothers had supplied all the meat at a generous discount and Tubby had specially fetched the fruit and veg that morning, guaranteeing its freshness. Mum was also pitching in to help and was arriving later with Nattie and Lily-Rose; they had promised to be back from Tenby within the hour. In an effort to mollify Nattie, Mum had suggested they go clothes shopping for her new job. Cruelly, they were all putting bets on Nattie finding a reason between now and her first day next week, why she couldn't actually take up the job. Nobody believed her when she said she would prove them wrong.

'I'll work for Adam to spite you all,' she'd said.

Cynically, Genevieve would believe it when she saw it.

Something else she was having difficulty believing was Dad going through with her plan. She had Adam to thank, really. The two of them had cornered her father at Angel Cottage as he was jet-blasting the patio that Gran had never allowed him to do; she'd always claimed it would destroy the lived-in look of the place, never mind that it was as skiddy as an oil slick with the build-up of moss and algae.

'What have you got to lose?' Adam had asked, after Genevieve had outlined what she'd thought was a stroke of pure genius on her part.

'My self-respect?' her father had muttered.

'You don't want to think of a little thing like that,' Adam had said. 'No one will have an ounce of it left by the end of the night.'

'But I've never sung in public before.'

'Nor have I, but it's not stopping me.'

The prevarication had been astonishingly short-lived and, slowly coming round to the suggestion, Dad had said, 'You're sure it would work?'

'Yes, Dad. It's the perfect way to prove how much you love her. And because she knows you so well, she'll know exactly how much courage it took. Trust me; you have to do it.'

'But what shall I sing?'

This was when Genevieve told him what had given her the idea. 'You have to sing a big Judy Garland number,' she told him. 'One of Mum's favourites. She'll love it.'

But Adam shook his head. 'I've been thinking about that, Gen. Those songs are better coming from a woman. How about the King? Elvis.'

Daddy Dean looked doubtful. 'Would I have to dress up like him?'

'All the way or nothing,' Adam said.

'Yes,' agreed Genevieve. 'It's got to be a show-stopping moment to bring a tear to Mum's eye.'

There were tears in Genevieve's eyes now: she was slicing onions for the vegetable lasagne. She slid them into the large frying pan on the gas hob, lowered the flame, added some crushed garlic and thought of her father, who should now be on his way home from Swansea with an Elvis outfit. There'd been nothing available locally, and with insufficient time to make one in secret, Adam had got on the phone and tracked down a costume hirer in Swansea.

'Where's your father gone?' Serena had asked earlier that morning.

'He's with Adam,' Genevieve had said.

'I know he's with Adam, but where have they gone?'

'For a walk, I think.'

'Then why hasn't he taken his walking boots with him?'

'Oh, hasn't he?'

'No, Gen, they're by the back door.'

'Perhaps it's not that kind of a walk. Just a leisurely stroll and a chat.'

Serena had looked at her suspiciously. 'Something's going on, isn't it? What's your father up to? And why does he always seem to be huddled in a corner with that woman?'

'Which woman?' Although, of course, Genevieve had known exactly who her mother was referring to.

'I'm talking about Donna,' Serena said impatiently. 'Has something been going on between those two while I've been away?'

Nattie had walked in at that moment. 'And what's it to you, Mum, what Dad gets up to? You didn't give a jam fig all those months you were away. Why be concerned now?'

There was no hostility in her voice, just a matter-of-fact tone that had made their mother drop her line of interrogation. 'Do you still want to go shopping in Tenby?' she'd asked.

Adding the salted and rinsed slices of aubergine, Genevieve stirred the pan and glanced across the kitchen to where Donna was peeling a mound of potatoes. It looked very much as though, without meaning to, their father had made his wife jealous. Serena's comment that he was always huddled up in a corner with Donna was an exaggeration, but it did contain an element of truth. The most professional singer in Angel Sands other than Polly, who was arriving home with Jonjo that afternoon, Donna was giving Dad singing lessons up at Adam's place. What Genevieve wouldn't give to be a fly on the wall during one of their sessions!

'Do you think that's enough potatoes?' asked Donna.

Knowing that Donna had a hundred and one things to do, Genevieve said, 'That's plenty. And thanks for your help. But feel free to disappear if you want. I've got it all under control here.'

'You sure?'

'Absolutely. Anyway, it's not fair of me to monopolise the star of the show.'

Donna smiled. 'I think you might change your opinion when you hear your father tonight.'

Having avoided asking the question till now, Genevieve said, 'He'll be okay, won't he?'

The smiled widened. 'He'll be fine, love. Beneath that reserve lurks a budding performer.'

Still worried and knowing she was responsible for putting her father through this ordeal, Genevieve said, 'People won't laugh at him, will they?'

'Trust me. He's got quite a decent voice on him. Shame he hasn't used it before. Mark my words, he'll knock everyone dead. Especially your Mum. I wouldn't be surprised if there was a drop or two of Welsh blood in him.' Washing her hands at the sink, she said, 'Now if you're sure there's nothing else I can do, I'll push off. I'll see you later.'

Encouraged by Donna's words, Genevieve thought of the others, apart from Donna, who knew about the surprise. Tubby and Adam, her sisters and Christian had all said the same when she'd told them about it. 'It's totally inspired, Genevieve,' Christian had replied to her email. 'I just wish I could be there with you to enjoy the moment.'

The disappointment that once again Christian couldn't spare the time to drive down hit Genevieve harder than she'd expected. There was no reason why he should want to witness an entire village making a fool of itself, but she'd invited him because, if nothing else, it would give them the opportunity to talk things through, face to face. Surprised how hurt she felt, she'd replied to his email with a businesslike update on everything, then told him how she'd been gazumped on the teashop. 'Turns out that my money just wasn't good enough,' she wrote.

'If it's any consolation, you did the right thing in not increasing your offer,' he answered. 'They could have strung you along trying to get even more out of you.'

It was exactly what Adam had said when Genevieve had shared her setback with him. He'd hugged her hard and said, 'And what will you do if the agent calls you because the current deal has fallen through?'

'I shall tell him to go to hell. Then offer slightly less than I did first time round.'

'Well done, Gen, you're learning fast.'

It didn't really feel like she was learning anything fast, but maybe Adam was right. He usually was.

Polly and Jonjo arrived home not long after Adam had dropped Dad at the front door, giving Serena no time to cross examine him on where he'd been or what he'd been doing. She was too busy anyway, what with meeting Jonjo for the first time and throwing all her energy into interrogating him.

Genevieve watched her mother assessing the man whom, in her own clichéd words, she'd heard so much about. They sat outside in the garden, a tray of drinks before them on the wooden table, where the not so subtle cross-examination was in full swing. Had she got it right that he ran a franchise of fitness centres? Jonjo took Serena's question, and those that followed, in his stride. Genevieve reckoned he'd met more than his fair share of protective mothers in the past, and had doubtless charmed each and every one of them. But of course, what Serena didn't know, and nor did their father, was that Jonjo was a serious contender for the role of son-in-law. Polly still hadn't mentioned anything to their parents about Jonjo's proposal and as far as Genevieve was aware, she still hadn't given him an answer.

Then the line of questioning took an unexpected turn.

'Genevieve tells me you're an old friend of Christian May,' Serena said.

Instantly Genevieve was on the alert and regretting she'd told her mother about seeing Christian again. Like Nattie and her father, she hadn't been exactly thrilled by the news.

'That's right,' Jonjo said, without looking Genevieve's way. 'I got to know Christian several years ago when he boasted he could have made a better job of designing my first fitness centre.'

'Really? That doesn't sound like the Christian we used to know. I don't recall him ever having a tendency to boast. Perhaps he's changed. Which might not be such a bad thing,' she added under her breath.

Genevieve cringed. But Jonjo, still not looking in Genevieve's direction, kept his tone even. 'I can't vouch for what he was like as a child. Apart from that one excusable blag he made to me, I'd say he's one of the most modest blokes I know. And completely reliable. Professionally as well as personally.' He put his glass down, before skilfully steering Serena off course. 'If you've got time, why don't I take you to look at the barn? The builders have made a start and I'm keen to see what they've done so far.'

Genevieve was grateful for his charm and quick thinking. 'That's a great idea, Jonjo,' she said. She shot her sister a glance, hoping for backup. 'Polly, why don't you go with Mum and Dad?'

Amidst the kerfuffle of decision making – could they really spare the time? – Genevieve leaned towards Jonjo and whispered her thanks.

'No problem,' he said. 'By the way, Christian sends his love. He said to be sure I got the message right. Not best wishes. Not regards. Not even fondest etceteras. But his *love.*'

Genevieve felt the colour rush to her cheeks. All she could think to say was, 'I was hoping he might make it down for the weekend.'

Everyone was on their feet now. Jonjo took Genevieve aside. 'Things are okay between you and Christian, aren't they?'

'We're fine,' she said brightly. But she suddenly heard the echo of the lie that had tripped so easily off her tongue. She remembered Adam saying that she always said she was fine. But she wasn't fine. She was confused. Christian seemed to be blowing hot and cold.

Keeping his voice low, Jonjo said, 'I got the feeling from Christian that he doesn't know where he stands with you. He hinted that he thought there was someone else in the background.'

'What? But that's absurd. He knows perfectly well there isn't. No, the trouble is we don't see—'

But there was no time to finish their conversation. Serena was bearing down on them.

After waving them off, Genevieve hurried back to the kitchen to finish preparing the food for that evening.

Genevieve had often seen the Salvation Arms so crowded it took for ever to be served at the small bar, but tonight it was the busiest she'd ever seen. Anyone wanting a drink had better be patient, she thought as she looked through the gap in the door from the kitchen to the public lounge. Every chair, bar stool and table had been claimed (extras had been brought in specially) and people were queuing at the bar getting their drinks in, stockpiling a round or two if they had any sense. And it wasn't just locals who had bought tickets. Plenty of visitors to Angel Sands had shown up, and some were participating.

With half an hour to go before Tubby, acting as master of ceremonies, would be getting the proceedings underway, Genevieve closed the door and checked on the joints of meat in the ovens. The two part-timers from the pub's bar and kitchen staff, those who weren't off sick, would be here in ten minutes, along with Serena and Nattie, who were going to help serve. Back at Paradise House, Kelly was babysitting Lily-Rose and had promised to be on hand should any of the guests need something.

Dad was booked to do his slot towards the end of the evening, after Adam. Genevieve had spoken to him before leaving the house and he'd seemed extraordinarily calm and philosophical. 'What will be, will be, Gen,' he'd said. He wouldn't let on which particular Elvis song he was singing and he'd sworn Donna and Adam to secrecy. Mum was still completely in the dark about what he'd been up to, though she kept throwing Donna narrow-eyed, suspicious glances. Perhaps Polly's original idea of finding a girlfriend for their father hadn't been such a bad one after all.

There was only one person who could open the show and that was Donna. She looked as spectacular as she sounded – shoulder-length blonde hair backcombed to within an inch of its life, legs wrapped in the tightest jeans Genevieve had ever seen, and wearing her own body weight in lipgloss and eye make-up. She tottered around on the small makeshift stage on her six-inch, baby-pink stiletto heels, a death-defying act of pure bravery. She gave a magnificent, gutsy rendition of Bonnie Tyler singing 'Holding Out For a Hero' and had the place in an uproar when she finished. The crowd went mad, hands clapping, feet stamping. Tubby looked on proudly.

Watching from the steam-filled kitchen, with the door wedged open, Nattie said, 'Bloody hell! That's an awesome act to follow. Pity the poor devil who goes next. Anyone know who it is?'

Serena shook her head and said rather primly, 'Is she always as showy as that?'

Genevieve smiled. 'She's playing a part, Mum.'

With a sniff, Serena crossed her arms firmly over her chest.

The plan for the evening was an hour of performances followed by a break for supper and then a further hour of performances.

'Expect things to run over a bit,' both Tubby and Donna had warned Genevieve. 'We'll do our best to keep it on track, but once people get a whiff of the greasepaint, there's often no stopping them from hogging the stage.'

Standing with her mother and sister, Genevieve looked across the crowded pub to where the panel of judges – the vicar of St Non's, the Reverend David Trent, Stan from the mini-market and Ruth from Angel Crafts – sat with their pieces of paper. She didn't envy them their job. The obvious outright winner would be Donna, no question. But who would make second and third? Perhaps not the man currently on his feet doing an appalling impression of Tom Jones singing 'Sex Bomb'. Genevieve didn't recognise him, so assumed he was a visitor, but as awful as he was – a scrawny, middle-aged comb-over wearing a shirt slashed to his waist, revealing more sunburnt hairless chest than was decent – she had to admit the crowd loved him and was urging him on to thrust his hips out of their sockets.

Nattie groaned. 'I know this is for charity, but there are limits.'

'Gran would have loved all this,' Genevieve said.

Serena smiled. 'She would have done a turn herself.'

The next act was Jane Davies from the pottery. Done up as Shania Twain, wearing a fabulously raunchy leopardskin number, she threw herself into a slightly off-key version of 'Man! I Feel Like a Woman!'.

By the time Tubby called half-time and announced that supper was served, they'd witnessed a warbling Mariah Carey, two Frank Sinatras – one singing 'My Way' and the other stumbling through 'Strangers in the Night' – a leather-clad Ricky Martin, and a bursting-at-the-seams Dolly Parton. Queuing for their food, everyone was in high spirits, talking and laughing about the performances. Judging from their comments, Donna was still way out in front to win first prize, with Ricky Martin close on her baby-pink stiletto heels. There was no sign of Daddy Dean. Or Adam. But then none of the singers, until they'd performed, were allowed to show themselves. Only when they'd sung could they sit with their friends and families. Those who had yet to sing were still upstairs, in either the dressing room or what Tubby jokingly referred to as the Green Room. Donna was currently ferrying trays of food up and down the stairs for them, which, Genevieve could see, was further annoying her mother. Serena had been amazed when Dad had told her he'd volunteered to help Debs get the performers down to the stage on time. Suspicious too.

'Let me take that for you,' Serena said to Donna now, as once more Donna came into the kitchen for a tray of food. 'You can't possibly manage the stairs in those shoes again.'

Gripping the tray of food, Donna laughed. 'That's okay Mrs Baxter, my feet are as tough as old coal scuttles.'

'Here, Mum,' Genevieve intervened – no way could they afford for Serena to go anywhere near the Green Room. 'Take this over to the judges. They look like they could do with a second helping of trifle.'

The first performer to take to the stage in the second half was Huw Davies. Dressed in a white singlet and ripped jeans, fake tattoos on his biceps, he got a massive cheer when Tubby introduced him as 'the cheeky lad from Stoke, Robbie Williams, singing "Let Me Entertain You".'

'Any time mate,' yelled out a woman from the back of the pub. But despite cries of 'Show us your bum!' he kept his trousers on right through to the end of his performance. 'I reckon he might knock Ricky Martin off the number two spot,' Serena commented.

'I had no idea Huw could sing so well,' Nattie agreed. 'It makes you look at these people in a whole new light, doesn't it?'

Genevieve knew that Adam was on next, and she wondered if Nattie might make the same observation of him afterwards. There was a short lull in the proceedings while Huw left the stage. Then Adam appeared – hair brushed back from his forehead, fake whiskers applied to his chin and a black leather jacket turned up at the collar. He stepped onto the small stage and exchanged a quick, nervous glance with Polly who was sitting at the piano to accompany him – everyone else had provided backing tracks to sing along to. Genevieve watched her sister closely, but Nattie's face was perfectly composed, giving nothing away.

Tubby introduced Adam. 'Put your hands together for none other than Mr Joe Cocker.'

A whistling, whooping round of applause went up, but when Adam leaned into the microphone and exchanged another look with Polly, the crowd fell quiet. The opening notes were Polly's and then Adam came in, his eyes closed, his voice low and husky.

'*You are so beautiful,*' he sang.

After all the raucous singing and booming backing tracks that had gone before, the audience was stunned into a pin drop silence.

'My God,' muttered Nattie, 'the bastard can actually sing.'

'And some,' whispered Genevieve.

'Ssh you two! You're spoiling it.'

'*You're everything I hoped for,*' Adam sang on, his voice cracking with a rich resonance.

Genevieve could hardly bear to listen. She felt weak all over, and all at once she realised that this was what she wanted from Christian. She wanted him to take her breath away, to make her feel she was everything he'd ever hoped for. She thought of what Jonjo had said. *Christian sends his love.* Did he? Did he really?

Adam's performance was mesmerising, and when he sang the words, '*You're my guiding light,*' he slowly opened his eyes and looked over to where Genevieve, her mother and Nattie were grouped in the doorway. For a heart-stopping moment Genevieve thought he was looking at her, but then she realised it was Nattie, standing just behind her, he was staring at. There was no mistaking that she was the whole focus of his gaze. Or that he was singing to her, and for her alone. She risked a glance at Nattie and saw that she was transfixed.

Only when the audience leapt to its feet, whooping and yelling its appreciation, did Adam look away from Nattie and take his bow.

In the din of noise, Genevieve clearly heard her sister say, 'Oh, what the hell! In for a penny, in for a pound.'

47

What happened next had the entire pub in an uproar of hysterical approval. Nattie pushed through the crowd, leapt up onto the stage and grabbed hold of Adam. She kissed him full on the mouth. He showed no sign of resisting – far from it – and just as Genevieve was wondering if she'd have to fetch a crowbar to prise them apart, Nattie pulled away. Grinning into the microphone, she said, 'Guess what folks, he kisses as well as he sings!'

Amidst more cheers and clapping, they stepped down from the stage, Adam leading the way to go back upstairs, but once again Nattie took matters into her own hands and propelled him towards the kitchen. As the door swung shut behind them, Genevieve caught a glimpse of Adam being pressed against the walk-in cold store.

'And about time too,' said Serena. 'That poor man's waited long enough for her to come to her senses. *Good God!* Is that your father? Oh, tell me it isn't!'

Despite the trademark Presley white fringed catsuit, the black wig, the sideburns, and the silver-framed sunglasses, the man now up on stage was unmistakably Daddy Dean. But what a transformation! He looked phenomenal; lip curled, one hand held out to the side to show off the sleeve fringe, the other holding the microphone.

'Tell me he's not going to sing,' murmured Serena. 'He's never sung in public before. Never!'

Hiding her own anxiety, reminding herself what Donna had said that afternoon, Genevieve said, 'Well, he's singing now, Mum.'

This time it wasn't Polly providing the musical accompaniment. The video CD up on the wall began with the backing track and 'Always On My Mind' started. Dad's eyes sought out Serena's face in the crowd. Her mother reached for Genevieve's hand, gripping it hard.

'*Maybe I didn't treat you quite as good as I should have . . . maybe I didn't love you quite as often as I could have.*'

He was singing from the heart and, amazingly, Donna hadn't exaggerated: he really could sing. But it was the sincerity in his voice that brought a lump to Genevieve's throat. That and the choice of song.

'*If I made you feel second best, girl, I'm so sorry I was blind . . .*'

Genevieve had never been more proud of her father. Had he known all along that this was how Mum had been feeling? When the music stopped and he took his bow to ear-splitting applause, she looked at her mother. Serena was openly sobbing, her face wet with tears. She tried to speak, but couldn't.

Genevieve put her arms around her mother. 'Now do you see how much he loves you, Mum?'

'But he only had to say.'

'It wouldn't have been enough, would it? You know as well as I do, you wanted something big from him. A grand, over-the-top romantic gesture. And they don't come much more romantic or dramatic than this.'

They both turned to look at the stage, to join in with the applause. Dad had already gone.

After Tubby had introduced the next act, Genevieve asked if he knew where her father was. 'I think Elvis has left the building,' Tubby joked. 'From the look of him, I'd say he went for some fresh air.'

Squeezing through the crowds, Genevieve and her mother made it to the door and outside. It was still light and easy to spot him. Down on the beach, dressed in his white Elvis suit, he looked a lonely, incongruous figure as he hurled stone after stone into the sea. Genevieve nudged her mother.

'Go to him, Mum. Don't let him suffer any more.' She watched Serena walk away, and knowing she'd done as much as she could, Genevieve turned and went back inside the pub to make a start on the washing up.

That's if the kitchen wasn't still occupied by Adam and her sister. She had no idea what was going to become of them – one snog does not a relationship make – but she felt happy for Adam. Surprised too, that, despite his conviction to put Nattie out of his mind, his feelings for her had clearly never left him. She also felt a twinge of sadness. If anything did come of this evening, there would be no more cosy evenings for her and Adam. The close nature of their friendship would inevitably change, and she would be the poorer for it.

Genevieve stopped for a moment to watch the next performer, a shockingly awful Tina Turner lookalike, possibly a man in drag. Cautiously she opened the kitchen door, in case the kissing had progressed to something the health and safety inspector wouldn't approve of. There was no sign of her sister and Adam, or the part-time kitchen staff who were supposed to be helping her. Instead, the unexpected sight of Jonjo brought a smile to her lips: he was standing at the sink up to his elbows in soapy water.

'Seeing as you've been abandoned, Polly thought you might like the extra help,' he said. 'There's a hell of a lot to get through, isn't there? Beats me why a pub of this size doesn't have a dishwasher.'

She picked up a tea-towel. 'There is one, but it's not working.'

'Oh, well, not to worry, you've got me instead. I'm doing my bit to assure Polly I'm the domesticated modern man she needs in her life.'

Genevieve laughed. 'I don't think Polly would mind one way or the other.'

'You mean she's so in love with me she'd put up with coffee cups left in the sink?'

'No, I mean she's like Nattie, not in the least concerned how things get done. I would have thought you'd have realised that by now.'

Rinsing a plate under the tap and passing it to her, he tutted. 'Modern girls, I ask you. What's the world coming to?'

From the other side of the door, the music had changed tempo and an unknown woman's voice screeched out the theme to *Titanic*, 'My Heart Will Go On'.

'I'm glad we're this side of the door,' Jonjo said. 'The punters in there could end up with blood pouring out of their ears if they're not careful.'

'You shouldn't criticise what you're not prepared to have a go at yourself,' she said good-humouredly.

'Some of us aren't as fair-minded as you, Genevieve. I haven't known you long, but I can't recall you ever saying a harsh word about anyone.'

'You haven't seen me when I'm rattled. I can turn nasty when I want to.'

He laughed. 'Yeah, about as nasty as Polly. You're two of a kind. No, make that three of a kind; you're both like your father.'

'Leaving Nattie out in the cold?'

'I don't think she currently feels out in the cold. The last time I saw Nattie, she and Adam looked decidedly hot. But never mind them, tell me about you and Christian. What's the deal there? You have such an amazing history, you owe it to yourselves to work things out.'

She reached for a clean tea-towel. 'Who said we have anything to work out?'

Jonjo switched off the tap and stopped what he was doing. 'You need to talk to him. Talk to him properly. He needs your reassurance.'

'But how can we talk? We never get to spend any time together. Not like you and Polly.'

He frowned. 'It's never a good thing to make comparisons. Not when Christian isn't as lucky as me. I can take time off whenever I want, to be with Polly. Next to Christian, I'm a right lazy bugger. His problem is that he's bloody good at what he does and is in high demand. He's also lousy at delegating and saying no. Which leaves him sod-all free time.'

She looked away uncomfortably. 'Stop lecturing me, Jonjo. Or you really will see the nasty side of me.'

'All I'm saying is, go easy on him. Who knows, he might just surprise you one of these days. He's not entirely lacking in sensitivity. After all, some of my perfection must have rubbed off on him along the way.'

She smiled. 'There's only the cutlery left to do. Let's take a break and go and watch some of the acts.'

He glanced at the clock. 'The job's almost done. Ten minutes' more and then we'll venture back into the fray.'

Surprised at his willingness to stick it out, she found another dry tea-towel and scooped up a handful of knives and forks, grateful that in Nattie and Serena's absence she had him to help her. How typically thoughtful it had been of Polly to send Jonjo to her rescue. And how good of him to oblige.

Jonjo was true to his word, and exactly ten minutes later, when they could hear a squeaky-voiced Britney Spears singing 'Baby One More Time', he pulled the plug out from the bottom of the sink.

'That's it. We're done here for now. Let's see if we can mount an attack on the bar for a drink. We've definitely earned it. You especially.'

There was no chance of getting a drink, the bar was much too busy, but Genevieve didn't mind. She was just happy to be out of the kitchen; she was beginning to feel like hard-done-by Cinders again.

With Britney off the stage, Tubby bounced back onto it. 'Well, ladies and gentlemen,' he boomed, 'that was to be our last performance of the contest, but we've had a late entry, one we simply couldn't refuse. So, if you'd like to put your hands together and give a warm welcome to this act, I think you'll agree a very special person is in for a treat. Ladies and gentlemen, I give you the Angel Sands Choir!'

'Angel Sands Choir?' repeated Genevieve. 'Who's that?'

Jonjo shrugged. 'Who cares? Do as the man says and put your hands together.'

She did, and watched with interest to see who would emerge through the curtain of sparkly red tinsel. But before anyone appeared, the backing track started. Genevieve recognised it straight away. It was 'The Wonder of You'.

She turned to Jonjo to tell him how much she liked this particular song, that it was her all-time favourite. But he wasn't there. Mystified, she looked around for him, but he'd vanished into thin air. How very odd.

Back on the stage, the curtain moved and people began to appear, first ... first Polly, and then ... Nattie with Adam, his hand on her shoulder. Next came her parents, hand in hand, followed by Donna with a crowd of other performers. Including Jonjo! How on earth had he got there so quickly? He flashed her a grin and a wave. Then, with one fantastic voice that made the hairs on the back of her neck stand on end, they all looked at her and sang the words she knew by heart.

> '*When no one else can understand me,*
> *when everything I do is wrong,*
> *you give me hope and consolation,*
> *you give me strength to carry on,*
> *and you're always there to lend a hand in everything I do.*
> *That's the wonder ... the wonder of you.*'

She knew who was behind this: Polly. Dear, sweet Polly. No one else would have been so thoughtful. No one else in her family would have known what the song meant to her. A flicker of sparkly red tinsel at the back of the stage caught her attention. As they began to sing the next line of the song – *And when you smile the world is brighter* – someone else appeared on the stage. Her heart leapt.

It was Christian.

He must have known where she would be standing because without hesitating, his eyes settled on her. And while everyone else swayed to the music and sang – '*You touch my hand and I'm a king, your kiss to me is worth a fortune,*' – they moved to let him through. And at '*your love for me is everything, I guess I'll never know the reason why you love me as you do,*' he stepped down from the stage and came slowly towards her. Again people made room for him to pass, and when he was standing right in front of her, he brought a hand forward and presented her with a single red rose.

'I couldn't serenade you in the way I'd have liked,' he said, leaning in to speak in her ear, 'so I roped in a few who could.'

She tilted her head back. 'You arranged all this yourself?'

'With a little help.'

The rest of the song was lost to her. Not minding that everyone was staring at them, she held the rose carefully between her fingers and threw her arms around his neck. She kissed him and kissed him. Then kissed him some more. Let them fetch a crowbar, she wasn't letting go of him for the rest of the night!

48

Gran used to say that miracles happen every day of our lives. 'And the reason we don't realise it,' she would explain, 'is that most of the time we are in too much of a rush to notice the angels going about their business.' After what had happened at the Salvation Arms, and what was happening to her now, Genevieve was inclined to agree with her grandmother.

Catching their breath outside the pub, Christian told her he was kidnapping her for the rest of the night, that he had a failsafe way to avoid anyone disturbing them. He led her to his car, which was parked outside Gran's house, and told her he wouldn't answer a single question until the time was right.

'Am I allowed to ask where we're going?' she said.

'It'll be obvious,' he said enigmatically. She thought he was taking her to Tawelfan beach, but soon realised she was wrong when he turned off down the narrow track to Ralph's barn. Or rather, Jonjo's barn. Parking alongside a large skip and a cement mixer, he switched off the engine and got out. He was round to her side of the car before she'd put a foot on the ground. 'You have to close your eyes,' he said, his face close to hers so that he could see her clearly.

'But it's pitch black, I can't see a thing anyway.'

Producing a torch from the back of the car, he offered her his arm.

Giggling with nervous excitement, she allowed him to lead her. She heard a door scrape and guessed they were going inside the barn. But why? After a few steps, he said, 'Now turn round, put your hands over your ears and keep your eyes tightly closed.'

What seemed like for ever passed, but was probably only a couple of minutes. It was long enough to feel tempted to sneak just one tiny glance. But she didn't. Then feeling his hands on hers, he uncovered her ears and said, 'You can open your eyes and turn round now.'

There before her was a sight so out of this world, she could hardly believe what she was seeing. The far end of the barn looked like something out of the Arabian Nights. It was a Bedouin wonderland – a magical canopied palace strewn with sumptuous rugs and cushions. And everywhere there were candles sparkling like brightly polished jewels in the glowing stillness.

She turned to Christian. 'It's beautiful. But what's it doing here?'

'It's for you, Genevieve. Somewhere I can have you all to myself and not worry about being interrupted.' He took her hand. 'Come and sit down.'

In a daze, a little disorientated, she did as he said. Could the night get any better? Could anything more miraculous happen to her? When she was settled on a low stool, he poured her a glass of champagne from a bottle sticking out of a wine cooler.

'Care of Jonjo,' Christian said. 'He told me he'd never forgive me if I stinted on what we drank.'

She took the glass from him. 'Jonjo knew about this?'

He sat next to her. 'I thought it wise to seek his permission. It is his house after all.'

'He never said anything. Not a word.'

He clinked his glass against hers. 'That was the general idea. The surprise was meant to take your breath away.'

'Any more surprises on this scale and I shall die of asphyxiation. When did you get here and arrange all this?'

'Around lunchtime with Polly and Jonjo. I followed them down and they helped get the main structure up.'

'I don't believe it. My sister was in on it as well?'

'Your parents too. Jonjo brought them to see it this afternoon. It was also the perfect opportunity, after all these years, to meet your mother again, properly. And maybe convince her I'm not the bastard she remembers me as.'

Genevieve saw now how she'd been thoroughly tricked. Jonjo hadn't offered to show Serena the barn to silence her mother's questions, it had all been part of a much bigger picture. What a devious bunch her family turned out to be!

'Is there anything else I should know about? Do you have any other surprises up your sleeve?'

In the soft candlelight, he suddenly looked serious. 'I might. But first I have to ask you something. I want to know what your feelings are for Adam.'

'For Adam? What a strange question. What's he got to do with anything?'

'Genevieve, he has everything to do with it. Don't you see that?'

Confused, she said, 'No, I don't. He's a friend. A really good friend.'

'But you're so close to him. And it's him you always turn to, isn't it?'

She hesitated. 'Only because he's always there.'

'Like he was the day your grandmother died.'

'You were there, too.'

'Yes, but when we were in the conservatory at Paradise House, while he was saying goodbye, I saw the way the two of you connected. And believe me, I felt you didn't want or need me there.'

Genevieve thought back to that day and picked her way through the jumble of events and emotions – the relief that Lily-Rose was safe, but the devastation that Gran was dead. With a flash of recall, she pictured the way

Adam had touched her arm in the conservatory, and how she'd kissed him goodbye, and the moment shortly after when she had told Christian she wanted to be alone with Nattie. Shocked, she saw the conclusion Christian must have reached, and it was hardly surprising.

'Is that why your emails tailed off?'

'Yes. I couldn't work out how you really felt about me. You seemed distant in your emails, businesslike and beyond my reach, as though you weren't sure we were doing the right thing. I decided to back off and give you some space.'

'But why didn't you say something? Why didn't you just ask me what I felt?' Even as she spoke, she knew how hypocritical she sounded. Since when had *she* been able to come right out and lay her emotions on the line?

He put his glass down. 'You Baxters aren't the only ones afraid to open up, you know. I was worried that if I put you on the spot, I'd get the answer I didn't want to hear, and I'd lose you.' He paused. 'But I'm asking the question now. I need to know, Genevieve. I know Adam is mad about your sister, but are you secretly in love with him?'

She put her glass next to his. It was time to be completely honest with Christian. And with herself. She moved in close, so there could be no mistaking her words. 'I do love Adam, I admit that. But I love him affectionately, like a brother. The only man I've ever truly loved and desired is you. There's never been anyone else who made me feel the way you do. I loved you as a teenager and I probably started to love you all over again that day you showed up at Paradise House looking for somewhere to stay. There, is that clear enough for you?'

A slow smile lightened the solemn expression that had clouded his face for the last few minutes. 'Crystal clear,' he said. And when, with exquisite tenderness, he kissed her, she knew that whatever doubts he'd been feeling, had now passed. He moved her to the soft-carpeted ground and put a cushion under her head.

'Do you think I'm finally going to get my wish granted?'

'What wish would that be?'

But he didn't answer her.

They made love slowly, neither of them wanting to rush what they'd waited so long for. And all the while, Genevieve experienced a sense of déjà vu. It was as though their bodies were completely known to them, as though they knew exactly where to touch each other to give the most pleasure.

Afterwards, lying in his arms, bathed in the wash of golden candlelight, as he told her how beautiful she was, she did indeed feel beautiful.

And loved.

49

In the weeks that followed, it was open season on the Baxter family. They had only themselves to blame, as Tubby was the first to say.

'If you must be so public in nailing your colours to the mast,' he teased Genevieve, 'what else do you expect, but for everyone to gossip about you?'

But for once, Genevieve wasn't bothered that her private life, a contradiction in terms these days, was being discussed so openly. Adam had just commented on this very point. They were up at St Non's; she was changing the flowers on Gran's grave and he, at Lily-Rose's request, was helping gather daisies to make a daisy chain to take home for Nattie.

'It wasn't long ago,' he said, 'that I recall a certain girl stamping her feet and throwing a tantrum when I dared to mention that folk were discussing her.'

Genevieve brushed away a fly that had landed on the angel of her grandmother's headstone. 'It all depends what people are saying. But luckily I'm not the only one they're talking about. I reckon you're of more interest to everyone.'

He went over to Lily-Rose, sitting cross-legged in the shade of the yew hedge in amongst the long grass, and gave her the daisies he'd picked. She was lost in her own little world, humming tunefully to herself as she laid out the flowers on her lap, lining them up like soldiers for inspection. Joining Genevieve again, Adam said, 'Any particular reason I'm the centre of attention?'

'Well, it's not every man who'd be brave enough to take on Natalie Baxter, is it?'

'At least they think I'm brave and not stupid.'

Genevieve smiled. 'So how's it going? Not regretting it, I hope.'

'No chance.' He hesitated. 'But how about Nattie? Has she said anything to you?'

'Oh, Adam, as if I'd repeat anything Nattie told me in confidence.'

'So there is something?'

Genevieve wished people wouldn't confide in her. She was hopeless when put under the spotlight. 'Look,' she said, 'it's not a big deal, and you must promise not to tell her I said anything, but . . .' she paused to glance across

978

to where Lily-Rose was still humming happily to herself, 'the thing is, she thinks you're holding out on her.'

He frowned. 'Holding what out on her?'

'You know.' Another glance across to Lily-Rose to check she wasn't listening. 'In the bedroom department. It's been three weeks since the talent contest and she's ... well you know ... wondering when it's going to happen.'

Adam's face suddenly broke into an enormous grin. But he said nothing.

'So, what's going on?'

'First off, it's no one's business but my own; second, it's unwise for her to go sleeping with the boss; and third ...' the grin widened, 'and third, I'm making her wait the way she made me wait.'

It was Genevieve's turn to smile now. 'You're braver than we all thought.'

'And bloody frustrated into the bargain!'

'How long do you think you can keep it up?'

'An unfortunate choice of words, Gen, but I get your drift. But the way she makes me feel, I don't think I can hold out for much longer.' He suddenly looked serious. 'I don't want to hurry things. I'm not interested in an easy-come, easy-go fling with her, I want the real thing. Love.'

'Then you're doing exactly the right thing. I doubt any man's ever given her this much consideration. The fact that she's worrying why you haven't got her into bed yet means she cares. Something she hasn't had a lot of experience of doing in the past.'

Two days after the talent contest, after Christian had left to go back to work, Adam had called Genevieve to say he wanted to talk to her in private.

'You must have thought it very odd what I did,' he said to her, 'singing that song for Nattie after everything I'd shared with you.'

'Just a little. But only because you seemed to have got her out of your system.'

'I gave it my best shot, but in the end, I couldn't do it.'

'And what about selling up and moving away? Is that still going to happen?'

Shamefaced, he'd admitted that it had been a lie. 'I'm sorry, Gen, but I told you that because I was banking on you telling Nattie sooner or later. I hoped it would make her think what it would be like if I wasn't around any more. And then, what with all the business with Lily-Rose disappearing, things sort of escalated in a way I could never have foreseen. Do you forgive me?'

She'd pretended to be hurt for all of two seconds. 'I'll forgive you,' she'd said, 'if you make me a promise. One that's in both our interests.'

'Name it and it's yours.'

'You must never, ever tell a living soul what we very nearly did that night at your place.'

'You mean, when we very nearly—'

'Strike it from your memory,' she'd interrupted. 'For Nattie's sake, and

Christian's, it must never be mentioned again. If Christian ever knew, I think it might eat away at him. And he doesn't deserve that.'

Breaking into her thoughts now, as she arranged the sweet peas Lily-Rose had specially picked for Gran's grave, Adam said, 'Nattie thinks you're avoiding me, Gen. Are you?'

'Yes,' she said, quite matter-of-factly. She didn't want to lie to Adam. 'Why?'

'Because you don't need an old chum like me hanging around and getting in the way.'

He'd looked at her sternly. 'You couldn't ever be in the way, Gen. I don't want things to change between us. And I don't think Nattie would want that either.'

Despite his words, Genevieve knew that their friendship had already begun to change. Today was the first time, since Adam had apologised for misleading her that they had been alone together. Well almost alone, they still, at Genevieve's contrivance had Lily-Rose with them to act as a chaperone. She'd had no idea that Christian had been feeling the way he had about Adam, and she would do anything to avoid hurting him.

With Lily-Rose wearing a daisy chain crown and carrying a matching one for her mother, Adam hoisted her onto his shoulders and they walked back down into the centre of the village.

After several days of grey skies and frequent showers, it was glorious again. The hot midday sun was high and bright in a flawless blue sky, and ahead of them the placid sea shimmered like an enormous blue jelly. The narrow streets were packed with smiling visitors – small, flush-faced children peering out from beneath sun-hats and waving fishing nets at one another, middle-aged couples strolling slowly arm in arm and groups of teenagers browsing the shops in search of trendy surfing gear. They passed Angel Cottage but didn't stop. Nattie, along with everyone else, would be waiting for them at Paradise House where Serena, having insisted that Genevieve take the day off, was preparing a special lunch.

'What do you think this lunch is all about?' Adam asked as they waved at Debs through the open door of the crowded salon – it always amazed Genevieve that no matter what the weather, women of a certain age were always prepared to sit under the hot dryer to have their hair done.

'I've a feeling Mum and Dad are going to make an announcement.'

'Any idea what it is?'

'If you'd asked me that a month ago I'd have said their divorce, but since you and Donna did such a good job of turning Dad into Elvis, they've barely let each out of their sight. Mum got what she wanted from Dad that night, a grand gesture of love, and Dad got a surprise – the realisation that the limelight's no bad place to be now and then.'

They stopped to help a young mother negotiate the kerb with a pushchair laden with beach paraphernalia, then carried on.

'Everything your father did that night was his own work,' Adam said.

'Donna and I had very little to do with his performance. When it's from the heart, it needs no extra encouragement.'

'In that case, the same must apply to your own performance. I've said it before, but you were show-stoppingly brilliant. It was a shame you couldn't have won joint first prize with Donna instead of making do with second.' To her amusement, a faint hue of red coloured his face. 'I had no idea you had such a fantastic voice,' she said, further embarrassing him. 'Why have you never showed it off before?'

'Because, just as I do in business, I like to keep a few tricks up my sleeve. Take them unawares is my motto. It never fails.'

'Then perhaps you should have done that sooner with Nattie?'

Holding onto Lily-Rose's ankles as she started bouncing on his shoulders and telling him to giddy up, he smiled. 'But the wait's been worth every minute. I've no regrets.'

It was early days, but Genevieve hoped her sister wouldn't disappoint Adam. Nattie had been her usual self, of course, taking on the chin the flak dished out by Tubby and their father.

'So what if I've changed my mind about Adam,' she told them. 'I was merely biding my time. I was being selective.' She told Genevieve and Polly that she had no intention of changing, though. 'Just because I'm going out with him, it doesn't mean I'm going to turn into something I'm not.'

'I think he'd be upset if you did, Nats,' said Polly.

'Yes,' agreed Genevieve. 'Goodness knows why, but it's the headstrong, difficult, stroppy you he's worshipped all this time, not some shallow, pliable girl without a thought in her head.'

But what amazed them most was Nattie sticking to her word and working for Adam, something they had never truly believed she'd do.

'I'm a woman of principle,' she said, coming home after her first day of being nice to people she probably despised. 'I made a promise and I'll see it through. Even if the job is as boring as hell.'

Lily-Rose, on the other hand, had had a fantastic day and was full of all the fun things she'd got up to: playing on the climbing frames, winning several swimming races in the park pool, and having her face painted. As the days passed and she came home each afternoon with a different face – a tiger one day, a tortoiseshell cat another – it was obvious she was having the time of her life.

As was Polly. Much to Jonjo's delight, and considerable relief, the night after the talent show, Polly had agreed to get engaged. Embellishing the story with infuriatingly little detail, Polly had told them the following morning, while he was upstairs in the shower, how he'd taken her down to the beach and, in the moonlight, had produced a ring he'd bought in Hong Kong. They'd all crowded round her hand to get a closer look at the cluster of diamonds, and had let out a collective whistle.

'It might have been nice for the young man to ask my permission first,' their father said when they'd run out of superlatives, and Nattie and Mum had stopped trying to squeeze it on their own much larger fingers.

'Oh, Daddy,' said Polly, genuinely upset. 'I'm sure he would have if the right moment had arisen, but –'

'It's okay, Poll, I'm only joking.' He hugged her warmly. 'I suppose this means you'll be moving to Buckingham?' Genevieve could see he was trying to be brave, that he hated the idea of losing her.

'Not for a while,' Polly said. 'And anyway, Jonjo and I will be here as often as possible staying in his new house.'

Even now, as Genevieve led the way round to the back door, she couldn't imagine Paradise House without her youngest sister's benign presence in it.

Lunch was an alfresco affair. Dad had set up two tables end to end in the dappled shade of the orchard. Mum had covered them with a couple of large white cloths, and then had artfully flung handfuls of rose petals in between the plates and glasses. It bore all the hallmarks of a grand Baxter celebration. But what exactly were they celebrating?

Luckily there were no guests hanging around. With the answerphone switched on so lunch wouldn't be spoiled by having to run to the phone every five minutes, Mum instructed them to sit down.

'Adam and Nattie, you sit with Lily-Rose between the two of you. Jonjo, you sit opposite Polly and next to Nattie, and Genevieve, you go at the top of the table, next to your father, and, well, Christian, I think it's fairly obvious where you should go, next to Genevieve. There now, that's everyone sorted. Well, Daddy Dean, what are you waiting for? Let's get these glasses filled!'

Looking happier than Genevieve could ever remember seeing him, her father moved slowly round the table, pouring out their wine. Sitting here with her family, each one of them hugging their own newfound happiness, it was once again easy for Genevieve to believe in her grandmother's theory, that while no one was looking, the angels had been meddling in the nicest possible way. If it had been left to us Baxters, she thought, it would have all ended in tears.

Across the table, she caught Nattie's eye as Adam showed Lily-Rose how to turn her paper napkin into a swan, another of his hidden talents. Nattie smiled at Genevieve and rolled her eyes in Adam's direction. But there was no scorn or malice to the gesture, just a look of happy indulgence. Had the inconceivable happened? Had Nattie been tamed? Had she come to realise that Adam would make the most wonderful father for Lily-Rose? And a devoted husband into the bargain. Even Nattie must have figured that one out for herself. Not that Genevieve could talk. Look how she'd totally misread Christian's feelings towards her.

She still couldn't get over the wonderful double surprise he'd pulled the night of the talent contest. Apparently, when Polly had been staying with Jonjo, and they'd had dinner with Christian, she'd seen how miserable he was and had encouraged him to come back with them so he could talk to Genevieve properly.

'Will it do any good?' he'd asked.

'You'll never know unless you try,' she'd told him.

A slight squeeze on her leg under the table had her turning to Christian. 'You okay?' he mouthed.

She reached for his hand and mouthed back, 'I'm fine.' There it was again. *I'm fine.* Yes, but this time she really was.

'Hey, you two!' said Nattie from across the table, 'no secret conversations. We had enough of that when we were children. The pair of you were always leaving the rest of us out.'

Christian missed what she'd said, so Genevieve repeated it for him.

'Perhaps you ought to learn to lipread, Nattie,' he said.

Adam burst out laughing. 'Steady on, Christian, she's got enough to do learning to be nice to me.'

Again Christian missed what had been said and after Genevieve had put him right, Serena raised her glass. She waited for them all to follow suit. She looked down the length of the table to where her husband was sitting.

'Here's to us all and what lies ahead.'

They responded to the toast and Lily-Rose, gulping down her apple juice too fast, let out an enormous burp and made them all laugh.

'Do you think we ought to tell them what does lie ahead?' asked Daddy Dean.

'I suppose we ought to,' Serena said, 'seeing as it affects them so directly.'

'Come on you two,' demanded Nattie. 'We've played along enough. It's time to hit the newsflash button and tell us what this lunch is all about.'

Serena looked at their father. 'Go on, then. You do the honours.'

With all eyes on him, Daddy Dean said, 'Your mother and I have decided we need some time away together and . . . and if it's okay with all of you, we want to go on an extended second honeymoon.'

'What a wonderful idea,' said Polly. 'For how long?'

'Um . . . We haven't decided exactly. But it'll definitely be longer than our first.'

'Perhaps a month, maybe two,' Serena added more assuredly.

Nattie whistled. 'Now that's some second honeymoon.'

'Where are you thinking of going?' asked Genevieve.

'New Zealand. Your mother wants to show me where she's been staying and then we'll go exploring somewhere new. Australia seems a likely bet. I've always been fascinated by the idea of Alice Springs.'

'Then perhaps you'd better make it two to three months,' suggested Jonjo.

'But what about us? And Paradise House?' Nattie's voice had taken a turn for the worse, like a child who didn't want to be left behind.

Serena said, 'You'll be fine without us, Nattie. You have a lovely new house to live in, a job, a gorgeous daughter and,' she cast a look in Adam's direction, 'a man who adores you. I'd say you have everything a girl could wish for. And as to Paradise House, well, that's slightly more complicated.'

She turned to Genevieve, and with a sinking heart Genevieve braced herself to hear the words she didn't want to hear. If there was one thing she was sure of, she didn't want to go on running Paradise House as it was. It was too exhausting. Too chaotic. With five guest suites, she needed regular help she could rely on.

'Genevieve,' her father said, 'your mother and I owe you a huge debt of gratitude for all the hard work you've put in since you came home, so before I say anything else, I just want to thank you. I, personally, don't know what I would have done without you.' Clearing his throat, he carried on. 'It's entirely up to you, but we wondered if you would want to take on the full responsibility of running Paradise House, but not as it is. So, we've come up with an idea we want you to consider. It would mean a total revamp of the place, someone to help oversee the work, and more importantly, someone special to put it on the map. And we think that special someone is you.'

Still holding Christian's hand beneath the table, Genevieve took a gulp of her wine and listened to what her parents had to say.

Genevieve was banned from going anywhere near the kitchen for the rest of the day. Not even to help with the washing up.

'Christian, I order you to take her for a very long walk,' Serena said. 'As far away from here as possible.'

'You don't have to do everything my family says,' Genevieve said, once they were away from Paradise House and standing outside the Salvation Arms, looking down onto the beach. It was early evening, the sun was dropping in the pale sky and most of the people on the beach had gathered together their belongings and gone. Only a handful of Power Boat People were left, as usual making their noisy exit, winching boats onto trailers, yelling and slamming car doors.

'Don't you mean *our* family? According to your mother I'm now an honorary member.'

She turned to face him. 'You're joking?'

'I'm not. Your mother said that now I don't have a family of my own, I'm to treat yours as mine.'

Genevieve cringed. 'Tell me she wasn't as insensitive as that.'

'Her exact words. So how do you feel about me being part of the family?'

'Outraged. She'll be handing over the priceless family silver next.'

'I'd rather have the best prize of all. You. OK, I know that was the cheesiest line ever uttered, but give me a break, I'm learning from the master, Jonjo.'

'Then stop it. Stop it right now. One charmer in the family is quite enough. Do you fancy a drink in the pub, or a walk?'

'Let's walk to Tawelfan.'

They walked hand in hand along the coastal path, in an easy, comfortable silence. Genevieve knew that Christian was tired from the strain of trying to keep up with so much hectic conversation during lunch.

Taking the steep path down to Tawelfan, they found they had the beach to themselves. The dunes were also deserted, and they sat on the warm, dry sand, staring out at the horizon. What little breeze there had been blowing in off the sea all day had now dwindled to nothing. Faint strands of clouds had formed in the sky around the setting sun and a chain of gulls flew along the shore, their wings hardly moving as they glided elegantly into the distance. In the perfect quiet of the moment, Genevieve thought of all that had been discussed that afternoon. Her parents going away for a second honeymoon; Jonjo saying he didn't want a long engagement – 'If I give Polly too much time to think about it, she might change her mind,' he'd said – and Polly admitting that she'd already applied for several teaching jobs in and around Buckingham so she could be with Jonjo. And lastly, there was her parents' idea to turn Paradise House into a smart, upmarket country house hotel, with a restaurant offering fine gourmet food. 'It's the way a lot of B & Bs are going these days,' they said.

They'd clearly put a lot of thought into it and had even been to the bank to see about a loan. 'We want to semi-retire,' her father said. 'We'll help as much as you want us to, but we want officially to sign over Paradise House to you three girls.'

What they had in mind was for Genevieve to have the marginally larger share, because she would be the one responsible for making it work. Initially, Genevieve was unsure. Would this be her dream? Or would it still be her parents'? She decided that the only way she could take it on would be if she had a full say in how things were run. She would need the right kind of help too, proper full or part-time staff. Donna, who'd already proved herself so invaluable, and had now moved in with Tubby, was the ideal candidate to be in charge of housekeeping. With someone so reliable on hand, Genevieve would be left to do what she enjoyed most – cooking. She might even go on a few courses, get a few fancy badges to her name.

The more she thought about it, the more excited she began to feel. She pictured the dining room having undergone a much-needed facelift. There would be candlelit dinners, with cocktails beforehand on the terrace if the weather was warm, and roaring log fires to cosy up to in the winter.

But to achieve any of that, there would have to be a great deal of upheaval. As her father had said during lunch, 'The worst bit will be living here while the work is being carried out. The layout will have to be improved; rooms knocked about, walls taken down, walls put up. For instance, you'll need a much larger kitchen. An extension's the answer. And if you got rid of the private sitting room you could turn it into a games room.'

'But where would we have our own private space? We can't lose that altogether.' Genevieve had said.

'You're forgetting the extension.'

'Sounds to me like you need an architect,' said Jonjo. 'A decent architect who comes with impeccable references. I wonder if anyone knows of one?'

Turning from the sea and looking at Christian, Genevieve said, 'You know that architect I might be in need of?'

'Yes.'

'Do you suppose he might be too busy with all his other commitments to help at Paradise House?'

'He might be. But on the other hand, he might not.' He shifted round so they were face to face, and reaching for her hands, he entwined his fingers through hers. 'I've come to an important decision, one that requires your approval before I take it any further. How would you feel if I lived more locally?'

'How locally?'

'Here in Angel Sands.'

'That's quite a commute. You'd have to be up early to be in the office for nine each morning.'

'True. Although it would depend where the office was. If, say, I worked for myself, I could work wherever I wanted.'

'Are you saying what I think you're saying?'

He stroked her cheek, traced her lips with a finger. 'I love you Genevieve, and more than anything I want to give *us* a real chance of working. We can't do that if we live so far apart.'

'You'd really do that?'

'In the blink of an eye. All I need to know is that you feel the same; that it's worth a go. But I'll warn you now, I've got it all planned. For the time being, I'm going to rent out my parents' house in Shropshire, sell my flat and rent a small cottage near you. That way we won't be rushing things. Oh, and as to work, to begin with I reckon I can make a living from all the barns in the area that are ripe for conversion. Tubby's already put me onto several further along the coast. And there are always holiday homes to create or renovate. So what do you think? Will it work?'

A euphoric surge of happiness filled her. 'I think it will work *fine*, Christian. But just to be sure, this isn't a double bluff, is it? You're not threatening commitment in the hope I'll do a runner?'

He laughed out loud. 'You're not running anywhere. In fact, you're staying right here.' He pushed her back onto the warm sand and kissed her.

As Genevieve closed her eyes, she caught sight of a faint ghost of a cloud floating directly above their heads. She was probably imagining it, but it looked just like one of Gran's angels gazing down on her.